GOSPEL

GOSPEL

WILTON
BARNHARDT

To JIM
with best wishes —

[signature: Wilton Barnhardt]

7/18/98

Picador USA ❧ New York

Picador® is a U.S. registered trademark and is used by St. Martin's Press under
license from Pan Books Limited.

Design by Jaye Zimet

Barnhardt, Wilton.
    Gospel / Wilton Barnhardt.
        p.   cm.
    ISBN 0-312-11924-0 (pbk.)
    1. Sacred books—Fiction.   2. Lost books—Fiction.   I. Title.
PS3552.A6994G67   1995
813′.54—dc20   94-46583
                                                                     CIP

First published in the United States by St. Martin's Press

First Picador USA Edition: March 1995
10 9 8 7 6 5 4 3 2 1

to my Blessed Trinity,
Mary Barnhardt, Joyce Carter,
and Betty Grigg

And in her friendship there is pure delight,
And unfailing wealth in the labors of her hands,
And understanding in the experience of her company,
And glory in the sharing of her words.

WISDOM OF SOLOMON 8:18

God does not die on the day when we cease to believe in a personal deity, but we die on the day when our lives cease to be illumined by the steady radiance, renewed daily, of a wonder, the source of which is beyond all reason.

—Markings
DAG HAMMARSKJÖLD

GOSPEL

NOTE TO THE READER: This is a work of fiction. All of the events, characters, and institutions depicted in this novel are entirely fictitious or are used fictitiously. However, all ancient sources, Biblical citings, apocryphal gospels, and historical information contained in the footnotes of the Gospel are true and accurate.

1

I had lost my faith, Josephus.[1]

2. It had parted as the flower falls from the wilting stalk, as the tide recedes to reveal the mud beneath the sea, gone as the moon behind a large cloud, as Helios in bed at Eridanus at nighttime's ebb.[2] So it was with me! I awoke to find what had once been certain now uncertain. And thus began my travels, my brother, and this magnificent history you are about to read—surely, I say, to be ranked among the most important of my works!

3. It is the sixth year [76 C.E.] of this monster Flavius Caesar,[3] whose avarice is boundless and cruelty legendary. However, I bring news to your deaf ears, for you, my brother, have done all but service this ogre in his bedchamber. Yes, and I assure you the Jews say worse about you. Such as, "First there was Aliturius

Textual Note: Throughout the gospel, the editor has arranged the text in paragraphs, punctuating as seemed reasonable, and using quotes in the dialogue for easier reading. The editor has endeavored to retain a bit of the self-importance and stilted tone of this confession, reminiscent of the Byzantine church historian Eusebius, but of an earlier era.

1. Ἀπέβαλον τὴν ἐμὴν πίστιν, "I had lost my faith." Faith, πίστις, as is commonly used by Paul in the First Century. Josephus is the Jewish historian "Flavius" Josephus (ca. 37–100 C.E.)

2. For this mediocre Greek poetry, see Appendix A.
   Eridanus is where Phaethon, the unfortunate driver of the sun's chariot, fell to rest, not his father, Helios.

3. Vespasian, the general who began the campaign to tame Judea in 67 C.E. and later Emperor, 69–79 C.E., was first of the Flavians.

upon the stage and now you too: Josephus who acts the Roman, betrayer of his people!"[4]

Mind you, Aliturius only committed his genital member to Caesar while you have flung your soul at him, as well as our beloved father's name, since you are now raised up as "Flavius" Josephus. Furthermore it is no small insult that you dally as an historian, a rival to me, your older brother, whose fame you shall not so easily eclipse by writing love letters to Roman generals! Truly, my brother, I would believe it if I heard that you had taken recourse to surgeons to erase that primal sign of covenant with our people.[5]

4. Perhaps you will throw this missive into the fire as you did my last one; certainly my tone with you does nothing for its chances. Indeed, Tesmegan, we shall soften my rhetorical blows when you read this back to me. (Tesmegan is my scribe, purchased here with my last monies, in what is surely the last act of my life. How it must delight you to know that you will never hear from me again!) But keep reading, for there are more delights in store for you, dear Josephus. For nearly half a century you have berated my association with the Nazirene Church[6] and it shall be among your final triumphs to know that I come to the end of my life with the Church at odds with me and I at odds with it; it is hard to know who is more disgusted and disappointed in

---

4. This snipe concerns Aliturius, a Jewish actor who performed in Rome and was a great favorite (and perhaps bedmate) of Nero. The author suggests Josephus played at being a Roman and was no less a traitor. In 67 c.e. Josephus commanded troops in Galilee against the Romans and was taken prisoner at Jotapata for two years. In that time he ingratiated himself with the soon-to-be crowned Vespasian and won his release, this time fighting on the side of the conquering Romans under Titus, destroyer of the Temple.

All Josephus texts throughout are the revised 1991 Hebrew University Press editions, editor-in-chief, M. Hersch. For a discussion of Josephus's reputed treachery to the Jews and responses to the attacks of Justus of Tiberias, see M. Hersch, *Josephus* (HUP, 1991), also S. J. D. Cohen, *Josephus in Galilee and Rome* (Leiden, 1979).

5. From the time of Antiochus IV, there was an operation that would render the circumcised apparently uncircumcised, which prevented social embarrassment when Jews and Greeks engaged in gymnastics. Years of Jewish unrest resulted from the clash of pro- and antigymnasium parties in the 100s b.c.e. See H. H. Ben Sasson, ed., *A History of the Jewish Peoples* (Harvard, 1976).

6. Nazirene (or Nazarene, as Paul claims for himself in *Acts* 24:5) is used throughout to denote the Jewish purity-cult (whose strictures are listed in *Numbers* 6), which evolved into the Christian sect of still-observant Jews in the 100s, also termed the Ebionite Church.

Nowhere in this gospel does the Greek term "Christian" appear. Εκκλεσία is the term used for the whole Church throughout; Συναγωγή for the individual church buildings.

whom. The Nazirene Church in the last twenty years has become a shambles, but I hardly need to tell you that, armed as you are with abuse for the followers of the Teacher of Righteousness.[7]

5. Mark my words: my faith in the justice of Our Savior's teaching has not swayed one bit—not a particle!

However, the ensuing riot of heresies that has affixed itself to the life-account of Our Master has forced me to stand to the side of the Movement He originated, so rife with blasphemies and innovations it has become. (Naturally, I your brother, scholar and historian, could be depended upon to root out all heterodoxies, but these days I am no more heeded than Micaiah before Jeroboam.)[8]

I propose to tell you now of the last ten years and my search for the truth concerning Our Master and His Disciples, and then lastly, how I come to the end of my life, here in the midst of Africa, alone, penniless, without companion or synagogue to support me. (Tesmegan insists that he be counted among my friends—very well, write that down but that is the last of your interruptions, young man.) Like Herodotus, I have come to my account of Xerxes.[9]

O Blessed *Sophia* be ever with me as I commit my last excellencies to posterity!

6. I recall you despised all of the fellow Disciples that you met, but you have more in common with them than you know, Josephus. Twenty years before the catastrophe of Jerusalem [50 C.E.], I wrote a three-volume Gospel that our Chief Disciple, Peter, quite intemperately burned, instructing me in his blunt, artless manner that I did no service to Our Church.

A similar fate was prepared for my *All Heresies Refuted* in Philippi, I was informed, though copies still exist in Damascus and in certain private libraries, along with my *Cosmos Explained*, which I feel to be immature and enthusiastic in its praise of

---

7. Interesting as well, nowhere in this gospel account does the proper name "Jesus" occur, though there could scarcely be any doubt the figure is Jesus. "Teacher of Righteousness" as a title appears in the Dead Sea Scrolls (the *Habakkuk Commentaries*, 1950 Burrows trans., St. Mark's Monastery) honoring an unknown master, and suggests a preexisting cult of persecuted rabbis that came to include John the Baptist and Jesus.
8. Micaiah warned Jehosophat, not Jeroboam. *2 Chronicles* 18.
9. The author reckons the history of Xerxes's campaign was the historian Herodotus's last volume.

Sophia, but not without many passages of merit, and my influential *Catalogues of Martyrdom*, which is a learned speculation upon the matters of the Throne, Crowns, the Chariot, Diadems, and the like. I have, it must be admitted, also distanced myself from that rather enthusiastic work (though my Greek garnered the praises of many).[10] I was delighted to note that Ephesus still possessed a copy of my *Odes of Arkady*, which was well received in many Alexandrian circles, I must say, as well as my splendid epic *The Hebraika*, which, I am resigned, will long outlive my theological dissertations.

(You will recall Zechariah bar-Sirach[11] himself considered *The Hebraika* the finest work of its sort since the Psalms of King David, and though you never mentioned it by name in our many letters, I have always suspected that you bore it begrudging admiration. Would that we could put aside these foolish pretensions!)

7. But now to my tireless history at hand: Clio, may thy steady hand be ever on my calamus!

Sadly, given your adventures with the Romans, who befriend us one moment to better crucify us the next, I have no way of knowing whether you are alive as I dictate this. I wonder if you have perished answering the outrages of more pots turned upside-down in Caesarean alleyways or died at the hands of the now-desperate Sicarii.[12] But there is no reason you shouldn't be alive and well-fed as you now sit enthroned in my former estate, our family's property that was rightfully mine and that you usurped from me—let it here be recorded!

8. I promise not to dwell upon this, the most recent of

---

10. None of these works is extant. Quite likely *All Heresies Refuted* was among the first *odia theologica* in a tradition followed by Irenaeus in his *Heresies Answered* (ca. 185 C.E.,) or Hippolytus in his *Refutation of All Heresies* (ca. 222 C.E).

11. It is tempting to speculate that this is perhaps a descendant of Simeon (or Jesus) Ben Sira, the greatest literary figure of the age, whose grandson in Alexandria translated and disseminated his Wisdom, *Ecclesiasticus*, in the 100s B.C.E.

12. The author mordantly refers to the quibble over a pot blocking the access to a synagogue in Caesarea, which began the war that destroyed Jerusalem; see *The Jewish War*, II.xiv.4.

   The Sicarii (after *sica*, for dagger) were the fanatical fringe of the Zealots of the First Century, who assassinated any dissenter or perceived Roman collaborator. They evolved to be little better than terrorists and robbers, forming and betraying countless alliances as they saw fit, fighting to their virtual extermination at Masada in 73 C.E.

our contentions, but though six years have passed, I feel no less heated about your being given the title to the estate as a reward by the Romans, and your expelling my Nazirene commune of charities from your property. Understand: it is not for me selfishly that I resented your intriguing with the Romans to give to you, the second-born, the property that was rightfully mine as the first-born.[13] My sadness was for the orphans and elderly, virgins and scholars that I had installed there.

Indeed, I smell the stale perfume and wine-breath of my unbeloved stepmother, my father's ill-chosen second wife, in all this! That woman, your mother, an ever-flowing fount of poison where I am concerned, was surely behind your action. Though she rarely left Jerusalem where she and our father spent their last decades, it nonetheless perturbed her that the country estate had been consecrated to this higher purpose. With Jerusalem in ruins, naturally, she set her eye upon the estate just as she had set her eye on our father's money. Your surprising choice to abandon the priesthood for a military career at the age of twenty-nine with no previous experience served to make her worse-tempered with, as she called it, my "distasteful Nazirene rabble," a sentiment she attributed to you.

Distasteful rabble? Coming from one who extinguished years fawning upon Nero Caesar and his whore-wife in that cesspit of all sodomies, Rome, mingling with a court for whom rabble is too good a name! Would that your dispossessed brother who shares your blood were as high in your sight!

But far be it from my purpose to start an argument.

9. Go and have the cursed estate, even with my blessing. Enjoy your desolate, ruined Judea. I shouldn't think the Zealots

---

13. A word about the respective ages of the two brothers.
   According to Josephus's own geneaology in the *Life*, par. 1, he was born in 37 C.E. ("the first year of the reign of Gaius Caesar"). It can be deduced from the following (see 2:11) that Josephus's brother, the putative author of this document, was born in 14 C.E., making a gap of twenty-three years between the brothers. Josephus writes in *Life*, par. 2, that "I myself was brought up by my brother," and seems to have been the offspring of his father's second marriage.

and rabbis and sons of Zadok and weekly messiahs that sprout like weeds in the rubble of the Temple should give you much peace. As Judeans they could for centuries not agree on a single matter until, of course, the matter of your infamy was before them. So since we find ourselves respectively reviled by the world we used to inhabit, surely then let us be as Jacob and Esau reconciled at Shechem![14] Having the estate in your possession—snatched like the girdle of Hippolyta!—let argument and strife be through between us and let us speak to one another as men of a family. Or better yet, scholars that we are!

10. And frankly it is little matter old as I am whether you love me or no, but rather, as with all that are aged, whether you attend what I have to say. I suspect you bear me, the one who raised you and encouraged you in your studies, no affection, still find me foolish and irresponsible, find my researches laughable and the values of Our Master doomed to extinction. At least then consider what I have seen, and that I have traveled to Tarsus and Tyre, Antioch and Alexandria, speaking to Celts and Caucasians, to Paphlagonians and Persians, and I write you now in dire circumstances from Meroe![15] Whereas you have marched with pomp into many a city and dealt with the rulers and sat at the fine tables, I entered often as a stranger, a beggar who took the kindness of the town, and believe I can write as true a history from my travels.

11. I exhort you,[16] my brother, to read on and learn!

You shall not believe the wickedness of the Nazirene's enemies. False messiahs abound! To take a life in these times is as nothing; no blasphemy is too foul, no lie is too absurd for it not to be believed and championed, no self-mutilation too horrid to practice. Though you have seen much in battle, you shall not sleep when I tell you that I myself, your own brother, was threatened with unchastity and sodomies[17] by the fleshpots of our

---

14. The author intends Seir, *Genesis* 33:14.
15. Meroe is 120 miles northeast of modern-day Khartoum in the Sudan.
16. παρακαλέω, an exhortatory constant for First-Century irenic writings.
17. πορνεία and "sodomies." Much has been written about the First-Century obsession with *porneia*; see the excellent R. M. Werner, *Die antiken Klassiker und die Unanstandigheit* (Freiburg, 1982). "Sodomies" should be taken as any improper act or inhospitality; a refusal to feed a stranger in this era could be termed a sodomy.

enemies! The Whore Helen, whose notoriety is deserved! (You know that virgin chastity, and freedom from submission to sin,[18] I have always felt, to be the only engine of refinement for the soul.) I dread even to think of her now, and her hellish loins. . . .

12. Ah, but young Tesmegan tires, and I will begin the tales of my travels tomorrow. How in fits and starts, over the last ten years, I began my wanderings to search for the true relation of Our Church's origins according to Our Master's first disciples, followers, and acquaintances.

---

18. μαλακία. This can mean "masturbation" but was also used by First-Century writers to mean any weak-willed descent into carnality.

BRITAIN

I never saw, heard, nor read that the clergy were beloved in any nation where Christianity was the religion of the country. Nothing can render them popular but some degree of persecution.

—"Thoughts on Religion," *Works,* vol. xv, R17 (post. 1765)
JONATHAN SWIFT

Let him who is fond of indulging in a dreamlike existence go to Oxford, and stay there; let him study this magnificent spectacle, the same under all aspects, with its mental twilight tempering the glare of noon, or mellowing the silver moonlight; let him wander in her sylvan suburbs, or linger in her cloistered halls; but let him not catch the din of scholars or teachers, or dine or sup with them, or speak a word to any of the privileged inhabitants; for if he does, the spell will be broken, the poetry and the religion gone, and the palace of the enchantment will melt from his embrace into thin air!

—*Sketches of the Principal Picture Galleries* (1824)
WILLIAM HAZLITT

[The Arian Heresy,] this poisonous error, after corrupting whole world at length crossed the sea and infected even this remote island; and, once the doorway had been opened, every sort of pestilential heresy at once poured into this island, whose people are ready to listen to anything novel, and never hold firmly to anything.

—*A History of the English Church and People* (721)
BEDE

So the Maker of Mankind laid waste this dwelling-place until the old works of Giants stood idle. . . . Therefore the Man wise in his heart considers carefully this wall-place and this dark life, remembers the multitude of deadly combats long ago, and speaks these words: "Where has the Horse gone? Where the young Warrior? . . . Where are the joys of the Hall? Alas, the bright Cup! Alas, the mailed Warrior! Alas, the Prince's glory! How that time has gone, vanished beneath night's cover, just as if it had never been!

—"The Wanderer," *The Exeter Book* (975)

hortly after the captain mentioned they were passing over Stornaway, that it was 45 degrees below zero outside, that they were at a height of 36,000 feet, that the weather in London was cloudy and drizzly and a good morning to all, he warned that due to a high-pressure cell over Great Britain it might be a little turbulent for the next hour or so, and after signing off—Buck, Chip, Dirk, Biff, whatever his name was, to Lucy he sounded drunk or at best half-awake—the little seatbelt sign lit up with a *ding*.

Lucy Dantan automatically put her hand to her seatbelt, which had never been unfastened, and steeled herself.

First flight.

With the excitement of a first trip to Europe, the unusual mission ahead of her and her terror of being airborne, Lucy reckoned she had acceded to just twenty minutes of tortured plane-sleep, awakening with every bump and wobble. It was 6:30 A.M. by her watch, 12:30 to the British people down below—technically Scottish, Lucy decided—and it wasn't too long now to London and Heathrow Airport.

As promised, here came the turbulence.

Lucy looked at the sleepy stewardess making her way down the aisle. The stewardess did this *all the time.* Several days a week, for months, *years* people did this. No problem, this turbulence. Absolutely common. Then there was a big *kalumph* as the plane dropped a hundred feet, a lurch Lucy found reminiscent of when the down elevator in the Sears Tower back home in Chicago puts on the brakes. A few people groaned, most shifted and readjusted themselves, still sleeping.

Time for more prayer, she vowed.

"Our Father, Who art in heaven, . . ."

(This again.)

". . . hallowed be Thy Name. Thy kingdom come . . ." Lucy trailed off, this being too pro forma. "Please don't let this plane crash, Lord. Jesus, if it does go down, forgive me of my sins. And Holy Spirit . . ."

(Yes?)

Lucy dried up on the Holy Spirit. "If we're all gonna die, please sustain me and allow me the peace to meet my end with dignity." What if the plane hurtled into the cold North Atlantic? Lucy imagined a crash-landing on the water. The plane would initially float and then panic would break out and there'd be a riot getting to the life rafts. "Give me the strength, Holy Spirit, to be of service through this coming ordeal. And if death is my lot . . ."

(The plane is not going to crash, My child.)

Then the plane hit a treacherous series of drops. A stewardess lost control of the orange juice she was pouring and a baby began to cry.

"Thy will be done," Lucy muttered, eyes pinched closed, hands clasped tight. "If You want me to drop out of the sky, twenty-eight years old in the prime of life, all right, I can't stop You. But I'll be happy to dedicate my life to something or make some kind of promise . . ."

(Over Newfoundland, you promised Us two years with Mother Teresa. What do We get now?)

"And please, Holy Spirit, be with the pilot and copilot and guide them and be with them so that we may all land safely."

(But I am with you always.)

There was a respite from the turbulence and Lucy was determined to distract herself. There were two allowable diversions: the in-flight magazine with every piece read three times except the mutual bonds article, and Lucy's own notepad with the details of her mission.

She reviewed: Dr. O'Hanrahan and his assistant, Gabriel O'Donoghue, her childhood friend and fellow grad student at the University of Chicago, had left the university on some kind of hush-hush expedition back in February. Gabriel and the professor were supposed to return in March. They didn't. Attempts to contact them by the Theology Department proved fruitless. Soon Gabriel stopped sending messages home. Soon the department had lost the trail of Dr. O'Hanrahan, but since he had the department credit card they had his receipts and some clue as to where he had been. Soon, a bill of $2,000 arrived and the department canceled the credit card.

While assuring Gabriel's parents that he was all right, and assuring Dr. O'Hanrahan's sister that the old man was all right, the Theology Department began to suspect that things were not all right: that this bitter, alcoholic, eccentric genius had taken the department credit card along with many other funds and trusts, and was blowing it in a last-ditch effort at revenge on the department he had built and, he felt, had betrayed him.

"You see, Miss Dantan," Dr. Shaughnesy had told her a week ago, as she sat in his oaken office, somber and muted as one expected a theological study to be, "O'Hanrahan is a great man with a great mind, but alas, with a great grudge against us as well. Poor Patrick suspects his ouster as chairman was the result of a Masonic plot."

Lucy asked, "If he doesn't listen to you, why would he listen to a stranger like me?"

"He may not, but at least the Theology Department will have done what it can to retrieve him. It is with the most abundant possible tact and diplomacy that we want you to approach him, and suggest . . ." Dr. Shaughnesy attempted a look of concern, human compassion never being his strength and always having to be slightly play-acted. ". . . suggest that he come back home to his loved ones and fellow colleagues. Don't let it end like this, in this . . . this childish display."

"Might," Lucy speculated, "he really be on to something? I mean, this was the man who worked on the Nag Hammadi digs, the Nimrut

Dag stele, who helped catalogue the Huntington Library fragments of the Dead Sea Scrolls. Maybe he'll walk in the door with another Dead Sea Scroll or something."

Dr. Shaughnesy looked somewhat pained and twisted the large onyx ring on his left hand; Lucy observed his pale, long fingers. "I don't think so, my dear. I have a file drawer full of hate mail from the man and I'm not sure he has any purpose but running up a tremendous bar and restaurant tab." The head of the Theology Department twisted his ring again uncomfortably. "And yet, I don't want to report him to the police for defrauding the department. I want to give him this warning—Patrick was responsible for hiring me, after all. We, his former colleagues and admirers, owe him this courtesy."

Lucy asked Dr. Shaughnesy why he was sure O'Hanrahan would be attending an upcoming dinner in All Souls College at Oxford University, Thursday night, June 21st, 1990. The Acolytes were a dining society for ecclesiasts from a number of faiths—Islam, Catholicism, and Protestantism, Judaism—who met once a year for a feast of fine food, rare wines, precious liqueurs, and an agreed-upon topic for learned, rousing debate.

"He's never missed one of these Acolyte Suppers yet," said Shaughnesy. "And I have contacted a colleague at Cambridge who is in the Acolyte Society and, being indisposed, has ceded his place to me, and I in turn have put forward your name to attend."

"Wow."

"You are free, of course, to decline this trip for the department," offered Shaughnesy, examining his bloodless hands.

"Oh no, sir," she had insisted. "What an opportunity. I mean, I've never really been anywhere at all. Is there . . . is there some reason you're picking me to do this?"

Shaughnesy smiled briefly. "We were going to send one of the faculty, but it occurred there was no one available whom Patrick might not take great exception to—so few of us are on speaking terms with him. And you are among the most mature grad students remaining in the department."

Lucy returned a wan smile. Her thesis: four years and counting.

So, of course, she had to go on this trip. When she said she'd been nowhere, she'd meant it. Indiana, Wisconsin as far as the Dells, all over Illinois, once down to St. Louis when the big arch was dedicated when she was a kid. Also, Lucy couldn't refuse the *one* thing ever asked of her in years of academic obscurity in this department. Especially with her thesis-extension hearing looming in September. And the fact that she'd been through three different senior advisers. No, there was no choice, politically. She had to go, and she had to succeed.

Lucy also had to go because it would be exciting—a whole other country. And there had been so little excitement in her life that if Lucy had turned this down she would be lying awake for months cursing this missed opportunity for an expenses-paid trip to Great Britain. Besides, she wondered sometimes if her life had the capacity to be exciting, if the years were fated to continue just like the previous ones, safe and dull.

A jolt from the turbulence brought Lucy back to the present.

Between the plane crashing and dealing with Dr. O'Hanrahan, whose ferocious presence Lucy had witnessed in lecture halls a time or two, her body pumped an adrenaline of incessant worry. What if Dr. O'Hanrahan isn't at Oxford as planned? What if he refuses to talk to her? What if he's insane? What if Gabriel's had a bad accident and O'Hanrahan is covering up. . . . Soon enough she would have her chance to learn the answers, Lucy thought as she looked out to see London in a soup of low-lying rain clouds. Oh thank you, Father, Jesus, and Holy Ghost, for delivering me safe and sound!

(No problem.)

Although, then again, most planes crash on takeoff or landing.

(This is not the fighting spirit We might have hoped for, Lucy.)

Touch down. Deceleration. Everyone alive.

Lucy was herded through Her Majesty's Customs and emerged with a minimum of hassle and customs folderol. Her luggage rode the luggage carousel and she grabbed her overpacked suitcase quickly, relieved to see it had come with her, afraid someone would run off with it, still suspicious of this Europe place.

Slowly she apprehended the foreignness of things. The sign: INFORMATION CENTRE. That's right, she remembered from somewhere, they turn around the *er*'s over here. Amid the Urdu and French and German snatches of conversation she recognized her own language, more clipped, sometimes more gracious and formal, sometimes incomprehensible but musical and bouncing. Yeah, she confirmed to herself, they even *look* English. Not all too different from the Irish she grew up with really, here and there. No bowler hats, though. No dreamy indolent boys from Eton, no chimney sweeps out of *Mary Poppins*, no royalty anywhere to be seen.

The signs led her to a plaza, where she discovered it was damp and cold; she congratulated herself on the warm clothes she had brought. And look, there rounding the corner was her first red double-decker bus, its sign announcing Victoria Station. There was a line, which Lucy didn't take notice of as she went to read the small posted schedule—

"Excuse me," said the protectress of the line, "there's a *queue*."

After a dumb second, Lucy joined the silent regiment of waiting travelers at the very back, glared at the whole way.

The bus wheezed into the dock and Lucy bought a ticket with a crisp blue five-pound note and sat by a window so she could look out; an elderly lady sat beside her. When the bus commenced the ninety-

minute trip, the windows fogged up and Lucy persistently used her
sweater shirtsleeve to wipe away a small peephole.

"It'll do that, it will," said the older woman in a whispered voice.

"I'm from America," Lucy explained herself, "I just want to see out."

"Yes, it's rather nice to see out."

That was it. First conversation in Britain.

Well, at least she can tell Judy when she gets back home she made
conversation, made *friends*, talked to people. Lived. It was important
to prove this to Judy, her housemate back on Kimbark Street. Judy
was adamant that Lucy never asserted herself or did anything fun. It
had just about *killed* her that Lucy was chosen to take this trip for the
department.

Her roommate Judy was her best college-era friend.

Both were Roman Catholic, both of them went to the non-Catholic
Chicago University, both were now graduate students, which mystified
their complaining parents. Perhaps university prisoners-for-life was
more like it, living in the grungy student ghetto in that biggest ghetto
of all, the South Side of Chicago. Lucy, after starting out as a classicist,
transferred to theology, specializing in Ancient Languages. No two
worlds could be more distant than the world of St. John's Greek and
the gauntlet Lucy regularly ran to class: the inner-city kids harassing
her, the drunken homeless she must step over or dodge, the brazen
drug deals at every corner obvious to the most naive policeman, the
rape whistle she always carried, the personal schedule of when not to
walk certain places, ride certain trains, be at particular bus stops.

About here her mom's scolding voice interfered with her memory:
"You should be living, like any proper young lady, at home."

To live away from home, according to Mrs. Dantan, as an unmarried
girl meant orgies and fornication. Lucullan banquets, Sodom and Go-
morrah, Lucy in the role of Valeria Messalina, coming home any
day pregnant and unbetrothed. I *wish*, Mom, thought Lucy, I wish.
Anything but the dullness of coming home to Judy. Judy was studying
psychology, which to Lucy was . . . ironic. That was always the way
with psychology students, she had observed, always in need of more
desperate messed-up people to talk to so they could feel like they had
the answers to their own disarrayed lives. No, that was cruel to Judy.
But Judy did undermine her.

"Can I wear your sweater?" she'd ask. "Your hand-knit thing? I
figure we're both about the same size and if it works for you it'll hide
all my flab too."

Judy was always on some form of unsuccessful diet and she was big
on announcing how she and Lucy were sisters in weight problems.
Lucy *was* a bit plump, twenty pounds overweight *max*, Irish-American,
freckled, white-girl plump, but she wasn't the cow Judy was.

"I just wish we hadn't been raised Roman Catholic," Judy would

declaim. "That's why our lives are decades behind other women's."
Judy went on: "I mean, you don't *really* want to be in theology, you're
just doing it out of guilt that you didn't become a nun like your mother
wanted."

Well, yes and no—

"And if we hadn't been raised Catholic, we'd have each had fifty
boyfriends before now. That's why we're neurotic about sex."

Yes, that was another ritual. Over the vegetarian casserole with the
TV local news blaring, drinking skim milk and having first courses of
plain yogurt to be followed by Weight Watchers frozen tuna lasagne,
the endless discussion of men men men. Lucy had never been the type
of woman to think night and day about men since, frankly, very few
guys she'd met had appealed to her. Catholic or not, she found most
men of the species loud and unkind and immature and, decisively, not
interested in what interested her.

Judy: ". . . and Vito Campanella, Gabe's friend? *Hold me back*, for
God's sakes. What a behind on that boy. I wish I could get him to
walk backward."

Judy had the rhetoric of horniness down to a precision not found
in Catullus. If there hadn't been constant sightings of good-looking
men and declarations of their great distance from Lucy, Lucy might
have lived quite happily. As if Judy was some great object of romance.
Okay. *Technically,* Judy was a little bit better looking in the face, though
given to putting on more weight. It was her personality that kept
men away, that and the nasalest, flattest Midwestern drawl. Besides,
Lucy knew that her roommate's true and everlasting love was Paws
the Cat.

Paws the Cat belonged to Judy, and Cattus—once part of a duo,
Felis and Cattus, but Felis got run over—was Lucy's.

"Lucy, I think we have to talk," Judy said the night before Lucy was
to leave on this trip, as if Lucy had a second to waste. "I notice that
you always give Cattus the same dish, but you put down any old thing
for Paws to eat off of. And another thing, why do you serve your cat
first when you dump out the Mr. Kittles?"

Because he's bigger and more aggressive.

"Because you always feed him first."

No, Lucy explained at the time, because if I put down food in Paws's
dish first, Cattus will think it's his and eat it.

"Only because he's used to being fed first."

Lucy was often subjected to Judy meowing, talking cat-talk to Paws.
"Big Cruel Lucy didn't feed yooooo, no she didn't! She doesn't care
if we live or die!"

Yep, that was about the size of it.

(A little more charity would not go amiss, My dear.)

It was just that Judy made her so mad. The first year they roomed together was all right—just all right, nothing brilliant—but this year had become pure misery. Why haven't I moved out? she wondered.

(Do you want an answer to that? You judge Judy for being a psychology major to observe others' distress and feel superior to them, but My child, that's what you do too. Always have. In St. Eulalia you usually gravitated to the girl who was less socially adept than you. Remember your friend Faith? Isn't that the real cause of your resentment of Judy, that you see in her your own faults, your own limitations?)

I don't want to think about Chicago anymore, Lucy decided.

She instead tried to make Berkshire and eastern Oxfordshire a little more like what she had expected. There were expressways and shopping malls and office parks and factories and no abundance of the thatched-cottage villages that she was hoping for. Every once in a while, too far from the highway to inspect, was an old Cotswold-stone church, a sturdy squarish bell tower amid a copse of trees and slate-roofed houses. Because the illusion and its beauty might have dissolved upon a closer look, she persuaded herself of its Englishness as the bus descended into another slight valley.

The road soon became more congested, and the bus leaned through a series of inevitable British traffic circles. Lucy looked at her watch and knew they were almost to Oxford. Lucy was giddy to be somewhere that had been previously confined to PBS specials and the Travel Channel on cable TV back home. The bus crossed Magdalen Bridge and the city of medieval monasteries came into view, its fortress gates, the bell towers and steeples, quaint ye-olde-Englande shops crammed between the stone bastions, bands of boisterous uniformed students gathered outside the Examination Schools celebrating the end of the term and exams with champagne and revelry. . . .

Lucy wanted off the bus so she could explore!

OXFORD
June 20th, 1990

The clouds subsided and the rain-soaked High Street was briefly displayed in the queer off-white, horizontal light Oxford alone seems to enjoy. Lucy stared fondly at the scene: the gradual hill of High Street, the road winding upward and left, fortified on both sides by the palisade of ancient colleges presenting spired, stone facades to the road, the Georgian evenness of Queens College and the isolated statue of some queen, *stylita*, under a stone canopy above the gate.

Lucy groped in her large carpetbag to unearth the guidebook she had bought, ready to decipher centuries of remainders and reconstructions. She walked to the middle of the square formed by St. Mary's Church, All Souls College, and the Bodleian Library. In the middle of the quad this big round five-story dome, the Radcliffe Camera, subject of most Oxford postcards, had been plopped down in the grass, it seemed, merely because it fit. No less impractical was another gate in the wall of All Souls College with its Indian mini—Taj Mahal dome, and two decorative towers shrieking up from the central building beyond it; farther down the street leading from the quad was a mock Bridge of Sighs at Hertford College, across from that there was a Greek Parthenon-like building, next to Christopher Wren's Sheldonian Theater . . . it was like a stone playground full of cherished architectural follies, and everywhere the much-lauded spires, wherever one could be affixed, at every awning and roofpoint.

Lucy felt despondent at being in Oxford and yet not being enrolled there.

She noticed a group of chattering British female students, dressed in shapeless sweaters, drab woollen skirts and black stockings, a fashion sense Lucy could love, but one much helped by an Oxford backdrop. All I got, mourned Lucy, is crummy old Chicago. Yeah, Chicago is a great university, but Rockefeller built a lot of the romanesque, Oxford-like buildings in the 1930s, for Pete's sake, and the local joke is that old John D. proved you could even buy history. But you can't. Because the University of Chicago is dignified and practical and indisputably boring, and Oxford, like history, is silly, impractical, and, she conceded, utterly romantic.

Her map led her to the grim Tudor facade of Braithwaite College where Dr. Shaugnesy had arranged for her to stay. Lucy showed her letters of introduction to the porter, a grumpy red-faced man at the gate, who grunted, looked up at her, grunted, made a phone call no one answered, grunted again, read the letter, another grunt, then put on his glasses in order to be authoritative.

"Can't say I can 'elp ye, miss," he said. "We got the Canadian Lawn Bowling Society in this week and rooms're tight. Ye'll have to take this up with the Bursary. Mrs. Miggins. And I don't envy ye none."

Lucy was given directions to get to the Bursary. Lucy quickly surveyed the square beyond this gate, a three-story quad with an even green lawn with several overlarge signs stating no one was to walk upon the grass. The signs had been allowed to become the most striking thing in this tomblike courtyard. She followed the cobblestone perimeter around the sacred grass until she came to a doorway with the numeral III above it, which opened to a dank passage leading to another square quad, replete with warning signs, a doorway that led to a masters' garden that no one but masters were to use, an outside stairway that led to a library that visitors were not permitted to see. Reminded of *Alice in Wonderland*—written by an Oxford don, Lucy recalled—Lucy finally found another passageway that led to a third and last quad and a doorway with the numeral XIII, The Bursary.

"We simply *cahn't* honor this," breathed Mrs. Miggins, setting down the letter, the pain of all martyrdoms in her voice. *"One,"* she enumerated, "you are here after the Bursary's hours of operations . . ."

Lucy noticed the silver hair plastimolded into an arc up above Mrs. Miggins's head, her gestures, and even the pinched, heartless meting out of the English language were familiar somehow. She's modeling her public technique on Margaret Thatcher, Lucy realized.

Two, there was no notification to the Bursary of a guest room being made ready for Lucy. Three, consequently there was no staff notification, hence a room could not be prepared. Four, perhaps the rooms had been booked for an American garden club that paid dearly to be here each and every summer, for her information. Five, these exchanges with the University of Chicago—who can't just barge in here thinking it owns the place merely because it virtually does—involve some degree of paperwork, which, as Lucy could see, is impossible now since the sign outside *clearrrrrly* states the office hours of the Bursary during which business may be conducted.

"I suppose you Americans think we need but snap our fingers and arrange things like that. See this stack of papers?"

Lucy looked at the five sheets to the woman's left.

"American graduate students applying for a place in the college *to live.* As if we're here to supply that sort of thing! Well, all I will say is that we have quite enough of the Americans, thank you very much, and there will come a time we don't have to use our fine institutions for hotels for Americans merely to meet our economic needs."

"Is there a guest room I could pay for?"

"As if we're a bed-and-breakfast? I suppose you think I have time to ring the lodge and investigate this for you?" Mrs. Miggins collapsed before the ordeal and pushed a single button connecting herself to the main gate. "Go back to the porter," Mrs. Miggins then directed, "and speak to John and he will try to find something for you, and tomorrow, if it will not be too much trouble for you, return to this office *during* the posted office hours and we shall try to undo this . . . this damage."

Lucy returned to the porter and:

1) filled out a form saying she had a guest room key and would give it back,
2) paid a £3 deposit and received a receipt,
3) filled out another form saying she had a doorkey to the college gate and would give it back,

4) filled out another form registering herself responsible for the guest room should any desecration occur in said guest room, and

5) handed over £6.25 for the guest room itself.

Lucy made her way through the quads and passageways to the gloomy, ill-lit Staircase IX. She trudged up to the very top of the groaning old stairs and found a door marked *Guest Room* staring her in the face ... beside a plaque delineating the "Rules of the Guest Room." Lucy turned the key to open the cold, dingy guest room with an old hospital bed and a rusted, dripping sink under a slanted attic ceiling. Oh well, she thought, what else can you expect from thousand-year-old rooms? How romantic! Perhaps a monk copied scrolls here once!

(The quad is 1925 pretending to be Victorian pretending to be medieval, but We're glad you're enjoying yourself.)

Lucy yawned as she sat on the bed and she realized if she put her head down she would fall asleep for hours, never to adjust to Greenwich Mean Time. She grabbed her guidebook with the map and headed out to explore All Souls College and see if Dr. O'Hanrahan was in residence.

All Souls College, she read as she walked: founded 1438 by Henry VI. The only college without students. All Souls is a collection of Fellows, reputed to be the cream of any generation, who gather to drink and talk and not too terribly much else. The test to be one of these elite was formidable. One needed to sit for exams in two of either Law, History, Philosophy, Economics, Politics, Literature, or Classics, submit three excellent essays, translations from an ancient language, and an oral quiz. Some fellowships must be forfeited upon marriage, as in the Middle Ages. And then there's the dining test. If you were bad company or a moron socially, that could blackball you. To hinder your path, a virtual obstacle course of difficult-to-eat foods was served: slurpable spaghetti, escargot with the shell-clamp, small game hen with knife and fork, and a dessert of cherries, which were passed to the candidate to see what he did with the pits. An insular, unaccountable place, All Souls College.

"Excuse me," said Lucy to the porter on duty at the entrance. "I'm looking for a visiting professor here, a Dr. Patrick O'Hanrahan?"

"Oh yes, miss," the porter said, nodding with concern. "The library, I suspect. If he's back from the Infirmary after last night. Or the Senior Common Room, near the sherry cabinet."

I see, thought Lucy, he's living up to his reputation. She had a faint memory of Professor Emeritus O'Hanrahan from her undergraduate days, when she took his Introduction to Hebrew. Dr. O'Hanrahan showed up plastered at the first lecture, telling wild stories of working on the Dead Sea Scrolls and being in Jerusalem in 1948 with bombs falling all around him. Not professorial behavior, but not a soul in the room didn't want to learn Hebrew by the time he was done. The next week a graduate student replaced him and the class returned to the predictable tedium of all language classes.

After a few wrong turns, Lucy asked directions again and was directed to a small door on the side of the quad beyond the chapel. She entered a little, reasonably appointed room of old leather-bound books, antique end tables, and vases. But nothing prepared her for the vista upon opening the next door: The Codrington Library, the greatest Georgian architectural expression of Oxford. A palatial hall paved with a checkerboard of black and white marble, enclosed by three floors of antique books and manuscripts shelved in towering old-fashioned, dark green–stained bookcases. Librarians and assistants climbed perilous ladders to reach the upper shelves, scooted along rickety ledges and railings, while below, symmetrically arranged down the marble avenue, were old scribe's desks, perfect for inkwells and quills and ledgers, with students laboring over modern books in absolute, heavenly quiet. A white-marble statue of some self-satisfied Jacobean grandee faced the students from the end of the long hall, as if to assure this tranquillity.

"May I help you?" whispered a heronlike librarian-lady. "You have to be a registered reader to study here."

Lucy snapped to. "I'm here to find a Dr. O'Hanrahan."

"Oh," she said, focusing unmistakable weariness into the syllable. "No, he is not here this afternoon, nor do I expect him . . ." But then she blanched. Lucy turned and saw a man bolt through the reference area and out into the main hall. It was just a glimpse, but it was Dr. O'Hanrahan, and his presence registered to Lucy as a shock.

O'Hanrahan took possession of a scribe's desk halfway down the cavernous room, and let his books, papers, and a briefcase drop with a thud, which startled the few drowsy students around him. Lucy uneasily edged forward, all the while taking the measure of his fearsome visage:

Patrick Virgil O'Hanrahan was 6′ 1″, around sixty-five years old Lucy figured, balding with a holy man's white hair combed forward and across, the pink excitable face of an unregenerate Irishman, and steely blue eyes that could sear the ignorant and inexcusable. Otherwise, he was standard academic professor-emeritus issue: a potbelly, a good suit now worn and creased around his girth, and even in repose an aura, his own weather-system swirling about him. Lucy recalled his oratorical booming voice that made his lectures legendary and his wrath a thing to be much avoided.

She took a step closer.

His left arm was in a light sling, without a cast or even a bandage to explain its injury. She watched him settle into the Victorian scribe's desk—a tight fit—and intemperately wrench off the sling with his good arm and hurl it to the floor. He slowly unstretched his bad arm, wincing slightly, exercising his five fingers, and then rubbing the injured elbow joint.

Lucy took another step closer.

Without looking up he said in a low tone, "Something I can help you with, my dear?"

"You're Dr. O'Hanrahan, I believe. Sir."

Still without observing her, he asked, "I'm sorry if I misbehaved last night but too much madeira will do that to a man. If the dress is ruined, just drop it off at the porter's lodge here at All Souls and I'll be happy to make reparation or have it cleaned."

"Uh, I believe you've confused me with someone else. I'm . . ."

He looked up, fixing her with a mildly curious glance.

"I'm a . . . here to see you, in fact. Sir."

O'Hanrahan didn't waver. "Short of my having fathered your love-child, young lady, I can't imagine what business we have to detain us longer."

"Lucy Dantan, sir. I'm from the department. I've been sent. To, uh, see how you're doing."

There was not even a minute change of expression as he held her there. "My health is fine, thank you," he said in a still voice. "My arm is a bit sore after last night's tumble in the quad and my stomach is a constant churning sea thanks to British tapwater, but aside from that I am in the golden prime of my autumnal years."

Here, he clambered to his feet, released by the surrounding desk. His voice grew more intense: "Now you know how I am. Now you can go away. Go far away, go back to Chicago, and tell mine enemies to call upon me no more." His white eyebrow arched, his countenance now exceedingly malign. "That clown Shaughnesy sent you, did he?"

"Well, yes sir, I—"

"You tell that impotence, that inconsequence, that imitation of a human being . . ."

Lucy reflected in mid-tirade that Dr. Shaughnesy had engineered the retirement of Dr. O'Hanrahan as department chairman in 1974. For O'Hanrahan's own good, it was said.

". . . that if he wants a piece of this action, thinks for a millisecond—which is surely as long as he can sustain cerebral processes—that the theological find of the century has one pitiful chance in hell of ever ending up in the Department of Theology's Patrick V. O'Hanrahan Library and Research Center . . ."

Lucy further reflected that the cost of unseating Dr. O'Hanrahan as department chairman had been naming the department library after him, which was just, since all of the treasures within it were acquired by Dr. O'Hanrahan. Lucy also noticed she was backing away and he was progressing toward her.

". . . then he is even more of a blackguard, cretin, and charlatan than I already know him to be. Is that clear? Good. Nice to meet you, Miss Dantan, and I hope you have a nice flight home."

"Uh, sir, I need to ask you about Gabriel O'Donoghue—"

As if an electric shock distorted him, he snapped, "*That* is a subject I have no interest in discussing!"

In the silence after this remark, Lucy had occasion to remember the tangled history of her friend Gabriel and Dr. O'Hanrahan. Last fall, to let him earn a bit of extra money and keep some of his office privileges, O'Hanrahan was summoned to Hyde Park to counsel a few students in their doctoral theses. Gabriel was assigned to Dr. O'Hanrahan, and for the whole year this adviser-advisee relationship had been the biggest source of stress in young Gabriel's life.

Gabriel's thesis—one of five topics last year—involved Alexandrian Greek, an O'Hanrahan specialty. Nothing Gabriel wrote, said, or thought suited O'Hanrahan, who thought his advisee was clearly an idiot. Nonetheless, if Gabriel threatened to cancel their monthly appointment, O'Hanrahan seemed distraught and insisted on seeing him. Gabriel once confessed by phone to O'Hanrahan that he hadn't done a lick of work since the last time they'd met, but O'Hanrahan said it didn't matter, they should meet anyway.

At some point it occurred to Gabriel that the old guy was lonely.

Then, out of the blue, January of 1990, O'Hanrahan asked Gabriel if he wanted to be his research assistant. It involved a month in Jerusalem, Rome, Germany, France, England . . . Lucy remembered vividly the savage winter day Gabriel ran over to the apartment to tell her about it.

"Sounds like a great opportunity, Gabe," she said.

"I know," he said, pacing in his hooded winter coat, shaking snow all over the carpet. "But two months with that ogre!"

"He's probably quite sweet underneath," said Lucy. "He must be companionable at some level."

Well, maybe I was wrong there, thought Lucy, back in the present.

She tried again: "Excuse me, sir, but back in Chicago no one knows if your assistant Gabriel is alive or dead—"

"I don't care if he *is* dead. And he's not my assistant anymore, the little Judas." He fixed her with an angry glare. "Now will you leave me be?"

Lucy began full retreat, nodding good-bye, as he stalked back to his desk. A few interested students had attended this scene and she met their glances hoping for a trace of sympathy, but none was there.

Stumbling out into Radcliffe Square again, into the cool damp air on this graying June day, Lucy sat upon a ledge of the domed library building. Her mission was going to be more difficult than she had imagined. And, Lucy wondered, what on earth is Dr. O'Hanrahan going to say when I show up to the Acolyte Supper tomorrow night? Maybe she should have mentioned that.

Oh well.

Feeling exhausted and ready for bed now, Lucy returned to Braithwaite College and her spartan cell. Lucy scouted out the dripping, mildewed toilet two floors below. She brushed her teeth at the sink in her room, discovering that the Hot faucet never yielded anything hot, and that once turned on, proceeded to drip in its discolored basin. Lucy then settled on the stiff, creaking bed, bouncing on it a bit hoping it would soften, and read from her guidebook by the light of the dim-watted bulb. And as tiredness overcame her, she mouthed a perfunctory Lord's Prayer and thanked God for delivering her safe and sound to a foreign land.

(Sleep well.)

"And Holy Spirit," she added, "don't let me be a failure on my one small mission for the university."

(Anything but that, My child.)

Lucy curled up in the rough, clammy sheets and stale-smelling doggy blanket provided for Braithwaite's guests. Not quite enough to defeat the chill. Lucy exhaled a few times, alarmed that she could almost see her breath. She got up and put on her sweater and climbed back in bed.

It was all so English! How exciting it was to be in Oxford!

JUNE 21st

Lucy awoke at dawn, still not adapted to her new time zone. She read some more in her guidebook and then made her way to the shower stall across the landing, a freezing mildewed compartment with a door that wouldn't lock.

Lucy later returned to her room to find a servant vacuuming it and her suitcase gone without a trace. The servant declared repeatedly, "Wouldn't know anythin' about it, love." Lucy, clutching her bathrobe and shivering, passed on the stairway an attractive, tall brunette in a beret, wearing a short skirt with her long legs in magenta stockings, on her way up, holding an empty champagne bottle, perhaps just now coming home from a party.

"I've been moved out of the room upstairs," Lucy said.

"How beastly," said the girl warmly, in a crisp, posh accent. "If he won't let you back in, come knock me up here and I'll give him a proper bollocking for you."

Lucy continued through the quads and confronted the new porter at the lodge.

"So you're the one in the Guest Room," he said accusingly. "We thought you'd gone off without paying your bill. Heh-heh, we've held your things for ransom . . ." With a sweep of his hand, she saw behind him, in the porter's lodge, her carpetbag and suitcase.

"May I have them, please?" she said, entirely annoyed, her teeth chattering with the chill.

Not before paying the £6.25 room bill, and for storing her things, an extra fine of £1, which Lucy grouchily paid to get her things back.

"You should've seen to this bill last night, miss," he mumbled.

"I *paid* yesterday, for your information."

"Is you stayin' tonight?"

"I suppose."

"So you're payin' me now for tonight, aren't you?"

"Are you going to give me my suitcase?"

The porter lugged her suitcase and carpetbag to the door and Lucy frowned at the prospect of carrying them up the stairs again.

"Oh, and miss?" he said. "I suppose you'll be wantin' a breakfast ticket."

She thought about it. Breakfast might be nice. Yes, an English breakfast, scones and richly brewed Earl Grey tea in pewter teapots . . . "How much?"

"That's £1.95, a real bargain, it is."

"Okay, I'll take one."

He pointed to the main stone edifice on the side of the well-groomed quad. "That's Hall right there, can't miss it. Be there at the door at 8:20 on the dot."

Lucy trudged back to her room, dragging her suitcase up the stairway, dressed hurriedly, put on two sweaters hoping for warmth, and ran down the stairs to report at the Hall at 8:20 on the dot. She heard the noises of students filing in, the clattering of plates and silverware, but the door she stood before wasn't open. She knocked, and as there was no answer, she circled the building and found a small, unheralded entrance on the other side.

"And where do you think you're going?" snarled another Dickensian relic, also with bulbous nose and red alcoholic cheeks.

"To breakfast?" she suggested.

"Let's see your 'alf-ticket."

Lucy showed him her ticket, untorn, with a dotted line down the middle.

"Ah, you can't use that."

Lucy met him with an impatient American glare. "Why not?"

"Well, ye didn't post one 'alf of it in advance. We dudn't know ye were coming, now did we? Not if ye don't post yer ticket."

Lucy explained that the porter had just sold her this, and she assumed it was good for breakfast.

"That it is, that it is, but not the breakfast fer today. And besides, 'tis after half past, too late to be seated anyways."

Just fine, thought Lucy, as she fled the portals of Braithwaite some time later and walked into the faint sun of the English morning, guidebook with map of Oxford in hand. Lucy spent the rest of the day sightseeing and snapping photos, half-distracted by the thought of the performance ahead. The Acolyte Supper. For god's sake, let's hope they don't ask me anything.

She started primping at 5:30. She combed out her often frizzy dark-red hair that the English humidity had made limp and oily looking. Lucy wore a conservative billowy black skirt, her one formal change of clothes, black stockings, and a white blouse; not far, she noticed, from the official *sub fusc* Oxford undergraduate uniform. She timidly checked in at the All Souls porter's lodge, punctually at 6:30. She was given directions to a wood-paneled upstairs room, where only three people had arrived.

Along the walls of this study were trophy cases displaying a variety of eclectic things, including three Nobel prizes, a reverend member's pipe, a wager on parchment written in Latin in the 1500s, a silver chalice, each, Lucy imagined, with its own venerable story to qualify for the cabinet. Elsewhere it was an elegant room of fox-and-hounds pictures, a sword above the fireplace, a long, dark-stained mahogany table loaded down with bottles and glasses, and two wordless servants awaiting the guests' pleasure.

"You must be Miss Dantan," said Dr. Whitestone, a tall patrician gentleman in a minister's collar, Anglican Vicar of St. Elizabeth's. "John Shaughnesy wrote that you were taking Father Ratchett's place, yes?" He clasped her hand with clammy fingers.

Relieved, she placed herself in his control and he escorted her to meet the guests. Lucy was introduced to a Dominican brother, Father Philip Beaufoix of Montréal and the American University in Cairo. Father Beaufoix was a short, compact man in his sixties, Lucy estimated, with a soft olive face with a large Gallic nose pitted by a life of convivial drink, which made him seem approachable and wise. Beside him was Sister Marie-Berthe, possibly fifty years old, a Josephine Sister from Québec as well, lately of the Sacred Heart Academy in Toulouse, France. Dr. Whitestone went to fetch a tray of liqueurs.

"Bon soir, mademoiselle," Father Beaufoix said, bowing, then the next moment wondered, "Dr. Whitestone tells us you are somehow associated with Patrick?"

"I'm from the University of Chicago. One of his . . . students, you could say."

"Are you over here," asked the sister, "assisting Patrick?"

"Well, no."

"Working on some book of your own perhaps?"

"Uh, no."

Sister Marie-Berthe glanced anew at Father Beaufoix and suppressed a smile. Oh, Jesus, thought Lucy, they think I'm his *mistress* now.

They moved along. "We're the Canadian contingent tonight," whispered the sister, in a perfect, nasal English. "Whatever tonight I say, Philip, you will agree with me, *non?*"

"Why should I make an exception tonight?"

The door opened and more Acolytes were admitted. Local scholars mostly, Lucy decided. One gratingly fey man, Dr. Crispin Gribbles, was introduced, a man in his late forties with a mouth that formed white foam at the edges. He was a scholar attached to St. Ann's College and was currently cataloguing the relics at St. Aloysius, the most popular Catholic church, he commenced to tell, for all the foreign students:

"Oh, it's dreadful, Vicar," Gribbles was saying to Whitestone. "All the Spanish and Italians and French, on their knees, *weeping*—what a show it can be when these foreign-student groups come through. Fifteen, sixteen years old, first time away from home, can't stand our food, can't stand our weather, so they come to St. Aloysius to weep."

Lucy took a small liqueur glass from the tray. It held a lavender aromatic liquor that seemed to taste of violets. It was called *violette*, explained the sister, a unique libation of Toulouse. "It was my turn this year to bring an aperitif. Each year," she added, "three of us bring a bottle of something extraordinary, with an ecclesiastical past. Three for the trinity," she added.

"Which is not a difficult task," added Father Beaufoix, "since most libation was originated by the Church at one time or another."

"Once, I recall," said Dr. Gribbles, "*dear* Patrick O'Hanrahan brought some moonshine from America, claiming we were to sample the wares of born-again Southern Baptists. Typical O'Hanrahan, I must say."

And speaking of the great man, he had arrived.

Reunited with his companions for this one rare time a year transformed Dr. O'Hanrahan; his blue eyes seemed to be in some afterglow of a dirty joke. He wore a gray crumpled suit with a black tie and Lucy smiled, noting that his top shirt-button had long lost the ability to fasten and the tie was not pulled tight either. Rumpled though he was, what a sight! He hugged his old friends, pinched at Sister Marie-Berthe pantomiming reaching under her habit; his eyes crinkled as he trumpeted his loud war-cry laugh.

Lucy hadn't been detected yet. She was suddenly fearful that he would see her and make a public scene, banishing her from the festivities. Maybe she should defuse the situation by announcing her presence. She crept up on O'Hanrahan, as he and Father Beaufoix were talking:

"Paddy," said the Dominican, "you know you want to tell me what you're after. Don't tell me you're chasing that worthless *Acts of Stephen* again. *Mon ami*, I have fifteen copies of that lying around in my office in Cairo."

"No," said O'Hanrahan, "no such latter-day riff-raff as Stephen for me. Nothing less than one of the Twelve."

Father Beaufoix laughed in O'Hanrahan's face: "Pooh! You don't believe you have found a real disciple's gospel, do you?"

"You'll read all about it one day, Philip, in the newspapers."

Father Beaufoix, despite the smiles, suddenly seemed to Lucy to be unpleasantly needling Dr. O'Hanrahan. "You're sure you are really chasing a lost gospel, dear friend, or is this another one of your schemes to bankrupt your department? I suppose, this research trip," continued the Dominican, patting O'Hanrahan's belly, "just happens to take you to Rome and Paris and every five-star restaurant in between."

O'Hanrahan mustered a good-natured laugh.

"And in any event," Father Beaufoix bellowed, without malice, but offensively nonetheless, "who is going to write your book for you? Don't tell me at seventy years old you will make your literary debut, *n'est-ce pas?*"

"You'll excuse me, Philip," O'Hanrahan said, turning aside to intercept a waiter and his drinks tray but only discovering Lucy.

"Hello again," she said with a weak smile. "Dr. Shaughnesy worked it out so I could attend."

"Lucy, wasn't it?" he breathed, with a trace of annoyance.

"Look, if you want me to leave, I'll leave—"

"Yeah, you can leave."

"I have to say, sir, that attending this banquet would be an unforgettable experience for me."

"What do you know about theology? Do you have a brain in your head?"

"Well, I *am* a grad student at Chicago."

"So I take it the answer's *no*," he brought out.

Lucy justified herself: "I've got a bachelor's in New Testament Studies, a master's in Greek, do a mean Latin, you taught me Hebrew. Those classes you showed up to, I mean—"

"All right, all right, then. Stay."

The *violette* was followed by a contribution from a Greek Orthodox archimandrite, Father Basilios, who was attached to London University.

"This elixir," he announced in a stentorian preacher's basso, "is an ouzo made by the monks at the Most Holy Monastery of St. Nikolas, but one in which a peculiar citrus blossom of the slopes of Mt. Athos has been allowed to steep. Enjoy, my friends, enjoy!"

Lucy took another small glass of a passing tray. "What a collection of liquor," she said politely to Dr. Gribbles.

"If I make it to 2001," he said, "I've been invited for the Night of the Mallard, where the All Souls Fellows gather around a member who is chosen Lord Mallard, enthrone him, and carry him around the quads and rooftops. Then this highly alcoholic evening is punctuated with a draught of punch including duck's blood as an ingredient."

"I think I'd pass on that, sir."

"It's a great honor to attend this, my dear," he added, already tipsy. "Only happens once a century."

Lucy noticed that O'Hanrahan had crossed the room to meet an old friend arriving, the Rabbi Mordechai Hersch, raised in Brooklyn as his accent would betray, currently an esteemed scholar at Hebrew University in Jerusalem. The rabbi, Lucy observed, may well have been O'Hanrahan's age but looked younger, more rested, with a hawk's glance and a trimmed gray beard he stroked in cogitation. The rabbi and O'Hanrahan reminisced and Lucy gauged the rabbi's New Yorker manner, practiced at nailing down inaccuracy or error or imbecility in ways a Midwesterner might find . . . gruff. He wore a conservative black suit and a yarmulke, the sole Jewish ecclesiast among the Acolytes this evening.

O'Hanrahan: "Look who we got here, Morey. A spy sent from Chicago to find out what poor old doddering Patrick O'Hanrahan is up to and bring him home."

The rabbi raised an eyebrow.

O'Hanrahan went on. "She says she'll go away if I tell her the details of our secret mission."

"No such luck, little girl," the rabbi said flatly.

Lucy sighed and said it was nice to meet the rabbi nonetheless.

"Charmed," Rabbi Hersch said indifferently.

There was a hush as it was announced: dinner was served.

Dinner was in the long hall of the Codrington Library. An oak table for twelve guests was laid sumptuously in the middle of the darkened hall, the only illumination being three candelabras. The Codrington had become an eerie vault of shadows against the silent scribes' desks and looming bookshelves. They all were seated, Lucy with Dr. O'Hanrahan to her right and across from Sister Marie-Berthe. A Father Keegan from University College in Dublin had yet to arrive and his place remained empty. A Moslem scholar, Dr. Mehmet Abdullah, sat on Lucy's left. A nondenominational blessing was offered from the Psalms of David.

(Maybe the only safe ground with this bunch.)

"Lord," Lucy added to herself, as the grace was being said, "allow me not to make a fool out of myself tonight."

(Why not? Where men and women gather to discuss doctrinal differences and church politics, what would be more in place?)

Dinner commenced. Lucy eagerly sipped the turtle soup and listened in on the professor and the rabbi talking across the banquet table. A servant meanwhile filled Lucy's wineglass with an amontillado. Later, as the *confit* of duck liver arrived with a Pinot Noir, Rabbi Hersch was sidetracked into a spirited discussion of future Jewish settlements in the Christian Quarter of Old Jerusalem.

"I hear now to my horror," said Dr. Abdullah, to Lucy's left, "that there is a large sentiment among Israelis to tear down the Dome of the Rock and rebuild Solomon and Herod's Temple."

"Mnyeh, just a fanatical handful," the rabbi assured him, having spent the last ten minutes berating Shamir and the Likud administration, the new pandering to the religious right wing. "We're talking about a government that has to check with Lubavitchers in Brooklyn in order to fix the potholes on our highways."

Sister Marie-Berthe spoke up, her Québecois accent loosened with the wine, "I wish they *would* knock down the Holy Sepulcher," she began, determined to stir the archimandrite. "It's a tasteless shambles, all the Christians ever do is to fight over who owns whatever dusty corner of it. Your Greek friends, Father Basilios, do not help matters. I think al-Hakim had the right idea," she added to the amusement of Dr. Abdullah.

"Dr. O'Hanrahan," murmured Lucy, "who was al-Hakim?"

"I'm not here to correct your many ignorances. Go look it up."

Venison followed with cranberries and a light gravy, with native English vegetables, swedes, brussel sprouts, and roasted parsnips, brought around by servants for the diners to spoon from silver trays onto their own plates. This was accompanied by a strong Rhône wine with the aroma of the oaken cask.

"What's this?" Lucy asked, nudging O'Hanrahan, holding a piece of swede aloft on her fork.

"After you look up al-Hakim, you can look up vegetables. It's under *V*."

The "pudding course" followed and Lucy was surprised to see a rich chocolate cake produced instead of what Americans take to be a pudding. Following that, cheese and crackers—"biscuits"—were put out as well as Bibles, many versions, in many languages for the upcoming discussion. Finally, a last pass by the servants produced decanters of port, madeira, sherry, sauterne, Beaumes de Venise. Lucy felt her unfocused glance wander and slide about their intended objects, and she knew she had consumed too much. She kept drinking water, determined not to belie her apparent sobriety.

"Here here," said the archimandrite, banging a gavel, ready to begin the discussion. "St. Paul, as you all know, is our topic tonight. Let us hope that it provides the rancor as did our topic last year, Shi'ite versus Sunni Islam."

Everyone laughed remembering what an acrid evening that had been, considering mostly disinterested Christians were arguing. The archimandrite asked for tolerance, open-mindedness, good humor, and reverence for the scriptures as well as the beliefs of one's fellow Acolytes. Lucy gathered this was a traditional statement of the ground rules. Then a toast followed. Lucy used her water glass and O'Hanrahan sneered to his side, "You're no apostle of mine, that's for sure."

"Let us start," said Father Basilios, "with Rabbi Hersch."

"Thank you, Archemandrite," said the rabbi, settling back in his chair, getting comfortable. "For this opening I thank all my fellow Acolytes. It may be the last word you let me have.

"First of all," he said, "the Apostle Paul is poorly understood by Christians because you have a written record of several Pauls. I can count three of them. You've got Paul the Jewish reformer we read about in the New Testament's *Acts of the Apostles*. Then there's the Paul we read about in the Letters, a sophisticated cosmopolitan man, former Pharisee, Roman citizen, who is inventing before his own eyes a new religion. Then there's the Pseudo-Paul of *Timothy* and *Titus*, which are con-jobs that attempt to discourage the more liberal aspects of the Church the earlier man claiming to be Paul created. Very anti-Semitic, this last guy."

"And misogynistic," said the sister.

"You see, Paul, like Jesus and John the Baptist, was a Nazirene. No, not someone from Nazareth—that is a willful misunderstanding of the Greek. *Nazairaos* is what Paul claims for himself, formed like *Pharisaios*, the Pharisee party. *Acts* itself in 24:5 says the Nazirenes are a sect . . ." The rabbi looked in a Bible he had pre-prepared during dinner. "Paul is characterized as *a ringleader of the sect known as the Nazarenes*. Now, can any of you gathered here think of one ancient movement named after the hometown of the founder? Of course you can't. It's a fact Christians hate to face, but Jesus and Paul are members of a historical Jewish movement."

"An interruption, Rabbi," asked Father Basilios. "If Jesus was not a Nazarene, meaning 'from Nazareth,' where was he from?"

"From Bethlehem. Jesus could never have been accepted to the degree he was if he wasn't one of David's descendants. Remember, tradition says Elizabeth lived in Ein-Kerim, outside of Bethlehem, where *your* Orthodox brethren, father, and the Roman Catholics both have shrines for the Visitation. That makes Mary's Visitation believable. Does anyone here honestly think Mary, pregnant, took a danger-filled hundred-mile donkey ride from Nazareth to Ein-Kerim, across the deserts of Samaria, a hated province, to see her cousin in Nazareth as Luke would have us believe? Ein-Kerim isn't ten miles from Bethlehem, that's more believable."

"And you think," asked Dr. Gribbles, making fast progress through stacks of crackers, leaving crumbs down his front, "Jesus and Paul and John and James the Brother were all of a failed purist sect called Nazirenes."

"*Nazir*. Hebrew for 'separated, special, consecrated.' The Nazirenes or Nazirites were ultra-observant and ascetic. Plus, the movement—like Jesus' ministry and Paul's—included women. It's all in Torah, *Numbers* 6. A Nazirene had to avoid wine, avoid corpses—even if your mother or father died you couldn't come near the corpse. Remember Jesus saying that he who would follow him can have no mother or father? He snaps at his mother Mary when she asks to see him, *Who is my mother? Woman, what have you to do with me?* So that explains the antifamily elements in Jesus. Also, the hair. A Nazirene, once consecrated and shaven, had to keep his hair long, like John the Baptist is described. *Judges* 13:7 tells how Samson is consecrated a Nazirite, and sure enough, when his hair is shorn God allows him to fall to his enemies."

"But," objected Dr. Whitestone, "how do you explain Jesus raising Lazarus from the dead if he was supposed to avoid corpses?"

"Neither *Matthew* nor *Mark*, the earliest gospels, include that miracle. I think it's odd Jesus raises someone from the dead and Mark doesn't find that showstopper worthy of mention. It's a legend that got edited in in Luke's time."

The rabbi smiled as he turned pages in *Acts*.

"Want more evidence that Paul was a faithful Nazirene? Turn to *Acts*, which is brimming with inconvenient evidence for you guys." The rabbi donned his reading glasses: "Paul says in *Acts* 26:5, *according to the strictest party of our religion I have lived as a Pharisee*. Sounds like a good Jewish boy to me. Then, as Torah directs, at the end of his consecration Paul fulfills the Nazirene rites laid out in *Numbers*. Sister, would you read 21:23 for me?"

Sister Marie-Berthe read the passage: "The elders of the Jerusalem Christians tell Paul, I'm reading, *take these men and purify yourself along with them and pay their expenses, so that they may shave their heads. Thus all will know that there is nothing in what they have been told about you but that you yourself live in observance of the Law.*"

The rabbi: "Read a bit further down, Sister."

"*Then Paul took the men and the next day he purified himself with them and went into the Temple, to give notice when the days of purification would be fulfilled and the offering presented for every one of them."*

The rabbi: "This is a Nazirene purification ceremony. Back to *Numbers* 6:18. *Then the Nazirite shall shave his long hair, the sign of his vow of separation. This shall be done at the entrance of the Tabernacle.* You get the idea?" ·

"An inconvenient fact for you, Rabbi," Father Basilios noted. "The Nazirenes forbade all alcohol. The prophet Amos, does he not tempt the Nazirenes of his day with wine? So explain *Drink no longer water, but use a little wine for thy stomach's sake,* which Paul writes in *1 Timothy*. Jesus' Last Supper involves wine, he turns water into wine, et cetera."

The rabbi smiled. "Paul didn't write *1 Timothy*, I think the Last Supper is an addition of the 200s—remember, it doesn't even appear in your *Gospel of John.* The water-into-wine shtick isn't mentioned in *Mark, Matthew,* or *Luke* so it's latter-day, and in any event, Nazirenes could drink when they weren't in their period of consecration."

"What," began Father Beaufoix, "if I grant you that John and Jesus and Paul sprang from a sect called the Nazirenes. What does that prove?"

"It proves," said the rabbi happily, "that the historical Jesus and the Christian Church at Jerusalem never intended to scrap Judaism, but rather wished to enlighten the Gentiles as they thought was their mission. The Law was never to be discarded. *Matthew* 5:17," he quoted, "*Do not think I come to abolish the Law and the Prophets, et cetera, For truly I say unto you, until heaven and earth shall pass away not the smallest letter or stroke shall pass away from the Law . . .* Most of Jesus' ministry is to Jews, and of course there's *Matthew* 10:5, when he sends out his people saying *Go nowhere among the Gentiles and enter no town of the Samaritans,* but go to the lost sheep of Israel."

The vicar said, "That was merely a phase of the ministry. Later Jesus did command his followers to go out among the world."

"Yeah, in those trumped-up resurrection passages I've never believed were genuine. How do you explain that the Twelve after Jesus' death are *not* preaching to the Gentiles? James is still attending the synagogue, right? Paddy, am I mistaken about this? Read the reaction of the disciples after Jesus ascends to Heaven from *Luke*."

O'Hanrahan turned to the end of *Luke*: "The disciples *returned to Jerusalem with great joy and were continually in the Temple, praising and blessing God.*"

The rabbi looked content. "This doesn't sound like a group that is rebelling against the Law. But then Paul starts his travels, starts having his visions. It's Paul that takes this ultraobservant sect and turns it into a new world religion. Paul invents Christianity."

O'Hanrahan concurred, "And the Jerusalem Church, those closest to the historical Jesus, hated Paul for it. Yes, Peter and Paul made peace according to *Acts*, but until the 300s there was a Jewish Jesus Cult, the Ebionites, that reviled Paul and thought he'd ruined everything. Do you remember the smattering of anti-Pauline texts quoted by Clement?"

Father Beaufoix volunteered, "Particularly Epiphanus's discussion of the Cerinthians."

Lucy observed O'Hanrahan glare at the Dominican.

"For 300 years," the rabbi continued, "before a church with the Emperor Constantine's gestapo to suppress the competition, the Early Christian Church is divided on Paul, the Jewish Christians finding him an innovator and self-promoter—the Paul, in other words, most modern Christians acknowledge. I submit, ladies, gentlemen, that it is *you* who for the last 1800 years have followed the wrong vein, followed doctored-up gospels and bogus Pauline letters, and that it was the Ebionites of the early centuries who best followed the tradition of the true Jesus, a rabbi and rebel Pharisee. Every one of you, excepting Dr. Abdullah . . . is in heresy!"

Amid the outcry, he went on provocatively:

"And it hasn't been the same for the Jews since! Dear God above, if you can save your Chosen People from one thing, deliver us from epileptics! Paul, blinded on the road, and we got the Christians. Mohammed, falling on the ground in a fit, and we got the Moslems. Have mercy!"

Dr. Abdullah announced above the din, "Of course it is offensive, you must realize, to attribute Mohammed's vision to epilepsy."

"Dr. Abdullah," pursued the vicar, Dr. Whitestone. "Who is to say epilepsy isn't a receptivity to the greatest of spiritual gifts? Might epilepsy not be God's way of making a prophet?"

"I apologize," said the rabbi, before the discussion was sidetracked, "for any offense, my friend."

Paul's role as defender of the Jewish faith raged on and Lucy excused herself to a small ladies' room to throw water on her face. I am not going to drink this much again, she told herself. And I ought to really try to make a point somewhere in this discussion. It would impress Dr. O'Hanrahan and maybe he wouldn't think I'm such a dolt. Of course, I could say something stupid and prove I *am* a dolt. She soon slipped back in her chair.

"Well, for my money," said Sister Marie-Berthe, "I could stand to lose a few of the bogus books attributed to Paul."

The men stirred, anticipating the drawing of battlelines.

"I love Paul," said the sister. "Rabbi Hersch defends the Paul of *Acts of the Apostles*, but I will defend the Paul of the Letters. The real Paul. Not the chauvinist in those Deutero-Pauline letters, although the insertions, I'll admit, were made by someone in a Pauline school. I suppose we better see if we can get agreement that *Romans* is the real Paul."

There was assent all around.

"Good," she said, thumbing through her Bible, the New Revised Standard Version with its sexism removed. "And can we agree that the epistle of *Timothy* is not the real Paul? No serious scholar these days, surely, would defend *Timothy* as true Paul."

The archimandrite quietly said, "I'm not sure you or our esteemed Jewish friend will get me to admit any canonical letter, even a Pastoral, isn't inspired scripture, sister."

She pursued her point: "Do you as a scholar, *Pater*, think the author of *Timothy* and the author of *Romans* are the same?"

"No, I do not."

"The real Paul," the sister continued, looking in her Bible, "wrote in *Romans* 16:1, *I commend you to our sister Phoebe, a deaconness of the church at Senkrae that you may receive her in the Lord as befits the saints.* A direct contradiction to *Timothy* 2:11, *Let a woman learn in silence with all submissiveness. I permit no woman to teach or to have authority over men; she is to keep silent.* So being a deaconness, contradictorily, is forbidden. You can tell the Crusty Old Bachelor Fathers were getting scared at the liberating implications of Christianity."

Lucy kept drinking her glasses of water. Her head hurt already but she had demoted her roaring-drunk down to tipsy-drunk.

"What, sister, do you intend to do . . ." asked Father Basilios, thumbing back, "about *1 Corinthians* 14:34?" He read: "*The women should keep silence in the churches. For they are not permitted to speak, but be subordinate, even as the law says.* And so forth. *For it is shameful for a woman to speak in church.* Surely you think *1 Corinthians* is Pauline, don't you?"

"Yes, but not that passage. It was added at the time of *Timothy*—"

"You can't just pick and choose what suits you, now."

"Father, may I refer you in the very same letter to 11:4. *Any man who prays or prophesies with his head covered dishonors his head, but any woman who prays or prophesies with her head unveiled dishonors her head.* This you see? Paul in the same epistle refers to women prophesying, which is presumably out loud, and not silent. Your later passage is an interpolation courtesy of the Crusty Old Bachelor Fathers. I would hope, just as no one takes too seriously Paul's edicts on head-coverings, that we could also put aside his sexism, which is just as quaint."

More irrelevancies ensued concerning ridiculous Early Church prohibitions. O'Hanrahan took the occasion to lean over to whisper to Lucy. "I don't suppose you come bearing more financing from Chicago, do you?"

Lucy realized the lure of Mammon might keep the lines of communication open. "Perhaps. It depends on what you're doing. And what you'll tell me."

"Too many people know already what I'm doing," he said, "and I have no intention of getting betrayed again."

"Did Gabriel betray you?"

"Yes. And I'm not going to talk about it."

The servant appeared at Lucy's side again, weary with the water pitcher; Lucy motioned for her to fill it up again.

She found herself staring at Sister Marie-Berthe. International scholar. Holding her own with, well, Crusty Old Bachelor men not unlike the old curmudgeons who wrote the Pseudo-Pauline letters. Where were you when we needed you back in the 100s and 200s? Lucy wondered.

(There were plenty of Marie-Berthes, We assure you.)

"Typical male thing to say," the sister said to the Anglo-Catholic Dr. Gribbles, who had been baiting her on whether female priests were allowable. "Jesus travels with women, ministers to women, liberates women. Suddenly with the invention of the Christian commune, and later the nunnery, a woman can free herself from being a male possession." Hoping to draw in Dr. Abdullah, with an eye to skewering Islam for its treatment of women, the sister asked, "Islam was liberating for women in the same way at first, is that not so, Dr. Abdullah?"

"Very liberating for the time," he concurred.

The sister continued, "Mohammed insisted that women and men were equal under religious law. A woman could sue her husband for divorce as well as a man could sue a woman. Tell me, Dr. Abdullah, what did they do, before the Prophet, with most female children?"

"Alas, they buried them alive, as Mohammed tells in his Holy Quran, Surah 16:60."

(Ah, the tears of Usmaan, later the Third Caliph. In the days before Mohammed he wept only once: when his little baby daughter wiped the gravel and dust from her father's beard, just as he put her squirming into the grave.)

Sister Marie-Berthe chided all the men with a stern finger: "But give the old boys time and they'll knock down all the advances the great men of religion gained for women. You couldn't pay me to be a Muslim woman now, Dr. Abdullah. Women who choose higher education in Pakistan get acid thrown in their face by fanatics at the universities. It's a crime for a woman in Saudi Arabia to drive a car; there are endless examples."

"I do not support what some in Islam have done to women," he began, "but it is difficult, is it not, to determine which traditions are inspired and which are uninspired. The *hadiths*, our traditional codes from the time of the Prophet, may peace be upon him, are half of our religion. The Holy Quran is the other half. Just as in Judaism there is a written Torah, but an oral Torah as well," he added, smiling toward the rabbi.

The rabbi grimaced to have his Torah so near to the Quran, but he nodded graciously back.

"I don't think it's so damn difficult," she said ornerily. "Just ask *me*, I'll tell you what is stupid and not of God."

I love Sister Marie-Berthe, thought Lucy. Where were these nuns when I was growing up? My mother might have gotten her way and I might have joined an order if there had been thinking, independent, activist nuns to emulate.

She let that bit of past history sink in anew.

Yes, my mother would have loved it if I had followed through. It started with my namesake, my Aunt Lucy, my mother's sister. I was the middle of the three girls, and I was named after Aunt Lucy and I was ordained to follow Aunt Lucy, Sister Lucy. I was to be the nun in the family since the intended priest-in-the-family, my brother Nicholas, fled for Notre Dame, then left the seminary for advertising and now lives in New York, comfortably, ecstatically far away from the grind of Dantan family life.

Lucy cringed as a vision returned to her:

She was six or so. Her mother was having a card party with seven other women, the ones in her Cardinal Newman prayer circle. Lucy came in, right before bedtime, in her little Yogi Bear footed-pajamas, and closed her eyes, got down on her knees, and said the Pater Noster for the nice ladies in perfect Latin and they all gave her a little kiss and made over her so much and told Lucy's mother what a little saint she was. And from this rush of approval much of her early childhood took shape, modeled on tales of St. Bernadette and St. Faith and suffering little virgins she could pray to, emulate. At least she stopped short of having conversations with Mary!

(What about Sister Hildegarde?)

Oh Jesus, thought Lucy, her heart sinking further. There was Sister Hildegarde's wake. The woman was eighty-five or so and never taught at St. Eulalia's while Lucy was there, but she had been a presence in that school since its inception. Well, she died. And Sister Miriam, the terror of St. Eulalia's, made an announcement that there would be a prayer service and vigil for Sister Hildegarde and every student who could make it Saturday afternoon between three and five P.M. should attend. As if any kid would spend a Saturday afternoon that way voluntarily!

(But you did, My child.)

Yes. I went. Me and Faith Kopinski, who was more pious than I was. Fourteen years old. I lay in my room for hours, trying to invent a good reason for not going, but I felt God and the Holy Spirit and Mary were watching, and I thought about poor Sister Hildegarde, old and frail and in Heaven now, looking down seeing not one student from the school she'd given her life to, not one willing to do lip service for her. And I went out to play with my sister Cecilia briefly, then I felt bad about it, lied, said I was going to watch TV with a friend, but secretly ran home, got dressed up, and appeared at the chapel where Sister Hildegarde lay. None of the sisters had shown up, though they probably had an earlier service.

(No, they didn't.)

And so I knelt, with Faith who showed up about ten minutes later, and prayed for the soul of Sister Hildegarde, whom I didn't even know, but I wanted her to be . . . prayed for. No one should go without some degree of—Lucy didn't know what word she wanted exactly— ceremony, valediction. Oh please, she thought, coming to, sick at such ripe, uninhibited piety.

(But there is no earthly good purer than the goodness of children.)

Lucy looked up, ending her reverie, to see an ancient, white-haired, kindly-looking man rush into the room in his raincoat and hat, ranting voluminously, while the others at the table stopped talking to welcome him.

"Jesus, I've missed the buckin' meal," Father Keegan mourned. "Awww 'tis me last time on that eeirline, I swear! I could've swum meself over the Irish Sea in the time that took. Gatwick was close to me vision of hell!"

Sister Marie-Berthe consoled him, "Yes, Father, but there's still drink on the table."

Father Keegan, before taking off his coat, grabbed the decanter of port to the amusement of all and poured himself a glass prior to claiming his seat. "Aye, the bounty of God before us here. What's in that bottle beside you, Paddy?"

"Beaumes de Venise, Father," said O'Hanrahan.

"Ey, scoot it over here, m'boy, and be quick about it!"

The discussion recommenced after the father's jolly display. If only the men in her family, thought Lucy, had an *ounce* of a sense of humor about their drinking. Often, Lucy had theorized, the sense of humor was the first thing to go in an Irish person once he or she got to America. The drinking and the religionizing certainly crossed the Atlantic undiminished, that's for sure.

"I'm telling you, Paul was not antiwomen until the Early Fathers of the Church made him so," said Sister Marie-Berthe, still arguing. "And I'm sure Miss Dantan here would agree with me!"

Lucy noticed O'Hanrahan was looking askance at her, sizing her up. "Excuse me, Dr. O'Hanrahan," she mumbled, "I wasn't listening. What was being discussed then?"

"The place of women in the Early Church," he whispered back, stifling a yawn. "What has been discussed for the past hour, it seems. Damn feminism."

"Well, it could be argued," began Dr. Abdullah, "that Paul knew next to nothing of Christ's teaching or opinions. He celebrates a conceptual messiah rather than the Jesus that existed. He says himself he went away for three years to think it all over, and purposefully didn't go to Jerusalem to talk to those who knew Jesus. Somewhere in the *Romans Letter, We do not know how to pray as we ought—*"

"Eight . . . 8:26," said the archimandrite.

"Think of it!" Dr. Abdullah continued politely. "Paul had not even heard of the Lord's Prayer."

"It is true that there are few direct quotes of Jesus in Paul," conceded Dr. Gribbles, who had been quiet this evening since annoying Sister Marie-Berthe, and who, having demolished all breadscraps, seemed not to be able to eat enough crackers, having begged everyone else's. "However, the gospels had not been written yet so what could Paul have read about Jesus? And in *1 Corinthians* 11:24, he quotes Jesus at the Eucharist."

"That's open to a lot of questions," said O'Hanrahan. "Paul quotes Jesus, 'Do this in remembrance of me.' Professor Jeremias back in the '30s proved, quite convincingly, the words in this passage were too modern for Paul. And of course, none of the gospels includes 'Do this in remembrance of me.' "

A number of clerics, including Dr. Gribbles, scurried to their Bibles, momentarily unsure that the most familiar sentence of the Last Supper, the centerpiece of the Christian ceremony, was indeed absent in *Matthew, Mark, Luke,* and *John.*

"Now we know," said O'Hanrahan, pleased with himself, " 'Do this in remembrance of me' was inserted into some Lucan manuscripts, once the Church increasingly fell in love with the symbols of communion, which, like confession, made their way from Persia. So in the 100s, 'Do this in remembrance of me' was inserted in some *Luke*s. But that suggests to me that it was also inserted at the same time into Paul, Dr. Whitestone. I'm not so sure Paul *really* knew about the Eucharist. I'm not even sure what Jesus may have thought of it, being principally antiritual."

The rabbi smiled. "*This is my body, which is for you,* says Jesus except there is no Hebrew or Aramaic equivalent of 'which is for you.' Which means it was originally Greek, and not spoken at any rate by Jesus."

"Ah," said Father Basilios, "but Jesus did speak Greek. He quotes the Septuagint. He preached in Gedara and in the Greek-speaking Decapolis."

"The point I'm making is that the Christians," added the rabbi sanguinely, "have nothing original. In *Genesis* 14:18 we see the Eucharist prefigured in Melchezidek, not that any of you know your Pentateuch. I think the Christian Eucharist is contemporary with *Hebrews,* which shows the early cult of Melchezidek, who is declared immaculately conceived in the New Testament, weirdly enough. An addition of the Second Century."

"Like the Cross and crucifixion itself," suggested Dr. Abdullah, to much objection and interested laughter.

Dr. Gribbles cleared his throat and took objection: "It seems to me that Paul does know a good deal about Jesus the man, more than our distinguished imam would admit. Christ's meekness is alluded to. Not a common trait for a messianic figure of that time. And Paul is certainly aware of the crucifixion. *Jews seek signs, and Greeks seek wisdom, but we preach Christ crucified. 1 Corinthians* 1:22."

"Odd you should use that one," said O'Hanrahan. " 'Jews seek signs.' According to all the gospels, written after Paul, Jesus *did* perform signs, healings, miracles. Paul doesn't seem to know about any of the miracles."

Dr. Abdullah shrugged serenely.

O'Hanrahan pursued, "As for crucifixion, Paul in more dependable texts isn't always so clear. Dr. Gribbles, do you have the RSV there?" O'Hanrahan fumbled for his reading glasses. "*Romans* 4:24," he requested.

Father Keegan, warmed by his speedy consumption of four ports, leaned over to his book and read it aloud: "*It will be reckoned to us who believe in him that raised from the dead Jesus our Lord who was put to death—*"

"Ah ah," said O'Hanrahan. "We all know what the Greek is."

"*Paredothi,*" said Lucy, debuting.

There was a brief acknowledging silence that she had spoken.

"Yes, *paredothi,*" confirmed Father Basilios.

"Which does not mean 'put to death.' " O'Hanrahan continued. "It is the same verb in *1 Corinthians* 11:23." He flipped the pages. "*Lord Jesus on the night he was betrayed took bread . . .* The word there is *paredidoto* and does not mean betrayed. The verb *paradidomi* means 'delivered up.' "

The rabbi interrupted: "As in the Septuagint *Isaiah,* the Suffering Servant is 'delivered up,' taken away."

O'Hanrahan went on: "Christians keep translating this word however they please—killed, crucified, betrayed, but Paul and parts of all four gospels in numerous places don't necessarily say those things. The original says 'delivered up.' Which is far more vague concerning the historical Jesus' death."

Dr. Abdullah with a half-smile suggested, "Perhaps the true interpretation is 'delivered up to Heaven.' As I was about to say a moment ago, Moslem scholars, myself included, believe *Isa Mesih,* the Prophet Jesus never went to the Cross but was assumed directly to Heaven. Maybe early texts of Paul, before all the later Christian alterations, confirmed the Prophet Mohammed's teachings about Jesus' death."

"Nonsense," said the archimandrite patiently but firmly. "Jesus most certainly went to the Cross and was later assumed."

"A lot of early Christians," began O'Hanrahan, "did not think so, *Pater*. The Basilidians and the Carpocratian gnostic sects."

"This was a Corinthian heresy too, along these lines," said the sister unsurely, then gaining confidence. "Wasn't that true?"

"Right," said Father Beaufoix, always ready to tangle with the know-it-all orthodox. "Your own Orthodox scholar Photius, as late as the 800s, had come across texts attributed to some of the apostles containing the story that Christ never went to the Cross, but was rather . . . delivered up. For such a heretical idea, it certainly has had a long life."

"Why bother being a Christian," said the Anglican vicar with distaste, "if you don't accept the sacrifice of the Cross?"

Dr. Abdullah was insistent: "You think Christ has no meaning unless there is a cross and God's prophet is put to death? Look at the shambles Catholicism—apologies, Sister, Father—has become: all tears and wounds and sacred hearts and suffering and bleeding statues. What has that to do with how to live and love God and help our fellow man, hm?" Dr. Abdullah folded his arms and leaned forward on the table, having everyone's attention:

"No, the Moslem has no part of the Cross, and nor did the Early Christian church. Moses, David, Elijah, Elisha, Mohammed—God does not allow his chosen to be crushed by his enemies! I assure you, vicar, some 800 million Moslems worldwide are quite edified by Jesus' teaching and not the heretical addition of the Cross, sometime, we think, like the 'Do this in remembrance of me,' in the Second Century. The Cross heresy so angered Mohammed, we read in al-Waaqidi, that Mohammed destroyed everything he could find with that symbol of error upon it."

Lucy felt brave enough to ask, "Dr. Abdullah, excuse me, but I thought there was a crucifixion in Moslem teachings."

"Oh, there was a crucifixion but Jesus did not suffer it. Simon the Cyrene or perhaps Judas himself, say some traditions. Surah 4:155. Uh . . . it's difficult in English . . . *Yet they crucified him not, but had no more than his likeness . . . No sure knowledge did they have of Jesus,* and on and on, *they really did not slay him but God took him up to Heaven.* In the traditions, it is thought a spy sent to entrap Jesus was crucified instead. No one *good,* surely, was crucified in his place."

"Let's hope not," said Dr. Whitestone lightly tapping the gavel, concluding the discussion, "or it should spoil our dessert."

Everyone pleasantly rose and walked slowly to the adjoining common room where dessert would be served with renewed, plentiful decanters of port, sherry, madeira, the chilled sauterne, chocolates and pastries, and brandy and cigars.

"I thought we *had* dessert," Lucy asked O'Hanrahan as they walked to the next room.

"That was pudding, this is dessert. Look it up in the encyclopedia."

"Yeah, yeah."

The rabbi pulled aside the professor. "Paddy," he said, "why don't we make a break and talk strategy with Keegan, hm? Leave Mata Hari behind?"

Father Keegan sidled up to O'Hanrahan and the rabbi, looking put out.

O'Hanrahan asked the Irishman, "Can't they get you anything from the kitchen, Father?"

"Of course not, not here in England. Kitchen's closed and rules are rules."

The rabbi suggested, "I think our fellow Acolytes will allow us to slip away to a pub and get the poor man something to eat, don't you, Patrick?"

"Why certainly," said the professor, matching the arched tone of the question. O'Hanrahan deigned to recognize Lucy. "Well, Lucy dear," he said, "we are going to fetch some victuals for Father Keegan and have a pint of something good for us."

"Aye," said the priest.

"So we'll be back in an hour or so, all right?" O'Hanrahan announced rather than asked. "And we'll talk then about many mysteries of the One True Church, hm?"

Lucy nodded numbly. "Yeah, okay. I'll be with the others."

Lucy returned to the paneled room they'd had drinks in earlier and she let her hand run along the wall to steady her. Too much alcohol. She used to be able to hold her booze but those were undergraduate days and since she was twenty-five or so she had cut back the boozing to nothing. First, alcohol went straight to her hips and belly and that was reason enough. The second motivation for abstinence was her father had become a worse heavy drinker as his recent retirement progressed. Not quite an alcoholic, she supposed, because he never fell down drunk or passed out, but he drank continually and the only thing worse than Mr. Dantan after a few stiff ones—obnoxious, spiteful, hypercritical, cynical, disapproving—was Mr. Dantan sober.

Lucy's mind flashed over a number of times in a traffic jam, at a family function, at a parents' day "thing" at St. Eulalia's, that her sisters and brothers and mother danced lightly around Dad because one wrong comment would be the detonation, the match on the gasoline that would create a scene and mortify them all. Lucy's mother would then rush her father home by way of a tavern and the pressure would be alleviated, meltdown contained. He was the same way about his food. Not on the table when he got home at five from the stockyards?

Hell would be unleashed, torrents of abuse, declamations of the insufficiencies of Mrs. Dantan, his children, how no one did any real work except him, no one contributed anything except him . . . and then like some dumb animal, he would be fed, and then he'd be all right.

Now that her dad had retired he had become a nuisance all day around the house instead of just at night, taking charge and "supervising," declaring that no wonder nothing got done given the worthlessness of the family, and thank God above he was there now to make things right. I have never, thought Lucy, regretted for a nanosecond moving out of that house and to Kimbark Street.

Forty minutes passed.

After enough small talk and conversation with the others, who were not so terribly interested in her life or her thesis, it seemed to be certain that O'Hanrahan had escaped.

"Dr. Whitestone," she asked. "Did Dr. O'Hanrahan tell you where he and Father Keegan were going?"

Dr. Whitestone looked wrily at her and Lucy gleaned that the O'Hanrahan's-mistress-misconception had made the rounds, courtesy of Father Beaufoix. But he answered, "Those fellows always finish these affairs by an appearance at the Turf Tavern."

Lucy got directions, buttoned her coat, and went out into the drizzle, walking under the mock Bridge of Sighs spanning the medieval street leading to New College, founded 1379. She backtracked and saw students slipping between two buildings down an alley not two yards in width. There was a streetsign: ST. BRIDGET'S PASSAGE.

She went down this alley past a streetlamp perfect for a Victorian Sherlock Holmes movie set in the fog, then turned to see the Turf Tavern come into view at the bottom of a slight hill, surrounded by the backs of Oxford townhouses and college buildings on all sides. The pub was a 13th-Century beam-and-plaster building with a ceiling less than six feet tall one must duck under, while outside there were picnic tables and stools where students gathered to warm themselves on this chilly spring evening before roaring fires. The pubyard was at the foot of the old city wall; the firelight cast ghastly, pagan shadows along the gray rotted stones and Lucy, squinting, sensed some former past-life, perhaps, amid the camps of Alfred with tomorrow a battle against the Danes to face.

After peering in various nooks and crannies, she discerned Dr. O'Hanrahan, wilder and more obviously inebriated, Rabbi Hersch, and Father Keegan, all being amused by one of Dr. O'Hanrahan's booming renditions of a tale:

". . . and *that*'s why," he was saying through hoarse laughter, "I never fail to go to Mulligan's when in Dublin, Father!"

"Ah," said the priest, "they did their duty by ye, m'boy. Carryin' ye all the way back to Dun Laoghaire like that. Just be sure you don't disgrace yourself before Father Creech and those bastards when you get over there."

O'Hanrahan nodded, "Don't worry, I'll be on my best behavior if it means getting the scroll . . ." He noticed Lucy and aborted this line of discussion. "Why, look! My darling daughter! Come to see your old papa!"

The Irish priest stood to shake her hand. "Why, Paddy, I'd no idea! Pleased to meet you, I'm Father Keegan."

"I'm *not* his daughter, Father."

Father Keegan looked mournful. "Aw Paddy, Paddy, at your age . . ."

"No," she snapped, "not the mistress either."

O'Hanrahan gleefully: "She's a spy from Chicago. She's the CIA."

"Lucy Dantan, Father."

"You can sit with us, lassie," said O'Hanrahan, "if you drink a pint of this heavenly brew."

"Oh, I don't think I'd better drink anything else—"

O'Hanrahan: "Then go away and haunt our revels no more!" O'Hanrahan thrust two pound coins into Father Keegan's hands. "Whadya think, Father? Dogbolter or Headbanger?"

"She's a wee one, Paddy. We'll start her off on Headbanger."

After Father Keegan's departure, Lucy turned to the rabbi while her drink was being fetched. "Don't you ever, Rabbi sir, show the effects of alcohol?"

"Never," answered O'Hanrahan for him, "he is the Hebrew Socrates. Drinks all night and never seems drunk—nay, he even gets more lucid, damn him. Whereas I . . ." O'Hanrahan was a bit unsteady as he matched his florid speech with ample gestures. ". . . get more colorful and ribald." He said the last word "ribbled" like the English say it.

"Sit still, Paddy," said Rabbi Hersch, pulling him back into the chair. "You're ribald enough without any help."

"Found your way, my dear, down St. Bridget's *passage*, did you?" O'Hanrahan asked it with a prurient emphasis. "St. Brigit, Virgin of Ireland, Morey," he went on. "Ne'er a man was there who e'er went down her passage, aye begorrah."

"Jesus, the Irish accent we're getting now," said Rabbi Hersch. "Now you know we're in trouble."

Father Keegan returned with her pint of Headbanger. "Here you go, m'dear. Now ye be careful with that."

Lucy sipped it to be polite, finding it soapy and strong. But not . . . not bad tasting, exactly. Well, she must drink this, really. English beer is very esteemed, even though it's warm and nauseating. I can't tell Judy I didn't have drinks at a ye olde English pub, now can I?

"Yes, good old Mulligan's," mused O'Hanrahan. "Shall we meet there, Father Keegan? Before our special mission!"

"Give us a call at the parish, 'fore ye depart, Paddy."

What mission? thought Lucy, remembering her own. Elsewhere in the pubyard, a band of young men in rowing sweatshirts and sweatpants whooped it up as one of their crewmen exposed his behind, before falling off his picnic table, insensibly drunk.

"Ah, to be in England," said O'Hanrahan.

Halfway to the bathroom, one of the spindlier rowers stumbled to a wall and threw up everywhere in the path.

"Ah, to be in England!" repeated O'Hanrahan. "Now it's your round, Lucy, dear Lucy the daughter I never had! Cordelia to my Lear, Ruth to my Naomi!"

The rabbi cackled for the first time all evening.

Father Keegan hid his laughter as O'Hanrahan warbled, "Go get us three of the same, O daughter mine, blossoming flower of mine seed . . ."

Lucy, feeling green herself, particularly after watching the boy over there get sick, steadied herself on the back of the priest's chair and aimed herself toward the pub building.

That's it, she thought, no more drink, not for me.

Lucy staggered into the hot, smoky pub and waited in the line to get her order. When she returned with the pints . . . the table was empty.

They'd gone and stiffed her.

"Hello there!" called a female voice.

It was the tall girl Lucy had seen earlier that morning with the beret and magenta stockings. She was sitting at a picnic table by a roaring fire surrounded by four young men, three of whom were moving on to a "drinks party," or so they announced. The tall girl waved Lucy toward her and Lucy got a closer look at the clear-featured handsome young man with rich black curls that hung before his eyes.

"Do you want these pints?" Lucy said instinctively.

Lucy set them down and joined the table.

"I'm Ursula Crewes," said the tall girl. She didn't introduce her brooding companion. "You're Julian's American friend, aren't you?"

Lucy paused long enough for Ursula to rush right in:

"You simply *must* come to Tessa's party—there'll be *stacks* of drink, I swear. There, I've done it. Everyone thinks I'm an utter selfish bitch, but I've just proven I'm not. You simply *must* come."

"Well I—"

"Oh, besides, it will terrify Alex when he gets back from London after the break! When he hears we've been friendly, comparing notes, saying horrible things about him, which we must. I'll go first. He's a dreadful lover, really he is. Too drunk or too quick, though maybe you have found the golden mean that eluded me . . ."

Lucy should have been correcting the mistaken impression that they had mutual friends, but Ursula was intensely devoted to what she was saying.

"No, there wasn't *much* between us; I just made a beastly fool of myself, threw myself upon him at the St. John's Ball. I was an *utter* slag-whore, I admit that! Oh he surely told you; I can't believe he's that gentlemanly, not to gossip about me."

"Well, actually—"

"You might as well call in later," Ursula said, "because the party's on our staircase and you'll be kept awake anyway."

"You can have parties all night in Braithwaite?"

"Heavens no, but Jim the porter's on duty tonight, always dead drunk, never susses. Three quads away. Well, we're off!" Ursula stood with her male admirer and reiterated the invitation kindly before sweeping her friend along toward St. Bridget's Passage.

That left Lucy alone with one pint.

"Still givin' 'em away, pet?"

She turned to see a young man with dark-blond, close-cropped hair, leather jacket, a T-shirt that had a caricature of Margaret Thatcher and something about FUCK THE POLL TAX.

"Sure," said Lucy.

The young man left his nearby table and sat at hers. "American?" he asked.

"Yep. From Chicago. My name's Lucy."

He was Duncan from North Shields, that was up north where no tourist ever went so he didn't expect her to know about it. Lucy was thrilled with the singsongy way he talked, up and down as if each sentence ended in a question. Had she heard of Newcastle, near where he was from? No, Lucy hadn't.

Duncan then asked, "How do you know Ursula?"

"I don't know her at all. She thinks she knows me from somewhere, I think. I'm staying in the guest room at Braithwaite and her room's on the same staircase."

" 'Tis the fuckin' end of civilization, that place." Duncan in a few swallows had drained the pint of beer.

"What college do you go to?"

"Braithwaite, so I knay what I'm talkin' aboot." Duncan suddenly patted Lucy on the knee. "Whadya say, pet? Fancy a kebab?"

Lucy was having trouble deciphering Geordie: he wants a bob? Which is some kind of coin, right? She reached into her suit jacket and produced a pound coin.

"Champion! Let's set out then . . ."

Lucy was led from the tavern, up the narrow alley and into Radcliffe

Square, which had been her main landmark. The scenery took a moment to settle when she looked at it—she was really hammered. The dome of the Radcliffe Camera and the spires of All Souls were surreal in a bluish light from the moon; there were millions of stars. She really ought to get to bed. Go back to the guest room and drink five glasses of water, take some aspirin.

"You're the first American I think I've ever talked to. I don't even like your bloody country. Not one decent band anymore."

"Who do you like?" asked Lucy, stung at having her country abused.

Duncan named half a dozen one-indie-hit wonders and Lucy lamely said she'd heard of a few of the bands but didn't know them well. Her last British record purchase was a Phil Collins cassette.

"Well, you can have him."

Lucy appraised Duncan out of the corner of her eye. You suppose this guy *likes* her? Lucy thought it over. A little short for her, a bit rough looking. But suddenly the idea of a rough boyfriend from the mean northern streets appealed; those late-movie British black-and-white '50s Kitchen Sink films starring Laurence Harvey replayed in her head. But she'd just met him! Well, she'd have to say no, cute accent or not. Well, why would she *have* to say no, come to think of it.

"Saw you talking to those wankers," he said, meaning Ursula and her friends. "God, I despise Braithwaite. Sodding snob-collection of public school gits . . ."

Lucy asked, if he disliked Oxford so much, why he was here.

"Maths. And they give me money to come, so I couldn't say nah. Fuckin' boring subject. Can't help it that I'm good at it, now can I? Better keep me voice down," he added, as some rowdy young men passed by across the street, "if I don't want me head kicked in."

Lucy deciphered as they walked. "There are students who'd beat you up just for how you talk?"

"No, the townies. Pulverize any bloke from outa toown, they will. Beat up the students. Not that ya blame 'em there. Not that ya blame 'em at all. We're a-taking our life in our hands coming out now; England's played Sweden tonight, qualifying round."

"Soccer?" Lucy guessed.

"Aye, football." Duncan surveyed the city streets, dead from pub-closing time after eleven. "Ah, shouldna worried. Closed down like a friggin' typical tomb, Oxford is." He scanned the High Street. "Now the van is usually here."

They decided to try St. Aldate's Street in front of Christ Church College, imperious as a prison, heavily presiding in the spotlights.

"But mostly," Duncan rambled on, "Oxford's fuckin' boring. Ah, if ye're like Ursula in the Tessa the Bloody Cow set and made of fuckin' dosh, it's allreeght for ya, otherwise this town's got fuck-all for titillation."

They spotted the van: AHMED'S DONER KEBAB.

Lucy approached the simple vending truck with its giant slab of lamb meat on a vertical spit. There was a line of three people waiting— a skinhead, a drunken damned-looking young man sniveling sadly in a stained tux, a pink-faced burly guy in a sweatshirt blazoned with the Guinness logo. All drunk. What an odd collection of humanity is Oxford, thought Lucy. Duncan guided her through the kebab-ordering process. Ahmed himself, a friendly Pakistani with bad skin, parted a pita bread and filled it with salad, tomatoes, onions, hot sauce, ground cheese, and some slivers from the giant cylinder of meat. Lucy gave him two pounds in return.

Lucy and Duncan talked some more and ate their kebabs as they walked back to the Braithwaite gate. Lucy heard herself tell Duncan some outrageous things . . . she knocked her age from twenty-eight down to twenty-three when Duncan said he was twenty-one . . . she said something about being Dr. O'Hanrahan's assistant, traveling the world over, chasing lost gospels across the Middle East . . . she had invited Duncan to come to visit in America and she said she'd help him pay for it. . . .

"You allreeght, lass?" he asked her, looking concerned.

Lucy discovered she was sitting on a damp stone wall. She felt worse than bad.

"You're gonna toss that kebab, I can tell."

"I'm perfectly fine," she said.

The last thing she said before she blanked out.

JUNE 22ND

Lucy awakened and felt ill. There were bells making a lot of unnecessary noise, too many for too long in the established Oxford fashion. She turned over and closed her eyes hoping she might retrieve her sleep.

No.

How does O'Hanrahan do it? she wondered, slowly lifting a hand to her pounding head. Apertifs in the paneled room, all that wine, the Headbanger at the Turf, and that kebab thing she ate . . . My God. Did she throw up in front of the one cute British guy that had given her five minutes of time? Lord, speak to me and assure me no, no . . .

(Yes, yes.)

Okay, she decided, maybe I'll just die in this bed. It was the most she'd drunk since a Theology Department party her freshman year. No wonder they close the pubs at eleven, she thought, if this is how they drink *until* eleven. It must be noon, thought Lucy.

(It's 7:45 A.M.)

After a merciless visit to the toilet to be sick, she dragged herself achingly to the bed, hoping to still her stomach and the revolving room. Two hours later she awoke again, only then knowing she had slept again. She dared herself to raise her head, and finally put feet to floor and stood up slowly.

From that act, Lucy risked standing on her bed to peep out her high window in the slanted attic roof of the Braithwaite College guest room: a gray and rainy morning. She opened the window for needed fresh air and listened to the British noise, extracting meaning as only a first-time tourist can do; the rain had a foreign rhythm, the snatches of British conversation, the European ambulance siren song, the rumble of trucks with differently revving engines.

She combed her hair, pulled on a sweater, and looked for a time in the mirror and thought: I am on the verge of failure. I can't report anything back to the department on O'Hanrahan's project, and I don't have a clue what has become of Gabriel. During the brushing of her teeth she felt an imminent nausea so she scurried to lie down again.

She fixated on the ceiling, sighing. Gabriel O'Donoghue.

Gabriel was in her kindergarten class back in Bridgeport, born and bred there like herself. He was a crybaby, she remembered, a weepy, pious Catholic boy who went through "phases." A rebel, a pious altarboy goody-goody, then getting in trouble for hitchhiking to Milwaukee, then announcing he was going to take vows as a priest, then for eleventh grade wearing an earring and being a hippie, then wanting to be an actor his senior year.

Lucy and Gabriel were reunited at St. Eulalia Catholic High School for four years, then Gabriel started seminary at Notre Dame, then dropped out, then went back to South Bend for a degree in geography, of all things, then applied for grad school at Chicago. He was bright, he was cute—though Judy disagreed—and Lucy had a crush on him when she was younger. He was tall and olive-complexioned, his eyes were very big and sad, and something about his hands turned Lucy on. There was something so unlikely about Gabriel as a sexual partner that Lucy thought about it all the time. Against all advice and her own inclinations, she had felt affection for him creep back as they spent their gradschool years together in Hyde Park.

"I don't see Mr. O'Donoghue making a woman very happy," Judy said not too long ago, "if you know what I mean."

He's had girlfriends, Lucy had said defensively.

"Yeah, and they were *just* friends," Judy went on. "Gabe seems to be the only one who doesn't think he's a fairy."

Fairy, thought Lucy. The prejudice as tired and old as that terminology.

"Christopher has more of a chance with Gabriel than you do," Judy concluded.

Christopher was a mutual friend in the department. A gentle, wispy Catholic boy—boy, hell, he was twenty-five for God's sake—who was even more timid and reedy than Gabriel, pretty in photographs but his lack of strong facial features made him less appealing in real life. Gabriel was always animated around Christopher, whom Lucy never could get to say enough to prove his being intelligent or stupid. Lucy would try to make Christopher say a few sentences in a row but often as not the result was Christopher saying, "*You* know what I mean, Gabriel. We were talking about it the other night."

Judy redux: "Gabriel may not know it himself but he wants to screw Christopher. You better watch it, Luce. You don't want to end up a fag hag."

Now that was just *typical* of Judy.

So supremely sure of what "category" a person was. Well, some people like Gabriel and, for that matter, herself, resisted such simple definitions. Gabriel was just unsure of himself and some day, Lucy figured, both of them at some unspecified, unpredictable time would stumble into some form of romance. Okay, that was a bit vague for a romantic wish, but that's what she wanted, that's what she'd hedged her bets for. For several years now.

(But that was not your only interest in Gabriel.)

No, there was an arrangement they'd discussed in the late hours of the night that Judy must never hear about—the ridicule would be endless. Lucy sort of envied Gabriel for deciding to join the Franciscans last year. At least, he belonged somewhere. There were so many important works to undertake and with the support of an order, think how rewarding it all could be. Lucy had suggested that she might be a Poor Clare and maybe she and Gabriel could start a homeless shelter together, a clinic for inner-city kids, maybe an AIDS hospice.

(There was nothing ridiculous in any of those ideas.)

But Lucy, upon continuing with grad school after her master's, had staked out a different path—she would never be a nun now. Being a nun meant defeat. It meant surrendering to Mother and her maiden Aunt Lucy and the Holy Roman Church and all the abominations of nunhood at St. Eulalia's Catholic High School. That's all the Church could proffer a woman: obedience, subjugation, humility, submission to God in Heaven and the Crusty Old Bachelor Fathers while on this earth.

"Women who become nuns," pronounced Judy, "are just scared of sex. They're like the invalids of the last century who took to bed rather than get out there and take control of their life. Or they're all lesbians."

God, Judy got on her nerves.

The truth of it was this: if Lucy was going to ditch a religious vocation, she should have made the break at eighteen when there was still time to exploit her youth to the fullest, for travel, for adventure, for men. I had one foot in and one foot out of the secular world, she realized, and the years began to fly by, 24, 25, 26 and I had missed out on too much life. Each year would pass and I would say, Okay girl, *this* year it will all change. And each year it never happened. I might as well be a nun for all my proximity to normal life, Lucy pined, a life most women take for granted. If I'd met Sister Marie-Berthe from the Acolyte Supper when I was younger and joined her thinking-woman's order, well, that would have made things simpler.

"I don't think you're going to see any action on the Gabriel front," predicted Judy upon hearing of Gabriel's desire to be a Friar Minor. "Why don't you stop looking in that goddam Theology Department? There's not a guy in that thing that isn't screwed up royal!"

For Judy's information, Lucy had a natural popularity with these effeminate church-types anyway. All the overmothered Catholic boys she knew from the Youth Group at St. Bridget's, the Drama Club would-be actors from St. Eulalia's, half of the seminary candidates en route to Loyola or Notre Dame, the young men of High Church leanings in the department—Lucy had an immediate bond with these guys. They weren't officially homosexual, perhaps, but something similarly different, an orientation with the fetid taint of Church. She was never short an invitation to coffee or to sit beside someone at a lecture.

You see, Lucy had worked up a persona: the cool, practicing-Catholic broad, 1990s style. Rebellious, antipapal, reform-minded, but mass-going and serious about it. Look, anyone could pull off this performance as a *lapsed* Catholic, but it was a tougher act to stick with the Church, and it seemed to underpin the trust young men like Gabriel and her fellow Theology Department pals had in her.

"I can talk shop with the boys," she told Judy once. "I have so many male friends because I don't have a female view of religion."

"And just what's that female view?"

"Something imprecise and spiritual and embracing and mysterious. See, Judy, I can talk theologians and doctrinal points, the nitty-gritty, with the best of them. It's like discussing the Standard & Poors with business majors or baseball stats with sports fans. I play on Augustine's turf."

"And you get to hang around a lot of faggy, repressed men who aren't going to sleep with you that way," Judy responded, not able to allow Lucy one, not one little social victory of any consequence!

Lucy was determined now to meet the English morning, queasy or not. It was nearly eleven.

Lucy first found herself strolling through Oxford's Covered Market, where none of the indelicacies of butchery are spared the customer. Game birds hung headless, upside-down calves were being stripped of their skin, entrails of swine were being publically chopped and arranged. Lucy examined a forlorn pig's head.

"I know how you feel today."

Feeling herself reel again, she decided to moor herself to a table in a workingman's café within the market, ordering a strong cup of tea. As she stared at her cup, she heard the dull march of her life back home on its mission to retrieve her, bolt the gates of new experience. Yep, Lucy decided, Judy's maybe got it right. That's my ol' stomping grounds: sensitive, repressed, intelligent men with a streak of some religious feeling.

(And only Catholics need apply?)

Not that she was anti-Protestant exactly . . . but she remembered Christopher had this friend Luke, who was raised Lutheran and she was attracted to him, since he was tough-minded and easygoing socially at the same time—*rare* in Theology Department circles—and it didn't hurt that he was on the soccer team and was a blond hunk. Lucy brought him by the house on some tissue of an excuse to drop off a book, but mainly for Judy to get a look at him.

"Now you're cookin' with gas," Judy whispered in the kitchen.

And emboldened, Lucy flirted rather successfully with Luke and might have even had a chance with him, but one night, over lots of wine, Christopher and Gabriel and Lucy and Luke got on to Catholic-versus-Protestant things and Luke quite cogently reviewed the last century of Catholic triumphalism and pronounced Roman Catholicism in severe decline and an amusing discussion of papal infallibility ex cathedra broke out, and while Gabriel and Luke talked and Christopher nodded, Lucy withdrew and thought: I know everything you say about Catholicism, Luke, is absolutely true, and I even agree with you, but you could never love me the way I have to be loved if you find the centuries of Catholic tradition that led up to the complicated person I've become as stupid as you say.

(Is it, My child, that you don't think your love would survive the controversy, or your Roman Catholicism?)

Darn it, Luke, she sighed, if only you were a dreamy semiagnostic with a misty New Age notion of universal order, open to weird mantras from the East and curious about all cults anywhere—*that* I could live with. But to be Christian and not Catholic is inevitably to be anti-Catholic and I'm not sure we could ever get around this.

"That's what I thought," Judy had lectured when Lucy had tried to explain this. "You're gonna let a chance with a god like Luke go by because," and here she sneered in the most demeaning imitation: "he's not Catholic like you. Tribalism. It's why they blow each other up in Northern Ireland, thinking like you think."

(Judy had a point, Lucy.)

Lucy sighed, vaguely ashamed of herself for arriving in the end at a position her sour old Irish grandmother would have fiercely defended: only eat, drink, live, and breathe among Catholics.

Fact was, Lucy had squarely informed herself, she'd made a botch of it with men. No argument, really. Her track record on romance was nonexistent—and it was her own fault. You wouldn't hear from Lucy the whiny denunciations of her upbringing or her Catholicism or her guilt-inducing mother, her romanceless life was of her own painstaking crafting, her infallible sense of missing opportunities, running when she should stay put, investing much in pursuits of long shots and dead ends.

Lucy, somewhat more melancholy, left the café determined to track down Dr. O'Hanrahan and discover the whereabouts of Gabriel. Outside the low clouds were bright white and made her squint. Lucy ambled along the narrow sidewalk while butcher's boys on bikes sped by in old-fashioned straw hats and striped aprons, ferrying carnage to the various kitchens, for other banquets and feasts. Deliverymen rolled kegs of beer to colleges, milkmen racks of clinking bottles.

Lucy arrived at All Souls College and was permitted passage through to Dr. O'Hanrahan's guest room. She knocked to no avail, and would have left but there were signs of life within, a grunt, a creak.

"What is it?" O'Hanrahan growled a second before answering the door.

Lucy smiled and surveyed the great man in the clothes he must have passed out in the night before: "Good morning, Dr. O'Hanrahan."

"Who are you?" he asked groggily but seriously. "*What* are you?"

"I'm Lucy Dantan, remember?"

He stared at her. "Did I molest you in a drunken stupor last night? Whisper sweet Latin nothings into your ear?"

Lucy colored slightly. "Uh, no, sir."

"Thank God; you're *really* not my type."

"Nor you mine," she risked. "I'm here for breakfast."

"Oh." He tried to focus again. "I set this up last night, did I?"

Lucy saw that a lie would be propitious here and said yes.

"All right, all right, let me throw some water on my face and get my coat, put on a tie."

"The one you've got on looks fine, sir."

O'Hanrahan surveyed his rumpled shirt and large belly not finding a tie. He reached behind his neck and retrieved the bedraggled tie that he had lain upon all night. "Lovely," he grumbled. "Do you have a place in mind for breaking our fast?"

"Any place you want. Sir."

With the Randolph Hotel as an announced destination, O'Hanrahan led the way briskly, Lucy following across the quads a step or two behind. Summoning all her bravery, Lucy tried to get personal and chatty: "You and Father Beaufoix seemed a bit, it seemed, like, um, combative last night."

"We're always like that, since we met in Beirut after the War."

O'Hanrahan considered maligning the man, but came up civil. "He's a genius about African languages, a truly . . . truly great man of his field. I just can't stand all the Marxist bullshit. What's the use of being a progressive radical scholar if you're only going to turn around and embrace a stifling orthodoxy like Marxism the next minute—and a defeated, discredited orthodoxy at that . . ." He suppressed a yawn. "We haven't gotten along really since he challenged me at a public lecture in Paris about the origins of the Holy Spirit. I said She was the oldest and most original part of the Christian Trinity."

"*She?*"

O'Hanrahan fumbled in his pockets for cigarettes and frowned to realize they were back in his room. "Just a minute," he said. Passing one of the many entrances to the Covered Market, he ducked inside and returned a moment later with a lit cigarette in his mouth. "Want one?" he offered halfheartedly.

"Uh, no," said Lucy. "I used to smoke cigarettes a bit back in school, but the nuns made life hell for me . . ." O'Hanrahan, Lucy sensed, couldn't care less. "The Holy Spirit is female?" she reiterated.

"Indeed She is. The Holy Spirit is a concept that emerged from the Jewish notion of *Sophia*, the Wisdom spirit of *Ecclesiastes*, the *Wisdom of Solomon*. She was so popular in Jesus' time that She was the only real rival Yahweh ever knew; Wisdom just about sank patriarchal monotheism. Christ would have used the words *ruah, shekanah*, both female gender to describe the spirit, the feminine glory and presence of God."

"Wow, what a cool idea."

"It is more than cool, it is historically correct," said O'Hanrahan, warming with the cigarette and the late-morning bustle of the passing crowd. "There are traces of Man for 35,000 years and traces of a Great Mother or Earth Goddess virtually all that time. Then we come to 1700 years ago, the age of Jerome and Augustine and Ambrose, and *pfffft!* Our Great Mother is gone. There was a Supreme Mother in the Early Church, the Holy Spirit. The greatest ancient church of Christendom, the Hagia Sophia in Istanbul, was built to the Blessed Wisdom, again of female gender. But the Fathers of the Church eliminated all traces of Her; She became the Spirit*us* Sanct*us* under Jerome, the old misogynist."

They shared an awkward silence to Cornmarket Street, the modern avenue of trendy storefronts and double-decker bus stops, swimming in exhaust and morning shoppers.

"Well," O'Hanrahan offered, determined to make conversation, not sure why. "What's your thesis again?"

"Oh," she said, taking a deep breath, "I'm interested in how the Corinthian alphabet shifted in the 300s B.C. Are you familiar with the evolution of some of the letters, like the Corinthian *lambda* and *sigma* about that time? It makes a difference, I think, a minor difference, to some of the translations and. . ."

She noticed O'Hanrahan yawning. Lucy felt a wave of tension pass through her again, at having mentioned the thesis that was to be reviewed in September.

"It's more interesting than I make it sound," she offered.

(Not really.)

Crossing George Street and passing St. Mary Magdalene's Church and graveyard, O'Hanrahan pointed out Balliol College, founded in the 1200s as penance for a dirty joke told before a bishop—or for kidnapping him, depending what you read—and to the left of those medieval bastions, St. John's College, the college that tore down Richard II's Beaumont Palace, birthplace of the Crusader Richard Lionheart and the niggardly King John, to use as foundation for its library filled with A. E. Housman's papers—

"The classicist? Housman's one of my heroes," interjected Lucy.

"God help you," muttered O'Hanrahan. "St. John's was the home of Edward Campion, cofounder of my beloved Trinity College in Dublin, who, speaking as one who has known the Jesuits, was a Jesuit's Jesuit. He almost got the hand of Elizabeth. In time the Church of England caught up to him, tore out his guts, quartered him, beheaded him, acting in that Protestant spirit of brotherly love."

As O'Hanrahan regaled Lucy with martyrdoms and ghastly deaths, she came to understand that friendly, ingratiating small talk from Patrick O'Hanrahan came in the form of copious, learned lectures.

". . . just as they did with Alexander Briant—the rack, the thumbscrews, the scavengers' daughter, needles under the fingernails. And Cardinal Fisher. 'Even,' mocked Henry VIII, 'if you send him a red hat, he will have no head to put it on!' "

Lucy decided O'Hanrahan was not without a Tudorian aspect himself.

"Henry VIII was determined to burn all papist art and my favorite story is that he took the wooden image of St. Gdarn from its Welsh village. The locals warned that the image was prophesied to set an entire forest afire, so he had John Forest, unrepentant Catholic, burned at the stake holding Gdarn's statue so the prophecy would be fulfilled."

"It's horrible to think of all the martyrdoms here," said Lucy soberly.

"Oh, what's a stake-burning every so often, hm? Keeps the rapacious churchmen on their toes. I can think of half a dozen prelates today crying out for the stake. Cardinal O'Connor in New York, Marcinkus and his mob connections, Mahoney in L.A., all John Paul's current hacks. All the TV preachers, while we're at it. Swaggart, Tilton, Bullins, Falwell, all of 'em to the flames!"

Lucy stood across from St. Mary Magdalene and beheld an excrescence called the Martyr's Memorial: a free-standing, three-story over-wrought Gothic spire that stood next to a bank of vandalized pay phones. A number of foreign exchange students congregated on the steps beneath the steeple, smoking cigarettes, striking poses.

Lucy looked at the spire. "More Catholics drawn and quartered?"

"Protestants this time. Bloody Mary at work."

The year was 1556.

"Bishops Latimer, Ridley, and Cranmer," O'Hanrahan recounted, "were all Cambridge men so they were served up by their college hastily when the Inquisition came to call. Mary sent Spanish friars up here to see to the Inquisition—you want an inquisition done right, you gotta bring in the Spanish. Latimer burnt quickly, since he was allowed to have a supply of gunpowder tied round his neck. An *explosive* Reformer."

"Oh, Dr. O'Hanrahan."

"Ridley," noted O'Hanrahan with seeming relish, "had one of the worst stake-burning deaths I've ever heard about. Hours went by and the wind blew the flames away from the top half of his torso while up to his waist he was burnt away. 'I cannot burn, God help me!' he kept crying out. A year later they got to Archbishop Cranmer, who had earlier recanted and said he'd convert back to Catholicism, though he was to be toasted anyway on general principle. But at the stake he renounced his recantation. He then thrust the hand that signed the recantation into the flames until it caught alight. Absolved, Cranmer committed the rest of himself to the fire soon after."

"Pretty gruesome."

"Cardinal Newman fought bitterly to have the Martyr's Memorial torn down, being a late-in-the-day Roman convert. Newman, Pusey, Keble, Hopkins—a whole generation of closet queens converting to Rome or at least a stratospherically High Church."

Lucy's eyes widened at his appraisal; her mom, after all, led a Cardinal Newman Study Circle once. O'Hanrahan assured her on the doorstep of the hotel, "Whenever you see good Protestant boys sucking up to Rome, or Catholic boys drawn to orders, you're talking a better-than-average chance of homosexuality, since Catholicism is *camp*, after all. The boys wanna play dress-up, swish about in the robes, kiss the rings, swing the censer. . ."

Lucy dourly reflected that Judy had an unlikely ally here.

O'Hanrahan held the door to the hotel open for Lucy to pass through. "In any event the Catholic orders have crept back into Oxford, despite all the human bonfires. More practicing Catholics in England than practicing Anglicans now. There are even more practicing Moslems."

"Really?"

"Let's hope Henry is rolling about in his grave, or in Hell or wherever he is."

(Hell.)

The Randolph Hotel. A rich person's stopover in Oxford, home of high tea and $150-a-night rooms, where young gentlemen rent private chambers and get wildly drunk on Bollinger $70-a-bottle champagne, swing on chandeliers, expose themselves to the other patrons, pass out, throw up, and write large checks afterward to the Randolph Hotel, swearing they won't do it again next year. The breakfast room was muted Edwardian splendor, and silently Lucy and the professor made their way between the uniformed waiters and ferns and Oxford's well-dressed, quietly breakfasting elite.

"English Breakfast tea," mumbled O'Hanrahan, rubbing his eyes, suffering more than he was used to, "is the *espresso* of tea. You can mainline the stuff."

Lucy smiled, not sure what mainlining was.

"Not like the flavorless bag of Lipton in a Styrofoam cup you get in many fine American establishments."

Under the influence of English Breakfast tea, served in a lovely urn, two kinds of sugar in bowls for his delectation, cream and then milk in precious mini-urns, O'Hanrahan's resuscitation accelerated. The menus were put before them. And Lucy saw that they would be lucky to escape for under £15. She figured she had £20 in change and bills and traveler's checks after that—

"My good man," O'Hanrahan announced to the long-faced waiter, "I'd like the herring in cream sauce to start, on a plate with a slice of cold cantaloupe melon, and to the side a cut of your sweetest Morvan ham—no, make that prosciutto. I'm missing *bella Italia*."

Lucy was inwardly tabulating: £6 plus £5, that's £11 plus—

". . . and, to follow, two eggs, poached. I think atop a crisp muffin, a rasher of smoked Canadian bacon to the side. And look, black pudding on the menu here! Let's have a patty or two of that, shall we?"

Maybe they would take her traveler's checks, thought Lucy, a big fancy place like this. Just whatever you do, damn you, don't get the steak—

"And yes, I think a *petite béarnaise*, a trifle rare, if you would."

"As you wish, sir. And for the miss?"

"Just grapefruit juice, I think, will be fine."

"Nonsense," snapped O'Hanrahan, taking her menu from her. "I insist. A traditional English breakfast for my daughter."

The waiter archly retreated, and Lucy looked at O'Hanrahan sheepishly. "So you remember me after all. At the Turf you were passing me off as your daughter."

"A bit of resemblance there, unfortunately for you," he added, laughing until it caused his head to smart. "You're Roman Catholic, aren't you?"

Lucy nodded.

"And you're, worse than that, *Irish* Roman Catholic, huh?"

She nodded again.

"Knew it," he sighed, "that dark red hair. And the way you blushed when I mentioned the mistress business last night. Dantan, Dantan . . . that's not an Irish name, is it? Oh, look!" A waiter was passing by with a pastry cart laden with a tableau of croissants and *gateaux*, strudel and *Kuchenstücke*, muffins and scones and crumpets and Danish pastries. "Excuse me," O'Hanrahan said to the man. "I'd like a strudel, yes, that thing there. Lucy?"

"The Danish, I guess," said Lucy, the bank broken for sure. "You're not going to have room for all you ordered, sir, if you pick your way through the pastry cart."

"I don't intend to eat all I ordered. I just want those bastards at Chicago to pay for it all. You were saying?"

"Dantan," she commenced, "is a Breton name. Somewhere in the late 1700s my great-great-grandsomething came over to Ireland."

"No doubt to avoid the French anticlericalism of the 1790s."

Lucy was embarrassed to know so little of her family history, let alone the history of the world that prompted it. "Yes, I suppose," she continued. "They made it to Ireland just in time for the famines. Then my grandfather came to the U.S. after World War One."

"Probably *instead* of World War One if he was true to Irish form. A lot of priests in the family, I bet."

"Fair number."

O'Hanrahan provided his own skewed take on Irish history: "The Bretons are the great Catholic prudes of Europe. Ireland used to be a fun-loving, copulating country before they imported a wave of Breton priests to help them survive the famine. By the time the Bretons were done, the average marriage age in 1850 for a woman was thirty-eight, for a man, fifty. And they were virgins too. Look at our island now! Thanks to your relatives, more puritanical than the Puritans."

Lucy noticed O'Hanrahan referred to it as *our* island. As did her father. Somewhere a line was drawn between her father's Irish-American generation and her own. She had never once been tempted to claim anything but America as home, and the troubles of Ulster held no romance at all. Who would lead the St. Patrick's Day parade in Chicago? A proper IRA-backing Republican—Kerry O'Casey from her father's union local, a man dubbed Uncle Kerry in the family— or some mealy-mouthed arse-kissing drunken ol' sod who'd say Your Majesty faster'n a lightnin' flash? Her father had noted a lack of Republican sympathy in his children and remonstrated with them for their apathy. When Lucy was nine years old her father as a birthday present made out a check to NORAID in her name. So she'd remember her ninth, and the nine former counties of Ulster. Thanks a lot, Dad.

Lucy got down to business. "I think I have an idea what you're hunting for, sir."

He raised an eyebrow, mildly interested. "You do, do you?"

Lucy cut her Danish into sections, trying to project nonchalance. "Yes. I think you're on the trail of a heretofore lost gospel. Something very old, Second Century maybe, by the sound of it, or you wouldn't be so excited. And it's attributed to one of the Twelve Disciples."

"Why do you figure one of the Twelve is the author of this supposed lost work?"

"Before I identified myself I heard you say as much to Father Beaufoix."

He grimaced. "Said that, did I?"

"Of course, maybe you've found a First-Century account. That would explain what the rabbi's doing here."

Now how the hell did she get *that*?

"I looked up Mordechai Hersch in the Scholarly Register at Braithwaite."

"I'm in there too, you know."

(Want to tell him the news, Lucy?)

Actually Lucy also looked up Patrick O'Hanrahan and didn't find his name, but diplomatically let the occasion to inform him pass. She reached into her carpetbag to her side and found her ever-present notepad. She went on, "Rabbi Hersch holds the Rosen Chair of Ancient Languages at Hebrew University. What would this man want, I figured, with some Greek Christian document? Perhaps, I got to thinking, this work is contemporary with Josephus, his specialty."

Good detective, thought the professor, before reminding himself never to discuss anything in public with anyone again on this subject. "Is that all?"

"No. I talked to the head of the Theology Department back at Chicago, Dr. Shaughnesy?"

"That moron? He did his lousy doctorate on Freemason rituals, copied it out of a book! I mentioned the Rosetta Stone to him one time and he thought it was the Hispanic cleaning lady who came in on Fridays. Reads everything in translation. A ninth-rate mind presiding over the first-rate department I created!"

(That's no way to talk about the man who conferred professor emeritus upon you. Out of kindness, let Us add, since you gave him nothing but abuse toward the end when he successfully got you out of the department and saved the entire program from ruin. What's more, you know the truth!)

"You got *nothin'*, baby," O'Hanrahan said momentarily. "A thousand scholars, such as myself, are hoping to acquire for their institutions a thousand scrolls at any given time. I've been involved in the papyrus trade for a half-century now."

This was Lucy's opening to read from the notepad again: "Dr. Shaughnesy says you have a sister who says you've hocked everything you own to pursue this project, including your house—"

"The old witch probably thought she was getting it when I die. Ha!"

"The university knows you've cashed in your life insurance plan. You began two months ago with the department credit card—"

"The bastards canceled it."

"—before they canceled it, and you racked up expenses of $2,243.86 in places such as Rome, Assisi, Jerusalem, Damascus, Trier in West Germany, Antwerp, Jerusalem again, Rome again—"

"God, they're getting off cheap! Only $2000 for a trip like that!"

"And they're worried about Gabriel—"

"I told you never to mention that little faggot to me again!"

Lucy hunched down in her seat, positive that "faggot" carried to the rafters. "And they're worried about your . . . your state of mind."

O'Hanrahan laughed richly. "So they think I hold the Alzheimer Chair in Ancient Studies, right? They'll wish they had treated me a little better when this whole thing is over."

Lucy reached into her carpetbag again and produced two letters. "This is from your sister, and this is from Dr. Shaughnesy."

"Burn them."

But Lucy held the letters out to him. He took the one from Dr. Shaughnesy, used his butter knife to open the envelope.

"Humph," he said, skimming. "Just what I expected. They want me to come back to Chicago, stop spending my money, the department's reputation, blah blah blah, they're worried for *my* reputation, et cetera et cetera . . ." He handed the note back to her. "Those swine wouldn't know an important scholastic find if the Hand of God led them to it."

At this juncture the *petite béarnaise* arrived with Lucy's English breakfast on an oblong, silly-looking trolley with a squeaking silver hood. Lucy looked down at her plate of bacon and fried eggs, fried bread—buttered bread deep-fried in the breakfast grease, she felt her arteries tighten—and this fried potato cake with shreds of cabbage inside it.

"That's bubble and squeak," explained O'Hanrahan, happy to switch subjects. "That's a banger, the link of sausage there. And *that* delicacy is black pudding." He pointed with his knife to the two black disks that Lucy mistook for American-style sausage patties.

"I'm sort of a vegetarian," Lucy confessed.

"Lucille, anyone who eats a vegetable now and then is 'sort of a vegetarian.' Are you telling me I ordered all this for nothing?"

"No, but I'd rather you had the bacon and the banger-thing. I think it's important to try other nations' cuisines."

O'Hanrahan ate steadily while talking. "England doesn't have a cuisine. Look at the word *cuisine*. They even had to borrow that."

Lucy slowly chewed a bit of her black pudding. Not bad, but it tasted odd somehow. "What *is* this?"

"Congealed animal blood with bits of fat and scratchings." Lucy swallowed quickly, irrevocably, and washed her mouth out with orange juice. Then went back on the offensive:

"Look, there are only twelve disciples. I virtually know what you're after, so why don't you tell me?"

"Because," he enunciated, as he cut his bacon, "I don't *know* you."

"I'm real trustworthy, honest."

"That's what Gabriel said."

She was dying to ask about Gabriel, but that seemed to be the dead end of all dead ends, so she held off. "If I guess what you're looking for," she asked politely, "will you tell me?"

Lucy imagined this would earn a quick rebuff, but O'Hanrahan stared at her oddly as he had a moment before. And surprised her: "Yeah."

"You would?"

"Because I know you'll never guess it."

"How many guesses do I get?"

"One."

"One's not very sporting."

"What would you suggest, Miss Dantan?"

"Ten would be nice." He didn't dignify this with a response. "Okay, six. Fifty-fifty chance."

He ran a piece of steak around in the *béarnaise* sauce. "With ten, you still wouldn't get it."

Oh yeah? thought Lucy.

"But what's in it for *me*?" said O'Hanrahan, now enjoying a mouthful of herring in sweet sour cream.

She hadn't thought about this. "I could go back to Chicago and tell everyone that what you're up to is very exciting and important and . . ."

O'Hanrahan pretended he was shaking a New Year's Eve party favor. "Whoopdie-doo. That would mean," he bent his head in sarcasm, "so very, very much to me."

"Well, let's make some kind of deal then," said Lucy.

"For allowing you six guesses?"

"Yeah, for allowing me six guesses."

He looked to the ceiling. "How much money do you have? How much can you get ahold of?"

"They gave me $500 spending money, and this breakfast will probably cost that."

"Just $500?"

"Maybe I can get more," she suggested weakly.

O'Hanrahan rose and patted his belly. "Miss Dantan, you make some phone calls and see what kind of additional funding you can get me. Then we'll talk, all right?"

Lucy nodded quickly and reached for her handbag. "Yeah, okay sure, but wait—wait, what about your sister's letter?"

"The flames, the flames!" he said, as he walked by her without ceremony.

And he was gone.

And so, moments later, was £60.32 . . . or, as she figured, $100. As Lucy walked down the historic Broad Street between the elegant Sheldonian Theater on one side and a row of quaint shops, a pub, and the venerable Blackwells bookstore on the other, she contemplated how to invent some money for O'Hanrahan.

There was, after all, her older sister's credit card.

Cecilia, the married, responsible sister who gave her mother all the angelic grandchildren the other daughters didn't. Ceece didn't want to surrender her MasterCard to Lucy, but Mrs. Dantan insisted, pleaded, was on the point of tears contemplating emergencies, near-deaths, terrorist acts, floods, natural disasters, and in a final calamity-saturated soliloquy worthy of Euripides coaxed Cecilia to lend Lucy the card for the duration of the trip. Credit limit $1000. Lucy could get an advance on the card and pay Cecilia back later when O'Hanrahan paid her back. . . . But let's face it, sighed Lucy, that may never happen. She decided she'd think it over at the Codrington Library.

Lucy reentered the grand hall, now returned to its Georgian prim-ness as a deathly quiet place of study. And sleep, Lucy noticed, spying a young undergraduate head down on the old-fashioned scribe's desk. She wandered into the card-catalogue room not exactly sure what she would do.

"May I help you?" asked a new woman behind the desk.

"Uh, yes," Lucy said, surprising herself. "I am Dr. O'Hanrahan's assistant from the University of Chicago."

"Oh, him."

"Yes, I am to collect for Dr. O'Hanrahan the books he ordered up yesterday and put on reserve."

"I see," she intoned.

"Of course," said Lucy, taking advantage of the universal dread of O'Hanrahan, "if you would rather set things up, I could have him come down here and tell you what he required himself—"

"I'll get the books right away," she whispered. Lucy surveyed the library staff, every last one of them wearing glasses with chains, older women without wedding rings in conservative English clothes.

The pile arrived. It included Sir E. A. W. Budge's *Contendings of the Apostles*, which Lucy noted was in Amharic. Copyright 1901. Next book: something by Flamion, in French, *Les Actes apocryphes de l'Apôtre André*, Louvain 1911. Next was a photostatic reproduction of an ancient book, which had the *Andreas* in Anglo-Saxon, and blazoned on its leather binding: Cynewulf, a Roman numeral showing the text was 1623. Origen's *On Luke*. Clement of Alexandria's *Stromateis*. The Collected Hippolytus, the Collected Sophronius. . . . She dutifully took down these titles on her notepad.

"Do you have a copy of the Bible?" Lucy asked the woman at the desk.

"About 546. Which century and language did you have in mind?"

"A current Bible will do."

The woman directed her to a reference shelf that had the King James and the RSV. Lucy flipped the page of her pad and listed the disciples according to *Matthew*:

Peter	Thomas
Andrew	Matthew
James bar-Zebedee	James bar-Alphaeus
John bar-Zebedee	Thaddeus bar-James Alphaeus
Philip	Simon the Caananite (the Zealot)
Bartholomew	Judas Iscariot

Unexpectedly, there was no list of the Twelve in John's gospel. What's more, *John* listed another disciple, Nathanael, who wasn't in the others. The Church considers Nathanael the same as Bartholomew, but Lucy wondered if O'Hanrahan knew something the Church didn't. Likely, his name was Nathanael bar-Tolomai. *Luke* listed an extra Judas, son of James bar-Alphaeus. So Judas must be Thaddeus. *Mark* and *Matthew* probably changed his name so it wouldn't be confused with Judas Iscariot. Lucy remembered an inkling of a Catholic prayer card to St. Jude, patron saint of lost causes: *St. Jude, glorious Apostle, faithful servant and friend of Jesus, the name of the traitor has caused you to be forgotten by many, pray for me who am so miserable*, and so forth.

Six guesses, hm?

Well, Judas Iscariot is probably out. The idea of a Judas gospel is intriguing but sure to be fictional, and even if he wrote one, who would believe it when they read it? Lucy suspected she could lose Simon the Zealot as well. Jewish independence propaganda wouldn't have been saved by the Church . . . unless he gave up his zealoting ways. And a Simon gospel could explain the rabbi's interest. Bartholomew, maybe. It seemed to her that there *was* an apocryphal *Gospel of Bartholomew* she had seen somewhere.

She looked up Bartholomew in an ecclesiastical encyclopedia. Sure enough, there existed a 4th-Century copy of a Greek *Gospel of Bartholomew*, but the writers of the entry cast doubt on its authenticity, as did an impressive list of Church fathers, Jerome following Origen. It was banned in the Gelasian Decree. Didn't look promising. But maybe O'Hanrahan had found an earlier copy of it, something more authentic.

"Hello, Miss O'Hanrahan," said a wry voice beside her, making her startle. It was Rabbi Hersch. "I see we have a list of the Twelve," he observed, taking a minute to look it over. "I wouldn't bet on your working it out."

"You never know," she said. "I might wiggle it out of Dr. O'Hanrahan yet."

The rabbi was looking casual today, tan and fit, a tweed coat with leather elbow patches, some remnant of late '60s academia. "Let's have some tea, shall we?"

They walked to the Queen's Lane Cafe on the High Street, across from the Examination Schools, where presently a flurry of uniformed students gathered to spray champagne on fellow examinees about to emerge. This little nook was crowded this lunchtime, but the rabbi and Lucy with brimming cups of tea pushed their way to a table by the window.

"Now let's get this straight," Rabbi Hersch began. "You're over here from Chicago to drag Paddy home? Slap his wrists?"

"Rabbi sir, you can imagine what they're thinking back at the department. I mean, he's climbed out on a limb really."

The rabbi motioned for her to go on and explain.

"Dr. O'Hanrahan sold his house. Cashed in his life insurance policy. Closed his bank accounts. Went through the department credit card and is now, as I see it, heading to the end of his own card's limit."

The rabbi rubbed his forehead. "Nu nu nu nu nu, why didn't he tell me? Sold his house, did he? On a grant—he tells me he was on a grant."

Oops, thought Lucy, the rabbi hadn't known any of this.

Lucy began, "No, I'm sure there's no grant involved. But if I could make a good report to Chicago, they might help him, maybe send him some money—"

"Bah, never! Too much bad blood there." The rabbi pulled on his neatly groomed gray beard. "He's sick, you know. Not well."

"Really?"

"His liver, his blood pressure, his arteries—well, how he enjoys himself you have seen."

"That's a shame."

"And I'll tellya something else, little girl. Since. . ." Lucy nodded, showing he didn't have to go into detail; she knew O'Hanrahan had lost his family, a wife and son, an only child, in some accident years back. ". . . since the accidents, he went into a tailspin. I thought he was a goner. But he's back! The risen O'Hanrahan, alive and full of energy as I've never seen him. I don't want to see that stop. Him squashed or held back, I don't want to see. On one level, I don't care if he ever finds this gospel, but as long as he has the hope of finding it he'll stay alive, have something to live for, you got that?" He pointed an accusing finger at Lucy. "*You* I don't want for to get in the way."

"No, sir."

He reached into his jacket pocket. Out came a slim billfold for traveler's checks and a wad of £20 notes. He counted out five, six . . . ten notes, £200. He pushed it across the table to her gingerly. "Now you tell him Chicago sent this as a goodwill gesture, okay?"

Lucy acquiesced, putting the money in her purse. "That's very kind, Rabbi." He started to get up and leave. "Uh wait, sir, can I ask you two questions?"

Rabbi Hersch sank back in the chair impatiently.

"One, what did you guys need to see Father Keegan for last night? It seemed very important."

The rabbi shrugged. "What of a Catholic priest should I know?"

Lucy didn't find this denial convincing. "Two, what happened to Gabriel O'Donoghue, his assistant?"

"I can't help you there. I really don't know what happened with that kid. A real nebbish, that boy." Lucy looked disappointed so he elaborated a bit:

"Something happened in Rome. Paddy, after months of arrangements, was supposed to purchase the scroll we've been hunting for from a shady antiques dealer, the . . . the, what was it, the Alberti Brothers. Crooks, through and through. This scroll, little girl, was bought by Hebrew University in July 1948 and stolen from us that September. It's had a dozen owners since then who never realized its value, and in Rome we sniffed it out one more time. Paddy raced to Italy to take a look at it."

"You were going to buy it?"

"Though Hebrew University was loath to pay for the thing twice, in this case we were willing. But I didn't want to buy a fake, so as I said, Paddy and Gabriel went to Rome to make sure it was for real."

Lucy sipped her tea. "What happened then?"

"The go-between in this sleazy hand-off was none other than your little friend Gabriel. He hands over the certified check, picks up the scroll, and is supposed to go back to O'Hanrahan's hotel room. He doesn't. He disappears."

"*Gabriel?*" Lucy couldn't reconcile anything so exciting with her old friend.

The rabbi continued: "Paddy was broken-hearted. He thought Gabriel had been shot or kidnapped. Or worse. He contacted INTERPOL, the carabinieri, the embassy. And then Gabriel called Paddy from the station and apologized for escaping with the scroll, but he didn't explain why."

"Doesn't sound like Gabriel at all."

"Ehh, who's to say what people will do, hm?" Rabbi Hersch decided to tell her a bit more: "Well, it didn't work. The antiques dealer had some, you know, family connections and Gabriel never made it out of the train station in Rome. The Alberti Brothers caught him, took the scroll back, and then wouldn't deal with O'Hanrahan or Hebrew University. In fact, they suggested Paddy leave town before with the cement shoes he ended up in the Tiber, right?"

"So who has it now?"

"It was purchased by a private collector, some rich German, two months ago. We don't know who, we don't know for how much, we're not sure if he's willing to sell."

Lucy thrilled to all this. To be a part of it! "How much were you going to pay for this scroll?"

The rabbi shrugged noncommittally.

"I just wondered with Dr. O'Hanrahan going broke how you guys were going to pay off this German guy."

"Ehh, we'd find the money," he said evasively.

"Hebrew University is that loaded?"

He thought a minute before saying this. "No, but the State of Israel is."

"This scroll is that important?"

"It's that important."

"But why would some Christian gospel—"

The rabbi was standing. "Nice to have the tea time and to schmooze with you, Miss Dantan, but I've got an appointment with Kaballah in the Bodleian collection before *shabbes* tonight. Give the loot to Paddy, now, don't forget." Lucy nodded, but was there some way to detain him? "And enjoy your flight back to America. If you're ever in the Holy City, should you be so blessed, gimme a buzz, hm?"

"Uh, yeah . . . thanks, Rabbi," she said faintly as he sprinted to the door, waving bye-bye, his mind already on something else.

Lucy went out and walked around Oxford aimlessly, thinking and talking to herself. She looked up to the churning gray sky overhead. Funny, it was almost sunny when she and the rabbi went for tea. What on earth have these old codgers got wind of? How could Gabriel betray Dr. O'Hanrahan? How could Gabriel do *anything* so . . . treacherous and daring?

Back to O'Hanrahan's chambers:

"Who is it?" O'Hanrahan sang through the door, "as if I didn't know." The professor opened the door, his eyes bleary and his white hair scattered about in all directions.

"I didn't mean to disturb your nap—"

"I wasn't sleeping," he said unconvincingly, "I was working. Or rather, trying to get some work done around here. I thought you wouldn't come back until '. . ." He saw her proffer a plastic traveler's-check billfold filled with pound-sterling bills. "Oh."

"About $300, sir." As he counted it, Lucy discreetly peered into the smoky chamber: texts were spread out on the desk, books of script opened and marked, a sloppy suitcase was opened on the bed with wrinkled clothes arrayed beside a large camera, next to notepads sprawled about, and a half-empty glass of Jamesons lay near the ash-tray and a smouldering cigar. "Well, well," he said, counting to himself. "And yet how insufficient this is when put against my vast expenses. You can go now," he added, ready to close the door.

"Wait! My guesses."

"You know," O'Hanrahan groused, "for 300 bucks, I think these six guesses of yours are a bargain. Did we agree to $100 a guess?"

"No. We didn't." She sighed as the door inched ever more toward closing. "I suppose . . . I suppose I could get some more money," she added hesitantly, inwardly volunteering Cecilia's credit card.

O'Hanrahan's features lightened. "By tonight, Miss Dantan? Five hundred dollars or so?"

"Uh, it would be more like $300, sir. Now as for my guesses. I figure since Hebrew University is so interested and the rabbi is so keen, it may well be a writing of Simon the Zealot you're after, since Jewish Nationalism was—"

"Wrong."

"Oh." That seemed so reasonable. She decided to get two-for-one by guessing James without saying which one she meant.

"Alas," said the professor, "neither *Maiorus* nor *Minorus*. There, you've had three—"

"No! I guessed *one* James."

O'Hanrahan looked weary as ever an old man looked.

"This is really someone mentioned among the Twelve in the Bible, right?"

"Yes, goddam it, he's right there in the New Testament, one of the Big Twelve. You just don't have the facility to work it out and our business is at an end!" He placed his hand daintily on the knob of the door, ready to slam it.

"About Gabriel, sir—"

"To shut you up," he said with strain, "I will tell you your little backstabbing friend has been following me since Rome. He's been everywhere I've been. I haven't seen him here in Oxford yet, but I haven't looked. So tell his parents, what manner of vermin they might be to sire such a rat, that their little Judas isn't dead. But he may be if he crosses my path again! Now to quote *Acts* 15:29, 'Farewell!' "

He slammed the door.

She breathed nervously. "Uh, Dr. O'Hanrahan?"

A roar from within: WHAT?

"When will I see you again? I mean, if I get the money for you. I mean, it's not actually *my* credit card . . ."

The door opened. He spoke in a beatific whisper to hide the blast that would follow if she didn't go away soon. "Save me the *invokata* of the Eleusinian Mysteries of how you get this money. I don't care. Sell your young, chaste body on the street. Return to me before the pubs open and you're likely to find me—*now can I get back to work?*"

"I'm going, I'm going . . ."

She turned and ran down the stairs and heard the sound of the slamming door again. You know, nasty as he was to her, she sort of liked him anyway.

(That's because you have a good heart, Lucille.)

Getting $400 from Cecilia's MasterCard required a passport, a second ID, and an unaccustomed, un-American half-hour wait in a line at the Barclays Bank despite only four people being in front of her. But she got the cash.

Lucy spent the next hour souvenir-mongering, buying some Oxford marmalade for Mom, she'd get a bottle of duty-free Irish whiskey for Dad, and she'd better pick up something for Cecilia since she was bankrupting her . . . and that meant Mary too, and her brothers Nick and Kevin. And postcards, postcards to everyone. See? I do *too* have an exciting life is what a postcard from Europe said.

> Dear Judy,
> Well wouldn't you know, two days in England and there's this guy, Duncan. From the northern part, cute—even you'd think so—and that accent!

Lucy read what she'd begun and put her pen down, not sure whether she'd send it or not. Maybe some real romance would happen and she could write something more substantial.

(You mean something more the truth.)

She looked at the embellished episode of Duncan and tore the card up. You lie a little bit and then you have to lie a lot when asked questions about it and before you know it you've created a whole false life . . . She would rub Judy's nose in some other adventure.

(What is this obsession with bettering poor Judy?)

A page in Lucy's address book had a list of potential postcard recipients. Maiden aunts and godparents and lots of old people who never went anywhere and didn't think anyone should live anywhere else but Bridgeport, Chicago, the 11th Ward, Mayor Daley country, paradise on this Irish-American earth. Her mother had demanded that half a dozen old prayer-circle biddies get cards from Lucy abroad.

"Old Miss McGill has never been anywhere," Mother lectured, "and think how she'd value a card from overseas! She has prayed for you and followed your growing up since you were the tiniest thing, and when you had your tonsils out she prayed for you, and for your confirmation she sent you two dollars and Lord knows she didn't have it to give. . . ."

All those tiresome old hags, Lucy thought.

(Lucy.)

Lonely, tiresome old hags, Lucy corrected. Old women with nothing and no one. Well, I could write them all the same card and hope they don't compare them . . . but of course they *will*. They'll be on the phone the second they get their cards, rubbing each other's noses in their importance at getting a European missive from Mary Dantan's little girl.

(Sounds almost as petty as you and Judy.)

It was four o'clock and new, darker storm clouds had arisen since her lunchtime tea with the rabbi. Before recommitting herself to playing detective in the library, she decided she needed a local expert. Maybe the friendly woman in the magenta tights who lived on the Guest Room stairway. Ursula. Lucy went to Braithwaite to avail herself of her newfound acquaintance who was majoring in English. "Reading English," as the British say, though Ursula soon assured her doing English at Oxford required very little reading whatsoever.

"What a relief, Lucy dear," said Ursula, clearing off a chair for Lucy to sit upon, "I was praying for someone to come by and prevent me from writing this dire little essay. I have an essay crisis concerning D. H. Lawrence. Considering what Lawrence uses the word 'crisis' for, I should think it best not to call it that, don't you agree?"

"I thought the term was over," Lucy wondered.

"Well, I fear I've been a bad little girl and they're making me stay and write papers for penance. I've been terrified for two years of being sent down but, I've decided, they've devised far worse for me by making me stay up."

Lucy took in Ursula's madcap room: Eastern carpets, a marble bust with an elaborate Edwardian lady's hat on it, knicknacks from around the world, onyx sphinxes, a small African mask, a kitsch ceramic Leaning Tower of Pisa, an impressive collection of empty champagne bottles along the window ledge.

"That was Trinity term," she said proudly.

Scattered elsewhere were veils, scarves, lustrous raiments and puff-pillows strewn about the obligatory dorm-room furniture, as well as numerous glamorous photos on her dresser of herself with a variety of handsome, tuxedoed young men. Ursula flopped down on the floor, papers and critical books around her and, thank God, Lucy observed to her relief: a Monarch notes!

"I won't bother you long, Ursula, but where can I talk to someone about Anglo-Saxon poetry?"

"Alas, around Braithwaite most people could help you. It's the trag-edy of the place." Ursula craned upward to her desk and tore a piece of paper out of one of her textbooks without remorse. "Here," she said, scribbling, "Dr. Renaldo, Staircase Ten. Our resident Anglo-Saxon don. He'd be more than happy to help you. God knows we, his charges, have as little to do with him and Anglo-Saxon as possible."

It was raining now. The wind found Lucy from all directions, car-rying the cold drizzle into her face. Looking dismally at her feet and walking stoically forward, she came to the stairwell. A roster of hand-painted signs, white on black, announced Room 5 was Dr. Renaldo's chamber. Ascending the groaning wooden stairs, centuries old, she passed student rooms with unidentifiable British house music seething on the tape players within. She found Room 5 and knocked on the door.

No sounds of life.

She knocked again, then took a step back and seated herself on the nearby stairs, to wait a bit. A moment later a female student enclosed in a tremendous bathrobe made her way down the stairs to a room nearby, yawning as she passed, just meeting the day at 4:30 P.M. It amused Lucy to picture an American university converted to the Ox-ford system, with student dorms, faculty offices, and professor's ac-commodations all bunched together. It would be about a week before revolution would ensue.

Lucy then heard a stirring from Dr. Renaldo's office. The door opened about a half-inch, and a steely eye peered through. "What do you want?"

"Dr. Renaldo?"

"You've been sent by the Common Room?"

"The Common Room?"

"Oh, wait, I know who you are. You'd better come in then, after all. Quickly quickly . . ." He opened the door and swept her inside. Lucy found herself ushered to a Victorian upholstered chair with the stuffing long pounded out of it.

Dr. Renaldo closed the door behind him and scurried to his big oaken desk to face Lucy, while Lucy assessed the museum of a room: dark-paneled walls, no light except the glow of the electric fire in the stone fireplace and the halfhearted daylight from the old, thick-glassed window, framed engravings by the score, a faded sepia globe, and piles of papers, tomes, and paperbacks lying amid the shadows and decades of long-absorbed pipe smoke.

"Come to face the music, have you?"

Dr. Renaldo was a tall, gangly man with a high, precise voice, about fifty but with a boy's full head of golden hair, a bit too long with uneven bangs hanging over his forehead, a mane Lucy suspected of being artificially lightened. She noted his dark green, crushed velour—what did you call those things?—smoking jacket with some monogram on the breast pocket, his light blue shirt without a tie, ancient blue jeans with a thick leather belt and a giant buckle.

"Now then," he said sharply. "Your essay, please."

"My essay?"

He gave a mocking laugh, as he twisted in his squeaking swivel chair and reached for his already lit pipe. "Ah, what is it this time, hm? Glandular fever—that time-honored excuse? Expiring relatives? Break up with the boyfriend?" And then with deliciously clipped British consonants: "Chapped lips, perhaps? I've heard them all, and most of them from you, Miss Campbell-Miers."

"Uh, excuse me, I—"

"Don't disappoint me, now. *Tears*, Miss Campbell-Miers! I want tears! Nothing short of your finest performance will do!"

"Uh, Dr. Renaldo, I think you have me mistaken for—"

"What?" he piped. "Oh, I do say indeed: an American accent! You simply surpass yourself! I take it we are working up to an amnesia scenario here?"

"My name is Lucy Dantan, sir, and really, I'm not one of your students."

He pursed his lips. "You're not?"

"No."

"You're positive you're not one of my first-years?"

"Yes, sir."

He pondered this while enjoying a taste of his pipe. "All the better for you, actually." Another taste. "No, you don't really look like Miss Campbell-Miers at that. I do my best to see my students as infrequently as possible, of course, so do forgive me . . . I don't suppose you'd consider *teaching* my first-years Anglo-Saxon, Miss Dantan?"

"I don't think I'm qualified, sir."

"That's hardly stopped the English faculty before." He looked genuinely dejected, but then sighed away this desolation. They shared a strange pause in which the silence seemed unbreakable. Then at last: "What, then, may I ask, brings you to this dread chamber?"

"Oh, I won't take up much of your valuable time, sir—"

"Valuable! What little you know!"

"—but I wondered if I could ask you a question or two about an Anglo-Saxon poem. I'm visiting from the University of Chicago." Suddenly Lucy felt insecure about her status and fluffed it up a bit. "I'm here to do research for the University of Chicago, and I won't bother you for longer than five minutes, I promise."

"Oh, you mustn't rush. Stay for hours, please. You must keep me from a deadly Senior Common Room function." The don sucked on his pipe with glee. "In fact, your visit has worked out splendidly. What poem shall we discuss?"

"Cynewulf's poem *Andreas*."

Renaldo almost allowed a smile. "Cynewulf didn't write the *Andreas*, for one thing. We can hardly imagine Cynewulf writing it, now can we?"

Lucy smiled in numb agreement.

"I'm rather surprised that you found a book that managed to attribute the *Andreas* to Cynewulf. For centuries that mistake has been corrected." Then he rolled his eyes wearily. "Though there is yet one old fool, at Cambridge naturally, who published a monograph suggesting otherwise in the face of incontrovertible proof and world opinion."

Lucy dug into her handbag for the little notebook. "Uh, it was, sir, a very old book. From 1623—"

"Yes, the Catherwood imprint of the Vercelli manuscript," he said with pleasure. "Taken from a copy of the Vercelli we no longer possess, full of mistakes, very old, possibly authentic. My, what led you to that? I myself have produced a small, unread monograph on the subject, in the *Anglo-Saxon Quarterly Register*, winter issue, 1972. You, no doubt, saw it prominently displayed in Chicago University's library."

Not sure if it was a joke, Lucy smiled.

"Here is the organ in question." Dr. Renaldo unearthed a slim academic volume from under the pile of papers before him. "You'll be kind enough to read aloud the features of this quarter's offerings," he added, handing it to Lucy.

Lucy scooted forward and read down the list of topics: "The Parousia in the Old English *Physiologus*. The Middle Cornish *Beunans Meriasek* and Arthurian Survivals. Theories on *Genesis B* after Line 441—"

"Grown men devoting their lives to this wretched matter," he said pleasantly. "There is a rumor afoot that the faculty intends to eliminate the Anglo-Saxon requirement from the English Literature bachelor's degree."

Lucy couldn't decide whether he was happy at the prospect.

"Of course, it's outrageous," he went on. "I had to learn this excruciatingly useless language, and I think it's only fair that everyone should suffer likewise; I hate to think of future generations having things so luxuriously. I made it my speciality, principally so I could be assured of an appointment. All colleges are reduced to hiring an Anglo-Saxon scholar of some variety. I would never have been hired if I developed expertise in my first and truest love."

"What was that, sir?"

"Late Stuart odes written in Latin."

The 1930s coal black phone on his desk rang.

"Oh, Miss Dantan, could you get that?"

"Me?"

"If you would."

Lucy picked up the phone. It was someone looking for Dr. Renaldo, the Senior Common Room meeting was about to begin and they were waiting for him. "Yes," said Lucy, "well, I'll check and see if he's here . . ."

I'm not here, he mouthed.

"No, he's not in his office," said Lucy. "No, I'm quite sure. What am I doing here? Uh, waiting for Dr. Renaldo. Yes. Bye-bye."

Dr. Renaldo was delighted watching her set the receiver down. "Good show! I suppose, indebted to you as I am, I should offer you some tea."

"That would be nice, sir." Lucy, no less chilled in this murky office than outside, welcomed a nice cup of English tea. English tea in an Oxford chamber brewed by an actual English don. To her disappointment, she saw him scoop some instant powder into a tea-stained mug.

"Milk?"

"Yes, please."

Dr. Renaldo bent over before a small boxlike refrigerator and removed from it a half-pint carton, holding it up to his nose. He winced. "Sorry, that seems to have gone off."

"Doesn't matter," said Lucy.

The don made do with some "coffee whitener" and stirred that in with some brown sugar clotted around the sugarspoon, which had doubled too many times as the stirring spoon. "I don't suppose," said Dr. Renaldo, proud of his creation, "that you would have preferred sherry."

"No thank you," said Lucy, ready after last night to take the pledge.

"I do believe it's all that will keep me from the abyss on this horrid afternoon," her host said, producing a bottle and wiping the dust off the tattered, ancient label. "The warmth of Andalusia," he said vagariously.

The phone rang again.

"Shall I?" asked Lucy.

"I'd ever so much appreciate it."

Lucy picked up the phone and answered a similar round of questions politely. ". . . No sir, I was expecting him for our class today—"

"*Tutorial*," whispered Dr. Renaldo helpfully.

"—for our tutorial. I'm sitting here with my essay, in fact," she added, observing a silent clap of approval from Dr. Renaldo. A pause as she listened. "Yes, I'm aware the term is over for undergraduates," she admitted, remembering Ursula, "but I've been bad this term and so Dr. Renaldo has demanded these papers from me . . ."

Dr. Renaldo joined his hands at his pursed lips, thrilled with her invention.

Lucy shielded the phone and whispered: "It's Dr. Blackwelder, who says to tell you that he knows you're sitting right here and they're not starting the meeting without you so you might as well come."

"They're bluffing."

Lucy reiterated Dr. Renaldo's absence, and suggested he might be sick.

After hanging up, Lucy asked, "Is attending this meeting so horrible?"

He held up his sizable glass of sherry to the gray light. "Most assuredly. It's all quite reasonable in America, isn't it? You hire businesspeople to do the business of the college. Security people to see to security. Academics in one building, the help in the other. We poor educators here at Oxford must double as disciplinary deans, quartermasters, supply officers, secretaries, and investment bankers. I'm in charge of Senior Common Room Dessert, amid my other travails here at Braithwaite—a college, dear girl, in utter decline."

"Yes, sir," she nodded.

"If the peaches aren't ripe I get stern letters from my colleagues. I am still in disgrace after the incident of the rancid grapes from Monday night. I say, am I to worry myself about the ripeness of fruit or serious scholarship?"

Lucy put aside her tasteless cup of tea. "I wasn't aware Oxford faculty had to double up so much."

"It's the meanness of Braithwaite, I promise you. I'm surprised they don't have us change the sheets and scour the loos. I suppose that indignity awaits, so I shouldn't suggest it too loudly."

The phone rang again.

Lucy suggested they let it ring and Dr. Renaldo agreed. But it kept ringing. Finally in annoyance he directed Lucy to pick it up.

"No," she began, "Dr. Renaldo is out, I believe—"

Dr. Renaldo snatched the phone: "Bloody hell, Blackwelder. In flagrante delicto, for Christ's sake. I thought it was perfectly understood that Fellows didn't interrupt the other Fellows in the throes of passion . . ." His face then brightened. "Oh hello, darling, it's you."

His wife.

"Darling, do be a love and call Blackwelder for me and tell him I'm much too sick to come in, would you? Yes, I shall have to sneak around for the rest of the day, I suppose. Perhaps you can send the boys over and they can secrete me out in a sack." His wife apparently agreed, and Dr. Renaldo hung up, looking content.

"About this poem *Andreas*," Lucy tentatively suggested.

"Yes, well. The source is a fairly old tradition that pops up a number of places in the Greek and Celtic world, really. The adventures of Andrew the Disciple and his pal Matthew, the Evangelist."

"Yes?"

"Well, they go about, performing miracles, going to sea, having adventures, finally dodging the cannibals in Ethiopia."

Ethiopia, thought Lucy, stirring. Where they speak Amharic, like one of the books called up by Dr. O'Hanrahan. "Is it based on an apocryphal gospel?" she asked.

"I suppose there is an *Acts of Andrew,* something like that. The legends of the disciples through the Early Church and Dark Ages were innumerable, really. The earliest copy of the *Andreas* is in Antwerp, it is thought. It was, for its time, an international best-seller."

Antwerp. Where some of O'Hanrahan's credit card receipts came from.

"Does the *Andreas* have any connection with Trier, West Germany?"

"Not that I know of."

There was a knock on the door. A muffled voice outside declared: "I know you're in there, Renaldo, so you might as well surrender!"

Blackwelder, mouthed Dr. Renaldo, wearily getting up out of his squeaky chair.

"I can hear your damned chair squeaking!" said Dr. Blackwelder.

Dr. Renaldo led Lucy around to sit in his chair while he shut himself up in a coat closet with his smoldering pipe. Dr. Blackwelder announced he was coming in, and the next moment he did.

"Hello, sir," said Lucy sweetly. "Can I help you?"

"Where is he? Where've you put him?"

"Dr. Renaldo, sir? I am waiting for him myself. Sitting at his desk and . . . reading."

Dr. Blackwelder was a short, stocky man in a beige woollen suit, bow tie, his face composed of pinks and whites, a man who could play Dr. Watson to Renaldo's Holmes in an amateur-theater production. Dr. Blackwelder loped about the office suspecting all cabinets, doors, areas under chairs and sofas. Then he walked behind Lucy and looked over her shoulder.

He read: "The 'Liges/Lifes' Controversy in the Old English *Phoenix* and *Guthlac B,* by Sholto B. Renaldo, Fellow of Braithwaite College, Oxford University." He stared at Lucy conspiratorially. "You can't honestly say, young lady, that you are reading something so preposterous and ill-researched as this collection of pretentious ramblings, are you?"

Blackwelder's fat face suppressed a laugh. He was trying to get Renaldo to reveal himself.

"I pity you literature students," Dr. Blackwelder went on, stalking around the room near the closet door that held Dr. Renaldo. ". . . forced to learn this useless drivel so a few minor intellects can hold their long-outdated posts, smoking pipes that smell of dried horse droppings . . . sipping the finest sherry in common rooms, wasting their college's precious delights."

"Yes, sir," said Lucy, trying to look away from where Renaldo was hiding.

"Of course," said Blackwelder, "recently, we here at Braithwaite would be hard-pressed to uncover but the meagerest of delights. One need never fear wasting the metallic treacle, as if distilled within a rusty culvert, that passes for sherry in the Senior Common Room *Dessert*." He aimed his diatribe at the area behind a worn sofa. "Not to mention the despoilt, maggot-ridden fruit strewn shamelessly before us each evening. Rotting. Rancid. As if gathered from some roadside tip . . ." Blackwelder aimed his rich recital at the closet door: "The emetic array of cloying sweets and stale biscuits, the unfailingly putrid cheeses, to be washed down with cheap cut-rate alcoholic swill no man of sensibility would use to unclog his drain!"

Blackwelder had tears in his eyes from suppressed mirth. He observed Lucy, hoping for a clue. "No," he concluded, "perhaps such a useless study as Anglo-Saxon depletes nothing from the already destitute commonweal, hm? Well, I shall report my dear colleague's absence to the Common Room and his friend Mrs. Miggins, as we vote on matters concerning him. Good day, young lady."

Having had his fun, Blackwelder left, and slowly Dr. Renaldo peeked outside of the closet in a plume of escaping pipe smoke. "Victory is mine, nonetheless," he said placidly. "Any hour away from Mrs. Miggins is a proof that there is yet a merciful God."

"I've met her, unfortunately."

"See what we've fallen to?" he asked, reclaiming his chair. "So eager to have anyone do our miserable accounting work that we turn over the college to these harridans and cower before them. She strides the narrow college like a *colossa* and we petty Fellows walk under her huge legs and peep about to find ourselves dishonorable . . . fruit," he concluded, mangling the Bard.

"Yes, well, thank you for your time, sir."

"Sure you . . ." He brushed the lapels of his green velour smoking jacket and cocked his eyebrows seductively. ". . . sure you won't stay for a bit of whiskey? Comfort from this miserable, loveless day?"

She'd heard about the dons at Oxford. Was this a lechery in the making?

He added, "I could turn up the heat for us . . ."

Greater love hath no Oxford don, thought Lucy. "No thank you, I really must be getting back to the library. But thank you."

"Oh, do call again," he said in his meek alto. "I'll be here."

Lucy broadcast a few smiles and slipped away. Out of Braithwaite, back to All Souls across the tundra and the howling winds, and up to O'Hanrahan's chambers. She knocked.

"Go away," he murmured groggily.

"Sorry to mess up your nap again, sir, but I—"

The door was yanked open, and he said intensely quietly, "I'm *not* taking a nap."

Before there could be more wrath, she quickly held out the bank envelope with $400. He examined it carefully.

"Not bad, huh?" she said. "$700 in an afternoon. You oughta make me your assistant."

"Thank you," he said begrudgingly. "When the great book is published about all this, I promise you'll get a footnote. And so, good night."

"Wait, my guesses!"

"Quickly, quickly . . ."

"Uh, Andrew?"

Nope.

"An earlier redaction of *Matthew,* I think. It—"

Nope.

She took a wild stab. "Guess No. 5, Bartholomew/Nathanael?"

Nope.

"Awww, I thought I had it."

The professor eyed her appreciatively. "You must have been going through the books I ordered up at the Codrington. Scheming with the librarians, I see, the Stymphalian Birds . . ."

"And you're sure it's not St. Bart?"

"His relics once were here in Oxford, you know," said O'Hanrahan.

(Poor St. Bartholomew, flayed in India, patron saint of all tanners and laborers who worked with skins. As a great favor to King Canute, a Danish thug canonized by the groveling church, an arm of St. Bartholomew was shipped to England and was the sensation of the 1000s, We can assure you.)

"Edward III built St. Bartlemas in Oxford, as I recall," said the professor, "which housed the flayed, blackened, peeled-off skin of St. Bart. What became of this relic, no one knows."

"I suspect the English mistook it for one of their breakfast foods and ate it. Now, sir, when can we talk about you-know-who and what I'm supposed to tell Chicago and Dr. Shaughnesy?"

O'Hanrahan looked down on her with unaccustomed patience. "Okay," he began, "what about tomorrow for breakfast? Twelve noon at the Randolph, this time it will be my treat."

"You mean it?"

"And I will tell you everything; all things will be made known. I shall imbue you with *gnosis,*" he added, making the sign of the Cross over her as a priest might, "and many gifts of the Spirit."

"Well, thank you, sir, I—"

The door slammed.

She cupped her hands to say through it: "Good evening, sir."

No response returned, but no matter. She would succeed on her mission at last! And who knows, she thought, with Dr. Shaughnesy sitting on my examination panel for my thesis, could my getting an extension be too difficult now? My stock will be at an all-time high among the faculty and how they'll enjoy the tales I'll tell about their colleague and nemesis, Dr. Patrick Virgil O'Hanrahan.

Lucy walked from All Souls up the High Street where she noticed a kebab van already doing business in the damp, gloomy early evening. She peered about in search of Duncan—primarily, to apologize for throwing up in front of him and being so drunk, and secondly to test the waters for friendship. Maybe romance even. Hey, Judy, I may send that postcard yet! Going back to the guest room in Braithwaite, Lucy changed out of her cold, wet clothes and lay on her bed thumbing through her Oxford guidebook. She became curious about the Franciscans. Checking the index, indeed, she found that the Franciscans did have a monastic hall here in Oxford, Greyfriars. She looked it up on the map.

Do you suppose . . .

Lucy shuffled back into her coat, grabbed her map, and went out into the night. The orange phosphorescent streetlights illumined the old colleges and threw titanic shadows of passersby upon medieval walls. A mist of fog and headlights sat low upon the road, and the end of Broad Street looked eerily suitable for Jack the Ripper to return. Indeed all the Oxford streets were quiet, a few hours into pub time, and all the more desolate for that.

Lucy found the right street and then the house number of Franciscan Greyfriars Hall, deep in Anglican Oxford. She backtracked to double-check, then stood intimidated before the large oak door.

She knocked.

Nothing. Maybe they're having a Friday service. Presently a young man in Franciscan garb peeked out from behind the barely parted door.

Lucy: "Gabriel O'Donoghue, please. It's quite important."

He looked at her innocently. "The American chap?"

"That's the one. He's expecting me."

The young Friar Minor went away, closing the door and not asking her in. She waited impatiently, checking her watch. Three minutes later he returned. "I don't think there's anyone here by that name."

Lucy was adamant. "No, I am sure he's around, and if you tell him it's Lucy Dantan he will come out, I'm sure."

"No, truly," he faltered, "there's no one by that name within."

Lucy heard more baritone mumblings from behind the door.

But then from behind her: "Lucy!"

Lucy spun around to see Gabriel in his familiar autumn jacket, T-shirt of their high school alma mater, and hole-ridden jeans approaching through the fog. He was eating a doner kebab from a van. The monk observed them both until Gabriel nodded that it was all right.

"What are you doing here, Lucy?"

"Gabriel," Lucy commenced, "everyone's been so worried about you. No one's heard from you in months!"

Gabriel rolled his eyes, his mouth full. And after he swallowed, he said, "You had one of these? They're great. You can get all kinds of junk on it—"

"Yeah, I've had one. Gabriel, *talk* to me."

"Damn," Gabriel muttered, distracted. "It's leaking . . ." He held up his pita sandwich and revealed soppy napkins of sauce and tomato-goosh. "I'm going to throw this away . . ." Gabriel idled back to the corner where there was a trashcan.

Lucy followed in annoyance: "Gabriel, answer me. It's me, your old pal Lucy!"

He dropped the disintegrating kebab in the garbage. "You go first. Why are you here?"

"The department sent me," she said as seriously as she could. "Dr. Shaughnesy figured you'd been kidnapped or something—murdered by Dr. O'Hanrahan."

He lifted his hand to his face to bite his fingernails. "That's still a possibility."

"What happened between you two anyway?"

Gabriel and his mobile face went through a highly visible performance of temptation and then resisting temptation, wanting to tell but deciding not to. "Uh, I can't talk about it, Luce. One day I promise I'll tell you the whole story."

Then from the fog there was a deep voice: "Brother Gabriel?"

Lucy startled and even Gabriel jumped. They turned to see a Franciscan in full attire approach them. A monk about thirty, with his cowl pulled up—all he needed, thought Lucy, was a scythe to resemble Death. In the weak light, Lucy judged him to be Mediterranean with dark beard stubble.

"Brother Vincenzo?" said Gabriel.

"Your presence ees required," said the friar with a trace of an accent. Brother Vincenzo turned and walked halfway back to the chapterhouse, but paused for Gabriel to follow.

"Gabriel," whispered Lucy, "are you in some sort of trouble?"

"No, nothing like that."

"Oh come *on*," she pleaded. "Tell me *something* to take back to Chicago. Look, I know O'Hanrahan found some kind of lost gospel that may be authentic and everyone wants it—see? I know virtually everything."

"Did you know someone's probably been killed for it?" he said quickly.

She merely opened her mouth.

Gabriel arrived at the doorway and Brother Vincenzo stood within, holding it open for him. "So why don't you get back to Chicago as fast as you can and tell them everything's all right. I called my parents yesterday so they're not worried anymore, and, uh, I'll be home soon, real soon."

"I thought you were going to leave the Franciscans," she said quietly.

"Yeah, I was. But my time here in Europe, thanks to Dr. O'Hanrahan, ironically, made me reconsider. The Franciscans are my family now."

"Gabriel," she said, pulling him closer to hug him good-bye, "you're not a hostage, are you?"

"It's Patrick who's the hostage," he said softly. Lucy was momentarily thrown by the reference to Dr. O'Hanrahan's first name. "The professor is hostage to some dream of academic immortality he probably won't live to see." His eyes held so much more he wanted to discuss. But he averted them. "Bye, Luce."

Lucy stood there speechless as Gabriel walked under Brother Vincenzo's arm and into the light. She heard the door thud. As she took a step away, she heard the door open again:

"Oh, wait a minute . . ."

A moment later Gabriel was back on the street putting ten postcards into her hand:

"Can you mail these for me?" he asked. "Got to leave early tomorrow for Ireland and I'm not going to be able to mail them from here."

"Sure," Lucy said numbly. "Our Mother Country, huh?"

"Right. Good-bye, now."

Aside from the mysteries, the frustration, Lucy found it wrenching to see an old friend in a foreign country and not go celebrate, talk old times, make some new times. Gabriel was no more energized by seeing her than he would have been to meet a mere acquaintance. This depressed her. And his being so tight with the Friars Minor again annoyed her in a petty way. Jealousy, she accused herself. He belongs somewhere, you don't. I didn't become a nun, she thought, because I know how little fun nuns are. But I know monks have a better time than they let on, the ultimate men's club. Whatever joys and comforts Gabriel has as a Franciscan that, like so many other things in his life, is a closed door to me, damn it.

As she walked up the High Street, Lucy decided she would read the postcards. Who knows? Maybe one had a secret message for help.

No such luck. They were all dull, dutiful, here-I-am-in-merry-olde-Englande cards, tailored for parents and friends. She scanned the addresses: Christopher, Luke, Dr. Shaughnesy. "Sorry I haven't checked in, but everything's all right," and so forth. There was a co-postcard to Judy and Lucy.

Dear girls,
My travels continue in ye oolde Oxforde, where I've fallen in
love fifty times already! If I weren't celibate I'd sleep with
anything with an English accent. How's those crazy cats??? I
expect to see this silly card on your refridgerator, okay? Keep
Chicago the same for me until I get back, end of the summer.
All the best,

                                                        Gabriel

Never could spell, thought Lucy, considering "refridgerator." The
card was one of those Oxford-typical-scene cards of a pretty couple
in *sub fusc* uniforms wildly riding a bicycle, being zany and youthful
in the sun. Never happened once around this rainy penitentiary, Lucy
assured herself. And what's with this Judy-and-Lucy business? Don't
I get my own *individual* card? she wondered.

More depressed, she read Christopher's and it was full of Gabriel's
more serious maunderings, descriptions of rain-soaked streets and
gray skies and old tomes in Oxford libraries he was thrilled to touch,
and hints of so much he had to tell Christopher when he got home.

Signed "lots of love."

I hate men, Lucy decided.

Damp and cold, she stood before her mirror back in the Braithwaite
guest room and unwrapped herself from her scarf. Briefly she held
the scarf over her hair and brought the ends down around her chin
so that she resembled a Holy Virgin, a righteous Puritan maid. With
the ceiling beams and old walls behind her she contemplated this
evocative image of piety: would she recant? Would she walk unbowed
to the stake? Who knows that such decisions weren't made within these
very walls and that she wasn't nudging to life the aggrieved ghosts of
the 16th Century? She felt a chill suddenly and she turned from the
mirror—enough of that!

Later, lying awake in bed, after she turned off the light and wrestled
with the faucet so it wouldn't drip, she stared at the pattern of light
on the slanted attic ceiling. I hate men for another reason, she continued: I hate men and all their little secret societies and mysteries and
codes and clubs and projects. It would kill Gabriel and Rabbi Hersch
and Dr. O'Hanrahan to let a woman in on their cloak-and-dagger
nonsense, I don't care what progressive semifeminist line they spew
about a female Holy Spirit, et cetera.

Well, Lucy assured herself, the good thing about being a woman is
that a woman doesn't give a damn after a certain point. She would
meet O'Hanrahan tomorrow at noon, hear the story, fly home, tell
the department what they wanted to hear, naturally embellished a bit,
and her duty would be done. A vacation to England all paid for. With,
she smiled, two or three extra days remaining to sightsee!

I'll do London, Lucy fantasized. I'll go see a show, I'll see Bucking-
ham Palace, the Tower, Big Ben. Or, I could go up to Scotland, which
is supposed to be gorgeous, or maybe over to France for a few days
and trot out my high school French. She felt herself giving over to
sleep, so with a wide yawn she dashed off a prayer by rote.

(Better than no prayer at all, We assure you.)

France sounded good. Or, of course, I could go to Ireland like
Gabriel. Yes, that would be a big hit with Dad and all the aunts back
home. Souvenirs from Cork, Irish kitsch for Mom, a bottle of duty-
free Bushmills for Dad from the actual isle.

Lucy listened to the bells all over town ring eleven. Strange people,
the British, Lucy thought, snuggling down into the bed. Oxford is
diffident and bureaucratic and formal . . . and yet, she sighed, there
is romance here in this damp, in the stones, in dismal old Oxford. Not
that it will find me, Lucy added wistfully. What a day, what a day, and
what an idea: a female Holy Spirit. I somehow always knew this.

(That's because We've always been close, My child.)

Those Crusty Old Bachelor Fathers of the Church have done us
ladies in, Lucy considered drowsily. I'd like to strike my own blow for
God.

(And We're going to give you that chance.)

Meanwhile, O'Hanrahan looked at his watch. 11:01 P.M.

He looked at his ticket to Holyhead where he would catch the ferry
across the Irish Sea tomorrow afternoon, being a man who never got
on an airplane. But even I, O'Hanrahan thought, will wish I were on
a plane when I set sail on that wretched body of water in this kind of
weather.

It was a bittersweet parting from Oxford.

And there is nothing more desolate than a British train station after
11 P.M., since most routes have ceased for the night and there is a
desperation about the final runs and last passengers who aren't already
in bed or finishing up at the pub but heading out into the rain. In the
gloom and chill O'Hanrahan had walked to the end of the platform
where one could see the night skyline of Oxford, Nuffield College's
green brass needle, and Lincoln College library illuminated there, and
St. Mary's and Christ Church thataway, and he had wondered: is this
the last time I'll ever see this blessed town? God's own prodigal, His
ever-wayward but brightest child?

(Come now, Patrick.)

Oxford, he mourned, is where I would have been a success! Not in
accountable American academia with the mandatory publishing and

office maneuvers and funding squabbles and 1990s political-correct-
ness litmus tests and the innumerable students with nagging personal
failures disguised as theses . . . No, in Oxford nothing matters but
good company and good wine and an occasional dabble of a column
in the *Times* to show, once a decade, you know your subject. And
certainly not those pesky students—here they fend for themselves!

(Why must you always dwell on some life you might have lived and
not on the life at hand? Did We give it to you for nothing?)

I would have been a don in the tradition of the medieval masters
whose rooms had windows that never looked outside the college, for
there *was* no world outside the college and its wine vaults and high
table and one's colleagues, worthy and unworthy. Moreover, Oxford
would have liked me back, thought O'Hanrahan. Here my not publishing a book would not have mattered. Dear Mordechai Hersch, a shelf
of scholarly books to his name. But not Patrick O'Hanrahan. No, he
left behind riotous evenings at bars throughout the world, the most
inglorious theater, the old Irishman, belly full of booze and head full
of stories. I have no family to carry on, no shelf of books to leave
behind, no lasting discovery. Ah, to be like that bastard Father Beaufoix, immortal by his scholarship and publications—what a crown I
might have worn!

(*Riches do not last forever; and does a crown endure to all generations?*)

Here now, in the drizzle, was the train.

O'Hanrahan looked once more to the spires and would have prayed
for a second chance to use his gifts anew, more wisely this time, more
productively, if he thought such a prayer would be heard, let alone
answered. Or if he thought prayer worked at all and wasn't the vainest
waste of words yet conceived.

(You have lost your faith, Patrick.)

"I have lost my faith," he said aloud to the rain-soaked night.

2

My dear brother Josephus, while in Alexandria last year [75 C.E.], most civilized of cities, I read what I could of your youthful history of our people's endless contentions. I see in it great promise and assure you that one day you shall compose a truly first-rate history! Predictably, you have omitted all that you might have written about Our Master and the Church that was your brother's home for decades. Such petulance, and what a disservice to your readers.[1]

2. And if I may be permitted a breath of criticism: I found it difficult to read your work for your incessant toadying for the good opinion of Titus. Titus devoted himself to the destruction of the Jewish race, indulging in every cruelty, debauchery, and sodomy available to mankind. When convinced that Jews had swallowed their own treasure upon the fall of Jerusalem, Titus watched as these citizens were disemboweled alive and their organs searched for gold and trinkets.[2] Such a man is to be flattered?

1. There are three Christian references in the thousands of pages of Josephus: 1) a passage declaring Jesus the Messiah (*Antiquities* XVIII.iii.3), which was unconvincingly interpolated by later Christians in one little paragraph in the middle of an irrelevant explanation. 2) Another reference to the fanatical high priest Ananus and his stoning of James, "the brother of Jesus who was called Christ" (*Antiquities* XX.ix.1), which is probably untampered-with except for the above quote. And 3) a final reference mentioning John the Baptist (*Antiquities* XVIII.v.2), which, though perhaps doctored, is almost surely legitimate. John the Baptist is mentioned as a martyr of Herod and his connection to Christianity is never noted. It can be truthfully said that there is no credible evidence Jesus existed in the most meticulous, if subjective, historian of the period.

   However, *Antiquities of the Jews* was written ca. 93 C.E. and it is odd to the point of suspicion that Josephus, a former priest of the Pharisee party (who attended every intricacy and subsect of Judaism), could fail to notice a sect that, at that point, was rivaling orthodox Jews in population in many Judean towns, had been the subject of Roman and, as with Ananus, Jewish persecutions, and had garnered ritual curses from famous, traditional Yavneh rabbis (from the Amidah, "May the Nazarenes and the *minim* [heretics] perish in an instant!" ca. 90–100 C.E.)

2. The author has not read Josephus's account attentively. Some 2000 deserters from the Siege of Jerusalem fell afoul of Arabian and Syrian troops who dissected them alive looking for swallowed gold (*Jewish War*, V.xiii.4). Josephus records that Titus forbade this practice and made the dissections punishable by death, but this gospel's account might be accurate because, as accused, Josephus wrote to curry Roman favor.

But let me not sow the seeds of argument.

3. Instead, let us return to the beginning of my troubles, during the twelfth year of Nero Caesar's ghastly reign [66 c.e.], when it did not take a Daniel to read that Judea was months away from war and total annihilation. Four years before, James, the leader of the Jerusalem Nazirene community, the blood brother of Our Master, was executed under Sadducean influence.[3] The Nazirenes never recovered from his absence. Now more than once, I your brother, scholar and historian, offered to rise to the patriarch's chair, but no, instead the Jerusalem mob chose an unlearned young man called Symenon.[4] This boy could not even remember my name from visit to visit.

Symenon mindlessly led the Nazirenes in prayer and in the lovefeast on Friday, and then to the Temple to sacrifice and worship on the Sabbath.[5] After being reminded that I was indeed one of the Master's original Twelve Disciples, Symenon welcomed me with kisses and touched my hands and pressed his tears to my hand, then streaked his tears across my feet, then wished to have our tears mingle—tears from my eyes that had seen Our Master with his tears, he who had never seen Him, and so forth, and this weeping and hystrionic continued for several minutes.

3. The execution of Jesus' brother, James (and many other Jews who disagreed with the Sadducees), in 62 c.e., led to a toppling of Ananus, the High Priest responsible, suggesting some degree of tolerance for Early Christians in the Jewish mainstream, or perhaps merely Roman ire at the Jews conducting their own executions.

4. Hegesippus (ca. 110–180 c.e.) is unreliable on many things, but he records a Simon/Symenon, son of Cleopas (*John* 19:25 and maybe *Luke* 24:18), as second bishop of Jerusalem. He was martyred, according to tradition, in 104 c.e. The elevation of Simon/Symenon shows a tendency of the Early Church to keep the bishop's throne in the actual extended family of Jesus, since *John* 19:25 also has it that Cleopas was Jesus' uncle, making Symenon Jesus' cousin. The Galilean Nazirene community claimed descent in Trajan's time from Jesus' second of three brothers, Judas (who is mentioned in *Matthew* 13:55).

5. One sees that many Jewish Christians (later termed the Ebionites) attended Temple and had a now-obscure ceremony before the Sabbath on Friday, the day of the Crucifixion.

  The Christian Sabbath was moved to the worship-day of the sun cult, Sunday, the Emperor Constantine's preference in the 300s. Jesus' birth was fixed on December 25th, the long-held birthday of the Sun god and Mithra, the Persian messiah-figure. Constantine continued to worship the Sun god and Jesus concurrently in his reign. As late as the 500s, Gregory the Great chastises his flock for sun-worship rites at St. Peter's. Justin Martyr, Ignatius, Clement of Alexandria, and Tertullian all found the common ritual of Sunday worship propitious for the spread of Christianity, since Christ himself said he was "the Light." The lighting of Advent and Christmas candles is a survival of the pagan festival of lights and has no Christian source.

4. My previous Nazirene mission possessed the aroma—let us be frank—of failure.

I had been mocked, run out of villages, and nearly stoned on one occasion in Hebron because we could not produce a miracle as if we were some market-day magus. A Macedonian, Epaphrodius, who whined and bickered with me for months, had been my assistant. He wasted no time in reviling me to Symenon and said I spoke over the heads of the Samaritans, which one can hardly help doing with the *Kuthim*.[6] I begged Symenon to release me from further missionary work and allow me to go to Alexandria where I was better suited to evangelize and teach, to which he said:

"My most blessed elder, it is not for us to go where it suits us or where we might be comfortable. You can never know what Our Lord can do for you until you put yourself in a difficult situation for His sake."

5. I told this upstart that I didn't see how much more difficulty the Master of the Universe could expect me to endure, given our reception in Gedara, a place where Our Teacher Himself brought the evangel.[7] Yes, I was critical of the Gedarene congregation and its ostentation and false religiosity during the *agápe* service. Strange tongues and fits as in demonic possession overcame the women who were all but denuded as they spat out prophecies and warnings and ecstatic raptures—this sort of nonsense.

6. Finally, I was done a violence at a wedding.

I remember from my youth weddings being holy and solemn affairs, but now it is considered fortunate if anyone is sober by the end of these things and the event is positively blessed by the Most High if at least five family members aren't carved up in the inevitable drunken brawling. Epaphrodius and I were invited and, to my disgust, we were not selected to preside over the ceremonies, though we certainly outranked anyone in that horrid, wealth-worshiping city.

---

6. Epaphrodius is perhaps Epaphroditus of *Philippians* 4:18. "*Kuthim*" was a favorite derogatory reference to the savage Samaritans.
7. *Matthew* 8:28.

The bride streamed forth in saffron, the orange veil and wreathes piled upon six ridiculous false tresses, exactly as the Vestals would prepare themselves. All but Zeus and Hera were invoked as the two babbled a number of vows and then, against my protests, a pagan centurion—for it is very fashionable now to have Romans at these affairs—was allowed to be auspex, and inspect the entrails of a tremendous ewe that was sacrificed with a scant line or two uttered to the God of Israel begging Him to align the intestines this way or that . . . can you imagine! Oh, these are Gedarene Jews all right—this is what we have fallen to in the outer provinces. The sordid bride's ring displaying the groom's family's newly minted wealth was shown to everyone, then came the feast, the orgy of flat, overwatered wine and bad entertainment—lewd dancing, of course, young men and young women together, a scene indistinguishable from camp followers after a battle! And finally, after much bawdy teasing, the groom took his young bride (I should die of surprise if she were unde-filed) to their new house and lifted her over the threshold in a hail of nuts.

7. It was during the hail of nuts, which, I don't have to tell you, resemble an aspect of a man's anatomy that is of some use to the more intimate union to come, that trouble began. Standing near the party, having made my moral res-ervations known throughout the evening, many of the boys thought it sport to pelt me with nuts and nearly did injury to my eye. As I chased them to reprimand, other youths joined in my persecution. I was tossed from the terrace of the mansion down a grassy hill, to the laughter of the throng, encountering ordure and dung before finally coming to rest in the reeking grainpile there to be consumed by the cattle on the morrow.

8. The Nazirene community in Gedara compounded their ignominy by demanding that Epaphrodius and I depart. I re-sponded like Jeremiah by decrying their sins, their great shows of being possessed by the spirit, which I suggested was more likely Belial than *Sophia*. (Though I have faltered in my faith in the Nazirenes, I still adore *Sophia*, and I believe She moves us to more practical and useful applications than frothing fits on the dusty floors of synagogues.)[8]

9. Upon our return to Jerusalem, the simpering Epaphrodius told Symenon, our child-hierarch, that he sympathized with these Gedarene impertinents. Symenon suggested that my faith was dry and in need of possession of spirit and this I rejected to his face, though I tell you now, my brother, it was somewhat true. Symenon looked at me for some duration and suggested I go to another disciple, Judas Didymus [Thomas],[9] who was ever-strong in the Faith and could counsel and revive my flagging hopes for the Nazirenes, and who could teach me the arts of evangelism.

Alas, Thomas never liked me nor I him. He was a boor and spoke before he considered what he had to say. He was, furthermore, against my inclusion as a Disciple, but more on that perverse sham in some future dictation [see 4:23–27]. Nonetheless, I decided I would go to Thomas, in part to complete my history that you are reading here. (Little did I know that my own little brother, not yet forty, would race first across the finish line with his own light historical work before my own treatise concerning the period!)

8. *Sophia* is the Hebrew spirit of Wisdom, whose Graeco-Jewish and Christian cult peaks from 100 B.C.E.–100s C.E.; she became popular enough to threaten the all-masculine theology of the time. The *Wisdom of Solomon*, a song of praise to this female spirit of wisdom (ca. 100 B.C.E.), was the most pervasive work concerning *Sophia* and elements show up in this document, in Philo and *John* (who both borrow the preconceived *logos*), and in Deutero-Paul's epistles *Ephesians* and *Hebrews*. *Sophia* and the Holy Spirit were synonymous for much of the Early Church; Byzantium's greatest church, the Hagia Sophia in Istanbul, built by the Emperor Justinian in 548, is not to a female St. Sophia (as was later claimed) but to the divine, female spirit of Wisdom.

9. Judas Didymus, or Judas the Twin, called Thomas to keep him from being confused with the other two/three Judases who were disciples. (The editor has rendered him "Thomas" throughout.)

Thomas is thought to have evangelized the Medians (modern-day Iraq) and the Parthians (Iran) as well as the Indians, and his tomb for 1500 years was preserved at Mylapore and later moved to Edessa, though Indian Christians say Thomas's relics are still with them. Syrian-descended Christian communities in India, among the oldest anywhere, claim Thomas as their founder; it is a church of the highest social caste, using Syriac as a liturgy and with Nestorian (anti-Mary) elements. Indian Christianity's very existence is one of the great fascinations of Church history; see L. W. Brown, *The Indian Christians of St. Thomas* (Cambridge, 1956).

Thomas's role as skeptic and doubter was fixed by the Second Century and the *Gospel of John* (ca. 110 C.E.), with its famous scene of Thomas doubting Jesus' resurrection, but also the less celebrated passages in *John* 11:6 and 14:5, where he cynically predicts Lazarus's death, and is confused concerning Jesus' mission. Tradition has him martyred by a spear in July 72 C.E., but no such martyrdom is alluded to in this gospel.

10. About the time of Nero's ascension [ca. 54 C.E.]—if it can be said one ascends to that squatting-place called the Roman throne—Thomas embarked on a journey to the Medians and the dread Parthians, savage peoples entrenched along the Tigris and Euphrates and the wastes beyond. There is an Arab trader, Duldul ibn-Waswasah from Sabaei, a dealer in essences, oils, and incense who had aided me on my previous travels throughout the Mediterranean. For a few shekels one could learn most anything one asks concerning trade routes and caravans, and for twice that one might even learn the truth.

After taking from me double the money I intended to pay him, Waswasah directed me to a community in Eleuph on the Gulf of the Arabs,[10] an endless trek across the Wilderness of Negev, through Nabataea where Thomas was known to be. I decided to employ an assistant to accompany me, and also decided to leave upon that Tebeth [December 66–January 67 C.E.] when the deserts would be milder.

11. To procure a traveling companion and scribe I decided to call upon a classmate from my youthful Grecian days[11] in Alexandria, dear Jason, who I knew had a surplus of sons. In fact, it was with Jason—a more beautiful youth did not exist in Judea—that I took my first journey as a man to Jerusalem without having to be accompanied by my tutor, Polycrates, who had developed a distaste for the Temple milieu and for the Teacher of Righteousness.

---

10. Modern-day Eilat on the Gulf of Aqaba, leading to the Red Sea.
11. Throughout this document, one can find ample evidence for how intertwined the upper-class Jews had become with Grecian ways and customs. The official Judean line on Greece had been enmity until the time of Herod the Great. The Maccabees spent their careers warring with Greeks; John Hyrcanus forcibly converted Greeks in Idumaea and Samaria, destroying Scythopolis for the crime of speaking the Greek language; Alexander Jannaeus pillaged the Decapolis. However, all this forcible conversion and intermingling, ironically, resulted in the Hellenization of the Jews.

  By Jesus' time, it was common for men to have Greek names, dress in Greek fashion, prefer Greek art and architecture, speak Greek, read their Bible (the Septuagint) in Greek, conduct trade, print documents and histories in Greek (as Philo), and have recourse to the Sanhedrin, a Greek-titled institution. Herod the Great appeased Hellenistic Jews and his own tastes by reviving the Olympic Games, building *gymnasia* and Greek theaters, and restoring the Temple of Apollo at Rhodes, though this pro-Hellene stance pleased only the wealthy class. Many scholars (see M. Hersch, *Josephus*, Hebrew Univ. Press, 1991, pp. 340–47) think the source of the Jewish Revolt that led to the destruction of Judea was less anti-Romanism than anti-Hellenism; the age-old Maccabean struggle against Jewish cosmopolitanism.

Jason and I were both in our seventeenth year [sixteen] and were determined to make this journey of twenty miles in the manner of grown men. We took enough weapons for a small army, which amused my father, as I recall. My father was more worried about our falling astray in the endless vice-filled alleyways of Jerusalem, that brothel, that once-great beauty prostituted from a lofty place, that multiplication of all harlotries.[12] However, no two purer young men ever rode more piously into Jerusalem.

Ah, and that was the fifth and final time that I witnessed the Teacher. . . . If I could only look in His face again, I am sure all my doubts would be as nothing, dispersed in the wind. There are so many questions I should have asked Him, so much He alone could tell me!

12. Jason married a Nazirene maiden from a good family—you remember your own Essene friend Tobias bar-Tobias, fellow disciple of that madman Banus you adored, with whom you went to the Wilderness of Judah when the rest of us were busy with harvest?[13] Jason married Tobias's half-sister, Pontica, and they had six sons and only managed to find employment for four of them, and so they were delighted when I approached them about traveling with their youngest son, Xenon, as my assistant.

(It is a shame Jason felt he had to marry but better that than *Gehenna*—one of the few things I agree with the Great Heretic about, it must be said.[14] Jason would have made a great evangelist of the Nazirenes, and to look at him on his farm, harassed by quotidian cares and squawling children of numerous widowed daughters due to the wars, I felt happy that God has given me the strength to stay the course of virgin celibacy!)

13. Jason directed me to the northern acres of his estate where I found the lad, a sturdy, square-jawed boy with dark-red hair, building a stone wall with some of the servants. I noticed immediately the rocks were piled thoughtlessly and against the

12. Echoing *Ezekiel* 16:33.
13. In his late teens, Josephus attempted the ascetic life under the hermit Banus, according to his *Life*, 2. It is unlikely, from Josephus's description, that Banus was an Essene.
14. As in all Ebionite scriptures, the Jewish Christians considered Paul the Great Heretic and innovator. For the author's more detailed attack on Paul, see below 3:11–12.

grain of how they lay in the earth, so I mentioned that the wall was sure in time to fall.

Xenon with the confidence of one in his sixteenth year said to me, "When it falls I shall come back to rebuild it."

I said to him, "But it is not likely to fall in your lifetime. It shall be for one of your brother's children to rebuild it."

"All the better then," he said to me.

I gathered this task was beneath him and his quick mind was in need of rigorous employment. I proposed my plan to take him as a scribe to foreign lands in search of the scattered fragments of the true Nazirene Church I longed to recover. I asked him, "You are a Nazirene?"

"My father is," he told me.

Very well, I thought. Best that he not be too religious, since that has led Our Movement to its current troubles. I asked him next if he was brave.

"Not particularly," he told me, "but I suppose I should rather die in Aethiopia than stack stones in this desert for my brother's children and my brother's flocks."

14. So it was agreed he should come with me and take my dictation. I soon learned on our journey back to my estate nearer to Jerusalem how inept his writing skills were, and upon seeing him render πόνος [laborious study] as the word πότος [intense drunkenness], I nearly returned to Bethzur to abandon him to his wall-building, but he said he would improve with practice, and I allowed this. Had I known what was to befall us it would have been better for him had he never laid his eyes upon me! No, that is too strong, for he is alive and well, but what a sacrifice this young lad made for me! But more on that as my epic history progresses.

It is no wonder, in retrospect, poor Xenon had little use for Our Master and His teachings, for southern Judea, with its Idumaean taint, was filled with the most pernicious heresies. At the risk of repeating much in my comprehensive *All Heresies Refuted*, I shall describe some of the damnable movements afoot between Jerusalem and Eleuph:

15. For one, there are the Children of Adam, who plague every decency by their insistence on nakedness. What commune of theirs has not been found to produce unmarried women-with-child by the score?

16. A particularly egregious group of heretics, always rumored to have died out only to return in greater numbers, are the Opheisians, located outside of wretched Ekron. This sect took Our Master at His word concerning the good of serpents, that time when Peter threatened to kill one near the house in Bethany.[15] Our Master hated to see harm befall any living thing. From this innocent source they commemorate Our Master by passing around the deadly snakes, though it is not long before unpoisonous ones are procured and the snake becomes the center of the rite itself. From Cyprus, Crete, Clauda, and Cyrenaica[16]—where any filthy thing is raised up and glorified—the ancient heathen rites creep back in, championed as always by credulous women.

Cretan women of great heft and size, Minotauresses, disrobe and oil themselves with balms and likewise the snake, which finds its way into dread orifices, during which the women, entered by God, fall into spasms and ecstasies—I prosecuted all these camps in my *All Heresies Refuted* so there is no need to prolong this recital of damnations. One is apt, however, to feel sorry for the snakes.

17. And everywhere, no less in Jerusalem, are the Heliogenesians and their attempt to recast the life of Our Master into that of Mithra. For example, they attribute the terrifying darkness and storm the day of Our Teacher's execution to the dimming of the Sun itself, with which Our Master was somehow consub-

---

15. The incident alluded to is unknown in the Scriptures. Ophists (from the Greek *ophis*, for snake) have a pedigree as old as Minos and Ancient Egypt; some degree of snake cults occurred wherever Judeo-Christianity and Egyptian or Cycladic cultures met.

　　One still finds the snake and the cross intertwined today in Haiti, Africa, in the *santería* of Brazil and Latin America, and in the Southern United States (the Holy Ghost People in West Virginia and Pentecostals in the Carolinas), where Christians practice snake-handling as sacrament, taking as their inspiration *Matthew* 10:16 (*Be wise as serpents and innocent as doves,*) as well as *John* 3:14 (*And as Moses lifted up the serpent in the wilderness so must the Son of Man be lifted up. . . .*) and the latter-day affixed ending of Pseudo-*Mark*, 16:18 (*They will pick up serpents, and if they drink any deadly thing, it will not hurt them.*) Paul escapes the consequences of a snake bite in *Acts* 28.

16. Crete and Cyrenaica had been centers of the Minoan snake and fertility. There is little difference today from the popular Mediterranean statuary image of the Virgin Mary treading upon a serpent (having redeemed the sin of Eve) and depictions of ancient Minoan priestesses (ca. 2000 B.C.E.) treading upon a serpent.

stantial. It is inconvenient enough that Mithra was resurrected after three days, and that the Nazirenes claim this of Our Master as well.[17]

18. I briefly mention a heresy making progress due to the Roman infusion in our world, particularly in Philistine Ashkelon where no loyalties to anything fine exist, and that is the Jews and Nazirenes who have freely absorbed the atrocious rites of Attis.[18] As He Who Redeemed Us died upon a tree in the prime of youth, the devotees of Attis feel Our Master is Attis returned. These Nazirenes conform outwardly to orthodoxy but one enters their homes to find a five- or six-cubit pine tree decorated in the corner, offerings underneath the boughs, candles lit all around it. How long, O Lord, will these pernicious survivals endure?

19. But onward, and to the worst of the heresies yet!

Xenon and I passed through Beersheba, beyond which the wastes and brigandages of the desert beckoned. We soon found a train of tradesmen under light Roman guard who were traveling to Eleuph to return with spices and incense bound for Rome itself. Lately this particular route had to be traveled with guards due to the dreaded Celepheans who live in the Negevian caves.

The Celepheans are the most insidious of the castration cults,

17. The semi-Zoroastrian cult of Mithra (from the 500s B.C.E.) was direct competition for Christianity, and hence Christianity compromised with it. Mithra, born of the Heavenly Virgin, was a Sun god, born on December 25. The Mithraic birth ritual involved the chant: "The Virgin has brought forth! The light is waxing!" Vermaseran (*Mithra the Secret God*, London, 1963) identifies the Communion-like meal with Mithra's prayer, "He who shall not eat of my body and drink of my blood . . . shall not be saved." Mithra performed miracles and healings, and the cult emphasized chastity, charity, and an afterlife. Underneath one of the earliest Christian basilicas in Rome, St. Clement, the catacombs have as their centerpiece a Mithraic altar, suggesting there was a Mithraic variation on "orthodox" Christianity.

The Church's line on Christian appropriation of Mithraism has never been convincing, i.e., Tertullian, who claimed Mithra and Attis were made to flourish before Christianity by design of Satan, so that future Christians would wonder about the similarities and have doubts!

18. Second to Mithra, the cult of Attis, a variation of Adonis, also influenced and detracted from the Early Church. Attis was the son of the Great Mother born through Nana, a virgin. Attis castrated himself under a pine tree and then bled to death in the prime of life. Three days later the divine Son was resurrected on March 24—the date most of the Early Church chose to celebrate Easter for centuries. All this coincided with the spring equinox and innumerable vegetation-god ceremonies for the renewed blooming of the land.

which, having infected first the Essenes and Baptists, have passed their abominations onto the Nazirenes.[19] The Celepheans do not stop at mere castration, however, and proceed to unthinkable mutilations in the name of Our Master.

20. The Celephean initiate endures a period of excessive punishment. The elders tie him to a post and beat him into confessing the lewdest of sins and, as a final act, the initiate is castrated and must preside, after this crude surgery, over the destruction of his own testicles, by hammer, by flame, by mincing knife, whatever.[20] This part of the ceremony is called the Second Baptism, the casting off of the old repositories of sin, and is the commencement of being born again, purification of sins, and like nonsense. In their most recent resurgence, the Celepheans have a female order in which the women, in surgery without intoxicants, have their wombs sewn shut with glowing needles hot from the forge to prevent their ever conceiving. Recognizing their potential for tempting the men, they submit themselves to the defeminization process in which their hair is shorn and their breasts are sheared off, and though one can't help but approve in spirit, these measures to limit the natural feminine wantonness and mischief-making, I assert, go too far.

(I see young Tesmegan smiles, because in Aethiopia women grow as big as water buffalo, have their fill of men in unseemly carnality, and then castrate the rest. As if with such as Sporus and Pindymion and Dareus there were not Roman mutilations

---

19. In an age when one plague, war, or earthquake could eliminate a people, an age in which fecundity was worshiped as the means to perpetuate the tribe, nothing could have been more radical and unthinkable than self-castration. Yet for all the patriarchal weight against it, it caught on in most ancient societies during the First Century, as did flagellation and masochistic rites. Jesus' suggestion that *there are eunuchs that have made themselves eunuchs for the kingdom of heaven* (*Matthew* 19:12) found a receptive audience among ascetic young men.

   Origen, it is thought, castrated himself to remain pure; Justin Martyr recorded many who volunteered to castrate themselves so that no rumors of sexual misconduct could obtain; see H. Chadwick, *The Sentences of Sextus* or R. Koenig, *Female Eunuchs and Castration* (New York, 1989), which shows castration-mania having its last peak in the 200–300s C.E.

20. Compare the rites of Attis in Rome. During frenzies of bloodletting and flagellation, the celebrants severed their genitals (penis *and* testicles, often) and flung them upon the revered pine tree or the image of the Cruel Goddess, jagged and blood-soaked. In the self-castration rites of Cybele in Syria, the celebrants would run through the town and hurl their organs into a house, which would mean the family had the honor of supplying the novice with new robes for his priestly role.

enough of subject peoples, that we should add to it.[21] Such tales about us Jews only endear us to savages, I am sure—yes, Tesmegan, write down what I say, every word of it.)

21. A word about their pseudo-messiah Celephus, the high priest of this movement. In an elaborate rite each Sabbath he would work himself up into a state of abjection and then stand before his mob for guidance, claiming the Son of Man would appear and touch the most offensive part remaining on him, and in solemn ceremony, while he fell into an ecstasy, a joint of a finger or a toe or some wedge of flesh from somewhere would be removed by pincers or saw, sending his congregation into spasms of flagellation and self-abuse. Celephus in his trance would be carried to his bed of thorns. Upon awakening he would wander the neighboring villages and be mocked, quite commonly mistaken for a leper, all in honor of the Greatest Martyr, our Son of Man, and then return to the compound and ask to be lowered into the latrines.

The only writings we have left to us—for most were burned under [the Procurator] Felix's orders—concerned which salves and juices provided the more pain upon open wounds. Mind you, he did not risk death as much as one might think, since he endeavored to recover sufficiently to continue to suffer. . . .

Ah, but enough, my scribe is wide-eyed with horror.

22. Of course, convinced of the efficacy of virgin celibacy, I feel one makes the gesture pointless by removing the stewing pots from which desire and temptations seethe and pollute our bodies. How else can we know the strength of Our Master, who never stained Himself by as much as an impure thought, if we are not frequently delivered from our own base concupiscence?

23. But to return to my histories:

Upon reaching Eleuph, Xenon and I beheld more brothel than city. Here ships and caravans from across Araby, leaving

---

21. Sporus had himself castrated for the love of Nero and disguised himself as the late Empress Poppaea (whom the Emperor had personally kicked to death); Pindymion is unknown, and Dareus is likely the boy-eunuch who accompanied Caligula (Gaius Caesar) in his costumed pageants, Bagaos to the Emperor's Alexander the Great. (See Suetonius, *Gaius* 19, *Nero* 28.)

For someone who declares himself above Rome and its degeneration, the author has an amazing depth of knowledge concerning her gossip.

for Parthia, India, China, and the Frankincense Kingdoms of the south met and traded information and monies. As one might expect in such a place, no prostitution or degradation could not be purchased, no mother's safeguarding of a daughter's honor could overcome the clink of mercantile coins.

As Xenon and I walked south to the port through the main thoroughfare, women with oiled, splayed breasts presented themselves in upper windows, male prostitutes[22] not in their fourteenth year, painted and lacquered as some Babylonian temple-prostitute, called out with services they were willing to render Xenon and myself. I clasped my hands over Xenon's ears until we came to a corner where on a rooftop terrace a woman the size of an elephant, her enormous stomach and breasts distended over her wretched sex, led the street rabble in a chorus of obscenity, hooting and throwing a shell necklace at Xenon that constituted some form of discount. I moved my hands to protect young Xenon's eyes in order to prevent the permanent tainting of his thoughts.

24. Upon reaching the dockside, we were directed to the nearest synagogue. The rabbi there spat when we asked about Thomas and it was obvious he thought little of us Nazirenes, but it can hardly be said that Eleuph knew God in any measure. However, this failed Pharisee did inform us that we could find Thomas's *harim* in the Old Quarter of the city. More filthy streets and execrable houses of base amusement presented themselves as we wandered into the complex alleys of the old city. Finally, with grudging help from the locals, who could be expected to do nothing without remuneration, we came upon the house of Thomas.

It was no small shock to learn that Thomas, whom I recall being newly married in the time of Our Master's epoch, had added another seven wives to his collection, including an Indian, a Parthian—who had erected a Zoroastrian shrine near the hearth, no less—and a tall aristocratic Negress from Barbaria.[23]

25. Thomas returned from the shipyards and welcomed me

---

22. Ἀρσενοκοῖται, which is not "homosexual" strictly, for which the ancients had no word or concept, but rather the passive male prostitute Paul condemns in *1 Corinthians* 6:9.
23. Probably modern-day Somalia, the Horn of Africa.

warmly, amused above all else to see me in such an outpost. After perfunctorily praising the beauty of his many wives, I asked him about the Law's restriction on such a brood.

"The Law is no more," he said to me happily. "If we learned nothing else from Our Lord it was that the damned Law could be dispensed with."

This kind of thinking is what I mean, dear Josephus, about the disregard for proper doctrine and codification! As if the Lord intended us to do as we please!

I reminded him, "But not one iota of the Law has fallen away,"[24] for Our Lord was observant of the Law.

26. He said brusquely to me, "I see you haven't changed. You wish to wear out the holy with debates of doctrine. You should go to Ephesus and wrangle with John, who has an endless supply of foul breath for all debates."

It was vain to suggest it, but I commenced a disquisition on the necessity of virginity and the difficulty of fully devoting oneself to the Most High while maintaining eight wives and as many families.

27. But Thomas only laughed and confessed he had four or five more wives in various ports around the Orient, and informed us it cost less than a rebah a month to keep up a Carmanian[25] woman with Roman currencies valued as they were—better yet, one was married to all the sisters of a Carmanian woman as well, and all were allowed to join in the marriage-bed festivities! He even had a widow in Ctesiphon who adored him.

I said to him, making the sort of brilliant jest for which I am known, "Be careful on your travels there, that you don't make your theatrical debut like Crassus!"[26]

Thomas claimed he had lost count of his other wives! (I only pass along my friend's baseness so that the type of man he was may be well recorded.) Thomas furthermore reminded me that

24. *Matthew* 5:18.
25. Carmania was the Iranian side of the Straits of Hormuz. A rebah had the importance of, say, the U.S. nickel.
26. Parthia was the irresistible magnet of Roman vainglory. Crassus, of the First Triumvirate, lost 20,000 men there ignobly, another 10,000 to slavery; was killed in 54 B.C.E., carved up, and his body parts used as props in a performance that night of Euripides' *The Bacchae.*

I alone of the Disciples was not married; even John, who we both agreed had made himself a eunuch for Our Lord, had as a younger man burdened some poor village girl with his espousal.[27]

28. Dinner was tasty enough with a multitude of unusual spices that only later, I discovered, sent my bowels reeling. Before confessing my own spiritual maladies, I thought it best to get to the truth concerning a famous episode in the Disciple Thomas's life. "Much is told when the tale is recounted," I said to him, "of your disbelief upon the final days of Our Lord."

Here Thomas laughed with a belch and poured himself some more wine. I noticed young Xenon was looking at us with an unsure gaze not used to the quantities of grape. Thomas answered me, "Yes, I doubted He had come back from the dead. Not sure I believe it yet!"

(I was, I should here record, quite absent attending to business on the estate during the days after the execution of Our Master, and I am not proud of this. Like others, who now pretend to have been at the trial and execution, I will confess to my weakness and disloyalty. And I also will tell my readers what few Disciples will admit, that the appearances and teachings of our Master after He returned from the dead are a matter of mystery and great confusion.)

29. Said Thomas to me, "I'm not sure He died on the cross. He was hammered to it, all right, but men last for days up there. He seemed to give up the ghost in a few hours."

Surely, I protested, you don't mean to say Our Lord was in any way party to a pantomime!

Thomas answered, "Ah, He may have seemed dead when He was put in the tomb. The women fixed up His wounds, He had a long nap, and He may have thought He died and came back, Himself. Who is to say?"

Your doubts must never be made public, I insisted.

"Of course I make them public! You think the Pharisees themselves do not speak these things? It does not matter to me what anyone says. What Our Teacher lived and taught is enough

---

27. *Do we not have the right to be accompanied by a wife as the other apostles and the brothers of the Lord and Peter? 1 Corinthians 9:4–5.*

for me. I leave the theologizing to you and John and his star-eyed catamites! Thanks to the Most High I was not a scholar, a cursed priest—thanks be to his Everlasting Mercifulness!"

30. I, as all know, am considered somewhat of a scholar and historian and I here reasserted the need for scholarship.

Thomas raged on thusly, "The rabbis have crushed the life out of the Bible and if you had your way, my friend, you would stomp the juice out of Our Master as in a vat of grapes."

And to another offering from the grapes our friend had recourse again, and was now quite inebriated. I inquired if Thomas had read my *All Heresies Refuted?* Thomas simplified far too much for my liking, I asserted.

Thomas said to me, "Plain old love and charity is simple, is it? Then why is it so difficult to get anyone to do it? What I think sours converts is John's talk of Eternal Sonship and whether the Word or the Holy Spirit came before the Father—as if Yahweh was a father like I am a father! Amazing that Yahweh does not strike us down for such an idea! I pity you, my friend, raised fancy to be a cursed Greek, Jewish blood in your veins, one foot in the Temple of Jerusalem, another in this new synagogue of ours, while living in the world of the Romans—you will never have a good night's sleep!"

31. Thomas went on to tell me that my selection as a Disciple was not without its corruption: "I'll tell you the damned truth and the others won't! You had money, you have an estate and a lenient father, you have an education so that you might be of use in letter writing . . . though I understand you have written nothing but kindling!"

By this remark I saw that news of Peter's destruction of my last gospel had reached even Eleuph. (I chose not to tangle with him on this, though I reminded myself to send Thomas a copy of *All Heresies Refuted* when I returned to Jerusalem and could assign Xenon the copyist's task.)

32. Thomas said to me, "So do not tell me it never occurred to you that it was your money and estate we were after, my fine fellow!" He said this while slapping me like some wine-tavern familiar. And then he said, "You were but sixteen! Did you think at that age we acquired you for your wisdom and maturity?"

And I hope, Josephus my own brother, you can appreciate how difficult it is to record that I was sought by the Nazirenes for my money, which I willingly gave them, and which you ridiculed me for. I hope you balance that satisfaction with pity for me for having fallen from the Nazirene Movement and to be at my age, homeless and confused. It is for the young to wander about in search of God, not for the weary and enfeebled, the old whose minds should be as stone tablets with the name of God indelibly engraved.

"No, go ask Peter," Thomas then said to me, "when next in Antioch and he will tell you why you were selected. Better for you, my friend, had you done as Jude has done, retired to his cloth shop in Beersheba."

As for Jude, and even John, whose scholarship repelled Thomas and me alike, I asked Xenon to record their locations and I began planning to travel to see them. Xenon began to hiccup and I saw that he could barely hold the quill. (Indeed a sip from his cup confirmed to me that Thomas had supplied my scribe with wine undiluted.)

33. Before I could protest, Thomas stood and got Xenon to his feet, preparing to take him for a walk. He boomed, "If it's gospels you want, why not peruse some of mine!"

I expressed amazement that he had recorded anything.

He said to me, "On the contrary. My wife Sepphora insisted upon it—she takes all my dictations!"

A woman! Xenon swayed unsteadily and so Thomas threw an arm around him and took him out for fresh air while I remained at the house and his wife, Sepphora, brought me some wretched Arab drink and a collection of scrolls for me to read.

I asked Sepphora, "Why did Thomas not educate one of his many sons to take his dictation?"

She said to me, "Why should he when we need our sons to work? Someone must work while he runs about preaching the Messiah has come, killed by the Romans."

I understood by this denegration that she was not a Nazirene.

She said to me, "No, but then I never met the man, and what I saw of John the Baptist was fearsome."

Yes, the Baptist was fearsome, but more on him momentarily

[see 5:5–6]. Sepphora said to me further: "Why should my husband hire a scribe when I am so skilled in the Laws of Moses and the Prophets?"

34. A woman speaking thusly to me! I becalmed myself by remembering that our abiding spirit of wisdom, *Sophia*, who pervades and penetrates all things by reason of her pureness,[28] is as female as the ground we walk upon. Scholarship is a task more fitted to a man, but a woman's learning surely does little harm, and does have the added effect of steeling young women against loss of virginity (without which any elevation of their wordly role is not possible).

I will quickly record that Thomas's ramblings were heterodox in the extreme. Not without a certain Aramaic flair, or without a certain honesty of spirit, but clearly too much from his travels has been stirred into the broth. I am the light that is darkness, the ice that is within fire, he that is first is last—this kind of Eastern tiresomeness.[29]

35. The next day after meeting a few of the paltry Nazirene congregation of ex-prostitutes and elderly, I was ready to pass out of that filthy town and on toward Beersheba to see Jude.

I asked of Thomas, "Is Jude involved in any ministry?"

"Not that I know," he said to me, "and good thing too, bad a speaker as he is. His horrible stutter."

But to do nothing!

"Perhaps it is his lot to do nothing," said Thomas. "Well, my friend," he then said, slapping my back as was his wont, "who knows if we shall see each other again? I am off to India, and at my age I can't see many more such voyages. I am off to finish what I started. Or rather, what He started."

36. Here I bethought it best to be honest and tell Thomas of

---

28. *The Wisdom of Solomon*, 7:24.
29. Thomasine writings all make use of the Apostle's journeys to India. Less authentic are an *Acts of Thomas* recounting Thomas's miraculous adventures in India (its origins are ancient but obscure); and there is an *Apocalypse of Thomas* (there is a 5th-Century Viennese fragment, probably originating from that time but some make a case it is quoted in Jerome in the 4th Century).

But more interesting is the Nag Hammadi *Gospel of Thomas*, which seems to have elements of the First Century, and is certainly no later than 140 C.E. Koester at Harvard suggests parts of *Thomas* may even precede the Synoptics; see *Nag Hammadi Library*, Koester's introduction to the *Gospel of Thomas* (New York, 1977).

my personal state. I envied him for the security of his faith, and I confessed I coveted it with an intensity that surely ranked as sinful. I would not have been surprised had he made sport of me, but he spoke warmly to me, which I took as a sign of his rustic good heart.

"I tell you what you do," Thomas said to me. "You need to spend time with the elderly and perhaps the sick, as He instructed."

My talents lie not there, I informed him.

"The prisoners then, when you get back to Jerusalem. We are to visit them, Our Master said. What you'd learn of the world when you see someone in the dregs of the Praetorian prison—those Roman swine!"

37. I said to him, "I am not suited for that enterprise as well. When I speak to people beneath my class they tend to laugh at me and mock me."

"And does not a prisoner need a laugh? Well, does he not? See the service that you might render, my companion?"

I record here that I was overcome with frustration when I said to Thomas: "You think me a total fool."

Then Thomas embraced me and gave me the kiss of *agápe*. "But as my brother before the Teacher of Righteousness, I love you with all my heart," he said to me. "I love you for the place you have in the scheme of things! I love you for the role that you were born to play!"

38. But what role is that?

How many times, though, I turned to God in prayer to put my case before Him. My learning, my scholarship, my literary gift, my impeccable Greek, my background in the philosophers—how best could He bring it to use? And I have never felt my heart move to the sure answer.

And that was the last I saw of Thomas.

39. Xenon and I began our journey to Beersheba and many of the women of the streets called to him familiarly and a horrible thought occurred that Thomas had taken him to one of these bowers of depravity! I charged Xenon to tell me the truth and he shyly insisted on his innocence, of which I was persuaded after many minutes of intense examination. A rascal, that

Thomas. Licentious as Thomas could be, I know he would not have done that to young Xenon out of regard for me, being aware, surely, of my insistence on virgin chastity as the engine of refinement for the soul.

The details of our trip to Beersheba are unimportant as that is clearly the dullest, hottest journey one can make in this land.

40. Jude[30] had a cloth shop where his wife commanded most of the business and commerce. "I have not a head for numbers," he said to me, as if it were a point of pride his wife should manage the business. Jude looked as I recalled him. His hair had remained dark and his eyes were a gentle man's; he was as retreating as I remembered and he still spoke only under great duress and, for the first few minutes, with his stutter.

I asked him if there were a Nazirene synagogue in Beersheba.

41. "There is none," he said with difficulty. "Though my wife will bring people over to pray. And there are pilgrims."

I inquired as to the object of pilgrimage.

"You, too, must know of pilgrims," he said to me. "They come because I knew The Teacher of Righteousness and was one of the Twelve. Once a week or more someone passes through this town to touch my hand or to have me pray with them."

I asked how he honored such requests.

He said to me, "Alas, I do not think the Lord has allowed me to be part of a healing, though once or twice I am sure I did some good. They ask about Him and I, in my way, stammer out what I remember, though my memory has blurred through the years. Do you not find it so?"

Yes, very much! It is the very reason, I told him, that I had embarked upon these travels! To recover the truth of those few precious years when He was among us.

---

30. The Disciple Judas/Jude/Lebbaeus/Thaddeus was the son (according to *Acts* 1:13 and *Luke* 6:16) or the brother (according to *Jude* 1) of James bar-Alphaeus. This gospel sheds no light either way. *Matthew* and *Mark* list him but do not give any relation. Jesus had a brother named Judas, too. "*Is not this the. . .brother of James and Joses and Judas and Simon?*" say Jesus' countrymen in rejecting him, *Mark* 6:3. As the Scriptures can agree neither on the name nor relation of this man, later attempts can only be legendary; hence, his being titled "the Obscure" and his patronage of lost causes. He and Simon the Zealot were supposed to have converted the Persians and to have been martyred there, but one gathers from this account that this never happened.

"You always had too much money," Jude said to me, I believe in jest.

42. Tell me, I asked of Jude, why haven't you gone with the evangel through the land?

He laughed. "The way I speak? Sometimes I am so unable to deliver my voice that I merely nod yes and no to pilgrims' questions. I wonder that I have given out incorrect information because some of the old and infirm have heard fantasies, have heard fictions. Two days ago a woman with an issue of blood, clothed in stained bandages, her face pale as new cotton, came to this house. She had heard that Our Master said that any who have such an infirmity are sure to reach Heaven for they are already washed in blood. You see how she was confused."

And you corrected this crone?

"No, I did not," Jude said to me, reclaiming his stammer.

From what I made out, Jude confirmed her mistaken notion of Our Master's teachings. Indeed, he was sure Our Lord would have told the woman the same thing or perhaps have healed her, although it was mysterious why some He healed and some He walked by. I recall Thomas asking Our Lord that if God were a God of love, why did Our Lord not visit the leper colony outside of the city and heal every sufferer? Our Lord made no answer. Mysteries too profound to consider!

43. Repeatedly Jude said to me: "Don't you see, my friend, it was enough that she had faith to come? It is such faith that God will reward. No, I could not help her, even after she walked from her village across the sands to my door. In the next world, though, she will walk into the Kingdom."

I confess here to a certain desperation with this laxity concerning Our Master's teachings. I do not feel good about it now, but I am afraid I was rather unpleasant to Jude and I asked if with his whimsical innovations of Our Master's philosophy, he had brought as much as a single soul into the Kingdom-to-come. What of Moses and his stutter—he delivered a people![31] Why was Jude at all chosen by Our Lord?

Jude gave me the brotherly kiss of peace. He then said, "Is

---

31. *Exodus* 4:10.

it not possible that the soul Our Lord intended to save was mine?"

44. I explained to Jude that it seemed unlikely with only Twelve Disciples to choose amid all the world, to commence all the chores assigned us before the coming End Times, that Our Teacher should be so inefficient but to gain only one small soul for the New Kingdom by Jude's selection.

"You think it a waste," Jude replied to me, "that only myself was gathered to Our Lord's flock by my selection. But I tell you, I believe that to be sufficient. Could it have been that Our Master looked out upon the world and saw me lost and brought me to Him the only way He knew how?"

But how impractical!

Jude laughed and said: "But that is precisely the sort of thing He was always doing." Jude then put a hand upon me and with his other hand touched his heart. "For all your learning, my brother, I believe it is I who knew Him better."

45. And as I left Beersheba that evening, I looked over at Xenon asleep on his mule plodding by my side, and I looked out upon the vast wastes of the Negev and wondered that God should send His True Prophet to personally redeem the likes of Jude and, if so, that the Most High Father must love His children very much indeed. But then to what purpose was I brought near Our Master as a Disciple? What did He gain through such a wretch as me?

IRELAND

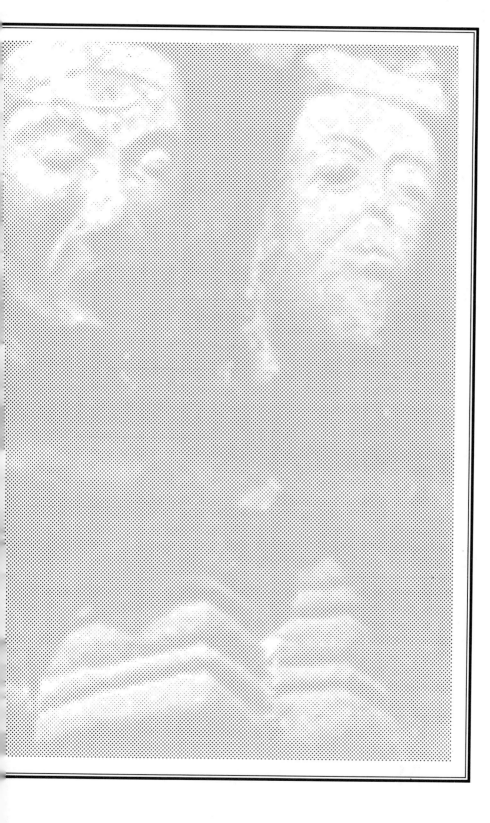

There was a beggar boy used to be in Burren that was very simple like and had no health, and if he would walk as much as a few perches it is likely he would fall on the road. And he dreamed twice that he went to St. Brigit's blessed well upon the cliffs and that he found his health there. So he set out to go to the well, and when he came to it he fell in and he was drowned. . . . It is likely it is in heaven he is at this time.

—An ancient Irish holy legend,
collected by LADY GREGORY (1906)

No single story would they find
Of an unbroken happy mind,
A finish worthy of the start.
Young men know nothing of this sort.
Observant old men know it well;
And when they know what old books tell,
And that no better can be had,
Know why an old man should be mad.

—from "Why Should Not Old Men Be Mad?"
Last Poems (1939)
W. B. YEATS

This morning from a dewy motorway
I saw the new camp for the internees:
A bomb had left a crater of fresh clay
In the roadside, and over in the trees

Machine-gun posts defined a real stockade.
There was that white mist you get on a low ground
And it was deja-vu, some film made
Of Stalag 17, a bad dream with no sound.

Is there a life before death? That's chalked up
In Ballymurphy. Competence with pain,
Coherent miseries, a bite and sup,
We hug our little destiny again.

—from "Whatever You Say Say Nothing," *North* (1975)
SEAMUS HEANEY

In name of the Former, and of the Latter
And of their Holocaust. Allmen.

—*Finnegans Wake* (1939)
JAMES JOYCE

baile áta cliat

L ucy found Dublin more modern-looking than she imagined, but still more of a large town than a city, which despite its recent thousandth birthday was not full of the ancient winding alleyways or cobblestones of quainter European capitals. It was staid and Georgian where it was grand and monumental, and shabby where it was not grand. Standing at the River Liffey and O'Connell Street she fought off disappointment that the legendary, much-invoked Dublin was not somehow more, well, Parisian or at least visually equal to Oxford, endearingly ancient.

(Give it time. Dublin grows on you.)

It was early evening. The airport shuttle bus had deposited Lucy at the Tourist Information office and there she acquired a simple city map upon which the nice woman circled Mulligan's Pub for her. Then she strolled by the modern fast-food franchises and the post office . . . was that *the* Post Office of the 1916 Uprising? She had crossed the main bridge over the Liffey, noticing the giant neon signs one finds in all Times Square equivalents, and then had turned to amble along the riverbank, listening to people talk—some of the Dublin speech sounded American and broad, surprisingly—and looking at the ruddy faces, the lovely pale women with yellow-blond hair, the redheads, and Ireland's great world export, the old drunk, with a creased caricature of a face, old sack clothes, scooting along at his own addled pace toward the next Guinness.

"Kin ye help me out, miss?"

"Sorry, no change on me." Lucy walked quickly by.

"God bless yer sweet heart anyways," he said, tipping his cap politely.

A few blocks from the river, in a shadowy, grimy alley was Mulligan's. Lucy peeped in, wondering if this was solely a male bastion of darts and pints quaffed by red-faced laborers, but to her relief there was a good mix of people within. Lucy noted the tin ceiling and tile floor, the ornate, dark wood liquor cabinet and frosted mirror that ran the length of the bar. Other countries invested their cathedrals with altarpieces and sculpture—here in Ireland, apparently, the greatest craftsmanship was expended on these baroque pub masterpieces. Aha. There in the back, Rabbi Hersch on one side, Father Keegan on the other side, and a young fellow at their table sharing their laughter, was her man.

"I refuse to believe it," the priest was saying, "that there'd be something ye can't work up a taste for, alcohol, I mean."

The rabbi insisted that *mou-tai* was undrinkable.

"In Korea," O'Hanrahan concurred, "the army captured a crate of the stuff from Red China. A whole platoon of drink-starved soldiers. We couldn't do it, Father. One taste would convince you."

"I am shocked," he said mournfully, "to hear *you* of all people taking this line with me, Paddy."

"Not just *mou-tai*, but *pulque* down in Mexico. In 1964, I was cataloguing the fascinating Jesuit Library at Guadalupe, Zacatecas, in which one can view—"

"Who gives a damn, man," said Father Keegan, single-mindedly. "What of this drink?"

O'Hanrahan: "It's called *pulque* and it looks like milk, made from the juice of the maguey plant, but this batch had moonshine-strength fermented cactus fruit in it as well. I was in this true, primitive cantina. Along the base of the bar was a trough, a urinal that drained in the street." The men roared with tipsy laughter. "You didn't have to move, Father. As you drank, you pissed right at the bar."

"Mother of God," said the priest, "they're ahead of us in technology now in Mexico, wouldn't you know?"

"You took Beatrice on such a trip?" asked the rabbi.

"No, left her in Chicago, like I always did," said O'Hanrahan.

"No wonder your marriage was in trouble," said Father Keegan, so plain-spoken that it was impossible to take offense, though it prompted a change of subject matter in O'Hanrahan:

"Whose round is it?"

Lucy cleared her throat: "It's mine."

O'Hanrahan stared up at her incredulously. "*You? Who* among my followers has betrayed me?"

"Aw," said Father Keegan, rising, "your daughter, Paddy. And a lovely young thing she is—"

"She's *not* my daughter."

Lucy explained that with all the talk of Mulligan's back at Oxford she figured O'Hanrahan would hardly be anywhere else. Privately she noticed the young man across from her, about twenty-six or so, with lightly freckled skin, vibrant red hair, gray-green eyes. He bowed his head to her, "Introduce me, Paddy." Was everyone on a first-name basis with Dr. O'Hanrahan but her?

"She's not staying long enough for you to meet," said the professor.

"My name's David McCall," said the young man unaided.

"Lucy Dantan. What are you guys drinking?"

Guinness!

"Right," she said. And as she left the table, she added, "When we get back we'll talk about St. Matthias."

That ought to keep them from running out the door, she figured as she made her way to the bar. But Lucy learned Guinness-pouring is a different matter in Dublin and it takes minutes to draw, settle, and refill up to the top, the publican wiping away the foam. So she placed her order and walked back to the table.

"You didn't give me my last guess, sir," she said, taking a low pub stool. "But that was just as well, because it made me take the time to figure out that the disciple in question was Matthias."

"You mean Matthew?" asked David, unclear what guesses she was referring to.

"I mean the *thirteenth* of the Twelve Disciples."

"Father," appealed David, "I thought I learned there were only twelve."

"*Acts*, Chapter 1, verse 20-something, Matthias was number thirteen," said Father Keegan, not too interested, wishing the conversation would return to the beverages of the world. "The replacement for Judas after he killed himself. Matthias is a what ye might call a New Testament trivia question."

"I called up," explained Lucy, "the books you ordered at the Codrington Library." She briefly noted O'Hanrahan's scowl. "I saw the *Andreas* and books in Amharic from Ethiopia. I also knew from credit-card receipts the Theology Department has back in Chicago that you were in Trier. I talked to this don about the *Andreas* and he said it was about the adventures of Andrew and Matthew—and you'd told me neither Andrew nor Matthew was the subject of this gospel.

"But then I started looking at some of the Greek apocrypha you ordered from the library, and I found in one volume a Fourth-Century *Acts of Andrew and Matthias*. Matthew and Matthias—the names got switched through the years since they were so similar. The Anglo-Saxon poem as well as the Greek *Acts* tells of Andrew and Matthias's adventures in Ethiopia."

"Oh, she's quite a detective," marveled David.

O'Hanrahan surrendered with a sigh. "Where's my Guinness?"

Lucy went back to the bar, paid for the beers and carried two back. Then David hopped up to get the other two, giving her a wink as he passed her.

Man alert, Lucy determined: he's cute.

"The rest fell into place," she told them, back in her chair. "The relics of Matthias were enshrined by the Emperor Constantine in Trier, West Germany. That explains your going there to look at the archives."

"I was checking out this year's Piesporter Riesling," O'Hanrahan said innocently.

"I'll drink to that," said the father. "Now as for this *mou-tai* libation, Paddy, you were referring to . . ."

Lucy opened her big carpetbag and pulled out the dog-eared notepad and flipped through pages covered with scrawled notes.

"Ah, mercy," said Father Keegan, "it's getting serious at this table. Now don't ye be forgetting our appointment, Paddy, at midnight."

"Who could forget?" said the professor. "You're not leaving now, are you, Father?"

"No no nooo," he said heavily, wishing perhaps he could.

Lucy began, "The *Gospel of Matthias* is mentioned first by Clement of Alexandria, so it's at least as old as 170 A.D. Clement mentions the work has a strict antisex morality—"

Father Keegan barely hid a belch. "Hmmm, so *that's* who we have to blame for that. Thought it to be an Irish doctrine alla these years."

Lucy went on. "There's a mention of St. Matthias in Irenaeus, but it's not very revealing. And then finally we have Eusebius, the first great Byzantine historian, circa 324—"

O'Hanrahan tartly: "We know who Eusebius is."

"He lists all the known gospels of the day. Of course, the New Testament as we know it didn't exist then and there were all kinds of gospels, heretical and otherwise, floating around. He classifies Matthias's as heretical, though it doesn't seem he actually read it. Which means in the next few decades probably all copies of it were burned."

Lucy put down her notebook.

"But I think we know," she said, having everyone's attention, "that if you want to preserve something forever, you ban it and drive it underground. The Early Church and, for that matter," she added, glancing at the rabbi, "the Mishnah and Talmud are examples of how writings of an intensely persecuted people endure. So I think someone translated the *Gospel of Matthias* into an obscure African language and the scroll survived."

"What makes you think that?" asked O'Hanrahan insecurely.

"Because you ordered up all those African books, and besides, the way you and Rabbi Hersch talk, I can tell it hasn't been translated. And you guys, between you, can read anything."

"What are we doing in Dublin then?" asked the rabbi, curious to see just how obvious their moves were to an outsider.

Lucy gambled. "Whoever had the scroll last after Rome—some German fellow you said, right, Rabbi? Whoever had that scroll must be willing to sell it to you. Though . . ." She looked sidewise at Father Keegan. ". . . Father Keegan I overheard saying that 'money wasn't necessary.' So maybe someone just wants to *give* it to you." It just occurred to her: "Or maybe is at such a loss to translate it themselves, they've contracted you guys to do it."

O'Hanrahan turned cross: "How do you know about the German guy and Rome?"

The rabbi patted his leg. "I told her a bit, thinking she was going home, Paddy. My fault."

David smiled, but then seeing the fearsome lack of levity of O'Hanrahan, he swallowed it.

Everyone remained quiet a minute.

"Not bad," said O'Hanrahan. "What do you plan to do with this illuminating report?" O'Hanrahan looked deep into his Guinness for guidance. "I don't suppose," he began, "you'd humor us by conveniently being hit by a bus and developing amnesia."

The festive spirit seemed to have drained away from the table and no one had anything to say. Father Keegan rose to be on his way, reminding O'Hanrahan portentously once more that they had a meeting, a rendezvous with fate and destiny!

"I'm bushed too, fellas," said the rabbi, also rising from the table. "I'll get a cab back to Mrs. O'Feagh's."

"That's where everybody's staying?" asked Lucy.

They glared at her as if to say: everyone but you.

"David, my boy," said O'Hanrahan, buttoning his overcoat, "I'll see you out front of Mrs. O'Feagh's tomorrow at eleven."

"I'll be there," he said.

O'Hanrahan and Rabbi Hersch departed, leaving David there with Lucy. Now there was another silence, but a friendlier one.

"Well, I could, uh, walk ye to the bed-and-breakfast, you know," said David helpfully. "I gotta check me posthole in college, see if anyone's dropped me a note, and then we could uh . . ."

"Walk over there."

"Yeah, that's what we could do."

Lucy was suddenly seized with an urgent need to look in a mirror. She excused herself and stood before a distorted reflection of herself in a small mirror attached to the hand-towel dispenser. Her auburn hair was windblown from her walks on the ferry deck and it looked accidentally stylish, wild and contemporary. Her long coat obscured the particulars of her figure and the scarf wrapped around her neck aided a slight double-chin problem, though she was expert in keeping her head erect in the presence of attractive guys. Oh, this was being ridiculous, wasn't it? Heck, she better get out there so he won't think she's primping like she's doing.

The streets of Dublin were loud and rowdy.

Lucy, still with her heavy bag, walked by David's side; he steered her clear of a teenage boy, his face the picture of all human suffering, kneeling in the gutter in order to be sick.

"Bet it's his birthday," said David, explaining. "It's painful to watch someone like that—I see meself there, you know?"

"Yes, that was me at Oxford, actually," Lucy confessed.

This topic of universities led to Lucy's mentioning she was at the University of Chicago and David's mentioning he was a student nearby at Dublin University, Trinity College. Lucy wondered aloud how David got to be so favored as to call Dr. O'Hanrahan by his first name.

"He's a longtime friend of the family, he is," said David, "and I can say what I please to him."

"How do you know him?"

"Near where I'm from, Ballymacross, up in the County Antrim, in the Northern part . . ." Lucy didn't seem to register the geography, but he went on. "There's this island, Rathlin Island. There used to be a retreat for the Jesuits."

"Rathlin Island."

"Back when I was growing up, before the Troubles, it was quite a retreat for brains like O'Hanrahan. Never been over to the island meself since I been grown, not that they'd want me in their church— I'm not the religious sort. Anyway, Patrick went over to Rathlin a dozen times or more, but he'd come back to Ballymacross to lift a few pints, of course, 'cause there's nothing on the island at all to do, no town, no pubs, no nothing. Me father used to run a boat over to Rathlin and back before he started working at the cannery, so Patrick and he met thataway and got on like nobody's business."

"I see," said Lucy.

"The last we saw of Patrick was about 1973 before his, you know, son was in that crash, God help him. I must've been no more'n seven or eight. And we got the Hare Krishnas over there now. The weather's so bad, I can't imagine shallyin' about in the light robes they wear, ye know?"

Lucy did some quick back-calculating: David must be 24, 25. Certainly legal marrying age.

David volunteered to carry her suitcase. Lucy surrendered the burdensome bag and David decided it was best to drag it, pulling it behind him by its leash. As promised, he led her through the elegant Georgian courtyards of Trinity College, by the grand, gray-stoned arches and neoclassical facades illumined at night, past the laughing, bustling groups of students, so much more alive and American-seeming than the oppressed, sniffling, pallid Oxford lot. David learned he had not received any mail so he and Lucy turned for the bus station and the bed-and-breakfast strip, down a slight hill during which the suitcase bit at their heels, rolling into them.

Lucy then asked, "What are Dr. O'Hanrahan and Father Keegan doing? This secret project at midnight?"

"Well, they wouldn't tell me exactly."

Lucy was sure. "They must be acquiring the scroll *tonight*."

She explained to David that she was on a mission from her university following O'Hanrahan and helping his department decide whether he was onto the find of the century or merely insane.

"No, I don't think he's insane," said David.

By the time Lucy finished relating the professor's adventure of the last three months, David was as curious as she was.

"Why don't *we* follow 'em?" suggested David. "I brought the car down last week from home, in order to drive Patrick up to see me folks."

Lucy quickly checked her bags in at Mrs. O'Feagh's Bed & Breakfast, while David went to a corner a few blocks away where he had parked illegally in a spot one never got a ticket. A few minutes later, he drove by the bed-and-breakfast, Lucy hopped in, and David drove to Father Keegan's church, Our Lady of Perpetual Sorrows.

They sat parked outside the church, waiting for midnight.

"This could be exciting," said David.

In ten minutes they were both a little cold. No excitement, subsequently, had presented itself in twenty minutes. Lucy listened to David as he told her about his agricultural engineering degree, concentrating instead on his handsome features in the bluish streetlamp light. Lucy found herself infatuated by his irresistible brogue and his gestures with his thick, freckled hands. And when he had something of interest to say how he'd squint as he spoke, then smile after he made his announcement, so naturally, so openly.

"So what do you think?" David asked her.

"Oh, I'm sorry . . . about what specifically?"

"About coming up with Dr. O'Hanrahan and the rabbi to Ballymacross tomorrow?"

"I'm sure they'd hate it," she said, hiding her delight.

"Patrick's a mangy cur, he is really. He's all bark. Ye mustn't give a thought to him—ye tell him you're going and that's that. Put them two in the backseat and you sit up front with me."

Where exactly *was* Ballymacross? It didn't matter, she'd go!

"But it's bound to be trouble."

"I'd tell ye if it were! I'd like ye to come, and plus I have an ulterior motive, you'll see."

Probably not the one I have in mind, thought Lucy.

"I'd like to go to the States," David said. "For a bit, ye know. Everyone goes but it's hard to get your visa 'cause once you're there you can work illegally and no one can detect you. We lose our accents like *that*," he added, snapping his fingers. "If I go to the States I'll need someone to stay with at first or show me 'round and Chicago's good a place as any. Only trouble with it, 's too many Irish there."

Lucy laughed.

"That's what's so good about the mission work in Africa. I wanna go somewhere where no one's got red hair and gets pissed and sings fockin' Molly Malone, ye know?"

Hope he does visit, thought Lucy. May have to kill Judy to get the apartment to myself but my conscience could accommodate that . . .

(Oh Lucy, really.)

Could bring this one home to Daddy and Mommy, she thought.

(Getting a bit ahead of yourself there, My child.)

Lucy wondered suddenly, since David came from Northern Ireland, whether he was Catholic or Protestant.

(It doesn't matter to Us, why should it to you?)

"Look," he said intensely.

Father Keegan and O'Hanrahan stumbled out through the chancery door, laughing about something.

"Must be gone to fetch his car," said David.

"You don't suppose they're taking a long trip, do you?"

"I don't have loads of petrol, so I hope not."

Soon a small black car emerged from the side drive, its clutch grinding and gears whirring. David waited until it reached the corner and turned, before starting his own car, turning on his lights, then following them.

"This is just like a television show," David enthused. "Bet you're used to this stuff all the time in America . . ."

He pulled up right behind the small car as Lucy ducked down needlessly in the seat. The two cars wound their way out of the valley of downtown Dublin until residential streets and rolling hills surrounded them, houses now dark and occupants sleeping. Before Dun Laoghaire, the road afforded a glimpse of the Dublin Bay, glassy smooth tonight with a reflection of moonlight, tankers and foreign ships anchored calmly, while the only motion on the bay was a car ferry, bound for Wales and laced with sparkling lights reflecting in the still black water.

"Getting down to an eighth of a tank," said David worriedly.

"I'll pay you back for the gas," Lucy mumbled.

" 'S not that I'm worried about."

But soon Father Keegan's car slowed before an old-fashioned Irish junction sign, pointed panels fanning out in all directions, black on white, announcing Wicklow was 17 miles ahead, Dublin 13 miles behind them, and up a small road, lined by hedges, was Enniskerry and St. Rodan's Chapel, three miles beyond. The father's car turned for the Chapel. David slowed and went beyond the turn, so as not to seem to be following them. He drove on another fraction of a mile, then turned around.

"St. Rodan's Chapel," said Lucy, considering. "Do you suppose the big handoff is going to take place there?"

(St. Rodan of the 570s. Battling a recalcitrant pagan king, Our inventive Rodan engaged in the greatest cursing contest of Ireland, reducing Tara to rubble, wishing the king the treatment of an animal skinned, a fish in a boiling pot, wishing a red-hot nail to fasten his tongue to the roof of his mouth, wishing that grubs and maggots and worms and sharp-jawed baby eels devoured the king from within. Christianity victorious, yet again.)

"I been there as a kid," said David. "It's an old Celtic church, 1000s or so, like Glendalough? Ruins of a roundtower, you know?" Lucy nodded, unclear about Celtic architectural features.

David and Lucy edged slowly down the country road to Enniskerry, a crossroads village, and then up a further, narrower lane until they came upon the chapel in a clearing of pines. Father Keegan's car was parked in front. And the front door of the chapel was ajar and a flickering light glowed from within.

David said, "Father Keegan's in charge of a lot of the holy places and shrines in these parts. A local historian, he is, always writing things for the paper. He probably has the keys to St. Rodan's."

They sat in the car not sure what to do next.

A chilling thought possessed Lucy: what if the parties involved were some of these rough-playing collectors or foreign dealers, armed and dangerous? What if Gabe wasn't merely being overdramatic about someone having been killed for this document? And what if Lucy and David's being there compromised this upcoming transaction?

"Maybe this was dumb," she said slowly. "Maybe we're just going to ruin the deal, being here."

David slipped out of the car. "Aw c'mon, let's go take a peek!"

"David," she hissed, getting out of the car herself. "No! What if we're messing up the big handoff? Dr. O'Hanrahan will kill us!"

"I've known Father Keegan for a bit and Patrick since I was wee, Lucy. They'll think it's a laugh we followed 'em. Ah, I tellya what, we oughta jump out and scare the shite out of 'em!"

"I really regret doing this now," said Lucy, fearful of O'Hanrahan's swift, assured wrath.

David stepped up to the chapel door and peered in. He motioned Lucy over. She reluctantly tiptoed across the gravel lot gingerly and took a look inside. It was a simple, dank stone church with spare decoration, a Celtic crucifix—a cross with a circle imposed on the transection—on the altar, and the interior illumined only by a few candles. Father Keegan was lighting another candle while chuckling about something but their echoing, indistinct voices couldn't be deciphered. O'Hanrahan stood holding a church candlestick, lighting up a small cigar with the flame. Father Keegan produced a rusted ring of old keys and unlocked a grate to a cellar beneath the altar . . . an ancient crypt! What a wonderful hiding place, thought Lucy. A foundation clear back to the lost Celtic mysteries of Ireland, the age of Patrick and Columkille. . . .

"The scroll must be in the crypt," Lucy whispered.

David looked amused.

"What's so funny?" she asked, smiling back.

"Nothing," he said.

But then they heard a triumphant yell from within. Lucy and David, huddled down low on the outside stairs, peered back into the dark church and Father Keegan was being helped from the cellar by O'Hanrahan. In the priest's hand was something like a gasoline can, like the container one uses back in America to fill a lawn mower. Then O'Hanrahan approached with a chalice from a nearby unlocked cabinet of Communion wares. David was snickering beside her.

"What are they doing?" she asked him.

"I knew it, I knew it . . ." David laughed.

Poteen, pronounced puh-sheen. The Irish moonshine. Distilled in many a church cellar in the golden days of 19th-Century ecclesiastical tippling, its production now nearly a lost art form. Trust Father Keegan to know where you get the stuff, explained David in whispers, and trust O'Hanrahan to quaff it down in the Holy Grail itself.

"I had a feeling," David concluded, sitting on the church steps.

"You let me think this had to do with the scroll," Lucy protested, swatting him lightly to scold him. "Making me look like an idiot."

"Nawww, I promise on me honor. But you see, they were talking about *poteen* before you came. That's what we were discussing, liquors of the world, you know? So I had a feeling that's what this was about."

Lucy smiled back. "Want to knock on the door and get a glass?"

"That'll make ya blind, it will," he said, shaking his head. "Or worse, keep a man from . . . ye know, functioning."

We can't have that, thought Lucy, scooting a bit closer to him on the steps.

David proposed: "We'll sit here and give 'em both a right scare when they come out." They both looked up to a clearing in the clouds, a window to a starry night. "Ah, it's nice for June but a bit cold. No rain, just a few clouds. You can see the moon behind that one . . . see? Not yet full."

Lucy was anxious about their lack of conversation. She racked her brain for tips from all the women's magazines Judy and she had lying around the apartment. She recalled it being sound advice to make the man talk about himself. "So," she began, "you were saying about, uh, agricultural engineering."

"Well, it's sort of boring to talk about," he said, stretching his legs down the stairs. "Master's degree. Agricultural Engineering for the Third World, Africa and all. How to help the Sudan or Somalia to feed itself. These places often have enough aid, enough base resources, everything but a decent government. And luck. I go with Austcare each summer for six weeks to a refugee camp and help out. All the people mad enough to go down there are really great—you'd love Georgie and Bobby. God, I bet you'd all get on."

"You go down with the same group each year?"

"Well, it's only my third year. I've volunteered for poor old Ethiopia. Those buggers have had the worst luck, since the Russians got rid of Haile Selassie."

"That crazy emperor," said Lucy, trying to remember what she knew about that part of the world.

"It's a Christian country, ye know. He wasn't just emperor, he was the Lion of Judah, descendant of King Solomon—we got a handful of Rastas here in Dublin, believe it or not, with the hair all braided up 'n everything, they think he's a god. And some will tell ye that since no body of Selassie was ever shown that he'll come back, right before the Judgment Day, and make Ethiopia the Kingdom of God."

Lucy was feeling happy to be with David sitting on the steps of an ancient church in the Irish moonlight . . . but also unhappy at seeming so provincial suddenly, so untraveled and unread and blah. "Must be something to see Africa," she said at last. "Must have to get a lot of shots."

"Christ, horrible ones—typhus is the worst. Like I said, Austcare sends us down in six-week shifts and that's about all me Western stomach can take. I spend the next twelve weeks recovering from it."

Almost an hour passed with Lucy following one question with another, interested in Africa but more in hearing David talk so warmly to her. Then the door to the chapel opened behind them and they heard a shriek from the father, followed by a string of Holy-this and Mother-of-that and importunings to St. So-and-So.

"Ye two scared me to death!" Father Keegan cried before regaining his smile. "Ah, but just as well you're here! I was nearly ready to set out for the town and fetch someone to help me with Paddy."

"Is he sick?" Lucy asked, springing to her feet.

"Well, I wouldn't say he's exactly sick, mind ye," said the priest. "He just needs to get back to the B & B. And recuperate."

David and Lucy went into the chapel and saw O'Hanrahan arranged along the first-row churchpew, snoring and red-faced.

"Ah, I told him it was strong," said Father Keegan.

Lucy and David examined the chalice and David stuck a little finger into the pinkish brew and tasted it. He made a noise like a horse exhaling. "Good God," David exclaimed.

"*Give wine to those in bitter distress*," quoted the father, "*let them drink and forget their poverty and remember their misery no more!* That, my boy, is the word of the Lord from . . ."

Lucy helped him. "Proverbs, Father." She remembered it being printed on an undergraduate Theology Department cocktail party invitation.

Father Keegan was tipsy and extravagant now, mussing David's hair. "Ah David, m'lad, you're a fine Christian boy, you are! Before the war they'd have paid you to be a priest, I tellya. Given you the whole see."

"I was raised Protestant, Father."

Lucy felt something inside her sink, her hoped-for union threatened.

"Ah, if ye're Irish ye're an honorary Roman Catholic," the priest persevered.

Between David and Father Keegan, they managed to get O'Hanrahan, babbling incoherently, to his feet. Lucy opened doors and blew out candles as the men dragged O'Hanrahan to the backseat of Father Keegan's car.

"O'Feagh's B & B, you say?" asked the priest, now winded and swaying unsurely.

"Why don't ye let me drive, Father?" volunteered David. Lucy sat in the back with O'Hanrahan, now snoring again. The father sat in the passenger seat and soon was insensate; David fished the keys out of his frockcoat and started the car.

"Oh, well," said David, "I'll have to come back to fetch me car tomorrow." He laughed. "I'll let Patrick pay for a taxi, otherwise he'll never get up to Ballymacross."

Lucy asked if it was merely a social call, O'Hanrahan going up to Northern Ireland to see David's folks.

"No, Patrick and the old Jew are up to something, but I don't know what. I think Father Keegan knows. He was talking about some sort of deal earlier tonight, but I'm afraid none of this talk meant a thing to me." As they turned the corner, which revealed the Irish Sea again, David added, "You're a brave girl."

"How's that?"

"Being so smart," he said. "Working with Patrick."

"I'm not working with him yet. But that would be nice one day. He's such a bear, though."

David waved this aside. "Nah, ye just have to know how to handle him."

I doubt I'll get the chance, thought Lucy, strangely sad about it.

ᴀᴏɴᴄʀᴀɪᴍ
JUNE 27TH

O'Hanrahan met the morning, his water-stained ceiling wavering into focus. Hm, he thought, I'm at Mrs. O'Feagh's Bed & Breakfast. Wonder how I got here? Without moving his head he reached to see if he was wearing his tie . . . He was. The rabbi, most likely. No, we lost him after Mulligan's. Father Keegan. Could be. Wait. No, Lord, please not the humiliation of *Lucy*, the inescapable St. Lucy, Virgin Martyr, her blessed and all-watchful eyes, *lux eterna*! But yet he had this unrelenting sense that she was somehow there at the chapel . . .

(Yes, let you remember: drunk again, making a fool of yourself, wasting what brain cells you have left.)

A knock on the door.

O'Hanrahan raised his arm to see what time it was. Couldn't be the maid quite yet. In raising his head to look at the door, he emitted a pained groan.

"Seeya downstairs for breakfast, Dr. O'Hanrahan," said Lucy through the door.

O'Hanrahan turned his head, right then left, stiffly. *Could* be worse. A hangover around five on the one-to-ten scale. The five cigars back-to-back were simply not called for, he thought judiciously, tasting his breath. Where's that mirror? O'Hanrahan had perfected grooming his white hair to a look of minimum baldness; he could wash, shave, brush his teeth without actually looking directly, irrevocably into the mirror. But today he did look. I see the skull beneath my face, he thought. Don't remind me, don't remind me . . .

(But you need reminding.)

O'Hanrahan stayed in Mrs. O'Feagh's Bed & Breakfast for the breakfast alone—God knows, like in most of Dublin's hostelries, there was never hot water or a comfortable bed or sufficient heating for the nighttime chill. But Mrs. O'Feagh laid it on the next morning, distinguishing her establishment. He made his way to a table in the breakfast room, like all Irish breakfast rooms, a museum of kitschy knickknacks and 3-D John Kennedy and Pope John Paul cards. He surveyed the other guests: an elderly couple, two loud-talking American guys with backpacks against the wall who were probably doing all of Europe in a month, and some old Irish crone in the corner.

(She's younger than you are, Patrick.)

"Here y'are, sir," said Mrs. O'Feagh's blemished granddaughter, who slid a plate in front of him and put down a pot of black coffee.

Oh look at it! Two eggs. An extra egg than usual, the way Americans liked it. Two links of proper Irish pork sausage—not that stuffed bread and paper-product roll of sawdust they called a sausage back in Her Majesty's United Kingdom—a slab of thick, cured bacon with the rind still on it, and two disks of black pudding, and a stack of toast and jams and marmalades in a diaspora before him—

"Good morning, Dr. O'Hanrahan."

With pain, he raised his eyes to meet her.

"Did you have a good sleep?" Lucy asked cheerfully, standing hesitantly before his table.

"What's it to you?"

"Well, I mean that stuff looked so strong you were drinking and you had . . ."

"So much of it?" O'Hanrahan began rearranging the table before him, pulling the jams and marmalades and even salt and pepper over to his half. "I am well past the point, Miss Dantan, of having to pay for my hangovers the next morning. I have a long-term account. When you're my age they hit you in the afternoon or maybe early evening, by which time . . ." He poured the rich coffee in a satisfying black arc into his cup. ". . . one is certainly drinking again. So I never pay for them, if you're wondering." His Paddy the Priest routine followed: "I'm a runnin' me tab which I'll be a payin' forrrr when the Great Almighty, saints presairve us, calls me to me heavenly home."

(Might be sooner than you think, Patrick.)

Lucy slipped into the chair across from him, waiting for his objection but he didn't have the energy to make one.

Mrs. O'Feagh's granddaughter returned: "Coffee or tea, miss?"

"Uh, tea, thank you." And as the granddaughter returned to the kitchen, Lucy asked O'Hanrahan, "How much is the breakfast you have?"

O'Hanrahan: "This is a bed-and-breakfast, Miss Dantan, you've already paid for it."

Lucy motioned for the young girl, and for once O'Hanrahan inspected Lucy. Same baggy sweater, bug-eye glasses, limp dark red hair hanging in her face in bangs. The granddaughter returned with Lucy's pot of tea and O'Hanrahan took a look at her, too: pale, plump, pimply, the baggy sweater, dark stockings. The Decline of the Irish Maiden.

"Do you have any cereal or bran flakes?" Lucy asked.

"I believe we have Corn Flakes. And we got some porridge, I'm sure. Do you not want the cooked breakfast, miss?"

Lucy whispered, "Well, actually, my stomach's been upset for a while and I think porridge might settle it better."

The granddaughter went in search of porridge.

"You're surely not," said O'Hanrahan, his voice an octave lower, ravaged by cigars, "going to eat *gruel* in front of me, are you? Disgusting, chalky Irish porridge?"

"Want me to move to a table over there, sir?"

"I want you to move to a table somewhere in Chicago."

"When it comes, I'll move." Lucy then picked up her giant brown handbag from the floor and started rummaging through it. "Now, about that letter from your sister—"

"I said destroy it!"

"Not even curious?" Lucy put it away and asked innocuously, "What's on Rathlin Island, sir?"

He looked lightly stunned, then his face relaxed. "So you've been talking to young McCall, have you?"

Lucy's porridge was set down before her.

"Well?" asked O'Hanrahan.

"Well what?"

"Aren't you going to move thy countenance from mine eyes?"

Lucy gathered up her things. "You're going to see me later anyway."

If O'Hanrahan had been in possession of a working brain at that hour he would have made his objections to her continued presence, but it was not until David pulled up before the bed-and-breakfast and the waiting O'Hanrahan and Rabbi Hersch, bags at the curbside, that it sank in that Lucy was accompanying them to County Antrim.

"I made up my mind, Patrick," said David, all smiles. "You can stop your bluster and get in the car."

After David's further threats to drive off and abandon them, there was a surcease of hostilities as David put everyone's bags in the trunk.

"Shaughnesy will pay for his meddling," swore O'Hanrahan.

The rabbi pointed a finger at Lucy. "*You,*" he barked, "are in the way more than you know."

David laughed unconcernedly, but Lucy saw they were genuinely upset. "But can ye blame me?" asked David, giving Lucy a wink. "She's gonna put me up on her sofa for six months back in Chicago, so she might as well see the splendors of Ballymacross."

Rabbi Hersch and O'Hanrahan grimly shared the back of the sedan and Lucy and David shared the front. The litany of complaints from the backseat gave way to road-punchiness and appreciation of the hilly, rain-soaked countryside around them. After an hour into the trip, a road sign offered a turnoff to Tara in a few miles.

"That's the real Tara?" Lucy wondered.

"As God is my witness," O'Hanrahan announced in a hokey Southern accent, "I will nevuh sit in the backseat again!"

"Yes," said David, confirming it was the Druids' famed capital, "the Dark Ages' St. Peter's."

"Or more properly, Jerusalem," said the rabbi. "You do know the persistent legend that Jeremiah fled here with the treasures of the Temple, including King David's harp, which is the source of the harp obsession in Irish lore."

"So I should think of the Covenant," asked O'Hanrahan intently, "each time I enjoy a Guinness with its harp logo?"

They passed the turnoff to Tara.

"Oooooh saints presairve us . . ." It was Paddy the Priest again. "To think we pass the very soil trod upon by his blessed feet, St. Padraig of Ireland, me patron and namesake!"

"Tell me a story, Paddy," said the rabbi.

"Okay. Back in the 400s St. Patrick was brought to Tara to vie for

Christianity against the Druids. The king had two houses built and a Druid disciple went into one and Patrick's Christian disciple went to the other, but the Druids cheated a bit because their house was out of green wood, which wouldn't burn easily. Then the king set both houses afire and only the Druid disciple burned to death. So the king was converted."

"A true Christian m.o. there," said the rabbi. "They were big on converting Jews before toasting them, too."

The road passed pleasantly enough, Irish towns to the left and right amid the rolling hills, gray slate villages with steeples and bell towers presenting themselves in the drizzle. Near a roadside there was a lifesize crucifixion scene, a plaster Christ on a one-story cross with the lurid wounds and drops of blood freshly painted in vibrant scarlet.

"Jesus-on-a-stick," commented O'Hanrahan.

A passing pub sparked another O'Hanrahan monologue. "It's comforting," he continued, "how among so many of the legends of the Celtic saints booze makes its appearance. St. Brigit discovered one day that there was too little booze in the house when St. Patrick himself came to visit, so that morning she rose from the bath and served Patrick and his attendant churchmen her bathwater, which was so pure and delicious that they thought it truly was the finest beer they ever had tasted."

"Yum," said Lucy. "I went to St. Bridget's in Chicago's Bridgeport, by the way."

"You grew up there?" asked O'Hanrahan. "That explains a lot."

Past the town of Dundalk, their car met a line with scores of cars.

They had come to the border with Northern Ireland.

"The queues are murder on weekends," said David as they inched forward to the checkpoint, a mile of cars visible in front of them. Lucy unhappily looked at the pillboxes and teenage soldiers with machine guns, the cement barriers in the road ahead. What was the IRA's newest thing? They'd hijack a car and its passengers, then threaten to kill the driver's family if he or she didn't drive dynamite into the checkpoint, making a human bomb out of some poor innocent.

A van ahead of them was being emptied, and she saw a fat, poorly dressed woman removed from the front seat, a trail of five sickly children streaming out behind her. Catholics. The man was being frisked.

"This a bad area?" asked Lucy, nervous in the presence of so much weaponry.

"Nowhere on the border's a good area," said David. "But the IRA are only killing soldiers these days, pretty much. They did blow up that marching band in England, but that was connected to the military. They can justify whoever—you remember they claimed Mountbatten and his grandchildren were a military target."

The road signs had changed, Lucy noticed. No more Gaelic under the English with kilometers, back to the British style and mileage. They inched toward a sign that informed them Newry was five miles.

"Remind you, Rabbi, of the West Bank a bit?" called out David cheerfully.

"It's sunnier there," he said, joining his hands and looking down at them, sighing.

"Ever been to Northern Ireland before?" asked David.

"First, and I suspect last time," said Rabbi Hersch. "This I can get at home."

Lucy looked over to see ten white roadside crosses. They approached the border guard . . . how old was he? Nineteen? He asked to see their passports, please, in a Northern British lower-class drawl.

"There oughta be no problem," said David quietly, not quite having the confidence to make it a prediction. "Three Americans and I've got me U.K. passport."

Lucy looked around at the pillbox beside them, the camouflage-colored tin and concrete walls on either side of them, in case a car bomb went off, and the video cameras that were filming them for evidence. And she glanced back at the indigent Irish family standing nervously to the side of the armed guards, the woman's tiniest child inches from the semiautomatic rifle, as their van was searched.

"I got caught at this very border one time for hours," said O'Hanrahan softly. "Coming to see your folks back in 1972. I was loaded up with research on the Celtic Church and these goons thought I was some kind of Catholic militant. Any American with a name like O'Hanrahan might well be bringing NORAID money into Ulster."

Lucy startled to hear NORAID mentioned, as if she belonged to it herself. Of course, thanks to Dad, there was a check somewhere in her name to the organization.

"What're you doing here?" sneered the guard, handing the passports back and motioning them forward, as another guard looked under and around their car for explosive devices.

David answered respectfully: "I live in Ballymacross and these are friends of me parents, coming up from Dublin. From America on their vacation and—"

"Ullroight," he said, waving them by, not interested.

Lucy scanned the dismal countryside for clues to life here. It looked placid enough. The roads were better paved than the Irish Republican ones. Forkhill was the first turnoff, more of a military base and armed camp than a town. As David explained, many of the southern Ulster towns had no income, industry had fled, but with the land cheap, the army had moved in. And then what was once dull and peaceful had become a battleground. Bessbrook was such a village in decline. In nearby Whitecross in 1976, three Catholic brothers were watching TV one night when Protestant terrorists burst into their home and shot them. Then later in Balldougan, Protestant terrorists arrived at a family reunion and blew away two brothers and an uncle in front of their children. So Catholics sidetracked this bus of Protestant workmen from Bessbrook, marched them out, asked whether they were Catholic or Protestant, then killed the eleven Protestants.

They were almost through the town of Newry. David would slow for a village and Lucy would spy a group of soldiers, in full battle attire, walking idly around a public square, a piece of graffiti SMASH BRITISH RULE with the orange, green, and white tricolor taking up a wall.

"So these towns are all divided?" asked Lucy. "Catholics on one side, Protestants on the other?"

"Not that many Protestants down here," said David. "It's mostly Catholics. It's sheer stupidity that the British decided to keep this county, for it's of no use. The Catholics and Prods pretty much got along until the Brits put the army bases here."

A big blue British-style sign reported that the motorway began ahead that led to the heart of Belfast. A city with a reputation only second to Beirut, Lucy thought grimly. The next minute she thought: but people live there, don't they? They go shopping and go to the pub and carry on their lives. All I'm doing is riding in a car through town.

"Shall we have a pint at the Crown, Patrick?" asked David.

"Oh," said O'Hanrahan, licking his lips, "Morey, you must see the Crown. Best pub in the United Kingdom."

Yep, thought Lucy resignedly, *that's* how we're gonna die. Blown up in a pub in Belfast so O'Hanrahan can have a drink.

"The tailor's shop is in Andersonstown," O'Hanrahan said, looking at his address book.

"That's a lovely place," said David unhappily. "If I'd known that's where this store was, Patrick, I wouldn't have volunteered to drive you."

"I've heard of that neighborhood from somewhere," said Lucy.

David recapped the history: In 1969 the Troubles were at their worst and some hundred British soldiers were killed, though they had come to protect the Catholics initially. Protestants had moved out of the shambling rowhouses and apartments during the riots. The city reallocated the public housing of Catholics, but the Protestants didn't want them even in their abandoned houses. A priest died, a 13-year-old girl was shot, ten British soldiers were then assassinated by the Provisionals that weekend, before the IRA set off 22 bombs in a one-square-mile area in downtown Belfast and the derailing of the Dublin-Belfast express train. Thousands panicked in the melee of bombs going off every few minutes and as hundreds huddled in a bus station terminal waiting for it to end, an IRA car bomb went off outside that killed six, spraying blood and body parts all over the waiting room.

David negotiated the car to the Falls Road, which had a renown no one in the car felt needed comment, and they all grew quiet.

"Paddy, why didn't you get this suit in Dublin?" asked the rabbi, looking at the grimacing residents on the sidewalks, dodging the rain.

"It's cheaper here, and they do good work," said O'Hanrahan. "I've bought two other suits from this guy." O'Hanrahan gauged his companions were all a bit nervous but no one wanted to say it because, statistically, the chances of wandering stupidly into sectarian violence were rare. "Look, people," he said with forced calmness, "I'll hop in the store, get my suit, hop out, and we'll be on our way. I tell you, you can't judge a place by its problems. Belfast is a blast."

"Yeah," said David as he drove along, "*kaboooom!*"

O'Hanrahan insisted: "The people are warm, they have a sense of humor, they're generous, and I find the lack of hearts-and-flowers, sugar-coated bullshit quite refreshing in Belfast conversation, so get that cringing look off your face, Dantan."

"Yes, the city's nothing like it was," reassured David.

Lucy saw the vacant lots pass with neighboring walls given over to one- and two-story painted slogans: OUR DAY WILL COME with a caricature of Mrs. Thatcher, dolled-up fascistically in jackboots, a combination of a swastika and Union Jack on her helmet, as she rises in triumph over a grave. The painted tombstone, thought Lucy, had an ever-changing epitaph that had been painted over several times. It now listed children killed by rubber bullets and the British Army.

At the next stoplight, Lucy read a streetlamp poster demanding STOP THE TORTURE, which detailed Amnesty International's charge of torturings, beatings, unlawful detentions, shootings on sight. This poster was accompanied by the motif of the 20th Century, a grainy black-and-white close-up of some poor prisoner's battered face.

"There's the place!" signaled O'Hanrahan.

David pulled the car to the curb. O'Hanrahan's destination was an ecclesiastical uniform shop on the other side of the street; a faded, smiling John Paul II poster hung in the window. Lucy watched O'Hanrahan dance through the puddles to the sidewalk and the shop, his suitcoat collar pulled up uselessly against the cold rain.

"Shall we stop at the Crown, Rabbi?" asked David.

"I wouldn't mind just getting it over with and getting on to Ballymacross, to tell you the truth," he said. "In this weather. Besides, the rush-hour traffic will start up."

"Aye, that's a point," said David, though it wasn't even two o'clock.

Lucy listened stoically to the rain hit the roof of the car.

At last, O'Hanrahan appeared with a black suit wrapped in cellophane on a hanger, running across the street, nearly being hit because

he failed to check the traffic from British left-side-of-the-road directions. As he slid inside, the rabbi announced good-naturedly, "Almost
another martyr of Andersonstown, Paddy!"

"Almost," he cackled.

They started up again and Lucy breathed a sigh of relief.

"Got you a present," said O'Hanrahan to Rabbi Hersch, handing
him a booklet of indulgences and rosary prayers, blessed by the priests
at Knock. Knock, O'Hanrahan reminded his friend, was the Lourdes,
Disneyland, and PTL Club of Ireland.

David drove with great relief down the Falls Road to the downtown
and pointed out the ever-cantankerous Divis Flats atop which an Irish
tricolor flew. It was an armed camp, vigilante-patrolled by Republican
groups, a no-man's-land for Protestants. And across the street from it
was the Hastings Street police station, the Royal Ulster Constabulary,
who rode around in silvery metal-plated Rovers, armed with semiautomatic machine guns and all the equipment necessary for a small
war. The police station could have been out of pre-1989 Eastern Europe. Barbed wire, television cameras, pillboxes manned with machine-
gun-toting officers.

As they entered the more Protestant north of town, the walls again
were brandishing giant political signs and slogans; a large red hand,
the Red Hand of Ulster, clenched in a fist, showing no sign of easing
its grip. Streets that would otherwise be a quiet neighborhood lane
had cement roadblocks and mechanical gates to stop a speeding car-
bomb driver. The traffic light ahead was red and David slowed to the
intersection. A car next to them pulled up and Lucy looked over. Lucy
saw two older men, the driver unshaven with a gray grizzle on a heavily
lined face, while the passenger seemed to be cursing under his breath
and yelled something that showed his missing teeth.

Lucy's blood froze.

"Oh jeez, here we go . . ." muttered Rabbi Hersch, looking to the
ceiling.

The rusted car revved beside them. No one said what was apparent:
the old, ill-tempered men doubtlessly had a firearm in the car.

"Nice fellows," said David quietly.

"Let's tell them we got a Jew in the backseat," said O'Hanrahan just
as quietly.

The rabbi: "Hey, bet I'd do better than you papists."

The light turned green and David pulled ahead slowly with the car
of old men going the exact same speed.

Lucy looked down at her feet, hoping that when she looked back
the old men would be gone. Old men looking for trouble. Looking for
an easy victim to report back to their Ulster Club, looking for those
free pub-rounds that come with being a hero and blowing a Catholic's

head off. No, Lucy told herself, it didn't happen every day, but it happened, and there were no rules about when it happened and why it happened, it just keeps happening, the mindless, automatic, unthinking willingness to go on with the killings.

After a grinding shift of gears, the old men sped forward with a screech of tires.

"Well," said David, "I guess they showed us, hm?"

Lucy looked over at a burned-out apartment building, like one sees in the South Side of Chicago. But, like in the dark spots of American poverty, people lived in this block of flats too. Starting on the third floor Lucy observed clotheslines and signs of life. The first two burned-out stories were boarded and bricked up so no one could shoot anything into the rooms or throw a grenade. And there was another entry in the continual war of graffiti: UFF RAMBOS IN STONE'S ARMY . . . SHOWED YOU FUCKIN BASTIRDS AT THE CIMITARY.

After a raw moment of shame for America's gift of *Rambo* to the world, Lucy stared at the misspellings, assessing the poverty and ignorance that saturated the problems here. "Stone's army," Lucy wondered aloud.

"You know," said David. "The Protestant guy who shot up those people at the cemetery. I thought the whole world saw that one on TV. Now we're off to see a castle," he emphasized hopefully, finding the motorway and accelerating beyond the reach of Belfast. "If we can change the subject here?"

"Yeah, let's change it," said Rabbi Hersch.

"Big castle it is at that, at Carrickfergus," David previewed. "And then we'll take the coast road to Ballymacross."

Minutes later, the North Channel of the Irish Sea came into view out the right of the car. The six-lane highway became just four lanes, then two, and the congested, winding road along the coast began. Soon hills, then mountains appeared, then little seaside villages at the foot of the cliffs, little towns gray and insular on this harsh day but not unwelcoming, the hanging pub signs swaying in the wind, the unbelievable spectacle of a group of pale boys playing soccer outside in shorts, pelted by cold rain.

"Oooh," said David, "painful to watch! I remember being out there on days like this meself."

The sky remained a blank, an almost-evening winter-white. The hills of Antrim were brown with only the sporadic farm or cultivated garden behind an isolated house striving for order against the mud-colored scrub. The passing fishing villages looked quiet and content, smoke from the chimneys, lights on behind yellowed curtains. Lucy pulled her coat a little tighter wishing she were inside somewhere. How much more peaceful it was after Belfast, how much more one could persuade oneself that violence and hatred had never troubled this outermost corner of Ireland. Lucy had been reading roadsigns automatically as they went by, but she came to full consciousness when she saw Ballymacross announced.

Ballymacross was a village of no more than 500, laid out like a "Y" with the one fork off the main highway, which led up a hill and soon degenerated into a muddy farm road. The houses, typical of the British Isles, were right on the street and some villagers' front doors opened to the road, with only a few feet of pavement and a slight dip that was the drainage gutter separating the living room from traffic.

"The Crown!" said O'Hanrahan gleefully, spotting the one of two pubs in town. "Let us off here, Master David."

Boy, these Prods sure love that *crown*, Lucy noted. Every town big or small had an alcoholic homage to Her Majesty.

David pulled the car beyond the town's one intersection and zebra crosswalk. The Crown Inn, founded 1723, according to the suspended sign creaking in the stiff coastal wind, was the one hotel of any sort in town. Everyone reluctantly stepped out of the car into the gale.

"That's the sea," David said, pulling up his collar, pointing down the hill of the main road. "Ye can't really tell, can ye, 'cause it's pissin' down so, but she's there."

O'Hanrahan got his suitcase and briefcase gathered to himself in the spitting rain, and the rabbi took a small flight bag from the trunk. They trotted inside to the Crown to get two of the five rooms at the inn above the pub.

"Davey, m'boy!" shouted a middle-aged man, who poked his head out of the Crown.

It was Mr. Robert McCall. David hurried to give his father a tentative pat on the shoulder and Lucy followed along and they huddled in the doorway to the pub. Mr. McCall was a dark-haired, tough-skinned man of rough handsomeness, the same squinting, laughing eyes as his son. He announced that he had gotten off early at the local cannery, but after apprehending that news Lucy found his accent impenetrable.

"Aye, son, who's the girl?" he said, after a brief catching-up concerning David's term at Trinity.

"Dad, this is Lucy Dantan."

Handshakes and well-wishing all around as Lucy feared conversation because of Mr. McCall's thick brogue. "How're ye tholin' this thrawn son of mine, eh?" he asked Lucy, who merely smiled.

"We'll come back down in a wee bit," said David.

David and Lucy got back in the car and traveled up the turnoff, the steep hill lined on each side with townhouses, which gave way to separate dwellings at the hilltop before the road itself turned to mud. Behind a fortress of low-lying trees and bushes there was the McCall house, a simple bungalow with a rusted steel roof and a stone foundation. They darted with their bags toward the side door.

The house reminded Lucy of her grandparents' because things looked comfortably used and out-of-date, old pictures, old books, the smell of the kitchen permeating the house, the noise of a crackling fire. David's mother, Mary McCall, was a pretty woman who didn't look fifty, with smooth white skin except for a warm rose in the cheeks, as only this weather could produce, and raven-black hair with the occasional strand of gray. She ushered Lucy to the bedroom of Fiona, David's sister a year younger who was away at Queens College in Belfast. Lucy sat on the bed and was presented with bathtowels and a barrage of friendly, nosy questions from Mrs. McCall, who spoke of her one trip to the United States and her piecemeal knowledge of Chicago. Then she excused herself to go lecture her son for losing his fifth scarf in a row.

Lucy leaned back on the tidily made-up sister's bed, the smells of damp from the old house and the smell of soap on the laundry mingled on the pillowcase near her face. Lucy was weary from exposing herself to the gale; she listened to the noise of the rain. With this weather, she fancied, no wonder the Irish stayed inside and sang and told stories and became the social people they were.

"Well," said David, leaning into his sister's room. "The Crown awaits!"

After a three-minute run with an umbrella down the hill, with most of that devoted to navigating the stepping stones through the mud, they arrived to find O'Hanrahan, the rabbi, and Mr. McCall installed by the fireplace and O'Hanrahan entertaining the whole bar, the seven other locals who had gathered to hear his storytelling.

"It's true," O'Hanrahan was saying, reviving another Celtic booze legend. "The first Celtic saint was a vintner. I wouldn't make this up."

Mr. McCall laughed, laughed very easily. "Ye're just tellin' us what we wanna hear, man!"

"I speak of the Most Blessed St. Theodotus, martyred May 18, 303."

Said Jack the innkeeper good-naturedly, "Doos that make him Catholic or Presbyterian then?"

"Orthodox," said O'Hanrahan diplomatically. "Theodotus was a Celt from Galatia, a town whose name translates to Celtic City, related to Gaelic and Gaul and *galloise* and Galway and Galicia in Spain and Portu*gal* and all other places we ancient Celts got around to. He owned a tavern and turned it into a home for the needy and destitute, the dregs of society."

"A lot like the Crown here'n Ballymacross," suggested Mr. McCall as the assemblage guffawed.

It was time for dinner. The sky was now clear as they headed out. Icy winter-sky clear, with the stars precise and innumerable. The weather often changed just like that, David explained as he unexpectedly ran ahead of O'Hanrahan, his father, and Rabbi Hersch, to take Lucy's arm.

"Hate this hill," he said. "After a few pints, it's like the friggin' Alps. When I get rich I'm building a tunnel from the Crown to under me house and then an elevator straight to me bedroom. Maybe put me bed right in the elevator, ye know?"

Lucy laughed and tried to make her arm light as air so he wouldn't release it. "Why not put your bed right in the bar—the pub, I mean."

"Ah, now maybe that's what we need. Ye don't like our Guinness?"

She had not finished her hefty pint glass. "No, it's all right . . ."

"Nyeh, you don't cotton to it, you can say so. When we go back we'll getcha a Harp. Eh, now you can get that miserable Budweiser stuff in Ireland, ye know. Can't see how ye drink the American beer."

"I'm not much of a drinker, really." Probably the kiss of death in Ireland, thought Lucy as she said it.

"Just as well. Ye keep your girlish figure that way, not drowning in Guinness every night. Not like our local girls."

This was the first unsolicited compliment her figure had ever gotten by a young man. The fact was to be etched in stone, in some most permanent, treasured part of her memory! Hear *that*, Judy?

"What're ye laughing like such fools aboot?" said David to the men behind, his accent more pronounced. Lucy looked back to see the men giggling like schoolchildren. "Oh, I see. That prayer pamphlet from Knock." The booklet O'Hanrahan picked up at the Catholic ecclesiastical store in Belfast for fifty pence.

"Knock?" wondered Lucy aloud.

David: "You know, Lucy, the whole village that got drunk and talked themselves into seeing the Virgin and Joseph and Angels and the Lamb of God. First time the Lamb had ever been seen. 1880-something. The pope's been there and they built this big barn—aww it's awful, ye can't believe it."

"Like Lourdes and all that?"

"Worse I'm sure, 'cause we're Irish and we got no taste. There's this sign there't has toilets this direction, holy water-tap that direction—ye can't make fun of it, it's doing such a good job making fun of itselflike."

When they returned to the house, Mrs. McCall announced it would be a half-hour *more* before dinner would be on the table, a dinner they could smell, chicken broth and leeks and cabbage that had been steeping together all day in the pot.

"Smells fabulous, Mary," said the rabbi, as they all sat in the parlor. "Sell my birthright for it."

David gave his mother some lip about why in God's name she called if it was still to be a half-hour 'fore they could get eating at it, and his father joined, demanding in his castle the meal should be a-waiting for him, a-handed to him on the plate as he walked in the door, but Mary McCall made short work of them, popping her son's backside with the soup ladle and chasing her husband "who smelled like a chip shop" to the showers before she deep-fried him and wrapped him in yesterday's newspaper.

"You heard of Ballinspittal?" asked David. "Back in 1988 there was a statue of the Virgin Mary there that moved and everyone saw it and they came from all over Ireland to see this thing, newspapers and television and *everyone* saw it. Even Protestants. And then every village was going after that. We had dancing statues, Mother Mary doing the bleeding hula dance."

His mother, leaning in from the kitchen, suggested a politer frame of reference was required to discuss the Woman Who Bore Our Savior.

"Well, anyway," David concluded, "the *Irish Times* decided that if you stared at something long enough with a lot of people around ye, it *would* move."

"Like Fatima," said O'Hanrahan. "Must be a thousand different accounts of what happened there, which isn't surprising when you get 70,000 miracle-starved Catholics staring at the sun for hours."

The rabbi was busy thumbing through the Knock indulgence prayerbook. The Joyful Mysteries, the Lady of Guadalupe, Our Lady of the Rosary at Fatima, the Blessed Visions of Medjugorje—not approved by the Vatican, but in the '80s it was Yugoslavia's number-one tourist attraction, with people setting up appointments at the children's homes to observe their daily conversations with Mary. Our Lady of the Scapular, pray for me, St. Catherine, pray for me, St. George, St. Christopher—all outlawed saints, according to Vatican II, but the racket's gone on too long in Ireland ever to put on the brakes.

The rabbi read out loud: "A single 'To The Blessed Virgin' gets you 500 days indulgence. Salve Regina gets you five years out of Purgatory. The Anima Christi can knock off 300 days—"

"But Morey," interrupted O'Hanrahan, looking beatific, "if you do the Anima Christi after Holy Communion, you get a whole *seven* years off. So said our founder, my guide, Ignatius Loyola."

Rabbi Hersch waved that aside. "Here's the ticket. If one as much as *hears* someone say the 'Three Very Beautiful Prayers for the Dying,' you get a whopping *400 years* indulgence."

David: "That'd be the one for you, Patrick."

Rabbi Hersch: "And if you say, 'Eternal Father I offer Thee the Wounds of Our Lord Jesus Christ to heal the wounds of our souls,' you get 300 days. Nu, just like that you get 300 days?"

O'Hanrahan clarified, "Only on the large-beaded rosary. The smaller rosary has another sentence assigned to it."

The rabbi marveled. "How do you actually know all this nonsense?"

He glanced at Lucy and read her expression of displeasure. Lucy sat apart from the group, not particularly amused with the familiar game of let's-tear-Roman-Catholicism-apart.

"Hey, Paddy," said Rabbi Hersch provocatively, "I think we're offending Lucy here. She believes all this stuff."

Lucy: "No one believes everything in those prayerbooks."

But Lucy knew in her heart that her own maiden aunts and their black-clad companions who made their daily processional to St. Bridget down Archer Street back home believed it all, every little ludicrous bit, offering up rosaries to the Blessed Child of Prague, however the hell that jewel-studded babydoll got so popular.

(Yes, We're somewhat mystified by that one too.)

"Give me something I can use here," requested O'Hanrahan. "Something that'll knock off centuries in Purgatory."

Mrs. McCall announced in the doorway, "You'll be needing those centuries if you keep this sorta talk going." She didn't, however, seem genuinely upset. "Not that we believe in Purgatory, but I'll thank you not to blaspheme in my parlor, Patrick."

The rabbi was unchastened: "Oh wait," he said, turning a page and skimming, "*St. Bridget of Sweden for a long time wished to know the number of blows Our Savior received during His Passion and Jesus, Our Most Holy Lord and Savior, appeared to her and said, 'I received 5480 blows upon my body.'* So here's the prescription. Fifteen prayers a day for a year equals almost 5480."

(If O'Hanrahan hadn't had three Guinnesses down at the Crown, he might have remembered that Pope Leo XIII approved the number 6666 blows directly to the Body, with 150 knocks to the Head, 108 kicks on the shoulder, 24 hair-pullings, 23 beard-pullings, and an array of thorn wounds—there were 72 thorns in the crown of thorns, piercing our Savior lightly 110 times with 3 mortal wounds on the forehead, 1008 separate mockings. Direct spittings in the Face were put at 180 and the pièce de résistance was Leo's drops-of-blood calculation: 28,430. These important calculations were worked out April 5th, 1890.)

"What's the Sacred Letter?" asked David, looking over the rabbi's shoulder at the next page.

Lucy watched the professor revive, his expertise appealed to.

"It was thought that Jesus may have committed something to paper in his final hours. When the Holy Sepulcher was discovered, supposedly in the crypt area was a letter written in Christ's own hand, in a silver box. It gave directions for how many Glorias, Paters, and Aves to say, for how much indulgence and time off in Purgatory. St. Gregorious adored the Letter and proclaimed anyone who carried a copy would come to no harm."

Enlivened by his two pints of beer, David blurted, "I can't see how Catholics can be so damn stupid!"

Lucy felt defensive. Worse, Lucy knew she was appearing to be prim and she didn't want David to think she was bound for the rosary brigade at the nearest Our Lady of Prompt Succor.

"But more interesting," O'Hanrahan continued, "is the continual Nestorian and Armenian claim that Jesus *did* actually write things in his lifetime and engage in celebrated correspondences."

O'Hanrahan told of Jesus' letter to Abargus the Toparch, which congratulated Abargus for converting his kingdom to Christianity, and promised to heal the king as well. When the king recovered, he adopted Christianity at his court in Edessa, from which the Armenian Church sprang. Jesus as an added bonus miraculously put his face into a handkerchief and divinely imprinted it and sent that to Abargus as well.

"All this is forgotten now," O'Hanrahan concluded, "but centuries passed and thousands died in battle over the possession of the Blessed Original Text and the Holy Handkerchief."

"Sort of like Tom Jones," suggested David. "And Elvis. You know how they had these towels they'd sweat upon in concert and then they'd throw 'em out to the screaming crowd. And women'd throw their panties and underclothes up to the stage, and Elvis'd wipe his sweaty brow on 'em and throw 'em back."

Rabbi Hersch: "Maybe something happened like that during the entry into Jerusalem."

O'Hanrahan nodded sagely. "There may be a Blessed Pair of Panties somewhere with Jesus' Face imprinted on it—"

Mrs. McCall: "All right, now I've heard enough from all of ye! If our house is struck by lightning tonight, we'll know why!" She was remonstrating against a room full of unrepentant schoolboys, with Lucy sitting to the side forcing a smile. "Oh, laugh at me? I may not serve ye supper, Patrick—you won't be afinding that so funny, will ye? It'll be ready in five minutes, and I 'spect not to hear another worda this talk."

But there was no going back now. David took his turn thumbing through the prayerbook. "Patrick, what's this stuff about the Sacred Shoulder Wound of Christ?"

O'Hanrahan gleefully explained. "St. Bernard, that old criminal, in a mystical conversation with Jesus asked him what his greatest unrecorded suffering was." O'Hanrahan read from the prayerbook: "*I had on My Shoulder while I bore My Cross on the Way of Sorrows a grievous Wound which was more painful than the others, and which is not recorded by men. Honor this Wound with thy devotion . . . .*"

"I wonder," Rabbi Hersch contemplated, "if Jesus stubbed his toe during His Passion. Paddy, there still might be time to make your mark."

"Yes, I could write the Oration to the Sacred Stubbed Toe of Christ. We could have a decade of rosaries, for each of the Ten Sacred Toes—"

Mrs. McCall cleared her throat unmistakably from the kitchen.

The rabbi answered back, "Paddy can't help himself, Mary. He's a Jesuit! Disobedience is in his blood."

O'Hanrahan: "Former Jesuit!"

This was news to Lucy. She sat up straight.

"No such thing, really, as a lapsed Jesuit," amended the rabbi. "A Jesuit's a Jesuit. It's almost like being a Jew. Doesn't matter if you're a good Jesuit or a bad Jesuit, you're still a Jesuit. Why I never met a decent Jesuit who *wasn't* a lapsed Jesuit."

Lucy was sorting out her thoughts from this revelation. O'Hanrahan *took vows?* Submitted to orders? A Jesuit, servant to His Holiness the Pope, Vicar of Christ on Earth, Scion of St. Peter?

(That's right.)

Well, pondered Lucy, it made sense, in a way. His personality, his skepticism. Priests in American theological schools, radical Dominicans, and most Jesuits she had met did a better number on Roman Catholicism these days than Martin Luther and Reverend Ian Paisley combined . . . And a man of O'Hanrahan's generation, and his intellectual skills, yes, he would have been a natural choice for Jesuit seminary.

Lucy couldn't imagine the young O'Hanrahan pledging eternal fealty to The One True Church, the long hours of prayer and discipline . . . Somewhere in his past he must have been, well, like me, thought Lucy. An earnest, practicing Catholic, maybe with a mother who wanted a priest for a son. A warm thought came to her: Dr. O'Hanrahan's so hard on me because I remind him of how he used to be, a Patrick O'Hanrahan who knelt and kissed the ring, a Patrick he'd like to forget!

Dinner was served. Everyone crowded hungrily around the kitchen table in the variety of folding chairs Mrs. McCall had brought in from the garage. Mr. McCall emerged from the back of the house, freshly shaven, hair combed down, and not smelling of the cannery. He plopped down the pub's secondhand newspaper beside his wife, who was ladling a helping onto O'Hanrahan's plate.

"Got the paper for you," Mr. McCall reminded his wife. "Still want to wrap me in't, do ye?"

Mrs. McCall tsk-tsked as she spied the Belfast headline, a feature about mothers who had lost more than one son to sectarian violence. Poor Mrs. Graham and her three boys shot out of pure malice by the IRA, for sport. "It's as bad as that poor Mrs. O'Malley in Derry," she said, putting the paper aside roughly, as if to disapprove of it. "She's lost four sons to the Troubles."

David helped his own plate. "Aww Mum, they should have some kind of pool for us to bet, ye know? Which of the old girls is gonna lose another one next."

Mr. McCall cackled from high in his chest. Lucy was stunned at the dark humor, but she noticed even Mrs. McCall hid a smile behind her hand. "David," his mother reprimanded feebly.

"It could be like the lottery it could," their son went on. "I mean, you could put a fiver down that Old Lady O'Malley was going to lose another boy by Christmas, that kind of thing."

"And if he merely gets knee-capped, it pays off half," encouraged his father.

Mary McCall: "Both of you two!"

"It's their own bleedin' fault," David said, taking his seat, and tearing at a soda-bread loaf. "And when they catch the boys who murdered the O'Malley boys they oughta try 'em twice, once for murder, and once for making us look at the same bloody television film of these old women wailing aboot their little gun-running, bomb-making angels!"

The rabbi, causing trouble: "What if a woman loses two sons, David?"

"Oh, pays off double, of course."

It occurred to Lucy that with Belfast and Derry in their vicinity the cynical streak of the Irish would turn unremittingly dark. Savage weather, savage history, savage humor.

After dinner and a great show of the men wanting to wash dishes but not actually doing it, the evening reconvened back down at the Crown. David and Lucy again walked down the hill unaccompanied by the others, who trotted thirstily on ahead.

"You see," he was saying, "I really do prefer it up here than to Dublin, old Begorrahsburg itself."

"You don't like Dublin?"

"It's great in its way, but if they could elect a leprechaun mayor they'd do it for the friggin' tourists, I think." Lucy smiled broadly as he ranted. "The town's like a Third World country for working phones, working plumbing—makes the British look good. I was walking down O'Connell and there was this leftover moth-eaten old hippie who had a sign around his neck, said for a pound he'd recite you a *bloody poem*." David made a cry of exasperation. "I asked him, taking the piss, what he could recite, and he started up a U2 lyric for God's sake. I mean, *that's* bloody Dublin right there. No, if there was a future in Belfast, I'd much prefer it, but there's not, so for now it's the Republic for me."

With all the bloody Catholics, thought Lucy.

She considered all the Catholic demerits: the IRA, the ignorant priests dictating local small-town policy in the Republic, the Visions of the Lamb at Knock, the dancing statues at Ballinspittal, the Republic outlawing divorce in the late 20th Century, preventing teenage rape and incest victims from securing an abortion, the Virgin Mary as Queen of Ireland, the electorate doing this particularly backward pope's bidding . . . and Lucy felt momentarily in the enemy camp. God, her name was somewhere on a NORAID contribution so technically she was. Now truly, she had never doubted that Protestants for five hundred years had treated the Catholics abominably on what had once been their land. But how did a credulous peasant rabble with their eleven kids per family and medieval papal triumphalism *expect* to be treated by modern, rational people from the 19th Century's most powerful nation? She coolly felt a lack of sympathy for Catholics, these weeping, ever-suffering professional victims, whining for recompense over something Henry VIII did.

Lucy also saw the complexity of cutting out an acceptable image for herself if she moved to Ireland. It was one thing to be an intellectual and practicing Catholic in the United States—a certain attractiveness, the consolation of an elite minority, a knowing quaintness attended the choice. It could be worn like an outfit for shock value or for temporary solidarity with fellow Catholics. But here in Ireland it merely demonstrated you weren't above the age-old superstition of the island, or worse, that you took sides in the hopeless Protestant-Catholic squabble. Living here would kill any religious feeling I ever had, she decided.

(No, but it might wreak havoc on your sectarian loyalty.)

Hours later Lucy arrived back in Fiona's room, once again escorted from the Crown on David's arm, and she found herself oddly awake and giddy, happier than she'd been in years. She combed out her hair and looked down at photos of David on Fiona's dresser, when he was younger, in faded, childhood birthday-party shots. Fiona's own picture was on the wall and she looked a bit plain, but Lucy saw in her expression that the McCall wit and irreverence had perpetuated itself.

Lucy crawled into bed and wiggled down underneath the many covers.

Old Northern Ireland wasn't going to let her alone, apparently. Not ten minutes could transpire without Lucy having to examine her own Roman Catholicism, her own near-miss as a nun. Lucy then thought of her buddy from St. Eulalia's Catholic Chamber of Horrors and High School, Faith Kopinski. I bet she's a nun by now.

(It hurt Faith that you dropped her as a friend after high school, Lucy. Your motives weren't exactly pure.)

Lucy felt a tinge of guilt even to think of Faith. Could that weepy, oversensitive girl have been her best school friend? Lucy smiled. Usually when you name a girl Faith or Chastity or Hope, she ends up, as any Catholic School graduate can tell you, a bona fide whore by high school, the school slut, selling drugs in the hallway. But the name paid off for Faith, who was as demure and sweetly pious as any girl at St. Eulalia's.

Faith was far from popular, but then neither was Lucy nor her inevitable partner, Gabriel, hounded mercilessly for his wimpishness and unathleticism by the guys, and Lucy instinctively congregated with fellow sufferers on the backside of school fame. Once in gym she glanced over to see Faith changing and was struck with how naked Faith looked when undressing, how white and thin and fragile she looked and how red her face was, blushing with a pure, intense shame for herself.

So Lucy stopped avoiding her sometime in ninth grade and sat beside her in the lunchroom. Faith wouldn't talk about boys except in the abstract and always as something other girls were better cut out for; she never saw movies, never went out, had no one but cousins that represented her social life, didn't know what records or TV shows were cool, and didn't seem to know she was missing anything, and in that Lucy and Faith were fundamentally different, because Lucy always had a precise knowledge of what she was missing.

Once Christian Hall sat near them at lunch period.

Christian ran true to form regarding the name rule, and Lucy was infatuated with his utter paganness. He was the jock of the school, the hero of the basketball team, broad shoulders and muscular, smooth upper arms and a St. Eulalia T-shirt that was tight enough to draw endless discourse from Lucy's slut sister Mary, the cheerleader. No, Lucy never had a chance with someone like Christian, and the only reason he alighted at their table that day in the lunchroom was because Lucy and Faith weren't considered to matter in the popularity game— they were lower than unpopular, they were *invisible*, they were nonpeople and if he sat near them it was because he looked right through them.

And Lucy felt, for Faith's benefit, that she had to speak to Christian because Lucy was always the more adventurous one and she relished her role of the more daring friend. So Lucy, in a choked, forced light way, said hi to Christian and congratulated him on his 22 points against Marie Curie.

"Uh, yeah," he said, mildly noticing Lucy and looking around to see if anyone else was observing them. Then after a minute: "You're Mary's sister, right?"

Yeah, said Lucy, and that was it for the longed-for conversation.

Lucy swore to herself she would kill her little sister if Mary was lucky enough to go out with Christian—well, Mary never "went out with" she just "made out with" and God-knows-what-else with by the age of sixteen. Anyway. Lucy would stare at Christian unobserved and adore his long arms and legs and try to imagine what it was to be his girlfriend and what it would be like to kiss him or hold him and she would contemplate the canyon between her life and his and how easy it was for him to be him and how difficult it was for her to be her, the cold consolation of a shared baloney sandwich with Faith.

When the dreaded Sister Miriam droned on about the sins of the Magdalene, it was always Christian who put on a mock-innocent expression and raised his hand.

"Hey, Sister?" he'd ask. "What exactly *were* the sins of the Magdalene?"

And others would titter and Sister Miriam would say that Christian knew full well what they were—

"No, honestly . . . I haven't read that part."

And Sister Miriam could believe any ignorance of Christian, whom she detested for his careless limbs that were an offense to her, his swagger in the halls, his violations of dress codes, and his loud laughing with the older boys. She glared at him with undisguised hatred for the sneering sixteen-year-old potency that mocked her. "She was a fallen woman," she breathed at last.

"Fallen? You mean she fell down?"

More titters. And Sister Miriam seethed as he pressed her for the exact details of Mary Magdalene's sin, capping it off with the unanswerable: "Where is it written in the Bible?"

For of course, it's not. There's not a word about Mary Magdalene being a whore. So Christian's final wise-ass victory was to be in his own way *smarter* than Sister Miriam. And Lucy envied more than his handsomeness, more than his popularity, more than his self-love, his untroubled soul, his sinless, guiltless world. Oh to be transported there in arms such as his.

But, conversely, what chance did Lucy have of becoming a Bride of Christ in this environment? The damage wrought by St. Eulalia's was terminal: Sister Belinda, so slow of mind and fat—the butt of a hundred jokes a day. The old addled sisters, the young Sister Hilda who was called Sister Hitler because of her disposition and it didn't hurt that she had a mustache. The only fun nun was the tippling women's basketball coach, Sister Victoria, always known as Sister Vickie, and her friend Father Kennedy, another lively boozer with a wild Irish love of practical jokes and malicious remarks about the nuns he was forced to work with . . . God, how did those two ever find their way into St. Eulalia's? But it was the wretched, sour old Sister Miriam who was a walking advertisement for Protestantism, Exhibit A for Reverend Paisley—maybe even for Paganism.

Sister Miriam, the woman who counted Kotexes in the girls' room dispenser, rounded up the girls and demanded to know who took one without clearing it with her first.

"I want you to know," she lectured seriously, "that whoever took that period-napkin, that this is a terrible, terrible thing you've done . . ."

Lucy wasn't sure whether she meant having a period or taking a Kotex, or both. Sister Miriam, the woman who got permission from the principal to go into the girls' lockers, who read their diaries late one night and then cornered the girls with their confessions, their filthy, sex-obsessed, perverse disgusting words, read back to them, held up to the scrutiny of Father Doogan, who would look at the girls with pity for their damnable actions.

God, what a war criminal she was.

Father Kennedy, full of life and intelligence, close pal of the pariah Sister Vickie, was Sister Miriam's mortal enemy. Sister Miriam would sniff the merest hint of whiskey-breath on the man and either commence a moral lecture, announce that she was to report him to the archbishop—one assumed it was never a real threat—or attempt one of her more useless tactics, break into his history class, sit in the back and glare at him righteously.

Father Kennedy in good form was incomparable, a natural Dominican, always ready to be carried away with his own storytelling, not having read the source materials in centuries, trusting his own mind and what he remembered or thought he remembered but had rewritten and improved. He would be especially red-faced and florid after lunch, hitting the wine with Sister Vickie, and Lucy and Faith and the class watched him bellow about what a big fat pig Aquinas was, the man who preached everything in moderation! When the funeral came, how it took twelve brothers and a box six by ten to fit the obese doctor into. Fatter, claimed Father Kennedy, than some of the sisters at St. Eulalia's! The class laughed and Father Kennedy, encouraged, continued to describe the fatness of Aquinas, doing a small imitation of Aquinas/Sister Belinda waddling about the halls.

And in the back of the room, her tissue out, was Sister Miriam quietly weeping, making a show of her sufferings. Until each child turned and saw her, until her tears were well recorded and at last a dense silence of embarrassment fell on the class.

"And what is your problem now, Sister?" the father would grumble, sobered and annoyed.

"Your soul," she'd wail dismally.

And apparently her threat to call the archbishop had some predicate, for one week as Lucy and Faith sat in their afternoon Church History class, Sister Miriam came in and stood regally, triumphal, *in gloria*, behind the podium: "Father Kennedy has been transferred," she said richly, and the class inwardly groaned, sensing deeper despair when it became known that Sister Miriam, justified, was to be his replacement. The father, it was rumored, was exiled to a rough, impoverished boys' school in Hammond, Indiana, to be a librarian, which was a demotion, a punishment; and not far behind was Sister Vickie, also shipped out. Maybe that beloved bit of schoolkid gossip concerning their affair had been passed on and taken seriously by the archbishop. Maybe it had been true.

So it was Church History with Sister Miriam, and out went the difficult learned texts, the *City of God* of Augustine, the *Summa Theologica* of Aquinas, gone were Pseudo-Dionysius, Justin Martyr, Origen, Tertullian, and Basil the Great, Isidore of Seville. Sister Miriam decided the text should be St. Alphonsus de Liguori's *Victories of the Martyrs.*

"Procopius," she said, during the five weeks devoted to the Virgin Martyrs, "not discouraged by St. Agnes's refusal to marry him, continued to pester her." She read from St. Alphonsus: *"Procopius continued with his ineffectual importunities until at last the saint, wishing to free herself from his unwelcome attentions, said to him, 'Begone from me, thou food of death! I am already engaged to another and a far better Spouse. He is the King of Heaven, to whom I have consecrated my entire being.'"*

Sister Miriam could partake of that high emotion. She sang out the refusals and rejections of the Virgin Martyrs' suitors as if she had had the occasion to issue the very words. And how she luxuriated in the eventual martyrdoms, St. Catherine's wheel bursting into flames before the inevitable beheading, the pincers and coals and grills and boiling pitch. And how when the Virgin Martyrs St. Lucy and St. Faith were mentioned, their namesakes, both red in the face, felt the glow of unwanted publicity as the class snickered at their God-ordained virginity.

"In 304," Sister Miriam noted seriously, always happy to justify her martyrologies as histories, "Agnes achieved her glorious martyrdom." She sighed heavily and delved into the book again: *"The governor then thought to intimidate Agnes by threatening to have her sent to an infamous place to be there . . . dishonored . . ."*

That must mean a whorehouse, thought Lucy, and dishonored means she was going to have to have sex. Deciphering St. Alphonsus's prim phraseology naturally made Sister Miriam's martyr-ridden history classes a good deal more sex-obsessed than Father Kennedy's proper ones.

"But if any man approached her," read the sister, *"with an immodest intent . . ."*

Fucking, thought Lucy, stealing a glance at Faith, who, though devoted to Sister Miriam's hagiographies, may have missed the baser points.

". . . he became so overawed as not to be able to look upon the saint. Only one rash young man attempted to offer her a violence, but as Cardinal Orsi here observes, the impure wretch soon experienced the jealousy with which the

Spouse of Virgins defends them, for a flash of lightning struck him blind and he fell dead upon the ground."

Sister Miriam serenely gazed out upon the next generation of Catholic youth, so fresh-faced and interested, never suspecting that they were stirred to the depths of their percolating adolescence, imagining Agnes chained down spread-eagle in a whorehouse, the young man buck-naked and ready to give it to her, before Christ ruined it all with His lightning bolts. Lucy glanced at Christian, whom she always cast as the pagan suitor. A boy just primed to offer a Virgin Martyr a violence, she was sure.

Half an hour later, Agnes was at the stake.

"The funeral pyre was accordingly erected, the saint was placed upon it and the fire enkindled; but the flames respecting her person divided themselves on either side of her and consumed many of the idolators who were assisting at the execution . . . "

Christian allowed himself a small, disbelieving snort.

As in all these stories, despite the lightning and blindings and miracles at the stake, the pagans persevered to behead the saint. Miriam here bleated the lines, moved by stifled emotion: *"The executioner trembled to give the stroke but the saint animated him saying, 'Haste thee to destroy this my body, which could give pleasure to others, to the offending of my Divine Spouse. Fear not to give me that death."*

Anything but sex!

Lucy once was talking to Luke, her Lutheran friend at Chicago, who swore he wasn't sure what a hymen *was* until he was in college. But no Roman Catholic would ever go in ignorance! Nooooo no no! As Sister Miriam lectured, the message came through: St. Agatha with her breasts sheared off, St. Dionysia watching her infant tortured to death, raked with scourges, the nun St. Febronia, her body as one wound, charred over a slow fire, her teeth extracted, St. Cecilia with her family massacred and herself put in an oven to roast and suffocate, St. Justina heated up slowly in boiling tar, St. Anastasia with her tongue pulled out, breasts removed by white-hot pincers, her every limb broken with hot coals implanted in her wounds, St. Faith, not even eleven, on the gridiron, and St. Lucy blinded and beheaded—but mind you, whenever the Virgin Martyrs were sent to a whorehouse or threatened with betrothal, angels descended, swords of flame appeared, men were struck blind and dead, the earth opened up, invisible walls were formed! The God of the Roman Catholics was quite clear on the subject: tear these pretty young things apart, any torture you like, but *not the hymen!* Not the precious, unbreakable hymen of blessed virginity! Lucy, one day while roaming the library at Loyola, pulled down Karl Rahner's theological essays—the rebel Jesuit, always a step away from excommunication, one of the Church's most progressive thinkers . . . and here, even *here*, was a consideration of the Virgin Mary's hymen and the implications of its remaining unbroken as she delivered Jesus, the theological *necessity* of its remaining intact, *in partum.*

O Masculine Father, was there no escape? Men were fortunate enough to have souls, but Catholic women only this ineffable membrane into which all worth or damnation or redemption was focused.

"And dearest, most beloved Agnes," Sister Miriam said, breathing deeply, crossing herself as she read the last, *"raised her eyes to Heaven and besought Jesus to receive her soul and this tender virgin . . ."*

Lucy saw Faith color at the word *virgin.* Lucy, back then, blushed too when talking of virgins. Not in the phrase "Blessed Virgin Mary," as that was automatic and well-worn, but in discussing virginity and an aspect of the proper female Christian life, and Lucy reddened particularly when she had to deliver reports in front of the class and could imagine her overamused classmates, could imagine Christian's unspoken ridicule.

". . . this tender virgin received the stroke of death and went to Our Savior to receive the palm of her triumph!"

Faith once leaned over to Lucy during a particularly ghastly account of St. Potamiena's martyrdom.

(Who begged to be lowered slowly into boiling pitch that she might suffer more for her divine spouse. How can We forget.)

Faith risked to Lucy perhaps her one irreverence: "If you didn't know any better, you'd think Sister Miriam was sad that she would never be burned at the stake . . ."

And Lucy showed enough surprise at hearing Faith say such a thing that Faith immediately blushed and receded to immediate regret. What do you bet Faith confessed this mortal sin that very evening to Father Doogan . . . and what do you bet Father Doogan secretly had to fight off laughter in the confessional?

(That he did.)

And in any event, poor Faith was wrong. Sister Miriam did not wish to have her convictions tested by martyrdom. To Sister Miriam, her entire life was an arduous martyrdom already.

Sister Miriam, on dispensation from the convent, lived at home with her mother, who was in her seventies, and incredibly, with her mother's mother, who was in her nineties: women who had grown bitter and cross with her, but women she could not have lived without. With every exasperation and indignity inflicted upon Sister Miriam by her elders, with every thankless wash of the bedpan, with every one of her mother's reminders of the future she would have preferred for her daughter, Miriam was confirmed and steeped in her martyrdom, known only to her and Our Lady, her Cross to bear, the way her youthful ugliness had been, the way her spinsterhood had been.

Lucy, the especial victim of the sister, dreaded the day when Sister Miriam's grandmother died because Sister Miriam's sufferings would know no bounds. Rather than accept that 90-year-old lives are likely to end, and maybe mercifully ended, all she would see was her loss, her desertion, the fact of a death visited upon her, an opportunity to focus the frustration and downright meanness of her life into a hallowed period of grief. And God help Sister Miriam, thought Lucy, when it came time for her own mother to die—that would be worth all the tortures, breast-shearings, pincers, and racks in St. Alphonsus. No one would ever suffer more or endure more bitterness. And how richer and deeper would be the recitals of the Virgin Martyrs in the Church History classes yet to be endured, to St. Eulalia students not yet born.

The one time Lucy had confessed acute hatred of Sister Miriam, Father Doogan had instructed her after the rosary to say a special and loving prayer for Sister Miriam. Rather blankly, superficially but not without kindness, Lucy prayed that when this disaster, these twin deaths that loomed over Sister Miriam's life, came to pass that the Holy Spirit would sustain her and help her cope.

(It's a dirty job, Lucille, but Someone's got to do it. And I'm proud of you. Miriam is unfortunate, but you have compassion in your way for her. Dear Lucy, sometimes you are truly a child of Mine.)

Poor Faith, Lucy thought, feeling sleep coming on.

No doubt Faith was with the sisters now. How they'd caress and adore her as she wavered between taking vows or not. How Sister Miriam would warmly befriend her, comfort her fears, describe the rewards of a life of chastity—that is, until Faith, with much tears and theatricality, had actually taken her vows and become a sister. Then how they'd descend upon her. "Just because you're new do not expect any special privileges!" How they'd be jealous of her youth and her popularity with the students, if she managed it. Yes, they would undermine Faith, discipline and criticize her, reduce and annihilate her until in middle age she would be their sister in bitterness. Oh, considered Lucy, it is surely the lowest ebb of female behavior in human experience: the bitchery of nuns.

And it was women like this that Lucy had once planned to make her life's companions! This was the path Lucy's own mother had hoped she would follow—her own mother who loved her! Who should have wanted only the best for her! To end up like her namesake, Aunt Lucy: as bad as any of them, capable of exuding righteousness and disapproval, capable of endlessly remembered scores to settle and grievances and pettinesses, incapable of radiating even the tiniest emanation of love. Better the slut circuit with her sister Mary, better Christian Hall and all he entailed!

(We understand how you'd see it that way.)

Yes, thought Lucy, as weariness overtook her, Christian sure looked good, but frankly he doesn't have a thing on David McCall.

JUNE 28TH

Around noon O'Hanrahan, Rabbi Hersch, and Lucy sat in the near-deserted pub of the Crown. They glanced at the clock, sighed, shuffled nervously, and the professor repeatedly read the same paragraph in a book about ancient African scripts.

"You know," said the rabbi, "Philip's book is the definitive one on that subject."

"This text is perfectly adequate." O'Hanrahan was not happy to see Father Beaufoix's eminence reasserted.

Lucy let out an audible exhale of boredom, hoping someone would talk to her. Most of the village's working men were at the cannery, she had been told, and lunch hour was not until one P.M., when the pub would become alive again.

Rabbi Hersch: "Where is this guy? Could Father Keegan have gotten some of his facts wrong, Paddy?"

"He's just a half-hour late."

Presently, the door opened and they heard the little bell tinkle. A slender, tall man in a long black overcoat, pallid with thinning brown hair and a somber expression, presented himself. Jack the publican eyed the man oddly but when he saw the stranger join the table with Dr. O'Hanrahan, he went back to polishing his pint glasses with a bar towel.

"Dr. O'Hanrahan?" the man said, looking at the rabbi first.

The professor identified himself.

The stranger eyed Lucy and Rabbi Hersch. "And who . . ."

O'Hanrahan: "This is Mr. Hersch, my associate from Hebrew University, and Miss Lucy Dantan, my assistant from Chicago University. Please, be seated." Lucy noticed that the professor did not advertise Mr. Hersch as a rabbi.

The pale man sat down without introducing himself; he began immediately speaking in a clipped, educated British accent:

"Needless to say this transaction must be conducted with the utmost secrecy and care. It was no easy thing to acquire this document and it is to be understood that you have been summoned by the Father General as our greatest hope of deciphering said document. It is and must remain property of the . . . of the order."

Lucy looked at the rabbi, whose glance darted to O'Hanrahan.

"Of course," said O'Hanrahan simply.

"I shall tell you a bit of the history of this scroll. Fortunately the collector who bought it in Rome, in April of this year, a German man, did not comprehend its value. In fact, one of our order posed as an assessor and informed him that the scroll was, indeed, an unimportant curiosity. This German collector put the scroll on the market soon after. Then we sent another of our brethren, Father Quinn, whom you shall meet on Rathlin Island.

"Father Quinn, posing as an antiques collector, displayed a mild interest in this document and in another scroll as well. We concluded by buying two scrolls, leaving the German gentleman with the impression that he had cheated us upon the second one, when all we desired was the first one."

"Commendable," said O'Hanrahan, impatiently.

"It is now with us upon Rathlin Island in our retreat." He paused and assessed how interested his listeners were. With a glance to the left and right to see if anyone else was listening, he continued: "You will hire a boat sometime this afternoon. Four P.M. would be most convenient. We shall meet with you, discuss the arrangements, and I hope, Father, you will join us in a service."

O'Hanrahan nodded serenely.

"Very well. I shall see you then."

Then the man pulled his coat tight and left.

Everyone shifted as the pub door closed, breathing more freely.

"*Father?*" Lucy asked the next second.

Rabbi Hersch: "Father Patrick O'Hanrahan, Society of Jesus, a Company man."

"Miss Dantan," O'Hanrahan began humorlessly, "these people are not likely to give this scroll to a lapsed Jesuit, so for the moment I am returned to my former profession. That's why we stopped in Belfast, to pick up my little priest costume. Morey, stop smiling."

"Heh-heh, it'll be something seeing you in a collar again. Not since Jerusalem in 1950 have I seen such a sight."

"I'm going to the island by myself, if you don't mind."

"Nonsense," said his friend. "It's my university's scroll and I want to make sure you get off the island with it."

"Do you really think, Morey," asked O'Hanrahan, "that your rabbinical presence is going to make dealing with these kooks any easier? Look, I met Father Creech in 1956 and he was a looney-tune then. He had a master plan to cripple the Soviet Union in order for the West to attack and reestablish a government there friendly to the Holy Roman Church. And . . ."

"Go on," said the rabbi.

"It is thought," O'Hanrahan said in a low tone, "that this order was instrumental in smuggling thousands of Nazis and war criminals out of Central Europe to Argentina at Pius XII's bidding—that's just a rumor but I wouldn't be surprised. Father Keegan keeps up with these guys more than I do and he says they still have a program for the Conversion of the Jews."

"Was that program or *pogrom?*"

Lucy said, "I didn't think the Jesuits were anti-Semitic anymore."

The men looked at her and then at each other.

"They're not exactly your card-carrying Jesuits," said the professor.

"Well, then, who exactly *is* over there?"

"They're a breakaway group," O'Hanrahan said slowly, "but beyond that, I couldn't tell you much more. We owe this meeting to Father Keegan, who is their go-between in Dublin, but he doesn't know very much about them either."

Lucy asked, "Do I get to come?"

"No," said O'Hanrahan.

"Yes," said the rabbi. "It'll take the heat off me if there's another in the party."

This was a shock to Lucy. Since when did her existence win the rabbi's approval?

O'Hanrahan stared out the window at the gusty day, the wind spitting the rain against the panes of glass. "Gonna be a lovely crossing," he said. "I'll see if I can get some Dramamine at that little corner shop." Then he stood up, and downed the rest of his Bushmills Black. "Aaaaah. Well, I better put on my penguin suit, and work up some Latin salutations for our hosts."

O'Hanrahan bowed to the table and went upstairs.

Lucy waited until he was out of earshot. "Thanks for letting me come along, Rabbi, sir," she said.

"I got my reasons."

"Do *you* know," she asked as delicately as possible, "who these people are on Rathlin Island?"

The rabbi looked down at his coffee. "Honestly, little girl, I'm not sure whom we're dealing with. Some breakaway group, as Patrick said."

"You think they're dangerous?"

"All fanatics are dangerous."

Around 3:30 Lucy emerged from her room, in her baggy sweater over a flannel shirt, her jeans, and a long overcoat that was David's sister's lent for her stay in Ballymacross. She also borrowed a knapsack from the McCall family closet and put in a more formal change of clothing, a dark skirt and blouse. O'Hanrahan emerged from his room in full priest's attire, and the rabbi soon followed, wearing something warm and nondenominational.

The rain had abated. They walked the half-mile down the main highway to the cliffs and the muddy path leading to some concrete steps and the jetty with the fishing boats moored there.

"I wish you two would stay here," said O'Hanrahan. "I'm going to be lying my head off from the time I leave, doing my Jesuit shtick, and I don't want you guys laughing."

"Believe me, Paddy," said the rabbi, "nothing about this strikes me as funny. I say we get our hands on the scroll and run for it."

"Run where? Once we're over there, we're stuck until they fetch us a boat."

"I have no intention of staying over there. Let's get Matthias and leave tonight."

O'Hanrahan returned crabbily, "I have no control over any of this, Morey."

Mr. McCall walked up from the jetty shaking his head. Too rough. His friend wouldn't take them over there, not upon a boat this small leastaways. However, there was a Mr. Sweeney in Ballycastle who went out in worse seas than this. Moments later, they hopped in the McCalls' sedan and Mr. McCall drove the trio twelve miles to Ballycastle and the piers. Sweeney the ferryman in late-summer months ran a boat service to Rathlin Island and, though not happy about it, he finally was persuaded for £20 to run them across before the incoming storm.

"You mean the storm isn't even here yet?" asked Lucy.

O'Hanrahan frowned. "Still time to back out."

"You're staying put, little girl," whispered the rabbi.

The three pilgrims felt their stomachs tighten looking upon their bobbing tiny craft.

"Aye, ah wouldnae set oot wi' me boot in this're muck," Mr. Sweeney said in Lucy's ear, above the howling wind. "Skelpin' doon the day. . . ."

"Excuse me, sir, but I don't speak Gaelic."

" 's English," said Mr. Sweeney.

Lucy frowned as she watched the little skiff roll up and down as the waves slapped the pier. Over to the west, at Carrick-A-Rede, the waves splashed against the foot of the cliffs, sending the birds scattering.

Sweeney stepped unsurely into his craft and started up his motor, amid his mutterings, predictions of doom. He tossed Lucy a damp life jacket that smelled of mold, and the rabbi and "Father" O'Hanrahan were thrown one too. Even stepping into the skiff was a challenge, and Lucy clung to the gunnels after the boat was away from the pier. Oh St. Christopher, she thought . . . nah, he's fiction. St. Clement, tied to the anchor and thrown overboard . . . not exactly a cheery thought in these circumstances. St. Paul? Everyone nearly drowned on that boat except the saint, and she was no saint, so she'd better go straight to the top, she thought, offering up an Our Father.

(We didn't ask you to get in that tiny boat in a storm.)

Holy Spirit, she concluded, her eyes tightly closed, grant us success on the voyage if it be Thy will . . .

(Oh, hold on tight.)

It was worse than she expected. She could see the waves rising toward the boat but there seemed to be no rule as to which ones tossed the boat like a seesaw and which troughs the boat fell into. Away from the shore now, the passengers felt the wind unimpeded; the gale harassed Lucy's face with Lucy's own salty, windblown hair. Sweeney told the rabbi something, which was passed on to O'Hanrahan then to Lucy, through cupped hands: Rathlin Island had a concrete pier and there was no way in these waves Sweeney was going to risk smashing his boat against the concrete.

"Bring us into the shallows and we'll jump off and run ashore," said the rabbi, determined.

The drizzle turned to driving rain. Supported by an icy wind, the rain stung Lucy's face and all her energies were focused on Life After This Boatride. "What?" she hollered above the squall. "We're swimming ashore?"

"Wading," said the rabbi, "or we don't get over there."

"By the sea, by the sea, by the beautiful sea!" sang O'Hanrahan.

Rathlin Island looked fearsome ahead of them, standing windswept and barren against a black afternoon storm-sky that rumbled and churned fiercely as if harboring the wrath of the Old Testament God, a disgruntled Scotsman, the clouds lit from within by pulses of eerie, summer lightning. With each gravel roll of thunder, Sweeney cursed this venture, calculating the proximity of the lightning and the storm's center. Lucy wiped the rain from her face to see a black-robed figure standing on the brown, treeless hill that led down to the rocky shore. Not the same man as this morning. This priest or monk stood perfectly still, observing dispassionately.

"Our welcoming committee," said the rabbi, huddling himself beside Lucy.

Lucy could see he wore an old-fashioned priest's cassock, as Sweeney brought the boat closer in the shallows, a crescent-shaped cove of agitated gray-blue water.

"Ah darenae bring her no closer'na this-here," he yelled. And then Mr. Sweeney handed Lucy a plastic grocery-store bag with a few letters in it, wrapped tight in rubber bands. "The post!" he yelled, and with a nod of his head directed her to take Rathlin Island its mail. As Lucy and Mr. Sweeney leaned to the one side of the boat, the rabbi, wincing, lowered himself over the other side into the three feet of water.

"Whoooooo!" he cried, laughing, moaning, screaming in agony simultaneously at the cold. He snapped his fingers for Lucy to follow.

"You wanna carry me?"

"Chivalry is a Christian idea," he yelled back, rushing to the shore.

O'Hanrahan, going second, rolled over the side and lost his balance, soaking himself completely. He bobbed up instantly in the icy water, emitting a shocked howl from his depths. Lucy smiled despite herself and even Rabbi Hersch, reaching the shore, bent over in unsympathetic laughter. O'Hanrahan beckoned for Lucy to jump in and take his hand. This is an adventure, Lucy told herself, hoping to make these next few moments tolerable. A wave hit the side of the boat and splashed up in her face, so figuring she wouldn't be much more wet she jumped into the water . . .

Excruciation! Misery!

Holding the professor's hand for support and her knapsack high above the water, they waded to the pebbly shore ten yards away. The rabbi peeled off his life jacket and gave it a fling back to the boat; O'Hanrahan did the same. Sweeney didn't catch them, but fished them into the boat with a pole. Lucy had tied hers so tight that she and the rabbi spent a few minutes untying the knot.

"I'm freezing!"

"You take Girl Scouts? Whadya call this Gordian knot here, Jesus H. Christ . . ."

"Hurry!" she cried, clutching her knapsack and the bag with the mail, her fingers turning blue.

Soon the rabbi had pitched her life jacket back to the boat and Mr. Sweeney of Ballycastle, now cursing no one but himself for this folly, sped away back to the mainland. Lucy, O'Hanrahan, and Rabbi Hersch walked toward the hill and the black-robed stranger who did not move to greet or help or guide them.

"Jesuit hospitality?" muttered Lucy.

"Just wait until you get inside this joint," O'Hanrahan replied.

As they approached the priest, Lucy saw that he was youngish, in his thirties; his beardless, waxen face did not seem to notice the rain streaming from his uncovered head and there were dark circles under his eyes as if in a permanent state of malnourished contrition. He viewed them noncommittally.

"We'll go now to the chapel," he said, turning and walking before them.

Across the heather they made their way to a gravel path as the rain pelted them and the wind blew through them. Pneumonia, thought Lucy calmly, and at the very least, flu. Ahead, at last, was a series of humble-looking, whitewashed stone croft-cottages, enclosed in a declivity, surrounded by gnarled, windblown trees and scrub. A second priest met them at the door—the man who had called on them in the Crown. Lucy took the mail out of the bag and handed it to them as cheerfully as she could, glimpsing the names on the envelopes: Rev. D. Quinn, S.J., and Rev. T. O'Reilly, S.J., and a few letters for a Father General, F. Theophilus Creech, one of which had a three-tiered miter and some inscription . . . But the letters were snatched from her before she could study further.

"Welcome," said the young priest without much feeling, "to the Chapel of the Holy Savior. I'm Father Quinn, if you need anything. I must admit, I believed you would come alone, Father."

While O'Hanrahan invented explanations, Lucy began to make out features in the dimness: she was in a foyer, not much warmer than outside, and through double doors there was a small stone-walled chapel. Behind them was a large dark wooden door that opened creakingly to reveal a short hallway with doors at carefully measured intervals; it could have been a small prison but, Lucy understood, this was a building of six monastic cells. The rabbi was shown to the end chamber and Lucy to the chamber across from his, and O'Hanrahan catty-corner to hers.

Father Quinn reached in and turned on the light, a small low-watt bulb from the ceiling. "The generator goes off at 7:30 after the supper is prepared," he said tonelessly, "but we'll get you a candle. The heat will be on until then, and I suggest you put your wet shoes and clothes on the radiator right away. I see you have a watch. Supper is at six in the refectory. There is a brief prayer service in the chapel but we ask you not to attend, being a woman." Then he left and closed the door.

There was a cot. A bedside table with a Bible and a drawer for one's very few belongings; there was a table and a chair against the wall, which had a small five-inch-wide gothic slit for a window. After draping and arranging her shoes, socks, jeans, and borrowed winter coat along the barely warm radiator, she changed into her dry clothes and lay down on the cot.

A nun I could be maybe, but never a monk, she thought flippantly. Been a monk ten minutes and I already hate it. Jesuit sexist pigs. She looked at her watch and saw it was 4:45 and decided she would take a nap, hoping some internal clock would wake her in time to eat.

It was Rabbi Hersch who woke her by knocking on the door.

"Dinnertime," he said softly. Lucy sat up and for a moment didn't know where she was. The rabbi opened the door and looked around it. "Paddy's been praying and helping at a Mass for the last hour, if you can believe it."

"No," she said, "but I can't believe any of it."

"Now I want you to listen, little girl, to all the claptrap talked at dinner and be sure to tell me what you learn."

Lucy looked at him oddly.

"It'll be in Latin mostly," he added.

"But you . . . you mean you don't—"

"When should a Jew need Latin, hm? I can read it but I can't speak it at a clip. That's where you come in."

"And that's why you wanted me along?"

"That's right."

Another pause. "So you don't trust Dr. O'Hanrahan to get the scroll and deal with these people?" she asked tentatively.

"Paddy, I trust. These people I don't trust."

Momentarily glad to have some rapport with the rabbi, she commented, "You know, sir, when I handed in the mail to these guys, I saw they had S.J. after their names, Society of Jesus, Jesuits. I find it odd these two priests, Quinn and O'Reilly, would go through seven years of schooling and rigorous education to be a Jesuit father only to serve this Father Creech fellow as sextons. It's a bit of a waste of Jesuit manpower, isn't it?"

"Yeah, but these don't appear to be your average Jesuits, huh?"

Lucy ran a brush through her hair, then accompanied the rabbi down the hall, stepping softly. They passed the chapel where the two attendant priests and O'Hanrahan, in vestments now, were at the Communion table, incense smoldering in the stationary thurible, the candles flickering. At the center of the rite, she assumed, was Father Creech, an ancient, drawn man, utterly bald but with gray flaring eyebrows that gave him the appearance of an owl. Rabbi Hersch and Lucy lingered out of sight in the shadowy doorway. ". . . *Et dimitte nobis debita nostra sicut et nos dimittimus debitoribus nostris*," intoned the elder priest.

"The Lord's Prayer," Lucy whispered to the rabbi.

"Big help you are. Everyone knows that one."

Soon the benediction was given and the ceremony was finished. The paten and chalice were retired, the thurible extinguished, and then the candles. The three fathers and O'Hanrahan emerged and Father Creech looked unsmilingly upon Lucy and Rabbi Hersch as they were introduced to him. "Blessings upon you," he said seriously as he noticeably didn't offer his hand. "Shall we to the refectory?" he said, turning in that direction.

O'Hanrahan, not breaking character, placidly followed.

" 'Shall we to the refectory,' " imitated the rabbi to Lucy as they followed the others. Lucy proceeded slowly, pausing to squint into the chapel and read the Latin motto above the altar: *Causam facti in nostro corde perpetue concludimus.*

Lucy looked quizzical.

"Mean something to you?" asked Rabbi Hersch.

"I've read that somewhere before . . ."

The Father General presided at the head of the long table. Father O'Reilly lit the central candles and turned off the low-watt bulb. Father Quinn went on to the kitchen to procure the slight meal: hard bread, a sliced, boiled leek, fibrous and metallic, a mold-ridden homemade blue cheese that was gritty, and a small, wallet-sized slab of boiled fish.

Father Creech began the blessing. In Latin he praised the beneficence of the Lord, the glories and treasures of the Roman Catholic Church, the One True Church, etc., and how this meal was one more sign of bounty . . .

The rabbi peeked at Lucy, scowling.

Lucy looked back at him. They both looked at O'Hanrahan.

O'Hanrahan rolled his eyes at them.

The long recitative went on another five minutes. Never let us fully enjoy Your blessings, said Father Creech in high-toned, rounded Latin phrases, never let us take for granted any morsel until our mission is completed on this earth, the restoration of the supreme omnipotent church headed by His Holiness, Pontifex Maximus, Bishop of Rome, and the reunification of the Church Triumphant under him, Vicar of Christ, Christ's Proxy on this Earth . . .

Lucy peeked again at Rabbi Hersch, who was sneaking a sliver of fish. The Latin had lost him a few paragraphs ago, she figured.

Then at last: ". . . *in nomine Jesu Hominum Salvator, Nazarenus, Rex Iudaeorum. Amen.*"

The rabbi winced at the King-of-the-Jews bit, as Lucy and the others began their meal in silence. Father Quinn rose to fetch a pitcher of acidic-tasting water, which Lucy decided was rainwater. With each gesture, Father Quinn turned to Father Creech and asked "*Permittetis?*"—asking his permission, but in the plural. Some equivalent, Lucy figured, of the "Royal We." Father Creech was the embodiment of the Order itself. Father Creech nodded his head solemnly to permit his minions to do what they asked, pour the water, take up the plates, and he even gave the men permission to eat this stingy offering. Lucy saw that ultimate, unquestioning obedience was the foremost ritual of this dinner. Again, she looked at the rabbi, who chewed his paltry portion miserably.

O'Hanrahan said quietly, "If I might speak, Father—"

"*Populus Dei est Romanus et lingua est Latina, Pater.*"

Informed that Latin was the only language going, O'Hanrahan began again, first asking pardon, and then if he might address an issue. Father Creech nodded. Lucy watched the Father General cut his tiny fish into ever-so-small bites and she felt revulsion as his tongue went out to meet the food like some reptile, savoring each tiny, precious morsel religiously.

O'Hanrahan in fluid Latin asked when he might view the wondrous scroll that they both valued so highly.

Perhaps after the evening prayers, answered Father Creech.

O'Hanrahan went on to say that the scroll, from what was known about it, was very difficult and the language obscure. He would need possession of the scroll in a number of the world's libraries in order to unravel its divine mysteries.

Father Creech was noncommittal. Then after a pause during which he sipped a sip of water—it occurred to Lucy then that he was counting his sips as well as his bites to conform to some holy number, twelve perhaps—the father said he could not part permanently with such a valuable scroll, its price being dear for them and it clearly being a manifestation of Divine Will that they should have received it while so many others wanted it. All to the Glory of the Pope, Christ on this Earth . . .

But it may be inauthentic, suggested O'Hanrahan.

Surely it is a pseudo-gospel, Father Creech suggested, surely it cannot be by the real St. Matthias as rumored.

"*Si inventum erit inutile*," O'Hanrahan next switched to the future less vivid tense and then to the subjective contrary. Lucy's head hurt trying to keep up; she noticed Fathers Quinn and O'Reilly were exercised too by O'Hanrahan's showing off at the outer fringes of grammar.

O'Hanrahan said it was his every intention to safeguard Father Creech's possession of the scroll, and all he required was to take it to the mainland—accompanied, of course, by one of the junior fathers—and to photograph it. From these photographs, O'Hanrahan explained, he could translate this mysterious artifact.

Why not bring the necessary equipment here? suggested Father Creech.

Lucy saw that O'Hanrahan was stumped briefly, but he recovered: because, he said, if the photos do not come out in sufficient focus, we will have to redo them. There is a photo lab, surely, in Ballycastle. The same day we make the photographs we can develop them and see that they suit our needs. Then, simply, Father Quinn or Father O'Reilly can return the scroll to Rathlin Island.

If it should require that, Father Creech assented, feeling—Lucy divined—papal in his extravagance. Father Creech further proposed that after dinner his guests should discuss the matter less formally in his study. Father O'Reilly was dismissed to go make a fire, and there were Latin permissions granted, a kneeling, a kissing of the Father General's ring, a rote benediction, before the lesser father scurried away to do his master's bidding.

Lucy looked at the rabbi, who was stifling a yawn, and then down at her plate. There was a faint Roman numeral above the simple blue line that ran the circumference of the plate: MDCCLXXIII.

Then suddenly the Father General stood, and the others stood after him. There was a benediction of several minutes, then following many scrapings and permissions sought, O'Hanrahan, Rabbi Hersch, and Lucy followed Father Creech to his study. Father Quinn and Father O'Reilly in a display of abasement crept from the study after completing the fire in the hearth.

Lucy surveyed the library, the warmest room yet revealed in the complex, walls of shelves of centuries-old leather-bound tomes, a worn carpet for the stone floor, several chairs by the fire, and a large window that rattled in its sill, shaken by the wind outside.

"Please, child," said Father Creech, speaking now in a baritone English. He pointed to the window with a gnarled, skeletal finger, "Look out upon the origins of this holy place."

Father Creech directed her to shield out the light with her hands and peer through the library window: it was not quite dark at this latitude, the horizon an otherwordly band of sky with an eerie lightless blue, this spoil of daylight an unwilling northern prisoner. Lucy listened to the wind howl and whistle about the eaves. She saw the silhouette of a stone altar, a fragment of stone wall, an iron Celtic cross planted in the midst of the ruin. Beyond this were trees rocking in the relentless wind, twisted and flailing, revealing but a moment of their centuries of torment. Lucy felt terror at the desolation of this ruin. How did anyone ever survive in this harsh weather?

(St. Bartholomew of the 1100s went out into the North Sea on a rock island of the Farne Islands, bird-covered and storm-battered, but Aelwin could be glimpsed on the horizon. One day Aelwin waded over through the icy seas and told Bartholomew to leave, but he didn't. Aelwin sulked off to another miserable location. But then the prior Thomas came out on the islands to freeze and nearly die and he and Bartholomew had to divide the seaweed and bird's eggs; they spent years praying that the other one would disappear or be swept out to sea so that they could be alone again. Alone, like St. Drythelm of the 700s, who would stand in a river until it turned to ice around him, trapping his legs while he was lost in prayer. Alone, like St. Pyron of Wales who built his oratory every day anew on the soft tidal sand so that each day his hut would be destroyed by the tide, reminding him of the impermanence of Man's world.)

"It was somewhat warmer a millennium ago," O'Hanrahan offered good-naturedly. "Greenland was Green, Newfoundland was called Vineland and she and England grew grapes for wine, the Shetlands and Orkneys were full of prehistoric peoples."

The rabbi offered, "But surely the storms were always this bad."

Then the lights went off.

The hum of the generator ceased.

The four of them stayed in place until their eyes adjusted to the coals in the fireplace while all about the house was the gale, shaking the rafters. The Father General's gaunt face looked ghastly and severe in the firelight.

"The Irish saved Christianity from extinction among the barbarian hordes," he droned, holding a book in his lap. "Great Britain was civilized twice by Rome, first by the ancient Romans, then by the Celtic Roman Catholics."

O'Hanrahan frowned at this too-tidy view. The Celtic Church and the modern Roman Catholic Church were worlds apart, the latter virtually wiping out the former at the Council of Whitby in 664.

Father Creech: "Even today, more than they will admit, England owes what humanity it has to the Celtic strain. They would have it the other way around, of course, but civilization spread from west to east. They claim that Patrick, evangel to the Irish, was British but this is a misreading. He was Breton, not British, and the Bretons are Celts."

Lucy was untouched by this parade of Celtic virtue.

"That altar outside, my daughter, is all that's left from the original Church of the Holy Savior founded in 562 by St. Columkille, the saint who evangelized Britain in 564. Remnants of his churches are throughout the northern isles."

Columkille, O'Hanrahan explained for Lucy's benefit, centered his ministry on the Holy Isle of Iona, off the island of Mull to the west of the Scottish highlands. "When he died," O'Hanrahan concluded, "they put Columkille on a bier and floated him away from Iona and he found his way back to Ireland where the ground opened between the bodies of Patrick and Brigit and received him."

But Father Creech looked sternly at O'Hanrahan, and O'Hanrahan quit in mid-legend.

"When the end of the world comes, and that will be soon," sighed the Father General, examining his veinous, bony fingers by the red firelight, "the Valley of Columkille, we think, in Donegal, will according to prophecy escape harm. In this final conflagration with Antichrist, it was prophesied by Columkille that Ireland would be spared, for the waters would rise and cover her." He uttered a mirthless laugh. "Already, with this global warming we read about the waters' rise. London puts up a barrier to hold back the ocean from rushing down the Thames."

"The prophecies of St. Malachy," added O'Hanrahan quietly.

"Signs of the End Times," nodded Father Creech.

Lucy asked, "Dr. O'Hanra . . . Father O'Hanrahan, what exactly are the prophecies of St. Malachy?"

He explained: Malachy was an Irishman who, starting with Pope Celestine II in 1143, began to compose Latin mottoes for all the popes until the end of the world. His third motto was *De rure albo* and sure enough, the third pope after Celestine, six years after Malachy's own death, was Nicholas Breakspear, the only English—Alban—pope, born near St. Alban's in fact. Gregory XII, Bishop of Nigripontis, was prophesied *Nauta de Ponte Nigro* (1406); the wicked Alexander VI, Bishop of Albano and Porto, was predicted *Bos Albanus in Porto* (1492); Benedict XV, pope through World War I, got *Religio Depopulata*, religion laid waste. . . .

(All in all a superb touch-up and con job by Cardinal Simoncelli and others through the centuries to make St. Malachy look good. However, despite the inapplicable mottoes, fraudulent alterations, and popes fashioning their coats of arms to include Malachy's motto so they would be more legitimate as Clement XI did in 1700, We have to admit there are some astounding coincidences.)

"And there are only two mottoes left," said O'Hanrahan quietly. "Just two more until the end. Depending how you count the past popes. Depending if you count the month-long John Paul I."

"The motto was *De Medietate Lunae*," said Father Creech. "Of the half-moon. It could refer to John Paul I's brief reign, no longer than the phase of the moon . . . or it could refer to John Paul II who will surely do battle with the Crescent Moon of the Middle East: Islam."

"After that?" asked Lucy, mildly despondent at the imminent apocalypse.

"*De Labore Solis*, from the toil of the sun," said Father Creech. "The environmental cataclysm to come. This is the motto of the papacy that should see the final war between Antichrist and the elect. Followed by *Gloria Olivae*."

"The glory of the olive," translated Lucy.

"The reign of peace before Christ Himself returns to the throne held fast for him through the centuries by the One True Church."

"Oh, brother," the rabbi murmured under his breath.

"Finally, *Petrus Romanus*," continued Father Creech. "Peter of Rome. The first and the last pope, who will return in glory to sit at the right hand of Jesus, Our Lord, as He judges this world of error."

Rabbi Hersch, with a forced smile, stood and stretched. "Well. If you'll excuse me? I'd like to read a bit and then turn in."

Father Creech did not wish the rabbi goodnight but rather replayed his pained smile and lifted an aged hand in some uncompleted, unfelt gesture. Then Father Creech returned to the book he had taken from the shelf. "Would you care to hear what befalls the English for their iniquities in the end, my daughter?"

Lucy took the rabbi's chair nearer the fire. This was like ghost stories at camp.

"Columkille from the 590s," began the Father General, "in translation, of course. *The pure Gael will fly away into exile into both the eastern and western regions of the world; the scantiness of land and oppressive debts, without a falsehood, shall bring decay unto them.* . . . And so it is true, is it not? The Irish have spread throughout the world, west to America, east to Australia. The English *shall be harassed from every quarter, like a fawn surrounded by a pack of voracious hounds shall be the position of the Saxons amidst their enemies.* Already their colonial misdeeds haunt them on their own shores. The scourge of Islam . . ."

Lucy and O'Hanrahan exchanged glances. She wanted very much to talk to him alone without Father Doom-and-Gloom around.

"The Saxons afterwards shall dwindle down into a disreputable people, and every obstacle shall be opposed to their future prosperity; because they did not observe justice and rectitude, they shall be forever after deprived of power, most of which is true now. Three English signs," he went on, closing the book, "foretell the End Times, according to Blessed Columkille. The burning of the Tower of London, the burning of the dockyards—both have historically happened—and finally, the destruction of the Bank of England, which has not yet happened. But with the union of currencies with the European Community, well, then all the signs shall have been accomplished."

"But if everybody's under water, it won't matter too much," began Lucy, but she saw that Father Creech had no levity in him. "I think," she said, standing to take her leave, "that I would like to read in my Bible a bit and I will see you tomorrow."

She hoped O'Hanrahan would come see her to the door so they could talk, but he remained seated.

"Good night, Father," she nodded to their host; "Father," she nodded to O'Hanrahan.

"Good night, my daughter," he said with a secret wink.

Lucy felt her way to the big oaken door and opened it. The hallway was lit by one votive candle under a Virgin statue in an alcove at the end of the hall. Outside the wind raked and strafed the roof and the shutters. She passed the icy Chapel of the Holy Savior where one red candle flickered in abysmal isolation, casting a shadow of the crucifix over the stone wall behind. Lucy, her hair standing up on end, felt like the End Times could begin now in this monastery, and she hurried away to her room. She fished in her pocket for the matches and struck one, then cupping the flame, walked briskly to her door and into her room. Looking up she saw the rabbi's face.

"Jesus!" she cried, dropping the match.

"I've been waiting for you in here—"

"You scared the *hell* out of me . . ." Lucy fumbled for her matches again.

"Sorry, I almost dozed off in here waiting for you. Cheery fellow, this Father Creech, huh? Why doesn't he just make a check out to the IRA and get it over with?"

Lucy, her heart still racing, sat on the bed and lit a new match. "He gives me the creeps. They all do."

"Contriving to make the world kneel before Rome is serious work," said the rabbi, rubbing his eyes.

Lucy lit the candle by her bedstand. "In fact, I thought Rome wasn't high on the Jesuits' hit parade this decade." Lucy continued thinking aloud. "Father Arrupe, the last Father General in Rome, spent most of his time undermining John Paul II. And that's another thing. Remember the mail I delivered? Another envelope was addressed to the

Father General, and all night long the priests were calling him that in Latin, Father General. Now, there's only one Jesuit Father General and he's supposed to be in Rome, and Father Creech isn't he. I'm not sure this is a breakaway group, Rabbi. I think these people think *they're* the real Jesuits and the modern Jesuits, the ones *we* acknowledge as Jesuits, are the breakaway group. These guys are what Catholics used to call Ultra-montanist."

The rabbi sounded out the word: "Across the mountains?"

"Yes," said Lucy, remembering her 19th-Century Church history. "The last century it was a term of derision for fanatical pro-papal clerics, movements and publications. Across the mountains, down in Rome and the Mediterranean, as opposed to Cismontanists, the progressive Northern European world."

A roll of thunder boomed about them and it seemed to linger in the damp stones of the hostel, echoing into a sustained gravelly hum. Lucy felt a chill and scooped up the rough wool blanket to pull around her.

"My God," said Lucy slowly, as rumors and gossip and years of hearsay fell into place. "He's . . . Creech is the Black Pope of the Ignatians."

The rabbi looked at her uneasily.

Lucy rambled, thinking of the Roman numeral on the plate: "Of course, 1773! You hear rumors about things like this but . . ."

He touched her sleeve. "Sssshh, quietly. Tell me what you think is going on here."

"And the motto in the chapel, 'The reasons for this act We keep locked up in Our Own heart.' "

The rabbi put an impatient hand on her arm. "Would you tell me what you're talking about?"

She lowered her voice. "In 1773, Pope Clement the somethingth . . . 14th, I think . . ."

"Go on!"

"Pope Clement disbanded the Jesuit Order, saying the words engraved over the altar in the chapel, 'The reasons for this act we keep locked in our own heart.' He banned them, it was thought, because the Jesuits were scheming too dangerously, maybe even scheming to replace him. But maybe that's not it."

The rabbi sat expectantly.

"Maybe the pope just wished to clean house and purge most of the Jesuit order of the day. But secretly, so the rumor goes, perhaps Clement funded an elite cadre of Jesuits to keep the order alive throughout the ban. The Ignatians—well, that's what they're thought to be called."

"The Ignatians."

"Exactly. I mean, by the 1770s Jesuits weren't welcome anywhere in

Europe, right? They had gone from being a secret intellectual police that controlled the fate of nations to this loathed band of corrupt monks—they were no longer effective in any conspiracy."

"So they went underground, huh? And here they are, still to this day?"

"And in the 19th Century, when the Jesuits were allowed to form an order again, the Ignatians must have kept going, preferring to think of themselves as the true, purist sect, committed in the spirit of Ignatius Loyola to the furtherance of the pope's bidding. God knows the other, official Jesuits are anything but friendly to the Vatican today."

(We'll say.)

Lucy listed some of the more notable Jesuit disobedience: fathers at American seminaries dismiss the pope's infallibility, Jesuits turn a blind eye to African magic and inclusion of lesser Hindu deities in the mass, James Carney, S.J., leads a guerrilla squad in Honduras, Jesuits were in the Sandinista cabinet, Jesuit influence was behind the jeering of John Paul II from a public mass in El Salvador in 1983, the radical Arthur McGovern, S.J., the Maoist-Christian movement led by Jesuits, the radical Karl Rahner, S.J., Jesuit calls for scrapping celibacy and the papal opposition to homosexuality, birth control.

"And the list goes on," Lucy said, before trailing off into thought. But everything now made sense, given how those tricky *real* Jesuits think. Who would look for the Ignatians off the coast of Protestant Northern Ireland on an inaccessible island? And those prayers through dinner: for a Catholic England, for a united Ireland, the homage to Mary, Queen of Ireland, the plans to turn Ireland into a Papal State with His Holiness as Priest-King . . .

The rabbi sighed. "We have got to get the Matthias scroll away from these clowns. Now what was all that talk at dinner? Paddy lost me once he hauled out the future perfect passive."

"They're going to let us take the scroll away just for the purpose of photographing it, providing we're accompanied by one of the fathers here. And I must say, Rabbi, Father Creech didn't sound like he had any intention of returning it to Hebrew University. The scroll, he vowed at one point, would never leave his sight or protection."

The rabbi stroked his chin. "The hell with that. That gospel is Hebrew University's property and we've got to swipe it."

Lucy wrapped herself more tightly in her blanket. "The Ignatians may be everywhere, Rabbi. Even in Jerusalem. They'll just figure out a way to steal it back."

Rabbi Hersch laughed. "If I get my hands on it, little girl, there's no chance they'll get it back. The Israeli Army will help me guard it, if necessary." He slapped his knee. "Okay. First things first, we got to get off the island with it. Part two, we lose the priest bodyguard. Part three-A, Paddy and I escape to Jerusalem. Part three-B, you go home back to Chicago."

Lucy was incensed. "Rabbi, I want to stay and help you guys. This would make my academic career! Why do I keep getting asked to leave?"

He looked steadily at her. "Rabbi Jacob Rosen, my predecessor in the Chair of Ancient Languages at Hebrew University." He paused. "He was probably killed. The scroll disappeared the day he fell down a flight of stairs to his death. That's how Hebrew University lost it in the first place."

Lucy's face went pale.

"So you see," the rabbi said, standing to leave, "it's not that we don't adore you, but we don't want you kidnapped for ransom, we don't want you threatened, we don't want you dead. You'll want to sleep on these pleasant thoughts," he added as he opened the door to leave.

Lucy decided she'd be lucky if she slept at all.

JUNE 29TH

The next morning Father Quinn knocked on her door to awaken Lucy.

"Pack up," he said, "you will be leaving before eleven."

Lucy had a headache and a cold nose. "I feel like I just got to sleep a few minutes ago," she complained out loud to herself.

After stuffing her barely dry clothes into her knapsack and after being led to the refectory for some more overblessed dusty bread and hot, bitter tea, Lucy was informed Father Creech was in prayer for at least an hour and she might enjoy wandering around the island. The rabbi was in Father Creech's library trying to entertain himself; O'Hanrahan had gone out for a walk.

"In an hour," said Father Quinn, "the Father General will bring the scroll from the vault. I am told you will be permitted to see it."

Lucy nodded her bland gratitude.

No window was large enough in the dim monastery to confirm Lucy's suspicion that the sun was out, but as she stepped from the monastery door she saw that the winds of the preceding night had swept the sky clean and she turned her face to the warmth of pure white sunlight reflecting from a calm, sparkling sea. It was the first sunshine she had seen in Ireland and her impression of the country was transformed: the green hills of the mainland were incandescent, the Atlantic an array of deep, intermingling blues, the noisy sea gulls, diving and swooping, were virgin white, even the brown scrub of the moors leading down to the sea was invested with tiny purple and reddish flowers.

Lucy walked down the path they had followed up from the beach the day before and digressed to a small overlooking mount. From this vantage she could see a strip of sand below, the pier for boats, a few whitewashed cottages to the west—it was not so lonely or forbidding an island, after all—and O'Hanrahan walking in his priest's uniform along the strand.

"Hello, Dr. O'Hanrahan," she called out some yards from him, startling him from his reverie.

O'Hanrahan acknowledged her presence with a brief smile.

Lucy, persuaded by the beauty of the scene, felt a personal question would not be out of place. "I didn't know you were a Jesuit, sir. When did you, uh, stop doing that?"

He paused and Lucy suddenly wondered whether she had offended him or, as bad, interrupted some private contemplation. O'Hanrahan said at last, "When I got married I renounced my vow. For some reason Ignatius Loyola preferred his orderlies to be unmarried."

Lucy felt she could balance the importunity by volunteering information about herself: "You know, I was almost going to be a nun."

"That's not too surprising," he said, walking a little in front of her at the water's edge.

She detected his scorn, but decided it was a joke. "No, really. Gabriel and I had this plan. He was going to be a Franciscan and I was going to be a Poor Clare and we were going to undertake some worthy ghetto project in Chicago, or maybe go to South America."

Trying to be as pleasant as possible, she had nonetheless wandered into unsafe territory by mentioning Gabriel. "Your pal Gabriel," said O'Hanrahan, "doesn't know what the hell he wants to do. He changes his mind each week, priest, monk, actor, academic—*thief*," he added.

Lucy tactically changed the subject. "Are we going to get the scroll, sir?"

"*We?*" he wondered aloud. He heard his own rudeness and was immediately more conversational: "The plan is as follows. Father O'Reilly will accompany us to Ballymacross where we're gonna take some photographs of the scroll."

"And then you're going to run off with it."

"Morey will. I'll explain to Father Creech that Rabbi Hersch merely stole property stolen from his university and that I had no idea he was going to do such a thing. Something like that. Then I'll hook up with Morey in Jerusalem, I'll translate the thing, then publish my findings."

"And then be world famous."

"Yeah, that's the plan."

Lucy deeply wished to be part of the team but she saw no opening in the scenario. She decided instead to impress Dr. O'Hanrahan with her deductions the previous night about the Ignatians. O'Hanrahan smiled as she recounted how she had deduced their identity from the year in Roman numerals on the dinner plate.

O'Hanrahan walked away from the shore. "You're a smart woman, Miss Dantan. Really wasted in grad school." From that remark, he began climbing up the trail to the top of the island's main hill. O'Hanrahan became red-faced and winded ascending the slight rise; Lucy wasn't in much better physical shape.

"See that?" he pointed, once at the summit. "That is the Mull of Kintyre, about twenty-some miles away. Scotland."

"Ireland and Scotland are that close?"

"In Bede's time the Irish used to be called the Scots. Long before Ulstermen had Protestantism and Catholicism to fight over, they fought here over other things, anything. One of the longest-running family squabbles in Europe."

And O'Hanrahan told Lucy the story of the Giant's Causeway, a volcanic basalt formation, like an oversized stairway, that sloped into the sea some miles west of here. It was the stairway of Finn MacCool who learned science from the Druid Master Finegas, who drank from the River Boyne into which the Nuts of Wisdom fell from the trees above, who had eaten the Salmon of Knowledge. Finn and his enemy Benandonner would fierce battle wage along this very coast, hurling boulders at each other, and one of Benandonner's throws missed the mark and splashed down between England and Ireland and is the Isle of Man, named after Mananan, the sea god who conveniently adopted the rock as his throne—that is, when he's not stirring up the water around Ireland to keep invaders away. "More important," O'Hanrahan added, "MacCool's house steward was converted to Christianity by St. Patrick.

(Patrick placed his hand on young Keelta's heart and it is what he said, *From myself to yourself, in the house or out of the house, in whatever place God will lay His hand on you, I give you Heaven.*)

Lucy was exhilarated. "Do you suppose Rathlin Island was a rock that missed?"

"Oh, there're legends for everything up here, every cove, every river. Much of it's lost thanks to my namesake. St. Patrick bragged that he burned thousands of volumes of legend and literature in bringing the One True Church to Ireland. That was 1600 years ago but it still steams me even now. What sin could this island have committed worse than that act?"

O'Hanrahan recounted his own favorite lore. How Ireland sainted three hundred different men named Colman in the 600s. How Colman of Kilmacduagh had a most blessed housefly to mark his pages for him in the Bible; and even unto his, O'Hanrahan's, grandfather's generation, it was believed that butterflies were souls waiting for an opening in Purgatory. St. Kenneth, who had to banish the mice from County Laoighis because they kept eating his shoes. St. Kieran of Saighir, who had a fox, a badger, and a wolf working for him, building his monastic cells and cooking the cabbage—until the fox ran off with his shoes.

"Shoes were apparently a major obsession," said Lucy.

"Few Celtic saints don't have associations with the animal kingdom," said O'Hanrahan. Poor St. Kieran of Clonmacnoise, who had a fox who carried his Latin lessons to his teacher until one day the fox ate the satchel. St. Kieran's wolf was a cousin of the she-wolf that suckled St. Ailbe as a child, before St. Ailbe, blessed adventurer, left for the Land of Promise, as did St. Brendan the Navigator of Tralee, who sailed amidst many tricks of the devil and jealous sea gods, and overcame many monsters. "As did dear St. Collen," added O'Hanrahan with a light Irish brogue, "who had to go to Wales to slay a giantess that would no ways leave."

(That tale is actually true, though.)

Lucy looked west over the cold Atlantic knowing the next land to be found was North America. She was then startled, turning back to see Father O'Reilly standing on the path before them, arms crossed, intolerant.

"It is time to view the scroll," he said unwarmly, rounding immediately back to the monastery. Lucy watched the wind pull his robe back, revealing his skeletal body underneath. He probably, she figured, stood out in this cold with that flimsy robe so better to humiliate what's left of his body. Catholics and their love of suffering. Lucy wished she could found an order in which you *ate to excess* for God.

(We've already got the Benedictines, thank you.)

O'Hanrahan, Rabbi Hersch, and Lucy gathered around a table in Father Creech's library; the other fathers lurked behind awaiting further abasements. Father Creech opened a two-foot leather cylinder scrollcase and slid out an airtight bag containing the papyrus. The Father General stepped back, deferring to O'Hanrahan, who had put on surgeon's gloves to avoid leaving a residue of oil on anything he touched. He expertly removed the dry papyrus and ever so slowly unwound it.

"It's in great shape," he whispered.

"I've got the spray back in Ballymacross," said Rabbi Hersch, who had brought an expensive fixative from the Jerusalem Museum that would help keep the scroll from crumbling, though, from the look of it, the scroll had been treated several times by previous owners.

"Beautiful," breathed O'Hanrahan as if he might cry.

Rabbi Hersch was reverent as well. "It's the one. I saw it only once in Rabbi Rosen's office but this is it, I'm sure." Lucy thought she detected the rabbi's lip trembling slightly. "Forty years ago," he added raspily.

Lucy eagerly edged her way between the two men to look over their shoulders.

Rabbi Hersch mused, "I have never seen anything quite like the script. Look at that," he said, pointing to a backward E. "I can't think of many post-Phoenician languages, save Hebrew, in which an E doesn't look like some form of an E . . . and yet what could the word be? E, something, E, E, something, something, E?"

"Some of the characters look Semitic," said O'Hanrahan. "This . . ." He pointed to what resembled a 4. "Bound to be an R, or maybe, like in Elephantine, a D. But what word would begin with two in a row like this?"

"Well, if it *is* Semitic, then the language has no vowels."

"Then why are the units so long?" O'Hanrahan pointed out that each "word" or unit of characters had a colon between them to separate them, and were often of nine or ten letters in length—pretty long for a Semitic language, though maybe not an Ethiopian dialect. In some places one could find back-to-back colons, which in some African tongues marked the end of a sentence, but if that were the case, some of the scroll's sentences were endless. Also, where were the small words that surely must be "the" and "and," that kind of thing? They stared at a line together:

$$\partial \Re \partial 3 : 4 \partial) 4 \Re : : \, \mathsf{H} 3 \beta \mathcal{E} \rho \, \mathsf{H} \mathcal{E}$$

"Or it could be like the Stele of Tyre," said O'Hanrahan, suggesting one of his fears. "I spent 1964 messing around with that thing. Where one culture has taken someone else's alphabet, Morey, and used it for their own phonetics."

"Nu, Master of the Universe, not that."

Similar to the Dead Sea Scrolls, there was no apparent punctuation except for the colons between word units—where sentences ended or began was anybody's guess. The text was organized in seven dense blocks down the scrollpage, or seven chapters as O'Hanrahan speculated. Most distressing, the last of the seven blocks showed the print running off the edge, as if the scroll had been torn before the writing had concluded.

O'Hanrahan stared glumly at the seventh text block. "It looks like a knife or something was used to break off this bit. As opposed to natural deterioration, I mean."

Rabbi Rosen, explained Rabbi Hersch, forty years ago began to decipher the scroll at Hebrew University, and he had told his colleagues that the last segment was loose and he had removed it hoping to carefully sew it back later.

"When Rosen died," said O'Hanrahan, finishing the tale for Lucy's benefit, "the scroll disappeared and so did the detached last chapter. Let's hope there's not a surprise ending," he added, irritated the whole thing wasn't in one piece.

Rabbi Hersch: "Jacob Rosen *did* say the last chapter particularly was a bombshell, but he never told me what was in it. I'm not sure he lived long enough to translate that far. Who knows? Maybe," he wondered, turning to Father Creech, "this German guy you bought it from is holding the last chapter hoping you'll pay through the nose for it."

Quite likely, thought O'Hanrahan. Once the Dead Sea Scrolls were confirmed in their importance the Bedouin traders parceled out the remaining fragments of papyri in exceedingly expensive doses, splitting and subdividing them for maximum profit. Perversely, as the Dead Sea Scrolls were translated the few remaining fragments were hoarded by academics in the same fashion, who hoped to increase their own importance by denying the public their scholarship. People are rotten, O'Hanrahan reminded himself.

"Well, let's get to the photo studio," said the rabbi.

The three pilgrims and the watchful Father O'Reilly went down to the concrete pier at a little after 10:30 A.M. The return crossing was calmer, or perhaps it didn't seem so choppy with the sun out. Mary McCall was telephoned and she drove to Ballycastle to pick them up.

Lucy went straight back to the McCalls', the professor and Rabbi Hersch with Father O'Reilly were dropped at the Crown.

"It's getting to be a resort around these parts, it is," said Jack the innkeeper and publican, explaining there was only one more available lodging remaining for this O'Reilly fellow, and that was the one of three rooms upstairs beside Rabbi Hersch and O'Hanrahan. "I do believe," he added, "we're becoming a tourist attraction. Americans everywhere."

Father O'Reilly, who did not register as a priest, merely put his small bag in his room and then ensconced himself in the most comfortable chair in O'Hanrahan's chamber.

O'Hanrahan opened his big suitcase and brought out a small camera. The rabbi shifted lamps and opened curtains to increase the light inside the room for a better picture. Every time O'Hanrahan and Mordechai Hersch made eye contact, they communicated a telepathic: what do we have to do to get rid of this guy? Until the chance came along, the professor spread out the scroll on a clean white linen sheet.

"We really need the tripod for it to be in focus," said Rabbi Hersch. "You, Paddy, with the shakes, forget it."

"I don't have the shakes—"

There was a knock at the door: "It's me."

"Go away," hummed the rabbi.

"If it's Lucy, in particular, go away," added O'Hanrahan.

"Ha ha. Open the door and I won't bother you anymore today." Having made her peace with her exclusion from this project, Lucy had decided to spend the day with David, whose company she preferred to the curmudgeons' anyway.

O'Hanrahan opened the door to his bedroom: "I asked the management to send up an Oriental girl skilled in all the erotic arts of the East. And look what I get."

"Will the East Side of Chicago do?" She inched herself into the room, sidestepping O'Hanrahan. She noticed Father O'Reilly wordlessly observing the makeshift photography arrangements. O'Hanrahan, his face turned away from the Ignatian father, rolled his eyes in frustration for Lucy's benefit.

"Father O'Reilly," offered Lucy, "do you want to have lunch or something? This can't be very interesting for you."

He summoned the energy to say he was fine just where he was.

Lucy then tried to project interest and professionalism: "So what are you photographing now, sir?" she asked the rabbi.

He mumbled distractedly, "Family vacation pictures I'm taking. This is Yellowstone."

Lucy absently wandered over to O'Hanrahan's little hotel-room desk and saw a variety of tomes laid out for study: a bibliography of what texts are in what world libraries, textbooks on African script, a book on Ge'ez and Nubian Christian dialects, Ethiopian etymologies, there was one in an Arabic title she couldn't make out . . .

"Excuse me," hissed Rabbi Hersch.

Lucy realized her standing by the desk cast a shadow across the scroll. "Oops, sorry." You would have thought he might have been a bit kinder after their midnight rendezvous of the night before, she thought.

"Why don't you go play with David today?" suggested O'Hanrahan.

She noticed he had a bathroom glass in his hand, filled with ice and a trace of remaining whiskey. "It's what I had in mind," she said. "Why don't you publish some of the pictures and see who might know something useful?"

The rabbi, for the first time in front of Lucy, laughed a sustained laugh; O'Hanrahan chuckled as well. "Are you that naive, Miss Dantan? You think we academics are one happy family, sharing our discoveries?"

"Okay, okay. Dumb question." She felt herself blush at her own lack of sense. She casually asked, "I don't suppose you'd let me have a copy of these photos—"

All three men in the room simultaneously: "No!"

She smiled anyway. "Never can tell. I might get lucky. Solve the whole puzzle. Someone let *you*, Dr. O'Hanrahan, view the Dead Sea Scrolls, remember, in 1948."

O'Hanrahan scooted her toward the door. "I'd love to let you help us but, alas, I would ruin your progress on that *seminal* thesis of yours on Corinthian script differences in Fourth-Century B.C. Greek. Would I do that to future generations of scholars?"

Lucy was shuffled to the hallway. "You think I should change topics, Dr. O'Hanrahan? I mean, if you would recommend another topic, I'd—"

"Yes, and if you take a flight from Belfast today you might get back in time to file for a topic change within 24 hours. Bye-bye now."

The door was slammed shut with a flick of O'Hanrahan's wrist, but he was not without a parting smile.

It was a sunny, white-light morning in Ballymacross and most homes were perfectly still, the fishermen or commuters to other villages having long departed. There was a trace of turf smoke from the chimney pots, a lingering medicinal smell that caught the nostrils. Lucy walked back to the McCalls' from the Crown, up the sloping hill past the identical white and pink painted homes, some brick, with differently colored doors for variety. She trudged upward feeling the warmth of the sun as well as the fresh sting of the sea breeze. Above her another band of sea gulls whooped and floated stationary against the wind, looking curiously at Lucy, as if they too shared the Irish fascination with the newly arrived.

"Come in, come in," enthused Mrs. McCall, her eyes full of welcome. " 'Course, wouldn't ye know, David's not risen yet, and here it is noon, Lord help us. Life of leisure, you students have! Ah, but I bet you're a girl who gets up early, right and proper."

"No," laughed Lucy, as she was shown into the parlor. "I'm just as bad, I'm afraid. Sleeping late whenever I can, like David."

(Lucy, you haven't missed a lecture in years at Chicago.)

"Daaaaavid!" his mother called out. "Outa yer bed, boy. Quit faffing about, company's here!"

"Uh, you don't have to wake him on my account—"

"David! Lucy's here!" Lucy heard stirrings as Mrs. McCall turned back to Lucy. "We spoil him, we do. He'll be off to Africa soon enough, I suppose, so we figure it'll do no harm to cosset him now."

"When does he leave for the mission, Mrs. McCall?"

"Oh, I'm sure I'd tell ye the wrong thing. You'd better ask David, and make sure ye get his address and write to him, if you would. His father is not a writing man, and my poor efforts are just that."

David in an R.E.M. T-shirt and boxer shorts, his red hair all scattered, loped into the room: "Morning, morning."

Mrs. McCall was incredulous he would show himself "in his pants" to company—no shred of decency anymore, it's what it proved. David demanded that his mother should fetch everyone some tea and before turning back to his bedroom, he tarried at the parlor to chat:

"Don't know why she's got so prim," he whispered, before yawning a cavernous yawn. "I'm not quite at meself yet. These are my best boxers—aye, with the shamrocks here, a real piece of Irish lore, this is—"

WHAPPPP! His mother unannounced gave him a slap on the bottom. "Get some clothes on yeself before I . . ."

"Lucy hasn't said she minded. I spied her lookin' at me, I did."

Mrs. McCall's eyes went huge: "I—just you—you're not so big I can't give ye a good joining yet!" After he went to find some clothes, Mary McCall confided, "It's Dublin thatsa done this to him. I raised him to have some cooth, I did. Send 'em off to university and ye see what happens."

There fell a rare quiet in the house.

"Tea's ready," said Mrs. McCall, returning presently to the parlor. "Had your breakfast yet, love? We got some pairtch on."

Pairtch? A fish? Oh: *porridge.*

"No ma'am, but thank you though."

Lucy craned to the edge of the sofa to look at some of the McCalls' children's photos. David as a kid looked about the same—more freckles, the red hair more fiery, but the same self-possession was already there. She imagined the circumstances: all of them surprised by a sunny day in the yard, David acting like a wise guy for his father, cocking a nine-year-old adult expression. The rectangular photo behind its glass had yellowed and the sky was now green, but David was David.

"Here's your tea," said Mrs. McCall, putting it down before her. "Now make David take ye to the Giant's Causeway. You'll want to be a-seeing that."

David bounded into the parlor, in a Trinity College sweatshirt and a pair of tired, farm-worked jeans, his hair still in all directions.

"Well, ye won't be setting out with your hair like a rat's nest no way," said his mother, looking as if she had discovered him in the gutter. "You're a tramp is what ye are."

"I thought I'd take Lucy up to the standing stone."

Mrs. McCall didn't approve. "You'll be up to your eyeballs in glar'n muck, if you set out up there. Mind you put on your boots; there's an extry pair in the shaid."

Lucy wondered why boots would be put in the shade. *Shed,* Lucy realized a moment later.

David borrowed his cousin Bruce's mini, since Mrs. McCall kept the family car for O'Hanrahan's chores, and drove Lucy around the sights of County Antrim. This land was a million miles from barbed wire and urban graffiti wars—not a blemish or a clue on the rolling green countryside. Lucy saw white cliffs like she had seen in pictures of Dover. Rookeries of seabirds. The Giant's Causeway of O'Hanrahan's tales with a long stop in the gift shop for another supply of postcards. Then they stopped by the Bushmills Distillery for a factory tour and a free sample that warmed Lucy internally. She picked up a bottle of the triple-distilled for her dad. Where whiskey was concerned he could forgive its Protestant origins.

"I bet Patrick would drink this place dry," David said. "It'd be their last tour, what do you bet? Let's pick him up a bottle of Black Bush, hm?"

That might ingratiate her further, so Lucy agreed.

"So it's all worked out all right?" asked David, as they concluded their tour amid a room of casks and bottles.

"Yep, they got what they came for," said Lucy, not really concentrating. "They're shutting me out, of course, so I guess I came up here for nothing."

"How can ye say that? We got to meet, didn't we?"

Lucy felt herself color and walk ahead of him so this schoolgirl behavior wasn't detectable. Lucy lectured herself for not at least uttering something appreciative and reciprocal. I'm a wimp, she conceded.

Back in Ballymacross, David went to prepare for the muddy slog up to the standing stone, and Lucy was dropped off at the Crown Inn, whose pub was closed through the afternoon. She entered a side door for the overnight guests and climbed the stairway to O'Hanrahan's room.

"It's me," she confessed, after knocking.

O'Hanrahan parted the door a millimeter and then spied the whiskey bottle. "Ah, you've been to the sacred fount, I see."

"For you," she said, holding it out.

Unable to be ungracious, O'Hanrahan let her in.

Lucy saw the room was back to normal and that Rabbi Hersch sat before a stack of slides and prints. She asked, "Where's the gospel?"

"Down in the pub safe," said the rabbi, holding up a slide to the light. "O'Reilly had the innkeeper put it in the vault, so we couldn't very well march down and demand that Jack hand it over to us. But we're working on options."

O'Hanrahan squinted at a photo print under a lamp. "We had Mary McCall drive us back to Ballycastle and had a rush job done on these prints . . . ehh, this is out of focus," he added, looking through a small eyeglass at the photo.

Lucy: "Where's Father O'Reilly?"

O'Hanrahan: "Eating lunch in his room. Bread and gruel, I suspect. We couldn't interest him in a drink." After a lull during which Lucy was made to feel in the way again, the professor directed, "Go play with David some more."

"I am."

O'Hanrahan looked at her wickedly. "You like him, don't you?"

"I'd tell you, but you'd probably find a way of embarrassing me with the information."

"How well you have come to know me," he said, before closing the door.

Back at his home, David was stretched out by the fire, his feet on a chair. "Let's get going," he said, "and make it to the standing stone before it pisses down."

Lucy and David pulled on the high rubber boots and clomped to the end of the road to stand before the stile, which was muddy on the north-facing side, puddles that would never evaporate. With much squishing and squealing, Lucy laughingly got a foothold on the stile and leaped over only to sink in further.

"Your mother was right!" she shrieked.

The short grass and turf were slippery and Lucy felt her foothold give several times on the hillside. In a moment of supreme confidence, as Lucy stepped toward a sure-looking imbedded stone, she slipped on the mud and hurtled down on her side. I look like such a dork, thought Lucy . . . until it occurred to her that she could be a damsel in distress.

"Are ye still alive?" David cried out, stomping over to help her.

Lucy suggested they hold hands the rest of the way up, which they did as David regaled her with tales of Viking raids. The Vikings would storm these shores and the men would lock themselves in the *dun*, or fortress. Down at the shore they put out their possessions. If the Vikings were weak from all the time at sea, they would settle for this easy theft. Then outside the castle the Celts put their women. The men stayed within and watched as their womenfolk were raped. Now if the Vikings wanted the castle, well then, the men would have to fight!

"The Irish gentleman," surmised Lucy.

But the very scenario seemed so surreal, David said he couldn't believe it. Imagine, men watching their daughters and mothers being raped. No, there had to be more to the story than that:

"I can see the men proposing to fight," David said, "and the women saying, no no, you mustn't risk the castle. We'll run down to the shore and sacrifice ourselves. And then when they got down to the shore, they yelled at the Viking boys, Sven, Erik, here fellas, over here!"

Lucy bowed her head, laughing.

"Well, face it, the Scandinavians were something to look at, ye know? Tall and handsome. And the Celts, bah, were short and runty, and no one in Ireland has sex anyway, I'm sure that's been the way for centuries. This was the girls' night out, when the Vikings came by."

(After St. Adoman's Decree in 556, the women were expected to take the Viking invasions passively or behave as St. Ebbe and her convent, who cut the noses off their faces in order to be unappealing for the Vikings. So better to preserve their precious virginity.)

Lucy and David reached the summit and Lucy walked forward to touch the menhir. "And there's our own standing stone," David said, out of breath. "Neolithic, Megalithic, I don't know. Two thousand B.C., something like that."

Lucy touched the striated cold granite. She noticed that a couple named Constance and Peter had scratched their declaration of love on one flank of the stone.

"People're so foul," muttered David, "writing on a monument like this."

Lucy was glad she didn't suggest LUCY LOVES DAVID for the other side.

Before the descent, which was surely to be one long slide on her behind, Lucy surveyed the whole valley beyond the town, the village, the broad green hills leading to the Atlantic, the winding stonewalled highway tracing the contour. It was sufficiently clear to the north to see a corner of Rathlin Island in view offshore.

"Got a boyfriend, Lucy?" David asked.

Panic.

"Oh. Uh, well . . ." She felt the possibilities of the moment slip away while something automatic welled up and found release: "There's this guy Gabriel, and we're sort of—well, not official anymore, nothing too official, really. We grew up together."

"Childhood sweethearts like?"

"Yeah, I guess, but it's not really, you know . . ."

"Ah, I figured you'd have someone back home waiting for ye."

They began the descent of the hill and Lucy sensed nothing but darkness! She replayed the exchange. She saturated her misstep in the bitterest acid of regret. After a hot moment of abjuration a familiar brooding settled upon her: you are a coward. What was the worst that could have happened if she'd said, "No one I couldn't dump for you, David McCall." And the worst, worst possible conceivable disaster that would have happened was that he might mildly reject her—how gently he would do it, how open-ended he would leave it—and she could pass herself off as having been unserious, flirtatious. . . . To some women these tactical skills came easily. Oh damn him, she thought while negotiating the muddy slope, damn my upbringing, damn me, damn everybody.

As evening approached, Lucy regained her equanimity. She and

David changed, threw their muddy clothes in the washer, and talked over two pots of tea. The conversation turned to Chicago and Lucy was ready at the drop of a hat to give David the deluxe, superduper tour. Yes, Chicago—*that's* where she'd make her move! Lucy began feeling more confident and happy from the moment she had solidly postponed this showdown.

Furthermore, all the talk of Chicago also made Lucy antsy to check in with Judy, or maybe call home. She hadn't called from Dublin as she intended, and now it was three days past that. She decided she'd hop down to the bus stop and make a call just to check with Judy and make sure there were no pressing messages for her back at the department.

"Use our telephone," said David, "it's all right."

"Nah, it's expensive. Look, I'll go get one of those phone-card deals and call long-distance at the bus stop."

So Lucy stepped back out into the windy afternoon to walk to the bus stop, which sold the phone cards and had a phone outside that utilized them as well. Above, a sentinel seagull cawed and rose in the gusts; beyond it the sweep of rainclouds moved as fast as they ever did in Chicago, bringing with their gray and drizzle an early end to this Irish summer day.

It was dead at the bus stop. It was 5:55 and there was a coach at 6:00 P.M. but no one was waiting to board it. There was a man, an odd-looking middle-aged man in strange attire: a bolo tie with an Indian clasp, yellow golf slacks and white spats, an ill-fitting, cheaply made pink-checked sports jacket, with a plaid cap. He was reading a tame Irish girlie magazine. Otherwise there was the newsstand proprietor. Lucy paid him for a £10 phone card and went to use the pay phone against the stone wall of the neighboring shop. She punched in the department number and waited for a connection to be made . . . instead she heard a series of clicks and hisses as technology attempted the impossible, a transatlantic call from a pay phone in Ireland.

She felt a tap on her shoulder.

"Hi, Luce."

It was Gabriel.

"Gabe!" she gasped, hanging up the phone immediately. "What . . . what are you doing here?"

He stepped back, holding one hand tightly in the other nervously, as he had done since he was a kid. "Is it really a surprise? I thought O'Hanrahan had spotted us and knew we were here." By *us* he meant the short, brutal-looking man of Mediterranean features with a scar on his lip and cheek, who stood beside two suitcases. Wait a minute, Lucy figured, this is the guy I saw at the Greyfriars back in Oxford.

She quickly stammered, "The innkeeper said the Crown was full of American tourists but how is it that we haven't run into you?"

"We're not at the Crown; we've been over in Ballycastle. Luce, it's good I found you, because now I don't have to leave Patrick a note." Gabriel shivered in his windbreaker, which was much too light for Northern Irish weather.

But this was going too fast for Lucy: "Wait, Gabe, can we have some tea or something? We gotta talk!" She put a hand on his arm to prevent his escape.

"I can't. We've got to get the bus back to Belfast and out of Ireland. With Brother Vincenzo."

Lucy glanced at the rough-looking man by the bags. "*He's* a monk? Looks more like a hoodlum."

Gabriel whispered, "He *was*. Before he found God. Best second-story man in Naples. He was in prison three years when—"

"Gabriel, *please*, what happened between you and Dr. O'Hanrahan in Italy? Did you really sneak off with the scroll behind his back?"

Gabriel shifted his weight. "You know, he'll thank me one day, I'm sure, when he finds out all the information."

The newsstand proprietor, acting very self-important as if this were a train platform and he a stationmaster, made an announcement to all of the three people assembled that the coach for Armoy, The Drones, Killigan Bridge and Ballymena, and Belfast was approaching. Lucy saw the bus distantly two hills away groaning and shifting gears along the narrow country road.

"Finds out what?" Lucy pursued.

But Gabriel's mind was elsewhere. "The *Drones*? Doesn't that sound like a great vacation spot?"

Lucy was near despair. "Gabe, what's going on?"

Gabriel turned as Brother Vincenzo coughed ominously to prompt him to be ready to meet the coach. "I'll tell you everything one day, but now it'll just mess up the works, but I can tell you this much now: *go home*. O'Hanrahan is in danger and if you stay with him so are you. That scroll is worth a lot and, like, some very dangerous people want their hands on it. It ought to be under armed guard, somewhere a lot safer than in O'Hanrahan's back pocket."

Lucy and Gabriel stood there awkwardly as the bus pulled to the side of the road, and a single young lady disembarked. The newsstand man put the men's suitcases in the underside of the bus.

Gabriel: "You'll be back in Chicago soon, huh?"

"Yeah, I guess. Aren't you coming back home too?"

"Well, I decided that my life . . ." Gabriel apparently decided not to squander the wealth of things to say with the bus panting there. "I've decided so much about my life in the last few months. I think after this is all over I'm going to South America, somewhere Third World.

I'm sick of academia, you know? I'm not John and Eileen's little boy on Halsted living above the paint store anymore."

Lucy remembered a few other times Gabriel had announced he had his life in order.

"Now here's the message for Patrick, which is very important. Tell him: I'll see him in Assisi, if he wants to come."

Lucy privately doubted that Dr. O'Hanrahan would be paying social calls on Brother Gabriel in Assisi, but she promised to pass it along. Brother Vincenzo wordlessly got on board the bus while Gabriel called back, "Come visit in Assisi sometime!"

She felt her head swim with unasked questions and unsatisfactory half-answers, but as she leaned forward to kiss him good-bye, Gabriel had quickly bounded onto the bus. He took a seat near a window and looked down at her.

"Bye-bye, Gabe," she said, waving faintly.

And soon the bus was bound for Belfast, and she watched it sputter away in a haze of bus exhaust, getting quieter and quieter as it moved to the bend ahead. Lucy stared until she realized she was looking at the distant hills of rough scrub, combed by the gusty saline breeze, no more color in the early-evening landscape than a black-and-white photograph.

Lucy put her phone card away and decided she'd better tell O'Hanrahan of this encounter. She wasn't sure just what to report—maybe merely that she'd seen Gabriel again. She turned and nearly ran into the man in the badly matched golfing clothes. He lifted his hat politely, giving her an intense, curious look before self-consciously reverting to his magazine.

Back at the Crown, O'Hanrahan had amassed a jovial crowd around him, Mr. McCall, the rabbi, David, Mrs. McCall nursing a half-pint, and a few other interested listeners.

"Lucille!" he cried, lifting a Guinness in her honor.

"Evening, Dr. O'Hanrahan." She noticed that Father O'Reilly, their watchdog, was missing. "Did you find the father?"

"Gone back to the chapel," said the professor, pointing beside his glass to a note Father O'Reilly had left them. "I was discussing with this ignorant man ..." He meant Mr. McCall, who was tipsy and laughing. ". . . that it is the O'Somethings rather than the McSomethings that put Ireland on the map."

"Total rubbish!" said Mr. McCall, as his wife restrained him by putting a hand on his arm.

The argument raged on with everyone in on the joke and Lucy distant from the discussion; she saw that David was also transfixed. She was tired from her bad night of sleep on Rathlin Island and wished to make it an early night. Maybe she would have a soft drink and then excuse herself.

"Lemme fetch ye a beer, love," offered Mr. McCall.

"Just a Coke," she insisted. "Do they have Diet Coke?"

Unheard of in these parts.

"Just a Coke then." Lucy picked up Father O'Reilly's note and folded it and then unfolded it, occupying her hands.

> Gentlemen,
> Unexpectedly I've had to return to the Church of the Holy Savior where many duties await me. I shall return by nightfall to discuss in full our business.
>
> Fr. O'Reilly, S. J.

Sure is proud of that S. J., thought Lucy.

"Dr. O'Hanrahan," she broke in, interrupting a lull in one of his stories. "There's something we ought to talk about—"

"Get back to me later, honey," he interpolated in his risqué tale of the moment.

"Jukebox," announced David, motioning to Lucy.

They went to the jukebox and scanned the pitiful song selection at the Crown. Some dance-club hits from a few months back. Lots of standard Irish numbers, the Dubliners, the Fureys, a brush with contemporary music featuring Sinead O'Connor, the Pogues, U2, all the regulars on the local Irish-bar jukeboxes back home.

The Pekingese by the fireplace barked as someone stepped too close to it. The old lady pulled the dog's leash and brought her little baby closer to soothe.

"God," said Lucy, "that woman has been here since this morning."

"Mrs. McCready, she lives in here, she does. She must go home from three to five because they close this place." The dog kept yipping despite its mistress' talking babytalk to it. "Now if I could only dress like that, me social life would improve," David added, nodding toward the man Lucy had seen earlier in a pink sports jacket. He looked to be waiting on the restroom, peeking restlessly around the corner impatiently.

David slipped a coin into the jukebox. "Now we got to pick something."

The titles were scrawled by hand: "The Flower of Sweet Strabane," and "The Brown Colleen (That I Met in the County Down)" and "Black's the Colour of Me Truelove's Hair."

"Ooh, that's a stinker," said David. "Let's play that one. Get the old men asinging."

Hold it, thought Lucy.

She interrupted the professor in midstory: "Dr. O'Hanrahan, could I see you a moment?"

She must have said it seriously enough that he resisted the temptation to yell at her. He left his coterie and walked to the edge of the bar beside Lucy. Lucy had Father O'Reilly's note. "Father O'Reilly's Irish, maybe English, right?"

"Yes."

"Then why did he spell 'Saviour' without a *u*?"

O'Hanrahan read the note and a troubled look spread over his face. "Morey, get over here," he called to the rabbi. The rabbi discreetly excused himself, joined them and examined the note as well.

"Excuse me, Jack," said O'Hanrahan to the innkeeper, working behind the bar. "Have you seen that O'Reilly fellow at all this afternoon?"

"Aye, before lunchtime with yourselves," he said.

"After he had you put that package in your safe?"

Jack said his wife delivered a coffee tray around 4:30 P.M. up to the man's room. Jack summoned his wife Martha from the kitchen. She came out, a hefty, red-cheeked woman, wiping her brow on her aproncloth, hot from assembling pub meals.

"Yes," Martha said, somewhat bothered. "He asked me to leave it outside his room. I went back in a bit and the tray was inside. I knocked him up to get me tray but there was no answer."

All five of the party looked immediately at the series of hooks where the room keys were. O'Reilly's key wasn't there, so it was still with him. He was still in his room.

O'Hanrahan tensely asked, "Do you have a skeleton key?"

Jack did. His wife took over the bar and O'Hanrahan led a group toward the stairs. Lucy noticed David staring at them quizzically. "Black's the Colour of Me Truelove's Hair" began to play.

O'Hanrahan with Rabbi Hersch and Lucy in tow reached the top floor and knocked on room no. 3. No sound inside. With a deep breath, Jack fiddled with his skeleton key and opened the door.

Father O'Reilly was stretched out on his bed, dead asleep in his clothes of that afternoon. The rabbi went over to him and shook him. "Father? Father?" But he wouldn't awaken.

"He's alive, isn't he?" asked Lucy.

"Very shallow breathing," said the rabbi, leaning in close.

O'Hanrahan examined the coffee tray. A remnant of the afternoon coffee was still in the cup. The remaining liquid had an odd film over it that caught the light prismatically like an oil stain. "Something's in this coffee," he said, smelling it. "This is drugged."

Jack: "Ah, me wife would never . . ."

O'Hanrahan: "No, Jack, we're not saying it's *your* coffee. It was sitting out in the hall for a while and someone could have dropped something in it."

Lucy looked at the rabbi, who seemed to be feigning great concern for this unlikable fellow. You don't suppose O'Hanrahan and the rabbi resorted to this . . .

Downstairs there was commotion. It sounded like a fight. Everyone heard Martha raising her voice to shoo someone out of the bar.

"What now?" Jack grumbled. "I'll call an ambulance," he then offered, as he made his way from the room, the others trailing behind.

"Jack!" his wife cried, meeting them at the bottom of the stairs. She was hysterical.

"It's all right, dear, we'll call a doctor—"

"No! The man on the phone," she wailed.

Lucy looked around the pub.

It was empty.

Everyone had been ushered outside. She looked out the window to the street and saw David waving her to come out. Jack picked up the receiver.

"Aye?" he said, the next moment faltering in his composure. "Seven o'clock, you say?"

Lucy instinctively looked at the pub clock. Three minutes till seven. Quickly, the wife opened the cash register and grabbed the money—

"No time for that," her husband snapped, slamming down the phone. "Let's get out of here!"

"What is it?" demanded O'Hanrahan.

"A bomb threat," he stammered.

Lucy felt the blood drain from her face. She and the rabbi and O'Hanrahan went immediately to the door. The innkeeper's wife followed, apron pockets full of cash, but Jack, disobeying his own orders, darted back inside to the back. His wife protested but he returned to the street in no time:

"I saw it!" he cried to the throng outside. "Get back from the glass! There's really a bomb in there!"

There were cries of panic, and everyone backed away a hundred yards.

"I think there was a man still in the loo," said Martha, wringing her hands. "And I doon't see him out here . . ."

"Not here," said Mrs. McCall, shivering beside her husband, clasping his hand. "Not *here*, too, please, God. I thought we'd outrun it."

"We've never had a problem here," said an older man bitterly. "It's all these newcomers in town—"

Mr. McCall spoke up sharply: "They're visiting me, Connor, and I won't have a word said against them."

"They're Taigs, aren't they? Catholics!"

Word spreads fast, thought Lucy, slipping a step back from the crowd.

Two minutes until seven. Lucy listened to the grumblings and the disbelief of the townspeople. People knocked on doors and phone calls were made to neighbors of the pub to get them out on the street.

O'Hanrahan put a hand on Lucy's shoulder and drew the rabbi closer as well, saying quietly, "This isn't sectarian violence. It has to do with the Matthias scroll. Which is, damn it, in that pub in the safe."

"Right," snapped the rabbi, "for goddamned safekeeping. We should have grabbed it and run, Paddy!"

One minute until seven.

"This is horrible," said Lucy. She thought: we've brought this to the town. Gabriel was right. This is dangerous. Matthias, whatever he has to say, is a troublemaker and I'm going home soon as I can get back to Dublin—I'll leave the Indiana Jones stuff to the old men. The gray stone Presbyterian church clocktower clicked into place for the hour. It began to chime.

Then, there was the explosion. A muffled one. A "pop."

Everyone jumped anxiously at the noise but it didn't shatter the glass in the front of the pub or make a fireball or any such thing. The crowd reaction was one of curiosity, more than outrage or horror. That little pop was like a cherry bomb on Guy Fawkes Day, someone said.

An old man with his wife mumbled, "Ah, that weren't worth gettin' out of me bed for, was it, May?"

Jack began to go inside, but many in the crowd cried for him not to. Maybe a bigger bomb had malfunctioned. Maybe this was a trap. A tiny boom and then we all go inside and then it really blows sky high. Call the police, Jack, they cried out. Call Special Services.

The crowd milled about, some drifting home for lack of new excitement, some because of the chill. O'Hanrahan and Rabbi Hersch removed themselves a few paces from the rest to discuss heatedly what they should do now—what they should have been doing rather than enjoying themselves and making merry. Lucy sullenly stood beside Martha.

"Oh thank God," she breathed, noticing the man in the garish golf clothes walking up from behind the houses next to the pub. "I thought he was in the loo, but he was out here to whole time."

Lucy followed with her eyes. The Man in the Cheap Suit fished out his car keys and got inside a white Cadillac. Lucy took a step closer. The man drove toward Belfast and Lucy quickened her step to glimpse the license plate and to see the country code of "D" on the back trunk. She immediately found O'Hanrahan and interrupted him:

"What country is D?"

The rabbi: "*Deutschland*, Germany."

"What's a German car doing in Ballymacross?" she wondered aloud, looking in the direction of the disappearing car.

"Stealing the scroll, that's what!" said O'Hanrahan, before moving quickly through the crowd to return to the pub. Now, everyone from the town was outside and talking about this incident, the first ever for this town. The Troubles, the Troubles! Jack stood guarding the door of the Crown.

"We shouldn't go in," he said, "until the police arrive."

"Jack," said the professor, "this wasn't sectarian, this was a *robbery*. They were after what was in your safe."

"I got nothing of that kind of value," he began.

"O'Reilly did," O'Hanrahan reminded him. "That package he gave you."

Jack relented. "Okay, let's be quick about it."

The pub's main room was undamaged and, aside from a spray of sawdust and the acrid smell of smoke, it was unchanged. Behind the bar, glasses were broken, bottles had overturned and come off the shelves, and the safe itself was wide open and the wood encasing charred.

"Well, would you look at that," said Jack, rubbing his head. "They left the deeds, the checkbook from the brewers—ah, they coulda had a time with that, they could . . . Now fancy that! They even left the money . . ."

The scroll was gone.

Soon the police arrived, and amid the milling, gossiping neighbors and curses of the bar staff, the amateur estimates of damage, the dark humor in the face of the robbery, two defeated figures made it up the back stairs to the rooms above.

O'Hanrahan, shaking his head, unlocked his room and went straight for the bottom desk drawer. The Bushmills Black, David and Lucy's gift. "I take it you'd like a sip too, Mordechai?"

"Make it a big sip," he said, wearily sitting on the side of O'Hanrahan's bed. O'Hanrahan washed out the room's glass by the sink, filled it and offered it to his friend. O'Hanrahan noticed himself in the mirror, and he looked unrecognizably ancient, tiredness verging on ruin.

"Almost," said the rabbi desolately, looking at the palm of his hand and its emptiness. "When Father O'Reilly disappeared this afternoon? That was our cue that something was up. That lousy kraut must have hired that goon to steal the scroll back."

"Slipped right through our fingers," O'Hanrahan stated pointlessly. He downed a swig of whiskey. "We at least have our photos to work from."

The rabbi nodded.

But this was no consolation. Even if they translated the gospel from the photos, without the original no one would necessarily believe them.

It even sounded like a good hoax: yes, it's a First-Century account of Christ and yes, it's revolutionary, but no, we don't have the original scroll—you'll have to take our word for it.

O'Hanrahan thought out loud. "My guess is you're right. The German guy caught on he'd been swindled by these Ignatian creeps and sent someone up here to steal it back. How long until he puts it on the black market?"

"Maybe he doesn't want to sell it ever again."

"He's got to translate it, right? If we're lucky, this rich collector will still need us to translate it, and will call us . . ."

"Forty years we chased after this. Forty years, Paddy."

"Matthias has slipped through our hands a dozen times already, and he may elude us a dozen more times."

Lucy cleared her throat to announce herself.

The professor tapped his whiskey bottle. "Oh, it's you, Luce. Get a glass and pull up a chair."

She started unsurely. "The scroll is definitely stolen?"

"Yes, Mr. Matthias is out of our hands again. Get a glass and pull up a chair."

"No, thank you," she said. "You know, that whiskey's so strong and my digestion has been . . ." O'Hanrahan's look of distaste for her constitution was fearsome. The rabbi had yet to acknowledge Lucy's presence. She got brave. "Uh, Dr. O'Hanrahan?"

"Hm?" he said, from deep in his glass.

"I think I know who took it."

O'Hanrahan reasoned she was making a dumb guess: "Let's hear it."

"The Franciscans."

O'Hanrahan looked at her.

"I think the Franciscans stole it, not wanting you and the Jesuits to have it."

The rabbi: "Any proof for this?"

"Gabriel."

O'Hanrahan stood up. "*Gabriel* was here in Ballymacross? You've seen him?"

"Yes."

At this the rabbi stood too. "Sit down, little girl, and start from the beginning."

O'Hanrahan repossessed the rabbi's glass, poured her a single, and pressed it into her hands. She was seated inexorably in O'Hanrahan's chair, as the rabbi closed the door.

Lucy took a deep breath. "Well, ninety minutes ago I ran into Gabriel. We met when I was making my phone call at the station—you know, checking in with Chicago. Gabriel and I talked—"

Rabbi Hersch: "Did you tell him we had the scroll?"

"I think he already knew." She tried to sound particularly female and desperate: "Well, if you guys had *talked* to me and let me in on one single *thing* you've been doing, I would've been able to make the right strategic move, so stop glaring at me."

O'Hanrahan, sitting again, leaned forward from the corner of his bed. "And did he tell you why he stole the Matthias scroll from me in Rome?"

"Well, not in so many words, but I think I know."

They were waiting.

"I think," Lucy began, "he was supposed to steal the scroll and take it to the Franciscans. He botched the plan down in Italy but I think he just got what he was after right here."

The rabbi shook his head. "That little nebbish? That boy couldn't tie his shoe without help. How would he blow up a safe?"

Lucy swallowed hard. "I think Brother Vincenzo actually stole it. But he didn't have to blow the safe. They came in while the pub was closed from three to five."

O'Hanrahan stared at her incredulously. "*Who* is Brother Vincenzo?"

"The guy who is traveling with Gabriel. You're right, Rabbi, sir, Gabriel couldn't break into a safe, but Brother Vincenzo could, without using an explosive." They continued to stare at her. "He converted to Catholicism after a life of crime in Naples, after prison. Now he's a Friar Minor." She added, "I ran into them both in Oxford. They just left on the six o'clock bus to Belfast."

The rabbi put a finger to his temple, considering.

Lucy: "But *they* didn't blow the safe, Dr. O'Hanrahan." She took a deep breath. "I think someone different, the man in the German car, was trying to steal it. And he blew the safe, but it was too late—Gabriel had gotten it already. As I said, Gabriel got on the six P.M. bus."

"And the safe was blown up," said O'Hanrahan, "at seven . . ."

Then after a pause, Lucy said slowly, "Gabriel said that we were all in great danger. That . . . that truly dangerous people were after it and might kill you, sir, and you, sir, and me, if I kept with you. He said the only safe place for it was under armed guard. And then he said . . ."

O'Hanrahan felt a smile play on his face, despite himself: "What?"

"He said, I hope you get to Assisi sometime, Lucy. You know Assisi, sir, that's where St. Francis founded the order—"

"I know where goddam Assisi is, Lucy—what else did he say?"

"And he said tell Dr. O'Hanrahan to look him up in Assisi."

The rabbi: "You're sure he was headed to Assisi?"

"Well, yeah."

Rabbi Hersch was revived. "I hope it's true, Paddy. I hope the Franciscans *do* have it!"

O'Hanrahan was rubbing his hands together. "We may not be dead yet!"

"Look, I gotta get back to Jerusalem before my department kills me," said Rabbi Hersch. "You check out Assisi. The *minute* you get your hands on the thing again, you call me and let me know how we're doing."

O'Hanrahan was already scooping up clothes and papers and putting them into his suitcase, now open on the bed. "You got it. If we move fast we can be in Belfast tonight and get a nightbus to Dublin . . ."

"Are you kidding?" cried the rabbi, stupefied: "Get on a goddam plane!"

"Mordechai Hersch," O'Hanrahan lectured, while throwing his shaving kit into the bag, "I did not come this far on this project to die in a lousy plane crash. For twenty years I haven't been on a plane. I'll take the ferry to Cherbourg, the train to Paris, and then—"

"What? Sometime in the next century you should get there!"

O'Hanrahan reexamined his shaving kit items. "Look, I got a copy of the photos, and you've got the slides. I want a little time to work on this mysterious script." O'Hanrahan spied a white medicine bottle and removed it and set it aside, adding nervously, "Of course, maybe the Franciscans won't want to give it back to us—"

"It's the property of Hebrew University. Tell them that!"

"They'll take us more seriously," said O'Hanrahan, pausing to lay the whiskey bottle tenderly, reverently upon the clothes, "if they think we've figured out the translation."

O'Hanrahan spun around to see Lucy sitting in the chair, her glass of whiskey untouched. He grabbed and downed it in a single gulp: "Aaaah! Well, at least you leave us, Miss Dantan, happier than when you found us."

"Thanks for the information," said the rabbi, perfunctorily. "And sayonara, little girl. And again, if ever you should be in the Holy City of Jerusalem, should you be so blessed, do stop in."

Said with absolutely no conviction, thought Lucy.

"And let *me* say," said O'Hanrahan, zipping his suitcase awkwardly, "that next time you make it your business to follow someone tracking down a scroll on the ecclesiastical black market, you might want to consider telling the people you work with *everything* you know, so these little incidents won't happen—"

"Dr. O'Hanrahan, you made it quite clear you didn't want to talk to me this whole day!"

"You should never get hung up on technicalities," he said, closing the suitcase at last. "Morey, meet you downstairs in five minutes."

"I'll call a cab, Paddy."

And after the rabbi left, O'Hanrahan reached over and took the white medicine bottle and put it in Lucy's hand.

"What's this?" she asked.

"Lomotil," he said. "For that ever-churning stomach of yours you're always going on about. A fair trade for the Bushmills, right?"

O'Hanrahan sat on the bed, catching his breath, a whirl of ideas in his head. The room was quiet, but from the street outside there was the noise of police sirens, downstairs the sounds of cleaning up of wood and plaster and broken beer glasses, customers returning to their pints in raucous, nervous laughter to erase the fear of some moments before.

"You're not mad at me?" wondered Lucy.

"Of course I am. You should have told me the second that twirp Gabriel spoke to you—you should have wrestled that little worm to the ground and held him there for me to pulverize." O'Hanrahan stood and lifted his case. "Well, Luce. All is forgiven, and I apologize for being so unsociable." O'Hanrahan gave Lucy the sign of the cross: "*Sine, Domina mea, sine me flere; tu innocens es, ego sum peccator.* Go in peace. And you keep checking the newspapers."

"What for?"

"When I get my hands on Matthias and translate him, my dear, I'll be front-page news around the world." He gave her a wink. "And in your own infinitesimal, little insignificant way, you played a part."

She smiled weakly. "Thanks a lot."

And O'Hanrahan was gone.

Lucy stood up and realized she'd have to go back to David's to get her things. Then down to Dublin to catch a plane home. As she walked down the stairs and into the bar, the smell of charred sawdust and plaster still in the air, she saw the spectacle of O'Hanrahan and the rabbi depart: the professor having purchased another half-bottle of whiskey at the bar, swigging it, laughing at something the rabbi said, frisky and revived as they could be. The old coots. Special Services had yet to arrive and the bartender was adamant that the old men stay and answer questions, but they had an unstoppable momentum.

Standing outside, she watched them scramble into a taxi and ride away. And Lucy was bereft, knowing the adventure continued without her.

JUNE 30TH

Lucy had an opportunity to make some kind of farewell I-really-like-you speech on the three-hour ride down in the car, but David and she talked about other things, and Lucy wondered if David was sensing the awkwardness too. Lucy had written a letter last night including her name, address, home number, all relevant details, and a short note saying how happy she was to meet him, how her sofa was open for business . . . she had paused and contemplated making a double entendre about her sofa *bed* being open for business too . . . No, not my style, Lucy figured. I could make the joke, but that's all it would ever be then: a joke. And for once, I don't want to be Lucy the Pal, Lucy with the jokes, the trusty female friend.

When they were on the outskirts of Dublin and began to see kilometers announced for the international airport, Lucy knew she was counting down the minutes.

(Why can't you speak what is in your heart?)

I'm a coward, I'm a failure. I'm not pretty enough to be entitled to make a move on someone . . .

(But you are beautiful in ways that he can see.)

She sighed as the motorway exit passed, then the parking lot entrance, then as they walked with her bags to the terminal, then as they walked through the concourse to check in her bags and purchase a ticket to London, where she would use her return ticket back to Chicago.

"I don't want to go back," Lucy said heavily.

"I was just thinking how much I wanted to get on the plane with you," David said smiling.

Was it that he wants so bad to see the U.S., Lucy wondered, or to visit me?

"Anyway," she said clumsily, knowing he had to get back to Dublin for an afternoon class, "here's a letter with lots of address things and my phone number . . . and stuff." Lucy knew her capacity to say anything more romantic was dwindling; she felt her heart darken in defeat.

(*For when dreams increase, empty words grow many.*)

So David said good-bye and patted her on the shoulder, uncomfortably. Then they found themselves stalling, talking nonsense:

"Come see me in Chicago if you get there sometime."

"Yeah, if I get there I'll come where you are."

David then kissed Lucy on the cheek and she waved good-bye. But then he ran back to say one more thing: "Whoa, how embarrassing, I forgot completely about *this*." He held out an envelope. "For Dr. O'Hanrahan," he said. "For some reason it came to our house."

Lucy looked at it. It had no stamp, she observed.

"Must have been hand-delivered from the Post Office down the street, special overnight mail or something."

Lucy wondered if she should open it. "Dr. O'Hanrahan's God knows where."

"Maybe you can forward it to the rabbi fellow."

"Yeah, there's an idea," she nodded, though she didn't have his address either.

"All right, good-bye this time."

"Yeah, have a good term and all at Trinity. And later on, take care of yourself in Africa. Don't get bitten by a—what are they? A tse-tse fly?"

"I'll bring me spray," he smiled.

And this time David left more memorably, waving happily, full of warmth for his new acquaintance. Lucy closed her eyes briefly: David. Oh, well, in another world you might have had an affair with someone like that, married him even, settled down and gotten fat in front of the TV together. But not this world.

She absently opened O'Hanrahan's telegram. Inside was a note from the Treasurer, she assumed of Chicago's College of Humanities, and . . . what do you know? A credit card.

DR. O'HANRAHAN:

ENCLOSED PLEASE FIND CARD FOR YOUR RESEARCH. WE DO REQUIRE REGULAR SUMMARY AND REPORT PLEASE. FAX: 312-555-2937

JOHN SMITH, TREASURER

Lucy looked at the VISA card, which had CORPORATE ACCOUNT emblazoned on it, and then PATRICK O'HANRAHAN engraved beneath that. Chicago finally came through for him! But that wasn't all. There was an international money order made out in her name for—good God— *one thousand dollars.*

Dr. O'Hanrahan, Lucy cried to herself, you left too soon! Lucy wondered how she could send it to him.

First, she went to the Bank of Ireland counter in the airport terminal and cashed her money order.

Second, she went to the travel bureau in the airport concourse.

"Excuse me," Lucy said to the lady at the Alitalia desk, "the board says there's an afternoon flight to Milan at 4:30 P.M. Are there seats still available?"

"Yes, miss."

"How much is it?"

Third, she went to a Eurail information desk and asked for a continental train schedule, which she offered to buy from the man.

"And so if my friend left on the Cherbourg ferry this morning, he'll get in Paris tonight, and then how does he get to Assisi?" she inquired, circling the possibilities on the timetables.

Lucy: "So no matter what, he's got to pass through Florence, right?"

Late that afternoon she sat in an Italian plane, taxiing to the runway.

Her wallet contained the cashed money order, minus the plane fare, and she gripped a stack of lire notes ready for a brief stay in Italy.

Thank the heavens above, Lucy Dantan was going to Italy! She'd always wanted to see it. She'd find the professor long enough to give him his credit card and sightsee at the department's expense and then turn right around. It was simply the most exciting thing, the most impulsive thing, the very best thing perhaps she had ever done in her life! Judy would be *green* with jealousy. "You went to Italy too!" she'd whine, condemned to a life on Kimbark Street ad infinitum.

The *Allacciate le cinture di sicurezza* sign dinged on, so Lucy fastened her seatbelt.

"Our Father, Who art in Heaven . . ."

Lucy, as always, prayed up a storm before flying. But here she was not alone: the Catholic contingent, St. Christopher medals by the score, was in evidence on this flight from Ireland to Italy.

". . . And bless David McCall and his family and all who showed me such kindness and generosity in Northern Ireland, and bless Northern Ireland itself and help in all its troubles and move people to be better in the future, Catholic and Protestant . . ."

The plane started its acceleration.

". . . and I ask the Holy Spirit to be with the captain and all the crew and passengers as we make this journey and keep us safe and free of harm."

(You got it, Lucy.)

"But as in all things, Thy will be done. Amen."

Takeoff. Those on the right side of the plane, now bathed in the intense afternoon light that made them squint, looked out over Ireland falling away beneath them.

Between the cumulus clouds and their fanciful shapes, under the blue sky and sea beyond, was the rain-lavished green of Ireland, performing now in the sunlight, verdant beneath the cloud shadows, emerald in the fields and smooth, gale-rounded hillocks of County Wicklow, a deep jade in the forests to the south, and different again like green glass held up to the sun along happier farms farther inland. And with tales of Patrick and Brigit, prophecies of Malachy and Columkille, the melange of hysterical Mariology and neurotic Blessed Wound tallies, and mostly, the blarney of O'Hanrahan in her head, she looked down to think: Yes, Eire, you are the perfect land for myth and legend, the right size for a fairy kingdom, and amid your bogs and loughs and glens, I can imagine the Celts and early Christians dancing amid the stone circles, telling lies by the fireside, and marveling at a magic not wholly of their own invention.

Turning from her window, she sensed something older and more decisive in herself, the sense of having learned a bit about what one is and what one need never be, where one comes from and where one hopes not to end up. She had bought an *Irish Times* to read on the flight and the bottom of the front page detailed a family of brothers in Derry. One had been killed, the other was in jail held by the British for some unspecified excuse, and the third brother had last night been knee-capped—held to the ground while someone drilled into his kneecaps with a power drill. The newest method, by IRA supporters who mistook him for an informer.

He was fourteen.

He was in the hospital and just wanted everyone to know that even though there'd been a mistake, he still was a friend of the IRA and there was Gerry Adams with various Sinn Fein party members and old despicable drunks in battle fatigues crowded 'round his hospital bed putting a beret on his head while the boy held a flower arrangement in the Irish tricolor, smiling for the photo.

And Lucy thought with some sadness: poor Ireland, you fucked up your island. The only one you have. For a thousand years you evaded the Romans, routed the Saxons and the Danes, dislodged the Druids, chased the British out for the most part, only to end up killing yourselves, mowing each other down in the alleyways of Ulster with British automatics and Libyan explosives. In the name of that God, no less, Who so favored you with those good hearts and fine talents for lyric and song, Who allowed you magic and superstition after He commanded it pass from the rest of the Christian world. Tolerant and loving He was to His Hibernian children. And now you make scars on the Body of Christ that will not heal.

Lucy looked out the window to the luminous Western sky and was not the first immigrant's child to think: thank God, someone got on a boat and let me be born in America and not the streets of Belfast.

3 Well may I be forgiven, I am sure, a recitation of my own poetry when I describe the exhilaration of travel upon the road to what once was Jerusalem. Everything that befell the polis was deserved, but who among us does not remember its beauty and former glory? I am sure you are familiar with this much-praised passage in the *Hebraika*:

> O golden towers! O streets of beryl!
> Whose stones would dance and sing with glee . . . [1]

2. Out of Negev, Xenon and I returned, past Bethzur, so that Xenon might give salutation to his parents and tell of his many adventures. Xenon's father, Jason, had decided the lad should begin a trade with his uncle in Ephesus rather than pursue mission work. It was determined that Xenon would accompany me that far.

My young charge and I ventured next to the environs of Jerusalem and to—what was then—my family estate, still a Nazirene commune. Things there were troubled, and I will admit that in the weeks I had traveled much petty bickering had broken out. A pair of Nazirene brothers had stolen monies accrued by the selling of our olives and so had to be expelled. (As you know, we live communally as Our Master would have us do, sharing everything, burden and bounty, and thereby avoiding the horrors of moneylending and rank commercialism Our Master so inveighed against.)

3. With the foolish, doomed Revolt surging and subsiding

---

1. For the Greek, see Appendix A. Matthias has lifted these notions from the far superior *Book of Tobit* (100s B.C.E.); i.e., *For Jerusalem will be built of sapphire and emerald/And her walls of precious stones/her towers and battlements of pure gold/and the streets of Jerusalem will be paved with beryl . . . and all her lanes shall say "Hallelujah"* (*Tobit* 13:16–18).

around us, Xenon chose to remain on my Nazirene commune through the spring and summer [of 67 C.E.]. There the enterprising young man learned our rules, befriending everyone with his simple ways, especially the womenfolk for whom he spared no effort to help with chores. O, to think of my noble band of Nazirenes now, weathering the storms and evils of the highway! Such is what you commanded with a wave of your hand when you usurped the property and evicted these living saints among us!

But let us not dwell on this time and time again.

4. No person, I determined, could better explain the mysteries of the time after Our Lord's execution than Joseph [of Arimathea] himself, who offered up his own tomb for the Teacher.

O exquisite oblation!

Joseph had died in the time of the monster Cuspius Fadus [Procurator, 44–46 C.E.], but I thought a trip to Arimathea would not be amiss to learn some record of the man. Again, I made a short journey to find Duldul ibn-Waswasah, who extorted from me many coins before revealing the whereabouts of Joseph's reclusive country estate. Joseph's own mansion had been turned into a meeting place for Nazirenes: a commune, much on the model of my own, thriving and splendid. Xenon and I joined a group of tradesmen and their soldiers, to avoid the bandits who were omnipresent in that era, and we found ourselves after two-and-a-half days walking into much-trampled Arimathea. Joseph's commune had become a rabbinical school for—steel yourself, my brother—Nazirene women!

5. The women resembled nothing more than Bedouins, with only their hands and face revealed. I imagined it would be a dowdy lot, filled with unmarriable daughters and penniless widows, but I was quite wrong. Some women could have entered marriage without dowries they were of such beauty, and I at once saw the necessity of the impenetrable defenses, given what marauding Romans might do to this panoply of Helens. I was reminded of my own lines from my epic *The Hebraika* in which the hero, King David, at first spies the Daughters of Jerusalem:

O cluster of henna blossoms, thy satchel of myrrh!
How from afar I drink in your odors and inhale thy nard![2]

Such were the beauties of this compound! How wise and appropriate that they did not sully their worth by entering into the marketplace of matchmaking and courtship, which turns all women into little better than tavern harlots. How much more beautiful the stainless path of chastity, the only wedding aisle a woman ever need traverse, her immaculate groom the True and all-fulfilling Church!

6. Sadly, I did not favor the leader of the convent, Maryam, the sister of Lazarus, the man Our Lord famously cured from a hopeless terminal bleeding.[3] Lazarus seemed a quiet and woman-dominated soul, an odd choice I thought for such strong attachment and friendship granted by Our Master. More intolerable was his sister Martha, a shrew and slave driver in the peculiar mix our race seems to propagate. Martha and I had battled a few times at various gatherings of the Teacher, in which she supervised all domestic matters—food, laundry, sewing, and the like—and, looking back, it was well the women took these matters in hand, as Our Master might well have walked through sandals and been naked for all the attention that he gave to such. From the time I was sixteen I never recovered Martha's good opinion after a harmless, precocious remark I made about some emetic broth she had stewed, one might have thought, from carrion and hay, such was its aroma.

7. Maryam, however, was the more decorous sister, but pitifully burdened with scholastic pretensions. She was, as I remembered her, handsome but serious-faced, a woman of the kind that is never at her chores or upon the tasks she is assigned, dreamy and indifferent to the household cares that God has made woman's lot. She announced, for example, "Some of your contendings are quite false, I assure you." (This she said in a

---

2. This is highly derivative of *Song of Solomon* 1:12–14, and one suspects the author had no clue as to the sexual nature of his borrowed descriptions.

3. There is no other interpretation that can be put upon the words ῥύσει αἵματος; one cannot construe this as a raising of the dead. The phrase is identical to the phrase used for the woman with an issue of blood in *Mark* 5:25. It is curious in any event that *Mark*, the first gospel, and *Matthew* (the orthodox rewrite of *Mark*) have no mention of Lazarus's raising; it is only in the later *Luke* and *John*.

made woman's lot. She announced, for example, "Some of your contendings are quite false, I assure you." (This she said in a tone as haughty as any woman had ever used with me.) "You contend, for example, that meditation upon the Most High in young women will lead, if their hearts are true, to a cessation of the menstrual flow."

(As is common knowledge.)

"It is God's design," Maryam said to me, "that we should be as we are; it pleases Him that we are so. In my own discussions with the Teacher, He made it abundantly clear that the Law, so relentlessly obsessed with our uncleanliness, was not of God but wholly of Man."

(But this is the sort of rhetoric one hears from women everywhere these days.)

8. Maryam continued "Our earthly fathers would have us be unclean more than we are clean. To touch a corpse is to be unclean[4]—but one never sees the men attend the dying family member or anoint the body of the deceased. Rule upon rule confirms we are tainted and unholy, but I found none of this in He Who Gave Himself."

You anticipate perhaps, my brother, that I should oppose this female community, raised up like the chastened schools of Yavneh,[5] but I shall not disparage these women who were in earnest. (Indeed I have changed somewhat regarding women and Our Church, but more on that when I tell of Mary of Migdal on my journey to Egypt [see 6:21–36].) No, the community shall receive muted praise from me because of their vow of virgin chastity (which I have always felt to be the engine of refinement

---

4. *Numbers* 19:11 declares a person unclean for a week if he touches or prepares a corpse; a task usually left to the women.

    If Jesus' "Nazirene" followers were indeed associated with the "Nazirite" movement, they were forbidden by the Law (*Leviticus* 21:11 and *Numbers* 6:6) to attend his funeral or execution (or for that matter, the funerals of their own mothers or fathers), explaining a near-total absence of his disciples from Calvary and the anointing ceremonies of the crypt.

5. Yavneh was the escape of the Sanhedrin while Jerusalem was under siege. Under the great rabbis Yochanan ben-Zakkai and Gamaliel II, Yavneh flourished as a peaceable intellectual community, and would have remained peaceful except for Hadrian's unfortunate decision to outlaw the Torah in 132 c.e., which plunged the obliterated region into another war.

    The Nazirene/Christian community fled to Pella.

for the soul). Furthermore, Maryam seemed intimately acquainted with my *All Heresies Refuted*, certainly no small mitigation.

9. Maryam guided me through her convent but felt it prudent that Xenon be taken to the most distant kitchens and away from the main life of the all-female community, and quite properly too! Two sisters led him away to see to his appetite while Maryam accompanied me to her chamber, lined with scrolls and copies of Holy Scripture, the *Ecclesiasticus*, a hastily copied *Wisdom of Solomon, Esther* (this heretical text one could expect in such an unorthodox enterprise), and many more minor works I noted. She asked if I would care to see Saul's latest missive. My defiant words convinced her I most certainly did not! That accursed Saul of Tarsus, the Great Heretic, held sway even here![6]

Maryam declaimed, "Paul accepts women as deaconnesses and as elders. The saintly man has built a Church of women all throughout the Great Sea. And it is upon womankind that the Church will grow and thrive."[7]

10. Jerusalem, I reminded her, still considered Peter chief among the disciples.

"What should anyone care about Jerusalem?" she replied to me in indifference. "The Church is wherever human hearts accept His Teachings, and the leader is whoever takes the beggar's hand and leads him to a warm meal. What? You would have that old fool Peter, thick and as unthinking as the rock he's

---

6. What follows is the classic Ebionite argument against Saul/Paul one finds in the late Second-Century *Kerygmata Petrou* (*The Preachings of Peter*; trans. R. L. Wilson, Hennecke's *NTA*, Philadelphia, 1965). In the "Homily," there is a fictionalized letter from Peter to James. *Jesus*, Peter recalls, *explained to us how the Evil One, having disputed with [Christ] for forty days, promised to send apostles in his retinue for the purpose of deception* (11:35).

There were anti-Paul numerological arguments as well, arguing that twelve apostles were perfect, and Paul as number thirteen was evil; see 4:23–24 below when the author considers this as well.

7. *I commend to you our sister Phoebe, a deaconness of the church at Senkrae so that you may welcome her in the Lord as is fitting for the saints. . . .* (Romans 16:1–2). *Give my greetings to the brothers and sisters in Laodicea and to Nympha and the church in her house.* (Colossians 4:15). In the earliest and undisputed Pauline letters, there are no prohibitions about women in leadership roles in the Church. Remember, the concept of "priest" was anathema to Early Christians, who wished to escape the theocracy of the Temple. In the Early Church deacons and elders, apostles and evangelists, and those with the gifts of prophecy (men as well as women, apparently) were the sole authorities—no priests.

named for, sit above us like an overstuffed Pharisee? I hear from my correspondent, a Nazirene sister of Rome, that when in the Romans' capital our Peter attends the pharisaic synagogue in the Jewish quarter, half-Nazirene, half-Pharisee, when it suits him. It is Paul alone among the men who grasps the breadth of Our Master's teachings."

11. Saul who had never met Our Master! As I made quite clear in *All Heresies Refuted*, I myself saw Saul lead the Temple rabble to execute five of our Gentile converts outside the city gate. I have heard him speak on Nazirene iniquities before the Sanhedrin, I have heard Saul plead with the Pharisees for our extermination, and what is more, I have former classmates from my own academy-days who studied with the great Gamaliel, as did Saul, and report him to be without a shred of human warmth—and to think he is now raised up before us, this Cilician, to do battle like Typhon![8]

"If you would but read his circulated letters," Maryam said predictably, "you would see a changed man."

12. But my argument, made many times before and since, was this: to credit this Saul of Tarsus with Divine inspiration and guidance was to make a mockery of Our Master's time on earth. It is as if to say that the life and mission of Our Savior were insufficient to form His Church, that the Most High miscalculated and had to resort to employing an extra person.

"And that is precisely what the Most High has done," Maryam said placidly. "Come now, do you believe that you Twelve have done the job well enough? James, before they killed him, was indistinguishable from a Pharisee; Jude, Philip, and Nathanael have not to my knowing advanced His Church past a handful of new converts, and the converts James bar-Alphaeus, John, and Thomas garner only render us ridiculous. And what of you, Matthias? What shall be written of you?"

I record this brazen speech in part to show you her nature, but in part to concur with this humiliating appraisal. The Chosen Disciples indeed proved a paltry lot. Need I punish myself by

8. The author, with untypical aptness, compares Paul to Typhon (both were Cilician, from Tarsus), one of the Titans who fought with Jove.

reminding you, Josephus, how none of us, save John, went to see the Teacher at His place of execution? (Mind you, John was twenty years of age but looked fifteen, and it was not the risk for him to be there as it was for others, so I weary of hearing about John and his sentinel at the Cross.) No, perhaps Our Most High Father trusted too much in Our Redeemer's judgment, just as the Redeemer trusted too much in the fallible, insufficient men he chose to keep the Light of Truth aflame in His absence.

13. Maryam said to me further, "Since I have been here in Arimathea, I have heard that Nathanael[9] was roasted over a spit, and we sisters prayed accordingly for God to forgive those responsible. Then some years back we heard he was in Greece and was lowered into boiling pitch. Consequently we prayed again. Then a year ago he passed through here on the way to Media and was quite alive and unsinged. Now there is word that he is delivered to his glorious martyrdom yet again, this time being eviscerated by the Parthians. You yourself, brother Matthias, have added to this sick-making obsession with martyrdoms and relic-cults with your *Catalogue of the Martyrs.*"

(One is forced to express a certain amazement at the erudition and well-read nature of this remarkable woman.)

14. However, she with some justice excoriated my youthful book, saying to me, "Half of what you record is total nonsense."

I let this remark stand because I have come to learn that my sources were dubious, though at the time I had no cause to doubt them. Certain sufferings, as I made clear in this work, won the Laurels of Heaven, others more complete and ghastly a Crown, with particularly horrid sufferings earning a Diadem in this Crown.[10] Some men, such as James, our first martyr, are allowed

---

9. Nathanael (found in *John*) has traditionally been associated with Bartholomew (*Matthew, Mark, Luke*). Eusebius has an account that places Bartholomew in India, like Thomas, but tradition has his martyrdom, by flaying, take place in Armenia.

10. This evangelist seems to have been an enthusiast for many of the cult obsessions of the day—Crowns, Diadems, the Chariot (the all-important *merkavah* of Ezekiel, source of much Jewish mysticism), and the Throne of God, traditionally the residing place of the human soul (female, and willful), either under or within YHWH's throne. The *Sefer Yetsirah* may be as old as the 200s, and is a culmination of these ancient preoccupations. Here is a particularly descriptive example of this literature from the 4th-Century "Heikhalot Rabbati" (see the brilliant Shafer trans., Leiden, 1981): *[Rabbi Nehunyah] at once revealed the secret of the world, the measure that appears to one who is worthy of gazing on the King, on his Throne . . . on the swift lightning, on the terrible Hasmal, on the River of Fire which surrounds his Throne, on the bridges, on the fiery flames that blaze up between one bridge and the*

to be in the presence of the Throne upon which Our Master now sits preparing to judge each of us.[11] I fear a certain enthusiasm overcame me as I recorded these gradations of martyrdom, and now older, I am not sure the mystical sources and rabbis who helped me compile this compendium are to be trusted. As for the long tracts of martyrdoms of our Church, I had James [bar-Alphaeus] to thank for that.

15. Maryam further pronounced, "Why is it this way with men? Is it not enough to do what Our Lord bade us do that you must construct these fantasies upon His Truth, a truth that could not be more plain and unadorned?"

I mentioned, as she well knew, that the Disciple James was the source of most of my accounts.

"You should go to Ptolemais then," she instructed, "for that is where the son of Alphaeus writes his tracts. What Church is so small or Nazirene community so insignificant as to escape the missives of James? And copied out by his own hand, I suspect! He produces martyrologies by the firkin, alternating with invitations to martyrdom, though we sisters observe he manages to live quite well and grow quite fat as the decades pass! He luxuriates in a fine estate inherited from a wealthy widow in his thrall."

Maryam concluded, "Were that not enough he has collected endless relics and scraps of Our Master's history and charges tribute for the privilege of kissing or touching these abominations to one's wounds and infirmities."

16. I determined then and there that I should go to James, if only to deliver a moral exhortation! But secretly I desired to know if, like myself, James had lost his initial fervor in the Faith, and whether his cynical industry was the result.

17. I attempted to find Xenon, who had disappeared. Only after a search of many moments did Xenon appear, coming up

---

next, on the dense smoke, on the bright wind that raises up from the burning coals the pall of smoke which covers and conceals all the chambers of the palace [the heikhal] of Aravot [the Seventh Heaven] . . . Etc. These mystical objects enthralled Jewish esotericists through the Middle Ages and to the age of Kabbalah.

11. In the Jewish martyrdom cult of the period, as through the Christian Middle Ages, a special Crown was awarded to the martyrs. Στέφανος, the name "Stephen," means crown. This convenient coincidence would seem to cast suspicion on whether a historical Stephen existed, or whether the Protomartyr was a composite Greek creation, invented to deliver the polished speech in *Acts* 7, and be awarded the martyr's prize.

from the stables with two of the sisters, himself rather humorously covered in hay, he having met some youthful accident therein. I asked him if he enjoyed his tour and requested a report upon the salient characteristics of the commune, which he could not do. (I am appalled at the inattention to detail in the young. They are not trained as they ought to be; I wonder if there will be a historian in their entire lazy generation.) Nor could he quickly recall what they had fed him to eat, or the names of the sisters that devoted so much time to his amusement while I talked with their superior. I had hoped their example of perpetual virginity—O insuperable triumph!—would have made an impression upon him but he blushed deeply as I referred to such things.

So innocent are these country lads!

18. By the next evening, we arrived in simple Apollonia and stayed with Nazirenes there for much of the next week.

Early in Tisri [September 67 C.E.] we caught a vessel that landed us in Ptolemais, which was amok with Romans newly arrived from Cyprus, ready as ever to crush the Jewish rebellions once and for all. You, my brother, had abandoned the priestly robes for the tunic of a general.

The Nazirene synagogue of Ptolemais was filled with hysterical old people convinced the End Times were beginning, for Our Master said His generation would see the destruction of Jerusalem and one imagined in those days that God would end His world rather than see the Temple fall to the pagans.[12] Tales of the earth opening to swallow the Great Sea were put forward by the elders; every mountain was suspected of being a volcano, every thunderstorm harbored fire and brimstone. It was said the week the Roman legion came, a calf was born to a ewe and a sheep was born to a cow, and both abominations were killed immediately and their heads sent to the son of Alphaeus for his collection of signs, wonders, and relics.[13]

---

12. Jesus joins the centuries of holy men to predict the destruction of Jerusalem (notably, *Mark* 13:1–9, *Luke* 23:28).
13. Like the Marys, there is a profusion of Jameses. By this gospel, it is confirmed that there are three main Jameses: 1) The James bar-Zebedee who was the brother of John, the first disciple to be martyred in 44 C.E. 2) The James of the pastoral letter in the New

19. Looking down from the most prominent hill behind Ptolemais is a vast estate; it seems to be several houses amid the cypresses and cedars. A Roman widow who had married a Jew, we were to learn, bequeathed it as a Nazirene meeting-place, and each Friday it became such. But otherwise it was merely the lavish personal home of James bar-Alphaeus, the most industrious and cunning of the Disciples.

Whereas many of the Twelve were rough men, such as Thomas or Simon or, for that matter, bumbling old Peter himself, James bar-Alphaeus belied his humble background and had made quite a private study of the Holy Scriptures. It is certain his mother wanted him to be a Pharisee but she underestimated the chasm between a man of his station from Galilee and the elite of Jerusalem.[14] Still, he had nonetheless found for himself the life of wealth and ease, as his slack form and acquired limp from gout betrayed. His eyes, however, remained as I remembered them, beady and observing, as if they contained his sense of hearing as well.

20. Xenon was tired and ate in the kitchen, fed by servants, and seemed to be enjoying coarse discussions with boys his own age. I left him to their care and their chambers in the cellar of James's estate. (I reminded myself that one's scribe must have some amusement on long voyages or he shall think ill of mission work.)

Meanwhile, James allowed me a view of his collection of relics. He had a variety of cloths that soaked up Our Master's blood during His execution, including an actual phial of blood that, though dried out, had healing properties when remoistened. Sandals, bits of robe, a walking stick grown from an offshoot of

Testament, and brother of Jesus, first bishop of Jerusalem, clubbed to death under the Procurator Albinus in 62 c.e.

There is no reliable account of 3) James "the Less," and for convenience the Church has grouped him with Jesus' brother James, though it is clear from *Luke* that James the Less is the son of Alphaeus. (For an array of iconography, see the complete R. P. Bedford, *St. James the Less.*) However, this document suggests that James bar-Alphaeus may well be the source of the *Protoevangelium of James* with surviving copies in Armenian, Coptic, Greek, and the oldest, Syriac. *James* was the most popular apocryphon in the Middle Ages, in which a birth narrative, legends of Mary, Hannah, and Joachim appear.

14. Mary, the mother of James bar-Alphaeus, according to *Luke* and *Mark* attended the funeral preparations of Jesus and went to the tomb on the day of the Resurrection.

the branch of the tree that yielded the Cross[15] as well as Moses' rod, and an array of clippings of hair and garments from Our Master's mother, whose relics are appealed to by desperate, barren Nazirene women hoping for a miraculous infusion of fertility.

21. James produced a tin container that he said contained the hand of the other, martyred James, the former leader of Jerusalem. He asked me, "Would you like to see it, dear brother, and kiss this precious remainder?"

This amputation had been soaked in a perfumed balm so as not to reek, but in its liquefaction I believe the fetid aroma of this new amalgam was worse. I informed James that the Law makes such unclean—one wonders if the Law ever conceived of such a profanation! I said I would not consent to look at the hand, and exhorted him to cease this grave-robbery.

"Ah," James then said to me, "I see this is not what moves you, my friend and Great Disciple. But for some this is a joy only less than entering Heaven itself."

22. James took no offense at anything I had to say to him, no matter how harsh. We moved past his household staff—young Syrian women, all!—and we talked of his writings and his scriptorium and assemblage of Nazirene texts. I noticed an inevitable collection of John's irrelevancies, of Janus-faced Paul, who lives to fill shelves with his exertions, and then James showed me my own missives and scrolls in his cabinet, which somewhat softened my polemic. I questioned, however, if he knew the dubiety of some of the sources for his, and later, my accounts of blessed martyrdoms.

"My source is the arena across the way," James said to me. "The more gruesome the finish, the wilder the crowd, the surer the legend. My letters and accounts are circulated throughout

---

15. Here we see an evidence of the pervasive obsession with the Tree from which the Cross was made. One of the oldest churches of Jerusalem, the Georgian Church of the Holy Cross (from the 400s), contends it marks the spot of the tree. In cultures as diverse as Anglo-Saxon-Germanic (see "The Dream of the Rood") and Ethiopian, Cross and Tree-of-the-Cross fetishism thrived. After the 80-year-old Empress Helena returned from Jerusalem in 326 convinced she had the True Cross, it was thought that a Piece of the True Cross upon touching a normal piece of wood made the normal wood holy as well (hence the proliferation of the True Cross all over Europe).

the lands of the Great Sea, dear fellow scholar. I feel it is no exaggeration to say I have brought many to our way of life. No, I shall claim something more: I have brought more souls to our Nazirene Church than any of the other Disciples, and I cannot be refuted on this."

Indeed, having traveled much, I would sadly admit that this is likely true.

23. There in Ptolemais, the international city of the Phoenicians outside the reach of Judean jurisdiction, innumerable impieties and wickednesses flourish, none worse than the holding of gladiatorial games, the torturing of prisoners, the feeding of holy men to beasts, all to satisfy the unslakeable Roman thirst for blood. James told me there were several accused Nazirenes among the criminals to die that next afternoon.

He said to me, "You, dear brother Matthias, should attend one of these games and see what passes as entertainment for our conquerors."

I said that my presence would merely allow them to make a quick martyr of me.

And James answered, "On the contrary, you are a man of wealth and prestige, and your brother is a favorite of the Empress.[16] Indeed, he was virtually the beloved of Nero Caesar."

(Despite your faint military efforts for our people, this sort of comment should show you how you were viewed, my brother.)

24. James continued: "No, it is safe. Metilius[17] only wishes to make an example of a few Nazirenes, not ignite the province in the hundredth internecine war. Besides, he thinks he can count on the Nazirenes, like the Samaritans, to fight against their Judean cousins who go to such lengths to despise them. And he may be correct."

What befalls our Nazirene brethren in the arena tomorrow?

He said to me, "It is bound to be quite tame compared to how

16. Josephus, *Life*, par. 3: *[I] became known to Poppaea, [Nero] Caesar's wife, and took care as soon as possible to entreat her to procure that the [Jewish] priests might be set at liberty; and when, besides this favor, I had obtained many presents from Poppaea, I returned home again.*
17. Metilius, a Roman commander in the region, mentioned by Josephus (*War* II.xvii.10).

I shall write it, that much is sure. The Romans have captured the thief Palidoros, an unlovable Syrian ruffian. The crowd should not side with the boy. I visited him this very morning and collected many relics from him, in return for some coins that shall be left to his mother."

His poor mother!

James said to me, "On the contrary, she is the worst drunkard and procuress on this coast. Neither of them is a true Nazirene, but they have been to the house a time or two. And there is a woman, the virgin Rachel."

I expressed outrage that they should put to death a virgin. Surely she would wear the Crown of Martyrdom bedizened with a Hundred Diadem!

25. But James told me, "Rachel, my brother, has been hoping to be martyred for some time now. They threw her to the beasts in Tyre, but the beasts refused to chew upon her."

In this do you not find miraculous designs?

James did not. He said to me, "Rachel is a woman past her bloom, well beyond her twenty-fifth year." He added the next as if it were some jest that we might laugh: "Traditionally the Romans take our virgins to a house of prostitution and let the legion desport themselves, but with Rachel they intend to move straight to the Arena wherein she will be unwound upon a spool."[18]

26. James then said to me, "You make a great show of disapproving of my martyrologies now, but in years past I sent you my martyrologies to circulate and evangelize upon. Were they not of service to you? What of Mariamne who was encased in a stove, her head free, as the metal confinement was heated up slowly? What of young Jonathan, not fifteen, staked to the ground, covered in rotting flesh and then seized upon by hungry birds of prey?

"Did you not see that it is by these executions that Our Church of the New Covenant grows by springs and leaps? I promise you, dear Matthias, that if you were to offer yourself up for

18. To be "unwound" was perhaps the most unimaginable torture the Romans devised, in which the abdomen was cut into, the colon was located and then nailed to a spool. By winch all one's intestines were wound out of one slowly.

martyrdom like Onias the Just and the Pharisees of earlier days[19] you should be the subject of many prayers. I predict that there would be lines of pilgrims here to mingle their tears with your blood-soaked cloak, yes? Or perhaps you do not believe what you wrote in your *Catalogue of Martyrdoms*. Do you not believe your own martyrdom, my friend, would enable you to sit at the Sixth Throne and cherish a perfect Crown of porphyry? Or was it chrisolite?"

(I could not, by this, determine whether James was mocking my earlier, youthful book, which I myself have taken pains to discredit, though some sections still have some merit and it is well admitted that the style of the Greek is exceptional in one whose adopted language is Greek.)

27. As for James's writings, I do not possess them here with me, but nonetheless, you have surely read the like of his tales:[20]

A young woman is led naked to the stake and exposed to the roar of the crowd, the very thing that arouses today's demeaned tastes. A bull is released from a pen, which threatens to gore her. "Be gone from me, O bedeviled beast," she sings out—or

---

19. Martyrs and their cults abounded in the Graeco-Roman persecutions of Judea.

Simon the High Priest, last of the Maccabees, was killed (with two of his sons) by his own son-in-law for the Ptolemies in 134 B.C.E. Under the despotic King Alexander Jannaeus (reigned 103–76 B.C.E.) some 800 Pharisees and detractors were crucified while he feasted with his concubines and looked on. As a final gesture, the Jewish King commanded that the pietists, while dying on the crosses, observe the throat-slitting of their own wives and children. He may be the model for the Wicked Priest of the Dead Sea Scrolls.

Onias the Just is perhaps the model for the Teacher of Righteousness of the Dead Sea Scrolls, inspiration to John the Baptist and perhaps Jesus himself. He was a miracle worker who delivered a tirade against the corrupt establishment and was stoned during Passover, 63 B.C.E. (Josephus, *Antiquities* XV.ii.1).

20. Josephus indulged in martyrology himself. *Racked and twisted, burned and broken, and made to pass through every instrument of torture in order to induce [the Essenes] to blaspheme their Lawgiver or to eat some forbidden thing, refused to yield to either demand, nor ever once did they cringe to their persecutors or shed a tear. Smiling in their agonies and mildly deriding their tormentors, they cheerfully resigned their souls, confident that they would receive them back again.* (*War*, II. vii. 3)

The early martyrdom of James, then Symenon, most of the Apostles, then Ignatius, bishop of Antioch, Polycarp, Justin, and the persecutions in Lyons and Scilli firmly established martyrdom as the currency of the newly emerging Christian faith. Forty years after Matthias writes, Ignatius embodied the desire for martyrdom in this letter written before he was killed in the arena: *Suffer me to belong to the wild beasts, through whom I may attain to God. I am God's grain and I am ground by the teeth of wild beasts, that I may be found pure bread. Rather entice the wild beasts to become my tomb, and to leave naught of my body, that I may not, when I have fallen asleep prove a burden to any man.* ("Epistle to Polycarp," 115 C.E.)

some such nonsense—and the bull licks her wounds. Then a lion is sent out, ferocious and hungry. "Be gone from me O noble beast and defy not the will of He Who Madest Thou," et cetera. And the lion turns on its Roman keepers and five guards die. And then a soldier is sent out to comb her flesh with hot irons. But upon looking in her eyes, the soldier is overcome and asks her, "Where, brave lady, drawest thou thy strength?" And she says, "From a higher love that is the God of Abraham and through the Son of Man of the House of David, Who waits to judge us all, Jew and Gentile." She delivers a homily until the executioner is converted and begs for martyrdom as well. The Emperor—and it is always someone important like the Emperor in these stories, not the second-rank clerk of the procurator that usually is drummed out to these affairs—in a fit of pique orders her beheaded. And there are more prayers before she is bravely, unflinchingly despatched.

These are the same stories the *perushim* used during the Tribulation of Antiochus IV, overstuffed and legendarized beyond belief. In Ashkelon one can kiss the rope of Simon ben-Sheta, which he used to hang eighty witches by his own strength; in Jericho one can place one's lips upon a lemon thrown by a Pharisee martyr during the desecration of that sinful sprout of Satan's vine, Alexander Jannaeus.[21]

I can confidently say, notwithstanding James's commerce, Our Church is sure to soon outgrow the trade of relics and legends and saints, God be praised.

28. Worse than his relic-mongering, truly, is the misinformation in his accounts and gospels. Among James's library is a gospel that concerns the life of Mary, mother of Our Lord, and the childhood miracles of Our Master—not a truth in the thing!

---

21. The *perushim*, Piestists (root of Pharisee), were persecuted under Syrian tyrant Antiochus IV beginning in 175 B.C.E.

The "sinful sprout" reference reflects *First Book of the Maccabees* 1:10. In an age where the merest slight could result in civil war, the five-year persecution (90–85 B.C.E.) of would-be priest-king Alexander Jannaeus was extraordinary, with some 50,000 pious Jews martyred for yet another Sukkot-based incident, in which the monarch was pelted with lemons after having botched the Pharisees' libation ritual.

Our Savior as A Child debates the rabbis as an infant, He makes birds out of clay like every other Jewish mystic for the last hundred years, He kills playmates and brings them back to life.[22] James ends this gospel with outrageous tales of the donkey Our Master rode into Jerusalem upon. Villagers followed Our Master out of town to collect the diamonds and gold coins that would appear miraculously in place of dung droppings. There is an account of the fish caught by Peter and Andrew when Our Lord was in the boat, that sang hosannahs. There are Roman spears that blossom and flower in Our Lord's presence; there is the Jordan that reverses its flow around Our Savior; there is Our Lord walking to meet John the Baptist in the Jordan, walking atop the water, and then John walks above it as well but is not the Anointed One of God and therefore sinks. . . . [23] One cannot list all the preposterous accretions.

29. One invention of James's led me to severe remonstration: Our Master's birth sanctified by Six Persian Magi. One scarcely knows how to protest strongly enough! To introduce the demonic magi of the Persians into the Life of Our Master, as if their consent to God's Holy Will was required![24]

"But my brother," James said to me, "we are making great

---

22. The *Infancy Gospel*, attributed to James sometimes, Thomas other places, are popular fantasies of the 100s, and in some Oriental Monophysite congregations are still given great credence.

 Jesus raises His fallen playmates from the dead (*Infancy* 7:1), Jesus rescues a bewitched man turned into a mule and converts him back into a man, only to have him marry a leprous woman He has also cured (7:12–35), Jesus cures a man of impotence with his wife by sleeping in his house overnight (7:1–3). Jesus as a boy meets nearly all the Disciples He will teach later, healing them and saving them as boys. Judas Iscariot comes over to play and hits Jesus and makes Him cry.

 No tale seems to have had a life of its own quite like the birds, and other animals, being made out of clay (15:6) just as Adam was formed from clay (*Job* 33:6). This Jewish showstopper lived on in the Jewish *Sefer Yetsirah* (ca. 200s?), where animals from clay could be given life, the Ebionite Christian *Pseudo-Clementines* (ca. 300s), where Simon the Magus's recipe for creating life is found, to Paracelsus's *homunculus*, Judeo-Arabic alchemy, and Jewish kabbalistic mysticism for 1500 years, even up to Meyrinck's *The Golem* and Grimm's Fairy Tales. Jew and Moslem alike credit Jesus with this, oddly enough: Jesus makes clay birds in the medieval anti-Christian Jewish tract *Toledoth Yeshu*, and the Prophet Mohammed mentions the episode in the Quran; Jesus says, *Now I have come . . . to you with a sign from your Lord: out of clay will I make for you, as it were, the figure of a bird. And I will breathe into it and it shall become, by Allah's leave, a bird* (Surah 3:44).
23. Compare the similar legend in *Matthew* 14:22–33.
24. The Three Wise Men are found solely in *Matthew*, its absence is suspicious in *Luke*, the most detailed of the canonical birth narratives.

progress in Persia, where they prefer Our Master to their own Mithra. I have sent them a piece of the swaddling cloth for their adoration in Gabae [Isfahan]. It is a harmless thing to add this little story! We may bring a nation to Abraham's bosom!"[25]

30. I believe my sarcasm showed when I noted that James's account had Our Master as a child flee to Egypt with His family.

"He must go to Egypt," James explained, "because the Prophet Isaiah said the Messiah must come out of Egypt. So I have written that, to escape Herod's rage, Our Master's parents fled with the babe to Egypt."

I protested, "Across hundreds of miles of barren desert to a hostile country? They could have escaped Herod's jurisdiction less than thirty miles away, here in Ptolemais! How could anyone expect such nonsense to gain credit and not be found ridiculous through the years?"

31. James then said to me, "Matthias, my brother, it is a matter of great debate, even amongst the Nazirenes, whether the Son of Joseph was the long-awaited Messiah. He is of David's family, indeed, and of Bethlehem, but many prophecies are unfulfilled by Him. It is important that what is written of Our Lord support the thesis, is it not? Our Teacher was not of humble birth, for example. We know that His father was a carpenter and made of money![26] His mother, the Sadducees are now saying, was with child before her marriage . . ."

What lies will they not tell?

James related to me, "His detractors say He was the bastard of a Roman and a prostitute from the Egyptian court. They say Mary gave birth alone and deserted by her customer, scorned

---

25. In the *Infancy Gospel* (ca. 100s) the Wise Men and the diapers of Christ are again associated (3:1–10). Mary gives them a piece of swaddling cloth, they return to Persia and *according to the custom of their country* [Zoroastrianism] *they made a fire and worshipped it. And casting the swaddling cloth into the fire, the fire took it and kept it. And when the fire was out they took forth the swaddling cloth unsinged, as much as if the fire had not touched it. Then they began to kiss it, and put it upon their heads and eyes saying, This is certainly an undoubted truth.* Later, more of this inexhaustible diaper is hanging upon a washing line (4:15–16) when it touches the head of a demonic child, who is relieved as crows and serpents fly out of his mouth. This precious relic found its way to Charlemagne's court where every seven years the Holy Roman Empire's mother church, Aix-la-Chapelle, displays the diaper to pilgrims, along with the loincloth from the Crucifixion and Mary's veil.

26. It is well to remember the bourgeois origins of Christianity. A woodcrafter in forestless Israel, like a fisherman who owned his own boat, would not have been thought of as poor or particularly humble, as it has suited the Church to think.

by her village and family, squatted and gave birth tied to a palm tree for support."[27]

32. I asked if God had any need of fictions in order to make the Son of Man more than what He was, when what He was is supreme!

James said to me, "The Nazirenes of John Mark's Damascus circle are convinced that the Messiah must be born of a virgin. A virgin, I mean, who has never known a man."

Of course, so He can be as Mithra, born of a virgin and Osiris, born of a virgin, and Tammuz, born of a virgin![28]

33. James asked me, "How are we to reach the Gentiles whose religions have these wonders, if not with the mysteries of Our Lord's birth? You yourself have heard His mother Mary talk endlessly about her little angel—try making a gospel from that! His birth is of no true interest, so what is the harm of making it so, to better persuade the Gentiles, who will simply believe anything, it must be said. How can we coax them to read, say, one of your learned tracts, my dear Matthias?"

But, I said, I still would prefer that we could bring them into the Kingdom by loving them.

James said in return, "Go try to love your fellow Romans and Syrians in Ptolemais tonight and see where it gets you. You're a fine one to preach. I have never known a more elitist man in my life than you, brother Matthias. You have made it quite clear

27. The centurion-prostitute genealogy had a credence of about three centuries, and became a staple of Jewish anti-Christian rhetoric, finding its way into pagan anti-Christian attacks, such as the tract by Celsus the Epicurean (countered by Origen, early 200s), where he identifies the soldier-father, downgraded from a centurion, as the Egyptian Panthera.

The palm tree legend lived on in Arabic Christianity and then into Islam. The lack of adverse comment about Mary's conceiving before marriage is surreal, given that era, and the Quran's account has something of isolation and banishment in it: *And she conceived him and retired with him to a far-off place. And the throes came upon her by the trunk of a palm. She said, "Oh would that I had died ere this, and been a thing forgotten, forgotten utterly!"* (Surah 19:22). Perhaps the true source of this notion is Homer and the description of the virginal Latona, selected to conceive by God/Zeus, and her delivery clutching a tree.

28. Pre-Christian virgin births abound: Nana gave birth to Attis, a virgin to Mithra, the worship of the Egyptian Osiris was associated with virgin birth and an ikon of madonna and child, but no preexisting myth is more similar than the Phoenician Tammuz. Born of a virgin, Tammuz died with a wound in his abdomen, rose from the dead from his rock tomb after three days. His cult had been popular in Jerusalem for some time, apparently: *. . . and behold, there sat women weeping for Tammuz. Then [the Lord] said to me, "Have you seen this O Son of Man? You will see still greater abominations than these"* (*Ezekiel* 8:14–15).

that you think yourself better than any of the Twelve, me included, me and my humble birth! So I shall wait for you to commence the conversion of the Gentiles by brotherly love."

34. My Josephus, you must know as a fledgling historian (as I, your brother, have known for some time), that it is not ten years after a man of consequence perishes in this ignoble land, whether prophet, king, or rabbi that he is not festooned with legend and myth like some general of old. Diligent though my own history may be, will I ever know what is the true account? O, that I had asked more questions of the Master! No word should have left his mouth without my hearing it!

As I wrote to you in our earlier letters, Josephus, I had only but one long meeting with the Teacher of Righteousness and with a sixteen-year-old's confidence I depended upon my memory—I curse myself for not bringing a scroll like Matthew or John and writing down his every utterance. In the one or two private moments the Teacher and I shared He was all human goodness, this emanation of love and purity as no man I had ever met. I was in such awe that all I could stammer were commonplaces and banalities. How little the Greatest One Among Us must have thought of your wretched brother.

35. Before the light of the next morning, I found James risen, pained by gout, limping along his marble terrace that overlooks the sea. I asked James if he had any of the True Church in his heart. Did he not recall the kindness and love of He Who Redeemed Us? What if the Teacher of Righteousness were to return, as He said He would, and were to behold James's shameless business of bribes to Romans, exaggerated martyrdoms, and certainly, the wealth and splendor that James had attained?

James said to me without hesitation, "You have judged me unfairly. What I do here is what all holy men do, just as Daniel and Elijah have tales woven around them, just as Ezra has culled the wheat to suit his whim. [29] It is by such tales we move the mob."

36. James took me to the terrace edge and we looked upon Ptolemais, beginning to stir in the foggy morning before the sun's arrival. The cocks crowed on the hillside and one heard

---

29. Ezra, the Chief Scribe, is thought to have single-handedly compiled the Bible's Old Testament as we know it, in 444 B.C.E.

the bells of animals as they shook themselves awake. In such a scene of peace, James was moved to say the following:

He said to me, "No, my brother. Our Lord has long since ceased to fill my heart in the way you mean. I look back at those days and find us hopeful and young and quite willing to see all that we saw. I wanted so much to be at the side of the Messiah— you cannot imagine! My mother had raised me for this. And when we rode into Jerusalem for Passover, when the crowds sang His name and bowed down before Him . . .

"But then He told the priests He could tear down the Temple and rebuild it in three days.[30] This did not happen and for once I saw Him as a mistaken man. Holy, possessed of enormous power, but mistaken somehow as to His role. And the mob, when they did not see this miraculous tearing down and building up . . . they were the same rabble who lined the streets to spit and jeer at Him as He was marched to the Western Gate with His cross. It is by my writing and my miraculous relics that I will avenge this, and bring this mob running back to Him. I will yet have their tears, their racked and pleading hearts."

37. And what of when the Teacher of Righteousness had risen from the tomb?

James said to me, "Those few hours in those strange days when He appeared again passed as in a dream. Just ask, Matthias, any of the Disciples. You will not hear the same story twice! No one can agree on what happened."[31]

---

30. The Pharisees make this claim against Jesus (*Matthew* 26:61, *Mark* 14:58), though Jesus isn't recorded in the Synoptics saying precisely that. *John* 2:19, written a half-century after the others, reports that Jesus does say it, but "He spoke of the temple of his body."

31. Nothing is more disheartening to the fundamentalist than the confusing, contradicting, and ultimately unreliable accounts of the Resurrection, in which almost no two assertions are in agreement. One is struck by the strangeness of the disciples' actions—does no one rush to the authorities with Jesus as proof? Would Peter and Andrew return to fishing, as in *John*, rather than stay with the Risen Jesus or preach His gospel? The original *Mark* (without Chapter 16) and "Q," the lost source of *Matthew*, do not have resurrection sequences at all.

In the added Deutero-*Mark* 16, the party that went to the tomb was the Magdalene, Mary-Alphaeus, and Salome; in *Matthew*, it's the Magdalene and the "other Mary"; in *Luke*, it's the Magdalene, Mary-Alphaeus, and Joanna; in *John* it's Mary Magdalene, later accompanied by Peter and John.

Mark and *Matthew* say there was an angel who spoke to the women; *Luke* and *John* say there were two angels; and *Matthew* has the guards faint in terror, while there are no guards in the other narratives.

Most incredibly, the gospels have no agreement on where Jesus was or what He said
Continued

Fearing the answer, I asked James if he felt the Lord's Resurrection was an illusion, or worse, a sham? For I was not there.

James said to me, "No, it was no illusion. I am quite sure it was He. Though, some nights I am not willing to believe it myself. It is curious. My having seen Him risen from the dead did not make it easier to accept."

Here he embraced me and gave me the brotherly kiss of peace.

38. And James said in parting, "Think, Matthias, of the millennia to come. Just as we revere Moses, they will revere Our Master, and how much more fortunate they will be. Never to have known Him! Free to suppose Him on clouds, borne by angels, light shining from His face, when we poor souls saw Him at His bodily functions, snoring beneath a tree, laughing after one of Peter's hopeless jests. You still disapprove of me, but I give future generations a belief in Our Master in a way they will understand. I construct the rudiments of faith for them."

And with our different views of ministry we parted peacefully.

39. Xenon and I then walked to the port. Xenon had slept in the cellar with the good-natured servants amid James's vast hoarding of wines and liqueurs and it apparently was no good accommodation, because the lad was violently ill all morning, irritable and unable to speak clearly or prevent himself from falling asleep all day long. (I am glad to be old and not so much in need of sleep as the young.)

---

after this resurrection, the very centerpiece of the Christian witness. Deutero-*Mark* and *Matthew* have Mary instruct the disciples to go to Galilee where Jesus meets them. *Luke* and *John* show Jesus never leaving Jerusalem, and *Acts* has Jesus insist that the disciples stay in the Holy City to await the Pentecost.

Luke has Jesus "part" from them, the others don't precisely say He ascends to Heaven except for Deutero-*Mark*.

No one seems to recognize Jesus. Mary Magdalene thinks He's the gardener (*John*), Jesus appears "in another form to two others," (Deutero-*Mark* 16:12, the vaguest piece of scripture in the New Testament); Simon and Cleopas don't recognize Him at the dinner at Emmaus, where Jesus then disappears like a ghost (*Luke*). To counteract this ethereal impression Jesus proves He is bodily resurrected in the episode with a doubting Thomas (*John*) and when He asks to be fed. After His "parting" in *Luke*, the Disciples, like good Jews, go to the Temple, home of the Pharisees who allegedly masterminded Jesus' execution, and give thanks!

To the detractors of Christianity, Celsus, the Gnostics, Jewish rabbis, Julian the Apostate, and others, the testimony of the four gospels has made the task of undermining the Resurrection a simple chore.

40. Yet, I tell you I am to this day haunted by James. A vision of him I have late at night, by his candle scribbling feverishly some new tale corresponding to some old prophecy, laughing as he takes a dog's bone and wraps it in a fine case and declares it a relic of a blessed martyr, all the while, supposing himself doing the work of religion. I appeal to you as a fellow historian and a believer-in-God, my brother Josephus: was this the way it has always been? Legends and miracle tales from anonymous holy men who meant well but did disservice to the truth?

ITALY

"... O lead me where you said but now awhile,
So that I may behold St. Peter's gate,
And those you say are so oppressed by grief."
Then he moved on: I followed in his steps.

—from *The Divine Comedy: Inferno, canto 1* (1320)
DANTE ALIGHIERI

The greatest travelers have not gone beyond the limits of
their own world; they have trodden the paths of their
own souls, of good and evil, of morality and redemption.

—*Christ Stopped at Eboli* (1947)
CARLO LEVI

Then the Magnifico Giuliano remarked: "We could add
to this what Nicoletto used to say, namely, that rarely do
we find a lawyer indulging in litigation, a doctor taking
medicine or a theologian being a good Christian."

—*The Second Book of the Courtier* (1528)
BALDESAR CASTIGLIONE

I am like God, as solitary as He, as vain, and as
despairing, unable to be one of my creatures. They dwell
in my light, while I dwell in unbearable darkness, the
source of that light.

—*Foucault's Pendulum* (1989)
UMBERTO ECO

Sometime in the dark early morning O'Hanrahan awakened, groggy from a half-pint bottle of brandy. The train was stopped. It was cold.

O'Hanrahan looked around the first-class compartment. A man under an overcoat, snoring lightly, sprawled over two seats appeared more tortured than restful. A teenage German backpacker in T-shirt and shorts, long skinny legs bristling with white hair, intellectual's glasses—he too, somehow, was asleep. Beside O'Hanrahan was a woman sitting in perfect stateliness, eyes closed as if in polite meditation, a veteran of the overnight train. Sitting by the window, the professor pushed on the glass to make sure it was closed all the way. They must be in the Alps, he figured. He stuck a finger behind the windowshade to peek out at the scene familiar to any train traveler on the continent: some border somewhere, fluorescent light towers, sleepy officials laughing and smoking short, filthy European cigarettes. Periodically there'd be a musical tone and a disembodied announcement made over the public address in some meta-language no one quite understood, another tone, then silence.

And now the whistle that meant they were pulling out. And as the train lurched to a start and the sleepers sank back into the rhythm of train sleep, O'Hanrahan saw the sign pass by, white letters on metallic blue: DOMODOSSOLA.

He smiled helplessly: again I am in Italy.

The presentiment of Italian sun and plazas and food and drink, the warmly held knowledge that, yes, the rest of functional Europe is behind now, I have arrived again in the land that speaks the language of the heart. One does not travel to Italy, one returns there. Once in a former, happier life, I made love here, I knelt in prayer here in this land where empires, churches, tyrants and *condottieri*, popes and princes, gods and temples rose and fell but always, always, the worship of the Beautiful persisted. *Cara Italia*, the first adolescent crush of the World . . .

When next O'Hanrahan awoke it was in Milano Centrale, Mussolini's fascist cathedral to the Italian railways. He had lost his traveling companions and gained a new one, a portly *signora*, grandmotherly, weighed down with shopping bags filled with breads and meats and cheeses. She nodded hello to O'Hanrahan and fell asleep before the train even left the station. As the train wended its way through Milan's crosstracks, O'Hanrahan noticed that someone had taken blue spray paint and removed the os from all the MILANOS. The work of anti-Italian-speaking Lombard separatists! O'Hanrahan smiled again. Oh Europa, you never get tired of renewing the old nationalistic struggles. Yeah, yeah, the EEC and 1992 and all that, but let an old man who knows your history retain a civilized doubt concerning your ability to get along for more than a few generations.

"*Signore?*"

O'Hanrahan turned to see a steward at the compartment door with a refreshment trolley.

"*Si, grazie,*" said O'Hanrahan, ordering a coffee, then a sweet roll in a cellophane bag. The steward moved along and O'Hanrahan noticed the sleeping *signora* rearrange herself to get more comfortable. First class makes all the difference in the world. That and the bottle of brandy he had picked up at the Gare de Lyon in Paris before boarding the overnight train to Florence.

"Excuse me, sorry . . ."

The professor detected a familiar voice from the corridor outside.

"Excuse me . . . *pardone* . . ."

He heard the sliding and unsliding of compartment doors. Then Lucy stuck her head into his compartment:

"Dr. O'Hanrahan!" Lucy beamed. "Thank God, I found you!"

O'Hanrahan was speechless. Lucy scooted her cumbersome suitcase into the compartment. She alley-ooped it halfway up to the luggage rack but couldn't quite budge it further. "Uh, could you help me with this, Dr. O'Hanrahan?"

He moved not an inch.

Finally, Lucy pushed her bag onto the hammock for luggage that was stretched above the seat. She sat down, still beaming, looking at him with those bugeye glasses he hated, two round circles like her round face. Her hair was really objectionable, straggly and hanging down in her eyes. And there was the *same* gray, poncholike, circus-tent sweater she apparently wore every living day.

"It'll be too hot to wear that sweater in Florence," he said at last. "We'll see at last if you brought a change of clothes."

She looked down at herself. "You don't like this sweater?"

"This isn't a conversation."

Lucy looked in her big carpetbag. "When I tell you what I brought you you're going to be happy to see me. Aren't you curious how I found you? I took the night flight from Dublin to Milan and then I took a cab to the train station, then I got on this train and waited until the sun came up to check each compartment. I knew you didn't travel second class."

O'Hanrahan crossed his arms, unimpressed.

She produced a train itinerary: "It didn't matter when you left Paris," she said, "you would have to come in on the morning Milan train—this one—or you coulda gone through Torino, see?" She held up the schedule. "In which case I would have caught you in Florence. See right here—this black line?"

"Stop waving that in my face. You'll wake up the *signora*."

Lucy fished through her carpetbag for her purse, and from the purse removed a wallet. She handed the credit card to O'Hanrahan: "You'll be happy when you see this. And here's the telegram that came with it. It arrived in Ballymacross after you left."

The professor stirred at last. "Let's see that . . ." A smile played at the corners of his mouth but was quickly restrained. "Positively surreal. Who'd have thought Chicago would have coughed up a cent?" He handed the telegram back to her and examined the credit card: PAT-RICK O'HANRAHAN with CORPORATE ACCOUNT emblazoned under the logo. "Who the hell is John Smith?" he asked, referring to the sender of the telegram.

"University treasurer?"

"Never heard of him, not that I could tell you who the university treasurer is. Sounds like a name you sign in with at a cheap motel."

"Yeah, I thought so too."

"What would you know about cheap motels?" O'Hanrahan lovingly added the VISA card to his wallet. "Wonder what the spending limit is?"

Lucy brought out his sister's letter. "And now, sir, since you're in a reading mood—"

O'Hanrahan snatched it, pulled down the window to throw it out, Lucy yelped "No!" and the *signora* awoke. She gave them both a disapproving glare and they remained in suspended animation until she closed her eyes again. O'Hanrahan whispered to Lucy, as he pushed the window back up, "I know every word in it without reading it. The old battle-ax is incapable of surprising me."

Lucy held it out to him, undeterred.

"All right, all right . . ."

> Dear Patrick,
> When news reached me that you had sold your's and Beatrice's
> house and closed your accounts at the bank

He grumbled, "*Yours* with an apostrophe, for Christ's sake. You see what I raised myself up from?"

> I was at first in a panic, thinking you were in trouble, emotion-ally or financially. But now I hear from Dr. Shaughnesy that you are in Europe, living it up, waisting your money and no doubt drinking it dry. If you think spending every cent you have is spiting me, then I'm afraid you are very much mistaken. You don't have to bankrupt yourself on my account because I don't want a cent from you.

"Hmmm, the Wicked Witch of Wisconsin thought she was going to get a piece of valuable Forest Park real estate." O'Hanrahan turned to Lucy. "I take it you've read this letter."

Lucy, never able to lie when asked something directly, nodded guiltily.

> And you are very much mistaken if you think that I'm going to bankrupt myself for you when you return. You are an ill man and you will need more than I have in the bank or your pension provides for you to see it through. Therefore this little spending spree in Europe has robbed you of any chance of a dignified treatment.

"Ehhhh," sneered O'Hanrahan, skimming the next two pages, "she just carps on and on like this."

Lucy asked quickly, "Are you really ill, Dr. O'Hanrahan?"

"Catherine O'Hanrahan has been trying to get me committed or chucked in a clinic since 1974 so she can run my life. Just like she ran my mother's for nearly twenty years—she's only comfortable at a deathbed. If I wanted to make her day, I'd end up in the gutter like she predicts so she could rescue me and attain her crown of martyrdom."

Lucy smiled agreeably though she was sure there was more to the story. She waited a moment more. "Rabbi Hersch said you were ill too."

"What *is* this, a conspiracy? Do I look like I'm on death's doorstep to you?"

"Oh no, sir, in fact for your age—"

"Normal retirement age," he ranted. Then, as if to himself, he swore he'd take the matter up with Rabbi Hersch next time he saw him. "I'm in perfect health, in fact."

"That's what my father says too, sir, and his system is one big ulcer. Ulcers run in our family, actually. Too much worry but that's very Catholic . . ." O'Hanrahan glared at her, so she asked instead, "Does your sister have a point, Dr. O'Hanrahan? I mean, if you're using up all your, you know, money, then what are you going to do when you get . . . I mean, when you do retire?"

O'Hanrahan wasn't going to discuss his retirement plans with Lucy. "The great Dr. O'Hanrahan is going out in a blaze of glory. Zion's glory, angelic realms of glory, a hoary head and a crown of glory— we're not choosy. This gospel I'm after means *everything*. I may even be excommunicated, the highest honor accorded by the Roman Catholic Church."

Lucy smiled, not meaning to.

"Grants, fellowships, appointments." He paused, aware he was not quite as sure as his words. "I'll be respected," he added.

"You're already respected, Dr. O'Hanrahan."

Yes, he thought, once upon a time, by people now mostly dead . . . And yes, in your little Theology Department circle I suppose I get a kind word or two, but what of The Ages? O'Hanrahan fell into thoughts of his former glories: Do you remember when you were a Jesuit novice at the American University in Beirut, Paddy? 1949? Do you remember what short work you made of the Thanksgiving Hymns in the Dead Sea Scrolls? Translated in part by *you*, the twenty-four-year-old kid, the goy! Professor Albright—that *genius*, who was among the first to recognize the value of the scrolls—do you remember the praise heaped upon you? Those Israeli masters, Sukenik and his son, those masterful Frenchmen, Dupont-Sommer and de Vaux . . . A head-turning swirl of adulation and promise that you'd eclipse them all!

(So what happened, Patrick?)

O'Hanrahan felt the adrenaline surge, that inescapable tension within: is there time enough? Time for me to join those ranks of academic immortality? Time to get a few points on the board? Lucy meanwhile was fading, her eyes getting heavy.

"Been to sleep yet?" O'Hanrahan asked.

"A bit. On the plane for a while, and back there in second class. What I am is starved."

O'Hanrahan proffered his sticky bun in the cellophane.

Lucy considered it and shook her head. "Better not," she whispered: "I've still got diarrhea."

The *signora* in the compartment repositioned herself with snorts and grunts.

"Why didn't you take the stuff I gave you?"

"I did, sir. It hasn't worked yet, all the traveling around. I think it was Mrs. McCall's boiled cabbage stew. You see, I don't really eat meat very much and—"

"*Scusi,*" said a man who opened the door of the compartment quickly. A short man, dark curly hair, almost Arab-looking. He stared at Lucy and then O'Hanrahan, and then looked at the luggage rack at O'Hanrahan's satchel. O'Hanrahan startled, wondering if he was going to grab it, but then all of them heard the conductor in the corridor, coming to check tickets. The dark man looked at the conductor approach and then cursing under his breath, hurriedly left the compartment, slamming the door.

Lucy looked at O'Hanrahan. "What was that about?"

"Friend of yours, Miss Dantan?" O'Hanrahan protectively retrieved his satchel and held it on his lap.

The conductor appeared. *"Biglietti, per favore."*

Lucy, in a strained whisper, asked the professor to explain in Italian that she would pay to upgrade her second-class ticket.

As they haggled and quibbled, the train continued across the flat Emilian farmland, which could have been the fields of rural Illinois, Lucy soon told herself, feeling the need for the familiar in yet another new country. Soon there was Parma, then Modena, cities Lucy knew from medieval church history or literature—what excitements and explorations waited beyond the train station signs . . . Then Bologna. She craned at the window to view the domes and towers and ochre highrise buildings as they left Bologna Centrale. O'Hanrahan fell asleep and she missed his narration . . . not that she would have incurred his wrath by awakening him.

But soon, up from the plains miraculously, were the Apennines. The train began winding its way through a series of dramatic tunnels, bringing temporary darkness and consternation, because Lucy greedily wished to look out and assimilate. A flash of a rich man's villa. A few seconds of the neighboring *autostrada*, a four-lane engineering marvel of stilted bridges and tunnels. Another break between tunnels revealed a farm and a vineyard and . . . could that be a mule and peasant cart laden with grapes? Could Italy have remained so quaint back in these hills?

As O'Hanrahan opened his eyes briefly, Lucy pounced with a question: "How long are we going to stay in Florence?"

He drowsily closed his eyes as if he didn't hear, then said, "Long enough to put you on a plane for Chicago."

FIRENZE
July 1st, 1990

Within the hour the train, after numerous stop-and-start delays, pulled into Santa Maria Novella Station. O'Hanrahan stood up and reached for his bag without speaking a word to Lucy.

"We're getting off?" she asked.

"Could be."

Lucy, in a panic, grabbed her suitcase and followed.

"Are we also going to Assisi?" she mumbled, dragging her suitcase a few paces behind him through the terminal.

"*We* are not going to Assisi. *I* am going to Assisi, after I talk to the Franciscans here. Florence is the traditional gossip-stop for Assisi since the Franciscans assigned here usually got drummed out of the big operation down the road. There's a library I want to look in as well, not that any of this has the remotest possibility of being your business."

Over the cobblestone streets buzzing with Vespas and *motorini* with teenage couples clinging to the seats, past the plaza's postcard trees and sea of Scandinavian backpackers, Lucy followed O'Hanrahan into the sun and down a narrow street of hotels a block from the station.

"I've got lots of work to do," he told her as he fished for the newly minted credit card. "So go play tourist. Not even *I* am so cruel as to put you on a plane without giving you a day in Florence to look around. Scram and don't bother me."

O'Hanrahan checked in at the Hotel Davide and accompanied Lucy in the lift to the third floor. Lucy, he noted with some fondness, was wide-eyed, eagerly drinking it all in, impressed with the tall ceilings and floor-to-ceiling windows and the small stone balcony outside . . . this was all so romantic and Italian to her, this average continental hotel room.

Lucy soon made her escape into the city.

She spent the middle of the day in the Uffizi, and then, brandishing a guidebook, ran around after 4 P.M., when churches were open again, to half a dozen she couldn't properly name now—madonnas and masterpieces happily whirled about in her head, too much to disentangle. Lucy trudged back to the hotel with a pocket full of postcards to write, and collected her room key from the half-attentive desk boy she could not catch the eye of. She rounded the hallway to see O'Hanrahan emerge from his room preparing to leave.

"Hello, Dr. O'Hanrahan!"

"Hmph."

"Just wanted you to know I was back from the Uffizi."

"You like it? All that art?"

"It was the greatest museum I've ever been to in my life!"

"Did you sign the petition for them not to tear it down and put up a Holiday Inn?"

Still believing anything possible in Europe, Lucy protested, "They *can't*—the building is so nice . . ." Then she saw by O'Hanrahan's expression that he was kidding. Of course, he was kidding. "Oh, sir, are we going to dinner?"

"No, we are not going to dinner. I am going to dinner with some friars and the custodian at the Biblioteca Laurenziana after having a peek at their index."

"I don't speak Italian, you know. And I don't guess my Latin's gonna go very far."

O'Hanrahan was not even looking at her.

"I'll have to go it alone out there and I'm short of money now—"

"Should have gone home while you had the chance."

Lucy put a right hand on her hip. "You wouldn't have had your credit card if I'd done that and we wouldn't be staying in such a nice hotel tonight, would we?"

Fair enough. He produced his wallet and slipped her a 50,000 lire note. "This oughta do you. Point to a slice of pizza in one of the bakeries. Get a gelato."

"I've had some gelato in Chicago. They have this place up on North Michigan Avenue—"

"Goooood," sang the professor, departing, "when you get back, it'll seem like you never left."

Lucy, however, discovered mumbling English at shopkeepers was no problem, and some were even nice to her. She had a 2500 lire pile of gelato: *stracciatella*, *zuppa inglese*, and *zabaglione*. She wanted to try what *sounded* the most exotic. Lucy then strolled around and admired the buildings and the *palazzi* and the mix of people, soon finding herself in Piazza Signoria before the Medicis' stronghold, the Palazzo Vecchio with its crenellated high tower—looking like a personal fortress ought to, thought Lucy. Underneath this golden medieval skyscraper was all of Florence milling about, buskers and Eurohippies and lots of American tourists, mostly college-age girls, with trains of Italian locals straggling behind trying to score with them, laughing at everything they each said. Policemen on horseback patrolled indifferently, tourists lingered before the postcard trees and souvenir stands, and there were also the Florentines themselves, beautiful and confident, walking home with their shopping or going out to dine and, everywhere, the cooing, mewling birds in possession of the square, the sudden fluttering eruptions of excitable pigeons.

I could stay forever, Lucy thought.

Having walked most of the old quarter enraptured, she surrendered to the hotel, tired in her bones. She thought she'd leave a note:

> Dr. O'Hanrahan,
> How was your night? Did you find anything important? If so,
> you can come and tell me about it, I'll probably be awake.
>   Lucy

Lucy lay in her room, exhausted, but awake with the wonders of the day. It was as if someone had whispered: see how much of your life you have wasted? *This has always been here, Lucille.* And like the students and twenty-something-year-olds wandering in the *piazza* tonight, you too could have been here years ago. She thought of the girls in the square—boy, did American voices, nasal and one-half too loud, stand out in other countries; she saw why foreigners complained about Americans. Those girls weren't any more attractive than she was when she fixed herself up, Lucy thought, and they were besieged with Italian admirers. Some of those guys were sleazy beyond belief . . . but everyone looked to be having fun. A little summertime romance. Something to talk about when they get back. Something she wished she could tell Judy.

Lucy then replayed her visit with David McCall in her head. She was fairly sure he liked her and was interested and she just did all the same old dumb usual stuff to make sure romance never came to a point, to prevent being rejected. Would it have been so bad to come out and announce her interest directly? God, she thought, having made a fool out of myself over this guy Vito in the Theology Department back home, what did I have to lose with David? Vito was a short, dark Italian guy with cheekbones you could slice bread with, generally adored by women—particularly his rear end, venerated especially by Judy the *connoisseuse* herself. And Lucy had once flirted with him to a degree that Vito, very gently, suggested he was not available. Nonetheless, Judy and Lucy were positive that Vito was attainable and furthermore none of his girlfriends was any better looking than either of them— worse, thank God, much much worse!

Vito's brother looked identical from behind and was often mistaken for Vito, and hence was called Deutero-Vito. In the winter with everyone bundled up, anyone short and Mediterranean resembled Vito as well and Lucy remembered the day she had everyone in the Theology grad student coffee lounge howling by identifying two or three Pseudo-Vito's. In addition, you see, to the Deutero-Vito.

Theology grad student humor there.

Lucy then heard the lift engage, faintly, at the end of the hall. She listened for footsteps. There was a pause. Was it O'Hanrahan reading her note? She heard a crumpling of paper, then the door being opened, and then it being closed. Lucy was curious. She slipped out of bed and stuck her head out in the hall to look: her note was crushed into a ball on the floor before his door.

I love Italy so far, she thought, back in her bed and looking at the ceiling, but I wish I weren't here alone.

JULY 2ND

Next day.

And what a day. The sky was a breeze-swept, clean and infinite blue, fit for going to sea like Amerigo Vespucci, fit for the mannerist blue on the pallet of Michelangelo or Pontormo, fit for the blue on the cerulean cape of the Most Blessed Virgin; and the sun was pure this morning, firing the earthen walls of faded yellow and deep orange, palaces and tenements alike—and for the lucky mortal who cared to raise his head there awaited the dizzying contrast of the baked ochre meeting the lapis lazuli of the sky. Lucy was intoxicated: is not this the weather that bore the Renaissance, cosseted the temperamental artists, soothed the poets, prodded the world to walk resplendent from the Dark Ages? Was it not on such a day that God made good His promise and sent an angel to inform Mary of what was to befall her—let's have the angel of Leonardo's *Annunciation* and let's have a Virgin by Botticelli, Lucy wasn't so choosy as to which one, and let's have the Christ Child by Michelangelo in his *Tondo Doni*.

(With or without the five male hustlers frolicking in the background? What that man got away with.)

Lucy's head was spinning with Renaissance and romance—what was with her this morning? Calm down, she told herself, looking in the mirror, combing down her hair. On with the sweater, glasses, baggy jeans, and in her purse the guidebook of yesterday and her automatic camera and some postcards she'd yet to write. The professor was waiting for her downstairs, having this morning volunteered grouchily to show her a thing or two, before abandoning her to a Chicago-bound flight. Out of the room, down the stairs, those smooth marble stairs and the cool metal railing, handing in the key at the desk, and then out into this wonderful life-restoring light, warm heavenly air—

"Goddam it," said O'Hanrahan, "are you going to tramp about in that lousy sweater and, aw geez, give me a break with those godawful bugeye glasses again—you told me you had contacts. I'm supposed to be seen with you? Didn't you bring anything else to wear, for Christ's sake?"

Lucy felt her face color completely, and she stammered, "Well, I thought I was going to England where it's cold, just for a weekend . . ." And she knew her lip was trembling and her eyes were tearing up. The *last* person she wanted to show a hint of emotion in front of.

"Well . . . don't get upset."

An awkward silence, as they both tried to ascertain Lucy's emotional state.

"Well, stop picking on me all the time," at last she sniveled, turning away.

"Look, I'm sorry, but I'm used to traveling solo, you see or . . ."

She wiped her eyes quickly, under her bugeye glasses. And at that moment a shriveled gargoyle of a Florentine, with a bicycle full of bread, coasted up and looked at them both with a caricature of a face, a cartoon person—

"Get outa here, you," said O'Hanrahan, waving him along.

Lucy laughed but it came out as a sob. That clown must have thought this was a lover's quarrel. Old geezer and not-so-pretty young thing.

"Where do they get people like that?" said O'Hanrahan, flailing for something neutral to say. "Look, uh, Luce. I'll declare a moratorium on treating you like shit for twenty-four hours. How's that?" He passed over his handkerchief to her.

"I don't think," she said, pausing to blow her nose, "that you can go twenty-four hours being nice."

"I don't either. But the first twenty minutes or so oughta be okay."

Lucy smiled, recovering. "It's my period," she said confidentially. "That always gets me all moody and sensitive."

O'Hanrahan cut her off, putting an arm around her shoulder. "I don't wanna hear about your period. Don't wanna hear about your diarrhea. What I want is to have a good time with you today in Florence, all right? We'll go to the market, how about that?"

Sniffing, she headed back to her room.

(Happy with yourself, Patrick?)

A memory returned to O'Hanrahan, a memory of how his late wife teared up and how her face reddened and her lip trembled when she cried. Which he had given Beatrice much cause to do.

(And not without some amount of pleasure.)

What a bully he had become—the most loathsome thing on earth, the cantankerous, bitter old wretch savaging the helpless, making the little girls cry.

Lucy, meanwhile, ran upstairs and reassembled herself, quickly put in the dreaded contacts, and was back in a flash, totally embarrassed but relieved somehow.

First stop. The Spanish Chapel of Santa Maria Novella and the cloisters with a fragment of a Uccello depiction of the Flood and Noah's ark and "God knows what kind of drugs the man was on," O'Hanrahan observed. Uccello, the first surrealist. Second stop, San Lorenzo. There is Brunelleschi's graceful nave and there is a Bronzino fresco of poor St. Lawrence on the grill, a hysterical cast-of-thousands psychedelic martyrdom. Next door, the Medici Tombs and Michelangelo's sacristy featuring his statues of Night and Dawn.

"The man could not do tits," elucidated O'Hanrahan.

In the shadow of San Lorenzo is the Florence Market, stall after stall of leather finery, jewelry, ceramics, loud bowling shirts and ludicrous scarves, souvenir T-shirts, noise and multicolored clutter in a marvelous Italian confusion. O'Hanrahan led the way through the tourist mobs with Lucy dutifully following, seeing a number of things she wanted. The professor halted before a stall featuring big, blowsy Italian dresses, sleeveless. He held out one for Lucy's approval, a white silky frock with blue polka dots. "You like?"

She giggled, "Me? It's not my style."

"You don't *have* any style," he gently corrected. "But then, I have only begun my vocation, my mission."

A man within the stall, wearing one of the dazzling chartreuse and magenta shirts hanging on the racks around him, put out his short cigarette and added to the discussion, "*Si, signorina* would look byootiful in the dress. Byootiful, byootiful."

After a brief discourse on what European size Signorina was, she slipped behind the stall to the changing room. The changing room was really a space enclosed by two sheets suspended from clotheslines. To the right you could look into the neighboring stall's changing-space. There an Italian boy was trying on a pair of jeans, advertised as 100% FROM THE USA by signs full of stars and stripes attractive to European customers. The boy looked over at her, smiling, shrugging, saying something in Italian, not embarrassed in the least to be observed in his boxer shorts. Not that he should be, thought Lucy, he's *gorgeous*. After his departure, Lucy slipped off the sweater and baggy jeans and put on the dress. There was a four-foot panel mirror leaning against a pole on the ground, which made it difficult to judge herself.

She couldn't go out in public in this. For one thing, her shoulders were whiter than white and she'd soon resemble a lobster. Not the most attractive upper arms in the world, a bodily region in recent years that had surmounted a challenge to the hips and thighs for fat-supremacy. Serious armpit stubble—

O'Hanrahan: "Come on! Stop temporizing!"

The dress was long enough to reach her knees, which was good because the thighs didn't need more exposure . . . she'd better get out there and get it over with.

"See?" she said, talking quickly, "it's just not me, and it shows off my fat butt—"

O'Hanrahan, astonishing her, slapped her backside: "It's a fine butt, *signorina*. This is the land of the big butt. Child-bearing hips turn a man on in these Mediterranean climes." He stood back to look at his creation. "Stop slouching. Get those shoulders back—this your first dress? Didn't your mother teach you comportment?"

She straightened her shoulders. "Hardly."

"What do you think?" O'Hanrahan asked the American yuppie tour-ist-couple in their late twenties who were also looking at goods in the stall.

"Needs a belt," said the woman seriously.

The couple was Steve and Donna, they were from Michigan. Really, where about? Birmingham, near Detroit? You're from Chicago, at the university? How long you been over here? Having fun? Isn't Florence nice? Yes, Florence is nice—

"Yeah, real nice," interrupted O'Hanrahan, cutting short the cant. "Donna, what color belt do we need with this dress?"

"Red . . . about this thickness," she said, demonstrating with her hands.

"How about green?" suggested Steve.

"Green with blue polka dots on white?" said Donna. "Good thing you don't work in fashion, sweetheart."

Lucy was sort of thinking green might be nice. But a red belt was decided on, which dictated a red hat.

"Dr. O'Hanrahan," she said, "you don't have to keep buying things."

"Silence," he insisted, reaching for a floppy, cardinal-red, woven-straw circular hat, a bit too big. "Steve, Donna. We need your judgment here."

Steve said the hat needed to be smaller in diameter, Donna said nonsense, it should be bigger and more audacious. It was Italian and meant to be excessive. There was a guy who looked Irish-American, ginger-headed with freckles, with a rural U.S. accent Lucy overheard as he tried to ask how much a wallet was. He had been sneaking glances at Lucy for some time, which O'Hanrahan noted. "Excuse me, young man," said the professor, "but we need your fashion advice here."

He turned to them, at their service.

"I think a reeeal big hat," he said, breaking the tie.

His name was Farley, from Louisiana, his first time in Florence. Your first time too? You been to the Uffizi? Some'n else, huh? Florence is nice, ain't it? Yep, Florence sure is nice—

"Well then," interrupted O'Hanrahan again, "I think we're just about presentable here . . ." Donna, Steve, Farley, and O'Hanrahan stepped back to observe the finished product. "Sunglasses," remarked O'Hanrahan. "This fashion plate from the pages of *Moda* needs sunglasses."

Leaving the others in a chorus of seeya arounds, have a nice trips, Lucy and her companion moved on to a sunglasses stall. Before a minuscule tiny mirror, they tried numerous pairs. To make Lucy laugh, O'Hanrahan found a pair of heart-shaped purple plastic spectacles and put them on: "Is it me?"

Laughing, she shook her head. "I dare you to wear them when you get to Assisi. Maybe in Rome too, for a papal audience."

"I think they suggest the dignity I deserve."

"You look like Elton John."

"Who?" He asked if Elton John had anything to do with the Baptist, the Evangelist, John the Presbyter, John Bishop of Rome, John of the Cross, John Chrysostomos, John the Silent, John the Almsgiver, John of God, Juan de Capistrano?

"You live in the wrong millennium, Dr. O'Hanrahan."

"*Here* you go," he said, handing her a big black pair of standard anonymous-making sunglasses.

"With the big hat and the sunglasses, people will think I'm a pop star hiding out, incognito."

"Tonight," promised O'Hanrahan, augmenting with Italian hand gestures, "the wolves, *i lupi*, will be out stalking the hot, reech *milionaria americana, capisce?*"

"I have my doubts anyone will be stalking me tonight. Too much competition from my countrywomen." Lucy bowed her head serenely, peering over the top of the sunglasses. "And of such dubious virtue."

Lunchtime.

"So what will it be?" said O'Hanrahan, scanning the menu. They were in an outdoor restaurant of the Piazza della Repubblica, a modern plaza of busstops that despite the most uncharming view in Florence, manages a formidable café life. "A little milktoast perhaps? Some oatmeal or gruel? Something to calm the ever-churning stomach?"

Lucy hid her smile behind the big menu.

"You're probably one of those American girls," he said vagariously, "who comes to Italy looking for a hamburger, some french fries . . ."

She put down her menu. "You order for both of us. Do your worst."

To the bored narcissistic waiter, O'Hanrahan ordered in Italian, a flurry of an order—Lucy tried but couldn't follow it. First, there arrived a bottle of chianti.

O'Hanrahan: "A glass, *signorina*?" And as he filled it:

"Whoa, sir, that's enough."

"You're not going to let me drink this nectar all by myself, are you?"

"Wine always upsets my stomach. I'm not a drinker, really."

O'Hanrahan smiled artificially. "I'd noticed."

First course, after Lucy polished off a basket of warm Italian bread, was *spaghetti aglio e olio*, so simple, so perfect, just oil and bits of fried garlic and that was splendidly simple and complete. The next course arrived and Lucy examined it oddly.

"They look like little octopuses. Octopi," she corrected herself.

"Squid," said O'Hanrahan, on his fourth glass of chianti. "*Calamari*, and a bit of octopus there, too. In vinaigrette."

Determined to be as cosmopolitan as her costume, Lucy bit into one with a positive attitude—*deliziosa*! she declared, before O'Hanrahan corrected the gender. She devoured her serving, even stealing one from O'Hanrahan's dish before the third course arrived and was set before them. Something orange and spongy and slimy.

"Hmmmmm," said Lucy, trying a bit. First it was delicious. Then, still chewing, she considered it again. "Strange texture." She swallowed with difficulty. "Not so sure about this."

"Five different cuts make up the world-famous Florentine tripe dish, as there are five different stomach tissues in the cow—that crisscross fleshy tissue there . . ." He pointed with his knife to the tripe slices in question. ". . . and this bit looks like tentacles almost, these little sucker pods here, see?"

Lucy, somewhat paler, nodded curtly.

"Ymmmmm," said O'Hanrahan, spearing a tripe piece, running it around in the tomato sauce and popping it into his mouth. "Fortunately, our Miss Dantan's no philistine. Sheeeee's not gonna turn up her nose at international cuisine, is she?"

"No," said Lucy, "she's not."

O'Hanrahan gazed around the square while breaking off a piece of bread. "It's a wonder beautiful as everyone is, good as the wine is, tasty as the food is, that Italy ever developed a cult of poverty and celibacy. *Il Poverello* and The Virgin Martyrs. Ever looked into your namesake?"

"St. Lucy?"

"*Santaaaaa Luciiiia,* he warbled.

She put her fork down, and recalled Sister Miriam's lectures at St. Eulalia. "Somewhere in Sicily?" she ventured. "Back in Roman days. Some girl who, given the choice of losing her virginity with some rich, good-looking Roman prince or dying in unspeakable tortures, took unspeakable tortures."

"Very good. Lucia, the Blessed and Most Holy Virgin Martyr of Syracuse, lived at the end of the 200s, and is often," O'Hanrahan went on comfortingly, "pictured with her eyes on a plate."

Lucy slowed in the chewing of her tripe.

"One legend said they were torn out by the Romans. But that's not the older, more beloved Sicilian legend."

"Which is?"

"She had this Christian boyfriend who wanted to marry her," said O'Hanrahan, reaching over to steal another square of tripe. "But," he added, raising his fork to make the point, "he would respect her spiritual marriage to Our Lord. But he kept getting tempted by her curvaceousness, her loveliness, her heaving Sicilian breasts—"

"I'm waiting."

"And he felt lust in his heart when he looked into her limpid blue eyes. So, like a good girl, she tore them out and presented them to him on a plate."

Lucy tore at a piece of bread, unimpressed. "Don't worry, Dr. O'Hanrahan, these eyes are staying right in here."

"You can go see her incorrupt arm up in Venice."

"Her incorrupt arm?"

O'Hanrahan poured himself the next-to-last glass of the chianti. "Lot of ol' girls around Italy refused to rot upon deliverance from their earthly ordeals. Up the road," he continued, "is Lucca. A lovely Tuscan city. You can see in some church whose name I've forgotten the Most Blessed Virgin of Lucca, Santa Zita, incorrupt from the 1200s, no formaldehyde, no taxidermy. She's on display in a glass case, all dried-up and dusty. Probably as she was in life."

Lucy was caught again with a full mouth of rubbery tripe.

"And every April something-or-other the old widow women and faithful line up down the block to come and *kiss* the mummy on her rotted, wasted maw. They stroke her withered, shriveled hands and feet. That's really good sauce, isn't it? And too bad you can't take in Cascia this trip."

(The Blessed and most Venerable Santa Margherita, Miracle Worker of Cascia, the Saint of the Impossible.)

O'Hanrahan regaled his companion: "While in the convent Margherita prayed for ordeals to befall her and, in His infinite mercy, God allowed a thorn from an altarpiece to float down miraculously to the praying Rita and pierce her forehead, producing an open, festering wound from which an unbearable putrescent odor would emanate all of her days. Such Divine Favor!"

(Watch it, Patrick.)

"On her death, light shone forth from this gash," he added.

"Do tell," said Lucy, resolutely continuing to eat.

"Now true incorruption, Lucy, has a Roman Catholic checklist of sorts, if you want to start planning ahead. Benedict XIV's *De cadaverum incorruptione*, which allows that the skin can be discolored and black or bruise-tinted, but the joints have to be flexible and limbs shouldn't snap off when moved. There should be a moistness to the body. Often, it is found that congealed or fresh blood will form on the saint's wounds, as holy men through the centuries carve up and divide the previous relic. Or go in for repairs."

"Repairs?"

"Some repairs are allowed," O'Hanrahan continued. "Santa Margherita's cheek gave way and sank into her face in 1650, but it was lovingly repaired with string."

"Fascinating," said Lucy.

O'Hanrahan gaily noted Teresa of Avila and her sidekick, Mother Maria of Jesus, whom he billed as "that great double-act of incorruption." While the various parts of Teresa exuded divine perfume, Mother Maria's remains have been known to flow with sacred ooze. Divine leakage was recorded when a loving priest amputated St. Teresa's hand for a relic, before cutting off one of her fingers, which he carried around with him as a cherished keepsake. One of Teresa's feet went to Rome, a cheek was hacked off and sent to Madrid and was stolen during the Spanish Civil War, as was her left hand, which ended up in Franco's personal collection.

"He must have thought," speculated O'Hanrahan, "that this blessed amputation would intercede for him before God for his many crimes."

(It didn't.)

"I've been to Teresa's convent in Spain, Alba de Torres, dear girl. And one can see her heart and left arm. You are familiar with Bernini's famous statue of St. Teresa in Ecstasy?" Lucy nodded. "The most overrated piece of sentimental schlock in Western art. Anyway, Teresa's heart was pierced by an angel's flaming dart during one of her transports and the nuns are able to show you the *precise* point the dart pierced her aorta."

(An autopsy in 1872 confirmed the piercing of her then 300-year-old heart. Science in the service of religion.)

"But that is not," added O'Hanrahan, far from exhausted, "the only sacred ticker on the block. What about the miraculous incorruption of Clare of Montefalco?"

Lucy looked grim. "What about it?"

"Her immaculate heart!"

(Clare insisted until her death at forty that the Passion of Our Lord had imprinted itself irrevocably upon her heart. Go ahead and tell it, Patrick.)

"As her blessed, sacred, most holy corpse was incorrupt—"

"Does anyone in this country know how to rot?" asked Lucy, putting down her fork for good.

"As her blessed relic was incorrupt," O'Hanrahan pursued, "they cut her open looking for the Lord's Passion, and indeed, there imprinted on her heart were the miraculous signs."

O'Hanrahan recounted: on Clare's abnormally enlarged heart is a white mound of tissue in the shape of a crucifix, the body perfectly outlined and completely white except for a livid scarlet puncture in the figure's side—Christ's spear wound. A small ring of hard nerve fibers forms a crown of thorns. There is a hard whitish nerve with knobbed ends—the dreaded scourge! There are dark, sharp fibers intruding into the engorged heart—the nails driven through Our Savior's hands and feet. Another hard nerve tissue with a soft tissue at the end has been pronounced the sponge of the crucifixion scene. Rummaging around the blessed Clare's incorrupt body for other miracles, three large nut-sized gallstones were found, of equal size, weight, and disposition.

"The Blessed Trinity!" pronounced O'Hanrahan.

"Yuck," said Lucy.

"Dessert?"

"Yes, actually," she responded, hoping to get the imagined tastes out of her mouth. A *mousse di cioccolata* was O'Hanrahan's choice, and a *cassata siciliana* for Lucy, in honor of Santa Lucia. And as Lucy began to enjoy her cake:

"Of course, we must consider the advice of John Damascene, that great Doctor of the Church."

"Must we?"

(In the 700s, John was able to provide an explanation for the wonders of leaking, sacred corpses: *Christ gives us the relics of saints as health-giving springs through which flow blessings and healing*, wrote John. *For if at God's Word water poured forth from hard stone in the wilderness . . . why should it seem incredible that healing medicine should distill from the relics of saints?*)

O'Hanrahan continued: "The Venerable Bede told of the trade in St. Chad's relics in Litchfield where the pilgrim was allowed to mix Chad's dust in a brew, or soak a bone in a broth for its healing medicine. Charles VI of Spain was so ill that the incorrupt body of a saint was fetched and nestled beside him in his sickbed. A miraculous recovery."

"Yeah, I'd wannna get out of that bed too."

For centuries, O'Hanrahan explained, pilgrims also made their way to the Capella di Sant'Agata in Sicily to behold the saint's sheared-off breasts preserved under glass. Cruel man, imitated O'Hanrahan in the role of Agatha pleading with her Roman torturer, have you forgotten your mother and the breasts that nourished you? But mind you, Lucy, those severed breasts were inlaid with jewels and precious stones, and pilgrims by the thousands came to drink from her scorched relic . . . that supreme seepage."

Lucy wondered if silence would prove contagious.

"Can you see them now, Lucy? The sick and terminally ill, with trembling, palsied hand, eyes closed in devotion, taking from the priest the goblet containing the thick black extract of her centuries-old corpse. How much were the wealthy willing to pay to Rome for such an invaluable sip?"

(The Arabs, My blessed children of Ishmael, upon conquering Sicily fortunately shut down that little operation.)

"You," said Lucy to the professor simply, "traffic in the most disgusting stories around."

"Aren't you proud of your fine ecclesiastic heritage?"

"Where's Oliver Cromwell when you need him?"

"Sicily's full of good things, Lucia. In Palermo, there's the Convent dei Cappuccini."

"Speaking of, can we have some *cappuccini?*"

Her merest whim, O'Hanrahan's duty today. Coffees were ordered, and to finish, O'Hanrahan ordered himself a Benedictine—would Lucy join him? No, she hadn't even gotten through her one paltry glass of chianti.

"Go ahead, Dr. O'Hanrahan. The Convent of the Cappuccinoes."

Believing quite literally in a bodily resurrection, he explained, as well as the efficacy of *memento mori*, in their elaborate system of caves and catacombs the monks have preserved the bodies of all that petition there. Rooms and chambers by the scores open before the visitor featuring *thousands* of embalmed corpses, lined on the walls, row upon row. Some are preserved adequately, some are rotting quite openly; all are brown and mummified, and all are dressed in the clothes of the period—here is 19th-Century Neapolitan splendor, here is 18th-

Century minor aristocracy, here is a fresh one from the '30s. Of most interest to the unfailing contingent of weeping, black-clad Sicilian women are the children, who mummify less unnaturally. The "brown little ones" seem to be sleeping, curled up next to their toys, simple flowers on their chests held by their tiny little hands. The women desire to place a blessed kiss on such a beautiful slumbering *bambino* . . .

"A stuffed baby, taxidermed centuries ago!"

"Yep," said Lucy, deciding it was time to make her break, "shame about missing out on that place. Well," she sighed as she gathered her things, "the churches will be opening again soon. The tourist is called to action."

"Oh. Going already?"

(What's the matter, Patrick? Are you remembering what it is to be warm to someone? Did this brief experiment in human relations disturb your years of gruff solitude? Tell Lucy that you wish she would stay and she will spend the afternoon with you.)

Lucy stood now, soliciting O'Hanrahan for suggestions of beautiful churches. "No leaking corpses, please."

"Hm. That narrows it down drastically in Italy. Have you seen the finest church in Florence? San Miniato al Monte?"

"Where's that?"

The professor matched his directions with elaborate gestures, across the Ponte Vecchio, up the big hill, etc. As for himself, he grimly thought about going back to the *pensione*. "I think the afternoon demands a siesta," he said of his own plans.

"I thought that was Spanish, not Italian."

The professor poured her undrunk chianti into his glass. "I get by," he said, "on a technicality. The Spanish and Charles V overran Florence in, uh, 1521."

(Charles V in 1529, in collusion with the Medicis from 1531.)

"A big nap for *il professore*," he said, anticipating a yawn. "Then, this evening I'm back to the Franciscan library, so I can intimidate our brethren down in Assisi tomorrow. You know, down in Naples, they call the siesta the *controra*. Napolitano for 'against the clock,' but then they had their share of Spanish influence as well. Remind me to tell you of the Golden Age of Spanish Catholicism—"

"Right, well, I better get started." Lucy made a gesture to contribute money.

"No, it's on me." He held up a finger of warning. "Remember though: it's back to normal tomorrow."

"Aye aye, sir. San Miniato," she added, checking the church name.

"Beheaded in the main square near the Duomo, in the Third Century by the Romans. After they beheaded him, Miniato picked up his head and walked to the mountaintop outside of town. There they built his church." O'Hanrahan exhaled deeply. Why, this had been the longest conversation he'd had with anyone in months. What a waste all his storytelling talents had been for him this last decade. No one to appreciate him. No audience to entertain, and O'Hanrahan prided himself on being good entertainment. But he surrendered, saying, "Seeya later."

O'Hanrahan watched Lucy depart and finished up her glass of wine, which left him sentimental and sad. Sometimes, he reflected, in still moments, with the remains of lunch before me, a little wine in me: I find myself desolate.

(You have only to ask Lucy to be your assistant. Lucy, who longs to be a faithful servant.)

Naaah, thought O'Hanrahan, inventing negative reasons. I know what type of woman Lucy is—Beatrice was that type, my sister Catherine was that type. A little Puritan soul who knows nothing of life, who as she gets older turns judge and puritan, a complainer . . .

(You don't think you could help her find another life?)

I've got missions enough, he concluded, reaching for his wallet.

Lucy had spotted O'Hanrahan's recommended church and now was in midstaircase, halfway up the mountain, winded and baking hot. The miracle wasn't San Miniato walking around with his severed head, thought Lucy, it was San Miniato climbing these stairs in one go . . . She noticed some of the tourists she'd been seeing all day long. On the discouragingly long stairway before San Miniato itself, she passed the couple who had offered fashion advice that morning, Steve and—what was it?—Donna?

"Hello again," they said.

"Doing the circuit, huh?" said Lucy, short of breath.

"Yeah, the great thing," said Donna, "is that from this church it's downhill all the way, no matter where you go."

Mild laughter as everyone continued in his own direction.

O'Hanrahan was right, thought Lucy before the door of the church, this was the church the other churches were imitating. Each square or archway of white marble was filled with inlaid designs of dark green marble, boxes within circles, trinities of patterns under the archways, and as one's eyes moved upward, one saw the Byzantine mosaic of gold set under the point of the roof and the surrounding flurry of green-white zigzags and checkerboards, a facade simultaneously amateurish and sophisticated, like the 13th Century that produced it.

The interior was geometry run wild, verdant squares within diamonds within circles within archways, on the floor, on the walls, and
leading to the apse above the altar. The church was dark and chilly
and Lucy pressed her cheek against the smooth marble of a column
as her eyes adjusted to the dimness. Then some tourist near the front
slipped a coin into a box and for thirty seconds the spotlight illumined
the mosaic in the apse, golden and incandescent. Christ enthroned
appeared, gazing down on the penitent with ageless Byzantine eyes,
staring with wise sympathy into the heart of the sinner. It was a Christ
of love, but also of judgment and sadness. *Thou alone, O Lord, knowest
my heart.*

"Nice, isn't it?"

It was the farmboy. Lucy ended her reverie. "It's Farley, right?"

"Farley, that's right," he said. "Sure is pretty."

Then the allotted time for the coin ran out and the church returned
to cool shadow.

"There's just too much to see in this town, Lucy," said Farley, lifting
briefly a *Let's Go* guidebook in evidence. "Take nearly a month to get
it all seen, I figure. I'll give the Catholics this, they could build 'em
some nice churches."

"You're not Roman Catholic, Farley?"

"No ma'am, Pentecostal. And proud of it."

Proud of what? Lucy wondered. Speaking in tongues, rolling on the
floor led by some untutored redneck minister on TV, building ugly
warehouse-churches until the congregation is broke or the minister
gets caught with some choirboy or teenage prostitute or married lady?

(Think of St. Clare's gallstones, My child. Have any of Our children
resisted turning Faith into a sideshow?)

"Well," Lucy told Farley, "not much in the way of Pentecostalism
down here."

"Nope. My daddy says there needs to be a Holy Ghost Revival, in
Europe. He says the whole continent needs to be born again."

Lucy suggested politely, "Florence *was* born again: the Renaissance."

"Huh?"

"Renaissance. Means Rebirth."

Farley nodded blankly.

"Oh well," she sighed, looking to the door. "I better be going—"

"Wanna walk back to the city with me?"

"Uh, that's not . . . I mean, I sort of was going to watch the sunset
from Piazza Michelangelo."

Farley brightened. "That sounds good. I sort of wanted to talk to
you."

"About what?" asked Lucy grimly.

"Well . . . I'm sort of on a mission for my Bible College and my church. My daddy told me to . . ." He was having trouble getting his words out. "Well, first, let me ask you one thing," he said suddenly. "Do you know Jesus as your personal savior?"

Oh boy. Just what she needed today. "Yep," she said, "I do."

"You do?"

"Yes. I'm a graduate student at the University of Chicago, Department of Theology. My specialty is New Testament Greek, I'm fluent in Latin, can fake Aramaic, read a mean Hebrew and all so I can read the sacred texts, Farley."

"Wow! Maybe you oughta come down to Louisiana and teach us all that."

"You never know," said Lucy, noticing this farmboy had a pretty sturdy build under his Myrtle Beach, S.C., windsurfing T-shirt. "I gotta be going, so, uh, seeya around."

"You got any plans for tonight?"

"Yes," she said, overly formal, "I'm going to pack since I'm leaving for Assisi tomorrow."

"Oh. That's a shame, 'cause I was hoping we could, maybe, you know, hang out."

Lucy tried another angle: "Look, Farley, you can't convert me, because I'm already on your side. There's tons of tourists here who don't know Jesus as their personal savior."

"Yeah," he said glumly.

"Well, bye-bye."

She stepped out into the sun, now dulled and yellow as it prepared to sink in the direction of Pisa. From the front porch of the church there was the grandest view of Florence, like the one from Piazzale Michelangelo a few hundred yards to the north, but this view allowed one to see the old city wall, the villas up on the neighboring hills. So little had changed from Late Roman times, the wealth amid the sartorial cedars, a sprawling eucalyptus over a red-tiled mansion, terraces of sandy-colored stone, urns upon graceful balconies, the cypresses the lone verticals on the mellowed hillsides. Beyond the villas, rows of vines arrayed on the steep hills, stopping only at a country lane—

"Sure would be great to live in one a them houses, huh?" asked Farley, appearing at her side.

"Blessed are the poor," reminded Lucy. "Well, one more time, Farley, seeya around."

"That's not really why I wanted to do something with you," he added, as she walked on. "Being born again, I mean."

Lucy pretended not to hear as she made her way down the steps and through the park toward the Piazzale Michelangelo with its view of the city . . . When it dawned on her: Lucy, that guy, with the pathetic are-you-saved routine was *trying to pick you up!*

See what a new outfit will do for you? That and pink shoulders, which she was vaguely aware of now. Poor guy, using Jesus as a pickup line! After Ireland and David, Lucy's taste in redheads had been upgraded, having seen the first-rate goods. All right, maybe Farley was cute in a goofy sort of puppy-dog way, but who could take that accent seriously?

Maybe she should have met him for a drink tonight.

Of course, she told herself, he probably doesn't drink any more than I do. I could have walked with him for a while and ditched him if he was awful . . . He *is* awful, I know that already. But then Lucy thought: I should fantasize and create an entire romance and write Judy about it, tell her he's a Southern gentleman, antebellum money—it would kill her. It would destroy her to think I had some kind of fling in Europe. She'd never get over it. I'll write her tonight.

More stairs, this time in the right direction, down.

Lucy strolled beside the Arno, across the Ponte Vecchio, and down the familiar streets to the hotel again. She arrived with hot, sore feet and longed to take off her shoes and walk up the glacial white-marble stairs barefooted. She took a cursory look at the man loitering in the lobby—

Uh-oh.

It was the man on the train yesterday. The man who stuck his head in their compartment and ran away when the ticket collector arrived. The swarthy man was hounding the teenage boy at the desk, who was distracted by a soccer match on his miniature TV. The boy glanced up to acknowledge Lucy and slipped her her room key. The man turned to look at Lucy, squinting, looked at the room number on her key, and looked back at Lucy as if he was trying to decide something. She studied him in a second as well: a formidable five o'clock shadow, dark, ill-fitting suit, a garish patterned tie, a movie gangster. Damn it, she didn't understand their Italian:

"*Se non ti é di troppo disturbo, mi chiami il Signore O'Hanrahan?*"

"*Spiacente, signore, ma é impossibile. Vuol lasciare detto a me?*"

Lucy decided not to wait for the lift. She briskly climbed the three flights of stairs, ran to O'Hanrahan's room and knocked.

"I'm not here . . ."

"It's really important—let me in!"

He growled, probably still siesta-ing.

She knocked again. "There's that guy downstairs we saw on the train. And he wants to see you, but they won't let him up."

Some rustling within. The door opened, and there was O'Hanrahan without his jacket on, his tie loosened. "Wants to see *me?*"

"That guy who walked into our compartment and looked at your briefcase like he might swipe it. That guy who looks like a crook," she added nervously. "I heard him say your name."

"No priest's collar? He's not a monk?"

But just then they heard the lift engage. Someone was in the lift. Perhaps coming up to their floor.

"The kid downstairs looked like he was about to give way," Lucy said tensely. "And the guy saw my key."

The lift whirred past the intervening floors and was headed for theirs.

"Come on," said O'Hanrahan, scooping her along down the hall to her room, after quickly locking his door. She fumbled with her key, trying to get it in the door. The lift, they could hear, stopped, the metal gate clanged open. Then shut. They heard footsteps . . . and as Lucy got her door opened, the man rounded the corner of their hallway. Quietly they closed Lucy's door behind her and Lucy bit her fingernails while O'Hanrahan knelt down and listened at the keyhole.

Silence. Then a knock on O'Hanrahan's door.

"That's him," Lucy breathed.

Another knock. Then a loud, impolite series of knocks, to rouse the dead. Angry knocks. Lucy felt a chill run up her spine. Then they heard whoever-it-was fiddling with the lock to O'Hanrahan's suite.

"What's he doing?" whispered Lucy.

"Trying to break into my room."

"Where's your briefcase?"

"In the hotel safe, thank God. I didn't get it out for our sightseeing spree this morning—"

They heard a crunch. He had jimmied the lock and was in O'Hanrahan's room now, two doors away. O'Hanrahan pressed himself to the door, trying to hear. He heard a lamp break. Then a bottle. Lucy put her hand to her mouth, shaking her head . . . that man was tearing O'Hanrahan's room apart. More noises, then a pause. O'Hanrahan stroked his chin pensively; he seemed to Lucy abnormally calm.

"What are we going to do?" she whispered.

"He won't find the gospel and he'll probably go away."

They heard the door close.

Lucy mouthed: "Well?"

O'Hanrahan shrugged.

Then there were more footsteps, slow deliberate ones. Coming toward them. Toward Lucy's room. He was right outside. Then the stranger walked on a little further and paused.

Silence.

"Is he gone?" Lucy said out loud.

O'Hanrahan blanched, turned and sssshed her in sign language— *he may have heard that*, his eyes told her.

Footsteps, this time back toward Lucy's room. He stopped outside Lucy's door. O'Hanrahan heard the squeak of his shoes.

Knock knock.

Lucy was biting her fingernail until it bled, and O'Hanrahan took a few steps back from the door, and then pulled Lucy closer to him as they stood next to the story-high Italian clothes cabinet. She looked around for a phone to call for help but, as in many continental rooms, there was none.

Knock knock again.

Neither of them breathed, frozen there in the corner of the hotel room. Lucy closed her eyes.

Then the man began to jimmy the lock, something like a screwdriver was stuck in the keyhole and he started wrenching it, shaking the doorknob—

O'Hanrahan whispered: "*Aiuto* is help, *stupro* is rape. When he breaks in, you scream your lungs out." Lucy began to whimper. "*Do it*," he hissed with unmistakable firmness, as he hid behind the dresser, out of view from the doorway.

Lucy stepped toward the door.

SMASH! The door sprang open: the swarthy man looked up and stared in surprise at Lucy. A momentary freeze. He took a step toward her and she knew somehow he intended to put a hand over her mouth—

"*STUPRO! AIUTO AIUTO! STUPRO!*" And then she let out a blood-curdling scream for good measure.

He looked quickly around the room, for whatever it was he was after, then he angrily fixed Lucy with a savage glance, one that promised revenge. Then he fled to the exit at the end of the hall.

"*AIUTO! STUPRO!*"

"No, darling, it's ah-ee-OO-toh, put some stress on the *u*," said O'Hanrahan, stepping from behind the cabinet, reverting to language teacher. "You can stop now, Miss Dantan."

O'Hanrahan left her room to see what had become of his own.

A panting chambermaid arrived: "*Cosa sta succedendo?*" Then she saw the broken lock. "*No no no . . . mamma mia . . . È ferita?* You American?"

Lucy joined the professor in his room—it was a mess all right. Lamp broken, clothes everywhere, cologne bottle smashed, O'Hanrahan's *Herald Tribune* scattered about. This burglar wanted to register his unhappiness with not finding what he was looking for. Then O'Hanrahan went into the bathroom:

"Damn that guy!"

"What is it?" asked Lucy, still trembling. The maid, right behind Lucy, noticed the jimmied lock of O'Hanrahan's room as well. "*Mi dispiace, signore . . . Maria . . .*" she muttered, astonished, before scurrying to tell someone downstairs.

"Damn that lousy two-bit hood to hell!"

"My God, sir, what is it?"

O'Hanrahan thundered, "He broke my bottle of homebrew grappa—I have been after that stuff for centuries, *centuries*, Luce. He did it out of spite, too! Smashed all over my bathroom floor—"

"You're upset about *that*? This guy wants to kill us and you're worried about your grappa?"

O'Hanrahan was calm again. "He doesn't want to kill us, he wants the *Gospel of Matthias*. Someone has hired him to steal the scroll from us, maybe the Ignatians—they're pissed off at us, I'm sure. Whoever it is," pondered O'Hanrahan, "doesn't know we don't have it."

Lucy's heart stopped beating so fast and she began to breathe normally. "I didn't bargain on this," she said. "I didn't bargain on . . . what are you laughing about?"

"Heh heh heh," he went on with his forced laugh, picking up some of his clothes only to scatter them for a bigger mess.

"Do you mind telling me what's so funny about this?"

"Nothing's funny. But there's something very reassuring . . ." He paused to turn his suitcase upside down and dump out the rest of its contents. ". . . in having someone be this interested in what we're after. Interested enough to hire a hood to steal it." O'Hanrahan laughed some more, in jubilant spirits. "And Lucy, brava! Brava!" He unexpectedly took her by her sunburned shoulders and kissed her on the cheek. "What lungs!"

"Is this what I have to expect if I keep traveling with you?"

"Heh heh," he said, delighted by the whole incident, "it'll get worse, I suspect." Lucy was out of her depth and looked it. "Aw, c'mon," O'Hanrahan added, "this is sort of fun, isn't it?"

"I didn't expect that we'd be pursued by hoods, Dr. O'Hanrahan. I think I better go home."

"Now *what* have I been telling you?"

She looked at the floor. "You've been telling me to go home all along, and now I see your point, sir. I'll go quietly. I guess you better take me to the airport."

O'Hanrahan almost agreed but he stopped short. He was aware of standing there, open-mouthed, drawing a blank. Damn it, he'd gotten used to his one-woman audience.

(Ask her to stay with you, then.)

Oh I can't, he thought, not after all my rant.

(Again, Patrick, you pay the price of pride. There are things that We have set in motion—get on with it!)

O'Hanrahan busied himself by trying to break a cheap vase on his nighttable left unsmashed by the burglar. And he thought: It's a shame Lucy's leaving, since frankly I could help that girl. She's a Roman Catholic disaster in the making, a future Beatrice. O'Hanrahan could see it all in perfect focus: she would marry the first Bridgeport lout who would have her, a loser whom she would romantically devote her life to correcting, and then when it became apparent this no-count mick was a rube for life, she would enter into the oldest and most ancient conventual order for the Irish female: the nagging malcontent, made miserable by marriage, made morally superior by the all-embittering One True and Holy Roman Catholic Church—

"Sir?" Lucy demanded, still waiting for an answer.

"I'm not taking you to the goddam airport," he snapped. "Go get a cab," he added, as he dumped out his shaving kit on the floor.

"Dr. O'Hanrahan," asked Lucy, matching his calm, "why are you messing up your room even more?"

"Stay tuned."

In a moment the hotel manager appeared, a thin bald man with a humorously thick mustache: "*Signore,* my apologies! I cannot believe!" He looked around and assessed the room, the broken lock, muttered something in Italian Lucy gathered had to do with the soon-to-be-fired desk clerk. "I can't believe thees happened in the Hotel Davide!"

O'Hanrahan in a mock rage lashed out at the man: *how dare* the establishment let a criminal up to rob the guests! Just wait until Fodor and Frommer and the *New York Times Travel Magazine,* which he worked for, heard about this! Where are the carabinieri? Of course, this hotel is liable for everything that was stolen . . .

"The carabinieri, *signore?*"

No hotelier wants the carabinieri around or the Frommer guide informed, so O'Hanrahan was led to the manager's office for a soothing glass of Amaro and to discuss this regrettable incident, this regrettable incident that surely the two of them could come to some form of—how do you say?—understanding about, no?

Lucy went to her room to relax and recover from all the excitement, and lay down on the bed until she felt calm. She propped a chair before her now-unlockable door.

"Rise and shine," said O'Hanrahan, in what seemed a moment later.

She must have napped. Lucy looked at the window and it was dark outside. "What's going on?" she asked, as O'Hanrahan shoved the chair out of his way.

To avert the publicity and keep himself out of court, the hotel manager had replaced O'Hanrahan's bottle of grappa with a fine brand purchased by his secretary, as they negotiated, and the stolen money—

"*What* stolen money?"

"The extra cash I told him I keep in my shaving kit. He was more than happy to reimburse me."

Lucy sat up on the bed. "I was feeling sorry for myself, but now I see I should feel sorry for the manager. You just . . . just invented that so you could steal money from the poor man?"

"Poor man? With what this clip joint charges? Besides, I expropriated this money for *you,* Miss Dantan. For traveling expenses. We can't put everything on the credit card."

She stood up and began packing her things, shoving the unwritten postcards into her handbag. "I don't want your ill-gotten money. Although, I'll take it if it'll help me to the airport."

"But you're not going to get a flight to America tonight."

She looked at her watch. "It's not late."

"It is for Florence's airport. You could get to London maybe, spend the night in a lounge chair and get something to the U.S. in the morning."

Lucy hurled her handbag into her suitcase. "Whatever it takes to get me out of the black market."

"How are you going to pay for your ticket?"

"Your credit card," she said hopefully.

"I'm not going thirty miles out to the airport so you can pay with my credit card, nor am I giving it to you. I'm going to Assisi on the eleven P.M. *locale*, and I'm not going to miss it."

Lucy's eyes flashed frustrated anger. "Then *how* am I supposed to get out of here? I'm not staying here with some goon breaking into my room every five minutes!"

"They don't care about you, it's *me* they want, and only because they think I've got the scroll *here*." By here, O'Hanrahan meant the satchel he was now holding tightly.

Lucy sat on the bed, not sure what to do. Hitting O'Hanrahan was among the options, kicking the old goat as hard as she could in the shins.

(Patrick, you could bring some comfort to this situation.)

"Lucy," he said begrudgingly, "this scroll may be a 5th-Century pseudo-gospel, it may be a medieval fake, it may be half a dozen things. But the Ignatians went to great lengths to get it, and now the Franciscans have gone to great lengths to steal it, and Mordechai Hersch and Hebrew University have spent forty years and a ton of money to track it down, and now we know someone else wants it, and good God, we've got a University of Chicago credit card so they want it too. Doesn't it suggest we're on to something?"

Lucy still didn't say anything.

"You know, honey, if you want to stay and work with me, you can, I suppose. Maybe . . . maybe you don't want to stay, I don't guess I blame you. You're not happy, you're not well. You're complaining all the time, you hate me—"

"I *am* happy, I *don't* complain all the time, Dr. O'Hanrahan, and . . . and I *don't* hate you. But can you understand that this cloak-and-dagger stuff is sort of scary?"

He shrugged. A shared silence. O'Hanrahan took a step or two away toward the hallway, and Lucy called out: "Wait!"

He stuck his head back in the room, this white-haired, red-faced, beaming old wreck of a man with irresistible eyes. "Yesssssss?"

"Is there an airport in Assisi?"

"Not really."

"Where do we go after Assisi?"

"Rome and the Vatican libraries, I suspect, if we get the scroll."

"Always wanted to see Rome."

"The Whore of Babylon," said O'Hanrahan gravely.

So a cab was called for the back entrance to the hotel, in the event the criminal element was waiting for them out front. Amid the scrapings and apologies and extreme unctuousness of the manager, they left in a huff, wound through a maze of alleys, and claimed their cab a block away.

"The train station's just right over there," Lucy pointed out.

"We're taking the long route to see if anyone's interested in following us," said O'Hanrahan, putting his suitcase in the back. "We won't have a very good night's sleep if some thug follows us onto the train."

Lucy slid down onto the backseat. "I still don't know about this . . ."

O'Hanrahan hopped onto the backseat as well. "You'll like Rome, I promise."

The driver: "Rome, yeys! It is a byootiful ceety, no?"

"*Bellissima*," said O'Hanrahan. "*Santa Croce, per favore, signore.*"

And then the cab recklessly took off, rattling across the cobblestones of dirty, overcrowded, touristy, unfriendly, arrogant, philistine Florence, the greatest city in the world, darting at an unsafe speed through the old quarter to Santa Croce. O'Hanrahan steadily gazed out the back, but so far no sign of followers, no hope for a chase scene. Upon arriving at Piazza Santa Croce, O'Hanrahan explained to the driver that his daughter wanted a last look at the church, and redirected him to the train station.

"Santa Croce ees very byootiful, yeys?" said the taxi man.

"Yes, very byootiful," said Lucy, before sinking lower in the seat, thoroughly ill at ease. "I guess my mother wouldn't forgive me if I got to Italy and didn't get the pope's blessing," she said.

"Yeys," said the driver. "Jahn Pool Two, ey?"

Said the professor, "You don't wanna miss that guy's act. He does a mean mass, I hear. Get your mother some kitsch souvenirs, some plastic crucifices." O'Hanrahan's coinage of the plural with the second syllable accented made Lucy laugh. She nudged O'Hanrahan the next second, prompting him to notice the glove-compartment shrine of the taxi: John Paul's picture, a small nativity scene, a crucifix, the ubiquitous Mary, and hanging from the rearview mirror, numerous medallions and a crucifix. A rosary was suspended from the meter.

"Rome's so full of shuck," said O'Hanrahan, "that you can get your mother a piece of the True Cross."

"She'd like that."

"Isn't it interesting, it's always a piece of the *True* Cross, and not merely a piece of the Cross. There were so many fakes around, even the Church had to insist on it." Lucy rose up a bit and looked over at O'Hanrahan, looked at his face as he was off on another ramble: "Santa Croce del Gerusalemme, one of the Seven Pilgrimage Churches of Rome, built by Constantine's mother in 327, fresh from her Cross-finding mission to Jerusalem. I have this mental picture of Constantine sending his mother as far away as possible to get her out of his hair . . ." O'Hanrahan stretched in the seat, a slight yawn, relaxed and philosophical.

"You may get on a plane in Rome, Miss Dantan, but remember I said this. Thinking Christians, scholars like yourself and even old heathen reprobates like me, have a challenge this century. Some of what we know of Christianity is garbage, some is certainly true. Some of the quotes in the New Testament of Paul and Jesus are the work of an overzealous Early Church, some quotes are accurate. Some doctrines of Christianity have the essence of divinity, other practices are corrupt, rotten, and certainly evil. We search, you and I," and here he put a hand on her shoulder, "scholars and wise men and wise women, we search through the toothpicks and the splinters and the driftwood and counterfeit kindling, because somewhere out there, some day, we may hold before us a piece of the True Cross."

They were at the station.

O'Hanrahan bade Lucy linger in the ladies' restroom while he bought two tickets, waiting in the interminable lines. While waiting, the professor surveyed the populace: everyone looked kosher, scantily clad teenage tourists, a carpet of backpacks, kids too cheap or out too late to find a hotel, intending to camp on the station floor. O'Hanrahan returned to the ladies' toilet and Lucy anxiously peered around the doorway: "Is the coast clear, Dr. O'Hanrahan?"

"What's the password?" hissed the professor.

Lucy emerged anxiously. "I'm scared and you think this is funny. Give me my ticket."

He gave it to her, before launching into an imitation of some raspy spy-movie hero: "If I don't make it, Lucy . . . you'll tell headquarters that Little Miss Muffet will have her hand in the cookie jar at ten o'clock singing 'There'll be Bluebirds over the White Cliffs of Dover.' "

Then Lucy dug her fingernails into O'Hanrahan's arm: "*Oh my God* . . . "

"What?"

Lucy pulled her companion behind a newspaper stall, ducking down. "That man there . . ." she whispered, "in the tacky suit."

O'Hanrahan, not ducking, scanned the terminal. "This is Italy, Luce, you'll have to give me a little more to go on."

Lucy hit him in the elbow, annoyed. "The tall man, blondish. Pink-checked jacket. Yellow pants, a bolo tie."

O'Hanrahan observed him, reading a paper. "So?"

"That's the guy who drove away after the safe at the Crown was robbed! The guy with the German car."

"You're sure?"

"Who could forget that suit?"

O'Hanrahan calmly announced: "C'mon, let him see us."

They walked audaciously right in front of him. O'Hanrahan faked a sneeze so the man would look up from his magazine, which he did, then O'Hanrahan took a sharp turn at *binario* 14, the track for Rome, the train sitting right there.

Lucy: "We're going to Rome now?"

"We'll get on the train just long enough to make our friend get on it too."

They boarded with their suitcases on the uncrowded first-class carriage and lingered near the door. O'Hanrahan walked into a compartment, put down the window and looked out to see when the train was ready to leave. Mr. Cheap Suit hurried to the train, presumably without a ticket, and hopped on several cars down. The conductor on the platform looked at his watch—one minute to go. Get ready, said O'Hanrahan, who had Lucy move their suitcases to the carriage door *not* facing the platform.

The conductor blew the whistle.

"Now!" said O'Hanrahan, and Lucy opened the train door that met the neighboring tracks, and she and her winded, huffing companion scrambled down to the ground. O'Hanrahan reached back for their luggage as the starting train clunked forward, then he and Lucy ran across the tracks to the next platform.

"Hide behind the schedule board . . ." wheezed O'Hanrahan, as Lucy ahead of him stepped up onto the platform, a foot off the ground, to the amused stares of the travelers watching this last-minute change of itinerary. He joined her behind the *arrivi* and *partenze* board which listed rail timetables, safely out of view of the departing train.

Soon, the Rome train was gone.

O'Hanrahan and Lucy searched the opposite platform for some sign of the Man in the Cheap Suit. Apparently, he was bound for Rome.

"What next?" asked Lucy as the red-faced O'Hanrahan caught his breath.

"After my heart attack," he coughed, finding a bench to sit down upon, "I'd say a drink is in order."

"I don't think," Lucy said absently, "a drink would be good for my digestion, sir . . ."

After a swing past the cafe for O'Hanrahan's shot, the next destination was the *locale* train to Assisi, making every stop between Firenze and Arezzo. From Arezzo, at 2:30 A.M. they were to transfer to the Perugia line, which would take them to Assisi by dawn. It was so slow and unpractical, this train, that no one would suspect they were on it. They found a first-class compartment to themselves and O'Hanrahan got out his cherished bottle of grappa.

"We made it," he said as the local train pulled out. "Say good-bye to Florence."

"*Ciao*," she said quietly, staring out the window intently, not that there was anything pretty to see.

"Let's get the Tuscan accent up to snuff," said O'Hanrahan, taking a swig of grappa, then shuddering. "Whoa baby," he said in response. "*Ciao* is fine, but don't think *c-h*. Can you say the *ci* like it's a *t*? *Tiao.* Like that?"

After O'Hanrahan's Italian lesson, he turned off the compartment light, drew the curtains, then stretched out and joined his hands on his belly and closed his eyes. Lucy, to calm herself, had been persuaded to drink a shot of grappa and, boy, was she feeling it now. She felt sleep coming on and she stared out the window as the lights of metropolitan Florence receded. On this bright moonlit night she could see the black silhouettes of the Apennines, and on these hillsides there was the occasional light from a peasant home, from a luxurious villa—she longed to see the scenery but her imagination was just as good. What am I doing here? she laughed to herself. And the next minute, looking over at O'Hanrahan, a slumbering Jupiter, she thought: should I ever go home? Have I ever been alive until these last weeks?

And she began a prayer that trailed into sleep and the sound of the plodding *locale* train, with a mix of relics, frescoes, postcards, saints, legends, and beautiful Tuscan faces mingling freely in her dreams. And for tonight, she had no need of prayer because, like so many before her, in her heart had been spoken the Blessed Name: *Italia.*

ASSISI
July 3rd

O'Hanrahan returned from the first-class compartment lavatory, all shaven and cologned, red-faced and awake as dawn was breaking.

"So," Lucy asked through a yawn, "Assisi's a nice place?"

"One of the greatest things in the country. The Basilica of San Francesco is a palace of a church. Spectacular."

(Even so, is there any of Us acquainted with Francis who, looking upon this palace of churches, does not hear him say: "All that money to build this church! Think of the poor it might have fed!" Jesus, after all, did say *the poor will be with us always* but one imagines Francis persisting, "Even so. All the more reason it shouldn't have been built.")

"In any event," O'Hanrahan lectured, full of incomprehensible energy at 5:57 A.M., "other venerated Franciscans have not fared as well as this. Are you listening?"

"Hmm," she nodded herself alert,"yes, I'm awake."

"Across the Apennines in Padova you can see the cathedral-pile erected for St. Anthony, a Franciscan who died five years after Francis. Anthony appeared in his native Lisbon and back in Italy at the same time, in order to get his father off a murder charge. He raised the murdered corpse up from the dead, had it accuse the true murderer, and then Anthony let him fall dead again."

(The most ungentlemanly miracle of the great saints.)

"Anthony was exhumed by Bonaventura, that tiresome hack, in 1263." O'Hanrahan knew this would enliven Lucy: "Only the tongue and upper bridge of Anthony remained incorrupt amid the putrefaction of the corpse."

"I can't believe you're doing this before breakfast," said Lucy.

"And Bonaventure took these fragments of Anthony's blessed mouth and brought the dried, swollen tongue to his lips to cover with kisses—"

"I had a feeling this would work itself around to something Italian and foul," said Lucy, as the train slowed down for the station.

"It gives a new spin to the French kiss, wouldn't you say? *Il bacio alla francescana*, so to speak, hm?"

The train slowly rumbled into the Assisi station.

Lucy and he stepped from their old-fashioned train car, lugging suitcases behind them. Lucy observed that they were two of only five people to disembark at Assisi this early morning. The station was dead, fog covered the green fields around the tracks. The conductor whistled and the train lurched forward, destined for Spoleto.

O'Hanrahan nodded his head in the direction of the north. "Over these mountains, Luce, is Loreto and the Sacred House of the Translation."

Lucy had heard of that one. "Mary's house, right? That flew over from Nazareth and ended up in Italy."

In 1294. The house in which the Blessed Virgin received the announcement that she would bear the Christchild began that year hopping around the Mediterranean. The *Casa Santa*, after touching down in Yugoslavia, picked up again and landed on a hillside outside of Ancona. Despite its suspiciously Italian appearance and construction from Italian bricks, a fact-finding team was dispatched from Rome to corroborate the story and sure enough, in Nazareth there was a gap where Mary's house used to be, and measurements were made to show there was no doubt.

(Pilgrims take heart from the Vatican: "*It is the House of Our Lady, the House in which she received the Annunciation. It is filled with the Holy*

Spirit. Mary lived there and dwelt here in Her holiness." That was John Paul II. In 1984.)

"And without a hint, an infinitessima of irony," O'Hanrahan went on, "Rome has made the Lauretian flying house and its madonna the patron saint of aviators." He chuckled. "You have to develop an affection for this kind of nonsense or you'd go crazy as a Catholic. It makes the empty triumphalism of Pius IX, worst pope since the Middle Ages, all the more damning. Did I ever go into—"

But rounding the corner into the depot lobby, O'Hanrahan froze, and Lucy looked up to see what had stopped him in middisquisition: Gabriel. Gabriel was in his friar's robes, asleep, slumped uncomfortably on a bench. His thin frame seemed lost in the rough brown robes. Lucy watched O'Hanrahan walk over to the bench and startle Gabriel awake by blasting *matins* at him at full volume:

"*Pulsi procul torporibus, surgamus omnes ocius,* you little Judas!"

Gabriel jumped awake: "Oh hello, Patrick . . ."

"Shall I sacrifice you here, or pitch you from the walls of the basilica?"

Gabriel tried to hurry himself awake. "Uh, can I explain—"

"I've been waiting two months for an explanation, you little runt," said O'Hanrahan. "Not that it will satisfy me!"

O'Hanrahan paced back and forth before his former assistant, emphasizing the occasional item with a sharp pointing of the accusing finger, which made Gabriel startle every time: "When you said you'd accompany me, it was clear that you swore allegiance to the project. Damn you, Gabriel, you told me you were going to *leave* the Franciscan order! How'd they get to you? They brainwash you? Pay you thirty pieces of silver? You *steal* the scroll from me, Gabriel? *Twice,* no less? I didn't think you were capable of this kind of deception . . ."

"Patrick, if you'd just—"

"The scroll *is* here, isn't it?"

"Yes, and they're expecting you at Santa Maria degli Angeli." Gabriel looked at Lucy and said, "I'll phone them and tell them you're coming too." Taking advantage of the brief calm in the tirade, he fished for a measure of sympathy: "I've been here for two days camping out, making sure I'd catch you."

"You caught me all right," snapped O'Hanrahan. "I'm off to Santa Maria and later this morning I'll see your superiors and find out what you people are up to. And as I don't need to talk to you, I don't think I will."

O'Hanrahan picked up his suitcase and satchel and stormed out to the front of the station. Gabriel looked up at Lucy sorrowfully.

"Guess Patrick didn't want to hear my story. He'll be happy when he hears the whole story. You know, Lucy, we've got to talk sometime."

Every mothering instinct rose to the surface at this scene, and Lucy felt joy at this reunion, a qualified determination that things were not distant between them after all, and a pang of desire. She really intended—no, really, she did this time—not to let their being together pass without demanding of her friend an account of their unspoken semiromance. Here in Italy was a perfect place to discuss everything. David McCall was just a dry run for this encounter—

"Luuuucy!" bellowed O'Hanrahan from the front of the station. He had found a taxi and poked its driver awake.

Lucy wanted to linger but the wrath of O'Hanrahan was worse, so she told Gabriel, "Find me and get in touch," then scurried with her suitcase to the waiting taxi.

Santa Maria degli Angeli is a suburb out on the flat plain before the medieval Assisi up on the hill. St. Francis wanted to get away from it all and founded his order here in the Porziuncola, a brick shack now overdecorated with a shimmering icon and other offerings; to the side of that is the chapel where Francis died, as a result of a botched medieval medical treatment, and in the neighborhood of that is the rose bush that St. Francis threw himself on in a bout of worldly tempta-tion. The flowers turned from white to red in honor of his blood, and the thorns immediately fell off as a sign of respect. All these sites are within the cavernous Basilica di Santa Maria degli Angeli, which is the official headquarters of the Friars Minor—Franciscans and Poor Clares. In this village of parking lots for tour buses, religious book-stores, souvenir shops, and hostels for visiting Minors and Minoresses is the bureaucracy of the holy order.

And as Gabriel promised, they were expected at the Franciscan headquarters. They were given rooms for as long as they wanted them, and they were given habits to wear.

"You're kidding," said Lucy.

"They have been issued for our own safety," said O'Hanrahan sim-ply.

"Do I have to wear it?"

"Here, take it, Sister Lucy," said O'Hanrahan, draping the habit over her unwilling arm. "You can't keep walking around in that giant red hat—we're sure to be spotted."

"I didn't *have* the giant red hat before yesterday, you'll recall."

"This is your key," he said, pressing one in her hand. "You Poor Clares are over there . . ." He meant the building across the court. "A cell to yourself. Watch it, though, we friars are going to stage a panty raid a little later tonight!"

She just looked at him, unamused.

"Of course, I hear Poor Clares are too poor to wear anything under-neath those habits, huh? Except those kind of pink crotchless panties you see advertised in the *National Catholic Reporter*?"

Lucy shook her head. *"One* lightning bolt is all it would take, Dr. O'Hanrahan. One bolt from above and you'd be gone."

"That's why I say these things indoors. Go."

So she went. She checked in with a pleasant sister who spoke a smattering of English. Lucy asked about laundry and there was a sister assigned to that lowly task, though she didn't collect Lucy's dirty clothes with the joyous smile her vow of humble obedience required. And Lucy, now in her second-floor room, overlooking the backside of the Basilica Santa Maria degli Angeli—ghastly, monumental thing!—sat on her bed and contemplated the habit.

Looks like Mother's going to get her way after all: Lucy in the habit, Sister Lucy, bride of Christ. She got undressed and slipped the habit on. A modern habit, stylish really, functional for charity work, a knee-length skirt, rather fashionable collar and bead belt, pretty snazzy actually. Nice lines.

†   †   †

O'Hanrahan ordered a light, unsatisfactory breakfast in the refectory, then donned his Franciscan robe and rode the shuttle bus into Assisi. It is a town of carefully stacked pink and white rock following the contour on the higher hills to the south, and culminating in the north at the huge bastioned fortress of the Basilica di San Francesco, ponderously imposing its will upon the Umbrian farmland beneath it. How long had it been since O'Hanrahan had wandered the shambling alleys and passages of rough-hewn crumbling walls, had ascended and descended the worn-smooth marble streets, this village baked each day into medieval preservation, a city of chaste white stone lifted against the deep blue Italian sky announcing its purity and sacred fame to the world.

Francescano, mused O'Hanrahan, etymologically related to "Frenchman." Ironic—the last epithet applicable to the least worldly of men. O'Hanrahan, now off the bus, ducked into a *bar-pasticceria* for a strong reorienting coffee and one of the many little pastries. Difference between France and Italy, thought O'Hanrahan: in Italy the pastries always taste as good as they look. A glance at the clock showed it was nine. Better get tangling with the Franciscans over with . . .

O'Hanrahan walked toward the Basilica di San Francesco, two showstopper churches, one sitting on top of the other: the Lower Church, a basement of vaults and shadows, dank and medieval; the Upper Church, the gothic perfection of Italy, a long nave capped by a ceiling of aquamarine blue worthy of the Sardinian coast, gold stars affixed, and along the walls, the famous frescoes by Giotto depicting the life of St. Francis, the renunciation of his inheritance before his father, the Dark Night of the Soul, receiving of the stigmata . . .

"*Professore O'Hanana* . . ."

"That's me," said O'Hanrahan, identifying himself to the young semi-English-speaking novice.

"You weel come? Here. Weeth me?" he requested unsurely.

O'Hanrahan followed the languid young man down a series of old corridors, across groaning wooden floors, by tapestries hung on the walls to hide the lack of repair, carpets on the slanted floors doing the same. The professor was deposited on a lumpy sofa in a room with a Minoress typing slowly on a manual typewriter. There was a modern tapestry from the '60s, no doubt thought to be very with-it then, but lurid and obvious now, bits of shag carpet sewn together. Along a wall, next to a bookcase full of tomes surely unopened since Francis's day, were a row of small statues, a plastic Mary, a kneeling, stigmatized Francis. Geez, thought O'Hanrahan, they have the artists of the world at their disposal and this is all they can do—

"*Professore,*" said a small man, standing in the doorway to a further office. "Welcome to Assisi, welcome!"

O'Hanrahan stood and received a brotherly pair of kisses from the father—Father Paco Vico, as it turned out, one of the chief librarians of the order. O'Hanrahan offered to speak Italian.

"Oh no no," sniffed Father Vico, "*mio inglese*—" He kissed his fingers. "*É perfetto!* We will have the good conversation, no?"

O'Hanrahan, reserving judgment, followed the friar inside his office, which was simple and appropriate, tan plaster walls, wooden beams above, shelves of books, a stark crucifix on one wall, and a window that looked out on the rolling countryside.

"You are an Irishman, yes?" said Vico, going behind his desk and sitting, swallowed by his much taller chair.

"Well, Irish-American."

"Theen you will like some tea in the morning, no?"

No. But O'Hanrahan politely said yes, that would be nice.

Father Vico pressed an irritating buzzer and the effeminate novice knocked quickly and entered. The novice, incensed for some reason, was ordered to fetch some tea.

"*Tè?*" the novice mumbled. "*Non ce n'é. Dove trovo il tè a quest'ora del mattino, padre?*"

"*Antonio, ora sono impegnato. Ma no sará cosí difficile! Ora va, per cortesia.*"

The novice made a sound like a horse, and turned to depart.

O'Hanrahan cleared his throat, "If it's a problem . . ."

"No problem, no problem. Thees," said Father Vico, with a swirling gesture, "thees is an international community. Cosmopolitan, ey?"

"Yes, Father." O'Hanrahan tried to commence business. "As for the scroll that young Brother Gabriel, uh, removed from the safe . . ."

Father Vico waved him quiet, "Sssssh ssssh, no, wait." He put his hand up for silence, smiling flatly, "Wait until your tea has arrived. I don't theenk young Antonio needs to hear, *capisce?*"

O'Hanrahan sighed compliance.

A minute went by. O'Hanrahan made eye contact with Father Vico once and they smiled at each other. Antonio entered presently with a paper cup and a tea bag in it.

"*Una coppa? Una coppa di carta? Che bella, Antonio—ma non abbiamo qualcosa di meglio? Antonio, Antonio . . .*"

O'Hanrahan watched them argue about the indecency of the paper cup, and look there's no milk. So Antonio was off in search of a proper cup and saucer, and O'Hanrahan's cold tea finally arrived in a souvenir mug with a design of Assisi on it. Antonio, grumbling, withdrew from the room at last.

"The tea ees all right?"

"Just fine."

"You are sure?"

O'Hanrahan wasn't about to recommence another round of tea making. "*É superbo, signore.*"

Father Vico, sat back, apparently satisfied. "*Bene, bene.*"

O'Hanrahan smiled politely.

Father Vico: "What ees this scroll, *esattamente*, hm?"

"Father, do *you* not know what the scroll is?"

"*Si, si*—of course, I know what it is *supposed* to be. What your assistant, Gabriel, said it was. He says it is," Father Vico here looked at the ceiling, "a gospel of the disciple Matthias, yes?" The father joined his hands together seriously. "But, surely. Ees not possible, eh?"

O'Hanrahan was wary of making the Franciscans value the scroll too highly and maybe keep it. "Naturally," began O'Hanrahan, "I do not know. It might be a fake, a pseudo-gospel written centuries after Matthias, it might be a worthless curiosity. I haven't had a chance to translate it. What with Brother Gabriel stealing it from me on two occasions."

Father Vico persevered. "The script is odd, is it not? We have tried ourselves here to—how you say—*decifrare?*"

"Decipher it."

"Decipher it, yes. We cannot. We have never seen the language before. Our Chief Librarian says it is like, what is it?" Father Vico searched his disorganized desk for a little slip of paper, he looked here, he looked there . . . ah, there it was. Now where were his spectacles? He looked in that drawer—no—and he looked in that drawer, not there either . . . He had them out a minute ago—perhaps, by the bookcase, no. Not in his habit, but he checked anyway. Ah, here they are, on the desk all along. He put on his glasses and took a look at the word he had written down so carefully: "Yes. Oxyree . . . ocheerick . . ."

"Oxyrhynchene," said O'Hanrahan, impatient to his depths. "Yes, it is similar—your librarian is very smart. But, alas, it is not Oxyrhynchene."

"No," sighed Father Vico, folding his paper. "It is not Oxyrhy . . . Oxyree . . ."

"Oxyrhynchene."

"Yes, it is not that."

Silence, for a moment.

"You *do* have the scroll, don't you, Father?" asked O'Hanrahan.

As if it were an afterthought, Father Vico nodded distractedly. "Um, yes yes, we have it. With the exception of an ultimate—how you say?—chapter?"

"Yes, a final chapter is missing."

"Yes, well, what there is, we have."

"It is, of course, the property of Hebrew University in Jerusalem," reminded the professor.

"Of course, they have lost it many times, have they not?"

"It was stolen, Father," said O'Hanrahan delicately.

"And now we have it here, is it not so?"

Father Vico sat back in his chair. He looked at the ceiling, the ancient wooden beams. He looked at the wall that contained the tapestry, St. Francis before his father, taken from the Giotto frescoes next door. Father Vico then looked out his window. "Of course," he said blandly, "we shall be happy to return the scroll to Hebrew University. In time."

"In time."

"Yes, in time. We would, *oseremmo insistere, professore*, insist that you yourself translate the scroll." Father Vico remained fixed on the window. "So many people are looking for it that should not possess it, we feel it is best that you work on it under our protection. In Assisi."

O'Hanrahan withheld comment.

"Thees cannot fall into the wrong hands, *professore*—the black market, a private collector. What if I were to tell you that we have learned that one of our Greek Orthodox brethren, in the spirit of the Gelasian Decrees . . ." He took a deep breath. ". . . has attempted to procure this scroll so he may destroy it, to put it in the flames. Yes, yes ees true."

This is the first O'Hanrahan had heard of this.

Father Vico: "Yes, a Mad Monk stalking Assisi—a thing to make worry for, no?"

"Perhaps you are mistaken," said O'Hanrahan, chilled at that prospect.

Father Vico, seeing he had O'Hanrahan's attention, continued, "Last month we had a visit from this monk. All up and down Italy he has been, every library, every ancient collection. He asks for the *Gospel of Matthias* by name."

O'Hanrahan was meanwhile thinking of the possibilities. O'Hanrahan had made a trip to the Athens library looking for Eusebius scrolls in late May, a trip to the Metropolitan's Library in Athens to look at their African scrolls in April . . . it's just barely possible a librarian might have put two and two together. Or more likely, thought O'Hanrahan, that he himself had blabbed too much. Oh, God. Who was he kidding? He'd been telling anyone who would listen for the last forty years that such a scroll existed and he intended to conquer it!

O'Hanrahan tried at least to console himself. "Perhaps your Mad Monk, Father, is not really a monk. Perhaps he is a collector disguised?"

Father Vico didn't think so. "Oh, no, he is a monk—this I know well. Gray beard, black robe, an old man."

A description that fit every Orthodox monk in the world, thought O'Hanrahan.

"He will be perhaps a problem," said Father Vico. "As will the Mafia."

"The . . . the Mafia?"

"Yes. That is why *we* stole it, so they would not."

"The Mafia?" the professor repeated dumbly.

Here Father Vico came to focus, leaning forward, lowering his voice. "It will not come as a shock to a man, as yourself, who knows the ways of Rome, that the Mafia will do the bidding of the Vatican. You have heard thees? It is not without a, eh, *particella* of truth."

The Mafia imagine themselves to be good Catholics, the father explained, and though the Vatican hardly sanctions their efforts or laundered money, neither do they reject what is given in the spirit of Christian atonement . . . "The process is inevitable, no? The pope makes his wishes known to his cardinals who mention it to the bishops who talk about thees at lunch in the *trattorie* in Trastevere," Father Vico continued, making an ever-turning wheel with his hands, "and soon the diocesan priest knows, everyone knows. What the pope wants is not a secret in Rome."

Might yesterday's afternoon caller in Florence have been an emissary of the Mafia? O'Hanrahan decided not to volunteer that information, because he didn't trust the Franciscans either.

Father Vico looked out his window again, chuckling. "The Mafia, 'Ndrangheta, the Camorra, whoever, thinks, you see, if they please the pope by bringing him thees scroll—ah, who is to say? Hundreds of years off in the purgatory, no?" Father Vico settled back in his chair serenely. "And the Vatican, however they get their hands on it, *want* it."

"Why do they want it?"

"To bury it," he said convincingly. "It ees very dangerous, no? A gospel of the First Century, the oldest existing gospel on earth." Father Vico, shrewder than he at first seemed, raised his eyebrows. "A gospel without a pope? Maybe . . . maybe thees scroll would make to revolutionize our notion of the Church. Maybe poverty, charity would be the message, as Jesus taught, as St. Francis taught. Perhaps there was never supposed to *be* a central Church, hm? What if thees work shows that Jesus had no Resurrection?"

Father Vico shrugged and joined his hands again.

"That, it may surprise you, would make little difference to our order, *professore*. Jesus is of God and whether he was a Begotten Son, to some of us today, makes little difference. To feed the poor. *That* matters. To clothe the naked. *That* matters. To rid the world of fascism and tyranny and poverty and oppression. *That* matters. If Christ were just a holy man . . ." He shrugged again. ". . . many here among us now would not falter in our mission." He looked O'Hanrahan directly in the eye. "But what a tremendous difference it would make to the pope, hm?"

O'Hanrahan felt a smile creep across his face. He'd missed this, the *Romanitá*: the wheeling and dealing of the Church. The Jesuit in him was aroused! And why shouldn't the Franciscans want to keep this out of papal hands? Since Pope Paul VI let everything go to hell, the Roman Catholic orders have been steadily mounting deep opposition to the all-demanding papacy—most acutely the Jesuits and the Franciscans—but also the Maryknoll Fathers, the Carmelites, virtually every American scholar of note in every North American seminary of note, Liberation theologians, scores of progressive left-wing and socialist Catholics.

"I see you are theenking thees over, no?" said the father.

O'Hanrahan nodded with a polite smile. Not since the disastrous, criminal Pius XII had there been a more conservative pope regarding his own divine authority than John Paul II. In addition to the intrusion into the Jesuit elections, he'd even toyed with the cloistered Carmelite order, demanding they return to the unworkable 1581 Constitutions of St. Teresa. John Paul's Cardinal Casaroli, hatchetman of the moment, had informed the nuns if they didn't like living in medieval squalor they could leave their order.

(It seemed to slip the infallible mind that Paul VI had approved the modernization of the Carmelites.)

The Dominicans, persistent in going their own way, elected Father Damian Byrne, fan of the papally unpopular Edward Schillebeeckx, in 1983. Then the struggle moved here, to Assisi and the 1985 Franciscan election for Minister General. John Paul then published a blunt open letter calling for the Franciscans to return to the obedience of the original rule. The election, held on the anniversary of John Paul's near-assassination, resulted in the California progressive, Father John Vaughan, being returned to office in a safe majority. His acceptance speech was full of Third World concerns, wars and refugees, an easing away from capitalism, materialism—the sole guide was "absolute fidelity to the Gospel."

Yes, O'Hanrahan now reflected, fidelity to gospel accounts and to the early communal Christianity, priestless and bishopless, would not go down well with Rome, and the *Gospel of Matthias* would definitely be a trump-card in any theological debate should the Franciscans continue to go their own way ... Father Vico was tactically astute: the Vatican can't be let anywhere near the scroll.

"We would like," Father Vico continued, slowly and carefully, "to oversee, if we may, your work on this. If ees revolutionary, thees new gospel, if it is genuine, we will support you and your conclusions. Rome, of course, will scurry to dismiss you."

A good bet, considering how the Vatican initially condemned the Dead Sea Scrolls, O'Hanrahan remembered.

"You'll forgive us the presumption ..." Here Father Vico smiled faintly at O'Hanrahan. ". . . of removing this from the Jesuits, hm? Many of the Society of Jesus, these so-called Ignatians, are quite conservative, no? Who remember their oath of complete loyalty to the Bishop of Rome."

O'Hanrahan smiled. "And after I translate the scroll, Father, it will be returned to its rightful owner, Hebrew University?"

"Of course," he shrugged. "After the truth of what ees there ees known. After the world knows."

"There is one problem, Monsignor," said the professor. "Assisi, I fear, does not have the resources for me to penetrate the mysteries of this scroll."

Father Vico nodded without expression.

"I must use, I suspect, the Vatican Library, perhaps the monasteries in Greece, I may have to go with the scroll to Jerusalem, to Cairo for all I know, since, I believe, it's written in some mysterious African language."

A faint smile from Father Vico. "It ees not a problem, *professore*. We have churches everywhere, no? You have made, I imagine, a photographing of the text of the scroll?"

The professor said he had. "But, honestly, my friend. I feel I must ask you if I may *see* the scroll now."

Father Vico weighed this, at last consenting. "Ah, it ees good that you trust no one in this. Not even me. Antonio!"

Antonio, fearing another beverage request, was instructed rather to bring in the safe. From the outer office Antonio produced a huge, jangling ring of keys and unlocked a closet door that had three locks. From this emerged a little combination safe on wheels. Antonio with difficulty rolled it across the cross-grained floor and edges of rugs, which offered resistance.

"It ees completely secure, *professore*," Father Vico said proudly.

O'Hanrahan stared at this ridiculous little safe. "Surely," he began, "this could be broken into . . ."

"I alone," said Father Vico, raising a finger, "know the combination and I alone possess the keys to the room it dwells in. Ask your assistant Gabriel. He himself saw me put our treasure into this safe."

O'Hanrahan insisted he would *still* like to see the document.

"Ah, very well . . ."

Father Vico creakingly got to his knees, groaning and cursing his stiffness, and after ordering everyone to look away, he dialed the combination, opened the safe, and presented O'Hanrahan with the scroll in a secure, clear plastic airtight envelope.

Yep, it was the one.

Father Vico: "We will follow you, wherever you must go, with the original manuscript, guarded by our brethren, safe and in our hands. Do you know San Francesco a Ripa in Trastevere?"

O'Hanrahan and the father arranged to meet again in Rome at this Franciscan fort in the shadow of Vatican City. Father Vico offered to O'Hanrahan that he and Brother Gabriel could stay there, in fact, if they so desired—

"I have no further use," clarified O'Hanrahan, "of his services. If he was capable of betraying me, he might well be capable of betraying *us*. He didn't have to steal the scroll, Father. If he had put it to me as you have, I would have given it to you."

Father Vico waved this aside. "Do not be too harsh on him. We did not explain anything to him. We just told him it was of the great urgency for him to bring us Matthias. We did not want to alarm him with tales of . . ." He made an empty gesture. ". . . *mafiosi*, and papal politics, hm? Now that you are here and the scroll ees here and we are all happy . . . there is no cause of anger."

O'Hanrahan bowed his head unenthusiastically.

"Your tea is cold—we have talked and I have not let you drink it. *Mi dispiace*, I shall give you some more tea—"

"No, that's all right."

"Ees no trouble—"

"No, I'm fine, really—"

"But it ees no problem—"

Etc.

Meanwhile in the town, Lucy saw the sights. She had taken a nap and had been awakened around eleven A.M. by a sister saying there had been a message. She eagerly bounded down to the desk to get it, hoping Gabriel had made contact, but it was only an O'Hanrahan phone message that commanded her presence by Assisi's basilica, lower entrance, at 1:30, on the dot.

"Lucy!" boomed O'Hanrahan.

"Dr. O'Hanrahan," she called out, rushing across the parking lot and forcing her camera in his hand. "Could you please? A picture in front of the basilica? In my nun's suit. It'll be good for a joke one day."

O'Hanrahan complied. Lucy couldn't fool him, though. She was thrilled to be posing there, in the uniform of the Poor Clares. O'Hanrahan returned to a thought he had entertained in Ireland: How do we do it? Take our young Catholic women and confine them, neuter them, harass them with chastity and renunciations. Poor girl, he thought, focusing the camera on Lucy. She had a set look for photos that wasn't flattering, a tense, unnatural squint.

"Relax your face," said O'Hanrahan.

"It is relaxed."

Screw it, take it anyway. O'Hanrahan was eager to get to lunch.

Lunch was in a place O'Hanrahan remembered from years ago. It had changed owners and menus and now took credit cards and was probably ruined but it was too hot to search for quaintness, so the little place in via San Ruffino would have to do. He immediately checked the wineracks along the wall.

"Rosé wine? We better seize the moment," said O'Hanrahan, motioning to the waitress and procuring a bottle of local Umbrian *rosato*. The waitress was ignorant when asked what vineyard produced this nectar. "*Il nombre della Rosé*," he joked, though Lucy didn't register. No matter, O'Hanrahan poured the pink wine. Lucy celebrated with half a glass.

"I see the spirit of denial has not abated," noted O'Hanrahan.

"If I drank a whole glass, I'd fall asleep, which I don't want to do because this town is so marvelous. I went up to Santa Chiara this morning."

"Did you see the veiled nuns?"

"Yes," said Lucy taking a sip of the *rosato*. "Clare's incorrupt body was there, dark and shriveled up. So I thought of you."

(St. Clare was less of a wimp than her pamphlet biographies of timid obedience would have one believe. When the indefatigable Frederick Barbarossa marched on Assisi, St. Clare placed the consecrated host in a monstrance and marched to the highest point of the city walls. The sight of her there, sickly, held up by her fellow sisters, against the wind, imbued with a power not of this world, caused Frederick uncharacteristically to retreat. Unarmed Assisi was spared.)

"There's so much legend," said Lucy, thinking back on her sightseeing. "My guidebook said the famous stigmata of Francis never existed.

He saw them, but they weren't present on his body. That's the most famous thing about Francis and it isn't even true."

"Same with St. Catherine of Siena," said O'Hanrahan, tearing at the bread. "Only she could see her stigmata as well. And her wedding ring." The professor fixed Lucy with a gleam in his eye.

Should she ask?

(You'll just be putting off the inevitable if you don't.)

Their pasta arrived and Lucy decided to risk a repeat of yesterday's unappetizing lecture. "Catherine's wedding ring?"

O'Hanrahan held forth: St. Catherine of Siena, who practiced the 14th-Century arts of masochism and self-flagellation, the first famous anorexic and bulimic, who would punish herself by throwing up whatever she had eaten, who gave new resonance to the phrase "eat dirt," because she did, was happy to share her mystical visions, which involved a marriage with Christ, the Virgin giving away her son with her blessing, and Christ walking down the heavenly steps to embrace her amid her raptures and ecstasies. As a sign of their union, Christ placed on her finger his discarded circumcised foreskin as a wedding ring.

Lucy slowed in her eating of the *ditali* in cream sauce. "You're doing it to me again, aren't you?"

"Now later in life, Sister Lucy, this ring that only she could see, as part of her divine humiliation, changed its aspect and she was blinded by its brilliance when she looked at her hand, so laden with the jewels of Heaven it was, so dazzling was Christ's ruby-encrusted, diamond-studded foreskin."

"This woman was made a *saint*?"

"Funny thing," said O'Hanrahan, enjoying his pasta, "one generation's crackpot, burned at the stake, becomes the next generation's saint. Trot out the foreskin story in Salem, Massachusetts, in the late 1600s and see where it'd get you. St. Anthony fed the consecrated host to a mule, to show how even the animals desire the eucharist while humans are lazy and don't go to church. The Church has killed thousands of Jews for lesser imagined profanations."

"Well, let's not talk about Divine Body Parts, if we could—"

"You mean, like The Holy Placenta?"

Lucy called his bluff. "No way."

"Yes indeed, there was a Holy Placenta relic and a Holy Umbilical Cord relic, both in the treasury of St. John Lateran in Charlemagne's time. One imagines if merely touching the hem of Christ's garment could get one healed, that there was a path beaten to the placenta. Ancient peoples and Mediterranean alike commonly eat the placenta as sort of a folk ritual. Maybe the placenta in the Lateran was a fake, and the real one was cooked up by Mary and Joseph. A little salt, a little garlic . . ."

Lucy chewed resolutely. "Would there have been a placenta in a Divine Birth by a woman who was immaculately conceived?"

"These are the types of questions—like whether Christ had a navel—that obsessed the medieval Church. You see icons and portrayals of the Crucifixion with and without navels, depending on the disposition of the artist toward Christ's humanity. More curious would be Mary's physiology." O'Hanrahan tore at the heel of the bread loaf. "Do you suppose a clitoris was provided for her?"

Lucy nearly spewed the wine across the table. "Sorry," she stammered.

"If she was conceived without sin and is held by the Greeks to be the *Theotokos* and the Catholic Church to be this half-holy, perfection-bearing vessel, one has to wonder if she had the capacity for such sinful stimulation."

"One does *not* have to wonder," said Lucy, who had found her voice. "Listening to you is enough to make you wanna turn Protestant."

"Curious you should say that in Assisi. St. Francis *was* the first Protestant, preaching fidelity to the gospels over Church tradition. Within a few generations, radical Franciscans were being burned at the stake for exhorting poverty to the pope. One of my favorite bits of Vatican-think was John XXII's 14th-Century *Quia vir reprobus*."

(A sterling defense of papal materialism, which insisted Christ approved of his apostles owning possessions. John decided that God gave Paradise to Adam and Eve as *property*, an investment, real estate that they were to own.)

"The papacy merely wished to return man to that prelapsarian state . . ."

"Whoo boy," said Lucy. O'Hanrahan poured himself another glass and Lucy allowed him to provide her with another half-glass while Lucy did some inner calculations: "You mean to tell me," she asked, "that there are no Pope Johns from the time of Avignon until the John XXIII who was pope when I was growing up?"

(Our beloved John XXIII, the briefly reigning pope of the 1960s, was a big St. John fan and he tried to rehabilitate the name, the most numerous of the papal nomenclatures, but also one of the most tainted. If he had lived longer Our John might have rehabilitated Catholicism.)

"John was an unlucky name," said O'Hanrahan, recollecting. John I went to Byzantium in 526 and got such a lavish reception that it made King Theodoric of Italy jealous—the pope was consequently imprisoned until his death. John III was chased out of Rome by the Lombards; John VIII is the first pope to be assassinated—first poisoned unsuccessfully, then clubbed to death. John XII turned the Lateran into a brothel with an oriental harem, surrounding himself with courtesans and virgins to defile. Several synods convened to depose him, but they needn't have bothered because his sexual appetites destroyed his health, and while performing in the papal bed with a married woman he suffered a stroke . . . at twenty-seven."

"Good going," said Lucy, impressed.

O'Hanrahan's list continued. "John XIV was deposed by a pretender to the throne, flung into prison, and allowed to starve to death. One Pope John, you'll be interested to know, was a woman."

Lucy was skeptical.

"Look in Siena Cathedral," he suggested. "Amid the gilt and barber-shop stripes of this temple of Ghibelline excess, is a statue of every pope up to the present time. There is among them a bust of a woman. Reformers like Hus and Luther and Calvin were familiar with Pope Joan and used it in their tirades against Rome's corruption. And Rome never denied it."

(Here's what happened: under all the robes, a young woman of great learning and piety was able to fool her fellow cardinals all the way to the papacy in the 800s. For two years she ruled, beloved by the people, only to be discovered as a woman when she gave birth during a public procession . . . the poor thing was so otherworldly that she wasn't aware of the mechanics of sex and was taken advantage of by an unscrupulous priest. At times, Pope Joan truly forgot she was a woman. But she is with Us now where there is no man and woman.)

"And to this day, papal parades avoid the old route between the Colosseum and San Clemente," O'Hanrahan concluded. "Where she dropped the kid."

"Cool," said Lucy, approving of an equal-opportunity papacy.

"John XVI," related O'Hanrahan with savor, "ran afoul of the Holy Roman Emperor's wrath and had his eyes put out, his tongue pulled out, his nose cut off, his lips torn off, his hands mutilated, and then he was put backward on a mule and paraded through the city where refuse and dung were hurled at him by the populace, always ready for a show. Then he was left to rot in a monastery. He lived on for years."

"I think we've had enough of Pope Johns, thank you," said Lucy.

"The ceiling fell in on John XXI."

"I don't care."

Soon, Lucy and the professor found themselves alone in the *trattoria* and they took the hint to leave from Mama, who emerged to gather crumb-covered tablecloths and sweep up, impatient but not one to overtly rush the *religiosi*. They paid the bill and stood outside for a moment and declared their afternoon activities:

"I'm going back to the monastery to look at the scroll," said O'Hanrahan. "It's a waste of time, but I thought I'd skim the library here and see if anything on Matthias or proto-Oxyrhynchene turns up."

"That term sounds familiar. Oxy . . ."

O'Hanrahan could live happily never saying the damn word again.

"Oxyrhynchus was a Roman city in Egypt and the African-influenced dialect of early Coptic writings is Oxyrhynchene."

"Sounds like an acne medicine." Then Lucy's face changed. "I *don't* believe it."

"What?" O'Hanrahan turned to see a beaming, waving figure approach. "That's uh, the guy from yesterday—"

"Farley," she said blankly.

"He likes you, Sister Lucy. I saw him stealing glances at the market. We'll be leaving Assisi soon, so you don't have much time. Gotta work fast if you want the big date."

Farley approached them and smiled, then wondered if he'd made a mistake because of Lucy's nun's habit. "Hi, Lucy, remember me?"

Lucy, slightly blushing, managed, "Hi, Farley."

"Man alive, you really *are* Catholic, aren't you?"

"What brings you to Assisi?" said Lucy, wishing the professor wasn't hulking there smiling at them both.

"Well, I was gonna go straight on to Rome, but you said Assisi'uz worth seeing, so here I am."

"What a coincidence," said O'Hanrahan, putting a fatherly hand on Farley's shoulder. "We'll be in Rome next, for a week or so. You'll have to drop in and see us. That is, when Sister Lucy isn't doing her special assignment for the pope."

"Sister Lucy?" said Farley, crestfallen. "Oh, hello to you too, sir. I didn't recognize you in your monk outfit."

O'Hanrahan went into his now-familiar hyper-Irish parish priest: "Ah, Lucy darlin', I must be off to mass and have a wee tipple with the bishop. Bless you, Sister." He made several signs of the cross over an unamused Lucy, then over Farley too. "And bless ye too, my lad. *Virgo virginum praeclara, mihi iam non sis amara.* Don't forget, Sister, confession at nine tonight. My room!"

And then O'Hanrahan headed downhill to the main square, leaving Farley perplexed, but more or less confirmed in his vision of Catholic mumbo-jumbo anyway.

"Pay no attention to Father O'Hanrahan," said Lucy, striking an air of beatitude.

"I didn't know you were, like, a nun."

"I may retire soon."

"You can do that?"

"With the pope's permission," she said, vaguely annoyed with herself for playing these games with her rustic acquaintance. Today Farley's fashion sense was down a notch in jeans and a T-shirt, a John Deere farmer's cap to shield him from the sun. But the kind of looks that grow on you, thought Lucy.

"My daddy says the pope isn't any more special'n anybody else and his being a big deal ain't really the work of Jesus."

"A lot of Franciscans at the moment would agree with you, Farley," she said, now looking for some escape. "Are you traveling by yourself?"

"Oh, no. I'm over here with some people from my school, my Bible College I was telling you about, back in Louisiana? We're gonna do Rome, Nazareth, Jerusalem."

"Right," said Lucy, stopping at the entrance to a small church. The sign in front announced San Francesco Piccolino. "I think I have to say my rosary now, Farley." Poor kid, she thought, he was really disappointed they couldn't be friends. Okay, he is not the end of the world, cute in his own Southern right-out-of-the-barn way, but you can do a lot better than this, your track record notwithstanding—

"Can I watch you doing it?"

"I beg your pardon?"

"Your rosary. I'm sort of curious. Do you pray to the Virgin Mary?"

Lucy crossed her arms. "You could, I guess. Jesus, God, the Holy Spirit whom I prefer, and the saints. Pray to any or all, mix and match."

Farley wasn't convinced, shook his head. "I don't think you're supposed to pray to people like St. Francis."

"John Calvin, the most radical Protestant reformer and enemy of the Catholic Church, held Perseverance of the Saints to be doctrine, Farley. *First Corinthians* 6:2, *Do you not know that the saints will judge the world?*"

Farley smiled widely. "Wow, you know your Bible, Lucy! Uh, Sister Lucy."

"But I agree the saint business *is* out of hand in a country like Italy. Close to idolatry."

"Yep," said Farley, not out of conversation ploys; he commenced a series of questions, with no sign of imminent depletion.

"What about you, Farley?" Lucy asked, hoping for a pause in her Catholic *summa theologica.*

She learned he was named after the TV preacher Farley Bullins, his brother was named Billy Graham for his first two names, his sister was named Katherine Kuhlman, and she just had a baby who was going to have the full name Jimmy Swaggart Jones but that was out now since Mr. Swaggart's lapse, but then Swaggart wasn't a very nice middle name anyway, huh? Louisiana is as hot as Italy but it was worse in Louisiana because it was more humid. Sometimes, over in Gulfport where his family goes on vacations, it gets so humid you can't go out of your motel room—

"Ah, those are the bells," said Lucy, noticing it was ringing four, and now time for mass. "Gotta go now," she insisted, figuring once the conversation had sunk to weather, that it was time to throw herself upon the mercy of the Church.

"Yep," sighed Farley, "I'm at the Albergo dee Spoe-letto. If you wanna come around tonight," Farley began, shuffling a bit, "we could, you know, go eat some Italian food or some'n." He looked momentarily panicked. "That is, if you're not doing some religious, some kinda *fast* or nothin'."

Persistent boy. Not letting the nun's habit discourage him. "Maybe I'll stop by later," said Lucy, before slipping into the church.

"Maybe see you in Rome?"

But Lucy was safe inside the church. And there she sat, worn out, sore from walking, but delighted with Assisi, looking forward to Rome, and sleepy because of her two half-glasses of Rosso d'Assisi. *Santuario.* These churches were sanctuaries from the unrelenting Italian sun. How soothing the caressing shade of the church was. In fact, if she didn't get back to the hostel for a nap, she'd go to sleep right here.

Before Lucy's nap, she dutifully faxed a progress report to Chicago as requested, saying all was going well and other vague things at O'Hanrahan's insistence. She also saw she had received a note, which the sisters presented her.

After her nap, Lucy determined to go into town and started fixing herself up. She sprayed herself with perfume . . . uh-oh, I bet that's out for the Poor Clares. Well, maybe no one will notice it.

She went to the window to look out on the backside of the Santa Maria Basilica, which was nicer than the front, the exterior so much nicer than the interior. And in the shadow of the early evening there were children playing below her window in the dusty churchyard below, arguing, squealing, tickling, bawling, the big one justifying why the little one was just hit. Children's play, apparently, had only so many variations. Lucy waved to the little girl—five years old? six?—amusing herself in the dust, reveling in it contentedly, wild and tan. The girl looked up and demonstrated that she could make a cross for the sister. Lucy crossed back approvingly. I'm a marked woman in this getup, thought Lucy, checking her appearance again in the mirror before escaping into the Umbrian evening.

Coincidentally, Lucy passed O'Hanrahan in the courtyard, he with two friars, one of them holding a decorative bottle containing an emerald-green liqueur.

"Whewwweeee, Sister Lucy!"

Okay, perhaps a little too much perfume. "I thought," she said performing a smile, "I'd go see the nightlife of Assisi."

One of the monks, an American, said, "Nightlife in this town? It hasn't improved since Francis's day."

O'Hanrahan sidled closer to Lucy, "Now, Sister Lucy, I think you know your vows don't allow such indulgence in the pleasures of the flesh."

"Good night, Dr. O'Hanrahan."

"Give Farley my best," called O'Hanrahan after her. "And remember, we're leaving for Rome at midnight."

Lucy then took the shuttle bus into Assisi; one of the young men offered her a seat. Across from her was a young couple, who had been entwined like all adolescent Italian couples, kissing every few seconds, hands on each other's legs, snuggling, playing in each other's hair . . . but they had cut it out when Lucy—Sister Lucy—sat across from them. The girl sweetly smiled at Lucy. Lucy winked back. She could imagine their conversation, once off the bus: Why did you stop kissing me? The girl would say she didn't want the *suora* to feel like she was missing out on romance, poor thing. Then they'd laugh. Then they'd start kissing again, for all the lost seconds.

Before she knew it, she was at the stop for the Piazza del Commune, the center of Assisi, a plaza with a few cafés, daytime souvenir shops, what seemed to be a medieval town hall with an old tower, and—as if Assisi needed another beautiful thing—a crumbling Roman temple. This must be the place, she sighed. She reached into her habit pocket for the note she had been given earlier . . . the Temple of Minerva, at 8:00 P.M. As if it read her note, the clock in the square began to clang the hour. She walked to the temple, now pleasantly surrounded by medieval buildings of the same height, which was sort of humorous. Minerva was the favorite virgin Daughter of God to the pagans; now the church was rededicated to Mary. She imagined O'Hanrahan's lecturing: no big difference.

She could hardly wait for Gabriel to arrive.

Lucy had survived her delusions with David McCall—he seemed as remote a possibility as someone standing across a chasm. No, perhaps, it was Gabriel she had better turn her attentions to again; a nice Catholic guy from Bridgeport who understood her—

"Long way from Archer Road, huh?" she heard from behind her.

Lucy spun around to see Gabriel, still in monk's robes, approaching with a smile. He hugged her and gave her a kiss on the cheek, and then stood there on the balls of his feet, virtually rocking with pleasure at seeing his old friend.

"It's all over now!" he said in his high-pitched voice. "My mission is finished, and now I can have the first decent night's sleep in several months! You know I wanted to talk to you in Oxford and Ballymacross but I just couldn't until all this was through, Luce."

"I understand," she said sincerely. "It seems to have worked out for the best with Dr. O'Hanrahan, huh?"

They strolled to a nearby café, not too far from where Lucy and the professor had dined that afternoon. There were only four tables outside, so they waited a bit; finally two teenage girls moved on, seeming to scurry away giggling about the brother and sister, imagining some plot out of Boccaccio, philandering *religiosi*. For that matter, Lucy was hoping for much the same thing.

"I love Assisi," said Gabriel. "It's been really *special* being here and seeing where St. Francis lived. I mean, you know me, what did I care about Francis? But he was like me in a lot of ways. He got depressed a lot, he wrote poetry." He looked comically to the heavens with his big brown eyes. "Hey, do you remember all my classics? All my great poems freshman year?"

"I remember," said Lucy.

This was a young person's café and the *ragazzi* seemed to resent the friar and sister invading their scene. The gush of bad, overorchestrated Italian pop music, interrupted by the same Madonna single every other song, blared forth with the video games from the bar behind them. A waiter indifferently brought them their orders, a cappuccino for Lucy, a lime *granita* for Gabriel, who sat there slurping his green half-melted ice drink through his straw.

"Anyway," he was saying, gesturing with his big, irrelevant hands, "some of the brothers you meet here are something else, Lucy. We got Marxists, we have Third World gunrunners, there was this Canadian brother who lectured and said it was our duty to assassinate people like Pinochet and Ceauşescu—can you imagine?"

He talked on and Lucy fell into an old practice: pretending to listen to Gabriel. Gabriel, she thought, hadn't changed much since his St. Eulalia days; paler than before, a melancholy olive, his large brown eyes more intelligent than he was, used primarily for his great show of being sensitive. Not that Lucy would exactly call that quality *goodness*.

". . . so anyway, in an effort to avoid my true feelings, I joined the order hoping to make myself proper again, in God's eyes, because I knew what a fuck-up I really was. You know, I've never been able to, like, empower my own self-esteem . . ."

Yeah, she'll always love him a little bit. A realistic, vintaged, removed-from-the-center-of-the-heart love. Judy, whom Gabriel ironically was fond of, trashed him relentlessly back at the apartment: "I can't see him," she had said, "making a woman very happy in bed, you know what I mean?"

Judy—world's expert on people in bed.

Gabriel was rambling, "I mean, it comes down to sex, doesn't it always? If you don't get that straightened out by eighteen or so, you really are in for a bad time, and I spent just more time than you know worrying over this thing . . ."

Poor Gabriel, thought Lucy. And poor me, as well. I should have dragged you when we were seventeen, kicking and screaming back to my bedroom, swept the stuffed animals off the bedspread, turned around the virgin statue on the ledge, and we should have started our lives then and there. How different, how unguilty our lives might have proceeded from such a moment! How normal.

". . . and so that's why I really had to see you, you know, to say all this. I mean, for years I thought I ought to quit, because I brought shame to the Franciscans, and then Father Gordon said that if I thought homosexuality was a sin, I should stay with the order and atone for it by doing good with my life. I don't think Father Gordon or a lot of the monks think it *is* a sin . . ."

What was this about homosexuality?

". . . and so I expect to be in El Salvador or Nicaragua this fall, with the mission, and I'll give you my address so you can write me and I've got your address, right?"

"Uh, waita second, Gabe. What was this about being gay?"

He took a restorative sip of his lime-green *granita*. "I think I am. I mean, I *know* I am. But you'd probably figured it out, huh? And I was sure Judy told you anyway."

"Judy?"

"I'd talked a little with her about it, because she's a psychologist and all."

Lucy stared at her cappuccino a moment.

Gee, what to be upset about first? The ascension of Judy as confidante or Dad being right about something after all—calling Gabriel from time immemorial "that little fruit." Goddam it, he's going to go back to Chicago and do it with that loser Christopher.

"It's not too much of a shock, is it?" he asked, looking down his straw. "I'm hoping you can, you know, support me on this."

Lucy merely asked, "But you're going to remain with the order?"

"Think so," he said. Lucy noticed his mouth and tongue were green from his drink. "How's Patrick?" he asked a moment later.

She still wasn't quite up to engaging in mental operations, still reviewing the facts: chaste, Franciscan, and gay. Mother told you this wouldn't end in marriage and Mother was correct. And Judy. God, the I-told-you-so of Judy will be heard round the world . . .

"Lucy? Dr. O'Hanrahan?"

"Oh," she said distractedly, "the same as always." It was too early to tell precisely how she felt; she wanted to go sort things out somewhere in private. "Dr. O'Hanrahan," she began, "was furious—*is* furious about your stealing the scroll. Of course, it seems to have worked out, so maybe you two can patch it up."

Gabriel took a deep breath, choosing his words carefully. "I was very uncomfortable working with him. He got very . . . fatherly."

"You don't think he was trying to . . ."

"Oh no, no, nothing like *that*. He's straight as an arrow, I'm sure.

Or used to be, you know there's lots of hanky-panky stories about him, him and secretaries, him and graduate students."

No, Lucy didn't know.

"Back in the swinging '60s," he continued. "I doubt he's up to very much now, you know what I mean?" Gabriel returned to why the professor made him uncomfortable. "I got the impression I was becoming his surrogate son, you know?"

Couldn't be, thought Lucy. O'Hanrahan reaching out for human contact?

Gabriel used his quiet and confidential tone he always said serious things in: "You know he lost his son and wife in accidents a number of years back, right?"

Lucy knew of it, but O'Hanrahan's general rollick and bluster had never suggested he might still be in mourning. "But that was in like, uh, 1973, wasn't it?" she asked.

"Yeah, but you don't get over losing your whole family, do you?"

"No, guess not."

Gabriel continued, "If I mistranslated any of the Greek in the indices we were using . . . well, he'd get *way* too mad at me. He kept talking about big plans for me, where he could get me an academic job, as if I were, you know, his little boy or something. And when I tried to run off with the scroll in Rome, he thought, I'm sure, that it was a personal stab in the back."

"Yeah, he did."

"He's a very unhappy man, Patrick."

"Dr. O'Hanrahan?"

"Yeah, can't you tell?"

Well, no. The professor seemed this thick impenetrable wall, this Titan, this walking encyclopedia of the ages combined with a dash of American philistine, a Socrates of toilet humor . . . no, Socrates was nicer somehow. Tertullian, someone like that. The truth was she was too scared and in awe of him to think he might be a human, let alone a grieving human.

Gabriel asked, "Ever seen a picture of his family?"

"No."

"His wife was a nurse in the Korean War. She left the sisterhood for him and he left the Jesuits for her. Did you not know this?"

"Not all of it."

"Anyway, in his wallet, there's a black-and-white of his son, a yearbook picture. We could be twins, really."

"You and O'Hanrahan's son?"

Gabriel finished his drink, slurping the last of it noisily through the straw. "Patrick's pretty ill too, I have a feeling."

Lucy sighed. The least informed person on the planet.

"Once in Rome he got in a really bad way. Have you seen this yet? His hands and feet lose their circulation and he gets doubled over. Cirrhosis or diabetes, or something." The plaza clock rang the half-hour. "Hey, I've got to go. Nine o'clock curfew at the monastery. Don't wanna get locked out or nothing." He added in a muted gay camp: "Who knows what's going on after the late mass tonight, hm?" Then he laughed at himself. "Just kidding, Luce."

Man, thought Lucy, do I ever know how to pick 'em.

Lucy walked him back to the basilica, and was rewarded with a firmly clasped hand, was told how "special" she was repeatedly, a chaste kiss on the cheek.

Good night Gabriel and good-bye, thought Lucy; a certain expectation and piece of the heart will be laid to rest, here in Assisi. With the moon rising and with the aid of the infrequent light spilling into the alleys from a door or window, she began trudging back downhill, careful not to slip on the steep cobblestones, polished slick by the centuries of faithful pilgrims. Assisi's white stone was cold and lunar, the back alleys threatening and inscrutable, but it wasn't fear she felt as much as isolation, the loneliness of being in too foreign a country, the feeling that precedes the turn for home.

Once back at her hostel, Lucy checked herself in the dresser-door mirror. This, she told her reflection, could be your future *yet*, Lucille. Finish your doctorate, join an order, and then park yourself at some Catholic seminary or some ritzy parochial school. You could be the *fun* sister, the one who goes out for burgers with the students, the cool Catholic broad whose theology classes are popular, Bridgeport's answer to Sister Marie-Berthe, the sister with the wisecracks and offbeat perspectives, a toned-down O'Hanrahan in drag. If you hated sisterhood you could leave. But you'd probably like it. It wasn't as if you were headed toward romance anyway. And Mother. Oh, Jesus, would Mother be happy:

Mom . . . Yes, it's Lucille . . . I'm in Assisi! Mom, the connection's bad I know, but guess what? I'm going to take the vow to be a Minoress, a Poor Clare . . . no, I'm not kidding, really . . . And then Mother would go into a patented mixture of laughter and disbelief and thanking God, thanking nuns who had raised Lucy, now departed, thanking Mary, thanking the Blessed So-and-So . . . She always knew! Didn't she always say her daughter would take the vow, hm? Didn't she? Like her own dear sister, her daughter's Aunt Lucy, a family tradition! Yes, Mother did in her own little way prod and push, but let's be careful not to take credit for that which Our Lord Jesus is most responsible for . . .

(That's right, My dear. Your mother would never be happier with you if you were to make this decision. To her discredit, you would completely and proudly be her daughter, maybe for the first time.)

Lucy hung her habit upon a hanger on her closet door. She stroked the wrinkles out of it, gently. She glanced more critically at the reflection of herself undressed.

She turned out the light and got in bed.

It certainly would be a stable life, she thought, Lucy Dantan and an ancient order, a rule of simplicity, of service, not open to the whims of the very human and impermanent hearts of others.

(It is a shame, My child, that you didn't make the journey to the Eremo delle Carceri, Francis's mountainside hermitage. It is a simple place, more or less as he left it, a small cell where he would sleep, while outside is an altar where he would pray and rejoice with the birds and animals that wandered from the woods. Around the hermitage is the forest he loved so, quiet and dark now, where you could listen to the faint wind in the upper branches, a gentle rustle causing the solitary candle in the saint's cell to flicker. *"Thou wishest to know why it is that God has raised me up,"* said Francis to a jealous brother. *"It is because He has not found among sinners any smaller man, nor any more insufficient and more sinful; he chose me because He could find no one more worthless and He wished here to confound the nobility and grandeur, the strength, the beauty, and the learning of the world."* His conscience led him to oppose his followers who raised a monastery in his honor—are the sick eased in their suffering? Will the poor be served? Francis was not listened to. So as Lucy and Gabriel and all the other children of Mine spend the night in serious thoughts, dreaming of the security of rules, orders, traditions, habits, the set routine from *matins* to *nones*, they would do well to consider the first Franciscan to resign his place in the order to continue the search for God: in 1220, St. Francis himself.)

ROMA
July 4th

Lucy decided that she would never listen to any more nonsense from her parents suggesting that old age slowed you down. Dr. O'Hanrahan, back in his priest's suit for convenience, and his itinerary verged upon the insane and Lucy was feeling the effects.

"I didn't get any sleep last night, Dr. O'Hanrahan," she muttered as they got off their night train, now arrived in Rome at seven A.M.

"You're weak, Dantan," he barked, two steps ahead. "Now keep up the pace."

They traversed the huge expanse of Roma Termini, a dwarfing stadium of a train station in which, Lucy noted, you could buy anything, televisions, cameras, have your hair done, and probably pick up drugs. She was accosted the next minute by a pleading gypsy woman with her dirty child. Lucy shirked away.

"You can tell we're farther south in Italy," O'Hanrahan said, before excusing himself to the men's restroom. Lucy in the interim bought a cheap 4000-lire guide of Rome, nothing special, just a small map and some suggested walking tours.

After much haggling with the driver about unannounced "special fees" and a death-defying cab ride, Lucy and O'Hanrahan were across the Tiber at an institution much beloved of the professor, the Hosteleria Santa Cecilia. The cab ride had taken Lucy past fountains, avenues that had magnificent churches beckoning at the ends of them; there were glimpses into market plazas, sun-warmed remainders of Ancient Rome, all mixed into the contemporary bustle of Roman life. Let her at it!

"We can go sightseeing in a minute, so calm down," O'Hanrahan said to Lucy upon checking in at the Hosteleria. "And remember to look pious. This hostel is for religious only. You'll have to be careful sneaking Farley up to the room."

"Stop with the jokes about Farley. He's a hayseed."

"You're gonna settle down and raise farm animals together."

O'Hanrahan and Lucy checked into adjoining rooms on the second floor that overlooked, uninterestingly, the front of the hotel and a bus stop. O'Hanrahan knocked on Lucy's door when he was ready to depart and she met him, camera, sunglasses, guidebook, and giant handbag all rearing to go.

"Ready for the Whore of Babylon?" he asked as they rounded the marble steps to the ground floor. "St. John, in my opinion, was entirely unfair to Babylon in his famous description of Rome. If it weren't for the Babylonian exile, we never would have the Bible—Isaiah, the prophets, Hebrew poetry—or the Talmud, or dozens of great, free-thinking Islamic philosophers, in the days when there could be such a thing. And while Christians persecuted Jews, Babylon was generally a haven for the Chosen, especially in Islamic times. Babylon always got bad press."

O'Hanrahan turned into the lobby, keys in hand, when they ran into Rabbi Hersch.

Surprise, surprise.

Rabbi Hersch: "Why aren't you in Assisi?"

O'Hanrahan: "Why aren't you in Jerusalem?

Rabbi Hersch: "Where's the scroll?"

O'Hanrahan: "What business would *you* have in Rome?"

Rabbi Hersch: "What's *she* still doing here?"

Ten minutes of summarizing the events in Florence and Assisi managed to placate the rabbi that the scroll was secure for the moment, kept in a safe by the Franciscans and on its way to Rome with Father Vico. O'Hanrahan mentioned the break-in but didn't mention the Mafia by name, so as not to frighten Lucy. Lucy, who'd be leaving soon anyway.

"In fact," the rabbi considered, "it may be just as well that the Franciscans guard it. We were sure to get it stolen from us. You actually *saw* the scroll, didn't you?"

"Yes, yes," O'Hanrahan said. "It's very secure," he insisted, despite a clear picture of the silly little safe on wheels. He turned to Lucy and gave her the keys and asked her to return them to the sister at the reception desk.

"What's the goil still doing here?" asked Rabbi Hersch in a Brooklyn *sotto voce*, Lucy out of earshot. "Tell me the truth. You having an affair with her?"

"Morey," he said, putting a hand on Rabbi Hersch's arm. "Maybe in the past I . . . Look, she's leaving from Rome," he offered, curious why he should be so adamant. "Just look at what Chicago sent me, Morey, look . . ." He took out his VISA credit card. "It arrived in Ireland after I left and Lucy brought it to me."

"Jesus," admired the rabbi, "I couldn't get one of these outa Jew U. if I spent a year on my knees."

"What are *you* doing here, Morey?"

He explained slowly as if to a child: "My flight went by way of Rome, so I decided I'd stop off and follow some hunches. You don't mind me working your turf, do you?"

Actually, O'Hanrahan minded it intensely. He thought: *I* am going to solve this mystery, and *I* am going to translate this scroll. But he pushed the pettiness aside.

"So, Paddy, gonna join me today in the libraries?"

"Nawwwww, come on," O'Hanrahan nudged him, not wishing the rabbi to get any closer to the solution before he got there. "We're going to play tourist. You've never been in Rome with me before. Look, I chaperoned Chicago's student group over here for four summers, I can *do* Rome."

"Mnyeh," squirmed his friend, preferring work.

Lucy soon reappeared to hear O'Hanrahan pleading for the rabbi's company for lunch. Lucy hoped Rabbi Hersch would go to the library and leave Rome to just the professor and herself, but out of politeness Lucy suggested, "C'mon, Rabbi, sir, it wouldn't be the same without you."

"Wellll," said Rabbi Hersch, "if the little girl insists, who I am to refuse? I have a price, Paddy, and that's lunch. Take me to one of the good places you know about. Good Italian you can't get in Jerusalem."

Another enticing, scenery-glimpsing taxi ride brought Lucy and her companions to the Piazza di Spagna, bounded on one side by the famous Spanish Steps. Everyone quietly wondered what everyone else was *really* doing there. But the cab ride wasn't the time to discuss any of it, and maybe not even today, this wonderful simmering day, not yet an inferno, the Roman *ponentino* lightly dipping down into the ochre streets, caressing the crumbling churches, softly assuring the ancient monuments, the wind that has turned the many pages of Roman history imperceptibly.

Lucy fumbled with her camera, trying to fit in her frame the hillside stairway laden with flower vendors and guitar-toting Euroyouth and bored American kids. She beheld the Spanish Steps, forcing their reality into her brain, trying to officially replace the image engendered by TV travel shows and Father Kennedy's slides of his two-week summer Italian vacation to meet Pope Paul, viewed in the gym at St. Eulalia.

"Wow, Dr. O'Hanrahan," said Lucy, walking alongside O'Hanrahan with her nose in her guidebook, "it says . . . it says that John Keats, the poet, John Keats—"

"Yes, I know who John Keats is."

"It says in the book he died in this square, I mean, a building here in this square—"

She had the book seized from her hands. "Yes, he died. He died waiting in the lines at the American Express, right over there. One day, but not today, you can return to Keats's house and pay to see where he croaked. Come back with your backpack and guitar and unshaven legs."

"Hey, I shave my legs."

"Ah, c'mon, Paddy," said the rabbi, "let her stay here with her own kind. We'll go to a bar and talk about the gospel—"

"I refuse to acknowledge this . . . this schism!"

Lucy, tripping on a cobblestone, stumbled along behind. "Uh, can I have my book back?"

O'Hanrahan stopped an oncoming American backpacking couple and put the cheap guide into the boy's hands: "*Here*," he said, "here, take this, learn something. And stop talking so loud."

The rabbi and Lucy were herded toward a subway entrance.

"Look, there's a McDonald's," Lucy dejectedly pointed out.

"I'm going to make you eat there if you don't be quiet and let me talk!" said the professor.

The Golden Age of Spanish Catholicism. 1480s–1520s.

O'Hanrahan, prompted by the Spanish Steps and the Roman Catholic ministry of Propaganda, built with the gold of the New World, expounded upon the ascension of Their Pious Majesties, Queen Isabella of Castile and King Ferdinand of Aragon, uniting by their blessed union two-thirds of Spain.

"Oh, yeah," said Lucy. "They're thinking of sainting the queen, right?"

"An absolute outrage!" said Rabbi Hersch. "She was responsible for an orgy of Jew-killing."

O'Hanrahan narrated. Isabella made for one hell of an Inquisition, led by Isabella's confessor, the fanatical Dominican, Tomas de Torquemada—alas, Mordechai, from a converted Jewish family—who in a decade would exterminate 300,000 citizens. Tens of thousands of Jews were burned at the stake, with minor tortures and maimings and wholesale confiscation of goods and property reserved for the 250,000 whose apostasy was correctable.

(Not surprisingly all inquisitees, We recall, forfeited their land and fortune to the Crown.)

"No one was immune from God's Holy Will," recounted O'Hanrahan, as they moved through the subway turnstiles.

Spanish Catholicism was spread by racks, pendulums, rats gnawing on various tender bodily appendages, hot coals, pincers, dismemberments, knuckle and finger breakers, and screws applied to spinal cords, recounted the professor. "Spain's sadism," O'Hanrahan continued, "was about to be exported to the New World, because the year is 1492 and Columbus is about to claim the New World for Spain—"

"Columbus was Jewish," interrupted the rabbi, now standing beside them in the subway car, hanging on to a strap. "The Sephardim were the greatest navigators of the age. If Chris had steered a little farther north, you know, he'd a hit Brooklyn, smack dab in the Promised Land."

O'Hanrahan cleared his throat, hoping to proceed.

The rabbi persevered: "First Christian wipe-out of the Jews on record is in Spain," he got in before he saw O'Hanrahan's pretended ire. "All right, just trying to educate the little girl, go ahead, Mr. Tour Guide, tell 'er about 1492, the Edict of Expulsion."

The Edict of Expulsion.

Ferdinand and Isabella marched into Granada at long last, giving them the southern third of the peninsula . . . and thousands of infidels to process, village upon village of Muslim women and men waiting for the stake, some 200,000 inconvenient Jews. What was Isabella to do?

(Pope Sixtus IV expressed mild disapproval with her Inquisition, but he was otherwise engaged with arranging for murderers to kill Lorenzo de Medici and his brother in Florence's Santa Croce, timed so they'd be bowed in prayer during the elevation of the Host. Not the pope, really, the situation called for.)

The rabbi explained that some 100,000 Jews wasted their time by going to Portugal but they were thrown out of there, too. And so began the wandering of the Sephardim and the end of Spanish Jewry, who had proud origins before the rise of Rome—gone, all gone.

O'Hanrahan: "But 1492 wasn't ready to say *adios* quite yet."

(We sense the Borgias coming on . . .)

"1492, that *annus mirabilis* saw the ascension to the Holy See of a Spanish pope—Alexander Borgia."

(An abysmal man, even for a pope.)

"At 62, syphilitic, debauched, swollen with every vice," said O'Hanrahan, beaming as if he might fit that description himself, "accompanied by his mistresses, catamites, and bastard children, His Holiness marched to his papal coronation in a spectacular Roman parade of pontifical money-wasting: garlands before him, the papal armies draped in the most expensive silks, his cardinals festooned with jewels, amid the music and noise, handfuls of ducats were thrown to the masses, and to the amazement of the crowd there were human statues, the pubescent breasts of the nymphs lacquered in silver for him . . ."

Lucy checked around to see if anyone looked like they could understand English. Yes, the entire subway car looked engrossed.

"How His Holiness's hand would grip the firm buttocks of the naked boys caked in gold! And what better celebration for the Old Basilica of St. Peter's than a bullfight in the inner churchyard. The Vatican was to become a brothel, a casino, a place of sport and murderous fights. Through extortions of every ingenuity, His Holiness plundered benefices, raking in the spoils of the Christian world."

O'Hanrahan lovingly described Alexander's spawn, the heartless Lucrezia, mistress of poison, incestuous orgiast, married off to a variety of noblemen to secure papal power. Her monstrous brother the Cardinal Cesare, responsible during his dad's reign for up to five murders a week, a man whose face was so eaten away by syphilis that he had to wear an executioner's hood in public—which was appropriate. Cardinal Cesare personally cut out the tongue of one man who repeated a joke about him. He will even come to murder his sister's husband, and after that, their little brother, Juan . . . whom Lucrezia always preferred.

"Oh, please now, not that you should leave anything out," said the rabbi.

Prisoners were brought into the churchyard of St. Peter's where Cesare, before a cheering drunken mob, practices archery upon them. He'll hit this one in the eye, that one in the groin . . . Alexander VI is too ghastly to behold, his skin blackened, his saliva white froth, as every disease of sexual degeneration wracks his ancient body—or was it that Lucrezia, tired of his grotesque furtive advances, is poisoning him?

"An absolutely *identical* description," interrupted the rabbi, "exists of Herod the Great, another fine moral presence. The sores, the disintegrating body, and the stench. Do you suppose it's merely legend about hated rulers or could it be that such really happens to you when you are very, very bad, hm? The blackened skin, the liquefying stomach that has to be bound up so as not to spill out . . ."

"Yuck," said Lucy. "You guys . . ."

Surrounded by his mistresses—always married women because he loved to cuckold the Italians—Pope Alexander opened the vaults of sacred treasure to those who could amuse him. "The Ballet of the Chestnuts!" proclaimed O'Hanrahan. Naked serving girls stoop and bend to pick up the chestnuts His Holiness has hurled across the marble floor of the Vatican. Soon his cardinals disrobe and help the girls, soon they are coupling and rolling about. Would His Holiness participate? No, he shall watch, just watch, and his hand slips under his papal robes to provide himself some last spasm of delight . . . Who among the young men retained by Alexander can perform the most times? The treasures of the Vatican for the most ejaculations!

"Can one imagine father and daughter, brother nearby watching jealously, commanding the church to be filled with the stallions of the Vatican stables? And the concubines of Rome—splayed upon the altars to receive the stallions?"

"You're making this up!" squealed an incredulous Lucy.

"No, it's all true," said the professor. "Polish up your Latin and get out your John Burchard, social secretary to the Borgias. *Whoa*, it's our stop, you two!"

(Alexander didn't have nearly the fun doing it that you did telling about it, Patrick.)

The trio left the train and a carriageful of Italians straining to understand O'Hanrahan's English at Laterano Station. O'Hanrahan and his charges walked up the stairs and emerged outside the city walls, before them the modern version of the most sacred of Roman roads, the Appian Way, now an eight-lane boulevard, traffic lights, newsstands, cafés, bus stops.

"And when the pope himself," said O'Hanrahan steering them along, "clutching the tiara, is helped to mount a gelding, his son and daughter cheering him on . . . ."

Rabbi Hersch: "*Anus mirabilis*, indeed."

"Well, you might have thought the very *end* of decadent imagination had been achieved."

"One might have thought," said the rabbi, distracted with crossing the impossible street and its maniacal traffic pattern.

"The Spanish, however, were just warming up. 1527, the Sack of Rome."

(Dark days for Us indeed. Charles V of Spain and the Holy Roman Empire had been double-crossed for the last time by the vain and incompetent Pope Clement VII. The emperor naively hoped for an organized and dignified assault on the capital, but the Germans were ready for plunder and rape . . . and rape they did, convent after convent was emptied and enslaved, sisters of every order stripped, humiliated, and defiled at drunken auctions, then passed around the marauding troops. The rich were kidnapped, held for ransom, their valuables taken, their infants roasted and eaten as a delicacy, their palaces burned, and then they were killed anyway.)

Churches were raided, recounted O'Hanrahan, jewels and gold scraped from the mosaics and altarpieces, and as for the priests and young monks who didn't strike the German contingent's fancy, they were massacred and thrown into the Tiber until the river was jammed with corpses. Only the arrival of the plague and the worst fire since Nero drove the troops away, convinced finally there was nothing left to plunder.

"But not before the Spanish troops had mocked the Church, Bride of Christ," O'Hanrahan concluded, "by crowning a harlot and putting her upon the Lateran throne, draping a mule in the papal robes and tiara and lashing it through the corpse-ridden streets. Meanwhile, with Rome so occupied, the King of England renounced popery, wanting to be rid of his shrill *Spanish* bride, and to the north, a man named Martin Luther was winning converts. In forty years, through Inquisition, Papacy, and Sack, the Golden Age of Spanish Catholicism winds to a close . . ."

A smattering of applause from the rabbi and Lucy, begrudging, and O'Hanrahan made a slight bow.

"And here we are at the Lateran," he announced, as they gazed upon one of the Five Great Basilicas of Rome. The front was a mass of columns and pillars and monumentality with three-story doors that reduced the poor pilgrim to nothingness.

"But first," said O'Hanrahan, "we must venerate the steps of Pontius Pilate's house."

The Scala Santa, across from the Lateran, is a church featuring a staircase taken from Jerusalem's Antonia Fortess, allegedly the stairs that Jesus descended after being judged by Pilate and the mob.

(Pilate, We hate to point out, lived in the Praetorium across town, and in truth their staircase was any old staircase, but what fun the Moslems had selling this pile of bricks and old wood to the Christians.)

There are twenty-eight steps in the Scala Sancta. The pilgrim, kneeling on each step, does twenty-eight rosaries until he or she finally reaches the top to glimpse the miraculous ikon, the *Acheiropoeton*, painted by St. Luke and finished by an angel. As one of the few actual portraits of Christ by the Evangelist it was carried by angels in the 700s out of Constantinople's grasp and arrived at the Lateran miraculously—proving once and for all Rome's supremacy.

Lucy stood in the doorway of the Church of the Scala Sancta, feeling uncomfortable, face-to-face with Eastern abasement for the first time. The old women in black, tearfully on their knees, prayed intensely— possibly the only eternal of religion, the old women in black. To the right of the door was the souvenir stand.

(The other eternal of religion, Lucy.)

Lucy listened:

"*Dolce bambina Maria*," said the nearest penitent, "*che destinata ad essere Madre di Dio, sei pur divenuta amantissima Madre nostra . . .* "

"Time to go," said O'Hanrahan, tapping her. "If we see the Lateran, then we can reward ourselves with drink."

Entering the Lateran's vast portals and letting her eyes adjust to the dimness, Lucy found the interior breathtaking. This, the true seat of the pope and not St. Peter's, is essentially an overdecorated box, an avenue of marble, giant statues in porticos under pediments under arches under mosaics and insignia—a jumble of every architectural trick since the Greeks.

"Do you know about Pope Formosus, Morey?" asked the professor.

"Tell me a story, Paddy," said the rabbi, contentedly looking at the splendor, impressed but not moved.

"The Trial of Pope Formosus," commenced O'Hanrahan. "Formosus was a man of great piety and learning in the 800s, one of the few popes to lead a strict ascetic life. But he was ambitious. And when he alienated a powerful Roman family, he made an enemy of the man who was to become Pope Stephen VI after his death. Pope Stephen's maniacal hatred of his predecessor led him to convene his cardinals and deacons. 'Exhume Formosus,' he commanded. 'He shall stand trial for his perjuries!'

" 'What's everybody standing around here for?' " re-created O'Hanrahan in a low, gravelly voice. " 'Go find his corpse,' Pope Stephen said! Nine long months and a rain-soaked winter had elapsed since the former pope's death. But workmen exhumed Formosus—gray, half-rotted . . ."

"This is another yuck story," moaned Lucy.

". . . and they brought the corpse to Stephen. Stephen had him propped in the bishop's throne. Now go get his papal vestments, his insignia, his ring, his miter! Stephen forced a deacon to stand behind Formosus and pretend to be the dead pope's voice, and this frightened deacon, about to pass out from the stench of the corpse, answered yes to all Stephen's rantings and accusations. His Holiness then declared all of Formosus's acts void, defrocking a fair percentage of the Church.

"Not able to slide the papal ring off the dead man's rigid fingers," O'Hanrahan informed them, "Stephen called for an ax and the pope hacked away at Formosus's hand; the three fingers Formosus had used to bless and pontificate fell one by one to the marble floor here." He smiled to see Lucy's pained expression. "With Formosus stripped and mutilated further, Stephen felt vindicated and had him reburied."

"Did he get away with it?" asked Lucy.

Understandably, Pope Stephen became anxious. Formosus's supporters were ready to riot; the cardinals, still in shock, were ready to lynch him. Stephen decided to hide Formosus's body, so there would be no evidence. Formosus was exhumed a second time and hurled into the Tiber, and his humiliated corpse, waterlogged and dissolving, floated downstream . . . where the mere sight of it caused miracles to occur. Downriver, healings were reported—a blind man could now see, a barren woman was with child in Ostia! Formosus was fished out of the Tiber and raised upon a bier! A tremor in 897 spelled the end of Stephen, and the Basilica of the Lateran fell into a heap. The town, convinced the earthquake was a sign of God's displeasure—

(Which it was.)

—rioted and demanded Pope Stephen's blood, but civil authorities threw him instead in prison. That night, in the dank cold and darkness, a priest came to His Holiness.

Are you here, asked Stephen, to hear my confession?

No, said the father, I come to deliver the judgment of God. And he strangled Stephen VI with hands that had recently held the Host. Formosus was buried once more. "*Only*," chuckled O'Hanrahan, "only to be exhumed one *more* time by Pope Theodore II for a proper burial in St. Peter's."

"Paddy, Paddy," said the rabbi, cutting him short, "do you think this dump has a toilet for us poor pilgrims?"

"Ask that man there," suggested O'Hanrahan, pointing to a sacristan, carrying a box of short memorial candles across the transept. Rabbi Hersch hopped away to interrogate him.

Lucy was mesmerized by the baroque ceiling—every intersection of every beam an excuse for gold encrustation, sculpted leaves, gilded excrescences, cherubim and seraphim, coats of arms . . . O'Hanrahan pointed to the baldaquin at the transept and explained the heads of Peter and Paul were kept in gold orbs there.

(What? No mention of the urn of manna, the rod of Aaron, tablets from the original Ten Commandments, a dress of the Virgin, John the Baptist's hairshirt, some fish left over from the Feeding of the Five Thousand?)

Lucy now wondered aloud, "Certainly surprising to see Rabbi Hersch, isn't it?"

O'Hanrahan didn't commit himself.

"He said he was going straight back to Jerusalem," Lucy reminded him.

"So, he changed his mind."

"Think he's up to something?" Lucy asked this remembering the sneaking around at Rathlin Island.

"No, but he might be *on* to something."

"If he's identified the script," began Lucy, now observing the rabbi shaking his head, thumbs down on his toilet mission, ambling across the expanse of the nave, "he'll surely tell you, right?"

"Sure," said O'Hanrahan, convincing himself. "Mind you, Lucy, it is his university's scroll. He can do what he likes with it." Then he said aloud in hopes of persuading himself: "I'm just along for the ride. Expendable at any point."

The rabbi returned. "Century upon century," he said, raising his hands to take in the whole of this former Roman palace, "and no toilet for tourists. See if I ever light a candle in here."

(Mordechai is too proud to admit he didn't understand the sexton's Italian. The toilets are off the cloisters.)

Time then, announced O'Hanrahan, to find a café.

They flagged a cab for the next pilgrimage basilica, Santa Maria Maggiore. The taxi let them out on the wrong side of the busy Via Merulana leading to the basilica, and so there was another life-endangering run, dodging the tramcars, threading the traffic on the wide avenue, until they found sanctuary at a small café, a few tables outside in the morning sun.

"We're supposed to *walk* to the basilicas," Lucy informed them, panting. "Not take cabs. We don't get the indulgence if we cheat."

"The only indulgence I'm interested in is a toilet," said the rabbi, making his way into the café's back rooms.

O'Hanrahan ordered three glasses of white wine, then said quietly to Lucy, "I meant to tell you something in Assisi. I saw, in the Lower Basilica parking lot, up on the hill? I saw the white Cadillac again with the German plates. I guess Mr. Cheap Suit figured out our train-to-Rome ploy after all. I suspect he walked the length of the train looking for us, then, not finding us, made his way back to Florence and started for Assisi. Where he'd been tipped off."

Lucy spoke in a needless whisper. "Tipped off? Who knew we were going to Assisi? You, me . . ."

"Gabriel?" suggested O'Hanrahan.

"Impossible," she said, pausing to collect her theory. "Mr. Cheap Suit and Gabriel couldn't be working together because back in Ireland Mr. Cheap Suit would never have blown up the safe and drugged Father O'Reilly if he knew Gabriel had just stolen the scroll."

"Then who's left?"

Lucy shook her head, and yet some information was teasing her from the edge of cognition. "Maybe the rabbi? He knew we were headed to Assisi."

"Now that's *really* absurd. Morey and that goon working together?"

But the rabbi was coming back, scooting through the narrow spaces of the tables inside. "Ah, Frascati!" he sang happily, sitting before his glass of chilled white wine. "*And I commend enjoyment, for man has no good thing under the sun but to eat and drink and enjoy himself . . .*"

". . . *for this will go with him in his toil*," finished O'Hanrahan, holding his gold-filled glass to the light. "This stuff only tastes good in Rome," he added. "I knew an Italian Carmelite who always called this stuff Montefiasco."

After this pit stop: the dazzling Santa Maria Maggiore of the 400s. The rabbi hadn't visited this church and, for his pleasure, a treat awaited him, the finest Christian homage to the Jewish fathers. Maria Maggiore is a long basilica, a vast hallway between two rows of Roman columns that support walls of the incomparable 5th-Century mosaics of gold and agate and glass and onyx and polished gems. There was Melchizedek greeting Abraham, Hamor and Shechem petitioning Jacob for the hand of Dinah, Moses marrying Sepphora.

Lucy went to stand in the magnificent Sixtus Chapel, a side chapel so spacious and tall, with each successive story more ornate and gold-strewn than the last, that she merely collapsed in amazement against a marble column, staring to the heavens agog.

"And guess whose relics were once thought to be here?" asked O'Hanrahan, hands around both the rabbi's and Lucy's shoulders. "Our old friend, St. Matthias. Lucy, you're the functional Catholic of the party. Go offer up a prayer to Matthias so that we might figure out his chicken-scratchings."

"You serious?"

The rabbi concurred. "Light one of them Catholic magic candles."

"Well, all right . . ."

(It might help, Patrick, if *you* offered up a prayer.)

While Lucy lit a candle and lined up behind some women from a Portuguese tour bus for kneeling space, the rabbi and O'Hanrahan walked away to view the apse.

Lucy's prayer was short and direct: "Thank you for allowing me the opportunity to work on this great discovery of the Church. And help us, Holy Spirit, to translate it . . . that is, if it be Thy will, and . . . Thou doesn't think that this gospel is going to cause too much trouble."

(The Holy Spirit has no fear of the truth, and neither should Her children.)

"Amen."

In another frenetic push, O'Hanrahan swept Lucy and the rabbi toward the metro station nearby, and they bought a subway ticket for the B line and their trip south of town to the next pilgrimage basilica, St. Paul Without the Walls.

"Morey brought up the subject of antipopes," said O'Hanrahan. "When you couldn't get the job legally, you'd bribe a few cardinals to come to Maria Maggiore and crown you there."

The professor mused on the most unfortunate antipope: Constantine of the 700s, pawn of the Roman aristocracy and the unscrupulous Duke Toto.

"Duke *Toto?*" Lucy wondered.

"I don't make this stuff up," said O'Hanrahan.

Having poisoned the reigning Pope Paul I, Toto had a mob take Constantine on their shoulders and rowdily install him as pope in the Lateran. The Lombards marched on Rome and Toto was slaughtered fighting in the streets, and poor, defenseless Constantine hid out in a monastery until a mob of Romans seized him, beat him senseless, and gouged out his eyes with the papal ring. Surviving this he was degraded in the Lateran, angering the inquisition by insisting on his innocence, so the cardinals took turns kicking and hitting the blind man in turn. He was exiled to solitary confinement in a forgotten monastery for the rest of his long life.

Antipope for a day: following this, the Lombards elevated their own pretender to the papal throne, Philip, so laughable a creature that the bishop who presided over his installation had to be forced at knife-point. Philip got no further than saying the blessing over a coronation banquet before the farce became too much and he was escorted to a nearby monastery so that a serious pope could be elected. In this brutal, bloody time, Philip never received as much as a cross word of punishment—perhaps the most likable buffoon ever to wander into the Holy See.

"Pope for a day," cried O'Hanrahan, "July 31st, 768!"

From the commuter station they began a brisk walk to the front of St. Paul Without the Walls. The rabbi made the inevitable joke, "How does the roof stay up without any walls then?" and Lucy was secretly glad she didn't ask the question in all seriousness, wondering if "Without the Walls" meant it was an open-air church.

The three pilgrims discovered that a stroll to the front of St. Paul's, the largest in Christendom until St. Peter's, was strenuous exercise on a hot Lazian day; on and on and on the rough brick walls and great stone foundations imposed themselves. Three Byzantine emperors, explained O'Hanrahan, decided to build Christianity's Big Mama throughout the 300s: four aisles of twenty massive columns, and a nave you could lose a football field in . . .

Lucy stood in the doorway of this gloomy expanse and let her eyes adjust. She watched tourists far away at the altar, people ant-sized against the hugeness. She looked to her left and right to see tourists obscured against the forest of columns and unlit chambers; a human being here felt nonexistent, reduced to a speck in the very throne room of Heaven itself.

(But of course, Heaven is an intimate place.)

Ahead of them in the transept, under the mosaics of the apse, was an altar under a gothic canopy, and under that, the simple rock that once marked Paul's grave, unmoved since his martyrdom in the year 66. Lucy was worried about the gift shop closing, which threatened her postcard collection, so she excused herself and began a brisk jog to the transept.

O'Hanrahan watched her depart, conjuring up a vision of an athlete running amid the ancient Roman columns, not the first time something pagan and lost would whisper to O'Hanrahan in a Christian sanctuary. He turned to his friend: "Whadya think? Jewish boy made good? St. Paul, the Rabbin Gamaliel's star student."

The rabbi nodded serenely. "The School of Hillel taught Jesus as a boy, and his grandson Gamaliel taught Paul, and later Gamaliel the Younger turned the Christers out of the synagogue and probably was first in line to stone them. He also ran out of town the followers of Rabbi Yochanan ben-Zakkai, the teacher who said *It is the unlearned who bring trouble into the world*, but wise as he was, he was wrong. It is the learned, Paddy—men like you and me—who start trouble. Men like Paul, Saul of Tarsus."

O'Hanrahan smiled in agreement. "Have you heard of the *Clementine Homilies* and the *Clementine Recognitions?* Not by Clement of Rome, but the name has stuck. Gnostic and latter-day texts and tracts, some in bizarre Syriac, some in codes; there are twenty homilies and ten books of recognitions—some, to this late, late day, untranslated."

"Sounds like a treasure trove," concurred the rabbi.

"Most of the work is in Greek, but the translations were by Rufinus in the 300s, who butchered and edited as he saw fit. God knows what these obscure African documents *really* say. I thought I'd hop over to the Metropolitan's Library in Athens and take a peek, and see if the Matthias script appears. And then I'll join you in Jerusalem."

"And you can walk right into Athens and read these things?"

The professor nodded.

"Go to it, then," Rabbi Hersch suggested. "I'll dig through the kabbalahs, some of the best of which, the Master of the Universe only knows why, are in the Vatican Library."

O'Hanrahan was querulous. "But Kabbalah is a thousand years older than the Matthias gospel . . ."

"Alphabets, Paddy," reminded the rabbi. "The *Sefer Yetsirah* is full of magical, mystical alphabets—22, in fact, one for each letter in Hebrew. I'll find Matthias's damn language yet!"

O'Hanrahan savored unwillingly the possibility that his friend would find the key to this gospel before he did. Yes, the rabbi would likely turn over all the work to him eventually, as a gift, as charity for old, doddering Patrick O'Hanrahan. To be the sole detective on this mystery, O'Hanrahan brooded, to solve this puzzle by myself, I would . . . I would sell my soul.

(Don't jest. Temptation lies ahead, Patrick.)

"Another thing," concluded O'Hanrahan glumly. "Father Vico, the Franciscan who's got the gospel, said that some Greek Orthodox monk came by the basilica in Assisi hunting for Matthias earlier this year.

Some monk who went up and down Italy; asked for it by name, too. He also said he got the impression this . . . this Mad Monk wanted to destroy it."

"Oh, just great. A Mad Monk on the trail too. This trail is getting pretty crowded, Paddy."

A sacristan and two sextons rushed around trying to shoo people toward the exit; the church was closing for lunch.

Rabbi Hersch: "When you getting rid of her?"

This caught O'Hanrahan off-guard. "Well . . . after she sees Rome."

"Tomorrow, then?"

The rabbi, thought O'Hanrahan, seemed oddly persistent. "She said she was leaving soon. She's gotta load up on trinkets for all the aunties back home, plastic Marys, et cetera. Of course, now that Gabriel's gone, I need an assistant—"

"Paddy, stop shmying around here. You can't take her to Athos, you can't take her to Wadi Natrun, if it came to that. What about Mar Saba and the library, hm? No women allowed. You're headed eastward and she'll be a millstone."

O'Hanrahan nodded.

"And that whole Gabriel business in Ireland; I can't say I trust her. Also, if there *are* big guns out looking for this, Mad Monks and aggrieved collectors, then she's in danger. You can't be responsible for her. What if someone kidnaps her? That kinda news you should want to break to her parents, huh? Think of the lawsuits."

O'Hanrahan acquiesced and said he'd get her packing within 48 hours.

"Good," he said. "How's the health?"

"No problems," said O'Hanrahan, the next moment tipping his hand a bit: "I guess the thought of translating that scroll keeps me alive, keeps the blood pumping."

But the rabbi didn't say anything. He just looked ahead at Lucy running up to them.

"Lunchtime at last?" she said.

Safely Within the Walls in central Rome, O'Hanrahan led his friends to an old favorite *trattoria* wedged against the back of Il Gesù, the spectacular baroque cathedral and headquarters of the Jesuit Order.

"This place has been here since Ignatius Loyola," said O'Hanrahan as they found a table in the back, amid a crowd of black-robed ecclesiasts, S.J. *Spaghetti all'amatriciana* to start—without the bacon for the rabbi, *per favore*—then Roman *saltimbocca* for Lucy and the professor. O'Hanrahan after lunch led them to a corner bar where he insisted, Lucy's protests aside, that they all have a Roman *sambuca*, that clear anisette, served flambé with a few Ethiopian coffee beans floating in the lambent blue flame.

"It tastes like mouthwash—"

"Drink it, Luce."

And then Giolitti, bastion of Roman gelato. Lucy smiled at the visage of two patriarchs eating ice cream out of little paper bowls with miniature spoons. "Rabbi," she asked, "can you eat ice cream after having fish in the meal we just had? Isn't that not kosher or something?"

"Hey Paddy, you listening to this? I'm getting *halakhah* from the little girl here . . ."

"And now," announced O'Hanrahan, depositing his paper cup and the dregs of half-melted *malaga* in a stuffed trashcan, "the Vatican!"

St. Peter's in Rome, atop the Vatican Hill.

The Superdome of Churches, thought O'Hanrahan standing before it—empty, vast, overdecorated mammoth that it is. St. Peter's, however, does a brisk trade in awe: awe as one approaches it from the via della Conciliazione, awe as one passes into the Bernini colonnade in Piazza San Pietro, awe as one climbs the steps beneath the balcony from which popes present themselves after the wisp of white smoke, delighted to hear *Annuntio vobis gaudium magnum: habemus papam!* and then, at last, awe upon passing through the overscale portals and into the largest church in Christendom. O'Hanrahan looked over his shoulder to watch Lucy, open-mouthed, approach this once-in-a-lifetime experience. As for himself, he sighed, he knew Rome too well to be taken in by the plunder. And yet it was this spot on earth that had shaped and harassed his life!

All around O'Hanrahan, also in awe, were prelates and monks and nuns, all living out the greatest moment of their lives, the pilgrimage, the impending audience with the pope, herded through the turnstiles like sheep. Look at them, sighed O'Hanrahan. From third world countries, from poor and hopeless conditions, from loneliness, from family exile, here it all pays off for them. This was not the religious life I longed for. Oh, let's admit it: the swish of skirts, the whispers in the back offices of the Vatican . . . What will *Stato* say to His Holiness? Is *Propaganda* conspiring against the Curia? Whose ambition shows too clearly? And under what quiet, ameliorative cardinal's exterior lurks another John XXIII, another John Paul I, a man who might sanctify this squalor? It was that world of Vatican politics I should have seized for my own.

(You didn't do so well with Theology Department politics.)

No, that's right. But that was only late in the game when my guard was down, and I was drinking after Beatrice and Rudy died and I let myself get unseated in 1974. Me and Nixon, out on our asses that summer. Until then, I was creating utopia! My cocktail parties were legendary, the faculty I brought in was first rate, we had our choice of students, there was travel and lavishly funded sabbaticals—I was beloved and reelected three times!

(That you were.)

I should have used that pulpit like Schillebeeckx and Hans Kung. I should have rocked the Eternal City with tract after tract. Oh, with my diligence and argumentative skills, I bet I could have toppled the pope after Vatican II, done away with the papacy! Or got myself excommunicated, which would have pleased me a lot.

(It sounds like you would have done anything to make Rome notice you. To make a mark, to engrave your name but once somewhere upon this city of marble.)

Yes, true enough. And what nonsense! O'Hanrahan reacquainted himself with the sight of St. Peter's, now nearly up to the portals. This church is only here because of the stupidity of Pope Julius II, who felt the original basilica built by Constantine in 326 wasn't big enough to house his tomb. Made senile by his syphilis, His Holiness wanted a place to house his monument designed by Michelangelo: three stories high, featuring forty statues, all dashed and racked with grief at Julius's passing. But he couldn't properly afford either his tomb or a new St. Peter's to put it in, so he sold indulgences . . . the ones that so angered Martin Luther. O'Hanrahan couldn't help but smile: my dear, ludicrous Rome! You tore down the foremost church in Christendom and built yourself the Reformation!

Rome, you old harlot, the Whore of Babylon! Faded though you are, and past your prime you still apparently have your way with men, you have made many mortals forget your livelihood, resplendent city of temple and cupola and ruin and monument, piled atop the bodies of sacrificed Christians, swindled Jews, enriched by the suppression and persecution of the known world and the harassment of Patrick O'Hanrahan! Silent beneath your makeup, the shimmer of your gleaming mosaics, seethes the anguish of the ages, the deaths of martyrs, saints unknown by name, innumerable bones.

And how I adored you, nonetheless!

Dr. O'Hanrahan, for Lucy's sake, agreed to be dragged around all the art of the Vatican. O'Hanrahan, Rabbi Hersch, and Lucy saw the Pietá, then trudged ever onward to the Vatican Museums, all the greatest rapine of Western Civ and Art History 101, the Apollo Belvedere, the Laocoön, room after room of Greek and Roman statues, chamber after chamber of crosses and candlesticks, halls one can't see the end of they are so long, map rooms, library rooms, each twist and turn revealing another infinity of wealth and ornament and gilt, not an inch of wall left unfrescoed. Lucy was speechless before such a hoarding, such beautiful obscenity.

Her two older companions showed their age, turning cranky, trashing all the great art, soiling the experience for Lucy, who was moved by what she saw—and the more sacrosanct her reaction, the more irreverent they sought to be. After a burlesque of the Raphael frescoes, dismissed as derivative hackwork by O'Hanrahan, they entered the humbling glory of the Sistine Chapel to the sounds of the taped message that plays continually:

"*Silènzio per favore* . . . Silence, please . . . *Sei still, bitte* . . ."

Nothing could wreck the sacred atmosphere more than that silly message, thought Lucy, gazing around at the newly cleaned and restored ceiling, the frescoes of electric yellow and hot pink and neon blue, the supporting work by Botticelli and Signorelli—

"Signorelli's a real *buttocks* man, you can tell," said O'Hanrahan.

Lucy, escaping him, drifted toward the Last Judgment, Michelangelo's swirling rhapsody on the final moments, the Damned never looking more damned—even Mary looks as if she can do nothing for them, Our Lady anxious at the coming ferocity. Her son Jesus, the still center of this divine storm of recompense, is resolute, darkly serene, the moment after every possible mercy has been allowed.

"It may be difficult," O'Hanrahan said to the rabbi, craning to see the ceiling, "having seen Michelangelo's *Creation* in countless books and reproductions to the point that we yawn when we see it, to remember that once someone turned to Michelangelo and said, Here's the assignment, kid: paint creation, the making of Man, God and Adam."

Lucy gaped at it. Michelangelo's depiction is the moment immediately after the touch of Creation is broken off. On the right is God the venerable, lifted by angels in the whirl of His pink gown, and on His face a fierce look of concentration, focusing all His divine energies into the supreme imperative: BE. To the left is Adam, postcoital, looking longingly at God as one would a lover, his hand limp and languid, aroused from an eternal sleep, awakening to Paradise—

"I see," said the rabbi, "Michelangelo knew about the small Jewish *pisher*."

"You'da thought," added O'Hanrahan, "that God might have done a little better by the prototype. Michelangelo's David back in Florence isn't exactly hung like a horse either, come to think of it."

"Here's a theory. Maybe, if you're like Michelangelo, if you like for to be shtupped up the wazoo, you're not looking for a schmucke the size of Aunt Goldie's pot roast—"

"*For God's sake*," hissed Lucy. "Is this the *best* you two can do? Before the greatest work of art ever done? This is as *high* as your thoughts can reach?"

O'Hanrahan pretended to be chastened. "You tell me, Luce. You like 'em large or small?"

"I'm not having this discussion." Lucy walked as far as she could get from them.

"Excitable girl," said the rabbi.

"Virgin," said O'Hanrahan simply. "Sure of it."

"Don't guess they're gonna let me smoke in here, huh?"

†   †   †

Nighttime in Rome on a summer evening:

The night was to be devoted to piazza-sitting, paying too much for drinks, eating a series of Roman delights—champagne ice, the famous *tartufo*, the Immaculate Heart of chocolate. The rabbi was fond of espresso ice, packed into a cold metal tankard drenched with fresh rich sweet *fior di latte*, the mouth delighting in the chill, confluent textures of fine ice and velvet cream. And what better place to end up than the Piazza Navona, staring at the tourist throngs and the Roman riffraff—plenty of it out tonight, observed Lucy—some beautiful people, some extremely loud and ugly people.

They strolled toward the the Bar Tre Scalini.

Lucy had observed that O'Hanrahan, after a drink, liked to touch and clasp his companions, and his hands were not above . . . above her waist, for that matter. She politely detached herself, assuming that his freshness was some remainder from his misspent middle years of womanizing. I could see how he'd pull the grad students, Lucy thought, a few years back, more hair, thinner . . . yeah, why not? All those kinky tales of his, all that brainpower. Probably worked like wildfire in 1969. There was a great warmth and generosity to the man, once you got him to the café. Aw, hell. She walked up beside him and allowed him to keep his hand around her waist for a brief, friendly moment, happy to have been approved of in their final days together.

They spied a trio leaving a café table and lunged for it, garnering a perfect view of Piazza Navona.

The rabbi: "Eighty-year-old man rushes into the confessional, he says, Father, Father! I just made love three times in one night to a woman one-fourth my age, I swear to God! Ooooh, says the priest, well, pal, you better say four Hail Marys and ten Pater Nosters. I can't, says the man, I'm Jewish. Priest says, What the hell you telling me this for? Man says, Are you kidding, *I'm telling everyone!*"

Groans all around.

"Moses," said O'Hanrahan, "came down from Sinai with tablets with that joke on it. John says in the beginning was the Word, but that joke, *that* joke, Mr. Catskills, is older than the Word."

"I got one," said Lucy, having allowed herself two whole glasses of amaretto. "What do you get when you cross an Irishman and a deck chair?"

Pause.

Lucy: "Paddy O'Furniture."

The men's stares consigned her to the outer darkness.

"Awwwww come on," she said, "that's *funny*! Sort of."

The rabbi, shaking his head, got up to use the restroom at this famous establishment. Lucy and O'Hanrahan watched him ungracefully scoot between the scores of little café tables as he made his way inside.

"Beautiful night," O'Hanrahan said.

"Yep, and no German white Cadillac either. Yet."

"Yet," O'Hanrahan repeated. "So you won't go on suspecting the rabbi has some ulterior designs here, let me inform you that the Man in the Cheap Suit knew we were in Assisi thanks to *you*."

"To me? I don't even speak German."

"The Man in the Cheap Suit is American."

She waited for the explanation.

"Last night in Assisi, as I was telling you before, I left the basilica around eleven P.M. and what should I find in the parking lot but the white Cadillac. The Cadillac is an *automatic*. No European drives an automatic. Also, on the windshield there was a sticker from Hertz Rent-a-Car. It's some American who's naive enough to want to drive a big gas-guzzling automatic-transmission car all over Europe. Now think hard, who was in Florence and Assisi that you told your plans to?"

Lucy winced. "Nawww . . ."

"It's a strong possibility."

"Farley? Associated with international black marketeers?"

The rabbi was seen in the vicinity, wending his way back. Lucy popped up, "My turn," making her way to the ladies' room.

Rabbi Hersch sat at the table and greasily laughed from deep in his chest, not quite out loud.

O'Hanrahan: "What?"

"Paddy O'Furniture," said the rabbi.

When Lucy returned from the toilet, O'Hanrahan was quoting something to Rabbi Hersch: "*Then shall begin the great Empire of the Antichrist in the invasions of Xerxes and Attila.* That's what the line is."

"So whadda we got?" asked the rabbi. "Iran or Iraq is Xerxes and Attila could be, one supposes, either China or Russia—"

"Or both, maybe. That would spell the end of the West: a coalition of Moslem powers, with the Chinese and Russians behind them, versus Europe and the U.S. and Israel."

Lucy took her seat. "What are you guys talking about now?"

Rabbi Hersch: "The End Times."

"Oh, not again!"

O'Hanrahan was quoting Nostradamus's prediction of the End, in a year with two eclipses in Leo, rising waters, and great natural disasters.

Lucy asked, "And is a year with two such eclipses coming up?"

O'Hanrahan: "1999."

"Great."

O'Hanrahan continued. The 16th-Century Nostradamus, who had described World War Two with uncanny accuracy, even naming the instigator "Hilter"—which is close enough to be impressive—predicts a coming war in Yugoslavia, the rise of the Mohammedans and China, a reborn Germany, and the fall of France to an Islamic population in 1998. None of that looks too unlikely all of a sudden, concluded the professor. "Serving Antichrist will be a 'Barbarian in a Black Head-dress.' "

"Sounds like an heir to Khomeini," said the rabbi. "Of course, *Daniel* and *Ezekiel* say the Beast was going to come out of Babylon, or modern-day Iraq. Nostradamus was thought to be a secret Jew and I'm sure he knew his Old Testament Prophets and Kabbalah."

Lucy asked, "Nostradamus was specific about which years this all was going to happen?"

"He didn't use a lunar calendar but a solar one, so there's room for play. But 1999 he mentions by name. And he also says there will be a great discovery of an early saint of the church that will rock the Vatican."

The rabbi crossed his arms. "Ah, perhaps Mr. Matthias is that saint."

"You guys," said Lucy, "are creeping me out."

"I taught a course for years at U.C.," said O'Hanrahan, "on Apocalyptics. That stuff does give you the creeps if you dwell on it too long. Enoch and Elijah will return to preach against the Antichrist, a False Prophet will appear, a False Prophecy will lead the Church to doubt, some woman or some nation perhaps is the Great Harlot. My bet is that's a reference to Miss Dantan here."

Lucy ignored this, asking instead, "So I've got about seven, eight years left before things turn nasty?"

The rabbi added, "Remembering that a day is as a thousand years with the Lord, some Ultra-Orthodox think there will be 6000 years of toil before the thousand years of rest, just as there are six days followed by the Sabbath. We all know the world was created in 4000 B.C., backtracking from the genealogies of the Old Testament. We're coming up on 2000 A.D. It's time for the finale, huh?"

O'Hanrahan enjoyed torturing Lucy. "So *Revelations'* millennium of peace is upon us. That is, after we go through the rise of Antichrist and the Tribulation."

"Hey," said Lucy, swirling the ice in her glass, "I'm too young for any of this."

Then suddenly at O'Hanrahan's side, a priest in a cassock cleared his throat to interrupt. "Excuse me . . ." The priest was North American. Possibly forty, but looking younger, with tender pink skin, sunburned from Roman sightseeing, with a pair of small gold glasses that made him look scholarly. "Excuse me, I hate to interrupt, but you're Dr. Patrick O'Hanrahan, aren't you?"

It turned out that this young man was a priest, Jim Vupolski, from Lorain, Ohio, first time in Rome, and he saw O'Hanrahan in the restaurant by Il Gesù at lunch, but was too shy to say hello.

"I've seen you lecture twice," Jim was saying, "once when I was studying at Notre Dame, you did the Patristic Fathers series, and this is probably ancient history for you, but I had an adviser who had a tape of your lectures twenty years ago in Bologna—"

"Bologna!" beamed O'Hanrahan.

"Yes, I think I enjoyed it more in Italian, actually. You did your lectures with such . . . you know, bravura. You're a real showman, Dr. O'Hanrahan."

O'Hanrahan was only too quick to agree, and proceeded to relive that lecture's reception for the rabbi's benefit.

"And this is my associate, from Rome," said Father Vupolski, during a breather in O'Hanrahan's banter, "Father Agnelli."

A short, pudgy Italian man, also about forty, with a pale face and a permanent shadow of beard, stepped into the conversation.

"Good to meet you," said O'Hanrahan, shaking hands. "Please sit down with us . . ."

"Well, I don't want to interrupt," said Jim.

"*La fotografia . . .*" said Father Agnelli, nudging Jim.

"Oh yeah . . . a bit embarrassing, but could we—could I ask to have your picture taken, with us, here? Father Agnelli really enjoyed the lectures at Bologna."

"*Naturalmente!*" cried O'Hanrahan. "You were there, Father?"

As the men relived O'Hanrahan's glory, Lucy was drawn into service. She took two pictures: both identical and flashbulb-marred, she imagined, the two grinning prelates and a red-faced O'Hanrahan, arms around one another's shoulders, old friends for years.

The conversation among the three raged on, and Lucy was thrown back on the rabbi for conversation. And none happened. A few polite questions back and forth. Lucy then listened to O'Hanrahan talk Italian with both men and she felt herself falling asleep, eyes getting heavy.

"Paddy?" asked the rabbi, momentarily, "are we going to talk about our, uh, project tonight or shall I go on back to the hotel?"

The two priests stood and apologized for invading like this, but actually, said Father Vupolski, they'd had a long day—up for prayers since four A.M.! They were headed back to the hostel near the San Callisto Palace.

"Good heavens," said O'Hanrahan, "we're practically neighbors! We're at the Santa Cecilia down the street."

"Great!" said Father Vupolski, "if you're going to be in Rome, then some of the fellows at the convocation would love to, well, you know, meet you and buy you a drink. Or two."

Hearty male laughter accompanied this suggestion.

Jim: "Can we give you guys a ride then? Father Agnelli has his car, thank God."

Lucy saw her chance to make a break and volunteered to come along. The rabbi and O'Hanrahan were abandoned to talk strategy.

Lucy: "Yes, you're sure it's not out of your way?"

"Not at all."

Soon their car was poking through Rome traffic, trying to thread its way to a major boulevard and out of the alleys. The Italian priest drove them, while Lucy sat in the back with Jim from Notre Dame.

What a day it had been: what an assault of the monumental and grandiose, the impossibly huge, ornate, and expensively wrought— Rome is certainly what it's cracked up to be. Lucy, with the guidebook fragments floating in her head, realized that still ahead there was the secular Rome of the palaces and art museums, the Imperial Rome of the Caesars and Capitoline Hill and the Forum, the café Rome where James Joyce worked on *Ulysses* and Keats and Shelley and Byron got drunk and Conrad and Henry James met for coffee, the Rome of fountains, the Rome of fashion, the Rome of food and drink and piazza-sitting. As she looked out her window she saw they were crossing the Tiber and that the moon made a path across the slow waters and she sighed the sigh of the tourist, for a moment touched by something ancient and immutable.

"Beautiful moon," she said.

"Just the perfect temperature, isn't it? After the hot days down here last week."

"Yeah."

She closed her eyes lightly, ready to cease consciousness. Her feet could have been amputated without her minding; all she wanted was to sink into the bed and sleep for a day or two. Tomorrow she'd have to load up for all the relatives—a dozen of those little crucifixes at least, and as much as she didn't care for them, some Mary statues because she had some older relatives who would care for them, particularly a Mary from Rome . . . that's odd, she noticed, they're crossing the Tiber again.

"Wait, uh, Jim?"

"Hm?"

"The place, the Hosteleria Santa Cecilia? It's on the Vatican side of the river, isn't it?"

But Jim didn't say anything.

"Uh, you know where I'm going, don't you?"

He smiled barely. "Yes. I know where you're going."

Something was wrong. "I think I better get out. Why don't you let me out right here and I . . ." She reached for the door handle as the car slowed at an intersection.

Jim grabbed her hand. "It really wouldn't be a good idea to get out of a moving car."

Lucy's heart began beating faster. "Jim, are we going somewhere else first?"

He cleared his throat. "My name's not Jim. But there'll be time for introductions soon enough."

Lucy swallowed hard. "You didn't really go to Notre Dame, did you?"

"No." Again the slight, unfriendly smile. "I didn't."

JULY 5TH

O'Hanrahan arose the next morning feeling no effects of the previous night's excess. He threw open the window and looked down upon the narrow avenue, into the Italian domesticity presented by the windows across the street. He looked up to see the perfect blue sky of Rome and felt the sun on his face. What a shame he had to go see Father Vico today.

After an elaborate shower and grooming session, O'Hanrahan passed by Lucy's room to see a DO NOT DISTURB sign hanging there, just as it was last night. Your loss, kiddo, he thought, Rome's out there just waiting for you.

"*Signore, taxi?*" said the mustachioed cabdriver in front of the building as O'Hanrahan stepped from the hosteleria. "Very good rate for you! Spanish Steps, eh, Villa Borghese, eh? San Pietro, you go to see the poop?"

"No, thank you," said O'Hanrahan, preferring to walk the short distance to San Francesco a Ripa. The inner offices of San Francesco a Ripa were more dilapidated and bare than the Assisi offices. Father Vico was enthroned in a plaster-cracked room with a slit window, again sitting in a chair that seemed to swallow him.

"Rome is like a foreign country to me," said Father Vico wistfully, after procuring O'Hanrahan a cup of badly made tea.

"After Assisi, I can see why," said O'Hanrahan, who politely sipped, knowing better than to complain.

"I have for you a sooo-prise," said the Father.

After a phone call to the ever-petulant Antonio, who had accompanied Father Vico and sat brooding in the outer office, an ancient man was shown into the room. The two Franciscans paid reverence to each other as Father Vico rose to his feet.

"This is Friar Luco Gatteoti, a brother attached to San Francesco for feefty years now," Father Vico said proudly, with a wave of his hand. O'Hanrahan observed this white-haired, funereal man. "Luco has full access to anything you may wish to see in the Vatican Library, and he shall accompany you."

"Where, Father," O'Hanrahan asked, "is our scroll now?"

"It ees safe," said Father Vico. "It ees safe in a, how you say? A safe. It ees safe in the safe, ha ha ha ha ha . . ."

O'Hanrahan pinched the bridge of his nose. "Where is this safe?"

"It is a very safe safe, ha ha ha ha ha . . ." Father Vico resumed his seat. "Antonio," he called.

Antonio, after some instruction, wheeled in the same asinine miniature safe Father Vico had presented in Assisi. O'Hanrahan cringed to hear the unoiled wheels screech in rhythmic triplets, squeak-squeak-squeak, squeak-squeak-squeak, as it was rolled across the uneven wooden floor.

"That really does not look very . . ." O'Hanrahan averted using the word *safe*. ". . . secure, father."

"Not even the Father General knows the combination, though I have been pressed to confess this secret. Nor did I commit our treasure to vaults and safes in Assisi or in a bank or a, what to call it?"

After some minutes, O'Hanrahan understood he meant a security deposit box.

Father Vico: "It is myself I trust alone. Anyone else might to be bribed, yes? The safe is in my power, so you do not to have the fear."

O'Hanrahan and Friar Luco left San Francesco and stood on the sidewalk. O'Hanrahan asked if the monastery had a car they could borrow or a driver to take them to the Vatican, and Luco didn't seem to know. How did Friar Luco go to the Vatican? O'Hanrahan asked. He walked, he said, all two miles, up the hill and down the hill. Annoyed, O'Hanrahan led his companion back to the Hosteleria Santa Cecilia.

"You want to the Spanish Steps to go?" asked the driver, awakened from a brief slumber.

"The Vatican, please," said the professor.

O'Hanrahan felt he had seen the cabdriver before . . . in a cartoon. Yes, that's right, Gepetto the Carpenter in Disney's *Pinocchio*. O'Hanrahan had taken Rudy when he was eight to see it. Same full mustache that could have been a bad theater department prop. O'Hanrahan turned to Friar Luco looking straight ahead, faintly smiling as if a taxi ride was a new, unaccustomed thrill.

"So," began O'Hanrahan, making conversation in Italian, "what is your field of expertise, Luco?"

He shrugged. "What I am told to do, I do."

Formalities were brief at the Vatican Library desk since Luco was trusted and familiar beyond suspicion, and permits were issued to O'Hanrahan for everything but the oldest and most valuable codices

kept in the vaults under the Vatican Palace. Friar Luco would be happy
to get O'Hanrahan anything he needed from down there, however.
On the chance that Luco might know something, O'Hanrahan removed from his briefcase a photo four-by-five print of a page of the
Matthias scroll.

"Brother Luco, does this script mean anything to you?"

"No," he said in a moment, not interested.

O'Hanrahan then wrote on a slip of paper a work he wished brought
up from the vaults: the 14th-Century vellum scroll of an Ethiopic
Contendings of St. Andrew. Brother Luco looked at the request, sighed
at the work expected of him, and went to locate it.

What a creature of the Vatican, the professor thought, thinking
again of the *Romanitá*, the Vatican mode of thought, which was part
Macchiavelli, part haggling in the marketplace, but also had a converse
aspect of utter, stupefying laziness and incompetence, the work of a
month, the inspiration of a moment, stretched to a slow death over
centuries.

O'Hanrahan seated himself amid the reference books, indices of
indices. His dream discovery: an early commentary of a father of the
Church, ignored, rarely read, that quoted an excerpt of the Matthias
gospel to agree with or disprove. Another useful discovery would be a
list of languages, primers of African tongues, ignored perhaps because
they translated, say, Nubian to Ge'ez. He hated to admit it but his rival
Father Beaufoix, the Dominican among the Acolyte Society, wrote a
compendium ten years ago concerning African Christian scripts. Ha,
O'Hanrahan swore he'd do it without Beaufoix's book. And that old
goat was publishing another tome next month—to hell with him!

Friar Luco returned, as if in slow motion, his shuffling, measured
old man's pace alerting O'Hanrahan a full minute before his arrival.
"Eccolo, eccolo," he sang as he put down the scrollcase before O'Hanrahan.

"Grazie," said the professor, opening the tube and sliding the medieval contents out.

"Il Trecento," mused Brother Luco, showing a mild interest.

O'Hanrahan explained it indeed was of the 1300s, but it was in scroll
form to appear older and therefore more valuable. However, like most
medieval fakes, it gave itself away by insisting too much on its accuracy
and prophetic qualities. Halfway through the prophecies of St. Andrew in Ethiopia, the Disciple launches a discourse about the triumph
of Latin rite over the East, the supremacy of Rome—in which Andrew
has a vision of Peter in papal tiara!—and finally a dire warning that
an Antichrist of the Gauls will signal the coming of the End Times and
come in the guise of Babylon, represented, as in *Daniel*, by a griffin.
This, of course, was a blatant attempt to coerce the Avignon, French-
controlled popes to return the papacy to Rome during the so-called

Babylonian Captivity, from 1309 to 1379. Pseudo-texts, before the age of linguistic scholarship and exact dating processes, wreaked havoc on the medieval Church; some clever forgeries, like the *Apostolic Constitutions* and, of course, the *Laudabiliter,* which gave papal approval for England's domination of Ireland, became bedrock documents of state. The *Gospel of Barnabas* of the 1200s, which pretends to have Jesus predict Mohammad, is still given credence by some Moslem scholars.

"Non ha nessun valore, eh?" suggested Friar Luco, leaning over the desk and breathing harsh cigarette breath on O'Hanrahan.

Yes, it's worthless scholastically, O'Hanrahan explained in Italian, leaning away from the breath, but a nice museum piece. O'Hanrahan took his *International Herald Tribune* and his morning's *La Repubblica* newspaper and rolled them into a scroll, while Friar Luco chuckled knowingly. O'Hanrahan placed the newspaper in the scrollcase and asked Friar Luco to return it, to act irate, and send the assistant back for another one as if he'd made a mistake. Meanwhile, O'Hanrahan shoved the 14th-Century scroll into his briefcase, careful not to damage it.

Lunch with Rabbi Hersch was next in the appointment book.

Upon leaving the Vatican Library and walking across the expanse of Piazza San Pietro, O'Hanrahan asked the friar where he went to eat in Trastevere and learned that Luco never missed a meal back at San Francesco a Ripa. Do they have a good cook? asked O'Hanrahan. The friar shrugged. The one Italian without taste buds. Father Vico's tea-making skills perhaps were indicative of a Franciscan lack of prowess in culinary matters.

(Not everyone lives for their stomach, Patrick.)

O'Hanrahan, parting from Luco, followed his nose toward San Crisogono and then turned into the warm, ochre alleyways and shambling streets of Trastevere, "across the Tiber," ancient dwellings supported by ivy and clotheslines, a peasant village within Rome.

"Reminds you of old times, doesn't it?" asked the rabbi, meeting O'Hanrahan at the Trattoria Maria, joining him at an outside table.

"Like Cairo in 1946," said O'Hanrahan while polishing off the breadsticks, referring to when the two men met for the first time.

In Cairo in 1946, the lost, verifiable *Gospel of Thomas* slipped onto the black market and among the dozen academic agents hunting for it in the alleys of the Khan al-Khalili were, one, a young Jesuit novice on a year abroad at American University in Beirut named O'Hanrahan and, two, a grad assistant at Hebrew University named Hersch, each there in hopes of buying it for their respective universities. The *Gospel of Thomas*, the previous greatest gospel find in 2000 years, had eluded the Coptic Museum in Cairo and all the authorities, and made its way before the shenanigans were over to, yes, America! Where *anyone* could have bought it if they had known what it was. A hero of O'Hanrahan,

Dr. Quispel of Utrecht University, nabbed it and it's in Utrecht to this day. But Quispel would be green with jealousy if he knew how close O'Hanrahan was to securing the *Gospel of Matthias*!

The *signora*—Maria, perhaps?—presented herself: a hulking woman, her eyes outlined in southern Italian–strength mascara, her emerald-green dress more appropriate for an opera diva. O'Hanrahan won her favor by quickly ordering a bottle of Montepulciano d'Abruzzo, not the cheapest on her wine list. She disappeared inside a curtain of blue beads, to a kitchen of clanging pots and Italian clamor, a young girl's repeated laughter and an older man's voice chastising her.

"You not gonna give me the last breadstick?" asked the rabbi. O'Hanrahan surrendered it. "Rabbi Eleazar said whoever fails to leave a piece of bread on his table will never see the signs of God's bounty and blessings." Rabbi Hersch then spoke of his adventures at the Vatican:

". . . and so this little man who has been there since they built St. Peter's Church came by and was very helpful. He said 'Signor Rabbi, do you want to see the back room, lots of Jewish, lots of Jewish.' "

Yes, thought the professor, half-attending. A book on Matthias— the oldest gospel ever found. It's the prize of the century, maybe the Dead Sea Scrolls included. What made you think, Paddy, that Morey was going to give you this privilege and not write the book himself?

". . . I love the New Ecumenism, it was please, Mr. Rabbi and Thank you so much, Mr. Rabbi—Rabbi Abba was right: once the door has been shut it is not soon opened, so you gotta take advantage of these opportunities. And then I got to look at . . ." The rabbi noticed his friend wasn't listening. "Then I got to look at St. Paul's First-Century personal pornography collection. Lots of naked Syrian boys, Abdul and his pet camel, a shvanze down to here and I'm not talking about the camel."

"What?"

"I'm talking to you, for Christ's sake. What's with you?"

O'Hanrahan shook his head, it was nothing.

The signora had arrived to take their order. A first course of *spaghetti alle vongole* for O'Hanrahan in which a *kashrut* discussion worthy of Quizzur Shulhan Arukh commenced over whether the rabbi was permitted under dietary laws to dip a piece of bread in the sauce on the fringes of the clam and tomato topping.

"Sorry if I seem distracted, Morey," said O'Hanrahan. He risked, "It's like you're looking over my shoulder. Sort of throws me having you here, working in Rome."

"Look, Paddy," his friend said momentarily, "Hebrew University will . . . will let the PLO use me for target practice if this scroll slips through our hands again, so I'm staying close, and besides, I can't finish my Josephus book until I read this thing." The rabbi eyed him knowingly, then quietly looked down in his lap and folded his napkin again and again. "It's your conquest here, Paddy; I'm not moving in on it. Look, I'm the wrong person to translate it. You're the Patristics man, not me. *You're* the man for it." He took a deep breath. "I just want to help you and make sure we don't run into any more trouble."

Two afterdinner glasses of Amaro Montenegro sundered the day for any serious work.

"Taxi, *signore?*" asked Gepetto the Cabdriver from his sentinel before the hostel. "Good rate for priest, for man of God!"

O'Hanrahan called back in Italian that it was siesta time, which the old man seemed to agree with, pulling his cap down over his eyes and getting comfortable in his front seat.

O'Hanrahan spread out upon his bed, sated. He looked at the ceiling and listened to the ebbing noise of the street as Rome closed her shutters and sank into beds of crisp cool linen sheets, leaving the empty carafes and breadcrumbs on the lunchtables, preparing to dream through the afternoon heat.

Lucy's key was gone downstairs and the DO NOT DISTURB sign was gone, so, he reasoned, she must be out cramming all of Rome into an afternoon. One life is not enough for Rome, says the old cliché, because half of her treasures are buried, or are uncelebrated, having eluded the guidebooks, or are shut up in private palaces, now sepulchers of old ghosts, clung to by the last bearer of a once-feared patrician name. And even if the veil were lifted, most of the treasures are too grand or ingenious to comprehend on the first viewing anyway . . .

If my faith was going to return to me, O'Hanrahan thought sadly, it should have happened here. This is probably my last visit to Rome.

(Indeed, My child, it is.)

This city stands for all that I've contended with and fought against all my life; from my childhood piety to my Jesuit vow, which I broke, to my latter-day crusades against the recidivist likes of John Paul II, who has preached this very year on Protestant error in Mexico, the necessity of celibacy, the sin of birth control, preaching against the errors of the Jews—God forgive him—and this year decrying "intellectualism." Lord, what a throwback.

(A typical pope, really.)

It was the atrocities, thought O'Hanrahan, of the last century of Catholic policy that made me permanently combative. Pius IX and his condemnation of free speech and thought, and the idiot Pius X railing against modernism, and the war criminal Pius XII not breathing a word against Hitler. All the Marian shrines, all the *mater dolorosa* Mediterranean sideshows, the Maria Gorettis!

Again, merciful God, what are we doing to our young women?

Every Catholic girls' school gets a dose of Maria Goretti. An eleven-year-old girl from Ancona. Accosted by a rapist, she refused him, then was stabbed, and then from her hospital bed she forgave him before dying. The spectacle of the cardinals, old celibate men, arguing, debating—*seven* volumes of evidence gathered—was she a martyr of chastity or not? She told the rapist that God disapproved, but she also said *Si si si*, which might have meant that she really wanted it after all. The long hours, the pros and cons . . . God's work in the world? Deciding if an eleven-year-old wants to be raped and enthroning her in the pantheon of saints if she didn't?

It is Rome who deserted *me*, the thinking Catholic. O'Hanrahan pulled the linen sheet around him and felt the consciousness of the afternoon slip away from him, his eyes getting heavy. My Church threw in its cards with the peasantry, the widows in black, the rosary brigade, the wound-counters, the indulgence-mongers. And yet. If my faith was to return to me, it should have happened here.

(Faith doesn't walk in the door and take you by the collar, Patrick. You must incline your heart.)

Then he felt something.

And as he was on the verge of sleep, he felt a pain in his side. A pain that had stayed away for some time now, not since the one bad night this spring in Rome, and the intimations of another one back in Florence. He opened his eyes and tried to predict from staring at the ceiling whether it would go away.

Then, like a knife, it cut into him again.

All right, enough discussion. He rose and got to his shaving kit and took out a bottle of pills. Two of these and he'd be out no matter what his body wanted to do to him. *Man wastes away like a rotten thing, like a garment that is moth-eaten.* He lay back in the bed, stoically ignoring his side. *His bones are full of youthful vigor, but they shall lie down with him in the dust.* It was his liver. Doctors say—hell, they'd told him a hundred times—your liver can't hurt, not like you say it does, Mr. O'Hanrahan. *An old man, and full of days.* But there it was, raging back at him for all the abuse and impertinence.

Soon the Percodan kicked in.

And the rock poured out for me streams of oil!

And then there were no more thoughts as the narcotic seethed within him in waves and all he knew was peace and absence of pain, a bliss and relief Heaven, it seemed today, was unlikely to provide.

O'Hanrahan was awakened by a knock on the door, and the rabbi called out: "Paddy, come see what's on TV."

He stretched in place on his bed. He fumbled for his watch: nine P.M.

Down the hall in the TV room the rabbi was transfixed before "*Colpo*

Grosso," a game show that featured topless Vanna White–equivalents, eight of them. Breasts presented themselves each and every question amid the incomprehensible workings of the show, and the contestants themselves competed for the right to strut down the runway and take it off, including the middle-aged Italian woman they were watching now.

"This is the kind of quality TV Israel needs," mumbled the rabbi.

"Look at the *rack* on that one," said O'Hanrahan of a chestnut-haired presenter; some ancient memory of young girl's breasts, circa 1971, telegraphing back to him. An undergraduate who fixated upon his lectures, and an expensive after-lecture dinner in which he plied her with booze, and then in the car they were revealéd, made manifest! Oh, there was much to edit out of memories like this: the fact that the next day she called up crying and said there would never be a repeat performance, the fact that all through dinner she said he reminded her of her own father—best not to follow the implications of that— the fact that Beatrice figured something was up when you got home and she wept silently beside you in the bed . . . No, let's not drag in all the peripheral stuff, let's remember those young, sumptuous, creamy nineteen-year-old breasts where you lightly reclined your head. In the car, motor running, windows fogged, outside her drab student apartment complex, and where you placed your tender kiss . . . Precious ikon! Bejeweled and resplendent as no holy relic ever was revered!

The emcee of the show was a stereotype of bad Italian show biz with his plastered-down jet-black hair, singing a tuneless song, while the topless women swarmed around him, representing all the countries of the world: a blond woman had a stein for Germany, a dark woman had a Carmen Miranda hat of fruit from South America somewhere, a wholesome slender blonde had a Lady Liberty hat.

"I go for Holland," said the rabbi.

She had a working windmill whirring atop her head as her breasts crowded the screen for attention.

O'Hanrahan and his friend then heard some light laughing of women, perhaps the Sisters of Jesus who were staying in the hostel for a convocation: St. Peter's was crawling with young, nubile third-world nuns. The rabbi dove for the channel and turned it as they passed the room. Anything on? they asked. Nope, just sports, O'Hanrahan said back in Italian. The nuns went away, and the rabbi turned the TV back to "*Colpo Grosso.*"

"I'm going to close the door," said O'Hanrahan, doing just that and locking them inside the public TV room.

Soon there was a knock. "Dr. O'Hanrahan, are you in there?"

"Go away, Lucy."

"Dr. O'Hanrahan, open up!" She sounded upset.

"I excommunicate you, anathema, anathema!"

But then she nearly beat the door down: "I said _open up!_"

"I'm coming, for God's sake, hold your horses . . ."

Lucy stood there out of breath and visibly emotional. Waiting a few yards from her was Gepetto the Cabdriver. That's odd, Lucy was in the same clothes as last night—

Lucy: "_Well_? Aren't you going to ask me where I was?"

"The Colosseum?"

"Dr. O'Hanrahan, I go missing for nearly two nights and you think I'm sightseeing at the Colosseum?"

"Missing?"

"Damn right . . ." He thought "damn" sounded funny coming from her mouth, as if she was trying out the word. She entered the TV room, raging at him: "Haven't you got the police looking for me? I disappear for a day and you don't even notice!"

O'Hanrahan explained about the DO NOT DISTURB sign and just assumed she was asleep or out on the town. Lucy looked near tears and she stood between him and the TV; on "_Colpo Grosso_" two women were making uh-oh! faces as their skimpy blouses fell away.

"_Signore_," pleaded the taxi driver from the hallway, who made a request for money.

"Jim wasn't a diocesan priest," Lucy snapped, "didn't go to Notre Dame, didn't see your lectures there or in Bologna, for starters."

"Who was he?" said the professor, leaning a little to the right to see the woman with the—

"_Could you turn this off?_" Lucy shrieked.

The rabbi turned off the TV and there was silence.

Lucy: "Jim turned out to be an Ignatian prelate. And they want their scroll back."

Inwardly, O'Hanrahan was relieved that it was only the fringe Jesuit group. The rabbi turned around testily in his chair. "What did I tell you, Paddy? Now what did I just say about the criminal element and Lucy here?"

O'Hanrahan: "Did you tell them we didn't have it?"

"They didn't believe me when I told them that, because they knew that the Ignatians had given it to _you_ back in Ireland. And until I convinced them, they thought you and the rabbi had merely staged the robbery in Ballymacross." She refused to be embarrassed about the next part: "I said the Franciscans had stolen it."

O'Hanrahan was horrified. "You told them everything?"

"They _kidnapped_ me, Dr. O'Hanrahan! I didn't know what they were going to do to me. The Jesuits toppled countries! They set up inquisitions."

"No, that was the Dominicans, but go on. Did they do anything harmful to you?"

Lucy regained her composure. "No."

The cabdriver leaned into the room. "*I soldi, per favore . . .*"

Lucy quietly interjected, "Could you pay the driver for me?"

O'Hanrahan dug into his pocket and gave the driver two 10,000-lire bills. The driver said it was more, but O'Hanrahan waved him away.

O'Hanrahan thought out loud: "So they know the Franciscans have it, and that we don't. No great harm done, I suppose—"

"No harm done?" snapped the rabbi. "The Ignatians have the resources to steal the thing from the Franciscans, don't they? How secure is it at the Franciscans'?"

O'Hanrahan felt defensive for the Friars Minor and their little squeaking safe on wheels. "Uh, it's pretty safe."

"I bet not safe enough to keep the Ignatians from stealing it back. And if the Ignatians *do* get it back, do you think they'll be eager to deal with us?" Rabbi Hersch creased his eyebrows and shot a disgusted glance at Lucy: "I knew you were going to be trouble."

Lucy shot back angrily, "I don't intend to be 'trouble' much longer, Rabbi. I'm getting on the first plane out of here."

O'Hanrahan smiled wanly watching this exchange. He would be alone again soon. Fair enough, Lucy had been a trouper. Above and beyond the call of duty.

The rabbi: "Paddy can take you to a travel agent tomorrow—"

Lucy: "Fine with me!"

And wouldn't you know, he had begun to get used to her. Her scholarship might have been helpful further along, her company appreciated. Good job, Paddy, he told himself. You had your chance to include her in the project, befriend her, but you were suspicious and selfish and inconsiderate of her feelings.

(A familiar story with people in your life.)

"I think that's an excellent idea," said the rabbi.

"First plane I can get on . . ." she predicted.

But then again, O'Hanrahan soothed himself, I've always been a solo act. Yes, even when married, even Beatrice smothered me when I was out in the field, on the trail of something. Your first expeditions and discoveries—you young buck, you—were solitary missions. And now it will end that way too, Patrick Virgil O'Hanrahan, the hermit, the modern-day monk poring over the tomes in the candlelit chamber. It is a noble ending. Decry us as you will, Sister Marie-Berthe, but it is we old crotchety bachelor men, alone and misanthropic through the centuries, in monastery and library: we have left the world civilized and enlightened! He sensed a sad foretaste of the lonesome hours ahead.

"C'mon, Luce," said O'Hanrahan. "You'll excuse us, Morey? I'm going to get Miss Dantan a calming drink of grappa."

"I don't want anything to drink, Dr. O'Hanrahan," she said, being led from the room, her face red from consternation. "It'll upset my stomach and I already have, you know . . . indigestion from all this."

The rabbi waited for them to leave the lounge, then turned on the TV set again as O'Hanrahan shut the door behind him. O'Hanrahan then put an arm around Lucy's shoulder. "You had me worried at first, there, Luce."

She didn't say anything as they walked to his room.

"I thought, Sister Lucy, you'd fallen into more criminal hands."

"Don't think that wasn't occurring to me, too."

"Where'd they take you?"

"We ended up at Il Gesù for the first night. Then we went to a church called Sant' Irene for lunch the next day and I talked to some very persuasive priests. They were the guys I told everything to. They were perfect gentlemen; the food was good. Then they let me go tonight. I got a cab from right outside the church and came straight back to here. Fortunately I remembered the name of the hosteleria—"

"What did you say?" O'Hanrahan looked panicked. "You found *that* cabdriver outside of Sant' Irene, *waiting* for you?"

"What about it?"

Both looked up to see Gepetto emerge from the shadows. He reached into his jacket and flashed a gun, and with a jerk of the head urged O'Hanrahan to unlock his door and go inside his hotel room. Lucy too.

"Tip not big enough?" asked O'Hanrahan.

"*Il vangèlo, signore,*" he requested shakily.

He's new at this, reasoned O'Hanrahan. Probably owes some Mafia family a favor and staking out this hotel, stealing my scroll is it. He's no murderer. I can tell by his face . . .

"Hurry hurry," he said in accented English.

O'Hanrahan would have preferred to play out a credible scene of resistance giving way to fear but he could take no chance that tonight's emissary might put the gun to Lucy's head. Slowly, O'Hanrahan went to his bed and creakingly knelt down. The robber cautioned him, reasserting the gun, not to do anything sudden or foolish. O'Hanrahan reached under the bed and slid from the slats of the bedbox the round tube of a scrollcase.

The robber grinned, almost laughing, his chore almost over.

"But Dr. O'Hanrahan," Lucy began to mumble.

"We have no choice but to give them the *Gospel of Matthias*, Lucy," said the professor, enunciating.

The robber opened the end of the scrollcase and slid out the vellum manuscript. "*San Matteo, si?*"

"*Si,*" O'Hanrahan performed, dejected, forlorn.

The man traced a small circle with the gun and O'Hanrahan knew he was expected to roll up the scroll and put it in the bag the cabdriver tossed to the floor. The cabdriver picked up the bag and kissed it, crossed himself. A relic of the Thirteenth Disciple didn't come along every day, thought O'Hanrahan, impressed by this operative's Catholicism.

Then the robber left after picking up O'Hanrahan's key. He closed the door and then locked Lucy and the professor inside O'Hanrahan's room. O'Hanrahan and Lucy listened until his footsteps could be heard down the hall.

"What did he just steal?" asked Lucy, one hand clutching the other, feeling faint.

O'Hanrahan sat on the edge of his bed. "A 14th-Century medieval forgery. Ought to keep the Mafia busy for awhile."

"The *Mafia?* Lucy cried. She touched her temples, then raised her face in cold serenity. "I want to go home immediately."

O'Hanrahan went to the window and surveyed the street. The man had scurried to his cab and driven off. O'Hanrahan thought aloud, "Next person who comes into the hostel, I'll shout down to. I'll tell them to get the hostelkeeper to come up and unlock us." He clapped his hands, trying out a smile. "Now, how about that drink I promised you?" he added, eyeing the grappa.

Lucy just glowered at him.

JULY 6TH–7TH

The next day O'Hanrahan escorted a very paranoid Lucy to a travel agent and discovered the day was completely booked for flights to New York connecting to Chicago, but come tomorrow TWA had a place. And so they reserved a seat with the omnipotent credit card, a five P.M. flight from Leonardo Da Vinci, and Lucy conceded that at last she was homeward bound.

On the day she was to leave, to her surprise, O'Hanrahan sought her out at nine A.M. and knocked on *her* door.

"Who is it?"

"International black market killers," he said.

When O'Hanrahan entered he could tell that Lucy had been up for hours and was all packed. She had put on the polka-dot dress he had bought in Florence.

"After a pastry and a cappuccino," he said, "I got a small itinerary planned. God, I hate days where you gotta travel. All that time to kill."

"Yeah," she said, "I hate it too."

They locked glances briefly but quickly turned away, both fearing a ceremonial goodbye. After all, thought O'Hanrahan as he watched

Lucy turn the key in her door, it won't do to have berated her company for three weeks and then suddenly beg her to stay.

O'Hanrahan knocked on Rabbi Hersch's door, who cried "Whadya want?" from within. The professor offered an invitation for a last coffee at a café, but the rabbi wouldn't join them because he had one more thing to look up in the Judaica section in the Vatican stacks.

"Oh, and Morey," said O'Hanrahan, annoyed that he had to talk through the closed door, "Lucy's flight is this afternoon like yours, from Leonardo."

"So?"

"You'll accompany her to the airport, won't you?"

An unwilling pause. There had been a great coolness since the taxi-driver incident as Rabbi Hersch made it plain that Lucy was an impediment and that he was counting the minutes until she left.

"Uh yeah, whatever," he said. "If it gets her on the plane."

O'Hanrahan whisked Lucy into the alleys of Trastevere, having a surprise up his sleeve, a wicked smirk which could mean anything. The surprise was an appointment at a student-frequented hairdressing salon near Santa Cecilia, radiating a trendy 1990s decor of chrome and stained wood, staffed by a brood of Italian prettyboys, all sporting frizzed-out and piled-up hair themselves.

O'Hanrahan: "I'm tired of your page-boy, Sister Lucy. You shouldn't look like Buster Brown."

"Who?"

"That hairstyle ain't you, Luce. Like that horrible sweater, that old tent-bag."

"Just for you, sir, I'm going to throw it away before I leave, okay?" She looked on at the flurry of activity, and the three beautiful Italian girls having their hair done, their long crossed legs, bracelets on thin tan arms, dressed in light summer yellows and oranges, chattering away as their earnest hairdressers in black cossack blouses fidgeted with their hair, coaxed and seduced it into shape.

Lucy asked how O'Hanrahan ever found this place.

"The *suora* downstairs has a teenage niece. This is *the* place in Trastevere, trust me."

"You don't have to—"

"Silence. My mission to make you over has been a failure. If I can't get you cussing, smoking and drinking, I can at least get you looking like the cosmopolitan beauty you are."

She felt her cheeks color. "Aw c'mon."

Lucy let herself be led away as O'Hanrahan fired orders at a devastatingly handsome twenty-year-old *ragazzo* with penetrating eyes, who certainly considered his hair designs as important as Michelangelo did his ceilings. Gay as Michelangelo too, figured Lucy complacently.

Soon the shapeless page-boy was doomed; hair fell on the floor

beside her, and through gellings and stylings and much Italian commentary, she was spun around in her chair to behold the mirror.

"Whadya think?" said O'Hanrahan.

Lucy's hair was higher on her head, in a helmet with the ends curling
toward her face. She quickly adjusted her face to match such a fashion-
model cut . . . Lucy caught her vulnerable attendant's eyes in the salon
mirror and smiled praise at him, wanting desperately to go somewhere
private to admire herself and make a true judgment.

Lucy and O'Hanrahan went forth into the Roman sun.

Up to the Piazza Santa Maria in Trastevere to settle upon a café, to
listen to the Roman fountain in the square trickle slowly, to look at the
smog-corroded mosaics emblazoned above the portico of the church.
A quick dart inside to see the walls of gold and agate, Our Lady
enthroned.

"C'mon, have a little drink for me," suggested O'Hanrahan, helping
her with her chair. "A Campari and soda? Hey, ever had a Cynar?
Fantastic—lemme get you one."

"Uh, please no, Dr. O'Hanrahan. I don't object in principle, but
before a flight, I might get all nauseated and . . . All right, all right,"
she conceded.

The drinks were ordered and O'Hanrahan, in need of one, began
to relax now that booze was on the way.

Lucy: "You know, sir, it's been an unusual time for me . . ."

"Don't start on the good-bye stuff, Luce. I'll be back in Chicago one
of these days and I'll look you up." Light dawned. "In fact, why don't
you tell me your thesis title and I'll wangle it so I can be the chief
examiner, how about that? Give you an easy A. What was it about
again?"

"Differences in 4th-Century B.C. Corinthian versus Athenian script."

"Ah, yes," he said, no more impressed than before. Their Cynars
arrived. He forced her to take a little sip and she rather liked it.

"Fermented artichoke," he whispered, as she registered amazement.
"They say this church," meaning Santa Maria across the plaza, "is the
first church in Rome, and not, as you might think, St. Peter's. They
claim Santa Maria was consecrated in 222, Roman persecutions notwithstanding . . ."

Lucy stared in her glass. She was going to miss this: the sun, O'Hanrahan's learned exordia, the drink, the food, the sights, each day so
many new things, untried things, that amassed to a new, barely tasted
life. What would Judy say when she saw her in this getup? Judy was
going to have enough to be jealous of for a hundred years, by the time
Lucy got through telling it!

She missed her mother. But going home meant going back to
mother's complaints and mother's grievings and mother's demands—
how much Lucy wished her mother could sit still for an hour, a half-

hour even, and *listen* and be happy for her daughter without her mind racing to the most negative implications. You drank what? You're going to be an alcoholic like Uncle Michael! You spent what? Don't cry to me when you're bankrupt! That old man bought you that dress? You know what he was after! But Mom, she'll weep inwardly, I was in Italy—*Italy!*

". . . Rome was so tolerant of everything," O'Hanrahan rambled on. "And yet here were these Christians, this communistic prosperous sect that took care of elderly and sick people—and they had such distaste for us! Claudius, a reasonable Caesar, persecuted us, Nero dipped us in pitch and used us for human torches, Pliny hated us, Hadrian hated us, Tacitus too. It's my theory we know nothing about how Christians behaved from 30 to 313 A.D. Maybe, after reading too many crackpot end-of-the-world books like *Revelations* we did burn Rome down as accused . . ."

Going back to Chicago, Lucy realized, meant going back to the thesis and the approaching deadline and the word-processing lessons so she could write it and edit it, and back to fighting over who got what cubicle in the Regenstein Library. Human beings didn't have souls at the University of Chicago, no love lives, no passions—they had cubicles. *That's my cubicle,* snarled the dark-haired female grad student with the faint mustache; the science nerd with the thick glasses, looking as if he might cry . . . But there were no books marking it, Lucy would say. *Doesn't matter,* the creature of the library would insist, *it's mine.* Lucy, fearing a display of mental illness, would back off. God, I wish I weren't going back, back to Judy and arguing over the cat-food piles, the gradual putting on of weight until all her small triumphs had been obliterated by Christmas.

". . . mind you, if Christianity was a slave cult, it could have been dangerous. Seventy-five percent of Rome in Paul's time were slaves, so a movement that spread among slaves was going to be trouble. Suetonius mentions that Jews rioted in Rome because of a man named Chrestus, and Chrestus was a slave name, easily confused with Christ, or perhaps it was followers of Christ who led riots and Suetonius got the name wrong . . ."

Oh, God, and then there was her father. Lucy swore she would talk to him seriously about the NORAID business. And he would tell her she looked like a lesbian—his branding women lesbians was a recent discovery—with her new haircut. And she would say she had the greatest time of her life in Europe. And he would say they were all worried sick and she spent too much and why couldn't she bring in a little more money for herself. And she would get to tell her maiden aunts about Rome and all the churches and show them her photos this coming Christmas. And her father, then imposing a silence from his retirement armchair, would turn up the wrestling or the football game louder to drown them all out, grumbling and uninterested and say something like, Our family spent a goddam fortune trying to get over to this country and here you spent a fortune to go back! And he'd hate her dress, too.

". . . there's Excommunication, which is just denying you mass, then Major Excommunication, which means no Catholic can even talk to you, and then if the pope really gets pissed off, Consignment to Hell. Sigismundo Mallatesti got this treatment, though I sort of like his gall. Taking over the town cathedral and dedicating it as a temple to himself! He kept marrying off his daughters to pretty young men so he could sleep with them, sometimes at the same time *with* his daughters. A close family." O'Hanrahan paused to glance at his watch and frowned. "Well. Time to go."

Lucy breathed in a slow, painful breath.

She and the professor passed for a last time through the time-softened alleys of Trastevere. And it figured, didn't it. Here she was, halfway home, and two Italian boys—complete jokers, no more than sixteen, swaggering along—pursed their lips at her and gave her a whistle.

"You know what I think you need?" said O'Hanrahan at the door of the Santa Cecilia Hostel. "You need a new roommate, maybe a new thesis topic. Hey, maybe you oughta can the thesis and do something useful, so you won't end up an old academic leftover like me."

She laughed lightly. "My parents would kill me, if I quit now."

"You told me yourself, you longed for some kind of service, something meaningful to devote yourself to . . ."

"Yeah, and you scoffed at me."

"Now that I know you, I'm not scoffing anymore. You're what? Twenty-six?"

She was twenty-eight, but let it stand.

"Tell Mom and Dad to go to hell. Get out of goddam Chicago if you have to. Go somewhere where you won't lose that tan. Ten years from now I don't want to hear you're still feeding the cats with Janie—"

"Judy." Desolately, it struck her how unlikely it would be that O'Hanrahan would be around ten years from now.

"There's an adventurer in there somewhere, Miss Dantan, someone not too different from what I am, what do you think?" She smiled hopefully. "As for me, I'll be taking tomorrow night's ferry from Brindisi to Greece, sailing on the S.S. *Argos*—God, it must be the twentieth time on that old rustbucket . . ." O'Hanrahan trailed off, already spiritually down the road, eyeing the next horizon. "Next time in Europe, you'll have to see Greece."

Soon the taxi arrived and the rabbi and Lucy put their suitcases—Lucy's unliftable and overstuffed to bursting—in the trunk.

Lucy would have given O'Hanrahan a good-bye kiss, but as she got in the car, he appeared a story above her, waving so-long from his bedroom window. He waved to them both, yelled a see-you-in-the-Holy-Lands to the rabbi, and watched as the taxi pulled away and the silver sedan rounded the corner. He clapped his hands as if to establish a new break, a page turning, and then it was back to work in his room.

But if O'Hanrahan had stayed at the window longer, he would have seen a white luxury car following them, with a German license plate.

    ✝   ✝   ✝

An hour later at the airport, the rabbi contributed a strained smile and shook Lucy's hand and said: if you should ever be in Jerusalem one day, should you be so blessed, look me up. Yeah, right, she thought. And brusquely he was off to check in for his ticket. Lucy waited an annoying half-hour in a line, confirmed her departure, picked up her boarding pass, and decided not to check through her bag until the interminable line for that service lessened. She went to sit in a passengers' lounge.

It was just 2:45 P.M. The taxi was fast.

You had to check in by 3:30 P.M. for the five o'clock flight. Well, if that will keep another massacre from happening: this is the airport, Lucy couldn't help reminding herself, where the Arab terrorists shot that little American girl. Every summer it seems something awful happens here. Great. Here she is stuck in Terrorism Central for another two hours. She wondered if the rabbi's flight left earlier . . . That's odd, thought Lucy, staring at the PARTENZE board, which listed departing flights: there's not a flight to Tel Aviv this afternoon or tonight.

Lucy supposed she had better call Judy in Chicago and get her to meet her at O'Hare tomorrow. She dragged her suitcase with the unworking tiny wheels to the Telecommunicazione desk, where she was assigned a booth to call from, the payment to be made when she was done. It would be . . . five, six, *seven* hours earlier there, so it would be 7:45-ish in Chicago, which was early, but Judy got up on Saturdays to do volunteer counseling at the Hyde Park Women's Clinic from 8:30 A.M., so she'd be awake.

"Hello Judy? It's me!"

Judy started in with a litany of concerns—

"Yeah, I know but Judy . . . Judy, I . . . Look, I'm calling from *Rome* . . . Yeah! Rome, Italy. Do you want to pick me up at O'Hare? Tomorrow night at midnight, but call and see if it'll be late before you drive out . . ."

Judy didn't say yes. Maybe Lucy's dad could drive out. Her father had been calling nightly.

"Yeah? Uh-huh . . . Well, you know my father."

And for variety there was her mother.

"Well, Mom'll be happy when she sees the stuff I bought for her."

Did she buy Judy a present?

"Uh, yeah, sure, Judy . . ."

She hadn't! Maybe there was time to hit the duty-free store and get something, anything.

"What? What about the cats? Judy I'm not going to buy a present for . . . No, it's expensive, I . . . Judy, come on, I—" It was no use. "Helllloooo, Paws. I love you pussy cat, and tell Cattus Mommy's coming home tomorrow night, okeee? Judy . . ."

Judy had some more comments. The rent was due, what about the electricity, what about the gas, and there was a bowl of something involving tuna in the back of the refrigerator that, one might have thought, Lucy would have had the decency to throw out before she left on a trip—

"Yeah, when I get home I'll deal with it . . ."

Judy had some questions, Was it hot? Did Lucy go everywhere? How about Romance?

"Uh, well, yeah, I do have . . . I have some stories to tell, Judy. But of course in person, when it doesn't cost a fortune." Judy was going to be so jealous! "What? Who? What about Vito Campanella?"

Vito, the resident Theology Department god.

". . . Vito, the guy in my seminar? That Vito, the guy with the behind, yeah . . . But how'd you ever . . . Really. Dinner and then you two went where? Did you have him back for coffee or did you . . . You had him back. To our place?"

Lucy listened.

"That's just great, Jude. Congratulations. Oh, I see. Yeah, if you two are doing something tomorrow night, I don't wanna mess anything up, I can take a cab . . . No, I don't—I don't really mind, no . . . Yeah sure, I understand and hey, it's costing a fortune, I'll see you tomorrow night when I get back. Heh heh, yeah, I won't wait up for you. Hope you guys have a good time."

And Lucy hung up and went back to the lounge to sulk.

Well, what do you know?

Judy finally got someone. Lucy got out of town and the next week, wham-blam, Judy got brave and asked Vito, Vito the cute Italian-American hunk with the Soloflex machine, the boring and shallow guy, the guy about to be flunked out of the department but Vito of the cheekbones and dimples, Vito who went out for dinner with Judy. Good for Judy.

Then Lucy thought: I want to die.

Not the note she would have ended her European adventure upon.

Lucy decided, in homage to O'Hanrahan, to go have a drink, a last drink of wine, just a glass, one little glass, which she hoped would calm her down, nervous about the flight, nervous about her parents and Judy and . . . Judy and *Vito*—just doesn't that beat all?

But if Lucy had not gone then to the bar she would have seen an old acquaintance, the Man in the Cheap Suit, loitering in the lounge by the magazine stand. He was wearing something just as attractive today, but different: a plaid sports coat, a yellow shirt with a bolo tie with a turquoise Indian design on it, a pair of green golf trousers under that.

And Lucy could also have seen Rabbi Hersch carrying his suitcase into the lounge, his ticket in hand.

The rabbi spotted the Man in the Cheap Suit. He walked over to him:

"Had a feeling you were nearby. From what my friends were saying, you can be identified a mile off in that getup."

The man looked up from his picture magazine, a topless European model his interest. "Hello, Rabbi. Funny seeing you in Rome. Didya get to see the pope?"

"Amusing, you're not. What are you doing here?"

PUGLIA
July 8th

O'Hanrahan had his little train vendor snack, a tin foil–wrapped package of dry biscuits, and a half-bottle of *acqua minerale* under his seat as the countryside of northern Campania, the feisty little province of Molise, and finally Puglia raced by.

When his train pulled into the Bari station, O'Hanrahan stared at the station sign and felt a tinge of affection for the old whitewashed city on the backside of modern Italy. Home of the Church of St. Nicholas, the 4th-Century Syrian Greek whose remains found their way to Bari. There was a butcher in his town whose appetites for young boys included chopping them into pieces and preserving them in brine. Nicholas, the patron saint of children, miraculously reassembled them. Best not to tell the kiddies the source of Santa Claus, O'Hanrahan mused with a smile.

Puglia, the land of Padre Pio, the Capuchin man of God! All along the Gargano, that inexplicable peninsula jutting into the Adriatic, O'Hanrahan had noticed the proud postcards of Pio displaying his stigmata. Remember that village high in the Gargano? The Greek-styled town of Monte Sant'Angelo, arranged like Santorini on the hillside, rows of white houses, the ubiquitous women in black patrolling the quiet streets. It is here that the Angel Michael appeared to some shepherds—what he said to them still remains a secret of the town.

(The usual stuff concerning the End Times.)

To prove he had been there, the Archangel left behind his red cape, on display in a cathedral in a cave beneath the town.

(No odder than the Virgin Mary dropping her girdle into St. Thomas's waiting hands, now on display in Lucca. Don't forget Joseph of Copertino, Patrick.)

St. Joseph of Copertino, the Flying Monk, laughed O'Hanrahan. He flew throughout the 1600s, observed by men of unimpeachable integrity, once before a group of doubting Lutherans, and severe Inquisition officials. Joseph would be struck by a vision of the beyond, fall into an ecstatic trance and levitate, once during an audience with the disbelieving Pope Urban VIII, who was then convinced.

. . . Ah, but there is a cure for Puglian nostalgia: Brindisi.

Brindisi, where the train was slowing to a stop, is sacrificed to the tourist-ferries-to-Greece racket. O'Hanrahan left the train and stood at the exit to the station and braced himself for the long haul, dragging his suitcase and his satchel. From the station to the port is an avenue of English and German signs—get your ferry tickets here, cheapest fare to Greece, gyp joints that announced a fixed-price menu for L. 5000 but don't you believe it. An Italian café owner accosting passersby, hawking them with a variety of languages: "American, yes? We love Americans here, special joost for you!" O'Hanrahan always hated that kind of thing. Reminded him of the world after the war, Europeans whoring for G.I. pocket change.

O'Hanrahan checked in at the terminal and booked his cabin on the *Argos*, the last one available. Then, with an afternoon to kill, he wandered along the seafront with an eye to having some wine; a perusal of displayed menus showed *turistico* prices were in effect. O'Hanrahan selected a café on the main drag so he could people-watch. The harbor was not exactly photogenic. The Brindisani . . . What was the adjective? Brindisani? Brindisese? . . . decided they should erect a monument to the Sailor, a giant concrete rudder, eight stories high.

Soon the wine arrived, the wine of the house but very good.

He sipped and enjoyed the mouthful. This is why I drink, he thought. This is what I cherish and misguidedly have all those other less successful drinks for, this: the sun, the blue sky, and gentle breeze, my work spread before me, around young people—and today, he couldn't even resent their youth and beauty—laughing, about to sail, all of us bound for foreign lands. O'Hanrahan complacently observed the pedestrian traffic to the ferries, the Eurobackpackers and the vacationers fool enough to holiday in Brindisi, sunning themselves near the marina. There's a pretty girl . . . California blonde, maybe Swedish. No, I think American. The way she uses her hands. You never had a girl like *that*, Paddy.

(You committed quite enough adultery for one man.)

And lookee there, thought Patrick, leaning forward, adjusting his glasses. There's an Italian beauty. Heh heh, she knows it too. Look at that disdain. Of course with the wolves in this country, walking around in a dress like that means 24-hours-a-day harassment. God, there's nothing like Mediterranean beauty . . . here today, gone by twenty-five. Enjoy it now, *carissima.* And look, there's Lucy—

"LUCY!" he cried, rising to his feet.

"Dr. O'Hanrahan," she said, dragging her suitcase behind her, beaming. "So glad I found you!" She lumbered up to his café table. "I figured you'd be near the ferry terminal. It was the *Argos,* right?"

"What happened to good-bye forever?" He sat down dazed, wondering if she was a product of too much wine and sun.

"You remember what you were saying in Rome? I think you need an assistant. You said you needed one."

He poured himself half a glass and tried to overcome his speechlessness. "Look, that's very kind, but I can get half a dozen assistants in Athens—"

"Yeah, but I know the background. You don't wanna break in a whole new person."

O'Hanrahan eyed her carefully. No, no he didn't. In fact, welling up inside him was a happiness that now he wouldn't be alone, a joy in dispensing with that half-hearted, bolstering rhetoric about being an old man of theology, alone, misanthropic but uncompromised. That's all he ever really wanted: an audience who could appreciate him! A willing listener to chart the complex play of his mind! If Beatrice had just *listened* to him . . . But O'Hanrahan became aware he was smiling and he immediately looked down. Mustn't let Lucy Dantan think she can just walk all over the old man, nosiree.

"Don't you agree, sir, that breaking in a whole new person would be wasted time?"

"I'm not through breaking in *you.*" He waved to the waiter. "*Scusi. Un'altro bicchiere per la signorina, per favore.*" O'Hanrahan dictated to her seriously: "You're going to help me through this bottle."

Out of breath from suitcase-dragging, she settled herself into the chair across from him, saying lightly, "I suppose it will please you to know I missed my flight yesterday because I had a bottle of wine that put me to sleep in the lounge."

"Aprocryphal tales, not to be believed."

"It's true, sir, a whole bottle. I was depressed. I suppose deep down I wasn't ready to go home. Wonder what my psychology-major roommate would make of that."

The glass arrived. The waiter put it down in front of her and O'Hanrahan began to pour. "Greek, I can do. Secretarial skills, I got. A drinking buddy, I don't got." He pushed the box of Winstons across the table. "Have a cigarette, Luce."

She wasn't going to blink here. She had smoked intermittently at St. Eulalia's to the distress of the nuns, who looked at her with pitiful the-Virgin-Mary-is-watching-you eyes, eyes that looked upon the damned once so beloved of Our Lady.

"You gotta light?"

O'Hanrahan leaned across with his lighter. "Some ground rules," he said, settling back into his chair. "You smoke. You drink. You don't lecture me about my health or my smoking or my drinking. You look pretty each day."

She shrugged. "Inasmuch as I can look pretty." As soon as she said it they both realized how automatic her self-put-downs were—

"And no more of that Catholic frump-talk either," he snarled. "I'd take it from you if you were a frump, but you're not. You're a lovely young woman."

But her face colored slightly from having been called out for her self-deprecations. It came from years of practice with Judy back in the Kimbark Street apartment: no, *I've* got the thighs of death, no, *I've* got the fattest behind, no, *I've* got less of a chance than you for going out . . .

"You're not listening, Miss Dantan," said the professor. "Did you hear what I just said?"

"I'm supposed to look pretty." Lucy suggested quickly, "Don't you think I ought to go book a ticket? I'm sure the ferry will be crowded."

He shook his head. "I wouldn't count on getting a seat or a bunk. You'll be sleeping outside on the deck tonight, buying a ticket this late in the day."

"Well then, I better go—"

"I'm not done with my ground rules. I don't want to see those insect glasses ever again. You got contacts, wear them. That lousy, welcome-mat, circus-tent sweater."

She interrupted: "I got rid of it in Rome already."

"No digestion reports. I don't care if you *drown* in your own diarrhea. I don't want to hear about it. Or periods."

They sat there a moment, staring at each other.

"Whatever you say. Do I get to stop calling you Dr. O'Hanrahan and call you Patrick like Gabriel got to?" She added immediately: "Sir?"

"No."

This was probably not the time to bring up sharing some credit on the eventual Matthias book with O'Hanrahan. And changing her thesis to a commentary on this very project. She would bide her time. "I accept your conditions," she said. "Partner?" Her hand remained un-shaken.

"A rather sudden and suspicious conversion. Perhaps you should break one of the Ten Commandments as a demonstration."

Lucy adopted the deadpan she used when giving back smart remarks to her mother: "Hmmm. Shall I make a graven image?"

"You blush easy. That's another thing, no more blushing."

Lucy stood up. "I'll work on it. After I get my ticket."

He looked up at her innocently, ready for his confirmation photo. "Oh, but look! You haven't finished your wine yet."

Lucy reached over and downed her glass in one, then grabbed *his* glass and downed it in one gulp as well.

"I'll be back," she said.

Lucy got her ticket tediously enough, and soon the afternoon and two more bottles with O'Hanrahan were also gone and Lucy found herself staggering onto a gangway, onto a ferry, someone taking her ticket, someone checking her passport, someone directing her to the upper deck, where she was going to spend the night. And at some point, after what seemed an endless wait with much folderol on the dock, yelling sailors, and lines being thrown and taken in, portly corrupt officials going on and off the ship, the S.S. *Argos* backed slowly from the pier and began a slow turn to the east. To Greece!

Lucy propped herself up at the rail, looking back on Brindisi, squinting at the intense streak of orange sun on the water, a sun that would soon set behind the olive groves and red earth of Puglia.

O'Hanrahan appeared. He proferred her a cup of strong espresso—a double. "Brought you something."

Feeling guilty, she figured, for intoxicating his new partner. Lucy took it and sipped the bitter brew.

"It's going to be a clear night, at least," O'Hanrahan said, looking eastward. "You won't get rained on."

"Where are you going to be?"

"In my first-class cabin, going over my notes."

Lucy noticed the duty-free whiskey in a duty-free shopping bag. He was probably going to familiarize himself with that too. Poor man.

"You feeling all right after all the wine?" he asked, not exactly strained with concern. "A little tipsiness is a plus on a boat. If it gets rough, you just rock along with it."

"It's not going to be rough, is it? I mean, is the Adriatic rough?"

O'Hanrahan calmed her—he had a new partner who was scared that luxury liner Mediterranean ferries were going to sink. What was she going to think of the West Bank? "Nope, almost never," he said, fatherly. "Never known this sea to be rough. But you want a little rocking," he added. "It's like the cradle. You never sleep better than at sea."

"In Rome you called this ship a rustbucket . . ."

He winced. "Ignore lots of what I say. I give you permission."

And soon they were a mile into the Adriatic, up to speed, Brindisi receding now, mingling with the dirty trail of the smokestack behind them. And the sea was wonderfully calm as it often is in the summer, glassy smooth, reflecting for a long twilight the dull violet of the sky. Then the night asserted itself, and the Evening Star revealed herself and soon others.

"I guess that's it for me," said O'Hanrahan some hours later, encountering Lucy again on the deck. He was yawning, and Lucy detected the faint aroma of licorice from whatever he was drinking.

"I've never slept outside before," she said.

"Not even in Campfire Girls?"

"My mother wouldn't let me be in those things, because the neighborhood was a bit rough. Rumors that the girls smoked cigarettes."

"You would have corrupted them all, Sister Lucy."

She laughed, still agreeably woozy. Lucy stole a brief glance at O'Hanrahan. He was staring mindlessly at the nighttime sea, the occasional shore light. "Did you ever . . ." Should she ask? Yes, she went ahead. "Did you ever really believe in God, Dr. O'Hanrahan?"

(Tell her the truth, Patrick.)

He looked at her kindly, but something within withdrew. You deserve an answer, sweet Lucy, but you won't get it tonight. Sometime, but not tonight.

(Tell yourself the truth, Patrick.)

He chuckled, "I *was* a Jesuit, young lady."

She giggled, looking down. "That doesn't exactly answer my question."

"I used to, yes," he said quickly. "And I'd like to again. I learned too much in between, that's my problem." But having said that, he refined the thought further: "No, more precisely, I've always believed in God. The problem with me was that . . . was that I grew not to like Him very much. But, interestingly, I have never lost an affection for the people handicapped by God. Do you know who I mean? There are, after all, people who get out of bed, marry and have children, laugh and live and go to the grave without giving God a second thought—moral, ethical, decent people."

"Yes."

O'Hanrahan struggled to explain. "And then there are the others. The old men who sat in the scriptoria for their whole lives copying out tracts, the nuns who can drink you under the table, old codgers like me who waste a lifetime reading theology. Maybe you're one of these people. These are my cronies, Miss Dantan, my partners in crime. We're different and we say it's because of God, but maybe we're just . . . just different, that's all."

Lucy stared toward the horizon, black meeting black, but the night warm and inclusive. "Do you think when you lose your faith . . ." Not that she'd lost hers exactly, but it was changing. "Do you think you can ever get it back?"

Now O'Hanrahan also looked away. "I'll let you know the answer to that when we find that last chapter and get the *Gospel of Matthias* translated. Ask me then, okay?"

She smiled gravely. "Well, good night, partner. Hope you can live with yourself, leaving me defenseless out here on the deck."

"Curl up with that Swedish contingent we saw in the snack bar. They looked pretty liberal. Europe's just one big orgy for you kids these days. Why, when I first came to Europe I was a bit younger than you, but it was after the war and . . ." But his ramblings weren't particularly directed anywhere. "Your generation doesn't realize how few epochs have been like this in history, how rare this is, traveling where you please throughout Europe—Eastern Europe too, now. You pack your backpacks and go. Sex for you kids is like drinking water . . ."

Lucy looked distracted but amused.

"Something wrong?" he asked.

She hid a smile. "I haven't been able to get it out of my head, Dr. O'Hanrahan, for three days. Catherine's wedding ring."

And then they both laughed. "That's a good story, isn't it? Stays with you. Night, Miss Dantan."

And he was gone. Accompanied by his duty-free.

Lucy took a final walk around the deck, going as far as she could go on both sides of the ship. There was room to walk, but just barely—one threaded an avenue of backpackers, teenagers in sleeping bags, there was a group of Italian boy scouts, every one of them a doll, talking loudly and sparring to the annoyance of the Germans beside them trying to sleep. There was a group of Americans trading home-town information, baseball talk, what college do you go to, what's your major . . . and after taking in these sights, she stood for a last time at the rail. No sign of land now. There was a light out there, but it looked like another ferry. It was comforting somehow, all these boats on the sea nearby, all going the same place.

It thrilled her anew: Greece!

After all the Greek she'd studied, to be upon the sea with Greece ahead! *Not the least shyness now,* she steeled herself in the place of Telemakhos, *You came across the open sea for this!*

Lucy returned to the top deck where she had set her suitcase beside some card-playing Australians who said they'd watch it for her. She staked out a space on the deck, and tried to use her suitcase for a headrest unsuccessfully, before opening it and removing some dirty clothes, piling them together for a pillow. She also took out a sweater, though it wasn't necessary because the night was warm and the sea was ever so gently swaying the boat and a dull glow on the horizon meant a moonrise was imminent.

And then she heard a groan and a grunt to her side, so she turned.

It was a couple making out.

The Lucy of a few weeks ago could have been expected to sneer, say something cynical for Judy's benefit—disgusting, wasn't it? Hey, give us all a break, take it to the bedroom, who wants to see it?

But not tonight.

She beheld them a moment longer, then looked away, rolling over on her other side, curling up smaller, holding herself more tightly, and she thought of Gabriel, *arrivederci, Poverello*, even of Farley—a passing glance, smiling—and then she settled on David. David, who took her arm so happily, David, who stammered and shuffled before giving her that farewell kiss. It was his clumsiness that Lucy replayed in her mind again and again because in it there was something beautiful for her, and if she had not been so expert at restraining her heart, it might have filled her with a longing so pure and sharp that she might have cried tears held in reserve for as long as she could remember and feel.

For she had prayed, Blessed Mary, very very hard for a very very long time not to end up alone. How the word echoes in any language: *alone*. She could see the vision with supreme clarity, taste its medicinal bitterness, the mandatory task of visiting maiden Aunt Lucy, with the fussy ways, not good with people anymore, just a little tea and toast please, the veinous trembling hands, the outdated, airless apartment of dust and mother's bedclothes and cameo photographs, the Irish spinster world of black and white, contagiously gray, and the only sound the ticking clock on the nightstand, ticking old maid time.

No, she thought. Not tonight, not now. I am melancholy, she thought, and I am lovesick and I am directionless in my life and I am half-drunk but tonight I choose to believe that Love shall find me or I shall find it, because Love is mostly the hope for Love, isn't it?

(Yes, My dear.)

Rocked to sleep by the *mare Adriatico*, charting a course between the bogus miracles of Italy and the crumbling glories of Greece, she awaited dreams with tender thoughts of Love.

(My dearest Lucy. You have never seen them above you, looking down, *con amore*, the ancient and all-permitting stars.)

4 And this, alas, brings us to a sorry episode, the once noble city of Tyre, now seat of every whoredom, a city where the stones themselves are wicked. Against our wishes we were put ashore in Tyre so ship repairs could be effected, intending in a day or so that we would be off to Antioch. Oh, poor Xenon! I blush to tell our miseries there—would that we had never left the boat!

2. As you may know, one enters Tyre through the Syrian quarter in which one is spared no rapacity. In a complete folly, dear Xenon and I entered the shop of a merchant who called to us: "Come, fine men of Judea, away from this godless street. You look in need of tea."

No sooner had we settled ourselves in his room and the tea was brought out, than a bolt of cloth stretched the length of the wall before us begin to shimmer with the gyrations of those behind it. Our host announced that what lay behind the Temple Curtain could not rival the treasure behind his own, and with that the curtain dropped from its hooks and we were presented with twelve bare-bottomed youths. The odious man proceeded to take a feather and run it along the laughing boys' posteriors, and he sang out some wretched song in Syriac to the effect of: "Tall ones, short ones, black ones, white ones," and such. I commanded Xenon to leave while I harangued our host for such an outrage. Xenon lingered to behold this spectacle until our host's veiled Syrian wife reached under Xenon's robe for a pinch of his buttocks. "Ah, an ample Jewish fundament," she sang, "that should catch many a shekel."

One sees by this illustration the state to which Tyre has fallen.

3. As Ephesus has given itself over to female whoredom, Tyre seems to have set up an equivalent trade in boys for the unending flow of sailors from the world over who must clutch at something while in a port. Many of the taverns have names like "Ganymede's Bower," which suggests the most depraved of Greek pagan myths. To dignify this trade with the purer, higher sensations of true *eros*, with Socrates and Alcibiades, with Hippotades and Aristogiton,[1] with Jonathan and David whose love lyrics I rendered in *The Hebraika*, (which, you recall, were foremostly admired in certain circles), does not bear pursuing.

4. Many dreadful heresies have sprouted here and the life-account of Our Master has degenerated to fable and hearsay. One sect, the Lapsarians, has decided that sin must be purged from the body by repetition. (This is what the pagans do with less pretension of course, but observe how these things thrive in Nazirene circles.) After endless orgies and saturnalia, the priest performs an exorcism and the demon, exhausted and spent (it is thought), is removed and the person free of any more sin. In no time, as one could predict, the demon comes back and the whole process is repeated.[2]

A variation on this occurs in nearby Sidon in which all the women of the commune are communal property, and not a day must pass without every man being satisfied in his lusts by every single one of the women.[3] In essence, these harlots must remain

1. The author means Harmodius and Aristogiton, the popular warrior-lovers of 6th-Century B.C.E. Greece.
2. There was no shortage of syncretic sex-and-Christianity cults in the early centuries of the Church, culminating in the Helvidians and Paternians of the 300s, known for their sexual excesses. A Gnostic sect by various names—Cainites, Contrarians, and others—allowed themselves great sexual license, having decided the God of the Old Testament had been defeated by the God of the New, meaning the prohibitions of the Pentateuch were ungodly. Some sects of the 1st–4th Centuries systematically tried to break every known Biblical rule. This author's reputation as a crusader against sexuality seems to have been all, previously, that survived him; e.g., Clement of Alexandria:
   For in obedience to the Savior's command . . . [a man has] no wish to serve two masters, pleasure and Lord. It is believed that Matthias also taught this, that we must fight against the flesh and treat it with contempt, never yielding to it for pleasure's sake, but must nourish the soul through faith and knowledge (Stromateis, Book III. ca. 210 C.E.).
3. Among the most notorious of the Gnostic leaders were Valentinus (who claimed a quite-likely succession from Paul), Cerdo, and Marcus, who, according to Irenaeus (in *Heresies Answered*, ca. 185), *fits out a bridal chamber and celebrates a mystery with invocations on those being initiated, declaring that what they are doing is a spiritual marriage on the patterns of the unions above.*
   Carpocrates may be referred to by the author here. This disciple of Simon the Magus was working in this period in Sidon (60–85 C.E.), and taught that until all sin had been experienced by the body, the body could not be expected to defeat these demons, hence every wickedness must be practiced. We hear of Carpocrates and his commune of shared women from Irenaeus of Lyons (130–200 C.E.). Polygamy seems to be inextricable from Christian Gnosticism up to more recent times with the American Mormon Church and Joseph Smith (1805–1844).

prisoners of concupiscence, barely having time to dress between their duties. Again, here, too, the priest has his way with whomever he wishes and then exorcises these imagined demons after he has had his fill.

5. In the days following Ptolemais, I was reminded painfully of my inadequacies as an evangelist—Thomas, Maryam of Bethany, and even James bar-Alphaeus had in their way bettered me. So I was determined that while in miserable Tyre I would regain the station worthy of a Disciple and set a fine example for Xenon, for indeed, Tyre held the greatest challenge a disciple could face, an enemy of the Nazirenes from earliest days: Simon the Magus.[4]

Xenon and I went to the empty Syrian marketplace, which stank of discarded fruits and greening meat scraps, and there we waited for the nightly appearance of the Magus. It seemed the whole of Phoenicia had gathered in usual expectation of glimpsing some illusion. At last the demon Magus and his entourage appeared, parting the crowd as he walked, awing them with simple tricks of producing flames and flowers, mumbling incantations no doubt learned from Belial himself. Ah, what a near-corpse Simon was, aged and stooped for a man of his years, sodden with the corruption that clotted his veins.

In his train was Menander,[5] once Simon's catamite and boy-whore, now a decrepit old ruin with more face paint than an embalmed Persian. Menander attended his master, calling the rabble to press nearer for the divine demonstrations. O but there was none more foul than the unspeakable Helen, his accomplice!

---

4. *Acts* 8:9–24 mentions Simon the Magus and shows Peter contending with him and eventually converting him to Christianity. No later account, strangely, mentions anything like this—Simon remains a fixed enemy for decades in the Early Church and long a figure of fascination, mentioned by Irenaeus, Clement of Alexandria, and Justin Martyr. In numerous apocryphal Acts and Contendings, Simon pops up to do battle with God, trick against trick, and always loses; in *The Passion of Peter and Paul* (300s?, attr. Marcellus), there is a contest before Nero in which Simon Magus flies and is brought down and breaks into four pieces. A Coptic version from the 300s of an early epistle warns *Cerinthus and Simon . . . are enemies of Our Lord Jesus Christ, for they do pervert the truth. . . . Keep yourselves therefore far from them, for death is in them and great pollution and corruption, on whom shall come judgment and the end and everlasting destruction.*

5. The Magus apparently spawned a dynasty of gnostic trickery, passing his "church" to Menander (who peddled earthly immortality), before it split into two camps of Saturninus (a mere magician) and Basilides, who wrote some 24 heretical gospels, inventing disciples as it pleased him, and (writes Eusebius) "monstrous fictions to support his impious heresies." We know of him from Agrippa Castor (90–150 C.E.?), who wrote a specific refutation.

But a teenage girl when the pair debated Peter some thirty years ago, she had grown into a creased, slatternly harlot, moist with disease and license, attired as no courtesan of Rome would dare!

6. Throughout the early moments of this theatrical Simon staged an invocation to the Higher Powers and performed sleights of hands any court magician can manage. With, I suppose, the help of some associates in the audience, he brought people upon his platform and pretended to read their minds, spouting hatred of Romans, hatred of Medians, all things to endear our race and bring unthinking hordes to slavish adoration, stirring the crowd into a froth of excitement and credulity.

Helen—that such a name as that Trojan beauty, or worse, the queen that fed our wretched nation in its need,[6] should be debased on this mantle!—Helen entered again wearing less than before. With her help, Simon the Magus produced a full-length Arabian saber from between her legs and illumined torches from what appeared to be her tongue, no doubt aided by some vile mechanism underneath Helen's immodest toga. Soon he brought out a tisane containing an essence that he mixed with great flourish into a bowl and with show poured and extracted, finally setting this unguent alight. When it had cooled he began to paint Helen, as if she were an Athenian statue, until she seemed a living idol herself, caked in gold.

"Behold," said the Magus. "I give you the New Ark of the New Covenant!"

7. Then the Magus undid the Slattern Helen's robe and exposed her nakedness, her breasts lacquered in gold potion. She fell into a trance, or pretended to, and Simon asked which of the Men of Tyre was man enough to touch the New Ark.

Said Simon: "Behold, my good men! Whereas My Father

---

6. Simon's accomplice Helen is mentioned in Justin Martyr's *Defense of Christianity* (ca. 150 C.E.) addressed to Antoninus Caesar. *And a woman named Helen who traveled around with [Simon] at the time and had previously lived in a brothel, [the gullible Samaritans] call the first Emanation from him.*

The author decries the irony that she should have the same name as Queen Helen, wife of Monobazus, who converted to Judaism and fed Judea during a famine (ca. 48 C.E.), mentioned in Josephus, *Antiquities* XX.ii.

once gave us water from the rock, manna from the sky, I shall give you a greater drink. He who receives it shall never thirst again!"

A man I assumed to be a coconspirator stepped forward, playing at being unsure. He began by berating the Magus, but this was surely part of the act. He put his lips upon this she-devil's breasts and sucked as a babe, as wine trickled from his lips. He cried out:

"The wine of Shiraz!"

8. At this harlotry, the crowd grew frenzied and some fell on their knees, some exclaimed they were not worthy to drink the Blood of the New Covenant. Xenon asked me how the illusion was done and I knew not—such sorcery might have the aid of Legion himself—indeed, Satan was more than present and wasted no time in revealing our whereabouts to his minion. The Magus pointed to my young charge and myself.

"You are Matthias bar-Matthias?" he asked.

Yes, I said, ashamed to have been discovered in this wretched circus.

He asked of me, "You knew the Nazirene, the Scion of David, did you not?"

Not one to commit the errors of Peter the Disciple, I answered loudly that yes, I knew and held My Teacher to be of the One True God and not to be a cheap carnival magician.

9. "A Nazirene," cried one spectator. "You bring the Romans down upon us. Curse you!"

"Where is your Messiah now, Nazirene?" yelled another ruffian. "Dead in the ground? Or secreted away by one such as yourself so that you might say he lives again?"

Another man called out: "I heard Your Deliverer went back to heaven like Elijah, leaving us no better than we were, still under the Roman lash! You call that a Deliverer?"

10. The Magus, incarnate of Hell, lovingly stroked his accomplice, the Whore Helen. "Come, learned Disciple! Come sup from the Breast of Life!"

I answered defiantly (while grasping Xenon closer to me lest there be violence) that I had no intention of participating in this devil's rite. But some in the crowd demanded that I should, my brother. Some roughly took me by the arms and shoulders and forced me toward the platform.

Then Helen, to the goading of the mob, began to perform an exotic dance of obscene writhings—and as I looked up she whisked away the strip of cloth and revealed to me the very maw of Hell! It was, my brother, the first time that I had confronted the female sex, this abyss of mankind. That my decades of virgin celibacy (which I've always felt to be essential for the refinement of the soul, indeed, the very engine) should be subjected to this!

11. But whereas my martyrdom was short-lived, I saw that Menander had grabbed Xenon and directed him to the Magus's table of libations.

"Unhand that virgin lad!" I said, while others laughed, such being the respect that chastity enjoys in this era. (Perhaps, upon reconsideration, the blessed state of my scribe might have been better left unannounced.)

"Magus!" cried one of the braying louts, "can you work a miracle? Can you change the lad from a virgin?"

Yes, I assure you, Menander intended to sacrifice me as well to this plot, but bravely Xenon said he would thrust himself in my place. Such stature in one so young! Menander and the Magus forced upon Xenon a phial from which he drank an admixture combinated to enflame the male member with the blood of passion. (Indeed, one may buy this elixir from many an Arab master of medicines for the assurance of a successful wedding night, or to enable further issue of late-marrying widowers.) Well, my brother, I need not relate the details of poor Xenon's disgrace under the effect of this diabolic poison. Some of the rowdies lifted him on their shoulders and carried him a few houses away to the brothels of Tyre—that *pornopolis*!—where his purity was sacrificed upon Satan's own dais.

12. "Perform a miracle like the Magus!" demanded one of the mob, clutching me by my robes.

"If your god is the real god," yelled another bucolic, "defeat the Blessed Magus in a contest!"

I answered them, "Thou shall not tempt the Lord thy God!"

"Heal this infirmity then," cried out one man, who held up a pus-filled stump where his hand once was. "I have seen Cephas," he said to me, "Apostle of the Judean, heal the blind! What say you?"

And then the crowd fell quiet as if I might be capable of such a miracle. O Josephus, I tell you, I prayed in my heart that the God of Abraham might work a sign through the Son of Man, Our Master, My Teacher! Come forward, I beckoned to the cripple.

13. With the purest of intentions and greatest of hopes, I looked squarely at this Phoenician criminal, who had obviously been caught stealing, had been punished by the exaction of his right hand, and was now left with a wound that would not heal, festering as the work of demons still within his body. I touched this injury with my walking stick to no avail. Then, I imagined that God would have me show my own faith by touching it with my own healthy hand, which I did.

"Place a kiss upon it," said the Magus to the crowd, "as I saw Your Master do many a time."

And this too the mob cried out for. What rigors! And I did kiss this abomination though nothing was changed! The power that is in other Disciples is not in me!

But I said to him, "Your heart is not pure, my friend. You have no love for your fellow man or for the Lord your God. Why should He heal you?"

14. Ah, but I was not listened to, instead I was lifted by the mob and deposited in a trough that the village women use for their laundry. (I was lucky not to be put down a well or thrown into the sewers, all of which I imagined quite likely, though yea, I was willing to endure that precious martyrdom and win for myself a Crown!)

However, it was not to be.

Wet and on the verge of illness, despairing, and bitter—yes, bitter, Lord, for Thou did not come to my aid when I was to do Thy work!—I made my way to the ship and the seafront. I recovered Xenon after his experience and threw myself upon his mercy, begging his forgiveness, for if it had not been for the Magus's recognition of me, then the perdition experienced by this young saint would not have occurred.

15. O fragile virginity!

But an evening's carelessness, an hour's indiscretion—and in Xenon's case—a few moments of villainy, and then all is lost! I had rather, I told him, that this martyrdom had happened to me, rather than to one so young and undespoiled. Xenon was moved by my tears and supplications and begged me to rise and speak no more of it. But I insisted on a prayer by which we asked the Most High for pardon and expiation from sordid and carnal deeds and asked He Who Will Judge Us All to examine our hearts where our every intention is chaste.

We remained in Tyre one more night, to my chagrin, and I felt it best to imprison, as it were, Xenon upon the ship so no further disgraces might befall him. It was only at the insistence of our captain, a noble Greek of great bearing and judiciousness, that I allowed Xenon, accompanied by our able captain, to go into the port for a meal and some harmless entertainment. I had told the captain about the tragedy that had befallen my charge and he proposed an evening of mild diversions in his care to remedy these depravities, far from the presence of women, where the captain assured me none but men would lay a hand on my young apostle.

16. At last, we sailed from Tyre, our ship landing in Seleucia, a lesser repeat of Tyre, and we moved upriver to Antioch on foot. Being inland, it is spared the worst abuses of race-mingling and cosmopolitanism, and is in fact a pagan place with more virtue than most; the scene, I recall darkly, of the Jews' first denial of Grecian ways and customs. Would that our race had become Greek and spared ourselves this last century!

Antioch possesses one of the loveliest synagogues I have ever seen, brightly furnished and floored with marble; while the Nazirenes still meet in a cave north of town, grubbing about like miserable Cappadocian cave-dwellers.[7] No care or interest seems

---

7. A cave church (now with a Syrian facade from the 700s) still exists north of Antioch (Antakya, Turkey) and has been revered as the site of Peter's first see from the very earliest times.

to be taken there, and a numbing laxity characterizes the congregation, with Nazirenes as soon going to a Pharisaic sabbath as to Mithra, Attis, Adonis, the Great Mother, as if their souls were shoppers in a marketplace, seeking some momentary distraction. One need only meet the hierarch of Antioch to understand everything else—Peter, the First Disciple, himself.[8]

17. Peter was expecting me for I had written him several times to warn him of my arrival. In fact, a bit must be said concerning my own history with Our Master's primal acolyte:

I had written a missive soon after the reading and circulation of *All Heresies Refuted* a year after Nero's installation [55 C.E.], inquiring as to Peter's health, his mission, and whether I might visit and lecture upon the tractates I had composed for his congregation. I did not receive a reply. I found this discourteous since it was I who displayed supreme magnanimity after he threw my first evangel, some years earlier, into the fire.

Next, I heard from passing Nazirene tradesmen that Peter's shrew of a wife had finally died. I sent a short epistle of condolence and received a reply from his lap dog Evoath, confirming what I suspected, that Peter could not write a cipher himself, having availed himself of no education. "Illiterate I was when Our Master chose me for the mission," he once said, "and illiterate I remain," as if that state were the result of divine promulgation and not remediable.

John Mark, once settled in Damascus, wrote to me about the time of the monster Nero's decade celebrations [64 C.E.] relating that Peter had married again, a much younger woman, who now commanded most of his attention and had her say in the finances. Peter, I learned, had also purchased two slaves for his growing fleet of fishing boats in Seleucia. Those worldly gains

---

8. Peter, traditional chief of the original Twelve, spokesman of the Jerusalem community in *Acts*. His historicity is obscure but undoubted. *Mark* is traditionally held to be from his perspective. *1 Peter* might well be a dictation of his; *2 Peter* is most certainly later than the time of Nero.

Though all Church sources are in agreement that he died in Rome, there is no telling when or how, and there seems never to have been any relics. Tradition holds that Peter was martyred in the Neronian Persecution of 64–68 C.E., but this document implies he is unmartyred as late as 76 C.E. (see 6:23) and much modern scholarship casts doubt upon the severity of Nero's persecution, instead crediting Domitian in the 90s with the first systematic purge.

were but the uppermost, visible signs of Peter's failings that I had always observed. (I admit to being lost on many matters, but none more so than the mystery of Our Master's having chosen Peter and raised him up as First of the Disciples.)

18. Finally, in the final year of Florus [66 C.E.] I wrote from Gedara to Peter again at Antioch, having heard he had made a successful tour of Rome. One can easily imagine the excess he gave himself to in the Rome of Nero, where no bodily vice went unassuaged. John Mark wrote back saying that Peter appreciated my correspondence but wondered whether I had "anything better to do"!

I had merely suggested that Peter might set an example, now that he was a widower, by steering a course of continence and celibacy, for as I have earlier explained, I feel virgin celibacy to be of dire necessity to the soul. So, our unhappy correspondence ended upon this, and I imagined that but twenty months hence [67 C.E.] I should get a cold welcome from this Disciple.

19. But not for the first time did Peter surprise me.

Upon recognizing me, the old man, unwashed for eons, flung his arms around me and breathed wine-breath into my face, nearly weeping with emotion—a quality not unknown to older men who indulge in the vice of wine. He showed me and Xenon around the chaotic river port of Antioch and proudly showed us his many sons mending nets and gutting fish (for it was the season when the Orontes was high) and discussed his plans for a fourth boat in Seleucia.

Peter said to me, "I hope to pass my ships on to another evangelist, since I am too old for much more travel. Though I have been a last time persuaded to return to Rome."

I prompted him to recall his adventures there. Did he speak before the Senate? Did he engage in discourse with the academies? What followed was a catalogue of great meals, haunches of venison and young calves fatted for his benefit, the hospitality of Rome's elite, afternoons observing gymnastics, bevies of dancing girls dangling grapes before his toothless mouth in senators' houses, pastries and sweetmeats, fine fowls stuffed with shellfish!

20. "You shall poison yourself," I said to him regarding the shellfish, which we are forbidden to consume.

He said to me, something of the sort: "Ooh, my friend, but an oyster in the oil of olives, salt, and lemon." He brought his fingers to his lips. "Oysters, my friend, harden the heart and that's not all they harden . . . Besides, I had a dream in which the Lord commanded me eat what I pleased."[9]

How convenient! It is a wonder your fine new Jewish wife will cook a cut of swine in all its uncleanliness for you. How she must love you! Peter confided in me that swine should be cooked over an open fire to let the fat drip away, then swathed in mustard seed and the must of white-wine cask—a dish, he reported, worthy of the Most High Himself. I risked an unkindness by suggesting he was more devoted to his own body than to the Body of Our Church. But he took no offense.

21. Peter said to me, "Our Teacher did not say we were forbidden to eat and drink and laugh and love our women and enjoy the gifts of God, my friend. I have told the same thing to John and his half-mad ascetics! Our Teacher indulged with us in all these things, save marriage. And perhaps, with Mary . . ."

The lewd suggestion that Our Savior, most Pure and Holy of Incarnations, stained himself with foul earthly lusts was more than I could bear. As I raged at Peter—a familiar scene, as we never did but argue thirty years ago—he laughed at me, more amused the more upset I became.

He went on in this vein, "Who is to say what passed between Mary and Himself? I noticed He spent a lot of time with Maryam, sister of Lazarus, yes? Though she's become an old frump in Arimathea, and it's my contention she would lay with a woman before a man, like the Greek ladies, you understand? And Johnnie, dear Johnnie, offered himself up to the Teacher countless times."

(I record this foul exchange, so that one might gauge the unnaturalness of this worldly man, so wrong for leadership of a new ethical and moral order.)

9. *Acts* 11:5–10.

He said as such, "Did a week go by that John did not anoint himself with Mary's sweetwaters and go into Our Master's chamber to sleep by His feet? Ah, the old queen ['ανδρογυγοζ] is in Ephesus now where he can sate himself with painted Asian boys, if he will. Tonight, my friend, I shall have Esther find us some lamb, lamb cooked in the fat of pork and broth of chicken, crowned with fresh olives and ground mint, sprinkled with cardoman!" Again he kissed his filthy fingers. "Ah, we shall eat tonight!"

22. And so to his home he, Xenon, and I went, accompanied in the street by his two slaves from Urartu [Armenia] as we traversed the alleys of Antioch. Esther, his young wife, was among the most fetching of Jewish women I had ever seen, and I pitied her having—no doubt in trying circumstances—to be married off to this old ruin. Alas, Aphrodite is always to Hephaestus wed! The wineskins were brought in. Peter was of that older, rural generation that preferred to suck from this teat of wine than transfer it into a civilized amphora and kylix, and it repulsed me to drink wine from the same orifice that Peter pressed his unclean snout upon.

23. Emboldened though, as this wine rushed to my head on this tiring afternoon, I confronted Peter with the information that Thomas claimed that my election to the Disciples was unfairly manipulated.[10] Peter remained a man who could never lie, but I attribute this to a lack of political art rather than any virtue.

He said to me, "Ah, Matthias, it is true. But what could it possibly matter now?"

I was on the verge of weeping to have this confirmed. I angrily suggested that Barsabbas be found and installed in my place, if he were the rightful Twelfth Disciple.

Peter said to me, "To limit our number to twelve hardly concerns us now. We have hundreds of disciples throughout the world, my friend!"

10. Matthias's election in *Acts* 1:23–26: *And they put forward two. . . Barsabbas, who was surnamed Justus, and Matthias. And they prayed and said, "Lord, who knowest the hearts of all men, show which one of these two Thou hast chosen to take the place in this ministry and apostleship from which Judas turned aside to go to his own place." And they cast lots for them and the lot fell on Matthias, and he was enrolled with the eleven apostles.*

Exhaustively, I explained to the simple man how important the number twelve was, it having many significances. Whereas the number of man was six, we, who are to serve man, are twice that, twelve. Twelve for the tribes of Israel, for the Testament of the Twelve Patriarchs, there are twelve ribs in the body, just as His Disciples form the ribs of His Body, His Church, not to mention the zodiac and its twelve signs.[11]

24. Peter waved this aside. He said to me, "None of this intellectual stuff, please. As I have said, it hardly matters now. I suspect we have, say, 53 proselytes here in Antioch. What do you make of that number?"

I said it is not for us to interpret every mystery of God, but that as sure as there is a God, the number has some significance and that value pertains to the situation at Antioch, and if we only knew how to read such things we would be well on the way to emulating God's knowledge. Forgive me, Josephus. I hardly need belabor the self-evident glories of numerology, as any street-sweeper of Alexandria could likewise report.

Peter said to me, "I leave these things to you, since your mind is tailored to these higher pursuits. Here, follow me."

25. We went into a small room, randomly cluttered with fishing tools, broken pottery yet to be mended, and a dank net mouldering upon other refuse in the back. From a small pouch he removed two dice and asked me to wager. I, of course, replied that just as God did not intend us to be usurious with one another, so did he not approve of gambling or profit without an investment of honest labor.

Peter said to me, "I do not recall any scripture in which gambling is proscribed, my brother. Furthermore, I remember amusing Our Master with these very dice, and telling him they were quite able to do the devil's bidding, to cheat for profit. Then Our Master looked at me and said, 'Truly, Simon, I say unto you that

11. Despite the prohibitions on astrology and the black arts throughout Judeo-Christendom, it was popular nonetheless and experienced great tolerance in this period and in the Byzantine world (numerous dome and apse paintings on Mt. Athos show Christ surrounded by the twelve signs of the zodiac).

these dice will yet do God's will, for much that is bad in the hands of man finds purpose with God.' Watch this . . ."

Peter threw his dice and continually they came up the highest number of twelve. Peter said to me, "Ah, there's a twelve for you! Do you recall what you said when you first rolled them, thirty-seven years ago?"

26. Then it occurred to me that these trick dice were the very dice that decided my election to the Disciples!

Yes, steadfast Barsabbas and I were the choices to replace Judas who left our band,[12] and these very dice Peter brought out in order to decide fairly between us. At the time it struck me as odd that I should be competing with the older Barsabbas, who had accompanied the Twelve for the entirety of Our Master's ministry.

Peter explained to me, "You see, when you let these tumble free they invariably show twelve or eleven. When you throw them against a board or a wall, like this, ah, you see that any random number can come up. We have a four now. By these dice we assured your election."

27. Peter put his hand upon me in comfort. "Dear fellow Disciple, it is in any event impossible to give your mantle to Barsabbas now, for he is martyred in Cyprus, land of his birth, some years back. He is most beloved of God."[13]

---

12. A note about Judas Iscariot.

Another universal archetype borrowed by Christianity is that of the betrayer, which can be found in the Orient, in Hindu, in Toltec and Mexican, in Native American, and in many Mediterranean heroic tales. The name Judas Iscariot is a corruption of Judah el-Sicarious, or of the party of the Sicarii, the extremist Zealots. With Simon the Zealot and Judas the Sicarii among Jesus' band, one can see how easy it was for Rome to execute him for political trouble-making.

The New Testament disagrees on what became of Judas: *Matthew* has him hang himself; *Acts* has the fanciful story that Judas *bought a field with the reward of his wickedness, and falling headlong he burst open in the middle and all his bowels gushed out (Acts* 1:18); and another codex says he merely *swelled up, burst open,* etc. *Acts* elsewhere, and more believably, says *Judas turned aside to go to his own place (Acts* 1:25), which as a Sicarii he might well have done, having had enough of pacifist Messiahs.

The incentive of the Early Church to perpetuate a Judas-Betrayer story is twofold: 1) It was necessary to get in the pieces of silver prophecy of *Jeremiah* 32:6–15, and the potter's field prophecy of *Jeremiah* 18:2–3—both prophecies a bit forced—and the clearer one in *Zechariah* 11:12–13.

And 2) as the Church became more Greek, anti-Semitism became more prevalent. Judas, which means "Jew," became useful symbolically—he is the wicked representation of his people who rejected the Son of God.

This gospel's author does not mention anything about Judas's betrayal.

13. Having missed his chance, Barsabbas disappears from Church history. Peter in this

It was the first I heard of this!

"He spoke too loudly against a governor, which Our Master was never foolish enough to do. Like John the Baptist and James—this impractical streak in so many Nazirenes . . . Nothing is a surer footpath to the cross!"

Poor Barsabbas, it was he that should have been among the Twelve, not me! If I took his earthly crown he surely wears a crown more radiant now! Among the legends and inaccuracies of Our Church, there had been a real martyrdom, a noble and brave one. How much more it displayed my worthlessness and folly! I took from Barsabbas his precious seat only to waste my days in indecision, to shirk the task of organizing the Nazirenes as I, the only one with a thorough education, was singularly qualified to do.

28. Peter said to me then, "As for you, we feared that your faith would fall away as its novelty wore thin, book-learned and young as you were. But not a one of us Disciples had a gerah to spend upon our mission, as you recall, and we had bankrupted ourselves and our trades in those years with Our Master. And you, of course, were terribly wealthy, and your father was blessedly indulgent. You could write, you could speak rhetorically in Greek, you understood some Latin. . . how could we turn away such as you? When it came time to decide, we wished Barsabbas to feel it was God's will, and we wished to spare his feelings."

29. And so my Discipleship was a sham!

Rather I was a fool who had been deceived for his money and influence. It gives me no pleasure to write this, Josephus, and confess these things before you, so I hope you have the humility to treat my distress seriously, just as I did not scoff or amuse myself at your expense when you spent your youth searching for a movement you could believe in, trying on Essenism as if it were a moth-eaten cloak.

Peter then said to me, "I shall give you these dice. I can feel sure you will never cheat anyone with them, and I'm not

gospel says Barsabbas was martyred in Cyprus as was, traditionally, the Apostle Barnabas (one of the 70, companion of Paul, founder of the Antiochene Church). One wonders whether there has been a conflation in later hagiographies.

sure I can say the same for me. They are temptation, so take them.

"An odd history these dice have. I gave them to Our Master since they amused Him and He gave them to Marcellinus, the centurion whose house he entered—very risky in those days, to enter a Roman's house. Anyway, the centurion, a rough and gaming man, lost them to another soldier, the one who was on duty when Our Lord was executed. In fact, he used these very trick dice to acquire the robe of Our Lord, for they cast lots for all criminal's garments, you see; it was foretold in the Psalms."

I didn't bother to correct Peter that the passage he referred to was in the Prophet Isaiah.[14]

30. Peter further related, "It was another centurion, Octavius, one of my first Gentile Nazirene converts, a companion to the monster Pilate himself! O, dear friend, you should have seen the scandal when he came to call! Simon [the Zealot?] almost had his head. Octavius knew the soldier in the crucifixion detail and acquired the dice from him and then passed them on to me. Thanks to him, a piece of Our Master's robe is now in James's marvelous collection of relics in Ptolemais."[15]

I have no use for these wicked dice, I said, or for James's sordid collection.

Peter seemed unoffended, and said, "Very well then, I

14. Peter is in fact correct. *Psalms* 22:18.
15. The reference to Pilate reveals some of the more evangelical tactics of the Early Church.

As Christianity became less a Jewish concern, and more a Greek and Roman possibility, anti-Semitic scriptural elements become more pronounced, and Romans increasingly become heroes and chaste converts. The dialogue of Pilate and Jesus in *John* (ca. 120 C.E.) is pure anti-Semitic propaganda, attempting to rehabilitate Pilate and the Romans, ending with Pilate insisting on Jesus' being identified as the King of the Jews on the Cross. Nowhere was Christian pro-Romanism more in evidence than in the litany of trumped-up Roman virgin and soldier martyrs (late 100s–300s C.E.) and the revised history of Pontius Pilate, who begins to appear as a virtual lawyer for Jesus' defense. *Tell me, how can I that am merely a governor examine a King?* Pilate pleads in the *Acts of Pilate* (ca. 300s?); *Jesus Christ of whom I recently wrote to you has been executed against my will. So pious and austere a man has never been seen, nor will be again!* insists Pilate in the "Epistle of Pilate to Tiberius" (concocted 100s?). The historically unsophisticated Middle Ages and its Crusaders were inspired by the anachronism of Tiberias ordering Vespasian to destroy Jerusalem to "destroy the enemies of Jesus" (the popular *The Avenging of the Savior*).

Nothing in Josephus suggests Pilate was other than a despised, corrupt, murderous procurator; see *Antiquities* XVIII.ii and iv.

shall keep them. Besides, now that I think about it, I think in some way Our Master would wish me to keep them. For both Our Departed Master and myself have some love of gambling."

How dare he impute such venality to the Teacher!

31. But Peter said to me, "Man gambles with such as these dice, but Our Master gambled with us. We are His 'twelve,' His trick dice! He had all the world to choose from and yet he asked an unworthy like myself to follow him."

He held my arm and beseeched me:

"Will Our Lord win his wager, Matthias? Are we another lunatic sect from this Messiah-hungry shore? Or is it entrusted in us to bring the Kingdom of Heaven to this world, to convert it to a place of love and charity and peace for all mankind?"

I could not answer these questions.

32. Peter went on, "Yes, I shall keep the dice. Each time I waiver, and I waiver often, my friend, I shall decide by these dice, yes? 'Twelve' means I go into the lion's den, into the arena, into the home of lepers and criminals and those who hate me. Any other number means I won't." Here the old man became weepy and sentimental as I remembered him. "God's love is like a loaded dice, is it not? No matter what our circumstances, His love shows on the roll time after time . . ."

33. Momentarily he recovered and surprised me by inquiring if I would accompany him to Rome. I said I had little interest in the capital of all evils and heresies, despite the talk of its many wonders. Instead, after leaving Xenon with his uncle and doing my researches in Ephesus, I intended to travel farther into Greece and among the Nazirene churches of the Aegean.

Peter said to me, "My, but we could use you in Rome. And you must see it: buildings four and five houses tall, I joke not! Flowing water and fountains, and palaces and arenas like you've never seen!"

Arenas, I said, for slaughtering Christians.

Peter said to me, "I see, indeed, you have been to see James.

But Paul has written me and Rome is perfectly tolerant of us. We are one religion among hundreds. Servants in Caesar's house are under Paul's sway."[16]

34. I despaired of the repeated recourse to the Great Innovator, the interloper. Is it Saul of Tarsus or Saul of Tartarus?[17]

Peter said of him, "No, I didn't like him at first one bit, but he is filled with *Sophia*, my friend. And I tell you, he would not have denied Our Master as I did—no, he would have fought the whole garrison, and likely won! Have you heard his missives read aloud? He has written twice to our synagogue at Antioch and takes me to task so horribly, I don't dare have them read to the congregation! I've hidden them actually . . . but I'm sure there will be more. Paul is staying at a senator's house[18] and has invited me to come and teach and reminisce about Him Who Taught Us, and that I am always willing to do. And a senator's house! Think of the food and wine!"

Peter then embraced his young bride and she giggled as a girl while he told her of the things that awaited her in Rome, promises of a new cloak and fineries that only such a hoarding place of rapine can provide. Esther kissed him unashamedly in front of me, then scurried to the kitchen to supervise the slaves in the making of our meal.

---

16. Tradition holds that Rome launched ten Christian persecutions—a suspiciously significant number—until Christianity compromised with the sun-worshiping, relative-slaying Emperor Constantine in 313 c.e. This cultish array of persecutions and martyrologies, as well as the total fiction of the Catacombs (which inconveniently do not bear but a handful of traces of Christianity), are fixtures of Early Church mythology.

     A Church endured in Rome and persecution was more exaggerated than actual in the first decades of Christianity. Paul, one may recall, began his mission calmly: "*And [Paul] lived [in Rome] two whole years at his own expense, and welcomed all who came to him, preaching the kingdom of God and teaching about the Lord Jesus Christ quite openly and unhindered (Acts* 28:30). Paul sends his love another time, writing *All the Saints greet you, especially those of Caesar's household (Philippians* 4:22). And this from *Romans* 16:23 is extraordinary: "*Gaius who is host to me and to the whole church greets you. Erastus, the city treasurer, and our brother Quartus greet you.*" If *Romans* is of the 40s, before Gaius (Caligula) Caesar became insane, might this be a conventional greeting of Caesar? Could someone as high up as Rome's treasurer have been a convert?

17. This rather weak piece of rhetoric concerns Saul being from Tarsus and its similarity in sound to Tartarus, one of the depths of Hell, where Cerberus sat outside the adamantine gate.

18. Again, could things have been so bad in Rome? We know a Roman Senator Pudens lent his home for the purposes of Christian gatherings, and this *titulus* has come down to us as the still-standing church of Santa Pudenziana. (From the 300s this church was misnamed, suggesting a female saint—some confusion over the Latin possessive).

35. How I would have reached out to Peter had I but only some point of shared experience with one such as himself, a former fisherman who means well but thinks not of the implications of the multitude of rules he breaks and the paltry excuses for his own weakness, put forward with the assurance of doctrine. How convinced he was that Our Master cared little about sins of the flesh or lapses in ritual, dogmas, and doctrines. That is fine if one has met the Teacher of Righteousness, but what of later generations who shall never know Him as we did? We must get to the business of strictures and codifying rules to live by, I explained to him, for our children and their children. Are we to found a Church without a single tradition?

36. Peter, I recall, began to look oddly at me. He asked me, "Matthias, dear brother, how stands it in the faith with you? Ah, I suspected as much. You have lost it, have you not?"

Here, I confess, though only some twelve years—ah, our number again—separate Peter and myself in age, I honored him as an avuncular presence, and wished to be comforted by him.

"You have healed people, have you not?" I asked of him.

"Why, yes," Peter said to me, "we all have. Lepers, invalids, lame people, blind people. But not always, no. It is odd when it happens and when it doesn't. Perhaps, it is like Moses at Meribah, his heart was not pure when he tried to perform the miracle and God knew it, yes? Although, there have been days when I was sure my laying on of hands would fail—days where I felt no love for the complaining old women I was to heal, and it worked nonetheless! So powerful is Our God."

I confessed I had never known even one healing, adding to my humiliation by telling him of my failures at Tyre.

37. Peter said to me, "Simon the Magus proved too great a match for me as well." He laughed, patting my shoulder. "God would not have us waste our time there, battling fruitlessly with circus demons."

I protested, God would not have us triumph over abominations?

"Of course," said Peter. "The abominations of hunger and disease, the abominations of being orphaned or alone and old.

The world is full of abominations over which we may safely triumph. If we but would!"

A moment later, upon reflection, Peter volunteered a confession to ease my feelings: "My brother Matthias, I've never spoken in tongues. Yes, John gets to jabbering and I nod along pretending I understand. I'm frankly embarrassed; it looks so silly. Even at the Pentecost, I didn't learn anything that I already didn't know. Some people get some gifts and others others. Like Paul. He's never healed a sore joint, to my mind—ah, but the difference he has made to us! A Roman and fine scholar that he is!"

38. And then I understood.

O bitter my revelation!

I saw clearly that it was to be *my* lot to teach and evangelize, to take my fortune and travel with the Nazirene message to the Gentiles, to dictate epistles like Saul's to be read throughout the Church, to be revered and studied. And I did not do it! And therefore Our Lord and Master, impatient but resolute, appeared by the grace of Our Father and recruited someone else— Saul of Tarsus! Mine enemy! The man I reviled! He was but fulfilling the mission that I did not complete![19]

I found myself weeping hopelessly before Peter. "I am a failure in the eyes of God," I told him.

"But so are we all, dear friend," he replied.

39. And so comfortless, bereft, I left the presence of another Disciple, but this time wiser to my failure. (My scribe Tesmegan is near tears for my sadness—yes, you may be recorded, dear boy, put it down if you like.)

40. Within that week Xenon and I began our trip to Ephesus where we would make our formal parting. All about us the news for Judea was bad—the Romans burned and marauded and we

19. Indeed, Matthias was virtually "replaced" by Paul throughout Byzantium and the Middle Ages, due to Paul's greater importance, but also because Matthias's relics resided in the northernmost apostolic shrines, in Trier (Germany), which soon fell to the barbarian world, effectively ending his cult. On Mt. Athos and in most pre-1400 Ascension scenes, one can count only eleven disciples gazing up at Christ; in medieval Pentecosts, one counts eleven disciples and Mary. On the porch tympanum of Malmesbury Abbey (from the 1100s) the Eleven Disciples and Paul ring the doorway, and this configuration is next to universal.

Paul, in the popular mind, became the Twelfth Disciple.

were told not to bother to return; Xenon worried greatly for his parents and we prayed much for their safety. I heard some years later that Xenon married and I counted this as a personal loss, but what other ending could there have been after such a despicable fall? I began to wonder if there was anyone or anything that I had made better in my time on earth.

Then again, thinking now of Ephesus and the brothel it has become, it seems to me that decline of all standards is worldwide, would you not agree, Josephus? The Jews of the Herodian age were not the fractious fanatics of our own; the Rome of the Republic had some scant honor; the Greeks of the age of Alexander were hardly the lust-driven voluptuaries of today. What chance, with or without me, did poor Xenon have? I attest even now: it is virtually impossible to maintain the ideal of virgin celibacy in such a land as Greece!

GREECE

Let us not make arbitrary conjectures about the greatest matters.

—Heraclitus (ca. 580 b.c.e.)

[Emperor Julian, the Apostate] ordered the priests of the different Christian sects and their supporters to be admitted to the palace and politely expressed his wish that they each might follow his own beliefs without hindrance or fear. The Emperor thought that freedom to argue their beliefs would simply deepen their differences, so that he would never be faced by a united common people. He found from experience that no wild beasts are as hostile to men as Christians are to each other.

—*Histories* (ca. 360)
Ammianus Marcellinus

Even God cannot change the past.

—Agathon (ca. 410 b.c.e.)

James shook his hard obstinate head. "It too, this spirit of Truth you talk about—it too will be crucified. You must realize, rabbi, that the spirit will be crucified as long as men exist. But it doesn't matter. Something is always left behind, and that, I tell you, is enough for us."

"It's not enough for me!" Jesus shouted in despair.

—*The Last Temptation of Christ* (1954)
Nikos Kazantzakis

P atrick O'Hanrahan stood at the rails and attempted to button his suitcoat. He unbuttoned the bulging jacket subsequently, preferring coldness to looking piteously rotund. There was an indistinct sun rising, *stepping up to her bright chair,* O'Hanrahan quoted to himself, behind the craggy mountains of Kerkira, "Corfu" to the tourists, looming before him in the blue-gray mists. *When primal Dawn spread on the eastern sky her fingers of pink light . . .* No, it will be a more spectacular day than that—he recalled his Homer in the Greek: *The sun rose on the flawless brimming sea into a sky all of brass, all one brightening for gods immortal and for mortal men on plowlands kind with grain.* That's how you write, folks, *plowlands kind with grain.*

Surrounding him at this hour were backpackers asleep on the deck, squirming into their sleeping bags for as-yet-undetected pockets of warmth, not quite ready to commence another day of hardcore tourism. O'Hanrahan tiptoed around a threesome of snoring young men, one of whom had wrapped his head in a windbreaker like a mummy.

O'Hanrahan settled himself on the leeward side of the ship.

On his left rose dreadful Albania, not so much mysterious anymore as simply weird, abandoned in the collapse of communism to its Marxist misery by an indifferent Europe. O'Hanrahan's mind was playful after two Greek coffees, and he smiled to think of how Albania disproved all rules of geography: a country smack between the West's greatest civilizations, Greece and Rome, with a final layering of Islamic culture at its Mameluke height. Albania should have been the showplace of the world's cultures, but instead it is the most wretched, backward land in Europe. Civilization, mused O'Hanrahan, is not contagious, not accidental, not a whim of geography. It doesn't spill over or infect; it is a deliberative act: we will have art, we will rise to advanced thought, we will surpass our normal venality, we will walk on the Western Slopes.

And such contemplations brought O'Hanrahan to the topography now distinguishing itself from the shoreline fog before him, only the fishermen awake at this hour, their boats now leaving the harbors. What number odyssey to Greece was this? His seventh or eighth, something like that. And possibly his last. And still so much that will now, he supposed, never be seen. Here on the Ionian side of Greece, so many treasures unvisited: Ithaka, for example, that astoundingly little islet where Western Civilization got a running start from Homer. *Someone immortal who cares for you will make a fair wind blow.* Alas, I never made it to Ithaka, sighed O'Hanrahan, no immortal willed my course to that far-famed Ithacensian shore, no seafaring Phaiakians granted me passage. *No other Odysseus will ever come, for he and I are one, the same; his bitter fortune and wanderings are mine,* mulled O'Hanrahan, feeling for the moment Odysseus-like and the only one on these waters who could feel such things.

Greece, O'Hanrahan addressed the mainland, for my entire scholastic life you have fascinated me, from mystery cults at Minos, the Delian League, the baptizing of St. Lydia, the first European Christian at St. Paul's hands, to your smoke-stained, imperious ikons of Byzantium glowering through the centuries. Now the Patriarch of Constantinople performs a weekly mass for less than a hundred faithful in what used to be the capital of Christianity, a sad old show of clinking censers and old men and women, mumbling the desperate prayers of age—such exquisite, bitter decline!

O'Hanrahan reasoned: Modernism betrayed you, Greece. It is the contemporary ugly country with its worthless trains and third-world plumbing, philandering presidents, deposed dictators, conniving restaurateurs who cheat on the bill, and polluted, rude Athens that annoys me. And yet, what affection you still inspire, the Western World's love, her greatest love . . . If Italy is the schoolboy infatuation of the Western mind, then you, Greece, are surely the enduring wife, our Penelope, outlasting all rivals and suitors, confident with maddening Greek arrogance that our world will return to you again, no matter how long it deigns to stay away.

"You're up early, sir," he heard Lucy say behind him.

"Ah," said O'Hanrahan, raising a hand in salute, "Amphitrite herself walks upon the waters, O gods!"

She sniffed back a runny nose. "Well, Amphitrite's got pneumonia now."

O'Hanrahan fished in his pocket for the key to his cabin. "Here," he said. "Go back to sleep in a nice warm bed."

"But I might miss seeing something."

"See the mountain there? Scrubby rock, a few houses, white church at the shore. It's that over and over again until Patras. I'll wake you."

That afternoon O'Hanrahan knocked on the cabin door, rousing Lucy at three P.M. Glancing at her watch, she sputtered a few half-awake apologies for sleeping so long and monopolizing his cabin. He said through the door that he would meet her in the ship's cafeteria.

Primping in the mirror, Lucy saw in the reflection that on an opposite shelf was O'Hanrahan's open suitcase. She turned cautiously to examine it; beside the suitcase, at a little writing desk, were some notes. She checked the door and made sure it was locked before poking still further: on a worn piece of paper, some kind of Xerox, was something O'Hanrahan had labeled in his fierce handwriting: J. ROSEN BOOKMARK.

The paper itself was a copy of a many-times-folded scratchpad of doodles and designs where someone had tried out a pen. Lucy surmised that this must be some fragment of what Rabbi Rosen of Hebrew University, translator of the Matthias scroll forty years ago, left behind after his not-so-accidental death. She glanced at the phrases and bits of words in Hebrew: *Jude* or was that "Jews"? *in Beersheba . . . All Heresies Refuted . . . Yochan . . .* John perhaps? *in Ephesus . . . The Harlot Helen, her dreaded teats! . . .* What was that about? *Benjamin the slave . . .* And what was this? *The Messiah's Bones.*

Lucy put that aside and examined O'Hanrahan's open suitcase with its contents slopped about. There was the edge of a golden frame of a five-by-seven black-and-white photo. With her hand trembling in anticipation, she pulled it from its surrounding of unwashed clothes. It was Patrick O'Hanrahan, slim with—good God—*dark* wavy hair, in a chaplain's uniform standing beside a squinting, worried-looking woman in a hospital sister's uniform, about twenty or so, much shorter, uneasily pulled close to O'Hanrahan. Mr. and Mrs. O'Hanrahan. Lucy felt a sudden untraversable gulf between her 20th Century and O'Hanrahan's, this wartime, all-American world saluting in patriotic black-and-white two Asian wars ago.

"Whatcha doing in there?" hollered O'Hanrahan outside the door, wanting his room back.

Lucy jumped, yelled something back too cheerily, and hid all signs of her investigations.

AΘHNA
July 9th, 1990

O'Hanrahan explained his acquaintance with the Matsoukis family while he and Lucy endured the obligatory two-hour bus shuttle from Patras to Athens. Lucy half-listened, desperate for fresh air, distracted by the *deedly deedly deedly* balalaika music shrilly piped throughout the bus.

The professor reminisced: Eleni Vlahos, Mrs. Matsoukis's maiden name, was the most brilliant girl in Athens and if O'Hanrahan had had any sense, according to O'Hanrahan, he would have married her and moved to a Greek island and written his books while she wrote hers.

(Your wife writing books, something you could never do, would have made for a marriage, Patrick, almost as tortured as the one you had with Beatrice.)

Eleni had written definitive histories of four of the Cycladean islands and taught at the American University, where she was a distinguished professor, a *Kathigitria*. But not only that, Eleni had been a beauty, piercing and dark. "God knows what she looks like now," wondered O'Hanrahan. "I suppose, though, many a beautiful Greek girl becomes one of those old Greek crones, so I ought to prepare myself."

Look who's talking, thought Lucy.

"Anyway, if I'd married her—"

"I thought you were a Jesuit back then."

"Details, details," he kept narrating. "Anyway, Eleni married this doctor, Dr. Matsoukis, a nice guy. Someone she could boss around, I think. And they have two kids, Theodora and Stavros. See? I've written it down in my address book so in my senescence I'll remember."

Once they arrived in Athens, O'Hanrahan telephoned the *Matsoukoi* and Eleni insisted he and Lucy come immediately to the house, and to banish all thoughts of a hotel. O'Hanrahan spent the next half-hour flagging a cab—no easy task in Athens where the taxis have a seller's market and ignore whom they wish—and subsequently sped with Lucy to Kolonaki, the beautiful-people's modern Athens of haute couture salons, chic art galleries, cafés where the plebeian ouzo and metaxa gave way to whatever cocktail was in vogue this summer in Europe. Kolonaki, speculated O'Hanrahan as the cab ascended the steep slopes of Likabettis, was a city state of the upper-middle- and upper-class Greeks, media and government people, artists and academics.

Eleni Matsoukis was hardly the old crone that O'Hanrahan had prepared Lucy for. She was sixty, striking and noble, with deep black hair pulled back tight to a bun, and her slim, tailored black dress brought out the soft paleness of her face. Except for the lipstick, Lucy found her remarkably monochrome, black and white. Dr. Matsoukis spoke little English, so after his visitors were escorted into a spacious marble living room, he sat there politely seeing that glasses were filled, O'Hanrahan's with ouzo, endless rounds, and Lucy's with mineral water.

Presently Theodora, a shorter, less regal version of her mother, breezed into the room in a blue turtleneck and designer jeans with a chartreuse scarf trailing behind her. Her English was excellent. Theodora went to the American University for some form of international business degree. Last to present himself was Stavros, who shlepped in unwillingly and only at the loud request of his father.

Stavros was a god, Lucy noticed.

Not the delicate, classical Praxitelean youth but the potent *kouros* from the Archaic period. Curly black hair in ringlets on either side of his large eyes, high cheekbones, developed neck and upper arms, a wonderful tan . . . Lucy was not personally drawn to this beauty, but she was damn impressed. Besides looking vain Stavros looked a little, well, packaged, Lucy decided, a little manufactured by spending too long with his blow-dryer or in some effete Eurohairstyling salon.

"Stavros is a business student," Theodora, called Teddie, explained with a sarcasm that communicated through all cultural barriers. "He's at Southwestern College."

Lucy gathered that was not the coup that attending American University was.

"He doesn't like Americans," Teddie continued. "He thinks he's a communist this month. The last one in Europe."

"Teddie, *parakaló* . . ." warned her mother gently.

Teddie: "He has one thought a month. It is all he can do."

"Sibling rivalry," smiled O'Hanrahan, willing things to remain light.

"He doesn't understand enough English to be offended by what I say," Teddie explained.

Stavros sauntered from the room while Teddie talked on of America and what she knew about it and an exchange program she hoped to participate in. O'Hanrahan and Mrs. Matsoukis talked in Modern Greek, which had come back to O'Hanrahan like an old friend, and Lucy was thrown back on the resources of Teddie for entertainment. Teddie grabbed her handbag and suggested Lucy and she go out to cruise Kolonaki. Stavros happened to pass through the room.

"No, you're not going with us," said Teddie.

On the way down the stairs, Teddie explained to Lucy that it was insupportable to be seen anywhere near her brother for there was a certain fourteen- and fifteen-year-old contingent that adored him and, worthless as he was, it was hard for a sister to watch.

Theodora: "You must think Athens is dreadful after Chicago."

"Not at all, Teddie. It seems great fun."

She made a dismissive noise.

Their first stop was a club called *1924.*

"What is so special about 1924?" asked Lucy.

"There is a *1900* and a *1920* so this came next. Someone probably died in 1924, I don't know . . ."

Lucy took in the surroundings. It could be anywhere in Europe, postmodern lines and decor, postmodern people, track lighting illuminating raging punk art on the walls. The pale waitpeople were clad in black, the men with ponytails pulled back and the women with short cropped hair, both frozen in a seriousness, a bleakness in their indifferent fulfilling of orders. Lucy looked at the female customers, all dressed similarly in browns and blacks, giant hoop earrings like Teddie's, and all lighter-skinned than she thought Greek people normally were.

"So tell me about Chicago University," asked Teddie, once the drinks were ordered. "Do you want some food?"

Lucy was starved. "I wouldn't mind a snack."

Recognizing *taramosalata* on the menu, Lucy ordered it at a steep 2000 drachmae, $12 or so. "Chicago," Lucy began. "Well, unfortunately the campus is in a slum, which is sometimes dangerous."

"Slum?"

"Ghetto?" tried Lucy. Teddie knew what that meant. "I live in an apartment with another student and we share expenses."

Teddie enthused for several minutes over the freedom of having one's own place. Until she got married, which she didn't intend to do since she hated Greek men, she would have to live at home with her parents and, until *he* got employed, which was inconceivable, with her brother Stavros as well. And what's more, all of Greece that was livable was in Athens. The rest was for the peasantry or for holiday-making. All the action was here, all the jobs, all the glamour, such Athenian glamour as there was anymore, all the connection to the new Europe. "If the EEC doesn't expel Greece," Teddie considered.

"Why should it do that?"

"Because the government a few years ago bought Yugoslavian wheat and sold it to the EEC as Greek wheat, cheating the EEC. And it will never get better for Greece, because the politics do not get better."

"Papandreou," checked Lucy, "was the one with the sex scandal, right?"

"Sex, business, corruption," she said, stirring her drink idly. "But scandal is better than elections. Because elections mean assassinations and worse. Even in this neighborhood, right on the street near our house a few years ago."

Lucy didn't know whether to believe her. This perfectly up-to-date cosmopolitan city . . . assassinations over local elections?

Teddie casually put an open box of cigarettes between them, offering Lucy as many as she pleased. Teddie went on, "I would love to live in America, New York City, for a while, no?"

"Yes, normal people get assassinated there," said Lucy.

The *taramosalata* arrived on a big black square plate, scooped into tiny fish-shapes atop that harsh, bitter red lettuce no one likes used by all trendy places worldwide. Discreet melba toast squares were stacked to the side. Not the dish of pink nirvana and the basket of pita bread Lucy would have preferred for 1000 drachmae less.

"It's not very good here," whispered Teddie. "Nothing is."

"Is there anything you like in Athens?" Lucy asked politely.

Teddie took a moment to think about it, and in that minute, Stavros and two good-looking buddies strode into the bistro, all with the same curly Greek-god hair, all with near-identical leather jackets with fake American army insignia or British air force patches.

"*Ohi ohi* . . ." wailed Teddie, spying her brother. "Look over there, that table near the . . . the . . ."

Lucy helped her: "The speakers."

" 'Speakers?' They do not speak, they play music. But there, the girl in the brown leather jacket."

Which one of ten? wondered Lucy.

"That is Jane, little sweet Jane, my brother's girlfriend."

Teddie explained the fondness for foreign nicknames, often as an escape from old-fashioned mouthfuls like Klytemnestra, Kassiopeia, Kassandra.

"I would not name my poor daughter Theodora," Teddie explained.

"But that's a lovely name—"

Teddie disgustedly exhaled her cigarette. "My father would call me his little Empress Theodora . . ." She rolled her eyes, then made a karate-chop gesture. "Named after a former prostitute who cut off men's penises for amusement."

Could be apt, thought Lucy.

Following a recent Madonna hit was a local Greek pop song, and then Madonna was back again, unchallenged pop queen of the Mediterranean. Stavros was threading his way through the tables to insult his sister. Lucy tried to listen in but Classical Greek against the Modern Greek left too few traces. Some serious Jane-insulting was followed by Stavros heaping abuse on his sister.

"Ehhh," Teddie concluded, motioning for him to go away. "You are a peacock—my friend Lucy does not want to know you."

"What ees peacock?" Stavros asked Lucy, suspecting something horrid.

"*Pagóni*," his sister said, before adding to Lucy, "except a peacock has a bigger *poutsos*."

Stavros arched his eyebrows in distaste, looking precipitously down from his high cheekbones. Yes, thought Lucy, one of the two or three best-looking, best-constructed men I have ever seen in my life. His stupidity is what would save a woman in a relationship with him. God help us all if he had genuine charm. She watched Stavros and his tight jeans saunter back to Jane the bimbo.

"Why don't we go?" suggested Teddie, leaving a 1000-drachmae note on the plate beside the bill. "This place is ruined now."

The evening outside was cool and the air still bad from the daily Athenian jam of diesel and leaded fuel–spewing vehicles. Lucy and Teddie walked along clean, prosperous streets and appraised women's fashions in store windows, Teddie deferring to Lucy's American, contemporary sense of what was in fashion and what was not: "What could we know here, after all? Athens probably gets the clothes no other country will buy . . ."

"Do you work?" Lucy asked.

"No," said Teddie, surprised at the question. Why should she work as parents regularly provided for their children on the slopes of Kolonaki?

A café or two more, all blaring American pop hits and atrocities from Northern European countries recorded in English trying to pass as American pop hits. Around midnight it was time to go home, Lucy yawning more than talking.

It was decided that Lucy should have Theodora's room.

"The couch is fine for me," Lucy pleaded, rather liking the look of the plush living-room sofa.

No, Lucy would get Teddie's bed and Teddie would bunk on the couch; Dr. O'Hanrahan was in the guestroom. He and Eleni were staying up late with a bottle of ouzo and intended to move to the balcony; Mr. Matsoukis, having nodded asleep several times, finally excused himself to the bedroom.

Teddie fluffed the pillows beside the sofa, all the while teaching Lucy how to deflate Greek leches. "They hate to be called *malakismeno*."

Her mother Eleni interrupted her conservation with O'Hanrahan. "Theodora, please . . . Why should you teach her that word?"

"Because we walked on the street and the *malakismena* made a comment. And if she goes to the islands she will need to know what to say."

Eleni warmly turned to Lucy. "Ignore them, Lucy. That is best."

Teddie was smiling and forcing a bit of laughter.

"What is so funny?" asked her mother.

"Lucy," Theodora explained. "Coming back from the café, the boys made fun of us and Lucy insulted them . . ." Here Teddie put her head back uttering what could almost be called a laugh.

"Whadya hit 'em with, Luce?" asked O'Hanrahan.

Lucy was persuaded to confess.

Dr. O'Hanrahan reeled, and Eleni put her hand to her heart laughing silently. "Brilliant!" she cried.

"You told them in Classical Greek to put a radish up their behind?" asked the professor.

"Aristophanes, *The Clouds*," she said quietly.

"A common punishment for adultery in those days, you know," said O'Hanrahan, who knew all. "A peeled radish would be quite a sensation, hm?"

"Call them *malakismena*," Teddie reminded, fluffing the pillow.

Teddie was to explain when things were more private that it was calling a man a masturbator, as opposed to a man with an actual sex life. It was worse than suggesting he was gay, though that was good too—Greek men suspect all foreigners have that impression, given Plato and the boys, et al., but then again, according to Teddie, so many Greek men *were* bisexual, whether they admitted it to women or not. Then Teddie launched into a recommendation as to which islands were one big orgy—Ios, for example—and which had to be seen to be believed, like Mykonos: "There are human creatures there that might be girls, might be boys, I cannot tell. I know they are beautiful *hermaphroditoi* . . ."

"Hermaphrodites," said Lucy. "We have your word in English."

"Of course you would have *that* kind of word from Greece," Teddie scowled.

Lucy bade her good night around one A.M., withdrew to Teddie's room and closed the door behind her. She sank into the cool sheets and kept the reading light on briefly, looking over some of Teddie's schoolbooks, the lovely Greek script gesturing balletically across the page. What a shame the Romans didn't abandon their blocky alphabet and adopt the Greek one, since they slavishly copied everything else Greek, littering their own capital with copies of Greek temples, copies of Greek statues. Perhaps no language has ever been such a simple, direct assault upon the complex; in what other language can so much emotion be uttered with such restraint? The model for a classicism, for a linguistic purity still sought after today.

Latin, Lucy had long ago decided, was authoritative, a language fit for Roman conquerors, precise to the point of small-mindedness. It never seemed to flow or sing like Greek. In *Genesis* 1:3, the Bible God creates light in Greek with

> *Kaì eîpen ho Theus 'genēthétō phōs.'*

Let there be light. But in Latin, it sounds like a proper order, barked by a centurion following Caesar's will:

> *Fiat lux.*

Latin renders the *Gospel of John* well enough; even the nonspeaker can appreciate the square, forthright rules-and-regulation Vulgate feel to John's opening, the *In the beginning was the Word* bit:

> *In principio erat Verbum*
> *et Verbum apud Deum,*
> *et Deus erat Verbum.*
> *Hoc erat in principio erat Deum.*

Maybe I'm not a good Roman Catholic, thought Lucy, but how much more I am moved by the Greek in which it was written. Aside from its meaning, the sound is . . . like an incantation, at once Western and philosophical, but at the same time sonorous with the mysteries of the East:

> *En archê ên ho Lógos,*
> *Kaì ho Lógos ên pròs tòn theón,*
> *Kaì theòs ên ho Lógos.*
> *Hoûtos ên en archê pròs tòn theón.*

Lucy turned off the bedside light and snuggled underneath the covers. My mind has never been more alive, she thought. I am full with thought. I want to live this mindfully always—yes, even if it means never going home. Forward, keep letting me move forward, to somewhere new. Let me, Holy Spirit, travel always . . .

(Sure about that, Lucy? You just might get your wish.)

JULY 10TH–14TH

In the leisurely days at the ever-generous Matsoukises, Lucy was permitted a few days of sightseeing and souvenir shopping amid the only days of true rest she and Dr. O'Hanrahan had had in weeks. Lucy got to visit the Akropolis with a bored and deprecating Teddie:

"The tourists are so ugly this year, uglier than ever before . . . It's too expensive to come up here to look at these broken-down things—look, over there, someone has brought his dog who has made a mess. People are less civilized now than ever before . . ."

O'Hanrahan, meanwhile, went to the library near the Metropolitan Church. Father Basilios from the Acolyte Supper had written him an all-purpose permission letter to wave in any official's face who stood between him and the valuable libraries of the Orthodox.

One morning at breakfast, Lucy asked O'Hanrahan how the search was going, and he said something patronizing, then drank and ate as if she wasn't there.

She stopped him afterward in the Matsoukises' hallway. "Sir," Lucy pleaded, "isn't there something academic I can do to help you? Why don't you take me to the library?"

"I thought you'd rather sightsee, Miss Dantan."

Well, the guilty secret of Athens, source of the Western World, is that you can do everything in two or three days. More important now, Lucy felt she had to improve her credentials in the professor's eyes, to be a full academic partner. After further entreaties, he relented. She tried to gush enthusiasm for long hours in the Metropolitan's library. "My guidebook says there's an excellent ikon collection."

"Fun fun fun," yawned O'Hanrahan, gathering up his satchel and trying out a wayward ballpoint on the outside of it, trying to make it write.

By noon they sat in a small assistant librarian's office waiting for a pass to be processed for Lucy. A monk then led them into another waiting room where O'Hanrahan's letters of recommendation were submitted to some unseen authority.

Minutes passed.

"Bet they don't let me in," mumbled Lucy.

They were led shortly into the gallery of famously celebrated ikons and illuminated manuscripts on display, which was due to open later for the tourists that afternoon. O'Hanrahan leaned over to stare at the miracle-working *Galaktotrophousa* from the 1000s. Lucy, peering over his shoulder, took a moment to work out the meaning of the name, but O'Hanrahan rushed to translate it in crisp tones: "Our Lady Who Gives Suck."

Lucy giggled, despite herself.

"Undoubtedly Our Lady's breast shown here, at some point, produced a drop of holy cream . . . Of course, Mary's milk, as endless Catholic theologians have assured us, was not like normal women's milk. So perhaps this ikon's milk was part divine effluvium, part real milk, sort of like Borden Half-and-Half."

"Ssssh, the monk's going to come back any minute."

"You no doubt recall that Aquinas in Naples was sitting beside a painting of Our Lady, who allowed him to catch three precious drops that spurted from her full, heavy breasts."

Lucy couldn't stop snickering and was reminded of being a young girl in church.

(Lucy, you *are* in a church.)

"Darn if St. Bernard didn't have the same thing happen. Droplets sprang from Mary's bosom and placed themselves on his tongue, one, two, three. I had in mind, once upon a time, to do an article on God's taste in art. To look at the minor painting that spurted on Aquinas or the crucifix in Assisi that spoke to St. Francis or all the plastic statues that weep and bleed throughout the Mediterranean. God could, if He wanted, speak through the Sistine Chapel but no, He always goes for the black velvet painting, the plastic Latino hood ornament, that lady in Mexico who had Jesus appear to her in the refried beans of a tortilla."

(Remember the story of Balaam's ass, Patrick?)

Lucy's eyes were teary from trying to suppress her unwarranted bout of the giggles, but she was determined to be under control—

"Our Lady Who Gives *Suck*," O'Hanrahan repeated richly. "See, I can get you to laugh at the word 'suck.' You're an easy mark today, Luce. Look at this ikon here, the *Glykophilolussa*, Our Lady of the Loving Kisses, or here's . . . yes, I've seen one of these before in a number of places, a *Myrovlitissa*, Our Lady Who Flows with Myrrh. Considering what her great-great-ancestor Solomon wrote about myrrh, I don't suppose we should contemplate whence floweth this myrrh—"

"Dr. O'Hanrahan, sssshhh!"

"Wouldn't you like to see one of these ikons go off at one time, streaming with myrrh, a bit of oil down the front, the lips smacking away, milk spraying in twin jets from the breasts—"

The monk-librarian: "Would you be so kind as to follow me?"

Lucy looked down to the floor and tried desperately not to laugh. O'Hanrahan moved calmly behind the father, who was now positive

these two pilgrims had no place in his library. Lucy and the professor
entered the rare book room pretending not to notice the glare of
the unwelcoming monk behind the desk. It was nothing like she or
O'Hanrahan expected: modern, clean, air-conditioned, and she
thought she discerned the hum of a computer terminal in the adjoining
office just out of the line of sight. The father grudgingly escorted Lucy
to a more public area of tables but informed her that since she was a
woman, he himself would have to fetch whatever book she requested
and bring it to her.

"Well, who can blame them?" said O'Hanrahan afterward. "You
don't know what you might drive these old monks to back in the stacks.
Consigned here for your own safety, I suspect."

"Sexist pigs," she whispered back.

Lucy took a table near a desk lamp, directly across from an ikon of
St. John the Theologian staring at her from the next world where,
Lucy was sure, the library would be coed.

(You got that right.)

O'Hanrahan reached into his satchel and produced a manila folder
filled with dog-eared loose sheets, Xeroxes of pages from all kinds of
books, in all sorts of scripts.

"This is my Matthias folder," he explained. "Every mention of Matthias I have ever been able to turn up in ancient writings I have
photographed or copied and collected here. Look it over and educate
yourself. Second, I've decided to give you an exercise to translate."

"Ooh, a test."

"That's right, a test. This is from the Louvain imprint of Flamion's
apocryphal texts, 1911—a virtual bible of biblical pretenders," he
added, pulling out a single Xerox of a page of Greek script, placing it
before her. "It's Alexandrine Greek of the 300s and it should give you
a few problems here and there. I want to see what conclusions you
draw from this."

Lucy was thrilled. "Got a pencil?"

"Maybe the *Panagia*, Blessed Virgin, will provide one," he grumbled,
as he delved into his satchel trying to scoop a pencil off the bottom
amid the paper clips and pocket change from several countries. "Make
sure you return it." He also sacrificed a few sheets from his legal pad
for her to work upon.

"What happens, sir, if I can't do this?"

"Chicaaaahgo, Chicaaaahgo, it's a wonnerful town," he sang.

As Lucy focused on the page before her, O'Hanrahan shuffled off
for the stacks, his old-fashioned, black-framed reading glasses squarely
on his face, ready for work. The professor jovially addressed the middle-aged monk behind the reference desk in Modern Greek. "I'm
looking for the photostats of the *Clementine Recognitions*," O'Hanrahan

said. "I realize you will not allow me to see the original ancient documents . . ."

No, the monk confirmed, that would be impossible without permission from the Patriarch himself. But alas, not even the large folio of photostats was available, having been recently shipped off to Megistri Lavra on Mt. Athos.

O'Hanrahan frowned. "And the material on the *Clementine Homilies?*"

"Sadly, that is also at Megistri Lavra," said the monk. "To what do we owe this rebirth in the interest in these uncanonical fragments?"

"Interest?"

"Indeed. A monk this very week called up these same documents, and the *Sermium Compendium*—"

"No," O'Hanrahan said in distress. "That was the very thing I was going to ask for next."

"That, sir, we have never owned. That has always been at Megistri Lavra." Megistri Lavra was the oldest and greatest of the Mount Athos monasteries, founded 963, a Byzantine showplace of frescoes and ikons, possessing a library adorned by the wealth of Eastern Christianity.

Professor O'Hanrahan smiled politely. "Do you recall who ordered these documents, Father?"

"The monk who read these scrolls did so here before me in this reading room, sir. As he was not removing them, there was no need to keep a record. Hundreds of scholars pass through here each year."

O'Hanrahan immediately thought of the Mad Monk of Father Vico's paranoia. O'Hanrahan pressed the librarian for a description.

"An old man, a beard, gray hair, monk's robes . . ." He laughed. "I'm sorry, it could be any of our fathers."

O'Hanrahan then wearily slumped at a reference table and drummed his fingers there, until told to hush by a nearby scholar. He thought: someone is on the same trail I am on. Then he dismissed the thought; there were many reasons to look at the *Clementine* documents besides looking for obscure alphabets and the *Gospel of Matthias.*

O'Hanrahan was hoping to go straight to Jerusalem after seeing these documents, which, frankly, he hadn't expected to be terribly revealing . . . but now that someone else was so interested, perhaps he had better see these documents at all costs. That meant going to Mt. Athos and living in the Dark Ages for a week. Because women are banned from the Athonite slopes, Lucy would have to wait behind in that little port city of Ouranopolis.

Oh well, O'Hanrahan sighed, while he was here in the library, he might as well cave in and look for Father Beaufoix's book on African scripts. He couldn't remember the name of it. A bland title like *African*

Scripts, something like that . . . O'Hanrahan stood and went to the reference shelf, determined to look up his rival's entry in the Scholarly Register.

Ah, the Scholarly Register; O'Hanrahan ran his hands over the searched-for volume with pleasure. What had started as a 19th-Century alternative to the Index of Banned books, the organ for right-minded Catholic thinkers approved by idiots like Veuillot and the stooges who wrote for *L'Univers*, had in one hundred years evolved into a hot Who's Who in the world of theology, a rank and file of the serious thinkers that the pope, in these times, did battle with. After Vatican II, the Scholarly Register expanded to list Protestant and Orthodox men of note as well, the outstanding Jewish ecumenicists too, hence the Metropolitan of Athens could look up his own name—indeed, so could Mordechai Hersch.

It was no small point of pride that Patrick Virgil O'Hanrahan was listed among these pages, listed as the former chairman of Chicago's Department of Theology, the renowned assistant translator among the original Dead Sea Scrolls team, adviser and editor to the Nag Hammadi Scrolls' critical editions, supervisor of the 1958 cataloguing of the Mar Saba Library, an all-around unforgettable, irreplaceable character . . . O'Hanrahan found the 1988 edition, as recent as they had, and looked up Father Beaufoix and found his works listed, ten or eleven of the finest contributions to 20th-Century Christian scholarship. Yes, there was the title: *Languages of the Nile*.

Should he do it? Should he look himself up?

Why not, he figured with a brief look over the shoulder to make sure he wasn't happened upon. Hey, there seems to be some problem here . . . *O'Hanrahan* is not in the index. Nor on page 489 between Cardinal O'Connor and Oldenbourg's history of the Albigensian Crusade.

Well, what do you know? I've been dropped out, he murmured aloud.

O'Hanrahan returned the book to the shelf.

When the hell did they drop his name? We'll just see . . . O'Hanrahan pulled down 1986, 1980, 1977. Again and again and again he wasn't included. I've been a nobody for over a decade, have I? This is what you get for your vanity! At last, in 1976, he found himself, his little reduced entry, former head of the Chicago Dept. of Theology, noted translator, particularly the Thanksgiving Hymn, Dead Sea Scrolls, 1949 . . . The entry concluded: Retired emeritus, 1974.

Why don't they just put that on the other end of my parentheses, go ahead and bury me! *Patrick V. O'Hanrahan (1925–   )*. He left the Registers scattered on the tabletop, too weary of heart to return them to the shelves.

Hell, he lectured himself the next minute, why *should* they keep you in? The wound was opened anew: where are your ten or eleven essential works? Idiots, cretins, morons, papal ass-kissers, and Protestant hacks are in this guide, possessing a tenth of your intelligence and knowledge of the Christian world, but they *wrote it down!* They wrote their drivel, for the world to read, and they exist to posterity! You and your laziness!

(*The way of a sluggard is overgrown with thorns.*)

Oh shut up! "It wasn't that I was lazy exactly . . ." he said out loud. "Ssssh!" said a monk, hushing him from a desk on the aisle.

I'm talking to myself, thought O'Hanrahan. I'm not only a has-been, but I'm senile to boot. I'm losing my mind in here . . .

That evening at the Matsoukises' dinner table a wild-eyed O'Hanrahan preached a crusade to Mount Athos by way of Thessaloniki where he could get proper forms for safe passage stamped and verified. Lucy considered what it would mean for her to wait for Dr. O'Hanrahan in Ouranopolis, the small fishing village and departure point for the holy peninsula. Days with nothing to do, just the Aegean sun to bask in, Greek café life to sustain her, a chance to get a tan, catch up on reading . . . Sounded good.

O'Hanrahan's first scheme was to rent a car and have Lucy drive him to Makedonia, but this plan faltered when Lucy confessed she couldn't drive a stick shift. O'Hanrahan then suggested volunteering Mrs. Matsoukis's Uncle Spiros, who had driven O'Hanrahan to the Meteoran Monasteries back in 1968, who at eighty-some might appreciate an outing.

"No," mourned Eleni, "he is fine around his village, but I would not risk your lives with him now."

"He was always a horrible driver," O'Hanrahan noted, hoping for nostalgia's sake to have again the old man's crude, bawdy company for one last expedition. O'Hanrahan moved himself to the living-room chair, ice tinkling in his evening glass of milky ouzo, and looked at Lucy. "Well, Miss Dantan, perhaps you'll get your chance after all to battle the Mediterranean roads. There's bound to be a car company that rents automatics somewhere in Greece."

"Uh, I don't know, Dr. O'Hanrahan," said Lucy. "I don't do a lot of driving back home exactly. Can't you drive, sir?"

He looked to the ceiling. "My license, in an unfortunate altercation with Chicago's Finest, was removed from my possession."

(DWI. October 2nd, 1979. Breathilizer went right off the scale.)

In the kitchen, Teddie and Stavros were spitting vindictive Greek at each other. O'Hanrahan cocked an ear and tried to translate . . . something about how Stavros never did a single bit of work at university and to send him to school was a waste of money. Stavros responded he was on break this summer and didn't see why he should feel compelled to study in advance of the school year or get any kind of job. Then, turning his attention, O'Hanrahan appraised Lucy in her bug-eye glasses, dressed in a nebulous blue dress shirt handed down from an older brother, her hair yet to recover from the recent sea voyage across the Adriatic.

"I'm going to procure for you," he said slowly.

(Oh Patrick, no.)

"What was that, sir?"

"Nothing, nothing . . ." he said, grunting to his feet and walking into the dining room to speak to Eleni.

July 15th

The next day the three of them, O'Hanrahan and Lucy, Stavros at the wheel for a prearranged sum, sped up Greece's major highway in a shiny yellow rented car at an unreasonable Mediterranean speed, wind rushing through open windows. Lucy sat in the backseat delighted with the scenery and the Greek roadsigns, presenting place names she knew from the classics.

O'Hanrahan rambled about nearby Thermopylae and the lopsided battle there—300 Spartans versus thousands of Xerxes' Persians—and the ridge of mountains culminating to the west in Mt. Parnassus, where the immortal poets dwell, where the muses hide. Unexpectedly, the road wound into a gray, sheer canyon and emerged upon the plains of Makedonia guarded by the *Oros Olimbos*, Mount Olympus itself. The isolated swirl of white cumulus around the peaks certified that the gods were home.

Stavros explained something in Greek to O'Hanrahan.

"A national park," O'Hanrahan supplemented. "Zeus and company. I'd watch out for swans, Miss Dantan."

"I'll keep an eye out."

Lucy let the miles pass while imagining a trip one day with a back-pack around the mountaintops: *In the bright hall of Zeus upon Olympos the other gods were all at home, and Zeus, the father of gods and men, made conversation.* Would Zeus talk to her upon that mountaintop?

(No, since he doesn't exist.)

Stavros broke this reverie by commenting upon two approaching female hitchhikers in the briefest of short shorts, by the side of the road. He wildly turned his head for a better view of thigh and cleavage, swerving the car. Whoa hoa hoa, Stavros uttered. O'Hanrahan, equally captivated, chortled approval. And then bilingual guy-talk broke out.

Lucy crossed her arms, frowning. Stavros Matsoukis is twenty-one and Patrick O'Hanrahan is sixty-five and though having nothing in common, having wholly different world views and levels of sophistication, they can unite here in this sacred, well-trodden Acadian grove where maledom adores a NICE ASS and BIG TITS, unifier of allllll mankind, bridger of all differences, from the cantinas of Latin America to the hashish joints of the Middle East: NICE ASS, BIG TITS. Pigs! And what woman, Lucy wondered, in her right mind would hitchhike in Greece in those shorts?

Stavros was saying something through O'Hanrahan's greasy, old-man's laugh, making gestures with his free hand, creating breasts in the air, speaking of *stitha amerikanida*. Something about American bosoms, Lucy figured. At this moment Lucy made up her mind not to lay so much as *a straw* upon the load of Stavros's male vanity, not to favor him with so much as a breath of interest, a glance of appraisal. Having sworn this she looked in the rearview mirror where she could see Stavros's eyes. He looked at her briefly and raised an eyebrow as if to say: looking at something you can't have? She quickly broke off eye contact.

In Thessaloniki, Stavros screeched to a stop in front of the Ministry for Northern Greece and O'Hanrahan hopped out to get his permission papers for Mount Athos stamped. Stavros idled in an active lane of traffic despite being waved away by a policeman and all of Thessaloniki honking and cursing behind him.

Lunch followed and for the first time Lucy tired of the inevitable bipolar choice of most Greek lunch specials: souvlaki or moussaka. What was that ever-rotating convex slab of meat anyway, exposed for months at a time to leaded European auto exhaust and flies? Certainly it wasn't one little lamb, undifferentiated and humongous . . . it must be lots of lambs, all ground up and reconstituted. Lucy had hoped to rely on salads to break up the culinary monotony, but the last sumptuous Greek salad in Athens was immersed in olive oil, and this had produced diarrhea, as one particularly long visit to the hole-in-the-ground Mediterranean toilet reconfirmed.

"The old diarrhea again, Luce?" said O'Hanrahan upon her return, roseate with an absorbed bottle of retsina. He waved the waiter away with the change from lunch.

"No, I liked squatting over that reeking hole in the floor so much I thought I'd stay for a while."

"Ah," intoned O'Hanrahan as they walked from the café, " 'twas Diarrhea herself that brought great Hercules low and bade him to his death. 'This is the *end*,' he said—"

"That's lame, old man. I did Classics as an undergrad," Lucy additionally informed him, getting into the car as Stavros held the door, "so there's no excuse for this second-rate material. And furthermore, I'd appreciate not having my diarrhea discussed publicly."

"Doesn't matter," he said. "Stavros loves you for who you are, don't you, Stavros?"

Stavros merely repeated the Greek word "diarrhea," unchanged through the centuries.

"Oh, please."

After Thessaloniki came the worst of the roads, the winding, badly engineered two-lane road to Ouranopolis, through the mountains of Chalkidiki. Accompanying the lurching right and left was the stopping and starting as Stavros came upon too quickly the back of a diesel smog–spewing truck moving 25 m.p.h. or a farmer and donkey cart blocking the road. Up, down, right, left, stop, start . . . Lucy's stomach churned with indigestion on the nauseating curves, and she at last demanded a rest break.

This garnered O'Hanrahan's opposition, though once they had stopped in a little village called Paleochori it allowed O'Hanrahan a chance to purchase more retsina, bottled in clear long-necks for easy drinking. Slightly recovered, Lucy got back in the car and Stavros drove on while O'Hanrahan swigged from the retsina as he talked.

"Yeah, they hate us," he was saying to Lucy, referring to Orthodox hatred of Roman Catholics, "and I'd hate us too if I were they." He turned to Stavros, asking in Greek, "What do you think of Roman Catholics, Stavros?"

He said something, as if about to spit.

"The enmity of the East," pronounced O'Hanrahan.

"Are they still sore over the *filioque* business?" asked Lucy, remembering Church History 102. In 451 the Council of Chalcedon, that fount of 1600 years of Christian bickering, confirmed that Christians would believe *in the Holy Spirit, the Lord, the Giver of Life, who proceeds from the Father*, etc. But eventually some prelates in Charlemagne's kingdom preferred the phrase *who proceeds from the Father and the Son, "filioque"* in Latin. The phrase was inserted in the Roman version of the Creed, despite the disapproval of centuries of popes, despite Rome's oaths to abide by the councils of the earlier, purer church, and despite that perpetual inconvenience for Rome, the Holy Scriptures: Jesus spoke of the Spirit, *who proceeds from the Father* in *John* 15:26.

(Nonetheless, Roman Catholics felt justified in branding the patriarchs of the East heretics, laying a bull of excommunication upon the altar in Constantinople's Hagia Sophia in 1054. The case was put forward by one of the great morons of Catholic history, Cardinal Humbert, who accused the East of *deleting* the phrase. Excommunications and anathemae flew back and forth and, much to Our disappointment, 900 years of hostility and schism ensued.)

"1054," said O'Hanrahan, "the same year as the Crab Nebula Nova, which lit the sky as a second sun, the heavens themselves in schism."

"Nice touch," noted Lucy. "Didn't Rome and the East try to patch things up?"

"Yes, but always with disastrous consequences, with Rome sending its stubbornest, stupidest men to the bargaining tables. It didn't matter, though, because Western behavior during the Crusades would make the schism complete."

O'Hanrahan swilled the last of the retsina and undid his seatbelt to better make room for his stomach, which he rested folded hands upon.

"It's significant," he narrated, "that in all these Crusades against the Moslem infidel, only two great cities were sacked and looted, and they were Christian: Constantinople and Alexandria. The Templars and Hospitalers cut all kinds of deals with the Moslems—Masonic secret orders practice bastardized Islamic rites to this day. And Mohammed, in any event, got on with Christians; some 12,000 Christians fought with him in his first great battle. If you paid the Moslems their tribute, like to the Caesars of old, they left other Children of the Book alone. No, the true target of the Crusades came to be the wealth of the East."

Lucy leaned forward during the lull. "Surely you're not pausing on the brink of atrocities, Dr. O'Hanrahan?"

"Forgive my after-lunch laziness," he said, sitting up straight: "On the First Crusade in 1095, would it surprise you to know that Romans, drunk and marauding, stormed Cappadocia, raped the women, killed the men, and then roasted the town's children on a spit for a banquet? In Caesarea, the European mob of homeless and destitute who came for plunder killed all the Moslems in their mosque, wiped out the Jews and all the Arab Christians they could lay their hands on, taking their property. Speaking of Jews, the Holy Roman Empire's Crusaders celebrated leaving Germany by the public slaughter of a thousand Jews, so they were well in practice by the time they got to the Holy Lands. Upon taking Jerusalem for the one and only time, the Christians rounded up the Jews, put them in a synagogue and burned it down with all inside. Mordechai can give chapter and verse on all the Jewish massacres."

"Yes," she sighed, "no doubt."

O'Hanrahan rambled, amassing the grisly highlights of the Crusades, the hypocrisy, the abject holocausts in Rome's name . . . Lucy observed her mentor, holding forth as if reading from a script, as if lecturing before an appreciative audience, a packed hall of students. She briefly regretted never having seen Patrick O'Hanhrahan in his prime teaching Church History back at the University. Lucy thought how thoroughly he *owned* the dark and shameful past, how tightly he held it to himself; not unlike a long-suffering son recounting his ne'er-do-well father's waywardness: do you see, God, what I have to remember and endure in order to love You?

". . . throughout France and Germany children would announce their intention to go to Jerusalem and parents would send their unwanted offspring after the knights, roaming in mobs as large as 20,000. The Pied Piper myths stem from this period; the original tale was of unwanted, unfed children being led away, not rats.

(Rats, alas, fared better then. These mobs never reached Jerusalem; they were sold into slavery in North Africa, sold to the child-brothels of Sardinia.)

"One also thinks of 1204 and the Sack of Constantinople by Roman forces. Three days of pillage were allowed, the jewels and gold of Byzantium began their slow trip to Venice—and not an Orthodox nun was allowed to go unraped for the glory of the pope. The relics were looted, including the Hand of John the Baptist, which is yet on display in Suleiman the Magnificent's palace in Istanbul. A prostitute was found and put upon the Patriarch's throne in the Hagia Sophia—"

"Excuse me, Dr. O'Hanrahan, but are there any episcopal thrones in the Mediterranean world that have *not* been occupied by prostitutes?"

"Now *there* is a thesis worthy of your time and attention, Miss Dantan. In any event the Hand was brought out and the prostitute upon the Patriarch's throne, shall we say, brought herself to pleasure with this most precious relic . . ."

(Patrick would fixate upon something like that.)

"The Baptist had to wait 1200 years for a feel, but if you hang around long enough, you see what can happen."

(Cover your ears, Lucy.)

"Well, to this day, the Sack is remembered," O'Hanrahan said sadly, "and after it no hope of concord was possible. Innocent II, on hearing that a Latin patriarch had been installed in Constantinople, declared the orgy of blood a *magnificat mirabilis*, a magnificent miracle, and announced that all the Crusaders were granted an indulgence that would permit them to go straight to heaven."

(The odd sense of outrage the Christian world has for how the Islamic world feels about it almost touches Us in its naiveté. If We have observed anything, it is that most crimes have a way of visiting themselves upon the countries who commit them; it is in this spirit that Moses wrote that sins of fathers are visited upon their children. If Islamic *jihad* and terrorism and anti-Western sentiment trouble the West, perhaps it should refer to its own 400 years of Christian state terrorism.)

"The greatest library of the Islamic world," mourned O'Hanrahan, "far superior to any pile of claptrap possessed in Europe, was in Tripoli, the Banu-Ammar. It was burned by Christian Crusaders in 1109. Christians are the world's great philistines; they've always had a Jesse

Helms streak. The best library ever assembled on earth was the Great Library at Alexandria, which puritanical Christians burned in 391, because there were possibly heretical and obscene works within it. Christian fanatics closed the School of Athens in 529, banning all universities and secular education. During Innocent III's Albigensian Crusade, the mere possession of a Bible in the home, which only priests were supposed to own, caused thousands to be burned at the stake."

(Woe to those who would spread ignorance!)

"Well," said Lucy, falling back in her seat. "I suppose it will take more than a rosary or two to make up for all that."

"I can tell," said the professor, "you're racked with guilt."

"Didn't the Greeks do anything bad?"

"Oh, tons. They pounce upon the West for heresy and updating conciliar creeds, but they did the same in 451 at Chalcedon, condemning monophysitism and losing the Copts, the Armenians, the Ethiopians, and the Syrians, who, technically, are more orthodox than the Greeks are. As for scheming and conniving, no sack or Hunnish invasion of Rome was ever as devastating as Byzantium's centuries-long plotting against Rome during the Dark Ages, all for the sake of a little real estate in southern Italy. Pope Silverius was tortured and killed by the bloodthirsty Justinian and Theodora . . ."

Lucy smiled to hear of Teddie's namesake.

"There was a roundup of Latin-rite Christians in Constantinople in 11-something or other . . ."

(1187.)

"Whom they massacred, Crusader-style. Plus, the Greek Orthodox treated their Arab-Christian brethren horribly, cheating them in war after war, treaty after treaty. If it hadn't been for all the bickering over personhood and substance, the naturally monotheistic Arab world might have remained Christian instead of being ripe for conversion to Islam. I have read intelligent men mystified, stymied by the spread of Islam, its speed and its thoroughness. Hell, if you had to contend with the Byzantine Emperor, you'd have converted too! The arrogance of Byzantium. One thinks of poor schmoes like Father Avvakum."

(Avvakum and the Patriarch Nikon argued over a theological point in the mid-1600s. Nikon had him exiled for ten years, but he didn't soften. Then he had him imprisoned for twenty-two years, moving him to a dank, lightless, underground cell. Avvakum still didn't agree with him. So the Patriarch burned him at the stake. At issue? Whether to make the sign of the Cross with two or three fingers.)

"But you like being Orthodox, don't you, Stavros?" asked O'Hanrahan.

"*Neh,*" he said, reaching under his T-shirt and bringing his pendant Greek Cross to his lips in reverence.

Lucy tried to get a clarification on whether *Neh* meant *no.*

The professor: "*Neh* means yes, and *ohi* means no."

" 'Nah' is yes and 'okay' is no?"

"That's right."

Lucy shook her head. "Of course, it should be that way. It's a foreign country."

A few more lurches of the narrow road and they came to a small mountain pass: on their left as well as far to the right was the Aegean, and in between rose a spine of mountains, the Athos Peninsula. The high ridge appeared heavily wooded and mysterious in the haze, and Lucy felt a small defeat in knowing its treasures were closed to her. Damn patriarchs.

"No women at all," she said, as if to herself.

"Nope," said O'Hanrahan. "Not even female animals," he reminded her. "That's why there's haze, because there are trees and plants. And there are plants and trees because there's no grazing. Sheep herds, goat herds—grazing has turned Greece into a rocky, barren place. In front of us, Miss Dantan, you see Greece as the ancients saw it, where Chloris fled from Zephyr. A tropical garden—"

"I don't want to hear about it."

"Jealous?"

It went without saying. Lucy, however, speculated: "I bet some woman's done it. Snuck onto the place."

O'Hanrahan answered, "I doubt any have gotten inside the monasteries."

(Want to bet?)

O'Hanrahan: "A Byzantine princess tried unsuccessfully."

(Empress Mara, wife of the conquering Sultan Murat, came to present the monasteries with money as well as the recovered relics of the Gifts of the Magi. As she stepped off the dock, there's the old story that the Virgin appeared to her and said it was her garden alone. She lost her nerve was what happened.)

"*Ohi gynaikes*," said Stavros, trying to participate. "Women, no."

Below them on the shore and the winding road down to it was the last reach of the 20th Century, Ouranopolis, a small town of a few blocks, L-shaped, just like the point of land it occupied. The nicer hotels faced the west; around the other corner of the L were a few junky beach shops, a pair of typical Greek restaurants, a newsstand with English and German newspapers amid the postcards, and a block behind those were three clubs—expanded bars, really, each with a disco ball hanging from the ceiling. The pebbly coast gave way to light blue water littered with numerous paddle-boats, windsurfing equipment, light sailboats. No harbor, judged Lucy, for expensive yachts or beautiful people, but rather for English and German couples on package holidays, whose greatest demand of the Aegean might be of floating upon an inflatable multicolored raft.

"Get that credit card out," said O'Hanrahan as they walked along the west front, surveying possible hotels.

Stavros asked if he should go stay in a *thomatia*, a cheap room in one of the local's homes, but O'Hanrahan said he should stay at the hotel. They needed a hotel with a phone, so O'Hanrahan could be in contact with Lucy.

"That is," added O'Hanrahan, faking concern, "supposing that I can even get ahold of Lucy by phone. I suspect she'll be out picking up Greek men at the local discos, meeting all the nice English boys."

Lucy sniffed, "I just might be at those discos, Dr. O'Hanrahan."

"Deeskos," said Stavros, smiling.

"See?" said O'Hanrahan, lumbering up the front steps of a hotel called the Hotel Poseidon. "You've even got a hot date for tonight."

"Hot deet, yays," said Stavros, strutting especially for Lucy, bounding up the stairs of the hotel with his and Lucy's bags.

Stavros's English wasn't all *that* bad, Lucy was surmising.

The Hotel Poseidon was near empty and overjoyed to see customers of any variety. The proprietor mourned the fall of the dollar's value, the inexplicable, fanciful fear Americans had of being blown up by terrorists in Greece . . . The oblong building had four balconied rooms on the second and top floor. Lucy got one of the rooms and O'Hanrahan and Stravros another. Lucy went out to stand on her balcony and O'Hanrahan went out to stand on his, separated by a thick wall.

"Howdy, neighbor," said Lucy.

As night approached the three had another meal at one of the two open-air, canopied cafés. Lucy had *kalamari* for a change of pace; O'Hanrahan and Stavros had souvlaki and happily absorbed two bottles of retsina. In a drawn-out trial Lucy was made to drink a whole glass without making a face.

"Tastes like turpentine," she coughed. "I don't have to worry about falling in love with that."

"You have failed my first test of holiness," intoned the professor.

"Oh!" said Lucy, reminded of her test of yesterday. She dove into her carpetbag and produced, folded in half, her yellow legal sheet with the translation of the Alexandrian text O'Hanrahan had set for her. "Tell me how I did," Lucy said, handing it over.

Stavros stood, bored and restless after a full day of listening to English being spoken. He excused himself for the hotel where he intended to adorn himself for the disco. As he left the café, the blond heads of the German female tourists turned to watch appreciatively his indolent saunter to the edge of the canopy, his striking a pose, and his finale, a slow stage exit to the hotel.

O'Hanrahan was impressed with Lucy's translation.

It was an Alexandrian Greek tale from *The Acts of Andrew and Matthias* of the 4th Century, this version much altered, featuring the Disciples

Andrew and Matthias, the source of the *Andreas* Lucy had investigated back at Oxford:

> *And a statue poured out water from its mouth as from a canal and it was bitter and corroded men's flesh. In the morning all the people of the town began to flee. The water killed their cattle and their children. And Andrew said, "Let Michael wall the city about with fire." A cloud of fire came and surrounded it and they could not escape. The water came up to their necks and consumed their flesh . . . And then Andrew went as far as the great vat and prayed and the earth opened and swallowed the water and the old man and the executioners. Then he bade them bring all who had been killed by the water but there were too many and so he prayed and revived them. Then he drew out the plan of a church and baptized them and gave them the Lord's precepts. And they begged the disciples to stay but Andrew refused saying I must first go to my disciples and he set forth and they were very sad. Then Jesus appeared in the form of a beautiful child and reproved him for leaving them and told him to stay seven days and then he should go with his disciples to the country of the Ethiopian man-eaters and then return and bring the men out of the abyss.*

"Not bad," said O'Hanrahan. "You even got 'vat' right. Matthias, you see, was meanwhile cooking in the cauldron."

Lucy wondered, "God kills all these people, then revives them, then the disciples leave, then Jesus says go back . . . whom could this ever have appealed to?"

O'Hanrahan handed the sheet back to her. "You have now learned, Miss Dantan, the first rule of apocryphal texts: most gospels disqualify themselves from serious consideration after ten lines. People like to think there are gospels out there somewhere just as valid as *Matthew*, *Mark*, and *Luke*, but the sad truth is most are of this variety. It's very rare that a useful, credible document shows itself. And until the greatest of all finds, 'Q,' the proto-gospel, turns up, the greatest find in ages will be the *Gospel of Matthias*."

Lucy: "Where did the *Gospel of Matthias* come from in the first place?"

O'Hanrahan shrugged. "I hope to investigate that in Jerusalem. I know Rabbi Rosen bought it from a Mustafa al-Waswasah, an acquaintance of mine from Dead Sea Scroll days. I'm going to go interrogate the old fox."

O'Hanrahan held forth about the whimsical ways gospels have turned up.

"Who knows where Matthias might have been hiding? In a museum or a library or in a private collector's case or in an attic. The thirteen Nag Hammadi gospels found in 1945 were discovered when an Arab in a blood feud killed his rival and tried to stash away the body. He dug a grave and turned up the scrolls. His mother that night used a few of the gospels for fire kindling to cook her soup."

Lucy closed her eyes in pain. "You're kidding."

"Nope, some of the Nag Hammadi gospels survived 2000 years only to go up in smoke for a pot of broth. Two kids were chasing a goat near Qumran's ruins and turned up the Dead Sea Scrolls. In 1958 a letter of Clement of Alexandria was found in the vaults of Mar Saba Monastery's library, mentioning a secret, second version of *Mark* passed only among church hierarchs. Consider, my dear, that archaeology and textual analysis are recent sciences. We in the 21st Century will have access to the First Century as no other century, even the Second or Third, ever had." He then yawned. "And I better get to bed since I've got to leave at seven A.M. Night night, and don't die of boredom here."

"I'll try not to, sir. Good luck."

O'Hanrahan entrusted her with the VISA card. "July 19th, four days from now, a phone call to the Hotel Poseidon, at high noon—if I'm not back before that. Unfailingly!"

Lucy watched him pad off to the hotel and wondered if she shouldn't have put out her hand or given him a hug or something. They were in an awkward stage of companionship. The next moment she saw Stavros, in a muscle shirt, ringlets newly arranged, tight jeans, leaving a plume of cologne behind him as he walked by on his way toward the thump-thump-thump of the disco.

Teddie's right, thought Lucy. What a peacock.

ΑΓΙΟΝ ΟΡΟΣ
July 16th

O'Hanrahan watched the town of Ouranopolis recede in the morning haze. Farewell to civilization for a while.

Or, on the contrary, maybe it was hello to civilization, the oldest and purest left, free from World Wars and common markets. Yes, also free of electricity, modern plumbing, sanitary kitchens ... O'Hanrahan walked over to the portside to stare at the stark peninsula of rock, the rocky hills becoming mountains as the boat motored eastward. He could see two houses, a fishing pier—no, this wasn't the Theocracy of Athos yet. O'Hanrahan patted his jacket; his wallet held several thousand drachmae in case a little old-fashioned bribery was called for among the elect of God.

As for O'Hanrahan's fellow passengers, they were the same as the time before, no doubt the same as men centuries before: priests on retreats, monks returning to their monasteries or new assignments, mostly old with long gray beards and black robes worn unwashed for ages, but a few young hopefuls in pressed shiny black, with silky, curly black beards and piercing eyes full of questions for the holy men. Were these . . . children, teenage boys, for Christ's sake, turning their back on the world? Were these young men here for a month of study or had they come to make a life in the 900s?

In a half-hour the boat came to a concrete pier.

On the shore a few monks waited to be taken back to Ouranopolis, their assignments done. Two backpackers—they looked British—had finished their allotted time as well; they looked parboiled in the full-length clothes Athos required. No shorts, no exposed arms, nothing but hands and face can be revealed. O'Hanrahan stepped off the boat and flashed his passport and letter of permission to the Greek customs official, who was barely interested, then he and the new pilgrims boarded Athos's one bus.

Already hot by nine, the pilgrims sweated and groaned and laughed as the bus clung to the perilous dirt road up the cliff; their driver nonchalantly made wide, leaning turns, providing those passengers in the back with the impression that they were going to topple thousands of feet down to the dock below—genuflections, laughter, a lively Greek pantomime of a near-miss followed each careening turn. Undoubtedly one of these days, thought O'Hanrahan, this bus *will* miss a turn.

(But not this day.)

It delivered them, shaken, hot, nauseated and thankful, to the capital of Athos, Karyes. Here, since 963, representatives from the twenty monasteries have met to vote on issues ranging from the decline of Byzantium, the invasion of the Turks, the occupation by the Nazis. O'Hanrahan's mind boggled trying to grasp the history viewed by the Protaton, the main church of Karyes, meeting room and "capitol." Monks and pilgrims made their way through Karyes's one street and here O'Hanrahan felt his soul stir, his heart fill with remembered affection for the East. The late Dark Ages before me! And God bless them, it was the same scene forty years ago when O'Hanrahan was first here, and eighteen years later when he was on his second visit. That, oddly, seemed more remarkable than the continuity for centuries; to have avoided the modernization and progress of the last forty years was truly to have rebuffed Humankind and the world.

"Oh, they've made some changes," said an Australian monk, a serious-looking man in his forties, the only English-speaker O'Hanrahan could discover from the boat. "A library burned down a few years back, so now, with great reluctance, they have a fire engine and they've cut some primitive roads to get to the twenty monasteries."

"Ah," said O'Hanrahan, "a worthy addition, if they had to make one. Of course, much of the best of Mt. Athos isn't in the twenty monasteries."

He was thinking of the *sketes*, mini-monasteries for the more serious monks attached to a larger monastery. In particular O'Hanrahan recalled a house called Prophet Ieremiou and a man who had haunted him since he had first met him in 1950, Father Sergius.

One of the few true men of God he'd ever met.

✝   ✝   ✝

Morning in Ouranopolis.

Lucy scanned the town's main newsstand on the promenade by the shore for news. There was a week-old *Time* magazine, a three-day-old *Herald Tribune*, which she'd read. What I want, she ascertained, is a romance novel. Classy, decorous . . . and failing that, a piece of utter garbage. Maybe something set in the ancient world, just because I'm here.

"You speak English?"

"Yes, sir," she said, looking up at the proprietor.

He reached behind the counter and produced some dog-eared paperbacks that had been read fifty times or more. A Fitzgerald translation of Homer, three plays by Aeschylus, a few orange-sided Penguin paperbacks left by holiday-makers who had taken something classy to read and sold it the first day to this newsstand owner, or traded it for *Valley of the Dolls, Hollywood Wives, The Other Side of Midnight,* previous decades' best-sellers in their final resting place in Ouranopolis.

"You read all thees?" asked the man.

Actually, yes, the classics and the trash. "Anything else, sir?"

There were some Mills & Boons and Harlequins, most without covers. Lucy took *So Hot the Sun* and thumbed through it to see if too many pages were missing. She checked the ending: *"A wedding ring? I'll take it, darling! Oh, yes, yes!" she cried, falling into Sir Gregory's arms, knowing now her desert nightmare was over and her dreams had just begun.*

Lucy's kind of ending. "I'll take it, yes," hearing herself echo unintentionally the book's last line. "How much?"

It was 1400 drachmae, eight bucks, which you'd never pay back in the States but English-language pulp was at a premium here. O'Hanrahan must never see this, she sighed, or the ridicule would form a continuum.

In fact, the spirit of O'Hanrahan must have been with her because she felt like a retsina, having reviled it the night before. An acquired taste that suddenly in the baking Grecian sun she seemed to have acquired. Maybe she would wander down to the shore and the restaurants, unbusy at this hour, and order a bottle of retsina and sit and drink it in the sun and feel like . . . Hemingway or someone like that.

The retsina arrived and, later, a Greek salad. Then Lucy automatically ate a stack of cellophane-wrapped, humidified crackers in a basket on the table before her, and she read lightly without attention. She glanced up to see a pleasant blond woman with a sunburned face laughing in her direction.

"No, I wasn't laughing at you," she smiled, speaking in a twangy, singsong British accent. "But the book."

"Well, it's not Plato, I admit—"

"No, I mean, I read it here last summer. *So Hot the Sun.* That bloody book'll be here twenty years from now, I'd wager."

Lucy put it down and introduced herself. The woman's name was Tracy, she was from Birmingham, England, mid-twenties, doomed to stay untan because she'd burned herself so bad the second day and now she was condemned to long-sleeved everything. Down here with her boyfriend Derek, they weren't getting on, they'd had four major rows: one over how silly Derek was, spending an hour each morning getting his hair to go spiky, as if any of his mates were gonna see him down here, having a row over her sunburn and whether she did it on purpose so she could whinge about it the whole time, a row about Derek not eating any of the Greek food and being peculiar about it and not getting into the spirit of their holiday, and a row this morning about his watching a football match on Greek TV for two hours rather than do anything romanticlike with her, now how do you like that?

"I would never waste my vacation time," said Lucy, assuming a pose, "with *my* boyfriend. You can have your boyfriend any old time, I figure, and my vacation is too short to throw away on him. I always go somewhere interesting by myself and do something I know will be fun."

"Brilliant, that is," Tracy said, scooting her chair closer, scraping the concrete floor. "You got the right idea there. Are you on holiday now?"

"Sort of."

Lucy noticed that Stavros was approaching the promenade, shirtless and exposing a perfectly chiseled chest supremely, evenly tanned to a *caffè latte* shade—she suspected him of grooming his chest hairs—and tight jeans out of fashion two years ago in the United States. He spotted Lucy and directed his beauty in her direction, cantering, absorbing all the nearby female adulation.

"Loocy," he said in his heavy accent, "you want to make to eat tonight?"

"I suppose so," Lucy said boredly.

"I come in your room, eh?"

"Okay—I mean, *neh*, yes."

Exit Stavros. Tracy was wide-eyed with admiration. " 'Scuse me, love, but that one's a bleedin' Greek god! And I thought you said you didn't travel with your boyfriend."

"He's not my boyfriend. I met him in Athens a few days ago."

"Bloody hell . . ."

Then Tracy, imitating Lucy, said she needed a drink even though it was eleven A.M. Tracy went inside the cantina to get the waiter, which one did here even in the midst of dinner, the waiters not being devoted to service as the day wore on. Lucy mentioned she had been to Great Britain, specifically Oxford.

"Oh, Oxford's *dire*. Bloody horrible place, dreadful people. The student-types are so damn snooty."

"How's Birmingham?" asked Lucy, pronouncing it as if it were the one in Alabama. Lucy felt she had been there by the time Tracy finished regaling her with its virtues; afterward, Lucy took a turn talking about Chicago. Then Derek the boyfriend, scowling, made an appearance:

"Oy, Trace. Thought we were going to meet for lunch."

Tracy: "You didn't want to talk last night so we made no plans that I recall. Besides, my friend Lucy here . . . Lucy, this is Derek; Derek, Lucy . . . decided to have lunch since you up'n disappeared."

Lucy stared at Derek. Concave chest, skinny, hairless legs burned on their backside like Derek's back, and though he was sort of cute in the face, the spiky hair needed a rock star under it to look convincing.

"This soddin' goat cheese again," he said, looking at their salads. "Enough olive focking oil to stick you with the runs for days."

Tracy refused to look at him. "Oh, lovely talk for the table, Derek. Do say some more pleasant things, we're only trying to bloody eat."

Derek: "And this meat here. You know what this is, don't you? Heeeeere kitty kitty . . ."

"Oh I'm sure."

Derek pouted. "I'm just saying worra bloody great mistake it was comin' here, that's all."

Tracy, after a few more smart-ass remarks at her boyfriend's expense, gave in and started to follow Derek back to the hotel, whispering to Lucy, "It's time for our daily row," before leaving with a wink.

Couples, thought Lucy.

Do I really want this? All men are more or less Derek, some smarter, some smoother, but all big babies who want their own way. And this male vanity thing . . .

At this juncture, Lucy turned to the harbor to see Stavros strutting about the German compound, all the healthy-looking German girls with white-blond hair and good tans enjoying Stavros's broken German, poking him with a rowboat paddle, one of them hopping to her feet, her perfect body covered with coconut tanning oil, bouncing and gleaming, trying to lead Stavros over to the windsurfing rental. Stavros put up a fake fight, pretending not to want to, so there could be much physical contact and tickling and dragging and a naughty threat concerning what the *Fräulein* was going to grab hold of to lead him away. I suppose, thought Lucy disinterestedly, that Helga (or whatever) will get Stavros to a deserted lagoon and have Eurosex in an aquamarine cove. Until the shark comes by to eat them, Lucy invented to render it poetic justice.

Lucy regressed into her romance novel but the heroine was being whiny and downtrodden and Lucy found herself yawning and wishing for the cool linen sheets of the hotel room and an afternoon nap.

The Athonite bureaucracy frees the pilgrim around one P.M., which gives him four hours to reach an accommodation. Doors slam and medieval bolts close the impregnable gates around five which is suppertime followed by bedtime for the monks, as in ancient days.

O'Hanrahan had been walking for about three hours and to his relief the golden onion-shaped dome of Skete Prophet Ieremiou poked above the trees ahead. O'Hanrahan, hot and short of breath, admired it: a monastic outpost for 1600 Russian monks in its heyday, the turn of the century. The Russians virtually supplanted the Greeks in the last century on Athos; the Russian Skete of St. Andrew had some 5000 monks and outnumbered any monastery of the peninsula, but Greek authorities wouldn't upgrade these houses into full-fledged voting monasteries for fear the Russians would take over. Which they would have done gladly.

Closer to the skete, O'Hanrahan smiled to see the many onion-domes, plated in a faded, dull-gold brass, and the whitewashed, crumbling cathedral-sized church beneath them. To the Russians, the first Rome had fallen in heresy and decadence. The second Rome, Constantinople, had fallen to the Moslems. And so the third Rome, Moscow, would assume Rome's role, and the Duke of Muscovy assumed a title fit for a Roman: Caesar, or *tsar* in Russian. But history also brought the Bolsheviks. And where there were once thousands of Russian aristocrats' sons and peasants here, eager for God, the numbers dwindled to ten here, seven there. Monks and religious leaders were put in Siberian concentration camps and the survivors on Athos began the task of praying for their unfortunate brethren. What had been a continual hymn of praise, a celebration, had turned into a requiem for the dead church of Russia.

Perhaps their prayers this very decade will be answered, thought O'Hanrahan. With state atheism and communism itself on the wane, the Orthodox Church again is sweeping the steppes, congregations are again returning to the *katholikon*; how soon before Athos populates itself again with ex-Soviet holy men? Or is it too late? Is this way of Eastern Christianity now too old-fashioned for the young of Russia and Romania and Bulgaria, so long kept from the modern world they yearn for? Have the old men who have fanned the small censers in the dark, abandoned chapels of Athos kept the candles burning for nothing?

O'Hanrahan stood before the two-story medieval gate to Prophet Ieremiou. O'Hanrahan pulled the bellrope. At last the door creaked open and O'Hanrahan recognized the man he had met forty years ago, Father Sergius.

"Father Sergius," said O'Hanrahan slowly. "You do not remember me—"

"Patrick O'Hanrahan, isn't it?" The father stroked his silver beard and squinted. "I told you when you left, we would meet again. Was I not right?"

"You were correct," said O'Hanrahan, marveling at the memory of the man in his eighties. He had last been here in 1950 and then in 1968—twenty-two years ago! "Do I have permission to enter your skete, *Pater*?"

"You betcha, come on in . . . I'll get the fellas up from the field."

Father Sergius was one of the last males to be oblated to Athos, left to a monastery as an orphan to grow up and serve the monks. He remembered as a child in the 1910s the Christmas treats courtesy of the Tsar and Tsarina, the despair at the destruction of the state church, the slow dwindling of monks through death, disease, and those who went back to Mother Russia to fight the Germans or Stalin. He had outlasted them all. And his English was pure Brooklynese. The only monks these days in the Russian sketes were Russian-American, grandsons of the original Russian-born Orthodox who had emigrated to America. It was from his seven monks, all from Brooklyn, that he had learned his English, tinged with the nasal street talk of Sheepshead Bay and Greenpoint.

O'Hanrahan was led into the quiet courtyard, where he could sense the stillness of a place meant for thousands, now down to seven. He was brought cool well water, and offered an ouzo from the still. O'Hanrahan put down his cup to peek inside the church. This sanctuary and the one at nearby Skete Prophet Eliou were the last great works of Russian ecclesiastical art patronized by Tsar Nicholas II.

O'Hanrahan beheld the *ikonostasis*, an icon wall from floor to ceiling of the vast whitewashed cathedral, every disciple, scores of Russian saints, the Tsar and Tsarina humbly kneeling in another panel, all bordered and decked out in gold leaf upon intricate woodwork. With what confidence the Romanovs built these great churches, never imagining that most would be in ruins within a decade, themselves executed, and God driven from the Russian heart with bureaucracy and secret police as the crushing substitute.

"Ah, there you are," said Father Sergius, discovering him in the chapel. "If you're praying don't let me stop you. Uh, hands off the ikons, though. I'll have to reconsecrate and that's a pain."

"I won't kiss anything, I promise," assured O'Hanrahan. "It's a beautiful church."

"You remember my showing you last time the samovar Tsar Nicholas gave to the skete? We almost got so poor that we had to sell it, but I couldn't do it."

The two men walked to the refectory to find O'Hanrahan something to eat. The Russians, as a rule, ate better than did their Greek counterparts. O'Hanrahan recalled there was mutual disrespect on Athos: the Greeks were a bunch of illiterate, lazy peasants, according to some Russians; the Russians lived like kings, the Greeks would accuse. O'Hanrahan preferred the Russians. The decay, the swarms of flies and open sewers that characterized, say, Pantokrator Monastery, were unknown in the Russian houses.

A brother set down some beet soup before O'Hanrahan, and after that a plate of lentils, no oil, no salt, a few chopped spring onions for flavor. Simple, so as to divorce the diner from the pleasures of the stomach and to better concentrate on God. Father Sergius had explained on O'Hanrahan's last visit that he had moved his, then, ten charges from their cells every few weeks, throughout the thousands of rooms. This kept up the whole place, and furthermore prevented the men from getting attached to the way the sun fell against the wall, the comfort of a particular bed.

O'Hanrahan ate the simple fare gladly and watched the monks, speaking only when it was necessary. Two Russian-Americans in their late-20s he could not tempt with tales of a World Series, the newest movies from Hollywood, what girls were wearing, who was president, whatever. They didn't care. Though raised in America they were able to walk away from the 20th Century. Of course, thought O'Hanrahan, as we end the 20th Century a lot of people might like the idea of walking away, since the United States is going to hell in a handbasket, but nonetheless, to commit themselves so young . . .

(Just as you committed yourself once.)

Yes, thought O'Hanrahan, just as I turned away from the world of marriage and career and normal American life when I took vows. He briefly tasted some of the high resolve, remembered the elevation he once hoped to attain.

"Brother Victor," Father Sergius then said happily, "this is the learned professor, Patrick O'Hanrahan, alas, a Roman Catholic—still an embracer of heresies."

Victor nodded hello as he made the tea by the fire.

The other brother set the table for the visitor and the abbot to have tea. O'Hanrahan imagined what it must be like to spend decades with other young men and never form a friendship, for this was forbidden. If one found oneself too fond of a fellow monk, one separated oneself—one's only loyalty was to God.

"What brings you to Athos again, my son?" asked Father Sergius, tearing at a hard piece of unleavened bread. "What are you hunting for this decade?"

"I am searching for the key to a new gospel I have found but it is in a very obscure language. I am hoping the *Pseudo-Clementines* may reveal the alphabet. If not that, then Megistri Lavra has some commentaries on the *Sermium Compendium*."

"Of 357?" Father Sergius asked while pouring some of their homemade olive oil onto a piece of rough bread.

O'Hanrahan marveled. "Yes, from the Council of Sermium. I know the book of alphabets has been lost but the commentaries may shed some light."

"It's the Matthias gospel, perhaps?"

"How did . . ."

"You mentioned it in 1950 when you were here before. That God has allowed by His grace such a gospel to resurface is the talk of Athos—not that much of that kinda talk reaches us up here in the . . ." He checked his vocabulary with Brother Victor before completing his sentence: "the boonies. I'd like a glimpse myself, I gotta say."

A Russian silver cup of tea was set before O'Hanrahan. O'Hanrahan resolved he would go tomorrow to Father Kallistratos at Moni Dionysiou, the great authority on the libraries of Mt. Athos, and ask about what is known concerning the *Gospel of Matthias*, and who might be searching for it. Now that Matthias was damnably common knowledge. What a big mouth, O'Hanrahan condemned himself.

It was becoming dark already. Shadows lengthened and the brothers opened the metal panels of the fireplace to allow the room to fill with firelight and faint warmth. A candle and glass was prepared for O'Hanrahan when he was to retire to his chamber. The younger monks were yawning and about to drop off, seven P.M. being quite past their bedtime. But Sergius was fresh and relishing conversation.

The abbot: "You know, Seraphim over at Prophet Eliou says the End Times are upon us, my friend. All the spirit-bearing men are in agreement, for once."

O'Hanrahan sipped his tea, glancing at the firelight shimmering upon the silver samovar. The professor assured his host, "History has never looked better, Father. Russia is dissolving, the Eastern Bloc is liberated."

"And nonetheless, up and down Athos the sense is that the End Times have begun. Russian history bears the sadness of the race. It shall not be so easy for her to find the light, my friend. And the Middle East will be at war soon."

O'Hanrahan smiled. "But you are not allowed to read the papers, Father."

Father Sergius's eyes crinkled. "We know more than you guys think up here. For God tells us much."

O'Hanrahan reflected this was one of the last places in the Christian world where mysticism was encouraged, fostered, listened to, revered.

The abbot: "I only bring it up so that you might have time to prepare, dear Patrick."

"Prepare?"

"Let me baptize you in the Orthodox faith, huh? You're an Eastern Christian at heart, I feel it—an absolutist in your way. Most of your churchmen have perished debating the role of the pope, for him or against him, a fight without end. But you, Patrick, search for the way it was, in ancient scrolls, in old texts, you look deeply into the Eastern eyes of the men of God, is it not so?"

Yes, he had always adored the remnants of the Early Church.

Father Sergius may have sounded Brooklyn but he spoke with that unmistakable lyrical directness of the Russian: "Come home to us, my friend. Be embraced by the True Church at long last—enough with the innovations and distractions. The Early Church of the Fathers is here in these walls. Let me baptize you anew this morning at our prayer service."

O'Hanrahan hesitated. "I appreciate it, Father . . . Tomorrow let us talk about it."

Father Sergius continued to stare a moment. Then the abbot bowed with a half-smile. "Okay. I'll take you to your room."

The monastery was now completely dark and the little candle barely progressed against the enshadowed vaults of the dank old corridors. O'Hanrahan was led by Father Sergius to a long hallway of cells, all empty now, ghostly and chilling. In O'Hanrahan's chamber was a pitcher of water and a basin for washing, a single linen sheet and a straw-stuffed pillow, and on the wall a faded, yellowed photograph of the Tsar Nicholas and Tsarina Alexandra, regal smiles from their irretrievably lost world—yet this very century!

"You recall what we ask here," Father Sergius mentioned as he stood with his own candle in the doorway.

O'Hanrahan: "A prayer for the restoration of the royal family to Russia."

"Indeed. No man should spend a night here without that fervent wish in his heart. How the True Church has missed his protection and guidance," the abbot added sadly. "We shall see you tomorrow! When you hear the woodblocks, come down and join us in the *katholikon* if you like."

The father blessed him, mumbled a Russian folk prayer to wish him a good sleep without danger or demons, and crossed himself and left.

O'Hanrahan lay on the stiff, cool bed and observed the candlelight softly illumine the old photograph of the last of the Romanovs. So, this is all that is left of that 2000-year-old idea called "Caesar." From Augustus and the Western Empire, passed to Emperor Constantine of the Byzantine Eastern Empire, then to Moscow through Nicholas II, and now kept alive in these Russian hearts, by prayers with Brooklyn accents, begging for Caesar to return. *Regions Caesar never knew thy posterity shall sway.* Maybe that would be the end to all the Russian troubles, to restore the earthly head of the Orthodox Church, patron and example to the people, but please, more beneficent this time, more humane and loving.

O'Hanrahan thought tiredly: no tsar will come back, no hero will rise up. There is just our own pitiful generation's longing for the more glorious history of another. As sleep filled the room, O'Hanrahan thought: no, I will not pray for the tsars, but I will pray for Russia and her people and her endless Slavic burdens, all the winters she has yet to face.

JULY 17TH

O'Hanrahan was awakened not by the morning call-to-prayer but by a knock on the door. He sprang awake not able to see a thing, and in the shadow he heard a match strike. It was Father Sergius lighting his candle.

"There we are," he said. "Ah, you are safe, my friend."

"Safe?"

"There has been a—how d'you say?—a break-in," he said glumly without overreacting. "A desecration. In our church. What do you call it . . . uh, the can of the paint that goes out in a hisssss sound, you know—"

"A spray can?"

"Yes, someone has come into the *katholikon* and spray-canned some Arabic profanities on the *ikonostasis*."

O'Hanrahan sat up in bed, and with his feet tried to position his shoes to be slipped into. "How horrible, Father."

"We never lock the door—why should we? An island of holy men, yes? But tonight, someone has come and done this thing. I shall have to reconsecrate everything. How odd that I joked with you about reconsecrations yesterday afternoon. Ah, perhaps God was speaking and I did not pay attention."

O'Hanrahan, while sitting on the bed, lit his own candle from the father's. "Was anything stolen?"

"Not that we can find, no." Though their conversation hardly seemed at an end, the father turned and left O'Hanrahan to get dressed. O'Hanrahan wondered if the father privately thought that he had something to do with it.

It was 6:15 in the morning, the sun not yet up and the sky a muted blue in anticipation. O'Hanrahan made his way downstairs and joined the seven resident monks, shaken and distressed, in the church where the damage was done. Someone had spray-painted red over the faces on the ikons and then sprayed an Arabic slogan or two.

"Can you read it?" asked Father Sergius, calmer than any of his charges, who were proposing violence, some tearful.

"Yes," said O'Hanrahan. He sounded it out. "Wasil ibn-Ataah—it's a proper name, I believe." O'Hanrahan had heard the name before. "There's more . . . something about graven images."

"An iconoclast Moslem," murmured Father Sergius.

It was a somber parting from Prophet Ieremiou.

Father Sergius wailed that the defilement meant getting a restorer up from Athens to clean the ikon wall. As a Russian, he hated dealing with the Greeks, who schemed to rip them off for everything.

"I wish I could do something," said O'Hanrahan.

(You could. What about the thousands of drachmae in your pocket?)

"Oh," said O'Hanrahan, not pausing to think of the consequences. "Perhaps this could help you, Father." He reached into his pocket and pulled out the money. Father Sergius at first refused, saying God would provide, but O'Hanrahan convinced him that God had led him here with this money that he could surely spare.

Father Sergius took it humbly. "But that," he said, "does not make up for the loss."

"Of course not. Those beautiful ikons—"

Father Sergius flashed an impatient glance. "I mean the loss of your faith, my friend. Are you sure I may not baptize you anew in the love of Jesus Christ? Let us pray together. Let us return you to your faith. For, you see, I know. I know it is not the orthodoxy that you object to, it is God. You are estranged from God, great scholar that you are. Too much time in libraries, not enough at prayer."

O'Hanrahan had nothing to say. Father Sergius had looked into his heart, had read him like a familiar text.

"I'll come back again, Father," O'Hanrahan awkwardly said, taking a step back.

"I do not think you will," said the abbot sadly, more concerned with O'Hanrahan than with the tragedy that preoccupied his monks, who were milling about vowing revenge on the culprit, for here was the more urgent concern of God. "I was hoping that we might discuss the great fathers at length, month following month, as long as it takes. I mean, of course, in the Next World."

O'Hanrahan felt himself stirred, drawn to the spirit of this man, this Man of God! But his heart hardened. "I will return, I promise. We'll talk about the baptism then, Father."

Father Sergius stroked his dry, gray beard and looked up at O'Hanrahan with the eyes of a boy, full of expression and care. "When we parted years ago I said we would meet again. I cannot say that this time with certainty, for my time on earth is coming to a close—and God be thanked, for the Time of the Tribulations is upon us . . ." He crossed himself and wished a blessing upon O'Hanrahan. "May God find you in your time on Mt. Athos," he said, turning, and closing the gate behind him.

(Dearest Sergius, We can refuse you nothing.)

All morning, Lucy had searched the town for a fax machine, but this technology was unknown and not even the greatest pantomime description of a fax machine seemed to register with anyone in Ouranopolis. Well, Chicago would just have to hold its breath, she surrendered.

Lucy put on her big red hat and sat down near the beachfront, against a gnarled cypress offering insufficient shade.

"Oh Gregory, hold me! Hold me!" said Priscilla in *So Hot the Sun.*

I've read this book, thought Lucy, putting the paperback down. It took until page 243, but I just realized I've read this book before. This is the one where she gets on this desert caravan in Egypt and gets abducted by Bedouins and raped and all that.

She looked up from her bench to see a screaming trio of girls beckoning and waving someone nearer to them. Stavros, in a brief bathing suit, walked into view. The Naiads, the Nereids perhaps, the Sirens, fill in the nymphs of your choice—make that: nymphos. Lucy supposed the Rhine Maidens would be more appropriate. She stood up and moved location, lightly wishing the splashing, giggling women would drown and pull Stavros down too.

Well, she said to herself. Only thirteen or fourteen more waking hours to spend in this town before I might naturally fall asleep. What next?

O'Hanrahan walked for a few hours until he came to Karyes. A supply truck that hauled the monks' produce and ouzo and ikons to the dock at Daphne drove by in a cloud of hot road dust. O'Hanrahan waved to them and the driver stopped. O'Hanrahan crawled into the truckbed in back and, minutes later, he was returned to the pier at Daphne, where the pilgrim in a hurry can pay for a fishing boat that will ferry him farther down the peninsula.

The boat arrived within the half-hour and two Greek fishermen right out of Hollywood's Central Casting for weathered, salty Greek fishermen, caps and cigarettes and pants rolled up to their knees, extended a hand to the professor to pull him aboard. O'Hanrahan went to the bow so he could observe the spectacular setting for the monasteries along the southeastern side of the peninsula.

Moni Simonopetra. The Monastery of Simon Peter, like the monasteries of Meteora, among the most daring, confident monasteries ever built, dangling on a promontory half a mile above the sea. Seven stories of rickety wooden walkways and balconies affixed to 14th-Century plaster and stone, craning out over the abyss. Never did make that climb, thought O'Hanrahan, knowing now it would never be done, and that he would never drink their once-miraculous ouzo.

St. Simon was Mt. Athos's own stylite and he had lived and prayed atop these cliffs and, after a vision, was commanded in the mid-1300s to build the monastery. His first set of disciples were so terrified of the heights that they abandoned him. One day, having persuaded another crew of monks to work for him, he prepared a reward of ouzo and sent his servant Isaiah out to deliver it. Over the wooden beams Isaiah walked and teetered, when a stone dislodged and he went hurtling over the side, thousands of feet below. After much praying and gnashing of teeth, who should they see a few hours later but Isaiah, who returned to them unhurt and with not one drop of the precious liquor spilled.

(Your kind of miracle, My son.)

The fishing boat stopped at Simonopetra's seaside pier and a few hearty pilgrims and a monk got out, being wished luck and blessings by everyone else, not envying that climb in the 93-degree heat. After that, the water turned a Caribbean blue, and the mountains rose and met the sea in spectacular cliffs, rich with verdure, colorful blooms, hanging vines, many species of flowering trees. And finally, Moni Dionysiou, the jewel of the monasteries, came into view. Again built in the 1300s, again on a precarious cliff overlooking the sea, mostly funded and patronized by the Moldavian Church, and featuring the eeriest of works: the Apocalyptic Frescoes.

O'Hanrahan, eager to talk to Father Kallistratos, began the steep climb from the dock to the entranceway. Heaving and huffing he made it, bathed in sweat, stopping to put on his suit jacket to cover his naked arms in this sultry heat. A guestmaster, all smiles, welcomed him and showed him to a room in the tower. Next to the brick-red multi-domed church, safely within the walls, stood an eight-story tower to hide within when the Moslems came calling, or worse, the Venetians.

O'Hanrahan was given a chamber to himself with access to a hall that led to the reeking hole-in-the-ground toilets and a bathing area, a laundry basin, and at the end of the hall a wooden balcony overlooking the cliffs and the lapping water below. O'Hanrahan stepped out on the spindly balcony, half-testing it to see if, having held for centuries, it had waited until now to crash down to the rocks. The sun was lowering and O'Hanrahan took in the scene, the endless textures of Athonite quiet, a world without modern sounds, where a distant bird or a fishing boat splashing through the glassy water could be heard for miles. What peace. What a place to listen for the ever-so-quiet directives of God.

(Where shall We begin?)

Feeling a sudden anxiety, O'Hanrahan turned away. He returned to the inner courtyard as the monks filed into the refectory for supper. He sat on a long bench and stared at the visionary frescoes of the End Times, painted in the 1500s. There was a mushroom cloud and scorpions and cockroaches wearing crowns—the only creatures that could survive a nuclear holocaust, the new kings of the world. Beyond was a fresco of world destruction: lamenting citizens hiding under the ground in caves while futuristic skyscrapers toppled and fell, as missilelike rockets streaked across the sky. The sun and the moon, with impassive faces, are surrounded by thick clouds: the world's first prediction of nuclear winter. Awesome, in the original sense of the word, thought O'Hanrahan.

(*Disaster after disaster! Behold it comes. An end has come, the end has come; it has awakened against you.*)

"It is not, Dr. O'Hanrahan, the whole picture, no?" An older monk, speaking excellent English, approached and sat beside him. "I'm Father Eusebio Kallistratos. Welcome."

O'Hanrahan looked at the thin, tall, frail man of gray hair and prodigious wrinkles, but still possessed of dark black eyebrows that aimed his glance with totalitarian intensity. "The famous librarian, *Pater*."

"It is not the whole picture," Father Kallistratos continued after acknowledging the compliment with a slight bow. "Everyone is awed by these paintings and they do not see the final frames on the wall over there . . . the triumph of God, the angels in glory. The victory of the Lamb."

"The victory scenes seem symbolic, Father," said O'Hanrahan, smiling. "A lamb on a throne. But the destruction parts we know could be quite real."

"It is not long, my friend." Father Kallistratos went on assuredly: "We are in the End Times. Many have come to Athos to await them. Can we doubt it can be much longer? For 1915 years after Christ was crucified, we have not had the power to destroy ourselves. But now we have and so, eventually, we will. Where will the Islamic horde stop in waging Holy War against us? How long before an attack on Israel and then Europe as predicted? Ah, it is soon, very soon." Before O'Hanrahan could speak, the father added, "You have heard what happened at the Skete Prophet Ieremiou?"

O'Hanrahan decided to play dumb.

"There is an Islamic fanatic on the peninsula who is defacing ikons with blasphemies and slogans. It is not the first time, of course. All through the Turkish occupation, we endured raids and sacrileges."

The professor nodded sympathetically.

"And that Islamic man, whoever he is, is quite stupid. For if he is discovered he shall be killed here. We are not under Greece's jurisdiction. He shall be as if he never existed. The monks will dispose of him."

"Not exactly turning the other cheek, Father."

"Are we not to fight even the Antichrist and his disciples? But enough of this." The librarian then asked, "What may I help you to find?"

"I am actually hoping to see the *Clementine Recognitions* and the *Clementine Homilies* and commentaries at Megistri Lavra, the *Sermium Compendium* as well. I have an alphabet I cannot decipher, Father." He asked the next with forced lightness. "Have you heard of others, Father, looking for a lost gospel?"

Father Kallistratos was informative. "Indeed, this very month. Perhaps it is the *Gospel of St. Matthias*? That is what a monk was searching for, quite recently."

O'Hanrahan cursed inwardly. "Can you describe this monk, Father?"

Father Kallistratos almost smiled. "He looks like every monk, sir. A gray beard, a black robe, an intelligent man." The father walked O'Hanrahan toward the dazzlingly frescoed refectory for his meal of white beans, pepper, a teaspoon of oil in a vague soup of hot water. "Of course," he added, "my patron, St. Eusebius, whose name I have taken as a blessing, first librarian of the Church, condemned the gospel by St. Matthias, did he not?"

"Yes, but perhaps he did not actually read it."

"But he knew, no doubt, people who had seen it and would hardly have declared it heretical without evidence, or for that matter, the guidance of the Holy Spirit, who rests with each Orthodox scholar."

(No, not all of them, Father.)

"If this gospel should come to light, it should be kept here on Mt. Athos where it may not confuse the faithful, or prove useful to the enemies of the Church, the False Prophet who is already born and lives among us."

"The End Times," sighed Dr. O'Hanrahan.

O'Hanrahan retired at an hour after midnight Byzantine time—about 8:30 P.M. in the outside world—knowing that the monks would beat rhythmically upon the wooden beams that hung near the tower, calling all to prayer at 3:00 A.M. Through the night for four hours they will pray and chant and touch their foreheads to the floor and adore the ikons and hear the words of Our Savior in the Greek language he may well have spoken. In this blessed quiet O'Hanrahan fell easily and deeply asleep, weary from his walk up the hill.

Then hours later, he found himself awakened.

There was running about in the courtyard, excited voices. He looked at his watch, which didn't quite glow bright enough to read. But at that moment the door to the dormitory room in the tower flung open and he was looking into a flashlight.

"Yes?"

Someone approached. Two monks talking in impassioned Greek. He tried to understand them. They yelled for him to awaken.

"I'm awake," sputtered O'Hanrahan. "What's going on?"

They began to look in his satchel by the cot.

"What are you doing?" O'Hanrahan sat up in bed.

The guestmaster was in the room the next moment: "Stefanos! Loukas! *Prosohi!*"

The two monks released the professor's satchel, chastised. The guestmaster told them to leave. Father Kallistratos walked into the chamber the next moment.

"I apologize for this invasion," he began, when the others had left. "But we seem to have been visited by the defacer."

"No," breathed O'Hanrahan. "Where?"

"Not in the main *katholikon*, God Most Merciful be praised, but in one of the outlying *kathismae*, by the vineyard."

O'Hanrahan stood up, rubbing his eyes. "Your outer gate is locked after five P.M., is it not, *Pater?*"

The guestmaster stared at O'Hanrahan. "Indeed. So there is no way you could have . . . Well, forgive the young men, they are outraged and not thinking clearly. You perhaps understand why the brothers impetuously came into your room, to see if you had . . . materials to do this wicked thing."

"Father, they're perfectly welcome to search me. But I would not do such a thing."

The father raised his hand. "Of course not. Please, go back to sleep."

"Was anything destroyed?"

"An ancient ikon, defaced," he mourned with cold, vengeful distaste. "We have a *kathisma* beside our vineyard. Father Paulos looks over the *Panagia Elaiovrytis* there, and begins his prayers there every morning at three before he joins us. This morning he found the ikon with an Arabic curse written upon it, that scrawl of the Devil!"

Elaiovrytis, O'Hanrahan considered, translating it to himself: Our Lady who flows with oil. As the father mourned the defaced ikon, O'Hanrahan became increasingly unsettled: was this happening all over the peninsula or just, inconveniently, where he was staying?

Father Kallistratos pulled the door behind him. The professor got out of bed and looked down from the rough-hewn stone window into the inner courtyard where torches had been lit. He saw, he assumed, Father Paulos, tearful and fragile, moved to deepest, wordless grief, inconsolably wringing his hands—to have this happen on his watch!

O'Hanrahan lay again on his bed: someone is following me or I am having the damnedest luck. Tomorrow I'll get to Megistri Lavra, the greatest library of Athos, and I'll be able to read what I wish, take my notes, then get the heck out of here before any more of this bizarre criminality happens and I'm caught up in it. Ghosts and curses and miracles and apparitions and visions of the End Times are common as houseflies here—not a place to run afoul of.

JULY 18TH–19TH

Megistri Lavra, the middle of the next night.

O'Hanrahan was again lying in another cell staring at the ceiling, unable to sleep.

"*Dedilosi!*" cried someone excitedly.

Monks were running about the courtyard, a commotion was beginning.

O'Hanrahan sighed. His old age had caught up with him yesterday. After the incident at Moni Dionysiou, he had lain down and gone back to sleep for eight hours, waking up at 1:30 P.M.—disastrous! He hurriedly flagged down a fishing boat and managed to run up to the gates of Megistri Lavra just as they were closing at 4:30. Could he please be permitted this late to see the library? No, they said, Wednesday was a night for a service consecrated to Mary their protectress, the Blessed Panagia, Theotokos. O'Hanrahan had been promised time in the library this coming morning, but the chaos outside suggested that he would never be granted this privilege.

Another monk near the window wailed "Desecration!"

Yes, it's happened again. Now there's no way I won't be suspected. O'Hanrahan thought calmly: I've demonstrated I can read Arabic, and been at the three places this has happened and even if some explanation is found, it will mean a questioning, a possible police interrogation—or worse than that, facing some 10th-Century Athonite form of justice. Some Turkish militant must be going where I'm going and committing these desecrations so they will have a fall guy to blame. A ridiculous unlucky break, to be picked as a fall guy by some Turk . . . but then again, the Turks don't write in Arabic. They write Turkish, since Ataturk, in the Roman alphabet. A Turkish Islamic scholar would know Arabic, though. But why would a scholar come all the way over here for this dangerous exercise in vandalism?

There was a knock on his cell door.

"Yes," he said, fearing the worst. The door opened and a fierce novice entered, glaring at him. Behind him was the short, scowling guestmaster. "Would you be so kind as to come with us, please?"

O'Hanrahan was already dressed. It occurred to him that being dressed looked suspicious. Better for him to have been caught undressed in bed dozing. He stood and reached for his suit coat, checking to see if his wallet and passport were there. Then he reached under the bed for his satchel. It wasn't there. He looked near the water basin, under the bed across from him, on the window ledge and, in desperation, out the window.

"My satchel is missing," he said.

"Come with us now, please," said the guestmaster firmly.

O'Hanrahan followed. Who could have taken it? He had left the briefcase in his room at dinner, and then he had left it again when he went to the latrines later that night to prepare for bed. This was a monastery, after all, and he even remembered smiling to himself: at least no one will steal it here. But someone did. Someone has the photos of the *Gospel of Matthias*, many of his essential papers . . .

O'Hanrahan was led to a small white-plastered room with a table and several chairs, a reception room where monks can meet their visiting brothers and male relatives. An older monk with a candalabra entered and sat across from him, pulling the table to himself, and the guestmaster stood behind him.

"I'm Father Irenaeus and I speak English," said the older monk, a tall thin man with white hair and beard, looking inaptly like Santa Claus. He spoke English with a European-taught British accent. "This is yours?"

A novice brought forth O'Hanrahan's briefcase, opened, and stained with red spray paint at the edge.

"Yes, *Pater*, it's mine. It was stolen from me."

"This was found in the Chapel of St. Basil the Blessed. One of our fathers entered to say a late prayer, and heard a man drop the paint can and dash for the exit. Your document bag was found on the floor beside the paint can. The ikon of St. Basil has been desecrated. All," he sighed, controlling an intense fury, "but St. John Evangelist, the Virgin, and Jesus have been defaced on the *ikonostasis*."

"That's because . . ." Damn it! Why did he open his mouth? "That's because," O'Hanrahan started again, "the Islamic people who did this consider John and Mary venerable persons along with Christ." The monks stared at him. "Look," O'Hanrahan went on, "this has been happening, I hear, all over Mt. Athos. These desecrations. I've seen two myself."

Father Irenaeus glanced down into his lap, frowning at his clasped hands. "There have only been three such incidents, all in places, sir, where you have been staying."

"Father, if I were to do such a horrible thing, do you think I would leave my briefcase as evidence?"

The young monk spoke heatedly: that the monk who had come upon the vandal surprised him and he might well have made a clumsy exit, knocking over the Bible stand as well.

Father Irenaeus shrugged slightly. "What are we to think? We have found out who you are. You are a learned, honored man, Mr. O'Hanrahan. We have relayed messages to and from Father Sergius at Skete Prophet Ieremiou who vouches for you completely and I am willing to believe him. Father Kallistratos at Dionysiou attests to your innocence as well. Indeed, we took in forty pilgrims this night, a large group from Thessaloniki, and amid this collection one man is not accounted for—it is perhaps this man who has done this thing."

O'Hanrahan was relieved.

"But wherever you are, for whatever reason, this seems to happen. So I must ask you to leave Athos."

O'Hanrahan was quiet a moment. "May I see my satchel?"

It was slid to him. O'Hanrahan looked inside. The notes were gone and, yes, so were the photos. Someone else now had the text of the gospel. "I have been robbed," said O'Hanrahan, "of my notes and research."

There is paint, said one of the younger monks, inside the satchel.

O'Hanrahan, understanding, snapped at him in modern Greek: You accuse me unjustly!

"I sympathize with your odd situation, sir," said Father Irenaeus, now standing. "But whoever has done this has done this, perhaps, because of you, and so you must depart immediately."

So close! "But Father, please, I have come for only one thing, to see the *Sermium Compendium* and commentaries of the Great Library of Megistri Lavra—"

"No, sir, I must insist. The Greek police have already been notified."

"Notified?"

"To escort you off Athos. For your protection, of course," added Father Irenaeus insincerely. "Since someone is following you with such malicious intent. Besides, some of the brothers would as soon stone a man associated with . . . with these crimes."

"Father, please. I have come all this way—thousands of miles, hun-

dreds of dollars." The men were unmoved. Oh damn, his bribe money
had been sacrificed back at Father Sergius's skete. "Have your monks
stand guard over me, watch me every second—"

"Sir, I believe you. You are not to blame for these godless acts of
desecration, but nonetheless, you see our position."

Day Four in exciting Ouranopolis threatened to be a rerun of Days
Three and Two, which were a rerun of Day One, which was a rerun,
Lucy suspected, of some day around the time of Homer. She rose at
ten A.M.-ish and walked out to the lagoon and read the same, frayed
newspapers that had been there on the stands yesterday, browsed
through the same paperbacks.

Lunch was predictable. Forget Skylla and Kharybdis, thought Lucy,
the modern Odysseus attempts to navigate beyond Souvlaki and Moussaka, the twin titans! Odysseus' men approach Kirke and are turned
into a reconstituted lamb slab on a gyro spit. The eye of the one-
eyed giant could be put out with a shish-kebab . . . Lucy wished Dr.
O'Hanrahan was around to develop these silly mock-epic ideas. She
missed him actually.

Lucy dutifully sat for an hour in the lobby of the Hotel Poseidon.
No phone call as arranged. The deskman said he would be happy to
take a complete message or send out an errand boy to track her down,
the village hardly being big enough to get lost in.

Sighing, slightly concerned about O'Hanrahan's disappearance,
she stood on the hotel porch and felt the intense blast of the sun,
searing, supreme. If her body were more presentable, she would
join the bronzed Teutonic maidens on the beach for a sunbathing
session, but that was too much exposure. She looked above at her
balcony. Private. Unobservable. Lucy then viewed with mild amusement Stavros's tanned, glistening body wavering and squatting on the
sailboard, trying to make the thing propel with too little wind. With
each awkward plunge back into the water, the attendant Nereids,
Helga and what's-her-name, giggling, bore him upon the surf and
bade him try again.

Lucy sauntered back through the lobby, got her key, and trudged
up the stairs. She hadn't thought to bring a swimsuit to England, so
consequently her sunbathing attire was underwear, or should she feel
more daring, no clothes at all. She'd never sunbathed nude. She
stepped out on her balcony. There was no higher building so there
was no possibility of voyeurism. Stavros was in the lagoon, O'Hanrahan
on Mt. Athos, so the only possible observation point, the neighboring

balcony with its solid concrete wall between, was not a risk. She studied her own balcony of white polished tile with the concrete wall—a virtual solar reflector.

Lucy went back in the room and undressed and removed from her purse some sunscreen, the strongest available. All right, she told herself, twenty minutes tops in this strong sun or I'll be a beet like Derek and Tracy. She lathered herself and gave herself one unaccidental glance in the full-length mirror on the bathroom door. Now I have lost some weight, she told herself. Not ready for the nude beach yet, but getting there.

It was hot, hot, hot.

Lucy lay on her back on a towel with an arm across her closed eyes. Sweat mixed with tanning oil swam at the edges of her eyes, so that she wiped her face with the corner of the towel constantly. Here I am, she told herself, nude-sunbathing in Greece. I'll tell Judy. I'll tell her I did it on a beach with thousands watching. Very European showing your breasts to strangers. She groped for the wristwatch beside her: I've been out here eight minutes, she discovered.

Then she turned over on her stomach. You know, she thought, I have never felt sun on these parts of my body before and it's not bad, not bad at all. There was the faintest breeze above the balcony and she sensed it above her, almost alleviating her glorious, luxuriant broiling—

"I seee yoo," said a familiar voice.

Lucy froze. Stavros was on the neighboring balcony, leaning around the concrete wall. Damn him. Well, she was on her stomach and better that than the other. No, she would not get up and run. He would go away and she would slip into her room quickly.

"Hello, Stavros," she said. "Please go away."

"I want to see."

"Well, you've seen, so now go away."

"You turn, uh . . . orange."

Orange is a familiar word because of American soft drinks. "Red. I might turn *red*, not orange."

"No," he laughed, "orange!"

She craned to look around at her feet and saw him leaning out around his balcony. "Are you going to go away?" she asked firmly.

He misunderstood. The next thing she knew he threw a leg around the partition separating the balconies and swung around to her side. He stood there dripping in his brief bathing suit, still leering at her. "Look what you do to me," he said, pointing at his bikini briefs.

Oh my God, thought Lucy.

She looked away and began to compose in her head a stern edict, when she saw his discarded bathing suit flung into the far corner of the balcony with a slap. The next second, on his stomach, he lay down beside her on the towel. "Halloo Lucy," he said.

Lucy shook her head. Well, maybe the worst was through. She wouldn't turn over, he wouldn't turn over, and what a story this would make! Judy, just wait till you hear about this!

Stavros spied the bottle of sunscreen on the far side of Lucy. He leaned over her, supporting his weight on her back and Lucy felt her breath become more shallow. "White, white, white," he said, commenting upon the expanse of Lucy's Irish coloring. He squirted some oil on her back before she could say anything. He rubbed it in with both hands, deeply kneading her back.

Lucy swallowed with difficulty. She sucked in her stomach as tight as she could, and lengthened her body as best she might, willing her appearance to thinness. You better get him out of here, she told herself, or it's going to end in . . . Yes. Maybe it should end the way it's going to end. She could feel Stavros's breath on her neck as he leaned over her shoulders. He rubbed oil on her upper back and his hands strayed perilously close to the edge of her right breast. She craned her neck around to see him, naked, amusing himself by rubbing oil on her.

Well, of course it's going to happen.

And I'm not going to prevent it, she heard herself think. It will be now. In such moments there is only the present; maybe the consequences fall to some other entity, but not the Lucy Dantan who is right here in this moment—

"You want?" Stavros asked.

He took her hand and squirted some oil into it and then pressed it to his chest and said something in Greek to her. He spoke again but she shook her head, not understanding. He touched her cheek, then stopped smiling as he took her shoulder and turned her over on her back. She closed her eyes in the searing sun, which had turned the day white and otherworldly; through her eyelids there was only the red and in her ears only a furious heartbeat and she fought to keep her eyes closed as he led her hand down to his waist, and his other hand traced a line down to her waist . . . Briefly there was flash of something ancient and dimly lit, a mother's face at church, an indistinct shape of sorrow, someone not quite recognizable, something not to be heeded, and though they all reached out, Lucy, throwing her head back, obliterated them in the sun. And she pulled Stavros, who smelled of oil and sweat, closer, and when he became more energetic and pressed himself upon her, she held him all the more lightly as if he might break or dissolve, and a drop of sweat from his forehead fell on her tongue with miraculous accuracy, the deliberateness of a nail through a hand—

Her heart beat furiously, the beating of wings, fallen angels cast out—they bore her aloft as a supreme selfishness welled within her, but she would not recant or be moved though fire consume her, though broken on the wheel, though tossed to wild beasts, she would now hold tighter, she would own this sin and commend herself to the sun above, the white-hot chorus of the Aegean . . .

Consummatum est.

O'Hanrahan, packed and ready to go, stood at the door of Megistri Lavra, now at midday. Father Irenaeus had assigned Brother Nikolas to stand guard over him while a boat could be procured, then to accompany him to Daphne where the police had been summoned.

"So," the professor protested politely, "I'm to be handed over, even though I'm innocent, to Greek authorities?"

Father Irenaeus: "Yes, to tell your side of the story, so that when this culprit is caught your witness will be on record."

I'm looking at three days down the tubes, thought O'Hanrahan. Greek police, Greek bureaucracy and of course, they may decide expeditiously that I *am* guilty of these things. Father Sergius wouldn't be able to come testify for me and no subpoena would be effective on Athos . . .

"Young Nikolas," explained the father, "will take you down to the dock now. The boat has arrived."

Nikolas, the earnest, fiery one with accusing eyes and a straggly teenage beard, said to his elders that he would be careful with O'Hanrahan and would soon return with news.

Oh yeah? thought O'Hanrahan. We'll see about that, little boy.

Nikolas escorted O'Hanrahan down the winding, rough cobblestone road on which O'Hanrahan had endured such dire prostrations ascending the day before. O'Hanrahan brooded briefly on the failure to see the *Sermium Compendium*. And what's worse was the mysterious Mad Monk had seen that very codex the week before. Bah, enough of this! First thing was to lose this twerp.

"Do you speak any English?" asked O'Hanrahan.

He didn't, he mumbled in Greek.

O'Hanrahan could make a run for it . . . Yeah right, huffing and heaving up this very road yesterday afternoon—what kind of getaway could he make? Maybe he should hit the kid over the head with— what, a rock? No, an act of violence would be taken as a sure sign of guilt. At the pier, an older fisherman in a tiny motorboat caked in blue-green peeling paint sputtered up to the concrete jetty.

"I am eager to get to Daphne," O'Hanrahan began. He then repeated it in Greek: "I want to clear up the whole trouble. And I hope they catch the fiend who did this."

"*Neh*," said the monk, eyeing the professor unsurely.

"All my research stolen! What a disaster my trip to your monastery has been. Accused of a horrible crime, my papers taken . . ."

The monk softened. "*Me sinhorite*," he sympathized.

"The policeman will meet me at Daphne, correct?" asked O'Hanrahan, hoping to get into the boat alone, where he might promise a bribe to the fisherman.

"Yes, I will be there to guide you," said Nikolas.

"You hardly need to trouble yourself, son," added O'Hanrahan, patting the novice on the shoulder. "Have no fear, I want to go to Daphne and assert my innocence."

"*Ohi*," he said sharply, "I will accompany you."

No dice. O'Hanrahan smiled sheepishly at the monk before stepping into the center of the boat; the monk, precariously, then stepped into the bow. The puttering motor was revived and the old fisherman began them on their journey around the end of the peninsula, back to Daphne.

Maybe the policemen would be understanding . . . This was dreaming! Then it occurred to him: whoever stole my photos has to escape from Mt. Athos too. At some point today he will have to go through Daphne and take the boat back to Ouranopolis, unless he wishes to walk the length of the peninsula, forty grueling miles. If I could get free then I could maybe intercept this criminal, see who he is.

"Beautiful!" exhaled O'Hanrahan, as the peninsula passed by to their right. "*Ti thaumasios keros!*" he said, hoping to initiate banter about the weather. He continued in Greek: "This is Karoulia, no? Where the monks live in caves?"

"*Neh, Karoulia*," the monk nodded in assent.

"Such blue water," continued the professor. "I would like to take a swim, ha ha!" O'Hanrahan looked back to see the fisherman piloting the boat was preoccupied scraping something off his shoe with a stick.

"*Apagorevete to kolimbi*," Nikolas said, shaking his finger.

"No swimming, huh?"

Nikolas explained that it is against the rules to swim in the Virgin's Garden, or to exhibit oneself undressed at any time.

"But you could swim with your clothes on?"

The monk looked at him oddly the second before O'Hanrahan lunged at him and pushed him over the side of the boat. "*Dio!*" cried the fisherman, not looking up until he heard the splash. O'Hanrahan leaned back and laughed heartily as if it were a joke. The fisherman, shaking his head horrified, stopped the boat, released the rudder, and stood to help the monk get back in. O'Hanrahan threw Nikolas the life preserver, though it seemed he could tread water. The monk with tears of rage fumed and called O'Hanrahan names. As the fisherman reached for the monk's hand, Nikolas watched O'Hanrahan swipe the cap off the fisherman's head; and as the fisherman tried to grab it back, O'Hanrahan pushed the older man into the Aegean as well, nearly capsizing the boat. O'Hanrahan glanced at the rocky cliffs. In one isolated cave an ancient monk looked on, cackling hysterically.

O'Hanrahan scrambled for the controls as the fisherman and the monk pawed at the underside of the boat trying to reach the gunnels. O'Hanrahan backed the boat away and waved farewell. He was free! O'Hanrahan looked at the Holy Mountain of Athos looming above the milky-blue, late-morning gleam of the Aegean. It would take hours for this to be reported. They would swim and then climb up the cliffs, where no boat could dock to get them, then walk hours back over these crags to Lavras . . . six hours, a day perhaps. No phones, no electricity, no walkie-talkies! God bless primitive Byzantium after all!

O'Hanrahan fixed the old man's cap on his head, put his head down in order to be inconspicuous, and motored steadily along the shore, passing the landmarks of the previous days, Dionysiou, Gregoriou, Simonopetra . . . and looked at his watch. Twenty, thirty minutes, he'd be back in Ouranopolis to explain to Lucy why he had missed his appointed telephone call. If the fuel held out. He might well make it back in Ouranopolis before the scheduled ferry and the possible culprit arrived—how's that for perfect!

But the fuel didn't hold out.

"Stavros," Lucy began, taking a deep breath, "I don't want you to think that just because . . ."

Stavros, sitting on the edge of the bed, looked up at her warmly.

". . . that just because what happened—"

"Ehhhhh," he said, not letting her finish, grabbing her, tickling her, rolling with her on the bed. "I know, I know," he said. "You love me more than all of the other of the boys, hm?"

She giggled. "Of course not."

"You don't? You don't?" More tickling. The tortures of the Greek inquisition until she recanted and said she loved him. "See," he said, "I knew you love me."

"Yes, and you love me?" she said lightly, her hand poised to attack him.

"Ehhhhh . . . maybe—"

She attacked. But he wasn't ticklish on his hard stomach or around his neck, so she resorted to pulling chest hairs.

"*Neh!* I love you," he said. A moment later he slipped an arm around her middle, nuzzling against her breasts, which she had shielded with the bedsheet. "I get to come visit you in USA?"

"Sure."

"You to make me stay with your home?"

"Yes, you're welcome."

He laughed victoriously. I'm glad everyone wants to go to America, Lucy thought serenely. "So," she asked him, "how many girls have you . . . have you done this with?"

"A meelion."

Lucy snorted in disbelief.

"*Kilia*—you have the word? Like kilometer . . ."

"A thousand," Lucy reasoned aloud. "That's just as believable as a million." But could it be true?

(Close to it.)

Lucy asked, "How many American girls?"

"One other American," he said. "From Canada."

"I see."

"But, eh, not as bootiful as you."

Now don't go and get kind on me, thought Lucy, or I really will fall in love with you. She mussed his hair that he had earlier styled in ringlets, arranged to perfection.

"Ehh ehh ehh!" he cried, jumping up and retrieving his flung-aside bathing suit. It was cold and damp now and Stavros made a great show of shivering as he pulled it up his legs. Lucy looked at his nakedness desperately, sensing that this sight she must not forget; soon it would all be gone and she would spend much of her lifetime longing to retrieve this proximate beauty—

"I go get food," he announced, checking the mirror for his hair.

Lucy wished she could get one more hug out of him, but no, she wasn't going to act . . . you know, the least bit needing or overly fond. She had to be as cool as he was or . . . or she just might get hooked on him and that would be the von Hindenburg, Krakatoa, the *Titanic*, the Johnstown Flood, the Chicago Fire.

"*Ieeah soo*," he said, closing the door behind him.

"Bye-bye."

Lucy lay on her back and looked up at the ceiling. I suppose, objectively, he's no Casanova, or whatever the Greek equivalent is—come on, stupid, you've studied this stuff for ten years: Adonis, Apollo, Hyacinthus . . . though that was sort of a gay myth, Lucy remembered. Anyway, lovemaking with Stavros, their initial act, lasted five minutes tops with her pretending not to be scared, nervous that he would see how inexperienced she was . . . or maybe that was what got him so excited suddenly. Anyway. It's done. That was it. And when he got up to take a shower and pulled her along behind him, that was great too, even better. She relived it. Lucy's impulse was to reach for a towel, cover herself up ... He ridiculed her modesty—so American, he laughed. Anyway, in the shower he was so tender and funny and as soon as they got out, Stavros was not sure whether he should leave or stay and that's when Lucy said stay, reaching over and, well, persuading him. Then they made love again on the bed, a bit more properly and leisurely. Lucy lay there contemplating the shameless, wanton things she had done without a moment's guilt or hesitation.

It was midafternoon now.

I'm alone again, she sighed, running her hands over the sheets. But this alone and the alone-before-Stavros have different textures. I am not *quite* as alone as I was when I was by myself before. Where's all the guilt I thought I'd be feeling by now? Yes, Lucy decided, somewhere deep down, there is a sense of regret—for *not getting here sooner!*

But, Lucy told herself, I couldn't have done it any sooner, not the way I was; it had to happen along my own scale of time. And yesterday I was ready and today I am ready again and forever, for love, for sex, for more travel and new faces, new sights, new thrills, and this brimming, overfull new person named Lucy who seems to have erased so much of what she was before in a single instant, who is born again with one unreasoned thought in her head: MORE. More of everything! More of this deep, boundless love I feel for ... well, not for Stavros, but for the world of love he represents, the wondrous universe I have been admitted into at last!

Lucy lifted her hand which had the scent of Stavros on it and placed it on her cheek, breathing in the aroma of salvation from the dreary path she would have traveled. Tears came to her eyes and she hugged herself, sweet giddy sensations: Thank God this happened. Forgive me, Lord, because I know it was all wrong and against what's in the Bible but I did not know what God's gift to Humankind was or the range of human feelings or this most common human moment—none of it until my travels, which You have been a part of, Lord, led me here. Forgive me for this, but thank You for my *fallenness*, my error, my sin ... Suddenly, I think it would be quite the worst thing imaginable to die, and I am panicked that it might happen so soon as to deprive me of other nights of yes, other sins.

(You have discovered the World, Lucy.)

Let me risk suggesting that You, Holy Spirit, maybe don't even disapprove so much ...

(You want to watch what you make a habit of.)

Lucy Dantan is bodily alive as she never was!

(But that must fade and tarnish.)

I am trying to dredge up some Catholic guilt but I swear I can't feel a hint of it! Oh, but think of the regret I would have felt if I had let this opportunity pass me by! It was now or never! My life was poised on a single fulcrum and that was it. Now my life will be different in some very sophisticated ways . . .

(You have eaten from the Tree of Knowledge.)

. . . and I'm not going to be such a moron about things from now on. No more shyness, no more false humility and insulting myself into failing. Imagine the emptiness and regret had I not seized that moment, had I sent him away from the balcony—how perilous it seems in retrospect! How he could have run away or how I could have thrown him off and protected my . . . my former, empty, dried-up life. Without him I would have been eternally wondering, bitter, joyless, and alone.

(No. I would have been with you.)

Such confusion, Lucy sighed, feeling all things at once. Lucy rolled about the cool white sheet and pressed the pillow closer to herself. God bless ridiculous, improbable Stavros, wretched me, and the man who led me here as Paul led Silas, dear, terrifying Dr. O'Hanrahan.

"Why, God, why?" O'Hanrahan yelled to the heavens as the boat muttered to a stop. He pulled, yanked, manipulated, kicked, and hammered at the motor but, here, a few yards offshore, miles from Ouranopolis, he was out of gas. "Is this Your idea of a joke?" he cried aloud. "How long, O Lord, how long? Damn You!" he added, kicking the motor.

(That's no way to talk to the Almighty.)

It's all those Virgin Mary jokes, O'Hanrahan thought, the years of blasphemy. Mister Smart-ass, had to tell Lucy the spurting-breast stories in Athens, and now the Old Bag has delivered you up for this! For God's sake, he lectured himself, think clearly, think clearly:

I am a wanted man. They'll soon find the boat . . . unless I pull it ashore and hide it. Then what? I better start walking the length of the peninsula and back into Ouranopolis. They hardly are going to comb the whole of Mt. Athos looking for me. Greek police don't care that much. He squinted at the shore behind him. I've just passed—what the hell was it?—Dochiarou Monastery. From there, I recall, I can get to the trail that runs the length of the peninsula. Ten, twenty miles? In this sun? And I can't stop in any monastery because there'll be some damn monastic equivalent of an all-points bulletin out for me. No water, no food. The rugged climbs.

He put his head in his hands. While he looked down he saw the fisherman's paddle. He took it up and began to paddle to the shore, the way the slight current was moving him anyway.

Of course, he thought, I could walk along the shore. No mountain-climbing, but I'd be in plain sight of anyone looking for me . . . no, the original plan was better: take the high road, in the trees, among the hills. Who knows? I might be able to find some remote skete or *kathisma* that would feed me, that hadn't heard about the desecrations—

And at that moment, far on the horizon, a military-gray Greek Coast Guard boat, flashing lights and sirens, passed by, speeding farther down the peninsula.

O'Hanrahan felt himself shudder: Could they be after me?

Surely not yet . . . But what if another fishing boat saw the men in the water and went to retrieve them and then radioed Ouranopolis—

Or worse.

Oh, Jesus God Mary and the All the Saints, worse, much worse.

O'Hanrahan felt a chill pass over him from his head down his arms where his hair stood on end: what if for some reason one of the men drowned? What if the old man had a heart attack? The young monk sank in his heavy, waterlogged robes? Desecrating ikons and stealing a boat and assault and battery and fleeing knowing a policeman was waiting to see me—O'Hanrahan swallowed though no saliva was in his mouth—and what if *murder* is now the charge? Oh Lord, why couldn't I have just gone along to the police, explained it and had it done with in a few minutes? Why has my life gone this way? Why do you bring me here in this wasteland to finish my life of error and pain?

(Get on with it, and stop whining. And when you talk to Us, Patrick, a bit more respect, please.)

He paddled again hurriedly, breathing quickly. Here I am trying to do something for God, having devoted my life to words about God and God can't do me one little goddam favor—

(You're not searching for Matthias for Us and don't pretend you are. You're doing it for yourself, some last bit of earthly glory. Money, fame, rubbing their noses in it, We've heard all your reasons. You've never once thought how We might feel about it.)

"Voices," he mumbled, now short of breath, sweat pouring down his brow, this whole Athos adventure being his first physical exercise in years."Greece and all the voices. You always hear voices . . ."

The shore approached. His thoughts again deteriorated: I'll never make it. After a few hours in this sun my heart will stop. That's how it will end, one big folly, O'Hanrahan's biggest and stupidest yet. Oh they'll enjoy this one back in Chicago! He died *how*? On Mt. Athos? After doing what? And what a shame about that young monk, drowning like that . . . Oh God, please don't let that have happened! Don't make me an accidental murderer!

(Selfish motivations, always. Not even a thought for young Nikolas, poor thing. Though he is a bit of a prig.)

The boat bumped the rocks in the clear lagoon. O'Hanrahan stepped out into the water up to his thighs and pulled the boat alongside him by the rope attached to the bow. He waded and hopped from rock to rock until he pulled the boat around the corner of this inlet. With all the perversity physical objects display when they are most needed to cooperate, the boat bumped, stuck, drifted in wrong directions, did everything but follow O'Hanrahan as he led it successfully to the cove, up into the mud, into the pines and the shade.

In this shade he sat down, sopping with sweat, and began lamely scooping up pine needles to cover the most visible side of the boat. He started laughing. What asininity!

This sixty-five-year-old in this ludicrous adventure of his own making. But he nonetheless felt some joy in this: if I get back and pull this off, what a story this will be! It'll make great reading in the *Trib*, wait till I tell Oprah! Yes, concentrate on the *fame*, the glory after this scroll is translated and the findings announced! And poor Lucy, going out of her head with boredom over there in damn dull Ouranopolis—wait till she hears about my adventure! It'll make her day!

One Ouranopolis disco bar was called the Argonaut Klub.

Since Stavros had not returned as promised with something to eat, Lucy got dressed after her intense, exhausted nap, fixed herself up nicely, and went into the town to hunt for him at his favorite night club. The Argonaut was near empty but it was early evening and people were just beginning dinner. The heart of the disco was a two-turntable music console and a teenage Greek boy in a too-large tie-dyed T-shirt and cyclist's pants who had two discrete piles of records stacked in a preferred order.

"And noow ees time for soom *real* rock'n rool," said the boy, before putting on "The Final Countdown" by the Swedish group Europe.

At some flip of a switch, the disco ball started spinning and flecks of prismatic light spun about the room. There was also a strobe light that alternated with the blue fluorescent light that turned everyone on the dance floor Martian green and purple.

This is a museum to the 1970s playing music of the 1980s, surmised Lucy. A bartender was glowering at her for not ordering a drink, so she ordered a Diet Coke that tasted nothing like the ones at home, in a smaller can, but with Greek writing on it. Interesting souvenir.

An even more sunburned Derek and Tracy appeared in the doorway. Tracy spotted Lucy and skipped over to see her; Derek sat at a table and began reading a rolled-up two-day-old British newspaper.

"I'm gonna bloody murrrrder the bastard," Tracy said, half-smiling. "He's getting on me nerves something awful . . . So how are you and, uh, what's-his-name?"

"Stavros," Lucy said nonchalantly. "Same story. Went out to get us some lunch, never was seen again."

"Well, I shouldn't tell you this then," Tracy confided, "but I saw him down at the sailboard rental place late this afternoon." Lucy imagined the mewling collection of German *Fräuleins* in attendance. Tracy put a conspiratorial hand on Lucy's arm: "He's something else, he is. Does he speak English?"

"Not very well," Lucy breathed. "But then he doesn't have to."

Tracy giggled and nudged Lucy who nudged back. "They're all a bunch of worthless layabout yobs, you know? Whatcha got there?"

"Diet Coke and, uh, rum."

Tracy turned to the bartender and ordered what she thought was the same. "See the bartender?" Tracy whispered. "Lucy, he's been giving me the eye since I bloody got here."

Lucy checked him out: standard Greek tan with a five-o'clock shadow, broad torso, trimmed mustache, convinced he was much better looking than he was. "He's all right," said Lucy. "Too bad about . . ."

"Derek."

"Yeah, Derek."

"I tell you what. Next year I'm coming back without the bloody millstone there . . ." Derek currently was making sure his spiked hair stood out straight in the faint reflection of the dark formica paneling. "It'd be a bleedin' Roman orgy if I hadn't dragged him along. And you can call me a right arsehole when I tell you I chipped in to pay for his coming here too. My own bloody hard-earned dosh. Oh Luce, look at that one there by the wall . . ."

Tracy indicated a fashionable Mediterranean man in his early thirties, smart navy-blue jacket, a small-collared white shirt, dark tie. A cigarette smoldered in an ashtray before him and Tracy pointed out that he must be a Greek with money because it looked like a Rolex on his arm. He looked up from the table and Lucy got a good look at his face: swarthy, deep olive complexion, large liquid brown eyes, a prominent aristocratic nose, and an intelligence, a discernment about him.

"Too good for this place, he is," said Tracy. "Maybe he's heir to some Greek shipping fortune. He's looking at us too," she squealed, turning her head into Lucy's shoulder. "Look what you've done! He's coming over here . . ."

Lucy and Tracy composed themselves.

"Hallo," he said in a rich baritone that made them both weaken. His accent was light and his vowels were rounded as if he had been educated in Great Britain. "I seem to have been stood up. So perhaps I will talk to you instead. If you would like."

So gentlemanly, noticed Lucy. Old world Mediterranean charm— no ass-pinching and hooting war cries like the lowest of the species. "Please join us," said Lucy, motioning to the neighboring barstool.

"Can I buy you a drink?" risked Tracy.

He laughed. "It is the man who should buy the drink for the woman, is it not?"

"It's a modern world," sang Tracy. But at this juncture, Derek was on his feet and standing a few yards from them.

Derek: "I thought you were gone to the bar for me drink not a focking hen party."

"I'm coming, I'm *coming* already—what bloody cheek."

"You got the bloody cheek . . ."

They retreated to the table to squabble. Not such a modern world for some people, thought Lucy.

The handsome stranger noted, "I have met that boy before."

"You have?"

"Many times, in England. Not him personally, just his sort."

"Yes," said Lucy, trying not to be nervous. "I've met him in England too a few times."

"You were in England?"

"I was . . . well, I had this, uh, visiting scholar teaching post at Oxford University." Suddenly she blanked out on names of colleges she could attach herself too.

"How unfortunate for you," he said consolingly. "For both of us. Unfortunate for you, because Oxford is what it is. Unfortunate for me, because I might have met you had you come to Cambridge."

Lucy smiled. "I wondered how you spoke such perfect English."

"Ah, it is far from perfect. Well. I must find my brother . . ." The stranger stood.

Lucy noticed out of the corner of her eye Stavros in his favorite muscle-shirt and tight jeans sauntering into the club. "Oh please," she said quickly, "won't you stay for at least a drink? I can't let you malign the honor of Oxford, a place far superior to Cambridge, as you surely know."

He laughed but did not sit down again.

Stavros had spotted them.

The stranger: "I must go, but perhaps I will return, yes?"

"Please do," she smiled, seeing that Stavros was glaring unhappily at her conversational partner.

The stranger bowed slightly and walked out of the club, passing Stavros, who in comparison looked immature and like an overmoussed adolescent. Stavros, frowning, joined Lucy.

"Who ees that?"

Damn it, she didn't get his name. "Just someone."

"Where were you this afternoon?" Stavros asked.

"Waiting for you to come back with food."

"I," he pantomimed knocking, "on yoor door. You are not there."

Well, she did fall deeply asleep. "I was there all afternoon," she said anyway, "and I didn't hear you knocking."

"I go to the room and sleeped myself, yes?"

"Was that before or after going down to see the German bimbos at the windsurfing stand?"

"Bimbos? I do not unnerstand . . ."

She repeated it until she knew he was pretending not to understand.

"I make many friends," he said in his defense.

"So do I," she said.

O'Hanrahan's Dark Night of the Soul.

He sat on the edge of a rock and assessed the trail before him. Shadows closed in and soon he would be wandering blindly. Perhaps if he had followed the shore and walked the coastline he would be able to see in the moonlight, but reaching the coast would be impossible now . . . Perhaps he could sleep on the ground. With the wolves. And the rattlesnakes—one of the last places they lived in Europe. Or he could just sit here, lean on this rock until he fell asleep and get going at the first hint of light.

Soon twilight gave way to darkness, which encompassed the woods. Only above him through the pines could he see the deepening blue of night. The pines rustled, leaves brushed, and he talked himself into hearing animals approaching. Eerily a gust of wind would rustle the treetops as if some consciousness were there, some angry, long-ignored Grecian deity.

(What about the long-ignored God of Abraham?)

I'm like friggin' St. Anthony of the Desert, thought O'Hanrahan, putting his hands under his arms to fight the chill. I'm starving, I'm seeing things and hearing things—

(When Anthony felt fear, he prayed to Us.)

No siree, I'm not going to pray. Lordy Lordy I'm so scared of the dark. More times than not, when a man turns to prayer and religion he's being stupid, insufficient.

(But men and women *are* insufficient.)

It's degrading. How can anyone believe in a religious experience when nine out of ten times one has it in extremis. Person A finds God when her plane is about to crash. Person B has got cancer and has six months to live and, whadya know, finds God. Person C is trapped in a mine for six days and, big surprise, finds God. I mean, isn't that the least little bit suspicious? No, I tell you what, when I'm on *top*, when I'm successful and thinking clearly, *then* maybe I'll give God a shot.

(Suit yourself.)

As my father said, "Be a man." I was scared of the dark when I was a child. I'd lie in my room whimpering, eventually getting my good sweet suffering mother, my dear loving mother . . .

(Your mother is here with Us.)

A picture of her soft, indulgent face floated before O'Hanrahan. He remembered: My mother would rise from her bed and come comfort me, read to me. She would look so old in the light of that little bedside lamp. She never cut her hair like many women of that generation, but rather arranged it every morning, neatly piling and braiding it atop her head. But in the night, in her faded flannel nightgown, without her spectacles whose absence made her face so vulnerable, she and her long, combed-out silver hair would look into my room and . . . and she seemed perpetually sad for me. Why isn't my little Paddy asleep and dreamin', she'd say. Well, what will it be, she'd ask, reaching for the Bible-stories book in the nightstand, the one with all the colorful pictures of miracles and Christ suffering and bleeding.

(So began your interest in Us.)

My father on the other hand was harsh, disciplining. Unloving, as his father had been.

(And what do you suppose your son would say of you?)

My father refused to buy a nightlight for me. And if he caught me with my bedside lamp on wasting valuable electricity, he would remove the light, cursing as his hands were burned on the hot bulb. And once . . . why does this come back to me now? Once he shut me in the closet, saying, "There, now be a man . . . And don't come out till ye can act like a man." And the closet wasn't really so dark and I wasn't scared, just humiliated, so I decided I would sit in there until I died. And I never would have come out except for the muffled sounds of my mother weeping, and to comfort her, I came out. Over a goddam half-century ago! Another lifetime!

(No, not another lifetime.)

I hated my father for a long time. Then I felt sorry for him. A son's love can survive hate and disagreement, violence and abuse, but no son's love can survive the emotion of pity for his father. I can say to my credit, my son Rudy never thought I was pathetic. He may have hated me, but never pitied me.

(Your son did pity you. Shows what you know.)

My father, Patrick O'Hanrahan, Sr., worked in the stockyards, loading and unloading freight. Despite a solid union wage we were always poor. He lent money to no-account relatives and friends over drinks in the bar, and he borrowed money just as liberally from loan sharks.

My mother hocked heirloom after heirloom, all junk, of course, Irish schlocky junk from the halcyon Old Country. As his son I was caught between him saying, "Ah, ye're not gonna have to slave yer life away like yer old bastard of a father, not on me life . . ." and conversely: "Workin' where I work wouldn't hurt ye none, or is it that you're too good fer us workin' folk . . . ?"

I could never win.

A good report card? I got "Ye think ye're so smart, do ye? Smarter than yer old man? Well, I can teach ye still a thing or two . . ." Around the house, never I, nor my mother, nor any of my brothers or sisters, received any evidence that he loved us, so it's hardly something to feel guilty about.

(Then why do you?)

God, how I dreaded family occasions, weddings and funerals. There'd never be a wedding without all three of his sisters and four of his brothers, jostling, getting drunk, bleating Irish songs until the union local catering staff asked them to leave, and there'd always be a fight. Someone would say something utterly, indescribably inconsequential and then my father would stand, wobbling on his feet, drunk:

"If ye say that . . . if ye say that again, then by God and the saints, I swear on Christ Almighty . . ."

And here my mother would restrain him, beg him to sit down, calm down, have some coffee, surely it was time to go home—

"By God, a brother of mine saying that . . . saying what ye just said . . ."

Even at this point, my father could not tell you, if his life depended on it, what exactly *was* said. It was merely an opportunity to hear himself roar and be manly, one more good-for-nothing bog Irish, dumb harp, millrat mick . . . I'll admit it, no argument here: I was thoroughly ashamed of him.

And funerals. Christ almighty, at funerals like some third-rate Irish vaudeville sketch, they'd weep one minute and sneak shots from the flask the next, then shove each other in the parking lot, then blame one another for the death of whoever had died, bar them from ever stepping foot in their houses again, swear by every saint and holy presence that they were no longer a brother/sister/in-law of theirs, that they were dead to each other! Dead as whomever they'd just ruined the funeral of! How I would run back to the car—yes, that was when we still had the car—and lock myself inside and put my head down on the backseat and shut it all out, all the emotional violence and drunk Irish grandstanding I didn't comprehend.

It was this life, this bad minor work by Eugene O'Neill too unbelievable ever to be staged, that loomed ahead as my destiny. To be lost in this sea of unreasoned Irish emotionalism, dockyard brawling, union politics, grabbing a bat after five shots of Jamesons to go down to the

yards with Grady O'Connell and Tom Kelly and Jacky Doyle to bust
the heads of the goons whom management had hired; my mother
pleading, sobbing for him not to go and get the hell beaten out of him,
which he went, and did . . . Not even my mother saw it as clearly as I
did. Her solution was that I should be a priest, and turn my eyes to a
higher calling, a better life.

(Because you loved God once.)

Don't take so much credit—it wasn't so much You as it was escape
from the South Side. I saw a world where men read and thought and
there was quiet and they lived in clean places and ate good food. It
was the only thing for someone like me to do.

(But you have forgotten that you wanted to do good, that you prayed
for a mission whereby others would be helped, raised up. Have you
truly erased what We once meant to you?)

I groan to see myself: how pious, how pale and weak and quiet. My
mother thought it was religiosity and was comforted, my father
thought it was unmanly but if one of his sons had to be a priest, it
might as well be me . . . And I thought that being a priest was the
answer, until I realized that that too was a trap, the same Irish conspiracy dolled up with a little incense.

My sister Catherine and I would walk to school together. Let's see,
I was twelve or so, she was a bossy fourteen. And she'd lead us out of
our way in order to go by the public school and look in at the other
kids, the Protestants. My sister would lean up against the open-link
fence and yell insults. I told her our mother said not to have anything
to do with them, and especially not to make fun of them. Do you know
why Mother said that? asked Catherine. Because they're Protestant
and going to hell. And I looked in at the guys playing stickball on the
asphalt playground and I dwelled fearfully on a God Who would send
these laughing boys to hell.

(You prayed about it that night for an hour.)

And then came the time when the parish closed our ill-educated,
understaffed parochial school and we were told we would have to go
several miles from our neighborhood if we wanted to stay in a Catholic
institution. So my father, in a horrific fight with my mother, ordered
that we go to public school, which he had, after all, paid for with his
taxes. And we took tests to see what grade we should be put in. And
I found my eyes smarting with tears and I felt rage inside me. Because
where were the questions about who was the Queen of Heaven and
who attended her Coronation? Where were the great saints, Christopher and George, what of the Joyful Mysteries, the four Archangels,
the Pater Noster in Latin? They wanted none of this, they wanted the
first eight U.S. presidents and for me to match animals with their
phylae and pair Longfellow and Poe to their famous poems' titles. And
I remember etched in my heart the woman receiving my test paper

and shaking her head, saying lightly to her colleague, "Another genius from Our Lady," and I was put back a grade.

(And you are still bothered by it fifty years later.)

Patrick Virgil O'Hanrahan, head of his class as long as he had ever been in school, put back a grade! Yes, I can still taste the bile. And so I had to play catch-up, which made me mad and bitter, and competitive . . . before it slowly seeped in, very slowly, ever so slowly occurring to me that to be Catholic at Kelly High in 1935 was to be one of the stupid back-of-the-yards mick kids.

And that's why there'd be no parish for me, no lousy rundown moaning diocese to see to, no old crones venting their family squabbles, no endless confessions from young women like my sister Catherine dredged up from a stunted, juiceless life . . .

No, Plan C: I would go to Loyola. I would be in the Jesuit elite. I would travel to other continents, anywhere in the world to do the pope's bidding if I must—anywhere but the South Side!

(Since when did you have the pope in mind?)

I was being facetious. I didn't care about furthering Rome's cause— far from it, I almost abandoned Catholicism after Pius XII sucked up to the Nazis through World War II. Nor did I wish to defeat Protestant error, because from my high school days, there were more Protestants than Catholics among my circle of friends—they at least had some sense of progress, of forward movement! Religion had little to do with my wanting to be a Jesuit. I was looking for that stamp of approval that Jesuit meant: I wanted to scream to the world I am a thinking, brain-alive Catholic man!

(You rewrite your own history. There was also an idealistic Patrick, who hoped to better the world, who loved a spiritual notion of God divorced from the ecclesiastical bunkum of the Church. You don't remember what a kind-thinking soul you had as a child, back in the days when you were confirmed.)

Oh geez, my Confirmation. The women on one side, all piety, all Marys and saints preserve us, all unloved, self-righteous frumps un-touched by their husbands in years; their men a loutish band of drunken, irreligious wrecks. Twenty minutes after the trumped-up fight at the reception at the church, there was a forced reunion, some-one would make my father and whoever it was—my father and Uncle Kenny usually—shake hands, then there was an embrace.

"Aw, Kenny my friend," my father would pine, and inevitably, "come take a look at me young man! Come see me pride'n joy! A smart one he is, gonna go far like his old man, ey! Paddy, Paddy my boy, come meet your Uncle Kenny, lad!"

And the introduction would be made for the third time that night, the hundredth time in my life, and I'd have my hair ruffled, whiskey breathed in my face all around, a prelude to some other relative trying to slip me my own shot of whiskey while the women howled in protest, and that was as good as I could expect: the only time my father owned me. Drunk out of his mind, his closest approximation to saying he loved me.

(What was your closest to him?)

Damn You, these accusing recitals of conscience, these voices of the night! What guilt should I feel? I honored him, didn't I? I loved him inasmuch as I could, being who I was. I never fought with him openly, always surrendered and ignored him. Gave him his respect that was due.

Besides, you could no more break through to him than you could talk with a cartoon figure on the screen. If he had *once* looked up in the kitchen over coffee and said, "Son, I don't know what life is all about," or if he had turned off the fights on the radio and said "Son, do you ever think there might not be a God above us?" I would have comforted him, talked to him, given all my poor wisdom to solace the man. But he never had a higher, deliberative thought in his life!

It was always "Yer old man knows how to deal with these city-fellow types, these big shots, ye let me do the talkin' . . ." right before the insurance man denied one of his claims. It was always "Jacky Doyle is the best man of his time and I stake me life and fortune on it—why, I wish I could only have lent the man twice the amount!" before Mr. Doyle went totally bust. It was always the same unoriginal, impossible, unending conspiracies behind my mother's back: she dumped the booze out, he'd sneak some back. He'd get solvent again, that night he'd lend the money out, being a big man at the bar, and lie about it when he got home. How can a man with a brain commit the same stupid mick mistakes a *thousand* goddam times in a row?

(Did he have to be perfect in order for you to love him?)

God, I see myself suddenly, prim and proper, soft-spoken like a funeral director, pious in my novice's collar, coming home from Loyola to see my mother. Was I that superior? Oh please, tell me I didn't go around like that, tell me I had more life in me than that, let's pretend I was always like what I am now. How I must have looked to him . . . At least my mother was proud of me—

(And what was it that she wanted from you before you went overseas to American University in Beirut?)

She wanted me . . . she wanted me to spend time with my father who was getting old and forgetful, she wanted there to be peace between us. And then years later when I was in Korea, she died, my blessed, worn-out mother. And my sister Catherine, who had nursed her and lived at home running her life for years, probably driving my father nuts. She wanted to be in charge of the family and correct the laxities of my mother, mete out judgment and scorn to my father, my poor father . . .

(A twinge of sympathy at last?)

And in six months after my mother's death, a woman he had misused and berated for 46 years, my father drank himself out of existence. I can see Catherine standing over his passed-out body lecturing him, rosary in hand. Although I didn't see it. I didn't go home to see any of it. I never asked for leave. I couldn't bear to watch. What did I have to say to him? My home was the place my mother lived, and when she was gone there was no home in Chicago for me.

Tears filled O'Hanrahan's eyes, in this deep darkness.

Oh, Patrick O'Hanrahan, Sr., how did you see your last days? How did you face the coming of the end, the half-fulfilled promises to yourself, the abject failures, the extinction of all possibilities? Did you know which of the bottles was your last? You never told your son how to do this part, this death business. Like everything I've ever done I'll have to do this, as you did it, alone. Why did you let it end so badly? A gutter in an alley beside the local bar that had cut you off . . . You just thought, Well here's me a place, I think I'll lay me down here and die tonight. I'd give anything to know what you were thinking.

(He was thinking of his son. His son he was proud of and so hoped to see again before he died. He was thinking: when I wake up tomorrow morning, my dear Paddy Jr. will be standin' over his dear old dad, comin' to give me his love and take his poor old father home.)

O'Hanrahan wept.

July 20th

Lucy, imagining O'Hanrahan had lost track of the days, waited in the Poseidon Hotel lobby for the appointed phone call at twelve noon.

Nope. No word today either.

Lucy went to eat a Greek salad and do the newsstand, beachfront, and the three side-by-side cafés walking tour again. Then she read a little more from *So Hot the Sun*. Then she went back to the Poseidon and asked again if there were any calls or messages. And there were none.

"Where do you suppose he is?" Lucy asked Stavros.

"Maybe the phone no work?"

Perhaps. It is a bit old-fashioned over there. Lucy didn't know what to do. If worse came to worst she could send Stavros over there to look around.

"No," he said, when she suggested it. "No religion, no." Then he nuzzled closer and put his hand on her behind indecently.

She pulled away laughing, having incurred a rude stare from an older townswoman. "No, not here," she said modestly.

"You get you tan today?"

"I might work on my tan, yes."

They walked back to the Poseidon Hotel again. Lucy had a sense that Stavros wasn't totally willing but he had balanced a guaranteed snooty rejection from one of the Valkyries against a sure thing with Lucy.

Lucy thought: I'm getting just a trifle addicted to this guy's company. I could make sex with this guy a habit, against my better judgment—well, who knows if he's even willing again. Lucy reached out to take his hand as they strolled down the seafront but Stavros clasped it for a moment then let it go, putting his hands in his pockets. Doesn't want to broadcast he's taken, thought Lucy, lest anyone else in town wants him. She felt a tinge of jealousy, then of inferiority and then let it pass. I'll deal with the consequences of all this later, she thought, closing her eyes, her face finding the sun.

"Time for you tan?" he asked.

She gave him an inviting look. God, he was beautiful. She wanted to devour him, for all the time he wouldn't be around in her future, for all the missed opportunities of her past.

"I was going to be a nun one time," she said, as they walked up the stairs to her room.

Stavros laughed. "Too late for you now."

And once in the room, she grabbed him playfully and pushed him against the door, nuzzling against his chest, undoing the buttons of his shirt. Erase that silly little girl who once was, she thought. Let's do away with her now and forever.

Lost! Thank you, Blessed Virgin! You appear to every teenage schizophrenic, sexually neurotic nutcase in the Mediterranean, and you can't even point out to Patrick O'Hanrahan a simple little direction!

(Is that any way to talk to the Handmaiden of the Lord?)

I should be nearly dead. Nope, no birds circling overhead yet, but dinner's almost served . . . O'Hanrahan laughed deliriously at himself. What a way to go. If I could just find water I would surrender to whomever, for whatever, however . . .

No.

No, that was a moment of weakness. I am being tempted by devils again. But God help me, look at this countryside. To go down and up the next mountain ahead will take the afternoon, in this heat, and what will be left of me? I could fall and twist my ankle, lie there and rot until the end of my life. The other direction is the same. I'm not even sure if this so-called trail I'm on is a trail or just the natural clearing across the top of this ridge. I'm too old for this kind of thing—maybe this comic death scene will be related in the Scholarly Register, that is, if I were still important enough to be listed in it. I'll be lucky to make the *Chicago Sun-Times* obituary page in fine print.

He arbitrarily decided on the right fork and began his descent into the valley.

I should have never left the Jesuits, O'Hanrahan thought. I should have parked myself in Jerusalem or Loyola at New Orleans and got tenure and kept out of the middle-class wife-and-family business. That would have been a hard decision to make in Eisenhower's America but I could have spared myself a lot of problems.

(And spared the woman you married.)

My life, thought O'Hanrahan, has been a series of choices in which I outsmarted myself: when I was 23 and about to be one of the youngest Jesuit Ph.D.'s I told myself it was unimportant and went instead to American University in Beirut to see if I could work on ancient finds. Having been brought onto the Dead Sea Scroll team when I was 24, by the time I was 27 I had been offered positions, grants, opportunities to associate my name throughout history to these documents . . . and nawwww, I rejected that, just so much *vanitas*, academic vainglory, all garbage. No, Father O'Hanrahan wanted to see *real* life, do something visceral and meaningful. Plunge his hands into third-world soil! Rescue the untouchables from the Indian streets. What pretensions!

(You were never more noble, Patrick. Never was your heart so full of charity for your fellow man.)

And so it was off to Korea in 1952, attached to the chaplaincy. What I knew of war, O'Hanrahan recalled, I knew from newsreels during World War II and black-and-white *Life* magazine pictures. But Korea was in lurid, nauseating color. A parade of dead were brought before me for last rites and often a final comforting word, which I was quite good at. The first week of duty was gut-wrenching but rewarding. But then there was a second week, and a third, and the dying and dead and maimed-for-life kept coming and kept asking larger questions—

(But you gave them answers.)

Yes! Thoughtless, memorized anodynes to death and loss, second-rate platitudes fresh from the Hackmeisters of the Church. Do you think I couldn't see it in their eyes? They came to me for justification . . . and I mouthed talk of Jesus and a Cross and something that happened a very very long time ago to people they didn't know. The only Transfiguration one boy knew was five fingers miraculously now an unsightly stump, hastily sewn up and patched in ten minutes so we could get another rearranged collection of human parts to the operating table. The young Polish Catholic kid who wanted a last Communion. Out of wine, out of grape juice, we made do with red dye and sugared water, blessed it, consecrated it, and gave it to him to sip desperately. It is His blood, okay? But what need had we of anyone's blood, summer 1952, the Iron Triangle, 38th parallel, day 36 of fighting. Blood, O Son of Man, we had in big supply there.

Then passed the sixth week, the seventh week.

Was it possible even carnage and human destruction could get tedious after a while? You want miracles? The perverse suspension of physical laws on the battlefield was more miraculous than all the legends of the saints combined: the guy who had been shot three times, one bullet after the other lined up end to end in the entry wound. The guy who had a .22 bullet crack his teeth but do no more damage than that . . . and then weeks later, he was back, having deflected a *second* bullet with his teeth. "Keep smiling, Johnny!" everyone joked. Who could believe these things?

(But some of those were Our miracles.)

And conversely there was the guy who got gangrene from a botched ingrown toenail do-it-yourself job and died. The corporal who drank so much Korean moonshine his last night of duty that he died from an alcoholic coma. The Turkish soldier who, upon hearing the full extent of his groin wound, calmly took out his combat knife and cut his own throat, as neatly as if it were a slice of melon.

I saw it all, God, I really did.

And, O'Hanrahan reasoned, if one reflected for a moment, one realized that one maybe gave some shard of comfort but mostly you were an impotence, a hindrance between a man and his death, a Soviet-style bureaucrat with papers and holy water and crosses and scriptures, cluttering up inevitable destiny.

Twelfth week, fifth month, almost a year.

The resentment began to build. After the first young man, his life spilling from innumerable shrapnel wounds, disintegrated before me I thought: well, of course all this religion-hooey is complete crap. Good on paper, but you can't take Christianity on the road. You need a suburb for this delightful we're-all-going-to-heaven parlor game, but "Excuse me, kid, I know the lower part of your body has been shot off and we're out of morphine but, more important, are your impure thoughts washed clean by the Blood of the Lamb because Jesus sits on the right hand of His Father" doesn't play so well.

"Heh-heh," O'Hanrahan announced out loud, "I've got you voices on the run now, don't I? What have You to say for yourselves when the subject of war and bodily pain comes up? This paradise You've made for Man!"

There was a Turkish battalion mowed down by the Chinese—Allah help me! A Persian brigade of wounded came in, a Zoroastrian among them—what of the eternal fire? No need to talk to the Jewish guy from New York with T-minus-five minutes left on this earth, his people gave up on Heaven some time ago. And as for the Lithuanian guy from Cleveland with bad English, clutching his Bible, kissing my Cross feverishly, craving absolution for—what? nineteen years of uncommitted sin?—feeling his body fail inside him, more than once did I feel like saying: oh *please*, have some dignity!

(So you doubted. Doubt is healthy. Jesus doubted from the Cross. Mohammed got discouraged, Moses disobedient, the Kings of Israel forgot about Us entirely. Do you not think We doubt sometimes? The worth of keeping the whole thing going? Where there is consciousness, divine or human, there is doubt. It is by doubt We know that We believe, but also that We think at all, that We are not stones, inanimate, content. If Humankind only knew how The Creator shared its doubts and discouragements!)

Unforgettable images returned. The Hispanic boy blown to bits, one eye closed by a wound, a good Catholic from New Mexico, begging him for a cure—a miracle, anything is possible, isn't it, chaplain? I believe in my heart if you lay your hands on me . . . And Patrick did as requested as the boy screamed and writhed his way out of this world in the course of the next hour, convinced his pain was his deliverance. Indelible, that. Almost as unforgettable as the Laughing Guy, as O'Hanrahan remembered him. This fellow was so relieved to be alive; he talked for a half-hour about what he would do upon getting back home to the United States, he showed photographs, he joked that his injury, a leg wound, had been his ticket out of the Punchbowl. And how when O'Hanrahan returned with coffee for them both, now laughing as well, the soldier looked up uneasily and said, "Something's weird, Father." And as O'Hanrahan sat down and adjusted himself and tore little packets of sugar into his coffee, the boy died. Just like that. And O'Hanrahan talked for a good minute or two before realizing it himself. He just tired from all the strain . . .

But it was Death, quietly efficient! How true to the old salve, it can be *just* like going to sleep: there one moment, gone the next, no tearing of the ether, no thunderclap from the heavens.

(Such death is a blessing, don't you think?)

Easy for You to say! O'Hanrahan wiped the sweat from his brow, gritty with the dust, scratching his forehead. So this is what I was brought out here for: to have my life pass before my eyes? A little *divertissement* of the All-Powerful, like Job's leprosy, like Jonah's misadventure with the leviathan—let this be a lesson to all who hear. If you see the burning bush, run from it! Turn away, for your very life! Get behind me, Yahweh!

(You haven't enjoyed Our little time in the wilderness?)

"You don't know when to leave well enough alone, do You?" O'Hanrahan cried out, screamed for relief and exhaustion and because he didn't have the energy to smash anything. He picked up a rock and hurled it hard as he could at the sky, hysterically laughing at himself while he was doing it.

I know what You Bastards want! You want me brought low, on my knees! You want me to pray my way out of this! You can taunt me with all the voices, all the memories You got in store, because this is one man who has known You and *turned away*, who finds Your Omnipotence braggadocio, Your Omniscience dubious, Your Holiness in bad taste.

(Very well. But why is it that you've never stopped believing in God? Most people who lose their faith, say We don't exist. You, perversely, say We exist but that you don't like Us. Reconcile yourself, My son: We are God and you are Human and you don't have many options.)

Ha!

O'Hanrahan at the bottom of the valley chose the trail to the left and began plodding up it with renewed energy. He mumbled, I'll take Hell with the libertines, drunkards, freethinkers. Lunch with the Renaissance popes, dinner at Mallatesta's, beer later on with Nietzsche, then stop by the palace at Julian the Apostate's for Roman orgies!

(There is a Hell. Every holy personage from the most liberal to the most severe, Jesus or Mohammed, told Humankind there is a Hell and there is still this fond fantasy that it doesn't exist. Well, it's not Our beloved Dante's vision, exactly, but not any more nice, We assure you. Certainly, We have mercy on most poor souls and the majority of mislived lives, but it is entirely possible nonetheless to end up in Hell and you really wouldn't like it, Patrick.)

Hey, don't wear me out with this. I've seen Hell. Right here on this earth. Right in my own house, looking across the dinnertable at me.

(Beatrice, your wife. She brought on most of her problems herself, but you committed many sins of the spirit—the only kind that matter, frankly—and soured her on living. No amount of charity you have ever had has balanced the zest and passion by which you determined to make her miserable, make her pay for not being your ideal.)

My ideal? Petty, bickering, shriveled up with ill-will, irritating, complaining, whining, malicious, hyperreligious old killjoy, uniting the worst of Irish prudery and self-righteousness with the worst of Womankind. It was she who made me unhappy every day we were married!

(I see We're going to have to bring it back fresh to you:)

O'Hanrahan nearly stopped in his path. She was so pale, even after seven months in Korea. So soft-spoken and docile. Not exactly kind, not exactly possessed of the soothing motherly qualities you want in a Sister of Charity if you're a wounded soldier, but her timidity passed as calmness to those who wanted to see it that way. Twenty years old, shy and hard to engage in conversation, she had been an orphan raised by the Josephine Sisters, and from there she worked part-time for her keep in a St. Vincent de Paul soup kitchen for the needy, before embracing sisterhood as a vocation herself.

No, wait a minute, Beatrice Helena McDidon wasn't really an orphan, that's right . . . she had been the last of thirteen children and the father, an Irish sot, had abandoned the family, and social workers decided that the children should be split up, the youngest to be put in orphanages. The nuns had been quite clear about it with Beatrice: your mother gave you up. The compensation: it must have been God's will that you become a sister like ourselves.

"Beatrice," O'Hanrahan said aloud.

Father O'Hanrahan went behind her back to learn who she was when he first saw her. It was at a mass. She had just arrived from a posting in Japan. She had dark brown hair, straight and pulled back, pale skin with freckles, tiny hands—she was porcelain, she was breakable. And that attracted O'Hanrahan, the twenty-seven-year-old man who had never known a woman. There was a woman who might understand, who might forgive my fumblings, who would revere my learning, whom I would impress and dominate—no, not in some boorish macho way, but . . .

(In what way then?)

But as a mentor. I could teach her, Paula to my Jerome, if you will, I could liberate her from the Roman Catholic abyss. I could show her what to read, show her how to think, save her from old-maidhood, from becoming like my own sister Catherine O'Hanrahan, that slow steeping in gall and vinegar that embalmed the Irish female heart . . .

(That was not really love, though, was it?)

Yes, it was! For me! For a man who had lived out of a book, who was more current with Tertullian and Justin Martyr than how to ask a woman to have a cocktail, to dance at the canteen? I flirted with her, I taunted Beatrice with apostasies, I sat and drank endless cups of bad army coffee with her in 1952, that endless hot, muggy summer of dirt and insects and slow death for the wounded. She'd sit in the canteen and I played the reckless, dashing Jesuit, dangerously modern, ridiculing Pius XII, calling him a war criminal, challenging all established precedents.

(Beatrice quietly defended her sisterhood, but all the while she was undermined. No man, Patrick, had ever taken the time to talk to her, to choose her for anything warm and human. She would go to bed each night, restless in the heat, sighing loudly until told to shush by the other sisters.)

Indeed, the Mother Superior pulled her aside and sternly wanted to know if she and that rascal O'Hanrahan were involved in something vow-breaking and illicit. O'Hanrahan recalled that once the idea of love had presented itself and attained the dazzle of the forbidden, it was only a matter of time. And he was there proffering temptation:

"I don't see any reason why a Jesuit shouldn't take a lover," he remembered saying in the canteen, in a low whisper. "Popes and cardinals do. Cardinal Spellman's got a boy on the side—yes, it's true!"

She was torn with indecision. Her fellow, secular nurses—the way they talked about men! The torn-out pictures of leading men from *Life* magazine taped to the interior lid of footlockers, the pictures of a boyfriend on the beach at Coney Island displayed on another nurse's nightstand, the tales from some of the coarser women about romance on leave in Tokyo, and those moving tales of men about to die, virgin boys, begging the nurse for a late-night tryst, a taste of earthly love before death. Yes, sometimes that pitch was a ruse, but sometimes it was true and sometimes nurses gave in. Beatrice was ashamed but that fantasy tempted her because the men would either die or be transferred home and that could be the end of it, no consequences, no scandal . . . Not that many of the men made passes at her, since she wasn't very pretty, although she was in a Sister of Charity uniform, so it could be that. Also very bothering: the older, married women who were separated from children and husband. Maybe they were the greatest objects of envy of all. And here she was just twenty, a prisoner of the Church! No, she would do the one reckless thing of her life. She would know love.

(Well, Beatrice certainly loved you, worshiped you, adored you. You replaced one vow with another, and in the place of the former authority of the Church you offered . . . what? You were going to order and uplift her life, but you lost interest.)

Because she was, once back in the States, quite apparently . . .

(Undereducated.)

Irredeemably stupid. She didn't care about anything I cared about. She didn't want to read. She didn't have an inkling of interest in ancient cultures, foreign languages, lost scrolls, treasures of the past. This was my life! She devoted herself to home and hearth and it was all right for a while, but even she knew we were badly matched. "I'm too stupid for you," she protested.

(You should have soothed her. You married her after all.)

But what she said was merely the truth. Two bumbling, Church-wrecked, hard-up, overaged virgins stumbled together in time of war. What possible future could that have once life returned to normal? All right, all right, she did love me and I never really loved her the way a man should love his wife. She was a concept, a ritual of passage, a way to dump the Church and change directions yet again in my life, one more lousy idea that led nowhere.

Oh and I was responsible at first now—You gotta give me that! How I wept about it. How I stared for hours at the backyard, all those rainy Sunday afternoons in Pennsylvania, thinking how can I salvage this, this disaster? A divorce would have been merciful. I got up the nerve to ask her about it.

(That was the turning point.)

I'll say. She began backfilling with religion. Back to church, back to daily mass, back to afternoons ensconced at the local St. Bridget's Church and its prayer circle and its food drives and a young Catholic faculty wives' group . . . and then a month later, she discovered she was pregnant. Carrying the child of the man who made her break her vow to God and then asked her for a divorce so she could fall into damnation twice.

"This marriage is my penance," she said stoically. "I bring a child into this world with an apostate and a drinker for a father."

Hell, lady, my drinking wasn't *anything* back in those days.

Just wait till I got to Hyde Park in 1961 when I was made an associate professor at Chicago. Everyone was happy for this promotion but Beatrice. She didn't want for us to leave Duquesne University because it was close to her sisters in Pittsburgh. Chicago was a million miles away, she didn't know anybody. Do you realize years passed without a warm word or any healing in this breach? Is it any wonder that I traveled as soon as any project was offered—when any grant was tendered, I was gone!

(So you escaped your wife, all right. And your son, Rudy. And in those few months and weeks you were home, you acted worse.)

Don't You see? She never once felt forgiven. She had taken a vow and then she'd broken her vow—to God. No amount of divine forgiveness was enough: she was purgatory-bound if not hell-bound and this she accepted coldly, with a quiet bitterness. I was the first cause of this sin. I was the apple from the Tree of Knowledge and Satan all in one—the living reminder of her Fall. And there was no way that her little angel, her Abel, her Benjamin, her baby was going to be tainted and corrupted by his father, the philanderer, the drunk!

(Not entirely inappropriate descriptions of this period, however.)

It was the '60s, for pete's sake. The mini-skirts, the topless sunbathers, the see-through bras, the young coeds who thought nothing of hopping into the sack with the learned professor. I could see them out there, pretending to take notes, thinking about it . . . There are few periods that wreaked more destruction on middle-aged men than that one; woe to men whose mid-life crises coincided with the Swingin' Sixties! The flowered open shirts, the sideburns, the rose-tinted glasses, the tweed jacket with leather elbow patches, the pipe—forty-four years old and a man of my . . . of my son's era! And I would stare at my class from the podium, amid the born-agains and Jesus freaks and Catholic human disasters that washed up in Theology 101, those few young women who came not for the course but rather for the dynamic, showstopping lecturer, for the polished erudition and memorized Aramaic, puns in Latin, beautifully pronounced Greek. The languages and histories of the past spun all the needed mystery and hocus-pocus of an aphrodisiac . . .

(News of your philanderings got back to Beatrice.)

Oh, but some of those undergraduates! I remember one in particular . . .

(How about this memory:)

Rudy was six years old and Beatrice was still settling in and griping
about being in Hyde Park. She declared at the dinner table in a scene
rehearsed all afternoon: "Fine. We won't have Christmas in this house
this year. I'll take Rudy and go to my sister's, and you can fend for
yourself!"

Rudy: "Mommy, don't cry . . ."

The child was hysterical every time Beatrice sought to make a scene.

So, Patrick recalled, I took her at her word. She said I could go to
hell and drink with my cronies at O'Connor's Bar and that's what I
did Christmas Eve, the next day, assuming she and Rudy had stormed
off to Pittsburgh and would be back after the holidays. I arrived home
to see the table set, the candles burned down, the turkey and all the
food picked at, and Beatrice indignant at the table.

"You said you were going . . ." O'Hanrahan mumbled, propping
himself against the wall, having really tied one on.

"Daddy?" It was Rudy in his little pajamas, peeping around the
corner. "Can we open our presents now? Please?"

He was trying, of course, to prevent the scene he knew would come.

Oh, but Beatrice, Our Lady of the Recriminations, would not be
denied! You see, *I* never wanted to fight in front of the child, it was
always at her instigation, until it became doctrine that when Daddy
was home there was always a fight. What chance did Rudy have to
know a decent father-son relationship: I was the villain, the reason
Christmas was a time of tears, the scourge of all clean-living Christian
folk!

Beatrice informed the boy, "Rudy, your father doesn't even have a
present for you." Heartless! Savage!

(Why didn't you have a present for him?)

I thought he was coming back after New Year's! Plenty of time to
get something! Hey, for every Christmas after that I showered him
with toys and books—

(But you never made up the hurt from that Christmas.)

No. No, I didn't. Every time I made an off-color joke or delayed
putting up the Christmas tree, *that* particular Christmas—more holy
to Beatrice than the one at the Nativity—was invoked: Father will ruin
Christmas, we are at the hand of Satan once again, my little angel . . .
The poison she poured into poor Rudy's ears about me! I'd have fared
better if she had left and taken the kid and let me visit now and then.
Without me as source material to work with, Rudy would in time have
come to see his mother for the manipulative shrew she was; I would
have had his sympathy.

(She offered to leave you once.)

Facedown, one winter night, on the living-room rug, O'Hanrahan decided rather than crawl into Beatrice's unwelcoming bedroom, he would stay right there and pass out. Next thing he knew she was standing above him with a suitcase.

"You want me to go to a hotel?" he asked.

"No, I'm leaving. Rudy is already in the car."

O'Hanrahan came to and heard the Pontiac idling in the driveway. The mantel clock said it was three A.M. Rudy must have padded out of his bedroom and seen his father there like this.

"Don't go," he said automatically.

She said, buttoning her winter coat, "I won't divorce you. You know I don't believe in it. But I don't have to live with you."

(There was your big chance. Why didn't you let her go?)

Because . . . well, not when I was on the floor like that—

(No, it was because you wanted to leave *her*, with the next available woman who'd have you.)

And I thought of Rudy, You have to give me that! I didn't want him shanghaied in the night, dragged to a life of her bitchy old sisters! All he would remember was me at my worst. So I made Beatrice a promise if she'd stay, that I'd go to some damn alcoholic clinic she'd picked out.

O'Hanrahan at this point in his reminiscence reached a rock ledge, the truly steep part of the climb was before him. He began a slow, step-at-a-time, breathless ascent.

And thought: there is something Protestant about the notion of an alcoholic clinic. Everything is counseled and confronted, talked about and reasoned with; the patient is submitted to a process from which he is to emerge purged and justified and whole, confirmed in his new life. It didn't seem to leave much room for backsliding into the gutter forty-eight hours after being sprung from the clinic, like any good Catholic could tell you would happen. Catholicism is founded, after all, on the notion that the human condition is a given; hence, pro forma confession and light slaps on the wrist. Protestantism persuades itself people can change, and that once a sin is identified and prayed about and fretted over it will go away if we really want it to; hence the fanaticism, Prohibition, antiabortion and antihomosexuality, antipornography and antiprostitution. And of course, Protestantism, though randomly well intentioned, is totally, completely misguided.

(Where reforming you was concerned, yes.)

The clinic Beatrice had set her heart upon was the Doster Clinic near Urbana, Illinois. She had talked to that sweaty, fat-faced priest about my problem—hell, she had taken out magazine ads, billboards! Told strangers at the bus stop about her drunk of a husband, her beloved cherished Cross to bear! Beatrice collected recommendation after recommendation for where to consign me. O Holy Mother

Church, support her in this Crusade! The Reform of Patrick O'Hanrahan. Her martyrdom could now take on the aspect of the supreme.

"Yes, I'm fighting for my marriage," she'd tell the church biddies, ennobled. "God would want me to do no less. For Rudy . . ."

Yeah, that was the putative excuse—for Rudy. Why didn't she think about the boy when she launched into her self-aggrandizing scenes at the dinner table, hm? Why didn't she give five minutes' thought to the effect that castrating his father nightly would have on the boy?

(But you went to the clinic, after all.)

Beatrice sat primly and erect in the driver's seat while O'Hanrahan sat in the passenger's seat, neither of them saying anything, as they drove through the gray farmland to Urbana. There was snow in the fields and mud under the snow where it met the potholed, rumbling state highway they headed down, with Urbana 45 miles ahead.

"If I hate it," he said, "I'm coming right home."

"You have to do this for a week, Patrick," she said cautiously, so near to her greatest victory. "I think these people will make you see what you're doing to your life. What you're doing to all of us."

"I'm not doing anything to you. You're provided for, you've got a roof over your heads, Rudy wants for nothing—"

"Except a sober father."

He wasn't going to argue, not here in the car. There'd be time for arguing after he got home unrepentant and started drinking again.

Because he had every intention of drinking again.

There was not a molecule in his body that wanted to stop drinking; there wasn't even a still small voice saying that it was a problem. Drinking was his *life!* It was what made him clever and funny, whence sprung the O'Hanrahan legend. When he gave a party, the entire Theology Department went through contortions to secure invitations because it would be the blowout they'd talk about all year long: O'Hanrahan in good form, O'Hanrahan the entertainer, the liberal mixer of delightful decoctions. Mind you, that was the 1960s when people really knew a good cocktail—the cocktail is gone with so many other once-hallowed American vices and improvements on the dreary run of daily life. *Puritans, you have conquered,* to paraphrase Julian the Apostate. And as for the passing out, the sloppy ending, every bit of that was done in the privacy of his own home—no one saw that stuff.

(Just your wife and child.)

"You're going to see," Beatrice was saying, her small mouth spitting out the words, brittle and factual, "what becomes of someone who drinks like you do. You'll meet lots of others there."

That was another thing. Whether it was the one A.A. meeting he attended or the week at the Doster Clinic, O'Hanrahan was always struck by how much *worse* a drunk everyone else was:

The teenage boy who could polish off two fifths of vodka before dinner and couldn't remember peddling his behind on the street for twenty dollars and another fifth. The woman who accidentally killed her baby daughter driving drunk, running into a telephone pole. The once-respected doctor who drunkenly misdiagnosed someone and got his license revoked and was in the midst of Illinois's most expensive malpractice suit. The man who owned an office supply company and drank himself out of power, out of his home, out of a family, out of his money . . . What *losers*! What cowards and morons!

Booze ruined their lives—it made mine tolerable, beautiful, it was Grace, it was the currency of social relations for me! You see, they were losers who became bigger losers with booze. In fact, I would not even have had to endure the clinic episode if I'd been born in Ireland, for God's sake, where my social role was honored, raised up, venerated!

"And you, Patrick?" asked the bald, lisping doctor hugging his clipboard, speaking in his cruise-director's soothing tones. "Will you say you're an alcoholic?"

"I'm a heavy drinker," he said, though he wouldn't have been embarrassed to confess murder and rape before this group-therapy circle of losers. "I don't think I could go a week without drinking but then I don't want to . . ."

No laughter, no conviviality, not with this crowd. They were huddled together here to compete in misery, to be magically cured of all their sins and insufficiencies. Suckers!

"But you are," said the doctor, "an alcoholic."

Who was this clown, this necrophile greedily picking over the corpses here assembled? What did he get out of this?

"I'm not sure I *am* an alcoholic," O'Hanrahan protested mildly.

A thin man who was, apparently, drunk and glassy-eyed just to come down from his room to this session, broke in: "That's what I once thought too. It's denial. You have to face it, Patrick." How did this bomb-out get on a first-name basis with me? "You have to look in the mirror and say it out loud: *I am an alcoholic.*"

After this sterling session, everyone ate a dreadful meal of healthy things, and retired to their chambers. O'Hanrahan got up in the night to walk down the hall to the bathroom and heard shiverings and withdrawal episodes, tears and sobs . . . Beatrice, you self-righteous old cow, can I come home now and get out of this funny farm? Oh Jesus God, six more days of this hell . . .

(It didn't do you one little bit of good, did it?)

Why should it have?

(In fact, you managed to corrupt the circle of patients there, drag them further down. You remember your friend Lila, don't you?)

Oh. I hate to think of her, actually . . .

(Let Us bring this fine episode back in vivid detail:)

Lila Gantry of Springfield, Illinois, wife to a state senator, started out drinking at parties being social, ended up a big political embarrassment. This was her fifth try at drying out here at Doster's. Lila didn't appeal to O'Hanrahan at first, but as these group-therapy-circle afternoons wore on she became more tolerable. She never said anything in the sessions. Just sat there and smoked; she was a product of smoking. That cured-ham tint of her skin, the leathery lips, the voice down in the Lauren Bacall range, sophisticated, taking no crap from anyone, least of all the doctors at this joint.

"Notice you don't say much," she said, setting her cafeteria tray down beside his in the solarium.

"Just counting the days," said Patrick.

"I bet I wouldn't shock you if I said I could get my hands on some hooch."

He laughed as he put down his fork before the vegetarian casserole. "You got my attention."

"I'm on the first floor," she whispered. "The window's narrow, but it can be climbed out of. There's a gas station that sells beer and, as I've discovered, a bit of the hard stuff. Half a mile, if you like a moonlit walk, sport."

"Sounds romantic," Patrick said lightly. But under the table he felt her stockinged foot climb up his pant leg and nestle in his groin. He looked across at her and saw her parted lips, smoke rising up from this frog-mouth. "Come by my room," she breathed, "after lights-out."

(And of course you did.)

It was a comedy squeezing O'Hanrahan through the window, scraping his arm and tearing his trousers, but he got through it. Lila climbed through next and the two conspirators trotted down to the truckstop along the U.S. highway. Had a decent meal at the diner, with beer in brown bags, so guiltily enjoyed, and then the man who ran the garage displayed a selection of half-fifths with no state tax stickers, direct to his regular customers from the truckers, who smuggled it from distributors farther south in Kentucky.

Lila had finished the bottle, virtually, by the time they were creeping back to the Doster Clinic, stumbling in the snow before the massive Victorian farmhouse. With much giggling and shrieking vulgarities—which no doubt gave their escapade away to the staff—he pushed Lila through the window and, insensate to injury, squeezed himself through as well. Before he could stand upright and dust himself off, she was all over him. Her talon hands raking his back and slipping between his stomach and his belt, her smoke-breath and hot mouth attacking his face.

Oh Beatrice! It was the only time I cheated on you with someone our age. Yes, there were silly little undergraduates, but after forty it's a man's *duty* to sleep with anything under twenty-five if the opportunity presents itself! But Lila was the indiscretion that made *me* feel guilty, that showed me my own depths. Her bony hips, her lovemaking sounds, so needing and guttural and animal, her repartee—she'd forgotten my name, it was just a catalogue of what she wanted done, faster, more, this, no that, her husband never touched her, never put his hand there, he had another girl on the side, the bastard . . . then somehow it was over, and she got up and strutted to her sink. Washed her mouth out. Washed her hands.

"You better go," she said in her baritone.

"I'm going," Patrick said, hurriedly grasping for his trousers and dressing in a rush.

"Maybe you ought to give up drinking," she said, not looking at him. "It takes its toll on a man, if you know what I mean."

Yes, that's how this kind of woman would be, he thought, trying to retie his tie, dying to be gone, feeling sick. Sick at the first booze in days, sick at the greasy diner meal, and this disgusting woman.

Lila was rushing him along so he wouldn't see her throw up blood in her sink: "Aren't you gone yet?"

In two more days the clinic released him, the ordeal was over and Beatrice came to pick him up. She'd driven down and her eyes were full of hope, a young woman's eyes. Oh, it was all going to be better now. She looked up at him with those eyes, not unlike when they had first met in Korea. She kissed him warmly, put him in the car, and seemed on the verge of singing, she was so happy. She sped down the highway satisfied, happy to be with her husband again.

"I really missed you," she said, adding, "dear," with all her bravery.

(And there was your chance, Patrick. The amount of chances people have with other people they love is surprisingly small, take it from Us. The possibilities of chance and good timing align themselves so infrequently that if you do not seize them you will find quickly a landscape of regret and impossibility. And that was where you should have mended the scars and told her you loved her, Patrick, and that you missed her too.)

But I turned away, remembered Patrick, to the indistinguishable winter fields rolling by, dead under the absent sky.

Lucy went down to meet the late-afternoon shipment of returning pilgrims from Athos. She stood at the dockside and watched the bearded monks walk off the four P.M. boat, the elderly priests helped off the ferry by the young men with many profusions of blessings in return for this small charity. A few tourists, looking worn and exhausted with 10th-Century living, aimed themselves with animal singularity toward the portside restaurants.

No Dr. O'Hanrahan. And the Poseidon Hotel had no message from O'Hanrahan as well. O'Hanrahan was now two days late for his telephone call, and Lucy had expected him back in person by now as well.

Lucy took her paperback, which she had abandoned and now wished to revive, under a shady tree until the sun got so low and mild that she began to prefer the waning light. Lucy then took a stroll on the pebbly coast, then once or twice around town, a groove she'd worn into the ground. She then went back to the room, having extinguished ninety languorous minutes since her last visit to the suite. Postcards, she informed herself: I should write another round of insincere postcards to lots of people who will never send me one.

Lucy flopped down on the bed and again removed the bookmark from *So Hot the Sun.*

In the final pages, true love won out. Lucy looked at the torn, trashy cover depicting an American redhead in modern dress and a veil, being embraced from behind by a shirtless sheikh, saber unsubtly prominent. She decided that this seminal work of literature was better on a second read; the complexities revealed themselves . . .

She heard a muffled sound of a door closing in the next suite.

Good! Stavros was back for his afternoon primp before his assault on the disco scene. But was that . . . was that girlish laughter Lucy heard as well?

Lucy went to the adjoining wall.

She pressed her ear to the plaster.

Well, she lectured herself, what if he *is* in there with another woman? You didn't want to marry him, after all. Though I could turn all this into a festival of self-doubt and self-persecution, I won't. I mean, I have this in perspective. It was only sex and that's hardly the biggest deal in the world.

(You seem to have changed your mind since the other day.)

Well, sex with Stavros isn't the biggest deal in the world. Lucy decided she would fix herself up and go to the disco as well and maybe meet someone new, scope out the guys with Tracy, have a few drinks. It's not really like me, she thought, as she applied lipstick before the mirror, making a clown-face to paint her lips.

(No, not like you at all.)

Night was beginning, in the tall trees, appearing under the bushes and shrubs, accompanied by noises of summer insects, frenetic, hissing and clicking, telling O'Hanrahan he was intruding.

O'Hanrahan had passed through the phases of hunger and was now merely sore inside. He had happened upon a *kathisma*, a lone hermitage and an abandoned well, but there was no device for him to bring up any water. He dropped a pebble down into it to torture himself with the sound of the splash. He then saw a long vine and then considered his shoe. Sitting on a tumbled-down stone wall he tied the green vine to the laces and tied the laces to the vine over and over—this was not going to end in the farce of his losing his shoe. He lowered this vessel and in a panic brought up some water, fearful the vine would break. The water was metallic and no delight, being borne by his rancid shoe, but this was survival. In fact, having drunk his fill he was inordinately pleased with his ingenuity.

The worst, he comforted himself, was over and the sea had been spotted again through a mountain pass. In the meantime, he would have his pick of any of the abandoned hermitages in this once-populous northern extreme of the holy preserve. O'Hanrahan found a shelter in the last light of the day; a simple stone room, a ledge for a candle, a worn place of ground for sleeping and at one point, before it had rotted, a wooden door. There was a primitive painting of St. John the Evangelist, and on the other wall Jesus and Mary, who would watch over him tonight.

That's right, he remembered, Holy Mt. Athos is John's fault.

St. John was steering the boat which found the storm and shipwrecked himself and the Virgin Mary on this peninsula. That's when the Old Girl fell in love with Athos and said something like "O beauteous Athos, how I admire thee—you shall be My garden alone, consecrated to My adoration and worship, forbidden to all women except My Resplendent Self, and those who pray and toil here I shall intercede for with the Son and the Father . . ." Knowing that prima donna, I bet she said just that, O'Hanrahan imagined, lying down upon the dusty floor.

Always hated St. John, thought O'Hanrahan sourly.

All that Greek crap. All the troublemaking passages. All that junk John has Jesus say about his Sonship. Jesus is the Messiah-deliverer and Christ-Anointed One in the other gospels; in *John* he's God's very own little boy, spouting theology about his trinitarian personhood. Rubbish like *the Son can do nothing of his own accord, but only what he sees his Father doing; for whatever he does, that the Son does likewise . . . The Father judges no one but has given all judgment to the Son, that all may honor the Son, even as they honor the Father. He who does not honor the Son does not honor the Father*, blah blah blah—this in the mouth of a man who told simple parables to the poor! Jesus never said anything like that!

(Sure of that, are you?)

I would have made a great Anti-Logoite. Dionysius, disciple of Origen, Bishop of Alexandria, who proved in 259, for pete's sake, that

Revelations ought to be thrown out of the canon. Paul of Samosata thought the *Gospel of John* heretical in declaring the Father and Son identical. As early as the late 100s, many fathers of the Church ignored *John,* and Justin Martyr was known to revere only the other three— heck, these guys knew people who knew the *real* John and they didn't want the *Gospel of John* in the Bible! It was Irenaeus, obsessed with having four gospels and a perfect number, who got his way and put *John* and all that Greek gobbledygook in the New Testament.

(How about this one? *If the Son makes you free, then you will be free indeed.*)

Oh, I get it. We've endured torments of Fathers and memories of my wife, the Virgin Martyr, and now it's time for the Son. Well, I'm stubborn on this. Rudolph and I never got on, never had a relationship. It is a dark thought: but it is a strange solace, since he is dead, that he despised me. Imagine the loss of an only son who adored you!

(But he didn't despise you.)

Could have fooled me. Yeah, even now I wonder how did Rudy get so fragile? In the house with all my noise and racket? Always so sickly and wounded as a child. He was smothered by his mother. Beatrice raised him to agree with her on all my faults. If I corrected Rudy, she defended him. If I suggested he get out and play with the other children in the neighborhood, she argued how unfit the other boys were for her son. I was always cast as the malcontent who picked on Rudy, who set standards he could not live up to. God knows I had no standards for him—

(That's not what you spent his adolescence saying, is it? You compared his own report cards to your own. He was going to be twice as smart as you or he was a failure.)

I never put it like that! A little fatherly pressure here and there—

(You took quite a patriotic line with him concerning Vietnam.)

No, I merely said he would have trouble getting a job one day if he didn't go if he got drafted. That no one wanted to hire a draft dodger. I'd been to Korea after all—

(And hated every minute of it, according to you the other day.)

Well, if I didn't actively say he shouldn't go it wasn't because I didn't care for him, it was because he was going to Princeton and that ended the speculation. He was a freshman in 1972 and the draft was winding down. Surely he knew I didn't want him to go to war—

(You quoted Caesar, Martial, Xenophon, Gibbon, and spiced it up with Herodotus and Aristotle, in a series of arguments persuading him of what a country could ask of its young men.)

Okay, I was an ass! But I would have said none of it if I thought he might actually have to go over there . . . Oh, God, how I must have looked to him though, what an old man I must have seemed, how loveless and arcane and goddam pretentious on top of all that. But look, he never tried to accommodate me either, did he? He never cared a damn for any of my pursuits. I sent him to college, put bread on his table, paid for his hippie phase—never once did he feign interest in my life!

(Yes, just like you didn't show interest in your father's unloading crates at the stockyards.)

It's hot and airless in this shack . . . I need some more water, I need cool air, I need food, I need a drink—I'll trade everything else for a drink. I am being tormented by devils again!

(O'Hanrahan in the Wilderness. Not forty years, but forty hours will do.)

A merciful God would let me have a drink about now, manna from the skies!

(You argued with Rudy about alcohol as well, didn't you?)

With Mrs. Temperance Union at the dinner table each night, what could you expect? I couldn't have a glass of champagne at a wedding without a lecture.

(Because in your whole life you never stopped at merely a glass of champagne. Taking after those family weddings you hated.)

Honor thy father and thy mother—remember that one? He had no right to speak of my drinking to my face. What kind of son calls his father an alcoholic?

(One with an alcoholic for a father.)

I did not destroy my family! We had plenty of money. Except for the Christmas debacle, I never missed birthdays, never pulled all the hard-core alcoholic antics. But in those days when they were trying to force me out of the department, I needed the drink to get me through it and maybe if I'd had some sympathy, some support, from my family I wouldn't have needed it! Besides, Rudy and I fought over marijuana. I caught him smoking marijuana in the garage, with that other long-haired creep friend of his . . . forget his name.

(Hypocrite! And you haven't smoked hashish in your Middle Eastern travels? Didn't turn up some narcotic-strength absinthe with the fathers at Montserrat in Spain? Your relations would have changed had you sat down and joined him! It was another excuse for you to play the authoritarian, ever-critical father, the one role you were least suited to. Speaking of drugs, what about the bottle of Percodan you're making your way through? And you forgot to get the prescription refilled in Athens, didn't you?)

O'Hanrahan panicked now that this shortage occurred to him: my precious Percodan! I've got only a pill or two left. Enough if my side acts up again. No sense worrying about it, or I will bring on the pain and I'll be even more miserable than I am now . . .

(And you had the nerve to lecture Rudy about drugs.)

Oh, poor Rudy. Look, no matter how bad I was to him, I am still

more to be pitied for having to endure his death, everything all unre-
solved. I hope he knew . . .

(Knew what?)

Knew how much I loved him.

(You never told him.)

How often I thought of him when I was at work, when he had
moved to Princeton to study, how I missed him—

(He never knew.)

If only . . . if only he'd had the slightest interest in my life. I'd regale
all those who'd hear with salacious faculty gossip, with bizarre lives of
the saints, with all the puerile things that amuse me to my taste, the
stuff I bombard Lucy with . . . He just didn't care. He'd stare at me
from his half-touched plate of food—and Beatrice never could cook
worth a damn—moping, brooding, can I be excused now? I embarrassed him, it seemed. It was an ordeal to sit with me. If I said something funny he would swallow his laughter, not wanting to give me the
satisfaction of amusing him. He was deeply ashamed of me in some
way. That was his mother's doing. I was being judged by them, nightly.
They'd go to all the high masses and I would stay home refusing to
go. That's it, perhaps, he thought I was damned, irretrievably lost.

(Most sons find their fathers irretrievably lost.)

He was a fag too.

(So?)

O'Hanrahan batting a thousand there! O'Hanrahan the loser once
again! Screwed up being a Jesuit, being a head of a department, being
a published scholar—you name it, befouled by Patrick Virgil O'Hanrahan's magic touch. Figures if he had a kid he'd turn out homo.

(Your heart is so far from charity, Patrick.)

You see, his mother effeminized him. Look, the concept of being a
queer doesn't bother me, not me the Hellenophile, the scholar of the
ancient Mediterranean world. Hell, half the priests and monks and
scholars I deal with are to some extent women-haters, some are out-
and-out screaming. Maybe I even had an unverbalized hankering back
a million years ago when I pledged to be a Jesuit novice, a life among
men, mentors and students, a thinly veiled rehash of the lover and his
beloved from ancient times. Christ never said a thing against homosexuality because there wasn't even a goddam *word* for homosexuality in
Christ's time. And what a word: Greek prefix and Latin root—what
moron thought that was proper? Look, I've given the lecture on tolerance to my classes a thousand times. It was natural in ancient times
that men should love men, David and Jonathan, the *Song of Solomon* is
flaming, the very idea of Christian male closeness, like Jesus and John
whom Jesus loved, probably *helped* spread Christianity through the
ancient world.

(Nice lecture. Rudy would have enjoyed it.)

But see? I'm no Bible-thumping, fag-bashing born-again. I'm educated, I'm rational, I'm . . . but I'm still sorry my son was queer. It
was one more separation between us, something we couldn't have in
common. I bet he did it to spite me!

(There's an intelligent thought.)

You know, Beatrice couldn't have survived if her little Rudy, her
ally, her witness to her martyrdom—forgive the etymological redun-
dancy—fell under the spell of another woman. So she made sure when
he was growing up that no other woman ever could get a foot in the
door.

(You can't *make* anyone gay, Patrick.)

And all his adolescent piety that went with it. Fifteen years old, other
kids were getting laid and playing sports—my boy was weeping before
tacky plastic crucifix chapels with Beatrice and the old ladies who doted
on him, shaped him, molded him into the little fruitcake he became.
He knew all the old ladies and their names and problems . . .

(With all the other human varieties, there's room for gay people in
the Church too. Always has been, always will be.)

How wrong and misguided all my attempts to communicate to Rudy
were, how I messed it up time and time again. Believe me, Rudy, I
didn't really hate your gayness or your liberal politics or your hippie
phase or your changing majors three times or taking your mother's
side, I didn't hate anything about you . . . it's just my way! It's my
manner to be argumentative and blustering. Why was I cursed with
the very type of son who would take offense at it, who would hate me
for it?

(Why didn't you look up Stephen?)

Stephen. That guy Rudy lived with his sophomore year, in that ratty
hippie house I disapproved of. The pale guy with the black beard,
Jewish maybe. Jewish named Stephen? Yeah, I guess it happens. Real
intellectual type, could spew Marx at you at ten paces in his belligerent,
self-satisfied way. I guess they *did it* together. I sicken to think of my
son putting . . . ehh, why pursue these thoughts? Maybe they were
happy.

I had to attend a conference at Princeton and since Rudy didn't
have a phone I couldn't warn him that I was dropping in. Perhaps I
wouldn't have warned him anyway. He and Stephen shared this upper
room of this near-condemned Edwardian house off campus, with
twenty-some long-haired, bead-wearing, unshaven, Afroed, psychedelic would-be revolutionaries living in the house as well. But he took
me up to his room and I remember the piles of books—that was good,
he read, he read a lot. I should have told him, right then and there,
how proud I was he was a reader, a studier. Even if it was some bullshit
like political science. Anyway, in pranced Stephen and said rather
argumentatively that it was his room too, and, what? I'm stupid?

One double mattress covered in Indian printed sheets in the middle of the room. So surprise, surprise. Rudy nervously walked downstairs and . . .

(You remember what he said?)

He said, "I don't care if you hate me, Dad. There's nothing you can do about it, I'm homosexual and that's all there is to it. But don't tell Mom, okay?"

My son said he didn't care if I hated him! I was such a dead loss, such a write-off, it didn't matter!

(But what did you do?)

I indulgently, deliciously, luxuriantly, playing out every baroque detail with relish and delectation, told my wife the truth and rubbed her pious, pinched old-woman's face in it. Take that! Happy now? So much for grandchildren, Beatrice O'Hanrahan!

(And what happened?)

Oh, the usual. A talk with the father—that weak-chinned, sallow Polish priest who had the facial coloring of a pirogi. Much lamentation, many prayers to Mary. And there was blame. I blamed Beatrice, she blamed me. And Rudy called to curse at me on the phone, which I deserved, and I suppose I said something backward and philistine—

(As a faggot, he was no son of yours.)

How kind of the day to bring it all back so clearly. My heart is ashes. Yet I dwell on it, pick it like a wound: I can't see my boy . . . I can't quite visualize him kissing that kid with that unruly beard . . .

(Stephen was at the funeral.)

Yes, crying his eyes out. I should have . . .

(Should have what?)

I should have gone over and consoled him, but . . .

(You glared at him instead, like he had been indecent to show up.)

But I'm not like that, damn it! I'm not that bad a person! I can be fun, I can be charitable, I can be warm and use my vast collection of tales to comfort and bring wisdom to people's troubles!

(Except when you dealt with the people you loved.)

I wonder if . . .

(You wonder if you might one day yet talk to Stephen?)

Yes, it's almost twenty years since Rudy's accident and Stephen's bound to have gotten over it, done something else in life. He might . . . I might sit down with him and say, Look, what was Rudy like? What was my son like? Tell me about him laughing. Tell me what he would be doing now, had he lived. Tell me if he . . . no, best not to ask if he loved his foolish, prodigal father. I suspect those two held each other tight enough to shut me and my generation out, to exile us as far as possible. All right, go ahead and hate me too, I'd say to him—I'm an old man, I'll be dead soon—but tell me how he was. Tell me Rudy was happy for a while and knew love during his unforgivably short life.

But of course, no father alive would do such a thing.

It's never done. Easier the loneliness than that kind of investigation! Would Stephen even consent to see me?

(He died last year of AIDS, shunned by his parents and, naturally, his church. At the age of thirty-eight.)

This Stephen, this stranger, wherever he is, holds what is left of my son in his heart, in his memory. This, somehow, gives me hope. Rudy is not entirely gone from this world . . .

(Patrick, poor Patrick.)

The half-English, half-Greek argument was highlighted by:

"After what the Germans did in Greece, I'm surprised you want to suck up to them so much."

"Eh! The Americans are worse, much worse! Greece is ruined by America today. I am a communist."

"The last one in Europe!"

Stavros strutted out as Lucy pretended to return to a page of *So Hot the Sun*. The door closed and Lucy fell back on the bed and rubbed her eyes.

Dumb move, girl. You couldn't just mind your own business, go down to the disco, flirt with the Handsome Stranger, talk to Tracy. No. No, that had prescience and self-discretion. You, Lucy, had to drink two glasses of wine, barge over to his room, knock till Stavros answered in a cheap hotel towel, some girl on the bed, so you could have a scene.

Her sensations from the fling were still warm and the fact that it had fizzled so quickly was . . . relieving in a way. Now the memory could be processed and shaped and packaged for her own endless consumption, and for replaying to Judy, of course. Ha ha, Judy! Guess what? And after a photo session yesterday afternoon, Lucy and Stavros leaning against each other, she would even have proof! She would blow up a photo poster-size and put it on the refrigerator. She wondered if Judy and Vito were actually going steady by now or if that had crumbled, or better yet, had never been anything but Judy's imagination.

(If we have not *karitas* we have nothing, Lucy.)

Lucy continued to think: who's to say my romantic life is over? Let's go find Tracy and Derek at the Argonaut Klub. After a second bout of beautifying and application of scent, Lucy strolled down to the disco wearing her Florentine sundress, carrying her large red hat in her hand. Maybe The Handsome Stranger would be there.

He was. It took a moment but he recognized her, smiled warmly, and crossed the club to join her at the bar. Georgios's turntable was still mired in the '80s with "Girls Just Want to Have Fun."

"I thought you maybe had left Ouranopolis," he said, beholding her with his steady, soulful eyes.

"No. I thought I'd be gone too. But Dr. O'Hanrahan, the professor I mentioned, he has yet to come back from Athos."

"My brother, I hope, is back tonight because we must leave for Athens tomorrow."

"Oh," she said disappointed, seeing endless dull nights in Ourano-polis stretch before her, even glimpsing a necessary rapprochement with Stavros.

"We are in the same hotel, no? The Poseidon?"

Lucy: "Why, yes, why haven't I noticed you?"

"I sleep very late," he admitted, laughing.

Same hotel, last night in town. Luce, old girl, you might be two for two if you play your cards right. And lookee there, who just walked in: Stavros. He seemed ready to come talk to Lucy but saw her companion, stiffened, and went to a table by himself.

"I have," he added, his back to Stavros, "however, seen your friend."

"Stavros? He just drove us here, accompanying the professor. I barely know him really." The Stranger seemed to half-believe that, but he seemed warmer as a result the next second.

"Do you want a drink?" she offered, trying to bury Stavros as a conversation topic.

"No thank you."

She'd have liked one, but decided if he wasn't she wouldn't. He offered her a cigarette.

"Thank you," she said, readdicted now thanks to O'Hanrahan. "I'm sorry, this is awkward, but I don't . . . I don't know your name yet."

He laughed, shaking his head, mocking himself. "How foolish. My name is Abdul. Abdul el-Hassami."

"Lucy Dantan," she returned. "Abdul is an odd name for a Greek."

"Excuse me, I am not a Greek. I am Arab."

"But . . ."

"I am from Syria."

How exotic! Lucy was more delighted by the minute. Lucy blew out a long, dismissive plume of smoke as if it had the taste of Stavros. "But why would you . . . I mean, Mt. Athos . . ."

"You think all Arabs are Moslems? Ten percent of Syria is Christian."

"The Antiochene Church, of course! How extraordinary. Is your brother with the Jacobite Church? What language is the liturgy?"

He laughed uneasily. "It is, naturally, in Aramaic."

"My God," she giggled. "I have never in my life met anyone who could actually understand Aramaic, the language of Jesus. You must speak it for me, a line or two . . ."

He stood. "No, you embarrass me . . . I don't speak it. I confess I am not religious like Hossein, my brother. You should ask him. In fact, yes, it is 8:30, time for me to meet him at the dock."

"May I come along?" she asked, noting that Stavros was seething in the corner.

"Yes," he said politely.

Perhaps, Lucy thought, Abdul did not want her along. But it was enough to exit the bar with him and irritate Stavros; once Abdul and his brother bid her good night she could make up any lie she pleased to tell Stavros about what happened between them. As the ferry sputtered into the harbor, Lucy stood back and let the two brothers reunite under the streetlight by the pier. Abdul walked forward and kissed a shorter, darker man on the cheek and began talking quickly.

Funny, thought Lucy, they don't look a thing like brothers.

A quick introduction was made and they walked back to the Poseidon and the brothers chatted in Arabic rather joylessly. No laughing or joking, it seemed to Lucy. Abdul's brother Hossein was carrying a knapsack as well as an envelope about which he seemed to be explaining to Abdul. At the hotel desk Abdul took the envelope and, presumably, because neither spoke Greek and Hossein spoke no English, Abdul explained in English to the proprietor:

"This envelope is for a woman in Room 13, please."

Lucy's pulse quickened. "Wait. I'm in Room 13."

Abdul turned to look at her oddly, and then handed the envelope to her. It was a white letter-length envelope with a return address of Karyes, the Athonite capital, on the back.

Hossein was saying something to Abdul, and Abdul translated for Lucy. "An old man gave him this and said it was very urgent."

Lucy went over to the light-blue vinyl 1950s lounge chairs in the lobby. Hossein got his key and went up the stairs and Abdul lingered to see if it was bad news.

> Lucy,
> I seem to be in big trouble. The police are after me and our entire mission is doomed unless I can get out of Greece. I have left Athos by fishing boat. Meet me in Athens tomorrow night, Hercules Hotel near the Plaka.

And "Patrick O'Hanrahan" was scrawled across the bottom. It was his handwriting, thought Lucy, not that she'd seen very much of it. How odd that there was not a mention of Stavros.

"I hope all is well," said Abdul.

"No, it doesn't look like it," she said. "There seems to be some trouble over there. And it looks like I have to go to Athens tomorrow."

Abdul gave a sympathetic smile. "Perhaps, you could come with us. We leave at nine tomorrow. I will be happy to give you every assistance."

"How kind," she said blankly.

JULY 21ST

Stavros said he would drive Lucy back to Athens, and she told him that she had had an offer from the Hassami brothers. Stavros reacted badly, launching into a stream of anti-Turkish invective that, Lucy imagined, Stavros thought applied to all people of the Middle East. On that note, she determined she would ride with the brothers after all, and snippily said good-bye to Stavros, holding out her hand for him to shake. In this final moment she could have abandoned this pretense and kissed him good-bye properly but the half-understood counterthreats between them had made this difficult.

The Hassami brothers were polite hosts and Abdul drove well.

She was quiet and sullen on the six-hour ride down. The trip slowed considerably as the urban sprawl and soot of Athens approached. Lucy was sufficiently jaded and despondent enough that the new views of the Akropolis and passing the ruins of the Temple of Zeus near the downtown park barely interested her.

The Hercules Hotel was not in the Plaka proper but in the modern city leading up to it. Lucy recognized some familiar landmarks around Constitution Square and she briefly revived, imagining that Dr. O'Hanrahan and she might go out that night, with O'Hanrahan telling his undoubtedly exciting story. Abdul and Hossein said the Hercules was too expensive and went elsewhere.

As she lay in her room, contemplating what she should do with her evening, the phone rang. She eagerly scooped it up and discovered it was Abdul: did she want to go to dinner in the Plaka? She decided she shouldn't, figuring O'Hanrahan would make contact soon. However, at 10:30 P.M. she was starved and bored and determined to go out for a quick bite.

"A message for you," said the hotelier when she returned twenty minutes later.

Lucy desperately stared at the simple phone message-slip, wanting it to reveal more. Patrick O'Hanrahan called, the note said in a strained Roman alphabet, an occasional Greek letter slipping in, and after that was the unrevealing message that "someone would be in touch again."

"That's all?" Lucy asked the deskman, who shrugged yes it was.

She wished she hadn't declined Abdul's invitation to the Plaka. It was the brothers' last night in Greece and tomorrow they flew back to Damascus. Abdul even seemed eager for her company, flirtatious for him. Maybe she should go attempt to find him, make a night of it.

Then the phone rang.

"Halloo?" said a heavily accented female voice on the other end of the line, as Lucy's heart beat faster. "I am calling for a friend . . ."

"Who is this?"

"My name is not important. Patrick O'Hanrahan," she said, mispronouncing his name completely, "is in hiding here and . . . I cannot talk . . ."

"*Wait*. What is going on here?"

"I will meet you tomorrow at the Piraeus metro station. Look for a woman in a black dress, dark hair, I will be carrying a white handbag. Tomorrow, 11:30 A.M."

And then she hung up.

Then Lucy again picked up the phone. If O'Hanrahan's in trouble, he would call Eleni Matsoukis, she was sure. Lucy found the phone directory and looked up the number. She dialed the first four digits. Then hung up. No, she convinced herself. If he was in danger he wouldn't risk scandalizing the Matsoukises.

And what if Stavros picked up the phone?

Lucy lay back on the bed and felt her stomach tighten. Something was very much wrong.

ΠΕΙΡΑΙΑΣ
JULY 22ND

Lucy assembled her bag, packed her souvenirs, and arranged her makeup kit and clothes for what could be the last time. It seemed that, at last, O'Hanrahan's luck had finally played out. Would he—or worse, he and she both, end up in the hands of the police? In the middle of her sleepless night she figured that the incorrigible Dr. O'Hanrahan had been caught stealing a scroll, or something like that—some last senescent gesture of bravura. And now he would have to answer to the Greek people and the Minister of Antiquities. And she would get on a plane soon enough and maybe, grimly, she would be in Chicago in forty-eight hours. She had prepared herself for the worst.

Lucy paid the bill with the VISA card and then handed in the key at the front desk. She saw Hossein and Abdul talking, their bags beside them. They had come to say good-bye to her.

"Well, Abdul," she said, handing him a slip with her Chicago address on it, putting out her hand to shake, "it has been a pleasure. And if you're ever in Chicago, do call."

"Likewise, I hope to see you one day in Damascus."

Hossein smiled broadly and Lucy felt uneasy.

"Have you got a cab to the airport?" she asked.

"No, you know how difficult getting a taxi in Athens is," he said glumly. "Hossein and I are taking the bus to Piraeus where there are many taxis and take a taxi from there."

She smiled. "I am going to Piraeus myself, on the subway."

Abdul was delighted. "There is an underground train to Piraeus?"

She explained and soon they all picked up their bags and began the trek five blocks, through the market and the tourists and the endless array of amphorae and fake red-and-black clay plates to the busy Monastiraki Station.

As they put their metro tickets in the automatic turnstiles, Lucy asked Abdul, "Could you ask your brother one more time for me under what circumstances he saw Dr. O'Hanrahan?" Abdul conferred with Hossein in Arabic. Abdul translated in pieces:

"Hossein says the old man was very unhappy and upset . . . They met at a monastery, he says . . . There had been some trouble with the police and . . . He had to escape Mt. Athos right away, and Greece as well."

Lucy nodded, convinced the professor had tried to steal a scroll. "Does Hossein," she asked, "have any idea where Dr. O'Hanrahan wishes to escape to?"

Hossein and Abdul talked some more, as Lucy heard the south-bound metro approaching.

"Hossein says very, very far away," Abdul related. "The professor said he would, however, have to go to an Islamic library."

"I see," she said, as the train slowed before the platform. "We both figured we might end up in Egypt."

Hossein smiled confidently, adding a detail. Abdul translated: "Yes, he said he could hardly wait to get on the airplane, yes?" Then he laughed as the train stopped.

Uh-oh, thought Lucy.

She looked over at Abdul, patiently returning her stare, handsomely groomed to perfection, and Hossein . . . who, she was now certain, was no relation to him, leering at some woman across the platform.

Lucy: "Oh, here's the train and I just forgot that—um, I mean, I think I forgot something at the hotel and I'd better run back and get it."

"We are happy to wait for you," he said smiling. "Is it important?"

Calm down, she told herself.

The train screeched to a halt and out poured a heavily cologned and perfumed pack of Athenian commuters. Abdul was busy putting her heavy bag inside the train, along with his own. Unfailingly polite, she thought, as she stepped inside and the doors closed behind her.

"No air-conditioning, no?" Abdul remarked, running a finger between his neck and his collar.

He couldn't name me one word in Aramaic, she remembered. Well, how many American Catholics could spout Latin anymore? She began weaving the facts through the pattern of coincidences. They go to meet the brother, he has the envelope, the announced trip to Athens, which conveniently these brothers had to make . . . Do you suppose Hossein has done something horrible to Dr. O'Hanrahan over on Athos? The note could be a forgery, the phone message from O'Hanrahan a fake, since I was out, and this woman I'm supposed to meet— God knows who she is.

Piraeus Station.

The train stopped and she stepped off and noticed her bloodless, clammy hand was shaking as she moved her own luggage.

"Again, nice to meet you. Bye-bye," she said hopelessly.

"Farewell," said Abdul, bowing slightly. He reached to kiss her hand and a shiver of revulsion ran through her.

They're actually letting me go, thought Lucy. Or else they're very confident of this woman I'm about to meet. She watched the brothers leave the station and hail a cab to the airport, ten miles outside of Piraeus. Lucy stood in the station amid the late-morning ebb and flow of tourists, commuters, and bored Athenian teenagers just hanging out. She saw booths for tickets, for passes, for reservations . . . and there in several languages was a stall for lost-and-found. And there was a woman, shorter than she'd imagined but quite beautiful, Arab-looking as well, with a white handbag, wearing a raincoat and sunglasses on this sunny day.

"You have a message," said Lucy guardedly, "from Dr. O'Hanrahan?"

The woman eyed her seriously, attempting to look sympathetic. "He is in great trouble."

Yep, figured Lucy. He's probably kidnapped by these Syrians . . . but then what would they want with me? The woman handed her a Greek newspaper folded to a photo. Today's paper. "You see this?" said the woman, pointing to the photo, which showed an ikon defaced with paint. "Your friend is wanted by the police for this."

"But," Lucy mocked, "he would never—"

"But he is wanted for this crime nonetheless. He has contacted us, his friends."

"Friends," Lucy repeated.

"We are old friends of Patrick O'Hanrahan."

No, thought Lucy, if he were to contact anyone it would be the Matsoukises, whom I was too damn pigheadedly stupid to call last night, scared of Stavros.

The woman reached into her raincoat. "I have this for you. We have arranged a flight out on a special chartered flight, which will avoid the customs and police, yes? He has bought a ticket for you both."

Lucy took the envelope and opened the flap, drawing out two second-class tickets on Iraqi Air to Amman, Jordan. Lucy felt her head grow light, she was breathing so shallowly. One, O'Hanrahan would never fly, even if it meant arrest, capture, imprisonment . . . or had he just been playing that up for her benefit? Two, the man wouldn't fly second-class . . . or was there no choice? Maybe the police knew to check the Matsoukis house and he had had to avail himself of these acquaintances. "The flight is in forty minutes," Lucy noticed.

"Yes, we must hurry."

Should she go with the woman? If she didn't, she'd never find out what had happened to O'Hanrahan. Perhaps when she saw him at the airport, all would be explained. And if he didn't show, she'd make a run for it, safely in front of video cameras and security officers.

"I have a car," said the woman.

"I prefer to take my own taxi," said Lucy.

"Whatever you wish," she said coolly.

Lucy hopped in a taxi and headed to the main terminal of the Athens International Airport. Well, if it's me they want, thought Lucy, they have missed a number of opportunities to abduct me.

And look, what a coincidence. At the Athens International Airport terminal, in the Iraqi Air check-in line, who should be there but Abdul and Hossein.

"Ah, we meet again," said Abdul, feigning surprise. "What brings you here?"

Lucy noticed, near the terminal entrance, the Arab woman had reappeared. "Oh, just these tickets," said Lucy icily. "Where is Dr. O'Hanrahan?"

"I wouldn't know."

"I suspect you do know, Abdul or whoever you are—"

At that moment, three policemen who had been quickly marching across the lobby, submachine guns at their belt, turned briskly toward the check-in line and tapped her firmly on the shoulder: "Meez Lucille Dantan?" one policeman demanded.

"Yes." Lucy turned to see the Arab woman hurriedly make her way to the exit.

An officer: "You are wanted by the police. Please to follow."

Abdul and Hossein stared at the floor, frozen in place.

Lucy was sure *she* was not who they wanted, but took a step forward. "What about my bag?"

"Leave it. INTERPOL wants you," said the man firmly. "Coom with me immediately."

Then, as she turned to Abdul and Hossein, she saw them stepping over the cordon for the check-in line and walking briskly toward the exit. Hold it . . . Now there were several men, some in uniforms, some in suits converging on the two Arab men . . .

Now everyone was running. Abdul was tackled halfway to the door. A security officer ran over and in the grappling Abdul was hit by the butt of the security man's rifle full across the face. Lucy was being dragged away by the policeman but kept turning to observe. Hossein had made it to the door and one of the policeman had pulled his gun. Screams. Panic. People dove to the floor, some ran, others scooped up their children. Lucy was open-mouthed, not sure where she should be, when the policeman pulled on her roughly: "I said, coom with me," he barked in bad English.

She was, in no time, led to a customs office with several policemen standing around looking at video monitors of the terminal. They eyed her dourly.

"Uh look," Lucy tried to explain as she was being shuttled down a hallway, "I'm not with those guys . . ."

And then horrible thoughts occurred to her: they were going to blow up the plane and they planted a bomb in my suitcase. I'm like those poor English women who marry Arabs and find they're walking time bombs for some Palestinian group. So this is how the adventure ends! In a Greek jail somewhere, shunned by my own embassy, front page of the tabloids—and won't Mom and Dad just love that.

Oh where, where, where is Dr. O'Hanrahan!

Lucy and her escort entered through some double doors to an older part of the airport, then climbed some steps to the second-floor glass-enclosed, unair-conditioned offices with desks piled with papers, wanted posters, customs documents, a Kafkaesque gathering of functionaries and customs rule–violators sitting sheepishly before bureaucrats explaining their crimes. She was told to sit in one cubicle.

A tall, middle-aged man with gray at the temples of his close-cropped hair appeared in the doorway. He wore an olive-drab Army uniform and held a Greek newspaper and a large manila file folder under his arm. It took a moment for Lucy to comprehend that it was an American uniform.

"I'm Colonel Westin," he said without looking up from the file folder. "I'm with U.S. Customs, attached to the U.S. Embassy in Israel." Then he looked up. "Lucille Dantan? House at 14320 Kimbark Street, Hyde Park?"

"That's me."

The colonel asked for her Social Security number, which she recited. Colonel Westin sat down on a spindly folding chair and leaned forward, hands on his knees, one hand clutching the newspaper. "IN-

TERPOL's been looking for you for *weeks*, Miss Dantan. We were beginning to think you'd been taken hostage. Flew up from Jerusalem because of you."

"I don't understand."

He didn't understand her confusion. "Where've you been? Chicago last heard from you two weeks ago. Someone checked with your roommate—"

"Judy," she said automatically.

"Who said you were due to fly home but didn't. This had us worried because . . ." He glanced back at his data. ". . . there was also a Gabriel O'Donoghue who traveled with this O'Hanrahan character before you. And he went missing for awhile, too."

"Someone's mistaken, Colonel, sir," she protested. "Until this week, I've been faxing reports every few days back to the University of Chicago."

Colonel Westin didn't seem to hear her as he pored over the sheets of paper in his file folder. He handed her the newspaper. "Seen this?"

She looked at the paper, a different paper from the newspaper the Arab woman had shown her. Lucy scanned the Greek, looked at the photo of some Greek officials, noticed a photo at the bottom of an ikon . . . a defaced ikon. Beside a mug shot of O'Hanrahan. "My God, Dr. O'Hanrahan!"

"Your companion seems to have found himself in trouble over on Mount Athos, something about defacing priceless ikons."

"That's completely impossible," she stammered.

"Yep," he said, not looking up again, sucking in air through his clenched teeth. "We thought so too. I flew up from Jerusalem because of him."

She thought he'd come from Jerusalem because of *her*.

"I'm trying to put it all together, Miss Dantan. You're on an assignment to England, your college told me, then you're in Ireland, Italy, Greece, then you leave with these Iraqi terrorists . . ."

He trailed off as another man entered the room. He was in his thirties, very short, with a light blue suit that didn't fit him, the sleeves too long and his pants cuffs a little high. He also had very thin brown hair, which he had tried his best to arrange over his bald head, and round, thick glasses.

"Howdy. Clem Underwood," he announced, putting out a small, ring-bearing, pudgy hand for Lucy to shake. "I'm with the State Department here in Athens. Hello, Colonel. Here's where you've gone to."

"Clem," said the colonel unhappily, closing his file folder.

Underwood showed keen interest in the colonel's file folder. "Oh, is that . . . is that the material on Miss Dantan, there?"

Colonel Westin: "This is classified. Involving a procedural communi-
qué re INTERPOL and, uh, reinterfacement with U.S. Customs access—"

Underwood: "Awww, just a little peek, heh-heh-heh . . ."

Colonel Westin: "I don't recall a directive issuing clearance for State
on our INTERPOL communications, Clem—"

Underwood: "I let you see the papers on Mr. O'Hanrahan downstairs."

Colonel Westin sucked in air through clenched teeth. "I have senior-
ity, Clem. My clearance access is Code 5, you're what? A 4? You get
me the paperwork, buddy, and I'll be happy to let you have a look-
see."

"Excuse me," said Lucy, "did I understand you to say that papers
on Dr. O'Hanrahan were downstairs or that Dr. O'Hanrahan himself
was downstairs?"

Underwood smoothed his thin hair toward his widow's peak, making
sure that the merest breath of wind hadn't blown his comb-over aside.
"Yes, miss, Dr. O'Hanrahan's downstairs."

The colonel stood, annoyed. "You might have told me, Clem."

Lucy was joyous. O'Hanrahan! Numbly she was led down another
hall and to a lounge with old chairs and sofas, shabby but clean, the
final resting place for the 1930s airport office furniture. And there,
yes!—she recognized the back of a silver, balding head, which turned
and cried out her name:

"Miss Dantan, you are among the living!" cried O'Hanrahan, struggling to his feet to greet her.

They hugged and Lucy sighed with a tremble, not until then realizing how fraught and shaky she was. "Where have you been?" she
demanded. "I thought that—I mean, I heard you—"

The colonel interrupted: "So you're Patrick O'Hanrahan?" The colonel was introduced to O'Hanrahan by Mr. Underwood of the State
Department. There was a foot in height difference between Underwood and the professor.

"What just happened?" Lucy asked of the assemblage at large, as
O'Hanrahan pressed a glass of strong Greek tea into her hand to calm
her.

"Tea?" she sneered at the glass. "Got any booze?"

O'Hanrahan gently rolled his eyes at her. "Do I have any booze?"
He reached into his sportscoat pocket to his flask. Lucy thought she
glimpsed an airline ticket in his inner pocket, of all things. He dumped
the tea in a trashcan callously, and poured her some metaxa in a
Styrofoam cup.

O'Hanrahan sat down and commenced his tale: "I had to walk back
to Ouranopolis, Luce. Ten, twenty miles, it seemed like the whole damn
length of the peninsula—in that heat, with no food, no water . . ." He

could see Lucy's eyes widen in amazement and no small portion of admiration. "As the colonel told you, someone framed me for those ikon desecrations. I suspect framing me was part of a larger plan to rob and debilitate me and eventually kidnap *you*. I get back to Ouranopolis, find Stavros packing to leave, and imagine my face when I hear you've gotten a ride to Athens with a bunch of Arabs."

Lucy defensively recreated the scene. "But . . . but they had a note from you. It looked like your writing. Your signature and every-thing . . ." She reached into her carpetbag to find the note. God, what a disaster her carpetbag was: tanning oil, a little that had spilled, half-finished postcards from Ireland with Italian stamps on them she thought she had mailed. There it was.

"Pretty good forgery," mused O'Hanrahan. "The guy in Ouranop-olis had an accomplice on Athos who was following me and getting me in trouble with this ikon vandalism, and he eventually stole the contents of my satchel."

"So the photos are gone?"

O'Hanrahan eyed the government men, whom he didn't want in-formed, and Lucy knew not to ask any question of substance. "Well, Morey has a copy."

This piqued the colonel's interest. "Copy of what exactly?"

O'Hanrahan lied seamlessly, "Just my notes for my next book, that's all! Of no value to anyone but me."

Still Colonel Westin was curious. "And this book's about?"

"The shift in Fourth-Century B.C. Corinthian script in Greek."

"Still sounds sort of dull, sir," Lucy said drily, recognizing her own thesis.

O'Hanrahan handed the supposed note from Athos back to Lucy to see both bureaucrats grab the paper.

Colonel Westin: "This is clearly germane to my files, Clem—"

Underwood: "This is a matter for the Athens Embassy, Colonel. And I got my hand on it first . . ."

Lucy and O'Hanrahan exchanged glances of mutual exasperation with their saviors and flashed to each other a desire to talk privately.

"If I may continue," said O'Hanrahan. "I was worried the police wanted me, so I had Stavros ask the hotelman for the names of the guys you left with. Stavros and I made our getaway and he drove me to the consulate in Thessaloniki, where Mr. Underwood heroically intervened between me and the Greek authorities."

Colonel Westin snapped, "You're not even with the Athens office, are you? You're in the goddam consulate in Salonika, man. You must be Code 2, if that—"

Underwood: "I am *not* Code 2, Colonel. We'll make a xerox of the note for both of our files."

O'Hanrahan went on, "As I was telling Mr. Underwood here . . ."

That silenced the colonel, who became all ears. "The men who were trying to get you on a plane to Amman, Lucy, and later to Iraq, were from the Ba'ath Islamic Seminary in Baghdad and belong to something called the New Mu'tazilahs."

Underwood, arranging his hair, burst in. "An intellectual extremist group with some very shady friends and supporters."

Colonel Westin: "Terrorists and contraversion units."

O'Hanrahan: "Not themselves so much, but they probably have no philosophical problem with bringing down planes, blowing up airports, that sort of thing. The original Mu'tazilah movement began in the 700s as a reaction to Moslems who preferred concentrating on the many attributes of God, which the Mu'tazilahs took as degraded Christian influence. Wasil ibn-Ataah was the founder and, like many great thinkers, he broke off from the school of Hasan al-Basri. You know, there's a story about al-Basri, that when he came to—"

The colonel, making notes on his file folder, cleared his throat. "Could we fast-forward this a bit, Mr. O'Hanrahan?"

"Yes, of course. They are fiercely anti-Christian purists, who feel—well, some do—that specific actions are not punished, and that the intent of one's heart to good or evil is all that matters to Allah, hence making terrorism an attractive option."

A Greek policeman appeared at the door to this little room and said something that warranted Underwood's attention.

"What is it?" asked the colonel.

"Oh, just some papers I have to sign to get our learned friend off the old hook here," said Underwood, trying to slap O'Hanrahan on the shoulder.

"I would appreciate, Clem, to be fully participated in this procedure."

Underwood and the colonel went to talk to the Greek authorities, with the colonel saying sternly, "You two stay here."

Lucy and O'Hanrahan waited a secure moment.

O'Hanrahan spoke quickly under his breath: "Have you told them about the Matthias scroll?"

"No."

"Good. Don't. I don't want these embassy hacks to interfere. Those Arab guys you went off with from Ouranopolis—"

"But they told me—"

"Let me finish. The plan, I think, was to steal the scroll—which they thought I was carrying—and frame me for the ikon desecrations. When they saw I didn't have it, they opted for what must have been the backup plan. Those guys were kidnapping you to hold for ransom."

"Ransom?"

"Yes, and the *Gospel of Matthias* was what they were gonna ask for in return."

Lucy sipped the metaxa. "I suppose you'd let them keep me, if it were me or the scroll."

"Baghdad's nice this time of year." O'Hanrahan hushed as he noticed a Greek bureaucrat and Underwood milling outside the door, talking seriously and looking through a series of papers, the colonel between them furtively looking over their shoulders. A Greek police officer was trying to be understood in broken English.

"Why would a Moslem group want a Christian gospel?" Lucy whispered as O'Hanrahan refilled her glass.

O'Hanrahan arched an eyebrow. "A First-Century account concerning the forerunner of Mohammed? An accurate record from the time of the Prophet Jesus, the *Isa Mesih*, fifth great prophet of Islam?"

Lucy nodded, beginning to understand.

"It is the Moslem contention," said O'Hanrahan, pouring himself some of the metaxa, "that Jesus never died on the cross, never rose from the dead and all that. The New Mu'tazilahs, I suspect, have no doubt this spectacular ecclesiastic find will bear out what the Quran says, but they don't trust the Christian world not to tamper with such a document—"

"What if the scroll really does?"

"Does what?"

"What if the *Gospel of Matthias* proves Mohammed right? What if at the end of Matthias's gospel he decides that Jesus was merely a man and not the Son of God?"

"We don't exactly have the last chapter anyway, do we?"

Colonel Westin and Mr. Underwood reentered the room, and the colonel cleared his throat for attention. "Well now. It seems we've explained to INTERPOL what an innocent you are, Miss Dantan. And our Arab friends are in custody. Illegal passports, terrorist ties, you name it, they're gonna pay, you betcha."

Lucy asked, "Will it be possible to go soon?"

"Soon?" asked the colonel.

O'Hanrahan could tell Lucy was acting. "Yes," she said, "I'm a bit shaken up and would like to go back to the hotel. I feel faint now and then."

"Yes," said Colonel Westin slowly, unhappily, "I'll see about it. It won't be more than another hour, I'm sure, though we will need to know where you're going to be staying. And you, Mr. O'Hanrahan, have to fill out some reports for the Greek police. You may be here for a few days."

O'Hanrahan needed the rest, but that also meant wasted time without copies of the photos, time better spent in Jerusalem. The Greek policeman was back with more questions, so the colonel excused himself and Underwood shlepped out the door behind him. "You heard that Chicago reported me missing?" Lucy then asked O'Hanrahan quietly.

O'Hanrahan's eyes sparkled. "How very remarkable. You've been faxing *someone* reports every other day."

"It was a Chicago area code 312 number. Remember the telegram that came with the credit card . . ."

Lucy bent down to pick through her handbag. Why shouldn't she have that too? She hadn't thrown one thing away yet . . . It was folded with a number of other papers and scraps in her Oxford guidebook.

O'Hanrahan: "Tell me *exactly* what you remember about receiving this telegram."

Lucy thought back. "I was at David McCall's house. He drove me to Dublin and to the airport, and we said good-bye. Then he ran up and said, Oh I forgot to give you this, it came for Dr. O'Hanrahan, at the house. I opened it and it was a telegram for you and the VISA card. And that's right, there was no postmark on the envelope, see?"

"As if it was delivered by hand," O'Hanrahan suggested, taking the telegram. He read over it again, this time paying attention:

DR. O'HANRAHAN:

ENCLOSED PLEASE FIND CARD FOR YOUR RESEARCH. WE DO REQUIRE WEEKLY SUMMARY AND REPORT PLEASE. FAX: 312-555-2937

JOHN SMITH, TREASURER

"Uh," he hummed, considering. "This isn't a Hyde Park prefix. When we get to a hotel we'll trace where this fax number really is. I *knew* those cheapskates at Chicago wouldn't have sent me a credit card."

"My God," Lucy cried in a delayed revelation, "No wonder Dr. Shaughnesy called INTERPOL. They must think I'm dead back home."

O'Hanrahan was distracted. "What mystery person in Chicago would want to pay for an expensive, possibly fruitless expedition after an obscure scroll?" he asked. He read the name from the telegram: "John Smith, treasurer. Should have known that was phony." He changed subjects: "Luce, the one thing I can't figure out to save my life is why you didn't call the Matsoukises? I was holed up there, and I left a message for you in the event you called. The second things got weird you should have called Eleni."

"Uh, I forgot about them, I guess . . ." Anything to avoid Stavros— what an idiot she was! "I mean, I forgot their last name and you try finding a needle in a haystack in a Greek phonebook."

"We stayed with them for a week and you forgot their last name?"

He brushed this aside, however, and reached into his sportscoat's inner pocket. "I took the liberty of . . ." He seemed distracted.

"What?"

"Borrowing from the Matsoukises, I was able to purchase a ticket back to Chicago. For tomorrow."

Lucy faltered. "We're going home?"

"You are." And before she could object, O'Hanrahan put a hand on her arm. "No. No more bravada. It's getting dangerous for both of us. And I'm going to Jerusalem where things will probably be even more dangerous. This Islamic group will try something again, I suspect. So I think it's time for you to go home."

"May I see the ticket?"

Dr. O'Hanrahan pulled out her Olympic Airway ticket, the details and gate numbers freshly marked in handwritten ballpoint pen. "Here, Luce. And I'll be back in Chicago before you know it and we'll still work together, I promise—"

Lucy tore the ticket in half.

O'Hanrahan jumped up: "*What* did you just do?"

Lucy said, "I'm not going home until I'm ready to go home, for the hundredth time. I've come this far and I'm not letting the find of the century slip through my fingers either." She added, "Sir."

"You're going home, baby, if I have to pack you in a suitcase myself!"

JULY 29TH

It was a warm night with a faint Saronic breeze. Lucy walked along the deck of their ship after settling in her private cabin. A cabin boy, fifteen or so, with an open, sweet face, showed her to her cabin, flirting brazenly. He demonstrated the mysteries of working the sink faucets and the air-conditioning and showed Lucy how to call him if she needed the least little thing.

Better watch it, my *kouros*, she thought, I might just call.

Both she and O'Hanrahan felt liberated to be on the road again after six days of bureaucracy and U.S. Embassy red tape. Lucy walked the deck and stared at the neighboring boats this evening in Piraeus Harbor as her ship slowly began the three-day voyage to Haifa, Israel, via Rhodes and Lakasia, Cyprus. Nearby was the hammer-and-sickle of the Soviet Black Sea luxury liner, the reward once for party officials, but surely, poor as Russia was, it dispensed few privileges this summer. Lucy stared out at the calm Aegean, satin and dull violet, the fading pink sky above the Sounion Peninsula now bedizened with evening lights from homes and streetlamps. At the end of the peninsula stood the Temple of Poseidon, but it would be dark by the time they rounded the tip, so it would have to wait for another visit. And there would be, she knew, another visit.

She heard from the deck above the distinct sound of O'Hanrahan clearing his throat. He seemed in one of his sour moods, brought on by too much inactivity induced by the afternoons at the embassy and with Greek authorities. He stood like a masthead looking out at the Saronic Gulf, no less Xerxes surveying the Hellespont, a bottle of ouzo, duty-free, in one hand, a Styrofoam cup in the other.

(Another night with the bottle, Patrick?)

Ah, the voices again. I don't care, he thought; annoy me as You will, goad me with my own past. I will be free of Greece soon and I will hear you no more.

(People hear My voice in Jerusalem all the time, so don't be so sure.)

This is my farewell to Greece, O'Hanrahan thought, filling the cup again. My last communion with *Ellas*—it is like losing a limb. *All strangest things the multitudinous years bring forth and shadow from us all we know.* And as the great tragedians knew so well, I am how Man ends, old and perplexed and alone, ennobled, if at all, by grief. *The long days hoard many things nearer to grief than joy.* And also *Not to be born is past all prizing best.*

(But you don't really feel that way.)

No, I have loved my life, You know that. And I have fooled myself while on Grecian soil, thinking of what could have been with Eleni. I wouldn't have been able to live up to her, to make her happy. I needed just what I got: a woman for whom I could be something spectacular, pitiful though that is to admit. Beatrice, even at her worst, kept at me about things. I mean, not just the usual nagging, the drinking, the ass I would make of myself at faculty parties, but my work, my writing. "I don't care how you treat me," she would say, "but for Christ's sake don't pour all of your God-given gift down the drain."

(And she spoke truly.)

Beatrice harped on lots of things but that she remained true to. That I had great talent—she never stooped to comparing me with those morons in the department; she never ridiculed my mind. She always was pushing me to write down my thoughts, in a paper, a magazine article, a book of essays one day. "Let me be proud of you again," she'd say. That's the problem, she told me in a lighter moment, "It's that you talked like a book that I fell in love with you, you know." And I did talk a lot of blarney, talked her into twenty years of misery with an old drunk, good-for-nothing unregenerate mick who might have been something if he'd just counted his blessings!

(So many blessings.)

How often I turned my step from the golden path—no sooner was it good than I fouled it up by outthinking myself, and I tell you, Beatrice, if only you, sweetheart, could have given me absolution be-

fore you left, then I could have done what I had promised you. I was
to keep faith with Homer and Virgil, I was to tend the pantheon in
which the lost worlds would speak anew! And now I'm a wash-out,
honey. I make jokes about women with big tits, spin tales I've told a
hundred times, I'm a vulgarian, a cocktail-party blasphemer. Oh, but
Beatrice, if you could just return and let me look you in the face one
more time I would rise up! You would lead me to tread among my
high places, I would take my stand upon the Western Slopes.

(Patrick, you do not know what is in store for you ahead. And nor
does Lucy. O My children, so much you have not counted upon.)

When I come back to Greece, thought Lucy, walking the deck,
running her hand along the rail, I will call up Stavros to get another
look at him, to see if he's grown up, maybe start a less rambunctious,
less immature affair. I don't exactly love him, she told herself, but I
love what happened and he was part of that.

"Halloo," said the sweet-faced baggage boy in his pressed white
uniform, waving to her as he hauled someone's suitcases to an upper
deck.

"*Iasoo*," said Lucy, making him laugh for her effort.

They're not so impossible and unobtainable, men. She decided:
They're much more simple than I thought, less complicated and implacable. That baggage boy, all of fifteen, could be *had*, for God's sake.

(A little young for you.)

No, of course she wouldn't seduce him, but such things *could* be
done, couldn't they? A gentle kiss, an invitation to her room when his
duty ended. I would be the older, rich American adventuress and he
would flatter himself in retelling the event to his friends for years to
come. I could change the course of his life on a whim if I wanted to;
I could scar him . . . or I could seduce him and ask for his address and
write him love letters for years and meet up with him again and,
indeed, change his future with minimal effort, deprive the Greek girl
that would have married him of her destiny, change Mediterranean
history, perhaps. All on a whim of an evening. I never knew humans
had such powers.

(All the free will in the world.)

And I see now, thought Lucy, how easy it would be to mess with
people, abuse your power with them, trifle with them and hurt them.
Like Stavros trifled with me. Although, I really think, his millions of
women aside, he did like me. Perhaps I will write him, after all.

(He won't write you back.)

And actually I trifled with him too.

(Not something to be so proud of, My child.)

Lucy then stopped at the rail and let the wind blow her dress between
her legs and rearrange her hair, tickling the back of her neck. To be
moving, to be at sea again, with Jerusalem ahead! But the Holy Lands

gave way to thoughts of the silly onboard disco, where there was no shortage of good-looking men on the ship to dance with . . . and who knows, Lucy smiled, I do have a cabin to myself.

(Yes, tonight you will dance and go to bed in a haze of exchanged flirtations, liberties taken by handsome Cypriot soldiers, a kiss, a squeeze, a fog of one too many metaxas. And it will be the first night at sea that you don't think to pray to Us and ask the boat not to sink, and it is good that you fear your world less and less. But will you forget Us entirely, My dear? We have lost so much good company through the ages.)

Oh, sighed Lucy, feeling the sweetness of this escaping day to her very soul, I must make it a point never to die. And to keep traveling and keep meeting new people, and I must make it a point to fall in love with frequency so I am never without this full, swooning heart. I do like this world, she thought, hugging herself in the growing Aegean chill, looking upon the Evening Star, feeling less in need of gods as she sailed to the mysterious and sanctified East.

5

O Ephesus, Mother of architecture, of mathematics and the sciences, greatest city of all that is Greek, why must you be so given to what is carnal and undisciplined in the human condition? In Asia [Western Turkey] any idea formerly noble and good finds some ardent attachment to wickedness—indeed, so much wickedness that it would take the strength of ten prophets to begin to discuss all the sins.

Praised be the Lord that He has made me up to the task!

2. In my youthful travels in the Aegean, I had seen everywhere the rites of Artemis, goddess of the hunt, not too different from our own former Temple sacrifices, really, if we are to be worldly about such things; a blood offering to the Divinity to show we appreciate the bounty of the land each spring. Ah, but here in Ephesus, the goddess and her Artemision [her temple] cater only to fornication and whoredom. Once-proud Artemis herself is transformed into a monstrosity weighed down by hundreds of breasts. (One sees little clay figurines for sale in the streets of Ephesus, this perversion visible to the saintly and children alike!)

3. Attis, Astarte, Cybele, all pagan gods that prey upon the desire for blood spectacle and *porneia*, every one of them beginning in some froth of blood and castration, ending in general lewdness, copulation, orgies of the nonpriestly celebrants. For this, throughout Asia and Phrygia, virgin girls are set aside to serve in the temples as whores, recepticals for every lust and disease known to the polities of the Great Sea. And yet, these festivals are holy and clean when one compares them to the secular Ephesus, which excels all other cities—except Tyre, the lowest pit within the many pits of Hell!—in entertainments for the most degraded of natures.

Carved into the stones of the streets themselves, advertisements give directions to the nearest brothel, shamelessly directing one to the "Pugixeinon," a disreputable orgy-chamber known as *Cras vives?* and a lovely bower known as *Quo Irrumbis?*[1] For less money than it would take to feed a mule in Judea, one can have three identical sisters of barbaric Moesia service one's every portal, or perhaps a parade of girl-children upon which one may obliterate the hymens until sated for a small price. One can take a mother and her infant into an alley where, for the price of a jar of olives, she has trained her infant to suck upon the members of men. This is not to mention the stench of the perpetual Dionysian festival upon the seafront in which entertainments of unthinkable lewdness transpire, no deformity of genital, no inconceivable size of organ or breast, no act so terrible, no pairing of races, children, numerous partners with animals cannot be observed for a simple remittance of spare coins.

And I merely relate what one can see from the street!

4. For myself, it was a strained parting from Xenon. I was sorry to be leaving him, while he remained stoic and controlled, though I reckoned him much moved within. The apprenticeship at his uncle's looked to be more slave labor than privilege and he saw a road of ordeals stretch before him. After several nights in Ephesus, I asked if he might rather join me in further evangelization of the nations, but he confessed his skills were elsewhere, I think, to save my feelings. It was unspoken between us that I had been a failure as a minister of the Righteous Teaching.

5. Presently, I was to make myself known to John [Zebedee]. A word about his former master, John the Baptist,[2] decrier of Jerusalem's evils, a Nazirene too pure for any congregation—

---

1. The ancient world thought little of these vulgarities and one finds them commonly in Catullus and other saltier writers. (The proper understanding of Latin and Greek, in this editor's view, never recovered from the prim bowdlerization of the Victorians.) The πυγιξεινον is a place of anal penetration; *Cras vives?* means "Will you live tomorrow?" and as a popular expression of *carpe diem* found its way into Martial's epigrams (*Epigrammaton*, book V, 58); and *Quo Irrumbis?* means "Who will put out their penis to be sucked?"

2. John the Baptist (ca. 4 B.C.E.–28 or 29 C.E.) All that we know of John is from the Synoptic accounts: a baptist-prophet figure who harangued Herod Antipas and his brother's wife Herodias for their adultery, and was beheaded at the request of Salome, who was granted any wish for her lascivious dance at Machaerus. While attempts to make him an Essene are improbable, his being a Nazirene (with long hair, and his father being given divine instruction to protect his son from wine in *Luke* 1:15) is virtually certain.

an impossible but I believe God-inspired man. My recollection of my first encounter with the Baptist was terrifying.

The debauchees of Herod's court would ride down from Machaerus or Herodion [Herod's palaces] and attend the Baptist's fanatical displays at the Jordan. I recall one woman, given to fat, painted in the Greek fashion. The Baptist called her out of the crowd and made her confess publicly her sins, her adulteries, her covetings, her willingness to cause trouble.[3] He spat upon her, slapped her, ripped her robe from her, and berated her fallen figure. "Behold your nakedness, harlot!" he cried as she wept. "Lavishing your harlotries on passersby![4] Here, woman! Here are strangers: splay yourself before them." When he had brought her to a final point of humiliation, he then held her head under water, dragging her up by the hair and using his rough, unwashed burlap loincloth to wipe away her facepaint; then back again into the water she would be submerged. John the Baptist had a strange gift for knowing how long one could endure before drowning; then his victim was brought up and allowed to live. He was so gentle and loving the next moment, that those who underwent this hysterical process often went away chastened and converted. Others returned that very sabbath to saturnalia, and were back again the next week for more repentance. Chariots and carriages from the city lined the hillsides for these spectacles.

6. I saw the Baptist, renowned son of Zechariah,[5] take a

---

3. The Greeks had more specific words for gradations of sin than we use now; there were many kinds of adultery, theft, apostasy, etc., and these crimes figure largely in Paul's rantings as well. Καπηλεύω is adulteration, as a merchant might water down his product, but could also describe the whoring of oneself in adultery for gain (as opposed to δόλος).

   The Baptist accuses the woman of covetings but does not use πάθος or ὄρεξις, both negative but cerebral, but rather ὁρμή which suggests a rapacious grabbing.

   πονηρός is to stir up mischief, rather than broadly evil, far which κακός was preferred.
4. *Ezekiel* 16:15. *But you trusted in your beauty and played the harlot because of your renown, and lavished your harlotries on any passerby.*
5. Here is another odd clue to the Zechariah puzzle of the New Testament, which seems to be a certain proof of words interpolated in Jesus' mouth.

   The Baptist's father in *Luke* 1:5 is the priest Zechariah. The Prophet Zechariah Barachiah of *Zechariah* and *Matthew* 23:35 was *slain between the sanctuary and the altar* according to Jesus. Josephus mentions the martyrdom of Zacharias Barachiah (*Jewish War*, IV.v.4) where *two of the boldest of [the zealots] fell upon Zacharias in the middle of the temple*. Finally, the *Protoevangelium* attributed to James also has the Baptist's father slain in the Temple. So here is a great puzzle: Jesus in *Matthew* thinks the Prophet Zechariah was martyred in the temple, with which no Jewish source concurs. However, the secular account of Zechar-

   Continued

young man, fallen to whoremongering, by the member, produce a knife, and threaten to cut it from him. I saw him beat upon a fat merchant, who wept as a baby, and take his purse and force him to hold the filthy Roman coins in his mouth, since his love for money was so great. An elder, given to indiscretions with young virgins, engendered a frenzy in the Baptist. He went to the shore and got a rock and taunted the elder with the stoning he would receive in this world, the perpetual never-ending avalanche of rocks he would endure in *Gehenna* [Hell], and said "Since you so love the sin for which you are to be stoned, I give you this taste of your eternity!" and hit him until he bled. Then the man was made to kiss and reverence the rock, then lick it clean, then take it and beat his own head with it, before the Baptist relented and was willing to baptize him. I was lucky because when I went to him he had just humiliated a lawyer, and so his wrath was spent for a young student as myself.

Yet for all his extremity, I always felt the Baptist to be sincere and quite possibly of God.

7. Among his followers was the Disciple John.[6] When I first met John he was a girlish youth of seventeen, formerly a prized student of the Temple. Brazenly, he castigated me for being a landowner and called upon me to eschew my worldly estate—I

---

iah (not the prophet) in Josephus has this sacrilegious slaying happen *34 years after the Crucifixion.* The explanation, though detrimental to Christianity, is that the composers of *Matthew* and the *Protoevangelium* were fond of the story of Zechariah's martyrdom [ca. 64 C.E.] and edited it in anachronistically, and that Jesus could never have said those words.

6. John the Disciple and Evangelist, ca. 10–110? C.E.

Apologists have strained to make the Evangelist John, traditional author of *1 John* and the *Gospel of John,* the John who was the "disciple whom Jesus loved." John the Elder (of whom nothing is known) claims to write *2* and *3 John.* No modern scholar thinks it conceivable that the *Gospel of John* was written before 100–120 C.E., and it is the editor's opinion that 120 C.E. is even cutting it close. That would have made John the Disciple an unlikely one hundred or more. Irenaeus claims John lived "to Trajan's time" (Trajan Caesar, 98–117 C.E.); Clement of Alexandria in his *Rich Man Who Finds Salvation* (late 100s) sets an account of John after the death of Domitian in 98 C.E.; Eusebius also says John lived past one hundred years. One wonders if the final comment of Jesus in *John* 21:22 was inserted to explain John's suspiciously long lifespan: *"It is my will that [John] remain until I come, what is that to you? . . ." The saying spread abroad among the brethren that this disciple was not to die; yet Jesus did not say to him that he was not to die.*

Not many, even in the times of the Fathers, think the John of *Revelations* is the same author as that of *John.* However, *Revelations* is, according to Irenaeus, a work of the 90s, in the time of Domitian (Caesar 81–96 C.E.), within John's probable lifespan. This editor suggests that it is *Revelations* that might be the work of the Disciple John, and the *Gospel* and *Epistles* the work of John the Elder—a very likely idea that has received little support through the centuries.

was a usurer, a swine. (By this we see he imitated the Baptist's rhetoric superbly. That is all, I tell you, my brother, I ever thought John bar-Zebedee good at: mouthing what his rabbi wanted to hear.) When he began service with Our Master he became a little lambkin and whispered back all the assurances of love and the Paradise to Come in the Teacher's own language, and for his trouble became the Beloved of Our Master, privy to His every utterance.[7]

8. John's monastery was, not surprisingly, in the wealthier suburbs of the polis. Young men, often self-made eunuchs, mostly Greek, lived here an ascetic life contributing their inheritances and worldly goods. These goods were invested by John in property along the seafront, from which John was assured a continuous profit for his order. Within the spacious country house, John's converts spent the better part of their day in prayer, in isolation, in fasting, which is the type of Essenic indulgence Our Master frowned upon, these great shows of holiness while there is so much charitable work to be done.

9. John was remarkably unchanged. He was beardless as a youth and remained so, though I wonder that he had some depilatory treatment by which he remains beardless, being that he wishes to preserve his looks from when he was the Beloved of Our Savior, or so he told me. John, who from a distance seemed to be ever twenty-one, showed his half-century upon closer inspection—I believe he used a dyed oil to blacken his hair, but I did not say anything because one who has made oneself a eunuch, for the Lord or otherwise, is less likely to age, having robbed his body of the corrupting manly fluids that make the rest of us elder and gray.

---

7. John is the disciple whom Jesus loved, *who had lain close to [Jesus'] breast* (*John* 21:20). Many ikons capture Jesus with John kissing or embracing him, repeating the familiar image (to the ancient world) of the Lover and Beloved, the Mentor and Pupil. John's Hellenistic Christianity and its popularity had more in common with the Academy of Athens than with the Temple rabbis (though current Dead Sea Scroll research shows much of the Father and Son obsessions of *John* may have a Jewish and not strictly Greek source after all).

The appeal to Grecian culture of *eros* between Master and Pupil was unmistakable in that age, and it is only prudery and homophobia that keep scholars from acknowledging it in this one. Jesus and John were to become a model of higher, chaste male love and devotion throughout the Middle Ages (see Aelred, *De speculo caritatis*, 1100s, in which John and Jesus have a spiritual "marriage").

Not surprisingly, John had surrounded himself with young men of his kind, for which no amount of discursive talk of doctrine and rabbinical cant was too much. I met his scribe Zossima, Pentheus to his Apollonius.[8] Like the Essenes known in our childhood, these young men looked as if they were in some trance of near-starvation in which a commonplace can appear to be a miracle, and John's doggerel worthy of remembering as Holy Scripture.

10. In the atrium I saw a young monk, not fourteen, weeping as he pulled up the weeds up from between the stones and began to eat these grasses.

"That is Andreas," John said to me, "and he weeps for the beauty of the weeds and honors them as if they were the yield of a rich man's garden, the fruits and vegetables of autumn. To the Glory of God!"

I recall Our Master discouraging fasting on many occasions, suggesting we should eat in moderation and drink wine and be content to live in the pleasurable moment.[9]

"Our Lord's eating and drinking," said John to me softly, "was but illusion, my brother, for his Divine Body had no use for this carrion and leafage we call food of this world.[10] He was fed by angels each night." John's eyes dazzled with potential tears. "The Cherubim fed him the sweetmeats of Heaven on beams of light, the Seraphim poured him celestial wine while

---

8. Prochoros (mentioned *Acts* 6:5) is traditionally the scribe who took down John's apocalyptic visions on Patmos, but this gospel lists a Zossima instead.

   Pentheus was, presumably, the disciple of Apollonius, one of the First Century's more interesting cult-rivals to Jesus: a youth so handsome and athletic, whose teachings were so wise and ecumenical, that he was taken to be a son of a Grecian deity. We know of him through Lucian (mid-100s) and in more detail from Philostratus (300s, and unreliable). Apollonius did his best to talk like Jesus and various Greek models, i.e., "What wonder is it if, while other men consider me equal to God, and some even consider me a god, my native place so far ignores me."

9. Attempts after the Dead Sea Scrolls were published to make Jesus into an Essene have been largely forced. Jesus talked to women, drank wine, had contacts with Gentiles, numerous disqualifications for the ascetic movements popular in his day. Though Jesus had his time of fasting and anguish during the forty days in the Wilderness, once his ministry began the trappings of asceticism were not visible. *Matthew* 9:14: *Then the disciples of John [the Baptist] came to him saying, "Why do we and the Pharisees fast much, but your disciples do not fast?" And Jesus said to them, "Can the wedding guests mourn as long as the Bridegroom is with them?"*

10. One of the most troubling heresies of the Early Church was "Docetism" (from δοκέηι in Greek, to "seem") and this gospel attributes docetic elements to John. Interestingly, the gospel *John* takes great pains to undermine Docetism. As late as the 500s, riots in Byzantium ensued over a bishop preaching Christ had no true bodily functions.

borne by the lyre music of David. Foods of every imaginable spice and color, arrayed before him on garnet and agate, bathed in the bejeweled Light from that one unconsumed, ever-burning Source of Light . . ."

(You see what jargon one must contend with in this era to have any discussion of theology.)

11. Nonsense, I protested. I remember in one encounter (I was accompanied by my tutor Polycrates) Our Dearest Master in Capernum being made ill by a piece of smoked fish. And I remember upon my second meeting with the Teacher, as John must himself, a feast in Cana in which he ate too many of the fowls cooked for us and made jest at His discomfort. And as a man, He joined us in endurance of all bodily functions. Or was all ordure wiped away by an angelic host?

John said to me, "This is all the more to the supremacy of the illusion by which we took Him to be as we are, simple mortal Men."

12. I asked of John, "So you think Him God and not Man completely?"

"I think him both," John said to me, "but partaking of different Essences at different moments. His Sonship is derived from the Father, conveyed by The Holy Spirit and Her Infinite Wisdom, which was preeternal. His Divine Essence was before the world and it will be after the world, uncreated and ever-proceeding and yet ever-originating. But such is the result of years of study here where I have made propounding such doctrines my life's work."[11]

I persevered. Even when Our Master spoke as no man before or since spoke, He was there, in the room before us—we could reach out to touch His flesh and feel the warmth of His body!

But John did not listen. "Too much has been revealed to me, some of which I can share, some of which was vouchsafed to me alone."

---

11. To whatever ends John succeeded here, his gospel was to be analyzed and argued over for the next 300 years because of his inscrutability concerning equality of Father and Son. Homoousians (Son and Father are one substance), Homoiousians (Son and Father are similar in substance), Antinomeans (the Son is not the Father), and Homoeans (the Son is similar to the Father), batted *John* back and forth through two centuries of bitter church councils.

(What, one wonders, was the point of the revelation then?)

13. John said to me, "First, as Our Master has said, Jerusalem will be no more, salt sown into the fields, the wells poisoned, the walls breached, and not one stone will be left standing of what once was the Temple. Already the signs are in place. Indeed, here in the synagogue in Ephesus, before a sacrifice, a cow was seen to give birth to a lamb, and a ewe to a calf. A sign of the abominations that await us!"

John further said to me, "I can tell you that in my time in the wilderness on a barren rock with nothing but the sun and air to eat,[12] I saw the final conflagrations and sufferings in the Woe to come, the destruction of all things, no soul not in anguish, no measure of our skin not seared with the heat of a thousand burning coals. A hunger will be visited upon the land such as has never been seen and man will turn on man; men will be as beasts consuming their neighbor's children."

I asked John if this would be before or after the searing of the hot coals.

14. He said to me, "All sufferings will be concurrent; we shall turn away from one but to see the visitation of another torment. And how much worse it shall be for those who cast doubt upon the Resurrection of Our Master."

I mentioned, nonetheless, that I indeed had doubts concerning this resurrection, not being of the party that saw Him, and furthermore, that no two Disciples seemed to have the same memory of it.

John merely said to me, "Having assumed the sins of all generations unto this one, having assumed within his Divinity all error and abomination, He fell through the many Hells until the seventh beneath Abadon, where for three days a worse ordeal than the Cross transpired."

15. Do you honestly believe, I asked of him, that God hurled his Greatest Prophet into a lake of fire with the fallen angels and Lucifer, Nero, Herod, and the like?

John said to me, "It has been revealed to me, my brother. I

---

12. Tradition holds that John ran afoul of authorities; some tales have him debate Domitian himself, and be exiled to Patmos, but all *Revelations* says is that he was on the island *on account of the word of God* (Revelations 1:9).

have seen but a fraction of this torment that when divided end-lessly, and subdivided again by a number equal to all the grains of sand, that even this small portion of misery revealed was more than I could endure. I would have torn my eyes from my head, had not Brother Zossima rushed to prevent me."

I turned again to see Brother Zossima, all of eighteen, emaci-ated and red-eyed from perpetual crying, a beardless castrate, I surmised, as well.

16. It was here that wearily I determined not to spend any more time in Ephesus with John and his ilk.

I commenced next a tour of our churches in Asia, Sardis, Pergamum, Thyatira, numerous small outposts in rural Lydia, decrying the abuses and misinterpretations the Nazirene Church had undergone in each of these towns. (Of course, I was follow-ing in the footsteps of Saul, who pelts our churches with all-knowing epistles, and though I was shown due respect, it was made clear that Saul and his seductive tracts were foremost in their hearts. As the year proceeded—let's see, Tesmegan, the glorious year in which the wretch Nero took his own hell-des-tined life [68 c.e.]—I composed a series of moral exhortations and diatribes I delivered in each of the Asian churches. I will try to recreate some of it here . . .

(On second thought, our time is limited. As Tesmegan re-minds me, he must soon leave me, so let us move ahead to my return to Judea and the main mission at hand. Quite right, young man, but it would not have done you harm to hear my moral exhortations. Yes, write all this down—all that I say.)

17. Very well then.

Late in the second year of the revolt [ca. January 69 c.e.] I returned by a tortuous route to the family estate to wait out the fighting and serve as a heroic leader to my Nazirene commune.

Repeatedly when I traveled through our ravaged land I heard tales of the Romans, always the Romans, how they are at war with us, what atrocities are committed in Jerusalem, only to arrive at the purported place of these outrages to find once again that it was merely we Judeans fighting ourselves, Jew against Jew once more. As for the Romans, it is only our national stupidity that prevented us from outlasting them: Florus, you will recall, demanded more taxes for his unceasing personal squalor and discovered some Jews had mocked him by giving him alms money, as if he were a beggar. Thousands died for this! The Romans marching through Jerusalem did not return the Jews' salute. To war! cried Judea. Nero and the brood of recreants requested a small sacrifice in his name and, naturally, could we Jews simply pay some pagan to conduct perfunctorily this meaningless rite and oblige the emperor? Of course not! We preferred to fight among ourselves and see our Jewish capital, greatest city of the East, razed than to endure these paltry, empty trifles![13]

18. Around harvest time, naturally, your Roman compatriots marauded the countryside, took what they wished, and set torches to our father's estate. My reduced band of Nazirenes, now down to twenty, marched off across the Jordan to hideous, provincial Pella where no Roman would trouble himself. Our father, Josephus, as you know, never liked life upon the estate and preferred to live in his residence in Jerusalem; your mother, his second wife, insisted on the pleasures of the city. I sent a message for them to leave Jerusalem before the siege and join us in Pella but they had hopes that your newfound influence with the Romans would protect them. As we heard reports of the siege, I gave up hope that our father in his eighth decade [his seventies] could be alive.

19. In fact, it was to discover the whereabouts of my father and, of course, to communicate with you, my brother, that I ventured from Pella after Jerusalem had fallen [September 70 C.E.] and, it must be admitted, partially for curiosity (being a historian of my repute).

So many reports of utter ruin and desolation had circulated that I thought it impossible such a grand and fortified city as Jerusalem could have been so annihilated. But indeed, standing at the gates, I beheld it was so—destruction unknown, I am sure, since the most ancient times of the Assyrians when vanquished cities were taken apart stone by stone until the ground was level!

No hill or horizon was spared row upon row of crosses and

---

13. These incidents of racial tension referred to are confirmed in Josephus's account. The great capital Matthias remembers is not legendary: Jerusalem, Tacitus estimates, had a peacetime population of 600,000, the largest eastern city of the day and the wealthiest.

gibbets. Indeed, downwind from the Mount of Olives there was no air that could be breathed and the night was tortured by the howls of hyenas and jackals as they leaped for the carrion hanging from cross and scaffold. Below the execution grounds there wailed a group of young scribes and rabbis, walking about in rags, flagellating themselves, cursing the Romans and then cursing themselves, making such an unworldly din that the Romans made frequent trips to silence them by sword. These shrieking rabbis would never make properly contrite slaves, and so they were killed rather than dragged back to Rome to march in chains in Titus's triumph, to be targets for Roman excrement and rotten foodstuffs. (Ah, such enormities your much-lauded history refused to observe lest your Latin patrons be embarrassed.)

20. In the bloodstained creekbed of Kidron I happened upon the fearful visage of the son of the Rabbi Yochanan bar-Yehoshua (who had not gone with the rabbis to Yavneh), his hair torn from his head by his own hands. He said that the Messiah would appear any moment upon the Mount of Olives in a host of angels descending and ascending and with a blast of the trump the earth would open and swallow the Romans, and then the Jews, butchered and decimated, would rise bodily from the ground and avenge this defiling. When shall we be weaned from these follies? *I turned you to ashes upon the earth! All are appalled at you; you have come to a dreadful end and shall be no more forever!*[14]

How weary I have become of Messiahs appearing to enact revenge for all man's evils! Sullen at the sight of fallen Jerusalem, I said to this tortured man that God has no interest in who gets what piece of land in His world. On this earth, we are surely our own Messiah and to wait for another mob-proclaimed one is to dwell fruitlessly on an unwaking dream, an unending tale, an unanswerable question. How much more difficult the question Our Master sought to answer! *How then, Lord, should we live*

---

14. *Ezekiel* 28:18. The agonies of the Siege and Fall of Jerusalem of 70 c.e. can barely be overstated. Josephus records 500 Jews a day were crucified in view of the city where "room was wanting for the crosses"; he gives a horrifying figure of 1,100,000 who died in the siege, with nearly 100,000 captives led away to Rome. He writes that the Romans came upon Mary, daughter of Eleazar, who had eaten her child and offered the Romans some of it as well, "*This is mine own son, and what hath been done was mine own doing. Come, eat of this food, for I have eaten of it myself . . .*" (*War*, VI.iii.3–5).

together in peace with our fellow man? Yes, how hard we must work for the answer to that!

21. So now we come to a piece of my history you know quite well. Through bribes and pretending that I was Greek (which I can speak as a native, as you know), I received a pass to the innermost depths of the Roman camp, near Titus's quarters where you, as if some favorite kept animal, could be found slavishly waiting upon his excellency's pleasure.

Our exchange was not pleasant. You seemed offended that I had not seen you when you were imprisoned, and my being out of the country seemed not a good enough excuse for you. As you won your freedom by fighting against our people with the Romans, I reminded you how my own (and our family's) standing and respect in Judea were ruined. It was in this, our last conversation, that I learned that the family estate was to be transferred to you and I was to become, for all you cared, one more of the impoverished refugees of Jerusalem.

"Go to your Nazirene friends," you goaded me. "See what charity you receive after having given to the Nazirenes all our family ever owned."

22. Am I wrong to say of our last meeting that in your eyes was something pained? Was there amid your sordid triumph some feeling for the wandering brother that you had not counted upon? That was surely the last time you will see me, the one who adored you, who gave you as untroubled a childhood as was ever had in Judea. How painful that our last encounter should have been such as that . . . Ah, but this path has no profit, let us forget it. Tesmegan, let us move on.

(We shall strike out all this later.)

23. Our father, badly shaken by the siege and malnourishment, as you know, passed away in this period.[15]

You might expect that I hold you accountable for this, but, dear brother, among the many injustices done to me by you, this

---

15. Josephus is taciturn on his family affairs during his traitorous march with the Romans, recording simply *"I made this request to Titus that my family might have their liberty"* (*Life*, 75). Not long after the fall of Jerusalem, he records, *I asked of [Titus] the life of my brother and fifty friends with him and was not denied.* When Titus became Caesar, Josephus was proud to include in his autobiography, the emperor *also made that estate that I had in Judea tax-free, which is a mark of greatest honor to who hath it.*

I have never claimed. No, he was an old man on the verge of not being able to care for himself. With Jerusalem razed and his estate plundered, I am glad that he could no longer think clearly and passed his last days like a child, fondly remembering his first wife and, in the end, calling out to his own mother as if she were in the room.

However, for the disasters that have befallen me, I am less forgiving. In the months following the fall of Jerusalem, dispossessed of my brother, my property, all my money, and shunned by the movement that I would have be my home, I threw myself on the mercy of Apollo, son of Erechtheus of Lod, who had a farm in the neighboring hills.

24. He was as destitute as I, but we were once schoolmates as boys in Jerusalem. Two of his daughters had starved in Jerusalem; his only two sons had rushed off to Masada to fight and meet the Messiah who would drive Rome from our land! How my heart broke for him. Apollo had no room with a roof over it for me (the Romans, your beloveds, had torched his estate) but I was content to make a place in the stable, cushioning myself upon the only straw not damp with blood, for the Romans had killed any animals they could not use for food or haulage.

For the winter months, I worked there as his accountant and tutor for his daughters' children, as I wrote you. You had fled to Alexandria where Jewish sentiment against you was not so high-pitched, and I heard you married also—a woman I have never met or could give sanction to. Again, I wrote you of my unease but you did not send monies to help me. It was not enough to displace and impoverish me: I heard from others that you were busy working on a history of your own treachery, writing frantically to better your older brother, and of course to clear your name and render your own behavior exculpable.

At that, dear brother, cursed as Tiberias Alexander by our people, you did not succeed.[16]

---

16. Tiberias Julius Alexander, procurator from 46–48 C.E. Matthias mentions this turncoat to goad his brother, who was often compared to him. Tiberias Alexander was a cosmopolitan Alexandrian Jew who had adopted Roman ways and sided with them, and wasn't much more popular with the Romans. Juvenal called him *that on-the-make Egyptian pasha who's had the temerity to gate-crash Triumph Row [in the Forum]: his effigy is only fit for pissing on, or worse (Satire* I:129–131).

25. I decided early the next year [spring 71 C.E.] to petition you in Alexandria and try again to redress my grievances. And *again* you did not consent to see me. (Yes, my scribe wonders that I write you even now subsequent to your former cruelty. Observe, Tesmegan, my insuperable Nazirene spirit of forgiveness!)

However, God was able to find a subsistence for me, His mercy be praised. It transpired for the next five years [71–75 C.E.], I gave myself passionately to teaching Greek in Alexandria. First to private families, to the children of former school friends of mine who took pity on me; and then for the last three years I taught in the Academy of Alexandria itself.

> O Alexandria! Where beauteous Alexander
>   bestrode the port
> His pharos huge and aflame for all to see!

26. Yes, but to mention Alexandria, that paradise, greatest of cities! And of course, it is no small pleasure to be so well known and received in such a town.

Between the ubiquitous Roman raids, I more than once had opportunity in a series of outings to the famous baths near the Serapium to recite from my own *Cosmos Explained* (an immature work, yes, but not without its supporters for its many precocious passages!) at many a *tepidarium* to great acclaim. It was all I could do to leave the fine tables and company of the capital—where, yes, even wives and serving girls are educated—and again set out upon the banks of the Nile to uncharted barbarities.

27. But set out again I did.

I had once hoped to end my life in the docile fashion I describe above, but it returned, you see: my sadness, my familiar emptiness. My curiosity! What of the Teacher of Righteousness and the entire phenomenon that had played itself out within my lifetime? Was I witness to God Upon This Earth or to my own illusions?

I had been once a man of God, but in Alexandria I had become a man of nothing—moorless, adrift. I would attend the Nazirene synagogue and hear ludicrous claims, untrue stories, tales of staggering miracles (so popular where a faith must compete with the theistic wealth of Africa), and I would wander to my lowly apartment through the noisy, dusty streets, dejected and without peace, keenly aware of how I had failed the Nazirene Church, how much yet my Church needed me to ascend to the scholar's chair. And more: how much my soul cried out for the guidance and assurance of God!

It is at that point, broken in spirit nearly to the point of refusing to rise from my pallet each morning, that by chance—no, it was by the Most High's doing!—that I encountered that scoundrel Duldul ibn-Waswasah who, like many merchants, had moved his business from obliterated Jerusalem.

28. Waswasah accosted me in the marketplace and ran to embrace me. From the din of the market he led me, still in the shock of surprise, to his home on the outskirts of the city where the Sabaeans had banded together in tent cities. Waswasah commanded one of his slaveboys—with a painted face, purchased for some unspeakable use—to make us some tea of mint and jasmine. Waswasah bade me lie down on his silks and cushions and kissed me fondly, heaping blessings and greetings upon my soul and my family.

He in time said to me, "You have decided your rebbe is not of God? You wish to go to Yavneh and make amends with the Pharisees? It can be arranged!"

I said that my affection for Our Master was strong but in my years of wandering and research I had yet found no part of his Church that reflected His True Teaching, no disciple that was His worthy heir.

29. Waswasah said to me, "It would be best for you and your people to forget their Messiahs before the Romans make an end of you. I have thought often of you, dear Matthias, with sadness, and I assumed in the siege you too had been made an end of."

With the torrid nature of the Arabian race, he seemed as if he might weep in his happiness to see me. But I now imagine he was overjoyed that more of my money might fall into his purse. I explained that I was but a poor tutor now and had no money to spend upon his services.

He asked, "What of your estate?"

Ruined in the Roman march, I said to him, and furthermore the deed was now in the hands of my famous brother, the general.

"Ah, the traitor," said Duldul ibn-Waswasah to me.

(I commit his opinion to print, in the interest of accuracy.)

30. I said to Waswasah that I was, as ever, curious about the last days of My Master. Was it possible to talk to any of the Roman guards who watched his tomb?

The Sabaean said to me, "My friend, those guards who let your master escape saw soon the cross themselves! And in any event, if they survived it was only to die elsewhere. It has been decades!" Then Waswasah amazed me, saying, "I have, I admit, taken advantage of you in the past, and this you know. While your money has held out I have sent you through the known world, taking a substantial fee for my arrangements and information. But now that there is no more to take I will reward you with the truth, for free. Your Master's body, as the Jews tell, was stolen from the crypt in Golgotha Field."

31. I replied, such is a familiar libel.

He said to me, "And if there was proof?"

I shouldn't believe any set of old bones, nor even a convincing collection of robes. Such shams are on display for every would-be Prophet. Aside from the horrors of James bar-Alphaeus's collection, I have myself seen the quill of Isaiah, the rod of Moses, even was once shown the skull of Elijah in an Idumaean marketplace, of all asininities.[17]

32. Waswasah said to me, "Joseph of Arimathea in the Sanhedrin asked for Your Master's body after the crucifixion, no? I knew Joseph very well as a fellow merchant and his trade in spices was important to me. He told me, in fact, that he expected Your Lord to be borne from the cross by the angelic host. Did you know that there were many portents the evening your Master died? Oh, yes! A tremor in the earth bode ill, and before the Temple a cow gave birth to a lamb—such things were seen."

Where are such things not seen?

---

17. Elijah, of course, was believed to have been taken bodily into heaven leaving no relics; see *Sirach* 47:9 and *2 Kings* 2:11.

33. Waswasah related the popular slander, repeated by the School of Shammai, Gamaliel the Younger, and others: "Joseph had a meal sent down to the Roman guards with a sleeping-draught in the wine."

My host leaned closer, though there was no one that could overhear. "But now comes the thing as a historian, a great scholar like yourself, will surely find interesting. Joseph sent his two slaves to the tomb to remove the body and this they did." Waswasah then asked of me, "Did you yourself, my friend, see Your Master upon his return from Hades?"

"No," I answered him, "but many Disciples I have talked to did bear witness. John and James bar-Alphaeus." Although as I made this answer, the untrustworthy natures of the men who so testified began to trouble me.

34. "I feel you are not so convinced," said my Sabaean host, "otherwise you should not have pursued your researches with such fervor. I merely save you much time and bring out the truth for you: the slaves who stole Your Master's body from the tomb took this relic to Egypt for safekeeping. It is there still! The bones of the Jewish Messiah."

"And I suppose," I said, displaying my learned sarcasm, "that you propose to show me a stack of old dog bones and thereby collect another fee for your services?"

But at this, Waswasah pulled back and it took many moments of ameliorations and blandishments to apologize for my rash comment. He said, having recovered, "I merely try to save you more trouble and worry. How you repay my kindness!"

35. I argued that there was a problem with his tale. If these slaves of Joseph indeed possessed such a relic and harbored such a secret, these slaves might surely profit richly by it. Indeed, the Pharisees and the Romans alike might pay handsomely for such a proof of Our Master's mortality.

Waswasah said to me, "You are quite wise. The slaves became as wealthy as you say! I do not recall the first man's name—but no matter, I am quite sure he is dead. But the other man, Benjamin, lives in Elephantine where Joseph paid him extravagantly to hide his secret. I knew Benjamin, you see, because he

gave a generous measure to his master's salt when we traded—
now I hear he is richer than any of us in Elephantine! How can
one explain such a fortune in a former slave? How can one
explain such a disappearance? I leave this analysis to a gifted
historian such as yourself."

He said further to me, "Benjamin was Bithynian. Why would
he go of his own will to Elephantine where his tongue and even
Greek is rarely of avail? Perhaps it was a condition of his freedom
that he hide there, yes? Hide there with the secret relics of Your
Master, of which I've heard rumors. Indeed, ghastly terrible
rumors concerning their nature."

36. I declared that Waswasah was a vessel of gossip and rumors. "What should it prove," I presently asked, "if I were to go
to Elephantine and investigate this report? I shouldn't believe
any old bones against the testimony of scores of people who saw
Our Master back from the dead." Although, I did not relate to
my host the conflicting and ethereal nature of most of these
sightings.

He said to me: "What if I were to tell you, dear Matthias, that
the death-relic is intact and incorrupt, like the mummies of old?"

Such abominations! No custom more barbarous or unclean
and against all that God in His Law forbade than the embalming
of corpses! And to think Waswasah suggested that our Master
met this fate!

He said to me, "Ah, but it is true. It was part of a larger plan,
my friend, to have Your Master appear at some distance from
a crowd and establish a resurrection. However, the Nazirenes
managed to invent their resurrection well enough without this
bit of helpful theater. But that, if Benjamin is still alive, is what
awaits you if you pursue your history to Elephantine."

37. Elephantine! Several hundred miles down the Nile into
the infernal Abyssinia to chase such a story! I said to him, "You
take me still for the fool I've been. You believe that my brother
will give me money for this expedition and that I am lying to
you about my poverty."

He did not get angry, but said to me, "No, I do not hope to
take money from you. I tell you this to ease your mind. Ah, I
pity you believers-of-Gods. What God there may be or may not

be I leave to others, yes?" He lifted his purse and rattled the coins within. "There is my God and I know that He exists. He is omnipotent and good to those who worship Him, yes? Go. Go build a new home, make a new family, sleep and forget, and wake to spend the rest of your days in the service of education— ah, buy yourself a beautiful boy like Kamaar there, yes?"

Waswasah's wretched little cup-bearer, obviously the prize of his master's aquiline eye, looked up at us with heavy lids. (The vices of the Sons of Ishmael know no bounds!)

38. There was a lull when at last Waswasah said to me, "However, if you must go to Elephantine, I have a way. O the upper reaches of the Nile are beautiful to behold! A poetical soul like yourself would surely be moved. Ah yes, I remember in addition to all your other skills and excellencies that you are a poet of the first rank!"

I inquired about this voyage with suspicion.

He said to me, "Each year I conduct business to buy spices and frankincense from my cousins among the Sabaeans, ivory and gold-dust from the Aethiope, and the like. I have attempted to entrust my order and letter of greetings to Romans and other couriers but in these times the posts are undependable. I need to entrust such an important document to someone I know who will go and return. If you were to go to Nubia for your stupendous history, my friend, you could deliver my letter."

39. I saw everything now: his story of Benjamin was an elaborate ruse to get me to do this chore! But when I said as much, he sighed and played hurt again to be so distrusted, though he warranted nothing else.

Waswasah said to me, "A caravan leaves in four days and as my agent it shall cost you nothing to ride along to Elephantine. As for your food and supplies, I shall give you a maneh, and for your trouble, a second one [6000 shekels]. Come. I would not make up such a story for my business's sake. It will be a simple thing for you to sail back down the Nile and I would have to face your wrath when you return, no?"

40. Yes, Josephus, it indeed proved my last folly. Perhaps, my brother, you turn your head and laugh even now as you read it, but I agreed to deliver Waswasah's letters and I boldly prepared to ascend the Nile. Because I had to know! Of course, I had to complete the life-account of Our Master for the generations of historians who awaited my work—to them I felt a duty, as a great scholar must. But also for myself! Had I followed mistaken paths yet again? Was I to learn by this investigation that the Nazirenes' claims of resurrection for Our Master were invention, calculated to keep his wondrous movement alive?

What responsibility suddenly rested with me. Here at the very last, old and beyond all plans and usefulness, the Most High had lifted me up to this task: to know, as no other Nazirene or Disciple, the truth of the final days after Our Master's execution. I assumed, naturally, that this was a groundless tale, another carefully crafted libel to discredit Our Master . . . but what if it were not?

41. Ah, Tesmegan, you should have seen me those last days in Alexandria! I became giddy as a young man; I was alive and joyous as if returned to a former happiness—it seemed I was not dead after all! And were there not Disciples left to search for? Matthew, who had evangelized the Nile decades before—might he be in Elephantine? Philip, who was said to be in the Faiyum. And I toyed with the thought of going to Mary of Migdal's illustrious convent (though I had had little success with Nazirene women and their willfulness).

42. But this greatest and last expedition was not undertaken without fear and a heavy heart:

I tried to imagine how I would feel were I to prove that Our Master's body was in fact held by the slave Benjamin! Would I continue to write and preach in favor of Our Master? Perhaps for the sake of the charitable Nazirene communes and all the good they do I would keep quiet if I found it were so. (Tesmegan, my dutiful scribe, smiles, for he knows the answer and what I found here in Meroe.)

43. And a worse, wrenching fear yet . . . God could dictate my life as suited His Will, but how I loathed the idea of perhaps having to one day return to Jerusalem to preach my discoveries, good or bad, before the Nazirenes and Pharisees alike! My Lord, anything but that! Alas Holy *Sophia*, Blessed Wisdom, it has seemed in these painful years no path would give peace, save one: the road leading away from Jerusalem, seat of all accursed and damned! Source of all enmity and war, destroyed as Our Master presaged, gone with its fanatics and troublemakers, zealots and hypocrites. Surely the Master of the Universe will never allow its irksome, smoldering rubble to rise again!

JERUSALEM

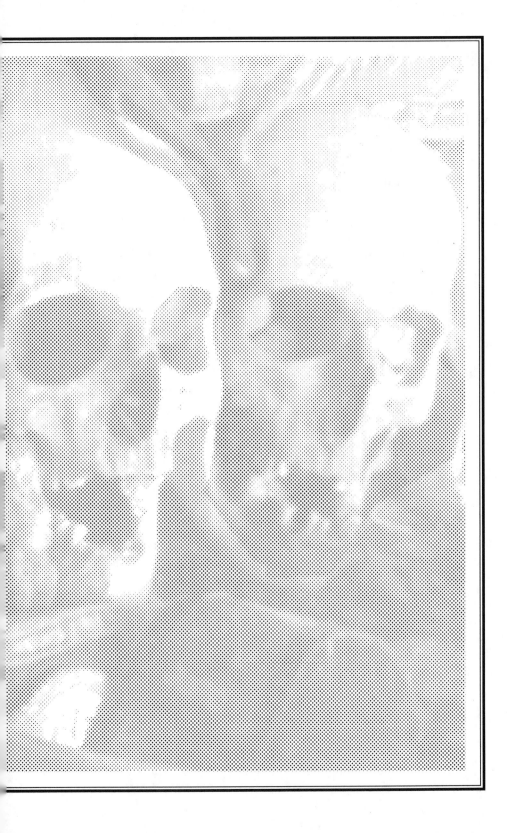

In less than thirty years the Israelis have produced a modern country. . . . It is both a garrison state and cultivated society, both Spartan and Athenian. It tries to do everything, to understand everything, to make provision for everything. All resources, all faculties are strained. . . . These people are actively, individually involved in universal history. I don't see how they can bear it.

—*To Jerusalem and Back* (1976)
SAUL BELLOW

There are miracles under my chair if I would bend over.

—attributed to Rabbi ELEAZAR

Here, in this carload, I, Eve, with my son Abel. If you see my older boy, Cain, son of Adam, tell him that I

—"Written in Pencil in the Sealed Freight Car,"
Selected Poems (1972)
DAN PAGIS

A Hasid asked the Seer of Lublin, "To the words in the Mishnah: *Man should thank God for evil and praise him,* the Gemara adds: *with joy and a tranquil heart.* How can that be?"

The tzaddik heard that the question sprang from a troubled heart. "You do not understand the Gemara," he said, "but I don't even understand the Mishnah. For is there really any evil in the world?"

—A tale (early 1800s) of
Rabbi JACOB YITZHAK, The Seer of Lublin

יְרוּשָׁלַיִם

Rabbi Hersch was incredulous when he received a call from O'Hanrahan that he and Lucy had arrived the night before and were registered at the King David, the palatial luxury hotel of Jerusalem. How did they get in from Haifa? They had booked a limousine. And if the phone call was to be believed, the rabbi had just been invited for a deluxe breakfast buffet. With champagne.

Rabbi Hersch made his way through the splendor of the lobby with its jewelry and fashion shops and gave a polite hello to the woman admitting diners into the grand dining room. Beyond the door he could see Jerusalem's businessmen and richer tourist elite helping themselves to sculpted fruit, trays of lox and seasoned fish, cheeses, bagels, pickles, and olives, the bounty of a kosher marketplace arrayed as if for King David himself.

"*Shalom,*" the woman said brightly, checking her list, "Mordechai Hersch . . . Yes, your friends are expecting you."

"Hmmm. What's it cost, my dear?"

"Your friends have paid so go right in. *Gut shabbes,* Rabbi."

The rabbi returned her wish for a happy Sabbath and entered the high-ceilinged hall, decorated like a lesser Hasmonean Throne Room, and soon spying Lucy and O'Hanrahan laughing at a corner table, plates of food before them. A silver platter of caviar, the expensive stuff. Champagne cooling in a stand beside the table. Lucy in sunglasses looking tanned and leaner. O'Hanrahan, also tan and decked out in a new navy sportscoat as well, an open shirt in the Israeli style with a scarf instead of a tie tucked in the collar, looking like some Miami Beach homes-of-the-rich tour boat captain. A waiter was standing nearby with a choice of cigars.

"So," said the rabbi, presenting himself, "who died and left you the mines of Solomon," reminded of his own hard-earned 200 pounds sterling sacrificed in Oxford.

"Morey!" said O'Hanrahan, springing to his feet. "Sit down, sit down. Some champagne, go get yourself some food!"

"It's 11:30," said the rabbi. "I had breakfast like the rest of the world at eight."

"Well, have lunch then."

One waiter pulled out a chair for the rabbi as O'Hanrahan reclaimed his seat and refocused on the cigar selection. The tobacconist recommended Cuba's finest Davidoff, the Dom Perignon.

Rabbi Hersch asked, "What's going on here, Mr. Rockefeller?"

"We're rich, that's what. You remember me telling you the department sent me a credit card in Ireland that Lucy was kind enough to bring to Italy." Lucy, serene behind sunglasses, toasted the rabbi with her champagne glass. "Well, as anyone should have been able to guess, the card was not from Chicago, not from my former department, which counts paper clips and rubber bands. It was from a mysterious benefactor."

O'Hanrahan traced this credit card, through many ruses of conversation with a toll-free operator, faking having lost his VISA then having found it again. The card originated from Merriwether Industries in Detroit, Michigan. The 312 number on the telegram to whom Lucy had been faxing reports was connected to the Medina Corporation, Chicago, Illinois. A trip of the library at Athens University turned up a Charles Merriwether who was the CEO of both operations—oil, shipping, chemical refining, and weapons. After racking up a large phone bill, after attempting to speak to anyone of importance at Merriwether Industries about why he should be issued a credit card, and after a few hostile middlemen declared him a crank and hung up on him, O'Hanrahan decided it was wiser to leave well enough alone and accept this generous funding.

"We are trying to spend our sponsor into bankruptcy," concluded O'Hanrahan, "hoping he will reveal himself and his motives."

"I see," said the rabbi, looking down at folded hands.

"So far," reported O'Hanrahan, "we can't seem to hit the card's limit. We spent a fortune in Rhodes. My new duds for starters."

Lucy began giggling. "Your clothes were ruined, after all." She turned to Rabbi Hersch: "Dr. O'Hanrahan fell into the bay and we missed getting back to our ferry and had to call ahead and get them to hold our luggage in Cyprus."

". . . and that's where I got this new coat, in Cyprus," O'Hanrahan said. "At the chichiest hotel."

"He thought he was the Colossos of Rhodes," explained Lucy, pouring herself champagne. "Trying to straddle the harbor."

"My dear, I *am* a Wonder of the World."

"A wonder of the *Ancient* World."

They pointed fingers and oohed at each other, Lucy bragging she really got him that time, O'Hanrahan vowing she'd pay for it!

"I don't suppose," began Rabbi Hersch drily, "that you should actually have managed to accomplish anything on this Mediterranean pleasure cruise?"

"Lucy was nearly kidnapped by an Islamic group in Greece, Morey . . ." And O'Hanrahan fondly replayed their Grecian adventures.

"I thought," said the rabbi, "that we had taken Miss Dantan out of harm's way."

"Rabbi, sir, I came to my senses. I realized my academic career would be made when Dr. O'Hanrahan translates the scroll and I'm his assistant. Where to? Harvard? Princeton?"

"No," said O'Hanrahan, "go west, Stanford or Berkeley. That's where I want to go, away from the snows and six-month winters."

The rabbi crossed his arms. "I see."

"Or," suggested O'Hanrahan thickly, "you could always go back to dear old Chicago . . ."

Lucy gave this a long Bronx cheer, and then O'Hanrahan did one as well and they both collapsed laughing, laughing too hard and sabotaging the effort to produce a Bronx cheer at the same time.

"I'm in a playpen here," said Rabbi Hersch.

Lucy: "I've been recording our trip with my camera so far. You'll have to let me take your picture, Rabbi, sir, so when *Life* magazine wants a full account of the *Gospel of Matthias* you won't be left out."

The rabbi stood unhappily, his champagne untouched. "Nu nu nu, I'll leave planning the fame-and-fortune part to you guys, while I will go back to doing what I've been doing without any help from anybody these last few weeks. Working very hard—"

"Would you *sit down?*" insisted O'Hanrahan. "And drink this stuff? This isn't exactly Manischewitz, you know." He turned to Lucy and suggested she have a puff from his cigar. "Now the thing about a cigar is this . . ." He fired up the lighter and roasted his Dom Perignon. "You let the smoke roll onto the palate—"

"I know how to smoke a goddam cigar."

O'Hanrahan withheld the prize. "When the hell did you ever smoke a cigar?"

"We snuck some out of my Uncle Liam's cabinet down at his farm in Kankakee and smoked them in the barn," she said. "Now give it here and stop wearing me out."

"Allow the smoke to ruminate on your palate—"

"Just give me the fucking cigar."

The rabbi said gravely, "Incorruption has put on corruption. To coin a phrase."

"What do you expect?" said Lucy, letting the smoke drift out of her mouth. "Just two months with the world's oldest living leprechaun, that's all." Lucy commenced a synopsis of their lost week in the Mediterranean with much embellishment and exaggeration. "To keep him from going ashore in Lanakia, I had to bring a bottle of metaxa to his room—"

Interrupted O'Hanrahan: "She appeared bottle in hand, in this diaphanous nightgown, woven as if by Alcyone for the King of Thessaly's return!"

Lucy almost let champagne come out her nose. "No, no, it wasn't like that!" She affected coyness, which didn't suit her: "It only occurred to me late that night," she said mock-innocently, "to get him drunk *on board* so he wouldn't go ashore and miss the boat the next morning. So I visited in my bathrobe, but it was hardly . . . diaphanous."

"The terrycloth clinging to her beauteous form; Aphrodite's *fine breasts that move the sighs of longing!*"

The rabbi pursed his lips as if he had a mouth full of something sour.

"Nonsense," Lucy went on, defending her honor. "Do you think I couldn't do better than an old goat like this?"

O'Hanrahan put a hand in his jacket like Napoleon, tipsily. "I could still rise to the occasion, darling girl . . ."

The rabbi slowly got out of his chair again. "I think tomorrow I'll come back when I should wake up and stop this hallucination."

"Sit down, sit down," said O'Hanrahan, tugging at the rabbi's sleeve. "What are you being an old humbug about? Someone, Morey, is underwriting our work!"

"Woik?" he exclaimed in sharp Brooklynese. "Work is in a library, like where I've been for the past three weeks! When you get through with your drinking binge, Paddy—and you, little girl, you I'm ashamed of. You're supposed to keep this . . . this *shikker* on track! After you get through buying all your $500 tchatchkes and wasting whoever's money, you can call me at Hebrew University. I'm off to the *Christian Science Monitor* before the Sabbath arrives, with my overdue review, if you don't mind."

O'Hanrahan telepathically knew what this review concerned. "Father Beaufoix's new book?"

"That's right—it's a masterpiece, and I'm saying so. The result of a lifetime of . . ." He leaned in his friend's face: ". . . serious, devoted scholarship. The kind that makes for published books!"

As the rabbi stood to leave, O'Hanrahan stood as well, chastened and repentant. "Morey, sit down. Look, on Athos I had my set of photos of *Matthias* stolen so I'll need you to make me another set. What could I do until I got to Jerusalem?"

"I'm not sure you *desoive* another set," the rabbi said, the New Yorker surfacing as he got upset. "If I print out another copy for you, where's this set gonna end up? In the Gulf of Aqaba?"

The rabbi walked away and O'Hanrahan gave chase, sweet-talking his old friend, answering each rebuff with blandishments. Lucy laughed to herself and put down her champagne glass. She looked at the Davidoff smoking, untouched for minutes, in the ashtray. She then breathed deeply, surveying the diners, the women in furs, the older Jewish-American moneymen with the spoiled daughters . . . No, this was not the life of serious scholarship.

Lucy rose and turned to the open double doors that led to the balcony of the King David Hotel, a grand balustraded plaza affording one of the great sweeping panoramas of the Middle East, the Old

City of Jerusalem, walled and fortified by Suleiman the Magnificent, ancient white bastions protecting the ecclesiastical hoarding within: domes, steeples, bell towers, minarets, the shrines of three great religions with the God of Abraham in common, this source, this staked claim of monotheism, this obsession of Western Civilization clutched firmly by the East. Looking upon these monuments and the pageant of pilgrims from around the globe, the spectacle of earnest scrapings, bowings, ululations, chantings, keenings, wailings, rituals in the service of competing faiths, how easy it is to come up short and wonder *why here*, why this place of all places?

(There is no river, no seaport, no mountain pass, no good farmland, no junction of trade routes, no incentive at all for Our children to put a city here. Except that it is a holy place.)

Lucy, gazing upon the medieval walls, wondered if the sun-baked white of this sacred city of gleaming stone was not the white of bones, the common pit of Judeans, Israelites, Greeks, Babylonians, prophets and libertines, Herodians, Essenes, Romans, Christians, Moslems, Crusaders, *jihad*-makers, and now Zionists, some 17,000 young Israeli soldiers to date, underneath this eternal altar of human sacrifice.

(That is not the worship We would have chosen.)

Lucy closed her eyes in the warm noontime sun and remembered it had been awhile since she had worshiped. Thank you, she meditated, Father, Son, and Holy Spirit for bringing me to this mountaintop, the Jewish and Christian and Islamic Olympus where I myself might walk where the holy walked.

(*I was glad when they said to me, Let us go into the house of the Lord. Our feet shall stand within thy gates, O Jerusalem.*)

Lucy turned around to notice O'Hanrahan talking to a waiter, probably ordering more libation. O'Hanrahan then strolled out to stand at the railing beside her. He glanced at his watch, then exhaled deeply.

Lucy said "Dr. O'Hanrahan" and O'Hanrahan said "Lucy" at the same time. Lucy motioned for O'Hanrahan to go first.

"Well," said O'Hanrahan, squinting at the view, "the great rabban has a point. We are in decline, Luce. *Quaeque ipse misserima vidi, et quorum pars magna fui.*"

"No argument there."

"We should return to our professional distance."

"If you'd like."

He raised an eyebrow.

Lucy corrected: "If you'd like, *sir*. Have you been in contact with Father Vico yet?"

O'Hanrahan rubbed his head. "I called him from Haifa and I received a phone message that he's deep in the Franciscan cloisters of the Holy Sepulcher. I suppose it's better than him hiding out in one of the numerous Franciscan kitschpiles throughout the Holy Lands."

O'Hanrahan's thoughts upon the visage of the Holy City were much different from Lucy's. She had the awe of the unacquainted; O'Hanrahan felt outrage at the atrocious, tasteless additions to Israel, campaigned by the insatiable Franciscans: Bethlehem's Church of St. Catherine adjoining the Basilica of the Nativity and its prize attraction, a ceramic, rosy-cheeked baby doll in a manger that reduces busloads of pilgrims to tears and is on sale in replicas around town. The nearby Church of the Milk Grotto, a cave with a chalky white powder that can be scraped from the walls and is sold representing Mary's own breast-drippings, featuring a chapel mannequin-Mary with exposed breast and life-size plastic Mary, Joseph, and donkey in another corner. The modern concrete Chapel Dominus Flevit, where Jesus wept. The cotton-ball sheep in the Church of the Shepherds of the Field. The airport-lounge modern of the Basilica of the Annunication in Nazareth, not to mention the Franciscans' modern insertions into, of all unmodern places, the Church of the Holy Sepulcher, where they unpopularly installed an organ to drown out the other sects' masses.

After his catalogue of aesthetic atrocities, O'Hanrahan announced, "I better go do homage to the rabbi this evening and soothe his feathers. So I can get another copy of the photos."

"He's not serious about denying them to you, is he, sir?"

"Ah, he was just being crabby," O'Hanrahan asserted less than convincingly. He tried to jump-start his brain: "Yes, this is perfect weather, isn't it? Perfect for work—and I'm eager to get back into it, Miss Dantan. We're getting soft, huh?"

She concurred.

A drinks-waiter in a tight uniform marched across the balcony and told Dr. O'Hanrahan there was a call for him, a Gabriel O'Donoghue.

O'Hanrahan said, "Tell him I'm not in, if you would."

The waiter did as ordered, and the professor turned on Lucy. "What do you suppose that good-for-nothing wants now?"

Lucy shrugged, not her brother's keeper in this affair. But Lucy was curious about something else: "How do they know who you are already in just 24 hours at this hotel?"

"A minor accident in the bar last night after you'd gone to bed. A little fire, of sorts."

"Of sorts?"

"I was merely demonstrating to this nice couple from Miami Beach the flammable qualities of a certain grade of arak. I was undone by a pillar of fire. A virtual pentecost!"

Lucy smiled as her mentor walked back to the hotel lobby, and she turned back to the Old City, the world's only inhabited ancient monument. The wonder is that there is not as much as a single square mile incorporated within Suleiman's walls, and yet the density of religious significance! Was there an unimportant inch in the Old City? A single brick that didn't mark a spilling of blood, a miracle, a site where some unsuspecting man or woman looked up from daily chores to hear the dreadful voice of God?

That afternoon, with the Sabbath looming and modern Jerusalem about to come to a holy standstill, O'Hanrahan and Lucy went in search of 2000 years of Christianity.

They taxied to St. Stephen's Gate, where one enters the Moslem Quarter of the city. The Temple Mount and its Islamic schools, the Dome of the Rock, where Abraham almost sacrificed Isaac, say the Christians and Jews, and Ishmael, say the Moslems; the site of the First and Second Temple, where Jesus argued with the Pharisees—the holiest of ground to nearly half the planet. From St. Stephen's Gate, where the Temple regulars rushed to stone Stephen and other heretics, one stands at the beginning of the Via Dolorosa. Lucy sighed: she had never been in a Catholic church anywhere that hadn't had along the walls the Stations of the Cross, and here she was! The Condemnation. The Accession to the Cross. Jesus Falls for the First Time. Jesus Beholds His Mother.

"I'm waiting," said Lucy staring at the crowds milling about and snapping pictures across from an Arab business called the Fifth Station T-shirt & Souvenir Shop.

"Waiting for what?" O'Hanrahan then saw the arch announcing the Armenian Catholic Church of Our Lady of the Spasm. "Oh, I see. You thought a church named Our Lady of the Spasm was going to foster a blasphemous joke on my part."

"It's not like you to hold back."

"I do feel compelled to point out that the 7th Century's St. John of Climax in his travels through the Holy Land doubtlessly performed the Stations of the Cross like all good pilgrims, and no doubt John *Climacus* felt a sympathetic shudder at Our Lady of the Spasm, a *simultaneous* multiple Spasm perhaps, he and the BVM. Very rare in ancient times."

Lucy hid a smile. "Erudite, but I think I prefer it when you go straight for the lowest possible remark."

"Yeah, so do I."

And now the Via Dolorosa led up the hill, past the Fifth Station where Simon the Cyrene took the Cross from Jesus, the Sixth, where Veronica wiped his face and occasioned the miracle of the Face imprinting itself upon her veil. Jesus falls for the second and third time at Stations Seven and Nine; he lectures the Daughters of Jerusalem at Station Eight. Few tourists track these down, having to go into dark, grimy Palestinian alleys to find a small Roman numeral on a plaque, but O'Hanrahan was, if anything thorough.

"Now to the Holy Sepulcher?" Lucy asked, thrilled to finally reach the place where the Crucifixion and burial took place.

"First, I'm going to take you to a holy place instead."

Winding down a dusty alley filled with construction materials, they reached the Ninth Station, an old column worn by the touches of millions of pilgrims that marked the exit of the Old City in Jesus' time. Through the door and down a step was the roof of the great Church of the Holy Sepulcher. Lucy walked along the smooth plaster, hearing hymns and chants and bustle beneath her. She walked over to a cupola and peered down at the worshipers below in the Sepulcher's basement at the Chapel of the Penitent Thief. *Truly I say unto you, today shall you be with me in Paradise.*

Lucy looked upward to see an even stranger sight. Huts. African huts, fashioned with white plaster. Beyond a wall were clotheslines with monks' garments hanging limp from them, huddled under the ruins of Gothic vaults. There were several little houses, one-room dwellings with leaning doorways and slanted plastered walls, like something out of the *The Hobbit* or Munchkinland.

"Who lives here?" she whispered.

"The Ethiopians," said O'Hanrahan.

When Ethiopia fell on hard times in the 1600s, the Greek Orthodox showed the Ethiopians the door when they couldn't make payments on the Moslem tribute.

(Right. It never occurred to the Orthodox that they should pay up for Our impoverished brethren.)

Lucy immediately reminded herself to write of this oddity to David McCall, probably now on his way to Ethiopia. From the 300s the Ethiopians had clung to this church through every rise and fall of Ethiopia, through every persecution in the Holy Lands, and they were still here, with their impenetrable musical liturgy in Ge'ez, their walking sticks that they leaned against through their long masses, the chants that phased in and out like an eastern mantra, a hum that would coalesce into words at intervals. Lucy lingered at the door to the nearby chapel, aside the stairway that led down into the rest of the Sepulcher complex.

"The Copts," explained O'Hanrahan, referring to those in the Egyptian Orthodox Church, "and the Ethiopians have been fighting over this stairway for centuries. The Ethiopians have it now because they changed the locks on the chapel in the 1970s and, after the Six Day War, no Egyptian could get a fair hearing in Israel. Fortunately, Moslems are in charge of the place and keep the peace."

"Moslems? You're kidding."

"Nope. Saladin's orders after the Crusaders were defeated. To this day the keys to the front door of the Holy Sepulcher, when it opens and closes and who gets in and who does what, are controlled by Moslems. They even do a lot of the repairs since the Christians can't be expected to do anything that might benefit another sect."

Lucy frowned, annoyed with her fellow Christians.

"All right," said O'Hanrahan. "You can die now, Sister Lucy, you're here at the Sepulcher where dispensations abound! I'm going to find Father Vico. I'll see you back at the hotel if I don't run into you. Wish me luck."

Lucy was left to wander down the dark Ethiopian stairway that led to the courtyard and simple doorway that led inside to the Church of the Holy Sepulcher. It was a mob scene. She snapped a picture although this famous church wasn't particularly picturesque. There was no facade to speak of, just a doorway in a tall wall of ancient sandy stone. The dreamed-of portals for two millennia of pilgrims, the crowning moment of a medieval man's or woman's life, the greatest of indulgences.

O'Hanrahan penetrated the inner recesses of the Church of the Holy Sepulcher. He asked in the Franciscan Chapel of Mary where he might find Father Vico, and was escorted to a small hallway. The place smelled of ruin and mold, though it was probable that the Franciscans were the best housekeepers of the six sects that shared this architectural pile-on. O'Hanrahan spied in a remote dank hallway the friar's assistant, Brother Antonio, appearing no more happy than in Assisi.

"Ah, *professore,*" said Father Vico emerging from the shadows. "Come to follow me . . . it is very dark, no? We cannot to make the electricity for to work here, eh?"

Father Vico had been given an office in the farthest reaches of the Franciscan vaults, virtually in the mosque next door. The room was airless and windowless, fitted with 19th-Century broken-down furniture one sees in poor parish offices.

"I have a soo-prise for you, *professore,*" Father Vico began.

"Oh boy."

Father Vico walked to the tall clothes cabinet and opened the door, removed a long overcoat from a hanger and reached into a secret lining. He produced a long scroll case, which looked familiar.

"You're kidding," said O'Hanrahan, recognizing it.

"No, we have our old friend from the *trecento* again, yes?" Father Vico had managed to recover the stolen 14th-Century vellum Ethiopian forgery from Rome. "The criminals dutifully returned it to the Church as I thought they would. A friend of the Franciscans passed it back to us. It is not without value, my friend."

"I'm sure it is worth thousands, Father."

"No one at the Vatican has missed it, so I suppose it will do no more trouble to let you to have it again. We have a word, *zimbello* . . ."

"A decoy, Father."

"Dee-coy, dee-coy, what a funny-sounding word." He returned to his desk. "Ah, but that is not all."

O'Hanrahan waited patiently.

"I had a dream."

O'Hanrahan bobbed his head, hoping he would continue.

"I had a dream of *you!*" Father Vico joined his hands and leaned back in his chair, inordinately pleased.

O'Hanrahan looked to the ceiling. "Was it . . . was it a nice dream?"

"Oh, I will tell you of the dream and then provide for you a interpretation, yes? I dreamed you were in the desert walking and walking, walking and walking, then you walked some more, walking and walking . . ."

The professor pinched the bridge of his nose. "Anywhere in particular?"

"No. And then a man whose face I could not see approached you within long robes, like an Arab, but not an Arab—very strange robes but very beautiful. And the man was beautiful too, very handsome."

"I thought you couldn't see his face."

"I could not but he had a possession of beauty, I knew without looking at his face. He held out to you a piece of bread and a vessel of water."

"Did I take them?"

Father Vico motioned with his hands like fluttering birds. "I woke up and could not tell you. It is significant, yes?"

No, thought O'Hanrahan. "I'm not sure I believe in dreams."

"Did I mention that the man had a tail?"

O'Hanrahan looked at the door that led out of the room and fantasized about passing through it. "You saw the tail?"

"No, I did not, but I *knew* of the tail, yes? You have this experience in the dreamworld? You know without seeing? Of course, it is the Devil perhaps. And you are to be tempted. Are you a man who can be tempted, *professore?*"

"Everyone can be tempted, Father."

"But you are not a . . . not a . . . *venalo, meschino* . . ."

"A venal man? I'd like to think not, Father."

Father Vico smiled at him placidly. "No, I think not also. I would hate for thees gospel to find the wrong possessor, and such a wrong person may to attempt to buy your favor, yes?"

"You have the gospel with you, Father?"

"Antonio!"

O'Hanrahan stared agog that the little safe on wheels had made it to Jerusalem. Squeak-squeak-squeak. Antonio rolled it from a locked closet in the antechamber into Father Vico's room.

"Here," said the father, "I shall open the safe and show you that *Matthias* is indeed with us in the Holy City. Ah, but you must turn your heads—yes, you too, Antonio. It is a very simple combination and anyone might see . . . ah, now what is it? Ha-ha, you are panicked that I have forgotten, yes? Of course I remember . . ."

Father Vico opened the safe and O'Hanrahan suspiciously examined the scroll case and slid the protective sack from it to glimpse the papyrus within. "Yes, this is it," the professor said. "I may have to photograph it again," he added, pessimistically contemplating a period of noncooperation from the rabbi.

"Ah," said the Franciscan father, "I see from your eyes you are not to be bribed by money from our agreed arrangements."

O'Hanrahan was certain that he could leave politely now. "You mustn't worry, Father. Nothing means more to me than translating our scroll." He then scooped up the *Pseudo-Acts of Andrew*, rested it in his satchel, and bade his host farewell. "Oh, I have a question." This slipped out before he thought about the implication of detaining himself with Father Vico.

"Yes?"

"Is the *Gospel of Matthias* safe here, amid the other five sects?"

Father Vico leaned forward and said confidentially, "None but the Franciscans will ever lay hands on it, and we will defend it, as we have defended thees church, to the death!" It struck O'Hanrahan that Father Vico rather titillated himself with thoughts of defending the scroll to his own demise. The father continued gleefully, "If someone were to pursue me, they should have no satisfaction! I am but a *zimbèllo*—what was your word? Dee-koo, Dee-koe . . ."

"Decoy, Father."

"Ah, I shall write that down . . ." Father Vico looked through his robe for a pen and could not find one, then every drawer of the desk, then the cabinet, then he called for Antonio, who also did not have a pen but went to fetch one, returned without a pen, was lectured, was sent out again, returned some minutes later with a pen.

"And now I am ready . . . ah! No paper! Antonio!"

Like all pilgrims, Lucy Dantan was initially disappointed in the run-down Holy Sepulcher, some chapels little better than storage rooms for debris, the Chapel of the Apostles, alive with frescoes from floor to ceiling, now a dumping ground for rotted lumber and rusted pipes. How, she wondered, did it ever get so dilapidated?

(The Syrians and their small caves in the back had had a fire—their fellow Christians cheering their misfortune. The Greeks and the Franciscans who have let walls and ceilings fall in rather than go to the expense of repairing something that might benefit another sect. A church that in 1834 had a fire during which a panic broke out among the Christian congregation and 300 people were trampled to death as the crowds rushed to save themselves. A church that in 1852 had a violent riot over who got to sweep the doorstep. A church in which a riot this century began over who had jurisdiction over the changing of an oil lamp. Monks have killed other monks over the issue of who gets to polish what. Godless place!)

Then the afternoon services began and the resulting cacophony Lucy found enthralling: the Armenian boys' choir with their atonal chanting was led in by pointed-hooded monks. The Syrians grouped around the backside of the Sepulcher itself and began a mass in Aramaic. Up on the mezzanine, as it were, at the site of Calvary, the Greeks began a ceremony. The Franciscans held Latin mass before the front entrance of the Sepulcher, which was encased in a gaudy marble hut under Constantine's much-restored dome. And at last the Ethiopians filed down from the roof and into the church and began touching their heads to the floor before the Stone of Unction, where Nicodemus and the women anointed the Lord's body with oils and balms. This echoing, ill-lit church in which one can barely see the ceiling reverberated with chant and rite and clinking censers that spread an Eastern perfume throughout the ancient hodgepodge.

It will take, thought Lucy, more than a few visits to decipher this labyrinth of catacombs: the Chapel of Adam, displaying the crack in the rock made during the earthquake as Jesus was crucified, his miraculous blood trickling down to the grave and bones of Adam—redeemed at last for his Fall. Down the stairs to a basement level, and down more stairs into a cave, was the Chapel of the Invention of the True Cross where Constantine's mother, Helena, was convinced she had found, 300 years after the fact, the real McCoy.

Lucy smiled. *Invenire,* "to find," in Latin; making the Latinized "Chapel of the *Invention* of the True Cross" a more cynical commentary than its namers had intended for us moderns. The Chapel of the Division of the Raiment. The Chapel of the Derision. The Chapel of Mary Magdalene on the spot she first beheld the Risen Christ. The Chapel of the Armenians where one can buy frankincense and myrrh from a nice monk—which she did—where one can view the 4th-Century pavement with Armenian letters in the mosaic, and see the Armenian Patriarch's throne, which looked amazingly like an easy chair in her mom and dad's living room . . . In fact it *was* an easy chair, discovered Lucy, inspecting it up close.

With clouds bringing an early darkness over the Holy City and the mosque across the courtyard sounding time for prayer, Lucy stepped out of the complex and into the open air, free of incense and chant, only the birds making noise. The inevitable horde of pilgrims, who lined up for hours for a solitary prayer in the Sepulcher or for the privilege of having a flash-photo taken at Calvary, where a silver plaque marks the spot of the Cross, had mysteriously thinned. There were no more than twenty people in the courtyard and Lucy lingered to look at the variety of Christians from East and West.

And from America.

Here came an American contingent of Baptists—they marched with a banner proclaiming THE PROMISED LAND and JERUSALEM MAKE-A-MIRACLE-HAPPEN MISSION 1990, as if their little banners would provoke God to action for the occasion. The Americans had availed themselves of Via Dolorosa, Inc., a group of untroubled Arabs who provided pilgrim groups with an oversize Cross they might carry along the Way of Sorrows. Lucy leaned against the dusty, chalky walls as this ostentatious group passed by in great solemnity. For one thing, thought Lucy, when Jesus carried his Cross it wasn't some chipboard, ten-pound prop like that—why don't you get a *real* Cross and see what the man went through? The Americans stopped before the front door to the church and an elder posed with the Cross for a picture.

"Mama," asked one drawn, middle-aged Southern woman, "have you had your time on the Cross yet?"

There'd be a chance for everyone to stand before the camcorder with the Cross before entering the Holy Sepulcher, the elder announced. We have rejected the ikon, thought Lucy, for the videotape souvenir played in the VCR, our modern altar. The Cross was passed to an overdressed Barbie doll of a Southern woman, all frills and calico ruffles, who wept profusely and had to surrender the Cross to someone less emotional. Next up was a young man . . .

"Farley," Lucy said with a jolt of recognition.

She decided to observe him secretly, and she scurried to the dark Ethiopian Chapel off the courtyard, to linger in the shadowed doorway. Farley with great seriousness carried the Cross, then turned to the video cameraman and said a few words, sharing his impressions for the folks who'd watch this, Lucy imagined, back home at Sunday school. Lucy scanned the Baptist mob for the Man in the Tacky Suit whom she and O'Hanrahan had decided was accompanying Farley. Suddenly it didn't seem very likely Farley was part of a master plan to steal the *Gospel of Matthias*.

AUGUST 4TH–5TH

Lucy left the Hebrew University Medical Center with a slow sense of impending unease. She had gotten yellow fever, cholera, and typhus vaccines in her left arm, a shot of gamma globulin in her behind, and had picked up two hefty containers of chloraquine antimalarial tablets. She cursed Dr. O'Hanrahan.

"It's just a bunch of shots," he had goaded her earlier at breakfast. "Stop being a baby. Your arm will be a bit sore for a few hours and then you'll be fine. *This* is a lot more worrying . . ." He showed her the headlines. Iraq had invaded Kuwait.

Lucy could care less at the moment, although she couldn't fail to notice how every headline, every newspaper, Arabic, Hebrew, and English, was blaring headlines about the international implications. Would Israel get dragged into this, one editorial wondered. Lucy stared coldly at the newspapers. Let's hope we're long gone before the answer to that plays out, she comforted herself. Of more immediate concern to her was her left arm, already throbbing in complicity with a slight fever; she reckoned a little bit of each of these killer diseases was swimming around somewhere in her body. That's right, she remembered, David McCall said the typhus shot was hell.

"I don't want *any* shots," she had firmly told O'Hanrahan that morning.

"All right, but when we start exploring monasteries along the Nile and the mosquitoes bite, don't come crying to me if you get yellow fever. Of course, you won't have any tears to cry with, since your 106-degree fever will have dehydrated every bit of moisture in your body, racked with spasms and sores—"

"*All right,*" she conceded.

Now all she wanted was to get back to the King David and crawl into bed, preferably lying on her right side. She raised her pulsing, wounded arm perversely to see if it was functional enough to hail a taxicab. She realized she would suffer for each and every movement.

O'Hanrahan was checking his phone messages at reception as Lucy passed by for her key. "How's our patient?" he asked cheerily.

"Regretting that she ever met up with you," she said, rubbing her shoulder. "The only recompense possible is that I can be around to see you get these shots too."

"I've had most of them already," he said lightly. "Did you get our malaria pills?"

She nodded, and even that hurt her arm.

"Look who keeps calling," said O'Hanrahan, sharing one of his phone messages. Lucy looked at the pink message-paper: Gabriel

O'Donoghue. Who came by the hotel at 11:36 A.M. Lucy glanced at the reception desk clock, which said 11:45 A.M.

"He must be nearby," she said.

"Yeah, and that's why I'm making my getaway for the library."

"How'd it go last night?"

He smiled, patting his satchel. "I've decided that the *Matthias* scroll is some form of Meroitic. Both Morey and I rejected that language earlier, but I've come back to it. Too many similarities, like the colons that separate the words. All the characters match up."

"Then what's the problem?"

"No one has ever deciphered Meroitic. It's one of the world's great lost languages. One of the reasons Morey and I rejected Meroitic is because Rabbi Rosen was reading this scroll in about a week and it's hard to believe he translated a mysterious language that scholars have been working on for a hundred years and then not tell anyone. But maybe he did just that."

O'Hanrahan noticed Lucy looking oddly at a giant rubber plant.

O'Hanrahan trailed off and turned in the direction she was looking.

A shambling, red-faced Clem Underwood sidestepped out from behind the fronds, as if he had been spying. "Heh-heh, well well well."

They stared at him.

"Long time no see, huh? What are you doing here, Mr. O'Hanrahan?"

O'Hanrahan and Lucy looked down as the five-foot Clem Underwood, the State Department lackey from their adventures in Greece, revealed himself. He now was wearing a light brown suit, again ill-fitting as if altered from a suit he'd got off the rack, a suit he persuaded himself looked tailored. His eyes were enormous behind thick circular glasses.

"I got the impression," said Underwood in his flat Midwestern drawl, putting out a pudgy hand to shake, "that you were going straight home. You sure gave our State Department sleepless nights. Miss Dantan," he added, nodding in her direction and extending his hand. Lucy noticed the ring on his right hand wasn't a wedding band but some fraternity ring.

"I'm a religious scholar," the professor said blandly. "Why shouldn't I visit Israel before going back to Chicago?"

Lucy looked at Underwood's sparse headful of hair that had been lacquered with some gel to form a point.

Underwood: "Hey, I hope you enjoy your stay here. And, heh-heh, if you need us at State don't, uh, hesitate to call."

O'Hanrahan was obdurate.

"Uh, I've got a meeting and I gotta fly," said Underwood, backing away. "Perhaps we can get together sometime for dinner, right?" Underwood picked up his briefcase, gave a lame military salute, and padded away.

"That was an odd encounter," said Lucy.

"Yeah. What's a two-bit functionary in the Thessalonika consulate doing down here in Jerusalem all of a sudden?" O'Hanrahan turned to the reception desk woman. "Excuse me, dear. Did that man, that short man, just check into the hotel?"

No, sir.

"Did he leave a message for me, perhaps?"

No, he didn't.

O'Hanrahan squinted, thinking about possibilities. "Okay, if it's not a coincidence and he's following us, we know two things. One, he's a very clumsy spy and a moron."

Lucy: "I got that impression back in Athens."

"And two, he knew we were here in Jerusalem and in this hotel. In Athens, did you say we were heading to Jerusalem?"

"No, you told me not to tell Mr. Underwood and Colonel Westin anything, so I didn't."

"Who knows we're here, then?"

Lucy sighed. "Rabbi Hersch knows. I called my mom. Apparently, Gabriel because of Father Vico knows we're here. Did you notice Mr. Underwood's ring?"

O'Hanrahan didn't.

"I could swear I've seen that design, that insignia before somewhere."

O'Hanrahan: "Well, you get some rest, Sister Lucy. And I'll keep plugging away at Meroitic and see what we get."

Lucy got her key and wandered to the elevator, her arm now aching with each footstep. Oh damn, she muttered, and lying down isn't going to help really. She needs sleeping pills. She needs to obliterate her consciousness for the next twenty-four hours until this goes away—

"Lucy!"

It was Gabriel. He ran up to give her a hug—

"Don't touch me!" she shrieked, turning a few strangers' heads, imagining a lover's spat. Lucy explained about the inoculations and Gabriel laughed.

"What are you still doing here? I thought you were back in Chicago."

"The chase continues," Lucy offered.

"Coming to Jerusalem was sort of my reward," Gabriel said, as tan as Lucy had ever seen him. "Father Vico said I could accompany him. Of course, he has no idea that I'm going to leave the Franciscans."

Lucy felt short-tempered due to the shots. She snapped at him, "One week you're in, one week you're out. Don't you get tired of yourself?"

Gabriel's big eyes went even bigger. "I'm trying to decide. I'm going through a lot right now."

Lucy tried to put this less sharply. "So going to South America and feeding the third world is out, for a while?"

"Oh, well, that wasn't very serious, feeding the world and all that. I think it's more important that I keep on with school." He began to discuss degrees he might get, programs he might consider, and Lucy found herself longing for the comfort of her hotel room. So Lucy invited him up—great view of the Old City from the window, she promised.

Lucy soon took to her bed, gently laying her left arm on a soft down pillow and turning to the chair where Gabriel had positioned himself.

"Can I have these?" Gabriel had discovered the chocolates left each night by the maids. Lucy, ever mindful of her virtuous loss of weight and never being a chocoholic like Judy, had stacked them neatly on the nighttable.

"Why do you want to see Dr. O'Hanrahan?" she asked.

"I'm hoping you'll help me. I mean, I think it's important to have resolution in your life, you know?"

Lucy listened, wondering why she had never detected so much New Age–speak in her friend's jargon before.

"And before I go home I want to sit down with Patrick and really *communicate* to him. I'm hoping we can secure some kind of bond before I leave because with all the bad things that have intervened between us, I still feel our time together was a really special growth experience for me and I want him to know that."

Hm, thought Lucy, I'd like to be a fly on the wall for that discussion.

"I was so depressed in Oxford," he was saying. "I'd have given anything to have someone to talk about the whole thing with . . ."

I was in Oxford, Lucy reminded herself.

"And I think I need to be free of the order for a while and pursue something for myself. You know, it's always been the Church—I don't do enough things for *me*."

Lucy yawned. "Gabe, I'm about to fall asleep, no offense."

Gabriel looked crestfallen. "Aw, we just started . . . How about getting together on Wednesday? I heard Dr. O'Hanrahan say that would be a free day because he's going to Tel Aviv to look up old friends. You and me can do the town."

Lucy said Wednesday sounded fine. Then he began a discussion of maybe being an art history major back at Chicago—

"Gabe, I've got to get some sleep. Rabbi Hersch is supposed to join us for dinner tonight and I always need to get my batteries charged before tangling with him."

Gabriel read more malice into the comment than she'd intended. "I hear that. The farther you and Dr. O'Hanrahan get from Rabbi Hersch the better, I think."

"Why do you say that?"

"I mean, I know Hebrew University owns the scroll and all, but I don't trust the old codger. Don't like him, and he didn't like me. He doesn't like any Catholics. Ever read his *Not the Messiah* book? It's really anti-Christian."

"He wrote a book called *Not the Messiah?*"

Gabriel declared it was the work of a Zionist fanatic. Then added, "You know when I tried to swipe the *Matthias* scroll in Rome back in April? The rabbi had said he was going to stay in Jerusalem, but then I saw him in Rome after all. I met with those art dealers and I was on my way out of the hotel where Patrick and I were staying, when Rabbi Hersch and I rounded the corner of an alley at the same time. I ran smack into him. I called out to him but he ran away."

Lucy reflected that the rabbi had shown up unexpectedly in Rome when she and the professor were there, too.

Gabriel noted, "And I never saw Patrick again to tell him about it. Doesn't matter now anyway, I guess."

Lucy found herself wide awake. "Interesting."

The next morning, following her five-hour afternoon nap and eight hours of sleep beyond that, Lucy was called upon to do some work. O'Hanrahan dug her out of her room where, enraptured, she was watching Israeli television and dragged her to a 7:30 A.M. breakfast with an emphasis on coffee. Then it was back to their adjoining rooms, where she was instructed to scoot her table against his room's table for a big work space.

"How's the arm today?"

"You're almost forgiven."

O'Hanrahan started right in: "Both Morey and I rejected out of hand that *Matthias* was in the Meroitic language earlier this year, but that was before I got out the newer German books last night and took a closer peek. Meroitic has 23 letters—four vowels, 17 consonants, and two diglyphs—with words separated by colons. So does our scroll, *exactly*. The Meroitic that Fletcher studied in 1909 was much different and that's the book Morey and I were using; but if you look at the Nubian manuscripts discovered when they started digging for the Aswan Dam in the 1960s, you'll find a later Meroitic, and it's a perfect match."

"I don't even know what kind of language that is."

"Join the club. No one's ever translated Meroitic."

"What's it like?"

"Nilotic Egyptian presumably, though it very quickly took on its own peculiar character. None of the Empire of Meroe's contemporaries could speak it either. Like all Nile languages, it evolved from a linear hieroglyphic to a hieratic alphabet around 200 B.C. to finally a more demotic written language."

"And it's totally indecipherable?"

"Hey. If the *Gospel of Matthias* is indeed written in some form of Meroitic, we'll be less famous for the gospel than for cracking this long-running mystery. People have been working on this goddam thing for over a century."

"Are there any clues at all?"

"Yeah. By comparing known pharoahs' names and gods and goddesses with their representations in Meroe, we can guess how the various letters are pronounced. We can sound the language out, but it means gobbledygook. And the grammar defies any known system. Here's what we're up against."

O'Hanrahan set down a yellow legal pad and scrawled some letters on the page:

NWSTHTMFRLLGDMNTCMTTHDFTHRCNTR

"Can you read that, Luce?"

"No," she laughed.

"This is a demonstration I used in my classes. It's an English sentence with no punctuation, and as in Semitic languages, there are no vowels. No clues to where one word stops and another one starts. This is what the Dead Sea Scrolls look like to the uninitiated."

O'Hanrahan let Lucy stare at the sentence for a moment, before he deciphered it, "*Now is the time for all good men to come to the aid of their country.*"

"Oh I see," she breathed. "Once you tell me I can see it, sort of."

"And so could the Hebrews who read the Qumran scrolls. They knew the material before reading it. They'd memorized it as if their memories were the sole, oral tradition, which was smart because in those days who could guarantee that papyrus or a scroll would survive. The Vedic Hymns from 2000 B.C. survive because still in the 19th Century Indians had memorized them perfectly—memorized them in a language dead for three millennia. Alexander the Great entertained his camp by reciting the entire *Iliad*. Man when he applies himself has a memory, what can I tellya?" O'Hanrahan sat down on the edge of his bed. "Fortunately we're not in total darkness, because Meroitic *does* tell us where words end with the colons. However . . ."

He leaned over to take out a brand-new set of prints of the *Gospel of Matthias*, courtesy of Rabbi Hersch.

". . . however, look at the first line of the gospel here."

𝟨𝖤4𝟥𝟨𝖠𝖴: 𝟪θ:4Δθ:𝟥Χ𝟩𝟪Χ:ΧU𝟥4𝟤𝖤𝟩

"Now," said O'Hanrahan, bringing out a yellow legal pad. "We know, if Rabbi Rosen wasn't deluded, that this is an epistle to Josephus and it is from Matthias. No epistle *ever*, in any archaelogical find I have ever heard about, fails to include in its opening the sender and the receiver. You never knew how many months or years it would take for the *grammatophoroi* to deliver mail in ancient times so you had to spell it out very clearly in the opening. Here is that top line with the Meroitic phonetics substituted . . ."

KVQGKJL: FR: QNR: VXMFX: XLMQSM

Lucy and O'Hanrahan stared at it.

O'Hanrahan: "Remember to read from right to left. I see nothing that sounds remotely like 'Matthias' or 'Josephus' or 'Jesus Christ' and I've converted half of the first block this way . . ." O'Hanrahan flashed the next and the next page in his yellow pad, revealing his transliterations. "I've read it up, down, sideways, you name it, trying to find one word that sounds familiar."

"Maybe it's just not in Meroitic."

O'Hanrahan crossed his arms pensively. "It's gotta be. Every character matches, with the most minor of variations, to the letter. And this colon business."

"So. What do I do?"

He smiled. "While I continue in the library, you go through the second and third chapter of *Matthias*, as far as you can go, and write the Roman equivalent of the Meroitic letters. It'll take a long time at first, but soon you'll just fly along."

O'Hanrahan left her with a chart with the 23 Meroitic characters and what sounds they equaled for her convenience. Lucy was eager to be of service . . . but what a long, dreary afternoon now presented itself.

Rabbi Hersch and O'Hanrahan and Lucy were in agreement for once: they all needed a break this evening from the drudgery.

O'Hanrahan returned to the King David Hotel at five P.M. with Rabbi Hersch, having detoured by way of the bar. O'Hanrahan was cross-eyed from reading everything about Meroitic in the library; the rabbi had spent the day sorting through library records to see what books Rabbi Rosen had once checked out. Lucy also suffered from cabin fever after making it most of the way through the second block of text, Chapter Two of the *Gospel of Matthias*, having in the process ordered up high English tea, a six-pack of Diet Cokes, and a pack of cigarettes from room service. She was wired.

In the Armenian Quarter, the three evangelophiles enjoyed two bottles of wine at an Armenian restaurant, ground lambsteaks with a wonderful red aromatic powder simply known as "Armenian spice," a finely diced salad Jerusalem-style, a confetti of spices and leaves, plates of *hummus* to be explored with warmed, blackened stone-baked pita bread, followed by a dessert of sugary, sandy pastries.

As promised, Rabbi Mordechai Hersch accompanied O'Hanrahan, with yarmulke, and Lucy, dressed conservatively in her long black skirt with black stockings, to the Wailing Wall, this remnant from Solomon's Temple. The pilgrim passes through a security station near the Dung Gate and looks down upon the marble plaza, a natural amphitheater leading to the Wall and its many supplicants there praying, chanting, men along one half, women at the other half, inserting their written prayer requests into the crevices of stone and mortar, this lapidary proof of 3500 years, marveled Lucy, of continuous faithfulness to Yahweh.

(Not entirely faithful, or else Solomon's Temple would still be there.)

There on top of the Wall and the Temple Mount was the al-Aqsa Mosque, one of the earliest mosques in Islam from 702, commemorating Mohammed's night journey to Heaven. And within view of both shrines in this realm of prayer, soldiers and Uzis and pillboxes and barbed wire.

(Remembrance and abomination, side by side, as it always is with Our children. Where is the Temple without the money changers? A mosque without the poison of fanaticism? A Church without hypocrisy?)

Lucy observed a young boy in the throes of his bar mitzvah, being whirled about on the shoulders of his father as the men formed a circle and danced and cried praise for another Jewish man brought into the tribe. The women in the family clapped, segregated to the side.

I am a creature, thought Lucy, unfashionable and politically incorrect as it may be in 1990, of the Eurocentric Western World, thank God. She was vaguely ill at ease with Eastern religiosity. Whether it was long-bearded Jews abasing themselves at the wall, Moslems ritually fanning the ground five times a day, or the myriad of Oriental Christian incense-sodden pieties, it was all in her final reckoning no different than Aborigines around the fire, American Natives before the totem, sun worship, stone worship, survivals of tribalism and primitivism. No, she preferred her intellectualized God of the grad-school coffee lounge, the reasonable American God of the Deists of the Enlightenment and Founding Fathers, benign and held at a safe distance just in case. I adore a private negotiable God of the heart, she realized.

They adjourned to Hurva Square for their after-dinner walk.

Hurva Square in the Jewish Quarter, narrated the rabbi, is the most successful Israeli architectural accomplishment. Bombed to ruin in the 1967 War for Jerusalem, and never much more than a slum before that, the rubble was cleared to make a plaza at once modern and respectful of the past, out of the same white stone of the ancient city. An arch, representing the dome of the great Hurva Synagogue, reminds visitors of the lively Jewish life that once was here—and is here again. O'Hanrahan observed some Israeli boys playing an impromptu game of soccer while two elder Orthodox rabbis walked through their playing field oblivious, committed to disagreement. They passed a series of columns exposed from an excavation on the edge of the square, Hadrian's Cardo, remnants of a once-grand Roman avenue.

At a café in the square, O'Hanrahan sat and, despite protests from his companions, who had had enough wine, ordered a bottle, something red from the slopes of Carmel.

The rabbi sipped and grimaced. "Yelllch. Next time get a bottle of California something-or-other. By the way, Paddy, come by the house sometime this visit and see if there's any of Shimon's books you want before I unload them all to the Christers."

"*That* is the most unseemly alliance made this century," O'Hanrahan declaimed. "Used to be Jews and liberals were the same thing in the U.S. but since the late '70s American Jews vote Republican, which they think serves Israel. They took Jerry Falwell and Jim Bakker's money, stood on platforms with redneck Baptists who ten years ago were burning crosses in Jews' front yards. And don't think a Yalie WASP like George Bush likes Israel, because he doesn't—"

"Hey," the rabbi shrugged, "Israel's gotta pay the bills somehow."

O'Hanrahan: "Tell Lucy about the library, Morey, if you can bear to utter the words."

The rabbi cleared his throat. "He acts as if I commit a crime. Rabbi Shimon Feldman, an inveterate bibliophile, left his library of thousands of volumes to the Hebrew University Capital Committee, of which I am a member. Feldman had over 5000 books of Old Testament commentaries, some, I am proud to say, the only existing English editions of the lesser medieval rabbis."

"So," interrupted O'Hanrahan, "guess who Morey's gonna sell it to? Guess!"

The rabbi remained calm. "I put feelers out and figured I could expect a few thousand bucks for it. Then I took out an ad in an

American Baptist Conference magazine and, boom—I'm up to $45,000 for the whole library at Bob Jones University. Got a damn good offer from Oral Roberts's place too."

The professor was disgusted. "Luce, can you imagine? Selling a first-rate library to Bob Jones? Why not a Judaica department in some small Brooklyn college?"

As they argued, Lucy contented herself with the parade of Israelis in the square, who ranged from secular and stylish to Ultra-Orthodox and severe. Two earnest Hasidic fellows were stopping American male tourists and asking them if they had a minute, and if they paused, they were asked if they were Jewish; if not, they welcomed them to Israel perfunctorily. If so, they were invited to a service and were immediately engaged in debate: Why wasn't a kipot on their head? Where had they been attending prayers? What were they doing for the Sabbath? Why hadn't they sought to study Talmud, Mishnah, the Pirke Avoth—why this decadence in America? And God help them if the innocents turned out to be Reformed Jews. Lucy thought: the rite of Judaism is argument.

"So these guys in suits come in and sit me down," the rabbi was saying. "And they ask me what I'm going to ask you: have you ever heard of the phrase 'Flight of the Griffin'?"

O'Hanrahan: " 'Flight of the Griffin'?"

"Just what I said. I asked why these Israeli government hacks wanted to know, and they said they couldn't tell me, just had I heard of that phrase. Weird stuff."

O'Hanrahan shared his own brush with mysterious authorities. "We got a strange visit this morning, too. A Clem Underwood representing the State Department in Greece. He helped get me off the hook after my trouble in Mt. Athos."

"What did he want?"

O'Hanrahan looked heavenward. "Who knows? I thought it was odd that some functionary from the Thessalonika consulate took a trip to Israel to ask about my health. So I went by way of the phone center and called Athens and asked to speak to personnel, pretended I wanted to send a letter of thanks . . . and what do you know? No one named Underwood works for the Greek embassy."

Lucy sat up in her chair.

All these fellow travelers irked Rabbi Hersch to impatience: "Can Father Vico be bought? I was thinking of bribing the guy to hand over the *Gospel of Matthias*. How long before someone else steals it?"

O'Hanrahan drained his glass of wine. O'Hanrahan wouldn't have admitted it if his life depended on it, but he preferred to have the scroll right where it was. In a place in which *he*, Patrick O'Hanrahan, was the go-between. Once Hebrew University gets it again, who's to say what will happen? It may be assigned to other scholars. Mordechai Hersch may call in a group of translators to help out, including Father Beaufoix. Rabbi Hersch was thoroughly unconcerned with who got the credit and glory; he just wanted it done so his Josephus book could be completed. O'Hanrahan clapped his hands as if to sidetrack this development. "Tell us a story, Rabbi."

Lucy, enjoying the cheap sweet red wine, feeling drunk and at ease on Mount Zion, put her legs up in her chair and got comfortable.

"All right," he said. "But I expect your interpretation, little girl. This is a tale of Elimelech of Lizhensk, who died in 1786, a disciple of none other than the Dov Baer of Mezritch."

This meant nothing to Lucy but she smiled familiarly.

"It was the Feast of Weeks and everyone was warm inside, all the students and rabbis, eating, and rejoicing and drinking, and the Hasidim were no strangers to drink, I can tell you.

"Elimelech is thinking, 'Ah, what a wonderful feast, what happiness,' until a brash pupil stood and said, 'Oh Rabbi, this is almost perfect. If only we had the Wine of Life that they drink in Paradise.'

"And Rabbi Elimelech considered this and said, all right kid, I will send you on an errand to fetch the Wine of Life. Get two buckets and a pole and balance the buckets at the ends of the pole and go down to the cemetery on this stormy night. Go into the very center of the graveyard and say, 'Salutations, spirits, Elimelech has sent me for the Wine of Life.' Now the spirits will help you and fill your buckets, though it may be invisible. In any event, you turn around and come back and be careful not to spill a drop. So the young man does as he's told, goes to the middle of the cemetery.

"And the wind blows and he feels a chill up his spine. He hears the voices of the long-dead moaning, moaning, saying, 'Give us a drop of the wine, we are so thirsty . . .' So he begins to run! Trying to keep the buckets steady he feels the hands of the spirits upon him, he feels his heart being touched by icy fingers, and all around him the wind carries moans of the dead to his ears! He trips and falls and breaks the pole and stumbles over the buckets, hurting himself. In terror, he runs through the door of the feast and slams it behind him.

"And the Rabbi Elimelech looks up and tells the young man, 'Fool, sit down.' "

That was it.

Lucy took a deep breath and ventured:

"It means . . . I think Rabbi Elimelech sent his student to the cemetery for the Wine of Life knowing he would get spooked and terrify himself with the idea of ghosts and graves and death in the dark. And thereby the student learned that graves and darkness and death await everyone . . . and that coming back to the table, into the warmth and light, with the food and drink and fellowship of men who love God, that *that* was the greatest pleasure, the Wine of Life that they drink in Paradise."

The rabbi bowed. "And is it not true?"

It was a mistake but the rabbi ordered a final carafe of wine.

The effect of the inoculations and too much wine had Lucy reeling. She propped herself against a stone wall of the café and had to be retrieved by the older men. "Take me home," she insisted, still managing a smile.

"Taxi!" called O'Hanrahan, laughing at his own joke, for no cars could drive into Hurva Square, or any of the narrow alleyways of the Old City. It would mean an arduous, uphill walk up those damn steps of David Street again. In the process of walking, the balance of power shifted and it was O'Hanrahan who proved too wiped out to walk a straight line.

"How'd he get insensate, for Christ's sake . . ." said Rabbi Hersch, struggling to support O'Hanrahan between himself and Lucy.

"He was so energetic a minute ago," Lucy said, taking the professor's other arm, aiming him down the closed market-street.

The Old City, once night fell, reverted back to the sleepiest of villages; bedtime was early since many of the populace got up at dawn to tend their stalls in the market or for the dawn services. It was deserted and a little scary.

"Is this the Via Dolorosa?" asked O'Hanrahan, recognizing a landmark.

Rabbi Hersch: "Just put one foot, then the next foot—"

O'Hanrahan broke free from his captors: "Our Lady of the Spasm!"

Rabbi Hersch: "We're almost up the hill now, that's it, that's it . . ."

"The Stations of the Drunk! Whoooops . . ."

(O'Hanrahan Falls for the Hundredth Time.)

That tumble seemed to wake him up. "Just a minute, guys," he said, upright again and swerving to a nearby alley. "Station Thirteen," he announced. "The Urination."

Lucy stood apart from this spectacle and, shaking her head, propped herself woozily against a wall.

O'Hanrahan: "The ostension of the relics!"

When a taxi appeared at the taxi-rank within the Jaffa Gate, Rabbi Hersch and Lucy deposited O'Hanrahan into the back of the station wagon, where he slumped over the whole of the seat. Lucy and the rabbi scooted into the front seat, uncomfortably intimate. As the elderly driver continually mumbled an ignored moral lecture in Yiddish, Lucy found herself virtually on Rabbi Hersch's lap.

"This can't go on," said the rabbi calmly.

"I know," she said. "But we got a lot done today. Really."

"A team of scholars would do better," he answered her. "We need half a dozen people I could name to fly in and brainstorm and figure this mess out."

Lucy shared O'Hanrahan's sense of loss at the prospect of renowned scholars descending on *their* project.

The rabbi said nothing until they arrived at the driveway before the King David Hotel lobby. O'Hanrahan came to and straightened his disarranged silver hair, his rumpled jacket. "Well," he said, tasting one too many cigars in his raw throat, "if you'll excuse me."

Lucy and the rabbi watched him trip on the curb and recover before falling. A bagman asked if he wished to be accompanied to his room, and O'Hanrahan waved him away. As soon as he disappeared inside the lobby, Rabbi Hersch said coldly, "I think, little girl, it's time to get Paddy back to Chicago before he self-destructs."

And her along with him, Lucy reasoned. "He's not *that* bad."

"Not that bad? The way you were describing him in Cyprus and Rhodes didn't sound so good. And tonight!"

"Rabbi, sir, *you* ordered the last bottle of wine. I don't think it's fair to keep filling his glass and have a good time and then at the end of the evening say, well, that's it, Dr. O'Hanrahan can't behave himself, let's send him home."

"You know what I'm taking about, don't pretend you don't." The cab driver asked if his presence was required any longer and the rabbi motioned him to hold on. Was he being paid for it, he asked. Yes yes, you'll get your money, the rabbi shot back. "Look," Rabbi Hersch continued, "I had hoped your presence would help Paddy reform just a little, but I know this guy. In a week he'll be back to his old antics and he'll walk all over the likes of you. He ought to go home, where if he gets sick he can be taken care of—"

"What home?" Lucy asked, as the rabbi seated himself again in the taxi. "He sold it, remember?"

"Maybe if *you* should go home, he'll follow you."

But Lucy didn't want to go home. "Why did you ask Dr. O'Hanrahan to come work with you in the first place if you thought he was undependable?" She then added, "You raised his hopes only to cut them off . . ."

The rabbi opened the car door again and hopped up, exercised though not angry. The cab driver muttered more Yiddish, pointing to the ever-running meter. "Little girl," he said firmly, "all his life Paddy has been on the cutting edge of his field only to fumble it—only to turn up a bottle, only to back away from the serious scholarship he was capable of. No one on this planet, if he put his mind to it, can give me more help than Paddy on this gospel, and he seems to be the last person who understands how serious this is! And how little time he has left."

Lucy said at last, "I'll help him walk the straight and narrow, I promise."

The rabbi was unpersuaded but ready to end this long evening. "And if he continues to carry on like this, will you also promise that you will help me put him on the plane to Chicago?"

Since it bought time, Lucy vowed she would.

"*Lela tov*, Miss Dantan," said Rabbi Hersch, at last committing himself to the taxi.

AUGUST 6TH

Monday morning was painful and hung over. O'Hanrahan looked stricken and unrested, and declined when the breakfast waiter asked if he might like the champagne–orange juice cocktail that was on special this morning.

"No," he sighed, resignedly. "Today is a work day, isn't it, Sister Lucy?"

"Yessir," Lucy replied, having miraculously avoided the ill effects of last night. The genetic Irish tolerance must be kicking in, she thought. I am my Daddy's little girl. She eagerly devoured a plate of succulent Middle Eastern fruits, a bowl of yogurt with some kind of bran dust sprinkled atop it, to the side of a butterless, hard bran roll.

"Very healthy this morning, I see," he grumbled.

"You've got a plate of cholesterol there, sir," she said, briefly pointing a spoon at his eggs and sausages. "I meant to tell you, all yesterday, that Gabriel kept calling. He wants to make peace with you."

"Fat chance."

"He's leaving the Franciscans again."

O'Hanrahan snorted. "That boy reminds me of my own son."

Lucy listened intensely; this was the first he had ever alluded to his ill-fated family.

"Rudy was the same way. Changed majors three times—each time he came up with something worse than the last time. Sociology, that kind of thing, political science."

O'Hanrahan was quiet and an impossible silence grew between them. He returned presently, saying, "We're meeting Rabbi Hersch at the Damascus Gate this afternoon, right?" He tried to remember how they had left it last night. Oh yeah, that's right: Rabbi Hersch threatening to bring in Father Beaufoix, which O'Hanrahan had heard as he played passed-out on the cab ride home. "Seen the Dead Sea Scrolls yet?"

"No, sir, I haven't got around to it."

"My greatest glory and you have not found time to pay homage?" He felt empty inside—his greatest trophy was nearly half a century behind him. Father Beaufoix's new book would be in the stores this week . . . Beaufoix and Elaine Pagels, actually writing *best-sellers*, making fortunes off this material that O'Hanrahan knew off the top of his head! "After the Museum," he added, "Mordechai said you should drop around Hebrew University, look him up."

That was the last thing she wanted to do. Just the rabbi and herself alone. Without O'Hanrahan there to intercede, what would they talk about?

"No, I'm ordering you to go," he went on. "I feel we need some damage control here. And I sense, despite my being a close friend, that Morey'd happily bring in someone else to replace us."

Right, thought Lucy, old Father Beaufoix waiting in the wings, fingernails sharpened for his grab. Unhappily, a more realistic vision of O'Hanrahan was taking shape: O'Hanrahan the almost-ran, the talker not the doer, the beloved but, sadly, dispensable scholar, no books on the shelf, no entry in the Scholastic Register. She would have been happier to think of him as invulnerable and titanic. But this, she reckoned, is the price of intimacy with one's idols.

"I told the rabbi," said Lucy, "that I'd make you take the pledge today. No alcohol at all. Will you swear?"

"Don't worry," he muttered, tapping his head.

Lucy, suspicious, questioned his day's activities.

"I'm going to see an important man in the history of this gospel. Mustafa al-Waswasah."

Lucy: "Who's that?"

"He's just about the wiliest old devil I've ever met. He sold a number of Dead Sea Scroll fragments to Israel for the moon—he's still living off the money. He's in East Jerusalem at the El-Khodz Hotel in one of those posh lobby stores where he can pawn off cheap brass coins left to sit in urine for a month as fabulous numismatic antiques."

"Urine?"

"He told me his way to age coins and get that green-blue brass effect."

"I'll remember that the next time I counterfeit Roman coins."

Promptly at ten A.M., they left the hotel separately.

Lucy spent the morning cashing traveler's checks O'Hanrahan had purchased for her with the all-powerful VISA card. She had been treated curtly at the bank, which offered no clue as to who approved what or how to proceed once one got approval; her every question was met with a long-suffering impertinence to tourists.

Lucy next wandered into a shop and was pressured by the over-solicitous Israeli merchant to buy a chessboard she did not want and finally made an escape rather than dare to look at the merchandise she did have an interest in.

She stepped up to a magazine store and bought a few postcards and discovered that Israelis who entered the line after her were served and dealt with before she was. For God's sake, she told herself, I'm trying to *give* them money, you'd think they'd want to take it.

Along the Jaffa Road she found a bookstore. She recalled Gabriel's characterization of Rabbi Hersch and his anti-Christian tract. Lucy stepped inside. The caretaker asked her something outright in Hebrew that she couldn't understand. She could read Hebrew at a snail's pace but she had no chance of speaking it. Only the Israelis could decide in the course of a generation to resurrect a language abandoned long before the time of Jesus, Lucy considered. Can you imagine America switching over to, say, Old Saxon in a generation, just on utopian principle?

She noticed the collections of Hasidic folktales and she took a few books from the shelf and perused happily. Edging toward the H's she saw a used copy of *Not the Messiah* by Mordechai Hersch. Just as Gabriel had said. Published 1974. Dedicated to all the students who have been swept up in Jews for Jesus, may your apostasy shame you into returning to the fold. Sounds more like Khomeini and his *fatwas* than Mordechai Hersch, she thought.

She flipped to a section titled: WHAT BRAND OF CHRISTIANITY SUITS YOU BEST? It was snide, taking the denominations of Christianity one by one and ridiculing them, with especial acid reserved for Catholicism. There was a chart of persecutions, and paragraph descriptions of who had done what historically to the Jews.

The Jewry of Brussels wiped out because Catholics testified that they overheard Jews sticking pins in the communion wafer and Jesus crying out. A consecrated host with blood on it was found and the thousands of Jews—who had, as always, built the town—were wiped out in horrible tortures and burnings. The countless churches to St. Chad and St. Hugh in England, little boys whose blood was drunk by Jews. A Gentile child disappeared and it was as good as certain that the Jews would pay for it—and of course all debts to the moneylenders would be erased. And Jews had to money-lend—they couldn't own property, practice any normal trade . . .

Catholicism invented fascism, wrote Rabbi Hersch, *and of course the papacy, the Pope, the papa and his Fatherland, are the original model for modern, infallible totalitarianism. Spain, South America, Italy—where fascism flourishes one finds the Catholic Church tied into it, and let us not forget Hitler rose from Catholic Austria and Bavaria. The Vatican signed concordats with Hitler, with Mussolini, and finally Franco in 1953; Pope Pius XII breathed not a word about the concentration camps despite the fact a smattering of Catholics were going to them as well—he even called on the Allies to stop their fighting the Axis as late as 1943.* There followed actual Nazi-Catholic liturgies with Hitler interwoven with the Father, Son, and Holy Ghost; a photo of Köln Cathedral with swastikas from the altars ... *With Western security forces, the Catholic Church under orders from Pius XII smuggled war criminals, many of them the priests, out of Europe to South America or to new identities in America—Barbie, Eichmann, the worst of the monsters! And his cardinal, the later Pope Paul VI, was his key operator in this filthy charade.*

Lucy stopped reading. What pathetic little defense could be offered up for all this villainy; what human could accommodate in one lifetime the requisite shame? Second, she wondered why Rabbi Hersch would write such a fondly detailed document against Christians.

(It's not as if what he writes isn't true.)

Lucy replaced *Not the Messiah* on the shelf, not sure she wanted to read 120 pages of unceasing accusation.

Then she took it down from the shelf again. She determined she would buy it and steep herself in all the guilt as part of her education for Israel. Lucy then browsed through the Mysticism section and thumbed through books of Kabbalah and magic, amused at this vast trove of secrets that had been cherished by the Sephardim and Hasidim, with a smattering of Christian, Islamic, and pagan mumbo jumbo sprinkled throughout—

"That you, Lucy?"

Lucy looked up to see Farley. "Hi," she said, off guard.

"Remember me? Farley, we met in Florence, I'm from Louisiana?"

"Yes, I remember. So your college group is in Jerusalem now."

Farley was enthusiastic. "Yep. See these books?" He had a grocery bag of paper pamphlets. He reached into the bag and presented Lucy with one titled THE ONLY HOPE FOR PEACE IN THE MIDDLE EAST, which was a tract full of elementary school–level prose with Bible quotes and large storybook pictures of Jesus performing miracles and looking kindly down upon his earthly children. If Israel would acknowledge Jesus, the text insisted, peace would automatically descend.

"We're passing 'em out to bookstores to give out for free, you know? We figure anyone buying religious books will wanna read it."

Lucy consciously hid the front of Hersch's *Not the Messiah*. "I don't think the rabbis in this town would be too enthusiastic, but good luck."

Farley magnanimously insisted that she keep that one for herself. "I know you don't need it," he said, "being Christian already but maybe you could give it to someone. You're not in your nun's uniform."

Lucy decided to be honest, with an ulterior motive of playing detective—she would rush back to O'Hanrahan with all the clues she would gather! "I'm not a nun."

"But you were dressed ..."

"Well, that was for Father O'Hanrahan's benefit. I didn't want to let the dear man know I wasn't a Poor Clare, you see." Not too convincing, but Farley seemed overjoyed to have Lucy returned to the secular world.

"That's great," he laughed. "You wanna come to lunch today?"

"I can't," she said truthfully, "I have to meet a rabbi friend today at Hebrew University."

Farley crestfallen: "You're not Jewish, are you?"

"No, I was telling the truth about being Catholic. And a practicing Christian," she added, before she was asked as to her born-again status.

"We're having a prayer service at the Baptist Mission in the New City, and my mom's gonna lead it this afternoon. You could meet my dad. I told him all about you."

"You did?"

"He said what I said, you oughta come teach at my Bible College."

Well, the job market *is* tight, thought Lucy, but I don't think it's come to that. "Actually, Farley," she said, looking at her wristwatch, "I had better be getting over to Hebrew University. See you around."

Lucy left the bookstore and dropped her pamphlet in the nearest waste can, walked a few steps further, went back and fished it out again, and reburied it under some deeper trash so Farley wouldn't be offended if he walked this way and saw it in the receptacle.

O'Hanrahan decided against taking a taxi with a Hebrew roof sign, since he was headed into East Jerusalem. Waswasah, the famed antiquities dealer, worked in the lobby of the plush El-Khodz Hotel, a Palestinian-run luxury hotel from the days when Jordan controlled the Holy City.

O'Hanrahan began a sunny walk to the Damascus Gate where one could find an Arab cab driver. He reflected on Mustafa Waswasah and the many Palestinians who profit by the Jewish intellectual and university community so many Arabs despise. What a philistine place Jerusalem had been before the advent of Israel. King Hussein of Jordan kept the Christian churches in shambles, presiding over their slow deterioration; Jews had no freedom of worship at the Western Wall; a suppurating Arab *fellahin* ignorance hung over the city then. Palestinian and Philistine are, O'Hanrahan considered, from the same root—proof that the Middle East only has a few conflicts, endlessly recast each new generation.

"El-Khodz Hotel, my friend?" checked the Palestinian cab driver.

O'Hanrahan was fairly gyp-proof with his conversational Arabic.

Since the driver was talkative, O'Hanrahan ventured, "So what do you think of Iraq in Kuwait and Saddam Hussein?"

"The world is a fool to think you can stop him," he said politely. "I think not even the Jews can stop him. He is a hero."

"He's a monster, you know."

"You know what your government tells you, the CIA . . ." But the driver was too smart to be satisfied with the delusional rhetoric Palestinians are so expert in. "No, he is very bad. But so is Shamir. Saddam may liberate the West Bank and destroy Israel. He is the hope in the world for the Palestinians—do you not see?"

Shamir and the Likud stiff-necks will never *really* negotiate with the Palestinians, unless it's for a very lopsided peace. Do not doubt it, O'Hanrahan told himself: many Palestinians, reported the morning *Jerusalem Times*, will go to Baghdad to die for Saddam Hussein since his pledge to use chemical weapons on Israel if any trouble started. This kind of evil they cheer.

"We are being followed," said the driver, just as lightly.

O'Hanrahan turned quickly to see a black Mercedes trailing behind them.

"You're sure?"

"Oh yes."

The cab driver turned into a narrow street marked for pedestrians only. His window was down and he nodded laughingly to all the people he inconvenienced in this narrow alley; Palestinian women and children took to the doorways, breathing in to let the car go by, perhaps, thought O'Hanrahan, familiar with this maneuver. The cab driver recognized three men sitting in a coffee shop. They waved, laughed, mock-insulted each other. A boy held three chickens, squawking and trying to release themselves from the twine that tied their feet together. O'Hanrahan glanced over his shoulder and indeed the black Mercedes had not attempted to follow.

The driver turned into an even narrower alley that had an exit onto a main road. A man selling Arabic newspapers, with a big, badly printed Saddam Hussein smiling heroically on the cover of several editions, moved his makeshift wooden stand to let O'Hanrahan's cab scrape through.

"Shukran," said O'Hanrahan, who elaborated further praise for the escape in Arabic.

"You are a friend of the Palestinians, yes?" asked the man. "You know the Arab tongue."

"Yes, I am a friend," said O'Hanrahan, feeling that did not commit him to PLO terrorist acts. "I am sympathetic."

"More and more Americans," he said, stopping the car before the side entrance of the hotel, "are beginning to see how we bleed."

"That's true," said O'Hanrahan, not imagining for a moment the hefty taxi driver had seen too much deprivation and hardship in his expensive taxi amid the Israeli prosperity.

He laughed. "Do not let Mossad catch you!"

O'Hanrahan wondered if the black Mercedes was indeed Mossad, the Israeli intelligence agency. No Mossad agent would stalk a car so obviously . . . or maybe that is part of modern Israel's strong-arm tactics, and like the old KGB, they opt now for the menacing, malevolent gesture. And Rabbi Hersch had mentioned he himself had endured a visit from some nebulous authorities.

"*Shukran,*" said O'Hanrahan.

"*Afwan eh ma'asalaama,* my friend."

Inside the lobby, O'Hanrahan observed things had declined from the 1950s, the glory days of the hotel. Tourists were far less likely to venture into this contested tear-gas zone, though the Palestinian welcome was warmer than Israeli officiousness and indifference, the prices cheaper, and even in some hotels, it was cleaner. A TV was blaring Jordanian news in the corner. There was President Bush mouthing forceful language about Saddam Hussein. There was a smuggled video of Kuwait being invaded, tanks in the street . . . there was a map and a graphics display of possible deployment of U.N. troops were Saudi Arabia to permit it.

Thought O'Hanrahan glumly: The End Times!

"Patrick, my brother," cried an aged Mustafa Waswasah, graying at the temples, but still a fit Arab man in an immaculately tailored Western suit.

"Mustafa," cried O'Hanrahan in return as they hugged and kissed. No, they were not best of friends but they were relics from each other's splendid youth, and so much had happened since those days, so many unaccountable years of wasted, bided time, that the sight of each other returned them for a moment to vigorous manhood. O'Hanrahan fought to not have his eyes fill with tears.

"Come," said Mustafa, "Come in to my shop . . ."

Hard times, thought O'Hanrahan. Without the flow of scholars and carefree tourists into East Jerusalem, only the brave ventured to the Hotel El-Khodz, mostly Moslems for whom the Christian ecclesiastical relics and parchments meant nothing. A collection of silver crosses unearthed in Madaba, Jordan. A Persian swastika that had eluded the Rockefeller Museum's collection from Hisham's Palace in Jericho. Alas, despaired Waswasah, it is a tough time, some of these treasures would be in these display cases at his death. Ah, but there were some profoundly important Roman coins in this case here, he asserted, pulling O'Hanrahan to the display—

"How long were these in your toilet?" the professor asked.

Waswasah raised his eyebrows, about to take offense, but then realized he had confessed his trade secret to O'Hanrahan a long time ago.

The men laughed then, rich, roaring laughs. "How well you know me!" said Waswasah, making his way to a storeroom excitedly. "I have for you a present, Patrick," he added with a gleam. From the back room he produced a dusty green bottle. "Arak of Damascus. For you."

O'Hanrahan had taken the pledge for today, but then again—

"You are pleased?" Waswasah asked.

But of course the sin of pride is a *worse* sin than drinking, O'Hanrahan considered jesuitically. Could I really insult my friend? "Just one glass, perhaps, Mustafa."

As they both sipped from small tea glasses, they talked of what all of Jerusalem was talking about.

Mustafa al-Waswasah: "To an Israeli I would say, 'Let Saddam Hussein sweep over this land and make the changes.' After all, he will not live forever, will he? With the West Bank back in Palestinian hands, it could not easily be taken back by the Israelis, yes?"

Well, thought O'Hanrahan, the Israelis easily took it the first time, in less than a week against three nations' armies!

"But to you, Patrick, I say he is a monster, a madman!"

As Westernized as Waswasah had become, O'Hanrahan wondered what would become of a Palestinian-dominated Holy Land. Arabs who'd prospered and become Israeli might well receive worse than the Jews. Although a master like Waswasah would certainly squirm his way out of trouble no matter what.

O'Hanrahan: "A word about the scroll you sold Rabbi Rosen in 1949 . . ."

"You know my code," Waswasah announced proudly, as he now without comment poured a little more arak into his tea glass. "I keep my clients and their affairs confidential. It is like a Catholic person and his priest, no?"

This fox would tell anyone anything for money, O'Hanrahan knew full well. "But this was forty years ago, Mustafa, and Rosen is long dead. My friend. Please. Do you recall the circumstances of Rabbi Rosen purchasing the scroll from you?"

"Hebrew University is willing to pay for such information?"

"It is not for Hebrew University. It is for me that I ask."

Mustafa looked pained. "My memory of something so long ago . . ."

"But I think some remuneration could be arranged from the University of Chicago . . ." O'Hanrahan glanced at the shop window and saw that VISA was honored.

"Yes then. I did not ask the man many questions myself. It came from Egypt and the National Museum, which was willing to sell it. They considered it untranslatable, a minor thing in any event."

"And before it was in Egypt?"

"It was in America."

O'Hanrahan was floored. "The *Gospel of Matthias* was in America?"

Waswasah looked a bit pleased. "I suspect this American collector came across this scroll after World War Two. Many treasures were stolen then, in North Africa, in the Middle East, in Europe. Much of what I sold in those days was taken by soldiers. Many European dealers would not touch stolen property, but we in this part of the world know the marketplace has no rules but two, those of selling, those of buying. I would tell you more of this man if I knew more. His last name was Merriwether."

Ah, the circle was closing in. "Now Mustafa, think carefully," O'Hanrahan pleaded, "is it true that Jacob Rosen, after he bought the gospel, brought the scroll to you to repair?"

The merchant's memory was truly quite sharp; he remembered every detail of a transaction. "He intended to."

Mustafa Waswasah, among his many talents in antiquities-faking and forgery, was an expert repairman. Many of the fragmentary Dead Sea Scrolls were reassembled by his judicious eye, sewn together with ancient thread unraveled from an antique cloth, or pasted together from a fund of old papyrus. His art was inspired by nothing more than the higher price the repaired article would fetch, but he restored nonetheless with the zeal of an artisan.

"Yes, Mr. Rosen called me and said the last segment of the scroll had come loose and that he had separated it from the rest. He proposed an appointment for me to repair it, but he never made the appointment."

"No?"

"No, a day after he called, he had fallen to his death."

A dark thought passed through O'Hanrahan's mind: could Rabbi Rosen's call to Mustafa have set off the chain of events that led to his death? Did this Arab trader sell the information to someone, who then knocked the poor man down the stairs and took the scroll? O'Hanrahan swept the thought aside—too complicating of his long-held good opinion of Waswasah.

O'Hanrahan confided, "The scroll has reappeared."

"So I've heard."

"The *Gospel of Matthias,* it is now called."

"A gospel! How wonderful for the Christians! Is Mohammed foretold in it?"

"I wouldn't put anything past this scroll." O'Hanrahan poured another arak and let the anisette fumes tingle his nose before sipping. "This gospel has reappeared but missing that final chapter. If you hear of anything, my friend, *anything,* concerning this last segment, contact me or Rabbi Mordechai Hersch."

O'Hanrahan paused.

"No. Better to contact me first," O'Hanrahan said slowly, feeling disloyal but convinced of his action. "Contact me at the King David. There is more money than you can imagine for the seller of that last chapter."

Waswasah's eyes glinted in anticipation. "I will take a personal interest in this project," he said, finishing his last shot of arak.

"Moslems would like it too, for some reason, and some groups I've been in contact with would think nothing of, shall we say, taking it from you without paying your price."

"Ah," he said simply.

"Whereas Hebrew University and myself will pay your price."

"I shall keep that in mind." Waswasah was distracted by a fat man in an expensive white linen suit who was turning his bulk this way and that and bending over cases, perilously capable of knocking a treasure to the floor. "See me again, my friend," said Waswasah, "before you leave Jerusalem. With the world as it is, who knows . . ."

No, he didn't have to finish the sentence. Considering their ages and Saddam Hussein, the Intifada and the crackdown, O'Hanrahan and Waswasah both knew the slim chances of another reunion. O'Hanrahan reached for his gift to discover only a little was left in the bottle. He attempted to leave it for his friend, but Mustafa would have none of this, so they finished the remainder in a quick shot after a toast and exchange of blessings.

O'Hanrahan stepped out into the street and wondered how long he would have to wander in this neighborhood to find a taxi. He could reenter the hotel and get them to call one, and as he turned to do that, he saw the hefty man in the doorway.

"Dr. O'Hanrahan?" he began in a soft German accent. "What a coincidence!"

Had they met before?

"We have not met, but I am acquainted with you fery vell. But we have almost met tvice."

Something dawned on the professor: this is the German who purchased the *Gospel of Matthias* in March and then let it slip through his fingers. He looked to his right and saw a BMW, white like the gentleman's suit.

The German offered, "Shall I give to you a ride back to New Jerusalem?"

After further wrangling with more shopkeepers and more rude treatment, Lucy finally hailed a taxi cab and requested the Jerusalem Museum. She had to raise her voice to the driver that *No*, she did not want to go to Yad Vashem, the Holocaust Memorial with displays of human soap and every ghastly artifact of the Holocaust, she wanted to go to the Shrine of the Book at the Jerusalem Museum. The man insisted that all non-Jews should go to Yad Vashem, that he had relatives at Bergen-Belsen, etc. Finally, she arrived at the Museum—the long way around, she was sure—and they argued over the fare to make their exchange even more unpleasant.

As Lucy listlessly plodded through the wonderful Jerusalem Museum, she considered whether it was anti-Semitic simply not to like the Israelis.

This, she told herself, is not the same thing as hating all Jews, which she didn't. But this country is rude. They're under the gun and anxious understandably, but if you're not Jewish they're not nice to you. Me, an American, Lucy reminded the air, me who subsidizes this country with my tax dollars. I don't expect an engraved thank-you letter but civility and politeness are not too much to ask.

After seeing the Dead Sea Scrolls, as impressive in real life as O'Hanrahan's legendarizing, she stood outside wondering if she could escape going to see Rabbi Hersch. I've had enough Israeli brusqueness for one day, she decided, but she dutifully trudged down and up the valley to arrive at Hebrew University atop the next hill, the Givat Ram campus.

After several twists and turns and security people as well as students directing her, she found herself before the whitewashed campus synagogue and in view of another domed structure that looked like a greenhouse, and between those two was the building where Rabbi Hersch had set up a temporary office to be near the National Library. Ordinarily, as the rabbi had explained, he was up where the action is at the Mt. Scopus campus, a disputed zenith by turns Jordanian, Israeli, Jordanian, and now Israeli but in the West Bank.

Lucy found the name Hersch on a bilingual roster. She approached his office and saw the door ajar and that a conversation was going on within. She waited a bit, not wanting to interrupt, but realized this Talmudic discourse might be destined for hours, so she made a humble knock.

"*Yavo*," said the rabbi.

"It's me," said Lucy, poking her head around the corner.

The rabbi sat behind an old wooden desk, a cubicle encased in books with venerable black leather–bound commentaries on the shelf at arm level. Lucy saw the tutorial involved a young Hasidic student in the black suit, white tasseled whatever-you-called-it, the wisps of a beard on his chin and the black forelocks hanging from his temples. The Hasid glanced at Lucy only to turn his head and look away.

"Gimme a minute or two," said Rabbi Hersch. "Sit down if you like."

Lucy scooted to the other chair in the room.

Lucy noticed there was to be no introduction. Of course not, she reasoned, being an unclean shikse, harlot of the Gentiles. The Hasidic boy obviously didn't want her to be there, and Lucy could discern she was being complained against in Hebrew. The rabbi answered him back unpleasantly, and directed the boy back to the Talmud. Lucy listened, not understanding.

The rabbi asked questions and the boy with dwindling confidence answered until finally the rabbi had him stumped. Rabbi Hersch reached behind him and pulled down a dusty commentary and read from it, pointing out a whole passage that the student might want to read—or perhaps, should have read. Lucy saw the young man blush deeply. Ha, she thought maliciously, shamed before me, the unclean one . . .

The rabbi must have said something to the effect of "that's it for today." At this cue, the student gathered his papers in his satchel and, taking special care not to make eye contact with Lucy, left the room in a show of hurriedness.

"Warm and friendly those Hasids," said Lucy.

"You think he disapproves of *you*? It's all he can do to take Talmud from *me*!"

"Why doesn't he go to a Hasidic university then?"

"Oh, Hebrew University is the big schamola and he knows it. He'll just have to put up with my *apiksorische*, pagan ways."

Lucy was particularly humorless about this. "Let me guess," she said, "I'm a *goya*—is that the female form?"

"*Sheygets* for boys, *shikse* for girls, *goyim* for both of you," he corrected. "*Goya*, huh? This ain't Italian, little girl."

"I'm a Gentile woman, and I might be thoroughly unfit in the eyes of God because I might be menstruating, that heinous act." The rabbi reared back, laughing. "Will it offend you, rabbi, if I say I think . . ."

"If as a 20th-Century woman you think that's crap?" the rabbi offered.

Lucy was emboldened: "The sexism is par for the course in religion, but smugly thinking you're superior to the Gentile race as well as other Jews seems racist. And some part of the reason Jews aren't liked by many people in the world."

"Including yourself," he stated cheerily.

"I'm not anti-Semitic," she said.

"Nuuuu, of course not," he said. "You just don't like any Jewish people you've ever met. They're pushy, they're arrogant, they would step on you for a dime—"

"I'm not saying that. I'm saying I think . . . Well, there's no point really in talking about it."

The rabbi still stood behind his desk, having locked his desk drawers and stacked all his papers in a pile. "No, there's every point in talking about it. Can't offend me. Not here. This is Eretz Yisrael. Unlike the U.S., we speak plainly and, as our guest, feel free to do the same."

All right, she would. "Rabbi, on Friday when I was in the Moslem Quarter I heard the Sabbath horn-thing—"

He cackled again. "I like that. We could market that, a *shabbatophone*, like the saxophone."

"And I was sitting there at the Third Station corner, you know, where Via Dolorosa meets whatever it is, uh—"

"I gotcha."

"And here comes all these Hasidic Jews up from the Jewish Quarter. Not through the Christian Quarter, which would be quicker, or out the Jaffa Gate, but up through the Moslem Quarter, their heads covered with shawls. They ran at great speed as they passed through this . . . this unclean territory of infidels. No eye contact, no attempt not to run over children or into old ladies. And O'Hanrahan said when they'd get to, wherever . . ."

"Mea Shearim."

"When they got to the synagogue, they would dust off their shoes because they had trod upon the soil of all these unclean people."

"So?"

Lucy felt the case was evident. "You just can't act that way in this world. Not anymore. I mean, that kind of arrogance will get you guys wiped out one day. I mean, what happens if in some reversal, the Palestinians take Mea Shearim?"

"Well, the Hasidim could get their asses kicked. Mind you, they got machine guns for days tucked away up there."

"I mean, this is no way to win friends and influence people."

"Welllll," he said patiently, "we were the cream of aristocratic Germany, Mendelssohn and the Rothschilds, and we were leading lights at all the secular universities, shone in society, and what good did it do us, huh? We got wiped out anyway in Europe."

Lucy nodded heavily. "Yes, that's true. But do you expect me to be happy about being considered so low as not to be acknowledged as a fellow human? God made me—it doesn't matter to Him that I'm Gentile or a woman."

"It matters to Torah."

"I guess that's what I'm saying, then. I'm not so crazy about the Torah if it can't be updated."

"Updated like a manual, like the sports scores," he chuckled, as he escorted Lucy from the office down the hallway. "Well," he argued simply, "go somewhere else, where Torah isn't being applied. There's plenty of the world left over. There's only twenty million Jews anyway, and most aren't observant and most of them aren't Hasidic and only a handful, a *handful*, cut through the Moslem Quarter, and so Jews are to be judged by this five-minute inconvenience, this perceived slight? Don't try to become pals with the Hasidim and you won't be slighted. Whadya want? The Welcome Wagon?"

"I will never win an argument with you, Rabbi—"

"That is true."

Irritated, Lucy continued, "But there are millions of Moslems and you are smack in the middle of them, and there are just a few of you. Maybe some *politesse* is called for."

The rabbi guided Lucy out the door with a gentle touch. "Assimilate, in other words. Like you were saying the other night. Be a little nicer, perhaps. Stop it with the everyone-else-is-a-*treyfener* chip on our shoulder, hm?"

Lucy and Rabbi Hersch walked through the tranquil Givat Ram campus toward the university's bus stop. "You know," Lucy went on, "my tax monies pay for this country's continued existence, and I think it would be politic to respond to my existence politely as one human being living on this planet to another human being in 1990."

"Interesting point, about the tax monies. You want your money's worth out of Israel, this . . . this Old Testament theme park here, right? Thank you evvvver so much, Miss Dantan of the Most Holy United States of America, for your selfless contribution to your only friend and strategical ally in the whole of the Middle East, to whom you give allll this money nobly without a thought to your own interests in the world. How can we thank you enough?"

Lucy surrendered. "As I said, you'll win if we argue—"

"That generally falls to the person who's correct."

Well, thought Lucy, we're into it now. "I can't believe there's not a part of you that doesn't think a nation founded on the basis of Zionism, a Chosen people, a theological Master Race, if you will, isn't racism pure and simple."

"Of course it's racism," he said, to the amusement of the students at the bus stop they were approaching. "Any Jew who pretends it's not doesn't know anything. This is big news? The French look after French interests, which are always against Jewish interests—no exceptions. The English do what they do to further the English people. Arabs can be united under a criminal like Nasser or a monster like Hussein like *that*," he announced, snapping his fingers, "because they imagine their racial interests are being furthered. However, there seems to be no room in your world vision for the Jews to do the same thing. As an Irish-American you ought to know better than most how us-versus-them determines the very texture of Irish life."

"But it shouldn't."

"In a perfect world, no. But we're in this one, so until it becomes perfect, if you don't mind so much, the Jews will look out for their own interests, culture, language, people, history, and land we are currently occupying, which happens conveniently this time to be our homeland. We got an art museum, a modern university, we care about reading, poetry, literature, classical music—more than your country, sweetheart—where else in this region do you see anything comparable? We got theater, we got a symphony orchestra. The Islamic world's idea of culture is a public flogging or a big, orchestrated million-person rally for Qaddafi or Hussein or Assad. Hey, burning American flags is great art, right? And those clever chants, 'Death to America,' 'Death to Bush,' 'Jihad! Jihad!' But where were you? Some things about Israel you thought were so terrible, hm?"

"Tribalism." She took a deep breath. "The reason the blacks are wiping each other out in South Africa right at the first breath of independence and liberation. Sordid, low-minded *tribalism.*" The rabbi was mildly amused at the rhetoric: "It's what cavemen did. It's what the Ku Klux Klan appeals to, and Louis Farrakhan, and Yasser Arafat and Meir Kahane—

"A lot of people hate Kahane in this country. I think he's a pig. But who among the Palestinians hates *their* extremist faction, Abu Nidal, Abu Abbas? Palestinian dissenters speak up, they die. That's the Arab way. Why are the Jews held up to some alpine scale of morality? You never hear Americans whine about Arab atrocities, which are innumerable, innumerable! One punk with a rock gets shot after battering soldiers all day with rocks—I hear the American newcaster already, 'They were only throwing rocks,' as if a rock couldn't kill you! It's a matter for the U.N.!

"King Hussein of Jordan wiped out 5000 Palestinians who inconvenienced him. I didn't hear a peep out of anybody, let alone the other Arab states who live vicariously through this Arab rabble that's accreted here to sponge off Israeli and Western prosperity. Israel invades Lebanon—granted, a mistake—and there's a massacre of Christians killing Arabs and what do the Jews do? Have a public inquiry to see if Sharon was responsible. You see this kind of conscience anywhere, *any place at all* in the Arab world? Can you imagine a tribunal on human rights from an Arab nation? Die on the spot, I would, if I should hear such a thing! Assad in Syria—he's killed a third of his country. Sadat, America's darling, wrote lavish praise of Hitler and just about did in the Christians there. The emirs in Saudi Arabia, America's new buddies—look at those dictatorships. As a woman, it may interest you to know that you can't go to the suburbs without an official note showing you have the permission of your husband to ride on the public bus. That appeal to you?"

"Rabbi," she interrupted, "I don't think life in an Arab-run country would be better for anybody in the 20th Century . . . Where are we going, by the way?"

"My house, and then lunch at Golda's. You who hate us so much should see Golda's, have some gefilte fish, borscht, a blintz—they do a cream-cheese blintz there that would circumcise the heathen . . ." Lucy noticed the woman standing next to them in the bus stop line hiding a smile.

"I *don't*," Lucy hissed under her breath, "hate the Jews, and would you stop announcing that to the whole country."

"Hear O Israel!" began the rabbi, before Lucy playfully hit him on the arm and they got onto the bus. The rabbi dropped in shekels for both of them.

"There," he said. "A little return on your whopping tax investment, okay?"

Lucy and Rabbi Hersch stood and let an older woman sit down in the last seat. "Are you this wicked with all your students?" she asked.

"Oh, I'm taking it easy on you. This isn't Jewish-strength arguing yet. If I opened up you'd fold like a house of cards."

Lucy smiled. "Yeah, I bought a copy of your *Not the Messiah* in a bookstore in New Jerusalem this morning."

The rabbi blanched and lost the smile in his eye. "Oh that. I thought those were all out of print."

"I bought it used. It's very instructive on how stupid the Christians were to think for a moment that Jesus could be the Messiah—"

"Hey, do me a favor, and gimme your copy, willya? I'll buy it from you. That should never have seen print."

Lucy discerned he was edgy about this pamphlet, produced twenty years ago. "You make a good case. A bit sarcastic and unkind, perhaps—"

"Please," he cut her off, "no more of this. Let me buy that book from you."

"What?" she asked, happy to discomfort him for a change. "Do I hear a recantation coming on?"

"Bah! Everything I wrote is true, I just shouldn't have written such a thing . . ." He trailed off, but Lucy waited for him to continue. "You see, little girl, in 1972, 1973, Jews for Jesus was making big inroads at Hebrew University and I had a nightmare vision of the Jewish state losing its youth. I wrote it in response to Moishe Rosen and the Jews for Jesus crowd but my attack . . . my attack made the rounds and found itself in publication. I didn't get a cent for it."

Lucy considered this. "But I thought you wrote a preface for this edition."

The rabbi, sinkingly, closed his eyes. "That's right. I have blocked this whole episode from my mind. A limited edition was brought out and—eh! To hell with it. You give it to me and I'll give you some money for it. It was not intended for a Christian audience."

Lucy decided she wouldn't annoy him about this further. But she also had no intention of giving him back the book.

O'Hanrahan in the white BMW now studied the man who was giving him a lift to the New City: a good-natured, spherical German with red cheeks and yellow hair with an unlikely golden beard in King Tut fashion. He was dressed in a continental white linen suit, painstakingly tailored to his bulk, and several of his fingers had ostentatious rings.

"Patrick O'Hanrahan, at lahst ve meet!"

The professor merely eyed his host cautiously.

The man laughed a laugh higher than his speaking voice, composed of clearly enunciated "ha" sounds. "*Zu treffen ist sehr gut, sehr gut . . .* Will you be so kind as to have a drink with me?"

O'Hanrahan had hoped to sober up, for after all, this day he had taken the pledge—

"A supreme white wine, I assure you, *ja?*"

"*Ich möchte, mein Herr. Viel Dank,*" O'Hanrahan agreed. Well hell, there was plenty of time to sober up before his reunion with Lucy, lest she ridicule him about his alcohol-free pledge so easily broken.

The white BMW made its way up the Mount of Olives to the Intercontinental Hotel, which overlooks the Old City and possessed a balcony famous for its sweeping view. O'Hanrahan let himself be led through the lobby to a terrace table with two chairs, all prepared as if they'd both been expected.

"I never travel without my wine cellar," the gentleman said, communicating the burden of his luxury. A Turkish young man of almost feminine beauty skipped out to see what his employer wanted. "Bodo, *der Trockenbeerenauslese, bitte. Ja.*" The fellow ran with great energy to fulfill this order. "Herr Professor, we have almost met twice and now the consummation!"

O'Hanrahan assented with an odd look.

"Thomas Matthias Kellner," he said, putting out a pudgy hand. O'Hanrahan noticed a very expensive gold watch on his pink wrist. "We met almost in Rome, *ja?* And almost in my own hometown of Trier, when you were there this year making your researches." Herr Kellner added coyly: "About you know whooo, hah-hah hah-hah . . ."

"I'm not sure I know what you are talking about."

"Oh but you do. Herr Matthias and his amazing document, *nein?* Of course, I know all about it. I am a former owner of the document."

O'Hanrahan reviewed the information: when Gabriel tried to steal the scroll in Rome and the Italian dealers swiped it back, the next buyer was a German man. The Ignatians bought it from him, before the Franciscans took possession of it. "Did you not get a good price, Herr Kellner?" the professor asked.

"Who can put a price on such a treasure?" he responded as the wine arrived. Bodo the houseboy set out glasses and assembled an ice stand. "As I said, I take my wine with me everywhere, lest I have to drink something local and dreadful. Palestine used to be famous for its grapes; still one can taste the Cabernet from Carmel, Special Reserve, but really, sir, you would with me agree . . . mediocrity. Now the making of wine is a scientific process, *mein Freund* . . ." Bodo uncorked a bottle of this exceedingly rare dessert wine of the Mosel from 1976 and poured a golden mouthful into Herr Kellner's glass to sip. "And where science is required, the Middle East eliminates itself . . . ahhh, *annehmbar*, not too presumptuous, as you might say." With a nod, Bodo was directed to fill O'Hanrahan's glass.

"Prosit," they said, toasting each other.

"Delicious," savored O'Hanrahan, never having had a more expensive white wine. He noticed the label listed the vineyard as Heilig Matthiaskirche and there was what looked to be a Byzantine imperial insignia.

"You are a vintner, sir?" O'Hanrahan guessed.

"Yes," he said, not elaborating. "Herr Tennyson's doggerel about having loved and lost is not true in antiquities collection, Herr Professor. This scroll vas in my hands, it vas out of my hands. I was convinced by an expert that the Matthias Gospel, for which I have searched for the last twenty years, was not what I bought. That I had been cheated. This expert claimed it was a pseudo-gospel from the 1200s."

"I'm sorry, Herr Kellner."

"So I thought I had been swindled in Rome," Herr Kellner went on. "How lucky then that I so quickly found a buyer for the thing. A simple Irish churchman attempting to build a library in Ireland, I understood. Ach! It was all a charade."

"Herr Kellner, there has been a man since Ireland in a German rented car following us through Italy and, I wouldn't be surprised, here to Jerusalem itself."

"No, he's not mine," he said, a little disappointed. "Oh, I do hope there are not too many people after this scroll."

O'Hanrahan delighted in torturing him. "Very many, sir. There is a Mad Monk, we think, following our every move, intent on destroying this blasphemous document."

Herr Kellner fumbled in his pocket for a German brand of antacids. "No, you mustn't tell me such things . . . Perhaps I shall accompany you? Two great minds are better, *ja*, than one, *glauben Sie nicht?*"

"Do you speak Meroitic?" asked O'Hanrahan, before devoting five minutes to encapsulating the century of vain effort that preceded them both.

"A lost language is a setback, I must admit," said Herr Kellner, now taking from his pocket some prescription medicine.

O'Hanrahan barely hid his amusement. "Well sir, I still do not possess this scroll, despite what you might have heard. I foresee a trip to Wadi Natrun outside of Cairo, to the national library at Khartoum. Moslem countries, *mein Herr . . .*"

His lip turned down in Hapsburg fashion. "Yes," he said mournfully, "where the barbarians do not allow the consumption of wine. The waste places!" Herr Kellner popped a handful of antacid tablets into his mouth, washing them down with wine. "You have no idea how deeply my folly is felt, Herr O'Hanrahan. Every part of my body is distressed. I sleep horribly, waking up to dreams of self-ridicule. My appetite is gone!"

O'Hanrahan imagined that particular hardship for his host.

"But I am brave. I shall join you in exploring this monastery in Cairo, you say? There are many fine hotels in Cairo."

O'Hanrahan hadn't painted a sufficiently grim portrait. "As pilgrims we should only be allowed to sleep outdoors in the caves of the Libyan Desert. And Khartoum, Herr Kellner? The rigors of the Third World?"

The German undid his bottle of prescription medicine. "Ach, perhaps I shall leave the travel to you," he conceded, changing tacks. "Let us broach then the subject of money. How much do you suppose this *Gospel of Matthias* would fetch in an open auction, hm? How much higher the price goes when one considers private collectors such as myself."

"Tell me," asked O'Hanrahan, "what possible enjoyment could you get out of simply owning this relic? It should be seen publicly, studied by scholars, put on display in a museum. How could you enjoy it collecting dust in a case in your library? Surely you don't want it merely because St. Matthias is your namesake."

"*Ja,* it is a small part of my interest. I was baptized in the Helig Matthiaskirche forty-five years ago, Matthias Kellner."

O'Hanrahan was struck by what a youthful ruddy face the gentleman had for being forty-five, if he was telling the truth, his fat somehow preserving him.

"*Ja,* I intend to put it in a museum. That scroll is the premier relic of the Holy Roman Empire, Herr Professor—perhaps of Christianity herself. But I tell you what you already know."

"No," said the professor, more eager to learn than to bask.

"Let us go back to the time of the Emperor Constantine and the 300s. Trier was the northernmost Roman capital, an ancient city of which there are yet a few remains, having avoided utter destruction for 1600 years by the Huns as well as American air assaults."

O'Hanrahan wondered if this pause was intended for him to apologize for America's role in World War Two.

"Constantine possessed numerous relics of the Disciples, any and all he might have wished, indeed. But the only Disciple's relic he chose to take north of the Mediterranean was that of the obscure St. Matthias, thirteenth of the Twelve Disciples. Constantine's own librarian, Eusebius of Caesarea, pronounced the *Gospel of Matthias* lost and heretical—an odd thing, to be so sure of the heretical nature of something one hasn't read, hm? The truth is, Eusebius possessed a copy of *Matthias*. It is my theory that he owned *all* the so-called lost gospels and kept them in an *apokryphon*, a secret library, *ja*? And I believe that that secret library was built by Constantine in Trier."

O'Hanrahan questioned, "But was placing an *apokryphon* in Trier wise, sir? With the invasion of the Huns and barbarians—"

"The exact opposite is true, forgive me. Trier was a perfect outpost for controversial matters. A few priests each generation made hidden the treasure of secret works, away from the Mediterranean squabbles and fights. Almost every library of note in the Mediterranean world was sacked or burned between 300 and 500, yes? The Huns wanted treasure—what did they care for scrolls and texts?" he added, as if he had been there. "I would like to point out to you an odd piece of *l'histoire trevaise*.

"It is said that a convent guarded the scroll, protected by the Masons and Templars from Crusader times, during which the scroll was first translated, and its authenticity realized. The women could be expected to protect it since it suggested matters very, *wie sagt Man*? Feminist. A female Holy Spirit, an ascendancy of Mary the Magdalene, tales of a secret library for Christian women alone where the true revelation of Christ existed . . . many curiosities, *ja*? And so it was guarded by the Matthiasine Sisters and the Masons through the ages."

This was all new to O'Hanrahan, and he wasn't sure he believed it. "So the contents of the gospel are known."

"Oh, the translation has been lost for centuries, and only a few fragments, rumors perhaps, come down to us. I merely tell you what my own mother . . ." Herr Kellner looked to the clouds briefly, deeply moved. ". . . my own mother, who spent her final years in the Matthiasine convent herself. And passed to me, on her deathbed . . ." Again, emotion threatened to overtake this recital. ". . . these centuries-held secrets. From that time I have made the procurement of the *Gospel of Matthias* my life's goal."

"Yes," said O'Hanrahan slowly, gently, "but might this gospel, Herr Kellner, after all our troubles prove to be as inauthentic as Eusebius said? A latter-day fake?"

His host seemed impatient. "But truly, Herr Professor, we both know that the gospel is not a work of fiction. And the Matthiasine Sisters and Masons who guarded the secret library knew it was not a fiction. Indeed, tragedy struck Trier simply because too many people knew of the *Gospel of Matthias* and its secrets. The Jesuits, no less antagonistic then as now. There came . . ." A sickened, disgusted look transformed Herr Kellner's appearance. ". . . that devil, Bishop von Schoneburg. He was to lead the assault against the women of Trier and the surrounding villages in what was the worst witch hunt in European history."

(The Trier Witch Hunt of 1587 to 1593 led by the Jesuits, Archbishop von Schoneburg and Bishop Binsfield, both currently reliving each execution exquisitely in Hell. In six years no woman remained untortured, some 368 witches were burned outright. Two women survived, an old woman they thought harmless and an orphaned idiot-child they thought ridiculous.)

Herr Kellner encapsulated the history of the Witch Hunt of Trier, concluding, "But the *Gospel of Matthias* was sewn by the old woman into the skirt of the idiot-child. Or so my dear mother . . ."

O'Hanrahan permitted himself to pour another glassful of the golden elixir while his host regained his composure.

". . . my mother told me in her fevered final revelations of her deathbed." A pink silken handkerchief was produced from his white linen jacket and he blew his nose. Then he said quite normally, "The convent there has known of these mysteries for 1700 years!"

O'Hanrahan was dismayed his own thorough research had missed this information. Why hadn't he visited the convent?

(Because it didn't occur to you that women could be the key to the *Gospel of Matthias*'s mysteries. Just the Crusty Old Bachelor Fathers.)

"Herr Professor," said the rich German seriously, "I invite you to research what I am saying. Jesuit accounts of the witch hunt reveal women claimed these so-called witches said the Holy Spirit was female and that God had a special mission for women—this sort of thing, with St. Matthias as the source. The secrets of Matthias were known only by a precious few after the witch hunt, but then we come to the World War Two."

O'Hanrahan wearily expected an SS connection brewing, from the Templars to the Matthiasine Sisters to the Masons to the SS. But he was wrong.

Herr Kellner said, "The usual wartime rapine and plunder went on. Not from British soldiers or Americans, no, but from the town. Very typical of a war-oppressed rabble. Jewelry stores, clothing stores, all looted and pillaged, and someone, some ignoramus found the treasury in the Matthiaskirche. It was not difficult with the Allied occupation to sell these jewel-encrusted relics, the Matthias scroll. I thought at first we had again the Templars to blame for the theft!"

"Does every bizarre thing in Europe have to do with the Templars?"

"That BBC reporter's book says it's the Priory of Zion, Umberto Eco suspects it's the Templars and Rosicrucians. Any Protestant can tell

you it's the Jesuits, any Italian can tell you it's P4 and—what's the
new one?—Gladio? Any European can tell you world conspiracies are
plotted by a handful of crypto-Nazis who have engineered the EEC
and 1992, the Germans' most diabolical plot so far. Any South American, the CIA. In Germany we used to say the Jews were behind all
conspiracies, so you can gauge the danger in believing these things too
much. However, it must be said that I do believe the Masons are
currently involved."

"The Masons? In America, *mein Herr*, Masons are like the Lion's
Club and Kiwanis and Rotary Club—do you know of these organiza-
tions?"

"Ooh, I think those are very dangerous too, but living in the Rhine-
land I am used to conspiracies. I would hate to think of a world without
them!"

"You were saying about the Masons?"

"Yes, an American Mason bought the antiquities illegally from the
thief who raided the church. For shame, an officer! He sensed the scroll
case was ancient and hoped somehow his find might be the centerpiece of
some Mason ritual. This major was from Detroit and that's where the
Matthias scroll stayed for a few months."

"Detroit?" asked O'Hanrahan, incredulous.

"He sold it to a very rich man who ascertained its value, a Chester
Merriwether II. A rival of my mother's! Throughout my dear mother's
life, she was plagued by this American collector with too damn much
money, as I am plagued by Mr. Getty in my own time . . ." Here Herr
Kellner laughed repeatedly. "Ah, but fate intervenes. Herr Merriwether was old, and his own son Charles takes over this multinational
company, leaving his aging father to his art collection. Before Chester's
death the son, a mere twenty-five years old and a thorough boor—but
Gott sei Dank—sells off everything, including the *Gospel of Matthias*
papyrus. It is purchased in 1948 by the National Museum of Egypt,
for they believe it is a document of their culture. In that time, a Jewish
fellow . . . ah, the name eludes me . . ."

O'Hanrahan: "Rabbi Jacob Rosen, I believe."

"Ah yes. This rabbi views this document through some Palestinian
agent and asserts it involves the Jewish historian Josephus and offers
a great sum to purchase it. And bribes are applied, of course. In 1949,
the gospel finds its way to Hebrew University, and then Mr. Rosen
falls down a flight of stairs the very day the scroll disappears."

O'Hanrahan sipped his wine. "And so that brings us to now, Herr
Kellner. You would like to engage me to help you get this scroll back
in your possession."

"But I think only of the public. Look at the tourist business the
Dead Sea Scrolls do at the Jerusalem Museum, at the '67 *Exposition du
Montréal*. I envision such a grand exhibit in Trier for St. Matthias. And

after the work is translated I think many American tour groups will add Trier to their itineraries. What one of your Southern Baptists would not want to see the writings of a real disciple, the words of one who looked into the eyes of Jesus, hm? The oldest Christian document in existence! Two hundred years before the Codex Sinaiticus! Scholars would pay fortunes to see this thing. Ah, think of the renaissance Trier could undergo!"

"And I suppose your wine sales would go up, Herr Kellner."

"Indeed, but my family has expanded beyond wine, my friend. Hotels, restaurants, spas. I own everything but the Youth Hostel, but I am working on that." He momentarily looked tragic, contemplating the Youth Hostel, an unowned property. "Do not mistake me! I wish for you to translate this thing and help publicize my scroll. I can assure you Trier is a marvelous place to work—the food, the wine, the weather, ah, not so nice this time in the spring, much rain, but better than Chicago in the winter, *ja*? This afternoon perhaps? You go where the scroll is hidden, ask to see it, put it up the sleeve of the coat, and present it to me and I shall give you a discreet sum of . . ." He had a pained look. "The vulgarity of speaking of money betroubles me. A million deutsche mark for your efforts, hm?"

"A million," O'Hanrahan repeated.

"This academic discovery will bring you fame, Herr Professor. But think of your former colleagues who worked upon the Dead Sea Scrolls. Did they make much money from their venture? Nor will you make much money from this without me. Oh yes, at most, fifty thousands dollar in book sales perhaps, but you are a young man! Not yet seventy! What will comfort you during the twenty years or so to come, eh?"

That's a lot of bread, thought O'Hanrahan.

(*Man does not live by bread alone*, Patrick.)

O'Hanrahan looked up to see Herr Kellner standing.

"I send for you a case of our finest Piesporter to the King David," he announced. "Enjoy, enjoy! Much more where that was made, *ja*? And I will be in touch, as you say. I know you have a big problem to lie to your friends here, this rabbi fellow at Hebrew University. But perhaps you can give him some of your money. I leave it for you two to arrange. As for me, I am haunted by those coins in the El-Khodz Hotel. I feigned uninterest but now I must go and buy them before anyone else—Mr. Waswasah's price was ludicrously low . . ."

"Perhaps they are not real," O'Hanrahan tactfully suggested.

"I know numismatics almost as well as I know ancient texts, *mein Professor*." He touched a fingertip to his tongue. "They have a certain taste. Ha-ha ha-ha, I put my tongue to one when you and the proprietor talked and I assure you it is authentic! *Auf Wiedersehen*." Thomas Matthias Kellner turned on his heels jauntily, and was gone.

(Well, Patrick?)

"I'd like a half a million dollars," O'Hanrahan said out loud to himself.

Lucy and the rabbi walked along his residential street in his quietly busy neighborhood on the edge of Mahane Yehuda.

"I didn't think you liked me very much," Lucy said. "You seemed to always want me to go home—"

"Nothing personal," he said, again shrugging. "Every time Paddy takes on a partner, disaster follows. However, Paddy needs someone to watch after him and you'll do." He nudged her. "Here's our street."

Lucy felt that giddiness at going somewhere foreign and cherishing an authentic experience, ascending to a higher tourist heaven than the tour bus droves. The rabbi knew his neighborhood well, apparently, waving to a hefty woman and exchanging greetings, waving to a shopkeeper and exchanging blessings. A Hasidic man with a wild topiary fur hat passed and they *shalom*ed and exchanged a few remarks in Yiddish.

"You know everyone," noted Lucy as they approached his door.

Rabbi Hersch dug deep in his pockets, fishing with change and keys and other impedimenta. "You want change you get keys, you want keys you get change," he mumbled. "Here," he said, asking Lucy to hold seventeen shekels in coins. "This jacket, for years, for years has a hole in it."

"I can sew," Lucy volunteered.

"Can you? Oh good girl," he allowed. "A town full of tailors," he said, finding his keys at last and opening his door, "and I can't find the time to go to one."

Lucy entered the rabbi's three-room flat, a large living room and library that extended to a dining table, a kitchen beyond that that opened on a back garden, and a bedroom off to the side. It was orderly around the shelves and the desk but each arm of his sofa was inhabited by opened, parted books. A small stack with bookmarks at half a dozen places occupied the most comfortable-looking chair. Decorations were simple. Eastern patterned rugs lay over the sofa, on the floor, a rug hung on the wall, there was a menorah on the bookshelf and a row of old black and white photographs of relatives, looking out from that lost *shtetl* world of longbeards and babushkas early in the 20th Century.

"Books everywhere," he grumbled, removing the pagoda of parted texts, seven books high, from the armchair. "You can go here," he told them, moving them to the sofa. "The cleaning lady has been in, Fatima."

"An Arab woman?"

"Yep."

"You're not worried she'll plant a bomb?"

He looked at her like she had no hope of understanding life in Israel. But then his face became more patient. "No, I'm not worried," he said simply. "Here's the damn sandalwood . . ." The rabbi took a woven plate-sized basket full of aromatic leaves, rose petals, sandalwood, and cinnamon. "She leaves this stuff here every Monday," he said, walking it to his kitchen trash can. "I was going to tell her to stop bringing this stuff because I go away for a week and the place smells like a spice shop and I sneeze for hours." He dumped it in the trash. "But she goes to the market in East Jerusalem and mixes this stuff herself so I give it a day and throw it out once she's gone."

Lucy felt the need to clarify. "I don't think everyone is Israel is rude and unfriendly, just . . . everyone I've met so far."

The rabbi chuckled. "Would it shock your Midwestern heart to learn there are people in the world who don't live for *nice*? Polite yes, serviceable and competent—I'll take that. Ten hours of small talk over bobkes, no thank you. *Nice*, little girl, means nothing. I'd rather have someone call me a kike to my face than Oh hello, Mr. Rabbi, how do you do, Mr. Rabbi, good day, Mr. Rabbi, then the knife in the back. I get you some coffee?"

"No, I overdosed on tea this morning. No thanks."

He was checking his cabinets. "No coffee actually, so it's just as well. Old Jew wine I got. Maneschewitz grape? It's probably turned to vinegar up there. I give it to Paddy. It's an armed camp here," he remarked, changing subjects without warning. "It's not everywhere you can hear machine-gun fire at night and turn over and go back to sleep. *Nice* won't work here, not with our history . . . which if those idiotic old terrorists who run this country have their way will end soon."

"You don't like Shamir?"

"Too old. Too old like I am too old, too intransigent. Jews are the best diplomats in the world, right? Disraeli, Kissinger—but for Israel we get Moe and Joe up there, not willing to talk to anyone who has ever talked to anyone who knows anyone that was a terrorist. This is Shamir talking! Blows up the King David Hotel, fifty British dead, a member of Irgun and he won't talk to terrorists. Mind you," he added, "the Palestinians have killed more of themselves than the Israeli Army has. And now, with Yasser Arafat taking time off from playing kissyface with the pope to play kissyface with Saddam Hussein, who's gonna talk now?"

The rabbi sighed wearily, stroking his beard.

"Bulldoze Palestinian homes," he began, "put 'em in camps, invade Lebanon, spy on the U.S., shoot a bunch of rock-throwing boys on prime-time TV, sell arms to Iran, put homesteaders in the Christian Quarter, alienate the U.S. and American Jews, develop friends like Mengistu and Pik Botha—what have we done right under these clowns? Meanwhile inflation through the goddam roof, the economy in shambles, we got hundreds of thousands of immigrants coming in like it's Ellis Island and we're made of money. As a product of a 4000-year-old culture, let me say *oy vey*."

"Well, it must be a little comforting to see how solidly the U.S. is behind Israel."

"Hey, I'm counting the days. You guys can't run your damn government on trillions of dollars, so when you go into a depression, that $3 billion to Israel will go pronto. You got a nation of *schvarzes* who love their welfare and have decided they'd get more if Israel didn't get any. Every time a black politician gets up it's anti-Israel, anti-Jewish, Hymietown, right? Jews who, for Christ's sake, went down there to Mississippi and Alabama and got their heads beat in for blacks to vote in the '60s. Talk about ingratitude, eh?"

"It doesn't help calling them *schvarzes*."

"What?" he asked, shrugging.

"It's a Jewish way of saying 'nigger.' "

The rabbi contemplated this. "No it's not. Okay, I won't use it anymore. Least around you."

"I think their resentment has to do with their image in Hollywood, which Jews controlled, and the record business, which the Jews still run, and you see, Israel sells all the weapons to South Africa—"

"Jesus H. Christ! Do you understand anti-Semitism, little girl? It always has a reason, an excellent, impeccable reason that sounds wholly rational—Jewish conspiracy of financiers, Jews and the Masons, they kill Jews because of plots to bring in Communism, the Soviets kill Jews because of plots to get rid of Communism . . . First comes the hate, then the rationalization." He changed subjects again: "How's the transliteration going?"

"I've gotten the second chapter of the gospel converted to Roman letters, but it's all nonsense so far." She sighed. "The gospel *can* be deciphered, can't it? You guys keep talking about Meroitic, and I looked it up, and the encyclopedia says it's a lost language."

The rabbi rubbed his eyes. "Heard of the Indus Valley Script? Every year someone's cracked it, publishes a paper, throws a party, and every year that someone is wrong. Etruscan. We got, what? Ten thousand words of the thing and we still can't manage their grammar. You better believe there are lost languages." The rabbi opened a small satchel and took out the existing books and began to insert others from another stack, while lecturing:

"And that's the damn thing about Meroitic. We can do some Kush, we can do most Axumite dialects, Ge'ez and Falasha-Semitic, Nubian scratchings . . . and here is this damn script, Meroitic right in the middle of the First Century. The Egyptians and the Greeks were there, the Romans, the Jews, then the Christians—they had trade with Persians, Indians, even the Chinese. A bunch of *schvarzes*—uh, Black Africans, but I promise you, the most cosmopolitan society of the age. With all those influences the language oughta be a cinch! But there's not a *hint* of anything familiar."

Lucy sighed. "So there's the possibility that Dr. O'Hanrahan and you will never solve it."

"No," said the rabbi heavily.

Lucy let him think a moment.

"Because Rabbi Jacob Rosen was reading this thing about two weeks after he bought it. But he was very secretive. He's the reason we know it was addressed to Josephus, the Jewish historian, and why we know it was purported to be by Matthias the Disciple. He said a lot more but who paid attention? Who knew he was going to die in the middle of translating it, let alone that the scroll was going to be stolen?"

"Did he make any notes?"

"There was *one* sheet from his legal pad—he filled hundreds of them—that escaped the theft. Used as a bookmark, I found it by accident. It had numerous phrases we assume are in the Matthias scroll but we don't know."

Lucy realized she had seen those notes in O'Hanrahan's bag before the Athos robbery, scrawled in Hebrew: *The Harlot Helen. Benjamin the Slave. All Heresies Refuted. The Messiah's Bones.*

"And there was the business of the last chapter," the rabbi added. "Rosen passed me in the hall and he seemed upset, which was odd, because he was always cheery. I was a graduate student, 1949, and hesitated to make idle conversation with the great man, but I asked what was wrong. He said the gospel was a very dangerous book. I asked what he meant. He said, 'If it's going where I think it's going, there's not going to be a *sheygets* alive who doesn't want to burn this thing.' Another thing he said, 'Do you suppose the Gentiles could survive it?' "

Lucy mulled that over. "So this final chapter has some unpleasant details about Christ, you think."

"I don't think Professor Rosen lived long enough to get to this final chapter himself."

"And now this last chapter is lost."

The rabbi didn't answer directly. "It's not attached to the scroll, I wouldn't say it was lost."

Rabbi Hersch decided to change sportscoats and went into his bedroom. Lucy stood and looked again at the old photographs. There was a man and wife, a rabbi and his young bride, hair pulled back under a babushka, but beautiful hopeful eyes. Her husband had Rabbi Hersch's eyebrows and knowledgeable stare. The place looked like a Central European town. It seemed to her that O'Hanrahan told her he was raised by his uncle in Brooklyn. But this couple could have been his parents. Why do you suppose he . . .

Oh of course. Oh no.

Not the Holocaust again. That gaping abyss that lurks behind daily life in Israel, only gone for a few happy distracted moments at a wedding, while caught up in a novel, but never really gone, that unrightable wrong, that criminal that got off scot-free. Lucy stepped back from the bookshelf and the photos; she didn't want to occasion the topic and hear Rabbi Hersch say the words, recite those litanies of dead relatives and people who couldn't get out of Europe in time, who instead poured their resources into smuggling out their children. This wrenching stab of sadness she felt—multiply by two, then three, for all of Mordechai Hersch's aunts and uncles, then by ten for the immediate family, then clutching something stable and solid, closing one's eyes, extrapolate by one, two, three, four, five, six million . . .

"Golda's you're gonna love," said the rabbi spryly, pausing to exile another stack of books from the sofa to the dining room table.

Lucy turned away. With what dignity he tends their memorial—at no point in their friendly argument did he prostitute their deaths, his own suffering. Had it fundamentally altered and shaped him? It must have. Is this why no wife or children, the fear of more loss? Is this why he had to be a rabbi—a great rabbi? To replace the father he never got to know, to have a life in common with him, to perhaps follow the same traces of thought and reason?

". . . you know it takes years off your life," he was saying, "but I can't do without the Golda's borscht. She serves it cold like a milkshake and then you watch her blend in sour cream—you feel the arteries harden, but . . ."

What can the world hope to say to a man like Rabbi Hersch? Only God can make a proper answer to his sufferings, proper recompense for his losses. His sadness lasts a lifetime, and for me, thought Lucy, it was only for a moment: but my eyes filled with tears, my heart trembled and I glimpsed vicariously one-millionth of an evil that could make you hate life and God Himself, I touched one bone in the pile, filled my mouth with ashes.

(Good. You now have all you need to know, My child, to understand the State of Israel.)

From the Intercontinental Hotel, O'Hanrahan gave a last glance at the Old City in the midday light, the gold Dome of the Rock and Temple Mount with the steeples of the churches near the Holy Sepulcher beckoning behind.

He left the hotel and found the lead taxi in the line and asked to be taken to the Damascus Gate where he was to meet Rabbi Hersch and Lucy in ninety minutes. The taxi driver pointed to another driver, who led him to another, back in the line . . . "Are you the right guy?" O'Hanrahan asked.

"Yes yes," said the driver, scrambling to open the door for the professor.

As they left the parking lot, O'Hanrahan saw a wealthy-looking woman emerge from the hotel and get into the taxi at the front of the rank as he had attempted. "Why did the other drivers send me to you, sir?" asked O'Hanrahan.

"Because we go somewhere."

"No, I do not need a tour," he said in clear Arabic.

"It is not a tour," said the man, still in English.

O'Hanrahan leaned back in the cab wondering where he was headed this time and who wanted to see him. Rather than descend the Mount of Olives, the driver seemed to be headed deeper into the West Bank toward al-Azzirya, a village known to Christians as Bethany, named by the Moslems for Lazarus whom Jesus raised from the dead. This was also the road to Jordan. O'Hanrahan looked out the back of the taxi to see a red Golf sedan following pokily behind. Added security, O'Hanrahan figured, in case I bail out and make a run for it.

"Where am I going?"

"You like to drink the coffee, yes?"

O'Hanrahan was let out at a simple café, iron tables, wooden stools, a blackened brewing pot that distilled strong Arab coffee near the door. The red Golf proceeded down the road, so O'Hanrahan dismissed his earlier scenario.

The sun was far enough west that the eastern-facing café was now in the shade. The shabby-looking men in Arab *kafiyeh* headdress, clones of Yasser Arafat, were indolent, the work for the day done, or more likely, done for them by their sons and wives. They observed O'Hanrahan with mild interest; the café dog, a mutt, sniffed up to O'Hanrahan's pant leg and showed slightly more enthusiasm.

"Patrick O'Hanrahan," said one youngish man with a prominent Arab nose, very slim and short, handsome in a black Western suit.

"Whom may I have the honor of speaking to?"

"Mohammed Baqir al-Taki, and the honor is mine. Your reputation precedes you, sir." The young man spoke excellent English in a high-pitched voice. He extended his right hand and displayed with his left the seat at the table intended for them both.

"Descendant," asked O'Hanrahan, "of the famed author of the *Haqqu al-Yaqin?*"

It seemed the next moment his host was fighting back emotion. "Oh sir, it is true what is said of you! Oh that you had been born to Islam! What honors we would have bestowed upon you! How the Christian world ignores the flower of the mind that Allah, most merciful and generous, has allowed to bloom."

O'Hanrahan nodded in complete agreement, as a small demitasse of Arabic coffee was set before him by the proprietor's eight-year-old son. "A Shi'ah deep in Sunni territory?" the professor ventured.

"Yes, though my Sunni brethren are objects of my daily prayers for reconciliation. My family is part-Palestinian, part-Iranian."

A helluva mix, thought O'Hanrahan.

"I am not of the blood of the Mohammed Baqir to whom you refer, but I was named in his honor, may peace be upon him . . ." The coffee-boy set a dish of date cookies between the two men and scurried away.

"You have brought me here to tempt me, Mr. al-Taki?"

He laughed freely. "Ah, to lure you and your scroll from the Western world you may see as temptation, my learned professor," he embellished, getting down to business with Arab indirection. "But is it temptation to put before a man such as yourself something that would produce mutual good? The people I represent would gain much by such a document as you possess: no less than the vindication of Mohammed's prophecies, may peace be upon him."

"May peace be upon him. You and whomever you represent will have to go a long way to tempt me," said O'Hanrahan, sipping the strong coffee, bitter and acid with a strip of lemon peel in it. "I was offered a million deutsche mark this morning."

"Such money we cannot offer, but rather a position of great honor."

"We?"

"My university."

O'Hanrahan was curious. "In the West Bank?"

"In Teheran."

O'Hanrahan was amazed but didn't show it. "A position for me in Iran? I take it it's in a prison somewhere."

Al-Taki shook his head, his large eyes liquid and expressive. "Oh, if the West could only know the true Persian hospitality!"

"Dear friend, I have been to Iran, but it was Iran under the Shah and I found the people most hospitable, as throughout the Moslem world. No people has a greater code of generosity to the stranger. But governments tend not to reflect this charity."

"That can be said of the U.S. as well, can it not? The government is one thing, but the people themselves are very, very good."

No, thought O'Hanrahan darkly, the Arab world would be saddened to know how uncharitable the American people have become—how our poor can rot on the street, how little we seek to correct perpetual social injustice, how the stranger in the West, rather than being welcomed into homes and given gifts in Moslem fashion, is considered dangerous and avoided. O'Hanrahan recalled visiting the Armenian churches of Turkey near the Soviet border, and he remembered that hotels did not exist because the locals would invite you into their homes and feed you. When O'Hanrahan unintentionally insulted a family once by trying to offer money, they assured him that it would balance out in the eyes of Allah, for one day they would come to the United States where this hospitality, of course, would be returned. If they only knew!

". . . for the Prophet, may peace be upon him," rambled al-Taki, expressively allowing his hands to rise and fall, "assures us that Allah is most generous to his servants, and how more so for the scholar . . ." Al-Taki arrived at his proposal: "We want to make you a professor at Teheran University, my learned friend," his host said, pausing, smiling. "You will have complete powers to teach Christian scripture as you wish, providing you do not refute the Holy Quran. You will have a house, servants. Life is very cheap in Iran."

Yeah, not the way he means, thought O'Hanrahan.

". . . and it is no exaggeration to say you will live like a king—a pasha, yes?" Mohammed Baqir al-Taki looked down at his cup, smiling humbly. "Even a wife can be found for you, should you require one. Many young women would be happy to have so eminent a husband."

A young wife?

Did he hear him right?

Appearing in his mind was a pair of eyes behind a veil, once glimpsed in Baghdad, when all the wonder and mystery of the East were rushed to his heart!

"You said," O'Hanrahan stammered, "a wife?"

"Yes, but of course. A virgin, I assure you!"

To have again in this world, as he hung on the very edge of his lifetime, as the abyss opened within view, to have a wife—no, he said, a virgin, a *young wife*, a girl! What was the Arabian Nights description of the smooth young thigh? Yes, the color of a sliced almond. *We will burn scent of nard and lie naked in its blue wizardry!*

(That was written for a prepubescent boy, Patrick.)

Oh the cruelty to hold out such a fantasy for an old man who had just made peace with putting such thoughts to rest! Ha, but why stop at one wife? Why not three or four? *Awake my children and fill the cup before Life's liquor in its cup be dry!*

O'Hanrahan said distracted, "My Farsi is a bit rusty—"

"There is much English spoken, and the texts are Arabic."

Yes, Persian Arabic, which is a whole different ballgame, but not an obstacle he couldn't overcome. "And this is your deal? A position, a rich life of a pasha, in return for the *Gospel of Matthias*? Why is it so important to you?"

"Because it will surely establish the truth of the Quran regarding *Isa Mesih*, Jesus the Christ, will it not? And with you presenting it to the world, we shall at last be believed. It will be no small measure of success for Iran amid the Moslem brethren to begin the uniting of the Christian peoples with the Moslem under the magnificent teachings of Our Prophet Mohammed, may peace be upon him."

"May peace be upon him."

Al-Taki looked pleased to have been underestimated. "Ah, but there is more. We could not lure a man such as yourself with paltry promises such as a wife. . . ."

Wanna bet, thought O'Hanrahan, already well on the way to evolving a complete fantasy, his freckled, aged hand brushing against her lower abdomen, the young girl's natural Middle Eastern modesty as the veils are removed, her breasts presented to her husband vulnerably as she calls upon Allah to make her worthy of the moment!

"Yes, a position, the life of a pasha, as you put it, but more, much more! We have a gospel for you to see as well. One that I think your scholars called 'Q.' "

O'Hanrahan was again stunned.

The date cookie fell from his hand and the dog scampered under the table to consume it.

"You have heard of it, yes?" asked al-Taki.

The professor almost swooned. It was like a thief before unguarded jewels, a miser before stacks of uncountable gold . . . Mohammed Baqir al-Taki had mentioned the one scroll for which O'Hanrahan would abandon Matthias! How could they have it? The Ur-Gospel . . . although attaching "Ur" to anything Judeo-Christian is a bit curious. The original, oldest gospel of significance! Long analyzed in absentia, and now found! No, it must be a fantasy.

"The Nestorians have many old gospels, yes?" Mohammed explained.

Yes, the Nestorians, reflected O'Hanrahan. A Christian sect closed off to us most of this century—all the fruits of 20th-Century philology and textual scholarship had yet to be applied to their vast libraries.

(Our poor Nestorians. Maybe the most persecuted sect of Christianity, having been on the outs since 430 when Nestorius insisted Mary could not be termed the *Theotokos*, the Mother of God. Yet they survive in Iran and in Northern Iraq as the Assyrian Church, though they were almost wiped out viciously by the Kurds in the 1930s, who have since understood what it is to be annihilated.)

Al-Taki: "Nestorius commanded his people keep the earliest of gospels to better argue the status of Mary. Our own Moslem scholars have dated the 'Q' to your First Century, and they have written much on it, but we are dismissed and have no credibility in the West. No Christian wants to admit a 'Q' gospel exists beyond hypothesis and conjecture. In our discovery, there is no Resurrection for Jesus. Although, mysteriously, there is no Ascension either."

O'Hanrahan was relieved to hear "Q" didn't follow Moslem orthodoxy, for if it did it was surely a latter-day fake. "Why didn't the Moslems burn the thing if it disagreed with the Prophet, may peace be upon him—"

"May peace and many blessings be upon him." The man finished his coffee down to the grounds. "Ah, it is the Christians who burn books, not the Moslems."

No, thought O'Hanrahan, you guys just issue *fatwas* and kill *authors*. But O'Hanrahan was enchanted: to go to Teheran was folly . . . but on the chance of "Q"! And the girl, let's not forget the girl! And if their "Q" was for real it would render this double find, "Q" and Matthias, the greatest one-two punch in ecclesiastical history . . . *and he could be the scholar who would present them* BOTH *to the world!* The unceasing academic glory through the ages unending!

"You must forgive our Iraqi brethren," said Mohammed, barely concealing distaste, "the al-Mu'tazilah who troubled you in Greece. So crude in their methods—Sunni, of course. What could one expect? Unforgivable. To you we offer a life that is worthy of you. You brought the first Moslem to the University in Chicago, did you not? You have always been a friend of Islam."

"A most beautiful religion," he said truthfully, bowing his head. The next minute adding to himself: it's a shame it's been so derailed by you fundamentalist clowns . . . O'Hanrahan noticed the young tea-boy going over to the growling dog and hitting it with a stick as hard as he could, trying to chase it away. The men in the café laughed, applauding this entertainment.

"I am not a man of the marketplace, professor," said Mohammed Baqir al-Taki charmingly. "I have made my offer. I shall accompany you to Teheran if you like. I will take you up the Great Minaret and you may look down over the wondrous place—your new home."

(*Then the devil took him to the holy city and set him on the pinnacle of the temple . . .*)

Al-Taki assured him, "None of our faculty is as fearsome as you believe! Teheran is not Qom; the university is not under the mullah's thumb."

Here, thought O'Hanrahan, you overplay your hand.

Of course, he had no intention of taking this academic position, but the thought did occur of going to Teheran, seeing "Q" and making a switch and then escaping . . .

(And when they catch you, it will be the last time your fingernails are attached to your body.)

And I might stay long enough to be married to a dark and nubile Persian virgin who doesn't speak a word of English . . .

(The Temptations of O'Hanrahan. What on earth, We wonder, are you going to do now?)

Lucy and Rabbi Hersch walked through Suleiman the Magnificent's Damascus Gate. Outside the Old City walls Arab tradesmen held up chickens ready to behead with a bloody knife, cookies and pastries and the ubiquitous sesame-pretzels were brandished before one, lambs and bleating goats stood tied together at another family's stall. Inside the gate, the passageway curved like an S, presumably, thought Lucy, to prevent a straight charge of an invading army. Lucy was taken further back in time by the sight of the Jewish money changers, hawking their exchange rates, shekels for dollars, for francs, for Jordanian pounds—a scene startlingly out of some anti-Semitic 1930s German propaganda film. She thought of Jesus and his angry reaction to this going on in the Temple itself . . .

"Are we supposed to wait inside the gate or outside?" asked Lucy, concerning their meeting up with O'Hanrahan.

"No idea," said Rabbi Hersch. "Let's go inside."

Passing through Damascus Gate, Lucy looked above her to see the guard patrols on the city walls, three soldiers with Uzis, two female, one male, fit and lean, smoking and staring intently at the day's pilgrims, ready to rain down vengeance for any atrocity.

The plaza around Damascus Gate slopes down past several Arab storefronts and splits into three pedestrian avenues; to the right Lucy spied a tea shop, next to a Palestinian pop-music record and CD store. Lucy dragged her older companion to the record shop and tried to communicate the want of a "greatest hits" cassette of contemporary West Bank pop music, and she was sold something amid many flourishes and smiles.

O'Hanrahan, meanwhile, weary and hot, edged toward the tea shop run by friendly Palestinians. "That's smart," he called out crabbily, "hiding in a shop where I can't find you."

Lucy scanned him up and down. "Did you make it?"

"Make what?"

"The whole day without a drop." Suddenly, she wondered if she should have brought up the subject with the rabbi in attendance.

"Of course I did," O'Hanrahan claimed, guiding them to the plastic lawn chair and tables in front of the tea shop. "My my, how much I would love a good strong cup of mint tea. Yum yum."

The rabbi and Lucy took their seats, neither apparently convinced of his pledge.

"No, really. This has been my alcohol-free day, Morey," O'Hanrahan insisted, as he groaningly took a seat at the one of two outdoor tables. "Not as if I have to have it every second . . ."

Lucy positioned herself to watch the packed, stopped passageways of Jerusalemites and goods and animals, mingled in perfumes and aromas, obscured by smoke from grills, vibrating with the noise of bargaining and the volunteering of advice about how to solve the frequent human traffic jams.

She noticed a peculiar vehicle designed just for the Old City and the Palestinian teenage boys who "rode" them. This vehicle was a cart, sometimes two wheels, sometimes four, and at breakneck speeds the boys would lift their feet and hang on the backs of the carts, careening through the alleyways and slopes of the worn-smooth stair-streets, clocking 30 to 40 m.p.h., screaming a battle-cry warning for all to get out of their way. When it came time to put on the brakes, a worn tire dragging behind the cart was jumped upon and the weight of the driver brought the cart to a screeching, tire-smoking halt. The rabbi, watching the spectacle too, reported that with years of practice on these carts, the only conveyance possible in these narrow streets of Old Jerusalem, the boys became masters, stopping and turning on a dime. Lucy watched a young man with a cart piled high with apples speed through the Damascus Gate and fearlessly part the crowds, who dodged him nonchalantly, without missing a word of their conversations.

It was evening. Lucy observed the orange light settling on the white polished stone of the City Walls, pursuing the tops of alleys into the Moslem Quarter, finding the white sheets of clotheslines. But no surface was as accommodating as the ancient, time-softened stone that seemed to hold the evening glow, hoard it, bask in it nobly.

"The gold dome of the Dome of the Rock really gets the sun nice, and the Mount of Olives behind it," said the rabbi. "Messiah couldn't pick a better place to return to, though I suspect He'll arrive in the morning."

"In order," mumbled O'Hanrahan, having ordered the tea by panto-mime, "to take aim on the Golden Gate."

"Through which Messiah must enter the city," the rabbi explained, seeing Lucy was confused.

"How do you keep some average person from walking through this gate?" she asked.

The rabbi: "Oh, it's sealed up with stone. It'll take a miracle to open it and when that happens, that'll be a good sign we're dealing with the real Messiah. And the Lubovitchers say it's coming soon."

Lucy rolled her eyes. "Please, not more End Times. You guys have got me spooked enough as it is. Everywhere we've been, they're saying it's the end of the world."

They fell silent, pursuing ominous thoughts. Would Jerusalem be standing six months from now? Where would the simmering Kuwaiti conflict end—nuclear missiles, biological and chemical exchanges? The Judgment Day?

A pot of mint tea arrived and three glass cups. The proprietor set down a plate of six thick almond cookies with a sprinkling of powdered sugar.

"Like I said," said Lucy for everyone, taking a cookie, "I'm too young to be judged."

Rabbi Hersch continued. "There's an amazing 13th-Century proph-ecy already much discussed here, that says the kings of Media, which would include Baghdad and Saddam Hussein, would turn on the kings of Arabia, which seems to be in the works, and they would bring down a king by the Jordan, which I take it means King Hussein. And that this would throw the world into a war that would begin the End Times and the arrival of Messiah and the triumph of Israel. The Lubavitchers have bumper stickers: WE WANT MESSIAH NOW."

"That ought to get God's attention," said the professor.

Lucy looked up to see the stone of the Old City had reddened, the sky warm and violet behind the City Walls. Odd, she thought, of anyone wanting to fight in this lovely, blessed place. And yet you saw the films on the news, the fighting in these streets, the tear gas in East Jerusalem. Everywhere amid this bustling, human scene were Israeli soldiers, ruthless and cocky, not loath to use their Uzis. What was the body count? 400-some Palestinians dead in this uprising so far, mostly teenage boys from wretched unimproved environments—environ-ments fostered by this occupation of what used to be Jordan, in a land that in 1917 boasted no more than 90,000 Jews. Yes, wave it away as the rabbi might, there were deep, irremediable differences, true injustices, children killed and homes bulldozed and people who've spent 25 years in horrible refugee camps.

And yet . . . it was more complicated than any outsider could imag-ine.

This morning, as Lucy walked around, she saw a souvenir stand full of local T-shirts, one of the many cavernous rooms off an ancient street, a place for wares for the last 3000 years. There was a Star of David and an Uzi with the clever slogan: UZI DOES IT. Now, thought Lucy, that's just not funny. 450 Arabs dead and you're poking fun. Here's another T-shirt: DON'T WORRY AMERICA, ISRAEL IS BEHIND YOU. A fine piece of irony, that. It manages to appeal to Israeli arrogance, cast aspersions on American fidelity—as if this little Zionist enterprise would have been possible without the $3 billion a year! You think the U.S. doesn't have better things to spend that on: killing Palestinians in their own centuries-held villages? And yet, look who's running the T-shirt shop. A Palestinian man in the Moslem Quarter, no more concerned with the content of what he sells than the alley cats he was shooing from his storefront.

And also last night, Lucy recalled, near the Mehane Yehuda neighborhood when she and the professor were coming back from a delightful Yemeni restaurant, the perfume of Yemeni tea persistent on their palates, there was a rock 'n roll club, which could have been in any Western city. And there outside were a group of Hasidic boys, in their hats and with their side locks and in their dark suits. One boy had his shirt rakishly unbuttoned. One boy, quite clearly stumbling and drunk and laughing loud, had his black suitcoat filled with buttons for rock bands and Zionist slogans. Were these kids sneaking out of Mea Shearim, outraging their parents, leaving at home some hand-wringing mother or some bellowing forbidding father? Somehow she thought not. They were just kids out having a wild post-Sabbath Saturday night. These kids, now dancing to Bon Jovi and Bel Biv Devoe, would grow up to run through the Moslem Quarter, heads covered, eyes on their feet, trying not to breathe the air of the infidel, joyously wiping the dust off when they got to synagogue in the New City. Again: Israel is endlessly more complicated than one's first, second, third, or, God knows, hundredth assessment.

The Moslems who coordinated their *muezzin* and call to prayer at the Mosque of Umar so as not to interfere with the bells across the alley at the Holy Sepulcher, though the Sepulcher is an offense to them.

The magazine article by an elderly Zionist who thought the oft-stated urge to tear down the Dome of the Rock and put up a Third Temple was foolish aesthetically, because he liked the Dome and could see it from his window.

The Little Sisters of Jesus closing up their religious articles store at the Seventh Station of the Cross in support of Arab solidarity and joining the strike, though it is to Israel they owe their security.

The Anglican school filled with Palestinian Moslem students, presided over by an Arab bishop.

The array of yarmulkes in a religious store, featuring Mickey Mouse and Bart Simpson as skullcap designs. When it matters so much that a man wears one, does it matter not at all what is pictured on it?

Though dependent upon a Christian country, earlier this year the Israeli government had secretly sought to install Jewish settlers in the Christian Quarter, causing an unnecessary rift between the usually allied Christians and Jews. For what absurd purpose was that plan hatched?

Is there anywhere else in the world so inscrutable?

"Look who we got here," said O'Hanrahan, eyeing the al-Wad Avenue from the heart of the Moslem Quarter: it was Colonel Westin and his countryman, the miniscule Mr. Underwood. "Try to duck down . . ."

"People you know?" asked the rabbi.

The colonel almost walked past O'Hanrahan and through the Damascus Gate, but then spied him, squinted to make sure, and took Mr. Underwood by the arm and led him to the table where the trio was sitting. "Well well well, if it isn't the intrepid Mr. O'Hanrahan! Clem told me you were in town and here you are."

"Here I am."

Underwood gave Lucy a special smile and she instinctively looked away.

Colonel Westin sucked air in quickly between clenched teeth. "Might we . . ." He paused as if the request was obvious. "You know? Have a word alone."

Warily, Rabbi Hersch and Lucy stood when it became apparent that O'Hanrahan had no intention of politely removing himself. "Let's get you some decent halvah, little girl," said Rabbi Hersch. "I know a place."

Lucy grabbed another almond cookie and accompanied the rabbi.

Underwood and Colonel Westin sat in their vacated chairs. Colonel Westin folded his hands and shook his head. "Apparently, Mr. O'Hanrahan, you can't keep out of trouble."

"I'm not aware I'm up to anything, Colonel."

Underwood and the colonel exchanged sophisticated, smug looks as if a joke had been shared.

"Something funny about that?" O'Hanrahan asked.

"You see, I know what you're up to, professor," Colonel Westin said confidently, sucking in air through his teeth. "Clem here didn't see it, but, uh, I filled him in. Your game is safe with me." While Underwood gaped knowingly, Colonel Westin reached across and patted the professor's arm.

O'Hanrahan: "Figured me out, have you?"

"Miss Dantan and you. Oh I approve, at your age . . . heh-heh. I've made some calls to Chicago. You abscond with department funds and a young lady, then do the beaches of Italy and Greece. Her parents and the university report her missing to INTERPOL and of course she's with you in a little love nest. If it hadn't been for that ikon defacement thing your little vacation would never've been discovered, right? I've got it pegged scenariowise, don't I?"

O'Hanrahan led him on. "Welllll, you make it sound so . . . sordid."

"As I said, heh-heh, at your age, sir! More power to you."

Underwood beamed approval as well.

Colonel Westin: "What I wanted to speak to you about was this. It would help us at Customs—"

Underwood: "And at the State Department."

Colonel Westin: "—if you would be so kind as not to associate with any more nefarious contacts, Mr. O'Hanrahan. You can imagine our concern."

"What nefarious contacts do you mean, Colonel?"

Colonel Westin sucked air in through his teeth and shook his head, as if to scold him. "You know who we mean. Mustafa Waswasah in the El-Khodz Hotel."

O'Hanrahan restrained his impatience. "He's not a dangerous man, Colonel. He trades in rare artifacts and antique texts. I've know him since Dead Sea Scroll days," he added, remembering the black Mercedes that attempted to follow him.

Underwood had produced a pad and a pair of reading glasses and assumed an authoritive air. "We have it on good authority from our sources . . ."

Colonel Westin made a show of pretending to clear his throat.

"What?" whispered Underwood.

Colonel Westin kept forcing uh-hummmms until Underwood realized he was being warned not to reveal the sources.

"I didn't tell him who told us," Underwood whispered back.

"Just don't say it out loud."

"I wasn't gonna."

"Well," Underwood regrouped, "never mind where we heard this, but, uh, we understand there are some illegally acquired antiquities that have been fenced by Mr. Waswasah, namely some Roman coins." Underwood sighed, gazing longingly upon the almond cookies with their light dusting of sugar.

"Roman coins," O'Hanrahan repeated.

"Yes," said the colonel, "not to say that his entire enterprise is illegal but he does claim trade in numismatics of an ancient time frame, I understand, and some of these objects clearly are not from the source he purports. We're not sure where he gets them, but when the Israeli government finds his source, well, there'll be consequences. We wanted to make sure you didn't get taken in."

"Gee thanks, gentlemen, for the warning."

"Those cookies," said Underwood, "are pretty good, aren't they?" O'Hanrahan wasn't moved to offer one.

The colonel stood up and Underwood did the same, and O'Hanrahan fought not to dwell on the Laurel-and-Hardy couple they made. "Keep your nose clean, Mr. O'Hanrahan," the colonel concluded, "and let us know if any other Islamic groups attempt to contact you. You do know that many of these antiquities dealers and Islamic merchants who make so much money from the academic black market have connections to terrorist cells and counterestablishment units—it's just best to steer clear."

"Greece is one thing," said Clem Underwood, running a hand through the sparse, carefully arrayed hair on top of his head. O'Hanrahan focused on the ring on his right hand, a black stone with a familiar insignia. Lucy had said she had seen it before, but as he squinted at it, O'Hanrahan was sure he had seen it recently too. ". . . but Jerusalem is another kettle of fish altogether," Underwood concluded uneasily, before asking, "Mr. O'Hanrahan, can I have a cookie?"

"They sell them inside," O'Hanrahan motioned to the ancient archway and the Palestinian tea-shop within.

"I'm gonna get some of these, John," said Underwood, sidling past and into the store. This left Colonel Westin and O'Hanrahan together.

O'Hanrahan decided he'd make things interesting.

"Colonel Westin," O'Hanrahan said confidentially. "I made a little call this morning to Athens. And there is no Clem Underwood that works for the mission in Greece, not in Athens, not in Thessalonika. The embassy was very thorough. Not in Treasury, not in Customs, not in State—nowhere."

Colonel Westin didn't flinch. "I know that," he snapped.

"You, Colonel, on the other hand, are indeed registered with the U.S. Customs office, so I feel I can trust you. Who is this Underwood guy?"

"We're, uh, still looking into that, professor," he said, as if discussing a secret wartime mission. "I think we'd best not talk about it at this juncture timewise—"

O'Hanrahan hid a smile. This guy didn't have a clue. This was the first he had heard of Underwood's false identity.

"Right," said Colonel Westin, obviously flustered. "This will all go into the official file concerning this matter, Mr. O'Hanrahan . . . sssh, here he comes."

"Got your cookies, Mr. Underwood?" O'Hanrahan asked in a tone verging on mockery.

"Uh-hm," he said, his mouth full of one.

Colonel Westin and Underwood moved along through the Damascus Gate, Underwood taking two steps for every one of the colonel's, and O'Hanrahan reached for one of the almond cookies himself.

The rabbi returned with Lucy.

"Who were those guys?" asked Rabbi Hersch.

"The tall one is some colonel put out to pasture, some poor diplomatic service bureaucrat; I checked him out. He's worried I'm going to smuggle out antiquities. The short one is pretending to be with the State Department and he's hooked up with the colonel for some reason."

Lucy reached for a cookie. "Did you notice the insignia on the ring?"

O'Hanrahan nodded. "Yep. Sharp eyes, Sister Lucy. I've seen it before too."

The rabbi scowled. "Too many people are interested in us lately. This isn't good." Rabbi Hersch stared intently at his friend. "You up to something I should know about?"

O'Hanrahan smiled back placidly, no sign that he'd been offered a million deutsche marks and, alternately, a *harim* in Teheran that very day to betray Lucy and Mordechai, who stood before him in perfect trust. "No," he said, lightly laughing. "Are you?"

AUGUST 7TH

Hours passed with O'Hanrahan breathing the familiar mold and dust of a fine library. He decided he deserved a break.

O'Hanrahan had not done what he was about to do in some time, but the temptation was irresistible. He backtracked a few aisles to the Prophets and the *pesharim*, the commentaries. A whole two shelves for Ezekiel, ditto for Jeremiah and Isaiah. Then the minor prophets. Waiting for him on the shelf was *Habakkuk: The Great Commentaries*.

A masterpiece. One edition in Hebrew, one in English, explicating the prophets and the commentaries, the commentaries on the commentaries, the *midrash*. Habakkuk in the Bible wrote three little chapters, and yet the author of this commentary was able to spin 450 pages out of it in the tradition of the best Jewish scholarship, where the original text comes to be less important than the play of an associative mind freely ranging over the material.

For centuries Jew and Gentile alike have opened their Bibles to the *Book of Habakkuk,* that great dialogue between God and his prophet, captive of the Chaldeans. Yes, we deserve your scorn, O Lord, but must it be at the hands of the Chaldeans who are so much more evil? How often this must have been remembered as the Jews suffered in later times at the hands of Greeks, Romans, Byzantines, Roman Catholics, Moslems, Nazis—*But the Lord is in His holy temple; let all the earth keep silence before Him*, which wasn't exactly the sought-for policy. O'Hanrahan turned the pages, skimmed a paragraph or two. The prose of this book was always immensely readable, learned. As in the best scholarly works, half the battle was in the choice of subject. *Habakkuk* was perfect. A small book, a minor prophet, about whom most people were content with what had been said.

Mordechai Hersch! How did you do it? You genius! You old bastard! Where did you find the patience, the discipline? If only God could have permitted me *one* of these to my name . . .

(You were given more than enough intellect to write one.)

I know, I know, thought O'Hanrahan, as he thumbed through the index. Look at the footnotes: every minor inflection of Hebrew tense is observed. Very important in prophetic scriptures—is God's wrath in the conditional or future perfect? Look at these acknowledgments . . . O'Hanrahan closed the book and held it reverently, the intellectual's modern equivalent of a relic. Thou shalt not covet thy colleague's work of scholarship, he told himself. Look at the About the Author: *Mordechai Israel Hersch teaches Hebrew and Comparative Religion at Hebrew University; he was made Rosen Professor* etc. etc., lists of awards and accolades, honorary degrees. *He is also the author of "The Azhkenazim of Prussia, 1880–1900."* His first book, not brilliant but thorough and worthy of notice, remembered O'Hanrahan. *New Revelations from Qumran*, his book following his work on the Dead Sea Scrolls. I spent double the time on the *Thanksgiving Hymn*, thought O'Hanrahan bitterly, and yet I didn't write a thing. *Not the Messiah*, a pamphlet diatribe directed against Jews for Jesus in the early 1970s, which stirred up worldwide attention—Mordechai! I even envy your follies! *Mr. Hersch is at work on his long-awaited biography and commentary on Flavius Josephus, the First-Century Jewish historian*, the paragraph concluded.

O'Hanrahan closed his eyes. *Habakkuk* 3:19, *The Lord is my strength; He makes my feet like hinds' feet, He makes me tread upon my high places.* Mordechai, you have trod upon the high places! I have stumbled and slipped . . . no, not even stumbled.

O'Hanrahan replaced Rabbi Hersch's book on the shelf.

No, not even stumbled, continued O'Hanrahan, I stayed at the bottom of the slope, never attempting an arduous climb. O'Hanrahan down in the valley, O'Hanrahan in *amousia*, the void in which no muses venture, buying drinks at the bar, holding forth to whomever would listen, pissing it away, talking it away, each night, each opportunity for study and serious accomplishment, all those evenings while Mordechai Hersch was writing, you, Paddy, were performing—you wanted an audience, you wanted to be the ringmaster.

(So you both got what you worked for.)

Right. O'Hanrahan the Clown, and Mordechai the Scholar. Enough of the library today. A stiff drink was what he needed.

(*Habakkuk* 2:16. *Drink, yourself, and stagger!*)

After a few quick shots in the King David hotel barroom, O'Hanrahan made his way to Rabbi Hersch's office and knocked on the closed door. The rabbi called out that he would be a minute, he was finishing up with two students. During the rabbi's travels there had accrued a backlog of thesis advisees seeking appointments, phone messages, correspondence, and department memoranda that Morey had allowed to stay taped to his door. O'Hanrahan scanned the Hebrew, practicing. Then he came upon a note that said: *Philip Beaufoix, returning your call, 11:30 A.M. 6/8/90.* Two days ago.

O'Hanrahan's heart sank further.

Yep, Mordechai's done it. He's called Father Beaufoix at the American University in Cairo. I'm being replaced. I've finally pushed it too far; he's finding another translator. And I probably deserve it, all the misadventures, the bad-boy behavior—

The door opened, two students walked out escorted by the rabbi, rosy-cheeked and chipper. "Where's the goil?" he asked, meaning Lucy.

"She said she'd be here at one," the professor said glumly.

Lucy had spent another day in the New City, making phone calls, faxing Chicago—the real number, this time—mailing postcards and having breakfast. Making another descent into the Old City had been less joyous with some trouble brewing in East Jerusalem near the bus station. Sirens, ambulances, noise, and she thought she discerned tear gas though the wind was away from her. The Old City, one moment lively and colorful, merchants and barkers calling out their wares and delicious savories, suddenly became grim: shopkeepers hastily closed up in midmorning, cursed and muttered as Israeli soldiers filled the streets.

Before the Fourth Station, Lucy watched the soldiers march in pairs down the Via Dolorosa. The Palestinian children ignored them, kicking a ball back and forth. Lucy watched the ball lodge itself behind a crate, behind a soldier. Kick it back to him, Lucy said inwardly. He's just a kid, what's the harm? But the soldier didn't, and the little Arab boy, his face nestling against the barrel of the Uzi machine gun, poked and manipulated the ball until it dislodged and the game commenced. Not even a *gesture* toward these people, Lucy thought frankly, looking at the immovable soldier, muscular and proud. She supposed darkly that this five-year-old is just the next decade's rock-throwing Intifadist.

After a cab ride to Hebrew University she met the professor and Rabbi Hersch on schedule in the appointed parking lot, both of them cross for some reason.

"I'm not going to discuss every phone call I make with you," the rabbi was saying. "He called me and I called him back and what business is it of yours. It had to do with the review!"

But the argument ceased when they saw her. The rabbi fumbled with his keys and took them to a standard light-blue sedan with West Bank plates, a university car, he explained. "Ready," he asked, "for your trip to Mar Saba?"

"I'm not sure I feel up to it," she moaned, rubbing her shoulder, still store from the typhus shot. "Is it going to be a bumpy road?"

"It's not too bad," O'Hanrahan muttered. "That is, if Morey isn't going by way of Cairo to pay further homage to this man—"

"Listen to you! You're consumed with jealousy!"

Lucy decided to make peace by announcing, "Mar Saba I'd love to see. Of course, the West Bank between here and there I'm not so sure about."

The rabbi: "Don't worry. It's just fifteen miles from here."

As they got in the car, O'Hanrahan asked, "And you're gonna wear that yarmulke, huh?"

Rabbi Hersch patted his head. "You want me to take it off? Maybe I should disguise myself as Yasser Arafat?"

"It's the West Bank, Morey, that's all I meant—"

"I'm not to look like a Jew in the land of the Jews? It's my country after all."

O'Hanrahan got in the front seat, Lucy in the back. "Try telling the Arabs along the road to Mar Saba that this is your country," grumbled O'Hanrahan.

The rabbi hopped in and started up the car. "The day I have to take this off in Israel is a day, if it be the will of the Lord, I never see."

O'Hanrahan hated it when his friend Mordechai went into Superjew mode, Zionist apologist. Most days Rabbi Hersch could be expected to bring his balanced view of things to all Arab-Jewish issues, but this wasn't one of those days, and it was O'Hanrahan's fault for lashing out at him for some perceived betrayal with Father Beaufoix.

"You want me to put on a *galabiyya* perhaps?" Rabbi Hersch mused, without humor.

"Well, why stop there, Morey?" O'Hanrahan said, escalating the matter. "Why not fit out the car in a *tzitzit*, paint the Star of David on the side, phylacteries around the tailpipe. We can paint a big bull's-eye on the windshield for the rocks."

"I am not going to be intimidated by the rabble," he said calmly. "These rock-throwing hooligans will be put down, I assure you."

If your country has to shoot every teenage boy in the occupied territories, thought Lucy to herself, sourly.

The ride progressed silently, everyone wishing an excuse to turn back and go their separate ways would present itself.

Before Bethlehem there was a refugee compound. Lucy had seen them on the news, but seeing them for real behind a two-story fence just yards from her car window was worse: open sewers, streets of mud, children playing in this mixture of sewage water and mud, flies, and garbage, the look of misery on the women's faces hauling water in jugs. Three ragged children pressed their faces against the metal fence and spit indignantly at passing cars, no hope of reaching their targets.

"That's a refugee camp, huh?" asked Lucy, not entirely innocently. She wanted Rabbi Hersch to apprehend the human tragedy in his country's occupied territories.

"There's plenty of the Islamic world for them to go to," he said. "From Morocco to India, 800 million strong. No, no one wants them, no one among their dear Arab brethren."

Lucy knew she could up the amperage in the conversation by asking if this is where Palestinian women and children went when the Israeli Army dynamited neighborhoods, bulldozed homes, wiped out blocks of houses because of rumors of misbehavior. In 1967, after the war, the Israelis evicted and destroyed homes of some 4000 Palestinians to "stabilize" the city. With these tactics, where wouldn't there be a home in all of Arab Palestine that didn't harbor sufficient hatred of the Israelis to be torn down?

The rabbi avoided Beit Shair, on the outskirts of Bethlehem, and began the single-lane, winding road across the barren, rocky hills to the mountainous canyons where the Mar Saba Monastery was located. *Where shepherds watched their flocks by night*, it occurred to Lucy, looking at the sparse grazing vegetation outside of David's Royal City.

The largest of the wretched little villages came into view along the ridge that defined the road. Young girls, Lucy surmised, didn't have to wear the veils, young women did; as the car passed, the Palestinian women raised their veils to prevent the strangers from viewing their faces. A dirty, energetic pack of young boys played by the entrance to the village, throwing up cupped handfuls of dust and dodging the mushroom cloud that ensued, laughing. They spotted the car and ran to the roadside scooping up pebbles.

"Delightful little boys," mumbled the rabbi, as a pebble or two, ineffectively thrown at the car, clinked and clattered against the trunk.

As they slowed through the town, Lucy anxiously looked at the hard, unfriendly faces that stared them down. The older women, who could abandon the veil again, looked fierce in what struck Lucy as war paint, those odd green tattoos of Palestinian women around the eyes and mouth, an earlier generation's beguiling beauty secret. Lucy saw the town's requisite all-male café, the men sitting by the road on stools and chairs, smoking the *sheesha*, and a poster of an idealized Saddam Hussein behind them, a newsprint Iraqi flag draped on the window. Lucy sighed. Saddam Hussein, who had killed more Arabs than Israel would ever have a chance to.

The car passed through the last village with another mob of jeering boys hurling small stones at the back windshield. They came to a junction.

"Do you know which way?" Lucy asked.

"The locals take down the signs," explained Rabbi Hersch, reaching for the glove compartment and pulling out a detailed map, "so all strangers can be lost and bribe them for directions . . . that is, the ones they don't rob." He ran a finger over a road on the map. "Here we go, right turn."

Immediately, as if from out of nowhere, two teenage Palestinian boys appeared and stood a few yards before the car. They put out their thumb as if for hitchhiking. They looked pleasant enough, their faces beseeching, could they get a lift down the right fork?

"Not on your life," said the rabbi, waving them off, as he turned the car down the road.

"Mar Saba!" they both cried out.

The rabbi accelerated, stirring up the dust. "Right. These Moslems want to go to a Greek monastery. Like hell they do."

O'Hanrahan: "Most Arabs around Bethlehem *are* Christian, after all."

"You want me to pick 'em up?" said the rabbi testily.

The taller one, about sixteen, wearing a green-red-and-white Palestinian flag–inspired T-shirt, ran after the car and banged a fist down on the trunk as he was left in the dust. They yelled something.

"When will," the rabbi asked, affecting a dainty tone, "the Arab mothers of the world teach their little boys some manners?"

O'Hanrahan was going to say something but didn't. His half-utterance was enough to set the rabbi off again: "What? You *really* want me to pick those guys up? They want our money, for Christ's sake . . . ehh, *look*, it's downhill all the way—why would anyone need a ride?"

"I'm glad you didn't pick them up, Rabbi," said Lucy, who would have had them beside her. "In fact, maybe this was a bad idea to come."

O'Hanrahan assured her that they'd be safe once they got to the monastic grounds. Lucy reminded herself how rarely one hears about tourists or pilgrims getting killed by Palestinians during the Intifada, not that that equalled assurance in the present day.

The road twisted and curved back on itself as it dropped a thousand feet toward the canyon's rim. There was not a bit of vegetation, not a plant, not a tree in this rocky valley. Lucy soon saw a parking lot of sorts, and a long wall with a single blue door in the middle of it. The three got out and O'Hanrahan went over to ring a bell suspended with a cord hanging down by the door. The rabbi and Lucy went to a slight promontory along a trail to better view the walled fortress.

"The Mar Saba Monastery," O'Hanrahan explained while waiting for someone to answer the door, "was founded by St. Saba, the father of monasticism in the area, Bishop of Jerusalem in 491."

(Where Saba kept a lion as a pet, until he ordered it to leave upon continued disobedience. Where dates grow without stones to this day, thanks to a miraculous command of Saba, who didn't care for the sinfully suggestive seeds in fruits. Home of Saba's sainted mother, Sophia, as well as John Damascene, Theodore of Edessa, Cosma of Majuma, Aphrodisius, John the Silent. What could anyone know now of their lost Byzantine world?)

"Curzon," said O'Hanrahan, hoping to lighten the mood, "the great Victorian explorer, said the Mar Saba Monastery's library was among the best in the Middle East. He saw ancient scrolls that have since disappeared; he talked about them lying on tabletops, texts 1500 years old, as if they were rags and towels. He walked off himself with a 9th-Century Old Testament. Did I tell you about working on the early redaction of *Mark* found here in 1958?"

"Yes," said Lucy, not meaning to be impolite though it had that effect.

The walled monastery was built for defensive purposes into the side of a cliff, suspended over this dry gulch of a canyon, not a tree or plant of any kind in sight down there either. From the slight rise, Lucy eagerly snapped off a few photographs of the Byzantine domes of the Church of St. Nikolas within.

Again: Damn these men and their exclusivity.

"You can't go in, of course," said O'Hanrahan to Lucy, seeming concerned about it. In fact, it was obvious after their mildly menacing drive he didn't want to be here, or for Lucy to be here. No curiosity within was bound to be worth the peril. This whole day, O'Hanrahan thought, is an exercise of Israeli macho from his friend Mordechai, who had insisted on demonstrating his *droit de seigneur* in the Occupied Territories. A monk at last came to usher the men inside.

"I suppose we could go in," said the rabbi, "in shifts."

"Really," said Lucy, acting brave for everyone, "you both go in. This is the middle of nowhere. I'll take a few pictures and sit in the car."

O'Hanrahan agreed. He stopped as if to say something to her, something about locking herself in the car perhaps, but he didn't want to alarm her. "Honk the horn if you need us," he said simply, then he and the rabbi turned to enter the doorway in search of the ineffably masculine mysteries within.

Lucy amused herself by walking to the brink of the canyon again and took some more scenery shots. Then a few more of Mar Saba perched on the abyss for good measure. Very exotic, this place. What you expect out of a desert monastery. Then she looked back upon the long road they had traveled from and she saw the two teenage boys walking down it. What do you know, she thought uneasily, they really did want to come down here. Then she saw, distantly, two more boys, younger, running along behind. She thought: they've gone back to the village, told about the offensive Jewish man driving the car down this dead end, and now they're coming to cause trouble.

Slowly, Lucy maneuvered the slippery, dusty slope of desert rock, taking the steep shortcut rather than the winding trail to return to the car. She could hear their cries. She went over to the blue door and rang the bell furiously. She stood there, torn between waiting for the door to open or going to the car. Knowing the monks, they wouldn't let her in . . .

(Get to the car, Lucy.)

She got inside the car and sat in the passenger seat. She locked the front and back doors. This was unnecessary panic perhaps. These guys might be workers at the monastery, sweepers or handymen for the garden; every Arab, after all, she had met so far had been friendly and generous. Suddenly the filthy refugee camp and the boys spitting at the passing cars flashed in her mind . . .

The boys walked to the driver's side and waved, leering. They tried the door handle and, again, with the same beseeching look, they seemed to want her to come out or let them in. Right, thought Lucy, her heart beating fast, I'm not in the mood to be raped by four dirty Palestinian teenagers this afternoon, no thank you—

"Shekel!" yelled one through the window, the youngest.

He repeated this. He wanted some money. He slammed his little fist against the window: "Shekel! Shekel!"

Then there was a boy, fourteen or so, at her window: "Shekel, shekel!"

The oldest boy pulled out a knife and threatened to scrape it along the hood and side of the car. He looked at Lucy and she understood: your money, or I'll do this. Lucy reached over to the horn and gave it a toot.

This angered the older boy. Lucy quickly saw the fourteen-year-old running for the stack of cut-stone bricks by the side of the monastery wall. He came running back, smiling, with two stones, almost too heavy for him to carry. Lucy honked the horn longer this time. The oldest boy began scraping the car, in a terrible metal-on-metal noise. He was laughing at her—see? She could have prevented this. "Shekel! Shekel!" She honked the horn again—

Uh-oh. The oldest boy tried to put his knife in the small crack of the driver's side window to force the window down. Then he tried putting it between the crack of the front door, hoping to trigger the lock. Lucy leaned on the horn, terrified.

"Hey there!"

Lucy lifted her head to see O'Hanrahan and Rabbi Hersch running toward the car. The boy snarled something and held out the knife for O'Hanrahan to see. The smallest boy took a stone and hurled it at the rabbi. It hit him on the shoulder. If I had a gun, thought Lucy, these little terrorists-in-training would learn their lesson.

(Weren't you the one who felt guns weren't an appropriate response to rock-throwers?)

They're sixteen and thirteen and fourteen, she wailed to herself, already impossible to deal with. They're just boys! We're three grown people terrified of these delinquents. O'Hanrahan stepped forward to confront the guy with the knife. O'Hanrahan knew Arabic and this seemed to placate the boy. O'Hanrahan, Lucy gathered, was calmly saying that they would be in great trouble concerning their parents and their homes if the Israeli Army was informed of this, so why didn't they run along . . .

The rabbi quickly went to the driver's side. Another rock from the young one was aimed toward the rabbi's head. He ducked and it hit the top of the car and slid off the other side—

Kallump! Lucy was startled by a big crash at her side: one of the boys had the stone brick and was smashing it against the passenger-side glass. He was yelling curses. The rabbi, fumbling with the keys, opened the car door and climbed in, slamming it and locking it at once.

"You all right, little girl?" he said with strange serenity.

"Yes. Were you hit?"

"Sandy Koufax the kid is not."

The rabbi knocked on the glass and got O'Hanrahan's attention. The older boy was unsure what to do now. O'Hanrahan quickly made his way to the right-side back door, the rabbi unlocked it, the professor hopped in, almost closing a boy's fingers in the door, which seemed to add to their fury. Now two boys with the two stones were starting on the front windshield. Bringing the great jagged rocks down and down again. On Lucy's side, the nicks began to form larger cracks.

"Happy with your little persecuted Palestinian angels now?" asked the rabbi.

O'Hanrahan bellowed: "Would you start the car and get us out of here?"

Rabbi Hersch started the car. Immediately, one of the little boys climbed onto the back. The rabbi accelerated forward, sending the boy sprawling in the rocky road. Lucy looked over to see the older boy laughing at this pratfall and thought flatly: they're even cruel to each other.

Lucy then looked to her side to see the fourteen-year-old ready to heave the stone brick. She made contact with his eyes. Hate, pure animal unreasoned hate. The rock scratched the glass but did not break it. The older boy with the knife ran to the car.

"He's going to slash the tires!" O'Hanrahan perceived.

"The little momzer's not gonna do anything," said the rabbi, turning the car sharply and heading away from him, only to have another boy standing in the road before him. "Don't dare me to run you over, I will," the rabbi swore.

But the rabbi didn't, and slowed.

And in that time, the boy who had been sent sprawling grabbed on to Lucy's door handle. He wouldn't let go. The rabbi accelerated up the hill, and the boy in front dove out of the way.

"He's still hanging on," said Lucy breathlessly.

"If I go fast enough, he'll have to let go."

They were dragging him. Pure will caused him to run alongside, then drag himself over the rocks. He cried out something. Then there was a loud thud. The older boy had hurled at great speed a rock that had dented the trunk. Here came another rock right for the back windshield. The rock cracked it and O'Hanrahan ducked down in the seat.

"Damn," he said.

The boy on Lucy's side still hadn't let go. The rabbi slammed on the brakes. The boy was flung forward, horribly, into the boulder-filled ditch. His body landed against the rocks, his head hitting a boulder. Lucy was sure he was seriously hurt.

Lucy stammered, "Rabbi, he's probably—"

"To hell with him!" said the rabbi, speeding away before more damage was done.

Lucy talked nervously. "I didn't have any shekels to give them," she said as if that were her responsibility.

"Why should you have to give those animals anything?" said the rabbi.

"That boy was badly hurt," O'Hanrahan stated quietly, feeling a premonition of pains in his hands and feet, brought on by the stress.

"*What?*" snapped the rabbi. "You wanna go back and give him mouth-to-mouth?"

"I wasn't pleading his case," said a tense O'Hanrahan. "It's just that they'll run up to their village and we're not gonna be very safe if the first village we pass through telephones ahead to the last, and some Palestinians are waiting for us—"

"I wasn't planning on dawdling in the next town."

Lucy looked down at her right hand shaking. She held it with her left and that steadied her but she noticed how cold and bloodless they both were. She slumped down in the car and looked at the floorboard. How regrettable this all was. All this naked, purposeless hate. And she was right in supposing that there were tens of thousands of such young men, raised in refugee camps and impoverished streets and slums the Israeli government had no intention of improving, and there would be more and more of them, until the army killed every one of them or the Arab world rose and eliminated every single Israeli or an impossible policy of Love Thy Neighbor was attempted.

Approaching fast: the village they had encountered on the way in. It was obvious from the state of the car that they had seen some trouble. And that seemed to incite the locals to cause more. Two teenage boys took some stones from a neatly piled supply by the road and hurled two at the car. One hit the taillight with the smash of glass and plastic.

"Ah well," murmured the rabbi, strangely serene again. "This is why I don't take my *own* car anywhere. Wait till the guys in Maintenance see what we're bringing back."

Another village was ahead and Lucy saw three little girls run up with their stones to throw. The rabbi smiled at them and waved them no-no-no with his finger and they obeyed. Lucy stared down at the floorboard wishing to be miraculously transported out of the West Bank—hell, out of Israel. I would get on a plane tomorrow, she thought for the first time. A rock from somewhere bounced on top of the car. She didn't look up or startle or turn to see who threw it and where it came from. Please, Lord, let this be over with soon.

(Alas, Beit Shahur approaches.)

"The army's sure to be up ahead," said the rabbi, steering this time to the village they'd bypassed on the trip in.

Lucy looked ahead to the roadblock. Israeli soldiers, lean and fierce looking, were stopping all traffic.

"Are you going to tell the soldiers about the injured boy?" asked Lucy.

"I'm going to tell the soldiers about those hoodlums, yes," he said.

Lucy realized these soldiers, now world famous for their rough treatment of suspected Palestinian troublemakers, would not deal lightly with these boys or their families. They would get files devoted to them, stern warnings, maybe a night or so in jail, their families identified and known.

"Maybe we shouldn't say anything," said Lucy unsurely.

Rabbi Hersch threw up his hands. "Look at the car! They're gonna ask what happened."

"I don't know," she stammered, "it's just if we get them in trouble, it'll be worse for the next group that comes through there to Mar Saba—"

"I hope the soldiers go and beat the shit out of those boys and that'll be a lesson to them."

Indeed, at the checkpoint, the rabbi described the hoodlums in clear detail. What they were wearing, their ages; he had coolly studied them to make this very report. But the soldier, a young, officious woman with no courtesy about her, was acting gruff.

She asked, "What were you doing there, *Rebbe?*"

"Going to the library at Mar Saba, with my associate here, Patrick O'Hanrahan, and his assistant, Lucy Dantan."

She said with a clipped Hebrew accent, "But there are no women allowed in Mar Saba."

"Yes," said the rabbi with forced politeness, "we know, but we thought she'd like to see the place from the outside."

The Israeli soldier stared at them impassively.

"Would you please get out of the car," she requested. "We're going to ask you a few questions."

"Oh boy," mumbled O'Hanrahan. "The third degree."

"It might not be so bad," said the rabbi, pulling the car to the appointed place. The rabbi would not criticize Israeli security because it was the world's best. A pain in the ass, yes, but planes didn't blow up and stores didn't go boom like in Northern Ireland.

"Where are we?" asked Lucy, before getting out of the car.

"Beit Shahur," said the rabbi.

(In the summer of 1989, the citizens of Beit Shahur, largely Arab Christians, decided to stage a passive resistance campaign. Why should they pay taxes to Israel where they were second-class citizens, their rights weren't recognized, and whose moneys went to shooting Palestinians. It was peaceful, nonviolent, and their manifesto was reasonable. An international team of journalists and peace activists gathered. All were arrested. Palestinian homes were looted by Israeli soldiers, valuables smashed, beloved objects burned, TV's kicked in—the idea was to do the equivalent amount of damage as in back taxes. When the multi-faith peace groups protested, they were arrested too. This was November 1989, a week after the Israeli Army had broken in and seized U.N. documents that gave them a further list of Palestinian troublemakers to crack down upon.)

O'Hanrahan's knuckles throbbed with circulation pains. He fumbled in his sportscoat pocket for his Percodan. At the first opportunity he'd take one. With his hand in his coat pocket he felt around for his passport. "I got some good news," muttered O'Hanrahan momentarily. "I got my wallet and my license and some ID, but my passport is in my other jacket at the hotel."

And this lapse meant an hour.

Sixty minutes of checking, double-checking, intensive questions, all cordial enough, all rational and understandable, but draining and invasive. Lucy's passport was in order and after a small interview she was released.

She left the small official building—once someone's home, seized by the army for whatever crimes had been alleged here—and glimpsed O'Hanrahan through a window, looking ancient, answering a series of questions. His political beliefs. Who belonged to the scribbled phone number he had in his wallet? It was an antiquities dealer, an Arab man in East Jerusalem. This suspicious fact opened up possibilities of antiquity smuggling and collusion with East Jerusalem terrorism, so another thirty minutes unfolded itself.

Lucy wandered into the street, hot with the dust-filled light of the late afternoon. There was a Palestinian fruitstand across the road. Lucy imagined she shouldn't be mistreated here, a hundred yards from the police checkpoint. She walked over and was informed a bunch of grapes was a shekel. Not bad.

"American you?" said the smiling, toothless Palestinian grandfather who was shopkeeper.

"Yes."

"Ah! Welcome to Intifada, eh?" he laughed.

"Yes," she smiled, amused at the blunt fatalism of his comment. She handed him the shekel.

"Many, many friends in America, no?"

She wasn't sure what the question was. "Excuse me?"

"Palestinians have many, many friends now in America, yes?"

"More and more, yes."

"You tell in America? You tell them about us, yes?"

Lucy took her grapes and the tattered paper bag, much reused, the shopkeeper had put them in. "Yes, I'll tell them," she said. "Many people want the Palestinians to have a homeland."

The man didn't seem to understand the word, but his wife from behind a veil translated for him and he beamed, exposing his wide, unhealthy mouth. He reached over the piles of fruit and found a lovely, juicy peach for Lucy and handed it to her.

"For me?"

"For you," he bowed. "You the American girl."

She made a nod of acceptance and turned back to the police station and the car. What to make of it all? This exhausting, ceaseless, relentless place. In one hour in Israel, one does more thinking about moral, religious, ethical, and political principles than one does in anywhere else in a decade. *I would like to erase my mind of this vexing place,* she thought, biting into her peach. Delicious. This blessed weather produced the most excellent fruit, true to its reputation.

It was soon five o'clock, time to get back on the road and hit the Jerusalem rush hour.

"I think I speak for all of us," said O'Hanrahan, revived after a cup of coffee, courtesy of his interrogator, "when I say it is time for a *drink.*"

After relaxing with some wine in a New City bistro, they went to a deli restaurant run by Parisian Jews where the rabbi, as if determined to show a softer side, picked up the check and ordered one of everything generously, and promised O'Hanrahan the best chopped liver in the city.

"This is as long as I've ever gone," said O'Hanrahan, returned to ebullience, "without an Israeli chopped-liver fix. I was on the verge of a *crise de foie*."

Lucy groaned and the rabbi pretended to ignore him.

"Some coffee?" the waiter asked. "French roast."

"A *consommation* devoutly to be wished."

"I see you're back to normal, Paddy," said the rabbi.

Then they trudged to a dessert café in the New City along Ben Yehuda, a pedestrian zone perfect for people-watching. Lucy, more paranoid than she was yesterday, wondered aloud if there was a chance of someone hurling a bomb in such a populous, much-enjoyed place.

"Of course there is," said the rabbi, pouring the three of them another glass of chilled South African white wine. "But we cannot live in fear. We must trust in God. We will not . . ." But the rabbi scrapped the inevitable manifesto to follow. Enough for today, already!

He changed the topic to more mystical, escapist topics: the *gematriot* of the Sephardim. The rabbi unfolded a napkin and wrote out the ten *sefiroth* and twenty-two consonants of the Hebrew alephbeth, singing as he wrote them, as if they were the ABCs: ". . . qoph, resh, sin, taw . . . and I've run out of song," he concluded at the 22nd and final letter. "Now each letter has a value. Aleph to yodh is 1 through 10, on to qoph is 10 through 100 by tens, and the last three are 200, 300, and 400."

"No values for vowel sounds?" checked Lucy.

"What vowels? Who taught you Hebrew? Can you read it without points?"

"Not very well," she confessed, needing the marks that gave away the vowel sounds between the consonants.

"Not very well, she says. You read it with points, it's not reading," the rabbi pronounced. "This is how they teach Hebrew at Chicago? Who was your teacher?"

Lucy pointed at O'Hanrahan.

"Paddy, you should retire all over again," said the rabbi.

"I can't help it," said O'Hanrahan, "if she didn't do her homework."

"I showed up for more classes than you did," said Lucy. Turning to the rabbi, she asked of *gematriot*, "Isn't this Jewish word-magic stuff all just coincidence? I mean, if you play with all words long enough can't you get them to signify something?"

"Yes," said the rabbi slowly, "but too many of these kinds of parallels and coincidences show up in Torah. Here's an example from *Habakkuk*, one of my specialties. "In *Habakkuk* 3:2 it says,'In wrath remember mercy,' or *rachem* in Hebrew, which comes to a value of 248. There are 248 Mosaic laws. The Law given to us by God is His greatest mercy."

"Do you think," asked Lucy, "that the Babylonian masters who compiled the Bible invented this word-magic and planted it in their revised editions?"

"Could well be," said Rabbi Hersch. "Can you imagine the effect that rediscovering this sort of thing had on a learned man in ancient times or the Middle Ages? It was all the confirmation one needed to see that Hebrew was the very language of God, in and of itself magical, spiritual. It was not a long step to imagine that the letters and words themselves had magical powers. God, it is said, created the world by pronouncing his name. The Jewish custom of wearing phylacteries—you know what a phylactery is?"

Lucy said yes, remembering one of her great embarrassing moments when referring to a phylactery in Old Testament History at St. Eulalia's as a "prophylactic." She afterward pretended to have done it on purpose to anger Sister Miriam.

"The *thephallin*, the *mezuzah*, a prayer cylinder that can be affixed to doors . . . this reinforces the belief in the power of the words of the Torah. The name of Yahweh, the four consonants, the holy tetragrammetron, the 42-letter name of God, the 72-letter name of God, whatever, were powerful spells to conjure with, hence, the necessity of the commandment not to take thy Lord's holy name in vain. This commandment may have less to do with disrespect than it does with the unknown, unpredictable powers of those letters. Moses killed the Egyptian with the *schem ha-mephorasch*, the spoken name of God," the rabbi noted. "And early mystical works kind to Jesus assumed he knew the *schem* to raise up Lazarus. But, little girl, don't pronounce this word unless you are pure of soul, perfectly chaste of body."

"Well, that leaves me out," mumbled O'Hanrahan.

"What happens?" asked Lucy.

"You die, of course. I'm not sure a woman can employ the *schem* in any event . . ."

(What of Lilith, first wife of Adam, Mordechai? For centuries rabbis held that Adam's first mate was not Eve but Lilith, a not-so-great creation who coupled with Adam frequently, giving birth to the demons that plague all women today. She was banished from Eden because she decided she wanted to be the boss and proved her defiance by speaking the *schem*. Then three angels ran her out of Eden and into Egypt where Lilith threatened to be nearby for every human birth to provide pain, make for stillborn infants, deformities, and deaths of the mother. That's why an amulet with the three angels Senoi, Sansenoi, and Samangeloph is still worn by Sephardic Jews in some lands. And there was another woman who used the *schem*, a Babylonian Jew named Ishtahar. The Angel Schamchasu had this plan to make her a prostitute—mortal man cannot comprehend the wickedness, the silliness, the bother of most of Our angels—and Ishtahar spoke the *schem* and was allowed to hide in a Lower Heaven.)

O'Hanrahan interrupted by signaling for the waiter and ordering another bottle of Johannesburg Riesling. "*That*," he insisted, "was word-magic."

The rabbi: "I was raised as a child by my uncle in Williamsburg, Brooklyn, with a strong distaste for this word hocus-pocus, because it was one more thing the Hasid believed and we didn't. My uncle said what you say, little girl, that you can prove anything with it if you try."

O'Hanrahan interrupted. "The name 'Jesus' and the word 'Messiah' both come to 74, which proves very inconvenient for the *gematria* crowd."

" 'Jesus' is Greek," reminded the rabbi. "It doesn't work with his Aramaic name. Anyway, in Brooklyn I heard the story from a Hasid about Rabbi Nehemiah who lived in a muddy little town by the name of Lodzuk in Poland. A Cossack-style raid in the early 1800s left the town burned to the ground and the people without a kopek. They turned to Nehemiah, their *tzaddik*, their Hasidic guru, if you will, and begged to know why God had allowed this to happen. The rabbi responded that it was God's purpose that they should be brought low so they might see the wonders of Torah. Ludzuk, L-D-Z-W-K came to 67, he explained, and when added to "Torah," 611, one got 678, which corresponds to Aravot, the Seventh and highest Heaven. Since *aravot* is also 'fields' he suggested the town return to them and begin planting their crops anew."

"Wow," said Lucy.

"As a kid in Brooklyn, I also heard tell of a nearby *tzaddik* who moved his whole congregation from the Sudetenland in the 1920s because of a chance remark an elder made that Hitler coming to power represented the writing on the wall. In Daniel, you'll recall the finger of God comes down and writes *Mene Mene Tekel Upharsim*, whose letters have a value of 1776, the year of the birth of America. On the basis of that, he told the village to pack up for America and good thing he did. Would that *that gematria* had been the rage in Middle Europe!"

"Claptrap is claptrap," said the doubting O'Hanrahan, "be it Roman Catholic relic nonsense or Jewish word-game nonsense. You gonna show Lucy how to make a golem, Morey?"

Rabbi Hersch began an explanation of how to create life:

"*Job* 28:13, as discussed in Midrash Tehillim, suggests that Torah was not in the exactly correct order, a letter or two out of place, chapters rearranged. If someone could reassemble it in the order God created it, then they too could create worlds and bring the dead to life."

Lucy was reminded of what little she knew about Jewish mysticism.

"And this is what kabbalists through the Middle Ages were trying to do?"

"You could make a man," explained the rabbi with a straight face, "if one recited the Hebrew and the other 21 Divine Alphabets—there were many formulas—but your man-made creature, though alive, could never talk or think or speak. That alone was for God to accomplish. However, if one stumbled upon Torah in the correct order, one could make a man who could talk and have the gift of language. Solomon ibn-Gabirol did in the 1100s and he created a woman who cleaned his house and cooked his meals."

O'Hanrahan: "Cheaper than buying one of those blow-up dolls, wouldn't you say?"

Rabbi Hersch: "Ignore this man."

O'Hanrahan: "Maybe you can get Rabbi Hersch to make *you* a man, Luce."

Lucy attempted to raise the tone. "And so, Rabbi, you've been looking in these medieval Kabbalah guidebooks for alphabets?"

"To go a long way around, yes, I've been looking in copies of the *Alphabet of Ben Zira*. Ben Zira was a man with a great reputation for making and unmaking golems. I'm trying to imagine what Rabbi Rosen looked at when he translated the *Gospel of Matthias* in 1949. Did you ever meet Rabbi Rosen, Paddy?"

"I glimpsed him at some dinner once. I knew who he was, and I certainly knew who his wife was."

Both he and Rabbi Hersch chuckled about this.

Lucy asked, "What's so special about the wife?"

"She was 23," said O'Hanrahan. "He was 84 or 85."

"She was 22," the rabbi corrected. "It was just a visa marriage, to get her out of the Soviet Union. 'Mrs. Rosen' was one of the most beautiful women that I have ever seen."

"She was 23," O'Hanrahan insisted. "I spent an hour trying to communicate with her at a party. Sumptuous dark Russian features. Anyway, she stayed at Rabbi Rosen's house until accommodation could be assigned for her and the jokes . . . well, you can imagine the jokes. A 23-year-old-bombshell and an 84-year-old man."

"Why do you keep correcting me?" Then Rabbi Hersch swallowed heavily.

"Something wrong, Rabbi?" Lucy asked. O'Hanrahan glanced up from his newspaper to see if the rabbi had become ill.

"No," said Rabbi Hersch tersely, distracted. "Jesus," he muttered to himself, "of course."

He stood up.

"I forgot an appointment," he added, seeming to curse himself. "I have stood this person up a hundred times—gotta go. Can't believe it . . ."

O'Hanrahan: "Why don't you make a phone call?"

"No," he said, taking his sportscoat from the back of the chair and putting it on. "Gotta be running along here."

Rabbi Hersch departed and O'Hanrahan and Lucy sat together in silence.

Lucy watched the rabbi shuffle through the crowd until she could see him no longer. Gabriel, she felt, had simply misjudged this man. Okay, so this spring he was in Rome where he wasn't supposed to be, seemingly working behind Dr. O'Hanrahan's back. He must have had some kind of reason.

"I've been meaning," began Lucy, "to ask you a question, sir. About what happened in Rome this spring. You know, with Gabriel and all that."

"Is this another attempt to get me to make it up with that worm?"

"No, this is a factual matter."

He waved her to proceed, though he withdrew his hand quickly, clutching it, hoping to numb a sudden pain. Ah, the pains again!

Lucy: "That day in April when Gabriel stole the scroll in Rome and ran away? Were you with the rabbi on that trip?"

"No, he was back in Jerusalem."

"You're sure?"

"I waved good-bye at the ferry terminal." He clutched his arm, discreetly. "You know differently?"

Lucy shrugged.

O'Hanrahan sipped the last of his wine and decided to pursue Lucy's question. Maybe she had discovered something . . . but just then a shooting pain pierced his left hand. He quickly set down the bottle unsurely and clasped his hand in his lap. Was Lucy seeing this? He looked up to see her unaware, borrowing his *Herald Tribune* to read.

O'Hanrahan felt in his jacket. Oh just great, just fucking great: his Percodan was at the King David Hotel. His passport had been in *this* jacket and when he switched jackets at the hotel the Percodan remained in the one he'd thrown on the bed. Well, perhaps these damn circulation pains would stop. His left hand throbbed and the right joined it in sympathy.

It was getting worse, his condition.

In the mornings he'd wake up and his hands would be ice-cold, and on some mornings he would have pains in his hands and feet. He would get out of bed and stand so the blood would flow into his feet and then rub his hands under hot water, but lately that was not stopping the conspiracy of fouled circulation, arthritis, labile blood pressure, blocked arteries, and whatever it was that was plaguing his liver.

(Is that such a mystery, Patrick?)

He looked at his glass of wine and lifted it to his lips in defiance. If cirrhosis is going to take me out, so be it! It's too late now. No liver transplant for such an old man—

The pain! He lowered his hand again. Yes, like clockwork, on cue, the arches of his feet commenced to ache. The more he feared an onslaught the more sure one was to arrive. Why does one's own body conspire against one?

(You conspire against it, Patrick.)

Well, he thought fatalistically, a bad episode was to be expected. He thought of his being lost on Mount Athos, straining every bit of his body's machinery, hearing voices behind every bush like a madman. And today's little West Bank antics . . . It's delayed shock.

"Something wrong, Dr. O'Hanrahan?" Lucy asked, identifying distress in his face. She stared through her round glasses, blankly concerned.

"No," he said, "just . . . just feeling horribly tired all of a sudden. It's been some day."

(Lucy can help you get a taxi to the hotel, Patrick.)

"You really don't look well," said Lucy.

"Thank you, thank you, my support staff," said O'Hanrahan rising from the table. "I saw an open drugstore back on the Jaffa Road. I'm going to go get some aspirin."

"I have a few in my purse—"

"I don't want any of that menstrual-cramps women's aspirin," he snarled. "I want some real aspirin, and besides . . ." His hand felt as if it would fall off, it ached so deeply. ". . . besides, I want a walk to clear my brain. I'll be back in a few minutes," added O'Hanrahan, not able to cover his acute distress any longer.

"Should I come with you?"

"No thank you," he uttered.

The pain in his side throbbed again. It had gone away at this point before and that was what he hoped now. No, there it was again. His liver would go for days without acting up, for weeks, then suddenly it would be like a knife wound, a twisting knife, vibrating and poking at some impossibly sensitive nerve tissue within. In between the jabs, which coincided with his heartbeats, there would be a deeper yet vaguer pain that would spread and subsume the whole body, until making a fist hurt, every joint could reflect in some way the pain in his side, each breath would be an effort. That is, unless he could make it back to the hotel room and get the Percodan.

He kept walking. Walking helped, moving helped, bending helped. When pain is constant you can confuse the nerves by rubbing the area, O'Hanrahan told himself. The ancients thought the soul was in the bowels and if you've ever known bowel pain you can understand this a bit, for pain there is hell and relief heaven, more sublime and ecstatic than . . . than . . . Jesus, how many blocks to go until the King David? Damn it, he breathed, almost panting now, taking carefully measured steps at a brisk pace—it's blocks from here, so a cab would be his salvation.

He attempted to turn around and scan the oncoming traffic, but in raising his hand to hail a cab the pain in his side nearly overwhelmed him.

Don't stop.

If I stop, he told himself, I won't start again. There was a passing group of laughing kids rounding the corner, a cat in the gutter drain picking at something: my final benedictory vision of this world!

The Ha-Malkah street met Gershon Agron and King David Street at the bottom of a hill; the Old City lit by spotlights, medieval and majestic to his left. See? Almost home, he told himself as if he were his own patient. Now just up this hill and we have it.

It might as well be Everest!

(Why were you such a stubborn old man, Patrick? Lucy could have run for help and you wouldn't be in this fix.)

Ah, the voices.

(You didn't listen to us about the drinking, about the unhealthy living, the smoking . . .)

I see we've got God the Puritan working tonight. I hate it, Lord, when You get like this . . . He laughed and allowed a tear to run down his face. He stopped and bent over. This might be *it*. Would anyone help me if I just fell over here in the middle of the night 200 yards from the King David Hotel? O'Hanrahan felt his forehead. Yes, delirium or something akin to it was coming on. Up the hill, one foot before the other.

He remembered the really bad times, he was so afflicted. In Chicago once, the episode that led to his getting the Percodan prescription from an old seminary buddy turned doctor. Then once with Gabriel in a shared hotel room in Rome. Murmurings all through Italy and Greece, and now in the Holy City of Jerusalem in the middle of the night on a deserted street with goddam Mt. Ararat between me and my bottle of pills—no, not Ararat with the dove and olive branch, but Pisgah, Mt. Nebo! With the Promised Land of his worldly ambitions glimmering at him from the valley, unreachable! And the Lord said to O'Hanrahan, This is the scroll that I swore to those before thee, and I will give it to thy rivals. I have let thee see it with thine eyes, but thou shalt not translate it and make a pile of money.

(Because you broke faith with Me in the midst of the people at the waters of Jack Daniels, in the Wilderness of Jamesons . . .)

God the Heckler, now. Catcalls from the cheap seats!

Then O'Hanrahan stumbled over the uneven sidewalk and fell without feeling it. He knew only the insistent, seething waves of pain from his side, his numb hands, the third and fourth fingers now insensible. It's a heart attack, isn't it? I read about this somewhere: burning in the throat, hands and feet go out. O'Hanrahan looked over to the other side to see a man walking briskly by. See what I mean, Lord? About how they wouldn't stop?

(*And no one spoke a word to him for they saw that his suffering was very great.*)

O'Hanrahan writhed on the ground. A car passed by. Then another. A police car if it saw him down here might stop. O'Hanrahan, doubled-over, was near a hedge and there was a small, muddy strip of grass between it and the sidewalk. He pressed his face into the cool grass— yes, the strip where people walk their dogs. *And he took a potshard with which to scrape his sores, and sat among the ashes,* he remembered. *I am full of tossing till the dawn. I will speak in the anguish of my spirit; I will complain in the bitterness of my soul.* Job cursed the day he was born, thought O'Hanrahan, but that's where our similarities end. You see, God, I love my own miserable mislived life, even in this rotten, broken-down body.

"Help me!" he cried out automatically as a pain pierced his side.

The *Book of Job* was O'Hanrahan's solace in his own agonies. *Let me alone that I may find a little comfort before I go whence I shall not return, to the land of gloom and deep darkness, the land of gloom and chaos, where . . .* O'Hanrahan felt consciousness slipping. *Where light is as darkness . . .*

Someone was standing above him.

"*Bevakasha,*" O'Hanrahan moaned.

"I speak English, sir. Do you need an ambulance?"

It was a person. O'Hanrahan fought to be conscious. It was a male soldier—so remember the different endings in Hebrew. No, wait, he said he spoke English, I'm not thinking straight.

"I'll call an ambulance," the soldier said. He was in his twenties, dark-skinned and handsome.

O'Hanrahan fumbled with Hebrew: "Take me to the hotel."

"But you need a doctor—"

"*Lo!*" pleaded O'Hanrahan, reviving under this ray of hope, "my heart medicine is at the hotel. King David."

The soldier stood in the road in the path of some headlights. The car slowed. The soldier explained the emergency—would the man in the car be willing to take this ill man to the hotel 200 yards up the hill? Leaving the car running, the driver and the soldier ran to O'Hanrahan and propped him between them. O'Hanrahan throbbed numbly and the pain wasn't so sharp now. A strange respite. His body knew, per-haps, the Percodan was moments away. O'Hanrahan was driven to the hotel and clutching his side he got out and went with the soldier to the desk and retrieved his key.

"You sure you will be well?" asked the soldier.

"Let me call you a doctor," said the deskman.

"No, I am a doctor," O'Hanrahan invented. Indeed, the deskman noted the *Dr.* Patrick V. O'Hanrahan registered in the books before him. "In fact, I'm fine now," the professor said, actually somewhat improved.

O'Hanrahan thanked the young soldier profusely, thanked the good samaritan who'd stopped his car.

Soon he was in the elevator, soon in his room, soon wrestling with the top of the pill bottle. Lying on his bed he knew he had come close to the end. Slowly the drugs suffused through his body, his hands felt light, then his side became a dull ache, then a second wave in which he seemed to float in warm shallow water, in which he was lifted above the indignity of bodily degeneration. Ah, he breathed, his health again, here is nobility, here is God. Here is Heaven.

(If We could only be sure that's where you were headed.)

AUGUST 8TH

O'Hanrahan was awakened by the phone. He came to consciousness with the sense the phone had been ringing for some time. He fumbled for it, alarmed anew that his fingers were so numb, his circulation so bad.

"Hello?"

It was the front desk checking if he was in.

"Here I am," he said crisply.

There had been since last night five or six messages, several from an urgent-sounding man named Father Vico. O'Hanrahan prepared to castigate the desk for waking him up at this hour but then he craned to see his alarm clock. 1:30 P.M. He had slept seventeen hours.

"Thank you," he mumbled. "I'll be down in a bit."

And as soon as he replaced the phone receiver, it rang again.

It was Lucy, calling from her adjoining room: "Do I need to get you a doctor, Dr. O'Hanrahan?"

"What do you mean?" he said, groaning the next moment from lifting his head off the horizontal. O'Hanrahan added in a ragged bass voice, "I am one with the divine."

"You didn't come back to the café, sir, and I didn't have enough to pay the bill—I had to leave my wallet with them. But more important, I came in to check on you last night because you didn't answer when I knocked and because the deskman said you looked gravely ill."

"Total overdramatization," he said, wondering if Lucy and a parade of others had stood around his bed while he was out cold. "I'd like to invite you to my *levée*, Miss Dantan, but the bathtub awaits. Unless you want to come scrub my back."

Lucy wasn't in a joking mood. "Rabbi Hersch's coming over for the lunch buffet and we'll be downstairs."

God, the thought of lunch sickened him. He hung up and fell back on the soft pillow. I probably should stay here all day, O'Hanrahan thought, except today promised to be an eventful day, with all that was set in motion . . .

As he shaved, O'Hanrahan wondered what Lucy and Mordechai were doing meeting for lunch. Two people he could be sure of never getting too chummy—were suddenly so chummy. Morey's trying to talk her into abandoning me, he figured. Mordechai wants her to go back to Chicago, drag me back there too, get me some counseling, another round of A.A. meetings or clinics, perhaps. Yeah, like hell.

(Wouldn't hurt, you know.)

If I can get through last night, Lord, I can survive anything.

(That was a close one, Patrick.)

O'Hanrahan at the mirror stared finally at his creased, sallow face, his eyes growing sadder with each month, the blue of the iris dimming, the circles deepening. Great, he sighed, splashing his face with cold water: once I lose Lucy to the enemy camp, I really will be alone here.

(There is an ally you have never availed yourself of. One Who has been with you always.)

If Morey packs me off to Chicago, what happens to me? I have no home, no car, no money or place to stay . . . I will join the ranks of homeless. Or to hell with everyone: I'll take Matthias Kellner's deutsche marks or spend my final years surrounded by my harem in Teheran—

There was a knock at his door.

"It's me, Patrick," Gabriel called out.

This very hour, O'Hanrahan figured, giving himself a last complicit look in the mirror, will determine whether Patrick O'Hanrahan should consider early retirement.

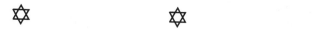

The King David Hotel dining room. Lucy had been to the buffet for fruit and some revolting liquid yogurt stuff, into which she had stirred nuts and fruit; Rabbi Hersch had a plate of roseate, lean roast beef with dabs of horseradish and mustard to the side, and a separate plate with salad.

Rabbi Hersch said, "I'm going to tell you a little secret as a reward."

Lucy brightened. "Really?"

"All this talk about *gematriot*, it jogged my memory. Do you remember Paddy and I disagreeing over Mrs. Rosen and whether she was 22 or 23? Suddenly everything fell in place—Rosen, the Kabbalah, the *Gospel of Matthias.*"

Lucy longed for him to explain further before O'Hanrahan arrived. She would love it even more if she got to be the one to tell the professor.

"You remember my mentioning the 22 Alphabets in the *Alphabets of Ben Zira*, that great kabbalistic work? Twenty-two Alphabets stemming from the 22 Hebrew letters." The rabbi slapped the table. "Some kabbalists thought there was a 23rd Alphabet, inspired by a secret 23rd Hebrew letter, a most dreadful and powerful symbol, known only to God and Messiah. Do you know who Shabbatai Zevi is?"

She shook her head.

"I'm glad you don't, actually." The rabbi dropped a sugar cube in his coffee cup and stirred it automatically. "A most embarrassing episode in Jewish history. In 1665 he declared himself Messiah and everyone fell for it, great rabbis, villagers, illiterates and geniuses, bowed down before him. He was mentally deranged and his disciple, Nathan of Gaza, was just as bonkers; Zevi's wife was a whore; he spoke the forbidden name of God everywhere. The Jewry of Europe and Asia rose up to be led to the Promised Land, but then the guy in 1666 goes and converts to Islam and lives on a pension from the Sultan."

"Oops."

"Oops is right. Anyway, Nathan of Gaza testified that this 23rd letter and 23rd Alphabet had been revealed to Zevi and to him. Rabbi Rosen, you'll recall, solved the mysteries of the *Gospel of Matthias* within two weeks, right? He was also, briefly, Professor of Kabbalah here. I always figured he must have had access to some kabbalistic book somewhere that gave the key to the Meroitic language. Little girl, in the forty years since Rabbi Rosen worked on *Matthias*, I went through every book in his office and in his house. I have gone through every library slip of every book he ordered from the library, and then as the years wore on and I checked each book for its index—tens of thousands of books—I kept thinking one day, *one day* I would turn up the page in the book that Rabbi Rosen must have known about that held the key to this impossible language."

Lucy was thrilled, breathing excitedly. "So now, with the 23rd Alphabet in mind, did you find the book?"

Both she and the rabbi noticed an exhausted Patrick O'Hanrahan plodding toward them, trying unsuccessfully to radiate ruddiness.

Rabbi Hersch: "No, the book I don't have. But I feel this is a breakthrough nonetheless. He must've known where the 23rd Alphabet was written and I bet you wherever *that* book is, we will find the key to whatever version of Meroitic the *Gospel of Matthias* is written in."

"Morning all," said O'Hanrahan raspily. "I think I'll go in search of coffee."

As he went to engage a waiter, Lucy turned to the rabbi and said quietly, "I think I better go home."

The rabbi folded his arms, suppressing a smirk. "You've lost your credibility with me, little girl. You say good-bye to me, it's a sure bet you'll be where Paddy is the next time I see him." Then he was serious. "But it's a good idea. Before the Middle East blows up. Not trying to scare you, but I'd bet money there'll be a war. Iraq versus the Saudis, Syria against Saddam Hussein—everyone against Israel, you can bet on that."

Lucy thought: that's not all that's going up in smoke.

O'Hanrahan looks on his last legs. I understand, she told herself, he can't go home to nothing, to his sister, to poverty, to ridicule—he'd rather die in the desert, given his last rites by a Coptic monk in a cave. But I can't keep following him down and even further down, Matthias or no Matthias.

"Rabbi, sir," she asked, "what will become of Dr. O'Hanrahan? Is he going to get to translate and write a book about the *Gospel of Matthias*? As you know, it's his dream. I think it actually keeps him alive."

Rabbi Hersch smiled wanly. "Don't hold your breath for that book— the man has trouble writing a grocery list. But I'll make sure what happens is for the best."

O'Hanrahan arrived at the table. "What's this about doing what's for the best?"

The rabbi didn't cower. "What's for the best is that you oughta go home and get some medical help."

O'Hanrahan treated this as a joke. "Aww, Lucy is just overreacting here—"

"And the deskman? And the soldier who left his name with the deskman, who I called."

O'Hanrahan, boxed in a corner, turned fierce. "Checking up on me, huh?"

"That's not all," said Rabbi Hersch, getting all the fireworks over with. "I've already contacted Father Vico and his Franciscan superiors. For an arranged sum they are willing to hand over the scroll to Hebrew University today."

O'Hanrahan stammered, "You ... you can buy them off? Okay, okay, that's good news, right? We'll work on it together at Hebrew University."

The rabbi did not flinch. "You might as well know that I've called Philip Beaufoix to come—"

"No!"

Lucy cringingly looked on as O'Hanrahan lost his demeanor and reason—he heard Father Beaufoix's name and all he could taste was betrayal. "So that's it, is it, Morey? You're going to rub me out of the whole project? Why did you bother asking me to help you in the first place?"

The table of diners beside them stiffened, sensing a scene.

"Because I thought you could help me."

"You should have left me where you found me," O'Hanrahan said, a catch in his throat. Lucy looked down at her plate. "You should have let me alone rather than raise my hopes—"

"Would you calm down," said his friend. "Who says you're off the project? You're still with me, working on this. Why are you overreacting so? We just need a little help to crack this language barrier . . ."

"Lucy," said O'Hanrahan, "it's time to pack up. We're leaving."

Lucy looked up, confused. "But—"

"On the four o'clock overnight bus to Cairo. We have an appointment with the Pope of Alexandria's library in Cairo." O'Hanrahan turned an accusing glance on the rabbi. "You watch us, Morey. We'll solve this mystery before you and Philip figure out the first sentence. God, as if . . . as if he didn't have enough books to his name already, enough glory!"

Rabbi Hersch threw up his hands. "You can still write the goddam book!"

"Right," said O'Hanrahan darkly, "I can have Beaufoix's *leavings,* what you two can spare me, like it's some academic hand-me-down. Lucy, let's go."

So it had ended as badly as Lucy had feared. She felt all the stares of the dining room upon her as she walked O'Hanrahan from the chamber. Lucy felt a sadness for the professor, not the least for his old friendship tearing under the stress of O'Hanrahan's failed dreams . . .

"Luce, I'm going on upstairs. Come see me when you get packed," he added lightly, as if nothing had transpired.

He's not thinking straight, she figured. His mind is out of control, just like his physical health—

"Hey, *there* you are."

Lucy spun around to see Gabriel, looking tan in a St. Eulalia T-shirt and jeans, sitting in a recessed room of the lobby behind a potted plant.

"Only a half-hour late," he said, motioning to his watch.

Lucy had forgotten about their Wednesday appointment; nothing could have been less important to her at this moment.

"I called your room and you weren't in, so I waited down here," he explained, lurking behind the flowers. "Hey, the rabbi's, like, gone, isn't he? I don't want to run into him."

"Look," she began, "the rabbi and Dr. O'Hanrahan have had a fight, so I gotta go upstairs . . ."

"What about us? I thought we were going to spend the afternoon together."

Lucy glimpsed the rabbi leaving the dining hall. "We can't, I'm sorry. Duck down, Gabe. Here comes the rabbi."

Rabbi Hersch turned at the reception desk, not even seeing Lucy across the lobby.

Gabriel: "He's going to see his friend outside, I bet."

Lucy slowed in her progress. "What friend?"

"Some two-bit hood he knows. I saw them . . . Lucy?"

Lucy briskly walked toward the plate-glass wall at the front of the lobby to see if she could see Rabbi Hersch depart.

"You're bound to have noticed him," said Gabriel, following cautiously behind her. "Worst dresser I've ever seen."

Lucy lingered behind a column. Outside, Rabbi Hersch was talking with the Man in the Cheap Suit. Money in an envelope was being fanned between them, counted. The rabbi pressed the money into the man's hands. Then the rabbi turned to go, but Mr. Cheap Suit said something and the rabbi got in the man's car, a red Ford Golf.

"This isn't good," said Lucy, watching the car drive round the circular driveway of the King David Hotel, departing for downtown.

The Man in the Cheap Suit had tried to steal the scroll in Ballymacross—was he working for the rabbi there? And in Florence, and Assisi? Was the rabbi spying on them?

Gabriel: "I spent a lot of time sitting in a car outside the hotel where O'Hanrahan and Rabbi Hersch were staying once I got working for Father Vico. Hersch and that guy would meet for coffee and stuff."

Lucy was heartsick. "That man has stalked us for weeks. He once blew up a safe in Ireland, after you and Brother Vincenzo cleared out."

Gabriel considered that. "See what I mean?" He then added, "Never trusted the old Jew anyway." Gabriel was bouncing at her heels like a puppy. "I want to take some pictures in the Old City, Luce. You and me over here? What will Judy say? Of course, no one will believe it's you. You look so different now."

Lucy regained herself, though still distracted. "Hm?"

"Hey, not that you were fat or anything," he said, protecting the compliment from any female objection, "but you've lost a lot of weight and you look great."

"Thanks," she said absently. She would have to go upstairs and tell Dr. O'Hanrahan about Rabbi Hersch and the Man in the Cheap Suit—

"But there's something else different. A glow in your cheeks," he joked. "Like my sister Liz when she had her kid!"

A very dark thought crossed Lucy's mind for the first time.

Ooooh, a very dark thought.

"So whadya say? Tea in the Christian Quarter?" Gabriel had a whole afternoon planned. "I wanna get some of those sesame pretzels—"

"Uh, Gabe," she said, breathing more shallowly, "I have to pack now and talk to O'Hanrahan. You'll forgive me for not going to take pictures with you?"

He looked like he wouldn't. Lucy leaned over and kissed him good-bye.

"Something wrong?" he asked as she made her way to the elevator.

Yeah, something could be wrong, she told herself.

She couldn't pursue *that* thought in all its implications!

In the elevator she became consumed, every cell in her body, to getting away from all the skullduggery and infighting, the intrigue and insecurity. She wanted to sleep in her own bed in Chicago again, see her mother, see Judy even. It would crush Dr. O'Hanrahan to be abandoned. But she was determined to confront this right away. She knocked on O'Hanrahan's door and identified herself.

"There's something very important we have to discuss," she began.

O'Hanrahan looked radiant, humming as he spritely packed his things. The phone rang.

"Oh," he said, suppressing a smile, "it's that ass Father Vico again. Can you get it for me and say I've gone out?"

Without thinking, Lucy did what she was told. It was Father Vico and he sputtered Italian into the phone with a bit of English.

"Wait, slow down, Father," said Lucy. "*What* are you saying?"

O'Hanrahan mouthed that he wasn't here.

"He's not here." She listened to the hysterical Franciscan. "The scroll is what?"

Lucy grew wide-eyed at what Father Vico was saying.

Lucy, shaken, beheld O'Hanrahan calmly packing. "Yes, I'll be sure to tell him, Father . . . Yes, I will tell him as soon as I see him, to get in touch with you. Yes, Father . . . Yes, I will pray too, Father, now . . . Bye-bye, Father," she said at last to the talkative man, setting the phone down and turning immediately to the professor: "Dr. O'Hanrahan, I've got some bad news. It seems the scroll has been stolen again!"

"Yep." He arched an eyebrow and said quietly, "I had it stolen."

Lucy let her mouth fall open.

O'Hanrahan lifted up his jumbled bathrobe in his suitcase, and underneath it was a scrollcase. "There she is. Stolen from the depths of the Franciscan chambers of the Holy Sepulcher."

"But who could have . . ." Then she breathed, "Gabriel."

"That's right. He told me he was going to leave the Franciscan order and that he didn't approve of them anymore, and I said, good, then steal back that scroll. It was an easy thing apparently—Gabriel had watched Father Vico take it in and out of the safe. Plus, Gabriel gets on with Brother Antonio and I didn't ask any questions. I suppose he swiped it this time to patch things up with me, so I said a few nice words and we hugged and . . ." He descended into a parody of Gabriel: "It was a very special growth experience."

Lucy asked simply, "Why didn't you let me in on your plan?"

"Because you and Morey were getting so chummy. Didn't want to risk it. Hey, did Gabriel mention to you what he was going to do for me?"

No, she thought selfishly. The world runs circles around me as usual. She mumbled, "And all that business downstairs with Rabbi Hersch . . ."

"I should get an Oscar, huh? Look, you saw for yourself, Morey intended to get the scroll back and buy off the Franciscans, and call in Beaufoix, which he's entitled to do."

"It *is* his scroll," Lucy reminded him.

"No ma'am." O'Hanrahan slammed the suitcase closed. "It's mine. It is my destiny, and no one else's with the possible exception of *you*."

Lucy was speechless.

"Are you still interested in an academic post, Miss Dantan?" O'Hanrahan walked about the room gathering papers for his satchel. "You know how hard it will be to get a job once you finish that worthless doctorate? You do have the sense God gave you to realize that the *Gospel of Matthias* will make your career, even as my assistant. And it is no exaggeration to say we might get rich and we might get famous."

And we might get killed, thought Lucy.

They looked at each other a moment.

"And," concluded O'Hanrahan, "none of those dreams can come true if we're one of twenty committee members to work on it, okay? Now that I've got *Matthias* . . ." He patted the suitcase. ". . . we have become, de facto, the most important people working on this project. Can't very well be told to go home now, can we?"

Lucy felt many things at once. There was a pull of loyalty to the rabbi . . . but hell, there he was connected to the Man in the Cheap Suit. Maybe no one was trustworthy, maybe O'Hanrahan's maneuver was the true salvation of the *Gospel of Matthias*. Up to now her role had been pleasantly decorative, she could sit back and enjoy the travel. But now it was getting serious. Briefly, she ached for home again, deep in the clutches of Chicago, back where things were simpler and dictated to her . . .

She raised her eyes to see O'Hanrahan looking at her with tenderness. God, she thought, on top of everything else, he needs me. If I leave him now, it really will be over for him. "I'll get . . . I'll get packed," said Lucy automatically, rising to use the connecting door between their suites.

"I knew you'd see your own self-interest."

But it wasn't self-interest at all! At this moment, nothing could be further from her motivations than academic posts and appearing in a thousand future footnotes. She walked into her room to see a bouquet of a dozen long-stemmed red roses.

O'Hanrahan poked his head into the room after her. "Oh yeah, those," he said, laughing. "Figures. I ordered them for you last week and they come today when we're leaving."

"Sir, they're beautiful."

Lucy opened the card, which read:

> *And everything upon which she lies during her impurity shall be unclean; everything also upon which she sits shall be unclean. And whoever touches her bed shall wash his clothes and bathe himself in water and be unclean until the evening.*

Shemoth 15:20–21

"What a lovely sentiment," she said, not getting the joke.

"See?" O'Hanrahan was saying, holding up the calendar page of his address book. "Here's what I've written: *'Lucy's period. Be nice to Lucy.'* See? I don't want any more unpleasant episodes, like in Florence. All through 1990 I've written 'Be nice to Lucy' across the same week of the month, heh-heh-heh. Hence the *Exodus* menstruation reference on the card with the flowers, heh-heh-heh . . . I gotta call the travel agent."

Lucy closed the door behind him, then lay down on the bed. It was going to be hard to abandon a man who wrote 'Be nice to Lucy' every day of her period.

Which she hadn't had yet.

Dear Lord in Heaven.

Lucy was paralyzed as the implications of a missed period overwhelmed her. Couldn't be. Couldn't happen. Of course it could be, of course it could happen. And as soon as the full horror of the idea expanded and touched every inch of her conscious mind, she raised her hands to her face and shut her eyes.

No! Oh, what folly. What a stupid girl you are, she told herself. And Gabriel saying she looked different, had a glow—she felt that she might tremble. Mother Mary, full of grace, I beg of you . . . But her prayer ran dry, seemed impotent and arid to her.

(That might be because it's been several weeks since you've actually spoken to Us properly, hasn't it been, My dear?)

I am with child, she said to herself, trying out the idea.

The second I thought of it, Lucy reeled, I knew it was true. The Fall! And a Fall it is, she thought, for that's what it feels like, a sinking, a hanging above an abyss by ten fingers, then five, then one, then a freefall into hopelessness that takes the very operation of the body with it, the heartbeat, the breathing. I have fallen from a life of light to some unforeseen damnation where my sin will define me, where my life would now reshape and recast itself.

". . . yes, that's right," O'Hanrahan was saying in the other room to the travel agent on the phone.

She calmed herself: no sense getting hysterical. A late period may be just that! You might well be fine.

"Uh-huh . . . two first-class seats, left side if possible. The smoking section of the bus, please." O'Hanrahan laughed. "Of course, where's my mind? This is the Middle East. Everybody smokes!" He laughed again. "Also, miss, you've been so helpful maybe you can help me with this. I have an American prescription that needs refilling here in Israel, since my trip has gone longer than I thought. Where could I . . ."

A pause, as he got the information he wanted.

That old man in there, Lucy thought, is running from the implications of the end of life. He doesn't ever really want to solve the mysteries of the Matthias scroll—not really. He wants a quest to beckon before him and keep eluding him so he never has to die. And I am part of his hopeless illusion. I, who want to run from the implications of life beginning, here inside me, which will grow at the expense of what used to be Lucy Dantan, now condemned.

Okay then, she decided, rising to pack stoically:

I'll run with you, old man. The wasteplaces are vast, this Wilderness of Sin, good enough for the wayward Hebrews for forty years. Lead me, you old charlatan, dealer in golden calves, Patrick Virgil O'Hanrahan!

(Go to the desert, Patrick and Lucy. The deserts of the Middle East are Our old stomping grounds, whence I have always talked to My children. You flee into My arms.)

6

Nilus! O great flow from Earth our mother,
From her Aethiopean bosom rolls the great torrent
Down past her Egyptian flanks
Until it finds release from her fertile delta
Discharged into the Great Sea!

I surely don't have to tell you, of all people, in what famous poem one will encounter that precious jewel!

2. I might have stayed in lovely Alexandria forever, as I was saying yesterday, but I was aided, however, in my quick exit by your friends the Romans, who arrived in our Judean Macedonia[1] to pillage, carouse, and deface the metropolis, in addition to rounding up suspected Nazirenes, and yet-rebellious Jewish sympathizers. Indeed, there has been no true peace for the Jews since the days of Cestus Gallus.[2] What frustration to know that even as you read this, your mind is busy inventing some justification for the Romans, some plausible motive to absolve them! Rome's greatest man, Julius Caesar, while smilingly patronizing the Jews with pillars and plaques, began his campaign in Alexandria by the burning of the *Museion* [the great library]—what more evidence need be given of the Romans' inhuman propensities?[3]

1. The Ptolemaic Greek rulers allowed Alexandrian Jews the pretension of calling themselves "Macedonians."
2. Cestus Gallus, Syrian governor during the Jewish Uprising of 66 C.E. After a successful massacre of Romans, Jews confidently rebelled throughout the Mediterranean. Two Roman legions and 5000 soldiers were summoned from Libya and allowed to rampage in Alexandria's Jewish Quarter, killing whom they wished and keeping what they found. Josephus, maybe undependably, says 50,000 Jews were slaughtered. The more dependable Tacitus's fragmentary account puts the Jewish dead over four years at an astounding 1.2 million. Also the census showed that Alexandria was 40 percent Jewish during Tiberius Caesar's reign; by 140 C.E. the city's Jewish population was almost nonexistent.

   The cataclysmic annihilation of Jewry in this period aided the conversion to Christianity as well as the extinction of Ebionite (pro-Jewish) Christianity that the author in this gospel promotes.
3. The Ptolemies granted Jews their own quarter so they wouldn't be defiled by Gentiles, and the Romans honored the agreement. *Julius Caesar made a pillar of brass for the Jews at Alexandria and declared publicly that they were citizens of Alexandria*, writes Josephus (*Antiquities*, XIV.x.1).

3. And so, in the seventh year [76 C.E.] of your beloved Vespasian's ignoble reign, I left Alexandria with the trade caravan Duldul ibn-Waswasah had arranged for me, with his letters and money to meet my expenses. The Romans had been spreading terror throughout the delta without adding a jot of security, hence robbers and brigands were afforded every opportunity of rapine. On our second day, the caravan was stopped by a band of Bedouins who neatly removed anything of value, including my purse where I made a great show of losing everything I owned. This clever theatric disguised a secret hoarding I kept under my robes wrapped tightly around my groin. I counted this small triumph to be an omen and I separated myself from the trade caravan, that slow-moving target, at the first opportunity in Ptolemais Hermiu.

4. I attended the Nazirene synagogue there where I observed that no article of Our Church had survived uncorrupted, and I sought to confirm the reports that a disciple—Philip, it was rumored, or perhaps Matthew, who was known to have traveled here—worked in the Faiyum. I heard that the Disciple Philip was indeed in a village near Oxyrhynchus, back down the Nile, maddeningly, from which I had come.[4]

I was persuaded to wait until the end of the week when a group of Nazirenes sought to make this simple journey together for safety's sake, though the crew assembled could hardly have withstood a pack of geriatric dogs—a caravan sent by God, I am sure, to test my patience. One Nazirene crone, impressed by my air of education, asked me if I were a Disciple and I told her, "If I were a Disciple do you think I should be crouched down here among you people, hiding from the Romans? I should perform twenty miracles and have them swallowed up by the earth," and that seemed to satisfy everyone. Surer yet, had I said

Matthias states Julius Caesar burned the *Museion* and its 700,000 scrolls on purpose, when it was certainly an accident during the battle for the city. Caesar commanded Cleopatra to reconstruct and replicate it, which she did.

4. Oxyrhynchus ("pointy-snouted thing") has an ecclesiastical history belying its absurd name. The gospel discoveries of 1896–97 and 1905–06 by Grenfell and Hunt yielded a trove of early gospels (copies from 400s–700s), the oldest substantial fragment of *John* (from the 200s), and the oldest known bound book on earth. Most scripts were in Coptic Greek with heavy demotic Egyptian influences.

I was a Disciple I should have been called upon for martyrdom, the way the old women were talking.

5. For this mob, Our Master was all miracle worker, doom prophet, and dispenser of secret mysteries; I do not think one of the group could remember a single charitable teaching of Our Master. Three old unmarried sisters—the Nazirene capacity for attracting unmarriable women remained insuperable—two old men, one quite senile, and a collection of orphans and ever-hungry young men who thought nothing of rampaging through a stranger's farm for chickens and small sheep. Some purity we Nazirenes maintained![5]

Escaping to the main road before dawn I met some Egyptians (who spoke no Greek) and with them I walked onward to the witlessly named oasis of Ammos ["Sand"] where Philip and his Nazirene commune reportedly resided.

6. I approached the gate of their small but high-walled village. No amount of persuasion was sufficient to let me inside. The hairy beast of a gatekeeper explained that virgins were within and I threw open my arms and asked if he seriously thought I was a threat to the girls' most precious compact. In time, a man, said to be the Nazirene hierarch of the village, arrived outside the gate.

I said to him, "I seek the Disciple Philip."

He said to me, "I am he."

7. Vividly you might imagine my surprise to discover, my brother, not Philip but an impostor! He was much younger than a True Disciple could ever have been, no older than his fifth decade [his 40s], with a shamefully shaven face and a bald head. If the rabble in the Faiyum had submitted his appearance to a moment's serious reflection they would have realized their error and banished this charlatan to the desert wastes.

"Ah, Matthias," he addressed me, as if familiar, "you perhaps do not remember me? I have taken the name after Philip, my own teacher."[6]

5. Again, a pun on N-Z-R (נ ז ר), "purity," derivation of Nazirene.
6. This was not an uncommon practice in the East, to have a most-trusted disciple continue teaching in the name of the more famous holy man. It is thought to perhaps play a part in the extraordinary long ages of Old Testament patriarchs as well as John the Evangelist, who, we are to believe, lived into the 100s C.E.

Upon hearing this, I was somewhat mollified, but still to pass himself off as a Disciple of which there could only be, of course, twelve. O splendid number!

8. He said to me, "I'm sure it could not matter to Our Master that others borrow the names of his original clan."

How preposterous! I insisted rightly that Our Lord and Master would have not tolerated this falsity for a moment.[7]

This impostor said to me, "Well, we shall disagree on this, I fear. I suspect it matters little to Our Lord in Heaven. These people of Egypt would not be convinced unless I came to them with some title, some rank. Examine, dear Matthias, the great store you yourself put by it."

9. I said to him, "But what of the real Philip? If you fall into heresy and disrepute you have besmirched that great Disciple's reputation."

(This was somewhat disingenuous for I never liked Philip and thought him weak-willed and fond of grand moments and self-promotion. I recall him rehearsing questions of such dexterity that Our Master was unfailingly impressed with his second-rate mind.) My suspicions as to Philip's character were well founded, for the next moment I was to learn, from Pseudo-Philip:

"The other Philip is quite happily retired from the ministry in Media, as you may know."

I informed him I knew no such thing. I had, however, heard tales of a great martyrdom in Armenia.[8]

"Oh, he is no more martyred than you or I. He has retired to his farm and is working to bring his estate in order so that his fifteen children might know some subsistence. I had heard, actually, that *you* were martyred in the fall of Jerusalem, my dear

---

7. The author seems not to have been aware of this incident in *Luke* 9:49, *John answered, "Master, we saw a man casting out demons in your name, and we forbade him, because he does not follow with us." But Jesus said to him, "Do not forbid him; for he that is not against you is for you."*

8. The Disciple Philip is supposed to have been crucified in Phrygia, but no Early Church source is positive as to what became of him. Wrote Luke in *Acts* 21:8–9, *We arrived at Caesarea where we went to the house of Philip the Evangelist, one of the Seven, and stayed with him. He has four unmarried daughters who were prophetesses.* Note that *Acts* identifies Philip as one of the Seven and not one of the Twelve—two different men—but neither Eusebius nor the later Church made the distinction, and legends concerning his prophesying daughters were popular. Also note that this passage of *Acts* was written before the influence of Pseudo-Paul in *Timothy*, who forbids women prophesying.

Matthias; I received an epistle to that effect from James bar-Alphaeus. But I see your treacherous brother has had your life spared."

10. I said to him, "Do you mean to tell me that you are in contact with other disciples who are unaware of your false identity?"

I must say Pseudo-Philip's capacity for a friendly countenance in the brunt of my searing indictments was admirable, but perhaps this show of humility and charity was just another sham to impress me with Nazirene virtue.

He said to me, "I am in contact with most disciples still alive. Shall I show you a missive from Peter?"[9]

Poor, senile old Peter—deluded by this impostor!

He said further to me, "I assure you, Peter is not beguiled in the least. His scribe writes to me as 'Crassus Philip,' combining my former name when I was Philip's assistant and my new chosen name. Dear Peter, though never having visited, is fond of our commune here and sent us money in the early days. Truly, Matthias, judge for yourself. It is among the largest and most prosperous of the Nazirenes'."

11. He suspected that I did not perceive the clue to his background. I said to him. "So Crassus is your former name. I take it then, you are Roman?"

He said to me, "Do not tell me you are of the circumcision party?"[10]

That of course went without saying!

12. I next threatened to expose Pseudo-Philip before his community for the fraud he was. He said to me after what he would have me interpret as a painful silence, "You are the only

9. Again, tradition says Peter was martyred no later than 68 c.e., but no mention of it is made here.
10. The author's Judean-centered Ebionite Church wished to remain within the Law and urged circumcision of converts. Paul is at first conciliatory toward Jewish feelings about circumcision and has his own disciple Timothy circumcised to please this faction, *Acts* 16:1–3, in the late 30s c.e. Later, Paul of the *Epistles* clearly eschews the value of circumcision: *Real circumcision is a matter of the heart—it is spiritual and not literal* (*Romans* 2:29). It seems he was not entirely persuasive to the Jerusalem Church and one senses that battle lines have been drawn by the late 50s when he writes in *Colossians* 4:11 that *[Mark and] Justus greet you. These are the only ones of the circumcision among my coworkers for the Kingdom of God and they have been a comfort to me.* Which would suggest Paul considered many of the circumcision faction a hindrance in his mission to the Gentiles.

Disciple who has found cause for complaint. Come and see how we live. Everyone has enough to eat, no one has more than anyone else. The elderly and sick are prayed and cared for; we harbor fugitives from the Romans, prostitutes who have turned away from that life."

I said to him, "You have great confidence in your own performance. I may yet go into the center of the commune and announce to the world that you are not Philip!"

Pseudo-Philip said to me, "You would not be believed."

13. I informed him that I should be recognized as a True Disciple.

He said to me, now most unpleasant, "How should that be? Where has been your ministry? Inside a library, I understand. The people will not believe you because they have seen miracles and they love the way of life here, the way shown by the Master."

Miracles? I examined Pseudo-Philip on this incredible claim.

14. He sighed as if he were weary—how well, you will observe, my arguments had tired him. He said to me, "I do not mean parting of seas or such. Elderly widows who no longer wished to live now embrace life. Children who were starving and racked with illness and demons are better. The man who let you in the gate, Levi? He beat his wife thoroughly, each and every night, though he observed the Law and was a member of the finest Alexandrian synagogue. Here, he has heard the teachings of Our Master and shared all he has with us. When he ceased to worry about money, he ceased to beat his wife and children. It is that sort of miracle to which I refer."

I saw by this clever twisting of rhetoric that I was left no choice but to expose him for the fraud he was. I asked to be taken to the central building of the village and, with resignation, he led me to the door of the synagogue. The elders were assembled and women came from their kitchens; I was asked to stand upon a rock near the garden of the synagogue.

15. Then something quite untoward happened that perhaps will shock you: as I spoke, claiming my lineage as a True Disciple, One of the Blessed Twelve, I was actually doubted! What is more, as I tried to convince this mob that Pseudo-Philip was not of the official rank he claimed and that he should be demoted,

Levi—the rough beater of women—was angered and decided to vent his wrath upon me. I was seized by the robes and thrown to the ground. I was told that I should perform miracles and do combat with Crassus and so reveal who God aids. As I refused, knowing that sort of demonstration has not historically been available to me, one man cried out "Why do you come to cause trouble?" and another "Go back to the rubble of Jerusalem, you Pharisee!" and this sort of thing.

I was carried outside the gate of the oasis and set down roughly in the dirt. The gate was locked behind me. As I lay there, injured and bruised, I considered that Crassus had seduced them like a draft of opium and controlled their minds. Crassus himself, nearly an hour after the scene with the mob, came to the gate with a young girl who dabbed my wounds with linen and warmed water.

16. He said to me, "What has your rank availed you, my friend Matthias?"

I said honestly, dejected in spirit, that it had brought me very little. Perhaps—it occurs to me now—better an impostor who follows the Lord's teachings than a Disciple who is useless. Silas, Linus, Timothy, Agrippa: the Nazirene Church was increasingly in the hands of people who were not Disciples, indeed, people who never met the Teacher of Righteousness.

I explained to Pseudo-Philip, "I am embarked on a journey to complete a full and comprehensive history; on my way to Elephantine to prove a scurrilous rumor about Our Master false. But perhaps we could start again? I could stay the night in Ammos and then try again to speak before your community."

He said to me, "I would rather you not. You have already sewn seeds of doubt among the village here—it was a mistake, after all, to let you speak. As long as my primacy was undoubted we could live without rancor, but already the elders compete among themselves for the hierarch's seat . . . Ah, what have you started? You have led us to doubt. They were not the doubts that plague every man, but forgive me, my friend, they were *your* doubts. It would be difficult to honor you among the leaders here when your own faith is uncertain."

17. I abased myself and said to him, "Then I shall be as the lowest among you!"

He refused, saying to me, "It should cause too much worry if a man who looked upon the face of Our Master and heard His voice has come to doubt. Perhaps you should talk to another of the great Disciples whose convent is not too far from here."

My heart leaped to think there was a Disciple I had failed to trace. Was it long-lost Matthew?

"Mary of Migdal, Chief of the Disciples," he answered.[11]

Mary! A woman, our chief! However, I asked, did he get that notion?

He said to me, "But is this not common knowledge? Was not she the Disciple closest to Our Master?"

18. My memories of Mary [Magdalene] were respectful. She was a wealthy woman and intelligent, in as far as the latter becomes a woman. I was sure that if she knew that this misinformation was circulating (that she, not Peter, was Chief of the

---

11. Virtually every gnostic sect (100–300s c.e.) of any popularity venerated Mary Magdalene: as a Disciple, as the keeper of mysteries passed from Jesus to her alone at the sepulcher, and in some African sects, the head of the Church instead of Peter.

   The *Gospel of Mary* (Third Century?), found by accident in 1896, is the prototype for the Magdalene in apocryphal texts. She sees the risen Savior first, as the canonical gospels attest, and she is shunned by the Twelve, who do not believe her. She is later believed and raised up to their circle. Matthew defends her, *But if the Savior made her worthy, who are you [Peter], indeed, to reject her? Surely the Lord knew her very well. That is why he loved her more than us* (*Mary* 18:15). In the Nag Hammadi gospel discoveries of 1945, Mary Magdalene is shown as possessing greater knowledge than the Disciples (*Dialogue of the Savior* 139:12). In the *Gospel of Thomas* 51:19–26, Peter—embodiment of the established Church—tries to banish Mary from attending a sermon by Jesus, who then says that through holiness Mary will become a man, and therefore equal. The *Gospel of Philip* 64:5, claims Jesus loved her more than the Disciples and kissed her on the mouth. When the Twelve complain, Jesus says that they should ask why it is He cannot love them as much as Mary. Whether Mary was pictured as a Spiritual Lover—theories about a secret marriage and children are latter-day and not how the Early Church thought, sexual and romantic imagery notwithstanding—or whether she was androgynous and made into a man in order to be equal, the goal was always the same: to escape the growing authority of the established Church run by apostolic succession, and the battery of bishops and theocrats.

   The orthodox Church struck back. A lost gospel quoted in the *Apostolic Church Order* (Second Century) has Mary denied Communion from Jesus in the presence of the Disciples because she had smiled. The Pastorals of Pseudo-Paul from this period, as does *John* (ca. 110), in which the fathers of the Church have inserted Peter and John at the tomb scene, who arrive first, discover the empty linens, and "saw and believed." This seems to short-circuit Mary's importance as the first witness of the Resurrection and derails any attempt to raise her above Peter or John; in the next episode we see Mary not recognizing Jesus. The 4th-Century *Gospel of Bartholomew* has Mary, Jesus' mother, go to the Sepulcher, expunging the Magdalene altogether.

Disciples) that she would write the necessary missives to clear up all confusions. Indeed, I saw that I might facilitate a published renunciation that she might sign before heresy had a chance to take root and grow! (Imagine my distress at having to shore up these ruins by adding mortar to the pedestal of that incompetent, Simon Peter! But yet it seemed then what God would have me do.)[12]

19. Reaching the outskirts of Thmuis that next week, I was taken by a Bedouin to the door of the convent. An Amazon of a girl stood atop the convent wall armed with bow-and-arrow and I am sure she would have thought nothing of skewering me. Mary herself, after some time, emerged at the doorway to talk through a sliding panel. She was enshrouded in a black robe, only her eyes revealed.

She said at last to me, "Ah, indeed it is you, Matthias. Why should I let you in?"

I said to her, "But dear Mary, I am a Disciple of Our Most Beloved Master and Teacher!"

20. Mary said to me, "You always despised and denigrated me. Any interest I showed in Our Master's teaching, you ridiculed, saying it was not a woman's place. I shall give you food and water, of course, but I do not see why I should entertain you."

---

12. A note about Mary Magdalene, the prostitute:

Matthias in this gospel regards her as a daughter of a great family; indeed, if she were a common whore of the streets the New Testament title "Magdalene," meaning that she was of a family of note from Migdal, would be absurd. The male disciples, fellow Galileans, are of the laboring and merchant middle class and not identified by city but by family, i.e., sons of Zebedee. The Bible merely mentions that Mary was possessed by demons (*Luke* 8:2), nothing more than illness in the medical notions of the time. In *Matthew, Mark* and *Luke* we see a nameless "woman of the city, a sinner" washing Jesus' feet with an ointment from an alabaster box; in *John* this woman has become Mary, sister of Lazarus (*John* 12:3). The Church would later be illogically content to associate Mary Magdalene via Mary of Bethany with the woman of the city. Such normally careful readers as Augustine, Gregory the Great, and Bede preferred to perpetuate the errors.

There are no doubt political reasons that Mary Magdalene was rendered a redeemed prostitute by the fathers of the Church, not all of them bad.

As a redeemed harlot, she holds out hope for the most fallen. Furthermore, great numbers of women without money or family became prostitutes through necessity and Christian convents provided, historically, their first humanitarian escape. Also: one of the earliest female-saint cults was that of Mary of Egypt who was a reformed prostitute, and once the Coptic and Eastern Churches separated from the Roman, a redeemed-prostitute saint was wanted and the Magdalene was conflated with Mary of Egypt. In theology Mary became symbolic of the harlot Israel (in *Ezekiel*) redeemed by the Savior; also Eve and Womankind redeemed for the Fall by Jesus.

I protested saying that I never meant to be unkind to her; indeed, in the company of Our Teacher I never gave her a moment of sustained thought.

She said to me, "That is exactly the unkindness to which I refer. You and John both: women-haters."

It is no exaggeration to say that I begged Mary for admittance and offered up a psalm, composed on the spot, of praise to her steadfast lifelong chastity.

At last she relented, saying to me, "Actually, I have been expecting you."

21. The door was opened and I heard a flurry of iron works and levers alter in the door. The women were well protected, as I suppose they must be in a Roman world! What locks are too secure for the guarding of that precious boon, virgin purity?

I was escorted through the compound and I observed the totally draped women, sexless and featureless except for hands and eyes that saw the light. One must be impressed by this show of holiness and Mary informed me that the women did not observe one another undressing or bathing, and most properly, all their hair was shorn so as never to be displayed should a wind gust remove their veils.[13]

13. Here as in many Early Church writings surfaces the obsession with women's hair and its exposure. *Any woman*, wrote Paul in *1 Corinthians* 11:5–13, *who prays or prophesies with her head unveiled dishonors her head. . . . For if a woman will not veil herself then she should cut off her hair; but if it be disgraceful for a woman to be shorn or shaven, let her wear a veil. That is why a woman ought to have authority on her head because of the angels. . . . Judge for yourselves: is it proper for a woman to pray to God with her head uncovered?* Incommunicative to the present age, Paul's dicta on hair covering and hair length was a fetish of the Early Church; in Paul it seems to be the sole justification for men dominating women. One would be tempted to dismiss this happily overlooked Pauline passage if only this document and the subsequent fathers of the Church were not equally obsessed:

Pseudo-Paul in *1 Timothy* 2:9, *Women should adorn themselves modestly and sensibly in seemly apparel not with braided hair. . . .* and *1 Peter* 3:1–3, *Likewise you wives, be submissive to your husbands. . . . Let not yours be the outward adorning with plaiting of hair.* Jerome was maniacal about exposed hair and wigs, citing a woman who wore a wig and his subsequent delight in the resulting slow death of her children, God's punishment. The normally sober Ambrose and Augustine thought nothing more shameful than exposed female hair; Cyprian wrote that it was worse to wear a wig than to commit adultery, which was a capital offense in many Early Church communities. Tertullian rages against the women of Carthage who expose their hair (*De cultu feminarum*), women who play with damnation thinking they can virginify themselves by unveiling their head (*De virginibus verlandis,* "On the Veiling of Virgins").

Consider in this light the shocking, improper nature of Jesus allowing his feet to be washed by a woman's loosened, exposed hair.

I was led to the kitchen where some food and wine were found for me.

22. Throughout the entire visit I saw nought but Mary's aged eyes—as to her form or weight beneath her robes, I could wager no guess. Like the Essenes of old, the true women-haters, she had managed to make the gross, shameful body invisible before men.

Mary said to me, "I have been expecting that you might travel here. Some years back I received a letter from Thomas's wife that you were writing a history and had become strained with doubts. Then Peter wrote some years ago, among other more important news, that you had lost your faith."

(I was horrified to learn my innocent questionings had become common lore!)

Mary said to me, "No, it is no use to lie to me. I can tell by your eyes that the light of faith has gone. I wonder that it was ever really there."

I ate the meal quietly, as she talked further.

23. She said to me, "We have come to Thmuis to avoid the menfolk."

Very good, lest the women become snares of temptation!

She said to me, "My brother Matthias, it is the so-called scholarship and prejudice of men that we wish to rid ourselves of. Look at what your fellow male creatures have made of Jerusalem and the Kingdom of Judea. The Romans proved the least of our enemies. Here we keep the true teachings of Our Master alive."

I informed her, "At Oxyrhynchus, dear Mary, some are possessed of the notion that you are Chief among the Disciples. I come, in part, to aid your renunciation of such a claim."

Those mysterious eyes stared hard at me, and at last she said to me, "If I am raised up it is not by my word or deed but by those who observe me. I leave the matter to you who are best suited for such trivialities."

24. Mary took me to a library in which the women were reading and copying—the women! Mary said to me, "These scrolls contain the words of Our Savior as I recall them. Maryam of Bethany too has contributed. I have taken a dictation of Mary, wife of Alphaeus, who talked often with He Who Redeemed Us. Joanna, Susanna, Leah and her sister Agrippina, and of course Procla.[14] Every lesson Our Deliverer taught to women, every parable I can remember I have set down."

What of the martyrologies of James, the Epistles of Peter, even the heterodox ramblings of Thomas? (Of course, I felt it unseemly, having admitted a loss of faith, to ask if my own *All Heresies Refuted* was within her vault.)

She said to me, "I have little of men here, for men distort and impose themselves and make a tale of it, or worse, aim an account to a place their minds are happy to go. Our Master spent most of his time in this world with women, and I have spent these forty years collecting their tales and reminiscences."

25. It must be said that the completeness of Mary's effort was daunting; why, it is not incorrect to say that her family's great wealth had been utterly squandered on this enterprise. I asked how she continued to finance herself.

She said to me, "The women themselves bring this money. Widows and their estates, prostitutes and their treasure."

Common harlots and courtesans, adulteresses and criminals, no doubt conveniently eluding capture and punishment, pretending to pore over these unorthodox texts as if it were the School of Gamaliel itself! Accounts scrawled by women with no training in the arts of rhetoric, history, theology, composition. And yet, as I have had more time to think of it, the accusations of Mary have stung me, and I have found this enterprise not entirely misguided—something Our Master may indeed have intended, such was His peculiarity about the worth of women and their minds.

(Ah, Tesmegan has interrupted to inform me that in *this* ludicrous kingdom all the teachers are women—how is that for outlandish?)

---

14. This historical Procla may be the source of the legend of Procla, popular in the 100s and 200s, as the converted Christian wife of Pontius Pilate, dreamer of the prophetic warning (*Matthew* 27:19). Pilate, rendered a Christian martyr, in a Greek apocryphal *Anaphora* prays, "*Number me not among the wicked Hebrews. Remember not evil against me or against thy servant [my wife] Procla . . . whom thou didst make to prophesy that thou must be nailed to the cross.*"

26. Mary then said to me, "While John and your lot argued over who was to be the first in the Kingdom[15] like spoiled children, I sat at His feet and asked questions. And moreover, He discussed matters with me He shared not with the Twelve for He knew I would not distort them or raise myself up by them."

I too sat down on the long stone bench, which was fashioned uncomfortably so that no ease would befall those who studied there. I began to read, in an elegant Greek (though the penmanship left something to be desired), Mary's account of the Teacher of Righteousness.

27. I do not possess her scroll to recopy it here, but I remember it well enough. What was revealed was a vision of Our Master vulnerable and pessimistic, and, dare I say it, confused and offended often, weaker than I remembered. Could it be He was brave for us, but confessed His insecurities to the womenfolk who would understand? Mind you, Our Master was ever-confident about God and His ministry—all the teaching and debating, I recall, showed Our Master to advantage, He being more skilled in the learned arts than any man I have ever met. But I encountered in Mary's history a man of misgivings, of profound cynicism even: I repeat, not about God or His Mission, but about *us*, His followers and the followers yet to be born.

How anxiously I scanned her text for fear that my name would appear and he would express a reservation about my inclusion on certain meetings, a doubt as to my fitness for the ministry. But though I found the other Disciples, I saw not a word about myself. Indeed, tears even come to my eyes now. Who was I that the Teacher of Righteousness, the One Who Was Delivered Up, should notice?

28. One of Mary's accounts has Our Teacher prophesy about the future of the Nazirenes: Our Savior foresaw a priestly caste as bad as the Pharisees arising from His followers, steeped in error and arrogance, and that the women who would object would be persecuted. Our Savior goes on to urge Mary to fight

---

15. *Luke 9:46. And an argument arose among [the Disciples] as to which of them was the greatest.*

this caste and never give back the better portion, which the women have taken in His ministry. Such mysteries!

Another collection of papers titled the *Amarantikon*[16] has the Teacher assure Mary that His Church would be in the hands of women, safeguarding its true virtues as the centuries progressed.

29. Mary said to me, "Our Deliverer came to fulfill the Law and to abolish it. We women are no longer to be the chattel of drunken husbands and greedy fathers."

(Well, now, here we had it all—typical female usurpation one finds in all Jewish women of money and position. But I shall record the rest of her rhetoric.)

Mary further said to me, " 'She that would follow Him must leave her father and mother, and cease to be wife and maidservant,' Matthias. Do you not remember His teachings? The men of the Temple mocked Him for not delivering them to a victorious military engagement, and they do not see that He was the deliverer for us, for women. When I think that alone of women He chose me to confide in completely . . ."

Here, tears filled Mary's eyes.

30. And I pronounced truly, "You were in love with Him!"

She said, "With all my heart and all my soul, I shall love Him always, and teach my sisters to love Him as I love Him, chastely and with reverence. My brother Matthias, you see He is the only bridegroom we can ever know? There is no other now. He has bade us express our love for all humanity. If it is sufficient for every man to be nurtured by his mother, why is it no less important for the Earth and all her children to be nurtured by the Female Wisdom in all female creatures?"[17]

31. You shall, predictably, find this sort of talk inane, Jose-

---

16. Ἀμαράντικον. The Never-diminishing book, literally. A popular First-Century word for "everlasting," as if composed of amaranth, i.e., *1 Peter* 5:4.

17. One must be careful with our genderless English language not to make this passage more protofeminist than intended.

Even in these patriarchal times there was no controversy that the Earth (אֶרֶץ) was feminine. Earth and Mother are linked commonly in the Bible, as in *Naked came I out of my mother's womb, and naked shall I return thither* (*Job* 1:21). Man was made of "dust from the ground" after the first rain (*Genesis* 2:6). It is also important to understand that the pagan and Christian Mother images, as in Gaia and the cult of the Virgin Mary, loving and fertile, are not the Jewish Eretz, who could be severe and judgmental, ruthless in natural disasters.

phus, but knowing what I did of Our Teacher, I had few doubts that He might have spoken such to her. Indeed, it explained a lot of His strange choice of companions—slave girls, prostitutes, adulteresses, widows wicked by reputation, all who have been much fodder for the enemies of the Nazirenes, who accuse Him, the Stainless One, of consorting with a *harim*, of fornications and sodomies, profligacy and license.[18] But perhaps, shall we consider, that God having made Man out of nothingness, having given Man the Law and appointed men earthly kingdoms, that now the Master of the Universe has sent One to lead the women? It all has the peculiar awkward fit of many of Our Master's ideas.

32. Upon the morning of my departure, I told Mary where I was traveling and for what it was I looked, Joseph of Arimathea's former slave Benjamin and the secrets of that famed sepulcher and that momentous night.

She said to me, "Yes, I have heard this tale. I am sure it is just a tale. I myself embraced Our Teacher after He rose from the dead."

However, it struck me—and I will maintain that my perceptions concerning people are quite acute, and indeed have been told so on many occasions—it seemed to me that Mary's voice was not confident. So I asked her, "Do you have doubts of this, my dear Mary?"

She said, "I have no doubts of my love for Our Master and the correctness of His teachings. But I must tell you that when I met Him again, after the tomb was found to be empty, I did not recognize Him. Your colleagues, the once-faithless Twelve, shunned me afterward and escaped with Him, and I never saw Him again. It is maintained that He ascended to the Seventh Heaven. Frankly, it does not matter to me what really happened."

33. I was shocked to hear this!

Mary explained to me, "What do the circumstances of His death change? I knelt at His feet and heard Him speak. That is enough. Think of the millennia that have preceded such a man

---

18. Ἀσωτία and ἀσέλγεια. The subtleties of these similar words are still debatable; this editor takes *asōtía* to be wastefulness, profligacy, and *asélgeia*, as in *Mark* 7:22, to have a sexual implication, of license and promiscuity.

and such an opportunity; think of the worthy women, so much more deserving than I, who never beheld the Deliverer. And yet it was I who was to spend years beside Him. We were, as you may know, to marry."

This I had heard. Arranged by the parents, Our Master of a chief family of Bethlehem betrothed to Mary, daughter of the chief family of Migdal. They were to be married in the synagogue in Capernum and all of Galilee was to celebrate.

Mary of Migdal said to me, "He proposed a higher marriage in which the mysteries of the soul and a foretaste of Heaven was given me. I cannot speak of it. Nor have I written of it. It was, I believe, for me alone."

34. Pursuing my own researches, I asked of her, "What was Our Master like as a youth?

She said, "Entirely beautiful, possessed of every grace and kindness. There was never another nature like His." Her eyes again filled with tears. She said then, "I often reflect upon our reunion in Heaven, where I wonder if there I shall be His bride. He said words that I could so interpret, but I do not dream of this for fear . . . for fear of blasphemy."

I concurred that this prohibition was very wise. And then with great reservation I asked of Mary, "Do you recall Our Master having said anything, good or bad, about me?"

35. She did not answer, but said to me in parting, "You go to Elephantine to prove a doubt true. Our Master would tell you that you would better make a journey to prove your faith true. As He told me, 'She that looks for reasons to doubt, will find much reward in this world. But she that looks for reasons to believe will find her reward in Heaven.' "

I confessed to Mary that I had no choice but to find out the truth of Benjamin and the slanderous tale of the sepulcher. How I longed for it to be untrue! But I must discover if I have followed false paths, if my life had been devoted to a mistake! What, after all, could explain a former slave of Joseph of Arimathea, ensconced like a king in Elephantine?

Then Mary said to me, "Do you know the Blessed Wisdom?"

36. I said I had read all of the Wisdom literature while a student in Alexandria.

Mary said to me, "Truly all you have read has done you little good, dear brother. Our Master once told me when I understood a parable without His explanation, that men read things and do not know them, whereas women know things they have never read."

She said further to me, "No, you must not know *Sophia*, or you would not go on this voyage of doubt to listen to other people's lies and misrepresentations. But go if you must. I will pray that She be with you. You cannot understand how She has sustained me here in the desert. I wonder sometimes, though I remember much of Our Master, whether I would understand anything if not for Her."

Then Mary retreated into the convent only to return some minutes later, handing me a sealed phylactery, tiny enough to fit into a pocket.

I asked of her, "What is this scroll?"

She said to me, "When you find your answer, and not before, I want you to read this. It is by a man now departed, one who once knew *Sophia*. You may prove this tale of the slave Benjamin untrue, learned Disciple, and still not find your faith. That only *Sophia* can restore."

37. Then impulsively, her eyes flashing, she said to me, "I have given my all for him. I have sacrificed my youth, then my young womanhood where I might have married, and under these robes my beauty. These robes hide scars, small cuts of the knife into which maggots were introduced burrowing in this cheek, leaves soaked in lye applied to my face and breasts . . ."[19]

I exclaimed, "Mary, no!"

---

19. The introduction of maggots to wounds, as done by Daniel the Stylite and a number of Egyptian anchorites, was a self-effacement and a pretaste of death in the ground where worms awaited, mortification in the truest sense. The legends of the desert holy women Mary Magdalene, Mary of Egypt (who became a hideous hag, wearing nothing but her overlong gray hair), Pelagia (whose eyes became, wrote the Deacon James, "a sunken pit through emaciation"), and Thais (who had herself immured in an airless, lightless cell so that she might starve to death) all were great favorites of the Early Church.

The First through Third-Century hagiographies of the Virgin Martyrs (Catherine, Agnes, Agatha, et al.), who are tortured exquisitely, show a deeply entrenched masochistic asceticism that Christianity, for the first time, made available to women. Indeed, having made it impossible for women to serve in any office in the institutional Church of the 200s–300s, the only way a woman could prove her worth to the Church was by spectacular martyrdom.

"This I did so no Roman might desire me should our convent ever be attacked. No, fear not, I shall not unveil myself to you—you need not fear. Ah, but old age would have done as good a job. Does it not? One day soon, in Heaven before Him, my beauty will be returned to me, I shall be fair as the angels . . . betrothed anew to a Celestial Groom."

Then she seemed to plead to me, "Matthias! If you should prove this tale true, this libel about the slave Benjamin and a stolen body from the tomb . . . Do not ever let me know. Will you promise?"

I gave her my word.

38. And so before the sun was fully risen, I left Thmuis with Mary's blessings. What a remarkable woman! It saddens me to know I shall never see her again.

Really, Tesmegan, what a variety the Lord has spread before us concerning womankind—from such pure souls as Mary of Migdal, and Maryam of Bethany, the charitable Queen Helen, and your own gracious sovereign here in Meroe, in contrast to that other Helen, that walking abomination! Oh, even now, thousands of miles from her splayings and writhings in the lowest cesspit of Hell, the thought of the Magus's harlot horrifies me.

Her dreaded paps!

AFRICA

Verily, they who believe [the Moslems], and they who
follow the Jewish religion and the Christians, and the
Sabaeans—whoever of these believeth in God and the last
day, and doeth what is right, shall have their reward with
the Lord: fear shall not come upon them, neither shall
they be grieved.

—Quran 2:59
MOHAMMED

One knocked at the door of God and a voice from within
inquired, "Who is there?"

Then he answered, "It is I."

And the voice said, "This house will not hold me and
thee." So the door remained shut. Then the Lover of
God sped away into the wilderness and fasted and prayed
in solitude. And after a year he returned and knocked
again at the door. And the voice again demanded, "Who
is there?"

And the Lover of God said "It is Thou."

Then the door was opened.

—from the *Meshnavi* (1200s)
JALAALU AD-DINU ARRUMI
founder of the Whirling Dervishes

Whatever share of the world Thou wouldst bestow on
me, bestow it on Thine enemies; and whatever share of
the next world Thou dost give me, give it to Thy friends.
Thou are enough for me!

—prayer (740s)
RA'BIAH of Basra

Whoever should kill any Moslem will go straight to
heaven.

—preaching the Second Crusade (1146)
St. BERNARD OF CLAIRVAUX

اسوان

L ucy awoke to the call of the morning *muezzin:*
"*Allaahu akbar! Allaaaaaaaaahu akbaaaaaarrrrrr!*"
She felt her heart racing from being startled awake.
And after a momentary panic of dislocation, Lucy remembered she was in Aswan, in Egypt, and the *muezzin,*
electronically amplified from the town's minarets, only
wished her to think of God, and how there was no God but God.

"*Ash-hadu an laa ilaaha illa 'llaah* . . ."

She was wide awake. It was still dark out, a deep before-dawn blue,
cold over the desert in the eastern sky. And yet the marketkeepers
and beggars and hotel washerwomen and lazy men of the cafés were
ambling down dark staircases, passing one another in the streets, exchanging elaborate Arabic blessings, wishing each other gardens and
perfumes and indolence in Paradise, waiting patiently for an opening
at the mosque's cleansing fountain to wash the sleep from their eyes
and enter God's house and face Mekkah and truly worship Him. Not
sit in a church pew politely Sunday morning, but abase themselves,
touch head to the floor on their knees and sob in abjection, five times
each day, every day of their lives: there is no God but God.

"*Ash-hadu an laaaa ilaaaaaaaaha illa 'llaaaaah* . . ."

O'Hanrahan was right, thought Lucy. What a musical language
Arabic is when talked, and how well this language adorns the prayer,
the incantation. There is no God but God: *Laa ilaaha il-la 'llaah.* A
divine tongue twister for the Western mouth, but said over and over
this creed, the Kalimah, becomes a trance, the phases of the short and
long *a*'s giving it a tidal rhythm. Each breath a prayer, the heartbeat
and respiration in tune to the worship of Him That Gaveth This Life.

"*As-salaatu Khairun mina 'n-naumi!*"

(It is better to pray than to sleep. What about it?)

Lucy rolled to her side, adjusting the thin linen sheet provided by
the hotel, not feeling so good. I haven't felt right, she thought, since
I arrived in Israel. I have horrible tortured sleep, bad headaches, and
this heat makes me swollen and irritable . . . Oh geez, now my bowels
are in an uproar too. I spoke too soon to Dr. O'Hanrahan, bragging I
had escaped all gastric evils. Lucy sat up on the side of the bed. Her
head swam as her stomach lurched and she tasted a nauseating acid
in her throat.

She ran to the toilet and vomited.

Moments later, having turned on the ceiling fan full tilt and spread
herself on the bed under the blast, she coaxed herself into feeling
better. Largely this was futile; sweat poured off her head and she felt

her forehead, clammy and sticky. There, she swore, that was the worst of it. She wiped her brow with the sheet.

Morning sickness.

She calculated: I didn't have my period but that could have been because of all the travel, heat, and distress. I'm swollen and grouchy but that could be due to the above as well. And now I've been sick in the morning . . . which could be Mohammed's Kebab Surprise the other night.

Or I could stop lying to myself.

Lucy imagined what it would be to pass a baby-sized object through her body. Out it will come and a nurse will put it into my arms, a boy or a girl . . . I think a boy. And I will hold it briefly and then the adoption people will take it from me. That's as unthinkable as the labor and delivery. As unthinkable as my returning to Chicago, having the kid and buying the bassinet and crib and decking out the apartment in baby things—maybe moving in with another single mother, sharing duties, baby-sitting. This little smiling thing that will waddle over to hug me when it's older, that will attempt to walk and fall down on its little diaper-padded bottom. Nope. No good—I can't stir an ounce of maternal feeling or sentiment into this situation. Lucy tried to picture herself holding a son, madonna and child: would I ever look at him and not think, well Lucy, this is what you get to do in this world instead of live your life.

"Hayya 'ala 'l-falaaaaaaah! Hayya 'ala 'l-falaaaaaah!"

She reached over on the nightstand and felt for her rosary beads. She had bought these in Rome for Aunt Lucy but now maybe she needed them more. Maybe they would lead her to the old Lucy, the one without this problem, the one who knew all the answers and had her life carefully proscribed and hemmed in where it couldn't get in any trouble—*that* Lucy Dantan.

(Wouldn't count on it.)

She began a Hail Mary automatically. Yes, it felt empty but, she told herself, eventually it will mean something . . . She felt her eyes moisten with tears. I've really done it now. I've messed up my whole life. And I've even messed up God for myself.

On the sunny vast porch of the hotel, O'Hanrahan had piled up a week's worth of now-outdated Western newspapers and was sitting in a wicker chair, drinking cups of tea, picking at a piece of bread, managing a smoldering cigar in the ashtray, temporarily a sultan.

"Dr. O'Hanrahan," Lucy announced herself, up at last at 11:00 A.M. "We've got to talk, sir. I feel like I ought to be getting home."

He studied a day-old *London Daily Telegraph*, which had detailed reports of Iraqi atrocities in Kuwait. Foreign workers were having trouble getting out of Iraq as well. "Hmm? Go home," he repeated distractedly. "It's just starting to get good."

"I'm worried about my health."

"You're taking your malaria pills, right? You're fine, if you don't drink the tap water." He glanced at her to see if she was ill. "Ah. Pharoah's Revenge caught up with you at last, heh-heh-heh. I had my bad day yesterday."

Lucy, appearing pale and red-eyed, sat down across from him, swatting at the flies that had immediately found her. "You still are determined to go to Khartoum overland?"

"Where else can I get to the invaluable material on the lost kingdom of Meroe, hm? If not at Khartoum University, and the archives at the National Museum, then where?"

"We couldn't have someone photocopy these things?"

"Between Sudanese photocopying and Sudanese mail and Sudanese uncooperation, that idea doesn't have a prayer." O'Hanrahan folded his paper. "Khartoum's the key for us, Luce. Professor Fletcher in the early 1900s began trying to decipher Meroitic and gave his whole life to it." O'Hanrahan lifted a finger to make a point. "But lots of scholars have shrugged and given up, taken it off the front burner. With all this new interest in Africa, someone's gonna figure it out any day now, so we've gotta get there first, Sister Lucy!"

Lucy could not be moved to share his enthusiasm. She glumly looked down at his newspapers, full of invasion news. A picture in *The New York Times* of General Colin Powell beside a chart showing the calling-up of American reserves. A photo of an open-mouthed Jesse Jackson protesting that too many black people were in the army. Surely we weren't going to war in the Middle East, Lucy thought darkly, standing.

"Whereya going?"

"Taking a walk," she said, patting her camera looped round her neck.

She wandered down a few dusty blocks, already 100 degrees in the sun, to the grand Cataract Hotel, a world-class joint decked out like a Moorish villa, overlooking Elephantine Island. Lucy asked at the desk if they had an international phone booth. A dark man whose face was a giant smile took her number and placed the call repeatedly until it connected:

"Rabbi Hersch?"

"What? Lucy! Where the hell have you guys been?"

"We're in Aswan. We're leaving for Khartoum tomorrow—"

"Khartoum?" Then there was a noise as if he had dropped the phone. "It all explains itself—you too are a meshuggenitzke! Is *the moon* on this man's itinerary?" The rabbi then came as close as Lucy had heard to raising his voice. "Nu nu nu, do you know anything about the Bashir regime in the Sudan there? I'm not gonna tell you, so that you'll sleep tonight, okay?"

There was a pause.

The rabbi said in a level tone, "Look. You might go back to Chicago and stop wasting your time. I got some bad news. The scroll's been stolen from Father Vico, and we're back to square one anyway."

Lucy paused a moment to prepare her response, but it was enough to confirm the rabbi's suspicions.

"I *knew it!*" seized the rabbi. "I knew that son of a bitch Patrick O'Hanrahan had the thing stolen—that nudzh Gabriel! Damn you two!"

"Rabbi, sir, I think you have to understand—"

"When you didn't call for a week I got suspicious! Surely, I said to myself, Paddy will stop pouting and check in with me; surely he needs to be close to the scroll . . . and then light dawns like the shmendrik I am that *Paddy* had it!" A few choice sentences in Yiddish-English followed this. When he raised his voice the satellite call hissed and crackled.

"If I could explain—"

Rabbi Hersch reversed himself: "No! I take it back: God bless you, let God bless showers and showers of blessings upon you! Blessings upon you and your issue unto all the generations! Blessings because at least you *have* the scroll. Tell Paddy, all is forgiven, if he'll just go back to Chicago and wait for me there."

"Chicago?"

"I don't trust Jerusalem. If Paddy hadn't swiped it, someone else would certainly have done it. Something's going on here. I had a break-in in my office. We had some weird guys harassing my cleaning lady at my house. I got a visit from Mossad again wanting to know about something called 'The Flight of the Griffin.' Something really big is up and, though I should be insulted, I'm actually glad you pulled this stunt." The rabbi reflected a moment. "I take it you're calling me behind Paddy's back."

"Yes, he said he was going to do it but I think he's chickened out. And besides, as far as I was concerned . . ."

The rabbi waited patiently.

"I didn't know if I could trust *you,* Rabbi, sir."

"Trust me?"

Lucy got brave and pursued the matters that had led her to call: "I saw you in front of the King David Hotel with the guy who was in Ballymacross and who stalked us in Florence. The Man in the Cheap Suit we've been calling him. I don't know if Dr. O'Hanrahan mentioned him to you, but I saw you and this crook exchanging money."

He was quiet a moment. "Ah. So this is why the silence. Okay, little girl, you remember when we discussed my selling a faculty member's library to the Bible-thumpers for $43,000?"

"Yes."

"He's from a Bible college, your Man in the Cheap Suit. He's been in touch with me for a few months or so and he's trying to undercut Bob Jones's offer for Rabbi Shimon's library. In Rome, I realized he didn't want my library, he wanted the *Gospel of Matthias* and was haggling for my library to cover his true intentions."

"I saw you hand him money."

"He gave me $1000 in an envelope if I would tell him who had the scroll. I handed it back to him."

"You then got in his car."

"He dropped me off at Hebrew University."

Lucy processed this.

The rabbi: "What? You think I've gone to all this trouble to find the *Gospel of Matthias* so I could give it to some hayseed back in the States?"

"What Bible college?"

"That TPL place down in Louisiana."

Lucy closed her eyes. So Farley and Mr. Cheap Suit *were* traveling together. Both were from a Louisiana pentecostal college. And Lucy felt her face color: Farley repeatedly wanted to have dinner, have drinks, get together, and talk to her *about the scroll*! Naturally, it wasn't about any romantic interest. Yep, she sighed, figures it couldn't have been that I'd swept him off his feet—

"You still there, little girl?"

"Yes. Another question."

"I am this untrustworthy? You gotta play detective here? Paddy thinks I'm up to something too, does he?"

Lucy persevered: "Gabriel told me about something that happened this spring—"

"That momzer?"

"He said when he and Dr. O'Hanrahan went to Rome to purchase the scroll from those dealers, that they left you back in Jerusalem. But then he ran into you in Rome trying to purchase the scroll secretly as well, behind Dr. O'Hanrahan's back."

"Do you blame me for that?" he said. "It doesn't look so nice, but my suspicions about Gabriel were correct, huh? Hey, I've lived in

Jerusalem for forty years, I got sources. I heard the Franciscans were gonna try and swipe it—was I right? Huh? So I came to Rome as a backup. Paddy left the hotel when Gabriel disappeared and I never got to make contact with him."

He collected his thoughts: "Look, little girl. *I* invited Patrick O'Hanrahan to work with me on this, remember? If I *had* gotten the scroll in Rome I'd have invited Paddy to Jerusalem to work on it there, together. Any imputation that I am scheming against him—when he's here because of me in the first place—is so much shlock!"

Indeed, the rabbi's instincts were correct about Gabriel . . . and probably right about O'Hanrahan losing control of his own life. Maybe the *Gospel of Matthias* was a job for Father Beaufoix, a job for a team of established scholars—not some crazy old man who had played upon the rabbi's strained sense of friendship, and not some undistinguished grad student from Chicago.

Rabbi Hersch; "So are you safe there?"

Lucy was aware she was sounding weepy and girlish but she almost let the rabbi know the worst of it: "Not really. We got our hotel room broken into in Cairo. O'Hanrahan carries the scroll on him most of the time, so whoever it was didn't find it. Then we moved hotels and the same thing happened the next day. We decided to stop using the credit card that Merriwether Industries sent us—somebody is using it to track our every move."

"So what are you doing for money?"

"Dr. O'Hanrahan is back to using his *own* credit card, which has gotta be pretty much up to its limit, since I bet he hasn't paid off his bill in months."

"This they love at credit cards. They probably raised his limit."

Lucy sighed and conveyed more news: "Oh and we had a near-encounter with the Mad Monk too. When we went to the Egyptian Orthodox monasteries at Wadi Natrun. We arrived to hear that a monk had preceded us by a day asking around for the *Gospel of Matthias* and books on Meroitic."

"The Mad Monk? The Greek Orthodox fellow Father Vico told us about; the guy trying to destroy the *Gospel of Matthias?*"

"I have no idea what his mission is. I do know that this monk fellow has shown up in Assisi, in Athens and on Mt. Athos, and now he's in Cairo. It's uncanny how he seems to know where to look. He's not following us because he gets places *before* we do."

"Look, tell Paddy for me to get what he needs at Khartoum, get the hell out of there, and we'll all reconvene in Chicago."

"Okay. Uh, Rabbi, apropos of nothing."

"Yeah, what now?"

"What's Israel's policy on adoption and abortion?"

Abortion, no. Adoption, yes, if the baby's Jewish, he explained, though there are no doubt special cases for both. "Why do you ask? You knocked up?"

Forced laughter. "Of course not!"

"You'd be taken care of in Israel, if that's what you want to know. I'd see to it. You're not knocked up? Paddy and you do something you oughta be ashamed of?"

"Rabbi, no!"

He didn't believe her now. "*Oy vey,*" he muttered. "Last time I have anything to do with a goddam Christian gospel! This has been one long kick in the toches!"

AUGUST 16TH–17TH

The tourists at this time of year were nonexistent, of course. Who would be crazy enough to travel up the Nile in the summer?

O'Hanrahan went to a bank in the morning and asked what the limit on Merriwether Industries' corporate VISA card was for cash advances and was told there was nearly $1000 he could have. O'Hanrahan thought this over. He could get the $1000 and spend it without leaving a trace ... except that he had gotten the cash advance in Aswan. Wouldn't the masterminds at Merriwether Industries assume Aswan was but a staging ground for a push to Khartoum? He didn't risk it. He used his own MasterCard for his cash advance in Sudanese pounds and committed Merriwether Industries' VISA permanently to his wallet, determined not to use it again.

Those traveling by ferry to the Sudan were numerous enough to book all but one of the first-class cabins on the steamer to Wadi Halfa, the Sudanese border outpost reached by the twenty-hour boat ride across Lake Nasser. O'Hanrahan as a peace offering had given Lucy the last first-class cabin, with its semblance of air-conditioning. He took a second-class cabin, paying for all the bunks so he could have it to himself.

Lucy awoke in the middle of the night to discover she was quite cold. Fumbling for the bedside lamp, she adjusted her eyes to the light and began trying every panel and knob of the air-conditioner unit, fiddling to stop the flow of cold air. Finally she unplugged it. Maybe it actually *was* cold. She opened the door to her room, which was on the top deck, and indeed, it was the middle of the night and quite cool. The lake was still and black as oil, the sky was clear with many stars, and only rarely could she find a light on the shore, perhaps a Nubian camp, or a village of the Shaiga peoples, or the Gaalyeen.

Here is Africa.

Peoples in tribes clustered around fires, speaking languages understood by them alone, people whose physical characteristics looked a
certain way, who dressed and sang and danced in specific patterns
honed by the centuries and the harsh conditions, the rise and ebb of
the Nile, the beneficence and indifference of the gods. People who
told stories, passed and embellished from the original tale told to their
ancestors by God Himself or God Herself. "Primitive" peoples: a term
a number of politically correct people back at the university found
insulting, but "primitive" from *primus* meaning first, meaning original,
meaning "here first"—that was not insulting. For this was where humankind began, remembered Lucy, in the headlands of this river, the
oldest-known bones of *Homo sapiens*. The first place on the planet to
host human life, and ironically, maybe the last place to become livable.

Lucy beheld the continent less fondly the next morning when she
and Dr. O'Hanrahan discovered there would be no train to Khartoum
before Saturday night, virtually a two-day wait.

"Where . . . is . . . the train?" enunciated O'Hanrahan carefully, his
handkerchief out to wipe sweat from his brow on this dry 110-degree
day.

"Eet is not to come." The man at the station, patient and smiling in
a perspiration-stained *galabiyya*, had introduced himself as Mohammed. As Lucy and O'Hanrahan were the sole crazy Western *'kchawa-
gahs* here this time of year, Mohammed had taken a piteous interest
in them.

"Can you find out when the train will come?"

Mohammed smiled inappropriately. "The phone ees not to work,"
he said in explanation.

"So you don't really know anything?"

"Saturday night, good sir, there will be a train. When there ees no
train on the Friday morning there is always a train on the Saturday
night. Oonless it is to come on the Sunday."

O'Hanrahan thanked the man and led Lucy away to the dusty main
street, such as it was. Wadi Halfa could have been a Mexican Wild
West town with shacks and adobe-style huts, abandoned buildings with
broken windows, and white dust hanging everywhere above the road.
The gas station was the locus, apparently, of all activity.

"We'll go by road," suggested O'Hanrahan, starting to haul his suitcase over to the gas station. "The train takes forever anyway." Sand
dunes block the track. Things break down. The train stops five times
a day for prayertime. "Let's hitch a ride."

They met a truck driver named Mohammed. He had a Bedford
truck for rough terrain with a canvas-covered bed full of ammunition,
chickens, goat hooves, plastic beach balls, and animal feed. There was
room for two passengers in his wide front seat, and if his guests found
that uncomfortable, they could stretch out with the chickens in the

back. The price was easily negotiated by O'Hanrahan, who had prefaced the deal with many elaborate Arab blessings and, as he told Lucy later, a semipromise to vouch for Mohammed's green card should he come to the States.

"In Europe and the second world they hate Americans," O'Hanrahan explained in the small grocery store as they loaded up on fresh bottles of water and prepackaged snacks. O'Hanrahan held one water bottle to the light and grimaced at the things floating in it. He examined the bottle top and figured well water or lake water had been put within and a new metal cap hammered on the bottle. "But in the third world, ironically, we get treated nice because they want to come to America. It's a cheap way to win friends but I'll promise anything to get out of this town."

Lucy raised a bottle to the light. "This looks clean . . ."

And so they were off, down the well-worn tracks alongside the narrowing Lake Nasser. The road soon degenerated and the pace slowed to 30 m.p.h. as Mohammed and his truck wavered and rolled precariously going down and up gullies. They had an air-conditioning of sorts; the truck had a fan that blasted hottish air upon them, in addition to the occasional breeze stirred by open windows.

Lucy looked at Mohammed, who kept sneaking looks at her. Lucy was dressed conservatively, long pants, long sleeves, but her neck and hair were exposed and that seemed to be of peculiar interest to Mohammed. Lucy was hot and weary enough to contemplate O'Hanrahan's dying of a heat stroke and then having to be Mohammed's sex slave all the way to Khartoum. Could be worse. He was about 35 or so, a smiling brown face, having gone a few days without shaving, had most of his teeth, big, moist, brown eyes, and that receding manner of many Arab men, a shyness borne of humility before Allah. Each truck voyage for Mohammed was a sign of God's grace. The next moment she grabbed the doorhandle to steady herself as Mohammed nearly tipped the truck over in a dry gully. Maybe, she thought, Allah *is* a major part of the completed journey.

(We help where We can.)

"I called Rabbi Hersch back in Aswan," she confessed.

Maybe it was too hot for O'Hanrahan to get particularly worked up.

Lucy wondered, "You're not upset?"

"No. Saved me from having to do it. You told him we had the scroll, didn't you?" O'Hanrahan explained he intended to call the rabbi in Cairo, then in Khartoum, but he had put it off so long he sort of dreaded the blast of accusations.

Hours were extinguished in the heat.

The road was so bad in one place that Mohammed took a detour down to the river bank, only to whir and slide about in the mud. Mohammed laughed as if this were high amusement.

Another hour passed and the lake had narrowed back to Nile-width and the desert on either side flattened out and was searing and endless. An hour might offer as entertainment nothing more than a two- or three-camel caravan, slowly moving along the riverbank, or a passing truck in the other direction, which was met with honks and shouted blessings, and once, when the Nile peeked through, a felucca idling against the current.

Lucy had memorized the truck cabin, which was affectionately cluttered with blinking Christmas lights, faded streamers, Arabic decals of holy phrases, a yellowed photo of Mekkah cut from a magazine and taped to the dashboard, photos of the driver's son, in ceremonial circumcision-wear, taped to the back of the visor. O'Hanrahan, noticing her interest in the photo, began a lecture on circumcision, that for boys it was often done at village fairs. Mohammed's boy was darling, thirteen, his eyes betraying terror of the public humiliation to come.

"And most natives," whispered O'Hanrahan, "circumcise the women around nine or ten. If not at birth."

Lucy worked on that a minute. Circumcise the women? "Wait, you don't mean . . ."

"That's exactly what I mean, removal of that organ of pleasure." O'Hanrahan enjoyed Lucy's fulminations and outrage, reviving them both as she railed against this butchery.

"The U.N. ought to stop it," she stammered.

"Heh-heh-heh, a woman who can't be ruled by sexual desire is a woman who can be trusted not to cheat on her husband with a better lover. I wonder how effective it is. You would think other body parts would step in as erogenous zones. Come to think of it, there are the Rasheda peoples in Sudan. Women's chins are their prize possessions, and are always kept hidden. You may see some in the *souk* of Khartoum. Anyway, women perform the operation, and there's no stopping the custom. A mother is heartbroken if her daughter doesn't have it."

That topic killed a good twenty minutes.

Lucy also contemplated the rough road and how, only a few hours into the big ride, she felt her bowels stir uncomfortably and her behind was sore. Maybe, she thought darkly, she would miscarry.

(Dark thought, indeed.)

Hey, it's my pregnancy. I can think darkly if I want to.

(A miscarriage would relieve you of a choice, you believe.)

It would make it easier.

(You want to risk hemorrhaging in the Sahara?)

No, I suppose not. Hey, I'm probably not even pregnant anyway.

(And if you are?)

This topic again? Well, she sighed, it has only been forty minutes since I last thought about it, so why not?

I confront the idea of raising a child by myself and what that would do to my life and I see a void, a cartoon scenario that has no reality, no shape, me miscast in a bad TV movie. Abortion's probably out. Yeah, if this were Judy I'd advise *her* to have one, but this is me and people can say I'm screwed up by Catholicism and guilt-ridden and all that stuff, but I know I could live with nine months of pregnancy more easily than with my having had an abortion. Besides. The pregnancy has the proper elements of punishment, of *ordeal* for my sin. That'll teach me, she set her mind to it coldly. I will undergo the tribulation as part of the penance for my sin of stupidity—

"Lake Nasser," said O'Hanrahan, mopping his sandy, sweaty brow, determined to resuscitate conversation, "has buried some one hundred monuments of historical interest. Nubia, Cush, the northern reaches of Meroe, a thousand clues under the water for good . . ."

My mom, thought Lucy. There's a happy thought. She felt her stomach tighten as she always did when thinking of her family. Her family, which was about to have a new member.

Actually, Lucy's mother would be the better parent about the news. Of course, there would be grieving and recriminations, but after a complete submission was made, her mother would then wear her daughter's unwed pregnancy proudly in her martyr's crown, another gift of suffering sent her way. Dad would see it for what it was, Lucy's stupidity and indifference to his good name. Her sister Cecilia would be woeful and superior, though faintly consoling. Her brother Nicholas would take the news the best—making a joke, relieved now to shift the black-sheep-of-the-family mantle off his shoulders. Her brother Kevin, younger and never particularly close, would bestow upon her "Smooth goin', Luce," and other slogans by which she would know she'd failed yet another test on his eternal adolescent coolness-scale. Her sister Mary would roll her eyes and whisper, "Why didn't you have an abortion?" because Mary probably had gone that route a time or two. And the reactions of the maiden aunt brigade, the prayer circle of St. Bridget's, her namesake Aunt Lucy—none bore contemplation.

Lucy let a small laugh escape. Actually, it was almost appealing: the idea of torturing the old harpies with her sin. *Here*, I should say, rub your superior ancient faces in it! Feel a disgrace and shame I myself couldn't possibly imagine!

"*Zauba'ah*," said Mohammed blandly.

O'Hanrahan chattering away: ". . . one thinks of the lost cities, yes, maybe even entire cultures themselves buried under this lake. It's changed the entire water table of the Sahara."

"I read somewhere it was unsafe, the Aswan Dam."

"Well, the Soviets helped build it, so what do you think? Khadaffi keeps threatening to blow it up, every so often. You realize if it broke, the whole of Egypt would be washed away into the Mediterranean.

Aswan, the Valley of the Kings, the pyramids perhaps, Cairo and its 15 million . . . an awesome thought. And yet without the flood control, a modern Egypt isn't possible—"

"*Zauba'ah,*" said Mohammed, shaking his head dourly.

"What's he saying?" asked Lucy.

"I have no idea," said the professor. "Not that the third world does very well with progress—the rain forests, the unlimited pollution, the rape of their environments. Like that smokestack plume ahead."

"Disgusting, isn't it?" said Lucy.

They stared at the plume of yellow and brown filth rising in a mushroom cloud above the distant desert.

"Did you see, when our train was leaving Cairo, the appalling pollution of some of those factories?" asked Lucy, stirring in the seat. "Some of the nearby houses were coated in that yellow chemical filth, and the river. They just dumped all that bilge into the Nile. Something wrong, sir?"

O'Hanrahan was grave. "Could swear that cloud came from the direction of the desert." O'Hanrahan's eyes widened. "Uh-oh."

"What?"

"It's a duststorm."

"*Zauba'ah,*" said Mohammed, pointing to the storm. "*Aywah, hennak . . . al-haboob.*"

The notorious *haboob* of the Sudanese Desert. It took up about a quarter of the sky, rising like a funnel cloud from a single point, then branching out in clouds of bilious yellow and brown and black, depending on what was being sucked up and how the sun hit it. Beautiful in its way, falling, rising, reconstituting its shape as if it were alive, Lucy thought, panicked by the sure doom of facing some part of it.

Mohammed slapped his steering wheel, disappointed but not particularly energized, muttering a prayer to Allah. He began to turn the truck around.

"What's he doing?" Lucy asked.

O'Hanrahan learned in Arabic. "There's a road a few miles back that leads to the Nile, a mile or two over. We're going to put the truck by the river and sit it out."

"Why?"

"Because," O'Hanrahan said, having reasoned it out himself, "if ten inches of dust are dumped on us, we want some bearings when it's all over."

As they drove north back to the turnoff, Lucy looked ahead at the clear blue sky in the direction they came from. But then eerily all the desert around them turned dim as the cloud passed before the sun, and the loose sand of the nearby dunes began to dance, agitated by the increasing wind. The wind began to whistle around the truck, rattling the canvas shell. Mohammed found the turnoff to the Nile and Lucy anxiously glanced to their right: no sky, no light, just an approaching curtain of churning sand, tossing itself and roiling like clouds of smoke.

"It was a perfectly calm day," said Lucy. "How . . ."

"Nothing needs a reason that happens out here," said O'Hanrahan, wrapping his handkerchief around his mouth.

Mohammed spoke, now more concerned.

"Mohammed thinks we'd do better in the back of the truck," said O'Hanrahan. Mohammed opened his door and the wind doubled its howl; he had parked the truck to protect the radiator grille so the back would bear the brunt of the storm. Lucy slid across the seat and hopped to the ground. A nettlesome blast of small sand particles stung at her, lashed her . . . she squeezed her eyes shut as Mohammed took her arm and helped her along. Upon rounding the back of the truck, she met the wind full force and she felt dust fly up her nose and, shocked, she breathed through her mouth, only to get a lungful of dust too. She tried to spit it out but Mohammed was pushing her up and over onto the floor of the covered truckbed. O'Hanrahan rolled in over the raised tailgate and then Mohammed himself climbed in and began to lash the canvas, sewing them up inside.

Lucy used her sleeve to wipe her eyes. Under her eyes, in her ears, up her nostrils, down her blouse, through the clothes, through her skin, the driving dust had penetrated everywhere. As soon as her eyes were accustomed to the dark she picked out a relatively clean place and huddled down behind the packages; with some amusement she saw O'Hanrahan settle himself beside the chickens in the coops. Mohammed continued muttering his prayers and rubbing his screwdriver, holding it up, kissing it . . .

"I'm curious but I'm not sure I want to know," said Lucy quietly.

"Something to do with a *jinn*," said O'Hanrahan.

Lucy brought up her legs and hugged her knees. "It's odd, isn't it, how even the most monotheist religions have all these little subgods and minidemons roaming about."

"Everyone else's religion is always quaint. I, for one, *like* the idea of genies. With earthquakes and sandstorms and famines out here, it is tempting to find God cruel. With accidents and injuries . . ." A faded photo he carried in his wallet of Beatrice and Rudolph was dimly illumined in his mind. He ignored them. ". . . but once it is explained that there are all sorts of mischievous *jinn* running about causing mayhem—"

"Like the Irish fairy people," inserted Lucy.

"Or the Scandinavian trolls . . ." His mind was half on this discussion as the truck began to rock. Mohammed beseeched the *jinn* causing the storm to accept his screwdriver. O'Hanrahan finally laid a hand on

Mohammed's shoulder and asked him what he was doing, perhaps Lucy and he could help.

"*Hadid! Hadid!*" he continued to yell at the sky.

"Uh-huh . . ." said O'Hanrahan as he listened, looking back at Lucy occasionally. "It is the *jinn* Zauba'ah who causes these storms and he is only scared of one thing and that's iron. So no harm will come to us if we . . ." With this O'Hanrahan stretched over to Mohammed's tool box. ". . . if we clasp to our bosom these iron tools." Mohammed, after a brief smile, bowed his head repeatedly, happy his charges would now be safe.

"*Hadid!*" yelled O'Hanrahan to the *jinn*. Lucy clutched a rusted wrench. "*Hadid*," she mumbled.

Lucy noticed in the next moment O'Hanrahan laughing to himself, and she began to smile too. Out in the middle of nowhere in a sand-storm, huddled with the chickens, scaring off the evil genie with a screwdriver.

Ten minutes went by.

It was possible, Lucy decided, to get bored in a sandstorm, now that she was sure her life wasn't threatened.

O'Hanrahan repositioned himself a little closer. "There are good genies, some are devout Muslims. If a snake crawls into a mosque during prayertime, he's a bad *jinn* in disguise; any other time, he might be a good *jinn* coming to privately worship Allah."

"I see."

(The tales of the *jinn*! The *Shiqq* is a horrible thing, half a human cut lengthwise, very kind to you until he turns and you see he is only one half a human—in your shock he will attack you. But he is not nearly as common as the *Nasnaas* genie, also half a human, an incredi-bly agile hopper. In Yemeni history one can read innumerable ac-counts of their being caught and eaten—the people of Hazramaut as late as the 20th Century swore that its flesh had a lemony, sweet taste. It, like the genies of Java, has a head tucked into its breast. *Tir* is unfailing in his capacity to cause wars, *al-A'war* is the genie of the erection, and watch out for *Dahsim*, who invents all marital strife, and that great Egyptian scourge, the *jinn Zalambuur*, who presides over traffic and intersections. The *Ghaddar jinn* lingers in dark caves and dark rooms and children are wise to be terrified of him. The most feared *jinn*, Iblis, the fallen angel, mentioned by The Prophet, often comes in female form, bearing forbidden wine, and this evil one excels at poetry and music, and he/she is thought to be the leader of all the other lesser *shaitans*. Or so Our Moslem children believe.)

"Shooting stars," remembered O'Hanrahan, "are explained by the people of the Sudan as Allah's attempt to nail an evil *jinn* with a divinely hurled stone. 'May Allah destroy the enemy of the faith!' they say, rather than making a wish when a meteorite falls."

"How much is this stuff believed nowadays?" asked Lucy.

"How many Christians worldwide believe there is a demon named Legion? An angel named Gabriel?"

Then suddenly it was quiet.

Mohammed, kissing the screwdriver, undid a knot of the canvas flap. It was clear, he announced, and began leading the escape from the back of the truck. When Lucy jumped down to the fine sand, filling her shoes with soft dust, she saw a new five-foot dune around the truck and above saw nothing but clear blue sky. She peeked around the truck, north, south, east, west . . . no funnel cloud, no sandstorm, just a calm azure afternoon.

O'Hanrahan shared her amazement. He looked at his watch, shook it, and cursed that sand had managed to get inside the watchface. He and Lucy observed how the other was coated in fine dust, looking Al Jolson–like. O'Hanrahan sang a halfhearted rendition of "Mammy," before Mohammed looked at him with a stare of concern. It had been cool during the duststorm, refreshing actually; now it was baking again, and Lucy and O'Hanrahan without eagerness returned to the cab and their lukewarm water bottles to quench their irremediable thirsts. Mohammed announced to O'Hanrahan that they would make Delgo by nightfall.

Back on the road.

Thought O'Hanrahan: this is what I live for.

He looked out the grimed window to the desert, the endless tract, monochrome yellow-beige in the middle of the 115-degree afternoon. A place to be by oneself, like the monks of Wadi Natrun and their caves. No place was ever more quiet. It takes a desert to invent religion—Islam, Christianity, Judaism, all products of too much time out here in the sun.

O'Hanrahan thought of the Grazing Monks who only ate as animals ate, grass and herbs from the ground. The Arboreal Monks who lived atop trees, begging to be scourged with storms, vultures, lightning. Coptic monks who interwove chains with their beards, so as to live in constant pain; some Copts spent a lifetime burdened with weights. Some took to cells too small to ever stand or sit in, forever writhing; the Hairless Ones who had every hair plucked to be sexless, featureless before God; and the Hairy Monks like St. Mekarius who let their hair grow long to cover their entire bodies, matted and infested; the Crucifixionists demanding nails be driven through all hands and feet. St. Moses the Black, St. John the Dwarf, St. Apollo of Scetis who before his conversion ripped pregnant women apart to molest the unborn children—saved and redeemed by the desert! The Anchorites of the rocks, the Hermits who lived out among the desert like Bola and Anthony, whose monasteries endure from the late 200s! European faith seems *arriviste*, nonchalant beside such a pedigree . . .

And the Stylites. Simon, who lived atop a desert column for thirty-seven years continuously, through duststorm and earthquake, who wore chains so tight that his skin was a raw breeding-ground for the maggots he introduced there, who wouldn't eat for forty days at a time. A pop star of sorts, a tourist attraction, raising his column higher and higher to avoid the throng that came to seek his guidance. His disciple Daniel, thrown out of all ordinary monasteries for being too masochistic.

(That took some doing in the 400s, We can assure you.)

O'Hanrahan laughed out loud at the thought—

"Something funny?" Lucy asked.

"No, nothing," he sighed, and they both returned to trancelike silence, staring straight ahead.

All this mortification of flesh, thought O'Hanrahan. Life expectancy being what it was, how could these saints have known that the great mortification, the supreme male humiliation, would elude them—*old age*. Saints Simon and Daniel should have taken a church post somewhere, a desk job and just waited, just held on until that 65th birthday rolled around. The sagging chest. The permanent gut until the hour of your death. Let's not even mention O long-dysfunctional Priapus—or worse, the *occasionally* functioning machinery. The creasing, drooping face, the lengthening, old-man ears, the loss of hair—the graying of the pubis! Yes I suppose one could alter these signs of mortality but what vanity! Never would Patrick O'Hanrahan be the clown with the hairpiece, the old-fart professor blackening his hair, corseting himself for that last undergraduette's felicities . . .

(We seem to remember some trips to the drugstore.)

Aw Jesus. Drink and corrode myself as I will, I still have the best damn memory in the world. Beatrice used to use this depilatory cream on her upper lip—she'd often as not send me down the block to the drugstore to get it, and happy to escape her house for any amount of seconds, I'd go. Then one day, disgusted with my ears, which were getting long like Lyndon Johnson's, I noticed the newest little surprise: hair growing out of my ears. Now *that* was a sign of ancientness, and it flashed back to me my father and the profusion of old-man ear-hair, gray and curly—never! So as Beatrice's bottle of Nair was on top of the toilet near her leg-shaving stuff, I would reach over and dab a bit on my ear. Then Beatrice had to go and die on me, leaving me to make the trip to the drugstore and buy a regular bottle of depilatory . . .

And once I felt accusing eyes upon me and I overexplained myself to the clerk: it's for my wife, you see. And the pharmacist, who knew Beatrice, who *of course* knew Beatrice, who had worked there for twenty years, regarded me with that sorrowful look you give to crazy old men. He thought that I bought bottles of Nair in order to pretend that

Beatrice was still alive. These are my humiliations and humblings! Pharoah got plagues and miracles and magic tricks, but you break my heart with emblems of *mediocrity*! So that you, Lord, can sup and take sustenance from my ridicule!

(You have no affection for human life and its frailties. Least of all your own.)

Well, my affection for myself is making a comeback.

I've had some time to think it all over since Greece: I was a bad husband, I was a bad father, I was a prejudiced and intolerant administrator of the department . . . You know what? I don't care. I felt guilty like a good Irishman, on cue like a good Catholic, but that guilt has solidified now to indifference in lieu of my life sentence of loneliness, which has risen up to atone for those previous transgressions.

"What time is it?" asked Lucy.

"Not half an hour since the last time you asked," O'Hanrahan said, glancing at his watch.

Yes, O'Hanrahan convinced himself, death by cholera in the wilds of Africa, far from friends and family, is preferable to one more goddam day puttering around with nothing to do in Forest Park. He thought: I'll happily avow that the only thing that could make old age worse is loneliness—which is a delightful little coincidence since the only thing that could make loneliness worse is old age.

Perhaps it's impossible for someone of Lucy's years to understand, or for that matter, for someone surrounded by wife and family: how each day takes forever to extinguish. To make it worse, you don't sleep as much; you can't even drown the day in sleep and afternoon naps. No. Wakefulness and insomnia, like my father had, thought O'Hanrahan, that has been the obstacle of the last ten years. Even the occupied, the semiemployed senior citizens I know, find it hard to get rid of all that time. I've seen my colleagues burn the hours away in card games, bridge addiction—bridge will kill off one's retirement years properly—gardening is good, organizing family photos, thereby allowing them to be thrown away with greater efficiency by the next generation . . . and still. All I was reduced to, the only real human contact I was allotted was my once-a-month advising of doctoral candidates back at the university. Those bastards. They first let me lecture, then cut me back to advising and grad seminars, then just advising . . . And that was hardly a salvation from the run of my daily life.

He returned in his mind to Forest Park, for the first time in months.

The morning. Awake again, still alive. O'Hanrahan would feel the weight of the unlived day upon him. Toiletries. To shave or not to shave? The only thing that made him shave and groom himself some days was the ghastly sight of white stubble, that bowery bum, staring back at him in the mirror. Look at the clock. Splendid: 7:30 A.M. A nice early start. The news shows. The anchorwomen so cute, perky, fresh, bright, laughing: both of you go to hell. Make some coffee. The kitchen is a nightmare, some dishes in the large two-basin sink will probably go unwashed until the day that he dies. Why bother, as there's never company. He eats out or eats frozen dinners so plates aren't important. It's the ashtrays that goad him. Always filling, overflowing. Not the kind of thing you think about in the middle of the day, emptying and cleaning those ashtrays, because one's nose is used to the stale, smoky air, but first thing in the morning there they are, staring at you, the cigar-stink of an old, old man's house. Maybe an old drunk man—look, there's the whiskey glass half full. O'Hanrahan will pour it back into the bottle he's working on, no sense wasting it. And now the TV has nothing but women's shows or greed-oriented game shows, nothing entertaining. Off goes the TV.

Congratulations, it's 9:30 A.M.

He reads. Yes, and a damn sight more than most people. But he has problems with books. Whereas an awful cop show on TV can occupy him, a well-written thriller often cannot because he takes the written word more seriously. If he's going to read, the book better hold him to the very core of his intellect. Literature, biographies, histories. He gave up contemporary fiction long ago, all the current product an advertisement for the superiority of the ancients.

How about a little exercise?

There's a convenience store six blocks away, Thomas and Roosevelt. Open 24 hours. Here comes Human Contact No. 1, the smiling, over-weight black girl, Zelda, behind the counter, calling him "professuh." He doesn't know Zelda's last name despite the fact they've been seeing each other in these circumstances for, what? Five years now? Before Zelda, there was Bob, who was white, zitty, painfully slow at the cash register, spent too much time reading drag-racing and motorbike magazines. You can get a 12-oz. cup of coffee for 59 cents. That and the doughnut of the day. O'Hanrahan, who had sipped cappuccino in Rome, espresso in Paris, Turkish coffee with ground pistachio shells with Moslem imams in Baghdad, *café brûlot* with rowdy Loyola novices in New Orleans . . . O'Hanrahan's great treat for the past ten years is nothing better than yesterday's Dunkin' Donut, now on special, 45 cents, and the 12-oz. convenience-store coffee. And a newspaper. Got to watch the money. If the headlines don't interest, he doesn't buy the paper—since there'll be Paul Harvey at noon on the radio and Peter Jennings on the nightly TV news, CNN, McNeil-Lehrer—god, considering it's a world I disapprove of and a country I think is in decline, I sure do keep up.

There, all nonalcoholic purchases made: total, $1.13 with tax. On Tuesdays and Saturdays, O'Hanrahan buys a bottle of spirits here. Before the humiliation of the Nair and the pitying looks of the pharmacist, he had bought liquor at great discount at the drugstore, but creeping back there is out of the question now.

(You really think anyone remembers this imagined humiliation?)

Oh ho, yes indeed, pharmacies deal in humiliation—that's their job: here is your prostate medicine, stuff for your diarrhea, your incontinence diapers, ma'am, all the successions of drugs that permit us to know our elder customers' bodily deteriorations, pinpointing decrepitude on our little graph that leads to the cemetery! No, I wouldn't give the pharmacist another excuse to pity me: How sad, he'd mourn, how tragic, Dr. O'Hanrahan is an alcoholic too . . .

(Well, you are.)

Anyway. Don't buy booze the same place every day or they stare at you like you're an alcoholic, but break it up a bit, and no one is too sure. Wouldn't want Zelda to think I was an alcoholic. Frankly, Lord, if it's any of Your concern, I was doing *well* to drink a bottle of spirits a day, quite often much less. Many drinkers are self-destroyers who if they could afford it would knock themselves insensate nightly, two or three bottles if they could manage it. Not me. An afternoon drink with lunch, a steady, regulated stream through the day.

What O'Hanrahan really adored was the middle of the night.

Now anyone who is up with him, in other houses, out on the highway, wherever, is alone like he is. 3:13 A.M. The lonely person's hour. But not without a hint of comfort, a trace of glamour, the threes—so much of the night left. The book one is reading is more interesting at that hour, the movies on TV more lost to another era. There's something desperate about the fours—will you get back to sleep or not? And the fives and sixes, when the working-class world awakens and the Eisenhower Expressway begins its rumble and O'Hare receives the day's first planes—it is no longer night.

Patrick O'Hanrahan never did his chores in the day, for all the idiots on the road, not to mention so many close calls for his short attention span for driving. He's not addled, nosiree, but driving a car never engaged him fully. The Antiochene Schism of the late 4th Century! The intrigues of the Tridentine Councils! These are worthy of his mind, but not suburban traffic. Anyway, at three A.M. there is no traffic. And he could drive as he pleased. He would drive to the Dominicks Supermarket, open 24 hours.

(In the days before they took your license away.)

Oh shut up, let me relive those glorious late-nights of freedom and carelessness. The world at 3:30 A.M. matched my old man's pace, my moodiness and reflectiveness. The half-awake check-out staff do not censure me for thumbing through the magazines. I settle on a *Cosmopolitan* or a *Vogue*, turn the pages slowly, looking at the youth of the women, women too pretty and young to lust after, because one would

have had to have some experience with women like this to even fantasize, to make it visceral for one. Why do I trouble myself? Why look
at what you can't have, never had, aren't going to have . . . Why this
ritual, this ceremony of taking in a dose of female beauty, 3:45 A.M.,
while the Hispanic boy sweeps the aisles with the wide broom, while
the black ex-athlete-now-cashier dozes on his feet. I am in my element.
You want a gauge of how many loners there are in society? Go to the
frozen-food coolers in November and right before Thanksgiving look
at what happens to the Lean Cuisine and Weight Watchers piles of
low-cal turkey dinners. Look how many fellow Americans are going it
alone with the diet frozen microwave dinners instead of getting with
their family. Each Thanksgiving I swore I'd buy lasagne, noodles,
anything but turkey . . . but then I'd break down and look for a Swan-
son's turkey dinner. How impossible was that solitary meal, how hard
to choke down, bringing back its memories of candlelit tables and
Beatrice bringing out the turkey. And Rudy who couldn't get enough
of that cranberry sauce from a can.

But let us leave the grocery store and escape back to the nightroad.

Those hours of driving. Glorious driving. Down to the Loop, out to
the airport, sometimes the toll road down to Indiana and back again
by the Skyway, a smile and a brief conversation with the toll keepers—
our stylites! What philosophers they must be to stay awake all night as
America zooms past them; what wisdom they must have as they observe
the nightworld *danse macabre* of people on half-speed, an unconscious
parody of America during the daytime. And it was on such a spree
that I got pulled over by a real fascist.

Where you going, "Pops"?

Where do you live?

Have you been drinking?

Well, he smelled as if he had, but he hadn't in hours—another
elderly disadvantage. Not good enough. His license was suspended
and he never bothered to fight to get it back. And there was the
indignity of a social worker coming out to counsel him: "Do you ever
feel suicidal, Mr. O'Hanrahan?"

No, but homicidal often, honey, in this city that can't leave the good
people alone, or stop the bad people.

(And if one day you drove truly inebriated and killed somebody?)

Thank You for Your support. I guess You're happy now, Lord, just
me and the clock. 3:30, 3:45, 3:58 . . . and then one more look: goddam
it, it's not four *yet*? The cigarettes, the reread books, the whiskey, the
warmly cantankerous older disk jockey playing big band on the radio:

How I shall end my days.

Until this! Until Mordechai called me with the rumor!

The *Gospel of Matthias* was on the black market—no, now Paddy, don't get excited, it's just a rumor, but it might possibly, possibly be true . . . Yes, the tantalizing discovery we only heard about in our twenties—it eluded Rabbi Rosen, God bless his soul, it eluded Dupont-Sommer and Albright and Quispel, and it's eluded every great scholar who has sought it, but is there a chance? A chance that Paddy O'Hanrahan and Morey Hersch, old devils, can succeed where man for 1900 years has failed?

And of course, Paddy, Rabbi Hersch claimed last December, you're the only person I can imagine translating the thing.

Not Father Beaufoix? he had suggested. You know, Morey, he's pretty good on African languages . . .

Do you remember? How you almost fumbled it away! Preferring for an instant the security of your sepulchral life of cable TV and old-timey radio—preferring the soft inner walls of the coffin! And I called Morey back that night, waking him up, saying yes, oh, God, yes, I am with you!

And there could be no debate, could there?

If it meant selling the house, cashing in the policies, pulling out the savings, all the insurance premiums paid for nothing for as long as he could remember? Do you think I'm going to die in a hospital? Does the world think if I got deathly ill I'd let doctors prolong this void? I'd lie down and keep drinking until it, life, went away. Yessir, in the time-honored family tradition. So screw the major medical, man. No beneficiaries. So of course, I cashed it all in! For *this*, Lord, this wondrous trip across the desert, the very life I was stupid enough to run away from!

Because, You see, that was my greatest offense to You: that I got off the track prepared for me. The Almighty practically brought down flashing neon signs and blinking arrows! But no, no, no, I listened to the *jinns*! I gave up what I loved most—the life of the adventurous, rambling, world-traveling scholar! Forty years of wrong turns and bad decisions and mislived, mistaken, misplayed moments, but now they will be redeemed.

(And if you had to go back home?)

Ah well, that's a sobering possibility. I will live on the street, I suppose. I will join the army of homeless, find a cot in the shelter, wander the street windblown as the scraps of urban trash, live as the anchorites of old, not eating, not finding any rest . . . It is haunting how that fate whispers to me, in the voice of my own father who foresaw I might repeat his failures, in the hectoring voice of Beatrice who said it was where I would end up, in the voice of my sister Catherine. Yet how I seem to recognize it, step resignedly toward it, how easy it is to see the alley and bottle and tattered overcoat of my destiny. With the other drunks and old men who screwed up or outlived their pensions or were simply unfortunate Americans in this indifferent age—indeed, how commonly my thoughts approach this horror: that perhaps it is with them that I *belong*, my true academic colleagues and equals.

"Delgo," said Mohammed, tapping O'Hanrahan to look ahead.

Yes, in the waning light there was Delgo, that oddest of notions: a Nubian truck stop. Forty vehicles, all Bedford trucks, were amassed in a central lot, around fires and pots over fires. There were a few real buildings, a guest house by the Nile bank, a police station, a garage and a gas station that looked, inexplicably, attached to what must be the mosque. The other dwellings were simple huts and makeshift accommodations, tents and pieces of sheet metal propped against sticks. Here was Nubia, with the inhabitants tall and dark black, seeming darker for the bleached, full-length white *galabiyyas* the men wore, their heads surrounded by the *emmas*, the loosely wrapped white turban-cloth.

To Lucy, Delgo seemed a bit untamed. Grizzled, sweat-stained men, raucous and then falling silent, gaped at Lucy and O'Hanrahan and Mohammed as they rolled past, no other women to be seen.

The truck wheezed to a stop. O'Hanrahan began to search for the cans of food in his bag but Mohammed knew people and no one would let these emissaries from the Western World go without the gifts of tea and food around their campfire. Lucy stood to the side, trying to project docility and allowing the truckers to admire her as O'Hanrahan's young bride—a charade that would save her from any harassment. She edged away from the main fire wondering how they could stand so near it when the afternoon heat was hardly abated.

Lucy and O'Hanrahan shared a room of cots in the guest house, being escorted there by a veiled old Nubian woman who was delighted with the foreign visitors and babbled on, unconcerned that she wasn't understood in the least. Mosquito nets were produced by the woman, and then a candle. Above the uneven wooden door, which did not meet the doorway, there was painted an Islamic slogan beneath a faded postcard of Mekkah. Lucy noted there didn't seem to be a lock or any way to prevent anyone from entering. But as all who travel in this part of the world, she surrendered to fatalism: one just can't fantasize about every bad thing happening. Besides, she sensed, these are more moral people than in the Western World. They believe Allah is watching.

Then it was night. After a few hours of stretching out and relieving her sore backside, and a meal of roast chicken brought to her by the woman, Lucy ventured out to O'Hanrahan, who was upon a box, sitting silently by the fire with a number of men. Now she longed for the fire in the desert night chill. A million stars shone above her.

"It's not an all-male fire, is it?" asked Lucy, a step back, her face in the shadows.

"Nah, I think it's all right," said O'Hanrahan. "I haven't said anything to anyone in half an hour, so unobtrusively make your way in here, Miss Dantan." He pointed to a flat place in the sand beside himself.

Lucy smiled, warmed by a tone that came from weariness with the day. He surprised her by kissing her.

"You're my wife, remember?" he whispered.

"Yes, master." She sat at his feet.

"I can't sit down on the sand like you," said O'Hanrahan, from his crate. "My circulation is so bad. They'd have to cut off my legs—I'm sure I'd never rise again . . ."

Uncle Liam, thought Lucy. He had this farm outside of Kankakee, south of Chicago, a small farm. When her father and his brother Liam were getting along, the family would take the bus down, getting up at some unnecessarily early hour, six A.M. or something, due to her mother's maniacal fear of lateness. And Lucy and her four siblings would play with their five cousins, two of whom, Danny and Sean, she was wildly in love with. With their cuss words and defiances and small attentions and white T-shirts that smelled of detergent when they'd play fort and wrestling would ensue in a leaf pile. And Uncle Liam would build a fire. She had conflated the memories of summer days with autumnal nights and herself in her hooded St. Eulalia's windbreaker that was too thin to ward off the chill but Lucy had decided she looked good in it, slim and like one of the guys, so she wore it even when told to go wear something warmer. Uncle Liam piled old barn wood and trash and doused it haphazardly with kerosene that smelled so intoxicating and all eleven Dantan kids would thrill and get giddy at the prospect of Uncle Liam sneaking up close with a lighted match . . . no, it didn't take that time. Then he'd try again as the girls would squeal, anticipating Vesuvius when the pile went off . . . sometimes Uncle Liam would get a piece of paper lighted and we all would wait for the rest of the bonfire to erupt, but the wind put it out.

Then suddenly the memory turned incomplete and confused. Her father and Uncle Liam had had one of those Irish family fights about something, something irreconcilable, something political. And Uncle Liam was dead from then on, and so was his family, and too much insistence on going to see Uncle Liam on their farm would occasion a scene at the dinner table. Lucy's thoughts turned bitter. What stupid, baseless argument did her father dredge up, raise to great heights in order to cut off that wing of his family, expunge that fellowship?

Sure, sure, in Irish fashion one day one of the men would be diagnosed with cancer and there'd be some kind of tearful reunion and a quick handshake, a reunion with Irish whiskey and bathos. But that's not good enough, Dad. It doesn't do *me* any damn good. What about all those bear hugs from Sean and Danny, what about all those bonfires your stupid need for enemies and Irish melodrama deprived me of?

She smiled. *That's* who Dr. O'Hanrahan reminded her of, in a strange way: Uncle Liam. It took awhile to place him, but they had the same bulbous nose and silver hair. And no wonder it all had come flooding back to her, since in the firelight the resemblance was even closer.

"Back in Korea," he began, "we were ten miles south of the Punchbowl. Mean anything to you, the Punchbowl?"

" 'Fraid not."

"General MacArthur, Harry Truman—heard of them?"

Lucy played dumb: "They made some *On the Road* movies in the early '50s?"

"Heh-heh, close enough. Anyway, the British were there, lots of British casualties. I like the British because I've seen them in wartime and they rise to the moment. Their army and officers are well educated too, the scholar and soldier and all that. At least it used to be that way."

"Korea. You were saying."

"As usual they had made a fine troop out of former colonials. Indians, Pakistanis, Burmese, Australians, the whole extended family. God, the Gurkhas were the most-feared warriors after the Turks. American soldiers would stumble upon a Chinese base where the Turks had been and find everyone beheaded . . ."

Lucy smiled at the rambling professor. He had seen a lot of life, she thought enviously. But as of this summer, so had she.

". . . and there was this Persian man from the Transjordan who guarded the fire each night. Everyone was trying to sleep, but no matter how late, he stayed up and watched it. Night after night, I'd be coming back from the hospital and there he was and I began to suspect some kind of racist thing, where the poor Middle Eastern guy had to tend the fire for the white man. But he was Zoroastrian, it turned out."

Lucy scooted closer and leaned against the crate he was sitting upon, hypnotized by the embers.

"And Zoroastrians," continued the professor, "think a fire is a sacred thing, a sacrament. It *is* mysterious, isn't it?"

Lucy nodded.

"The world within is fire, as the Persians knew, the stars above are fire, God is light, our souls are a fire within us. No, the Zoroastrians never could put a fire out—that was heresy, an interruption of the communion with God's blessing upon us, the gift of flame. A fire had to die down on its own, in God's own sweet time."

"And so this soldier . . ."

"This soldier stayed up later than the others every night to make sure no one put it out. There in Korea, Janists and Buddhists, born-agains and atheists for company, he guarded the eternal flame. I saw him almost kill a fellow Jordanian who, drunkenly, attempted to piss on the fire to put it out."

"Not a mistake I'm likely to make," she said. Lucy held out and examined her hands, her fingernails dirty, her hands in the firelight looking like an old woman's hands. "I don't know anything about Zoroastrianism, Dr. O'Hanrahan. I didn't even know any were left."

"Quite a few. They have another custom I like. The Jews once had it to a degree, but the Zoroastrians took it most seriously: when you die, you're not really dead for three days."

"Yeah?"

"The body is gone, but the soul dwells among the family and friends for three days. If you have anything you want to clear up with the departed, you have three days to talk it out, apologize, tell whoever how much you loved him or her. And then, at the end of three days you have a ceremony and officially say good-bye."

Lucy felt chilled and wrapped herself a bit more tightly in the coat, then said, "I like that too. Think of all the Catholic mamas lighting candles and wailing that they didn't get to say how they really felt about their long-lost family members. But," she sighed, "even after three days you still have to say good-bye."

Dr. O'Hanrahan looked into the fire and thought of when Beatrice and Rudolph died. How did he commemorate those three days? In a barroom, day one. Being sick, day two, and going out and buying more booze. Day three, getting drunk again and wrecking the living room, smashing photographs, those stuffy kitschy heirlooms in that precious glass-doored chest of antiques and objets d'art . . . A proud scene. O'Hanrahan asked himself without mercy: do you suppose in all that time, just in case, on that outside Zoroastrian chance they might have heard you, did you tell them how much you loved them?

"Dr. O'Hanrahan?"

He swallowed hard, and took a deep breath. "Hm?"

"I wondered if you were asleep sitting up. You just stopped talking."

"No," he said, creaking to his feet, "but sleep isn't a bad idea. Let's go drop you off at the *lokanda*. Nighty night; don't let the bedbugs bite. Because around here they'll be scorpions."

"Aw, scorpions, great," she muttered, standing, and to her surprise, finding O'Hanrahan taking her arm and leading the way. "I'm going to dream about *jinns*, thanks to today."

They came to the *lokanda* doorway beneath a large fluorescent hissing light surrounded by mosquitoes and gnats and flies. "Home sweet home," he said. "Spray yourself again, get under the net. Now that I'm on my feet, I'm not going to turn in quite yet."

Lucy stood there feeling like she should say something.

Apparently, O'Hanrahan also felt the need. "Here you are in the goddam Sudan. Sleeping on a flea-bitten mattress. Risking typhus, cholera. Sandstorms. If it all goes wrong, forgive me."

"Dr. O'Hanrahan—"

"No, I feel responsible. What if we never get to the bottom of this scroll? What if it's all a waste of time . . ." In the blue-white fluorescent light O'Hanrahan looked deathly, his expression like some oriental mask of tragedy.

"Dr. O'Hanrahan," she began, "I wouldn't miss market day in Dongola tomorrow morning for anything. I don't get to the capital of Nubia very often. I may die of something out here. But I'd rather be here than anywhere in the world." No, that wasn't all that she had meant. "With you," she added. "And don't laugh. But I think God is with us."

That gave him pause.

"I think," she went on, "Allah, or whatever His name is in these parts, is with us and wants you to decipher that scroll."

He was touched. But he prevented the sensation from penetrating deeper. "Well. I've no doubt that He must be looking out for you," he said, stepping back, "because I don't think He's very fond of me."

(We are looking out for you, Patrick. We sent you Lucy, didn't we?)

AUGUST 18TH–19TH

After the sweltering, colorful market of Dongola, it was back in the truck along a route rougher and bumpier than the day before. Lucy, sitting between Mohammed and O'Hanrahan, tried to make up for a miserable mosquito-taunted night by drifting in and out of a sweaty, dusty road-sleep. After the ordeal of the mosquitoes she then dreamed scorpions were crawling all over her, and the merest movement of a hair on her arm startled her awake, flailing pointlessly.

Nine o'clock resembled noon, which resembled three, more desert, more bumps. And what was merely sore and tender from yesterday's bumpy ride became deeply aching and excruciating today. But nothing could be done about it.

And then, to cap the day off, right in the midst of the heat, the right tire went flat, and Mohammed parked the truck on a level place near the Nile, overlooking a few *feluccas* of fishermen. One of the boys from the boats jumped into the Nile, swam over, and ran up the path to be friendly and in the way. Meanwhile, Lucy and O'Hanrahan adjourned to the shade side of the vehicle, leaning against a dusty tire, listening to the squawking chickens within the truck.

"I thought you said in Aswan there'd be no mosquitoes out here in the desert," she complained, scratching her wounds of last night.

"Of course there are mosquitoes. You were working yourself up into a snit about malaria so I told you that so you could sleep. Today I'm less charitable. Those malaria pills you're taking only cover certain strains of malaria, and if you get chloraquine-resistant malaria you get to take the Fansidar in my bag, which has the possible side effect of stopping your heart."

"Death is some kinda side effect."

"But I wouldn't waste time worrying about that here where there's cholera, bubonic plague, yellow fever, typhus, polio, rabies to consider between famines, droughts, earthquakes, floods, and one of the longest running civil wars on the planet."

The boy from the river was finally shooed away by Mohammed, so he came to take a look at Lucy and O'Hanrahan. He smiled at them and they smiled back and he asked for something but it was clear he wasn't exactly begging.

"He wants a pen," said O'Hanrahan. "Always mean to pick up a box of crayolas and some cheap Bics when I get down to this part of the world. It's apparently a real commodity."

Lucy dug into her handbag, which was becoming as dirty as a vacuum cleaner bag, and pulled out some of her perfume. "Come here," she motioned.

The boy held out his arm, thrilled to be touched by someone with unusually white skin. Lucy rubbed some perfume into his wrists and then held his hands toward his nose so he could smell. A wide smile broke out across his face, a simple, unmodern happiness. Here where there is nothing, the currency of human affairs is gesture, a small gift, a gentle competition for well-wishing between fellow travelers, the purchase of a glass of tea, a shared cigarette, all traded about with smiles and elaborate blessings that long ago passed from the West. How humankind used to be.

The boy then scampered back to the boat where his father and his friends were patiently waiting—the utter absence of work ethic, thought Lucy. And then he returned with a gourd.

"Uh-oh," said O'Hanrahan chuckling. "He's gonna give us some water. These people eat bilharzia and tapeworms for breakfast."

The boy arrived and joyously held out the gourd to Lucy.

"Fake it," O'Hanrahan said through a pantomime of grateful smiles.

Lucy spilled some down her front as she pretend-drank, taking a long, satisfied sigh afterward, then handing it to the professor.

"Thanks so much, sweetness."

"Not at all, my husband."

He emptied some into his hand and patted himself on the face, then faked a sip. "Not the kind of drink I want," he mumbled. Soon the boy was gone, leaving his untroubled smile lingering in the memory of the day.

Back on the road.

More of the same, more sand, more tepid breeze, more roasting through the windshield of the truck in the setting sun. And at last, as the desert glowed orange at 5:30 P.M., Abu Dom came into view. Lucy had assumed each one of the last five villages was the one that meant the end of the misery.

Since there was fresh water in town, they could waste the lukewarm water in their purchased bottles. Lucy stepped into the shade of the truck and poured the superfluous water over herself, washing off successive sedimentary layers of fine Sudanese dust.

Lucy: "I want a Seven-Eleven. You know the Big Gulp specials they have? You know these big, 48-ounce cups and you put the ice in and then all that Coke, a vat of Coke—"

"No baby, you know what I'd like."

"Yes, I know what you'd like," she said, her eyes possessed as she circled him. "Gettin' a little thirsty, Doc? A nice *cold beer* hit the spot about now? A nice cold Harp lager. Extra Strength, the condensation running down the side of the glass—no, a specially prepared frosted mug."

O'Hanrahan, propped against the side of the truck, closed his eyes, crossed himself. "Get away from me, Great Satan, away!"

"Or maybe a shot of Jamesons? How about that Black Bush triple-distilled?" she continued, remembering the factory tour with David back in County Antrim. "Maybe you'd break your rules and put an ice cube or two in the glass. I can hear it tinkling in the glass, the sound of whiskey and ice mingling, tinkling, tinkling . . ."

"God," he muttered, "you know you're in trouble when someone can torture you by describing the *sound* of booze." Then he laughed the next minute. "It all awaits, Sister Lucy, at the Khartoum Hilton. A western oasis of hamburgers and, yes, pizzas—"

"Jesus," she said, a knife plunged into her entrails. "Pizza—you bastard, you had to say *pizza.*"

"A juicy American hamburger, lettuce, tomato, a disk of onion . . ."

"Oh and a room with a shower."

"Air-conditioning. Blissfully subarctic hotel air-conditioning."

At the gas station in Abu Dom, Mohammed brought them the news that the regular boat was running several days late, which meant it had arrived the day before. Why didn't it merely wait a day, O'Hanrahan asked, and get back on schedule? No, he is a week behind, explained Mohammed, and the captain must rush to get back on the timetable . . . However. A trucker friend of his would take them to Khartoum, driving through the night. They'd be in Khartoum tomorrow afternoon, since the drivers preferred doing this hellish desert stretch, some hundred miles inland from the Nile, at night.

Lucy and O'Hanrahan looked at each other, at the lack of accommodations, and at a nearby charcoal spit with green chicken pieces surrounded by flies neighboring a beheaded chicken hung upside down, draining out the blood. Black children with once beautiful faces now ravaged by rashes, unhealthy teeth, and a life of uncleanliness reached out their hands and Lucy withdrew within herself.

"Let's go," she said.

One hundred miles from Khartoum:

"To be clean again!" Lucy suggested.

"A bottle, an entire bottle of, oh, what? What should it be? Bourbon, Wild Turkey, fifteen years old? Which single malt shall I begin with—Balvenie, no Clynellish. Or should I go to the Islands malts . . ."

Lucy focused dead-ahead on the road, which had nice new pavement as of the last military checkpoint. Nothing else mattered but Khartoum appearing front-and-center before the truck's hood ornament. "Khartoum has all that fancy whiskey?"

"This former bastion of English colonial empire? There are 19th-Century gentlemen's clubs in Khartoum, dear—not that they'd let you in."

"What will the Hilton be? $100 a night?"

O'Hanrahan talked as if in a trance, hypnotically. "Who cares if it's $500 a night. To touch the first world, even for a moment, is worth anything. Everything!"

Fifty miles from Khartoum:

Dr. O'Hanrahan: "I will sell myself on Khartoum's main street into white slavery for some ice cream and chocolate sauce, chocolate of any variety . . ."

Rusted signs probably erected by the British a century ago announced that Omdurman was in 10 miles, and Lucy saw the beginnings of shacks and village sprawl. Omdurman was a bustling, dirty city in its own right, though everything in this valley was termed a suburb of Khartoum, spread about the junction of the White Nile and the Blue Nile.

Their new driver, also named Mohammed, pointed out a beige mosque with a metallic dome that resembled an upside-down cocktail shaker, home of the whirling dervishes. Their driver, translated by O'Hanrahan, told of the humor of watching the novices without proper practice spin round and round until they collapsed sick from dizziness, vomiting and retching. Mohammed in recounting this laughed and laughed . . . Lucy found the concept of whirling until an otherworldly trance was achieved foreign and a little terrifying.

(Your country, My child, was settled by Quakers, Stompers, Ranters, and Shakers dancing up a storm.)

The metallic dome they passed was the tomb of al-Mahdi, O'Hanrahan explained, the Ayatollah Khomeini of his day, a messianic figure rising up to make *jihad* with the West. The British in the 1870s had acquired the Sudan by way of mercenaries; the hope was an East Africa to offset the French West, solidly British from the Suez down the Nile to Kenya and finally to Johannesburg. They would have gotten by with it if so many Christian missionaries hadn't streamed in to convert the heathen Moslem. The Islamic Sudanese rose up. They killed the governor of Sudan, General Gordon. Their hero, the Mahdi and his successor the Khalifa, fought the Egyptians and the Ottomans, Italians, Belgians, Ethiopians, the Dafur Sultanate. Brimming with affronted dignity for the rejected Queen Victoria, the British under Kitchener steamed up the Nile and made short work of the Mahdists, tearing down the Mahdi's shrine where far too many miracles and healings had already occurred.

But now the truck crossed the Nile again—Lucy had actually missed seeing it! Children swam along one of the shores, naked and uninhibited. Lucy was ready to join them.

Then at last the Hilton.

Thanking Mohammed and impatiently dispensing blessings and thanks, O'Hanrahan gathered his suitcase and satchel with the gospel, and Lucy her carpetbag and suitcase, and they intemperately ran at a trot across the air-conditioned lobby.

"Two rooms, please," said O'Hanrahan, discovering sand in the inside of his wallet. He extracted his own MasterCard and put down his passport by its side.

"Maybe I'll just order one of everything from room service," Lucy said. "I don't think I can sit down in a restaurant. I don't think I'll sit ever again. I want to soak my butt in a bathtub."

The receptionist asked for O'Hanrahan's MasterCard in proper British-accented English. Lucy blanched, realizing her "butt" comment was perfectly understood.

"It will take a minute to confirm, Mr. O'Hanrahan," said the plumblack Sudanese deskman, impeccably attired in a white suit. Nearby, to assure calm, there was a muscular, compact soldier also taking an interest in them.

Lucy examined a sample menu with color photos showing the delights of the restaurant, the buffet worthy of a sultan . . . and below that was a menu listing Western delicacies. The hamburger, the pizza, the ice cream sundae—

"I'm sorry, sir," said the receptionist, "but the card has been refused."

"But that's impossible," said the professor. "Will you try again?"

The clerk did patiently, with the same result.

"Does it say why?" O'Hanrahan asked feebly.

"Sir, we have no way of knowing."

Lucy and O'Hanrahan took a step back from the desk and conferred. Should they use Merriwether Industries' VISA card after all? It would just give their position away and they could expect more secret visitors. And this was a fairly lawless society anyway—maybe the goons-for-hire would just shoot them and take their time hunting for the scroll.

"No," conceded Lucy, "don't use the Merriwether card."

O'Hanrahan said they could use his wad of money but the Hilton meant Western rates and that would eat up his capital pretty quick.

Lucy's will was ice-cold. She knew what she must do. It was something she wouldn't have suggested anywhere under any other conditions but being stranded in Khartoum, the Sudan, in the middle of summer when she wanted a shower. "I have, Dr. O'Hanrahan . . ." She found her voice with difficulty. ". . . I have my sister's MasterCard."

O'Hanrahan was agog.

"Yes, it's true."

"You . . . you . . ."

"I got money for you back in Oxford on it, and I haven't mentioned it since."

The minaret microphone hissed into action and it was the afternoon call to prayer. O'Hanrahan continued to stare at her, emboldened by the *muezzin*'s call to face God and judgment.

"Oh, stop looking at me like that," Lucy said, walking out of the air-conditioned lobby ahead of him into the furnace. "If I'd told you sooner, you'd have used it. No, worse, stolen it from me, abandoned me, gone through all the money!"

"I am . . . am hurt, Miss Dantan, that you would think that I—"

"Save it, old man. I want a shower. I want the shower I have wanted for the last 800 miles of desert. We'll use your Sudanese pounds for a taxi and we'll go downtown, somewhere, where it's cheaper and this credit card can go further. Don't know how much credit we have left."

That "somewhere" was the more downscale Hotel El Qasr on the boulevard of the same name. A simple mansion built in the days of colonialism and now a bit seedy. The unctuous proprietor, bowing and scraping, showed them around; the rooms of the El Qasr were spacious, the ceilings tall, the windows wide open but closable with shutters, and there were ceiling fans and sinks in each room. Lucy made a grim reconnaissance of the toilet situation: there was one for each floor, sharing its room with a rusted bathtub under a dripping cold shower. The toilet stank but was better than usual, a seatless bowl with a little fountain-device to allow the Sudanese to wipe with their left hand while enjoying a plash of water upon their backside. As for the shower, there was no hot water anywhere in the Sudan, the proprietor swore.

"I don't *want* any hot water," she said tiredly.

"So you take two rooms?"

O'Hanrahan said yes, he and his daughter wanted adjoining rooms. He reached into his wallet for his rejected MasterCard again, all innocence. "You take this, sir?"

"Yes, MasterCard, yes!"

The proprietor didn't check O'Hanrahan's canceled card. They watched the proprietor take out an American Express imprinting-device and put the MasterCard upside down in it, the carboned receipt wrong way around, slide the thing feebly over the card, then fill out the bill in Arabic, non-Western numbers.

Then, at long last, under a fan, O'Hanrahan with loosened collar, shoes kicked in a corner, sank into the stiff, stuffingless mattress. It hardly mattered—this was the Ritz compared to Delgo and sleeping through the night in the front seat of Mohammed's truck. The hotel had an aged retainer, an old man content to occupy himself in the service of customers between prayertimes. He tried to communicate in some nonlanguage, and then O'Hanrahan assured him by speaking Arabic.

The retainer asked, "Would the good sir like a beer?"

Allah is most good, assented O'Hanrahan.

AUGUST 20TH

O'Hanrahan lay groaning, sweating under the light covers, still wearing his short-sleeved blue shirt, his jacket lying across a chair, his tie, his trousers, and socks on the floor where he had hurled them.

"Want me to get a priest?" Lucy asked.

"I want you to get me a drink," he moaned.

"That's a no-no according to my guidebook," she said authoritatively. "You see, alcohol depletes the body's already-precious water supply . . ."

"Damn *foul*."

"Don't be too hard on yourself, sir—"

"I said *foul* not 'fool.' The bean thing I had last night with gobbets of unidentifiable flesh. Why aren't you dying?"

"Don't know. I had diarrhea all through the first world. Now that I'm here I'm fine."

"It's all that bran dust and yogurt you eat. Your body wouldn't recognize real food. Luce, please, go to a pharmacy and say the word *ishail*."

Lucy practiced the word for diarrhea two or three times until he gave her the nod. She whispered, "Sure it's not dysentery, sir? Is there blood in your . . . in your stool?"

"My stool's none of your business! And get me a *Herald Tribune*!"

Lucy gave him a last concerned look. She noticed beside him on the bed was the scrollcase and the *Gospel of Matthias*. He sure wasn't letting it get too far away from him.

This was Lucy's third or fourth venture unaccompanied out on the street in a Moslem country—maybe the Sudan would be better than Cairo and Aswan. She stepped from the Hotel El Qasr and into the sun of the street, calmly walking with the directions the hotelman had given her to a pharmacy two blocks away. The fine dust stirred by the traffic of military transport vehicles on the crumbling city streets lingered in the air and she breathed it, tasting the ashen, chalky taste.

Two teenage Arab boys in Western jeans sustaining a hum of constant laughter followed behind and made kissing noises.

"How are you?" cried the boys. "What's your name?" they offered after that, the official conversation-starter of the Nile.

Lucy found a newsstand and bought a paper, then discovered the pharmacy on the corner as promised. Soaps, razors, drinking water, diapers—an array of products stacked and crammed, lining the walls of the pharmacy. None of the veiled women spoke a word of English.

"Ishail," she tried, in every accent and emphasis.

The women fetched a dapper Arab man in a white coat, with trimmed beard and large, knowing brown eyes. A handsome race, Lucy admitted.

"May I be of assistance?" he asked. Educated in the United States, he happily supplied her with Nile-strength diarrhea medicine and two bottles of drinking water. It cost 50 cents, as Lucy converted in her head. While she was in the store one of the veiled women had the doctor ask if she needed a place to stay for the night. Lucy said no thank you, regretful that she wasn't free to take up the invitation. What whisperings behind the veil, what mysteries behind the *mashrabiyya* in the women's quarters would be revealed to her? The veiled women retreated and Lucy went back into the street. We in the West hate the unknown, imprecision, anything that deprives us of fact, thought Lucy, but the Islamic world cultivates mystery, suspends veils, whispers secrets too forbidden to speak of further . . .

"You need a guide?" asked a dirty Sudanese boy with a wide smile.

"No thank you."

"You need place to sleep?"

Another scrambled to her side, "You American?"

The two smooching Arab boys turned the corner and delightedly approached her again: "What's your name?"

Back in O'Hanrahan's room, as she dabbed him with a cold towel:

"A single woman on these streets is public property," she said, nearly laughing. "I don't know what was worse, the flies or the boys."

O'Hanrahan looked at her hand. "They didn't see a wedding ring, so you were fair game."

Lucy had forgotten to wear today a cheap ring purchased for that purpose in Cairo. She had hoped that her conservative dress, long skirt, long sleeves, scarf over the head with her hair pulled back—which she cursed as supremely unflattering—and dark stockings would meet the local requirements for modesty. She tossed O'Hanrahan the *International Herald Tribune* of a day ago. He rummaged through it, ignoring the headlines.

"We at war yet?" asked Lucy.

"I bet your parents must be fit to be tied," he imagined.

"Fortunately, I called the department collect and had the department secretary call my parents. I'm not telling them I'm in Africa; they can just assume I'm still in Jerusalem. My mom objected to *Italy* as too dangerous."

O'Hanrahan didn't respond, finding what he was looking for. "Yep. Yep, here it is . . ."

A review, glowing, worshipful, of Philip Beaufoix's latest work, *Silent Partner: The Contribution of Egypt to the Formation of Christianity.* 625 pages . . . and here was a black-and-white photo of the bastard, smiling knowingly in pressed black monastic wear. Since when does a Dominican wear black? wondered O'Hanrahan. "Bet that photo got touched up with an airbrush the size of a Douglas fir," he mumbled. And what shill, what stooge coughed up this puff-job of a review? When O'Hanrahan saw the name, he groaned. The review written by Sr. Marie-Berthe Comeaux, special to the *Herald Tribune.*

"See?" he snapped. "The Acolytes all stick together."

Lucy foraged for something positive. "Yes, and they'll rave over you too when you publish your book on the *Gospel of Matthias.* With a footnote," she joked, hoping it was a joke, "by Lucy Dantan."

"I may let you dot the *i*'s." He struggled to sit up, ready for action. Upon sitting up straight, his head swam and he fell back onto the pillow.

"You're not going anywhere," said Lucy maternally. "Actually, you probably need to go ahead and be sick."

"I will be sick if I eat any more of . . ." He trailed off, referring to what the proprietor's wife had brought him as a cure-all, *zabadi,* a mildly spiced yogurt dish. Lucy looked at it, oleaginous and strong-smelling. She reflected on some of their most preposterously unclean meals at the Egyptian Orthodox monasteries near Cairo—unpasteurized goat cheese, hard bread where one shook the small bugs free, treacle and wild onion sprigs for flavor. Then the grilled meats in Degoma they could not politely refuse.

"You'd make a good nurse," he said quietly.

"As a little girl I always wanted to be one," she said. "Being in such a needy country makes me want to, you know, do something for them."

"Yeah, that's right," O'Hanrahan chuckled. "The ol' nun routine. You told me in Ireland you were going to be a nun."

"And you told me not to be one."

O'Hanrahan recanted. "I was just being dismissive. If it appeals to you, do it. Hell, I wish I'd stayed a Jesuit in some ways. Some people aren't cut out for Father-Knows-Best, all that family crap. The Middle Ages knew this, they provided for people like us, people who longed to study or do something more meaningful than be a merchant or milk the cow."

Lucy became vagarious. Do you realize, she told herself, this is the first time in my life anyone I respected ever stuck up for my childhood plan of wanting to be a nun? Was anyone aware of the years of ridicule and deprecation it had automatically received, and here was her idol, Patrick O'Hanrahan, saying go for it, Sister Lucy.

Her heart sank. She'd forgotten. She was probably pregnant.

"I wanted to do something good with my life too," O'Hanrahan rambled, "when I was your age. There was no Peace Corps back then for my generation. I went to the Korean War as a chaplain—did I ever tell you that?"

"Yes, you told me."

He patted the *Herald Tribune* lying beside him. "Read me something."

Lucy opted, after the *Herald Tribune* was plundered, for a pamphlet she'd picked up in Cairo concerning the Coptic saints. She thought O'Hanrahan would be amused. She read portentously, "Our next selection is from this fine work of literature and, no doubt, thoroughly factual history *The Glorious Holy Saints and Martyrs of the Copts*. The Miracle of St. Bishoi," she announced.

O'Hanrahan just made a low groaning sound.

"Sitt Bishoi after a great fast and show of piety received a rare and precious vision from Our Lord. The Lord appeared to him upon the Cross, then descended from the Cross borne by angels, blood streaming from his hands and feet. Bishoi was allowed to contemplate the agony of the festering, infected wounds of the stigmata . . ."

"This better improve."

Lucy enjoyed herself. *"Sitt Bishoi was allowed to wash the feet of the Savior, and lovingly, with his own tears and perfumed water, cleaned the pus-*

filled wounds, washed the dirt and dung from the Savior's feet, until the water
was brown with dirt and spilt blood. Then as a kindness from our Lord, he bade
Bishoi to drink this heavenly broth, which Bishoi did gladly."

O'Hanrahan felt the gorge in his throat rise, and rolled off the bed
and hurried to the toilet. Lucy put her hand to her mouth, horrified
but helplessly laughing at the vision of him scurrying in his boxer
shorts and black socks pulled up to his knees.

"Oh, God, I'm sorry, sir!"

She winced as he retched in the other room.

"I was just . . . just getting you back for all those stories in Italy."

Lucy crept from the room before Dr. O'Hanrahan could avenge
himself!

AUGUST 21ST

Lucy steadied O'Hanrahan on the stairs from the hotel leading down
to the street. Full of medicine, aspirin, and, as she suspected, a dose
of Percodan, he was determined to flag a taxi and get to the National
Library. The *Gospel of Matthias* was in his satchel.

"You were saying about al-Hakim?" she prompted, once in the taxi,
having requested a lewd Sudanese story.

"Al-Hakim?" the professor said, brightening. "I thought I gave you
the goods in Cairo on this guy."

"You started, but something came up."

"Depending on the accent his name means 'a just ruler,' which
he was anything but. Like me he was sort of a night-person. In the
1000s as the Fatimid caliph of Cairo he outlawed daytime and everyone
had to creep about at night—you would be put to death by his secret
police if you went out in the day. He hated women, and outlawed them
too."

"How did the chores get done?"

"They didn't. The empire went to hell, he burned cities on a whim
like Nero, decapitated holy men without a second thought. He was
Saddam Hussein meets Caligula meets Herod the Great. He only liked
his pet mule, named Moon, *Qamar.* Indeed, if I had time I'd research
to see if the notion of 'lunacy' took its cue from his moon-obsession.
And Hakim adored his Sudanese slave, the result of an intensive search
in these climes for a very specific quantification of length. . ."

"You don't have to elaborate, sir."

"His slave Masoud was found to have the largest member of any
black man alive. I'm sure given the proclivities of the Arabs Masoud
was discovered after a not entirely joyless search. Not unlike the survey
of Africa made by Tiberius for the same reason, his 'collection' at
Capri."

Lucy added, "Lampridius writes that Elagabalus Caesar sent out emissaries to Africa for the same purpose."

O'Hanrahan was momentarily silenced. "Lucille! Is this what you have done with your learning, read Late Empire filth like Lampridius?"

She put her head back and laughed. "That's the only reason *anyone* does Classics, sir—the filth."

"I'm going to have to regard you in an entirely different light. What was all that blushing earlier in our acquaintance?"

"You were saying, sir."

"Masoud had this tremendous organ that when at last aroused was used to mete out justice—that's m-e-t-e, Sister Lucy." Lucy hid her face in her hands, laughing. "Hakim would stand on the offending man's head as the accused was sodomized. You can see why behavior of this sort convinced a number of holy men he was a messenger of Allah."

"I beg your pardon?"

"You've heard of the Druse Militia in Lebanon? The Druse who live in northern Israel and Syria? That's the source of their Islam-based religion, that one day, al-Hakim, who rode off on his mule not to be seen again, was the Last Manifestation of God and will come back to see who has doubted and who has believed."

Now Lucy was speechless. "What—you—Syria really wants these Druse people in the army?"

"Oh, they're very loyal. When the Golan Heights became Israeli property they stopped fighting for the Syrians and took up arms for the Israelis. They swear a deep oath of allegiance to whatever country they find themselves in. It's probably why they're still around."

O'Hanrahan winced as the cab driver peeled an onion while waiting in traffic. The professor continued:

"Al-Hakim was an iconoclast's iconoclast. He was the only human crazy enough to go to Mekkah and smash the *Masjidu al-Haram*, the Mosque of the Black Rock. There are all kinds of apocryphal tales about fragments of this holy stone making their way to Europe to be used as philosopher's stones in Kabbalah and—well, you can imagine. Then Hakim went to Jerusalem and smashed the Holy Sepulcher. Only one true fragment of the original slab Jesus lay upon remains, thanks to that. He persecuted his own people but had especial hatred for Christians and Jews; he was surely the most fearsome of persecutors. If it hadn't been for him, one wonders if St. Bernard would have had such good material for whipping up a crusade."

"I don't feel so bad for the Crusades now that you've told me about this guy. How could he be championed as a messenger of God?"

"It's in Islamic Law that insane people are not to be held accountable for sins and heresies, indeed, they are considered inspired beings. Isaiah, Jeremiah, Ezekiel, John the Baptist, and maybe Jesus as well:

all crazy to outward appearances. Mohammed the Prophet and his headaches, going into trances and spewing poetry. Think of medieval saints and their masochism and insane apocalyptic ramblings—religion has more than a toe in the water with insanity."

O'Hanrahan said the Moslem world today was not very different. "The mob rises up in the street for a butcher like Saddam Hussein and we in the West can't figure out why. They'll never understand the Eastern mind, because we don't understand the ancient mind."

The taxi cab driver spoke: "Yes, Saddam Hussein!"

Both O'Hanrahan and Lucy froze, having assumed the driver only spoke Arabic. "You speak English, sir?" said O'Hanrahan after a moment.

"Oh yes!" the rotund driver said proudly, chomping now on a leek.

Lucy leaned back having detected the pungent oniony smell. She realized their discussion about Sudanese black men imported for their propensities had been attended.

"Saddam Hussein, a great man, a very very great man!"

"You think," said O'Hanrahan, "that he perhaps is the Mahdi?"

"A very great man," he repeated. "Perhaps the Mahdi, yes."

Hmm, thought O'Hanrahan, I don't want to be responsible for starting up *that* kind of idea!

"You want to go to Mahdi Tomb?" he asked quickly, thinking of the money to haul them back across the two Niles and north to Omdurman. "See whirling dervish?"

O'Hanrahan declined, asking, "Sir, why do you eat that leek? Is it very tasty?"

"No," he said, factually, "it is not for to eat good." He patted his perfectly spherical belly. "It has no ... what you say?" He said the Arabic phrase for "no calories" and after some Arabic explanation, O'Hanrahan communicated this diet to Lucy. The driver, nearly swerving into a curb, held up a small bag of spring onions. "Thees is no calories too, yes?" He bit down happily into the onions and continued eating right up to the green ends.

O'Hanrahan grimaced, rediscovering his nausea.

"So far I lose lots and lots of weight, very much weight." He patted his belly again. "For my young wife, yes?"

O'Hanrahan smiled. "You have more than one?"

"Oh yes, I have three, and the new one very very young."

Lucy considered the prospect of being married off as this man's third wife. As O'Hanrahan and she had discussed, this was the Moslem solution to divorce and broken families. You could have up to four wives if you could afford it but you must treat them all equally, buying the recently displaced wife a home. O'Hanrahan had said there are many songs and tales of wives luring young women into shops for their husbands to marry, so they might get an apartment and happily pass on their wifely duties to a younger woman. Once the older, first wife was in her own home and unobserved, then she too could play the field. A conservative society, yes, but not at all a sex-hating, puritan one.

Lucy snapped to attention when a leek, half-chewed, was pointed toward her face by the driver. "You want?"

"*La, shukran,*" she said, having mastered no-thank-you.

"She is very very young your wife," said the driver.

"She is my daughter," O'Hanrahan answered, in a mood to vary the charade.

"Does she have a husband? I have five sons!"

Lucy said *la shukran* again, imagining his five handsome devils would one day expand to sphericality like their father.

O'Hanrahan and Lucy got out at the university and the professor paid the driver, who said he would just as soon wait for them to finish and drive them back.

"But we may be hours, sir," O'Hanrahan said.

The driver shrugged. A sure fare in two hours was better than wasting gas, driving aimlessly.

Waiting, as expected, was Dr. Ibrahim Mehmet, perhaps the last of the internationally respected Sudanese philologists, former member of the Acolyte brotherhood before transferring from Cambridge to Khartoum University in an effort to save the institution from the *sharia* and the tide of Islamic fanaticism replacing independent thought in his homeland.

What did poor 70-year-old Dr. Mehmet make of these years?

Having been raised with tales of his grandfather fighting with the Mahdi, having seen the colonial powers leave in 1952, having danced and celebrated independence only to watch his country deconstruct into civil war, only to watch the elected leaders eliminated by military dictators with phony medals down their chests. There was hope in the '70s, briefly, with one of these generals, Jafaar Nimieri, Sudan's Nasser. There was flirtation with investment and massive irrigation, land reform and progress, but this, like all things in this doomed African century, failed, became an embarrassment, made his country a synonym for hopeless tinpot African backwater . . . and so rose the Moslems to impose Islamic law on the Christians and tribal peoples to the south, having exhausted all other practical notions. O'Hanrahan empathized with Dr. Mehmet: to have spanned that first taste of independence, to have taught and dwelt in the first world and to have brought back those hopes for his reborn country, only to see the dark ages reenacted—the old 7th-Century battle cries, defeat of the infidel! Then the famines and ever-lengthening war, so much death.

O'Hanrahan looked into his old acquaintance's eyes and saw the worry, the lines on a face that had borne the sorrows of the continent. They embraced and exchanged Arabic blessings:

"As-salaamu 'alekum," said O'Hanrahan, concluding the cascade of well-wishing.

"Wa 'alekum as-salaam wa rahmatu 'llahi," said Dr. Mehmet, kissing O'Hanrahan's right hand, moved to see him. And after Lucy was introduced and praised and blessed, the learned Moslem guided them to his office. Dr. Mehmet's black skin was ashen and his gaunt face very creased; his eyes were yellowed and weak. The Sudanese man walked with great dignity with a walking stick, but very slowly.

"I have a strange version of Meroitic for you to look at," said O'Hanrahan walking beside him, keeping Dr. Mehmet's pace.

"All versions of that language are strange," he sighed. "In my youth I promised myself to decipher its mysteries, but this Allah has not allowed. *Walk not proudly on the ground,* says the Quran, *truly thou canst by no means cleave the earth."*

O'Hanrahan smiled. But what old man who has given his life to the holy books does not suspect he will one day rouse the attention of God?

"Meroitic is very popular, no?" asked Dr. Mehmet.

Both Lucy and O'Hanrahan faltered in step. O'Hanrahan asked feebly, "Someone else, Ibrahim, has made inquiries?"

"Why, yes. Two days ago. An orthodox monk was referred to me from the National Museum. Something about a Christian gospel in Meroitic. It is surely the only one—what a precious artifact! You yourself, my friend, should attempt to find such a thing!"

The taxi driver returned Lucy and O'Hanrahan to their block. O'Hanrahan had left some of the *Gospel of Matthias* photographs with Dr. Mehmet though he didn't expect any miracles. How did that rascal Rabbi Rosen translate this thing so easily? And how did this damn Orthodox monk stay a step ahead of them?

Lucy and the professor strolled down the sidewalk, seeing the hotel ahead. Ragged children cavorted upon El Qasr Boulevard, kicking a deflated soccer ball with the lines worn off it, all of Khartoum their soccer pitch. O'Hanrahan saw a tobacconist shop that beckoned to him: ah, cigars from Cuba, one of their allies. Lucy longed for her hotel room, washing her face, scrubbing away the dirt, lying in her underwear under the ceiling fan.

"Patrick O'Hanrahan?"

Lucy looked up to see the short, sturdy dark Arab policeman in the white uniform who had observed them at the Hilton. Behind him were two tall, indifferent African soldiers, submachine guns dangling from their belts, waiting at the door of the hotel.

"May I help you?" asked O'Hanrahan, his expression darkened by the prospect of dealing with the authorities.

"Coom eenside to de hotel wi' me," the officer said in a beautiful African-lilted English, which was spoken in Khartoum by most educated Sudanese, a vestige of colonialism. "I am Major Mohammed Ali Nessim of Internal Security."

Inside the lobby the hotelkeeper and his wife met him with a look of concern. "We are sorry, Mr. O'Hanrahan," said the proprietor, "but there is a problem with the credit card, yes?"

The gig is up, thought Lucy.

"Nonsense," bluffed O'Hanrahan, elaborating that his MasterCard had been accepted everywhere they had gone.

"Excuse me, sir," said the officer, "but alas eet ees not so. I was present at de Hilton Hotel and I was to see dat de card was no good for you there."

Lucy attempted a rescue: "Well, no matter. I have a credit card, sir. Father dearest," she directed at O'Hanrahan for authenticity. Lucy fished through her handbag and handed the proprietor her sister's MasterCard.

"You mus' coom wi' me, sir, I am so sorry to say."

"But if my daughter's card is good, which it is, why is there a problem, sir? A simple mistake, after all . . ."

The compact man was implacable, offering justification after justification. O'Hanrahan's heart sank, realizing this trifling situation was merely a pretext for an arrest, which meant the officer could revel in reporting a Western criminal to his superiors, and, of course, bribery for all around. No doubt they had been stalking him since the folly at the Hilton, the lone Americans in town this summer, imagining him made of money, scouting for his first infraction.

"Is there some way," began O'Hanrahan, "that this entire episode can go away?"

"Many serious charges we have, sir. You have in your room an empty bottle of alcohol, no?"

The proprietor, whose retainer had procured beer for O'Hanrahan, swept in with rabid denunciations of demon alcohol, the wisdom of the Prophet in banning it forever, the glory of the government in enforcing the prohibition, so vigilant and just the government!

The officer brushed the hotelkeeper aside. "I theenk also that de woman here is not at all your daughter, sir."

O'Hanrahan kept his calm. His calm would mean the difference between a small *baksheesh* bribe or a major investment to scrape away the attentions of the Islamic authorities. "My stepdaughter, Major Nessim. That is why our last names are different. I accompany her so she can see your marvelous country. She is a student of Islam."

This gave the officer pause. Lucy smiled feebly, panicked that something Islamic would be asked of her. Suddenly, the hotelkeeper's wife stood at the telephone desk and said something in Arabic—to the effect, Lucy realized, that her sister's card had been rejected too.

Now they were broke.

"I theenk it is best dat you coom now to de station, sir."

O'Hanrahan's eyes narrowed, his shrewdness surfacing. "After a phone call, I would be glad to accompany you, Officer." He turned to the hotelkeeper and said, "My friend, you shall not be reimbursed for your loss if I cannot secure new finances. A phone call will have my money wired here by tomorrow and you will be paid. Do I seem like a criminal to you?"

The man shook his head, no happier about the attention of the police in his hotel than O'Hanrahan. "A local call?"

"Yes, to the U.S. Embassy."

The hotelkeeper looked at Lucy and O'Hanrahan, considering . . .

"Or perhaps," O'Hanrahan whispered with a tense smile, "I should tell the officer about your refrigerator and its wondrous collection of libations, hm?"

The proprietor relented with a bow. The wife dialed the number, easily found in the Khartoum phone book. Meanwhile, O'Hanrahan casually placed his satchel in Lucy's hands; she now was entrusted with hiding the *Gospel of Matthias*.

O'Hanrahan's call was put through to the U.S. Embassy. "Hello, connect me to In-Country Emergencies, please."

AUGUST 22ND–23RD

Colonel Westin sucked in air through his teeth, shaking his head in patronizing disappointment. "Patrick, Patrick," he said. "May I call you Patrick?"

O'Hanrahan begrudged to his rescuer, "If you like."

"We have a discretionary fund through the State Department, as you might imagine, for unexpected materiel, emergencies of nationals in-country, and miscellaneous actualities, uh, contingency-wise."

The professor tried to smile. He diverted himself by looking at the grinning, affable portrait of George Bush in this U.S. Embassy office. Westin had flown down from Jerusalem to bail him out, and clear up any red tape and difficulties—which seemed way beyond the call of duty. No one was more shocked than O'Hanrahan to see Colonel Westin within 24 hours of this trumped-up interrogation in Khartoum. Money was distributed, apparently, and the matter disappeared. O'Hanrahan had been released by the police but he had had to surrender his and Lucy's passports, so they couldn't leave Khartoum.

"What about our passports, Colonel?"

"We have them," he said helpfully. "An assistant is getting them stamped with an Ethiopian visa."

"Ethiopia?"

"As I was saying about our discretionary fund, Patrick, we have a bit of petty cash to work with, and we've been able to book you and Miss Dantan on a local flight to Addis Ababa in Ethiopia. We'd send you to Cairo but Egypt and the Sudan seem to be about to engage in hostilities. Besides, Addis is closer and there are connecting flights to the United States. A colleague of mine in Addis will meet Miss Dantan and provide her with a ticket on Ethiopia Air to Chicago, back home, safe and sound." The colonel paused, expecting to hear objections. "That's all right with you?"

"Perhaps," said O'Hanrahan, forgetting to prop up the love-nest charade so dear to the colonel. "And as for me?"

Colonel Westin stood and grabbed a desk chair and put one highly polished boot on the chair, leaning forward on his knee. "I've also got a ticket to Addis for you, Patrick, but first I want some straight talk."

"Of course," said O'Hanrahan, priming himself to invent a new round of lies.

"You met with a Mohammed Baqir al-Taki, did you not?"

O'Hanrahan impulsively decided to tell the truth here, however. "Yes, he offered me a position at Teheran University. You had me followed while I was in Jerusalem, Colonel?" O'Hanrahan recalled the black Mercedes and the red Golf. It was also clear to O'Hanrahan that Colonel Westin was in reality surprised about the job offer in Teheran.

"No Patrick, I assure you, this didn't find us in a state of nonexpectation. Did you know Baqir was among the students who were instrumental in the taking of the American hostages in 1979?"

O'Hanrahan wasn't surprised, but feigned innocence.

Colonel Westin: "Was that the whole purpose in your contact?"

"I know, Colonel, a great deal about Islamic texts. They were offering a position to teach about Christianity in Teheran, as Jesus is reckoned the Fifth Prophet of Islam. For an old man, retired, such excitement is very tempting. As a master there I would have my meals and lodging provided, and there was talk of a young wife."

"You old dog, you." The colonel slapped his knee. "You dog!"

O'Hanrahan smiled wanly.

"Hell, Pops, you just don't run out of steam! You're getting more than I am, that is for damn sure." He leaned in: "What's your secret?" Not waiting for an answer, he asked, "You'll consider taking it, of course?"

O'Hanrahan had yet to see Colonel Westin's motivation, so he answered cautiously. "Well, I'm worried about the danger. I know the Iranians want a better relationship with the West but the mullahs are still in power and I'm not exactly confident. Besides, I must finish the project I'm working on."

"The U.S. government, Patrick," said the colonel in a whisper, "wants you to take this position."

Now O'Hanrahan understood. "And spy for the U.S.?"

Colonel Westin joined the fingertips of his hands daintily. "Ssssh, ssssh, we don't know if the Soviets have bugged this place but use of the word 'spy' is problematic connotations-wise. We just need an intelligent man's report now and then."

You know, this deal didn't exactly repulse O'Hanrahan.

"The tickets," Colonel Westin said, reaching into a jacket pocket and producing two. "These are for tomorrow, Patrick."

O'Hanrahan was giddy. Life was perversely presenting him with both the *Gospel of Matthias* and "Q" and don't forget the *harim!*

(Aren't you forgetting someone?)

The colonel produced a manila envelope with 400 Sudanese pounds. "This should square all hotel debts and provide a bit of food money. The less time spent here the better, professor. A lot of curious people from known paraterrorist and contraversion units seem to find you out. Nor do I wish one American citizen to be in harm's way with the crisis in Kuwait building. We have reports that missiles are being shipped in from Iraq for the purposes of shelling the Aswan Dam."

"Jesus," muttered O'Hanrahan, inwardly cursing the stupidity of the Sudanese government.

"I will personally see to it, Patrick," Colonel Westin was saying, "that you find yourself on the flight to Ethiopia tomorrow morning. We'll send a hired car for you and Miss Dantan tomorrow at six A.M., which will give you plenty of time to make your flight. Oh, there is a small bit of bureaucratic wrangling we were not able to help you with. These exit visas need a stamp from the Ministry of Transportation. Not even the U.S. government can help you there."

Colonel Westin explained that the Ministry of Transportation was open until six P.M. so he and Miss Dantan had better get a move on. The colonel concluded with a bemused laugh, "So they're gonna fix you up with a regular harem, huh? You old devil."

(We would call that a fair characterization.)

An embassy car dropped off O'Hanrahan on El Qasr Boulevard a half-block from his hotel. As he walked by the merchants and the surplus of children in the street this afternoon, he felt warmly toward them in their shambles of a country. Such good-natured people. Such a stupid government. Per capita income of $325 a year. Designated a *fifth*-world country by the U.N., incapable of subsistence. In the ravaged south, there is one doctor per 90,000 people. Millions died in the 1985 famine; they say 27 million will be affected by the next. Meanwhile the Sudan goes $10 billion in debt so they can buy arms to put down the 21-year-old civil war against the Christians and tribal Sudanese who have watched their country become fanatically Islamic, militaristic, and inconceivably corrupt. It figures in the coming big blowout they'd back Saddam Hussein, who was mounting an effort to get himself shot off the map.

Ah, next to his hotel was the tobacco shop he had admired the wares of two days ago.

O'Hanrahan stepped inside to a world of aromatic tobaccos, for pipe and hookah, and indeed, the prize was there: Cuban cigars . . .

"You like, sir?" asked the proprietor of the shop. A white foreigner was rare enough to attract his whole family, who lingered in a beaded doorway to observe this transaction.

O'Hanrahan lifted a Dom Perignon under his nose and inhaled—oh, precious incense! The tobacconist, short of customers this season, could barely contain himself and his greed, imagining the unloading of his expensive stock. O'Hanrahan in his marketplace play of interest and disinterest glimpsed out the window to the street. He saw Clem Underwood walking by the store outside.

"Excuse me!" he said in a rush, bolting for the door.

Underwood, holding a small gym bag, nonchalantly stood at the curbside, looked left then right—not seeing O'Hanrahan—and proceeded to step into the street, searching for a taxicab. O'Hanrahan was upon him the moment before he turned, babbling, "Oh, Mr. O'Hanrahan, hello there—"

O'Hanrahan snatched the gym bag from his hand.

"No!" Underwood clutched the gym bag and at one point was being led by it; it resembled a man leading his dog around him in a circle, the dog's teeth firmly attached to a rag.

"Whadya got here, Mr. Underwood?" panted O'Hanrahan, getting red in the face.

"Just some stuff . . ."

O'Hanrahan broke free and to the amusement of everyone on the street, made his way to the alley between the tobacco shop and a deserted travel agency.

"You no buy cigar?" cried the dispirited tobacconist, running from his store.

Underwood, surrendering before O'Hanrahan's bulk, stood aside glumly as O'Hanrahan opened the gym bag in the alley. Inside, as

O'Hanrahan was relieved to find, was his decoy, the 14th-Century *Contendings of St. Andrew.*

"I'll give you some money for it," said Underwood sheepishly.

O'Hanrahan grabbed Underwood by the lapels of his ill-fitting suit and pressed him against the wall: "*Why* did you steal my scroll?"

"Don't hurt me!"

Recognizing a weakling, O'Hanrahan shook him an extra time and donned his fiercest madman's expression hoping to terrify Underwood, rather enjoying his own performance. "You're from Merriwether Industries, right?"

Underwood's thick round glasses fell from his face. "Yeah, sort of . . ."

"What does a multinational conglomerate want with my ancient scroll?"

O'Hanrahan relinquished his grip, but kept one hand on Underwood's lapel. "You see, Mr. O'Hanrahan, my client wants it—"

"*Who?*"

Underwood seemed unwilling, but O'Hanrahan raised an eyebrow in ire and Underwood crumbled: "Charles Merriwether, Chairman of the Board."

O'Hanrahan had learned from Mustafa al-Waswasah back in East Jerusalem that Chester Merriwether II, the industrialist's father, formerly owned the *Gospel of Matthias,* having acquired it shadily after World War Two. "All right, you tell me, Clem, why does Charles Merriwether wish to get my scroll back in the family?"

"He's going to give it to a friend."

"What friend?" Underwood didn't know and O'Hanrahan wouldn't accept that he didn't know, so Underwood received another bone-disconnecting shake from O'Hanrahan. No, really! cried Underwood. He didn't tell me who he wanted it for! O'Hanrahan threatened, deviously, to stomp on Underwood's glasses, then tear out by the roots his dwindling supply of hair. Underwood flailed and hit O'Hanrahan in the face—by accident probably—with his sharp black ring.

"Oops," said Underwood, immediately horrified of the consequences.

"Why, you little . . ." O'Hanrahan lifted Underwood off the ground: "What friend—tell me!"

Underwood moaned, "Awww, c'mon. He's not gonna tell someone like me."

O'Hanrahan relented.

The professor: "What do you think the Sudanese authorities will say about your little theft?" He belatedly thought of Lucy. "You didn't harm my assistant Miss Dantan in any way, did you?"

No, never! he pleaded.

O'Hanrahan turned to the entrance of their alley to see a number of curious African and Arab faces staring intently. The next moment the crowd parted and the same compact Sudanese soldier appeared. Major Nessim. Two soldiers with submachine guns lurked behind him. "Mr. O'Hanrahan," he said, "you seem too very much to find trooble."

"This man is a thief!" O'Hanrahan declared.

Underwood straightened out his crumpled suit and immediately rearranged his hair to its most propitious pattern.

"My stepdaughter," O'Hanrahan asserted, "will be more than cooperative in testifying for the police that this man is a thief, Major. He broke into my room and stole this ... this document that I have brought to Khartoum to use in my studies."

The Sudanese officer was impassive. O'Hanrahan couldn't detect a flicker of interest or predisposition behind his eyes. After a moment the major ordered his men to lead Mr. Underwood away, and suggested that O'Hanrahan return to the El Qasr Hotel and stay there until he arrived for further questioning.

Lucy was waiting for him in the hallway outside his room. "Dr. O'Hanrahan!" she smiled. "Good news, in a way." She started right in, pleased that she had withstood some excitement while he was gone. "I saw Clem Underwood from my balcony out on the street and I ran to your room and fixed it so the decoy gospel was hidden under your bed."

O'Hanrahan was out of breath from his adventures in the alley and from walking up the stairs. "Good girl." O'Hanrahan held up the inconspicuous cardboard tube that held the *Contendings of St. Andrew.* "As you see, Mr. Underwood ran afoul of me in a nearby alley and he is now in the hands of the police. Now Lucy, where's the real *Gospel of Matthias?*"

"I was afraid to keep it in my room. I mean, I couldn't tell if all this police attention you've been getting is part of a big scam to arrest you, and then search our rooms thoroughly."

O'Hanrahan patted her on the shoulders. "You're learning to outthink these people, good for you. Now where is it?"

Lucy whispered, "In the maid's closet down the hall, behind a box of diapers and some cleaning fluids."

O'Hanrahan wished to check on it. They walked to the end of the hall. Their nostrils registered the bathroom mildew and the reeking toilet chamber ahead. Beside these fixtures was a little room for the maid's supplies. Lucy turned the handle on the door, but it was locked. She panicked for an instant. "The maid must have locked it," she said.

O'Hanrahan went down to the desk. The hotelkeeper and his wife were suspicious and resentful of O'Hanrahan since he had caused the police appearance at their little establishment earlier. Where is your maid? O'Hanrahan asked. She may be finished with her work and she may have gone home, the proprietor's wife said. O'Hanrahan ascended the stairs again.

"I found her!" said Lucy, referring to a short, stooped woman who vainly lifted a moth-eaten veil before her aged face, her toothless mouth, when O'Hanrahan approached. She mumbled in Arabic.

O'Hanrahan listened, deciphering with difficulty. *"La la,"* he assured her in Arabic, we don't think you've stolen something from our rooms. May we see your supply closet?

They followed this poor woman down the hall, with O'Hanrahan wondering how a woman so old and slow managed any amount of work. As they approached the stench of the toilet chamber, he decided that maybe she didn't manage very much work after all. She turned and examined them both, remembered her veil and raised it coquettishly, then turned her key in the closet door.

Lucy stepped around her, as O'Hanrahan apologized for their use of the woman's domain. Lucy moved aside the cleanser and some towels . . .

"It's not here," she said bloodlessly.

O'Hanrahan anxiously asked the woman if she had seen a small leather case, a foot-and-a-half long. No, she shook her head. O'Hanrahan wondered if she was after money . . . she didn't seem capable of such a complicated maneuver. "Fatima!" she called out presently.

Lucy didn't meet O'Hanrahan's glance.

An insolent twenty-year-old woman appeared in more modern attire, a longish black dress, no veil. She met the older woman's eyes with annoyance. Must be mother-daughter, thought Lucy. The women exchanged irate Arabic with one another and wearily the younger woman led O'Hanrahan, Lucy, and the maid to a trash bag.

"It's in there?" O'Hanrahan asked in horror, imagining how a delay of a few minutes might have seen this bag on its way to the incinerator.

The young woman, while berating her mother, opened the garbage bag and O'Hanrahan, spotting the leather tube, reached through wet rags and food scraps and removed the scrollcase.

"Thank God," breathed Lucy.

The older woman harangued her daughter. The daughter must have assumed the foreign object in the closet was one of her mother's many affronts.

Back in O'Hanrahan's room, the professor handed Lucy the cardboard tube while he wiped off the scrollcase. Then he spread out the *Gospel of Matthias* upon the bed, still in its clear-plastic airtight envelope, to see if it was damaged. Their whole Khartoum mission had gone off the rails with this arrest and now their hasty departure the next day. It would be good to see Ethiopia again—possibly the only country on earth in worse shape than the Sudan, he thought grimly. But they have a good library too—

There was a knock on the door.

The hotelkeeper cried out that it was he, with some new towels.

Lucy opened the door. Behind the hotelkeeper was Major Nessim in his immaculate white uniform and his two submachine gun–toting soldiers. Bringing up the rear was Clem Underwood, who craned to look into the room. "Miss Dantan," he nodded, filing past her.

O'Hanrahan drily, "Can I help you?"

The hotelkeeper scampered away, wanting to be out of gunfire range, no doubt. Major Nessim looked to Underwood. Underwood looked at O'Hanrahan, and said, "I think we'd better take that scroll there, Patrick."

Having scammed bribe money from O'Hanrahan, then the U.S. government, reasoned O'Hanrahan, our Major Nessim has figured out that Underwood is attached to some mighty big purse strings too. O'Hanrahan wondered how much the major was offered to lend his soldiers to this scroll-napping enterprise.

"Hand it over," goaded Underwood, his pudgy fingers moving like some sea creature's tentacles.

O'Hanrahan glanced at Lucy, who was willing herself to be invisible. O'Hanrahan moved to the *Gospel of Matthias* laid out on the bed. "I'm not sure I'm going to let you have it, Clem. Are you prepared to kill me?"

Underwood squirmed apologetically. "Awww, it's not gonna come to that, Mr. O'Hanrahan," he said, nervously twisting his ring.

Lucy clutched the cardboard tube with the *Contendings of St. Andrew*; she noticed her knees were shaking. Well, they had had a good run, but it was over now. I suppose the wished-for outcome at this point was to get out of the Sudan without ending up in jail—

"Move away!" yelled the major. His lieutenant cocked his Kalishnikov.

Lucy felt faint. Expectations were lowering fast: she'd settle for getting out alive.

O'Hanrahan, with his hands up, backed away from the bed.

Underwood approached the bed and examined the *Gospel of Matthias* in its airtight envelope. "You know," he mumbled, "this doesn't look like . . ."

Lucy thought of something!

She bolted for the door, pushing aside one of the soldiers.

"Stop her!" cried Underwood. One soldier stayed with his gun trained on O'Hanrahan, and the other darted for the door after Lucy. He grabbed her in the hallway, tackled her to the floor—the cardboard tube with the *Contendings of St. Andrew* flew from her hand and rolled down the hall. The old maidservant rounded the corner, invoked Allah in terror, and tottered away.

"No!" screamed Lucy, as the tall, thin African soldier, more annoyed than angry, pressed her to the floor. Lucy put on a show, she screamed, she begged him not to take the gospel . . . but she was led back to the room sobbing and miserable. Underwood gentlemanly handed her his handkerchief.

Underwood recognized the cardboard tube. He slipped out the 14th-Century vellum and laughed contentedly, handling it gingerly. "Very nice, very nice," he cooed. "You're a clever man, Mr. O'Hanrahan. You almost had me going for that scroll, whatever it is, all laid out on the bed just waiting for me."

"You bastard," O'Hanrahan seethed, adding as he could to Underwood's mistaken impression.

Lucy, acting upset in a bravura performance, noticed an insignia on the handkerchief, like the one on Underwood's ring. The symbol she and Dr. O'Hanrahan had both encountered before . . .

Underwood: "I knew you were clever when you stopped using Mr. Merriwether's credit card."

"Because you were following us using our receipts," O'Hanrahan said. "Nothing too clever about that . . . but how did you know we were in Khartoum?"

Underwood was cocky. "Miss Dantan has been kind enough to send in reports of your whereabouts every few days."

Lucy recoiled in shock. O'Hanrahan stared hard at her—it occurred to them both at the same time: Dr. Shaughnesy.

"The ring," Lucy mumbled. "It's the same ring!"

She remembered where she'd seen the insignia now: on the ring on Dr. Shaughnesy's long, sepulchral fingers. Dr. O'Hanrahan had raved for years that his unseating from the Theology Department was part of a Masonic plot—my God, his paranoia may have been justified!

"Dr. Shaughnesy," she said. "You guys are Masons."

"And not just any," he said, chuckling. "Scottish Rite but with an added Persian ceremony known only to our elite brotherhood. Mr. Merriwether, one of our members, has quite a few people looking for this and there's a $20,000 reward for who gets it first!" He was delighted like a child. "So thanks for the money, Mr. O'Hanrahan. Dr. Shaughnesy is a fine lodge brother and for his help Mr. Merriwether is going to show his appreciation. I'm sure," he added to O'Hanrahan, "that must warm your heart to at least know one of your own former colleagues will make out well on this too."

O'Hanrahan looked as if he might spit.

The three military men and Underwood left, smugly grasping the *Contendings of St. Andrew.* O'Hanrahan sat on the bed to steady himself. Lucy quietly closed the door and locked it. Only then was she confident enough to turn around and silently cheer, clenching her fists and jumping a little. O'Hanrahan laughed more deeply: "You, Sister Lucy, are a genius!"

"I *knew* I'd seen Underwood's ring before."

"That moron Shaughnesy," O'Hanrahan grumbled. "Figures, really. Looking back, it's a bit difficult to believe Shaughnesy would spend any department money to retrieve me, any more than he'd really send me out with a credit card."

"Let's get out of Khartoum," she requested.

He put a hand on her shoulder, fatherly. "It just so happens I've got two tickets, thanks to Colonel Westin, for Addis Ababa tomorrow morning," he reported.

Ethiopia? Another country? "And then we're going back to Jerusalem?" she hoped. She had thought it all out: she would find out whether she was pregnant the *day* she got back to civilization and then decide accordingly. If pregnant, she would confess her sin to O'Hanrahan and Rabbi Hersch and, hell, after everything they'd all been through, these guys would think of something to help her. She could go to a kibbutz or something. Give the kid up for adoption in Israel—it might be possible. Or have it in Israel and bring it back to the U.S. and place it in adoption back home. The important thing is *not to go home*. For the next eight months.

Whom, after all, could she trust? Judy would tell Gabriel and it would get back to her parents. There was nowhere to hide out, and she knew as well as she knew anything her life would be without value as a pregnant unmarried woman in the sphere of the Dantan Family and her maiden aunts; oh, even at the University of Chicago they'd yuck it up, have a good laugh on the frumpy Irish girl who came back from a summer with O'Hanrahan, pregnant and sunburned.

"Sir?" she prodded. "We *are* going back to Israel, aren't we?"

O'Hanrahan slowed in his answer. Actually, he was content to put her upon a plane and pack her off home while he pursued "Q" and his harem, of course, in Teheran.

(You selfish man. This woman is your salvation!)

He hadn't thought about what to do with Lucy.

(Never anybody else. It's always your own desires!)

"Sure, I suppose," he said, postponing the suspension of his disciple's duties until the last minute. "Goodness, look at the time!"

"We've got to get our stamps from the Ministry of Transportation or we're never getting out of this place!"

The Ministry of Transportation.

A building only Kafka could have imagined.

Six stories of a square plan, each office identical, each waiting area and service window identical, and the bureaucrats themselves, mostly soldiers—it seemed the whole country was in the army—ignoring all pleas and bribes. Emaciated Africans, families of eight, huddled in piles in stinking, dirty clothes wearing expressions of hopelessness, trying with what life was left in them to get an emigration stamp, a permit for something, a pardon, a bending of the rule . . . and weeks could transpire before these wishes, if ever, were fulfilled.

Lucy saw a man in some final stage of bureaucratic humiliation tug on a soldier's pantleg and weep, beg for some silly stamp on a crinkled paper he waved as if it were a surrender flag. The Arab private shook his leg and lost the pest, walking on obliviously. There was no fresh air, no working lights above, and little natural light in the building—the air was thick with harsh blue tobacco smoke that hung like smog.

"We'll never get out of here," Lucy moaned, after forty-five minutes of impatient waiting. "This is pointless. This is Hell."

Each time a certain veiled woman passed by, O'Hanrahan leapt to his feet with twenty others and screamed at her, cried out like sellers in the commodities market back in Chicago, sacrificing any dignity for attention. This icy bureaucrat would coldly choose one and promise him or her that it would be just a moment, five minutes more.

Then it was prayer time.

The *azaan* blasted forth over the p.a. system.

All the people waiting would spread out a straw mat and for the next forty-five minutes there would be afternoon prayers. O'Hanrahan noticed many of the black Sudanese didn't pray and presumably weren't Moslem—hence, their inhuman wait for attention, for days, for weeks. Or maybe they were just bereft of hope, in the bosom of African bureaucracy and beyond the reach of Allah.

"Now? Please! *Laosah mahtee!*" O'Hanrahan cried to the all-important woman, on her next appearance after prayertime. "We must go to Ethiopia tomorrow!"

She took his and Lucy's passports and disappeared.

For the benefit of tourists downstairs there was a laughably ill-equipped tourist information station. Lucy left O'Hanrahan and went down to it, read an outdated brochure, then asked impulsively where the nearest phone center was. Across the street, she was told, in the Marriott Hotel.

Lucy longed to hear what the rabbi would advise them and, committing her remaining Sudanese pounds, she had the Marriott Phone Center operator place her call to Hebrew University.

The voice was a gravelly whisper. "This Lucy?"

"Rabbi Hersch, is that you?"

Silence.

Lucy: "Is something wrong?"

"Yes, to answer your question, everything's wrong. I don't trust the phone in my office so I'm having my calls bounced to my colleague's office, where I am now. My office got broken into again and so did my desk safe . . ."

Lucy's heart beat faster. "Who got into it?"

"I don't know, but they must have great connections. Hebrew University is an armed camp against terrorism and Intifada—you can't just walk in there and break in a safe, break in an office, unless you're . . ."

"Someone else in the university?"

"God Himself," he contemplated, a strong note of frustration in his voice.

Lucy offered her own uncheery report. O'Hanrahan had been arrested, the embassy got him out of trouble, Mr. Underwood stole their scroll at gunpoint, but got the wrong one, the Mad Monk showed up in Khartoum two days before they did. "We seem to be falling two days behind him now," Lucy sighed.

Rabbi Hersch took a deep breath. "What good is this monk's research doing him? He doesn't have the scroll."

"Not yet. I'll talk quick. We're leaving for Addis Ababa tomorrow and then I guess we'll fly from there to Jerusalem."

"Wouldn't do it. Let's get to Chicago or New York maybe—I got friends there."

But Lucy really didn't want to go home. Rabbi Hersch was messing up her Operation Secret Baby in the Holy Lands plan—

"Can't believe Paddy O'Hanrahan is getting on a plane," the rabbi said softly. "After Rudolph died in that crash at O'Hare, Paddy swore he'd never get on another one."

Lucy felt her head lighten. "I thought it was a car accident . . ."

"No, Beatrice died in a car accident speeding hysterically to O'Hare in seven inches of snow and ice to see if Rudolph survived the plane crash. It was a 727, slid off the runway, everyone injured and just ten deaths but Paddy's kid was one of them. And then Beatrice went crazy . . . didn't anyone tell you any of this?"

"Not the details."

The rabbi: "So. Does Addis have a Hilton? When and where can I meet you guys?"

"Well, Dr. O'Hanrahan says . . ." There had been a click. "Hello? Hello?"

And now a repeating dial-tone noise.

Lucy went out into the late-afternoon light, which had turned the Ministry of Transportation a warm desert orange. She found O'Hanrahan where she'd left him. After passing on the highlights of her phone call, she asked, "Any progress on our rubber stamps?"

"A lady just told me it would be two minutes, tops."

Ten hopeful minutes gave way to an impatient fifteen, twenty, then the anesthetized blank stares returned as an hour evaporated in the heat and stench of the building. Finally, two toothless men, smiling, laughing, enjoying it vicariously—they had been waiting days for such a moment for themselves—pulled on O'Hanrahan's sleeve, rousing him to life: *as-sikriteera!* they shouted. The omnipotent secretary was knocking on the glass of the service window. O'Hanrahan clambered to his feet and received the passports . . . his own and some other white woman's, not Lucy's.

"But this is not her," he insisted.

She shrugged. What's the difference?

O'Hanrahan wrote out "Lucy Dantan" and put an Arabic equivalent next to it. Please, he begged, for the love of Allah! Find her passport and put a single Sudanese half-pound, 17-cent, stamp on it.

O'Hanrahan returned to the dark stretch of floor in a hallway that Lucy had marked as her own. He looked at the place he had formerly sat and there was a chicken there, scrawny, undernourished. As he shooed it with his foot, a woman came running for it, shaking her finger at him, scooping up her prize possession.

"I don't suppose," said Lucy, "I want to know what the toilet is like in this building."

"I can assure you you don't."

There at the end of the hallway came a drinks seller, hawking bottles of water for two pounds apiece. The poorer Sudanese watched sadly as the glistening bottles of liquid passed, not able to afford them. The Arabic Sudanese bought some bottles, as did the soldiers. O'Hanrahan asked for two. Is it clean? he asked. Oh yes, he was assured. Lucy and he stared at the bottle. It was room temperature. O'Hanrahan held it up to the dim light. No, damn them, better not drink it. Lucy gave hers away to the ragged family of eight, her idea of a leper colony, hunched silently across the hallway from them. She studied how they each had a sip gratefully, and then passed it on to another indigent family—three mouthfuls of water stretched to sixteen people.

O'Hanrahan's legs were falling asleep so he got up to wander the hallway to the end and then turn around. Between two connecting hallways he noticed that the tile-cement floor had been chipped away as if hit by a mortar in this one spot. It was filled with brownish, brackish water. Five stories up: a mud puddle in an office building.

Africa!

ሞንደር:

August 24th

On the limousine ride to the airport at six A.M., O'Hanrahan was anxious, wiping his brow repeatedly like a tic.

"You fly all the time, don't you?" he asked her.

Lucy didn't fly all the time but she would not have joked with him, knowing that his son had met his death that way. "All the time," she reassured him. "There's nothing to it. And this isn't a long flight to Addis, is it? Just think if we were flying from here to Chicago, how long that would be. This is just a little hop."

"Yes," he said, swallowing her answer like medicine.

In the pause, she was of two minds about her bringing up his son's death: in a human way she wanted to know the details and commiserate, but another facet wished to keep O'Hanrahan invulnerable—too much had conspired to make her mentor and idol, her Moses in the wilderness, fragile and fallible. She longed briefly for their inequitable relationship in Ireland, his great somebody to her meaningless nobody. There was some comfort, after all, in his Jovian domination of events.

(So you think it best not to give comfort where you can.)

She sighed. And before she could retract it, she said, "I'm sorry."

"Hm?"

Lucy looked at the shambling, outlying shacktown passing by, the open sewers gurgling up brown water, the roosters atop trash piles crowing the dawn. "I'm sorry about what happened to your son."

Oh, registered O'Hanrahan. The McCalls or the rabbi probably satisfied her curiosity. "Yes, I'm sorry too."

"I mean, there's nothing I can say . . ."

"I appreciate," he said mechanically, "that you said something at all. It was a long time ago, of course," he added, wondering why.

"But you must be reminded. You know, getting on this plane."

He nodded, back in touch fully with the old sadness, the lifelong ache. There ought to be, he thought, a moratorium on sympathy past a certain point—within six months of the funeral, fine. But after that, why bring it back anew?

(But Patrick, this is all humankind has. Sympathy, if everyone practiced it, would save your world tomorrow from most pain and woe.)

True. And there were people, he reflected, men he had appointed to the department and given tenure to, women in the administrative pool who'd typed hundreds of letters for him and owed their Christmas bonuses to him who did not say a thing to him, who sent no card, who turned their heads at his bereavement. *All my intimate friends abhor me, and those whom I loved have turned against me.* He said at last, "He was a good kid. Rudolph."

Lucy repeated the name, "Rudolph."

"We called him Rudy. You'da liked him, Luce."

Hoping to lighten the mood, she flirted in absentia. "Was he good-looking?"

O'Hanrahan mumbled, "An acquired taste perhaps, but I would say so." He scooted forward and edged out his wallet from the back pocket. Deeply enfolded within was a photo, the photo Gabriel must have seen.

He held it up and looked at it but not intensely, not to make eye contact with the eyes in the photo.

Lucy gingerly held it.

Indeed, Lucy thought there was a resemblance between Gabriel and Rudolph. Or maybe mostly it was the monastic haircut. It was a senior high school official photo, the one that went in the yearbook, circa 1971 or so, with wide lapels on a corduroy jacket, a wide brown tie, too much hair. In contrast to the yellowing photo and the pale, unsmiling face staring back at her, perhaps unhappy with the photo being taken, O'Hanrahan was forcing a cheery spiel:

"A bit unathletic perhaps, but that's because he read all the time. He was a scholar like his old man. Sure do miss the talks—I mean we used to . . . sure do miss the long talks we used to have. If he'd lived he'd have probably done something in academia, against my sternest warnings."

"What subject?"

"Of course, theology." He closed his eyes, fighting nausea. Where was this stuff coming from? "A real ladies' man," he heard himself say. "You'da had to watch yourself, I think. Sister Lucy."

"I was a real nothing in high school," she said, handing the photo back, "so he would've steered clear of me."

"Oh I doubt that. You remind me a bit of one of his girlfriends, really . . ." He mopped his brow, wondering if he had lost his mind. He was talking about his son with no more reality than if he were a TV-advertised product . . . But he was inexpert at this. For the mourners of Beatrice he had a prepared set piece: what a good wife she was, how he missed her, what a splendid woman, and that satisfied all parties. But for Rudolph he was flailing, he had no patter to throw as a sop to the world, who would not leave his injuries alone!

But did you hear me, Rudy? Hm, did you hear your father there? All right, so I took a few liberties but I owned up to you, didn't I? All the approval you were looking for, all the love—did you hear it? And yet . . . yet in the pit of my bowels I feel something has been torn out and a great emptiness put back in its place.

(The truth will set you free, Patrick.)

At the dilapidated airstrip, Lucy and O'Hanrahan joined the line of sleepy travelers, mostly Arab and a few refugee Ethiopians. They were guided to a desk where no one presided, then to a counter where a woman insisted she had nothing to do with anything, then they were led outside in the cool morning shade of the hangar to await the authorities.

"Maybe," suggested O'Hanrahan, ever ready to figure out a route overland, "we could go down to Kassala and get the Red Cross to take us in by jeep . . ."

He trailed off as he saw the 1950s Soviet-built propeller plane bouncing along the tarmac to the terminal. Black smoke plumed from one of the propellers, not that anyone official-looking on the field found this alarming. Religious designs, the intricate weaving of holy phrases in Arabic into geometric shapes, graced the exterior on faded decals.

"Insha'allah Airways," O'Hanrahan said almost in a whisper. "If God wills it."

There was a cardtable desperately leaning to one side, where a fat Sudanese army officer and a bureaucrat of some sort in a dirty *galabiyya* sat organizing passports, papers, and tickets, arguing with whomever was brought before the table. A toothless man raged vehemently with the officials, showering them with little sprays of spit that made them wince, stamp his passport and wave him on—but not before demanding his knife. The man reached into his boot and produced a shockingly long dagger and put it on the table. Guns, knives, sabers, stilettos, one by one the passengers disarmed themselves and the army officer swept them into a ratty suitcase for distribution after they landed.

Lucy swallowed with difficulty. "At least there's some security."

O'Hanrahan was stricken.

Then there was a pop and two men emerged from behind the plane to yell at one another, while there appeared another man in a uniform ... My God, thought O'Hanrahan, that shambling man with khaki pants from one uniform and a blue jacket from another is the *pilot*. The pilot ordered the two men to the garage and soon it became apparent that one of the plane's wheels had gone flat. A steady hiss underscored the workmen's conversation as the plane slowly tilted toward the leak.

"I'm sure," said Lucy, horrified herself now, "that in order to fly they must have been in the Sudanese Air Force. I mean, you can't just *be* a pilot with no qualifications, can you?"

O'Hanrahan laughed darkly. "You're handing me the Sudanese Air Force? That sure makes me feel a whole goddam lot better."

Soon a group was waved through and O'Hanrahan found himself at the leaning cardtable with the heavily mustached army officer, who looked like a browner Saddam Hussein. He disinterestedly examined their passports and visas and set them aside. "You go to Gonder?" he asked in Arabic.

"*Insha'allah*," O'Hanrahan said.

"Indeed," the officer nodded, reverting to English. "No is safe Ethiopia. Very bad, very bad. You daughter?" he asked, meaning Lucy.

"Yes," he said.

"Two names not the same name."

"She is a widow," O'Hanrahan invented.

"Ah," he said, then mumbled a blessing upon widows from the Quran. He stamped their passports.

Takeoff would be as bad as feared. The plane rumbled and bumped along to a *dirt* runway, though no reason for avoiding the paved one was given by the pilot. Each announcement deteriorated into a crackle of static because of a broken public-address system. O'Hanrahan and Lucy were buckled up, grimly preparing for death. O'Hanrahan noticed the *fellahin* on board were doing the same, prayers, mutterings, tears, hands outstretched imploring Allah. The round-faced African man in the dashiki across the aisle smiled at him however, impossibly serene.

The plane sped down the gravel road, leaned to the right, then the left, then nosed up, then touched back down, all at a leisurely speed that seemed to defy attaining lift. Finally they were off, though they hovered close to the ground for what seemed ages before gaining any altitude; O'Hanrahan wondered briefly if the pilot intended to bounce all the way to Ethiopia, touching down every one hundred yards.

Lucy crossed herself.

They were airborne.

Khartoum looked like a junkyard from the air with two swaths of green near the mud-colored rivers and beyond that an endless void of soft yellow sand. It was not long until a range of reddish-brown, sun-baked mountains appeared. The mountains, thought O'Hanrahan, that kept the Romans out of Ethiopia. It was not until the 19th Century that an overland route was found through these mountains. Strange emissaries periodically escaped—like Prester John, the legendary Ethiopian king who rode in the Crusades bedecked in gold and silver armor, leaving rock-sized gems in his wake, who no sooner appeared than disappeared again, back to this inscrutable land of Jews the world's Jews barely recognize and Christians the world's Christians have forgotten. Yes, down below the mountains and canyons that warped this land, the peaks two miles high, the chasms impossible to traverse, the terrain that allowed Ethiopia to fall off the earth, the land of abysses, Abyssinia.

Just as a modicum of ease had begun to set in, there was turbulence and the plane rapidly raised and lowered itself, rattling and creaking. This set off a new round of supplications to Allah.

"God," said O'Hanrahan, sweat pouring off his forehead, his silver matted hair hanging in his face distressfully, "this is how it was in the days before jets. I went over to Korea in a bigger version of this."

"And you survived." Lucy was grasping at any assurance.

The plane swooped up and down and all the fastened seats and tray tables seemed as if they might detach themselves. Lucy, who had bravely undone her seat belt, fastened it again with bloodless hands.

O'Hanrahan: "Lotta good that will do."

Then there was a sound like a siren, a high-pitched arc of noise.

O'Hanrahan speculated, "Probably a warning sound meaning the tail section's fallen off."

On the left side of the aisle many of the men were agitated and pointing out the windows, raising their voices. O'Hanrahan disbelievingly watched one man leave his seat and abase himself in the aisle, feet twisted in prayer position, bowing his head to the floor over and over . . .

"Uh-oh," said Lucy, afraid to seek more information.

Then another 4th-of-July-noisemaker sound, this time from behind them on the right. Lucy looked out the window to see what looked like a child's smoke bomb falling down into the canyons below.

"What on earth?" said O'Hanrahan, crowding her at the window.

"Did that fall off the plane, sir?"

Then they heard the sound of marbles and ball bearings being loosed on a sheet of tin. Something was scattering itself under the floor in the belly of the plane.

O'Hanrahan, resigned, fell back in his seat and said quietly, "Speaking of Korea. We're being shot at."

It was the end, Lucy thought absolutely.

O'Hanrahan was not merely a doctor of the faith, he was a prophet— he said they would die, and now they were going to die. Thanks to the Sudanese Civil War or the Tigrean resistance or the Eritrean rebels or the Loyalist forces of Mengistu or, since this is Africa, maybe someone is just using the plane as target practice—

"Jesus," said O'Hanrahan, clinching the armrests as the plane received a thwack on its underside. He noticed the plane was ascending as well as it could in the turbulence. The Moslem passengers were keening and howling prayers now—Allah is good, Allah is merciful, Allah is all-powerful! The professor listened and thought with coldness: I don't know, boys. Allah is pretty tough on you people in this part of the world. Not exactly your hands-on deity.

(It would be much worse than it is, if not for Us.)

I suppose, thought O'Hanrahan, thanks are in order, Lord, for this quick death. I can say it'll be a helluva lot better than what would have happened had I never left my armchair back in Forest Park. There's some justice to all this that must please You. Dying in a plane crash, like my son. An equivalence. If Rudy could endure it, then I can endure it. I don't know if he was brave or in a panic or maybe never knew what hit him, but in case he's watching from up above, I'll meet the end with dignity. I dedicate this death to my son.

(Gestures of love are for the living, Patrick.)

O'Hanrahan glanced at Lucy who was tensed in prayer, reciting Hail Mary's over and over. Not me. I'll meet the end eyes open.

The propeller out the right window that had been putting out black exhaust now was slowing, having been hit by anti-aircraft fire. White smoke now joined the black, thickening smoke. The plane was descending, angling to the right, toward an expanse of desert. O'Hanrahan decided not to look for villages or landing strips. What was going to happen was going to happen—infected, sighed O'Hanrahan, in his final moments by Arab fatalism.

Lucy reached over and grasped his hand.

My God! It hadn't occurred to him. Lucy! Would she be here if not for you and your stupid quest? *Her death is on your head!* O'Hanrahan felt tears well in his eyes. This young life sacrificed to my follies!

He pressed her hand back.

Oh, forgive me! Your youth and the life ahead of you, the loves and triumphs of Lucy Dantan snuffed out in this . . . Ah, now that could get me Hell, after all. Good going, old man. Taking everyone down with you! O'Hanrahan prayed, earnestly and determinedly for the first time in seventeen years: let me die if You Guys want—but *not Lucy, for the love of God!* As for me, Lord, I don't, even now, feel any need to beg for forgiveness! I adore and venerate my sins! Unrepentant to the end, O God! But if You have one little shred of decency, save this girl!

(You've had plenty of chances to look out for her safety.)

He raised his head and saw Lucy looking over at him.

"It's going to be all right," she said. "Whatever happens."

The rocky hills were window level. Down, down . . .

"Even if it's not I want to say . . ." She was fearless with a calm from deep within. "Thank you for allowing me this trip."

"Please," he wailed, "if you hadn't come with me—"

She cut him off with a sharp squeeze of his hand. "I love you, sir."

The valley floor or scrub and hard-baked earth was feet below.

(And you can't even respond in kind, can you, Patrick?)

"Yeah," he said, wiping his brow, hyperventilating. Ah, the feared words! The magic, mystical name of God that he was too scared to speak! What couldn't be said in twenty years of married life or eighteen years of fatherhood, nor be said to sister or father or mother or colleague or friend—not that simply and nobly as Lucy had said it—

KA-THUDDDD . . . With bouncing and rumbling, the plane touched down, lifted up again slightly, came down with a greater thud and it occurred to everyone in the plane who had made their peace with death that perhaps, in this one second, the possibility of living had been revived. Now the passengers were united in an almost bemused anticipation: will the plane crash or flip or turn over or just slow down and give us our lives again? They decelerated crushingly, and O'Hanrahan leaned over to the window to see a ditch parallel to the plane's course. They were landing on a gravel road.

They slowed, and slowed some more . . .

And then they stopped.

The pilot and copilot appeared in front of the cockpit door and smiled; a man up front knelt before them and kissed their hands. Not necessary, not necessary, the pilot shooed him away. The pilot announced in Arabic: we must send to Bahir Dar for a repair truck, and then we will take off again and get to Addis Ababa. He announced this with such casualness that O'Hanrahan was momentarily confused as to their ever having been in serious trouble. Was this a common happening on this air service?

The round-faced gentleman in the dashiki across the aisle asked O'Hanrahan in musical West African English, "You thought we were to die, mon?"

"Yes."

"Ah, my daughter is to marry dees next week and it has been foretold dat I should be at her side, mon. So we could not die."

"Wish I'da known that," O'Hanrahan said, breathing more normally.

"No no," the man said cheerily, getting a bag down from the compartment above him. "There was no doubt, sha."

Lucy fell back in the seat and put her head down, exhausted.

O'Hanrahan then let go of Lucy's hand. He was mildly troubled, then ashamed that he could not declare his love for her in what could have been a last gesture. I am stone inside, he thought plainly, I am desert.

(*And I will take away your stony heart and I will give you a heart of flesh.*)

"You all right, Luce?" he asked, still shaken.

She nodded.

Up front, many passengers were going to the door of the plane and lowering themselves in the open doorway for a survivable jump to the ground. Once there, the ground was kissed and the earth praised, then they stood with outstretched arms to the sky and praised again the wondrous Allah, the Exalted, the Evident, the Deferrer, the Enduring, the Incomparable, on through the 99 Holy Names. They cried aloud: is He not a good God?

(Well, Patrick, what do you say?)

"I say," he said to Lucy, "we're getting off this plane. No more surprises. We're in Ethiopia and we can hitch a ride from here to Gonder and get a bus to Addis."

"But maybe we should—"

"No more plane rides," he issued.

"Okay, just a minute," said Lucy. "I need to sit for a moment and . . . I feel weak." She reached into her handbag with shaking hands for her water bottle and took a long sip. She watched O'Hanrahan go to the front of the plane and receive assistance, comically, from several Sudanese men who helped lower his heft to the dirt road below. Lucy closed her eyes and experienced peace, breathing deeply and rhythmically.

I know, Holy Spirit, what You're up to, she prayed.

(Yes, My child?)

A moment ago all I could see ahead was death and the end of things. Now I am alive and my future has been returned to me. What a small burden it is to me now whether a child is part of it. How happy I should be to bear it and give it life!

(You know We are with you always.)

So forgive me when I inform you that I am unregenerate. I still don't want to be pregnant. Having come so near death, now, more than ever, I want my freedom.

Then from out of nowhere, she imagined David McCall. Somewhere in this land, out in this vast scrub. He could be the key to my future happiness, she decided calmly. I will confess my sins to him, put it in his beautiful hands. She found herself looking at the man in the dashiki and kofi upon his head who was grinning in radiant joy:

"My daughter is to be married, yah? Lemme tellya sha, God tole me I was to dance at de feast, and God do never lie. No sha, God do never lie."

Lucy opened her eyes to the sound of helicopters flying over. She wondered where she was briefly, then she flashed back to the plane going down, the short trip to the Degoma refugee camp where they had been offered lodging, then she doubted it had ever happened . . . She sat up straight in bed, realizing it had. She was in the nurses' barracks and a crack of light shone under the heavy canvas tent flap.

Lucy sat up on the creaking bed and, careful not to disturb a sleeping nurse two beds away, went over to the tent entrance hung with thick black material. It was still light outside; very late afternoon. Jeeps and medical supply trucks drove in and out of the camp replacing the dust, stationary in the air. She surveyed the camp. The aid-workers and tent hospital were on one side of the road; on the other in a scrubby field began the tent villages of the refugees.

Lucy observed a line of miserably thin Ethiopians being marched to an aid station, just arrived, the bawling children, the silent mothers still too scared to hope for food even though they were now so close, the men who were expected to provide for their families marching automatically in some trance of utter humiliation and surrender. She observed this line of people, strangely patient and unexcited, plodding along, and Lucy comforted herself that at last there was food for them, that they were saved, and she warmed herself with this thought until her eyes happened upon an emaciated woman limping behind the others, fingerless, and—with a shock it registered—no nose on her face.

She turned away. Leprosy. A treatable thing now, but perhaps her village, wherever it was, whoever destroyed it, didn't know that. Her children, altering their pace only to swat at a fly, followed blankly. Surely they had the disease too, but there was time for them. What must they think, observing their mother; had their little minds made their peace with that any more than they had found some way to accept their homelessness, this eternal war, the atrocities, the numerous brothers and sisters they had already lost?

"Leprosy," said a nurse at Lucy's side, standing near the tent flap.

"Yeah, so I guessed."

Lucy and the nurse, who was about Lucy's age, with short hair, sort of mannish, exchanged names. Lucy learned the nurse had served a summer with World Vision, and now was here with Catholic Relief Charities. "Though I'm no Catholic, these days," she added.

Lucy shared her thoughts. "They look so . . . indifferent."

"That's the hunger," said the nurse. "A phase of starvation. They spend all day in these camps staring off into space, barely able to move, even when there's food a few yards away. We can't assume they'll come get it even when it's right next to them. We've had mothers starve to death in sight of food. They don't think straight." The nurse turned to go inside the tent, her shift over. Lucy was struck by her passionless assessment: "But then a woman loses a kid and you see her cry. They're still alive in there." The nurse averted her eyes from Lucy as she said, "There's a woman in the east tent city who just lost her seventh child this morning. Imagine."

The nurse ducked into the tent and Lucy stood there watching a next wave of refugees file by. Lucy was miffed that O'Hanrahan had deposited her for that well-deserved nap of deep, postcrisis sleep without leaving a clue to his whereabouts. She turned and walked to where she imagined the headquarters of this camp to be, and where O'Hanrahan might be.

The headquarters was an abandoned service station, the pumps long ago removed. Where a large glass pane once was, canvas flaps hung down. There was a crowd of Ethiopian aid-workers milling around the door with an array of problems, waiting wordlessly and patiently, inhumanly calm . . . or maybe it was some deeper philosophical patience that took its source from Africa itself. She wondered if she should wait in this line, and then reasoned it might be days before these people's needs were met.

Lucy shyly stuck her head in the doorway, into the surprisingly clean front office. "Anyone speak English?" she asked.

One aid-worker did, and directed Lucy back to the street and told her to walk into the village, such as this road junction was, and find the stone building with *Scuola* engraved upon it, a school building from the brief Italian colonial days of the '30s. O'Hanrahan would be there near the only working phones.

Lucy dodged two snarling wild dogs that, after a bark or two, had no interest in her. She forded the rutted street, muddy with dung and filth, to enter the council building.

"Lucy, over here!" cried O'Hanrahan.

He sat in the back of a vast warehouse that was once an auditorium, now filled with aid-workers and local bureaucrats. Two black phones, with small lines to use each of them, stood at one table and a policeman between them, listening in; there was also a radio set against the other wall with a doctor yelling to make himself heard into the microphone. O'Hanrahan, chipper and alert, a paper cup of something in his hand, waved her back to his table.

"You managed to find a cocktail out here?"

"It's not that bad," he said, looking into the cup at the brownish mixture. His tone suggested it was that bad. "It's *swa*. Made from fermenting bread. An inventive people, the Tigreans."

A policeman nearby looked quickly at O'Hanrahan, who had spoken the name of the forbidden rebel faction.

"Wanna sip?"

"No thank you."

"I've called the U.S. Embassy in Addis and they were relieved to hear we had survived. They're sending someone up to fetch us from the capital. By car, thank God."

Lucy now noticed an older priest who was rambling in some language to himself, Abba Selama. Lucy noticed the extraordinary face of the priest: he was obviously old in his eyes and in his gray beard, but his face and princely cheekbones seemed young, as if a young black actor had not too persuasively pasted an old man's beard on his smooth face.

"Abba Selama has been kind enough to come down from Debra Istafanos to vouch for me," explained O'Hanrahan, "since the police here think it's best for us not to go anywhere until the people from the U.S. Embassy arrive. We didn't miss getting arrested by much. Anyone who drops in like we did is thought to be a spy, and they can be shot without a trial."

"You sure know how to make me feel secure, sir."

O'Hanrahan shuddered uncontrollably.

Lucy feared a convulsion. "Are you all right?"

"It's the *swa*, Luce. Brrrr, this packs a punch! Sure you don't want a sip? A little sip?"

Lucy tersely: "No thank you."

The priest turned to Lucy, put his hand briefly on his heart, took Lucy's hand politely, then returned his hand to his heart, smiling.

"Consider yourself blessed, Miss Dantan." O'Hanrahan braved another sip of the bread brew. "Good God in heaven . . ."

"Stop drinking it," she snapped, irritated, "if it's so awful." Lucy eyed the radiophones. "How's the phone situation here?"

"The black phones are strictly third-world. The trick is to wait in line for time on the radio set and make a satellite call. You calling those African datelines again?" Lucy's impatience prompted him to be helpful. "See that man there? The doctor in the filthy white coat, black guy with a hundred pens in his pocket? That's the head of this show down here. Ask him if you can place a call. And, Lucy, pretend it's life-or-death business so they'll give you time on the radiophone."

She nodded gratefully.

Lucy took from her handbag the address of the Austcare camp that David McCall had given her and showed it to the chief aid-administrator. This man knew quite a bit about the ups and downs of refugee camps and aid stations during this phase of the rebellion. It turned out that David's Debra Zebit camp had moved due to the war. What's more, he told her, foreign-aid supply lines had been cut off by President Mengistu because this villain didn't want to risk feeding any of his enemy and so had confiscated the supplies of international aid and sold it to other poor countries for profit in order to purchase more Russian and Cuban arms. Austcare had moved westward to Debra Tabor and was working with an existing camp set up by the Red Cross and CARE.

Having learned this information and the Debra Tabor frequency, she asked the radio operator to place an outgoing message to David McCall. She got a doctor who spoke broken English, then an American nurse who knew that Australians had joined their camp but had never heard of him, then two people who spoke something thoroughly unrecognizable. And then the next second:

"Hello?"

"Uh, David?"

"Yes, who is this?" He sounded worried. Surely no one would call with good news, or just to say hi.

"Lucy Dantan. You remember from a couple months ago?"

"It must be costin' you a fortune to call me here!"

"I'm in Ethiopia. Right down the road."

"Naawwwww . . ."

"Yes, about five miles out of . . ." She asked quickly for where this was. "Degoma, near Gonder."

"Well, that's not too far from me. About sixty miles?"

"Yeah, well, I wanted to call. If it was near, I hoped I could visit, hitch a ride with some aid people."

"I have a Jeep," he said lightly, as if picking her up was no more trouble than a run down to the store back in Chicago.

"Yeah, but you have work to do—"

"I'll just go pick up our supplies a day early in Addis Zemen and bop up there."

"But the war . . ."

"Oh, we're fine for now. They even ran bus-tours up to Lalibela last week."

"I'd love to see you."

"Well, I'd like to see you too." He laughed freely, putting the phone aside. "Hey, John, Georgie—guess what? That girl I's tellin' you about, she's in friggin' Ethiopia!" Then he put the phone to his mouth again. "Is Patrick with you?"

"Believe it or not, yes."

"Christ almighty!"

She wanted credit for her adventurousness. "Our plane got shot down by the SDLP and we ditched it near a town called Aykel and have hooked up with the Degoma camp until someone from our embassy comes to fetch us."

David squealed with delight. "Lord Jesus, our poor little evacuation pales beside that! Well, welcome to Ethiopia! 'T only get worse!"

"Not if I see you."

The sun was setting and it began to be cool, a high-elevation mountainous cool that Lucy, walking back to the nurses' tent, found restorative after the excruciation of the Saharan heat. Sensing she was a burden the aid people didn't need, she found the nurse she had spoken to earlier and volunteered for chores, engendering the first smile she had seen on this difficult day. After an hour of sorting plates and cups in the aid-workers' mess, counting bags of flour, washing up in the remarkably well-equipped kitchen for mass production of bread and grain meal, Lucy felt better about being in Degoma.

You know, she lectured herself, you used to do things like this when you were at St. Eulalia's. Weekends at the St. Vincent de Paul store, sticking price tags on secondhand goods sold for charity, writing them on a sticker with a ballpoint pen while Sister . . . what was her name? Hispanic woman, Sister Assumpta—something like that. I could barely understand her English and I was sure that each Saturday she would discover I had copied down the wrong price and had bankrupted St. Vincent. Somewhere along the line I got the idea—wait, it was my sister Mary: "That's only for losers. Whyntcha get a life like normal people? Wanna hang around a bunch of nuns all your life?"

Wiping her brow, Lucy took a break by taking a brief stroll of the area. She passed by a tent where little children sat covered with flies in surreal motionlessness, staring up at her with big eyes in sunken faces. Lucy walked across the road to the defecation field, the stretch of desert designated as the refugees' latrines. Every few minutes several of the thousands gathered at Degoma would go to the field to excrete. This field was thought to be far enough out to lead the vermin away and not poison the water supply—when there was water in the creek.

There was a shotgun blast. In the fading twilight, Lucy saw that an emaciated man had fired a shot over the field and hundreds of crows, picking at the ordure for any scrap of nourishment, fluttered into the sky with aggrieved cries. It could be a mountain in Western America, the field could be a dustbowl field anywhere, the sky is the same violet blue of autumnal evenings in Illinois . . . and yet this is Ethiopia, she said, closing her eyes.

"You watch," said O'Hanrahan, appearing at her side. "An Ethiopian won't kill a wild bird, not even to eat. Birds were all-important in the Christians defeating the Moslems early in this century."

When Ras Tafari, Haile Selassie, was fighting the vicious Moslem regime for power after World War One, he got the Abun, Archbishop of Ethiopia, to excommunicate the other side, cursing them officially and promising them the reprobation of Judas. Then Moslem troops from North Africa joined to attack the Christians. They were able to get a messenger with essential information through Ras Tafari's lines to another battalion poised to crush the Christian forces . . . but then thousands of bees swarmed and stung the messenger to death before he could relay his information.

O'Hanrahan, recalling the fantastic history, noted, "He would have lost again except for the birds."

"Haile Selassie controlled the birds too?"

"He was a god, remember? No, you're too young, you don't remember. Emperor, King of Kings, Lion of Judah, Haile Selassie, declared a god by Marcus Garvey and millions of Jamaicans." O'Hanrahan chuckled. "In 1966 I almost went down for the department to attend the visit of Haile Selassie to Jamaica. This was supposed to be where the Black Messiah would show himself, and a number of militants were ready to heed his call to arms and take on the white world. Selassie ignored the Rastafarians, really, told them to get their own countries in order before coming back to Africa."

"What about the birds?"

"Oh yeah. The enemy Moslem troops got in close to the Christian camp, and if they'd attacked they would have won. But the birds in the nearby swamp gathered and swooped and cawed and woke Ras Tafari up. The enemy was spotted and defeated."

"This is documented?"

"Yep. Iyasu, the Moslem commander, was let to wander the desert for five years, then was sought for and led back to Addis Ababa in gold chains, where he spent the rest of his life locked in a prison. With his harem, however. The Ethiopians aren't savages, as you can see."

O'Hanrahan led a leisurely amble toward the village.

"There are thousands of pothead Jamaicans waiting for Ras Tafari, Haile Selassie, the Lion of Judah, to come back, since his body was never shown after his 1977 assassination. And the Druse are waiting for al-Hakim to come back since he was never found; and the Sudanese the Mahdi to come back, and the Christians want Jesus to come back, and the Jews want Messiah any day now, and the Shi'ah want the Eighth Imam to return . . . a whole planet crying out for a rerun of God." He looked down to kick at a clod of dirt. "The world awaits a Savior."

They strolled down into the ransacked, near-deserted village at the crossroads of the rough highways. A few boarded-up homes, a few occupied huts, a shiny, well-kept-up police station—of course—though no soldiers were in sight. The war was elsewhere this week. Lucy and O'Hanrahan stopped before a church.

"Oh, look at her," whispered O'Hanrahan, as they watched a thin woman in a deep indigo-blue drapery emerge from the church, around her neck a polished silver Ethiopian cross, and a wrap of some kind, but on closer inspection as she shyly walked by, it was a sheepskin scroll with painting and words upon it.

"It's like a phylactery," said O'Hanrahan, "but with more magic powers. I remember when I was last in Lalibela I saw an abba chastise a woman for wandering aimlessly around the marketplace. Her beauty so unguarded was sure to let one in for a *ganén*. An evil spirit."

"This doesn't sound particularly Christian," said Lucy.

"We don't sound Christian to them," defended O'Hanrahan.

The *dabtara*, or unordained cleric associated with her church, instructed her to go to a *zartaenqway*, the cult specialist who goes into a trance over her problems. A *zar*, the good angel, will speak through his mouth and call out the name of the demon responsible for her mishaps. And then comes the prescription, the most holy words, the most Holy Name of God and the mystery of the written holy words. The *dabtara* will prepare a magic scroll with a picture of Michael and Gabriel, her guardian angel, and perhaps a favorite beloved saint. Maybe St. Liqanos, who in the 500s came to Tigre where the serpent Arway tyrannized over the people and was killed by the saint with

Michael by lightning bolts. Maybe the Holy Alexander the Great, the long-remembered Emperor of the World, who bred an eagle with a horse and rode the wingéd offspring to the edge of the world where he met the Angel of Darkness, guardian of the end of each day, the blackest African one could ever meet, who deep within his robes hides the darkest of all nights. St. Alexander the Great, conqueror and patron of Abyssinia, there met Enoch who invented the Ethiopian script and was told of the One Who Would Come, Jesus Christ.

"What happened to the beautiful woman?" asked Lucy. "Did she get rid of her demon?"

O'Hanrahan explained that the woman must sacrifice a sheep on her own land, and the color of the sheep is important depending on what ill has befallen her. A pit she must dig behind her house and dance around it three times for the Father, Son, and Holy Spirit; and the blood of the lamb must be poured over her in some cases, for the demons love the blood of the lamb, and as it flows over her nakedness, the demons exit from her body to taste the blood and they follow it into the hole, where the blood and bones are quickly buried, the exorcism complete. The meat must be cut into twelve pieces for the Twelve Disciples and eaten.

"The Western World has pounded the magic out of religion, hasn't it?" said Lucy, tired from her day of chores, leaving her open and unjudging.

"You know, Luce, that's going to be the misfortune of the 21st Century, maybe the central intellectual tragedy of postmodern man. Africa will one day be full of free-market Methodists and Episcopalians, and they'll get decent governments and VCRs and dubbed American sitcoms, and *this*, the disease and famine and ignorance and corruption, will lessen, and their quest will be complete: a proud, united continent of first- and second-world nations. But will it be Africa anymore?"

They walked the perimeter of the field. On the other side of the road the sprawling refugee camps teemed with activity; smoke began to rise from fireplaces for warmth, for the cooking of meager rations, the boiling of water.

"Ethiopian angels," said O'Hanrahan in the tone of voice that warned something salacious was on the way, "have two eyes, two hands, two feet, and two penises."

"They have two, do they?"

"A sacred mystery," O'Hanrahan demurred, "too inscrutable for one such as myself. Other traditions hold that the angels have no genitalia. Demons not angels, most Ethiopians would agree, have penises. I saw an Ethiopian ikon once of a saint doing battle with this huge-membered demon. A demon's penis is always erect."

Yep, thought Lucy, that's been my experience.

"Well," said O'Hanrahan, calling it quits, "that's all the Abyssinian filth I know. I'll get working on it."

Lucy and the professor circled back toward the dung field.

A skeletal woman rose from her squat and rewrapped her dress about her. Moments later crows flew to the spot and began to pick at her leavings, competing with the rodents and the ever-circling vultures for this wretched sustenance. Again, a man set off his shotgun aimed at the air to scatter the birds. The shotgun's report echoed about the violet-shadowed mountains.

O'Hanrahan remarked, "Abba Selama told me that some birds are eternal because they actually rested on the Cross itself."

The man in the field fired another shotgun blast.

"As I said, an Ethiopian won't kill a bird lightly."

Lucy smiled faintly, "But they could eat it and feed their families."

O'Hanrahan looked at her and then at the darkening blue of the sky. "What would that be worth if you believed you had killed a magic bird that had alighted on the Cross of the Savior? What if you could believe, in this land abandoned by God, in such things?"

AUGUST 25TH

Lucy spent the morning talking to her friend the nurse over cups of coffee. They had introduced themselves yesterday but Lucy had forgotten her name and was fearful of giving offense by asking so late in their acquaintance.

A young woman, around thirty. A white woman, with strong black eyebrows and short cropped hair—so nothing can live in it, she joked—with her khaki clothes from military surplus hanging loosely on her, Lucy assumed, from loss of weight.

"The Ethiopians," the woman laughed, "keep mistaking me for a man. They're not good on white people." The nurse could be mistaken for a man because she was broad-shouldered and muscular from lots of crate-carrying, but inspection showed she was a woman with delicate hands actually, with nail polish. She was divorced, one kid. She had worked a year at the local hospital back in Minneapolis, and then her mother died, the last of her living parents. So, with their sure objection out of the way, she indulged a whim and called up the American Refugee Committee, which ran camps in the Sudan and Ethiopia.

"I'd sent checks, you know," she said, spraying her hands with mosquito repellant at the tent's edge, careful not to breathe it. "And I knew someone who had come here for three months and I always told myself I ought to do it, just for a summer. Then I've come back again and again."

Lucy felt unvirtuous. "I know . . . but you actually *did* come over here, and few people do *that* much." Again, how often Lucy had planned on this type of summer activity, collected brochures from the Union, talked to people who had done it, and it always came to nothing, dead from her damn laziness and passivity . . .

"I think you're pretty heroic," Lucy blurted out.

Lucy watched the nurse as she put up the spray, locking it in the cabinet, interrupting herself to explain how the men will steal anything that's not tied down—to sell, of course, for their families. The Ethiopians are not ordinarily criminal. Said the nurse, "The work to do here is bottomless. Your three months are absolutely nothing, half of a drop in the bucket."

Lucy wouldn't stand for it. "It's three months more than most people give."

"No, any thoughts you might have of all the good you're doing are eaten up by the enormity of it. What are they saying? Seven million people starving in this country. The Tigrean rebels captured a convoy of U.N. medical and food supplies and destroyed everything but what they could sell to the Sudanese government . . ." She sighed. "And the Sudanese, who are looking at a famine of twenty million, refuse to admit there's a problem. They think the CIA is behind every bag of oatmeal."

There were hundreds of stories. It was truly a case of demons running governments, agents of some immense, incontrovertible evil hijacking food, cheering the famine on for the other side; nations with nothing fighting over next-to-nothing. Ethiopia's 28-year-old civil war. In 1985 Mengistu's men lined up children in one village near Gonder and shot every other one according to height. Such random evil, such whimsy. In one Tigrean town, the Ethiopians bade the women and children lie down before a Soviet tank, which ran back and forth over them, making a human pavement. Add to this the ignorance. The locals cured cholera and malaria by scores of tiny cuts, leeches, and bleeding—which aided death. In the west, the nurse heard that they thought demons caused illness and one had to burn them out. She told Lucy in cold, realistic terms the tale of a nine-year-old being forced by his parents to swallow a burning coal.

"No," the nurse concluded, "you always know you can get on a plane and then that's *it* for you, it's all over. It all goes away, and you can get back to your hot shower and run down to the Safeway whenever you're hungry. Then late at night, just as you're on the edge of sleep you see a face, a child's face. With those flies that can burrow under an eyelid, a child looking up at you, holding out a little black hand for food. That's your reward," she said flatly. "Those weekly, sometimes daily reminders that millions of people you've met are probably dying. Or are dead by now."

Lucy was drawn to this unsentimental woman. "You said you had a kid?"

The nurse looked blank a moment. "Jason. He's seven."

"With your parents passed on, who baby-sits while you're, uh—"

"His father got custody," she said matter-of-factly.

Lucy pondered how that could happen. This charitable soul, caring mother to the world's needy, somehow had had her child put in the father's care. But this is a present life. Maybe in some past life she was not so good. A drinker? Suicidal? A dark thought, but abusive or neglectful of her child? Was this time in the wilderness an atonement?

Lucy instinctively said, "You're a good person."

The nurse, gathering up her light jacket before leaving, looked at Lucy oddly and said, "Not really. That's the funny thing." She reached into her pocket. "Here." She presented Lucy with a card with the American address for Médécins Sans Frontières, the French relief organization. "Here's another," said the nurse, digging deeper. This card had an address for Catholic Relief Charities. "I pass 'em out to whoever will take them, journalists, U.N. observers, and I say 'Do what you can.' "

The nurse gave Lucy a friendly, patient squeeze of the arm.

"Thanks," said Lucy, blushing for some reason, staring hard at the addresses.

Lucy returned to the coffee pot, big rusted thing, circa World War Two, and filled her Styrofoam cup. This is the cup she had been given and told: don't lose it, it's the only one you get out here.

"There she is!"

Lucy turned to see O'Hanrahan, remarkably pressed and uncrumpled, smoking an American cigarette.

"God, doesn't it feel great," he said. "We're back in the land where booze is legal! Civilization! Got this Winston from a nurse, what about that? Gimme that coffee," he said, playfully taking it from Lucy's hand.

"That's my cup. Don't lose it."

"You all packed up?"

Lucy faltered. "What? We're leaving already?"

O'Hanrahan sat at one of the long mess-hall benches at a table. "The guy from the U.S. Embassy is driving up and oughta be here by lunch."

Lucy walked to the position at the table across from him, the long way around the long table. Oh no, she thought.

"I called David McCall yesterday, sir," she confessed. "You know, just to see if he was nearby. He is. He's supposed to show up this morning."

"Young McCall, huh? It'll be good to see that boy."

Lucy frowned, thinking of O'Hanrahan inserting himself.

"Actually," he said, "you call me when he shows up. I'm going to get

Abba Selama to give me a crash course in Coushita. One dialect I don't speak, read, or know a damn thing about. I just *love* this," enthused O'Hanrahan finally. "A new language. God, give me seventy more years and I'll know everything worth knowing in the world!"

And with that, he left.

Lucy looked into her cup to see O'Hanrahan had absently used it as an ashtray. "He could at least have given me a drag," she said out loud, disgusted, though hankering for a cigarette.

But just as well, she thought. Not good for the baby.

She sighed. Lucy had gone ninety minutes this morning without remembering the baby-to-be. But, as on every other day, it caught up with her, tagging her from behind at a moment of calm and repose. Frankly, this morning the abortion forces within were winning all the arguments. I so much wanted to press that nurse, Lucy thought, for information on how to join Catholic Relief Charities for a summer, how does one apply, what qualifications one needs . . . But I'll need all the charity and aid I have to spare in about eight months. This child not only kills any chance of doing something with my life, but of doing something *good.*

(Raising a child is a good thing.)

But I could do better things.

(Like that thesis of yours?)

No, I mean the down-and-dirty business of running a camp like this. Getting in there and doing what has to be done. The will to be of service in this world has always been strong but I wonder if I would feel so strongly if I hadn't been brought here to see it firsthand for myself. Maybe the plane going down near here was God's doing.

(Could be.)

But again, this is all empty talk. Ethiopia amid all the diseases is no place to have my child. She reflected dourly on the parade of emaciated women, their breasts shrunken and leathery, their faces haunted with an animal despair for their children, the hundreds, the thousands, the thousands more to come. Each woman would give her life so that her children could live—no, more than that: each woman would trade her life so that her children could eat for *a week.* And what am I considering? Having some doctor suck it out of me with a vacuum cleaner and toss whatever, whoever, on the pile. Of course, David might fall in love with me, marry me, and think it's his . . .

(Lucy.)

Just kidding. But I am going to tell him. He's good and level-headed. I can't tell Dr. O'Hanrahan—the shame, the ridicule! No, really, even he would be good about it. He would, after the fireworks, be fatherly, authoritative. And I bet he'd cover for me, let me spend the last months hiding out with him or something, help me lie to my folks . . . but offsetting this avuncular fantasy, I would never in his eyes be the young bright scholar again, the girl who read Lampridius. I would be the craven little repressed Catholic girl, slattern at the first opportunity—

"Lucy Dantan?"

At the tent flap there was a mechanic she'd seen around the camp. "There are some doctors here to see you."

Lucy stood, surprised that David and his friends had made it so soon. She panicked! She scurried toward the coffee pot, which gave her a dim fun house–mirror reflection, and pathetically she attempted to arrange her hair and prettify herself . . . Hopeless! She then went to the tent flap and peeked out.

There he was.

David McCall in a pith helmet, accompanied by a long-haired youngish man in medical sweats, and a sunburned, officious-looking woman in a long white skirt like a 1920s tennis player. David was telling a story and had them both laughing. Lucy committed herself and walked to meet them, waiting for him to turn around, recognize her, and—what? Sweep her up in his arms, whirl her around?

"Lucy!" David shook his head in disbelief, not quite over the novelty of seeing her in Ethiopia. He did run to greet her. He did hug her and give her a slight lift off the ground. "Where's Patrick?"

"Somewhere nearby, chasing a bottle of Ethiopian moonshine," she laughed, happier than she thought she'd be to see him. He was everything! A familiar face, a calming voice, now leaner and burnished by the sun.

"Aw damn, I wanted to lay me eyes on the man!"

"David, I'm *so* glad to see you. I have something to talk over with you . . ."

All smiles, he snatched the pith helmet from his head and temporarily put it on Lucy's. "Gotta getcha one of these, Lucy. It'll fry your brains out here, the sun will."

"I hope I'm not staying long enough. You know—"

David interrupted her so as not to be rude to his traveling companions: "Ah, you must first meet me mates."

Lucy was led by his strong hand to stand before the somewhat hippie-ish young man in an aquamarine orderly's shirt. David introduced him as, "This is Bobby O'Connell from Cork—a fact that we overlook."

Bobby took a tube of stacked plastic cups in a plastic bag and bopped David on the head for revenge. "Lucy, pleased to meetcha," he said. "Look, I'll catch you later, Davey. I've got to set out for Addis Zemen and fetch the supplies. Don't anyone go away now, 'cause I wish to be around when you open the you-know-what."

David explained he had an unopened bottle of Bushmills, previously saved for the farewell week, but this was special!

"He's told me lots about you," said Bobby, pointing a finger at Lucy.

"I'm goin' to move in, back in Connecticut on her sofa," said David.

"Chicago," reminded Lucy. She noticed Bobby had a camera round his neck. "Going to see the castles in Gonder?" she asked.

"Ah yes, play tourist a wee bit," he said, putting himself in the driver's seat of the Jeep. "Nothin' back in the camp fit to take a picture of, all the poor little buggers . . ." He didn't have to elaborate.

"I'm Georgie Shelton," said the woman, putting out her hand, "since Davey can't bring hisself to own up to me."

Lucy tried to place her accent. "English or . . ."

"Australian," she supplied. "From Perth."

David: "Oh, say *g'day* for Lucy, Georgie! Don't deny the lass."

Relenting, she said an archetypical Aussie *g'day*.

While Lucy laughed, David sidled up to Georgie and gave her a squeeze. "I guess Lucy here'll be the first in the outside world to know. Georgie and I are engaged!"

The driver of the 1988 Ford Tempo stopped for a shepherd and his flock of sheep spread across the dirt road to Addis Ababa.

"I promise," said Mr. Conrad Thorn of the U.S. State Department and diplomatic mission to Ethiopia, a forty-year-old man, sandy hair, a cross lapel pin. "Promise, that once we get to Debra Markos the road gets better. Paved all the way to the capital."

O'Hanrahan, in the backseat with Lucy, was content. "I'm just happy to be in one piece after the plane went down."

"That happens all the time," said Thorn, beeping the horn lightly to scatter the sheep, inching the car forward. "Local planes land in Lake Tana, on the highways—seems everywhere but at the airports. By the grace of God, I think, these planes stay in one piece."

O'Hanrahan laughed politely. He glanced at Lucy, who looked ill. "You all right?" he asked quietly.

"Something I ate," she said huskily.

"I guess David can eat what the locals eat by this time, after five weeks, huh?"

"I guess."

"Didn't he look good?"

Yep, thought Lucy.

Their State Department friend spoke again. "You two have a file on you *this* thick."

This kind of thing fed O'Hanrahan's ego. "Really?"

"There's a special directive issued by a Colonel Westin—"

"Ah, good old Colonel Westin," said O'Hanrahan, leaning forward. "He's not too happy with me, I'm sure." Go on, O'Hanrahan seemed to be saying, tell me more of my own legend!

"It's my job . . . uh, this is awkward, I guess I better just come out and say it . . ."

"Please."

"To obligate Miss Dantan to return at once to the United States and out of danger. And you, sir, to a predetermined location . . ."

"That's right. Go and set up a shop for you boys in Teheran."

Mr. Thorn shook his head. "That's extraordinary, sir."

It *was* really extraordinary when said out loud so simply. O'Hanrahan couldn't leave it alone! "I suspect I'm the first Westerner to be offered a post. Perhaps, in my way, I could help restore our diplomatic ties with our long-lost Persian friends."

Lucy sneered to herself: what's this about a post in Teheran?

"You know I envy you, sir," said Thorn, now back to full speed after the obstacle of the sheep. "We poor civil servants spend a lifetime in these places and never get an opportunity to really further our country's cause."

O'Hanrahan was suffused with self-congratulation.

"What's this about Teheran, Dr. O'Hanrahan?"

He looked to the floor, managing a weak air of pleasantry. "Well. I've been recruited to go to Iran, it seems."

Lucy turned away to the window. "And I'm to go home, huh?"

"Oh, I'm gonna join you right away, after I check out Teheran, you see. We'll get right back to the *Gospel of Matthias* like we'd planned. But they've got 'Q,' Luce! I have to go check it out!"

She felt tears in her eyes. Of course, this was the ending. Anyone could have seen it coming, really. He's tired of this little dalliance with the scroll, and is moving on to some other adventure, and you, Lucy Dantan, have exhausted your usefulness. You were just someone to talk to, keep him from getting bored. But now it's time to shuffle on along, dump the dead weight.

"It'll just be a month or so," he said, laughing insincerely the next minute, passing it off as nothing.

Lucy stared out her window feeling betrayed in every sense, no less by her talent for believing what she wanted to believe, about Stavros, about David, about Dr. O'Hanrahan, about her own life and future. She was not fit for this world where people lied and fooled you. Yes, others got the hang of living, but not her. She should never have left Kimbark Street, never have put before herself any more complex issue

than what flavor yogurt Judy and she should have for dinner before
they put on the aerobics video, fed the cats . . .

Soon the outskirts of Addis lay outside Lucy's window.

Shacks and fires and slums gave way to boarded-up shops, crumbling
tenements, a city rotting from the top down. Troops were everywhere,
20,000 Cubans, according to Mr. Thorn. Most of the downtown was
spread out illogically over a number of hills in no grid pattern, sort of
an African Washington, D.C., with circles and monuments now torn
down or defaced. There was a glimpse of the ravaged Presidential
Palace, Haile Selassie's looted pleasure dome, and throughout, as in
Eastern Europe or Maoist China or Iraq, the large five-story mural of
People's Art: a smiling Mengistu beside a smiling Gorbachev beside a
fierce, saintly Lenin happily waving to the adoring Africans over a
tableau of tanks parading through the streets. Famine, natural disasters, endless civil wars, a ruined economy, over a quarter of a million
killed by this regime, but never fear, Marxists of Ethiopia, your future
has been assured: $12 billion in Cuban and Russian arms!

O'Hanrahan and Lucy were taken to the Hilton Hotel, where the
State Department *strongly* insisted they remain, since the capital was in
a bout of improvised curfew and the population of drunken soldiers
out after dark was not to be underestimated. The Cubans, said Mr.
Thorn, of whom a fresh shipment had just come in from Angola, were
drug addicts and drunkards—not to be wondered at since they were
losing this civil war and utter annihilation awaited them. If Americans
and their diplomats had any ease of mobility at all, it was because the
government realized that Americans, *not* their Soviet patrons, were
instrumental in famine relief and as long as there were Americans
around, the government wouldn't have to lift a finger to help its own
people.

The Hilton had seen its best days, as had Addis Ababa, in the 1960s.

O'Hanrahan exchanged his 400 Sudanese pounds for Ethiopian
birrs, paid for the two rooms, and made empty conversation with the
receptionist, fearing that moment that he and Lucy would be alone.
Mr. Thorn, scurrying back to the safety of the embassy before dark,
wished them Christ's blessings—it paid to advertise his Christianity
down here, Lucy figured, given the Muslim insurgencies—and hoped
to see them tomorrow.

Lucy was silent in the elevator.

"What are you thinking?" the professor risked.

"How you've been lying to me."

"Now, Luce, I am just as excited as ever about finishing the *Gospel
of Matthias*, but Teheran is a once-in-a-lifetime opportunity. I was
offered a position back when we were in Jerusalem—"

Lucy was bitter as she left the elevator. "Thanks for telling me! So
what was Khartoum and Degoma? Just a little vacation before you

dropped all this, dumped me on a plane with Colonel Westin and headed off for Teheran on another adventure?" She slammed her key in the lock. "That's great for you, isn't it? You don't even intend to finish the *Gospel of Matthias* project, do you?"

"Of course I do—"

"No you don't. You're not a finisher of things, I see that now." She spun around to accuse him to his face: "You dabble. You stand beside the people who do things and get your picture taken with them, but you don't . . ."

O'Hanrahan shamefacedly put a hand consolingly on her arm—

"Let go of me," she pulled back.

"I just want you to hear me out—"

She rushed into her room and slammed the door in his face.

Lucy, near tears, paced before the mirror, checking her flustered appearance, which seemed to increase her anger. She went back to the door, hearing that O'Hanrahan was right outside. She turned the lock. She had been ready to endanger herself for this man who would lie to her, steal from her, *use* her however he would just to distract himself from his . . . his own mortality. She leaned against her door and heard the professor go to his room, unlock his door, and gently retire within. I hope he's disappointed in himself, she thought. I don't care if I've hurt him.

Lucy flopped down on the bed.

She was, as she had always been, *alone*. Patrick O'Hanrahan had never really been an ally. She was part of *his* life's dream, she hitched a ride for a while. For a time it seemed it was hers too but no more. And David McCall. How so much hope was wagered—what an edifice, what a St. Peter's and the Pyramids and Holy Sepulcher was built upon so little information! As in most of my life, I saw what I wanted to see, heard what I wanted to hear. What a fool, what a colossal embarrassment I am to myself.

All the more reason it should be me in those refugee camps near Gonder dishing out food, doing what I can for those people whose needs are so obvious, so painful—me, the woman whose life doesn't count with anybody else.

Outside in the streets, ten stories below, she heard gunfire.

Curious, she went to the window. Few streetlights worked anymore; she could only make out some scattered people below, ragged, running in packs. There was a truck filled with fruit, followed by another with more people in the back than she had thought possible, countless skinny arms and legs wrangling and bouncing over the broken asphalt of once-fine Addis Ababa, the 1960s showplace of the New Africa, birthplace of the OAS, jewel in the crown of black nationalism and African independence, now a Soviet client state overrun with terror and evil and Cuban drunks shooting out windows for fun at eight P.M., longing for Havana.

She lay back on her bed: much of this world is a terrible place.

አዲስ ፡ አበባ ፡

AUGUST 26TH

Lucy awoke and gave thanks briefly for this modern, luxurious, clean bed at the Hilton, her island of the Western World. Slowly her old life crept up on her. Deserted by O'Hanrahan. Pregnant. Thesis due. Parents ready to kill me for having a life. I need an ally, she figured coolly. I'll call Rabbi Hersch at his home and see if he can advise me— I'll tell him everything. Maybe there's still a chance I can have this kid in Jerusalem out of public view.

"Can I make an international call?" she asked the woman who picked up the phone at the reception desk. "It's to Israel, but I don't know the home number of the person I'm calling."

The woman informed her she would have to come downstairs to their bank of phone booths and meters.

Lucy picked up her key from the bedside table. Quietly she turned the doorknob and peered into the hall. Stealthily, she closed and locked her door, barely breathing lest O'Hanrahan discover her, and she skipped quickly to the elevator bank.

The lady at reception greeted her with a smile. It was 10:30 A.M. and the few guests were in a spare breakfast room off the lobby, drinking coffee and choosing with tongs from a mountain of croissants.

"We spoke about an international phone call," Lucy announced.

The receptionist, the woman who'd registered O'Hanrahan and Lucy last night, was a tall woman of Somalian features, with a perfectly oval head with large circular eyes. She knelt beside a stubborn drawer that opened with difficulty. Inside were numerous phone books from various African capitals, a few European cities, New York, Los Angeles . . .

Lucy: "Do you have Jerusalem?"

"Oh yes," she said, rummaging.

"Your English is very good," said Lucy, feeling the urge to make friends with this woman of such striking beauty.

"I studied in America, Michigan State University."

"East Lansing, sure," Lucy said, having never been there.

"Last night was a night of Americans at the hotel."

Lucy glanced up at the hundreds of keys dangling at the boxes, few venturing to travel to Ethiopia amid the war. Or perhaps, those who did come to Ethiopia—aid-workers and volunteers and returning ex-patriates—would not stay at such an expensive place. "No businessmen stay here?" asked Lucy.

"No one comes anymore," she said, setting aside Athens and Paris. "That is why it is odd, three Americans last night. We do not get many Americans these days. You, the doctor . . ." She meant O'Hanrahan, who had registered himself as Dr. O'Hanrahan. ". . . and the monk."

"The monk."

"An American monk . . ." The woman unearthed the Jerusalem phone book, tattered and coverless. "It had no front, see? Impossible to find," she laughed.

"A monk, you say."

"Yes, he checked to see if your friend . . ." Her eyes glanced down to the guest register for the name she wanted, ". . . to see if Dr. O'Han-rahan was staying at this hotel but when he asked you had not arrived. The monk is with your party, yes?"

Lucy's heart beat faster. "Yes."

"Axum is closed to tourists because of the war. But Lalibela some-times, sometimes is open." She plopped the book on the counter and kicked the bottom drawer closed. "Many Christians used to travel to Ethiopia—it is sad."

"The monk is my uncle," invented Lucy. "What room did you put him in, again? I'll go call on him for breakfast."

The woman's lovely face looked to her register with heavy lids, perfect arcs. "Oh yes, 416."

Lucy opened the Jerusalem phone directory and looked up Morde-chai Hersch's home number, then copied it down. Then she excused herself, promising to be right back to make her phone call. The woman said Lucy would have to deal with Rashawn, who was coming on duty in five minutes.

In the elevator Lucy pushed "4."

When it opened on the fourth floor, Lucy stepped out into the empty corridor. What did she have in mind to say? Was this man *their* Mad Monk who had been following them? She would pretend she had the wrong room, but she'd get a good look. She went a few doors in the wrong direction, then backtracked counting down the rooms, 420, 419, 418, 417 . . .

She stood before the door.

Which was ajar.

"Hello?" she tried.

Nothing. Lucy pushed the door foward ever so gently.

"Hello? Uh, maid service, excuse me."

Still nothing. Lucy leaned in and looked into the room. It was a shambles. A suitcase on the bed lay in shreds, the sides and bottoms ripped apart by some rough blade. Papers were scattered everywhere, a black robe was in tatters. Her heart was beating quickly as she surveyed the mess. There was an airline tag hanging from the remains of the suitcase, El Al, and the name on the luggage was Mordechai Hersch.

"Lucy," said O'Hanrahan, looking exhausted after his restless, sleepless night, "please come in. Look, let me apologize. I don't know what I was thinking. Teheran is out. I must have been crazy . . ."

Lucy quickly stepped inside to his room of spent smoke and an emptied half-pint whiskey bottle.

"Better sit down," Lucy warned him, beginning to pace.

O'Hanrahan sat on the edge of his bed. "What?"

"By merest chance I learned there's a monk in the hotel who was looking for us yesterday."

O'Hanrahan's eyes widened.

"The trusting woman at the desk gave me the room number. She said he was an American. I got curious, I went to Room 416 and it was ransacked. And the suitcase inside belonged to Rabbi Hersch."

O'Hanrahan lightly touched his forehead. "So . . . he did say he was going to meet us here . . ."

"Do you think Rabbi Hersch could be our Mad Monk?"

The professor muttered, "Jesus," and began thinking, reviewing the whereabouts of their nemesis. The Mad Monk had first surfaced in Assisi, according to Father Vico . . . and, yes, the rabbi was in Italy where he wasn't supposed to be, in Rome. So he could have preceded them to Assisi.

Then the monk was at Athens and on Mt. Athos. Conceivably, Morey could have not gotten on a plane to Tel Aviv and flown to Greece days ahead of them.

No sign of the monk in Jerusalem, damningly enough, and then at Wadi Natrun and the Coptic Library, then at Khartoum . . . Why would Morey do such a thing? He and Lucy considered every possibility, going over and over the scanty collection of facts.

"Let's go down to the reception desk," said O'Hanrahan, standing. "There is one way we can tell where Morey's been for sure."

In the elevator Lucy looked anxiously at the professor. "What are you gonna do?" she asked.

"Let's hope all old white men look alike to Ethiopians."

O'Hanrahan went to the reception desk and talked to a honey-colored, smiling man, very eager to please. "Excuse me, sir," said O'Hanrahan. "I need my passport to cash the last of my traveler's checks. Could I have it? Room 416."

A moment of truth. Would O'Hanrahan look enough like Rabbi Hersch in his passport photo to fool this young man? But the man handed the passport of the guest in 416 to O'Hanrahan without checking, an American asking for an American passport. Lucy approached the professor as he flipped through the pages.

"Of course," mumbled O'Hanrahan. "Morey was raised in Brooklyn and has dual citizenship in Israel. No Israeli could travel easily in the Sudan so, of course, he'd travel on this American passport . . ."

Lucy remembered he used this passport at the Northern Irish border.

"Here he is in the U.K., in Ireland, stamped at Dublin on the right date, here's Italy, Milan . . . Damn it, here's Greece! He *was* there the day before we were there! So he *didn't* go back to Jerusalem after Rome. Didn't you see him get on his plane when you guys went to the airport in Rome?"

"No," she shrugged. "I was getting drunk in the lounge, remember?" But the thought occurred: "But that's right, I didn't even see a flight for Tel Aviv. I recall that now."

The man behind the counter now squinted at them suspiciously.

"Changed my mind," said the professor. "I'll do it tomorrow." The professor noticed that the key for 416 was missing. They doubled back and took the elevator to the fourth floor.

"If his key's out," said O'Hanrahan, "he might have come back."

This time the door to 416 was closed.

O'Hanrahan knocked.

The rabbi was there. He cautiously, as if expecting the former vandals, asked, "Who is it?"

"Morey," O'Hanrahan said somberly.

"Hello, my friend," sighed the rabbi glumly, opening the door. Looking burdened, he sat on his bed. "Come in, pull up a broken chair."

"So you're the Mad Monk?" said Lucy, hurt deeply for a reason she couldn't put into words. Betrayal? Being wrong about someone yet again?

"What's going on here, Mordechai," said O'Hanrahan, still standing.

"We're all in a lot of trouble, is what's going on," he said.

O'Hanrahan found an overturned chair, righted it, and sat down. "All right, Morey," he said carefully. "I'm not going to say anything until I hear what you have to say. It looks bad."

Rabbi Hersch stroked his beard with his typical composure, but less serene somehow. "Now Paddy, you listen to me and don't get upset.

All right, so I dressed up in the monk's outfit—you yourself gave me the idea in Rome. It was the most painless way to look at some of these indexes and books of alphabets in Athens. No harm done—"

"Except that you didn't trust *me* to do it. Morey, what am I to think? You call me and say come from Chicago and work on the scholastic find of the century, then when I'm here, ready to give the rest of my life to this project, I find you sneaking around behind my back, trying to beat me to it! What am I to think?"

"You think what is the truth: I had to find the key to that language. Yes, before you did. I asked you to help me *before* I had thought out all of the implications of this gospel."

O'Hanrahan was speechless.

"Listen to me, Paddy. Since April all kinds of strange things have been happening. Visits from Mossad, visits from government officials. I found listening devices in my phone. Last week, my office and my safe were broken into. The bearer bonds from my Uncle Leopold they left, the gold coins minted by the tsars from Uncle Sasha—*that*, they left. Whoever it was has resources beyond our imagination."

O'Hanrahan thought of the limitless credit card once at his disposal, the million deutsche marks offered by Herr Kellner.

"These people, I figured, were looking for the *Gospel of Matthias*, not knowing the Franciscans had it. Then you took it, and they still kept breaking in. And then they broke in my house, still looking for something. It occurred to me. They were looking for the missing last chapter, and they thought that I had it."

O'Hanrahan and Lucy watched him as he stood.

"And," said the rabbi, "I *did* have it."

"You have the missing last chapter . . ." breathed O'Hanrahan.

"Rabbi, no!" said Lucy automatically.

"For several years now. I wasn't sure, because I needed the first six segments to know if what I had was the seventh. When I examined the larger part in Northern Ireland, I was sure. The alphabets matched up, the papyrus was the same—no doubt in my mind. A few years back I looked up Mrs. Rosen and sure enough, it was among her things. He had taken the last segment home with him the day before he had his accident."

"*Why* didn't you say anything?" O'Hanrahan demanded.

Rabbi Hersch: "You're not going to understand this . . ."

"I think I get it!" said O'Hanrahan, now standing too. "It wasn't enough that you had a shelf of books to your name! You wanted to make this discovery your own as well! Of course, you have the right—your university owns the thing. But why did you string me along? Get my hopes up! I had planned on this—sold my worldly possessions, Morey. *This was my life!*"

"Calm down, Paddy, please, let me—"

"Or was it money?" O'Hanrahan was particularly convincing in his accusation, having fingered tempting sums himself. "I was offered a million deutsche marks to steal that scroll and hand it over to a private collector and I didn't. Was that it? You wanted to cash in?"

"I think *I* understand it," said Lucy, a trace of harshness in her voice. "It had nothing to do with money, Dr. O'Hanrahan."

"The little girl's right, Paddy—"

"It has to do with Christianity. I've been thinking about the rabbi's book, *Not the Messiah,* and the sustained effort, the discipline that writing that kind of 200-page attack on Christianity required. I've heard Rabbi Hersch say he didn't trust the Jesuits or the Franciscans or the Catholic Church to publish the *Gospel of Matthias* unexpurgated and unedited. He figured this last chapter had proof that Jesus was . . . was merely a deluded fool and his disciples shady accomplices. And he didn't want to risk that last chapter being destroyed."

"Oh, you think that's it, do you?" said the rabbi, bristling.

Lucy finished, "Isn't this why Israel has gone to such trouble to get this thing? That it contains the last stroke of the Jewish argument made for 2000 years? That Jesus is a fraud."

"You had your little speech, little girl? May I talk now?"

Lucy's face was stinging from her own argument, which was more emotional than reasoned. She stood behind the chair of Dr. O'Hanrahan for solidarity.

The rabbi surprised them by shouting:

"Hypocrites! You, Paddy, with your delusions of grandeur! Cover of *Time* magazine, front page of *The New York Times,* money and new position—did you hear yourself in Jerusalem? Not just Jerusalem. For as long as we've known each other the *Gospel of Matthias* was going to be your ticket. It was going to make up for everything that had gone wrong in your life. A panacea, a philosopher's stone!"

The rabbi, pacing measuredly, turned on Lucy: "And *you,* little girl. Did you hear yourself, bagel in your mouth, at the King David? Princeton, Harvard, Columbia—what to do with all the big offers coming your way? Oh yes, this scroll meant you got to see the world, got to take a Greek cruise, buy some pretty new schmattes, get rid of that thesis you hated. Both of you, think about it! You never once have thought about the implications of this scroll! Never *once!*"

Both Lucy and O'Hanrahan remained quiet.

"You didn't care if this gospel caused a war? You didn't care if this gospel shook the faith of millions? I never once heard you consider such a thing. And you, Paddy, you yearned for it to be a firebomb. I've heard you *delight* in the possibility that you could dismantle the Vatican, upset housewives all over America—you *prayed* for this to turn Christianity on its ear."

The rabbi's voice weakened with strain: "I'm sorry I wrote that book, *Not the Messiah*. It was unworthy of the gifts that God has entrusted to me. You don't believe me, little girl, though I have spoken honestly with you. But I don't care what you think anymore. I tell you . . ."

The rabbi sat down on the bed, he too showing the strain of the recent weeks.

"I tell you," he continued softly, "I think about God all the time. When I wake up in the morning—you, Paddy, may mock—but I praise God for the day and that I am alive in it. And when I go to sleep, I go to sleep praying—God is the last thought I think. And through the day, I make a sandwich. I take out the garbage. I make the bed. And I think then too of God."

Lucy now wished she hadn't spoken. She wanted to say something but it was impossible. Because she used to be that way too.

". . . but it is how I am," the rabbi went on. "And as I get older, I come to see the world as a great challenge laid out to us by God. Moslem, Jew, and Christian all adoring the God of Abraham. If we kill each other in war after war, I am convinced God will have done with us! If we learn to love and respect each other and praise this God of Abraham together, then we will be worthy of His world, and not until. And that is why I held back that last chapter. Just in case it did upset the apple cart, hm?"

Rabbi Hersch stared directly at Lucy, looking tired but his eyes piercing and purposeful as ever.

"Because, little girl . . . I wouldn't do that to you. The bleeding Sacred Immaculate Wounds of Mary's little toe—I think a lot of your religion is full of crap. I respect it—*this* much . . ." He held up a pinched finger. "Which is nothing. To hell with the church, to hell with your religion, but I would not shake your *faith*. I would not do that to you because you are a good person, Lucille. And if you find God in what you believe then I am not going to have it on ledger: the Rabbi Mordechai Hersch took that away from Lucille Dantan. No one who believes in God . . ." He looked to the ceiling. ". . . should cause others to disbelieve in this godless world. I would never do that to you."

Then he turned from them and paced toward the hotel room window. "Besides," he mentioned, "it's a dangerous thing finding out what happened in the First Century with this man named Jesus, hm? Maybe the evidence makes it *woise* for the Jews, huh? Maybe it will launch a wave of anti-Semitism by the Catholics—who can say? Or maybe it proves Jesus is a fraud. And the Orthodox and the Ultra-Conservative Jews will celebrate and demand that Christian shrines in Jerusalem be torn down, the land ceded to Jewish settlers, and Israel waves good-bye to its American support." He sighed heavily. "Throw it in the fire before any of that."

"Where is the last chapter now?" asked O'Hanrahan quietly. "Did the thieves get it?"

"No, in Jerusalem I had been keeping it in a friend's safe. Before I left I sewed it into these, uh, robes—what used to be robes here . . ." The rabbi lifted a shredded garment near his suitcase and let it drop. "Everywhere I went in Jerusalem someone was following me, so since the girl told me you were headed for Addis Ababa, I hopped on the plane to find you people and run to Chicago. This morning I went to the U.S. Embassy and entrusted the chapter to their valuables safe, figuring their security's pretty good." He laughed darkly and turned to them. "For all I know, it's been the American government after this thing all along . . ."

There was a noise at the door.

"The CIA," Colonel Westin said, leaning into the doorway, "is a pretty good guess, Rabbi."

The trio spun around to observe Colonel Westin in his dark green uniform and Mr. Thorn in a black suit entering the room.

"You're a smart man, no doubt about it. It took us a long time to figure out where that last chapter could be, but eventually we traced all our sources back to Hebrew University and we figured it never left that location. Holding out on your partners, I see, Mr. Rabbi." The colonel sucked in air quickly, shaking his head. "Ah, the shrewdness of the Jewish mind. One learns to appreciate that, yes indeed—"

Colonel Westin turned to lock the door behind him.

"You fellows made it too easy," said the colonel. "What with Patrick here calling the embassy first sign of trouble, I was able to keep track of him. And then you, Rabbi, bringing us the missing puzzle piece, pretty as you please . . ." The colonel uttered a porcine, snorting laugh. "Oh, and I like how you stiffed Underwood with that two-bit scroll. Looks like no $20,000 bonus for him!"

"What could the American government possibly," began the professor faintly, "possibly want with this gospel, Colonel?"

"Why, we want you to translate it, Patrick," he said cheerily. Colonel Westin sucked in air through his teeth. "Agent Thorn?"

"Yessir?"

"Get the needle."

As Lucy and Rabbi Hersch and O'Hanrahan felt their blood freeze in their veins, Agent Thorn opened up a doctor's kit and produced a syringe and a bottle of clear liquid. Thorn stuck the needle into it and drew up the liquid into the hypodermic.

"My God," mumbled the professor.

"What are you going to do?" asked the rabbi quietly.

"Rabbi rabbi rabbi," began Colonel Westin lightly, as if some parlor game were being played. "You have been of service, yes indeed, but now you are in the way—"

O'Hanrahan stood: "If you harm him, so help me God, I'll testify about this to a Senate subcommittee and get you clowns put under the jail they should have put Oliver North in!"

"Relax, Patrick," said Colonel Westin, taking the syringe from his assistant. "I just need the rabbi to sleep and stay out of my hair for about 48 hours . . . No sense him running back to Israel or the press or the authorities of any variety while we're trying to get out of this Soviet hellhole, hm?" A jet of liquid spurted from the top of the hypodermic as Colonel Westin held the device up to the light. "It's just a sedative, Rabbi. And by the time you get up we'll be long gone—"

O'Hanrahan: "You hurt him and I'll . . . My cooperation is not assured, Colonel! If anything bad happens to him, you'll never get a moment's cooperation from me!"

"Well, that's where Miss Dantan comes in," said the colonel, as his assistant went to restrain the rabbi. "Don't make us use Miss Dantan as . . . how shall we say," he sucked in an intake of air, "leverage?"

The rabbi was absent of expression, the look of inevitability and weariness that connected him to centuries of moments where God allowed his Chosen to fall prey to the godless. Rabbi Hersch turned to O'Hanrahan, who gasped at him, speechless. Was this their final meeting? The rabbi's resigned expression burned itself on Lucy's memory—poor man! If only she could recant her accusations . . . Lucy, her eyes tearing up, turned away. Westin rolled up the rabbi's sleeve and Thorn held the syringe. Then the rabbi suddenly attempted to get free but was restrained roughly by Agent Thorn, wordlessly, like a robot following orders. Thorn mumbled something piously to himself, and then concluded, "In Jesus' name. Amen."

It was done.

"Make sure he's resting comfortably," said Westin. "He'll be in that position for some time, we don't want anything to lose circulation."

"Paddy, I . . ." The rabbi felt a wave of sleep wash over him.

"Everything will be all right, Morey, I promise," said O'Hanrahan desperately. Lucy looked down at her hands to see them tremble, as weak as her knees.

"We have a 12:30 P.M. flight we have to meet, my friends. Agent Thorn will be happy to help you pack."

O'Hanrahan: "And what about—"

"Yes," said the colonel, reading his mind. "We have been through your luggage, Patrick, and have the first six chapters in our possession. The *Gospel of Matthias* is now complete."

The rabbi groaned, and O'Hanrahan looked as if he might charge Colonel Westin like a mad bull.

But Westin spoke quietly. "And do I have to be so crude as to, well, say that if you prove uncooperative or try anything rash that we have people here permanently in Addis who could make your Hebrew friend's escape from this third-world sideshow very, very difficult. What if, shall we say, cocaine found its way into his luggage here . . . What's left of his luggage. Looks like you need a new set of Samsonite, great rabban, heh-heh-heh."

"I get your point, Colonel," said O'Hanrahan. "Where exactly are you taking us?"

He fixed the professor with an oblique smile. "Would you believe The Promised Land?"

With Thorn at the wheel and Colonel Westin in the passenger's seat, O'Hanrahan and Lucy in the back, the diplomatic limousine came to a stop on the runway of Ethiopia's international airport.

"Right on time," said the colonel as the expected plane loomed above the runway approach. Wordlessly, the foursome watched the plane descend, land, and turn so that the afternoon sun was full upon it. The Boeing 737 jet was gleaming white with a light blue line running its length. On its tailfin was a light blue cross and the initials TPL. Lucy and O'Hanrahan watched it turn from the landing runway and drive across the tarmac toward the terminal. In the berth that was its destination O'Hanrahan noticed a stack of wooden crates set out on the tarmac marked MEDICAL and FOODSTUFFS.

"TPL," murmured O'Hanrahan. The Promised Land Ministries. "That's the holy-roller program back in the United States."

Colonel Westin didn't say anything.

"You got these Bible-bashers fronting for the CIA, Colonel?" pursued O'Hanrahan.

"Reverend Bullins is a man of God, Patrick," Colonel Westin said at last.

The four passengers in Westin's car watched the plane noisily come to a stop in the airport berth, the engines' pitch dying, octave by octave.

"I saw on 'Prime Time,'" O'Hanrahan began, "where Reverend Bullins has a personal tax-free fortune of $100 million and the IRS is after him. Not to mention the Interstate Commerce Commission, which is investigating his religious products, and the Postal Service, for mail fraud."

"Regrettable, really," said the colonel, staring placidly ahead.

"We used to have people we could depend on," Thorn sputtered. "You can bet President Reagan wouldn't have allowed the IRS . . ." But Colonel Westin with a turn of his head had silenced his assistant.

O'Hanrahan chuckled. "Ah, that's right. Good ol' Uncle Ronnie's administration let those TV Bible boys get by with murder, in return, of course, for a stream of contributions." O'Hanrahan hoped another round of questioning would this time produce some answers: "What on earth could you want with an old scroll, Colonel?"

"It's not just any old scroll, of course." Colonel Westin reared back in the seat, looking very military and confident. "And the time for explanations is not yet at hand. Suffice it to say that this phase of our assignment has virtually come to an end. It was but one of a two-prong operation, the other half being still in an unfolding mode, and still classified—"

"The Flight of the Griffin," said O'Hanrahan, taking a stab, remembering the rabbi asked about the phrase in Jerusalem.

Colonel Westin did not immediately acknowledge this. "Well, we will have to interrogate you, Patrick, on how you came by this piece of information."

Not wanting the third-degree, O'Hanrahan explained that Rabbi Hersch had asked him about the phrase, having himself been examined by Mossad agents.

"Make a note of that, Thorn," babbled Colonel Westin. "Mossad can still be an impediment, though we assumed they were actuality-neutralized as regards this operation, uh, implementation-wise."

Lucy noticed O'Hanrahan seemed paler than a moment before.

"Wait a minute," he said. "Does this have something to do with Iraq? The Griffin, the wingéd lion of Babylon, in *The Book of Daniel*."

"All I can say, professor, is that events, though unexpected, seem to be concurring with our timetable. Since the Iran-Iraq war ended two years ago, we in the West have allowed a steady stream of munitions and ordnances to accumulate in Saddam Hussein's stockpile, once we identified him for who he was."

Lucy falteringly asked, "For who he was?"

O'Hanrahan: "Is the CIA involved in the Iraqi invasion of Kuwait? I hope to God that's not the case, because if it's true I'll gladly have you and your people before a Senate subcommittee faster'n you can say Admiral Poindexter!"

"We've never even met Poindexter on this," snapped Colonel Westin unconvincingly. "And as for the invasion of Kuwait, the plan was . . . well, I mean we figured that he would attack Israel. Perhaps Kuwait is just a distraction for the big push into the Valley of Jizreel. Knock out Tel Aviv, leave Haifa unguarded to the Syrian north, the West Bank and Gaza to the Arabs in the south . . . Divide and conquer."

O'Hanrahan in disbelief: "On the plains of Armageddon. As it is written in *Revelations*," O'Hanrahan added somberly. The mix of biblical apocalyptics and covert operations swam before him. "And what's an old crook like Reverend Bullins got to do with all this?"

Thorn protested. "If you knew Farley Bullins like we do, you wouldn't repeat these scurrilous charges."

Both Lucy and O'Hanrahan chilled at the mention of the first name: Farley. Lucy briefly pressed her palm to her forehead. "Uh, Colonel," she stammered. "Reverend Bullins's family . . ."

"Fine people, fine people."

"Everyone," smiled Thorn, "knows Lila Mae Bullins."

Lila Mae Bullins, favorite target of the *National Enquirer* and *People* magazine and Johnny Carson's monologue. A tone-deaf harpie with a mile-high bouffant known for her outlandishly tasteless little-girl frills-and-ribbons ensembles, worn late into her fifties, and her spending habits that put her in a league with Imelda Marcos—her close personal friend, by the way.

"A son and two daughters," Colonel Westin continued. "Farley Junior will probably one day take over the ministries."

Lucy closed her eyes tightly. Farley Jr.! Recovering, she turned to O'Hanrahan, who merely muttered, "Great."

"Although," added Thorn, "I doubt any of us will be around for that day. Farley Junior will be looking down from the clouds, like the rest of us."

Lucy was confused. "I'm not sure I understand what you mean."

O'Hanrahan looked from his window to see two airport maintenance men roll a huge mobile-stairway to the cabin door of the TPL jet-liner.

"*And we who are alive and remain shall be caught up together with them in the clouds to meet the Lord in the air, and thus we shall always be with the Lord,*" Thorn said reverently, before the colonel silenced him with another headturn.

O'Hanrahan sank back in his seat. "Mr. Thorn is referring to the Rapture."

Lucy blurted out, "You mean that born-again nonsense about being taken up before the end of the world?"

Thorn was exercised, despite Colonel Westin's restraint. "It is *not* nonsense, Miss Dantan! It would behoove you to read your Bible and see what it promises. *There will be a great tribulation such as has not occurred since the beginning of the world until now, nor ever shall!*"

"That's enough, Conrad," said the colonel, undoing his seat belt, preparing to meet the plane's passengers.

"Are you telling me the godless CIA has swiped this thing," O'Hanrahan blurted, half-laughing, "because of the *Rapture*, Colonel?"

Thorn: "I beg your pardon! The CIA is far from godless. In fact, the founder of Operation Rapture, that saint, that man of God, William Casey—"

Colonel Westin: "That's enough, Conrad!"

"—William Casey, I heard him many times say the CIA was more than the Central Intelligence Agency, that we should think of ourselves as Christ in Action."

"Operation *Rapture?*" checked O'Hanrahan.

"Agent Thorn," hissed the colonel, "what have I told you about speaking in the open of these things? I swear sometimes . . ."

O'Hanrahan had the calm to ask, "Are you telling me that that senile nincompoop Ronald Reagan sanctioned a covert operation to oversee the implementation of biblical prophecies concerning the Rapture?"

"I think it is well established," said the colonel, annoyed and clenched tight with displeasure at his assistant's big mouth, "that Ronald Reagan believes in the Rapture—"

Thorn: "As do forty percent of Americans, don't forget that!"

"And with so many of the signs coming into place for these Final Days, the President made his will known concerning the many exigencies contingency-wise for America." Colonel Westin seemed to overboil the next moment: "I mean, good God, man, if this End Times thing is just around the corner, what leader would want his country to be caught off guard? Make no mistake, it is in the national interest that we prepare for the worst—the Bible itself instructs us to prepare the way of the Second Coming. And we want to make damn sure this is an *American* apocalypse and we're not caught with our military and spiritual pants down round our ankles."

O'Hanrahan almost laughed.

"I assure you, Patrick, the Antichrist and his minions know who *they* are. Gorbachev, with the mark of the beast on his forehead, and Saddam Hussein . . ."

O'Hanrahan steadied himself against the dashboard.

Colonel Westin took a long breath through his teeth, and produced his smile again. "It is very difficult to say, Patrick, just what Reagan approved and what he didn't approve specifically-wise, per se. However, it was quite clear from the directives he signed and the money we've had to work with that Operation Rapture has been a top government priority. In Casey's absence, it was left to me to find the men who believed our greatest spy manual, professor, is the Holy Bible itself."

O'Hanrahan: "Does President Bush know about you guys?"

Colonel Westin winced pleasantly again, "Well, I believe the former Vice President was . . . out of the loop."

O'Hanrahan looked at the gangway, now at the door of the plane. Then Underwood appeared, his comb-over immediately blown to the side, and both hands darting up to sculpt his arrangement back into place.

"The gang's all here," growled O'Hanrahan.

"That Underwood fellow's a royal pain in the butt," said Westin, shaking his head.

"I thought you were working together," O'Hanrahan prompted.

"I suppose we are. I just wanted this to be an all-Company operation and then Merriwether starts poking around."

Thorn: "Mr. Merriwether has been a generous contributor to our operations . . ." Agent Thorn turned on his superior, who was sulking. "That's no secret. I can tell him that, can't I?"

"Conrad, I swear . . ." The colonel then asked for everyone to get out of the car, in preparation for the great man of God.

Lucy and O'Hanrahan leaned against the government limousine, viewing the TV-familiar girth of Reverend Bullins emerge from the plane. Reverend Bullins stayed put as two video cameramen in light blue warm-up suits, TPL and a white cross emblazoned on the back like a team logo, ran down the gangway to record Bullins's dramatic arrival in Ethiopia. Moments after him, there appeared Lila Mae. An attendant followed before the cameras began filming to spray down her big silver-white dome of hair, a light-blue foot-wide ribbon supported in the tresses.

At the base of the stairs, one of the cameramen led two young Ethiopian children toward the welcoming red carpet. Action. Farley and his wife, waving as if to a large crowd, made their way down the stairs and scooped up the spindly black children in their arms. Reverend, yelled a cameraman, let's have you and the boy and the lollipop. As the kid made pleading, imploring eyes at the laughing, broad-faced Southerner, Reverend Bullins made a great tease out of offering a lollipop, taking it away, giving it back. The boy greedily put it in his mouth, wrapper and all.

"There's your friend," said O'Hanrahan.

Lucy looked to the top of the stairs to see Farley Jr. waving frantically, trying to get her attention. He was wearing a robin's-egg blue pastel suit, white ruffled shirt, and string tie that would befit a country & western star.

Both Lucy and O'Hanrahan noted the Man in the Cheap Suit stick his head out right behind, say something to Farley Jr. before both retreated inside. Then Underwood, holding his hair together from the swirl of jet engines, left the videotaping area and crossed the tarmac all smiles, his hand held out in anticipation of being shaken: "Howdy, folks!"

Neither Lucy nor O'Hanrahan extended hands.

"Awww, now don't be like that. I'm the one who oughta be sore. You stuck me with the wrong scroll." He handed O'Hanrahan the cardboard tube with the *Contendings of Andrew* within, while Thorn and Colonel Westin audibly snickered at Underwood's imbecility.

All heads turned to see Reverend Bullins wrapping up his video spot, surrounded now by five Ethiopian children, raising his voice, praising Jeeeeezus, arms outstretched and face heavenward. Farley Jr., standing to his daddy's side, waved at Lucy.

"Sickening," she breathed.

"I think you'll really get to like Reverend Bullins," Thorn predicted. "He's a scholar, like yourself, professor. Oh, don't let his fiery preaching put you off, he's a real showman, yes indeed, but first and foremost he's a living Christian example of charity."

O'Hanrahan scoffed, observing Bullins being filmed before the crates marked MEDICAL and FOODSTUFFS, holding the Ethiopian boy and girl shoulder-high.

"Those crates were there before the plane landed," noted O'Hanrahan drily.

"Well, that's just for, you know, the cameras," said Underwood. "The real stuff is on the plane."

No one, however, was unloading anything from the plane. Lucy noticed that the one mechanic was refueling the jet.

When she turned back to the ceremonious Reverend Bullins, she saw that filming had stopped and he was crossing the tarmac to greet them. Bullins, all grins, approached and grasped O'Hanrahan's hand: "Greetings and God bless!" he called out, his trademark opening of each Promised Land Bible Hour. "So you're Patrick O'Hanrahan. My my, it's good to meet you at last, following your adventures secondhand these many weeks."

"Lucy!" called out Farley Jr., running to her side.

"Son," said Farley Sr., "this must be Miss Lucy, yes ma'am," he exhaled, forcing a blast of Southern charm. "Why don't you take Miss Lucy and her bags and the professor's . . . Colonel, would you help us here? Into the plane, that's right. We'll be leaving for New Orleans tonight."

O'Hanrahan was severe. "Leaving for *where?*"

"For The Promised Land, my friend. It's a thirteen-hour flight to New Orleans, with a fueling stop in Accra, I think they told me. Then we'll drive on from there. Plenty of time, plenty of time."

Mr. Cheap Suit held out his hand to the professor. "Good to finally meetcha, sir," he said with a twang. "John Smith, the name."

Something caught in O'Hanrahan's mind.

"Yes," said Smith, "I hate to bring it up, but if I could have Mr. Merriwether's credit card back? The one we sent you for your travels?"

O'Hanrahan fumblingly reached into his wallet. John Smith, Treasurer. It *was* his real name.

Lucy asked Farley Jr., "You said you were named after Farley Bullins, the minister. *Why,* Farley, didn't you tell me you were his actual son?"

He shuffled and shrugged. "Well shucks . . . Didn't want you, you know, to think I was braggin' or nothin'."

Lucy was speechless.

"You know," Farley said, "I do the Bible Study segment on the telecast back in Philadelphia, Louisiana, and people treat me different, in stores and shops and stuff, and I just . . . just wanted you to like me for who I was."

Before Lucy could protest, Reverend Bullins was taking O'Hanrahan by the arm and leading him away: "Miss Lucy," the minister said, "we have some refreshment in the lounge on board, if you'd like. I would enjoy a word with Dr. O'Hanrahan here."

As the others scattered, Reverend Bullins put his arm around O'Hanrahan's shoulder, man to man. "Good to meet you at last, sir. I consider it a blessing, a blessing indeed. A scholar of your reputation. I tried to find out about you. I went to the library to check out your books, but it doesn't seem you've written any, heh heh heh . . . You're like me! You're a talker. A preacher. And a helluva translator, I understand. The best. Oh, we shopped around and checked out lots of alternates, like your friend Philip Beaufoix at American University in Cairo, but you're the man for the job."

"What job?"

"Translating this antigospel." Here Bullins paused, savoring the details deliciously. "The second our scouts heard tell of a First-Century gospel on the market, well, you can bet we naturally wanted to get our hands on it! Bob Jones, Oral Roberts—had to beat 'em to the punch! I am sure you will bear out our contention that the *Gospel of Matthias* is the False Prophecy that is foretold. The tool of Antichrist himself, and his minion, the False Prophet. We assume, of course, the False Prophet will be the pope, but there's still room to move on this thing. We'll know better when more of the signs manifest themselves."

O'Hanrahan tried to be reasonable with the man. "Look, Reverend, heretical gospels have come to light before. Several this century. What makes this scroll the False Prophecy of *Revelations*?"

"What else could it be? The fathers of the Church condemned the Matthias gospel as heretical and dangerous. You're telling me it's a coincidence that 1900 years pass by and then now, just now, when so many of the signs are in place, when Babylon is on the ascendancy and the Jews have returned to Israel, that *just now* this wicked manuscript returns to us. Oh no, Dr. O'Hanrahan—this is Satan's final ploy, his program for the minds of the faithless!"

It took all of his courage for O'Hanrahan to utter fearfully, "And you want to destroy this gospel?"

Reverend Bullins took a step back from the professor, staring at him oddly as if trying to recognize a stranger. And he said with an unnerving quiet: "No. On the contrary. Would I stand in the way of the Coming of Jesus?" The reverend seemed strained with emotion: "Oh it will be a horrible thing, really it will. To see so many of my own congregation perhaps, my own extended family, turn away, fall away into doubt and apostasy. But many will turn away before the Rapture. So many . . ." Reverend Bullins was genuinely moved by their plight: ". . . so many otherwise good people, left behind. Left to the Tribulations."

Reverend Bullins clutched at O'Hanrahan's arm:

"*Daniel* 12:4: *For these words are concealed and sealed up until the End Time.* Also it says *that those who have insight will understand.* In the End Times, sir, the world is to be besieged with the lies of Antichrist. *Second Thessalonians,* you'll recall. *Therefore God sends upon them a strong delusion, to make them believe what is false, so that all may be condemned who did not believe the truth but had pleasure in error.* The great False Prophecy, the Ultimate Lie of the End Times, will be written from within the Church, apparently by one of the very apostles of Christ."

"The very apostles?"

"*Second Corinthians* 11:13, the deceivers at the end of the world are *false apostles, deceitful workmen, disguising themselves as apostles of Christ.* And that's what we've got here, isn't it? The antigospel banned by the early fathers, supposedly by Matthias, an apostle of Christ himself! Oh so long I wondered how these particular prophecies would come to pass, but then I heard from my friend Charles Merriwether that his father once owned such a heretical scroll, and that this heretical scroll had now found its way to the black market, purported to be by one of the Twelve! Well, it couldn't very well be anything else! I realized that this was *my* mission. My little humble contribution to the preparing of The Way." Bullins looked off distantly at the fringe of forest near the runway.

"What with the impending end of the world, Reverend," said O'Hanrahan drily, "do you think there's time for me to translate the . . . this False Prophecy?"

"About nine more years," he said confidently. "This skirmish is merely the drawing of battle lines. Saddam will emerge from this coming conflict to fight another day."

"If we go to war, Reverend," laughed O'Hanrahan at the absurdity, "I sincerely doubt anyone's going to do anything as idiotic as leave Saddam Hussein alive!"

"He must plague Israel, *Revelations* suggests, for three and a half years, professor. You know that! 1993, 1994, somewhere in there he will make his most destructive move on Israel—either he or his successor in the Moslem world. We're not sure on that." Then Bullins gave O'Hanrahan a friendly press on his shoulder. "Come with us to The Promised Land and you'll have all the help you can use to translate this."

O'Hanrahan was somehow relieved. Bullins wasn't going to burn it. In fact, he was appallingly sincere. Jesus, thought O'Hanrahan,

Gorbachev, the Mark of Cain, Saddam Hussein on the warpath, Israel vulnerable—what if he's actually correct about . . . Nahhhh.

"I have your cooperation, professor?" Bullins asked.

As O'Hanrahan smiled noncommittally, he thought: it has happened. The last chapter was reunited now with the first six. What do you know? The *Gospel of Matthias* may actually get translated and published! O'Hanrahan had never seriously let the thought settle for a moment in his brain: translated by *me*. Yes, Lucy was right, I'm a dabbler, a messer, a mucker-about. But I will rise up! I will meet this challenge!

(So you got what you wanted.)

Yes, Lord, but did you know I was immortal and indestructible as long as I kept pursuing that next place, that next monastery! For you see, Holy Spirit, I knew it was my destiny to translate it. Therefore, as long as it eluded me I remained alive. And now a new worry: will I live long enough to finish this translation?

(That's up to you.)

O'Hanrahan stared at the TPL plane and the camera crews scrambling about the scene taking pictures, first Farley Jr. holding up a milk bottle, then his mother Lila Mae attempting to read off the cue cards. She got carried away and began crying, running her thick mascara.

"For God's sake," said Reverend Bullins impatiently with a false smile, "Lila, read what's on the goddam card and let's get the show on the road."

A makeup girl in the uniform blue TPL jogging suit rushed in to repair the facial damage.

"When I think," said Lila Mae, fighting tears, "of all the hungry people in Ethiopia, it just makes me wanna bawl, Farley, just cry my eyes out! But there is a worse hunger. The people that don't know Jesus, Jesus Christ . . ." She closed her eyes as more tears streaked a black mascara trail down her lacquered cheek.

Reverend Bullins snorted disapproval, and turned to O'Hanrahan with a male-complicitous smile: women, what can you do with 'em? "All right, honey," he conceded. "Let's forget it. We'll do it back in Philadelphia—"

"But I was witnessing, Farley," she said, wiping her eyes and allowing herself to be hugged by her husband. "I can't do anything right," she said, taking a first step on the gangway.

"Nawww, honey. You're just a bit tired, that's all."

O'Hanrahan, amusingly, was the last person to board the plane. Two Ethiopian airport mechanics—the fathers, O'Hanrahan surmised, of the prop children used in the TPL video—stood at the gangway platform ready to roll it away as soon as he got on board. Colonel Westin and Agent Thorn waved farewell beside their limousine.

(A chance to make a run for it.)

Not anymore. No more running. Poor Ethiopia, he thought, looking back in the direction of downtown Addis, the African utopia turned hellhole. I should keep you, Ethiopia, in my prayers.

(We would like to hear some of those prayers, Patrick.)

But O'Hanrahan would not pray. Not this close to finding out the true answers. When he knew what Matthias had to tell him he would pray or not pray—but not until!

7

But my scribe Tesmegan is eager for his own appearance in this important history, so let us proceed on this last day of dictation, to Meroe, this mysterious African kingdom, so beautiful and welcoming, so unpredictable and . . .

(Ah, but here Tesmegan is frowning, fearing my bad opinion of him and his people. I shall say what I wish, my boy—yes, yes, write down all I have said.)

2. In Elephantine, that temple-sodden island of paganism stubbornly rising out of the Nile after the Cataracts, I mingled uneasily with those who call themselves Sons of Abraham, though I question their Jewish pedigree. In one home I heard a ritual rejoicing that the Temple of Jerusalem was destroyed, a vengeance allowed by God for the centuries of persecution and arrogance Jerusalem had come to represent for the Elephantinians.

In this village of seething ignorance, I found the merchant that Duldul ibn-Waswasah would have me find—they were twins in mischief and double-dealing, I could tell in a moment. But what Arabians are anything else?

3. With my trade documents delivered and my mission completed, I asked the locals about the small Nazirene commune established by the Disciple Matthew in his evangelistic travels in these parts.[1] The Nazirene converts, I learned, had died, moved, or converted back to the odd, paganish Judaism that inhabits the island—so that concludes that proud episode!

It takes God Himself, apparently, to establish a new church,

---

1. Matthew (Ματθαῖος) and Matthias (Ματθίας), differing so little in Greek, became intertwined and inextricable very early in Church history. Most accounts say Matthew first evangelized Egypt (except Jerome who puts him in Persia) and then went south to face the cannibals in Ethiopia. There is a Greek *Acts of Matthew and Andrew*, which is almost identical to a Syriac *Acts of Matthias and Andrew*, both dating from the 400s though no extant copies of it are that old. The much-adored Anglo-Saxon *Andreas*, a tale of miracles, seamanship, and cannibal-vanquishing, was based on these apocryphal, secondary acts.

and here with community after community failing or falling into heresy, I realized that nothing but an act of the Most High could conspire to make the Nazirene Church survive another twenty years.

4. The marketmaster was sympathetic as I told him the story of the slave Benjamin and his unexplained wealth. He was a kind man who was not opinionated upon religions, having seen so many flow up and down the Nile.

He said to me: "This Matthew fellow banished a number of good people from this island for one reason or another. He finally lost his will to fight the heretics, as he called them, and moved on himself though I know not where. But not before banishing the person I believe you seek to the realms of Cush.[2] A rich man you say?"

I discussed what I knew of Benjamin, former slave of Joseph, and the marketmaster nodded and said with great certainty that his name was not Benjamin but Belshazzar, like the king. (Indeed, it was common in Joseph's generation to rename slaves after former overlords of Israel, as an ironic reversal of fates— I was much encouraged by this!)

Belshazzar had traveled farther up the Nile and that was all that was known of him, the marketmaster reported. In parting, he said to me, "My Judaean friend, you do not want to go as far as Meroe. Whence even the Romans do not return!"[3]

Herein you can see my bravery, Josephus!

2. From *Genesis* 10:1 and 6 there is a jumble of place names masquerading as genealogy: *These are the generation of the sons of Noah, Shem, Ham, and Japheth; sons were born to them after the flood. . . . The sons of Ham: Cush, Egypt, Put, and Canaan . . . Cush became the father of Nimrod; he was the first on earth to become a mighty man."*
   Cush, the short-lived but glorious 25th or "Ethiopian" Dynasty of Egypt (728–664 B.C.E.) eventually ceded Lower Egypt but continued to rule in the Sudan, first at Napata (653 to 525 B.C.E.) until trouble with the Persians moved them farther south up the Nile to Meroe (near modern-day Khartoum). The First Century saw Meroe at its height.
3. Meroe, by Roman times, was considered untakeable. Herodotus and other Greek sources tell of futile attempts to take Cush by the Egyptians, who eventually would lose their own kingdom to the Cushites. The gospel's author seems to reflect the Meroitic xenophobia for visitors. Herodotus records the ingenuous response of an Aethiopian king: *The king of Persia has not sent you with presents in order to foster a friendship. You have come to get information about my kingdom; therefore you are liars and your king is a bad man.* Romans toyed with a mission in the 60s C.E. but the scouting party disappeared; indeed, the few historical contacts with Meroe suggests that did not let ambassadors or emissaries leave.
   Rome's Egyptian Province bordered upon Meroe, and was the one border in their empire they did not defend (after an attempt at Qasr Ibrahim), choosing to garrison troops in fractious Alexandria where they could be more usefully applied.

5. (Oh, my scribe is distressed again. It is a most horrible thing in Meroe to commit an insult or an unkind opinion of a person or place to paper, where it is said to have a life of its own. Tesmegan, stupid boy, I must record things as they are . . . yes, I am waiting for you to write down every word I say. Yes, include the word "stupid." What little time we have left!)

6. I confess to a brief, foolish flirtation with the adventures of my youth, my brother. I lay awake at night, in the camps of other travelers, looking at the desert night sky and imagining that I should go into the court of Meroe and perform miracles as Moses before Pharoah, that I should win over a kingdom where Matthew before me had failed. And that finally my gospel alone would touch another man's heart and that the world might change ever so slightly toward the good and that it be *my* words and faith that engendered this inclination. I see, alas, in looking back it was always myself at the center of these dreams. And he who would bring God to others must put the Most High before all else. How clear it seems now . . .

7. O what wonders were those Nubian towns! (With another life before me I should write a *Nubiad*.)

In Sarras I saw as strange a slave market as ever I saw. Types of men were gathered from all races and colors and sizes and I beheld a man no higher than my waist, and many taller than [seven feet]. I was told the people called the Pygmies were used by Carmanians in powering their barges for the rich upon the Euphrates, for a larger man cannot be fit into their crafts. Aethiopians[4] had been collected for their great height from Dongola, although they did not seem particularly strong. A Greek merchant wished to have them trained as lookouts for the army; an old Persian eccentric had demanded one of these men in order to reach the highest shelves of his papers and scrolls, being too arthritic to mount a step stool. As in all towns where slave-trading is the prime means of subsistence this village had an air of desperation.

---

4. Aethiopica, the land of burned faces, is not to be thought of as modern-day Ethiopia, but rather the southern Sudan. Nor, confusingly enough, is modern-day Merowe (which was Napata) to be thought of as Meroe (whose ruins are near Khartoum), nor is present-day Dongola in Nubia the site of ancient Dongola.

Then I came to Napata, a town in which modesty has been abandoned completely. The women, stately and ebony black, walk around with their breasts exposed, and merely a thin belt of reeds disguises their sex! The men are near naked as well except for metal ornament, golden and highly polished against their black skin. What is unusual is that, in time, this affront of the exposed, shameful parts becomes as normal, and I could be persuaded that sexual sin was less in such a society. But deep into Africa, as everyone knows, the people are innocent and highly honorable, though naturally they are much misguided about religion and the need for chastity, which I, your brother, have always felt to be the engine of refinement for the soul.

8. And so, getting on with my tale: with a month of much walking, two hired mules, and eventual good winds, I was allowed a relatively quick passage to the junction of the Astapus tributaries that confluent make up Nilus, O Greatest of rivers![5] O haughty river that the God of Moses did once turn red as the pomegranate![6] Flow to the sea as you will, O Nile, we evangelists shall brook your flow and ford your shallows, embracing your very source in our search for souls who thirst to hear of the God of the Nazirenes and His most holy prophet and Messiah, He Who Gives All Strength.

(That was a bit of just-invented verse, my brother—I hope you may delight in that even until the end of the poet within me knows no suppression!)

9. The trading portion of the capital city of Meroe, which rivals perhaps all but Alexandria, is along the riverfront, stretching for miles. No scattered houses outlie this monument to commerce, leaving one with the impression that Meroe is nought but a trading post and all else desert.[7]

---

5. The author imagines he is at the meetings of the two Niles, White and Blue, near modern-day Khartoum, but it is the Astaboras, which flows into the Nile near Meroe, not the Astapus. The Meroitians and Greek-speakers probably called the Astaboras "the Atbara," which confused the author.

6. *Exodus* 7:20–21, the Plague of Blood.

7. Meroe is not well excavated or well known about, due to its impenetrable language and its location in the harsh realms of the Sudan, whose modern government is not always cooperative with intellectual undertakings within its borders. However, some is known of their astounding trade. Meroe's foreign contacts were as vast as Rome's, whose coins have been found in digs throughout Meroe. The capitals of Meroe and Napata traded with

Continued

I acquainted myself with a Greek-speaking assessor of tariffs who declared that no tradesman was allowed in the capital city itself, set some miles beyond the riverbank. I said to him, "I am not come to sell wares, dear sir, I am here to bring the God of the Nazirenes to the good people of Meroe!"

This noble Nubian, a cubit taller than myself and quite an excellent choice to enforce tariffs with intimidation, broke into the smile of a young boy and said I was to accompany him. I was taken with great courtesy to a neatly swept little house where his wife—like all women of Meroe, tremendously fat and polished black with a charcoal dust to make their skin the color of deepest Indian jet—prepared a fine if simple repast of fruits and breads. A messenger was dispatched to the capital to tell of my arrival as if I were some ambassador or important personage.

(Only now does it occur, where Greek is so prevalent, that my *Hebraika* or even my *Cosmos Explained*, which despite their ignorance of theology might have been appreciated on a rhetorical level, had perhaps won a place in the poetic heart of this marvelous city. Ah, Tesmegan smiles as I say this, so it must be that.)

10. A chariot was sent for me and presently I arrived at the most splendid stone gate I have ever seen! Meroe looked to be a square walled city of at least two miles a side. No windows looked out of this fearsome wall, indeed, I know now there are no windows to the outside world. A great staircase, bounded by stone lions and baboons and familiar Egyptian idols and a Sebastian from the age of the first emperor,[8] led to a gateway of

Ethiopians farther south and the sub-Saharan nomads; indeed, the seeds of the Great Sudanese Empires of West Africa, Ghana, Mali, and Songhay derive much from these primitive trading routes. Near the Red Sea, the Meroitians traded with India, Parthia, later the Kushans (no relation), and indirectly with the Chinese. The society seemed to adopt whatever pleased them from Egypt, the Ptolemies, the Jews, the Romans, and eventually, when the Axumites overran them in the 300s for sure, but probably earlier, the Christians.

For all this, their language, despite 800 textual examples and a phonetic code deciphered in 1909, is still mysterious, resembling no known Indo-European or African tongue. The Egyptian hieroglyphs the Meroitians used before developing their own written language are turned backward and read differently—as if from the very beginning their language had been composed to be a mystery to the outside world.

8. The Greeks called Augustus Caesar "Sebastian," and the proliferation of his image as an ideal youth were "sebastians" as well. A head of Augustus, curiously, was found purposefully embedded in one of the Meroitian palace doorways. Whether this was reverence (as suggested by this document) or disdain (after the Meroitians sacked Roman Aswan in the 20s B.C.E.) is hard to say.

three arches, all ornate and magnificently carved. Once reaching the top of this stairway, I discovered I was to wind my way through any of several doors that stretched for several yards, requiring the entrant to twist and crawl, at one point, down on my aged knees through a passageway. No advancing army could make a run through this gate.

11. And Meroe itself! Well may it please my scribe that I declare a paradise opened before me! Lushly strewn with flowers and plants; every other street in this supremely organized city had a canal of still, clean water with ever so often a fountain erupting. All homes, identical in size and wealth, were draped with flowers and hanging plants. Tesmegan tells me that fifty miles away the [Astaborus] is diverted through a series of aqueducts until it flows through this city, providing canals and fountains, baths, and a subterranean sewer system not unlike the *cloacae* of Rome.

And if I am not mistaken, no wonder of the world was not itself there imitated or bettered. Meroe's central palace is the Athenian Akropolis as if done by an Egyptian with a hypostyle court before the main chambers. It sits atop three concentric plateaus, each which afford verdure, hanging plants trailing over the railings and balconies as in Babylon. Nowhere does one see filth or ordure as one must wade through in other city streets; everywhere is the smell of flowers and perfumes! How Jerusalem is put to shame! Ah, but again I have forgotten—poor Jerusalem is no more.

12. I knew that Meroe was a matriarchy and consequently I expected the worst: a squalid court of castrated eunuchs and men retained for libidinous purposes; one usually finds the queen has raised herself up as a deity and presents herself as an incarnation of fertility, or some such debased thing. But Meroe is unique.[9]

Tesmegan has explained to me that women rule as a safe-

---

9. The Meroitians had a notoriety for the fatness of their queens. Their cult of the large black woman, aside from the universal earth-mother connotations, had its roots in Cush/Egypt (Egyptians called themselves *kamit* or "black") and attained its height in Meroe. Most female gods of the Nile had "black" as a divine attribute; indeed, the Mediterranean has no shortage of venerated Black Madonnas even now. A large black woman was thought to embody the virtues of Isis, who was commonly rendered in hieroglyphic as "the great black woman." No ancient society of the period was so thoroughly a matriarchy as Meroe, though mother-son and husband-wife coregencies are recorded in what little we know of Meroitian history.

guard against tyranny. Nor can any woman rule in Meroe unless she has several grown children, which in principle should lessen her desire to send them to wars; also she must be past bearing children to prevent her scheming to engender heirs and coregencies. Tesmegan, with childlike clarity, explained that no man could sit upon the throne following the Century of Debacles[10] in which men ruled this nation, made ridiculous expenditures, caused countless wars, and fell among fighting within their ministers for unrivaled powers.

What is more unusual, and takes its source from the Ptolemies, is that the office of Candace is an elected office that lasts five years, or until her death. There is no Assembly or Sanhedrin or Senate that might counsel the Candace, so it is the election of a beneficent autocrat. I asked my young scribe why no deliberative body existed, and he replied that no such senate ever accomplished anything but rancorous argument and fell easily to corruption. Better a single all-powerful queen who would rule as she would, for good or bad, but in any event, merely five years. There is an army but only used for defensive purposes, repelling intruders or punishing crimes, including usurpation.

13. Just as remarkable in this extraordinary kingdom—or queendom, rather—is a total lack of orthodoxy concerning religion. Of course, in Alexandria and Ephesus one finds all faiths being practiced by various devoted enthusiasts. But nowhere have I seen a more eclectic society, which takes from any faith what pleases them. Every seven days there is a festival of someone or other—Isis, Aphrodite, Jupiter, whomever. Consequently each sabbath is a riot of food, color, dance, and, often, carnality, though there seem to be inscrutable rules concerning this sort of behavior as well.

14. Upon being fed and then shown to an isolated bath by a pale Germanic slave[11]—who was kept inside to cultivate his pal-

---

10. This "Century of Debacles" is lost to history, but during a period where at least three men ruled consecutively (ending by 12 C.E.) the Romans, under the vicious governor Petronius of Egypt, managed to avenge the sack of Aswan by razing Napata, the second-greatest city of the empire.
11. A note about the slaves: Though the Nubian slave was valued in antiquity [see above 7:7] for his strength and size, racial slavery is a latter-day concept and ancient nations enslaved each other regardless of nationality, and freed them more readily as well. The Meroitians, confirmed in this author's account, seem to have been a black nation with

lor, which was a novelty here—I was told that I was free to leave Meroe now, but were I to stay and meet the court it is unlikely I should ever leave easily. Indeed, in the indecipherable written language of these people (who also speak Greek as we all do in public) there was a motto above the city gate that the guard was kind enough to translate: *No trouble has ever befallen the city who welcomes all guests; only misery will befall the city who lets a false friend depart.*

At the time, I was sure bribery would be efficacious here, should I want to escape, but I was to discover that the Meroitians direct all bribes to the Candace, who must decide all things. And truthfully, after what I did, there was no way I should be allowed to leave.

15. But now, I shall speak of the court and the Candace. I had been instructed it was Meroitian custom to change the form of honorific in each address to their queen, and contests were held late into the evening to see which of the competitors could greater fabricate panegyric. This presented no ordeal for a poet of my rank, you can appreciate.

The Candace Shanakdekhete VII[12] was a tremendous creature, made all the more fearsome by a robe that extended over her throne and several steps of her dais. I had believed no woman could be so fat, and I believe, though Tesmegan refuses to comment, that pillows and cushions surround her under this raiment to support her titanic appearance. No shortage either of fine gems and jewelry was noted, though I suspected some of the gems for their improbable size of being glass.[13] Nothing in her manner gave one a hint of malice; indeed, her court

white slaves, a situation that has not seen enough research, considering the derivation of "slave" (from the use of white Slavs) suggests white slavery in empires of color was at some point a norm. See the Victorian historian G. A. Hoskins's quaint and fascinating *Travels in Ethiopia* for many evidences of white slavery in Upper Egypt and Abyssinia.

12. Shanakdekhete was a historical and repeated name of the candaces but this particular queen is unrecorded. Shanakdekhete's namesake was a candace of the 160s B.C.E. who appears to have been the first sole female ruler of Meroe; her name appears on the Meroitic hieroglyphs at Naga, among the earliest examples of Meroitic known.

13. The jewels of Meroe, like its gold, was a legend with a source in truth for once. Ferlini in the 1830s raided the Meroe funeral complexes, hence the splendors of the Berlin and Munich museums. Meroe led the ancient world in gold mining—they were expert miners, having taken iron smelting to its highest-known state. Entire Meroitic temple interiors were caked in gold leaf.

seemed—and I shall speak as I please without your whining and sniveling, Tesmegan—ridiculous.

16. As I stood before this throne, I saw that two exotic feathers protruded from her nostrils. These feathers, dyed blue, went about a cubit and turned upward, as if giant tusks on an elephant beast. She and her court of about twenty retainers fought to remain unlaughing and it seemed there was no business but this joke.

She asked of me, "Kneel before the Candace of Meroe and introduce yourself. Do you not find me beautiful?"

I said to her that she was most lovely, a radiant flower of the Nile.

She said to me, "Beautiful, even with these feathers up my nose?" She then removed them, shaking with laughter, transfixed entirely by the entertaining of her court. At last she said to me, "You bring a religion of some sort?"

17. I began to speak of Our Master and his many excellencies, when she turned to a miniature statue of Caesar and asked if the man I spoke of was he.

I said to her, "No great Candace, Insuperable One, that is merely a ruler of Rome, Sebastian, who is long since dead."

She said to me with some horror, "I thought he was a God!"

I said to her, "Indeed, Your Glory, he declared himself such but he was merely a ruler upon a throne. No greater, indeed, than Your Majesty."

The queen joined her hands and seemed to moan, rocking back and forth. She said to the court, "Ah, what a lovely god he was, but if he is dead, then we shall have to do without him. Bring you, gentleman of Judea, a god to replace the one you take away?" Then she gasped as if in a sudden revelation: "Oh, of course, you are of Judea and the God of Abraham! The jealous God who will not have any of the others! I'll thank you not to pray to Him while you're with us thereby giving Him our location, bringing His wrath upon us. I would be an easy target for brimstone from the heavens, not able to leave my palace."

18. I saw by this that like the Sabaean [Sheban] queens of old, she was prisoner of her court.[14] Indeed, I was to learn that the tale of the Queen of Sheba in the court of King Solomon was as popular here as in Jerusalem, though it had been extensively added to and embellished. Thanks be to the Most High that I was not subjected, balm in hand, to make Solomon's ministrations upon this Candace![15]

19. I said to her, "Yes, O Beneficence, but I have new information concerning Our Lord. The God of Abraham has sent us in addition to His Law a great prophet and teacher, Who speaks of peace, of love, of sacrifice but also of redemption."

The Candace considered this and said to me, "How much sacrifice?"

I said to her, "Our Master, He Who Redeemed Us, sacrificed His life for us, Your Splendor."

"Keep in mind," she said to me, "that we already have Attis and Adonis and the like. We would prefer something different."

I asked of her, "Your Radiance, is it the habit of Meroe to worship *all* the known gods?"

She said with serenity, "Not knowing which God is most powerful or most likely to benefit us, would a sovereign advise her people otherwise? We are concerned lest we should neglect a deity and cause Her or His ire. In your religion, do those who have not heard of your God suffer punishment for their ignorance?"

Of course not, I said.

"But if one has heard your God revealed and then not accepted, then horrible judgments are bound to follow, correct?"

14. The Sabaeans (modern-day Yemen and Djibouti) had the custom of never allowing the queen or king to leave their palace; indeed, the Queen of Sheba (Sabaea) in her trip to King Solomon was a rare emissary. If identified out of their palace, the king or queen of the Sabaeans would be stoned by their subjects. The source of this predisposition to regicide might well be ancient Cush, in which the priests could advise a king to commit suicide and were unflinchingly obeyed (except for one Greek-loving Meroitian king who had the priests killed, according to Diodorus Siculus!).

15. The author's odd reference to magic balms derives from an odd bit of Old Testament apocrypha in which Solomon impresses the Queen of Sheba by showing her a depilatory cream that removes the hair from her legs. *Your beauty is as the beauty of women,* Solomon informs her in the Ethiopian *Kibre Negest, but your hair is as the hair of a man!* Curiously, some fragment of this tale made its way into the Quran, in which Sheba's legs are bared before Solomon, *Surah* 27:44.

I said to her that this was true.

She said to me, "Ah, you see the wisdom of our ways. One can never be too careful with other people's strange gods."

20. An adviser (or male courtesan for all I knew) suggested that I had but brought Osiris down the Nile again, but I protested, describing in full the genealogy and pedigree of Our Teacher.

She said to me, "As to this sacrifice, if we follow your God we ourselves do not make this sacrifice?"

I told her that the sacrifice of lives was not necessary, lest she confuse the Nazirene Church with some Eastern barbarity. Instead, I mentioned, some sacrifice of wealth was required so that God's children might live communally and be clothed and fed.

She said to me, "But we live already communally and share whatever we have between us. All extra wealth is accumulated in this palace for the glory of the Candace, as well as for disasters and famines, which, sadly, are common here."

21. Our Master, I said to her, said to love one's enemies. To turn the other cheek if we are struck.

She said to me, "We have no wars. Should anyone declare one, it is not long before they lose interest or undo themselves. We are very skilled at hiding our money and treasure, you see, in the many catacombs beneath Meroe. We have an army in the event someone wishes to destroy us and raze the city but not since the Persians has anyone traversed this far up the Nile with an army intact."[16]

Then the Candace seemed to grow impatient with me.

She said to me, "Please, my Judean gentleman, tell us of the festivals! How do we celebrate this new prophet?" She snapped her fat fingers and a minister approached showing her an unrolled papyrus. "We have nothing for the first winter month. A

---

16. Twenty-fifth Dynastic temples and Cushite legendary cycles resemble that of the Greeks on the subject of the marauding Persians. They too tell of Darius and Xerxes attempting to take their kingdom and failing. Having launched an arrogant raid to the "land of the cannibals," the Persians, ironically, starved before reaching Meroe and turned to eating each other. This much-recounted Persian disgrace bolstered popular notions that no northern or Eurasian empire could harm them. Indeed, it was the Axumites from the south who defeated them unexpectedly.

fourteen-day gap with nothing religious. We tried to celebrate the Sacred Fire then but no one could be troubled to stand around a fire in this part of the world, as you may understand."

22. At great length, I explained that it is ritual itself that we Nazirenes have eschewed as worthless.[17]

I persevered and was at last able to introduce the subject of why I had come. I said to her, "Your Lustrousness would not know then of a man named either Benjamin or Belshazzar who claims to possess a great secret about the Teacher of Righteousness?"

And at this the entire court fell quiet, as if I might have given offense. (Yes, I see Tesmegan is hushed as I retell it.)

One of the more clothed of the attendants rushed to my side to whisper that the talk of secrets always annoyed the Candace deeply, but soon the Candace spoke for herself:

"As a newcomer to Meroe you could not know that we never speak of secrets here. To have secrets, secret pacts and groups, secret societies and schemes, is the beginning of all evils, my determined Judean. If the man you search for did come here with a mystery and my court voted to make it a secret, then there is no way you shall ever know it."

23. The minister by my side counseled me not to say much more, this topic of secrets was of such great sensitivity. Indeed, once something was proclaimed a secret, the originator was consigned to his house forever, a guard posted at the door, and in serious cases of dreadful secrets, he was killed. Someone unfortunate enough not to have a house was confined to the Palace of Secrets, a most dread prison filled, according to open gossip, with schemers for power, would-be usurpers, a magician who refused to tell the Candace how he did a particular illusion, and an array of secret and inconvenient lovers of great personages.

The Candace entered her own opinion, saying to me, "What is said in Meroe must be said for all to hear."

Indeed, one must credit a society highly that bans secret factions and agencies. Your own modest history, my brother

---

17. It is curious, and confirming what many patristic scholars have long suspected, that the Early Church, and Matthias here, know nothing of any Christian ceremony, i.e., the Eucharist.

Josephus, shows that our former Judea was a society doomed by scheming and deal-making. I said to the Candace, "Alas, O Beauteous One, Your Greatness is telling me I shall never know if Benjamin and his libelous information have passed through Meroe. I suppose I have committed myself to come here in vain."

24. She said to this, "But of course you have not. I hope to see you often in our court where we make much sport of newcomers; we have barely begun with you! And you may have the honor of adding a theological document to our library. Our ministers will study it repeatedly until we shall find something of your Nazirene God to admire."

Then she added, as I was waved away (I believe it is a private matter, her moving from her throne, having all her attendants bring the pillows and stuffings that lend credence to the illusion of her bulk)—she said to me, "Besides, in time we shall get to know you and once you are deemed unthreatening and not a Roman spy, you may bribe your way out of the city, a gift to our Treasury. Nothing in these parts cannot be managed if one is skilled in bribery!"

25. I was then taken to a banqueting hall, atop the tombstones of lesser nobles and older Meroitian families—for it is impolite not to include the departed, they think, in all festivities and gaiety; the ritual uncleanliness of this custom barely needs elaboration. After this impossibly spicy fare (the court competes, I am told, among who can swallow the hottest morsel), I was shown to a spacious mansion used for visitors, and introduced to—yes yes, he is so happy he can barely write it down—my dear young Tesmegan, my scribe.

26. And here I have written down my history.

My passion for my mission faded, of course, as I surmised that I should never impress upon the Meroitians the need for only one God; all I might ever do is provide some trinket by which they can create a feast or a special holiday. They use God to merely decorate the calendar.

Ah, dear Tesmegan. How I wish I had stayed in his company alone, my brother, but I felt the need to wander among the citizens and investigate this marvelous place. I trifled with the idea of writing a book upon the unvisited Meroe and so I occupied many weeks with meeting the inhabitants and perusing the library and its numerous Greek works. (I confess to finding the Meroitian language totally indecipherable; nor would anyone give me as much as a clue to reading it—impossible people!)

Of course it was not long before I discovered the house of a wealthy man who was said to have been Judean, guards posted at his door, a man condemned to his home for harboring a secret deemed malevolent by the Empire of Meroe. The more the locals refused to answer my questions, the more information perversely I was to garner. I asked the guards one day if any visitation of the man inside was possible, and I learned there was such a day granted, upon each full moon. But, they told me, this man had existed many years without visitors; they would not even speak his name to me.

27. Dutifully, thinking only of my history . . . no, that is not true. Thinking only of my own faith, my brother, hoping for a final proof, my own powers of prayer and faith quite dry, I waited until the next full moon to pay a visit.

The guard knocked loudly on the bolted door of what looked to be a pleasant house. In many minutes there was no answer, and so the guard beat the door again. I feared briefly that the prisoner had expired, but then I heard him call out to us, "Leave the food inside the door, I shall get it later!"

"It is a visitor," called back the guard.

Then there was more delay as the man had run to change into something appropriate for company. He was, upon appearing, a man of sixty-some years, still with dark beard and large, mournful eyes. He came to the window in the wall. He was dressed well but it did not disguise his weariness and unhappiness. And what a strange sensation, here in Meroe to speak in Aramaic! (Do not worry, Tesmegan, I shall continue in this language.)

28. He said to me, "I wondered if I should ever see another visitor."

"Are you Benjamin," I asked, "the former slave of Joseph of Arimathea?"

He was very cagey, this man. "Do I look like a slave?"

I said to him, "I mean, of course, a freedman who was once a slave."

"In this prison, I am hardly a freedman now."

I told Benjamin that I would appreciate his cooperation. I was an historian, in addition to my fame as a poet, and I was also a Disciple of Our Beloved Teacher. But he merely wanted to know one thing, asking me, "Are you rich?"

I said to him, "I was born into a noble family and have possessed great wealth within my lifetime."

He asked me, "Are you rich enough to get me out of here?"

I said to him, "I understand there is no escape."

He said to me, "But there is. Only at the changing of the Candace, which should be in six months. A new Candace can hear my case. You cannot imagine my rage, my bitterness at this foolish land!"

29. I decided to outwit this rascal by proffering the hopes that I might fund such an enterprise. I said to him, "I might well pay the sum if it is not too much, if you are willing to speak honestly with me. A former slave of Joseph of Arimathea was made rich by his owner, who sent him away up the Nile on the condition that he not tell a secret concerning the death of Our Master, the Teacher of Righteousness."

He interrupted me, saying, "You mean the Nazirene."

I said to him, my heart fully racing, "Yes, the One Who was crucified and buried."

He said to me, "And is said to have risen from the tomb."

I explained to him, "Yes, Joseph's family tomb, in fact. It is said that a slave was paid to secrete away the body and, as a reward, was sent to Elephantine with quite a lot of money to ensure his secrecy. Again, sir, is your name Benjamin?"

30. He said at last, "Why of course it is. Yes, that is I."

I asked him to swear that this was true and he willingly gave his word in the solemnest of oaths. I asked him finally, "Have you some proof of what became of Our Master's relics?"

He said to me, "We brought the body to Egypt. Shall I show him to you?"

Such heresies hinted at: the bones of the Messiah! I said to him, "Do you expect me to be convinced by a display of bones, a fetid pile of grave clothes?"

He said to me, "One cannot, my friend, believe what men say

is true, but perhaps you will believe your own eyes. Remember the secrets of the Pharaohs, the art of embalming? If you could get inside this house I would take you to the cool cellar where Your Master awaits."

Of all the unclean abominations—the mummies of the Egyptians! To think that Our Master, rather than ascended bodily to sit in the presence of the Throne, encrowned with the Seven Diadem, was rotting in this vile man's cellar like a preserved foodstuff!

31. Overcome with emotion, I said to him, "I should know in a moment if it were He, the One Who Brought Us Life. Just to look upon him . . ."

And here this villain laughed, saying to me, "To look upon what is left of his face, you mean?"

I declared this talk all blasphemous and beyond what even the scripture had thought to condemn! What good was it to even entertain such pollutions in the mind, as I could never be admitted to examine this ghastly relic.

But he said to me, "Because no one wishes to break into this house it would not be difficult for you to slip inside when a meal is delivered and the guard not looking. It is getting out that would require delicacy."

I said to him, "Apparently it is too great a trick to escape, otherwise you would have done so already."

"I am known to be imprisoned here, but you are not. Were you to be seen again on the street no one should care."

32. I hoped to avoid the risk of lawbreaking. Still unsure, I asked him questions to verify his identity. Did he remember anything said or done by Our Master? He did not, not being a Nazirene, he said. Could he tell me particulars of the estate at Arimathea? He described an estate and large house generally enough (honestly, no country estate is so dissimilar from another). What was Joseph's wife's name? He did not remember, but I must say it was lost in my own mind.

He said to me, "Choose your course, Disciple. You have only this day to visit or you shall wait another month. I shall make a crashing of crockery, turn over a table, and feign that I have obtained an injury. Inform the guard you are a physician bringing medicine; he shall let you in briefly. The guard will change in the evening. After some minutes we will knock to let you out and the evening guard will suppose you newly arrived. I shall dissemble convincingly for you, for these guards have grown to like and trust me. But there is a price!"

And of course I knew that price, the ransom for his escape. It should mean all my remaining monies, except what I had laid aside to pay my scribe.

"And you are truly Benjamin?" I begged of him again.

"Who else would I be?" he insisted.

Giving this scoundrel my purse would mean never having money to bribe my own way out of this city, and since no trade would be allowed me, I should never leave this land unless rescued. But at my age . . .

33. My brother, you now know the choice I made. I risked being caught and punished. I gambled with my last monies, assuring that I should never leave this place.

For I had to know!

I had lost my faith, Josephus, and even if this Benjamin were a base charlatan, a deceiver intent only upon my money, what other life did I have? And if this mummy turned out to be Our Master, I thought, then what business did I have continuing to be alive? I tried to conceive what Peter would have me do. Thomas, who would have urged me to kill this slanderer, James bar-Alphaeus, who would have spun some legend out of it, broken up the mummy for relics, no doubt! But they had pursued their faiths in directions unknown to me, and here God had delivered me to this. It was for me alone! It was I who would hold the future of the Nazirene Church in my hands! I alone would know the truth!

34. I went to my lodgings and got my money, some pieces of silver stacked so they would not clink within my belt. I fabricated a bottle of rose-water, which I feigned to pass off as physic, and that very day I returned to the house and slipped inside.

It was more than a simple cellar, I discovered. Meroe had built itself upon another city with catacombs and caverns, like the cities of Cappadocia. I asked of Benjamin, before me, holding our torch, "In all your years here you have not found a way out of the city through these passages?"

He said to me, "For years I have wandered, there are hundreds of passageways, chasms, and abysses to the very center of the earth. But never a ray of light to lead to freedom."

I admit to being afraid, wondering if he might murder me for the money and run to an exit he had in reality discovered. Deeper and deeper into the labyrinths we wandered!

I asked of him, "How do you keep the vermin, which I hear all around me, from consuming this . . . relic of ours?"

He said—how horribly!—to me, "I'm sure they have a feast now and then? Perhaps with each bite they are cured of all their rat diseases, yes?"

Such were his infernal jests!

35. Then we came to the door of the chamber where this hideous apostasy, this death-relic of Our Master was supposed to be secreted . . .[18]

---

18. About fifteen lines are lost due to a tear in the papyrus here. The manuscript continues at 7:37 below.

THE PROMIS

ED LAND

Why should the taxpayers have to spend money to cure diseases that don't have to start in the first place? Let's help the drug users [with AIDS] who want to be helped and the Haitian people. But let's let the homosexual community do its own research. Why should the American taxpayer have to bail out these perverted people?

—From a 1983 newsletter issued by
JERRY FALWELL's Moral Majority

"Oh, why is God letting this happen to us? We haven't done anything wrong—oh, I cry and pray every night that God will allow the truly guilty people to be punished for what they've done to Jim and Tammy Ministries. . . ."

—TAMMY FAYE BAKKER (quoted AP 6/30/87
before the conviction of her husband
of embezzling $158 million from PTL contributors)

Yes, I believe all dancing, by whatever name it may be called, is sinful and harmful. For example, all television dance programs show performances designed essentially to incite and arouse lust in people's minds and hearts. The contortions they display are all too similar to the perversions of the heathen nations who lived so long ago. . . . I can see where it would be a temptation for young girls to want to learn tap dancing or ballet dancing. I cannot, however, recommend it for Christian girls. I would even put gymnastic dancing in the same category. . . . Neither should we resort to bodily movements that provoke lust in others or set a bad example.

—*Straight Answers to Tough Questions* (1987)
JIMMY SWAGGART

Beware of the scribes who like to go about in long robes and to have salutations in the marketplace and the best seats in the synagogues and the places of honor at feasts, who devour widows' houses and for a pretense make long prayers.
They will receive the greater condemnation.

—*Mark* 12:38–40
JESUS

Farley drove the station wagon down a slight hill under a canopy of live oak trees draped with Spanish moss, limply stirring in the humidity. Lucy noticed a Louisiana state highway sign with the number illegible from rust and a shotgun blast.

"Here it is," said Farley. "Where it all started."

It was a brick box of a church, three feet above the ground on cement blocks in the event of high water. PHILADELPHIA FIRST PENTECOSTAL, said the rotting wooden sign, black letters on white peeling paint. There were white double-doors in front, a squat steeple on the roof that resembled a bird feeder, also white. Lucy felt the gravel lot crunch under the station-wagon tires.

"Does anyone use it anymore?" she asked.

"The Senior Center does," he said, motioning across the road to a simple series of one-story brick apartments in an L-shaped building. "Dad will still come up here once a month to be with the seniors and longtime members and prayer-partners."

Prayer-partners, Lucy had realized, meant people who had given sums of money from the very beginning of The Promised Land Ministries.

Farley explained to Lucy that, chronologically, there were four other churches between this humble building where Farley Bullins, Sr., felt the anointing and the "God-Dome," the Bullins Seminary complex in Philadelphia that from the air—as a popular postcard showed—resembled a crown.

"We've got a bigger Senior Center in Philadelphia," he explained, "one that you have to pay a bit for. This one's free."

As the station wagon wheeled in the lot recircling through its own scattered dust, Lucy gave it another glance. She imagined a younger, less jowly Reverend Bullins exhorting and thumping his Bible, bullying Satan in this unattended box of a church. She saw it all: his fervent prayers to be delivered unto a great congregation, the private moments no less agonized than Gethsemane when the funds ran out or the cable service in some Southern city was canceling his telecast. For this was a man, she told herself, who knew even at the Philadelphia First Pentecostal that his mission would be worldwide, and God, apparently, did not interfere in his dreams.

(Give Us time.)

Farley had been a dutiful tour guide. He had already shown her the Poverty Outreach program, the Feliciana Parish Homeless Mission, the rambunctious children–filled playground dedicated to Obadiah Bullins, the reverend's father, also a preacher.

Near the Mississippi River, Farley drove down a dirt road over the levee down to a quaint but impoverished row of wooden houses. A group of dark black children stopped their ballgame in the middle of the road to let Farley cruise through. This was Catfishtown. Like all towns on the river, there was a seedy shacktown that met the docks on the riverside of the levee. With each flood the slum would be washed away, only to be rebuilt when the water went down again. One such flood in 1948 had washed away Obadiah Bullins's home where Farley Sr. was raised, where he and Lila Mae Bullins, married at sixteen, spent their early years.

Farley happily talked at length, allowing Lucy to drift into her own thoughts. After the long flight, a day of combativeness from O'Hanrahan and a series of phone calls that revealed Rabbi Hersch had made it back to Israel in one piece, Lucy had time to remember: I am actually back in the United States.

Frankly, thought Lucy, Louisiana didn't look so terribly American anymore after Europe and Africa. Yesterday afternoon, a TPL deacon had arrived to greet them at New Orleans International and had brought the Bullins family station wagon. Farley put Lucy's bags in the back and offered to drive her "the long way home" through New Orleans. It was late in the day and the light was lengthened by humidity, but still intense in the yellow sky. Americans black as the Africans of Khartoum lingered on wooden front porches of brightly painted shack-houses motionlessly observing children in underpants giddy with a flailing garden hose. Farley spoke of welfare fraud—highest welfare percentage of any American city—and rampant criminality as he found the wide avenues of live oak trees, branches laden with moss, the parade of stately homes covered in hanging ivies, dangling flowering vines, bougainvillaea . . . indeed, it struck Lucy that after the initial effort to raise New Orleans all subsequent human and floral accumulation had been permitted to droop, fall to ruin and listlessness. Lucy saw the famed Spanish ironwork of the balconies, the French mansard rooves and street names, and she factored in as well the peculiar Southern gestures overlaying the colonial accomplishment, something that whispered the sins of the Confederacy, something not of an America she recognized.

Yet, there was the Circle K Convenience Store, the Exxon station, the American flag flying from homes now that troops had been called away to the Persian Gulf. Lucy felt strangely assured by the shield-shaped Interstate 10 sign that seemed to connect her with highways back home.

Farley had driven the station wagon—windows rolled up and air-conditioning blasting—through the French Quarter, stopping constantly for uncareful tourists. Lucy had craned to look at this foreign city within American borders as Farley pointed out St. Louis Cathedral in Jackson Square, choked with sunburned tourists, wide white women in terry-cloth shorts, red-faced retirees broiling in the tropical sun, European backpackers uninformed about the stifling heat and humidity when they had planned their American summer odyssey. . . .

"There's all kinds of black mumbo jumbo stirred up in the Catholic Church down here," Farley regretted, shaking his head.

"The whole of Christianity is an accretion of other cultures' mumbo jumbo, Farley."

(O'Hanrahan could tell you of St. Tammany, beloved in St. Tammany Parish, but in reality named after the graft-ridden Tammany Club of New York. The Bienville brothers who founded New Orleans named two streets after their own names, adding a "St." as did a town planner who gave New Orleans St. Adrien. And yet no local saint is as beloved as St. Expedite, named for the word "expedite" that was stamped on Italian shipments of religious statues. Whenever a statue was hard to identify it was decided to be St. Expedite. There are even Protestant churches to St. Expedite in New Orleans.)

Farley had driven them past Bourbon Street, giving her a momentary glimpse, confirming for Lucy why O'Hanrahan longed for the ten blocks of rowdy bars and Creole restaurants with jazz spilling competitively from the neighboring clubs. Farley told her that each Mardi Gras, he and the TPL Young Americans for Jesus group, about a hundred of them, were bussed in to Bourbon Street—the destination sign on the bus read "Heaven"—to hand out pamphlets for God, picket in front of the gay bars and topless joints, preach through a megaphone above the boisterous din.

"Does it do any good?" she had asked.

"I think the young people who participate," he had said, as if he himself were much older, "really grow from the experience."

Typical, thought Lucy.

The point is not really to "save" the revelers but rather to procure an "experience" for the self-satisfied youth-mob haranguing the partygoers. Yes, she reasoned, how they must swell with pride when the gay couples yell back, when the sinners taunt them, when the topless dancer tells them to go screw themselves—how steeped and ennobled becomes their martyrdom. Catholics, Lucy thought at the time, keep this vice for martyrdom behind closed doors in the family context where it belongs—Pentecostals take it to the street.

Lucy got curious about the geography of bayous and parishes, which substituted for counties in Louisiana. She opened the glove compartment, put aside a Bible—"That's for when Daddy has to make a house call," said Farley—and looked up Philadelphia on a tattered 1981 Texaco service-station map. Farley meanwhile was pointing out a street in outlying Philadelphia, Louisiana, named for Flora Hicks Johnson

Pratt, one of the first prayer-partners to contribute to the TPL ministry. The old girl had left Reverend Bullins all she had and the town
fathers decided a run-down street of nearly condemned houses should
be named in her honor. Currently there was a brouhaha between the
only black man on the council—despite Philadelphia, Louisiana being
60 percent black—and the town over whether to name the street near
the TPL Medical Center after Martin Luther King, Jr.

"Next stop," said Farley, truly at home playing tour guide, "we'll go
to the Newlife Covenant Center."

An hour into this afternoon of touring, Lucy could not be bothered
to generate a polite question of interest as to what the Newlife Covenant Center did. She instead amused herself thinking of O'Hanrahan
currently at the TPL Bible College Library, trying to transliterate the
Gospel of Matthias with the unscholarly resources collected by Reverend
Bullins. She could hardly wait for his commentary. Lucy and her
mentor, on the flight from Israel, got to sit with Reverend Bullins's
party in first class, two seats off to themselves. O'Hanrahan, trying to
hide his terror at being on a plane, took out a cocktail napkin and
made a proposed itinerary in New Orleans, oysterhouses and posh
hotel restaurants, neighborhood dives and ancient jazz hangouts.
He assured Lucy that she would get his deluxe tour, including a
little church in East New Orleans in which absinthe was yet distilled
illegally . . .

But none of this was to pass. The professor and Lucy had been,
so far, prisoners of the Bullinses, pleasantly confined to their grand
antebellum mansion on the Bullins TPL Bible College campus, surrounded by fresh all-American Bible College students, considerate,
well-groomed young men, beauty-contest-pretty virginal young
women, all with distinctive TPL crosses dangling from fine gold chains.

Last night, O'Hanrahan had spent hours trying to reach Rabbi
Hersch's home number and finally around 1:30 A.M., the rabbi, safely
back in his house, picked up his phone. The sleeping serum had only
lasted through the night and the rabbi had been awakened by the hotel
cleaning staff. Once awakened, he flew back to Israel and, according
to the phone call, told Mossad everything he knew and received assurances that Flight of the Griffin and Operation Rapture and all other
shenanigans were soon to be investigated and hopefully halted. The
rabbi promised to fly to New Orleans and make his way to Philadelphia
as soon as he could get away.

"Well, here we are," Farley announced, as a series of condominiums
came into view. There was the omnipresent TPL logo in a circle with
the sign Newlife Covenant Center underneath. "It's the home my
daddy set up for unwed mothers," he added.

Lucy felt her stomach tighten.

"I mean, it's well and good to be against abortion like a lot of TV preachers, but if you don't have an adoption outreach program, it's sort of hypocritical, don't you think?"

Lucy smiled blandly. At some point, she realized, I am going to have to escape the minions of The Promised Land ministries and get to a drugstore and buy one of those home-pregnancy tests.

"A lot of girls get in trouble," Farley went on, explaining the obvious, how girls often get pregnant and have nowhere to go.

"How does the clinic work?" asked Lucy quietly.

"Oh well, it's all free. It's open to born-again Christians mostly but we'll take anyone and preach at them later," he added, laughing. "We find a Christian home for the child and then the adoption papers are all signed. The TPL Newlife Center is the second-biggest adoption agency in the state, after the state itself."

"How about . . ." She focused her thoughts. "What about the women keeping their children?"

Farley pulled the station wagon into the parking lot.

"They're just *girls*," said Farley. "Fourteen and fifteen, that kind of thing. Can't take proper care of a kid, you know."

Lucy found it a bit cruel to pose such a thing to a teenager. On the other hand: childless couples were made happy, the children themselves could have a better home, better opportunities. Then again, Southern Baptist morality runs these girls out of town, out of their homes in the first place, saying: give up the baby and we'll help you pay for all the shame and trouble you caused. Then the girls get saved and born-again to convince themselves it was the right thing to do.

(Might not it be the best thing, My child?)

Yes, Lucy thought starkly. It is perhaps the unselfish thing to do.

"But they don't get to see them," said Farley.

"What?" Lucy asked, caught not listening.

"The girls don't get to see the babies. Because then it's just too difficult to give them up. So a lot of the girls want the baby to be taken right after they give birth. I mean, they get to find out what it was, boy or girl and all that. And they get to write a letter to their child that the child can open when they're eighteen years old, saying, you know, why the mother gave him up and that kind of thing."

Lucy closed her eyes, imagining the emotional violence of the process. The physical pain of childbirth wouldn't be as great as the absence afterward, Lucy saw. A mother might well cherish the humiliation of being tossed out of her pious Christian home, might well venerate the sickness and labor pains of pregnancy: that was the time, my child, we were together.

The Newlife Covenant Center headquarters was an angular four-story building that looked like it might be a suburban office complex, perfect for a dentist or insurance firm. Lucy fought a feeling of dread as Farley and she entered the lobby, a sunny waiting room with a nurse

behind a desk. Farley said many irate parents—once a disgraced Dad
toting a shotgun—barge in to see their fallen daughters and are firmly
turned away.

"I don't know why people have to be like that," concluded Farley.

"One day," said Lucy, "and it's already happening, a woman can be
a single mother without a community thinking it's any of its business."

"You think? What would *your* mother say," he asked playfully, "if
you came home pregnant?"

Lucy didn't say anything.

Posters in the lobby of the Newlife Covenant Center advertised the
"TPL Fullness Festival," posters that were ubiquitous in Philadelphia.
Along one wall there were framed photographs of parents with
adopted children and laminated letters mounted on polished wood
thanking God for sustaining the mother in her ordeals and delivering
a child to them at last. Lucy looked at one mother, middle-aged, hefty
and careworn in Southern cat-eye glasses, flowing like an ikon of Mt.
Athos with love and feeling for her precious adopted child.

Lucy noticed the woman behind the reception desk wore a lapel pin
of two baby feet, tiny and toylike. Farley explained the pin was an idea
from Jerry Falwell's center in Lynchburg on which this center was
based; the tiny feet were the size of a fetus's feet at nine weeks. Lucy
felt hot revulsion for this fetus-re-creation, the crassness of the appeal.
Farley, meanwhile, was being accosted by three pregnant teenage girls
who recognized him from TV:

"Farrrrrley," sang one chunky, wide-faced country girl, laughing,
"there's still time to marry me, honey, and make this baby legit!"

Lucy observed the girls.

How many times would they regret this decision? As they got older
and saw a world that didn't stigmatize the single mother . . . would
they not replay these months again and again in their head? Wouldn't
they want to write the agency and meet the child? Or maybe that's
where the strength of religion comes in; the constancy of faith that
says: God led me to this decision and it is done. Forever and ever.

As Farley and Lucy went back to the station wagon for the rest of
the grand tour, she found herself admitting that Reverend Bullins
and his operation weren't entirely, as first suspected, wholly a money-
grubbing scam. Misguided and self-serving, she wouldn't deny, but it
was at some level . . . at least sincere. And Farley and his father seemed
to be led by some sort of vision. She was pleased by the ease and
laughter Farley had with the pregnant girls, so free from judgment,
so eager to radiate charity and love, so no girl would feel she was the
exiled sinner in the TPL family. Catholicism, admitted Lucy, has none
of this community . . . though she wondered if it were more a function
of the close-knit Deep South rather than Pentecostal Christianity.

"And now to the main campus," said Farley, back at the wheel, slowing for a speed bump.

Lucy surveyed the population, changing classes now at three o'clock. The kids seemed normal. Unusually good-looking and fresh-scrubbed perhaps, but normal. She wasn't sure what she'd expected. Speaking in tongues and healings in front of the dorms, perhaps. Several students recognized Farley and waved vigorously. Farley, despite the air-conditioning, rolled down the window and fielded good-natured jibes and questions. How was Jerusalem? Did he bring them all a souvenir?

My gut instinct, thought Lucy, is to try to find the cynical underside to all this sweet-faced goodness and fellowship, but there probably is none. Southern kids from rural Christian homes and parents wishing their kids to meet a nice girl or boy, save sex until they are married, have a polite courtship in an atmosphere of prayer and counseling for the Christian marriage to come, and then upon graduation, a big wedding with the whole school turning out, everyone happy, everyone smiling and full of *agápe* and *karitas*.

A question occurred to Lucy:

"What about evolution, Farley? Do they teach that here?"

"No ma'am."

"So they actually teach that the world is 6000 years old, rocks and fossils notwithstanding?"

"That's what the Bible would have us believe," Farley said untroubled, "and either it's 100 percent correct or it's the biggest lie ever."

"Farley," said Lucy, riled, "that's, forgive me, somewhat . . . ridiculous. The spiritual truth of the Bible can be intact without every fact or historical tale being true—"

Nope, Farley and his daddy know the Bible is infallible. Every little word.

"Do you think," asked Lucy, "that your father is led by the Holy Spirit in many of his sermons?"

"I know he is."

"Does that make him infallible?" She decided to appeal to his antipapalism: "Does that make the pope or any minister infallible?"

He paused. "No."

"Then why should the writers of the Bible be held to be infallible? It's the same thing. They were inspired but they were still human."

Farley insisted the infallible Bible was a different matter.

Lucy: "And the men who compiled it and chose which books got in and which were out, in the 300s—they were infallible too?"

"No, but . . ."

"Do you think the Bible just fell out of the heaven typeset by God? In vernacular 20th-Century English?"

Farley fell back on, "I just know that the Pentecostal Assemblies of God, the TBN broadcasting family, and the Southern Baptist Conference all hold the Bible to be infallible."

"Oh and that settles it? I could quote many contradictory passages from the Bible, Farley—some that are direct opposites of each other."

"Each gospel to some extent corrects the one that went before."

"So you're saying there are human errors in the scriptures."

He was quiet a moment. "Just differences in details, that's all. Nothing important."

"Nothing important?" Lucy repeated. "*Acts* has Jesus insist, the Savior himself, that the disciples stay in Jerusalem to await the Pentecost, and *Luke* and *John* show Jesus never leaving Jerusalem."

"That's right."

"But *Matthew* has Jesus meet up with everyone in Galilee. 'Nothing important,' Farley? Only the details of the Resurrection. Got a question for you. Remember Jesus in the Garden of Gethsemane? All his disciples fall asleep."

"That's right," Farley nodded, back on surer ground.

"Then who overheard Jesus' prayer in the garden? Who took down his words if everyone was asleep?"

"I guess . . . I guess an angel must have appeared to Matthew or Luke and told them everything."

"The same angel that messed up the details of the Resurrection?" Lucy smiled, amusing herself mostly. "So nothing in the Bible is figurative, is fictionalized, is purely symbolic? You don't believe Adam and Eve are to some extent a poetic symbol, a fable of man's relation to God in a non-Edenic world?"

"No ma'am, they historically really existed."

"Jesus is said to be the Lamb of God. *Worthy is the lamb.* Do you think that means Jesus came to the earth as a man or as a four-legged lamb?"

Farley laughed. "That's clearly a symbol!"

"So what *you* think are symbols are symbols and anything you and the Southern Baptist Conference don't think are symbols aren't. My, how has Christianity flourished for 2000 years without you guys to explain it all perfectly and infallibly for us?"

Farley laughed, shaking his head. "You're some'n else, Lucy. I'll have my daddy get back to you."

$ $ $

A young coed, early 20s, blond, makeup a bit thick, in a stylish pink summer business outfit met Dr. O'Hanrahan at the door to the auditorium. Her name was Jessica, and she was an adorable li'l ol' thing, smiling and laughing easily, speaking in a charming, uncalculated

Southern drawl. Jessica was sent down to meet O'Hanrahan and lead him through the maze of offices and studios to Reverend Bullins's office in the center of the crown-shaped complex.

"Hot enough for you, professor?" she chirped.

"Hell, it wasn't this bad in the Sudan," he said, drenched in sweat due to the dense humidity. The air-conditioning made him swoon as he walked into The Promised Land's main building, the God-Dome.

"Dr. O'Hanrahan!" said Bullins, as Jessica led him into Bullins's palatial office. "Welcome to Mission Control, as we call it."

O'Hanrahan looked around at the lavish office. A wall of books—probably never opened—three TVs side by side and a top-of-the-line VCR underneath, sculpture and paintings, mostly of mawkish Bible scenes, adorned the walls, and Bullins's redwood desk was worthy of a major corporate chief executive officer, which, O'Hanrahan supposed, he was.

"Sit down, over here where it's more comfy," motioned Bullins, leading the professor to leather chairs by the giant plate-glass window that overlooked the TPL development. We must be, deduced O'Hanrahan, in the highest point of the crown. Bullins took a seat behind his desk, looking regal.

Jessica: "Is that all, Reverend Bullins?"

"Thank you, darlin'," he quipped, waving her away. He paused to watch her saunter out of the room, her shapely calves, narrow waist. "Heh heh," he added for O'Hanrahan's benefit, "you can't touch but the Lord surrrrely doesn't mind us sneakin' a peek!"

How much time, O'Hanrahan wondered, before Reverend Bullins and some female student, or some tramp, are caught in adultery?

(It didn't take you one month after arriving at Chicago, Patrick, to cheat on Beatrice.)

"I read in the *Times-Picayune* today," O'Hanrahan began, "where the chairman of the board of Merriwether Industries was going to speak to oil executives in New Orleans this morning."

"A fine man, Charles Merriwether! A good Christian, and a soldier for the American Right."

"Why did he bankroll your search for the *Gospel of Matthias*?"

"As a favor to me, a personal favor," said Reverend Bullins. "I've helped him with some things, and now he has helped me. But come, come, let's talk about this gospel. We've had a look or two at it and damn if we can get anywhere on it. I've had my Greek scholar give it a shot and, I gotta tell you, that is some kinda mystery, professor, some kind of mystery."

O'Hanrahan didn't need to be reminded. "I have every intention of translating it, but I also have every intention of seeing the scroll returned to Hebrew University, its rightful owner."

Reverend Bullins looked out over his empire. "Oh, my friend, within the next year there may not be a Jerusalem standing. Not if what the Lord foretells comes to pass . . . However, for a price Hebrew University can have it back—after you've done your bit, Patrick. After this college and your work are famous the world over. And after the False Prophecy of the End Times has begun its necessary work, leading astray the lukewarm of the Church Triumphant, the doubters, the insincere. What power we have, my friend!" Reverend Bullins rose and paced, talked of the Rapture and his ascension through the clouds, before stopping to lay his hand on O'Hanrahan's hand, trembling and unsteady since morning. "We are active partners in the End Times, you and me!"

O'Hanrahan was distressed his hand was shaking so. He raised his head to meet the eyes of Reverend Bullins, who had a look of concern. O'Hanrahan knew he was jaundiced and his eyes an unhealthy color. Some African malady kicking around inside.

"Our medical center is the finest in the Baton Rouge area," the reverend said gently. "Yes, over on Philadelphia Drive. We'll getcha over there while it's still called that," he added morosely.

"What do you mean?"

Bullins explained as if O'Hanrahan were a natural ally. The sole black city councilman in Philadelphia, Louisiana, had staged a loud protest, packing the city council chamber with "his people" all demanding a street named after Martin Luther King, Jr. "If it just weren't going by my hospital," said Bullins disgustedly.

"Let me guess," said O'Hanrahan in a feisty mood. "You don't like Dr. King, though, I'm sure, some of your best prayer-partners are black."

"Don't get me wrong, racism is a vile sin, but that man should not be lifted up. He was an adulterer."

"Hell, half you TV preachers *are*. Aimee Semple McPherson, Jim Bakker, Jimmy Swaggart, Elmer Gantries all!" O'Hanrahan was satisfying himself if no one else. "It must be something in the American water. Even ol' John Wesley, founder of Methodism, couldn't keep from getting run out of Georgia, caught with his pants down with the mayor of Savannah's niece."

Reverend Bullins ignored him. "Your Dr. King was also a plagiarist."

"You know, one thing really mystifies me about you crackers," said O'Hanrahan. "The way good Christian white Americans treated the black man in the '50s we're lucky we have *one* city left standing, and Martin Luther King was a man who could have said, all right, people, go to it, burn this country down. But he didn't. And all you can do after some white trash shot him, is run him into the ground."

(Martin Luther King was a prophet of God. One of the few America has ever known. Do the Ed Meeses and Jesse Helmses, the Pat Buchanans and David Dukes, Ronald Reagan with his cabinet's jokes about "Martin Luther Coon"—does no one think there will be a judgment? Do they not even sense the reckoning to come?)

Bullins arranged some papers on his desk, not looking up. "I wouldn'ta figured you for a liberal, Patrick. I take it you're for quotas, discrimination against the white man and all that."

O'Hanrahan wasn't going to waste his breath on this man.

"*I'm* penalized," Reverend Bullins added emphatically, "by the U.S. government. None of my students can get a government-sponsored loan to come here. Why? Because, like Bob Jones University and many others, we forbid interracial dating. It is a sorry day in the history of America when good Christian men and women can't be supported by their government in Bible College because liberals in Washington put pressure on us to dilute the races." Bullins changed the subject quickly, looking in O'Hanrahan's eyes as a physician might. "You're jaundiced. Tomorrow, let's say you and me go over to the TPL Medical Center and have 'em take a look-see."

O'Hanrahan stiffened his resolve to avoid doctors.

"Demons working within your body, my friend. The demon alcohol. And your medication—our cleaning woman saw the pill bottle by the sink . . ."

Before any more moral exhortations, O'Hanrahan lumbered to his feet. "I think I'll see the scroll now, Bullins."

He was ushered to a small library with a large oaken desk, the private study of Reverend Bullins. Again, O'Hanrahan noted it smelled freshly painted and plastered, didn't look truly utilized but rather assembled for show.

Bullins sincerely wished to be helpful. "If you need any book, call it up on the computer and Jessica down the hall will see to it that it's brought over from the main library." He directed Jessica to bring in the scroll from the valuables vault.

O'Hanrahan noticed an armed security guard standing in the doorway, a retired, donut-eating, Southern ex-cop in his sixties. He had a gray crew cut. Reverend Bullins beamed, "Oh, hello, Tom. Patrick, this is Tom. This scroll is perfectly safe within this room—no thief or rival collector will bother you here." With a less than hidden tone, Bullins assured O'Hanrahan the scroll would in *no way* leave the room with the culprit unscathed.

O'Hanrahan nodded, "I get the idea, Bullins."

The reverend blessed the enterprise and left to attend to other business. Presently, Jessica brought in the scroll and set it before O'Hanrahan, leaving a trail of her splendid perfume. O'Hanrahan spread out the papyrus in its clear plastic sheath, not exposing the actual papyrus to air. O'Hanrahan was content to work with the many legal pads Lucy had filled with transliterations of Meroitic script. Page after page of letters, senseless, indecipherable. He stared at the first line again:

> 𐤃𐤄4𐤄 6𐤠𐤒 ꞉𐤚 θ ꞉ 4 𐤠 θ ꞉ 𐤄 ⵝ ꞉ 𐤚 ⵝ ꞉ ⵝ 𐤒 ꞉ 4 𐤚 𐤄
>
> KVQ6KJL꞉ FR꞉ QNR꞉VXMFX꞉ XLMQBSM

Hopeless! Reams and reams of this stuff. Perhaps he should enter it all into a computer and ask the computer to identify any of the 800 known Meroitic names, hoping by some coincidence a Pharoah or Candace was mentioned in the gospel somewhere.

"My oh my," said Jessica, who brought him a cup of coffee dutifully. "I can't make head or tails out of that. What language is it, professor?"

Rather than elaborate, he shrugged. "No idea, honey."

"What's the Bible say? It's Greek to me?" she laughed.

O'Hanrahan rolled his eyes and like Reverend Bullins watched her saunter from the room. Tom the Security Guard watched her walk down the hall as well. "It's Greek to me" is Shakespeare, honey.

O'Hanrahan was alone with the scroll again.

It's just you and me now, he said to himself. God, I wish you *were* Greek, he thought. If you were in Greek, Mr. Matthias, I'd be reading you this very week. Just as Rabbi Rosen read this scroll in under a week.

Wait.

Maybe it is in Greek.

Maybe that's how Rabbi Rosen read it so quickly. Rosen realized this scroll had nothing to do with Meroitic and that the language was merely a *code*, merely a code for Greek letters . . . but, no, no, O'Hanrahan calmed himself, steadying himself at the table. That can't be. Greek has 24 letters, Meroitic 23. . . .

Wait.

As if an intoxicating drug spread through his body, O'Hanrahan felt his head lighten, his fingers tingle. Oh God, that's it, isn't it? The *colon* isn't a word-separator: it too is part of the code. It's a letter! A Greek letter! This damn thing's in *Greek*!

He stood up, laughing. O'Hanrahan's head darted around wildly. Who was looking at him? Any hidden cameras? Could anyone observing him steal this revelation? In triumph, he allowed himself a deep, restoring breath.

Oh, but what geniuses the transcribers of this gospel were, what masters of deception!

They encoded the *Gospel of Matthias* in a lost language—lost and mysterious to the First Century even! They knew! They knew every pitfall of those who would come after! They knew any linguist attacking the thing would try to solve the mysteries of Meroitic—for 2000 years they led scholars to this dead end! Those geniuses! Those devils.

O'Hanrahan smiled: of course, the 23 Meroitic characters and the colon make 24, one symbol for each of Greek's 24 letters. Dimly, like Eurydice falling back into the shadow-world, hands outstretched, the Empire of Meroe and its unknowable language darkly withdrew, never to be deciphered this generation, not by O'Hanrahan. The Nile would keep this mystery.

An hour of work, trial and error, and he had a pretty good idea what figures were *sigma*, and once *Iosephus* was picked out, the code unraveled in no time. The colons were *nus*. The first line read:

$$6\mathcal{E}456\mathcal{P}\mathsf{U}\cdot 8\theta\cdot 4\Delta\theta\cdot\mathcal{E}\mathsf{X}\ddagger 8\mathsf{X}\cdot\mathsf{X}\mathsf{U}\ddagger\mathcal{C}\mathsf{X}\ddagger$$
APEBALONTHNEMHNPISTINIOSEPHUS

O'Hanrahan marveled at it: *Apebalon tin emin pistin, Iosephus.* "I had lost my faith, Josephus." A disciple writing of a loss of faith? His hands began trembling anew with the import and gravity of such a find!

And nor would he share this new revelation with anyone, not even Lucy or the rabbi—well, not at first. With this information, any fool could decode the gospel and render himself, the rabbi, and Lucy superfluous. No, it would be just his alone now.

(Not even a thank-you. Not even a small hosanna?)

O'Hanrahan now with a new sense of wonder and awe before this epistle from the 100s turned over a new leaf in the legal pad with trembling hand—Matthias, he said, a tear coming to his eye, you old comrade. What have you to tell me, my friend?

$ $ $

In the midst of the campus was an antebellum plantation home, three stories with Greek columns, a grand portico and a staircase leading to the front door. The driveway was cobblestone and wound up to the slight rise of the mansion as if it were the White House, designed for a procession of limousines.

"We call it home," said Farley.

The tolerance Lucy had surprisingly found for the TPL empire was beginning now to slip away. This house costs a million, figured Lucy, stepping out of the station wagon.

"A big place."

"Well, we get important visitors so it has to be a bit of a showplace," Farley explained, not bothering to lock the car in this Christian community. "President Reagan, when he was running in 1980. That sure was exciting! I got to shake his hand and everything. He came down to help dedicate the Bullins Rapture Center. What are you, Luce? A pre-Tribulationist or a post-Tribulationist?"

"I think the Rapture is a bunch of hooey," she said. "You guys are doing what the Catholics did in 1956 with Mary being assumed to heaven. You've seized upon a symbolic sentence or two in *Thessalonians* and invented your own theology around it."

Farley shook his head, "I'll be waving down at you from the clouds."

"That's where Heaven, is, Farley? Up above us. How far into outer space? When you go up up up, where will you stop? Pluto? Or after the big special effect, will God fast-forward you to Heaven several zillion light years away?"

Lucy was escorted through the lavish, marble-floored vestibule to stand before an antebellum staircase that wound to the upper floors, past soft flattering pastel portraits of Reverend and Mrs. Bullins staring beatifically to the promised land of verdant fields fresh in the light of sunrise.

Lila Mae Bullins was a dynamo of energy at 5'4" with her hair teased up high for another three inches of added height, lightened to a lavender-silver, a face thick with makeup, apparently true to the un-written rule that TV evangelists' wives have to do their best to represent the *vanitas* of the world, stopping this side of clown face-paint. But aside from her cosmetic-surgeried caricature of ageless Southern-belle charm, she seemed to Lucy somehow fragile, ready to weep at any given opportunity, like on Bullins's often hysterical revival telecasts. Lucy was deposited with Farley's mother in the kitchen while Farley ran upstairs to get some promised treat.

"We have many prayer-partners in Chicago," said Mrs. Bullins, groping for commonality with Lucy, while fetching her guest a Diet Coke from one of two large refrigerators. "You know," she added confidentially, "we have Catholic Pentecostals now too."

Yes, Lucy had heard of this. It was an attempt to keep black Catholics particularly from streaming out of the staid, unchanging rote of mass and into the more ethnic and exciting African-American Protestant denominations. Lucy thought of Reverend Stallings in Washington, excommunicated for the African elements in his mass . . . and yes, that bishop in Africa she had read about, Emmanuel Milingo, thrown out as well for allowing dance and no small amount of folk-healing to mix in with what John Paul II commanded. Mind you, thought Lucy cynically, when it's Polish culture and Solidarity rallies, the pope mixes culture, politics, and Church just dandy. It's a small wonder the Host hasn't become a kielbasa by now . . .

"Lovely house, isn't it?" asked Mrs. Bullins, proud of it.

"It's quite a lavish mansion you live in," said Lucy pointedly.

"Yes," she enthused, "it's antebellum—that means before the war. Of course when we Southerners talk about 'the War' we mean the Civil War, not World War Two!" Mrs. Bullins laughed alone. "1836. Over

400 slaves at one time; the Pettigrew family who built it raised sugar cane and cotton—very hard work in those days."

Not for the Pettigrews, thought Lucy.

"I'm happy to say that Augustus Pettigrew was a minister who had been to seminary in Scotland. Very influential in his day. I feel," she breathed with sincerity, tears held back, "that God has been a long time in this house."

"But the Reverend Pettigrew owned 400 slaves," Lucy repeated.

As her Diet Coke was poured over the ice cubes in a tall glass, Mrs. Bullins nodded her head positively. "Slavery was a horrible thing but it was the way Our Lord chose for the black man to come to know Jesus Christ."

The notion was so sealed and complete Lucy hardly knew where to begin to comment upon it.

"Black people in this country have been made a special revelation to go with their special sufferin'," continued Mrs. Bullins. "And it is through Jesus Christ that they will rise up in this country and be done with drugs and poverty and all that Satan has thrown in their path. Now you just help yourself to anything in our refrigerator—we have plenty of everything. Camilla sees to that, don't you, honey?"

Lucy turned to see a maternal black woman in a maid's uniform emerge from a pantry, a can of black-eyed peas in her hand: "Thaz right, Miz Lila."

"Camilla's making her special Cajun meatloaf tonight. It's a *vayry* special occasion, having you and Dr. O'Hanrahan as our guests."

"Don't you forget your meh'cine now, Miz Lila."

Eagerly Mrs. Bullins took a bottle of prescribed medicine from atop the spice rack and emptied two pills into her hand, greedily swallowing them, remarkably, without the aid of water. "Cayn't forget my pills now can I, Camilla?" She flashed a guilty look in Lucy's direction. "My medicine. You see, I have to take these . . . my medicine."

Farley returned and led Lucy to a wood-paneled office with a large desk stacked with pamphlets and letters to sign by the window, and a large television screen and VCR opposite in a paneled cleft.

"I'm not like showin' off or nothin' but I thought at some point you might wanna see me in action," he snorted, turning an embarrassed pink. "This is, uh, 19 . . . 1985, my first telecast. You gotta see my long hair to believe it, and that horrible ol' pink suit. And this tape, this one here, is this year. I led the prayers for young people in the Spring Revival. I'm gonna let you look at 'em while I go take a shower. I can't stand to see myself, I look like such a hick!"

Lucy let her arms be laden with video cassettes.

"And this is our Mardi Gras tape you were askin' about. This is where we stood outside this gay bar and, uh, the language gets a little blue but you can see the kind of sin we're up against."

Lucy was left to play with the videotapes in this huge office by herself, presumably Reverend Bullins's home office. She played the Mardi Gras tape first and there was a younger, paler Farley stopping two men in Panama hats and Guatemalan ponchos with tall plastic cups of fruit-flavored drinks in their hands, telling them that *The party's thataway, but Heaven's thataway, my friend,* pointing upward. This received a predictable response. The video caught one lipsticked fellow in halfhearted drag who tried, as Lucy had tried, to argue with the group in vain. *You say Mardi Gras is pagan,* he said, *but you don't realize that Easter and Christmas are full of paganism too. Who am I? I'm a graduate assistant at Tulane and I study ancient history and . . . No, I'm not going to pray with you, I'm going in this bar and . . .* And the debate went on, the Pentecostal Youth impervious. Farley looked sadly at the camera after the exchange was over and sighed: *Satan, you've got another one, but Devil, we're gonna getcha! We're gonna get you and kick you all the way back to Hell!*

Lucy, bored soon enough, left the video running and got out of her chair to wander around the office. Here was the 1980 photo of Ron and Nancy looking benevolent beside a thinner Reverend Bullins and Lila; both ladies' face-lifts vacuously smiling to the breaking point, stretched to Kabuki. Here was a photo of Gavin McLeod, the guy on "The Love Boat" turned born-again booster. Here was a country & western singer whose name she thought she recognized.

Lucy spotted the array of Bullins pamphlets on the bookshelf. He had no actual books, but on the shelf as if they were books was a video series. His photograph was always on the cassette, glasses down his nose, looking scholarly and authoritative. Lucy wondered if Bullins had ever heard of Augustine, read a word of Luther or Calvin, St. Teresa or Catherine of Siena, anything of the Church that had gone before. She saw Jimmy Swaggart's *Straight Answers to Tough Questions* and took it down from its place.

(Oh please.)

Lucy and Luke and Gabriel and Christopher would sit around the TV on dull Sunday nights and jeer this man who bashed every known denomination, put Jews and Catholics in Hell, bashed gays, bashed feminists, bashed intellectuals, sang paeans to President Reagan, the nonchurchgoing, divorced Hollywood has-been with the estranged family, racist cabinet, and West Coast morals who had persuaded every born-again in America of his deep personal holiness. On the inside cover there was a flourished signature and generic message from Swaggart to his Louisiana rival Farley Bullins. She thumbed through the book:

Is aerobic dancing sinful? "For Christians to get their aerobic exercise to the beat of this same music is to expose themselves to the pollution of the world." *What do you think about mixed swimming?* Swaggart's against it. *Movies?* "It is wrong for Christians to associate themselves with worldly entertainments such as movies." Here's a goodie: *Is oral-genital sex scripturally permissible between husband and wife?* Of course not. *Homosexuality?* They're not born that way, according to Swaggart, but rather entered by Satan . . . "These individuals would like to be in a position where they could recruit young men and boys (or girls) into their life of debauchery and filth." *Evolution?* "I think that it is clear that no true evolutionist can be a Christian or a believer in the Bible." Lucy indulged herself, flipping through the book. Cremation is a sin, capital punishment, of course, is *not;* and as for women, "Any husband who is Christlike in conduct and attitude should be reverenced by his wife and she should submit to him as unto the Lord. She should submit in everything, knowing that everything he demands will be scriptural, godly and Christlike."

Gee, Jimmy, I have a question, thought Lucy, replacing the book on the shelf: *what does God think about sneaking out on your wife in your $1.5-million mansion, going to a sleazy motel and renting a room with a prostitute whom you've paid to spread her legs and play with herself while you masturbate nearby?* She thought of the triumphal facts on the book jacket: a following of 2.2 million households on TV, a weekly worldwide television following of 500 million. The number-one preacher on the tube, until his little misadventure; a man worth *millions*, Farley Jr. had explained, to the local economy of Baton Rouge. How could even *one* million people want to hear *these* opinions? How could so many of her fellow Americans be moved to hand over their hard-earned money in support of these politics and sentiments?

What hope do we women have? she thought blackly. Where Christians are concerned, it just hasn't changed one little bit—

"Lucy?"

She turned to the door to see Farley.

"Dr. O'Hanrahan's here and supper's almost on the table."

In the foyer, she was reunited with O'Hanrahan, who looked like a melted wax sculpture of himself. "I'll take the Sudan to this humidity any day," he grumbled, wiping his red forehead.

She looked into his yellowed eyes, which he averted. "You don't look very well, sir."

"I don't feel very well," he admitted, for once.

Reverend Bullins was seen next sweeping through the front doors, waving his driver and the white Mercedes-Benz with the TPL logo to be parked in the garage, depositing his suitcoat into his servant's waiting hands. "Thanks, Camilla. Yes, I'm tellin' you, Patrick. You *ought* to see a doctor."

"Maybe tomorrow," he said, flashing her a signal he had something to tell her.

In one of the long stately rooms off the side of the central high-ceilinged hallway was an equally long old-fashioned oaken table. The room was a soft yellow with many wall-ridgings and plaster excrescences in antebellum style; a crowded chandelier sparkled above the table, and a portrait of Farley Bullins with an American flag imposed upon a dawn breaking beyond him hung over the room's unused fireplace.

They milled around the table and Camilla wheeled in a tray with her meatloaf steaming on a silver platter. She industriously prepared everyone's iced tea, squeezing the lemon and asking who took sugar and would Miss Lucy like Sweet-'n-Low.

"So, how do you find our little library?" asked Mrs. Bullins, as her husband was seating himself at the head of the table.

"Inadequate and philistine," said Dr. O'Hanrahan.

Lucy hid a smile. She had encountered O'Hanrahan frequently in this mood when nothing could please him and there was nothing nice to say about anything.

Lila Mae: "Well, I'm sorry you—"

"You've got a fair collection of patristics but of course not one scientific work of textual analysis. Since you people fear truth and science."

Lucy noticed O'Hanrahan swayed unsteadily taking his chair. He was drunk perhaps . . . But where would he get booze around here?

". . . that library is a pile of stupefying ignorance on biblical interpretation and scriptural infallibility. Of course, you believe each word is divinely dictated by the Holy Spirit, which attributes the many mistakes in the biblical text to God instead of Man. I'm sure God appreciates that."

Farley Jr. and Mrs. Bullins turned their eyes back on Reverend Bullins, their patriarch, their savior from the crummy little three-room shack under the levee in Catfishtown, their miracle worker. Reverend Bullins cleared his throat, "You are right to suggest I have no truck with secular humanism, Dr. O'Hanrahan. Or modernism or science-ism or whatever-you-want-ism you so-called scholars want to call it—"

"Stupidity-ism?"

Reverend Bullins buttered his cornbread. "I can understand some resentment, Patrick, on your part. But we Pentecostals merely intend to return here to the sanctity of the Early Church."

"I'm sure that's true," Lucy spoke up, ready to tangle as well, "where the place of women is concerned."

O'Hanrahan laughed. "Early Church? In this million-dollar mansion you've got for yourself? And the tax-free salary? And the two Mercedes-Benzes and the private airplane—"

"God will provide for His servants." The subject of servants reminded him to ask Camilla to go to the kitchen and fetch him another slice of lemon for his iced tea.

Mrs. Bullins set her drawn, face-lifted countenance to O'Hanrahan and displayed empathy, shaking her head so slightly. "This anger inside you, Patrick . . . Come to Jesus. Put your burdens on Him."

Reverend Bullins: "Lila, if you'd allow *me* to continue."

"Come to Jesus," she got in one more time.

"Do you know what your pious husband is up to here?" O'Hanrahan asked Mrs. Bullins. "One of my greatest friends and one of the world's greatest Hebrew scholars had a hypodermic needle full of sedative stabbed into him so he'd stay out of your husband's plan."

"Of course it's not like that, Lila—"

"Your husband is aligned with fanatics and kooks and dangerous men who are bringing a war upon this world!"

Reverend Bullins had nothing to fear from Lila Mae, who had been lobotomized long ago to a "Come to Jesus" and "Jesus is love" and "God is good" frequency that kept her close to tears . . . although a doctor could recognize that was more to do with her regular and increasing doses of depression medication.

Reverend Bullins: "No bad will come to those who preach Jesus as he is in the gospels, Patrick. I was ordained at the age of thirteen . . ."

O'Hanrahan pinched the bridge of his nose. Lucy noticed the red color of his face had not blanched to its usual healthy pink. Perhaps he was sunburned, but it looked more fevered.

". . . which is why," Reverend Bullins concluded some moments later, "I'm proud to call myself a fundamentalist."

"*Mentus* means 'mind.' *Fundus* to the Romans meant 'anus.' Fundamentalist: a mind like an anus. I'm surprised anyone prefers the sobriquet."

"Well, I am proud," Bullins said imperturbably, as Camilla returned with his slice of lemon. "Heh-heh, as a Roman Catholic you must be tired of finding yourself on the losing team. You see, what your anger is really directed to is our success. Look about you. We were in 1.8 million American homes last year."

Farley Jr. interrupting: "We're beaming our program into all the Eastern Europe countries. We're gonna bring Russia to Jesus." Farley and his father pronounced Russia *rusher*.

"Jeeeezus," his mother repeated, by increments leaving her present world.

"We were mobbed," said Reverend Bullins, "on our last trip to Russia. In Africa our ministry is growing—and they're not going to be Catholic or Lutheran, they're going to be Pentecostal. We're growing by leaps and bounds!"

O'Hanrahan, steadying himself at the table: "What are you hawking in the third world? Get rich quick, get a big shiny car like Reverend Bullins?"

Reverend Bullins rested his hands on his belly, basking. "We have triumphed, the televangelists will take Jesus to the Indian heathens, the godless communists, the pagans worshiping sticks and stones in Africa—oh, thank you, Camilla . . ." Camilla had slipped a slice of her meatloaf onto his plate. "Mexico," he continued, working up to his familiar TV crescendo. "There wasn't a single Protestant ten years ago. Now ten percent of Mexico is Protestant, and so goes South America—*our* kind of Protestant, Pentecostal with a living, healing, breathing faith!"

"Jesus be praised . . ." said Mrs. Bullins, almost weeping.

"You look at TPL, Patrick, and you see the future of Christianity. Oh, what a gift God has given us when He allowed the television and radio to come into our minds. So at the last, at the very last, we could get the message out: God is coming! 1999 say all the signs! The End Times! The End Times! God is onnnnnn the way!"

Lila Mae: "Praise Jesus!"

Farley Jr.: "Mom, it's all right . . ."

O'Hanrahan: "How long has your wife had a religious mania, Bullins? She needs help, you know."

Mrs. Bullins, glassy-eyed: "Come to Jeeeezus." Then she lifted her upturned hands and glanced to the ceiling, closing her eyes, deep in ecstasy.

"Mama," Farley Jr. tapped her arm, slightly embarrassed.

Camilla wordlessly—used to much worse—put a slab of meatloaf on Mrs. Bullins's plate while her mistress indulged her transport.

"Perhaps you ought to go lie down, Lila Mae," said Reverend Bullins without much concern. "Her demon is not as strong as yours, Patrick. *Nor drunkards, nor revilers, nor extortioners shall inherit the kingdom of God.*"

"Well, 'extortioners' takes you out. And you're a reviler too. I've watched your broadcasts in Chicago. You send the whole damn country to hell. You don't preach love, you don't preach Jesus—"

"*Neither fornicators nor idolators, nor adulterers nor homosexuals.* Those are the cold, cruel facts."

"You're quoting Paul out of context of his society," said O'Hanrahan, mopping a fevered brow.

"Dr. O'Hanrahan," asked Lucy, "are you all right?"

"The adulterers shall burn!" pronounced Lila Mae, gawking maniacally at her husband. "Isn't that right, honey?" Lucy wondered suddenly whether Mrs. Bullins was accusing her husband of this sin.

"Mama, calm down," said Farley Jr.

"The central message of Christianity," O'Hanrahan said, "is redemption. Yes, redemption for all those people Paul listed." He looked down at his plate with no appetite. "My late son was a homosexual."

This briefly brought conversation to a halt.

Lucy recalled some of the things O'Hanrahan had said in Khartoum about Rudolph. Oh, but here was the truth. She glimpsed a fraction of the struggle of Patrick O'Hanrahan, a man of his generation with a gay son . . . now a dead son.

"AIDS," intoned Reverend Bullins, "is God's vengeance upon those who would pervert God's design. I'm sorry if that is how your son met his death. But *vengeance is mine sayeth the Lord.*"

O'Hanrahan stood up to leave the table in disgust . . . but wavered. Fell back into his chair, his eyes rolling up into his head. O'Hanrahan in steadying himself overturned his water glass, which had hit the edge of his plate and broke; a water stain spread under his plate.

"Sir!" cried Lucy, rising to her feet.

O'Hanrahan held on to the back of his chair but then he passed out, falling to the floor.

Lucy ran around to him. "My God, call a doctor!"

"The full quote is as follows. *Do not be deceived,*" quoted Reverend Bullins with a cold superiority before his fallen guest, not moving a finger. "*Neither the fornicators nor idolators, nor adulterers nor homosexuals, nor the greedy, nor the drunkards—*"

"For God's sake, he's having some kind of seizure!"

Camilla put down her tray and ran to the kitchen phone.

"*Nor revilers, nor extortioners will inherit the Kingdom of God.*"

Mrs. Bullins stood and pointed an accusing finger at O'Hanrahan, now groaning in pain on the carpet. "Satan has come upon him for his unrighteous works! I cast out the demon in the name of Jeeeezus, in the holy blessèd lovely . . ." She teared up, her voice cracked in the familiar way one can see several times a week on Bullins's telecast. ". . . most beautiful saintly name of Jeeeezus! I say *out*, devil, come out of there!"

Lucy rounded on Farley, near tears herself: "He's not drunk, *for God's sake,* he's had a heart attack or something!"

Camilla called out: "Ambulance on the way, miss!"

Lucy screamed to Farley, "Would you help me move him?"

Farley Bullins, Jr., scion to the $100-million TPL Empire, sat in his place stymied, one hand clasped in his raving mother's hand. He glanced at his father for advice and his father looked back serenely. Farley gaped at Lucy, unable to know what to do.

$ $ $

As advertised, the TPL Medical Center was a large, well-equipped hospital in the tradition of a number of Baptist and Pentecostal hospitals through the South. Lucy was struck, traversing the lobby, with the Southern look of the people, the old heavy women, the obesity of the blacks, the scarecrow men out of Margaret Bourke-White '30s photographs, the polyester shifts, dusters, pullovers, the anxious, over-

madeup teenage girls with fire-red nail polish looking chunky in halter
tops . . . As she arrived on the ninth floor in the Bullins Tower, O'Hanrahan's floor, she saw a waiting room full of drawn Louisianans, smoking up a storm, a father sipping beer from a discreet paper bag, an
overweight grandmother with hamhock arms all gathered for news of
Grandpa.

"Patrick O'Hanrahan, please," said Lucy at the desk.

She was informed she could visit him without accompaniment but
not to tire him out. Room 923. Oh, she dreaded this. Maybe the old
guy had at last played out his hand. She felt her breathing become
more shallow as she determined not to pause but to go straight into
the room.

"The vultures circle," grumbled O'Hanrahan, looking, to her relief,
like himself but bloodshot and jaundiced. His stomach, grotesquely,
was notably swollen, rounded.

"Hello, sir," she tried tentatively, before returning to their familiar
form. "You look . . ."

"Like garbage, don't lie to me. I suspect foul play, Sister Lucy.
They're poisoning me so they can walk off with the scroll."

Lucy noticed that by his bedside on the rollaway table were stacks
of photos of the *Gospel of Matthias* and several empty notepads. O'Hanrahan scrawled a message on one of them: *The room may be bugged.*
Then another message: *I figured out the gospel!*

"You—" Lucy cut off her own enthusiasm. "You sure?" she whispered.

O'Hanrahan nodded. Yes, he looked gravely ill but his eyes held
triumph! "Hepatitis A, they say," he whispered to Lucy. "Survivable.
But we need to work round the clock to finish this, in case I . . ."

Lucy didn't supply the phrase.

"I will *not* have my best-selling edition of this gospel be posthumous.
Sheer meanness and bile will keep me alive."

(Those qualities you have in abundance.)

Lucy went to the windows. There was a playground down below
and a large stadium-style light near it so kids could play after it became
dark, which would be soon. She noticed a swarm of gnats, mosquitoes,
moths darting and flitting around the lights.

"You missed Camilla's Cajun meatloaf," said Lucy.

He laughed faintly. "Didya get a load of that plantation house? I
suspect if we'd made dessert we'd get to see three nappy-haired boys
tap-dancing for our evening enjoyment and . . ."

Inconveniently, a black nurse appeared in the doorway, silencing
O'Hanrahan to a mumble. Oblivious, she announced that this wing
ceased visiting hours at nine P.M. and Lucy had to leave. Then the
nurse removed the pen from O'Hanrahan's hands and put his pad

away. No more work now, Mr. O'Hanrahan, she requested in a gentle nurse-tone.

It was not until Lucy was walking down the chemical-lemony, antiseptic hallway that O'Hanrahan's vulnerable condition registered. The great man reduced, debilitated. She wanted some time alone and decided to skirt the ever-present TPL limousine and the attentive Farley who loitered in the waiting room. She walked down the stairway, all nine floors, and let herself out an emergency-exit door in the parking lot, out into the orange-fluorescent-illumined rows of cars. She returned to the visitor's entrance and got a taxi to take her back to the TPL Bible College campus. No sooner had the taxi deposited her than she realized that she could have asked the driver to take her into town and by a drugstore.

So she could buy that home pregnancy kit.

Lucy walked across the campus. It was a pleasant evening, seventy-five degrees, a little after 9:30 P.M. now, although it seemed to her it should be midnight, so much had happened these last two days, all of it suspended in a haze of jet lag and surreality.

"Excuse me," she asked, stopping a Promised Land undergrad, "but can you tell me where a nearby drugstore is?"

The girl smiled warmly and gave directions, and even offered to come along by car since there was one tricky turn going into Philadelphia. It became obvious to Lucy it was really too far to walk.

"Something I can help you with?" the girl offered. "I've got a closet full of stuff back in the dorm."

"No, I don't think so," said Lucy, "thanks anyway."

"Is it a medical problem?"

"Uh, no, just hygiene things."

"Are you a student here?"

Lucy suddenly found the friendliness encroaching. On the other hand, after months of old men and their crotchets it was tempting to make a female friend . . . in fact, in her tired, exasperated state, Lucy might well tell this girl with the friendly face everything. But imagine! The kindhearted, well-meaning pieties, the return visit to the Newlife Covenant Center, the prayers and earnest beseechings for God's will.

"No, I'm a guest of the Bullinses."

"Wow," she smiled, tossing her long, straw-colored hair back, "at the White House—that's what we call that big mansion."

"Yeah, they've got me in there . . ." Lucy was aware she'd trailed off.

The young woman put forward her hand and touched Lucy's arm. "Something's wrong, isn't it?"

Lucy stiffened. "No. I just wish the drugstore wasn't so far away. It's a small thing. Sorry to have bothered you."

"My boyfriend Scott? He's got a car and we can take you—"

Lucy broke away and turned resolutely to walk in the other direction. "No, that's very kind, but no thanks. Good evening."

The woman looked a little hurt, but also secure in the knowledge that something was wrong. "My name's Patsy! Seeya around . . ." she added, hoping to backtrack to an introduction.

How did she know something was wrong? Lucy wondered as she walked away.

(Anyone could tell to look at you.)

Damn, these Christers sure can spot a lost soul.

(Patsy's a sweet girl, and she could have helped you.)

I'm scared of these born-agains, thought Lucy, keeping her head down as she passed an auditorium that was emptying scores of students holding Bibles and talking impassionedly about Isaiah, prophecy, yes—she heard it—the End Times, being announced even in Philadelphia, Louisiana. There's something wrong with them around the eyes, Lucy decided. Patsy was living in a dream world. Christian innocence plus monthly contributions to Reverend Bullins's evangelization machine.

(You find that less substantial than the saints and rosary routines of Roman Catholicism, do you?)

How close she came to being taken back to Patsy's suite and crying and confessing everything, being prayed over and counseled and . . . Oh, God, how close I came to that kind of circus. To be beholden to Patsy, that twenty-year-old goody-goody with no life experience, no concept of anything but her suburban, comfortable God—

(Sounds like you a few months ago.)

Lucy leaned against a bus-stop sign. After what she had seen in Ethiopia, after all the disease and suffering she had beheld—and surely there was no shortage of it here in Louisiana—how could all these people pour millions into this feel-good, self-indulgent medicine show of Reverend Bullins's delusions of grandeur . . . Actually, it was no different, though infinitely less beautiful and lasting, than St. Peter's in Rome and the gaudy, gold-encrusted palace of the Vatican. It was all so goddam irrelevant, really, to what Jesus would have wanted.

(What are you going to do about it?)

Look, I'd leave this world in a second, leave academia, leave my life in Chicago as well, for Africa to stand beside that nurse, to stand beside people who really might need me instead of what I have here: no one who needs me. Except Dr. O'Hanrahan. And damn it, he's dying.

Lucy returned to the mansion and was let in by a black servant at the side entrance. Camilla in the kitchen was up making Reverend Bullins's favorite pastry for tomorrow morning's breakfast, yes she was, she told Lucy in a languorous Louisiana accent. Bet he pays her shit, thought Lucy, climbing the stairs. This TPL empire, despite a smattering of black students, is just one more White Fantasyland, Lucy decided, another luridly compelling production from the part of the world that gave us Scarlett O'Hara, Graceland, Mardi Gras, "Way Down Upon the Suwannee," and the Confederacy.

Lucy found her way to the bedroom and shut and locked the door before Farley or any late-night prayer vigil could descend upon her. She crawled into the guestroom bed, which was deeply comfortable— surely the first really comfortable bed since . . . well, since she left Chicago in June. A digital desk clock was the only light, with a cobalt blue TPL and a cross centered above the time.

I suppose, she sighed, I could march over to the Newlife Covenant Center or some such equivalent. Go home to my folks before my child started showing, do some song and dance about working on the Matthias scroll in Louisiana, have the kid, give it up, go back to my life and allow him or her to be brought up—

Her thought stopped there: *him* or *her*. It was the first time she had given the *it* in her body that much of an identity. No matter, she thought stoically, it will have to be given up. Don't even like kids that much, and my sister Cecilia's monsters drive me crazy, the bawling, the whining, the selfishness that has to be tamed with loving caution. But here they would make me write that letter. That letter the child could read at eighteen when Lucy would be . . . let's see, well into another unrecognizable, uncharted life at 46. Dear Daughter, or Dear Son. You're probably wondering why I gave you up . . .

No.

You must know that if things were different I would not have given you away . . .

No.

You will never understand, perhaps, why I felt it best to give you away but since you're eighteen maybe you can see how much having a child would change your life, or maybe you're the kind of woman who welcomes that, but, dear daughter—or son—whoever and how- ever you are, with your Southern accent and your mother's bad Irish skin through adolescence, can you believe just one thing? That, trust me, I did you a big favor. And forever after this letter you must know that somewhere your one-time mother loves you, wanted the best for you, which was not me, but hopes you're very happy with the wonder- ful, mystifying life before you as it once was before me . . .

Better the silence than such a letter! My God!

$ $ $

O'Hanrahan awoke to dull pain. He blearily focused on the room and saw that it was dark outside the window and only one light in his room, a table lamp, was on at its lowest wattage.

The nighttable clock said it was nearly midnight.

It was, he surmised, a homey little room, probably the Bullins Center's best luxury suite. To his side was a bedstand with a variety of medical gadgets and between him and this table was his IV tree with three full bags of something-or-other filtering into him. He raised his left arm, which was straightened against a lightweight splint so he wouldn't bend his elbow and disrupt the IV drip. Imagine getting poked with all those needles and being so out of it you had no idea, he considered.

Also on his bedstand were three Dom Perignon cigars in individual humidors. Surely Lucy didn't leave those . . . or Bullins, maybe?

"Cigars, Mr. O'Hanrahan," said a gravelly, assuring voice from across the room.

O'Hanrahan raised his head weakly. Sitting by the lamp was a gentleman in his sixties with full silver hair styled as for a politician, a sturdy but not heavy man dressed impeccably in a conservative dark suit. He was half-attentive to an article in a neatly folded *Wall Street Journal* on his lap. A bottle of some kind of whiskey was beside the stranger on the tabletop, shrouded in a brown paper bag.

"Dom Perignons, as you no doubt recognize," said the man. It was a cigar-smoker's tenor voice given a false bass rasp.

"Thank you," said O'Hanrahan, distressed at how feeble he sounded. "I take it then you're not a doctor."

He set aside his *Wall Street Journal*. "No," he said, volunteering no new information. "This bottle here is a Kentucky Bourbon I thought you'd enjoy. Special Reserve, Old Confederate—private stock, only a few barrels of the stuff ever made. They tell me you've got hepatitis and a number of complications, but when you get better I thought you'd appreciate it."

"Maybe I won't get better."

The gentleman examined his fine, manicured hands. He stood, picked up the bottle and walked closer to put it down on O'Hanrahan's bedside table. O'Hanrahan noticed the youth of the man's hands, like a teenager's, not a liver spot or a crease. The man stood at the bedside and they both looked at each other a moment. "Well, my friend, if indeed the end is near, it wouldn't hurt to drink it. Our vices, Mr. O'Hanrahan, support us in our old age; they are the guardrails we cling to, our constants in an impermanent world." He paced back to the easy chair. "Vice is endangered in this country in this era."

O'Hanrahan smiled faintly. "I agree."

After a pause the man opened a cigar case and motioned, "Do you mind?"

"Not at all." O'Hanrahan wondered if he would have to answer to the head nurse for the lingering cigar smoke in his room.

"You're sure?"

O'Hanrahan lifted his splinted arm and gestured a be-my-guest as well as he could.

"A man my age is defined by his vices. To the club for a dinner of high-cholesterol prime rib, port in the library, cigars with the fellows, a warmed brandy by the fire, a bit of gambling from time to time, cards. A visit to the mistress, much younger—you see what I mean." He barely smiled, raising a hand gracefully. "They have become the sum of me."

It occurred to O'Hanrahan, still struggling with the sensation of having seen the man before, who his visitor was. "You're Chester Merriwether, aren't you?"

The gentleman lit his cigar and availed himself of a paper cup as an ashtray. "I'm *Charles* Merriwether, Mr. O'Hanrahan. But you've got the right idea. Merriwether Industries, chairman of the board."

O'Hanrahan felt fevered and weak, relieved his guest was up to doing the talking.

"Chester was my father. Or Chester the Second, I should say. My grandfather, founder of the original steel enterprise, was Chester the First." He paused, puffing on his cigar.

"Chester the First was a man of God. Led the factory in collective prayer, each Sunday. Mind you, his workers would work for pennies until an industrial accident did them in, children and women too, inhuman hours, unspeakable conditions. Before my grandfather's eyes was a sea of laboring-class misery that he alone was responsible for, but in all those prayers, in all that piety, in all that talk of . . ." He said the name with distaste: ". . . of Jesus, he never could perceive a contradiction. With men of God like Chester the First, unions became inevitable—and our nation pays the price for this now. Chester the Second, my father, was a lover of fine things. Art, old masters, porcelain from China, suits of armor from the Middle Ages, and scrolls, collectibles, antiquities."

"He once owned the *Gospel of Matthias*," O'Hanrahan said.

"A prized possession. We had, in fact, a falling-out over my selling it to another collector. My father paid more attention to his hoarding and rapine than to our family's corporation, which funded his dilettantish pursuits. When I got power of attorney over my father, I began selling off the bric-a-brac. It was easy capital and rendered unnecessary our outrageous insurance payments to protect a bunch of old paintings and potsherds. My retired father became estranged. Never forgave me."

O'Hanrahan stopped short of asking why he himself should be privileged to hear this recital of family history. Mr. Merriwether continued:

"There was a Chester the Third, my older brother."

O'Hanrahan had heard of this brother dimly, an article once in *Look* magazine, a playboy, a jet-setter in the 1960s, convertibles and French actresses with lots of hair . . .

"Having no interest in the family business, he wasted lots of money and died drunk, from a failure to negotiate the road along the cliffs of Menton. A thorough waste of a life, my brother."

"Seems to me he enjoyed his life," O'Hanrahan offered. "A man of vice, like yourself."

But at this Mr. Merriwether erupted: "*Not* like myself. There is a difference in the practice of vice and the practice of self-destruction, of ruination! Any fool," Merriwether thundered, "can die at thirty, Mr. O'Hanrahan." He relaxed his fist and examined his hands, smoothing them as if to calm them. More quietly he continued, "To ration the pleasures of life to old age is a sign of classical temperament, also something endangered in this country in this era. Chester . . ."

O'Hanrahan said nothing as his visitor trailed off, thinking of his older brother. But soon he began again: "My father hoped to pass the company to my brother but had to make do with me, I'm afraid."

"You've done quite well," said O'Hanrahan, scooting up on his pillows to better have a conversation, though a conversation was by no means Merriwether's evident program. "Your multinational is in the Fortune Top 30, is it not?"

Merriwether nodded. "I expanded a series of dying rust-belt steel production plants to a multinational corporation with assets in the tens of billions, Mr. O'Hanrahan. Which brings us to Chester the Fourth." Merriwether sank back in the chair, morosely examining his right hand now, reaching absently for a small silver nail file from his inner suitcoat pocket.

"Your brother's son?"

"No. My son." Without any emotion or change of tone, Merriwether rambled on easily, "You lost your son, did you not, Mr. O'Hanrahan?"

"Yes."

"And your wife?"

"Yes."

"Not to minimize your grief, my friend, but one can suffer these losses in ways other than death. My wife walked away from our marriage with millions—it would have been billions, but I paid my lawyers a fortune, a fortune I would as soon have put into the garbage than allow her to possess. And my son is lost to me. Chester."

O'Hanrahan felt brave enough to venture, "Doesn't want to follow in your footsteps?"

Merriwether put down the nail file and leaned back in his easy chair, placing his hands on his stomach. "He's on the board. I have spent the last forty years pretending my only child is not an idiot, and I have prepared the way for him, I have hired the best advisers for him, I have sent him to the best schools and bribed the best colleges for degrees . . . but what's the use? He lost his first trust fund, the largest, in his first divorce. That castrating debutante was followed by a Brazilian dancer, I kid you not—she too made off with a bundle. His third wife was a drugged-out socialite, his children, my grandchildren, are in and out of psychiatric clinics. Two weeks ago his oldest boy tried to kill himself and made a botch of it—blew the side of his head off . . . More money changed hands to keep this tidbit about young Charles . . ."

Mr. Merriwether's own namesake, thought O'Hanrahan grimly.

". . . from tabloid TV shows, the Neanderthal national media at large."

A pause. There was nothing O'Hanrahan could think to say.

"The board will politely wait until I retire and then they'll force out this nincompoop son of mine and the once-proud Merriwether Industries will cease to have any Merriwethers."

"You could decide not to retire," said O'Hanrahan, his strength fading. "Like Paley and Getty, keep hanging on."

"I deal in actualities, Mr. O'Hanrahan. If I don't step down upon my proposed retirement my board members will retire me themselves—I have no illusions about this. Although, I have sown the seeds of my renascence."

O'Hanrahan rallied his strength to challenge his visitor. "It's hard to believe you deal only in actualities, Mr. Merriwether."

Merriwether buffed a thumbnail. "Really. What would lead you to say that?"

"Because you're hooked up with a lunatic who is planning to broadcast live from the Rapture. And a rogue CIA agent who's trying to bring on Armageddon, and your cohort on the scene is a silly little man who quoted Masonic drivel to me in Khartoum. You don't strike me as the type for Masonic plots, Mr. Merriwether."

Merriwether laughed gently. "Bullins isn't a lunatic, Mr. O'Hanrahan, he's a charlatan. Believes about one-half of the nonsense he spouts, and the other half of the time he's got his eyes on his profit margin. You don't build a personal fortune of $100 million tax-free dollars if you're a lunatic. That scroll of yours is worth a few million more. No matter what he tells you, don't think that fact has escaped him.

"The good reverend is connected in Louisiana as few people are. We had a business deal. I was to get him the *Gospel of Matthias*, this so-called False Prophecy, for his nonsensical end-of-the-world ministry and his nutcase CIA sidekicks. In return, he was to facilitate my purchase of nearly one-third of existing oil leases in the Gulf of Mexico."

O'Hanrahan said presciently, "And since Iraq invaded Kuwait and gas has gone up to . . ."

"Gone up to $1.35 and climbing. $24 a barrel. Already some 80,000 Louisiana riggers have gone back to work. This little brouhaha in Kuwait is good for American business."

"I imagine your investment has paid off royally, Mr. Merriwether. But if these men whose mischief you're underwriting ever really start a big war in an attempt to make a red-white-and-blue Armageddon, how will you feel then?"

Mr. Merriwether laughed. "Come now, Underwood and Colonel Westin can barely tie their shoes. I'm afraid any attempt to postulate a vast conspiracy theory in which I commence the trumps of Armageddon is doomed, sir." The idea of Colonel Westin amused him. "Down in Langley they have shredded every document with Westin's name on it. They don't want to know."

O'Hanrahan had taken the measure of his visitor, and said sourly, "And it doesn't matter to you that there might be thousands of deaths as Saddam's war machine sweeps through the Arabian Peninsula."

"What did I tell you? I deal in actualities, Mr. O'Hanrahan." Merriwether folded his hands again on his stomach. "War," he said lightly, "is a constant in that part of the world. They fight wars, that's what they do. With or without our arms, with or without our involvement, war in the Middle East will happen; Arabs like killing other Arabs. Now we can choose to wring our hands like Jimmy Carter and say ooooh isn't it all so terrible, or we can choose to affect the outcome and, failing that, profit by it, derive some good from it."

"And it doesn't trouble you that Saddam Hussein is evil?"

Merriwether allowed a look of weariness to cross his face before regaining his polite affability. "Good. Evil. These are medieval terms of magic and superstition, words used by men who do not have sufficient perspective on the workings of the world. There are only plans that work, Mr. O'Hanrahan, and plans that don't work."

O'Hanrahan nodded. "And buying up the Gulf of Mexico is your plan. So even if Merriwether Industries gives you the heave-ho, thanks to Bullins you still have the wherewithal to form another company, perhaps, start all over."

Merriwether stood. "If only I could start all over—start everything over. New wife, new children." He seemed distracted, looking at the window. "There's not enough time, of course, to father another heir, that . . . no, that's not a possibility, I suppose."

"If you have your health."

"I don't," he said in cold simplicity. Merriwether looked to the window again. "Well, not for much longer."

More interesting to O'Hanrahan than the mystery of Merriwether's schemings for oil profits was why Merriwether was here at all, telling him all this. But now Merriwether was to address this:

"I wanted to meet you, Mr. O'Hanrahan," he said softly, approaching the bedside, leaving the cigar behind. "I followed your adventures secondhand all summer. I knew in addition to being a scholar and living a manly life of mild excitement, shall we say, travel and some degree of intrigue, I knew that you were a gourmand, a man of rich tastes, refined opinions, a man very much of this world. A man, if I may be so presumptuous, like myself. Though you have had a much different calling."

O'Hanrahan examined his troubled soul . . . was he like this civilized, rational, charming villain? Had he not been as ruthless with his own family? Had he not preordained his son Rudolph a life like his own and withheld his love when things didn't go according to plan? O'Hanrahan thought back upon his office-politics schemes for getting to be department head, his lies and misrepresentations to get what he wanted out of Mordechai Hersch, out of Lucy. Why even now he would rather take the secret of the Matthias scroll to his grave than give it to someone else! If O'Hanrahan had been born with millions at his disposal might this not be the man he would have become, with a gospel of economics instead of an interest in gospels of theology. Of course I'm different, he insisted to himself.

"And so I have come to ask you," Merriwether said seriously, bending over slightly, "an important question."

O'Hanrahan unsteadily met Merriwether's steely gaze.

"My grandfather's religious hypocrisy, and my own father's dilettantish, bloodless Christianity never took with me. I have no interest, Mr. O'Hanrahan, in art, in music, in religious experience. It was my first premise, sir: that there was no God. All things followed from that for me, and as you see, I've done well for myself and well for my country. I find myself at this juncture, with this illness . . ." He slowed temporarily but resumed: ". . . I find myself alone, which is how I always was and how it will end. I do not mind the loneliness, do not mistake me, but that too followed from my first premise, that there was no God. Many things I've done to get where I am . . ." No, this was more of a confession than Merriwether had intended, so he changed directions. "Let us say, if I could bring myself to find some merit in the argument that there was a God, or failing this, that perhaps there was, as you quaintly think, merely good and evil . . . well, I might well have lived a different life."

O'Hanrahan was surprised when Merriwether sat on the edge of his bed.

"You're sick like I'm sick. I had to meet you to ask you this: is there a God after all, Mr. O'Hanrahan?" As if embarrassed by the question, he rushed on: "You've given your life to this subject. You've prayed at Him, you've found Him in gospels and ancient texts, you've seen God in all His supposed variations beseeched and invoked around the world by millions of men. Now in all that time, can you honestly tell me . . ."

Merriwether was all cold granite but his eyes, his eyes flashed the briefest vulnerability. "Do you think there's . . . there might be a God?"

O'Hanrahan averted his stare.

(Are you going to deny Us again, Patrick?)

O'Hanrahan reflected. He says we're the same, but we're not the same. If only it comes down to the answer to this question that distinguishes us! "Yes," he said, meeting his visitor's glance, "I believe there is a God."

Merriwether stood up, his reverie broken. "Eh, what other answer could I have expected from you . . ."

Merriwether returned to the chair and reclaimed his cigar, reached for his light overcoat, replaced the nail file in his jacket pocket, picked up his *Wall Street Journal,* saying, "I don't know why I thought . . . why I thought I'd hear something different. You're just another believer, entranced by the medicine man before the fire, scared by the ghost stories, worried about the bogeyman."

O'Hanrahan frowned. The bogeyman was not half so terrifying as rich men and their secret societies and their secret plans with other rich men, men with too much love of money and too much free time, the source of the better part of mischief in this world! But why had Merriwether asked about God if he hadn't wanted a positive answer?

(He is running from the answer. He has spent a life running from the voices.)

Merriwether stood in the doorway. "I wish you luck in your recovery, sir, and I hope you have the leisure to enjoy the cigars and bourbon one day." He almost faltered, adding, "If you would drink to my health."

O'Hanrahan gravely nodded.

Then Merriwether paused in the doorway, momentarily speechless.

"I suppose it makes no difference really," said Merriwether, as if he really wished to stay but was being pulled away. "Whether my first premise was wrong, whether God is looking down, as we speak. How could I alter what's been done? How can I change this late in the game? Even if you could have proven God to me, I'm not sure I want to have anything to do with Him." He looked for a last time out the window into the black of night. "Such an inefficient Deity, really. Wasteful, irrational, incompetent, to judge by His world."

(Just wait until the next one, Charles.)

"Oh well," sighed Merriwether. "Forgive this long imposition, Mr. O'Hanrahan. I see we are not like each other after all."

And as he left, O'Hanrahan closed his eyes. No, not after all: I am not Charles Merriwether. Didn't miss it by much, perhaps, but those old masks of the shaman do obtain: good and evil. Maybe that is what it is to be in the Elect of God, to be able to discern a moral core in this chaos of the world, to have such things matter to one. But even to have evolved that far, to know of good and evil and know that a choice exists, how impoverished and irrelevant is our performance, how paltry our effort, what a dead weight we are, how even the good among us are worthless against the squalor of the whole.

(No, not worthless.)

O'Hanrahan turned on his side hoping to sink from this sadness into a rescuing sleep. *If I only had more time to show there was good in me, to retrieve it from the soul I've submerged and diluted with the world's nonsense.*

(There is time. But will you know what to do?)

AUGUST 30TH

Lucy awoke about 10:30 A.M. due to some vacuuming in the house. A wretched night of sleep; even her exhaustion counted for nothing as stress and concern for Dr. O'Hanrahan marred her rest. She hurriedly got dressed, peeked outside of her guest room, and made her way to the stairs. She rounded the curved, antebellum stairway to the foyer only to see Farley, who must have been waiting for her.

Lucy: "Can you get me a car to the hospital?"

"I'll take you myself—"

"I'd prefer a taxi, please."

But Farley drove the station wagon around to the front and Lucy hopped in, determined not to speak a word.

"My mother was just tryin' to heal him—"

"I don't have anything to say to you!" she spat out.

They concluded the trip in silence.

Farley Sr. was in the lobby signing autographs and being venerated by elderly people who had just emptied their life savings into his medical center or made a contribution to his ministries. Lucy slipped out of sight, walked out of the hospital to make a small pilgrimage to the shopping center across the six-lane boulevard not as yet named after Martin Luther King. There was a drive-thru bank and an automatic teller machine. She hadn't used her bank card in three months but if God was on her side she would be able to access her funds in her home account.

It worked. She checked her balance: $625.

Enough, at least, she thought darkly, for the fee at an adoption agency, if it comes to that. She withdrew $200, the limit. Suddenly she wondered, *Do you even pay at an adoption agency?*

This shopping center was circa 1959, long horizontal storefronts and outdated slanted, zippy lettering on the signs, big green-glass plate windows. Many stores seemed to be closed for good. Lucy spotted a pay-phone booth. There were numerous ordeals by phone awaiting her. She ought to call Judy and see how she'd managed roommateless for two more months than she'd planned.

Lucy stepped into the booth. All over the glass at eye level were decals for some Satanic-sounding heavy metal rock band, which Lucy smiled to discover in the heart of Bullins's mission fields, and a 24-hour help line for depressed people. There was also a yellow decal for a women's center:

RAPED? PREGNANT AND ALONE? BATTERED?
NEED HELP? NEED COUNSELING? NEED MONEY?

And below that was the number in a suburb of Baton Rouge, twelve miles away.

Lucy lifted the receiver, dialing the number with false calm.

"Hello," she said tentatively.

The woman on the switchboard was Ruby, who sounded like what one would expect from the name, a sensible black woman in whom all things might be confided. The center was a 24-hour women's hotline, a shelter, an abortion clinic—that is, until the legislators of Louisiana got their way any day now! Ruby insisted on a first-name basis.

"I think I'm pregnant," said Lucy.

"You don't know, honey?"

"Well . . . okay Ruby, it sounds stupid when I say it but I'm afraid to do the test. I'm not married, I don't believe in abortion, so that means adoption and I'm not exactly thrilled about—"

"Hold it, hold it, child," Ruby laughed. "You go test yourself with the kit and you call me right back, and then we're gonna talk."

Lucy was widely relieved and soothed by this near-meaningless exchange. "And I can call back?"

"You sho' can, baby. I'll be here."

Lucy gently replaced the receiver. She took a pen from her carpetbag and jotted down the Feliciana Parish Women's Center's number.

How much, she thought, I have needed to hear a comforting voice. She decided to call Judy, who ought to be in at noon . . . Of all things, Lucy had a bad hankering to talk over *everything* with Judy. They'd never had much success talking over events and crises in Lucy's life— Judy went into psychiatrist-mode with Lucy, threw around terms she used in her studies, took every opportunity to berate, belittle, or condescend to Lucy, the irrational basket case, before Judy's omnipotence. But then they had also never had a *real* crisis to deal with, like Lucy being pregnant. Maybe.

"Hello, Judy?"

Judy was excited to hear from Lucy, accepting the collect call. You're where?

"Louisiana, a place called Philadelphia."

Judy began to talk and spew gossip mingled with news of people who had left messages on their answering machine for Lucy. Lucy was a little depressed by the slim recital of friends: Gabriel, over and over, screaming how urgent it was, her parents, her mom in a snit, her father in a snit, Cecilia her big sister calling for her parents who were in a snit, Gabriel again, Luke to say hi, Margery who wanted her notes from the summer-session seminars—Judy told Marge Lucy was away so you don't have to call her back—and Dr. Shaughnesy.

"That's it?"

Wait a minute, said Judy. Someone was over at the apartment and Judy was talking to her. No, it was a him.

"Is that Vito?"

Yes it was.

"I have something to talk to you about real important, Judy."

So do I, she said, laughing. We may not even be roommates when you get back!

"What?"

Vito and she had decided they ought to move in together, things were going so well.

"It's a little soon, isn't it?" Lucy asked, wishing she hadn't called. In an avalanche of pent-up emotion, she could discern the greater waste of years with this woman, propping up a one-way friendship, the false declarations of solidarity. Lucy said at last, "Don't you wanna give this time, use our apartment as home base while you explore the future of the relationship?"

Judy wanted very much to use the apartment as home base.

"Well, Judy, there's hardly room for three of us there—"

Judy explained.

"I see."

Judy did, after all, hold the lease in her name, and the phone, and the utilities. Lucy had for years felt relieved that nothing pragmatic was expected of her. But when it came to one of them moving out it also made Lucy the logical choice. Oh, said Judy, but this is nothing definite yet . . . Vito was tickling her or molesting her and she was giggling now. Stop it, stop it!

"Okay. We'll talk when I get back."

Judy didn't even ask when that might be.

Lucy hung up the phone.

This new information mixed with the Louisiana humidity conspired to make her feel sickly. She almost called Ruby back—or maybe she ought to call the Depression Hotline . . . All she had really wanted, she now realized, was a reassuring sound of a friendly voice. Maybe one of her brothers or sisters would be home. In fact, the longer she let the call to home go untended the worse it would be. Maybe the voice of her mommy, if Lucy could just hit her on a good morning . . .

"Operator, a collect call from Lucy Dantan, please."

A pause.

"Mom? Yes, it's me, I'm . . ."

Lucy twirled her hair, a nervous gesture from childhood revived with each phone call home.

"I don't know my calling-card number. I know it's . . . no, could you listen to me? Mom . . ."

A discussion of the expense of a collect call.

"I don't care if it is cheaper, I can't read the number on this pay phone so you can't call me back . . . I'll pay you for the damn collect call when I'm home . . ."

Her mother began a disquisition on girls who say "damn" to their mothers. And speaking of home, young lady—

"I'll be there very soon. Can we not argue? I'll be up there in a week or so. Is Cecilia there, I'd really like to . . ."

Her father, you should hear her father. Speaking of Cecilia, Cecilia got her credit-card bill and someone has been running up expenses all over Africa, for God's sakes. That's why Cecilia canceled the card.

"That was me, I went to Africa."

Why had she lied? Jerusalem's one thing, but Africa? It's lucky she wasn't killed by all the crazy niggers with guns—and if she gets some horrible African disease, don't expect them, nosiree, to foot the bills. For did she have health insurance? Noooo, ma'am, she certainly did not, spending her life in school, writing a thesis when other girls her age were raising families! Like her sisters. How God had cursed her to give her a daughter like this—

Lucy hung up.

I really am alone in this world, she thought lucidly. I really am all alone.

She walked back toward the hospital across the wide, hot parking lot, the countless specks of broken glass catching the sun, making the pavement appear embedded with diamonds. And she thought: is this pathetic collection of bickering, small-minded people and their grievances *my life*? Is that how it was before I left? I should have given Gabriel a call, she figured. At least he's sympathetic to people with problems, generating so many of them for himself. It began to bother her—Judy said Gabriel said it was urgent to call him. Might this be scroll-related?

Once in the staggering air-conditioning of the hospital, she made her way to a bank of pay phones and gave Gabriel a collect call. Noon, and he was still asleep.

"Gabe? It's me, Lucy."

As he groggily came to consciousness, Lucy related how Judy planned to throw her out.

"Well," said Gabriel mildly defending her, "you haven't been available to pay rent or anything for three months." Yep, that was also typical Gabriel, always the reasoned spokesman for the other side, Judy's side. Lucy wondered when there'd come a day when someone was *her* champion, unthinkingly, automatically. Gabriel went on: "Hey, but can you believe it about her and Vito? Lucky girl. Vito's sorta dumb but what a hunk. You know, I'm real proud of her. She's come out of her shell and been able to empower herself, you know?"

"She can go to hell," said Lucy. "I don't want to come home to find my furniture on the street." Lucy pictured this, doubly depressed by the shoddiness of her used, thirdhand, St. Vincent de Paul thrift-shop collection of furniture. "Oh Gabe, I gotta go actually, but what was so urgent—the thing you needed to tell me?"

"It's going to take a while to get into the topic. I've really lost a lot of sleep over it. Are you ready?"

"What is it?"

"I've decided to get a master's in art history."

$ $ $

The jowly, unsettlingly ignorant face of Oral Roberts disappeared and an ad began, pushing some forty-song record offer of some ancient man warbling the old Protestant standards. If you order now you got another album of contemporary Christian music. A choir of fifteen men and women, black and white, singing a bland, soothing wash of tuneless Jesus-music appeared. The camera panned their faces, wide-eyed, full of holiness, empty of everything else, singing the selection "His Love Is There for Me," the elevator music of Christianity.

"Where once ruled Bach and Mozart and Beethoven," sighed O'Hanrahan, "is now this. That's what saddens me more than anything about American Christianity. The lack of learning in the ministers, the clichéd sermons and backward politics, the shoddiness of the churches, the vapid emptiness of the music . . . With the wealth of this nation in which nine out of ten citizens claim to be religious, we could have a Sistine Chapel in every city, a Brahms *Requiem* composed each decade. But for our country's Christians, art and architecture and scholarship and music are the enemy camp."

O'Hanrahan looked at Lucy, sitting in a vinyl chair across the room.

"Hell, maybe Bullins is right, this easy-listening anesthesia is Christianity's future. Maybe people don't want to be elevated or have anything expected of them, they just want thoughts-for-the-day any idiot can appreciate. These new megachurches with 20,000-people congregations—they have day-care centers and medical programs and discount stores for the faithful but where . . . where is the reflected glory of Zion? Where is beauty and mystery, the incalculable, the incomprehensible? It is enough to make me run screaming for the Ethiopic Rite!"

Oral on TV was hectoring his viewing public—why hadn't they sent that check yet? They'd have to answer to God for it!

"Oral's on the way out, I hear," said O'Hanrahan.

Oral Roberts, whose healing ministry of the 1950s got him in hot water—the Detroit woman who left his crusade convinced by Roberts she was healed of diabetes, who died three days later after throwing away those insulin shots. Recently, Roberts hit the airwaves, envisioning an 80-foot Christ who talked to him. His masterpiece was his prophecy that God would take him up if he didn't get 4.5 million bucks. A mystery donor coughed it up in the end, he claimed, but not before his antics lost him half of his viewers. As Richard Roberts, his son, ascended the stairs with the cameras to Oral's death-chamber to tell his father the good news, lightning hit the tower, zapping this spectacle into oblivion.

(We couldn't resist.)

Lucy at one time dismissed all this silliness as Bible-belt nonsense, but Oral's 80-foot Jesus she now filed as another of Christianity's never-ending surprises—Agnes's sheared breasts, visionary stylites, milk droplets from an ikon, Haile Selassie and his obedient Christian menageries, and Oral's Tower of Power. Only difference, she commented, is that the other lunacies reflect the beloved, treasured folklore of those countries.

"But, it's the same in the United States," insisted O'Hanrahan. "Charlatans like Oral Roberts and Jim Bakker reflect America's trademark cultural obsessions as well: money lust and show biz." O'Hanrahan thought aloud: "Reverend Ike who said 'I can love the Lord a lot better when I've got money in my pocket.' Kenneth and Gloria Copeland and their 'health and wealth, you name it you claim it gospel.' Robert Tilton, up to his eyeballs in tax-free money, $80 million some estimate—his private villa alone worth $5 million."

The professor raised his head from the yellow legal pads to look squarely at the TV and the source of the bland wash of music. Richard Roberts was now pushing some cassette tapes for a $120 contribution: *"And if you plant your love-seed today,"* Roberts the Younger was saying, *"we'll rush to you this five-set cassette tape package of the New Testament dramatized. Just like being there!"*

O'Hanrahan looked out of the corner of his eye at Lucy. "Get out your checkbook," he said as Lucy punched the remote.

Someone on the next Bible station was hawking a checkbook folder with the TBN, Trinity Broadcasting Network, logo on it. *"When you write those checks,"* said a lively young man, *"you'll look down and have a little reminder of the TBN family when you send that love-gift . . ."*

"Love-seed, love-gift," groused O'Hanrahan, grappling for the remote control.

"Wait," said Lucy, not wishing him to zap the TV.

It was the new and improved Praise The Lord Club, with Jan and Paul Crouch. Lucy thought for a moment that Tammy Faye Bakker had found her way back onto TV but it was Jan Crouch, a new and improved Tammy Faye, a good bit older, with even higher, whiter hair and the same charcoal-smudge eye makeup. Paul and Jan descended a pair of intertwining staircases, each descending a stairway to meet and kiss happily at the bottom. They settled into the talk-show set, a cozy, frilly, velveteen and velour collection like the worst thing in a furniture showroom.

Lucy: "I saw these guys last night with the bodybuilder guy."

"I woke up at five A.M. and they were showing that. Almost called you, too."

John Jacobs, who breaks cement blocks for God on TBN, does power lifts. Everybody prays and cheers him on and then God makes for a miracle and he breaks a record number of bricks. Not on the first try always, but eventually.

"I almost called you at the Bullinses'," O'Hanrahan confessed. "To make sure *I* saw it. The most fevered *delirio*, however, can't touch American TV."

"You sure you're feeling all right, sir? If I'm tiring you I could leave—"

"Nahhh, that got me so doped up I don't know how I feel."

"Making headway?" Lucy asked, referring to the legal pads filling up with Greek.

"Yeah," he said glumly. "And you've got to keep smuggling this out to a safe place."

"Why don't you give me the key to the code, sir—"

"Forget it. This baby's my last hurrah and I'm not dying just so you can make your career on it."

Lucy was offended, but chalked it up to his usual bluster. Maybe he had to talk that way to convince himself he wasn't all that sick.

Jan Crouch on TV was in one of her periodic near-hysterical retellings of her daddy's deathbed scene: *". . . and I turned to him and held his leetle head in my hands, my leetle poppy in his leetle pajamas, and I said oooooh my leetle poppy, I love you so very very much and we will be united in heaven, poppy, my leeeeeetle tiny poppy . . ."*

"Jesus," muttered O'Hanrahan, flicking the channel.

It was the ACTS Network, the Association of Christian Television Stations. And they were showing a movie. You can always tell one of these Protestant born-again movies, thought Lucy, because of the woodenness of the villains, the appearance of the one strong holier-than-everyone young teenager who won't have a sip of beer because he is saved. There was a scene where the young Christian man was having to persuade his girlfriend not to have a can of Budweiser with her cool friends. The hairstyles, Lucy figured, suggested 1975 or so. *Everyone else is doing it*, the girlfriend inveighed.

O'Hanrahan: "Would you bring me the brown paper bag nearby my satchel there . . . there, in the chair."

Lucy found a crumpled bag and looked inside it. There was Merriwether's gift of Old Confederate. "I think I ought to pour it down the drain, sir."

"Just a little medicinal sip, I'm not going to turn up the whole bottle."

No, she said, having her brief revenge on his crass accusation of her ruthless ambitions the moment before.

The Christian TV movie had progressed and the ex-girlfriend of the Christian boy was now in extremis, ready to do anything to get someone to buy her some liquor at a convenience store. *You'll do anything?* the old man asks greasily, leering and evil. *Yes*, she breathes, all shame and misery.

"See, sir?" said Lucy. "That's where you'll end up."

"Getting sex from teenage girls in return for bottles of alcohol? Sounds great. Now give me the bottle."

Lucy returned it to the bag, not quite nervy enough to pour it down a drain. O'Hanrahan saw the bottle was safe and so he didn't make an issue of it, for fear she might do something rash. Lucy stared at him with concern.

"I'm *fine*," he said. "I've felt exactly this lousy for the last three months. Give me my Percodan and a drink and I'm good as new. They're keeping me here for nothing. No, worse than that, Luce, it's part of their plot. They're going to keep me drugged and on the verge of death so I can't escape and they'll get the scroll translated."

That was almost believable, thought Lucy. But he looked horrible, deathly ill, his face transformed in color and tiredness.

A nurse came in with an orderly and so Lucy left him, hypnotized with the Contemporary Christian rock videos, and went in search of the white-haired doctor she had talked to briefly the other night. Lucy found her at the floor's reception desk looking down a clipboard and scowling, turning to walk away—

"Dr. Stewart?" Lucy asked, hoping to arrest her escape. "I wanted to ask you about Patrick O'Hanrahan."

She professionally smiled, stopping to talk. "His fever is still with him, his blood has every chemical imbalance known to man, his blood pressure is through the roof, his cholesterol level is off the scale, and last night after the paramedics brought him in, he was in such pain in his hands and feet, which even his high blood pressure can't supply with blood, that we had to give him morphine."

"Oh," said Lucy. "Is it . . . very bad?"

She said firmly in a lower voice, "It is after all hepatitis A."

Lucy nodded nervously. "That's the good one, isn't it?"

The doctor set down her clipboard, with a faint smile. "Neither A nor B is exactly good, but yes, A is more easily curable with rest and antibiotics. But getting well depends on having a liver that can pull you through, dear. And I . . . I am led to believe his liver is pretty much gone."

Lucy blanched and wished she'd poured the liquor down the drain. "I have another question," she added slowly. "A friend of mine has missed her period. I mean . . ." Lucy suddenly had cold feet. The doctor might be born-again and maybe premarital sex was verboten down here in Bullinsland. ". . . but she's missed this period and I just wondered. She's traveled all across Europe and Africa and had strange food and different climates and lots of stress . . ."

The doctor nodded. "It's certainly possible she might skip a period. Is your friend with you? She can buy a home-pregnancy test in the pharmacy, right next to the gift shop."

"Yes, I'll suggest that," said Lucy smiling falsely. "To my friend."

Lucy turned to the elevator banks.

Well, are we gonna get this over with or what?

In the hospital pharmacy she picked up some toothpaste, a magazine, neutral things for the home-pregnancy kit to hide behind. She read the instructions on the box . . .

But Lucy couldn't do it.

She thrust the kit into her carpetbag. I'll do it back at the Bullinses', she told herself. And as she walked out of the pharmacy:

"That you, Miss Dantan?"

Lucy turned, not believing her eyes at first. It was Rabbi Hersch!

He sauntered down the hall, his familiar gait, his venerable tweed coat with the leather patches, necessary in the hospital's arctic air-conditioning. Lucy ran to him and gave him a hug.

"Hello," he said, shying away quickly, awkward about the affection.

"Rabbi, you're alive! I'm so glad to see you!" Lucy talked incomprehensibly. "I'm sorry I had such suspicions; you see, when I found out that you had been the Mad Monk I thought that—"

He raised his hand. "No, enough! It is I who had suspicions and didn't trust you either. We're a fine trio. But cautious, and cautious is good. We are where we are because we are cautious. Paddy is getting better?"

Lucy shook her head glumly, and repeated the doctor's prognosis.

"Ehh," said the rabbi, shaking his head. "This I knew should happen. And I told him as much. He's finally done it."

Lucy turned to walk Rabbi Hersch to O'Hanrahan's room. The rabbi turned and looked over his shoulder, hesitating a minute as if expecting someone.

"Someone following you, sir?"

"Yes, actually. This fat moron who thinks he's playing spy. He stands out a mile . . . Too stupid to be a real secret agent. Feh! Let's go to Paddy's room."

In the elevator to the ninth floor, Lucy began a synopsis of the odds and ends she knew about Merriwether and Bullins and O'Hanrahan's tales of oil leases in the Gulf, about Colonel Westin and Operation Flight of the Griffin. They arrived at O'Hanrahan's room.

Rabbi Hersch: "What's wrong, little girl?"

"This is his room and he's not here."

"You don't got the wrong room?"

"Excuse me," said Lucy, flagging down a nurse. "I was here not twenty minutes ago and a Patrick O'Hanrahan was in this room."

"Reverend Bullins hisself has taken an interest," the hefty nurse said with the ubiquitous muddy accent, which Lucy realized was nearly the same for black and white people. "We wanna be very careful, now don't we? We've moved him down to Intensive Care."

"That necessary?" asked the rabbi.

"Fever of 104," she said. "Delirium, the shakes, irregular heartbeat. They're gonna hook him up to a monitor."

The rabbi and Lucy looked at one another, allied in a common sadness.

$ $ $

Lunchtime, late in the afternoon.

Lucy took a brown plastic tray and scooted it along the metal grill before the steam tables. Large black women in crisp white uniforms and hairnets stirred steaming piles of black-eyed peas, tubs of mashed sweet potatoes, and a tray of fried breaded okra under a heatlight. Lucy bravely pointed at the Southern vegetables, ready to give them a try. After paying, she turned her tray toward the sunny rows of tables and saw, as expected, Rabbi Hersch reading a newspaper. They had taken turns seeing O'Hanrahan in Intensive Care since only one visitor at a time was allowed in. O'Hanrahan, so perky that morning, had faded seriously into fever and delirium. He came in and out of focus, not sure if Rabbi Hersch was a vision or a reality. Lucy went into the room second, and agreed to meet the rabbi downstairs for a late but long-awaited lunch.

"No improvement," she said, as the rabbi read through his paragraph, then folded up his newspaper. "He was awake again but I didn't like what I saw. Delirious, high fever, ice packs, and monitors all hooked up . . ."

"So he's worse."

"Yes, he's worse," said Lucy simply. She wondered suddenly if he hadn't downed the bottle of bourbon and sent himself into this tailspin. She cursed her indecision about pouring the bourbon in the sink.

Rabbi Hersch looked around him, and leaned toward her. "Keep your voice down. You see that shlemazl three tables away? That's the clown who was on my flight from Jerusalem. Two rows behind me on the plane."

Lucy scanned the culprit briefly: a fat man in a white suit, yellow shirt, and pale blue tie that matched his pocket handkerchief; a panama hat sat atop a pink baby's face with a dark blond, groomed King Tut goatee.

Lucy wanted to ask what would happen should O'Hanrahan . . . die. Would Rabbi Hersch volunteer to take over, committing himself to Bullins and the enemy camp? He probably would, long enough to grab the *Gospel of Matthias* and make a run for it back to Israel. But wouldn't the Masons or Merriwether just come looking for it again? In any event, Lucy would be an unnecessary appendage, and it would be back to the old thesis . . . A sick feeling came over her thinking of it, all the little four-by-six notecards with little factoids on them, waiting to be compiled into a several-hundred-page thesis. Oh, and what would it all matter really, if poor Patrick O'Hanrahan died and left her alone in this deeply indifferent world she'd built for herself. If he would come out of his fevered sleep, Lucy was confident that he would assure her that he, if no one else, cared passionately about what she, his last disciple, did with her life.

Lucy said slowly, "I should have been stricter with him. I could have stopped him from a lot of his excesses, if I'd put my foot down. Not at first, perhaps . . ."

The rabbi waved this consideration aside. "What could you have done? I, on the other hand, I should have trusted him and been open with him about the last chapter . . ."

A spoon fell to the floor, and the fat man made an unconvincing display of craning closer to pick it up.

"And," continued the rabbi, almost whispering, "maybe if I'd have been more open he wouldn't have felt so paranoid about everything and turned up so many bottles—although that's the way he is. Maybe," he took a deep breath, "maybe I shouldn't have called him in the first place. Maybe I should have left him where he was in Chicago and not tried to be the savior here, raise his hopes."

Lucy risked putting a hand on his hand briefly. "No sir. That was a good thing to do."

He withdrew his hand, embarrassed.

She smiled faintly. "I would never have got to meet him otherwise. Or meet you."

Still to be spoken, Lucy knew, was a better apology for her quick and too-easily-made accusations in the hotel room in Addis Ababa. How seamlessly she was able to ignore what she knew to be the good heart of this man and become filled with righteous indignation for herself and O'Hanrahan, and—she cringed—the glories of the Christian faith. For a moment, and it had only been a moment, she had sided with the Inquisition. It is in those little waverings of basically good people, she understood, that the evil of the world is done.

"And you wouldn't have got to see lovely Philadelphia, Louisiana," he added.

She shared a brief smile with him. Also unspoken were some nagging questions . . . These, however, she could now ask:

"Rabbi sir, there's a question that's been bothering me for days. I understand how you could have got to Athens before us in your Orthodox monk suit—"

"Not that again!"

"But the day that we went to the National Library in Khartoum we learned the Mad Monk had been there. But I called you in Jerusalem two days after that. So you hopped a flight that night?"

He stared at her uncomprehendingly. "I've never been in Khartoum in my life."

"What about Wadi Natrun in Egypt?" she asked. "Our Mad Monk was there too. And Cairo."

"Look, I just put on the damn robe *once*, for Christ's sake. For a little checkup trip to the Patriarch's Library in Athens, and I mostly did it to cut through the paperwork. Paddy gave me the idea. In Rome he told me some monk was after the scroll, so it seemed a good way to cover my tracks."

A greasy, raspy sound came from the direction of the man in the white linen suit, as if air was escaping at intervals from a tire. The large, cherubic-faced man tried to turn away and hide his evident amusement.

"So," checked Lucy, now confused, "you weren't in Wadi Natrun or Khartoum—"

Then the rabbi blasted the fat man impatiently: "*What* the hell do you want?"

"You are refarrrink to me?" he said, disclosing his German accent.

"You've been on my ass since Ben-Gurion. Now, please to tell me: what do you want?"

Lucy noticed the man's face transform from pink to a healthy crimson. Then he suppressed his wheezing, silent laugh that vibrated his frame. "I know who you are ... You are the venerable Mordechai Hersch of Hebrew University, *ja?*" The man picked up his tray with a pudgy, ring-covered hand and moved to Lucy and the rabbi's table. "And you are the assistant of the Dr. O'Hanrahan, yes? I haff been overhearing your discussion, forgive me, forgive me ... I am Matthias Kellner of Trier."

"A one-time owner of the Matthias scroll," deduced the rabbi.

"It was myself," he beamed proudly, putting a hand on his heart, "who was in Wadi Natrun and Khartoum! I had for myself made a robe of an Orthodox monk, yes?" He paused as if he might be congratulated on his cleverness. "Your mentor," he nodded to Lucy, "told me that a monk was in pursuit of the scroll and it occurred to me to undertake this adventure, *ja?* And Herr O'Hanrahan was good enough to recite his entire itinerary for me, never to be suspecting that I had the genius to follow, yes?" He laughed and patted his thighs in short sharp pats. "I am happy to report that I was entirely believable and aroused suspicion nowhere. Alas, I did not find the final missing segment of the evangel in question, or clues to the language in which it was written."

The rabbi was impassive. "May I ask what you're doing here now?"

"I assume," he said, "that you have in your possession the entire gospel now and are engaged in its translation. Hence I have come to offer you a pretty sum, Mr. Hersch. And yes, something for you as well," he added to Lucy.

The rabbi collected his coffee cup and rose to get another cup, saying, "Well, Mr. Kellner, I am sorry to disappoint you but we are not the people you must do business with. We don't have it, and wouldn't sell it to you if we did."

"For a million dollars?"

The rabbi paused, weighed it, tilted his head one way and then another, then pronounced, "We could talk about it. Maybe the Matthias Kellner Wing of the Jerusalem Museum featuring the ancient *Gospel of Matthias* scrolls displayed—"

"No, it vill return to its home in Trier!"

The rabbi absorbed this and went to fetch his coffee. "We'll talk."

Herr Kellner immediately, furtively turned to Lucy. "Steal it for me, young lady, and I vill make you rich! *Rich!*"

Lucy smiled as she allowed herself at last to eat a bite from her plate of vegetables. "So you're the Mad Monk?" she asked, not entirely without condescension.

He tapped her on the arm. "I was very industrious, no?"

Lucy slowed in her chewing. "So you have been crossing our path as far back as Assisi?"

"No," he said, now attacking his slice of pie. "Assisi? Why should I go there?"

Perhaps, thought Lucy, amused and relieved, Father Vico made up the whole Mad Monk story to begin with.

$ $ $

O'Hanrahan felt the cool damp cloth being laid on his forehead. It seemed to him as if he was burning, and he imagined a sizzling sound as this cloth was laid on his forehead. His eyes focused on a long black sleeve and an older hand that was tending him. His consciousness was swimming, about to plunge him back to sleep when he then focused on the bedside table and the clock. Six in the afternoon. Then he refocused on the black-clad figure standing near his bedside.

"Glasses," he uttered drily, hardly a voice left.

The blurred figure in black swayed before him and he thought he made out a black bag in his hand. The figure set the black bag on the bedside table and opened it, removing a bottle of something. O'Hanrahan heard it clink on the table. Then a little bowl was produced from the bag and some liquid was poured into it.

"Who is it?" O'Hanrahan moaned, now curious.

Next he saw the figure reach for the glasses case on the table and slide them out. The man in the monk's outfit put them on O'Hanrahan's face gently.

"Ah, it's you," O'Hanrahan breathed softly.

Father Sergius from Prophet Ieremiou on Mt. Athos looked kindly down upon him.

"This is a dream . . . you have come so far," O'Hanrahan said.

"Ssssh," said Father Sergius. "I heard from my Orthodox brethren in Jerusalem what had happened. Fortunately the Franciscans cannot keep a secret. For you, my friend, I have left Athos again."

O'Hanrahan looked up weakly into Father Sergius's strong blue eyes. He thought deliriously that he might have died and that God was Father Sergius, long white beard, countenance of kindness, Himself putting the cool cloth upon his fevered head. "Left Athos again?" O'Hanrahan wondered aloud.

Father Sergius nodded seriously. "Yes, for you I would leave my beloved home, for you and St. Matthias. And his gospel. I hoped first to procure this gospel in Assisi, but it was not to be."

O'Hanrahan strained to refine his thoughts, barely able to make a fist in his weakness. He must concentrate! "You remembered me speaking of the *Gospel of Matthias?*"

"My friend, from the 300s, from the time of Constantine, thanks to

Eusebius, all of the East has known of Matthias and his heretical gospel." Father Sergius moved to O'Hanrahan's luggage, which sat in one of the uncomfortable orange vinyl armchairs for visitors. Sergius began to rummage through O'Hanrahan's papers and notes, photos and yellow legal pads. "And you yourself told me of the *Gospel of Matthias* and its discovery by the Rabbi Rosen when you were much younger. When we met for the first time."

Yes, thought O'Hanrahan. My first trip to Mt. Athos in 1948. To impress Father Sergius, O'Hanrahan, a lowly Jesuit novice, had mentioned Rabbi Rosen and his finding of the *Gospel of Matthias* in Jerusalem. A conversation over forty years ago.

"You remember everything, *Pater*."

"What I remember," he said, "God has allowed me to remember." Father Sergius discovered the brown cardboard tube and the ancient scroll it contained. He lifted it from O'Hanrahan's suitcase. "These are the End Times, my old friend."

O'Hanrahan watched Father Sergius examine the scroll, reroll the vellum into a cylinder and put it back in its tube. Then he put the scrollcase into his own satchel.

"This world, so near to its end," Father Sergius said calmly, "will use this for wrong, I fear."

"Do you think it is the False Prophecy of the End Times?"

"I am sure that it is," he said. "But the End must not come now, Patrick. Man is not ready. Mankind has so much that it must do. Think how we will have failed God should the world end tomorrow. I do not wish to see God fail . . . No, I will hide it, and if God wishes it known, He will see to it. I am willing to answer for this in Heaven." Father Sergius's face looked at some distant otherworldly realm. "Just as Moses and Ezekiel begged the Lord to stay his wrath, so I too must hope the Lord will postpone His day of judgment. To the East it shall return to disappear from history again."

Father Sergius returned to O'Hanrahan's bedside and his own black bag. O'Hanrahan was not directly able to see the tabletop to his side and he heard more liquid flow into the bowl.

"But this time not for another 2000 years," said the monk. "Maybe what I do is futile! Who knows that the End will not commence before I return to Athos? War is coming in the Middle East, an Antichrist is before us in Babylon . . ."

O'Hanrahan thought deliriously of the apocalyptic frescoes of Dionysiou, the missiles, the masses huddled in underground shelters—

"You must never attempt to get this back," said Sergius somberly. "No one must. Indeed, no one must know that I was here." He returned to his mixing bowl and mumbled some prayers in Russian.

O'Hanrahan felt his heart beat faster. "What are you doing, Father?"

Father Sergius took the damp washcloth on O'Hanrahan's head and began to soak it in the bowl. Holding the bowl in one hand, and the cloth in the other, he sat on the edge of the bed.

"What . . . What is it?"

"Ssssh," said Father Sergius calmly. "Did you really think I would fail in my mission to baptize you anew in the Faith?"

O'Hanrahan felt his eyes become full.

"Did you think, my friend, I was to do without your company in Paradise? Think of all we will talk about, all we will discuss." Father Sergius dabbed O'Hanrahan's brow, pressing the sign of the Cross into his forehead.

Yes, this is just as well, thought O'Hanrahan: at the end reconciled to the East. It is where my absolutist heart has always been—it was my Western mind that caused all the trouble. He was comforted by Sergius's Russian-accented Greek: *Ego men udati baptizo umas, erchetaide o ischuroteros mon* . . . Ah, this is the deathbed I would have selected. Sergius alluded to Ignatius of Antioch contemplating death: *My birth now approaches; let me receive the pure light!* And no, I shall not tell him that the scroll he has taken from me is the 14th-Century tract I stole from the Vatican, returned to me once by Father Vico and once by Clem Underwood.

"You sleep in peace now, my friend." Father Sergius kissed his Greek Cross and then, lightly, supported by a trembling arm, O'Hanrahan's forehead. "We shall not meet again on this earth."

O'Hanrahan closed his eyes for a moment.

Father Sergius gathered his things, returned the holy water to a phial, and with a final Russian blessing, crossed himself. The old men looked into each other's eyes a last time.

Then Father Sergius left.

O'Hanrahan did sleep only to find himself awakened by Gregorian chant. Opening his eyes, he was still in the hospital room. The drugs must be doing their job, he thought, as he had the strength to sit up, then put his legs to the floor, then stand. From the dark private room of Intensive Care he peeked around the doorway to see a long, torch-lit vaulted hall. Where was this? He had seen it before . . . that's right, Karak Castle in Jordan. He was there in 1948 before the U.N. Mandate. He remembered: Morey drove me there. It was built by Baldwin I in 1132, the luckless Crusader who set himself up as King of Jerusalem and built this very castle. O'Hanrahan ran his hand along the hewn stone walls. An old dusty place, many ghosts, many ghosts. I remember now: thousands of Frenchmen and Englishmen and Germans and Spaniards were camped within, awaiting the showdown with Salaadin. O'Hanrahan heard the chant dwindle as the sound of the *muezzin* took over. Yes, this is in Moslem Jordan today, O'Hanrahan realized, and it is the time of prayer. He heard the Arabian carpenters making little boxes outside the castle. He looked out from one break in the ramparts and down below, half a mile down this treacherous, unscalable cliff where the Moslems, in such bright robes and flashing turbans, were constructing hundreds of little boxes. For Salaadin had taken Baldwin's castle and they were preparing to execute the Crusaders; an officer with the face of Saddam Hussein looked back at O'Hanrahan, telling him to mind his own business. O'Hanrahan returned to the long, cool, vaulted hallway and heard the rattling of chains. He turned into a darkened cell . . . Morey? Was that you? Morey wordlessly nodded. He had been branded with the Star of David—burned into his face! Of course, I must apologize and see if I can get him out of this mess, thought O'Hanrahan, turning to run for help. But the faster he wished to run the slower his steps. I must get help and explain to Mordechai that I am not a part of the Crusaders who branded the Jews, massacred the women and children and hauled the men about as slaves, keeping the smart ones alive for doctors and advisers . . . I must explain to him . . . *François, you will see*, said one young soldier, not fifteen. Oh, a lovely boy, out of a medieval painting I saw once. *You will see, François, the Virgin Mary will rescue us. Before we hit the ground a band of angels will fly from the clouds commanded by the Queen of Heaven.* Oh no, I must tell these boys, these children, what is to happen here— they must fight again or bribe their Moslem conquerors . . . *St. George will save me*, said one young soldier, with an American accent. Why it is . . . it looks like . . . *St. George will ride on his fiery steed and prevent us from falling and he shall smite all our enemies and they shall be as dust . . .* Rudy! Is that you? Why did you come on this Crusade, I never wanted you to go to war! Come, we will escape . . . No, no, Salaadin has bid them come forth and the Moslems are attaching the boxes they made to each Christian soldier's head. Ah, the boys are crying now, large boys' tears on their cheeks, calling for their mothers; some are in prayer. *The Queen of Heaven will rescue me . . .* One soldier weeps into a medallion of the Virgin, who in this rendering bears a resemblance to Beatrice, my wife. Ah well, women are no help in these situations, condemned to sit and watch us men fill the earth with murder and persecution. It is a bright hot day and thousands upon thousands of boys will be pushed from this ledge. It's odd, really, they let me get up so close to see all this—clearly, they will not mistake me for a Crusader. I do hope Rudy got away . . . and Morey, I must see to him . . . The Moslems built little boxes to fit around the boys' heads so that their long fall will not break their neck in flight, and so they might never predict when they shall hit the ground half a mile below, but feel it when they do. Look at that spattered wreckage below, and it seems an airplane has crashed and scattered about the foot of the cliff . . . There goes François, praying while he falls—the little box prevents me from hearing him well. Such ingenuity, such effort for these young men's deaths. Ah, and there is Salaadin: *Jump my poor Christians, see where your God is now! See how He doesn't come to your rescue!* But listen to me, God never comes to the rescue—no barbarity can move Him anymore and we are left to ourselves for redemption! What are they doing? Yes, well, of course, they are nailing a box around my head now. Attractive race, the Arabs. These boys are fourteen, if that, smiling broadly with such white teeth. Considerate, these kids—does your box fit, they ask? Is it too tight, dear sir? Ah, listen to the music of that lovely medieval Arabic. Shame I don't have time to persuade them to write some down for me . . . And now they are pushing me to the edge. It will be this step or the next and then I will be falling. I hear the young man next to me, choking sobs, calling upon Mary, calling upon the Angel Michael and his flaming sword, for surely this is not how it is supposed to end, surely our God was to triumph here. Ah, another step. And—ouch— a kick in the backside . . . I am airborne. These boxes are ingenious, after all. I'm going to hit bottom *now.* Nope. A little longer. My clothes wrap around me, the wind buffets this little box; I feel the scrape of rock—it's quite close. It's odd, but how familiar is this fall. Have I lived, perhaps, a whole life of this? Oh, here's the bottom, coming up to meet me, tingling my feet in anticipation, one–two–three . . .

O'Hanrahan came to.

He looked at the bedside clock, saw it was night again, and determined that it was ten hours since he had last come to. The days and nights are burning away in fever, he thought. The last days of my life and I am sleeping through them. He looked at the water glass on the table: tepid, milky water, direct from the Mississippi. There was the limp flower Lucy had brought in a simple dimestore vase. And next to that lay a Bible. *We bring our years to an end as it were as a tale that is told. The days of our years are threescore years and ten,* and I may not even make seventy, thought O'Hanrahan as an addendum.

So be it. We fear and dread the throes of the end, we grumble at God for the pain and awfulness of final hours, and yet it perhaps takes a bit of agony to convince us that we would do well to move along to the next world, whether that world be unfeeling sleep or the bourn of angels, this one no longer can please us. In which case there is a dark wisdom in these agonies. They are really but a moment in the whole span, a last exaction before surcease, a small price for having lived at all. And then the thing itself—will there be an instant where my dwindling consciousness shall glimpse the millennia of nonexistence upon which I embark? Will there be a pure emanation of light, as some have glimpsed near death, or will that light slowly turn cold and dim as the darkness rushes in ineffable, supreme. *The womb shall forget him. The worm shall feed sweetly upon him. He shall be no more remembered.*

He thought back to Korea, how the men would revive, the terminal cases, often, to say a final word or utter a mother's name. And perhaps this is what is happening now, this returned consciousness. O'Hanrahan's eyes in his immobile head looked around the room and fluorescent light of the cork ceiling and the vinyl chair in the corner, my own little death-chamber. *Be with us, O Lord, now and unto the hour of our death.* Is this the hour of my death?

(It's looking that way.)

Well, O'Hanrahan thought, how to spend it? A little TV? I thought at this point I would feel defeated and broken. The scroll outlived me, after all. The Great O'Hanrahan goes to an ignominious grave, slightly better than the gutter his father went to. But you gotta hand it to me, Lord: I got one last, irresponsible adventure out of the world, didn't I? One last fling with my true romance, the rubble of the past, the wisdom of the ancients, the aged, bearded companions shielded by cross and Torah and crescent, the supernal mysteries—all 4000 years of them put upon this earth by God for me to dabble in and amuse myself. O Holy Spirit . . .

(You remember Me after all.)

Do You know how much I have loved this life? Have any of Your children had such fun as I? All right, all right, I'm an apostate and blasphemer, I'm aware, but it was to *amuse* You as well as me! I have always thought God was in on my jokes—surely You're as cynical as I am at this point.

(True, One has to have a sense of humor in this job.)

Forgive me, but even at this late date, I could never believe You were perfect. That you were God and greater than I, indubitably. But perfect? You're doing well to keep your head above water lots of times—Auschwitz, Hiroshima, World War I, and all that—and am I mistaken or do You need us lowly humans too? We're the best creation You could muster and, face it, there's a lot of hackwork. I objected to the pious infallible papal God, the God of omnipotence and omniscience . . . You're none of those things. Beatrice and my Rudy dying in a plane crash show there are cracks in this creation of Yours.

But I, Patrick Virgil O'Hanrahan, accepted your terms!

Of course I know my failures. My wife should have known how much I loved her. My son should have gotten bored with the constancy of his father's love. And there I failed. Failed, failed, screwed up, crapped out—no argument from me on this. But for the last twenty years I have lived in a hell of my own making, and perhaps that will check any more of hell off my list. I'm feeling faint now. This must be delirium, because here I am talking to the Holy Spirit and She's right in the room with her beautiful face of light with shining hair of stars . . . if I could only focus and look right at Her, but I feel sleep coming on again . . . My eyes grow heavy. A last thought, then: if I could keep on with this preposterous life I would, and I would find a way to make amends for my selfishness and lack of love to my wife and son. I know You must get tired of bargains but there it is. I would continue with a better heart.

(But We love bargains. We make them all the time.)

August 31st

Lucy was the first one to find the chapel this morning at Bullins Medical Center.

Inside the foyer was a variety of pamphlets, all produced by Bullins, many with his wide face and outstretched hands beaming from the cover. "When Death Comes to Call." Here was one called "Prayer and Miracles," which peddled miracles that happened to good Pentecostal Christians every single day, yes they did!

Lucy parted the chapel doors and saw it was empty. Considering it was a Bullins production, this chapel, nondenominational and modern, was in pretty good taste. Several short rows of pews led to a raised platform and a communion table of some kind, though no paraphernalia was about. A simple cross in blue stained glass behind the table sufficed. Lucy slipped into the last pew and breathed the still air of the little chapel; the hellish racket of life-support machines, ambulance sirens, and the ever-rasping intercom calling doctors and nurses for various codes and emergencies did not penetrate this peaceful room.

She reached in her pocket for her rosary.

Lucy knelt and bowed her head, weary of spirit, exhausted at the thought of a hundred Our Fathers or whatever assignment she had set for herself when she awoke after yet another wretched night of bad sleep.

(You could ditch the Our Fathers, and just talk to Us.)

Lord, she thought, half-praying, I've fallen back to the faith I had as a child, except going through these rituals doesn't register anymore. But I don't know what else to do. I feel very distant. *Our Father Who art in Heaven, hallowed be Thy name. Thy kingdom come . . .* I'm hoping if I do these things by rote enough times, I can, you know, jump-start myself into the faith I used to have. That rascal Dr. O'Hanrahan! He's undermined me, or rather, the unshakable confidence I once had. Not in God, I know You're up there, but in which version of Him . . . Coptic, Moslem, Orthodox, Pentecostal, an academic faith like the Theology Department back in Chicago, an emotional, blinding, all-pervading faith like Patsy the TPL college student, religion as a sickness like poor Mrs. Bullins . . . Look, I don't want to feel this confused.

God, complete with instructions, would come in real handy about now. I guess I don't know what I believe anymore. There you have it.

I'm going to go to the restroom and use the pregnancy kit and if I am knocked up, I am aware it's my own damn fault, and I will take what's coming to me but am I crazy here? I also—forgive the arrogance—think that I was destined for something *else* in this world besides being an unwed mother. I know, I know, what service could I possibly perform that might matter to You . . .

(Innumerable things. We wish religious people didn't think this way.)

. . . but I feel that I am on the threshold of something, just beginning to know myself and what I can do in this world. And here I go and louse this up with a kid. Maybe I'll keep it and stick it out and be disowned by my family and my friends and retire to some dark corner of Chicago sharing a house with some other single mother and work out some baby-sitting schedule to alternate with my classes. Jesus, Blessed Savior, that sounds like hell on earth what I've just said. I don't feel very forgiven, even after this talk.

(Why don't you forgive yourself first?)

With the arrival of two talkative white rural women, Lucy rose up and surrendered to a feeling of emptiness. She walked slowly to the Intensive Care Unit, in no hurry to face the lobby of miserable, anxious relatives.

No one can help me now, she figured calmly. Sister Miriam has triumphed!

(No, My child.)

No really, she has. She said sin would lead to ruin and disgrace, and she was right. All her sourness, all her accusing glares and pointed fingers were justified. She sensed I was a loser and now I've gone and proven it for her. It didn't take a lifetime of sin, either. *One* little lousy slip in twenty-eight years of clean living and *whammo*—

"Excuse me," said a nurse at Lucy's side, as she entered the Intensive Care Unit. "You were with Mr. O'Hanrahan, weren't you?"

Lucy froze.

Oh, please. Please God. She prepared herself for the worst possible bad news.

"I've been looking for you, Lucy—it is Lucy, isn't it?" The nurse was a small woman, petite and perky, who could turn on enthusiasm and bedside optimism with ease. "Mr. O'Hanrahan has been asking for you."

Lucy brightened. "He's out of his delirium?"

"He seems to be. The fever broke in the night and he was awake this morning. We're changing his sheets right now, but we'll be moving him to a regular hospital room within the hour. But give us, say, fifteen minutes, and then come visit with him, all right?"

An ammonia-smelling hallway led to the lounge, where a despairing lot was assembled. A small family huddled awaiting news of Dad's heart attack. An old woman halfway to widowhood reading her Bible and looking up at the TV when someone got a letter on "Wheel of Fortune." A young wife sliding her wedding ring back and forth on her finger nervously, a variation of wringing one's hands, trying to concentrate on a *National Geographic* magazine. Lucy sat in the corner, sinking into the squeaky vinyl overstuffed sofa, insultingly lemon-yellow and cheery.

"Excuse me," said an elderly lady who sat down beside Lucy.

"Yes ma'am?"

"The nurse there said you were with Patrick O'Hanrahan?" The woman was orderly and prim, her gray hair pulled back; she was slender, dressed in a conservative navy blue. Lucy assumed she was sent over by the TPL people. She handed Lucy the fifth of bourbon.

"The nurse said for me to give it to you. Patrick is a trial, isn't he? Always has been. Would you like some orange juice?"

The woman had two Styrofoam cups and she reached into a large bag and produced a small carton, from which she poured Lucy some. "You," she noted, "must be the graduate student paired with Patrick. My, you must have had some adventures. I thought Gabriel would be a boy, of course—"

"Oh," corrected Lucy. "Gabriel was a boy. Is a boy. I'm Lucy Dantan, Gabriel's replacement. And you're . . ."

"Catherine O'Hanrahan," she said, smiling.

Patrick's sister. The Witch of Wisconsin! "From Wisconsin," Lucy mumbled.

"Yes, I'm a retired postal worker there, in Madison. He may have told you."

This woman was no harridan, Lucy surmised in an instant, no grave-robbing, testament-seeking relative. Another deranged characterization from Dr. O'Hanrahan. They walked to his new room, a happier place than before, curtains pulled back and sun streaming in.

O'Hanrahan was awake. He groggily looked at his sister entering the room: "Good heavens, they must think I'm on my deathbed! Calling in you, Cathy!"

His sister became more reserved. "That you almost were, but no such luck." Lucy noticed her Irish lilt was more pronounced around her brother, the both of them returned to the accents of childhood.

"Lucy," noted Miss O'Hanrahan, "has been entrusted with your private stock."

Lucy saluted her mentor by holding up the bottle.

"I expect not a drop to be missing from the precious grail, Miss Dantan. When they spring me from this clip joint, I'll relieve you of it."

Miss O'Hanrahan looked at Lucy for sympathy. "He was never like this when he was young, you know. Quiet and shy and never spoke a word—"

"Good God, woman, you'll ruin my reputation! That what you came down here for?"

They argued good-naturedly over the letter and whether Patrick got it. Patrick denied he got it and accused Lucy of losing it—

"I did not! I gave it to you on that train—"

"Silence!" demanded O'Hanrahan. "I will not be intrigued against."

Catherine enjoyed his distress: "I hope, since you've bankrupted yourself, what it was that you were chasing was worth it."

O'Hanrahan, looking redder in the face, shifted his pillows behind himself. "Let me sit up and take a look at you. Hate to admit it, but you look good, Cathy—I look like shit, don't bother informing me."

"I don't use that language, but 'tis how you look all right."

"Yes, if you must know, we found what we were looking for." O'Hanrahan talked excitedly as a teenager might: "Get a load of this, Cath. A First-Century gospel, earliest in existence, by an actual disciple."

Lucy now noticed the small silver cross on the navy blue blouse, no ring on the unmarried Miss O'Hanrahan's smooth hands. There goes me had I been born in that generation, Lucy reckoned: lucky for me I'm knocked up and a soon-to-be total Catholic outcast. Lucy noticed that Patrick rested his hand on his sister Catherine's hand, though they continued to battle and willfully misinterpet each other. I suppose in thirty, forty years this will be one of my family in the hospital bed, maybe even me, Lucy thought. Will aged versions of Nicholas, Cecilia, Kevin, and Mary come filing past, send get-well cards, do their duty? Inconceivable, that we should ever be so convenient and close. Maybe it takes an almost-death to unite Irish-American families. How little solidarity we Dantans have . . .

Catherine O'Hanrahan had to move her car from the thirty-minute zone and her brother cheered her departure provocatively. O'Hanrahan barked out some errands, forays for toiletries and razors and cough drops. "And pick up a fifth of Maker's Mark, while you're at it."

"So you can brush your teeth with it?" she asked without a smile.

"So I can soak my dentures in it."

Lucy and Dr. O'Hanrahan sat there silent a moment as she left the room. Catherine wasn't one to laugh out loud or openly appreciate her brother, but the routine they participated in, his outrages, her stoicism and concealed smiles, this was their sibling currency, this was their love.

Lucy offered, "Not my idea of the Witch of Wisconsin."

"Ehhhh, she's all right," said O'Hanrahan, joining his hands on his belly, sighing. "Perhaps, just maybe, I was a trifle unjust."

Another silence.

"You're alive," said Lucy. "It didn't look so good last night. Fever of 105. You were delirious."

"I'll say. I had these crazy dreams and conversations with God . . . Luce, look in my satchel for that scrollcase I've been carrying around."

Lucy rummaged through the dirty laundry and crumpled notepads. "You mean that cardboard-tube thing?"

"Yeah. You remember, that 14th-Century fake Ethiopian gospel I stole out of the Vatican Library."

"It's not here."

O'Hanrahan laughed. "Then I didn't dream that. It's in the hands of Father Sergius of Mt. Athos."

Lucy thought she had seen him in the halls. "Tall guy, ancient. Beard down to here?"

"That's the guy. Our Mad Monk, in part."

"Our other Mad Monk is a Mr. Kellner—"

"Matthias Kellner. Is he here too?"

"Was here. This morning I saw the monk fellow and Mr. Kellner chasing each other across the parking lot. I asked the rabbi, but he didn't have an explanation."

"I will explain all to you in time." O'Hanrahan felt joy well within him. His old friend Morey was here, his sister, Lucy. Oh, let them all make peace and reconcile.

"The rabbi's sleeping off jet lag, sir," Lucy informed him. "Said he'd make it over here by lunchtime. He prayed a Hebrew prayer over you last night, so expect him to claim that Yahweh is the One True God."

"Yahweh *is*, I'm prepared to admit it." O'Hanrahan flashed back to the vision of a dank, enshadowed cell of Karak Castle, and Morey branded with the Star of David, looking out silently and accusing— dreadful dream! Dredged up from some dark quarter of shame! No, he would make amends, they would again embrace, and O'Hanrahan vowed to speak of his love for the rabbi.

O'Hanrahan then looked at Lucy.

What had he done to her, dragging this nice American girl all over creation . . . had they really been in England, in a boat off Northern Ireland in a storm, dodging mafiosi in Florence, driving around with that ass Stavros in Greece, scurrying from Palestinian hoodlums in the West Bank, then Cairo, then the Sudan across the desert, then a crash landing in Ethiopia—

"It's sort of dull now, huh?" she said telepathically. "Now that we're back in the States."

"Don't know why you say that," he said, pulling a chair round to his bedside so she could sit near him. "A war brewing with Iraq, CIA plots,

the End Times and a Rapture due any minute. This country knows
how to entertain. Called your parents?"

"I'm disowned. This morning we had weeping, and gnashing of
teeth and how I didn't respect them, how my mother has taken to the
bed, my father won't speak to me, which is a state I frankly prefer."
Lucy felt a wave pass through her, almost of nausea, a yearning to
speak the truth about her possible pregnancy, to confess to Dr. O'Hanrahan.

"The gospel is about one-quarter done," O'Hanrahan was saying.
"Now that I'm alive—and who knows when I'll get ill again—I stand
to be the most famous person in classical scholarship, theology. I recant
all earlier remarks about vain old men; I'm going to get a hairpiece
for the cover of *Time*. Ha! Can you see them incontinent with despair
back at Chicago! Shaughnesy the Pretender, our Anti-Chairman! Oh
that God would allow me to see their faces when . . ."

(Patrick.)

Yeah I know, I know. I was just hearing how it sounded, marching
out the brass band one more time. I know what I have to do—what I
want to do. And so do You.

"You were saying, sir?"

He looked at the clock on his bedstand. "But that's not really how
it's going to happen. There'll be vine-leaves of glory, Miss Dantan, but
I will not wear the crown."

Lucy wondered if he was thinking straight.

O'Hanrahan shrugged deprecatingly. "So I get my name in the
paper, what's that worth? So I make it back in the Scholastic Register.
Whoopdiedo, that moron Shaughnesy's in there, what kind of honor
is that? I'm not going to waste my final years—if I got *that* long—on
some dry old book. I'm handing over the reins."

Lucy saw herself suddenly exiled from the project altogether. And
then his meaning became clear as she met his eyes.

"You mean . . ."

"I'm giving it to you, Luce, the *Gospel of Matthias*. I want you to do
the final edit of the gospel and publish the findings as your thesis."

Lucy had trouble finding her voice. "Dr. O'Hanrahan."

He held up his hand. "No, listen to me. That will make your career,
young lady. You will be as famous as Father Beaufoix and Morey and
that crowd, and you deserve to be that famous, because you have a
mind in that head of yours. And if you go back to work on that void
you're currently shilling as a thesis, you'll rot in academia—trust me.
I had a mind and I got caught up in academia and little by little what
was good about me got ground down by drink and petty infighting
and budget squabbles and anxiety over publishing and I was hell to
live with—my wife, my son, if you only knew how . . ."

He slowed, feeling his throat tighten. No, he was not ready to look that so completely in the face yet, not in front of Lucy at least.

"Anyway, Luce, I'll talk to Morey and he can oversee you. And I'll call that anus Shaughnesy and get his approval and you can start your young life out where it ought to be. On top."

"Sir, I . . . I can't."

"Sure you can. I proclaim it; I'm speaking ex cathedra here."

"But you worked so hard—"

"Yeah, but you know what the goddam truth is? I'm no writer. Never was. All my life I wanted a shelf of books across my office, like Morey, something to leave behind, when the truth is: all I am is a good teacher, a talker, on a good day Socrates, on a bad day some con-man who should have run for Congress. And Socrates never wrote anything down either, right?" He saw Lucy might cry or get emotional so he headed it off: "So dedicate the thing to me. Make me . . . you make me a footnote."

But the last request had sounded hollow and sad, and Lucy sniffed back a tear. "We'll talk about it when you're feeling better—"

"I'm better already!"

A nurse in the doorway: "No, you're not. Miss," she added, meaning Lucy, "you're gonna have to let our li'l patient rest now!"

Lucy blankly faltered toward the door. "I'll come back this afternoon. That'll leave you time with your sister."

"Not that!" he cried in mock despair. "Check her bag for arsenic!"

The nurse fluffed his pillows and a very tired O'Hanrahan sank back into them. Lucy glanced at him before leaving. Of course, who doesn't look deathlike in those flimsy hospital gowns in this fluorescent splotchy lighting? Poor man, thought Lucy. And the next moment as she walked down the sterile hallways past other scenes of grief and wretchedness: and if this child is a boy, I'll name him Patrick. One gesture deserves another. One gesture of love, that is—oh, she thought, blinking back a tear and bravely taking a deep breath, not slowing her pace, I hope you don't die, old man.

(Which is just what Patrick was thinking.)

All alone now.

The curtains drawn, no lights on, no nurse, no Lucy, no Catherine.

It is done, O'Hanrahan said with a sad certainty. You've given away your ticket to immortality. Take down the pedestal on the Western Slopes, boys, I'm not coming after all. But that was the right thing, wasn't it? I do the right thing so rarely I'd forgotten it has a certain weight and shape in the heart and though it is not easy or happy-making particularly, there is a sense of connectedness and order. Ehh! Who wanted to write out all those damn footnotes anyway? It's just too bad the fun is over. He closed his eyes, feeling unusually weary.

He snuggled down under the blankets, as he felt his knuckles and feet throb again, but dully. The pain in his side poked at him vaguely. Into *Your* hands, he thought looking at his gnarled, veinous old man's hands, freckled and palsied, I commend my spirit.

(But you know what, Patrick? We are going to let you live. A few more good years, and maybe even longer. After the bypass surgery, when you get out of here, get the diet on track, do the exercises they tell you, take the drugs—and not that Percodan stuff—you will have the time you need to find "Q." Yes, it will mean going to Teheran and you'll have adventures, to put it mildly, and as always, We'll be with you. But Lucy will not. For Lucy another destiny awaits.)

Lucy decided to go discuss O'Hanrahan's generosity with the rabbi and so she went down to look around in the cafeteria and she found herself standing beside the door to the women's room.

There it is.

She lectured herself: have one-tenth of the courage shown by O'Hanrahan who, facing death, has sacrificed what kept him alive for the likes of worthless little you. Let's get this over with.

Lucy went to the Ladies' toilet and looked in the mirror. She heard a flush from one of the stalls. A woman left and Lucy was all by herself. Lucy filled her cupped hands with cold water, splashed and looked at her face. This was not the young woman who had left Chicago in June.

She went into one of the stalls and with a nervous hand locked herself in. Her breathing was shallow and she sat on the toilet and breathed deeply for a bit, calming herself down. She read the instructions, collected with minimal awkwardness the urine sample, put in the stick, and held the kit in her hand. Please, please, God! It occurred to her that maybe there was a sister in the Early Church in the midst of a pregnancy scare waiting for her period who coined "saved by the blood, washed in the blood." Had it been ten minutes?

Here Lucy felt her life measured in heartbeats, which were loud in her head. She pulled out the stick. It was pink. What did that mean?

She read the back of the kit: she was pregnant.

Oh, God.

But that can't be.

We'll do it again. Tears silently falling from her face, she left the bathroom, patching herself together. She marched directly to a water fountain and drank and drank. The cold water gave her a momentary neuralgia, hurting from the roof of her mouth through her whole skull. She slowed down but soon was compulsively drinking again.

The test, twenty minutes later, showed the same thing.

Is there a loophole to this? Some percentage of error?

Lucy looked at herself in the mirror, but this time the look returned was resolved and knowing. Could she follow through on the plan now in her head?

"Yep," she sighed to the mirror. "It has to be."

$ $ $

Lucy looked into her carpetbag and checked for the money she had withdrawn.

"You say Lafayette Road, didn't ya?"

"Yessir," she told the taxi driver, a gray-headed black man, paunchy in an open white shirt that was a size too small.

"That women's clinic, right?"

"That's right."

She was calm, after all. By the end of the day she would be, physically, who she was before this whole summer began. And the facts presented themselves with great limpid clarity: I am not cut out to be a mother, not even to endure the childbirth part for another woman. And while pregnant I drank, I smoked, I took small doses of cholera and typhus vaccines and no doubt this fetus is compromised. But even if I hadn't done those things, more important: I have never wavered from the notion that one day I would give myself to great service, great devotion to some aspect of God. For a while that meant being a star student at St. Eulalia's to win the nuns' approval. Then for a while it meant becoming a nun. Then I decided it meant writing a thesis on a religious subject. Now it means what it should have always meant: a life of service.

She looked down at her fist, clutching the business card of Catholic Relief Charities. On the phone a half-hour ago, they had been very enthusiastic, and if the training and preparation could start in October she could conceivably be back in Africa by Christmas. Whoo boy, what an argument that's going to be: Mom and Dad on the subject of why their little girl didn't come home for Christmas, dropped out of school, turned down that offer from that nice Mr. O'Hanrahan. I'll be in Africa, with any luck, celebrating a truer Christmas, attending in some small hopeful way to the mass of starvation and misery.

(You are meant for great service.)

What did I promise God during this pregnancy scare? How many years of charity work in the Sudan? Well, after what I am about to do, God will have the goods on me. This will be the greatest sin I have ever committed, but that will not derail my life . . . no, this will not change me as much as the life to follow. *That*, not this, is the defining act. And I do see what that aid-worker in Ethiopia meant: those faces haunt you.

(Go to them, then.)

She briefly faltered. I'm not Mother Teresa—

(Lucy Dantan will do. Go for a summer, or a year. We don't ask for lifelong service, Our demands are not that great. But how few people can even manage a summer, a week, a day of charity?)

Yeah, but You know me. I'll get over there and get started at something and then I'll feel like I have to stay until it's finished, and a summer will become a year, which becomes two years, which becomes a life. And I can see myself getting all politicized and speaking at the U.N. and campaigning for money with corporations and meeting with corrupt government officials and all the stuff you do when you're committed.

(Yes. We can see it too.)

And one day maybe I will be working in some refugee camp like that nurse whose name I could not remember, and someone will wonder about me the way I wondered about her: why did you do this with your life? And I will not tell that interrogator any more than that nurse told me, because this is my sacrament. No one but myself and God will understand why I am going back to Africa and why I feel I have to. It is not for anyone else to judge or indulge in speculation. It is no doubt this independence from people's opinion and this dependence on God alone that the saints must have known—oh, Holy Spirit, let me be so sure always! I pray that my resolve will not weaken.

(It might. So many good intentions, so many chances for a happy world have passed away, so many just kingdoms, so many acts of kindness that would have changed life as it's lived today . . . all vapor, as someone practical talked Our children out of their dreams and missions.)

Lucy looked at the poor outskirts of Baton Rouge, dirty and despair-ridden. I'm hurting and I'm grieving, but I am not afraid of the procedure to come. Or of Africa.

(We can't promise you that planes won't go down or you won't get cholera or that death squads won't find you. We do what We can, but there are no guarantees. But We can promise you joy. Lasting and constantly renewing, the only happiness that endures.)

Just so you know I'm not a good person—

(But you are. And that's all that survives of you when you die, My child, the good that you have done. So much bad theology and empty talk about faith over works. Better the dispirited cynic complaining as she dishes free food in the soup kitchen than the pieties of cloistered prelates, theologians, purveyors of empty rituals, thesis-writers, makers of religious regulations. If you've done no good for anyone in your life, then to Hell with you! Simple as that.)

Sinners such as I can do Your work?

(The murderer Moses. The illiterate Mohammed. Jesus the Sabbath-breaker. The womanizing Martin Luther King. The fanatic Paul. The drunkard Noah. O My child, you do not know as We do, how you shall rise up.)

Lucy stared again at the card of Catholic Relief Charities. Promise, Holy Spirit, if I do this, You'll be with me?

The taxi stopped outside the Feliciana Parish Women's Center.

And promise, Holy Spirit, even though it's probably a sin to ask, that you'll be with me at the clinic through this procedure to come as well?

(But We have always been with you. And who is to say, My children, whether you invented Us or whether We created you. We hear each other's voices, do We not? All We can tell you is that We are true, as you are true, as love is true. And that We'll be with you always. Now, and until the end of time.)

[. . . and Benjamin brought me to the door of the chamber where this hideous abomination, this death-relic of Our Master was supposed to be secreted.][19]

37. And here, my brother, you shall no doubt find it strange—but I stopped and refused to go forward.

Benjamin brought the torch into the chamber and bade me follow but I stood frozen in my path! He approached what looked to be an embalmed body and began to unwrap the reeking linen and I demanded he stop and take me back upstairs.

He said to me, "But the soldiers are here now. They are sure to find you."

I don't remember what happened precisely, owing to being beaten upon the head. I know that Benjamin attacked me, thinking I was trying to escape my payment to him. He hit me and took my belt and the money I had brought. I merely wished to be gone and in my excitement, clambering up the ladder to the house, crying out from my being attacked, my presence became known to the guards.

38. I had no delusions, and I was well aware of the risks I took, so I did not debase myself by begging for mercies that I knew shouldn't be granted me. But something of my innate dignity must have impressed itself upon the Candace, because Her Opulence, tears flowing down her huge face, was so moved by my sentence that she has paid for me to retain my scribe, Tesmegan here, until my addition to their library was complete . . .

19. For speculation over the missing paragraph, see my paper in *The University of Chicago Theologian*, vol. XXVIII, no. 1. Patrick V. O'Hanrahan, "Textual Problems in the *Gospel of Matthias*."

(My dear Tesmegan is confused. He is sitting here muttering—yes, write it all down, I'm almost done.) The young boy cannot understand my having incurred imperial disfavor and to have been sentenced, only to have run from the very prize I risked all for! Ah, my earnest scribe, we are all, all of us, sentenced to one death as it is, the same death, maybe today, maybe decades from now, but it will come. Do we truly wish to know what might leave us crushed and emptied? Do we wish to deprive ourselves of comforts in our saddest days of loss, in our struggle with great questions, in our final hours of earthly life?

39. I tell you, young Tesmegan, press not too closely upon what you believe, ask not too much of it. By some accident had I seen it was indeed the Teacher of Righteousness in that horrid cellar, I believe, upon contemplation, that I would not have told anyone of the truth. Because what does Truth matter beside the good that we Nazirenes will bring to the world? It may be absurd but I believe one day Rome may surrender to the Nazirenes, all its armies and wealth of empire will fall into the service of He Who Showed the Way. And O what a world we will live in then!

So why then did I turn away before all answers were revealed? Why, for myself.

40. I preferred, dear brother, in this final gesture, Faith to Truth. I recall it is said that at His shameful trial, Our Master was asked by the Roman procurator, "What is Truth?"

Our Master made no answer.[20]

I would not be surprised if God Himself was equally silent on the matter—why should God tell us such a thing, as He alone has the power to be certain of Truth? The Master of the Universe's gift to us is not Truth, which we clearly don't have the capacity to perceive; it is instead the capacity for Faith. These past years I have allowed my obsession with what was true to lead me down faint, irrelevant paths. One cannot retrieve Faith by a world of proofs, facts, histories, and tracts, as if it were Truth one had lost.

I began this gospel by admitting that I had lost my faith. Now I tell you it is found again. But very different, this time, this

---

20. *John* 18:38.

faith: not the raging inferno of my passionate youth or the fiery tractates of my middle years. It is a small spark now, fought for and sheltered, fanned with constant attention, but it shall not go out in these last hours.

And it is warmth enough.

41. Here I risk your censure, Josephus, but you too will return to your faith, though perhaps not to the priesthood that once was your life. Admire as you will the Romans and their Empire and their management of it—even in Man's history if there is none greater—I know you shall discover Rome to be so much dust, for that is all she is. She has rearranged the stones, no more, no less; her mighty arches and viaducts are ruins in the making.

I cannot say what form of faith you will return to.[21] Odd, sitting here watching my last day turn to night, I have found the serenity to wonder that which faith we lift up does not matter; God must expect some confusion concerning our lowly notions of Him. But God would not forgive our indifference, let alone our persecuting each other over it.

42. You know, I tell you my brother, as I have recounted my travels here to Tesmegan—what's that, my boy? Tears for my paltry life sputtering to its end? (Oh, even at the end I must endure nonsense and incompetence.) As I was saying, I have in these days relived the last years of my life, and it seems, now that death is certain on the morrow when the Meroitians will

21. Josephus's later work, *The Antiquities of the Jews*, was accompanied by an autobiographical *Life* that in many places contradicts his account of his actions in his earlier *The Jewish War*. In the earlier work one reads of his superhuman diplomacy and martial skills, but one finds a humbler Josephus in the *Life*, i.e., *And on this [escapade], I suppose, it was that God, who is never unacquainted with those that do as they ought to do, delivered me still out of the hands of these my enemies. . . . (Vita, 15)*. This editor is not convinced there was a wholesale conversion from the pro-Roman life back to observant Judaism. It seems where before his own magnificence brought him rewards, in the *Life* it is because Josephus is God's own warrior that he succeeds. His egotism remains undimmed.

More curious in the *Life* is his insistence on his compassion. For example, *They also came to me to Taricheae with four miles of loadings of garments and other furniture, and the weight of the silver they brought was not small and there were five hundred pieces of gold also. . . . And it is prohibited by our laws even to spoil our enemies (Vita, 26)*. Certainly loving one's enemies was no part of Hasmonean or Herodian Judea. When a faction insists on persecuting another Jewish sect for their heresies, Josephus says he said, *"Everyone ought to worship God according to his own inclinations and not to be constrained by force" (Vita, 23)*. Might he, in later years, have truly investigated the Ebionite Christianity of his brother?

See S. J. D. Cohen, *Josephus in Galilee and Rome*, appendix 1 (Leiden, 1979) or more recently, M. Hersch, *Josephus*, "Vita" chapter (HUP, 1992).

bake me or burn me or some ingenious thing, that less and less have I been able to take to my breast our ranting prophets or ancient Mosaic rules or even the confident voices of Peter or Gamaliel, and, alas, the face of Our Master, once clear and embossed upon my mind, even that has faded somewhat as the years have dulled and distracted me.

No, as Mary predicted, it is the Holy Spirit I have come to cherish, Blessed *Sophia*, guiding me with a calm and discernment that I have mistaken most of my life for the memory of my blessed mother, the woman's-voice of my own conscience.

43. Oh yes, speaking of *Sophia*, Mary pressed a missive into my hand, as I believe I mentioned, to open upon my discovering the truth in Meroe. I opened it with trembling hand, wondering if it might be a scrawling from the Teacher of Righteousness Himself! But no, it was merely the words of a young man not seventeen, full to brimming with a love of God and His world:

I have come to think that God is surely no more luminous than a mother tending her children, the rituals of the kitchen and successful harvest, the hearth of a home at peace. The foolish men look to the skies, My Sophia, when it is down around us, yes, even to the womenfolk that we should look. How well they have cradled Love through the ages while we men have raged in tongues unknown to God, persecuted one another for piles of twigs, hurled pebbles at the silence of the night.

That, you will recall, is from my *Cosmos Explained*, an immature work full of enthusiasms, but not without some small merit and well regarded, despite some superficial deficiencies of style, in many quite reputable Alexandrian as well as Damascene circles. Mary has scribbled upon the bottom of the papyrus that she recalled Our Master having regarded this passage very highly.

Hosanna, at the last, the very last I am to know that He Who Is Beyond Compare found in me some thing to love!

44. Might *Sophia* grant me a final blessing?

Should this scroll never reach my brother Josephus bar-Matthias, may it one day be found by, I pray, a fellow scholar, a lonely soul such as myself who may have misplaced the consolation of God, who found his faith passing with his youth, who searches for the light of brotherly love amid the confusion and darkening muddle of this world. I leave it, Holy Wisdom, in Your capable hands.

You Who can do all things!

45. And what have I ever really known? Perhaps even now, the True Temple is being rebuilt in the new Jerusalem. Gamaliel and Peter have become reconciled, holding hands and leading our redeemed nation in prayer! And you, Josephus, returned to our people . . . why, maybe it is you who will lead the Nazirenes away from their fondest heresies, using your skill as a leader (since, dear brother, your inaccurate histories cannot make your career or fame, I am sad to say). Blessings, many blessings, and farewell! Investigate for yourself the teachings of Our Master— but be sure to do it quickly, quickly:

For we are living in the End Times!

ACKNOWLEDGMENTS

The epics of old invoked the muses for inspiration and gratitude . . . we have acknowledgments pages.

BRITAIN. Let me thank John and Chris Kelly for the best that was in Oxford, the monks at Blackfriars, late-night theological discussions with Gordon and Jonathan, Tania Glyde on general principle, and St. John's College and their legendary Arabist Freddie Beeston. IRELAND. Apologies to Cormac about the name; many thanks to David and his folks (and Bruce and Andrew) in Belfast and their splendid hospitality in contrast to my little encounter with the Royal Ulster Constabulary. Utterly indispensable was James Logue for his savvy and guidance. ITALY. *Ciao*, Enrico, love to my muse Elisabetta, an enormous *grazie* to Davide, with thanks to Tom, who lost everything with me after the robbery in Rome. GREECE. Nothing was possible without the assistance of Father Timothy Ware, who got me onto Mt. Athos where I enjoyed the charity of monks in Dionysiou, Pantokrator, Megistri Lavra Monasteries, and most especially the skete of Prophet Elias and its abbot Father Seraphim, a true man of God (I hope nothing herein gives offense, *Pater*). Love and gratitude to Henrietta Miers, who endured the night we hit the flock of sheep on the freeway, James Delingpole for his heroic endurance by my side, and the Stamboulopouloi for their incomparable Athenian hospitality, with exceeding thanks to the lovely Artemis for all the dirty Greek words. JERUSALEM. The unflappable Christina Gerstgrasser at the wheel for her superb rock-dodging in Hebron, Occupied West Bank (and Hertz for being so forgiving about the windshield), my old pal Jacob, the one and only Mimi Stark, George Moffat at the *Monitor*, my friend Khaldoun, and countless kind Palestinians along the way. AFRICA. James Fergusson for his company up the Nile, the American University in Cairo, Father Matthew at the Monastery of St. Bola, who lovingly revealed the splendors of the Coptic faith, and the monks of Deir el-Muharraq, and the guestmaster of Deir el-Suriani who took me to the desert and prayed with me in the cave of Pope Carolus where the Holy Spirit dwelt, where one looked out upon the wastes seeing the occasional light from the fires of the lone monks, some of them out there thirty years. . . . Blessings upon the aid workers gathered in the Metropole Hotel in Khartoum, the Holy Spirit abides with you! Innumerable thanks to my African friends Sele and Rashawn for extricating me from many a bureaucratic scrape. Peace upon your lands!

Also, closer to home, thanks to Henry Dunow, Danetta Genung, Mary Pendergraft of Wake Forest University, the tireless Cal Morgan, Amelie Littell, Leslie Sharpe, Ian Sturgess, Jeremy Drake, Loie Kostelich, Greg Kelly, Rev. Stimp Hawkins, Don Campbell (fastest xeroxer east of the Mississippi . . .), and my support staff in Chicago: Leslie, Ceece, Cynthia, and Judy. And of course and always Thomas McCormack, through whom all things flow, the munificent, the deferrer, forgiver of failed deadlines, who is with me always. . . .

Oh yeah. And to Lux Rent-A-Car, the Bashir and Mengistu regimes (one down, one to go), to the Ethiopian Tourist Commission, and to American Express, who canceled my card *when I was in the friggin' Sudan* after a review showed I had "insufficient salary" to deserve renewal, I execrate you: *Anathema! Anathema! Anathema!*

INDEX

My publishers thought that readers might care to review some of the more unusual information in the book, so I have provided an index of the purely factual matters herein. Disciples can be found by their names; only the true facts concerning Matthias are below, not the gospel that I've made up. Look under "Epistles" for any letters, "Gospels" for any gospels. Except for a few, all the saints are under "Saints." Emperors and empresses are under "Emperors (Byzantine)" or "Caesars."

ABOUT THE AUTHOR

WILTON BARNHARDT was born and raised in Winston-Salem, North Carolina, and studied at Michigan State University before writing his master's thesis on Henry James, attending St. John's College, Oxford University. He has worked as a reporter for *Sports Illustrated* (auto racing, his specialty), and his first novel, *Emma Who Saved My Life* (1989) was published by St. Martin's Press. He divides his time between New Orleans, Louisiana and Long Beach, California.